THE WORKS
OF
MARK TWAIN

Tom Sawyer

Huckleberry Finn

The Prince and
the Pauper

A Connecticut Yankee in
King Arthur's Court

Fenimore Cooper's
Literary Offenses

LONGMEADOW PRESS

This edition is published by Longmeadow Press,
201 High Ridge Road, Stamford, Connecticut 06904

Reprinted by permission of Running Press Book Publishers,
Phila., PA from the UNABRIDGED MARK TWAIN, copyright © 1976
by Running Press.

ISBN 0-681-41002-7

10 9 8 7 6 5 4 3 2

Manufactured in the U.S.A.

TABLE
OF
CONTENTS

THE ADVENTURES
OF
TOM SAWYER

THE ADVENTURES OF TOM SAWYER

PREFACE

Most of the adventures recorded in this book really occurred; one or two were experiences of my own, the rest those of boys who were schoolmates of mine. Huck Finn is drawn from life; Tom Sawyer also, but not from an individual—he is a combination of the characteristics of three boys whom I knew, and therefore belongs to the composite order of architecture.

The odd superstitions touched upon were all prevalent among children and slaves in the West at the period of this story—that is to say, thirty or forty years ago.

Although my book is intended mainly for the entertainment of boys and girls, I hope it will not be shunned by men and women on that account, for part of my plan has been to try to pleasantly remind adults of what they once were themselves, and of how they felt and thought and talked, and what queer enterprises they sometimes engaged in.

THE AUTHOR.

HARTFORD. 1876.

CHAPTER I

"Tom!"

No answer.

"TOM!"

No answer.

"What's gone with that boy, I wonder? You TOM!"

No answer.

The old lady pulled her spectacles down and looked over them about the room; then she put them up and looked out under them. She seldom or never looked *through* them for so small a thing as a boy; they were her state pair, the pride of her heart, and were built for "style," not service—she could have seen through a pair of stove lids just as well. She looked perplexed for a moment, and then said, not fiercely, but still loud enough for the furniture to hear:

"Well, I lay if I get hold of you I'll—"

She did not finish, for by this time she was bending down and punching under the bed with the broom, and so she needed breath to punctuate the punches with. She resurrected nothing but the cat.

"I never did see the beat of that boy!"

She went to the open door and stood in it and looked out among the tomato vines and "jimpson" weeds that constituted the garden. No Tom. So she lifted up her voice at an angle calculated for distance, and shouted:

"Y-o-u-u *Tom!*"

There was a slight noise behind her and she turned just in time to seize a small boy by the slack of his roundabout and arrest his flight.

"There! I might 'a' thought of that closet. What you been doing in there?"

"Nothing."

"Nothing! Look at your hands. And look at your mouth. What *is* that truck?"

"*I* don't know, aunt."

"Well, *I* know. It's jam—that's what it is. Forty times I've said if you didn't let that jam alone I'd skin you. Hand me that switch."

The switch hovered in the air—the peril was desperate—

"My! Look behind you, aunt!"

The old lady whirled round, and snatched her skirts out of danger. The lad fled, on the instant, scrambled up the high board-fence, and disappeared over it.

His aunt Polly stood surprised a moment, and then broke into a gentle laugh.

"Hang the boy, can't I never learn anything? Ain't he played me tricks enough like that for me to be looking out for him by this time? But old fools is the biggest fools there is. Can't learn an old dog new tricks, as the saying is. But my goodness, he never plays them alike, two days, and how is a body to know what's coming? He

'pears to know just how long he can torment me before I get my
dander up, and he knows if he can make out to put me off for a
minute or make me laugh, it's all down again and I can't hit him a
lick. I ain't doing my duty by that boy, and that's the Lord's truth,
goodness knows. Spare the rod and spile the child, as the Good Book
says. I'm a laying up sin and suffering for us both. *I* know. He's full
of the Old Scratch, but laws-a-me! he's my own dead sister's boy,
poor thing, and I ain't got the heart to lash him, somehow. Every
time I let him off, my conscience does hurt me so, and every time I
hit him my old heart most breaks. Well-a-well, man that is born
of woman is of few days and full of trouble, as the Scripture says,
and I reckon it's so. He'll play hookey this evening,* and I'll just be
obleeged to make him work, tomorrow, to punish him. It's
mighty hard to make him work Saturdays, when all the boys is
having holiday, but he hates work more than he hates anything else,
and I've *got* to do some of my duty by him, or I'll be the ruination
of the child."

Tom did play hookey, and he had a very good time. He got back
home barely in season to help Jim, the small colored boy, saw
next-day's wood and split the kindlings before supper—at least
he was there in time to tell his adventures to Jim while Jim did
three-fourths of the work. Tom's younger brother (or rather,
half-brother) Sid, was already through with his part of the work
(picking up chips) for he was a quiet boy, and had no adventurous,
troublesome ways.

While Tom was eating his supper, and stealing sugar as
opportunity offered, Aunt Polly asked him questions that were full
of guile, and very deep—for she wanted to trap him into damaging
revealments. Like many other simple-hearted souls, it was her pet
vanity to believe she was endowed with a talent for dark and
mysterious diplomacy, and she loved to contemplate her most
transparent devices as marvels of low cunning. Said she:

"Tom, it was middling warm in school, warn't it?"

"Yes'm."

"Powerful warm, warn't it?"

"Yes'm."

"Didn't you want to go in a-swimming, Tom?"

A bit of a scare shot through Tom—a touch of uncomfortable
suspicion. He searched Aunt Polly's face, but it told him nothing.
So he said:

"No'm—well, not very much."

The old lady reached out her hand and felt Tom's shirt, and said:

"But you ain't too warm now, though. And it flattered her to
reflect that she had discovered that the shirt was dry without
anybody knowing that that was what she had in her mind. But in
spite of her. Tom knew where the wind lay, now. So he forestalled
what might be the next move:

*South-western for "afternoon."

"Some of us pumped on our heads—mine's damp yet. See?"

Aunt Polly was vexed to think she had overlooked that bit of circumstantial evidence, and missed a trick. Then she had a new inspiration:

"Tom, you didn't have to undo your shirt collar where I sewed it, to pump on your head, did you? Unbutton your jacket!"

The trouble vanished out of Tom's face. He opened his jacket. His shirt collar was securely sewed.

"Bother! Well, go 'long with you. I'd made sure you'd played hookey and been a-swimming. But I forgive ye, Tom. I reckon you're a kind of a singed cat, as the saying is—better'n you look. *This* time."

She was half sorry her sagacity had miscarried, and half glad that Tom had stumbled into obedient conduct for once.

But Sidney said:

"Well, now, if I didn't think you sewed his collar with white thread, but it's black."

"Why, I did sew it with white! Tom!"

But Tom did not wait for the rest. As he went out at the door he said:

"Siddy, I'll lick you for that."

In a safe place Tom examined two large needles which were thrust into the lappels of his jacket, and had thread bound about them—one needle carried white thread and the other black. He said:

"She'd never noticed if it hadn't been for Sid. Confound it! sometimes she sews it with white, and sometimes she sews it with black. I wish to geeminy she'd stick to one or t'other—*I* can't keep the run of 'em. But I bet you I'll lam Sid for that. I'll learn him!"

He was not the Model Boy of the village. He knew the model boy very well though—and loathed him.

Within two minutes, or even less, he had forgotten all his troubles. Not because his troubles were one whit less heavy and bitter to him than a man's are to a man, but because a new and powerful interest bore them down and drove them out of his mind for the time—just as men's misfortunes are forgotten in the excitement of new enterprises. This new interest was a valued novelty in whistling, which he had just acquired from a negro, and he was suffering to practice it undisturbed. It consisted in a peculiar bird-like turn, a sort of liquid warble, produced by touching the tongue to the roof of the mouth at short intervals in the midst of the music—the reader probably remembers how to do it, if he has ever been a boy. Diligence and attention soon gave him the knack of it, and he strode down the street with his mouth full of harmony and his soul full of gratitude. He felt much as an astronomer feels who has discovered a new planet—no doubt, as far as strong, deep, unalloyed pleasure is concerned, the advantage was with the boy, not the astronomer.

The summer evenings were long. It was not dark, yet. Presently
Tom checked his whistle. A stranger was before him—a boy a shade
larger than himself. A new comer of any age or either sex was an
impressive curiosity in the poor little shabby village of St.
Petersburgh. This boy was well-dressed, too—well-dressed on a
week-day. This was simply astounding. His cap was a dainty thing,
his close-buttoned blue cloth roundabout was new and natty, and so
were his pantaloons. He had shoes on—and it was only Friday. He
even wore a necktie, a bright bit of ribbon. He had a citified air
about him that ate into Tom's vitals. The more Tom stared at the
splendid marvel, the higher he turned up his nose at his finery
and the shabbier and shabbier his own outfit seemed to him to grow.
Neither boy spoke. If one moved, the other moved—but only
sidewise, in a circle; they kept face to face and eye to eye all the time.
Finally Tom said:

"I can lick you!"

"I'd like to see you try it."

"Well, I can do it."

"No you can't, either."

"Yes I can."

"No you can't."

"I can."

"You can't."

"Can!"

"Can't!"

An uncomfortable pause. Then Tom said?

"What's your name?"

" 'Tisn't any of your business, maybe."

"Well I 'low I'll *make* it my business."

"Well why don't you?"

"If you say much I will."

"Much—much—*much*. There now."

"Oh, you think you're mighty smart, *don't* you? I could lick you
with one hand tied behind me, if I wanted to."

"Well why don't you *do* it? You *say* you can do it."

"Well I *will*, if you fool with me."

"Oh yes—I've seen whole families in the same fix."

"Smarty! You think you're *some,* now, *don't* you? Oh what a
hat!"

"You can lump that hat if you don't like it. I dare you to knock
it off—and anybody that'll take a dare will suck eggs."

"You're a liar!"

"You're another."

"You're a fighting liar and dasn't take it up."

"Aw—take a walk!"

"Say—if you give me much more of your sass I'll take and
bounce a rock off'n your head."

"Oh, of *course* you will."

"Well I *will.*"

"Well why don't you *do* it then? What do you keep *saying* you will for? Why don't you *do* it? It's because you're afraid."

"I *ain't* afraid."

"You are."

"I ain't."

"You are."

Another pause, and more eyeing and sidling around each other. Presently they were shoulder to shoulder. Tom said:

"Get away from here!"

"Go away yourself!"

"I won't."

"*I* won't either."

So they stood, each with a foot placed at an angle as a brace, and both shoving with might and main, and glowering at each other with hate. But neither could get an advantage. After struggling till both were hot and flushed, each relaxed his strain with watchful caution, and Tom said:

"You're a coward and a pup. I'll tell my big brother on you, and he can thrash you with his little finger, and I'll make him do it, too."

"What do I care for your big brother? I've got a brother that's bigger than he is—and what's more, he can throw him over that fence, too." [Both brothers were imaginary.]

"That's a lie."

"*Your* saying so don't make it so."

Tom drew a line in the dust with his big toe, and said:

"I dare you to step over that, and I'll lick you till you can't stand up. Anybody that'll take a dare will steal sheep."

The new boy stepped over promptly, and said:

"Now you said you'd do it, now let's see you do it."

"Don't you crowd me now; you better look out."

"Well, you *said* you'd do it—why don't you do it?"

"By jingo! for two cents I *will* do it."

The new boy took two broad coppers out of his pocket and held them out with derision. Tom struck them to the ground. In an instant both boys were rolling and tumbling in the dirt, gripped together like cats; and for the space of a minute they tugged and tore at each other's hair and clothes, punched and scratched each other's noses, and covered themselves with dust and glory. Presently the confusion took form and through the fog of battle Tom appeared, seated astride the new boy, and pounding him with his fists.

"Holler 'nuff!" said he.

The boy only struggled to free himself. He was crying,—mainly from rage.

"Holler 'nuff!"—and the pounding went on.

At last the stranger got out a smothered "Nuff!" and Tom let him up and said:

"Now that'll learn you. Better look out who you're fooling with next time."

The new boy went off brushing the dust from his clothes, sobbing, snuffling, and occasionally looking back and shaking his head and threatening what he would do to Tom the "next time he caught him out." To which Tom responded with jeers, and started off in high feather, and as soon as his back was turned the new boy snatched up a stone, threw it and hit him between the shoulders and then turned tail and ran like an antelope. Tom chased the traitor home, and thus found out where he lived. He then held a position at the gate for some time, daring the enemy to come outside, but the enemy only made faces at him through the window and declined. At last the enemy's mother appeared, and called Tom a bad, vicious, vulgar child, and ordered him away. So he went away; but he said he "'lowed" to "lay" for that boy.

He got home pretty late, that night, and when he climbed cautiously in at the window, he uncovered an ambuscade, in the person of his aunt; and when she saw the state his clothes were in her resolution to turn his Saturday holiday into captivity at hard labor became adamantine in its firmness.

CHAPTER II

Saturday morning was come, and all the summer world was bright and fresh, and brimming with life. There was a song in every heart; and if the heart was young the music issued at the lips. There was cheer in every face and a spring in every step. The locust trees were in bloom and the fragrance of the blossoms filled the air. Cardiff Hill, beyond the village and above it, was green with vegetation, and it lay just far enough away to seem a Delectable Land, dreamy, reposeful, and inviting.

Tom appeared on the sidewalk with a bucket of whitewash and a long-handled brush. He surveyed the fence, and all gladness left him and a deep melancholy settled down upon his spirit. Thirty yards of board fence nine feet high. Life to him seemed hollow, and existence but a burden. Sighing he dipped his brush and passed it along the topmost plank; repeated the operation; did it again; compared the insignificant whitewashed streak with the far-reaching continent of unwhitewashed fence, and sat down on a tree-box discouraged. Jim came skipping out at the gate with a tin pail, and singing "Buffalo Gals." Bringing water from the town pump had always been hateful work in Tom's eyes, before, but now it did not strike him so. He remembered that there was company at the pump. White, mulatto, and negro boys and girls were always

there waiting their turns, resting, trading playthings, quarreling,
fighting, skylarking. And he remembered that although the pump
was only a hundred and fifty yards off, Jim never got back with a
bucket of water under an hour—and even then somebody generally
had to go after him. Tom said:

"Say, Jim, I'll fetch the water if you'll whitewash some."

Jim shook his head and said:

"Can't, Mars Tom. Ole missis, she tole me I got to go an' git dis
water an' not stop foolin' roun' wid anybody. She say she spec'
Mars Tom gwine to ax me to whitewash, an' so she tole me go 'long
an' 'tend to my own business—she 'lowed *she'd* 'tend to de
whitewashin'."

"Oh, never you mind what she said, Jim. That's the way she
always talks. Gimme the bucket—I won't be gone only a minute.
She won't ever know."

"Oh, I dasn't Mars Tom. Ole missis she'd take an' tar de head
off'n me. 'Deed she would."

"*She!* She never licks anybody—whacks 'em over the head with
her thimble—and who cares for that, I'd like to know. She talks
awful, but talk don't hurt—anyways it don't if she don't cry. Jim,
I'll give you a marvel. I'll give you a white alley!"

Jim began to waver.

"White alley, Jim! And it's a bully taw."

"My! Dat's a mighty gay marvel, *I* tell you! But Mars Tom I's
powerful 'fraid ole missis—"

"And besides, if you will I'll show you my sore toe."

Jim was only human—this attraction was too much for him. He
put down his pail, took the white alley, and bent over the toe with
absorbing interest while the bandage was being unwound. In
another moment he was flying down the street with his pail and a
tingling rear, Tom was whitewashing with vigor, and Aunt Polly
was retiring from the field with a slipper in her hand and triumph
in her eye.

But Tom's energy did not last. He began to think of the fun he
had planned for this day, and his sorrows multiplied. Soon the free
boys would come tripping along on all sorts of delicious
expeditions, and they would make a world of fun of him for having
to work—the very thought of it burnt him like fire. He got out his
worldly wealth and examined it—bits of toys, marbles, and trash;
enough to buy an exchange of *work* maybe, but not half enough to
buy so much as half an hour of pure freedom. So he returned his
straightened means to his pocket, and gave up the idea of trying to
buy the boys. At this dark and hopeless moment an inspiration
burst upon him! Nothing less than a great, magnificent inspiration.

He took up his brush and went tranquilly to work. Ben Rogers
hove in sight presently—the very boy, of all boys, whose ridicule he
had been dreading. Ben's gait was the hop-skip-and-jump—proof

enough that his heart was light and his anticipations high. He was
eating an apple, and giving a long, melodious whoop, at intervals,
followed by a deep-toned ding-dong-dong, ding-dong-dong, for he
was personating a steamboat. As he drew near, he slackened speed,
took the middle of the street, leaned far over to starboard and
rounded to ponderously and with laborious pomp and circumstance
—for he was personating the "Big Missouri," and considered
himself to be drawing nine feet of water. He was boat, and captain,
and engine-bells combined, so he had to imagine himself standing
on his own hurricane-deck giving the orders and executing them:

"Stop her, sir! Ting-a-ling-ling!" The headway ran almost out
and he drew up slowly toward the side-walk.

"Ship up to back! Ting-a-ling-ling!" His arms straightened and
stiffened down his sides.

"Set her back on the stabboard! Ting-a-ling-ling! Chow! ch-
chow-wow! Chow!" His right hand, meantime, describing stately
circles,—for it was representing a forty-foot wheel.

"Let her go back on the labboard! Ting-a-ling-ling! Chow-ch-
chow-chow!" The left hand began to describe circles.

"Stop the stabboard! Ting-a-ling-ling! Stop the labbord! Come
ahead on the stabboard! Stop her! Let your outside turn over slow!
Ting-a-ling-ling! Chow-ow-ow! Get out that head-line! *Lively* now!
Come—out with your spring-line—what're you about there! Take a
turn round that stump with the bight of it! Stand by that stage,
now—let her go! Done with the engines, sir! Ting-a-ling-ling!
Sh't! s'h't! sh't!" (trying the gauge-cocks.)

Tom went on whitewashing—paid no attention to the steamboat.
Ben stared a moment and then said:

"Hi-*yi! You're* up a stump, ain't you!"

No answer. Tom surveyed his last touch with the eye of an artist;
then he gave his brush another gentle sweep and surveyed the
result, as before. Ben ranged up alongside of him. Tom's mouth
watered for the apple, but he stuck to his work. Ben said:

"Hello, old chap, you got to work, hey?"

Tom wheeled suddenly and said:

"Why it's you Ben! I warn't noticing."

"Say—*I*'m going in a swimming, *I* am. Don't you wish you
could? But of course you'd druther *work*—wouldn't you? Course
you would!"

Tom contemplated the boy a bit, and said:

"What do you call work?"

"Why ain't *that* work?"

Tom resumed his whitewashing, and answered carelessly:

"Well, maybe it is, and maybe it ain't. All I know, is, it suits
Tom Sawyer."

"Oh come, now, you don't mean to let on that you *like* it?"

The brush continued to move.

"Like it? Well I don't see why I oughtn't to like it. Does a boy get a chance to whitewash a fence every day?"

That put the thing in a new light. Ben stopped nibbling his apple. Tom swept his brush daintily back and forth—stepped back to note the effect—added a touch here and there—criticised the effect again—Ben watching every move and getting more and more interested, more and more absorbed. Presently he said:

"Say, Tom, let *me* whitewash a little."

Tom considered, was about to consent; but he altered his mind:

"No—no—I reckon it wouldn't hardly do, Ben. You see, Aunt Polly's awful particular about this fence—right here on the street, you know—but if it was the back fence I wouldn't mind and *she* wouldn't. Yes, she's awful particular about this fence; it's got to be done very careful; I reckon there ain't one boy in a thousand, maybe two thousand, that can do it the way it's got to be done."

"No—is that so? Oh come, now—lemme just try. Only just a little—I'd let *you*, if you was me, Tom."

"Ben, I'd like to, honest injun; but Aunt Polly—well Jim wanted to do it, but she wouldn't let him; Sid wanted to do it, and she wouldn't let Sid. Now don't you see how I'm fixed? If you was to tackle this fence and anything was to happen to it—"

"Oh, shucks, I'll be just as careful. Now lemme try. Say—I'll give you the core of my apple."

"Well, here—. No Ben, now don't. I'm afeard—"

"I'll give you *all* of it!"

Tom gave up the brush with reluctance in his face but alacrity in his heart. And while the late steamer "Big Missouri" worked and sweated in the sun, the retired artist sat on a barrel in the shade close by, dangled his legs, munched his apple, and planned the slaughter of more innocents. There was no lack of material; boys happened along every little while; they came to jeer, but remained to whitewash. By the time Ben was fagged out, Tom had traded the next chance to Billy Fisher for a kite, in good repair; and when *he* played out, Johnny Miller bought in for a dead rat and a string to swing it with—and so on, and so on, hour after hour. And when the middle of the afternoon came, from being a poor poverty-stricken boy in the morning, Tom was literally rolling in wealth. He had beside the things before mentioned, twelve marbles, part of a jews-harp, a piece of blue bottle-glass to look through, a spool cannon, a key that wouldn't unlock anything, a fragment of chalk, a glass stopper of a decanter, a tin soldier, a couple of tadpoles, six fire-crackers, a kitten with only one eye, a brass door-knob, a dog-collar—but no dog—the handle of a knife, four pieces of orange peel, and a dilapidated old window-sash.

He had had a nice, good, idle time all the while—plenty of company—and the fence had three coats of whitewash on it! If he hadn't run out of whitewash, he would have bankrupted every boy in the village.

Tom said to himself that it was not such a hollow world, after all. He had discovered a great law of human action, without knowing it —namely, that in order to make a man or a boy covet a thing, it is only necessary to make the thing difficult to attain. If he had been a great and wise philosopher, like the writer of this book, he would now have comprehended that Work consists of whatever a body is *obliged* to do, and that Play consists of whatever a body is not obliged to do. And this would help him to understand why constructing artificial flowers or performing on a treadmill is work, while rolling ten-pins or climbing Mont Blanc is only amusement. There are wealthy gentlemen in England who drive four-horse passenger-coaches twenty or thirty miles on a daily line, in the summer, because the privilege costs them considerable money; but if they were offered wages for the service, that would turn it into work and then they would resign.

The boy mused a while over the substantial change which had taken place in his worldly circumstances, and then wended toward head-quarters to report.

CHAPTER III

Tom presented himself before Aunt Polly, who was sitting by an open window in a pleasant rearward apartment, which was bed-room, breakfast-room, dining-room, and library, combined. The balmy summer air, the restful quiet, the odor of the flowers, and the drowsing murmur of the bees had had their effect, and she was nodding over her knitting—for she had no company but the cat, and it was asleep in her lap. Her spectacles were propped up on her gray head for safety. She had thought that of course Tom had deserted long ago, and she wondered at seeing him place himself in her power again in this intrepid way. He said: "Mayn't I go and play now, aunt?"

"What, a'ready? How much have you done?"

"It's all done, aunt."

"Tom, don't lie to me—I can't bear it."

"I ain't, aunt; it *is* all done."

Aunt Polly placed small trust in such evidence. She went out to see for herself; and she would have been content to find twenty per cent of Tom's statement true. When she found the entire fence whitewashed, and not only whitewashed but elaborately coated and recoated, and even a streak added to the ground, her astonishment was almost unspeakable. She said:

"Well, I never! There's no getting round it, you *can* work when your'e a mind to, Tom." And then she diluted the compliment by adding, "But it's powerful seldom you're a mind to, I'm bound to say. Well, go 'long and play; but mind you get back sometime in a week, or I'll tan you."

She was so overcome by the splendor of his achievement that she took him into the closet and selected a choice apple and delivered it to him, along with an improving lecture upon the added value and flavor a treat took to itself when it came without sin through virtuous effort. And while she closed with a happy scriptural flourish, he "hooked" a doughnut.

Then he skipped out, and saw Sid just starting up the outside stairway that led to the back rooms on the second floor. Clods were handy and the air was full of them in a twinkling. They raged around Sid like a hail-storm; and before Aunt Polly could collect her surprised faculties and sally to the rescue, six or seven clods had taken personal effect, and Tom was over the fence and gone. There was a gate, but as a general thing he was too crowded for time to make use of it. His soul was at peace, now that he had settled with Sid for calling attention to his black thread and getting him into trouble.

Tom skirted the block, and came round into a muddy alley that led by the back of his aunt's cow-stable. He presently got safely beyond the reach of capture and punishment, and hasted toward the public square of the village, where two "military" companies of boys had met for conflict, according to previous appointment. Tom was General of one of these armies, Joe Harper (a bosom friend,) General of the other. These two great commanders did not condescend to fight in person—that being better suited to the still smaller fry— but sat together on an eminence and conducted the field operations by orders delivered through aides-de-camp. Tom's army won a great victory, after a long and hard-fought battle. Then the dead were counted, prisoners exchanged, the terms of the next disagreement agreed upon and the day for the necessary battle appointed; after which the armies fell into line and marched away, and Tom turned homeward alone.

As he was passing by the house where Jeff Thatcher lived, he saw a new girl in the garden—a lovely little blue-eyed creature with yellow hair plaited into two long tails, white summer frock and embroidered pantalettes. The fresh-crowned hero fell without firing a shot. A certain Amy Lawrence vanished out of his heart and left not even a memory of herself behind. He had thought he loved her to distraction, he had regarded his passion as adoration; and behold it was only a poor little evanescent partiality. He had been months winning her; she had confessed hardly a week ago; he had been the happiest and the proudest boy in the world only seven short days, and here in one instant of time she had gone out of his heart like a casual stranger whose visit is done.

He worshiped this new angel with furtive eye, till he saw that she had discovered him; then he pretended he did not know she was present, and began to "show off" in all sorts of absurd boyish ways,

in order to win her admiration. He kept up this grotesque foolishness
for some time; but by and by, while he was in the midst of some
dangerous gymnastic performances, he glanced aside and saw that
the little girl was wending her way toward the house. Tom came up
to the fence and leaned on it, grieving, and hoping she would tarry
yet a while longer. She halted a moment on the steps and then moved
toward the door. Tom heaved a great sigh as she put her foot on the
threshold. But his face lit up, right away, for she tossed a pansy over
the fence a moment before she disappeared.

The boy ran around and stopped within a foot or two of the flower,
and then shaded his eyes with his hand and began to look down
street as if he had discovered something of interest going on in that
direction. Presently he picked up a straw and began trying to
balance it on his nose, with his head tilted far back; and as he moved
from side to side, in his efforts, he edged nearer and nearer toward
the pansy; finally his bare foot rested upon it, his pliant toes closed
upon it, and he hopped away with the treasure and disappeared
round the corner. But only for a minute—only while he could button
the flower inside his jacket, next his heart—or next his stomach,
possibly, for he was not much posted in anatomy, and not
hypercritical, anyway.

He returned, now, and hung about the fence till nightfall,
"showing off," as before; but the girl never exhibited herself again,
though Tom comforted himself a little with the hope that she had
been near some window, meantime, and been aware of his
attentions. Finally he rode home reluctantly, with his poor head full
of visions.

All through supper his spirits were so high that his aunt wondered
"what had got into the child." He took a good scolding about
clodding Sid, and did not seem to mind it in the least. He tried to
steal sugar under his aunt's very nose, and got his knuckles rapped
for it. He said:

"Aunt, you don't whack Sid when he takes it."

"Well, Sid don't torment a body the way you do. You'd be always
into that sugar if I warn't watching you."

Presently she stepped into the kitchen, and Sid, happy in his
immunity, reached for the sugar-bowl—a sort of glorying over Tom
which was well-nigh unbearable. But Sid's fingers slipped and the
bowl dropped and broke. Tom was in ecstasies. In such ecstasies that
he even controlled his tongue and was silent. He said to himself that
he would not speak a word, even when his aunt came in, but would
sit perfectly still till she asked who did the mischief; and then he
would tell, and there would be nothing so good in the world as to see
that pet model "catch it." He was so brim-full of exultation that he
could hardly hold himself when the old lady came back and stood
above the wreck discharging lightnings of wrath from over her
spectacles. He said to himself, "Now it's coming!" And the next

instant he was sprawling on the floor! The potent palm was uplifted
to strike again when Tom cried out:

"Hold on, now, what 'er you belting *me* for?—Sid broke it!"

Aunt Polly paused, perplexed, and Tom looked for healing pity.
But when she got her tongue again, she only said:

"Umf! Well, you didn't get a lick amiss, I reckon. You been into
some other audacious mischief when I wasn't around, like enough."

Then her conscience reproached her, and she yearned to say
something kind and loving; but she judged that this would be
construed into a confession that she had been in the wrong, and
discipline forbade that. So she kept silence, and went about her
affairs with a troubled heart. Tom sulked in a corner and exalted
his woes. He knew that in her heart his aunt was on her knees to him,
and he was morosely gratified by the consciousness of it. He would
hang out no signals, he would take notice of none. He knew that a
yearning glance fell upon him, now and then, through a film of tears,
but he refused recognition of it. He pictured himself lying sick unto
death and his aunt bending over him beseeching one little forgiving
word, but he would turn his face to the wall, and die with that word
unsaid. Ah, how would she feel then? And he pictured himself
brought home from the river, dead, with his curls all wet, and his
sore heart at rest. How she would throw herself upon him, and how
her tears would fall like rain, and her lips pray God to give her back
her boy and she would never, never abuse him any more! But he
would lie there cold and white and make no sign—a poor little
sufferer, whose griefs were at an end. He so worked upon his feelings
with the pathos of these dreams, that he had to keep swallowing, he
was so like to choke; and his eyes swam in a blur of water, which
overflowed when he winked, and ran down and trickled from the end
of his nose. And such a luxury to him was this petting of his sorrows,
that he could not bear to have any worldly cheeriness or any grating
delight intrude upon it; it was too sacred for such contact; and so,
presently, when his cousin Mary danced in, all alive with the joy of
seeing home again after an age-long visit of one week to the country,
he got up and moved in clouds and darkness out at one door as she
brought song and sunshine in at the other.

He wandered far from the accustomed haunts of boys, and sought
desolate places that were in harmony with his spirit. A log raft in the
river invited him, and he seated himself on its outer edge and
contemplated the dreary vastness of the stream, wishing, the while,
that he could only be drowned, all at once and unconsciously,
without undergoing the uncomfortable routine devised by nature.
Then he thought of his flower. He got it out, rumpled and wilted,
and it mightily increased his dismal felicity. He wondered if *she*
would pity him if she knew? Would she cry, and wish that she had
a right to put her arms around his neck and comfort him? Or would
she turn coldly away like all the hollow world? This picture brought

such an agony of pleasureable suffering that he worked it over and
over again in his mind and set it up in new and varied lights, till he
wore it threadbare. At last he rose up sighing and departed in
the darkness.

About half past nine or ten o'clock he came along the deserted
street to where the Adored Unknown lived; he paused a moment;
no sound fell upon his listening ear; a candle was casting a dull glow
upon the curtain of a second-story window. Was the sacred presence
there? He climbed the fence, threaded his stealthy way through the
plants, till he stood under that window; he looked up at it long, and
with emotion; then he laid him down on the ground under it,
disposing himself upon his back, with his hands clasped upon his
breast and holding his poor wilted flower. And this he would die—
out in the cold world, with no shelter over his homeless head, no
friendly hand to wipe the death-damps from his brow, no loving face
to bend pityingly over him when the great agony came. And thus
she would see him when she looked out upon the glad morning,
and oh! would she drop one little tear upon his poor, lifeless form,
would she heave one little sigh to see a bright young life so rudely
blighted, so untimely cut down?

The window went up, a maid-servant's discordant voice profaned
the holy calm, and a deluge of water drenched the prone martyr's
remains!

The strangling hero sprang up with a relieving snort. There was a
whiz as of a missile in the air, mingled with the murmur of a curse,
a sound as of shivering glass followed, and a small, vague form went
over the fence and shot away in the gloom.

Not long after, as Tom, all undressed for bed, was surveying his
drenched garments by the light of a tallow dip, Sid woke up; but if
he had any dim idea of making any "references to allusions," he
thought better of it and held his peace, for there was danger in
Tom's eye.

Tom turned in without the added vexation of prayers, and Sid
made mental note of the omission.

CHAPTER IV

The sun rose upon a tranquil world, and beamed down upon the
peaceful village like a benediction. Breakfast over, Aunt Polly had
family worship; it began with a prayer built from the ground up of
solid courses of Scriptural quotations, welded together with a thin
mortar of originality; and from the summit of this she delivered a
grim chapter of the Mosaic Law, as from Sinai.

Then Tom girded up his loins, so to speak, and went to work to
"get his verses." Sid had learned his lesson days before. Tom bent
all his energies to the memorizing of five verses, and he chose part of
the Sermon on the Mount, because he could find no verses that were

shorter. At the end of half an hour Tom had a vague general idea of
his lesson, but no more, for his mind was traversing the whole field
of human thought, and his hands were busy with distracting
recreations. Mary took his book to hear him recite, and he tried to
find his way through the fog:

"Blessed are the—a—a—"

"Poor"—

"Yes—poor; blessed are the poor—a—a—"

"In spirit—"

"In spirit; blessed are the poor in spirit, for they—they—"

"Theirs—"

"For *theirs.* Blessed are the poor in spirit, for *theirs* is the
kingdom of heaven. Blessed are they that mourn, for they—they—"

"Sh—"

"For they—a—"

"S, H, A—"

"For they S, H—Oh I don't know what it is!"

"Shall!"

"Oh, *shall!* for they shall—for they shall—a—a—shall mourn—a
—a—blessed are they that shall—they that—a—they that shall
mourn, for they shall—a—shall *what?* Why don't you tell me Mary?
—what do you want to be so mean for?"

"Oh, Tom, you poor thick-headed thing, I'm not teasing you. I
wouldn't do that. You must go and learn it again. Don't be so
discouraged, Tom, you'll manage it—and if you do, I'll give you
something ever so nice. There, now, that's a good boy."

"All right! What is it, Mary, tell me what it is."

"Never you mind, Tom. You know if I say it's nice, it *is* nice."

"You bet you that's so, Mary. All right, I'll tackle it again."

And he did "tackle it again"—and under the double pressure of
curiosity and prospective gain, he did it with such spirit that he
accomplished a shining success. Mary gave him a bran-new
"Barlow" knife worth twelve and a half cents; and the convulsion of
delight that swept his system shook him to his foundations. True, the
knife would not cut anything, but it was a "sure-enough" Barlow,
and there was inconceivable grandeur in that—though where the
western boys ever got the idea that such a weapon could possibly be
counterfeited to its injury, is an imposing mystery and will always
remain so, perhaps. Tom contrived to scarify the cupboard with it,
and was arranging to begin on the bureau, when he was called off to
dress for Sunday-School.

Mary gave him a tin basin of water and a piece of soap, and he
went outside the door and set the basin on a little bench there; then
he dipped the soap in the water and laid it down; turned up his
sleeves; poured out the water on the ground, gently, and then
entered the kitchen and began to wipe his face diligently on the towel
behind the door. But Mary removed the towel and said:

"Now ain't you ashamed, Tom. You musn't be so bad. Water won't hurt you."

Tom was a trifle disconcerted. The basin was refilled, and this time he stood over it a little while, gathering resolution; took in a big breath and began. When he entered the kitchen presently, with both eyes shut and groping for the towel with his hands, an honorable territory stopped short at his chin and his jaws, like a mask; below emerged from the towel, he was not yet satisfactory, for the clean territory stopped shirt of his chin and his jaws, like a mask; below and beyond this line there was a dark expanse of unirrigated soil that spread downward in front and backward around his neck. Mary took him in hand, and when she was done with him he was a man and a brother, without distinction of color, and his saturated hair was neatly brushed, and its short curls wrought into a dainty and symmetrical general effect. [He privately smoothed out the curls, with labor and difficulty, and plastered his hair down close to his head; for he held curls to be effeminate, and his own filled his life with bitterness.] Then Mary got out a suit of his clothing that had been used only on Sundays during two years—they were simply called his "other clothes"—and so by that we know the size of his wardrobe. The girl "put him to rights" after he had dressed himself; she buttoned his neat roundabout up to his chin, turned his vast shirt collar down over his shoulders, brushed him off and crowned him with his speckled straw hat. He now looked exceedingly improved and uncomfortable. He was fully as uncomfortable as he looked; for there was a restraint about whole clothes and cleanliness that galled him. He hoped that Mary would forget his shoes, but the hope was blighted; she coated them thoroughly with tallow, as was the custom, and brought them out. He lost his temper and said he was always being made to do everything he didn't want to do. But Mary said, persuasively:

"Please, Tom—that's a good boy."

So he got into the shoes snarling. Mary was soon ready, and the three children set out for Sunday-school—a place that Tom hated with his whole heart; but Sid and Mary were fond of it.

Sabbath-school hours were from nine to half past ten; and then church service. Two of the children always remained for the sermon voluntarily, and the other always remained too—for stronger reasons. The church's high-backed, uncushioned pews would seat about three hundred persons; the edifice was but a small, plain affair, with a sort of pine board tree-box on top of it for a steeple. At the door Tom dropped back a step and accosted a Sunday-dressed comrade:

"Say, Billy, got a yaller ticket?"

"Yes."

"What'll you take for her?"

"What'll you give?"

"Piece of lickrish and a fish-hook."

"Less see 'em."

Tom exhibited. They were satisfactory, and the property changed hands. Then Tom traded a couple of white alleys for three red tickets, and some small trifle or other for a couple of blue ones. He waylaid other boys as they came, and went on buying tickets of various colors ten or fifteen minutes longer. He entered the church, now, with a swarm of clean and noisy boys and girls, proceeded to his seat and started a quarrel with the first boy that came handy. The teacher, a grave, elderly man, interfered; then turned his back a moment and Tom pulled a boy's hair in the next bench, and was absorbed in his book when the boy turned around; stuck a pin in another boy, presently, in order to hear him say "Ouch!" and got a new reprimand from his teacher. Tom's whole class were of a pattern—restless, noisy, and troublesome. When they came to recite their lessons, not one of them knew his verses perfectly, but had to be prompted all along. However, they worried through, and each got his reward—in small blue tickets, each with a passage of Scripture on it; each blue ticket was pay for two verses of the recitation. Ten blue tickets equalled a red one, and could be exchanged for it; ten red tickets equalled a yellow one: for ten yellow tickets the Superintendant gave a very plainly bound Bible, (worth forty cents in those easy times,) to the pupil. How many of my readers would have the industry and application to memorize two thousand verses, even for a Dore Bible? And yet Mary had acquired two Bibles in this way—it was the patient work of two years—and a boy of German parentage had won four or five. He once recited three thousand verses without stopping; but the strain upon his mental faculties was too great, and he was little better than an idiot from that day forth— a grievous misfortune for the school, for on great occasions, before company, the Superintendent (as Tom expressed it) had always made this boy come out and "spread himself." Only the older pupils managed to keep their tickets and stick to their tedious work long enough to get a Bible, and so the delivery of one of these prizes was a rare and noteworthy circumstance; the successful pupil was so great and conspicuous for that day that on the spot every scholar's heart was fired with a fresh ambition that often lasted a couple of weeks. It is possible that Tom's mental stomach had never really hungered for one of those prizes, but unquestionably his entire being had for many a day longed for the glory and the eclat that came with it.

In due course the Superintendent stood up in front of the pulpit, with a closed hymn book in his hand and his forefinger inserted between its leaves, and commanded attention. When a Sunday-school Superintendent makes his customary little speech, a hymn-book in the hand is as necessary as the inevitable sheet of music in the hand of a singer who stands forward on the platform and sings a solo at a concert—though why, is a mystery: for neither the hymn-

book nor the sheet of music is ever referred to by the sufferer. This
Superintendent was a slim creature of thirty-five, with a sandy
goatee and short sandy hair; he wore a stiff standing-collar whose
upper edge almost reached his ears and whose sharp points curved
forward abreast the corners of his mouth—a fence that compelled a
straight lookout ahead, and a turning of the whole body when a side
view was required; his chin was propped on a spreading cravat which
was as broad and as long as a bank note, and had fringed ends; his
boot toes were turned sharply up, in the fashion of the day, like
sleigh-runners—an effect patiently and laboriously produced by the
young men by sitting with their toes pressed against a wall for hours
together. Mr. Walters was very earnest of mein, and very sincere and
honest at heart; and he held sacred things and places in such
reverence, and so separated them from worldly matters, that
unconsciously to himself his Sunday-school voice had acquired a
peculiar intonation which was wholly absent on week-days. He
began after this fashion:

"Now children, I want you all to sit up just as straight and pretty
as you can and give me all your attention for a minute or two. There
—that is it. That is the way good little boys and girls should do. I
see one little girl who is looking out of the window—I am afraid she
thinks I am out there somewhere—perhaps up in one of the trees
making a speech to the little birds. [Applausive titter.] I want to tell
you how good it makes me feel to see so many bright, clean little
faces assembled in a place like this, learning to do right and be
good." And so forth and so on. It is not necessary to set down the
rest of the oration. It was of a pattern which does not vary, and so it
is familiar to us all.

The latter third of the speech was marred by the resumption of
fights and other recreations among certain of the bad boys, and by
fidgetings and whisperings that extended far and wide, washing even
to the bases of isolated and incorruptible rocks like Sid and Mary.
But now every sound ceased suddenly, with the subsidence of Mr.
Walters' voice, and the conclusion of the speech was received with a
burst of silent gratitude.

A good part of the whispering had been occasioned by an event
which was more or less rare—the entrance of visitors; lawyer
Thatcher, accompanied by a very feeble and aged man; a fine,
portly, middle-aged gentleman with iron-gray hair; and a dignified
lady who was doubtless the latter's wife. The lady was leading a
child. Tom had been restless and full of chafings and repinings;
conscience-smitten, too—he could not meet Amy Lawrence's eye, he
could not brook her loving gaze. But when he saw this small
new-comer his soul was all ablaze with bliss in a moment. The next
moment he was "showing off" with all his might—cuffing boys,
pulling hair, making faces—in a word, using every art that seemed
likely to fascinate a girl and win her applause. His exaltation had but

one alloy—the memory of his humiliation in this angel's garden—
and that record in sand was fast washing out, under the waves of
happiness that were sweeping over it now.

The visitors were given the highest seat of honor, and as soon as
Mr. Walters' speech was finished, he introduced them to the school.
The middle-aged man turned out to be a prodigious personage—no
less a one than the county judge—altogether the most august
creation these children had ever looked upon—and they wondered
what kind of material he was made of—and they half wanted to hear
him roar, and were half afraid he might, too. He was from
Constantinople, twelve miles away—so he had traveled, and seen the
world—these very eyes had looked upon the county court house—
which was said to have a tin roof. The awe which these reflections
inspired was attested by the impressive silence and the ranks of
staring eyes. This was the great Judge Thatcher, brother of their own
lawyer. Jeff Thatcher immediately went forward, to be familiar with
the great man and be envied by the school. It would have been music
to his soul to hear the whisperings:

"Look at him, Jim! He's a going up there. Say—look! he's a going
to shake hands with him—he *is* shaking hands with him! By jings,
don't you wish you was Jeff?"

Mr. Walters fell to "showing off," with all sorts of official
bustlings and activities giving orders, delivering judgments,
discharging directions here, there, everywhere that he could find a
target. The librarian "showed off"—running hither and thither with
his arms full of books and making a deal of the splutter and fuss that
insect authority delights in. The young lady teachers "showed off"
—bending sweetly over pupils that were lately being boxed, lifting
pretty warning fingers at bad little boys and patting good ones
lovingly. The young gentlemen teachers "showed off" with small
scoldings and other little displays of authority and fine attention to
discipline—and most of the teachers, of both sexes, found business
up at the library, by the pulpit; and it was business that frequently
had to be done over again two or three times, (with much
seeming vexation.) The little girls "showed off" in various ways, and
the little boys "showed off" with such diligence that the air was thick
with paper wads and the murmur of scufflings. And above it all the
great man sat and beamed a majestic judicial smile upon all the
house, and warmed himself in the sun of his own grandeur—for he
was "showing off," too.

There was only one thing wanting, to make Mr. Walters' ecstacy
complete, and that was a chance to deliver a Bible-prize and exhibit
a prodigy. Several pupils had a few yellow tickets, but none had
enough—he had been around among the star pupils inquiring. He
would have given worlds, now, to have that German lad back again
with a sound mind.

And now at this moment, when hope was dead, Tom Sawyer came

forward with nine yellow tickets, nine red tickets, and ten blue ones, and demanded a Bible. This was a thunderbolt out of a clear sky. Walters was not expecting an application from this source for the next ten years. But there was no getting around it—here were the certified checks, and they were good for their face. Tom was therefore elevated to a place with the Judge and the other elect, and the great news was announced from head-quarters. It was the most stunning surprise of the decade, and so profound was the sensation that it lifted the new hero up to the judicial one's altitude, and the school had two marvels to gaze upon in place of one. The boys were all eaten up with envy—but those that suffered the bitterest pangs were those who perceived too late that they themselves had contributed to this hated splendor by trading tickets to Tom for the wealth he had amassed in selling whitewashing privileges. These despised themselves, as being the dupes of a wily fraud, a guileful snake in the grass.

The prize was delivered to Tom with as much effusion as the Superintendent could pump up under the circumstances; but it lacked somewhat of the true gush, for the poor fellow's instinct taught him that there was a mystery here that could not well bear the light, perhaps; it was simply preposterous that *this* boy had warehoused two thousand sheaves of Scriptural wisdom on his premises—a dozen would strain his capacity, without a doubt.

Amy Lawrence was proud and glad, and she tried to make Tom see it in her face—but he wouldn't look. She wondered; then she was just a grain troubled; next a dim suspicion came and went—came again; she watched; a furtive glance told her worlds—and then her heart broke, and she was jealous, and angry, and the tears came and she hated everybody. Tom most of all, (she thought.)

Tom was introduced to the Judge; but his tongue was tied, his breath would hardly come, his heart quaked—partly because of the awful greatness of the man, but mainly because he was *her* parent. He would have liked to fall down and worship him, if it were in the dark. The Judge put his hand on Tom's head and called him a fine little man, and asked him what his name was. The boy stammered, gasped, and got it out:

"Tom."

"Oh, no, not Tom—it is—"

"Thomas."

"Ah, that's it. I thought there was more to it, maybe. That's very well. But you've another one I daresay, and you'll tell it to me, won't you?"

"Tell the gentleman your other name, Thomas," said Walters, "and say *sir.*—You mustn't forget your manners."

"Thomas Sawyer—sir."

"That's it! That's a good boy. Fine boy. Fine, manly little fellow. Two thousand verses is a great many—very, very great many. And

you never can be sorry for the trouble you took to learn them; for
knowledge is worth more than anything there is in the world; it's
what makes great men and good men; you'll be a great man and a
good man yourself, some day, Thomas, and then you'll look back
and say, It's all owing to the precious Sunday-school privileges of my
boyhood—it's all owing to my dear teachers that taught me to learn
—it's all owing to the good Superintendent, who encouraged me,
and watched over me, and gave me a beautiful Bible—a splendid
elegant Bible, to keep and have it all for my own, always—it's all
owing to right bringing up! That is what you will say, Thomas—and
you wouldn't take any money for those two thousand verses—no
indeed you wouldn't. And now you wouldn't mind telling me and
this lady some of the things you've learned—no, I know you
wouldn't—for we are proud of little boys that learn. Now no doubt
you know the names of all the twelve disciples. Won't you tell us the
names of the first two that were appointed?"

Tom was tugging at a button hole and looking sheepish. He
blushed, now, and his eyes fell. Mr. Walters' heart sank within him.
He said to himself, it is not possible that the boy can answer the
simplest question—why *did* the Judge ask him? Yet he felt obliged
to speak up and say:

"Answer the gentleman, Thomas—don't be afraid."

Tom still hung fire.

"Now I know you'll tell *me*" said the lady. "The names of the first
two disciples were—"

"DAVID AND GOLIATH!"

Let us draw the curtain of charity over the rest of the scene.

CHAPTER V

About half-past ten the cracked bell of the small church began
to ring, and presently the people began to gather for the morning
sermon. The Sunday-school children distributed themselves about
the house and occupied pews with their parents, so as to be under
supervision. Aunt Polly came, and Tom and Sid and Mary sat with
her—Tom being placed next the aisle, in order that he might be as
far away from the open window and the seductive outside summer
scenes as possible. The crowd filed up the aisles: the aged and
needy postmaster, who had seen better days; the mayor and his
wife—for they had a mayor there, among other unnecessaries; the
justice of the peace; the widow Douglass, fair, smart and forty, a
generous, good-hearted soul and well-to-do, her hill mansion the
only palace in the town, and the most hospitable and much the
most lavish in the matter of festivities that St. Petersburg could
boast; the bent and venerable Major and Mrs. Ward; lawyer
Riverson, the new notable from a distance; next the belle of the
village, followed by a troop of lawn-clad and ribbon-decked young

heart-breakers; then all the young clerks in town in a body—for
they had stood in the vestibule sucking their cane-heads, a circling
wall of oiled and simpering admirers, till the last girl had run their
gauntlet; and last of all came the Model Boy, Willie Mufferson,
taking as heedful care of his mother as if she were cut glass. He
always brought his mother to church, and was the pride of all the
matrons. The boys all hated him, he was so good. And besides, he
had been "thrown up to them" so much. His white handkerchief
was hanging out of his pocket behind, as usual on Sundays—
accidentally. Tom had no handkerchief, and he looked upon boys
who had, as snobs.

The congregation being fully assembled, now, the bell rang once
more, to warn laggards and stragglers, and then a solemn hush fell
upon the church which was only broken by the tittering and
whispering of the choir in the gallery. The choir always tittered and
whispered all through service. There was once a church choir that
was not ill-bred, but I have forgotten where it was, now. It was a
great many years ago, and I can scarcely remember anything about
it, but I think it was in some foreign country.

The minister gave out the hymn, and read it through with a
relish, in a peculiar style which was much admired in that part of
the country. His voice began on a medium key and climbed steadily
up till it reached a certain point, where it bore with strong
emphasis upon the topmost word and then plunged down as if
from a spring-board:

> Shall I be car-ri-ed toe the skies, on flow'ry *beds* of ease,

> Whilst others fight to win the prize, and sail thro' *blood*- -y seas?

He was regarded as a wonderful reader. At church "sociables"
he was always called upon to read poetry; and when he was
through, the ladies would lift up their hands and let them fall
helplessly in their laps, and "wall" their eyes, and shake their
heads, as much as to say, "Words cannot express it; it is too
beautiful, *too* beautiful for this mortal earth."

After the hymn had been sung, the Rev. Mr. Sprague turned
himself into a bulletin board, and read off "notices" of meetings
and societies and things till it seemed that the list would stretch out
to the crack of doom—a queer custom which is still kept up in
America, even in cities, away here in this age of abundant
newspapers. Often, the less there is to justify a traditional custom,
the harder it is to get rid of it.

And now the minister prayed. A good, generous prayer, it was,
and went into details: it pleaded for the church, and the little
children of the church; for the other churches of the village; for the
village itself; for the county; for the State; for the State officers;
for the United States; for the churches of the United States; for
Congress; for the President; for the officers of the Government; for
poor sailors, tossed by stormy seas; for the oppressed millions

groaning under the heel of European monarchies and Oriental despotisms; for such as have the light and the good tidings, and yet have not eyes to see nor ears to hear withal; for the heathen in the far islands of the sea; and closed with a supplication that the words he was about to speak might find grace and favor, and be as seed sown in fertile ground, yielding in time a grateful harvest of good. Amen.

There was a rustling of dresses, and the standing congregation sat down. The boy whose history this book relates did not enjoy the prayer, he only endured it—if he even did that much. He was restive all through it; he kept tally of the details of the prayer, unconsciously—for he was not listening, but he knew the ground of old, and the clergyman's regular route over it—and when a little trifle of new matter was interlarded, his ear detected it and his whole nature resented it; he considered additions unfair, and scoundrelly. In the midst of the prayer a fly had lit on the back of the pew in front of him and tortured his spirit by calmly rubbing its hands together, embracing its head with its arms, and polishing it so vigorously that it seemed to almost part company with the body, and the slender thread of a neck was exposed to view; scraping its wings with its hind legs and smoothing them to its body as if they had been coat tails; going through its whole toilet as tranquilly as if it knew it was perfectly safe. As indeed it was; for as sorely as Tom's hands itched to grab for it they did not dare—he believed his soul would be instantly destroyed if he did such a thing while the prayer was going on. But with the closing sentence his hand began to curve and steal forward; and the instant the "Amen" was out the fly was a prisoner of war. His aunt detected the act and made him let it go.

The minister gave out his text and droned along monotonously through an argument that was so prosy that many a head by and by began to nod—and yet it was an argument that dealt in limitless fire and brimstone and thinned the predestined elect down to a company so small as to be hardly worth the saving. Tom counted the pages of the sermon; after church he always knew how many pages there had been, but he seldom knew anything else about the discourse. However, this time he was really interested for a little while. The minister made a grand and moving picture of the assembling together of the world's hosts at the millennium when the lion and the lamb should lie down together and a little child should lead them. But the pathos, the lesson, the moral of the great spectacle were lost upon the boy; he only thought of the conspicuousness of the principal character before the on-looking nations; his face lit with the thought, and he said to himself that he wished he could be that child, if it was a tame lion.

Now he lapsed into suffering again, as the dry argument was resumed. Presently he bethought him of a treasure he had and got

it out. It was a large black beetle with formidable jaws—a
"pinch-bug," he called it. It was in a percussion-cap box. The first
thing the beetle did was to take him by the finger. A natural fillip
followed, the beetle went floundering into the aisle and lit on its
back, and the hurt finger went into the boy's mouth. The beetle lay
there working its helpless legs, unable to turn over. Tom eyed it,
and longed for it; but it was safe out of his reach. Other people
uninterested in the sermon, found relief in the beetle, and they eyed
it too. Presently a vagrant poodle dog came idling along, sad at
heart, lazy with the summer softness and the quiet, weary of
captivity, sighing for change. He spied the beetle; the drooping tail
lifted and wagged. He surveyed the prize; walked around it; smelt
at it from a safe distance; walked around it again; grew bolder, and
took a closer smell; then lifted his lip and made a gingerly snatch
at it, just missing it; made another, and another; began to enjoy
the diversion; subsided to his stomach with the beetle between his
paws, and continued his experiments; grew weary at last, and then
indifferent and absent-minded. His head nodded, and little by little
his chin descended and touched the enemy, who seized it. There
was a sharp yelp, a flirt of the poodle's head, and the beetle fell a
couple of yards away, and lit on its back once more. The
neighboring spectators shook with a gentle inward joy, several faces
went behind fans and handkerchiefs, and Tom was entirely happy.
The dog looked foolish, and probably felt so; but there was
resentment in his heart, too, and a craving for revenge. So he went
to the beetle and began a wary attack on it again; jumping at it
from every point of a circle, lighting with his fore paws within an
inch of the creature, making even closer snatches at it with his
teeth, and jerking his head till his ears flapped again. But he grew
tired once more, after a while; tried to amuse himself with a fly but
found no relief; followed an ant around, with his nose close to the
floor, and quickly wearied of that; yawned, sighed, forgot the beetle
entirely, and sat down on it! Then there was a wild yelp of agony
and the poodle went sailing up the aisle; the yelps continued, and
so did the dog; he crossed the house in front of the altar; he flew
down the other aisle; he crossed before the doors; he clamored up
the home-stretch; his anguish grew with his progress, till presently
he was but a woolly comet moving in its orbit with the gleam and
the speed of light. At last the frantic sufferer sheered from its
course, and sprang into its master's lap; he flung it out of the
window, and the voice of distress quickly thinned away and died in
the distance.

By this time the whole church was red-faced and suffocating with
suppressed laughter, and the sermon had come to a dead stand-
still. The discourse was resumed presently, but it went lame and
halting, all possibility of impressiveness being at an end; for even
the gravest sentiments were constantly being received with a

smothered burst of unholy mirth, under cover of some remote
pew-back, as if the poor parson had said a rarely facetious thing. It
was a genuine relief to the whole congregation when the ordeal was
over and the benediction pronounced.

Tom Sawyer went home quite cheerful, thinking to himself that
there was some satisfaction about divine service when there was a
bit of variety in it. He had but one marring thought: he was willing
that the dog should play with his pinch-bug, but he did not think
it was upright in him to carry it off.

CHAPTER VI

Monday morning found Tom Sawyer miserable. Monday
morning always found him so—because it began another week's
slow suffering in school. He generally began that day with wishing
he had had no intervening holiday, it made the going into captivity
and fetters again so much more odious.

Tom lay thinking. Presently it occurred to him that he wished he
was sick; then he could stay home from school. Here was a vague
possibility. He canvassed his system. No ailment was found, and he
investigated again. This time he thought he could detect colicky
symptoms, and he began to encourage them with considerable
hope. But they soon grew feeble, and presently died wholly away.
He reflected further. Suddenly he discovered something. One of
his upper front teeth was loose. This was lucky; he was about to
begin to groan, as a "starter," as he called it, when it occurred to
him that if he came into court with that argument, his aunt would
pull it out, and that would hurt. So he thought he would hold the
tooth in reserve for the present, and seek further. Nothing offered
for some little time, and then he remembered hearing the doctor
tell about a certain thing that laid up a patient for two or three
weeks and threatened to make him lose a finger. So the boy eagerly
drew his sore toe from under the sheet and held it up for
inspection. But now he did not know the necessary symptoms.
However, it seemed well worth while to chance it, so he fell to
groaning with considerable spirit.

But Sid slept on unconscious.

Tom groaned louder, and fancied that he began to feel pain in
the toe.

No result from Sid.

Tom was panting with his exertions by this time. He took a rest
and then swelled himself up and fetched a succession of admirable
groans.

Sid snored on.

Tom was aggravated. He said, "Sid, Sid!" and shook him. This
course worked well, and Tom began to groan again. Sid yawned,
stretched, then brought himself up on his elbow with a snort, and

began to stare at Tom. Tom went on groaning. Sid said:
"Tom! Say, Tom!" [No response.] "Here Tom! *Tom!* What is the matter, Tom?" And he shook him and looked in his face anxiously.

Tom moaned out:
"O don't, Sid. Don't joggle me."
"Why what's the matter Tom? I must call auntie."
"No—never mind. It'll be over by and by, maybe. Don't call anybody."
"But I must! *Don't* groan so, Tom, it's awful. How long you been this way?"
"Hours. Ouch! O don't stir so, Sid, you'll kill me."
"Tom, why didn't you wake me sooner? O, Tom, *don't!* It makes my flesh crawl to hear you. Tom, what *is* the matter?"
"I forgive you everything, Sid. [Groan.] Everything you've ever done to me. When I'm gone—"
"O, Tom, you ain't dying, are you? Don't, Tom—O, don't. Maybe—"
"I forgive everybody, Sid. [Groan.] Tell 'em so, Sid. And Sid, you give my window-sash and my cat with one eye to that new girl that's come to town, and tell her—"

But Sid had snatched his clothes and gone. Tom was suffering in reality, now, so handsomely was his imagination working, and so his groans had gathered quite a genuine tone.

Sid flew down stairs and said:
"O, Aunt Polly, come! Tom's dying!"
"Dying!"
"Yes'm. Don't wait—come quick!"
"Rubbage! I don't believe it!"

But she fled up stairs, nevertheless, with Sid and Mary at her heels. And her face grew white, too, and her lip trembled. When she reached the bedside she gasped out:
"You Tom! Tom, what's the matter with you?"
"O, auntie, I'm—"
"What's the matter with you—what *is* the matter with you, child?"
"O auntie, my sore toe's mortified!"

The old lady sank down into a chair and laughed a little, then cried a little, then did both together. This restored her and she said:
"Tom, what a turn you did give me. Now you shut up that nonsense and climb out of this."

The groans ceased and the pain vanished from the toe. The boy felt a little foolish, and he said:
"Aunt Polly it *seemed* mortified, and it hurt so I never minded my tooth at all."
"Your tooth, indeed! What's the matter with your tooth?"
"One of them's loose, and it aches perfectly awful."
"There, there, now, don't begin that groaning again. Open your

mouth. Well—your tooth *is* loose, but you're not going to die about that. Mary get me a silk thread, and a chunk of fire out of the kitchen."

Tom said:

"O, please auntie, don't pull it out. It don't hurt any more. I wish I may never stir if it does. Please don't, auntie. *I* don't want to stay home from school."

"Oh, you don't, don't you? So all this row was because you thought you'd get to stay home from school and go fishing? Tom, Tom, I love you so, and you seem to try every way you can to break my old heart with your outrageousness." By this time the dental instruments were ready. The old lady made one end of the silk thread fast to Tom's tooth with a loop and tied the other to the bed-post. Then she seized the chunk of fire and suddenly thrust it almost into the boy's face. The tooth hung dangling by the bed-post, now.

But all trials bring their compensations. As Tom wended to school after breakfast, he was the envy of every boy he met because the gap in his upper row of teeth enabled him to expectorate in a new and admirable way. He gathered quite a following of lads interested in the exhibition; and one that had cut his finger and had been a centre of fascination and homage up to this time, now found himself suddenly without an adherent, and shorn of his glory. His heart was heavy, and he said with a disdain which he did not feel, that it wasn't anything to spit like Tom Sawyer; but another boy said "Sour grapes!" and he wandered away a dismantled hero.

Shortly Tom came upon the juvenile pariah of the village, Huckleberry Finn, son of the town drunkard. Huckleberry was cordially hated and dreaded by all the mothers of the town, because he was idle, and lawless, and vulgar and bad—and because all their children admired him so, and delighted in his forbidden society, and wished they dared to be like him. Tom was like the rest of the respectable boys, in that he envied Huckleberry his gaudy outcast condition, and was under strict orders not to play with him. So he played with him every time he got a chance. Huckleberry was always dressed in the cast-off clothes of full-grown men, and they were in perennial bloom and fluttering with rags. His hat was a vast ruin with a wide crescent lopped out of its brim; his coat, when he wore one, hung nearly to his heels and had the rearward buttons far down the back; but one suspender supported his trousers; the seat of the trousers bagged low and contained nothing; the fringed legs dragged in the dirt when not rolled up.

Huckleberry came and went, at his own free will. He slept on door-steps in fine weather and in empty hogsheads in wet; he did not have to go to school or to church, or call any being master or obey anybody; he could go fishing or swimming when and where he

chose, and stay as long as it suited him; nobody forbade him to
fight; he could sit up as late as he pleased; he was always the first
boy that went barefoot in the spring and the last to resume leather
in the fall; he never had to wash, nor put on clean clothes; he could
swear wonderfully. In a word, everything that goes to make life
precious, that boy had. So thought every harassed, hampered,
respectable boy in St. Petersburgh.

Tom hailed the romantic outcast:

"Hello, Huckleberry!"

"Hello yourself, and see how you like it."

"What's that you got?"

"Dead cat."

"Lemme see him Huck. My, he's pretty stiff. Where'd you get
him?"

"Bought him off'n a boy."

"What did you give?"

"I give a blue ticket and a bladder that I got at the slaughter
house."

"Where'd you get the blue ticket?"

"Bought it off'n Ben Rogers two weeks ago for a hoop-stick."

"Say—what is dead cats good for, Huck?"

"Good for? Cure warts with."

"No! Is that so? I know something that's better."

"I bet you don't. What is it?"

"Why, spunk-water."

"Spunk-water! I wouldn't give a dern for spunk-water."

"You wouldn't wouldn't you? D'you ever try it?"

"No, I hain't. But Bob Tanner did."

"Who told you so!"

"Why he told Jeff Thatcher, and Jeff told Johnny Baker, and
Johnny told Jim Hollis, and Jim told Ben Rogers, and Ben told a
nigger, and the nigger told me. There now!"

"Well, what of it? They'll all lie. Leastways all but the nigger. I
don't know him. But I never see a nigger that *wouldn't* lie.
Shucks! Now you tell me how Bob Tanner done it, Huck."

"Why he took and dipped his hand in a rotten stump where the
rain water was."

"In the day time?"

"Certainly."

"With his face to the stump?"

"Yes. Least I reckon so."

"Did he *say* anything?"

"I don't reckon he did. I don't know."

"Aha! Talk about trying to cure warts with spunk-water such a
blame fool way as that! Why that ain't a going to do any good. You
got to go all by yourself, to the middle of the woods, where you know
there's a spunk-water stump, and just as it's midnight you back up

against the stump and jam your hand in and say:
>   "Barley-corn, Barley-corn, injun-meal shorts,
>   Spunk-water, spunk-water, swaller these warts."

and then walk away quick, eleven steps, with your eyes shut, and
then turn around three times and walk home without speaking to
anybody. Because if you speak the charm's busted."

"Well that sounds like a good way; but that ain't the way Bob
Tanner done."

"No, sir, you can bet he didn't, becuz he's the wartiest boy in this
town; and he wouldn't have a wart on him if he'd knowed how to
work spunk-water. I've took off thousands of warts off of my hands
that way Huck. I play with frogs so much that I've always got
considerable many warts. Sometimes I take 'em off with a bean."

"Yes, bean's good. I've done that."

"Have you? What's your way?"

"You take and split the bean, and cut the wart so as to get some
blood, and then you put the blood on one piece of the bean and take
and dig a hole and bury it 'bout midnight at the cross-roads in the
dark of the moon, and then you burn up the rest of the bean. You see
that piece that's got the blood on it will keep drawing and drawing,
trying to fetch the other piece to it, and so that helps the blood to
draw the wart, and pretty soon off she comes."

"Yes that's it Huck—that's it; though when you're burying it if
you say 'Down bean; off wart; come no more to bother me!' it's
better. That's the way Joe Harper does, and he's been nearly to
Coonville and most everywheres. But say—how do you cure 'em with
dead cats?"

"Why you take your cat and go and get in the graveyard 'long
about midnight when somebody that was wicked has been buried;
and when it's midnight a devil will come, or maybe two or three, but
you can't see 'em, you can only hear something like the wind, or
maybe hear 'em talk; and when they're taking that feller away, you
heave your cat after 'em and say 'Devil follow corpse, cat follow
devil, warts follow cat, I'm done with ye!' That'll fetch *any* wart."

"Sounds right. D'you ever try it, Huck?"

"No, but old mother Hopkins told me."

"Well I reckon it's so, then. Becuz they say she's a witch."

"Say! Why Tom I *know* she is. She witched pap. Pap says so his
own self. He come along one day, and he see she was witching him,
so he took up a rock, and if she hadn't dodged, he'd a got her. Well
that very night he rolled off'n a shed where' he was a layin drunk,
and broke his arm."

"Why that's awful. How did he know she was a witching him."

"Lord, pap can tell, easy. Pap says when they keep looking at you
right stiddy, they're a witching you. Specially if they mumble. Becuz
when they mumble they're saying the Lord's Prayer back-ards."

"Say, Hucky, when you going to try the cat?"

"To-night. I reckon they'll come after old Hoss Williams
to-night."

"But they buried him Saturday. Didn't they get him Saturday
night?"

"Why how you talk! How could their charms work till midnight?
—and *then* it's Sunday. Devils don't slosh around much of a
Sunday, I don't reckon."

"I never thought of that. That's so. Lemme go with you?"

"Of course—if you ain't afeard."

"Afeard! 'Tain't likely. Will you meow?"

"Yes—and you meow back, if you get a chance. Last time, you
kep' me a meowing around till old Hays went to throwing rocks at
me and says 'Dern that cat!' and so I hove a brick through his
window—but don't you tell."

"I won't. I couldn't meow that night, becuz auntie was watching
me, but I'll meow this time. Say—what's that?"

"Nothing but a tick."

"Where'd you get him?"

"Out in the woods."

"What'll you take for him?"

"I don't know. I don't want to sell him."

"All right. It's a mighty small tick, anyway."

"O, anybody can run a tick down that don't belong to them. I'm
satisfied with it. It's a good enough tick for me."

"Sho, there's ticks a plenty. I could have a thousand of 'em if I
wanted to."

"Well why don't you? Becuz you know mighty well you can't.
This is a pretty early tick, I reckon. It's the first one I've seen this
year."

"Say Huck—I'll give you my tooth for him."

"Less see it."

Tom got out a bit of paper and carefully unrolled it. Huckleberry
viewed it wistfully. The temptation was very strong. At last he said:

"Is it genuwyne?"

Tom lifted his lip and showed the vacancy.

"Well, all right," said Huckleberry, "it's a trade."

Tom enclosed the tick in the percussion-cap box that had lately
been the pinch-bug's prison, and the boys separated, each feeling
wealthier than before.

When Tom reached the little isolated frame School-house, he
strode in briskly, with the manner of one who had come with all
honest speed. He hung his hat on a peg and flung himself into his
seat with business-like alacrity. The master, throned on high in his
great splint-bottom arm-chair, was dozing, lulled by the drowsy hum
of study. The interruption roused him.

"Thomas Sawyer!"

Tom knew that when his name was pronounced in full, it meant trouble.

"Sir!"

"Come up here. Now sir, why are you late again, as usual?"

Tom was about to take refuge in a lie, when he saw two long tails of yellow hair hanging down a back that he recognized by the electric sympathy of love; and by that form was *the only vacant place* on the girl's side of the school-house. He instantly said:

"I STOPPED TO TALK WITH HUCKLEBERRY FINN!"

The master's pulse stood still, and he stared helplessly. The buzz of study ceased. The pupils wondered if this fool-hardy boy had lost his mind. The master said:

"You—you did what?"

"Stopped to talk with Huckleberry Finn."

There was no mistaking the words.

"Thomas Sawyer, this is the most astounding confession I have ever listened to. No mere ferule will answer for this offence. Take off your jacket."

The master's arm performed until it was tired and the stock of switches notably diminished. Then the order followed:

"Now sir, go and sit with the *girls!* And let this be a warning to you."

The titter that rippled around the room appeared to abash the boy, but in reality that result was caused rather more by his worshipful awe of his unknown idol and the dread pleasure that lay in his high good fortune. He sat down upon the end of the pine bench and the girl hitched herself away from him with a toss of her head. Nudges and winks and whispers traversed the room, but Tom sat still, with his arms upon the long, low desk before him, and seemed to study his book.

By and by attention ceased from him, and the accustomed school murmur rose upon the dull air once more. Presently the boy began to steal furtive glances at the girl. She observed it, "made a mouth" at him and gave him the back of her head for the space of a minute. When she cautiously faced around again, a peach lay before her. She thrust it away. Tom gently put it back. She thrust it away, again, but with less animosity. Tom patiently returned it to its place. Then she let it remain. Tom scrawled on his slate, "Please take it— I got more." The girl glanced at the words, but made no sign. Now the boy began to draw something on the slate, hiding his work with his left hand. For a time the girl refused to notice; but her human curiosity presently began to manifest itself by hardly perceptible signs. The boy worked on, apparently unconcious. The girl made a sort of non-committal attempt to see, but the boy did not betray that he was aware of it. At last she gave in and hesitatingly whispered:

"Let me see it."

Tom partly uncovered a dismal caricature of a house with two

gable ends to it and a cork-screw of smoke issuing from the chimney.
Then the girl's interest began to fasten itself upon the work and she
forgot everything else. When it was finished, she gazed a moment,
then whispered:

"It's nice—make a man."

The artist erected a man in the front yard, that resembled a
derrick. He could have stepped over the house; but the girl was not
hypercritical; she was satisfied with the monster, and whispered:

"It's a beautiful man—now make me coming along."

Tom drew an hour-glass with a full moon and straw limbs to it
and armed the spreading fingers with a portentous fan. The girl
said:

"It's ever so nice—I wish I could draw."

"It's easy," whispered Tom, "I'll learn you."

"O, will you? When?"

"At noon. Do you go home to dinner?"

"I'll stay if you will."

"Good,—that's a whack. What's your name?"

"Becky Thatcher. What's yours? Oh, I know. It's Thomas
Sawyer."

"That's the name they lick me by. I'm Tom when I'm good. You
call me Tom, will you?"

"Yes."

Now Tom began to scrawl something on the slate, hiding the
words from the girl. But she was not backward this time. She begged
to see. Tom said:

"Oh it ain't anything."

"Yes it is."

"No it ain't. You don't want to see."

"Yes I do, indeed I do. Please let me."

"You'll tell."

"No I won't—deed and deed and double deed I won't."

"You won't tell anybody at all? Ever, as long as you live?"

"No I won't ever tell *anybody*. Now let me."

"Oh, *you* don't want to see!"

"Now that you treat me so, I *will* see." And she put her small hand
upon his and a little scuffle ensued, Tom pretending to resist in
earnest but letting his hand slip by degrees till these words were
revealed: *"I love you."*

"O, you bad thing!" And she hit his hand a smart rap but
reddened and looked pleased, nevertheless.

Just at this juncture the boy felt a low, fateful grip closing on his
ear, and a steady lifting impulse. In that vise he was borne across the
house and deposited in his own seat, under a peppering fire of
giggles from the whole school. Then the master stood over him
during a few awful moments, and finally moved away to his throne
without saying a word. But although Tom's ear tingled, his heart

was jubilant.

As the school quieted down Tom made an honest effort to study, but the turmoil within him was too great. In turn he took his place in the reading class and made a botch of it; then in the geography class and turned lakes into mountains, mountains into rivers, and rivers into continents, till chaos was come again; then in the spelling class, and got "turned down," by a succession of mere baby words till he brought up at the foot and yielded up the pewter medal which he had worn with ostentation for months.

CHAPTER VII

The harder Tom tried to fasten his mind on his book, the more his ideas wandered. So at last, with a sigh and a yawn, he gave it up. It seemed to him that the noon recess would never come. The air was utterly dead. There was not a breath stirring. It was the sleepiest of sleepy days. The drowsing murmur of the five and twenty studying scholars, soothed the soul like the spell that is in the murmur of bees. Away off in the flaming sunshine, Cardiff Hill lifted its soft green sides through a shimmering veil of heat, tinted with the purple of distance; a few birds floated on lazy wing high in the air; no other living thing was visible but some cows, and they were asleep. Tom's heart ached to be free, or else to have something of interest to do to pass the dreary time. His hand wandered into his pocket and his face lit up with a glow of gratitude that was prayer, though he did not know it. Then furtively the percussion-cap box came out. He released the tick and put him on the long flat desk. The creature probably glowed with a gratitude that amounted to prayer, too, at this moment, but it was premature: for when he started thankfully to travel off, Tom turned him aside with a pin and made him take a new direction.

Tom's bosom friend sat next him, suffering just as Tom had been, and now he was deeply and gratefully interested in this entertainment in an instant. This bosom friend was Joe Harper. The two boys were sworn friends all the week, and embattled enemies on Saturdays. Joe took a pin out of his lappel and began to assist in exercising the prisoner. The sport grew in interest momently. Soon Tom said that they were interfering with each other, and neither getting the fullest benefit of the tick. So he put Joe's slate on the desk and drew a line down the middle of it from top to bottom.

"Now," said he, "as long as he is on your side you can stir him up and I'll let him alone; but if you let him get away and get on my side, you're to leave him alone as long as I can keep him from crossing over."

"All right, go ahead; start him up."

The tick escaped from Tom, presently, and crossed the equator. Joe harassed him a while, and then he got away and crossed back

again. This change of base occurred often. While one boy was
worrying the tick with absorbing interest, the other would look on
with interest as strong, the two heads bowed together over the slate,
and the two souls dead to all things else. At last luck seemed to settle
and abide with Joe. The tick tried this, that, and the other course,
and got as excited and as anxious as the boys themselves, but time
and again just as he would have victory in his very grasp, so to speak,
and Tom's fingers would be twitching to begin, Joe's pin would
deftly head him off, and keep possession. At last Tom could stand
it no longer. The temptation was too strong. So he reached out and
lent a hand with his pin. Joe was angry in a moment. Said he:

"Tom, you let him alone."

"I only just want to stir him up a little, Joe."

"No, sir, it ain't fair; you just let him alone."

"Blame it, I ain't going to stir him much."

"Let him alone, I tell you!"

"I won't!"

"You shall—he's on my side of the line."

"Look here, Joe Harper, whose is that tick?"

"*I* don't care whose tick he is—he's on my side of the line, and
you shan't touch him."

"Well I'll just bet I will, though. He's my tick and I'll do what I
blame please with him or die!"

A tremendous whack came down on Tom's shoulders, and its
duplicate on Joe's; and for the space of two minutes the dust
continued to fly from the two jackets and the whole school to enjoy
it. The boys had been too absorbed to notice the hush that had stolen
upon the school a while before when the master came tip-toeing
down the room and stood over them. He had contemplated a good
part of the performance before he contributed his bit of variety to it.

When school broke up at noon, Tom flew to Becky Thatcher, and
whispered in her ear:

"Put on your bonnet and let on you're going home; and when you
get to the corner, give the rest of 'em the slip, and turn down through
the lane and come back. I'll go the other way and come it over 'em
the same way."

So the one went off with one group of scholars, and the other with
another: In a little while the two met at the bottom of the lane, and
when they reached the school they had it all to themselves. Then
they sat together, with a slate before them, and Tom gave Becky the
pencil and held her hand in his, guiding it, and so created another
surprising house. When the interest in art began to wane, the two fell
to talking. Tom was swimming in bliss. He said:

"Do you love rats?"

"No! I hate them!"

"Well, I do too—*live* ones. But I mean dead ones, to swing
round your head with a string."

"No, I don't care for rats much, anyway. What *I* like is chewing-gum."

"O, I should say so! I wish I had some now."

"Do you? I've got some. I'll let you chew it awhile, but you must give it back to me."

That was agreeable, so they chewed it turn about, and dangled their legs against the bench in excess of contentment.

"Was you ever at a circus?" said Tom.

"Yes, and my pa's going to take me again some time, if I'm good."

"I been to the circus three or four times—lots of times. Church ain't shucks to a circus. There's things going on at a circus all the time. I'm going to be a clown in a circus when I grow up."

"O, are you! That will be nice. They're so lovely, all spotted up."

"Yes, that's so. And they get slathers of money—most a dollar a day, Ben Rogers says. Say, Becky, was you ever engaged?"

"What's that?"

"Why, engaged to be married."

"No."

"Would you like to?"

"I reckon so. I don't know. What is it like?"

"Like? Why it ain't like anything. You only just tell a boy you won't ever have any body but him: ever ever *ever,* and then you kiss and that's all. Anybody can do it."

"Kiss? What do you kiss for?"

"Why that, you know, is to—well, they always do that."

"Everybody?"

"Why yes, everybody that's in love with each other. Do you remember what I wrote on the slate?"

"Ye—yes."

"What was it?"

"I shant tell you."

"Shall I tell *you?*"

"Ye-yes—but some other time."

"No, now."

"No, not now—to-morrow."

"O, no, *now.* Please Becky—I'll whisper it, I'll whisper it ever so easy."

Becky hesitating, Tom took silence for consent, and passed his arm about her waist and whispered the tale ever so softly, with his mouth close to her ear. And then he added:

"Now you whisper it to me—just the same."

She resisted, for a while, and then said:

"You turn your face away so you can't see, and then I will. But you mustn't ever tell anybody—*will* you, Tom? Now you won't, *will* you?"

"No, indeed indeed I won't. Now Becky."

He turned his face away. She bent timidly around till her breath stirred his curls and whispered, "I—love—you!"

Then she sprang away and ran around and around the desks and benches, with Tom after her, and took refuge in a corner at last, with her little white apron to her face. Tom clasped her about her neck and pleaded:

"Now Becky, it's all done—all over but the kiss. Don't you be afraid of that—it ain't anything at all. Please, Becky."—And he tugged at her apron and the hands.

By and by she gave up, and let her hands drop; her face, all glowing with the struggle, came up and submitted. Tom kissed the red lips and said:

"Now it's all done, Becky. And always after this, you know, you ain't ever to love anybody but me, and you ain't ever to marry anybody but me, never never and forever. Will you?"

"No, I'll never love anybody but you, Tom, and I'll never marry anybody but you—and you ain't to ever marry anybody but me, either."

"Certainly. Of course. That's *part* of it. And always coming to school or when we're going home, you're to walk with me, when there ain't anybody looking—and you choose me and I choose you at parties, because that's the way you do when you're engaged."

"It's so nice. I never heard of it before."

"O, its ever so gay! Why me and Amy Lawrence—"

The big eyes told Tom his blunder and he stopped, confused.

"O, Tom! Then I ain't the first you've been engaged to!"

The child began to cry. Tom said:

"O don't cry, Becky, I don't care for her any more."

"Yes you do, Tom,—you know you do."

Tom tried to put his arm about her neck, but she pushed him away and turned her face to the wall, and went on crying. Tom tried again, with soothing words in his mouth, and was repulsed again. Then his pride was up and he strode away and went outside. He stood about, restless and uneasy, for a while, glancing at the door, every now and then, hoping she would repent and come to find him. But she did not. Then he began to feel badly and fear that he was in the wrong. It was a hard struggle with him to make new advances, now, but he nerved himself to it and entered. She was still standing back there in the corner, sobbing, with her face to the wall. Tom's heart smote him. He went to her and stood a moment, not knowing exactly how to proceed. Then he said hesitatingly:

"Becky, I—I don't care for anybody but you."

No reply—but sobs.

"Becky,"—pleadingly. "Becky, won't you say something?"

More sobs.

Tom got out his chiefest jewel, a brass knob from the top of an andiron, and passed it around her so that she could see it, and said:

"Please, Becky, won't you take it?"

She struck it to the floor. Then Tom marched out of the house
and over the hills and far away, to return to school no more that day.
Presently Becky began to suspect. She ran to the door; he was not
in sight; she flew around to the play-yard; he was not there. Then
she called:

"Tom! Come back Tom!"

She listened intently, but there was no answer. She had no
companions but silence and loneliness. So she sat down to cry again
and upbraid herself; and by this time the scholars began to gather
again, and she had to hide her griefs and still her broken
heart and take up the cross of a long, dreary, aching afternoon, with
none among the strangers about her to exchange sorrows with.

CHAPTER VIII

Tom dodged hither and thither through lanes until he was well
out of the track of returning scholars, and then fell into a moody
jog. He crossed a small "branch" two or three times, because of
prevailing juvenile superstition that to cross water baffled pursuit.
Half an hour later he was disappearing behind the Douglas
mansion on the summit of Cardiff Hill, and the school-house was
hardly distinguishable away off in the valley behind him. He
entered a dense wood, picked his pathless way to the centre of it,
and sat down on a mossy spot under a spreading oak. There was
not even a zephyr stirring; the dead noonday heat had even stilled
the songs of the birds; nature lay in a trance that was broken by
no sound but the occasional far-off hammering of a woodpecker,
and this seemed to render the pervading silence and sense of
loneliness the more profound. The boy's soul was steeped in
melancholy; his feelings were in happy accord with his
surroundings. He sat long with his elbows on his knees and his
chin in his hands, meditating. It seemed to him that life was but
a trouble, at best, and he more than half envied Jimmy Hodges,
so lately released; it must be very peaceful, he thought, to lie and
slumber and dream forever and ever, with the wind whispering
through the trees and caressing the grass and the flowers over the
grave, and nothing to bother and grieve about, ever any more. If
he only had a clean Sunday-school record he could be willing to go,
and be done with it all. Now as to this girl. What had he done?
Nothing. He had meant the best in the world, and been treated like
a dog—like a very dog. She would be sorry some day—maybe when
it was too late. Ah, if he could only die *temporarily!*

But the elastic heart of youth cannot be compressed into one
constrained shape long at a time. Tom presently began to drift
insensibly back into the concerns of this life again. What if he
turned his back, now, and disappeared mysteriously? What if he
went away—ever so far away, into unknown countries beyond the

seas—and never come back any more! How would she feel then!
The idea of being a clown recurred to him now, only to fill him with
disgust. For frivolity and jokes and spotted tights were an offense,
when they intruded themselves upon a spirit that was exalted into
the vague august realm of the romantic. No, he would be a soldier,
and return after long years, all war-worn and illustrious. No—
better still, he would join the Indians, and hunt buffaloes and go
on the warpath in the mountain ranges and the trackless great
plains of the Far West, and away in the future come back a great
chief, bristling with feathers, hideous with paint, and prance into
Sunday-school, some drowsy summer morning, with a
blood-curdling war-whoop, and sear the eye-balls of all his
companions with unappeasable envy. But no, there was something
gaudier even than this. He would be a pirate! That was it! *Now*
his future lay plain before him, and glowing with unimaginable
splendor. How his name would fill the world, and make people
shudder! How gloriously he would go plowing the dancing seas, in
his long, low, black-hulled racer, the "Spirit of the Storm," with
his grisly flag flying at the fore! And at the zenith of his time, how
he would suddenly appear at the old village and stalk into church,
brown and weather-beaten, in his black velvet doublet and trunks,
his great jack-boots, his crimson sash, his belt bristling with horse-
pistols, his crime-rusted cutlass at his side, his slouch hat with
waving plumes, his black flag unfurled, with the skull and crossbones on it, and hear with swelling ecstasy the whisperings, "It's
Tom Sawyer the Pirate!—the Black Avenger of the Spanish Main!"

    Yes, it was settled; his career was determined. He would run
away from home and enter upon it. He would start the very next
morning. Therefore he must now begin to get ready. He would
collect his resources together. He went to a rotten log near at hand
and began to dig under one end of it with his Barlow knife. He
soon struck wood that sounded hollow. He put his hand there and
uttered this incantation impressively:

    "What hasn't come here, *come!* What's here, *stay* here!"

    Then he scraped away the dirt, and exposed a pine shingle. He
took it up and disclosed a shapely little treasure-house whose
bottom and sides were of shingles. In it lay a marble. Tom's
astonishment was boundless! He scratched his head with a
perplexed air, and said:

    "Well, that beats anything?"

    Then he tossed the marble away pettishly, and stood cogitating.
The truth was, that a superstition of his had failed, here, which he
and his comrades had always looked upon as infallible. If you
buried a marble with certain necessary incantations, and left it
alone a fortnight, and then opened the place with the incantation
he had just used, you would find that all the marbles you had ever
lost had gathered themselves together there, meantime, no matter
how widely they had been separated. But now, this thing had

actually and unquestionably failed. Tom's whole structure of faith
was shaken to its foundations. He had many a time heard of this
thing succeeding, but never of its failing before. It did not occur
to him that he had tried it several times before, himself, but could
never find the hiding places afterwards. He puzzled over the matter
some time, and finally decided that some witch had interfered and
broken the charm. He thought he would satisfy himself on that
point; so he searched around till he found a small sandy spot with
a little funnel-shaped depression in it. He laid himself down and
put his mouth close to this depression and called:

"Doodle-bug, doodle-bug, tell me what I want to know!
Doodle-bug, doodle-bug tell me what I want to know!"

The sand began to work, and presently a small black bug
appeared for a second and then darted under again in a fright.

"He dasn't tell! So it *was* a witch that done it. I just knowed it."

He well knew the futility of trying to contend against witches,
so he gave up discouraged. But it occurred to him that he might
as well have the marble he had just thrown away, and therefore
he went and made a patient search for it. But he could not find it.
Now he went back to his treasure-house and carefully placed
himself just as he had been standing when he tossed the marble
away; then he took another marble from his pocket and tossed it
in the same way, saying:

"Brother go find your brother!"

He watched where it stopped, and went there and looked. But
it must have fallen short or gone too far; so he tried twice more.
The last repetition was successful. The two marbles lay within a
foot of each other.

Just here the blast of a toy tin trumpet came faintly down the
green aisles of the forest. Tom flung off his jacket and trousers,
turned a suspender into a belt, raked away some brush behind the
rotten log, disclosing a rude bow and arrow, a lath sword and a
tin trumpet, and in a moment had seized these things and bounded
away, bare legged, with fluttering shirt. He presently halted under
a great elm, blew an answering blast, and then began to tip-toe
and look warily out, this way and that. He said cautiously—to an
imaginary company:

"Hold, my merry men! Keep hid till I blow."

Now appeared Joe Harper, as airily clad and elaborately armed
as Tom. Tom called:

"Hold! Who come here into Sherwood Forest without my pass?"

"Guy of Guisborne wants no man's pass. Who art thou that—
that—"

"Dares to hold such language," said Tom, prompting—for they
talked "by the book," from memory.

"Who art thou that dares to hold such language?"

"I, indeed! I am Robin Hood, as thy caitiff carcase soon shall know."

"Then art thou indeed that famous outlaw? Right gladly will I dispute with thee the passes of the merry wood. Have at thee!"

They took their lath swords, dumped their other traps on the ground, struck a fencing attitude, foot to foot, and began a grave, careful combat, "two up and two down." Presently Tom said:

"Now if you've got the hang, go it lively!"

So they "went it lively," panting and perspiring with the work. By and by Tom shouted:

"Fall! fall! Why don't you fall?"

"I shan't! Why don't you fall yourself? You're getting the worst of it."

"Why that ain't anything. *I* can't fall; that ain't the way it is in the book. The book says 'Then with one back-handed stroke he slew poor Guy of Guisborne.' You're to turn around and let me hit you in the back."

There was no getting around the authorities, so Joe turned, received the whack and fell.

"Now," said Joe, getting up, "You got to let me kill *you*. That's fair."

"Why I can't do that, it ain't in the book."

"Well it's blamed mean,—that's all."

"Well, say, Joe, you can be Friar Tuck or Much the miller's son and lam me with a quarter-staff; or I'll be the Sheriff of Nottingham and you be Robin Hood a little while and kill me."

This was satisfactory, and so these adventures were carried out. Then Tom became Robin Hood again, and was allowed by the treacherous nun to bleed his strength away through his neglected wound. And at last Joe, representing a whole tribe of weeping outlaws, dragged him sadly forth, gave his bow into his feeble hands, and Tom said, "Where this arrow falls, there bury poor Robin Hood under the greenwood tree." Then he shot the arrow and fell back and would have died but he lit on a nettle and sprang up too gaily for a corpse.

The boys dressed themselves, hid their accoutrements, and went off grieving that there were no outlaws any more, and wondering what modern civilization could claim to have done to compensate for their loss. They said they would rather be outlaws a year in Sherwood Forest than President of the United States forever.

CHAPTER IX

At half past nine, that night, Tom and Sid were sent to bed, as usual. They said their prayers, and Sid was soon asleep. Tom lay awake and waited, in restless impatience. When it seemed to him that it must be nearly daylight, he heard the clock strike ten! This was despair. He would have tossed and fidgeted, as his nerves

demanded, but he was afraid he might wake Sid. So he lay still,
and stared up into the dark. Everything was dismally still. By and
by, out of the stillness, little, scarcely preceptible noises began to
emphasize themselves. The ticking of the clock began to bring
itself into notice. Old beams began to crack mysteriously. The
stairs creaked faintly. Evidently spirits were abroad. A measured,
muffled snore issued from Aunt Polly's chamber. And now the
tiresome chirping of a cricket that no human ingenuity could
locate, began. Next the ghastly ticking of a death-watch in the wall
at the bed's head made Tom shudder—it meant that somebody's
days were numbered. Then the howl of a far-off dog rose on the
night air, and was answered by a fainter howl from a remoter
distance. Tom was in an agony. At last he was satisfied that time
had ceased and eternity begun; he began to doze, in spite of
himself; the clock chimed eleven but he did not hear it. And then
there came mingling with his half-formed dreams, a most
melancholy caterwauling. The raising of a neighboring window
disturbed him. A cry of "Scat! you devil!" and the crash of an
empty bottle against the back of his aunt's woodshed brought him
wide awake, and a single minute later he was dressed and out of the
window and creeping along the roof of the "ell" on all fours. He
"meow'd" with caution once or twice, as he went; then jumped to
the roof of the woodshed and thence to the ground. Huckleberry
Finn was there, with his dead cat. The boys moved off and
disappeared in the gloom. At the end of half an hour they were
wading through the tall grass of the graveyard.

It was a graveyard of the old-fashioned western kind. It was on
a hill, about a mile and a half from the village. It had a crazy board
fence around it, which leaned inward in places, and outward the
rest of the time, but stood upright nowhere. Grass and weeds grew
rank over the whole cemetery. All the old graves were sunken in,
there was not a tombstone on the place; round-topped, worm-eaten
boards staggered over the graves, leaning for support and finding
none. "Sacred to the memory of" So-and-So had been painted on
them once, but it could no longer have been read, on the most of
them, now, even if there had been light.

A faint wind moaned through the trees, and Tom feared it might
be the spirits of the dead, complaining at being disturbed. The
boys talked little, and only under their breath, for the time and the
place and the pervading solemnity and silence oppressed their
spirits. They found the sharp new heap they were seeking, and
ensconsced themselves within the protection of three great elms
that grew in a bunch within a few feet of the grave.

Then they waited in silence for what seemed a long time. The
hooting of a distant owl was all the sound that troubled the dead
stillness. Tom's reflections grew oppressive. He must force some
talk. So he said in a whisper:

"Hucky, do you believe the dead people like it for us to be here?"
Huckleberry whispered:
"I wisht I knowed. It's awful solemn like, *ain't* it?"
"I bet it is."
There was a considerable pause, while the boys canvassed this
matter inwardly. Then Tom whispered:
"Say, Hucky—do you reckon Hoss Williams hears us talking?"
"O' course he does. Least his sperrit does."
Tom, after a pause:
"I wish I'd said *Mister* Williams. But I never meant any harm.
Everybody calls him Hoss."
"A body can't be too partic'lar how they talk 'bout these-yer
dead people, Tom."
This was a damper, and conversation died again. Presently Tom
seized his comrade's arm and said:
"Sh!"
"What is it, Tom?" And the two clung together with beating
hearts.
"Sh! There 'tis again! Didn't you hear it?"
"I—"
"There! Now you hear it."
"Lord, Tom they're coming! They're coming, sure. What'll we
do?"
"I dono. Think they'll see us?"
"O, Tom, they can see in the dark, same as cats. I wisht I hadn't
come."
"O, don't be afeard. *I* don't believe they'll bother us. We ain't
doing any harm. If we keep perfectly still, maybe they won't notice
us at all."
"I'll try to, Tom, but Lord I'm all of a shiver."
"Listen!"
The boys bent their heads together and scarcely breathed. A
muffled sound of voices floated up from the far end of the
graveyard.
"Look! See there!" whispered Tom. "What is it?"
"It's devil-fire. O, Tom, this is awful."
Some vague figures approached through the gloom, swinging an
old-fashioned tin lantern that freckled the ground with
innumerable little spangles of light. Presently Huckleberry
whispered with a shudder:
"It's the devils sure enough. Three of 'em! Lordy, Tom, we're
goners! Can you pray?"
"I'll try, but don't you be afeard. They ain't going to hurt us.
Now I lay me down to sleep, I—"
"Sh!"
"What is it, Huck?"
"They're *humans!* One of 'em is, anyway. One of 'em's old Muff

Potter's voice."

"No—tain't so, is it?"

"I bet I know it. Don't you stir nor budge. *He* ain't sharp enough to notice us. Drunk, same as usual, likely—blamed old rip!"

"All right, I'll keep still. Now they're stuck. Can't find it. Here they come again. Now they're hot. Cold again. Hot again. Red hot! They're p'inted right, this time. Say Huck, I know another o' them voices; it's Injun Joe."

"That's so—that murderin' half-breed! I'd druther they was devils a dern sight. What kin they be up to?"

The whispers died wholly out, now, for the three men had reached the grave and stood within a few feet of the boys' hiding-place.

"Here it is," said the third voice; and the owner of it held the lantern up and revealed the face of young Dr. Robinson.

Potter and Injun Joe were carrying a handbarrow with a rope and a couple of shovels on it. They cast down their load and began to open the grave. The doctor put the lantern at the head of the grave and came and sat down with his back against one of the elm trees. He was so close the boys could have touched him.

"Hurry, men!" he said in a low voice; "the moon might come out at any moment."

They growled a response and went on digging. For some time there was no noise but the grating sound of the spades discharging their freight of mould and gravel. It was very monotonous. Finally a spade struck upon the coffin with a dull woody accent, and within another minute or two the men had hoisted it out on the ground. They pried off the lid with their shovels, got out the body and dumped it rudely on the ground. The moon drifted from behind the clouds and exposed the pallid face. The barrow was got ready and the corpse placed on it, covered with a blanket, and bound to its place with the rope. Potter took out a large spring-knife and cut off the dangling end of the rope and then said:

"Now the cussed thing's ready, Sawbones, and you'll just out with another five, or here she stays."

"That's the talk!" said Injun Joe.

"Look here, what does this mean?" said the doctor. "You required your pay in advance, and I've paid you."

"Yes, and you done more than that," said Injun Joe, approaching the doctor, who was now standing. "Five years ago you drove me away from your father's kitchen one night, when I come to ask for something to eat, and you said I warn't there for any good; and when I swore I'd get even with you if it took a hundred years, your father had me jailed for a vagrant. Did you think I'd forget? The Injun blood ain't in me for nothing. And now I've *got* you, and you got to *settle,* you know!"

He was threatening the doctor, with his fist in his face, by this time. The doctor struck out suddenly and stretched the ruffian on the ground. Potter dropped his knife, and exclaimed:

"Here, now, don't you hit my pard!" and the next moment he had grappled with the doctor and the two were struggling with might and main, trampling the grass and tearing the ground with their heels. Injun Joe sprang to his feet, his eyes flaming with passion, snatched up Potter's knife, and went creeping, catlike and stooping, round and round about the combatants, seeking an opportunity. All at once the doctor flung himself free, seized the heavy head board of Williams' grave and felled Potter to the earth with it—and in the same instant the half-breed saw his chance and drove the knife to the hilt in the young man's breast. He reeled and fell partly upon Potter, flooding him with his blood, and in the same moment the clouds blotted out the dreadful spectacle and the two frightened boys went speeding away in the dark.

Presently, when the moon emerged again, Injun Joe was standing over the two forms, contemplating them. The doctor murmured inarticulately, gave a long gasp or two and was still. The half-breed muttered:

"*That* score is settled—damn you."

Then he robbed the body. After which he put the fatal knife in Potter's open right hand, and sat down on the dismantled coffin. Three—four—five minutes passed, and then Potter began to stir and moan. His hand closed upon the knife; he raised it, glanced at it, and let it fall, with a shudder. Then he sat up, pushing the body from him, and gazed at it, and then around him, confusedly. His eyes met Joe's.

"Lord, how is this, Joe?" he said.

"It's a dirty business," said Joe, without moving. "What did you do it for?"

"I! I never done it!"

"Look here! That kind of talk won't wash."

Potter trembled and grew white.

"I thought I'd got sober. I'd no business to drink to-night. But it's in my head yet—worse'n when we started here. I'm all in a muddle; can't recollect anything of it hardly. Tell me, Joe—*honest,* now, old feller—did I do it? Joe, I never meant to—'pon my soul and honor I never meant to, Joe. Tell me how it was Joe. O, it's awful—and him so young and promising."

"Why you two was scuffling, and he fetched you one with the head-board and you fell flat; and then up you come, all reeling and staggering, like, and snatched the knife and jammed it into him, just as he fetched you another awful clip—and here you've laid, as dead as a wedge till now."

"O, I didn't know what I was a doing. I wish I may die this minute if I did. It was all on account of the whisky; and the excitement, I reckon. I never used a weepon in my life before, Joe.

I've fought, but never with weepons. They'll all say that. Joe, don't
tell! Say you won't tell, Joe—that's a good feller. I always like you
Joe, and stood up for you, too. Don't you remember? You *won't*
tell, *will* you Joe?" And the poor creature dropped on his knees
before the stolid murderer, and clasped his appealing hands.

"No, you've always been fair and square with me, Muff Potter,
and I won't go back on you.—There, now, that's as fair as a man
can say."

"O, Joe, you're an angel. I'll bless you for this the longest day I
live." And Potter began to cry.

"Come, now, that's enough of that. This ain't any time for
blubbering. You be off yonder way and I'll go this. Move, now, and
don't leave any tracks behind you."

Potter started on a trot that quickly increased to a run. The
half-breed stood looking after him. He muttered:

"If he's as much stunned with the lick and fuddled with the rum
as he had the look of being, he won't think of the knife till he's
gone so far he'll be afraid to come back after it to such a place by
himself—chicken-heart!"

Two or three minutes later the murdered man, the blanketed
corpse, the lidless coffin and the open grave were under no
inspection but the moon's. The stillness was complete again, too.

CHAPTER X

The two boys flew on and on, toward the village, speechless
with horror. They glanced backward over their shoulders from time
to time, apprehensively, as if they feared they might be followed.
Every stump that started up in their path seemed a man and an
enemy, and made them catch their breath; and as they sped by
some outlying cottages that lay near the village, the barking of
the aroused watch-dogs seemed to give wings to their feet.

"If we can only get to the old tannery, before we break down!"
whispered Tom, in short catches between breaths, "I can't stand it
much longer."

Huckleberry's hard pantings were his only reply, and the boys fixed
their eyes on the goal of their hopes and bent to their work to win
it. They gained steadily on it, and at last, breast to breast they burst
through the open door and fell grateful and exhausted in the
sheltering shadows beyond. By and by their pulses slowed down,
and Tom whispered:

"Huckleberry, what do you reckon 'll come of this?"

"If Dr. Robinson dies, I reckon hangin 'll come of it."

"Do you though?"

"Why I *know* it, Tom."

Tom thought a while, then he said:

"Who'll tell? We?"

"What are you talking about? S'pose something happened and Injun Joe *didn't* hang? Why he'd kill us some time or other, just as dead sure as we're a laying here."

"That's just what I was thinking to myself, Huck."

"If anybody tells, let Muff Potter do it, if he's fool enough. He's generally drunk enough."

Tom said nothing—went on thinking. Presently he whispered:

"Huck, Muff Potter don't *know* it. How can he tell?"

"What's the reason he don't know it?"

"Because he'd just got that whack when Injun Joe done it. D'you reckon he could see anything? D' you reckon he knowed anything?"

"By hokey, that's so Tom!"

"And besides, look-a-here—maybe that whack done for *him!*"

"No, 'taint likely Tom. He had liquor in him; I could see that; and besides, he always has. Well when pap's full, you might take and belt him over the head with a church and you couldn't phase him. He says so, his own self. So it's the same with Muff Potter, of course. But if a man was dead sober, I reckon maybe that whack might fetch him; I dono."

After another reflective silence, Tom said:

"Hucky, you sure you can keep mum?"

"Tom, we *got* to keep mum. *You* know that. That Injun devil wouldn't make any more of drownding us than a couple of cats, if we was to squeak 'bout this and they didn't hang him. Now look-a-here, Tom, less take and swear to one another—that's what we got to do—swear to keep mum."

"I'm agreed. It's the best thing. Would you just hold hands and swear that we—"

"O, no, that wouldn't do for this. That's good enough for little rubbishy common things—specially with gals, cuz *they* go back on you anyway, and blab if they get in a huff—but there orter be writing 'bout a big thing like this. And blood."

Tom's whole being applauded this idea. It was deep, and dark, and awful; the hour, the circumstances, the surroundings, were in keeping with it. He picked up a clean pine shingle that lay in the moonlight, took a little fragment of "red keel" out of his pocket, got the moon on his work, and painfully scrawled these lines, emphasizing each slow down-stroke by clamping his tongue between his teeth, and letting up the pressure on the up-strokes:

"Huck Finn and Tom Sawyer swears they will keep mum about this and they wish they may Drop down dead in their tracks if they ever tell and Rot."

Huckleberry was filled with admiration of Tom's facility in writing, and the sublimity of his language. He at once took a pin from his lapel and was going to prick his flesh, but Tom said:

"Hold on! Don't do that. A pin's brass. It might have verdigrease on it."

"What's verdigrease?"

"It's p'ison. That's what it is. You just swaller some of it once—you'll see."

So Tom unwound the thread from one of his needles, and each boy pricked the ball of his thumb and squeezed out a drop of blood. In time, after many squeezes, Tom managed to sign his initials, using the ball of his little finger for a pen. Then he showed Huckleberry how to make an H and an F, and the oath was complete. They buried the shingle close to the wall, with some dismal ceremonies and incantations, and the fetters that bound their tongues were considered to be locked and the key thrown away.

A figure crept stealthily through a break in the other end of the ruined building, now, but they did not notice it.

"Tom," whispered Huckleberry, "does this keep us from *ever* telling *always?*"

"Of course it does. It don't make any difference *what* happens, we got to keep mum. We'd drop down dead—don't *you* know that?"

"Yes, I reckon that's so."

They continued to whisper for some little time. Presently a dog set up a long, lugubrious howl just outside—within ten feet of them. The boys clasped each other suddenly, in an agony of fright.

"Which of us does he mean?" gasped Huckleberry.

"I dono—peep through the crack. Quick!"

"No, *you*, Tom!"

"I can't—I can't *do* it, Huck!"

"Please, Tom. There 'tis again!"

"O, lordy, I'm thankful!" whispered Tom. "I know his voice. It's Bull Harbison."*

"O, that's good—I tell you, Tom, I was most scared to death; I'd a bet anything it was a *stray* dog."

The dog howled again. The boys' hearts sank once more.

"O, my! that ain't no Bull Harbison!" whispered Huckleberry. "*Do*, Tom!"

Tom, quaking with fear, yielded, and put his eye to the crack. His whisper was hardly audible when he said:

"O, Huck, IT'S A STRAY DOG!"

"Quick, Tom, quick! Who does he mean?"

"Huck, he must mean us both—we're right together."

"O, Tom, I reckon we're goners. I reckon there ain't no mistake

---

*If Mr. Harbison had owned a slave named Bull, Tom would have spoken of him as "Harbison's Bull," but a son or a dog of that name was "Bull Harbison."

'bout where *I'll* go to. I been so wicked."

"Dad fetch it! This comes of playing hookey and doing everything a feller's told *not* to do. I might a been good, like Sid, if I'd tried— but no, I wouldn't, of course. But if ever I get off this time, I lay I'll just *waller* in Sunday-schools!" And Tom began to snuffle a little.

"*You* bad!" and Huckleberry began to snuffle too. "Consound it, Tom Sawyer, you're just old pie, 'longside o'wshat *I* am. O, *lordy*, lordy, lordy, I wisht I only had half your chance."

Tom choked off and whispered:

"Look, Hucky, Look! He's got his *back* to us!"

Hucky looked, with joy in his heart.

"Well he has, by jingoes! Did he before?"

"Yes, he did. But I, like a fool, never thought. O, this is bully, you know. *Now* who can he mean?"

The howling stopped. Tom pricked up his ears.

"Sh! What's that?" he whispered.

"Sounds like—like hogs grunting. No—it's somebody snoring. Tom."

"That *is* it? Where 'bouts is it, Huck?"

"I bleeve it's down at 'tother end. Sounds so, anyway. Pap used to sleep there, sometimes, 'long with the hogs, but laws bless you, he just lifts things when *he* snores. Besides, I reckon he ain't ever coming back to this town any more."

The spirit of adventure rose in the boys' souls once more.

"Hucky, do you das't to go if I lead?"

"I don't like to, much. Tom, s'pose it's Injun Joe!"

Tom quailed. But presently the temptation rose up strong again and the boys agreed to try, with the understanding that they would take to their heels if the snoring stopped. So they went tip-toeing stealthily down, the one behind the other. When they had got to within five steps of the snorer, Tom stepped on a stick, and it broke with a sharp snap. The man moaned, writhed a little, and his face came into the moonlight. It was Muff Potter. The boys' hearts had stood still, and their hopes too, when the man moved, but their fears passed away now. They tip-toed out, through the broken weather-boarding, and stopped at a little distance to exchange a parting word. That long, lugubrious howl rose on the night air again! They turned and saw the strange dog standing within a few feet of where Potter was lying, and *facing* Potter, with his nose pointing heavenward.

"O, geeminy it's *him!*" exclaimed both boys, in a breath.

"Say, Tom—they say a stray dog come howling around Johnny Miller's house, 'bout midnight, as much as two weeks ago; and a whippoorwill came in and lit on the bannisters and sung, the very same evening; and there ain't anybody dead there yet."

"Well I know that. And suppose there ain't. Didn't Gracie Miller fall in the kitchen fire and burn herself terrible the very next

Saturday?"

"Yes, but she ain't *dead.* And what's more, she's getting better, too."

"All right, you wait and see. She's a goner, just as dead sure as Muff Potter's a goner. That's what the niggers say, and they know all about these kind of things, Huck."

Then they separated, cogitating. When Tom crept in at his bedroom window, the night was almost spent. He undressed with excessive caution, and fell asleep congratulating himself that nobody knew of his escapade. He was not aware that the gently-snoring Sid was awake, and had been so for an hour.

When Tom awoke, Sid was dressed and gone. There was a late look in the light, a late sense in the atmosphere. He was startled. Why had he not been called—persecuted till he was up, as usual? The thought filled him with bodings. Within five minutes he was dressed and down stairs, feeling sore and drowsy. The family were still at table, but they had finished breakfast. There was no voice of rebuke; but there were averted eyes; there was a silence and an air of solemnity that struck a chill to the culprit's heart. He sat down and tried to seem gay, but it was up-hill work; it roused no smile, no response, and he lapsed into silence and let his heart sink down to the depths.

After breakfast his aunt took him aside, and Tom almost brightened in the hope that he was going to be flogged; but it was not so. His aunt wept over him and asked him how he could go and break her old heart so; and finally told him to go on, and ruin himself and bring her grey hairs with sorrow to the grave, for it was no use for her to try any more. This was worse than a thousand whippings, and Tom's heart was sorer now than his body. He cried, he pleaded for forgiveness, promised reform over and over again and then received his dismissal, feeling that he had won but an imperfect forgiveness and established but a feeble confidence.

He left the presence too miserable to even feel revengeful toward Sid; and so the latter's prompt retreat through the back gate was unnecessary. He moped to school gloomy and sad, and took his flogging, along with Joe Harper, for playing hooky the day before, with the air of one whose heart was busy with heavier woes and wholly dead to trifles. Then he betook himself to his seat, rested his elbows on his desk and his jaws in his hands and stared at the wall with the stony stare of suffering that has reached the limit and can no further go. His elbow was pressing against some hard substance. After a long time he slowly and sadly changed his position, and took up this object with a sigh. It was in a paper. He unrolled it. A long, lingering, colossal sigh followed, and his heart broke. It was his brass andiron knob!

This final feather broke the camel's back.

CHAPTER XI

Close upon the hour of noon the whole village was suddenly electrified with the ghastly news. No need of the as yet undreamed-of telegraph; the tale flew from man to man, from group to group, from house to house, with little less than telegraphic speed. Of course the schoolmaster gave holiday for that afternoon; the town would have thought strangely of him if he had not.

A gory knife had been found close to the murdered man, and it had been recognized by somebody as belonging to Muff Potter— so the story ran. And it was said that a belated citizen had come upon Potter washing himself in the "branch" about one or two o'clock in the morning, and that Potter had at once sneaked off— suspicious circumstances, especially the washing, which was not a habit with Potter. It was also said that the town had been ransacked for this "murderer," (the public are not slow in the matter of sifting evidence and arriving at a verdict), but that he could not be found. Horsemen had departed down all the roads in every direction, and the Sheriff "was confident" that he would be captured before night.

All the town was drifting toward the graveyard. Tom's heart-break vanished and he joined the procession, not because he would not a thousand times rather go anywhere else, but because an awful, unaccountable fascination drew him on. Arrived at the dreadful place, he wormed his small body through the crowd and saw the dismal spectacle. It seemed to him an age since he was there before. Somebody pinched his arm. He turned, and his eyes met Huckleberry's. Then both looked elsewhere at once, and wondered if anybody had noticed anything in their mutual glance. But everybody was talking, and intent upon the grisly spectacle before them.

"Poor fellow!" "Poor young fellow!" "This ought to be a lesson to grave-robbers!" "Muff Potter'll hang for this if they catch him!" This was the drift of remark; and the minister said, "It was a judgment; His hand is here."

Now Tom shivered from head to heel; for his eye fell upon the stolid face of Injun Joe. At this moment the crowd began to sway and struggle, and voices shouted, "It's him! he's coming himself!"

"Who? Who?" from twenty voices.

"Muff Potter!"

"Hallo, he's stopped!—Look out, he's turning! Don't let him get away!"

People in the branches of the trees over Tom's head, said he wasn't trying to get away—he only looked doubtful and perplexed.

"Infernal impudence!" said a bystander; "wanted to come and take a quiet look at his work, I reckon—didn't expect any company."

The crowd fell apart, now, and the Sheriff came through,

ostentatiously leading Potter by the arm. The poor fellow's face
was haggard, and his eyes showed the fear that was upon him.
When he stood before the murdered man, he shook as with a palsy,
and he put his face in his hands and burst into tears.

"I didn't do it, friends," he sobbed; "'pon my word and honor I
never done it."

"Who's accused you?" shouted a voice.

This shot seemed to carry home. Potter lifted his face and looked
around him with a pathetic hopelessness in his eyes. He saw Injun
Joe, and exclaimed:

"O, Injun Joe, you promised me you'd never—"

"Is that your knife?" and it was thrust before him by the Sheriff.

Potter would have fallen if they had not caught him and eased
him to the ground. Then he said:

"Something told me 't if I didn't come back and get—" He
shuddered; then waved his nerveless hand with a vanquished
gesture and said, "Tell 'em, Joe, tell 'em—it ain't any use any
more."

Then Huckleberry and Tom stood dumb and staring, and heard
the stony-hearted liar reel off his serene statement, they expecting
every moment that the clear sky would deliver God's lightnings
upon his head, and wondering to see how long the stroke was
delayed. And when he had finished and still stood alive and whole,
their wavering impulse to break their oath and save the poor
betrayed prisoner's life faded and vanished away, for plainly this
miscreant had sold himself to Satan and it would be fatal to
meddle with the property of such a power as that.

"Why didn't you leave? What did you want to come here for?"
somebody said.

"I couldn't help it—I couldn't help it," Potter moaned. "I
wanted to run away, but I couldn't seem to come anywhere but
here." And he fell to sobbing again.

Injun Joe repeated his statement, just as calmly, a few minutes
afterward on the inquest, under oath/ and the boys, seeing that the
lightnings were still withheld, were confirmed in their belief that
Joe had sold himself to the devil. He was now become, to them,
the most balefully interesting object they had ever looked upon,
and they could not take their fascinated eyes from his face.

They inwardly resolved to watch him, nights, when opportunity
should offer, in the hope of getting a glimpse of his dread master.

Injun Joe helped to raise the body of the murdered man and
put it in a wagon for removal; and it was whispered through the
shuddering crowd that the wound bled a little! The boys thought
that this happy circumstance would turn suspicion in the right
direction; but they were disappointed, for more than one villager
remarked:

"It was within three feet of Muff Potter when it done it."

Tom's fearful secret and gnawing conscience disturbed his sleep for as much as a week after this; and at breakfast one morning Sid said:

"Tom, you pitch around and talk in your sleep so much that you keep me awake about half the time."

Tom blanched and dropped his eyes.

"It's a bad sign," said Aunt Polly, gravely. "What you got on your mind, Tom?"

"Nothing. Nothing 't I know of." But the boy's hand shook so that he spilled his coffee.

"And you do talk such stuff," Sid said. "Last night you said 'it's blood, it's blood, that's what it is!' You said that over and over. And you said, 'Don't torment me so—I'll tell!' Tell *what*? What is it you'll tell?"

Everything was swimming before Tom. There is no telling what might have happened, now, but luckily the concern passed out of Aunt Polly's face and she came to Tom's relief without knowing it. She said:

"Sho! It's that dreadful murder. I dream about it most every night myself, Sometimes I dream it's me that done it."

Mary said she had been affected much the same way. Sid seemed satisfied. Tom got out of the presence as quick as he plausibly could, and after that he complained of toothache for a week, and tied up his jaws every night. He never knew that Sid lay nightly watching, and frequently slipped the bandage free and then leaned on his elbow listening a good while at a time, and afterward slipped the bandage back to its place again. Tom's distress of mind wore off gradually and the toothache grew irksome and was discarded. If Sid really managed to make anything out of Tom's disjointed mutterings, he kept it to himself.

It seemed to Tom that his schoolmates never would get done holding inquests on dead cats, and thus keeping his trouble present to his mind. Sid noticed that Tom never was coroner at one of these inquiries, though it had been his habit to take the lead in all new enterprises; he noticed, too, that Tom never acted as a witness,—and that was strange; and Sid did not overlook the fact that Tom even showed a marked aversion to these inquests, and always avoided them when he could. Sid marveled, but said nothing. However, even inquests went out of vogue at last, and ceased to torture Tom's conscience.

Every day or two, during this time of sorrow, Tom watched his opportunity and went to the little grated jail-window and smuggled such small comforts through to the "murderer" as he could get hold of. The jail was a trifling little brick den that stood in a marsh at the edge of the village, and no guards were afforded for it; indeed it was seldom occupied. These offerings greatly helped to ease Tom's conscience.

The villagers had a strong desire to tar-and-feather Injun Joe and ride him on a rail, for body-snatching, but so formidable was his character that nobody could be found who was willing to take the lead in the matter, so it was dropped. He had been careful to begin both of his inquest-statements with the fight, without confessing the grave-robbery that preceded it; therefore it was deemed wisest not to try the case in the courts at present.

CHAPTER XII

One of the reasons why Tom's mind had drifted away from its secret troubles was, that it had found a new and weighty matter to interest itself about. Becky Thatcher had stopped coming to school. Tom had struggled with his pride a few days, and tried to "whistle her down the wind," but failed. He began to find himself hanging around her father's house, nights, and feeling very miserable. She was ill. What if she should die! There was distraction in the thought. He no longer took an interest in war, nor even in piracy. The charm of life was gone; there was nothing but dreariness left. He put his hoop away, and his bat; there was no joy in them any more. His aunt was concerned. She began to try all manner of remedies on him. She was one of those people who are infatuated with patent medicines and all new-fangled methods of producing health or mending it. She was an inveterate experimenter in these things. When something fresh in this line came out she was in a fever, right away, to try it; not on herself, for she was never ailing, but on anybody else that came handy. She was a subscriber for all the "Health" periodicals and phreneological frauds; and the solemn ignorance they were inflated with was breath to her nostrils. All the "rot" they contained about ventilation, and how to go to bed, and how to get up, and what to eat, and what to drink, and how much exercise to take, and what frame of mind to keep one's self in, and what sort of clothing to wear, was all gospel to her, and she never observed that her health-journals of the current month customarily upset everything they had recommended the month before. She was as simple-hearted and honest as the day was long, and so she was an easy victim. She gathered together her quack periodicals and her quack medicines, and thus armed with death, went about on her pale horse, metaphorically speaking, with "hell following after." But she never suspected that she was not an angel of healing and the balm of Gilead in disguise, to the suffering neighbors.

The water treatment was new, now, and Tom's low condition was a windfall to her. She had him out at daylight every morning, stood him up in the woodshed and drowned him with a deluge of cold water; then she scrubbed him down with a towel like a file, and so brought him to; then she rolled him up in a wet sheet and put him away under blankets till she sweated his soul clean and "the yellow stains of it came through his pores"—as Tom said.

Yet notwithstanding all this, the boy grew more and more melancholy and pale and dejected. She added hot baths, sitz baths, shower baths and plunges. The boy remained as dismal as a hearse. She began to assist the water with a slim oatmeal diet and blister plasters. She calculated his capacity as she would a jug's, and filled him up every day with quack cure-alls.

Tom had become indifferent to persecution by this time. This phase filled the old lady's heart with consternation. This indifference must be broken up at any cost. Now she heard of Pain-killer for the first time. She ordered a lot at once. She tasted it and was filled with gratitude. It was simply fire in a liquid form. She dropped the water treatment and everything else, and pinned her faith to Pain-killer. She gave Tom a tea-spoonful and watched with the deepest anxiety for the result. Her troubles were instantly at rest, her soul at peace again; for the "indifference" was broken up. The boy could not have shown a wilder, heartier interest, if she had built a fire under him.

Tom felt that it was time to wake up; this sort of life might be romantic enough, in his blighted condition, but it was getting to have too little sentiment and too much distracting variety about it. So he thought over various plans for relief, and finally hit upon that of professing to be fond of Pain-killer. He asked for it so often that he became a nuisance, and his aunt ended by telling him to help himself and quit bothering her. If it had been Sid, she would have had no misgivings to alloy her delight; but since it was Tom, she watched the bottle clandestinely. She found that the medicine did really diminish, but it did not occur to her that the boy was mending the health of a crack in the sitting-room floor with it.

One day Tom was in the act of dosing the crack when his aunt's yellow cat came along, purring, eyeing the teaspoon avariciously, and begging for a taste. Tom said.

"Don't ask for it unless you want it, Peter."

But Peter signified that he did want it.

"You better make sure."

Peter was sure.

"Now you've asked for it, and I'll give it to you, because there ain't anything mean about *me;* but if you find you don't like it, you musn't blame anybody but your own self."

Peter was agreeable. So Tom pried his mouth open and poured down the Pain-killer. Peter sprang a couple of yards in the air, and then delivered a war-whoop and set off round and round the room, banging against furniture, upsetting flower pots and making general havoc. Next he rose on his hind feet and pranced around, in a frenzy of enjoyment, with his head over his shoulder and his voice proclaiming his unappeasable happiness. Then he went tearing around the house again spreading chaos and destruction in his path. Aunt Polly entered in time to see him throw a few double summersets, deliver a final mighty hurrah, and sail through the open window, carrying the rest of the flower-pots with him. The old lady stood petrified with astonishment, peering over her glasses; Tom lay on the floor expiring with laughter.

"Tom, what on earth ails that cat?"

"*I* don't know, aunt," gasped the boy.

"Why I never see anything like it. What *did* make him act so?"

"Deed I don't know Aunt Polly; cats always act so when they're having a good time."

"They do, do they?" There was something in the tone that made Tom apprehensive.

"Yes'm. That is, I believe they do."

"You *do*?"

"Yes'm."

The old lady was bending down, Tom watching, with interest emphasized by anxiety. Too late he divined her "drift." The handle of the tell-tale tea-spoon was visible under the bed-valance. Aunt Polly took it, held it up. Tom winced, and dropped his eyes. Aunt Polly raised him by the usual handle—his ear—and cracked his head soundly with her thimble.

"Now, sir, what did you want to treat that poor dumb beast so, for?"

"I done it out of pity for him—because he hadn't any aunt."

"Hadn't any aunt!—you numscull. What has that got to do with it?"

"Heaps. Because if he'd a had one she'd a burnt him out herself! She'd a roasted his bowels out of him 'thout any more feeling than if he was a human!"

Aunt Polly felt a sudden pang of remorse. This was putting the thing in a new light; what was cruelty to a cat *might* be cruelty to a boy, too. She began to soften; she felt sorry. Her eyes watered a little, and she put her hand on Tom's head and said gently:

"I was meaning for the best, Tom. And Tom, it *did* do you good."

Tom looked up in her face with just a preceptible twinkle peeping through his gravity:

"I know you was meaning for the best, aunty, and so was I with Peter. It done *him* good, too. I never see him get around so since—"

"O, go 'long with you, Tom, before you aggravate me again. And you try and see if you can't be a good boy, for once, and you needn't take any more medicine."

Tom reached school ahead of time. It was noticed that this strange thing had been occurring every day latterly. And now, as usual of late, he hung about the gate of the school-yard instead of playing with his comrades. He was sick, he said, and he looked it.

He tried to seem to be looking everywhere but whither he really was looking—down the road. Presently Jeff Thatcher hove in sight, and Tom's face lighted; he gazed a moment, and then turned sorrowfully away. When Jeff arrived, Tom accosted him, and "led up" warily to opportunities for remark about Becky, but the giddy lad never could see the bait. Tom watched and watched, hoping whenever a frisking frock came in sight, and hating the owner of it as soon as he saw she was not the right one. At last frocks ceased to appear, and he dropped hopelessly into the dumps; he entered the empty school house and sat down to suffer. Then one more frock passed in at the gate, and Tom's heart gave a great bound. The next instant he was out, and "going on" like an Indian; yelling, laughing, chasing boys, jumping over the fence at risk of life and limb, throwing hand-springs, standing on his head—doing all the heroic things he could conceive of, and keeping a furtive eye out, all the while, to see if Becky Thatcher was noticing. But she seemed to be unconscious of it all; she never looked. Could it be posssble that she was not aware that he was there? He carried his exploits to her immediate vicinity; came war-whooping around, snatched a boy's cap, hurled it to the roof of the school-house, broke through a group of boys, tumbling them in every direction, and fell sprawling, himself, under Becky's nose, almost upsetting her—and she turned, with her nose in the air, and he heard her say. "Mf! some people think they're mighty smart—always showing off!"

Tom's cheeks burned. He gathered himself up and sneaked off, crushed and crestfallen.

CHAPTER XIII

Tom's mind was made up now. He was gloomy and desperate. He was a forsaken, friendless boy, he said; nobody loved him; when they found out what they had driven him to, perhaps they would be sorry; he had tried to do right and get along, but they would not let him; since nothing would do them but to be rid of him, let it be so; and let them blame *him* for the consequences—why shouldn't they? What right had the friendless to complain? Yes, they had forced him to it at last; he would lead a life of crime. There was no choice.

By this time he was far down Meadow Lane, and the bell for school to "take up" tinkled faintly upon his ear. He sobbed, now, to think he should never, never hear that old familiar sound any more—it was very hard, but it was forced on him; since he was driven out into the cold world, he must submit—but he forgave them. Then the sobs came thick and fast.

Just at this point he met his soul's sworn comrade, Joe Harper—hard-eyed, and with evidently a great and dismal purpose in his heart. Plainly here were "two souls with but a single thought."

Tom, wiping his eyes with his sleeve, began to blubber out
something about a resolution to escape from hard usage and lack
of sympathy at home by roaming abroad into the great world never
to return; and ended by hoping that Joe would not forget him.

But it transpired that this was a request which Joe had just been
going to make of Tom, and had come to hunt him up for that
purpose. His mother had whipped him for drinking some cream
which he had never tasted and knew nothing about; it was plain
that she was tired of him and wished him to go; if she felt that way,
there was nothing for him to do but succumb; he hoped she would
be happy, and never regret having driven her poor boy out into
the unfeeling world to suffer and die.

As the two boys walked sorrowing along, they made a new
compact to stand by each other and be brothers and never
separate till death relieved them of their troubles. Then they began
to lay their plans. Joe was for being a hermit, and living on crusts
in a remote cave, and dying, some time, of cold, and want, and
grief; but after listening to Tom, he conceded that there were some
conspicuous advantages about a life of crime, and so he consented
to be a pirate.

Three miles below St. Petersburg, at a point where the
Mississippi river was a trifle over a mile wide, there was a long,
narrow, wooded island, with a shallow bar at the head of it, and
this offered well as a rendezvous. It was not inhabited; it lay far
over toward the further shore, abreast a dense and almost wholly
unpeopled forest. So Jackson's Island was chosen. Who were to
be the subjects of their piracies, was a matter that did not occur to
them. Then they hunted up Huckleberry Finn, and he joined them
promptly, for all careers were one to him; he was indifferent. They
presently separated to meet at a lonely spot on the river bank two
miles above the village at the favorite hour—which was midnight.
There was a small log raft there which they meant to capture.
Each would bring hooks and lines, and such provision as he could
steal in the most dark and mysterious way—as became outlaws.
And before the afternoon was done, they had all managed to enjoy
the sweet glory of spreading the fact that pretty soon the town
would "hear something." All who got this vague hint were
cautioned to "be mum and wait."

About midnight Tom arrived with a boiled ham and a few
trifles, and stopped in a dense undergrowth on a small bluff
overlooking the meeting-place. It was starlight, and very still. The
mighty river lay like an ocean at rest. Tom listened a moment,
but no sound disturbed the quiet. Then he gave a low, distinct
whistle. It was answered from under the bluff. Tom whistled twice
more; these signals were answered in the same way. Then a
guarded voice said:

"Who goes there?"

"Tom Sawyer, the Black Avenger of the Spanish Main. Name your names."

"Huck Finn the Red-Handed, and Joe Harper the Terror of the Seas." Tom had furnished these titles, from his favorite literature.

"Tis well. Give the countersign."

Two hoarse whispers delivered the same awful word simultaneously to the brooding night:

"BLOOD!"

Then Tom tumbled his ham over the bluff and let himself down after it, tearing both skin and clothes to some extent in the effort. There was an easy, comfortable path along the shore under the bluff, but it lacked the advantages of difficulty and danger so valued by a pirate.

The Terror of the Seas had brought a side of bacon, and had about worn himself out with getting it there. Finn the Red-Handed had stolen a skillet and a quantity of half-cured leaf tobacco, and had also brought a few corn-cobs to make pipes with. But none of the pirates smoked or "chewed" but himself. The Black Avenger of the Spanish Main said it would never do to start without some fire. That was a wise thought; matches were hardly known there in that day. They saw a fire smouldering upon a great raft a hundred yards above, and they went stealthily thither and helped themselves to a chunk. They made an imposing adventure of it, saying "Hist!" every now and then, and suddenly halting with finger on lip; moving with hands on imaginary dagger-hilts; and giving orders in dismal whispers that if "the foe" stirred, to "let him have it to the hilt," because "dead men tell no tales." They knew well enough that the raftsmen were all down at the village laying in stores or having a spree, but still that was no excuse for their conducting this thing in an unpiratical way.

They shoved off, presently, Tom in command, Huck at the after oar and Joe at the forward. Tom stood amidships, gloomy-browed, and with folded arms, and gave his orders in a low, stern whisper:

"Luff, and bring her to the wind!"

"Aye-aye, sir!"

"Steady it is, sir!"

"Aye-aye, sir!"

"Steady, stead-y-y-y!"

"Steady it is, sir!"

"Let her go off a point!"

"Point it is, sir!"

As the boys steadily and monotonously drove the raft toward mid-stream it was no doubt understood that these orders were given only for "style," and were not intended to mean anything in particular.

"What sail's she carrying?"

"Courses, tops'ls and flying-jib, sir."

"Send the r'yals up! Lay out aloft, there, half a dozen of ye,—
foretopmaststuns'l! Lively, now!"

"Aye-aye, sir!"

"Shake out that maintogalans'l! Sheets and braces! *Now,* my
hearties!"

"Aye-aye, sir!"

"Hellum-a-lee—hard a port! Stand by to meet her when she
comes! Port, port! *Now,* men! With a will! Stead-y-y-y!"

"Steady it is, sir!"

The raft drew beyond the middle of the river; the boys pointed
her head right, and then lay on their oars. The river was not high,
so there was not more than a two or three-mile current. Hardly a
word was said during the next three-quarters of an hour. Now the
raft was passing before the distant town. Two or three glimmering
lights showed where it lay, peacefully sleeping, beyond the vague
vast sweep of star-gemmed water, unconscious of the tremendous
event that was happening. The Black Avenger stood still with
folded arms, "looking his last" upon the scene of his former joys
and his later sufferings, and wishing "she" could see him now,
abroad on the wild sea, facing peril and death with dauntless heart,
going to his doom with a grim smile on his lips. It was but a small
strain on his imagination to remove Jackson's Island beyond
eye-shot of the village, and so he "looked his last" with a broken
and satisfied heart. The other pirates were looking their last, too;
and they all looked so long that they came near letting the current
drift them out of the range of the island. But they discovered the
danger in time, and made shift to avert it. About two o'clock in the
morning the raft grounded on the bar two hundred yards above
the head of the island, and they waded back and forth until they
had landed their freight. Part of the little raft's belongings
consisted of an old sail, and this they spread over a nook in the
bushes for a tent to shelter their provisions; but they themselves
would sleep in the open air in good weather, as became outlaws.

They built a fire against the side of a great log twenty or thirty
steps within the sombre depths of the forest, and then cooked some
bacon in the frying-pan for supper, and used up half of the corn
"pone" stock they had brought. It seemed glorious sport to be
feasting in that wild free way in the virgin forest of an unexplored
and uninhabited island, far from the haunts of men, and they said
they never would return to civilization. The climbing fire lit up
their faces and threw its ruddy glare upon the pillared tree trunks
of their forest temple, and upon the varnished foliage and
festooning vines.

When the last crisp slice of bacon was gone, and the last
allowance of corn pone devoured, the boys stretched themselves
out on the grass, filled with contentment. They could have found
a cooler place, but they would not deny themselves such a

romantic feature as the roasting camp-fire.

"*Ain't* it gay?" said Joe.

"It's *nuts!*" said Tom. "What would the boys say if they could see us?"

"Say? Well they'd just die to be here—hey Hucky!"

"I reckon so," said Huckleberry; "anyways *I'*m suited. I don't want nothing better'n this. I don't ever get enough to eat, gen'ally—and here they can't come and pick at a feller and bullyrag him so."

"It's just the life for me," said Tom. "You don't have to get up, mornings, and you don't have to go to school, and wash, and all that blame foolishness. You see a pirate don't have to do *anything*, Joe, when he's ashore, but a hermit *he* has to be praying considerable, and then he don't have any fun, anyway, all by himself that way."

"O yes, that's so," said Joe, "but I hadn't thought much about it, you know. I'd a good deal rather be a pirate, now that I've tried it."

"You see," said Tom, "people don't go much on hermits, now-a-days, like they used to in old times, but a pirate's always respected. And a hermit's got to sleep on the hardest place he can find, and put sack-cloth and ashes on his head, and stand out in the rain, and—"

"What does he put sack-cloth and ashes on his head for?" inquired Huck.

"*I* dono. But they've *got* to do it. Hermits always do. You'd have to do that if you was a hermit."

"Dern'd if I would," said Huck.

"Well what would you do?"

"I dono. But I wouldn't do that."

"Why Huck, you'd *have* to. How'd you get around it?"

"Why I just wouldn't stand it. I'd run away."

"Run away! Well you *would* be a nice old slouch of a hermit. You'd be a disgrace."

The Red-Handed made no response, being better employed. He had finished gouging out a cob, and now he fitted a weed stem to it, loaded it with tobacco, and was pressing a coal to the charge and blowing a cloud of fragrant smoke—he was in the full bloom of luxurious contentment. The other pirates envied him this majestic vice, and secretly resolved to acquire it shortly. Presently Huck said:

"What does pirates have to do?"

Tom said:

"Oh they have just a bully time—take ships, and burn them, and get the money and bury it in awful places in their island where there's ghosts and things to watch it, and kill everybody in the ships—make 'em walk a plank."

"And they carry the women to the island," said Joe; "they don't kill the women.''

"No," assented Tom, "they don't kill the women—they're too
noble. And the women's always beautiful, too."

"And don't they wear the bulliest clothes! Oh, no! All gold and
silver and di'monds," said Joe, with enthusiasm.

"Who?" said Huck.

"Why the pirates."

Huck scanned his own clothing forlornly.

"I reckon I ain't dressed fitten for a pirate," said he, with a
regretful pathos in his voice; "but I ain't got none but these."

But the other boys told him the fine clothes would come fast
enough, after they should have begun their adventures. They made
him understand that his poor rags would do to begin with, though
it was customary for wealthy pirates to start with a proper wardrobe.

Gradually their talk died out and drowsiness began to steal upon
the eyelids of the little waifs. The pipe dropped from the fingers
of the Red-Handed, and he slept the sleep of the conscience-free
and the weary. The Terror of the Seas and the Black Avenger of the
Spanish Main had more difficulty in getting to sleep. They said
their prayers inwardly, and lying down, since there was nobody
there with authority to make them kneel and recite aloud; in truth
they had a mind not to say them at all, but they were afraid to
proceed to such lengths as that, lest they might call down a sudden
and special thunderbolt from Heaven. Then at once they reached
and hovered upon the imminent verge of sleep—but an intruder
came, now, that would not "down." It was conscience. They began
to feel a vague fear that they had been doing wrong to run away;
and next they thought of the stolen meat, and then the real torture
came. They tried to argue it away by reminding conscience that they
had purloined sweetmeats and apples scores of times; but
conscience was not to be appeased by such thin plausibilities; it
seemed to them, in the end, that there was no getting around the
stubborn fact that taking sweetmeats was only "hooking," while
taking bacon and hams and such valuables was plain simple
stealing—and there was a command against that in the Bible. So
they inwardly resolved that so long as they remained in the business,
their piracies should not again be sullied with the crime of
stealing. Then conscience granted a truce, and these curiously
inconsistent pirates fell peacefully to sleep.

CHAPTER XIV

When Tom awoke in the morning, he wondered where he was.
He sat up and rubbed his eyes and looked around. Then he
comprehended. It was the cool gray dawn, and there was a delicious
sense of repose and peace in the deep pervading calm and silence
of the woods. Not a leaf stirred; not a sound obtruded upon great

Nature's meditation. Beaded dew-drops stood upon the leaves and grasses. A white layer of ashes covered the fire, and a thin blue breath of smoke rose straight into the air. Joe and Huck still slept.

Now, far away in the woods a bird called; another answered; presently the hammering of a woodpecker was heard. Gradually the cool dim gray of the morning whitened, and as gradually sounds multiplied and life manifested itself. The marvel of Nature shaking off sleep and going to work unfolded itself to the musing boy. A little green worm came crawling over a dewy leaf, lifting two-thirds of his body into the air from time to time and "sniffing around," then proceeding again—for he was measuring, Tom said; and when the worm approached him, of its own accord, he sat as still as a stone, with his hopes rising and falling, by turns, as the creature still came toward him or seemed inclined to go elsewhere; and when at last it considered a painful moment with its curved body in the air and then came decisively down upon Tom's leg and began a journey over him, his whole heart was glad—for that meant that he was going to have a new suit of clothes—without the shadow of a doubt a gaudy piratical uniform. Now a procession of ants appeared, from nowhere in particular, and went about their labors; one struggled manfully by with a dead spider five times as big as itself in its arms, and lugged it straight up a tree-trunk. A brown spotted lady-bug climbed the dizzy height of a grass blade, and Tom bent down close to it and said, "Lady-bug, lady-bug, fly away home, your house is on fire, your children's alone," and she took wing and went off to see about it—which did not surprise the boy, for he knew of old that this insect was credulous about conflagrations and he had practiced upon its simplicity more than once. A tumble-bug came next, heaving sturdily at its ball, and Tom touched the creature, to see it shut its legs against its body and pretend to be dead. The birds were fairly rioting by this time. A cat-bird, the northern mocker, lit in a tree over Tom's head, and trilled out her imitations of her neighbors in a rapture of enjoyment; then a shrill jay swept down, a flash of blue flame, and stopped on a twig almost within the boy's reach, cocked his head to one side and eyed the strangers with a consuming curiosity; a gray squirrel and a big fellow of the "fox" kind came skurrying along, sitting up at intervals to inspect and chatter at the boys, for the wild things had probably never seen a human being before and scarcely knew whether to be afraid or not. All Nature was wide awake and stirring, now; long lances of sunlight pierced down through the dense foliage far and near, and a few butterflies came fluttering upon the scene.

Tom stirred up the other pirates and they all clattered away with a shout, and in a minute or two were stripped and chasing after and tumbling over each other in the shallow limpid water of the white sand-bar. They felt no longing for the little village

sleeping in the distance beyond the majestic waste of water. A
vagrant current or a slight rise in the river had carried off their
raft, but this only gratified them, since its going was something like
burning the bridge between them and civilization.

They came back to camp wonderfully refreshed, glad-hearted,
and ravenous; and they soon had the camp-fire blazing up again.
Huck found a spring of clear cold water close by, and the boys
made cups of broad oak or hickory leaves, and felt that water,
sweetened with such a wild-wood charm as that, would be a good
enough substitute for coffee. While Joe was slicing bacon for
breakfast, Tom and Huck asked him to hold on a minute; they
stepped to a promising nook in the river bank and threw in their
lines; almost immediately they had reward. Joe had not had time to
get impatient before they were back again with some handsome
bass, a couple of sun-perch and a small catfish—provisions enough
for quite a family. They fried the fish with the bacon and were
astonished; for no fish had ever seemed so delicious before. They
did not know that the quicker a fresh water fish is on the fire after
he is caught the better he is; and they reflected little upon what
a sauce open air sleeping, open air exercise, bathing, and a large
ingredient of hunger makes, too.

They lay around in the shade, after breakfast, while Huck had
a smoke, and then went off through the woods on an exploring
expedition. They tramped gaily along, over decaying logs, through
tangled underbrush, among solemn monarchs of the forest, hung
from their crowns to the ground with a drooping regalia of grape-
vines. Now and then they came upon snug nooks carpeted with
grass and jeweled with flowers.

They found plenty of things to be delighted with but nothing to
be astonished at. They discovered that the island was about three
miles long and a quarter of a mile wide, and that the shore it lay
closest to was only separated from it by a narrow channel hardly
two hundred yards wide. They took a swim about every hour, so it
was close upon the middle of the afternoon when they got back
to camp. They were too hungry to stop to fish, but they fared
sumptuously upon cold ham, and then threw themselves down
in the shade to talk. But the talk soon began to drag, and then
died. The stillness, the solemnity that brooded in the woods, and
the sense of loneliness, began to tell upon the spirits of the boys.
They fell to thinking. A sort of undefined longing crept upon them.
This took dim shape, presently—it was budding home-sickness.
Even Finn the Red-Handed was dreaming of his door-steps and
empty hogsheads. But they were all ashamed of their weakness,
and none was brave enough to speak his thought.

For some time, now, the boys had been dully conscious of a
peculiar sound in the distance, just as one sometimes is of the
ticking of a clock which he takes no distinct note of. But now this

mysterious sound became more pronounced, and forced a recognition. The boys started, glanced at each other, and then each assumed a listening attitude. There was a long silence, profound and unbroken; then a deep, sullen boom came floating down out of the distance.

"What is it!" exclaimed Joe, under his breath.

"I wonder," said Tom in a whisper.

"Tain't thunder," said Huckleberry, in an awed tone, "becuz thunder—"

"Hark!" said Tom. "Listen—don't talk."

They waited a time that seemed an age, and then the same muffled boom troubled the solemn hush.

"Let's go and see."

They sprang to their feet and hurried to the shore toward the town. They parted the bushes on the bank and peered out over the water. The little steam ferry boat was about a mile below the village, drifting with the current. Her broad deck seemed crowded with people. There were a great many skiffs rowing about or floating with the stream in the neighborhood of the ferry boat, but the boys could not determine what the men in them were doing. Presently a great jet of white smoke burst from the ferry boat's side, and as it expanded and rose in a lazy cloud, that same dull throb of sound was borne to the listeners again.

"I know now!" exclaimed Tom; "somebody's drownded!"

"That's it!" said Huck; "they done that last summer, when Bill Turner got drownded; they shoot a cannon over the water, and that makes him come up to the top. Yes, and they take loaves of bread and put quicksilver in 'em and set 'em afloat, and wherever there's anybody that's drownded, they'll float right there and stop."

"Yes, I've heard about that," said Joe. "I wonder what makes the bread do that."

"Oh, it ain't the bread, so much," said Tom; "I reckon it's mostly what they *say* over it before they start it out."

"But they don't say anything over it," said Huck. "I've seen 'em and they don't."

"Well that's funny," said Tom. "But maybe they say it to themselves. Of *course* they do. Anybody might know that."

The other boys agreed that there was reason in what Tom said, because an ignorant lump of bread, uninstructed by an incantation, could not be expected to act very intelligently when sent upon an errand of such gravity.

"By jings I wish I was over there, now," said Joe.

"I do too," said Huck. "I'd give heaps to know who it is."

The boys still listened and watched. Presently a revealing thought flashed through Tom's mind, and he exclaimed:

"Boys, I know who's drownded—it's us!"

They felt like heroes in an instant. Here was a gorgeous triumph;

they were missed; they were mourned; hearts were breaking on
their account; tears were being shed; accusing memories of
unkindnesses to these poor lost lads were rising up, and unavailing
regrets and remorse were being indulged; and best of all, the
departed were the talk of the whole town, and the envy of all the
boys, as far as this dazzling notoriety was concerned. This was fine.
It was worth while to be a pirate, after all.

As twilight drew on, the ferry boat went back to her accustomed
business and the skiffs disappeared. The pirates returned to camp.
They were jubilant with vanity over their new grandeur and the
illustrious trouble they were making. They caught fish, cooked
supper and ate it, and then fell to guessing at what the village was
thinking and saying about them; and the pictures they drew of the
public distress on their account were gratifying to look upon—from
their point of view. But when the shadows of night closed them in,
they gradually ceased to talk and sat gazing into the fire, with their
minds evidently wandering elsewhere. The excitement was gone,
now, and Tom and Joe could not keep back thoughts of certain
persons at home who were not enjoying this fine frolic as much as
they were. Misgivings came; they grew troubled and unhappy; a
sigh or two escaped, unawares. By and by Joe timidly ventured
upon a round-about "feeler" as to how the others might look upon
a return to civilization—not right now, but—

Tom withered him with derision! Huck, being uncommitted, as
yet, joined in with Tom, and the waverer quickly "explained,"
and was glad to get out of the scrape with as little taint of chicken-
hearted home-sickness clinging to his garments as he could.
Mutiny was effectually laid to rest for the moment.

As the night deepened, Huck began to nod, and presently to
snore. Joe followed next. Tom lay upon his elbow motionless, for
some time, watching the two intently. At last he got up cautiously,
on his knees, and went searching among the grass and the flickering
reflections flung by the camp-fire. He picked up and inspected
several large semi-cylinders of the thin white bark of a sycamore,
and finally chose two which seemed to suit him. Then he knelt by
the fire and painfully wrote something upon each of these with
his "red keel;" one he rolled up and put in his jacket pocket, and
the other he put in Joe's hat and removed it to a little distance from
the owner. And he also put into the hat certain school-boy
treasures of almost inestimable value—among them a lump of
chalk, an India rubber ball, three fish-hooks, and one of that kind
of marbles known as a "sure 'nough crystal." Then he tip-toed
his way cautiously among the trees till he felt that he was out of
hearing, and straightway broke into a keen run in the direction of
the sand-bar.

CHAPTER XV

A few minutes later Tom was in the shoal water of the bar, wading toward the Illinois shore. Before the depth reached his middle he was half way over; the current would permit no more wading, now, so he struck out confidently to swim the remaining hundred yards. He swam quartering up stream, but still was swept downward rather faster than he had expected. However, he reached the shore finally, and drifted along till he found a low place and drew himself out. He put his hand on his jacket pocket, found his piece of bark safe, and then struck through the woods, following the shore, with streaming garments. Shortly before ten o'clock he came out into an open place opposite the village, and saw the ferry boat lying in the shadow of the trees and the high bank. Everything was quiet under the blinking stars. He crept down the bank, watching with all his eyes, slipped into the water, swam three or four strokes and climbed into the skiff that did "yawl" duty at the boat's stern. He laid himself down under the thwarts and waited, panting.

Presently the cracked bell tapped and a voice gave the order to "cast off." A minute or two later the skiff's head was standing high up, against the boat's swell, and the voyage was begun. Tom felt happy in his success, for he knew it was the boat's last trip for the night. At the end of a long twelve or fifteen minutes the wheels stopped, and Tom slipped overboard and swam ashore in the dusk, landing fifty yards down stream, out of danger of possible stragglers.

He flew along unfrequented alleys, and shortly found himself at his aunt's back fence. He Climbed over, approached the "ell" and looked in at the sitting-room window, for a light was burning there. There sat Aunt Polly, Sid, Mary, and Joe Harper's mother, grouped together, talking. They were by the bed, and the bed was between them and the door. Tom went to the door and began to softly lift the latch; then he pressed gently and the door yielded a crack; he continued pushing cautiously, and quaking every time it creaked, till he judged he might squeeze through on his knees; and so he put his head through and began, warily.

"What makes the candle blow so?" said Aunt Polly. Tom hurried up. "Why that door's open, I believe. Why of course it is. No end of strange things now. Go 'long and shut it, Sid."

Tom disappeared under the bed just in time. He lay and "breathed" himself for a time, and then crept to where he could almost touch his aunt's foot.

"But as I was saying," said Aunt Polly, "he warn't *bad*, so to say—only mische*e*vous. Only just giddy, and harum-scarum, you know. He warn't any more responsible than a colt. *He* never meant any harm, and he was the best-hearted boy that ever was"—and she began to cry.

"It was just so with my Joe—always full of his devilment, and up to every kind of mischief, but he was just as unselfish and kind as he could be—and laws bless me, to think I went and whipped him for taking that cream, never once recollecting that I throwed it out myself because it was sour, and I never to see him again in this world, never, never, never, poor abused boy!" And Mrs. Harper sobbed as if her heart would break.

"I hope Tom's better off where he is," said Sid, "but if he'd been better in some ways—"

"*Sid!*" Tom felt the glare of the old lady's eye, though he could not see it. "Not a word against my Tom, now that he's gone! God'll take care of *him*—never you trouble *your*self, sir! Oh, Mrs. Harper, I don't know how to give him up! I don't know how to give him up! He was such a comfort to me, although he tormented my old heart out of me, 'most."

"The Lord Giveth and the Lord hath taken away,—Blessed be the name of the Lord! But it's *so* hard—Oh, it's so hard! Only last Saturday my Joe busted a fire-cracker right under my nose and I knocked him sprawling. Little did I know then, how soon—O, if it was to do over again I'd hug him and bless him for it."

"Yes, yes, yes, I know just how you feel, Mrs. Harper, I know just exactly how you feel. No longer ago than yesterday noon, my Tom took and filled the cat full of Pain-killer, and I did think the cretur would tear the house down. And God forgive me, I cracked Tom's head with my thimble, poor boy, poor dead boy. But he's out of all his troubles now. And the last words I ever heard him say was to reproach—"

But this memory was too much for the old lady, and she broke entirely down. Tom was snuffling, now, himself—and more in pity of himself than anybody else. He could hear Mary crying, and putting in a kindly word for him from time to time. He began to have a nobler opinion of himself than ever before. Still he was sufficiently touched by his aunt's grief to long to rush out from under the bed and overwhelm her with joy—and the theatrical gorgeousness of the thing appealed strongly to his nature, too, but he resisted and lay still.

He went on listening, and gathered by odds and ends that it was conjectured at first that the boys had got drowned while taking a swim; then the small raft had been missed; next, certain boys said the missing lads had promised that the village should "hear something" soon; the wise-heads had "put this and that together" and decided that the lads had gone off on that raft and would turn up at the next town below, presently; but toward noon the raft had been found, lodged against the Missouri shore some five or six miles below the village,—and then hope perished; they must be drowned, eise hunger would have driven them home by nightfall

if not sooner. It was believed that the search for the bodies had
been a fruitless effort merely because the drowning must have
occurred in mid-channel, since the boys, being good swimmers,
would otherwise have escaped to shore. This was Wednesday
night. If the bodies continued missing until Sunday, all hope
would be given over, and the funerals would be preached on that
morning. Tom shuddered.

Mrs. Harper gave a sobbing good-night and turned to go. Then
with a mutual impulse the two bereaved women flung themselves
into each other's arms and had a good, consoling cry, and then
parted. Aunt Polly was tender far beyond her wont, in her
good-night to Sid and Mary. Sid snuffled a bit and Mary went off
crying with all her heart.

Aunt Polly knelt down and prayed for Tom so touchingly, so
appealingly, and with such measureless love in her words and her
old trembling voice, that he was weltering in tears again, long
before she was through.

He had to keep still long after she went to bed, for she kept
making broken-hearted ejaculations from time to time, tossing
unrestfully, and turning over. But at last she was still, only
moaning a little in her sleep. Now the boy stole out, rose gradually
by the bedside, shaded the candle-light with his hand, and stood
regarding her. His heart was full of pity for her. He took out his
sycamore scroll and placed it by the candle. But something occurred
to him, and he lingered considering. His face lighted with a happy
solution of his thought; he put the bark hastily in his pocket. Then
he bent over and kissed the faded lips, and straightway made his
stealthy exit, latching the door behind him.

He threaded his way back to the ferry landing, found nobody at
large there, and walked boldly on board the boat, for he knew she
was tenantless except that there was a watchman, who always
turned in and slept like a graven image. He untied the skiff at the
stern, slipped into it, and was soon rowing cautiously up stream.
When he had pulled a mile above the village, he started quartering
across and bent himself stoutly to his work. He hit the landing on
the other side neatly, for this was a familiar bit of work to him. He
was moved to capture the skiff, arguing that it might be considered
a ship and therefore legitimate prey for a pirate, but he knew a
thorough search would be made for it and that might end in
revelations. So he stepped ashore and entered the wood.

He sat down and took a long rest, torturing himself meantime
to keep awake, and then started wearily down the home-stretch.
The night was far spent. It was broad daylight before he found
himself fairly abreast the island bar. He rested again until the sun
was well up and gilding the great river with its splendor, and then
he plunged into the stream. A little later he paused, dripping,
upon the threshold of the camp, and heard Joe say:

"No, Tom's true-blue, Huck, and he'll come back. He won't desert. He knows that would be a disgrace to a pirate, and Tom's too proud for that sort of thing. He's up to something or other. Now I wonder what?"

"Well, the things is ours, anyway, ain't they?"

"Pretty near, but not yet, Huck. The writing says they are if he ain't back here to breakfast."

"Which he is!" exclaimed Tom, with fine dramatic effect, stepping grandly into camp.

A sumptuous breakfast of bacon and fish was shortly provided, and as the boys set to work upon it, Tom recounted (and adorned) his adventures. They were a vain and boastful company of heroes when the tale was done. Then Tom hid himself away in a shady nook to sleep till noon, and the other pirates got ready to fish and explore.

CHAPTER XVI

After dinner all the gang turned out to hunt for turtle eggs on the bar. They went about poking sticks into the sand, and when they found a soft place they went down on their knees and dug with their hands. Sometimes they would take fifty or sixty eggs out of one hole. They were perfectly round white things a trifle smaller than an English walnut. They had a famous fried-egg feast that night, and another on Friday morning.

After breakfast they went whooping and prancing out on the bar, and chased each other round and round, shedding clothes as they went, until they were naked, and then continued the frolic far away up the shoal water of the bar, against the stiff current, which latter tripped their legs from under them from time to time and greatly increased the fun. And now and then they stooped in a group and splashed water in each other's faces with their palms, gradually approaching each other, with averted faces to avoid the strangling sprays and finally gripping and struggling till the best man ducked his neighbor, and then they all went under in a tangle of white legs and arms and came up blowing, sputtering, laughing and gasping for breath at one and the same time.

When they were well exhausted, they would run out and sprawl on the dry, hot sand, and lie there and cover themselves up with it, and by and by break for the water again and go through the original performance once more. Finally it occurred to them that their naked skin represented flesh-colored "tights" very fairly; so they drew a ring in the sand and had a circus—with three clowns in it, for none would yield this proudest post to his neighbor.

Next they got their marbles and played "knucks" and "ring-taw" and "keeps" till that amusement grew stale. Then Joe and Huck had another swim, but Tom would not venture, because he found that in kicking off his trousers he had kicked his string of rattlesnake rattles off his ankle, and he wondered how he had escaped cramp so long without the protection of this mysterious charm. He did not venture again until he had found it, and by that time the other boys were tired and ready to rest. They gradually wandered apart, dropped into the "dumps," and fell to gazing longingly across the wide river to where the village lay drowsing in the sun. Tom found himself writing "BECKY" in the sand with his big toe; he scratched it out, and was angry with himself for his weakness. But he wrote it again, nevertheless; he could not help it. He erased it once more and then took himself out of temptation by driving the other boys together and joining them.

But Joe's spirits had gone down almost beyond resurrection. He was so homesick that he could hardly endure the misery of it. The tears lay very near the surface. Huck was melancholy, too. Tom was down-hearted, but tried hard not to show it. He had a secret which he was not ready to tell, yet, but if this mutinous depression was not broken up soon, he would have to bring it out. He said, with a great show of cheerfulness:

"I bet there's been pirates on this island before, boys. We'll explore it again. They've hid treasures here somewhere. How'd you feel to light on a rotten chest full of gold and silver—hey?"

But it roused only a faint enthusiasm, which faded out, with no reply. Tom tried one or two other seductions; but they failed, too. It was discouraging work. Joe sat poking up the sand with a stick and looking very gloomy. Finally he said:

"O, boys, let's give it up. I want to go home. It's so lonesome."

"Oh, no, Joe, you'll feel better by and by," said Tom. "Just think of the fishing that's here."

"I don't care for fishing. I want to go home."

"But Joe, there ain't such another swimming place anywhere."

"Swimming'a no good. I don't seem to care for it somehow, when there ain't anybody to say I shan't go in. I mean to go home."

"O, shucks! Baby! You want to see your mother, I reckon."

"Yes, I *do* want to see my mother—and you would too, if you had one. I ain't any more baby than you are." And Joe snuffled a little.

"Well, we'll let the cry-baby go home to his mother, *won't* we Huck? Poor thing—does it want to see its mother? And so it shall. *You* like it here, *don't* you Huck? We'll stay, won't we?"

Huck said "Y-e-s"—without any heart in it.

"I'll never speak to you again as long as I live," said Joe, rising. "There now!" And he moved moodily away and began to dress himself.

"Who cares!" said Tom. "Nobody wants you to. Go 'long home and get laughed at. O, you're a nice pirate. Huck and me ain't cry-babies. We'll stay, won't we Huck? Let him go if he wants to.

I reckon we can get along without him per'aps."

But Tom was uneasy, nevertheless, and was alarmed to see Joe go sullenly on with his dressing. And then it was discomforting to see Huck eyeing Joe's preparations so wistfully, and keeping up such an ominous silence. Presently, without a parting word, Joe began to wade off toward the Illinois shore. Tom's heart began to sink. He glanced at Huck. Huck could not bear the look, and dropped his eyes. Then he said:

"I want to go, too, Tom. It was getting so lonesome anyway, and now it'll be worse. Let's go too, Tom."

"I won't! You can all go, if you want to. I mean to stay."

"Tom, I better go."

"Well go 'long—who's hendering you."

Huck began to pick up his scattered clothes. He said:

"Tom, I wisht you'd come too. Now you think it over. We'll wait for you when we get to shore."

"Well you'll wait a blame long time, that's all."

Huck started sorrowfully away, and Tom stood looking after him, with a strong desire tugging at his heart to yield his pride and go along too. He hoped the boys would stop, but they still waded slowly on. It suddenly dawned on Tom that it was become very lonely and still. He made one final struggle with his pride, and then darted after his comrades, yelling:

"Wait! Wait! I want to tell you something!"

They presently stopped and turned around. When he got to where they were, he began unfolding his secret, and they listened moodily till at last they saw the "point" he was driving at, and then they set up a war-whoop of applause and said it was "splendid!" and said if he had told them at first, they wouldn't have started away. He made a plausible excuse; but his real reason had been the fear that not even the secret would keep them with him any very great length of time, and so he had meant to hold it in reserve as a last seduction.

The lads came gaily back and went at their sports again with a will, chattering all the time about Tom's stupendous plan and admiring the genius of it. After a dainty egg and fish dinner, Tom said he wanted to learn to smoke, now. Joe caught at the idea and said he would like to try, too. So Huck made pipes and filled them. These novices had never smoked anything before but cigars made of grape-vine and they "bit" the tongue and were not considered manly, anyway.

Now they stretched themselves out on their elbows and began to puff, charily, and with slender confidence. The smoke had an unpleasant taste, and they gagged a little, but Tom said:

"Why it's just as easy! If I'd a knowed *this* was all, I'd a learnt long ago."

"So would I," said Joe. "It's just nothing."

"Why many a time I've looked at people smoking, and thought well I wish I could do that; but I never thought I could," said Tom.

"That's just the way with me, hain't it Huck? You've heard me talk just that way—haven't you Huck? I'll leave it to Huck if I haven't."

"Yes—heaps of times," said Huck.

"Well I have too," said Tom; "O, hundreds of times. Once down by the slaughter-house. Don't you remember, Huck? Bob Tanner was there, and Johnny Miller, and Jeff Thatcher, when I said it. Don't you remember Huck, 'bout me saying that?"

"Yes, that's so," said Huck. "That was the day after I lost a white alley. No, 'twas the day before."

"There—I told you so," said Tom. "Huck recollects it."

"I bleeve I could smoke this pipe all day," said Joe. "*I* could smoke it all day. But I bet you Jeff Thatcher couldn't."

"Jeff Thatcher! Why he'd keel over just with two draws. Just let him try it once. *He'd* see!"

"I bet he would. And Johnny Miller—I wish I could see Johnny Miller tackle it once."

"O, dont *I!*" said Joe, "Why I bet you Johnny Miller couldn't any more do this than nothing. Just one little snifter would fetch *him*."

" 'Deed it would, Joe. Say—I wish the boys could see us now."

"So do I."

"Say—boys, don't say anything about it, and some time when they're around, I'll come up to you and say 'Joe, got a pipe? I want a smoke.' And you'll say, kind of careless like, as if it warn't anything, you'll say, 'Yes, I got my *old* pipe, and another one, but my tobacker ain't very good.' And I'll say, 'Oh, that's all right, if it's *strong* enough.' And then you'll out with the pipes, and we'll light up just as ca'm, and then just see 'em look!"

"By jings that'll be gay, Tom! I wish it was *now!*"

"So do I! And when we tell 'em we learned when we was off pirating, won't they wish they'd been along?"

"O, I reckon not! I'll just *bet* they will!"

So the talk ran on. But presently it began to flag a trifle, and grow disjointed. The silences widened; the expectoration marvelously increased. Every pore inside the boys' cheeks became a spouting fountain; they could scarcely bail out the cellars under their tongues fast enough to prevent an inundation; little overflowings down their throats occurred in spite of all they could do, and sudden retchings followed every time. Both boys were looking very pale and miserable, now. Joe's pipe dropped from his nerveless fingers. Tom's followed. Both fountains were going furiously and both pumps bailing with might and main. Joe said feebly:

"I've lost my knife. I reckon I better go and find it."

Tom said, with quivering lips and halting utterance:

"I'll help you. You go over that way and I'll hunt around by the spring. No, you needn't come, Huck—we can find it."

So Huck sat down again, and waited an hour. Then he found it lonesome, and went to find his comrades. They were wide apart in the woods, both very pale, both fast asleep. But something informed him that if they had had any trouble they had got rid of it.

They were not talkative at supper that night. They had a humble look, and when Huck prepared his pipe after the meal and was going to prepare theirs, they said no, they were not feeling very well—something they ate at dinner had disagreed with them.

About midnight Joe awoke, and called the boys. There was a brooding oppressiveness in the air that seemed to bode something. The boys huddled themselves together and sought the friendly companionship of the fire, though the dull dead heat of the breathless atmosphere was stifling. They sat still, intent and waiting. The solemn hush continued. Beyond the light of the fire everything was swallowed up in the blackness of darkness. Presently there came a quivering glow that vaguely revealed the foliage for a moment and then vanished. By and by another came, a little stronger. Then another. Then a faint moan came sighing through the branches of the forest and the boys felt a fleeting breath upon their cheeks, and shuddered with the fancy that the Spirit of the Night had gone by. There was a pause. Now a wierd flash turned night into day and showed every little grass-blade, separate and distinct, that grew about their feet. And it showed three white, startled faces, too. A deep peal of thunder went rolling and tumbling down the heavens and lost itself in sullen rumblings in the distance. A sweep of chilly air passed by, rustling all the leaves and snowing the flaky ashes broadcast about the fire. Another fierce glare lit up the forest and an instant crash followed that seemed to rend the tree-tops right over the boys' heads. They clung together in terror, in the thick gloom that followed. A few big raindrops fell pattering upon the leaves.

"Quick! boys, go for the tent!" exclaimed Tom.

They sprang away, stumbling over roots and among vines in the dark, no two plunging in the same direction. A furious blast roared through the trees, making everything sing as it went. One blinding flash after another came, and peal on peal of deafening thunder. And now a drenching rain poured down and the rising hurricane drove it in sheets along the ground. The boys cried out to each other, but the roaring wind and the booming thunder-blasts drowned their voices utterly. However one by one they straggled in at last and took shelter under the tent, cold, scared, and streaming with water; but to have company in misery seemed something to be grateful for. They could not talk, the old sail flapped so furiously, even if the other noises would have allowed them. The

tempest rose higher and higher, and presently the sail tore loose
from its fastenings and went winging away on the blast. The boys
seized each others' hands and fled, with many tumblings and
bruises, to the shelter of a great oak that stood upon the river bank.
Now the battle was at its highest. Under the ceaseless conflagration
of lightning that flamed in the skies, everything below stood out in
clean-cut and shadowless distinctness: the bending trees, the
billowy river, white with foam, the driving spray of spume-flakes,
the dim outlines of the high bluffs on the other side, glimpsed
through the drifting cloud-rack and the slanting veil of rain. Every
little while some giant tree yielded the fight and fell crashing
through the younger growth; and the unflagging thunder-peals
came now in ear-splitting explosive bursts, keen and sharp, and
unspeakably appalling. The storm culminated in one matchless
effort that seemed likely to tear the island to pieces, burn it up,
drown it to the tree tops, blow it away, and deafen every creature in
it, all at one and the same moment. It was a wild night for
homeless young heads to be out in.

But at last the battle was done, and the forces retired with weaker
and weaker threatenings and grumblings, and peace resumed her
sway. The boys went back to camp, a good deal awed; but they
found there was still something to be thankful for, because the
great sycamore, the shelter of their beds, was a ruin, now, blasted
by the lightnings, and they were not under it when the catastrophe
happened.

Everything in camp was drenched, the camp-fire as well; for
they were but heedless lads, like their generation, and had made no
provision against rain. Here was matter for dismay, for they were
soaked through and chilled. They were eloquent in their distress;
but they presently discovered that the fire had eaten so far up under
the great log it had been built against, (where it curved upward
and separated itself from the ground,) that a hand-breadth or so
of it had escaped wetting; so they patiently wrought until, with
shreds and bark gathered from the undersides of sheltered logs,
they coaxed the fire to burn again. Then they piled on great dead
boughs till they had a roaring furnace and were glad-hearted once
more. They dried their boiled ham and had a feast, and after that
they sat by the fire and expanded and glorified their midnight
adventure until morning, for there was not a dry spot to sleep on,
anywhere around.

As the sun began to steal in upon the boys, drowsiness came over
them and they went out on the sand-bar and lay down to sleep.
They got scorched out by and by, and drearily set about getting
breakfast. After the meal they felt rusty, and stiff-jointed, and a
little homesick once more. Tom saw the signs, and fell to cheering
up the pirates as well as he could. But they cared nothing for
marbles, or circus, or swimming, or anything. He reminded them

of the imposing secret, and raised a ray of cheer. While it lasted,
he got them interested in a new device. This was to knock off being
pirates, for a while, and be Indians for a change. They were
attracted by this idea; so it was not long before they were stripped,
and striped from head to heel with black mud, like so many
zebras,— all of them chiefs, of course—and then they went tearing
through the woods to attack an English settlement.

By and by they separated into three hostile tribes, and darted
upon each other from ambush with dreadful war-whoops, and
killed and scalped each other by thousands. It was a gory day.
Consequently it was an extremely satisfactory one.

They assembled in camp toward supper time, hungry and happy;
but now a difficulty arose—hostile Indians could not break the
bread of hospitality together without first making peace, and this
was a simple impossibility without smoking a pipe of peace. There
was no other process that ever they had heard of. Two of the savages
almost wished they had remained pirates. However, there was no
other way; so with such show of cheerfulness as they could muster
they called for the pipe and took their whiff as it passed, in due
form.

And behold they were glad they had gone into savagery, for they
had gained something; they found that they could now smoke a
little without having to go and hunt for a lost knife; they did not
get sick enough to be seriously uncomfortable. They were not likely
to fool away this high promise for lack of effort. No, they practiced
cautiously, after supper, with right fair success, and so they spent
a jubilant evening. They were prouder and happier in their new
acquirement than they would have been in the scalping and
skinning of the Six Nations. We will leave them to smoke and
chatter and brag, since we have no further use for them at present.

CHAPTER XVII

But there was no hilarity in the little town that same tranquil
Saturday afternoon. The Harpers, and Aunt Polly's family, were
being put into mourning, with great grief and many tears. An
unusual quiet possessed the village, although it was ordinarily
quiet enough, in all conscience. The villagers conducted their
concerns with an absent air, and talked little; but they sighed often.
The Saturday holiday seemed a burden to the children. They had
no heart in their sports, and gradually gave them up.

In the afternoon Becky Thatcher found herself moping about
the deserted school-house yard, and feeling very melancholy. But
she found nothing there to comfort her. She soliloquised:

"Oh, if I only had his brass andiron-knob again! But I haven't
got anything now to remember him by." And she choked back a
little sob.

Presently she stopped, and said to herself:

"It was right here. O, if it was to do over again, I wouldn't say that—I wouldn't say it for the whole world. But he's gone now; I'll never never never see him any more."

This thought broke her down and she wandered away, with the tears rolling down her cheeks. Then quite a group of boys and girls,—playmates of Tom's and Joe's—came by, and stood looking over the paling fence and talking in reverent tones of how Tom did so-and-so, the last time they saw him, and how Joe said this and that small trifle (pregnant with awful prophecy, as they could easily see now!)—and each speaker pointed out the exact spot where the lost lads stood at the time, and then added something like "and I was a standing just so—just as I am now, and as if you was him— I was as close as that—and he smiled, just this way—and then something seemed to go all over me, like,—awful, you know—and I never thought what it meant, of course, but I can see now!"

Then there was a dispute about who saw the dead boys last in life, and many claimed that dismal distinction, and offered evidences, more or less tampered with by the witness; and when it was ultimately decided who *did* see the departed last, and exchanged the last words with them, the lucky parties took upon themselves a sort of sacred importance, and were gaped at and envied by all the rest. One poor chap, who had no other grandeur to offer, said with tolerably manifest pride in the remembrance:

"Well, Tom Sawyer he licked me once."

But that bid for glory was a failure. Most of the boys could say that, and so that cheapened the distinction too much. The group loitered away, still recalling memories of the lost heroes, in awed voices.

When the Sunday-school hour was finished, the next morning, the bell began to toll, instead of ringing in the usual way. It was a very still Sabbath, and the mournful sound seemed in keeping with the musing hush that lay upon nature. The villagers began to gather, loitering a moment in the vestibule to converse in whispers about the sad event. But there was no whispering in the house; only the funereal rustling of dresses as the women gathered to their seats, disturbed the silence there. None could remember when the little church had been so full before. There was finally a waiting pause, an expectant dumbness, and then Aunt Polly entered, followed by Sid and Mary, and they by the Harper family, all in deep black, and the whole congregation, the old minister as well, rose reverently and stood, until the mourners were seated in the front pew. There was another communing silence, broken at intervals by muffled sobs, and then the minister spread his hands abroad and prayed. A moving hymn was sung, and the text followed: "I am the Resurrection and the Life."

As the service proceeded, the clergyman drew such pictures of the

graces, the winning ways and the rare promise of the lost lads, that
every soul there, thinking he recognized these pictures, felt a pang in
remembering that he had persistently blinded himself to them,
always before, and had as persistently seen only faults and flaws
in the poor boys. The minister related many a touching incident in
the lives of the departed, too, which illustrated their sweet,
generous natures, and the people could easily see, now, how noble
and beautiful those episodes were, and remembered with grief
that at the time they occurred they had seemed rank rascalities,
well deserving of the cowhide. The congregation became more and
more moved, as the pathetic tale went on, till at last the whole
company broke down and joined the weeping mourners in a
chorus of anguished sobs, the preacher himself giving way to his
feelings, and crying in the pulpit.

There was a rustle in the gallery, which nobody noticed; a
moment later the church door creaked; the minister raised his
streaming eyes above his handkerchief, and stood transfixed! First
one and then another pair of eyes followed the minister's, and then
almost with one impulse the congregation rose and stared while
the three dead boys came marching up the aisle, Tom in the lead,
Joe next, and Huck, a ruin of drooping rags, sneaking sheepishly
in the rear! They had been hid in the unused gallery listening to
their own funeral sermon!

Aunt Polly, Mary and the Harpers threw themselves upon
their restored ones, smothered them with kisses and poured out
thanksgivings, while poor Huck stood abashed and uncomfortable,
not knowing exactly what to do or where to hide from so many
unwelcoming eyes. He wavered, and started to slink away, but
Tom seized him and said:

"Aunt Polly, it ain't fair. Somebody's got to be glad to see Huck."

"And so they shall. *I*'m glad to see him, poor motherless thing!"
And the loving attentions Aunt Polly lavished upon him were the
one thing capable of making him more uncomfortable than he
was before.

Suddenly the minister shouted at the top of his voice: "Praise
God from whom all blessings flow—SING!—and put your hearts
in it!"

And they did. Old Hundred swelled up with a triumphant burst,
and while it shook the rafters Tom Sawyer the Pirate looked around
upon the envying juveniles about him and confessed in his heart
that this was the proudest moment of his life.

As the "sold" congregation trooped out they said they would
almost be willing to be made ridiculous again to hear Old Hundred
sung like that once more.

Tom got more cuffs and kisses that day—according to Aunt
Polly's varying moods—than he had earned before in a year; and he
hardly knew which expressed the most gratefulness to God and
affection for himself.

CHAPTER XVIII

That was Tom's great secret—the scheme to return home with his brother pirates and attend their own funerals. They had paddled over to the Missouri shore on a log, at dusk on Saturday, landing five or six miles below the village; they had slept in the woods at the edge of the town till nearly daylight, and had then crept through back lanes and alleys and finished their sleep in the gallery of the church among a chaos of invalided benches.

At breakfast, Monday morning, Aunt Polly and Mary were very loving to Tom, and very attentive to his wants. There was an unusual amount of talk. In the course of it Aunt Polly said:

"Well, I don't say it wasn't a fine joke, Tom, to keep everybody suffering 'most a week so you boys had a good time, but it is a pity you could be so hard-hearted as to let *me* suffer so. If you could come over on a log to go to your funeral, you could have come over and give me a hint some way that you warn't *dead,* but only run off."

"Yes, you could have done that, Tom," said Mary; "and I believe you would if you had thought of it."

"Would you Tom?" said Aunt Polly, her face lighting wistfully. "Say, now, would you, if you'd thought of it? "

"I—well I don't know. 'Twould a spoiled everything."

"Tom, I hoped you loved me that much," said Aunt Polly, with a grieved tone that discomforted the boy. "It would been something if you'd cared enough to *think* of it, even if you didn't *do* it."

"Now auntie, that ain't any harm," pleaded Mary; "it's only Tom's giddy way—he is always in such a rush that he never thinks of anything."

"More's the pity. Sid would have thought. And Sid would have come and *done* it, too. Tom, you'll look back, some day, when it's too late, and wish you'd cared a little more for me when it would have cost you so little."

"Now auntie, you know I do care for you," said Tom.

"I'd know it better if you acted more like it."

"I wish now I'd thought," said Tom, with a repentant tone; "but I dreamed about you, anyway. That's something, ain't it?"

"It ain't much—a cat does that much—but it's better than nothing. What did you dream?"

"Why Wednesday night I dreamt that you was sitting over there by the bed, and Sid was sitting by the wood-box, and Mary next to him."

"Well, so we did. So we always do. I'm glad your dreams could take even that much trouble about us."

"And I dreamt that Joe Harper's mother was here."

"Why, she *was* here! Did you dream any more?"

"O, lots. But it's so dim, now."

"Well, *try* to recollect—can't you?"

"Some how it seems to me that the wind—the wind blowed the—the—"

"Try harder, Tom! The wind did blow something. Come!"

Tom pressed his fingers on his forehead an anxious minute, and then said:

"I've got it now! I've got it now! It blowed the candle!"

"Mercy on us! Go on, Tom—go on!"

"And it seems to me that you said, 'Why I believe that that door—' "

"Go *on*, Tom!"

"Just let me study a moment—just a moment. Oh, yes—you said you believed the door was open."

"As I'm sitting here, I did! Didn't I, Mary! Go on!"

"And then—and then—well I won't be certain, but it seems like as if you made Sid go and—and—"

"Well? Well? What did I make him do, Tom? What did I make him do?"

"You made him—you—O, you made him shut it."

"Well for the land's sake! I never heard the beat of that in all my days! Don't tell *me* there ain't anything in dreams, any more. Sereny Harper shall know of this before I'm an hour older. I'd like to see her get around *this* with her rubbage 'bout superstition. Go on, Tom!"

"Oh, it's all getting just as bright as day, now. Next you said I warn't *bad,* only mischeevous and harum-scarum, and not any more responsible than—than—I think it was a colt, or something."

"And so it was! Well, goodness gracious! Go on, Tom!"

"And then you began to cry."

"So I did. So I did. Not the first time, neither. And then—"

"Then Mrs. Harper she began to cry, and said Joe was just the same and she wished she hadn't whipped him for taking cream when she'd thowed it out her own self—"

"Tom! The sperrit was upon you! You was a prophecying—that's what you was doing! Land alive, go on, Tom!"

"Then Sid he said—he said—"

"I don't think I said anything," said Sid.

"Yes you did, Sid," said Mary.

"Shut your heads and let Tom go on! What did he say, Tom?"

"He said—I *think* he said he hoped I was better off where I was gone to, but if I'd been better sometimes—"

"*There,* d'you hear that! It was his very words!"

"And you shut him up sharp."

"I lay I did! There must a been an angel there. There *was* an angel there, somewheres!"

"And Mrs. Harper told about Joe scaring her with a fire-cracker, and you told about Peter and the Pain-killer—"

"Just as true as I live!"

"And then there was a whole lot of talk 'bout dragging the river for us, and 'bout having the funeral Sunday, and then you and old Miss Harper hugged and cried, and she went."

"It happened just so! It happened just so, as sure as I'm a sitting in these very tracks. Tom you couldn't told it more like, if you'd a seen it! And *then* what? Go on, Tom?"

"Then I thought you prayed for me—and I could see you and hear every word you said. And you went to bed, and I was so sorry, that I took and wrote on a piece of sycamore, *'We ain't dead—we are only off being pirates,'* and put it on the table by the candle; and then you looked so good, laying there asleep, that I thought I went and leaned over and kissed you on the lips."

"Did you, Tom, *did* you! I just forgive you everything for that!" And she siezed the boy in a crushing embrace that made him feel like the guiltiest of villains.

"It was very kind, even though it was only a—dream," Sid soliloquised just audibly.

"Shut up Sid! A body does just the same in a dream as he'd do if he was awake. Here's a big Milum apple I've been saving for you Tom, if you was ever found again—now go 'long to school. I'm thankful to the good God and Father of us all I've got you back, that's long-suffering and merciful of them that believe on Him and keep His word, though goodness knows I'm unworthy of it, but if only the worthy ones got His blessings and His hand to help them over the rough places, there's few enough would smile here or ever enter into His rest when the long night comes. Go 'long Sid, Mary, Tom—take yourselves off—you've hendered me long enough."

The children left for school, and the old lady to call on Mrs. Harper and vanquish her realism with Tom's marvelous dream. Sid had better judgment than to utter the thought that was in his mind as he left the house. It was this: "Pretty thin—as long a dream as that, without any mistakes in it!"

What a hero Tom was become, now! He did not go skipping and prancing, but moved with a dignified swagger as became a pirate who felt that the public eye was on him. And indeed it was; he tried not to seem to see the looks or hear the remarks as he passed along, but they were food and drink to him. Smaller boys than himself flocked at his heels, as proud to be seen with him, and tolerated by him, as if he had been the drummer at the head of a procession or the elephant leading a menagerie into town. Boys of his own size pretended not to know he had been away at all; but they were consuming with envy, nevertheless. They would have given anything to have that swarthy sun-tanned skin of his, and his glittering notoriety; and Tom would not have parted with either for a circus.

At school the children made so much of him and of Joe, and delivered such eloquent admiration from their eyes, that the two

heroes were not long in becoming insufferably "stuck-up." They
began to tell their adventures to hungry listeners—but they only
began; it was not a thing likely to have an end, with imaginations
like theirs to furnish material. And finally, when they got out their
pipes and went serenely puffing around, the very summit of glory
was reached.

Tom decided that he could be independent of Becky Thatcher
now. Glory was sufficient. He would live for glory. Now that he was
distinguished, maybe she would be wanting to "make up." Well, let
her—she should see that he could be as indifferent as some other
people. Presently she arrived. Tom pretended not to see her. He
moved away and joined a group of boys and girls and began to talk.
Soon he observed that she was tripping gayly back and forth with
flushed face and dancing eyes, pretending to be busy chasing schoolmates, and screaming with laughter when she made a capture; but
he noticed that she always made her captures in his vicinity, and that
she seemed to cast a conscious eye in his direction at such times, too.
It gratified all the vicious vanity that was in him; and so, instead of
winning him it only "set him up" the more and made him the more
diligent to avoid betraying that he know she was about. Presently she
gave over skylarking, and moved irresolutely about, sighing once or
twice and glancing furtively and wistfully toward Tom. Then she
observed that now Tom was talking more particularly to Amy
Lawrence than to any one else. She felt a sharp pang and grew
disturbed and uneasy at once. She tried to go away, but her feet were
treacherous, and carried her to the group instead. She said to a girl
almost at Tom's elbow—with sham vivacity:

"Why Mary Austin! you bad girl, why didn't you come to Sunday-
school?"

"I did come—didn't you see me?"

"Why no! Did you? Where did you sit?"

"I was in Miss Peter's class, where I always go. I saw *you.*"

"Did you? Why it's funny I didn't see you. I wanted to tell you
about the pic-nic."

"O, that's jolly. Who's going to give it?"

"My ma's going to let me have one."

"O, goody; I hope she'll let *me* come."

"Well she will. The pic-nic's for me. She'll let anybody come that
I want, and I want you."

"That's ever so nice. When is it going to be?"

"By and by. Maybe about vacation."

"O, won't it be fun! You going to have all the girls and boys?"

"Yes, every one that's friends to me—or wants to be;" and she
glanced ever so furtively at Tom, but he talked right along to Amy
Lawrence about the terrible storm on the island, and how the
lightning tore the great sycamore tree "all to flinders" while he was
"standing within three feet of it."

"O, may I come?" said Gracie Miller.

"Yes."

"And me?" said Sally Rogers.

"Yes."

"And me, too?" said Susy Harper. "And Joe?"

"Yes."

And so on, with clapping of joyful hands till all the group had begged for invitations but Tom and Amy. Then Tom turned coolly away, still talking, and took Amy with him. Becky's lips trembled and the tears came to her eyes; she hid these signs with a forced gayety and went on chattering, but the life had gone out of the pic-nic, now, and out of everything else; she got away as soon as she could and hid herself and had what her sex calls "a good cry." Then she sat moody, with wounded pride till the bell rang. She roused up, now, with a vindictive cast in her eye, and gave her plaited tails a shake and said she know what *she'd* do.

At recess Tom continued his flirtation with Amy with jubilant self-satisfaction. And he kept drifting about to find Becky and lacerate her with the performance. At last he spied her, but there was a sudden falling of his mercury. She was sitting cosily on a little bench behind the school-house looking at a picture book with Alfred Temple—and so absorbed were they, and their heads so close together over the book that they did not seem to be conscious of anything in the world besides. Jealousy ran red hot through Tom's veins. He began to hate himself for throwing away the chance Becky had offered for a reconciliation. He called himself a fool, and all the hard names he could think of. He wanted to cry with vexation. Amy chatted happily along, as they walked, for her heart was singing, but Tom's tongue had lost its function. He did not hear what Amy was saying, and whenever she paused expectantly he could only stammer an awkward assent, which was as often misplaced as otherwise. He kept drifting to the rear of the school-house, again and again, to sear his eye-balls with the hateful spectacle there. He could not help it. And it maddened him to see, as he thought he saw, that Becky Thatcher never once suspected that he was even in the land of the living. But she did see, nevertheless; and she knew she was winning her fight, too, and was glad to see him suffer as she had suffered.

Amy's happy prattle became intolerable. Tom hinted at things he had to attend to; things that must be done; and time was fleeting. But in vain—the girl chirped on. Tom thought, "O hang her, ain't I ever going to get rid of her?" At last he *must* be attending to those things—and she said artlessly that she would be "around" when school let out. And he hastened away, hating her for it.

"Any other boy!" Tom thought, grating his teeth. "Any boy in the whole town but that Saint Louis smarty that thinks he dresses so fine and is aristocracy! O, all right, I licked you the first day you ever saw this town, mister, and I'll lick you again! You just wait till I catch you out! I'll just take and—"

And he went through the motions of thrashing an imaginary boy—
pummeling the air, and kicking and gouging. "Oh, you do, do you?
You holler 'nough, do you? Now, then, let that learn you!" And so
the imaginary flogging was finished to his satisfacton.

Tom fled home at noon. His conscience could not endure any
more of Amy's grateful happiness, and his jealousy could bear no
more of the other distress. Becky resumed her picture-inspections
with Alfred, but as the minutes dragged along and no Tom came to
suffer, her triumph began to cloud and she lost interest; gravity
and absent-mindedness followed, and then melancholy; two or
three times she pricked up her ear at a footstep, but it was a false
hope; no Tom came. At last she grew entirely miserable and wished
she hadn't carried it so far. When poor Alfred, seeing that he was
losing her, he did not know how, and kept exclaiming: "O here's a
jolly one! look at this!" she lost patience at last, and said, "Oh,
don't bother me! I don't care for them!" and burst into tears, and
got up and walked away.

Alfred dropped alongside and was going to try to comfort her,
but she said:

"Go away and leave me alone, can't you! I hate you!"

So the boy halted, wondering what he could have done—for she
had said she would look at pictures all through the nooning—and
she walked on, crying. Then Alfred went musing into the deserted
schoolhouse. He was humiliated and angry. He easily guessed his
way to the truth—the girl had simply made a convenience of him to
vent her spite upon Tom Sawyer. He was far from hating Tom the
less when this thought occurred to him. He wished there was some
way to get that boy into trouble without much risk to himself.
Tom's spelling fell under his eye. Here was his opportunity. He
gratefully opened to the lesson for the afternoon and poured ink
upon the page.

Becky, glancing in at a window behind him at the moment, saw
the act, and moved on, without discovering herself. She started
homeward, now, intending to find Tom and tell him; Tom would be
thankful and their troubles would be healed. Before she was half
way home, however, she had changed her mind. The thought of
Tom's treatment of her when she was talking about her pic-nic came
scorching back and filled her with shame. She resolved to let him get
whipped on the damaged spelling-book's account, and to hate him
forever, into the bargain.

CHAPTER XIX

Tom arrived at home in a dreary mood, and the first thing his aunt
said to him showed him that he had brought his sorrows to an
unpromising market:

"Tom, I've got a notion to skin you alive!"

"Auntie, what have I done?"

"Well, you've done enough. Here I go over to Sereny Harper, like an old softy, expecting I'm going to make her believe all that rubbage about that dream, when lo and behold you she'd found out from Joe that you was over here and heard all the talk we had that night. Tom I don't know what is to become of a boy that will act like that. It makes me feel so bad to think you could let me go to Sereny Harper and make such a fool of myself and never say a word."

This was a new aspect of the thing. His smartness of the morning had seemed to Tom a good joke before, and very ingenious. It merely looked mean and shabby now. He hung his head and could not think of anything to say for a moment. Then he said:

"Auntie, I wish I hadn't done it—but I didn't think."

"O, child, you never think. You never think of anything but your own selfishness. You could think to come all the way over here from Jackson's island in the night to laugh at our troubles, and you could think to fool me with a lie about a dream; but you couldn't ever think to pity us and save us from sorrow."

"Auntie, I know now it was mean, but I didn't mean to be mean. I didn't, honest. And besides I didn't come over here to laugh at you that night."

"What did you come for, then?"

"It was to tell you not to be uneasy about us, because we hadn't got drowned."

"Tom, Tom, I would be the thankfullest soul in this world if I could believe you ever had as good a thought as that, but you know you never did—and *I* know it, Tom."

"Indeed and 'deed I did, auntie—I wish I may never stir if I didn't."

"O, Tom, don't lie—don't do it. It only makes things a hundred times worse."

"It ain't a lie, auntie, it's the truth. I wanted to keep you from grieving—that was all that made me come."

"I'd give the whole world to believe that—it would cover up a power of sins Tom. I'd 'most be glad you'd run off and acted so bad. But it aint reasonable; because, why didn't you tell me, child?"

"Why, you see, auntie, when you got to talking about the funeral, I just got all full of the idea of our coming and hiding in the church, and I couldn't somehow bear to spoil it. So I just put the bark back in my pocket and kept mum."

"What bark?"

"The bark I had wrote on to tell you we'd gone pirating. I wish, now, you'd waked up when I kissed you—I do, honest."

The hard lines in his aunt's face relaxed and a sudden tenderness dawned in her eyes.

"*Did* you kiss me, Tom?"

"Why yes I did."

"Are you sure you did, Tom?"

"Why yes I did, auntie—certain sure."

"What did you kiss me for, Tom?"

"Because I loved you so, and you laid there moaning and I was so sorry."

The words sounded like truth. The old lady could not hide a tremor in her voice when she said:

"Kiss me again, Tom!—and be off with you to school, now, and don't bother me any more."

The moment he was gone, she ran to a closet and got out the ruin of a jacket which Tom had gone pirating in. Then she stopped with it in her hand, and said to herself:

"No, I don't dare. Poor boy, I reckon he's lied about it—but it's a blessed, blessed lie, there's such comfort come from it. I hope the Lord—I *know* the Lord will forgive him, because it was such goodheartedness in him to tell it. But I don't want to find out it's a lie. I won't look."

She put the jacket away, and stood by musing a minute. Twice she put out her hand to take the garment again, and twice she refrained. Once more she ventured, and this time she fortified herself with the thought: "It's a good lie— it's a good lie—I won't let it grieve me." So she sought the jacket pocket. A moment later she was reading Tom's piece of bark through flowing tears and saying: "I could forgive the boy, now, if he'd committed a million sins!"

CHAPTER XX

There was something about Aunt Polly's manner, when she kissed Tom, that swept away his low spirits and made him light-hearted and happy again. He started to school and had the luck of coming upon Becky Thatcher at the head of Meadow Lane. His mood always determined his manner. Without a moment's hesitation he ran to her and said:

"I acted mighty mean to-day, Becky, and I'm so sorry. I won't ever, ever do that way again, as long as ever I live—please make up, won't you?"

The girl stopped and looked him scornfully in the face:

"I'll thank you to keep yourself *to* yourself, Mr. Thomas Sawyer. I'll never speak to you again."

She tossed her head and passed on. Tom was so stunned that he had not even presence of mind enough to say "Who cares, Miss Smarty?" until the right time to say it had gone by. So he said nothing. But he was in a fine rage, nevertheless. He moped into the school-yard wishing she were a boy, and imagining how he would trounce her if she were. He presently encountered her and delivered a stinging remark as he passed. She hurled one in return, and the

angry breach was complete. It seemed to Becky, in her hot
resentment, that she could hardly wait for school to "take in," she
was so impatient to see Tom flogged for the injured spelling-book. If
she had had any lingering notion of exposing Alfred Temple, Tom's
offensive fling had driven it entirely away.

Poor girl, she did not know how fast she was nearing trouble
herself. The master, Mr. Dobbins, had reached middle age with an
unsatisfied ambition. The darling of his desires was, to be a doctor,
but poverty had decreed that he should be nothing higher than a
village schoolmaster. Every day he took a mysterious book out of his
desk and absorbed himself in it at times when no classes were
reciting. He kept that book under lock and key. There was not an
urchin in school but was perishing to have a glimpse of it, but the
chance never came. Every boy and girl had a theory about the nature
of that book; but no two theories were alike, and there was no way of
getting at the facts in the case. Now, as Becky was passing by the
desk, which stood near the door, she noticed that the key was in the
lock! It was a precious moment. She glanced around; found herself
alone, and the next instant she had the book in her hands. The title-
page—Professor somebody's "Anatomy"—carried no information
to her mind; so she began to turn the leaves. She came at once upon
a handsomely engraved and colored frontispiece—a human figure,
stark naked. At that moment a shadow fell on the page and Tom
Sawyer stepped in at the door, and caught a glimpse of the picture.
Becky snatched at the book to close it, and had the hard luck to tear
the pictured page half down the middle. She thrust the volume into
the desk, turned the key, and burst out crying with shame and
vexation.

"Tom Sawyer, you are just as mean as you can be, to sneak up on
a person and look at what they're looking at."

"How could *I* know you was looking at anything?"

"You ought to be ashamed of yourself Tom Sawyer; you know
you're going to tell on me, and O, what shall I do, what shall I do! I'll
be whipped, and I never was whipped in school."

Then she stamped her little foot and said:

"*Be* so mean if you want to! *I* know something that's going to
happen. You just wait and you'll see! Hateful, hateful, hateful!"—
and she flung out of the house with a new explosion of crying.

Tom stood still, rather flustered by this onslaught. Presently he
said to himself:

"What a curious kind of a fool a girl is. Never been licked in
school! Shucks. What's a licking! That's just like a girl—they're so
thin-skinned and chicken hearted. Well, of course *I* ain't going to
tell old Dobbins on this little fool, because there's other ways of
getting even on her, that ain't so mean; but what of it? Old Dobbins
will ask who it was tore his book. Nobody'll answer. Then he'll do
just the way he always does—ask first one and then t'other, and

when he comes to the right girl he'll know it, without any telling.
Girl's faces always tell on them. They ain't got any back-bone. She'll
get licked. Well, it's a kind of a tight place for Becky Thatcher,
because there ain't any way out of it." Tom conned the thing a
moment longer and then added: "All right, though; she'd like to see
me in just such a fix—let her sweat it out!"

Tom joined the mob of skylarking scholars outside. In a few
moments the master arrived and school "took in." Tom did not feel
a strong interest in his studies. Every time he stole a glance at the
girls' side of the room Becky's face troubled him. Considering all
things, he did not want to pity her, and yet it was all he could do to
help it. He could get up no exultation that was really worthy the
name. Presently the spelling-book discovery was made, and Tom's
mind was entirely full of his own matters for a while after that. Becky
roused up from her lethargy of distress and showed good interest in
the proceedings. She did not expect that Tom could get out of his
trouble by denying that he spilt the ink on the book himself; and she
was right. The denial only seemed to make the thing worse for Tom.
Becky supposed she would be glad of that, and she tried to
believe she was glad of it, but she found she was not certain.
When the worst came to the worst, she had an impulse to get up
and tell on Alfred Temple, but she made an effort and forced
herself to keep still—because, said she to herself, "he'll tell about
me tearing the picture sure. I wouldn't say a word, not to save
his life!"

Tom took his whipping and went back to his seat not at all
broken-hearted, for he thought it was possible that he had
unknowingly upset the ink on the spelling-book himself, in some
skylarking bout—he had denied it for form's sake and because it
was custom, and had stuck to the denial from principle.

A whole hour drifted by, the master sat nodding in his throne,
the air was drowsy with the hum of study. By and by, Mr. Dobbins
straightened himself up, yawned, then unlocked his desk, and
reached for his book, but seemed undecided whether to take it
out or leave it. Most of the pupils glanced up languidly, but there
were two among them that watched his movements with intent
eyes. Mr. Dobbins fingered his book absently for a while, then
took it out and settled himself in his chair to read! Tom shot a
glance at Becky. He had seen a hunted and helpless rabbit look
as she did, with a gun leveled at its head. Instantly he forgot
his quarrel with her. Quick—something must be done! done in
a flash, too! But the very imminence of the emergency paralyzed
his invention. Good!—he had an inspiration! He would run and
snatch the book, spring through the door and fly. But his
resolution shook for one little instant, and the chance was lost—
the master opened the volume. If Tom only had the wasted
opportunity back again! Too late. There was no help for Becky

now, he said. The next moment the master faced the school.
Every eye sunk under his gaze. There was that in it which smote
even the innocent with fear. There was silence while one might
count ten, the master was gathering his wrath. Then he spoke;
    "Who tore this book?"
    There was not a sound. One could have heard a pin drop. The
stillness continued; the master searched face after face for signs
of guilt.
    "Benjamin Rogers, did you tear this book?"
    A denial. Another pause.
    "Joseph Harper, did you?"
    Another denial. Tom's uneasiness grew more and more
intense under the slow torture of these proceedings. The master
scanned the ranks of boys—considered a while, then turned to the
girls:
    "Amy Lawrence?"
    A shake of the head.
    "Gracie Miller?"
    The same sign.
    "Susan Harper, did you do this?"
    Another negative. The next girl was Becky Thatcher. Tom was
trembling from head to foot with excitement and a sense of the
hopelessness of the situation.
    "Rebecca Thatcher," [Tom glanced at her face—it was white
with terror,]—"did you tear—no, look me in the face"—[her
hands rose in appeal]—"did you tear this book?"
    A thought shot like lightning through Tom's brain. He sprang
to his feet and shouted—"*I* done it!"
    The school stared in perplexity at this incredible folly. Tom
stood a moment, to gather his dismembered faculties; and when
he stepped forward to go to his punishment the surprise, the
gratitude, the adoration that shone upon him out of poor Becky's
eyes seemed pay enough for a hundred floggings. Inspired by the
splendor of his own act, he took without an outcry the most
merciless flaying that even Mr. Dobbins had ever administered;
and also received with indifference the added cruelty of a
command to remain two hours after school should be dismissed—
for he knew who would wait for him outside till his captivity was
done, and not count the tedious time as loss, either.
    Tom went to bed that night planning vengeance against Alfred
Temple; for with shame and repentance Becky had told him all,
not forgetting her own treachery; but even the longing for
vengeance had to give way, soon, to pleasanter musings, and he
fell asleep at last, with Becky's latest words lingering dreamily
in his ear—
    "Tom, how *could* you be so noble!"

CHAPTER XXI

Vacation was approaching. The schoolmaster, always severe, grew severer and more exacting than ever, for he wanted the school to make a good showing on "Examination" day. His rod and his ferule were seldom idle now—at least among the smaller pupils. Only the biggest boys, and young ladies of eighteen and twenty escaped lashing. Mr. Dobbins's lashings were very vigorous ones, too; for although he carried, under his wig, a perfectly bald and shiny head, he had only reached middle age and there was no sign of feebleness in his muscle. As the great day approached, all the tyranny that was in him came to the surface; he seemed to take a vindictive pleasure in punishing the least shortcomings. The consequence was, that the smaller boys spent their days in terror and suffering and their nights in plotting revenge. They threw away no opportunity to do the master a mischief. But he kept ahead all the time. The retribution that followed every vengeful success was so sweeping and majestic that the boys always retired from the field badly worsted. At last they conspired together and hit upon a plan that promised a dazzling victory. They swore-in the sign-painter's boy, told him the scheme, and asked his help. He had his own reasons for being delighted, for the master boarded in his father's family and had given the boy ample cause to hate him. The master's wife would go on a visit to the country in a few days, and there would be nothing to interfere with the plan; the master always prepared himself for great occasions by getting pretty well fuddled, and the sign-painter's boy said that when the dominie had reached the proper condition on Examination Evening he would "manage the thing" while he napped in his chair; then he would have him awakened at the right time and hurried away to school.

In the fullness of time the interesting occasion arrived. At eight in the evening the schoolhouse was brilliantly lighted, and adorned with wreaths and festoons of foliage and flowers. The master sat throned in his great chair upon a raised platform, with his blackboard behind him. He was looking tolerably mellow. Three rows of benches on each side and six rows in front of him were occupied by the dignitaries of the town and by the parents of the pupils. To his left, back of the rows of citizens, was a spacious temporary platform upon which were seated the scholars who were to take part in the exercises of the evening; rows of small boys, washed and dressed to an intolerable state of discomfort; rows of gawky big boys; snow-banks of girls and young ladies clad in lawn and muslin and conspicuously conscious of their bare arms, their grandmothers' ancient trinkets, their bits of pink and blue ribbon and the flowers in their hair. All the rest of the house was filled with non-participating scholars.

The exercises began. A very little boy stood up and sheepishly recited, "You'd scarce expect one of my age to speak in public on the stage, etc"—accompanying himself with the painfully exact and spasmodic gestures which a machine might have used—supposing the machine to be a trifle out of order. But he got through safely, though cruelly scared, and got a fine round of applause when he made his manufactured bow and retired.

A little shame-faced girl lisped "Mary had a little lamb, etc.," performed a compassion-inspiring curtsy, got her meed of applause, and sat down flushed and happy.

Tom Sawyer stepped forward with conceited confidence and soared into the unquenchable and indestructible "Give me liberty or give me death" speech, with fine fury and frantic gesticulation, and broke down in the middle of it. A ghastly stage-fright siezed him, his legs quaked under him and he was like to choke. True, he had the manifest sympathy of the house—but he had the house's silence, too, which was even worse than its sympathy. The master frowned, and this completed the disaster. Tom struggled a while and then retired, utterly defeated. There was a weak attempt at applause, but it died early.

"The Boy stood on the Burning Deck" followed; also "The Assyrian Came Down," and other declamatory gems. Then there were reading exercises, and a spelling fight. The meager Latin class recited with honor. The prime feature of the evening was in order, now—original "compositions" by the young ladies. Each in her turn stepped forward to the edge of the platform, cleared her throat, held up her manuscript (tied with dainty ribbon), and proceeded to read, with labored attention to "expression" and punctuation. The themes were the same that had been illuminated upon similar occasions by their mothers before them, their grandmothers, and doubtless all their ancestors in the female line clear back to the Crusades. "Friendship" was one; "Memories of Other Days;" "Religion in History;" "Dream Land;" "The Advantages of Culture;" "Forms of Political Government Compared and Contrasted;" "Melancholy;" "Filial Love;" "Heart Longings," etc., etc.

A prevalent feature in these compositions was a nursed and petted melancholy; another was a wasteful and opulent gush of "fine language;" another was a tendency to lug in by the ears particularly prized words and phrases until they were worn entirely out; and a peculiarity that conspicuously marked and marred them was the inveterate and intolerable sermon that wagged its crippled tail at the end of each and every one of them. No matter what the subject might be, a brain-racking effort was made to squirm it into some aspect or other that the moral and religious mind could contemplate with edification. The glaring

insincerity of these sermons was not sufficient to compass the
banishment of the fashion from the schools, and it is not
sufficient to-day; it never will be sufficient while the world stands,
perhaps. There is no school in all our land where the young ladies
do not feel obliged to close their compositions with a sermon;
and you will find that the sermon of the most frivolous and least
religious girl in the school is always the longest and the most
relentlessly pious. But, enough of this. Homely truth is
unpalatable.

Let us return to the "Examination." The first composition that
was read was one entitled "Is this, then, Life?" Perhaps the
reader can endure an extract from it:

> "In the common walks of life, with what delightful emotions
> does the youthful mind look forward to some anticipated scene of
> festivity! Imagination is busy sketching rose-tinted pictures of joy.
> In fancy, the voluptuous votary of fashion sees herself amid the
> festive throng, 'the observed of all observers.' Her graceful form,
> arrayed in snowy robes, is whirling through the mazes of the joyous
> dance; her eye is brightest, her step is lightest in the gay assembly.
> "In such delicious fancies time quickly glides by, and the
> welcome hour arrives for her entrance into the elysian world, of
> which she has had such bright dreams. How fairy-like does every
> thing appear to her enchanted vision! each new scene is more
> charming than the last. But after a while she finds that beneath
> this goodly exterior, all is vanity: the flattery which once charmed
> her soul, now grates harshly upon her ear; the ball-room has lost
> its charms; and with wasted health and imbittered heart, she turns
> away with the conviction that earthly pleasures cannot satisfy the
> longings of the soul!"

And so forth and so on. There was a buzz of gratification from
time to time during the reading, accompanied by whispered
ejaculations of "How sweet!" "How eloquent!" "So true!" etc.,
and after the thing had closed with a peculiarly afflicting sermon
the applause was enthusiastic.

Then arose a slim, melancholy girl, whose face had the
"interesting" paleness that comes of pills and indigestion, and
read a "poem." Two stanzas of it will do:

A MISSOURI MAIDEN'S FAREWELL TO ALABAMA.

ALABAMA, good-bye! I love thee well!
　　But yet for awhile do I have thee now!
Sad, yes, sad thoughts of thee my heart doth swell,
　　And burning recollections throng my brow!
For I have wandered through thy flowery woods;
　　Have roamed and read near Tallapoosa's stream;
Have listened to Tallassee's warring floods,
　　And wooed on Coosa's side Aurora's beam.

Yet shame I not to bear an o'er-full heart,
  Nor blush to turn behind my tearful eyes;
'Tis from no stranger land I now must part,
  'Tis to no strangers left I yield these sighs.
Welcome and home were mine within this State,
  Whose vales I leave—whose spires fade fast from me
And cold must be mine eyes, and heart, and tête,
  When, dear Alabama! they turn cold on thee!

There were very few there who knew what *"tête"* meant, but
the poem was very satisfactory, nevertheless.

Next appeared a dark complexioned, black eyed, black haired
young lady, who paused an impressive moment, assumed a tragic
expression and began to read in a measured, solemn tone.

A VISION.

Dark and tempestuous was night. Around the throne on high not
a single star quivered; but the deep intonations of the heavy thunder
constantly vibrated upon the ear; whilst the terrific lightning
revelled in angry mood through the cloudy chambers of heaven,
seeming to scorn the power exerted over its terror by the illustrious
Franklin! Even the boisterous winds unanimously came forth from
their mystic homes, and blustered about as if to enhance by their
aid the wildness of the scene.

At such a time, so dark, so dreary, for human sympathy my very
spirit sighed; but instead thereof,

"My dearest friend, my counsellor, my comforter and guide—
My joy in grief, my second bliss in Joy," came to my side.

She moved like one of those bright beings pictured in the sunny
walks of fancy's Eden by the romantic and young, a queen of
beauty unadorned save by her own transcendent loveliness. So soft
was her step, it failed to make even a sound, and but for the magical
thrill imparted by her genial touch, as other unobtrusive beauties,
she would have glided away unperceived—unsought. A strange
sadness rested upon her features, like icy tears upon the robe of
December, as she pointed to the contending elements without, and
bade me contemplate the two beings presented.

This nightmare occupied some ten pages of manuscript and
wound up with a sermon so destructive of all hope to non-
Presbyterians that it took the first prize. This composition was
considered to be the very finest effort of the evening. The mayor
of the village, in delivering the prize to the author of it, made a
warm speech in which he said that it was by far the most
"eloquent" thing he had ever listened to, and that Daniel
Webster himself might well be proud of it.

It may be remarked, in passing, that the number of

compositions in which the word "beauteous" was over-fondled,
and human experience referred to as "life's page," was up to the
usual average.

Now the master, mellow almost to the verge of geniality, put
his chair aside, turned his back to the audience, and began to
draw a map of America on the blackboard, to exercise the
geography class upon. But he made a sad business of it with his
unsteady hand, and a smothered titter rippled over the house.
He knew what the matter was and set himself to right it. He
sponged out lines and re-made them; but he only distorted them
more than ever, and the tittering was more pronounced. He
threw his entire attention upon his work, now, as if determined
not to be put down by the mirth. He felt that all eyes were
fastened upon him; he imagined he was succeeding, and yet the
tittering continued; it even manifestly increased. And well it might.
There was a garret above, pierced with a scuttle over his head;
and down through this scuttle came a cat, suspended around the
haunches by a string; she had a rag tied about her head and
jaws to keep her from mewing; as she slowly descended she curved
upward and clawed at the string, she swung downward and
clawed at the intangible air. The tittering rose higher and higher—
the cat was within six inches of the absorbed teacher's
head—down, down, a little lower, and she grabbed his wig with her
desperate claws, clung to it and was snatched up into the garret
in an instant with her trophy still in her possession! And how the
light did blaze abroad from the master's bald pate—for the
sign-painter's boy had *gilded* it!

That broke up the meeting. The boys were avenged. Vacation
had come.

NOTE.—The pretended "compositions" quoted in this chapter are taken without
alteration from a volume entitled "Prose and Poetry, by a Western Lady"—but
they are exactly and precisely after the school-girl pattern and hence are much
happier than any mere imitations could be.

CHAPTER XXII

Tom joined the new order of Cadets of Temperance, being
attracted by the showy character of their "regalia." He promised
to abstain from smoking, chewing and profanity as long as he
remained a member. Now he found out a new thing—namely,
that to promise not to do a thing is the surest way in the world
to make a body want to go and do that very thing. Tom soon
found himself tormented with a desire to drink and swear; the
desire grew to be so intense that nothing but the hope of a chance
to display himself in his red sash kept him from withdrawing
from the order. Fourth of July was coming; but he soon gave that
up—gave it up before he had worn his shackles over forty-eight

hours—and fixed his hopes upon old Judge Frazer, justice of
the peace, who was apparently on his death-bed and would have
a big public funeral, since he was so high an official. During
three days Tom was deeply concerned about the Judge's condition
and hungry for news of it. Sometimes his hopes ran high—so high
that he would venture to get out his regalia and practice before
the looking glass. But the Judge had a most discouraging way of
fluctuating. At last he was pronounced upon the mend—and then
convalescent. Tom was disgusted; and felt a sense of injury, too.
He handed in his resignation at once—and that night the Judge
suffered a relapse and died. Tom resolved that he would never
trust a man like that again.

The funeral was a fine thing. The Cadets paraded in a style
calculated to kill the late member with envy. Tom was a free boy
again, however—there was something in that. He could drink and
swear, now—but found to his surprise that he did not want to.
The simple fact that he could, took the desire away, and the charm
of it.

Tom presently wondered to find that his coveted vacation was
beginning to hang a little heavily on his hands.

He attempted a diary—but nothing happened during three
days, and so he abandoned it.

The first of all the negro minstrel shows came to town, and
made a sensation. Tom and Joe Harper got up a band of
performers and were happy for two days.

Even the Glorious Fourth was in some sense a failure, for it
rained hard, there was no procession in consequence, and the
greatest man in the world (as Tom supposed) Mr. Benton, an
actual United States Senator, proved an overwhelming
disappointment—for he was not twenty-five feet high, nor even
anywhere in the neighborhood of it.

A circus came. The boys played circus for three days afterward
in tents made of rag carpeting—admission, three pins for boys,
two for girls—and then circusing was abandoned.

A phrenologist and a mesmerizer came—and went again and
left the village duller and drearier than ever.

There were some boys-and-girls' parties, but they were so few
and so delightful that they only made the aching voids between
ache the harder.

Becky Thatcher was gone to her Constantinople home to stay
with her parents during vacation—so there was no bright side
to life anywhere.

The dreadful secret of the murder was a chronic misery. It
was a very cancer for permanency and pain.

Then came the measles.

During two long weeks Tom lay a prisoner, dead to the
world and its happenings. He was very ill, he was interested in

nothing. When he got upon his feet at last and moved feebly down town, a melancholy change had come over everything and every creature. There had been a "revival," and everybody had "got religion," not only the adults, but even the boys and girls. Tom went about, hoping against hope for the sight of one blessed sinful face, but disappointment crossed him everywhere. He found Joe Harper studying a Testament, and turned sadly away from the depressing spectacle. He sought Ben Rogers, and found him visiting the poor with a basket of tracts. He hunted up Jim Hollis, who called his attention to the precious blessing of his late measles as a warning. Every boy he encountered added another ton to his depression; and when, in desperation, he flew for refuge at last to the bosom of Huckleberry Finn and was received with a scriptural quotation, his heart broke and he crept home and to bed realizing that he alone of all the town was lost, forever and forever.

And that night there came on a terrific storm, with driving rain, awful claps of thunder and blinding sheets of lightning. He covered his head with the bedclothes and waited in a horror of suspense for his doom; for he had not the shadow of a doubt that all this hubbub was about him. He believed he had taxed the forbearance of the powers above to the extremity of endurance and that this was the result. It might have seemed to him a waste of pomp and ammunition to kill a bug with a battery of artillery, but there seemed nothing incongruous about the getting up such an expensive thunder storm as this to knock the turf from under an insect like himself.

By and by the tempest spent itself and died without accomplishing its object. The boy's first impulse was to be grateful, and reform. His second was to wait—for there might not be any more storms.

The next day the doctors were back; Tom had relapsed. The three weeks he spent on his back this time seemed an entire age. When he got abroad at last he was hardly grateful that he had been spared, remembering how lonely was his estate, how companionless and forlorn he was. He drifted listlessly down the street and found Jim Hollis acting as judge in a juvenile court that was trying a cat for murder, in the presence of her victim, a bird. He found Joe Harper and Huck Finn up an alley eating a stolen melon. Poor lads! they—like Tom—had suffered a relapse.

CHAPTER XXIII

At last the sleepy atmosphere was stirred—and vigorously: the murder trial came on in the court. It became the absorbing topic of village talk immediately. Tom could not get away from it. Every reference to the murder sent a shudder to his heart, for

his troubled conscience and fears almost persuaded him that
these remarks were put forth in his hearing as "feelers;" he did
not see how he could be suspected of knowing anything about the
murder, but still he could not be comfortable in the midst of
this gossip. It kept him in a cold shiver all the time. He took
Huck to a lonely place to have a talk with him. It would be some
relief to unseal his tongue for a little while; to divide his burden
of distress with another sufferer. Moreover, he wanted to assure
himself that Huck had remained discreet.

"Huck, have you ever told anybody about—that?"

"Bout what?"

"You know what."

"Oh—'course I haven't."

"Never a word?"

"Never a solitary word, so help me. What makes you ask?"

"Well, I was afeard."

"Why Tom Sawyer, we wouldn't be alive two days if that got
found out. *You* know that."

Tom felt more comfortable. After a pause:

"Huck, they couldn't anybody get you to tell, could they?"

"Get me to tell? Why if I wanted that half-breed devil to
drownd me they could get me to tell. They ain't no different way."

"Well, that's all right, then. I reckon we're safe as long as we
keep mum. But let's swear again, anyway. It's more surer."

"I'm agreed."

So they swore again with dread solemnities.

"What is the talk around, Huck? I've heard a power of it."

"Talk? Well, it's just Muff Potter, Muff Potter, Muff Potter
all the time. It keeps me in a sweat, constant, so's I want to hide
som'ers."

"That's just the same way they go on round me. I reckon he's
a goner. Don't you feel sorry for him, sometimes?"

"Most always—most always. He ain't no account; but then he
hain't ever done anything to hurt anybody. Just fishes a little, to
get money to get drunk on—and loafs around considerable; but
lord we all do that—leastways most of us,—preachers and such
like. But he's kind of good—he give me half a fish, once, when
there warn't enough for two; and lots of times he's kind of stood
by me when I was out of luck."

"Well, he's mended kites for me, Huck, and knitted hooks on
to my line. I wish we could get him out of there."

"My! we couldn't get him out Tom. And besides, 'twouldn't
do any good; they'd ketch him again."

"Yes—so they would. But I hate to hear 'em abuse him so like
the dickens when he never done—that."

"I do too, Tom. Lord, I hear 'em say he's the bloodiest looking
villain in this country, and they wonder he wasn't ever hung

before."

"Yes, they talk like that, all the time. I've heard 'em say that if
he was to get free they'd lynch him."

"And they'd do it, too."

The boys had a long talk, but it brought them little comfort.
As the twilight drew on, they found themselves hanging about
the neighborhood of the little isolated jail, perhaps with an
undefined hope that something would happen that might clear
away their difficulties. But nothing happened; there seemed to be
no angels or fairies interested in this luckless captive.

The boys did as they had often done before—went to the cell
grating and gave Potter some tobacco and matches. He was on the
ground floor and there were no guards.

His gratitude for their gifts had always smote their consciences
before—it cut deeper than ever, this time. They felt cowardly and
treacherous to the last degree when Potter said:

"You've been mighty good to me, boys—better'n anybody else
in this town. And I don't forget it, I don't. Often I says to myself,
says I, 'I used to mend all the boys' kites and things, and show
'em what I could, and now they've all forgot old Muff when he's
in trouble; but Tom don't, and Huck don't—*they* don't forget
him,' says I, 'and I don't forget them.' Well, boys, I done an
awful thing—drunk and crazy at the time—that's the only way
I account for it—and now I got to swing for it, and it's right.
Right, and *best,* too I reckon—hope so, anyway. Well, we won't
talk about that. I don't want to make *you* feel bad; you've
befriended me. But what I want to say, is, don't *you* ever get
drunk—then you won't ever get here. Stand a little furder west—
so—that's it; it's a prime comfort to see faces that's friendly when
a body's in such a muck of trouble, and there don't none come
here but yourn. Good friendly faces—good friendly faces. Git
up on one another's backs and let me touch 'em. That's it. Shake
hands—yourn'll come through the bars, but mine's too big. Little
hands, and weak—but they've helped Muff Potter a power, and
they'd help him more if they could."

Tom went home miserable, and his dreams that night were
full of horrors. The next day and the day after, he hung about the
court room, drawn by an almost irresistible impulse to go in, but
forcing himself to stay out. Huck was having the same experience.
They studiously avoided each other. Each wandered away, from
time to time, but the same dismal fascination always brought
them back presently. Tom kept his ears open when idlers
sauntered out of the court room, but invariably heard distressing
news—the toils were closing more and more relentlessly around
poor Potter. At the end of the second day the village talk was to
the effect that Injun Joe's evidence stood firm and unshaken, and
that there was not the slightest question as to what the jury's

verdict would be.

Tom was out late, that night, and came to bed through the window. He was in a tremendous state of excitement. It was hours before he got to sleep. All the village flocked to the Court house the next morning, for this was to be the great day. Both sexes were about equally represented in the packed audience. After a long wait the jury filed in and took their places; shortly afterward, Potter, pale and haggard, timid and hopeless, was brought in, with chains upon him, and seated where all the curious eyes could stare at him; no less conspicuous was Injun Joe, stolid as ever. There was another pause, and then the judge arrived and the sheriff proclaimed the opening of the court. The usual whisperings among the lawyers and gathering together of papers followed. These details and accompanying delays worked up an atmosphere of preparation that was as impressive as it was fascinating.

Now a witness was called who testified that he found Muff Potter washing in the brook, at an early hour of the morning that the murder was discovered, and that he immediately sneaked away. After some further questioning, counsel for the prosecution said—

"Take the witness."

The prisoner raised his eyes for a moment, but dropped them again when his own council said—

"I have no questions to ask him."

The next witness proved the finding of the knife near the corpse. Counsel for the prosecution said:

"Take the witness."

"I have no questions to ask him," Potter's lawyer replied.

A third witness swore he had often seen the knife in Potter's possession.

"Take the witness."

Counsel for Potter declined to question him. The faces of the audience began to betray annoyance. Did this attorney mean to throw away his client's life without an effort?

Several witnesses deposed concerning Potter's guilty behavior when brought to the scene of the murder. They were allowed to leave the stand without being cross-questioned.

Every detail of the damaging circumstances that occurred in the graveyard upon that morning which all present remembered so well, was brought out by credible witnesses, but none of them were cross-examined by Potter's lawyer. The perplexity and dissatisfaction of the house expressed itself in murmurs and provoked a reproof from the bench. Counsel for the prosecution now said:

"By the oaths of citizens whose simple word is above suspicion, we have fastened this awful crime beyond all possibility of

question, upon the unhappy prisoner at the bar. We rest our case
here."

A groan escaped from poor Potter, and he put his face in his
hands and rocked his body softly to and fro, while a painful
silence reigned in the courtroom. Many men were moved, and
many women's compassion testified itself in tears. Counsel for the
defence rose and said:

"Your honor, in our remarks at the opening of this trial, we
foreshadowed our purpose to prove that our client did this
fearful deed while under the influence of a blind and
irresponsible delirium produced by drink. We have changed our
mind. We shall not offer that plea." [Then to the clerk]: "Call
Thomas Sawyer!"

A puzzled amazement awoke in every face in the house, not
even excepting Potter's. Every eye fastened itself with wondering
interest upon Tom as he rose and took his place upon the stand.
The boy looked wild enough, for he was badly scared. The oath
was administered.

"Thomas Sawyer, where were you on the seventeenth of June,
about the hour of midnight?"

Tom glanced at Injun Joe's iron face and his tongue failed him.
The audience listened breathless, but the words refused to come.
After a few moments, however, the boy got a little of his
strength back, and managed to put enough of it into his voice
to make part of the house hear:

"In the graveyard!"

"A little bit louder, please. Don't be afraid. You were—"

"In the graveyard."

A contemptuous smile flitted across Injun Joe's face.

"Were you anywhere near Horse Williams's grave?"

"Yes, sir."

"Speak up—just a trifle louder. How near were you?"

"Near as I am to you."

"Were you hidden, or not?"

"I was hid."

"Where?"

"Behind the elms that's on the edge of the grave."

Injun Joe gave a barely perceptible start.

"Any one with you?"

"Yes, sir. I went there with—"

"Wait—wait a moment. Never mind mentioning your
companion's name. We will produce him at the proper time. Did
you carry anything there with you."

Tom hesitated and looked confused.

"Speak out my boy—don't be diffident. The truth is always
respectable. What did you take there?"

"Only a —a—dead cat."

There was a ripple of mirth, which the court checked.

"We will produce the skeleton of that cat. Now my boy, tell us everything that occurred—tell it in your own way—don't skip anything, and don't be afraid."

Tom began—hesitatingly at first, but as he warmed to his subject his words flowed more and more easily; in a little while every sound ceased but his own voice; every eye fixed itself upon him; with parted lips and bated breath the audience hung upon his words, taking no note of time, rapt in the ghastly fascinations of the tale. The strain upon pent emotion reached its climax when the boy said—

"—and as the doctor fetched the board around and Muff Potter fell, Injun Joe jumped with the knife and—"

Crash! Quick as lightning the half-breed sprang for a window, tore his way through all opposers, and was gone!

CHAPTER XXIV

Tom was a glittering hero once more—the pet of the old, the envy of the young. His name even went into immortal print, for the village paper magnified him. There were some that believed he would be President, yet, if he escaped hanging.

As usual, the fickle, unreasoning world took Muff Potter to its bosom and fondled him as lavishly as it had abused him before. But that sort of conduct is to the world's credit; therefore it is not well to find fault with it.

Tom's days were days of splendor and exultation to him, but his nights were seasons of horror. Injun Joe infested all his dreams, and always with doom in his eye. Hardly any temptation could persuade the boy to stir abroad after nightfall. Poor Huck was in the same state of wretchedness and terror, for Tom had told the whole story to the lawyer the night before the great day of the trial, and Huck was sore afraid that his share in the business might leak out, yet, notwithstanding Injun Joe's flight had saved him the suffering of testifying in court. The poor fellow had got the attorney to promise secrecy, but what of that? Since Tom's harrassed conscience had managed to drive him to the lawyer's house by night and wring a dread tale from lips that had been sealed with the dismalest and most formidable of oaths, Huck's confidence in the human race was well nigh obliterated.

Daily Muff Potter's gratitude made Tom glad he had spoken; but nightly he wished he had sealed up his tongue.

Half the time Tom was afraid Injun Joe would never be captured; the other half he was afraid he would be. He felt sure he never could draw a safe breath again until that man was dead and he had seen the corpse.

Rewards had been offered, the country had been scoured, but no

Injun Joe was found. One of those omniscient and awe-inspiring
marvels, a detective, came up from St. Louis, moused around, shook
his head, looked wise, and made that sort of astounding success
which members of that craft usually achieve. That is to say he
"found a clew." But you can't hang a "clew" for murder and so after
that detective had got through and gone home, Tom felt just as
insecure as he was before.

The slow days drifted on, and each left behind it a slightly
lightened weight of apprehension.

CHAPTER XXV

There comes a time in every rightly constructed boy's life when he
has a raging desire to go somewhere and dig for hidden treasure.
This desire suddenly came upon Tom one day. He sailed out to find
Joe Harper, but failed of success. Next he sought Ben Rogers; he had
gone fishing. Presently he stumbled upon Huck Finn the
Red-Handed. Huck would answer. Tom took him to a private place
and opened the matter to him confidentially. Huck was willing.
Huck was always willing to take a hand in any enterprise that offered
entertainment and required no capital, for he had a troublesome
superabundance of that sort of time which is *not* money. "Where'll
we dig?" said Huck.

"O, most anywhere."

"Why, is it hid all around?"

"No indeed it ain't. It's hid in mighty particular places, Huck—
sometimes on islands, sometimes in rotten chests under the end of a
limb of an old dead tree, just where the shadow falls at midnight;
but mostly under the floor in ha'nted houses."

"Who hides it?"

"Why robbers, of course—who'd you reckon? Sunday-school
sup'rintendents?"

"I don't know. If 'twas mine I wouldn't hide it; I'd spend it and
have a good time."

"So would I. But robbers don't do that way. They always hide it
and leave it there."

"Don't they come after it any more?"

"No, they think they will, but they generally forget the marks, or
else they die. Anyway it lays there a long time and gets rusty; and by
and by somebody finds an old yellow paper that tells how to find the
marks—a paper that's got to be ciphered over about a week because
it's mostly signs and hy'roglyphics."

"Hyro-which?"

"Hy'rogliphics—pictures and things, you know, that don't seem to
mean anything."

"Have you got one of them papers, Tom?"

"No."

"Well then, how you going to find the marks?"

"I don't want any marks. They always bury it under a ha'nted house or on an island, or under a dead tree that's got one limb sticking out. Well, we've tried Jackson's Island a little, and we can try it again some time; and there's the old ha'nted house up the Still-House branch, and there's lots of dead limb trees—dead loads of 'em."

"Is it under all of them?"

"How you talk! No!"

"Then how you going to know which one to go for?"

"Go for all of 'em!"

"Why Tom, it'll take all summer."

"Well, what of that? Suppose you find a brass pot with a hundred dollars in it, all rusty and gay, or a rotten chest full of di'monds. How's that?"

Huck's eyes glowed.

"That's bully. Plenty bully enough for me. Just you gimme the hundred dollars and I don't want no di'monds."

"All right. But I bet you *I* ain't going to throw off on di'monds. Some of 'em's worth twenty dollars apiece—there ain't any, hardly, but's worth six bits or a dollar."

"No! Is that so?"

"Cert'nly—anybody'll tell you so. Hain't you ever seen one, Huck?"

"Not as I remember."

"O, kings have slathers of them."

"Well, I don't know no kings, Tom."

"I reckon you don't. But if you was to go to Europe you'd see a raft of 'em hopping around."

"Do they hop?"

"Hop?—your granny! No!"

"Well what did you say they did, for?"

"Shucks, I only meant you'd *see* 'em—not hopping, of course— what do they want to hop for?—but I mean you'd just see 'em— scattered around, you know, in a kind of a general way. Like that old hump-backed Richard."

"Richard? What's his other name?"

"He didn't have any other name. Kings don't have any but a given name."

"No?"

"But they don't."

"Well, if they like it, Tom, all right; but I don't want to be a king and have only just a given name, like a nigger. But say—where you going to dig first?"

"Well, I don't know. S'pose we tackle that old dead-limb tree on the hill t'other side of Still-House branch?"

"I'm agreed."

So they got a crippled pick and a shovel, and set out on their three-mile tramp. They arrived hot and panting, and threw themselves down in the shade of a neighboring elm to rest and have a smoke.

"I like this," said Tom.

"So do I."

"Say, Huck, if we find a treasure here, what you going to do with your share?"

"Well I'll have pie and a glass of soda every day, and I'll go to every circus that comes along. I bet I'll have a gay time."

"Well ain't you going to save any of it?"

"Save it? What for?"

"Why so as to have something to live on, by and by."

"O, that ain't any use. Pap would come back to thish-yer town some day and get his claws on it if I didn't hurry up, and I tell you he'd clean it out pretty quick. What you going to do with yourn, Tom?"

"I'm going to buy a new drum, and a sure-'nough sword, and a red neck-tie and a bull pup, and get married."

"Married!"

"That's it."

"Tom, you—why you ain't in your right mind."

"Wait—you'll see."

"Well that's the foolishest thing you could do. Look at pap and my mother. Fight! Why they used to fight all the time. I remember, mighty well."

"That ain't anything. The girl I'm going to marry won't fight."

"Tom, I reckon they're all alike. They'll all comb a body. Now you better think 'bout this a while. I tell you better. What's the name of the gal?"

"It ain't a gal at all—it's a girl."

"It's all the same, I reckon; some says gal, some says girl—both's right, like enough. Anyway, what's her name, Tom?"

"I'll tell you some time—not now."

"All right—that'll do. Only if you get married I'll be more lonesomer than ever."

"No you won't. You'll come and live with me. Now stir out of this and we'll go to digging."

They worked and sweated for half an hour. No result. They toiled another half hour. Still no result. Huck said:

"Do they always bury it as deep as this?"

"Sometimes—not always. Not generally. I reckon we haven't got the right place."

So they chose a new spot and began again. The labor dragged a little, but still they made progress. They pegged away in silence for some time. Finally Huck leaned on his shovel, swabbed the beaded drops from his brow with his sleeve, and said:

"Where you going to dig next, after we get this one?"

"I reckon maybe we'll tackle the old tree that's over yonder on Cardiff Hill back of the widow's."

"I reckon that'll be a good one. But won't the widow take it away from us Tom? It's on her land."

"*She* take it away! Maybe she'd like to try it once. Whoever finds one of these hid treasures, it belongs to him. It don't make any difference whose land it's on."

That was satisfactory. The work went on. By and by Huck said:—

"Blame it, we must be in the wrong place again. What do you think?"

"It *is* mighty curious Huck. I don't understand it. Sometimes witches interfere. I reckon maybe that's what's the trouble now."

"Shucks, witches ain't got no power in the daytime."

"Well, that's so. I didn't think of that. Oh, *I* know what the matter is! What a blamed lot of fools we are! You got to find out where the shadow of the limb falls at midnight, and that's where you dig!"

"Then consound it, we've fooled away all this work for nothing. Now hang it all, we got to come back in the night. It's an awful long way. Can you get out?"

"I bet I will. We've got to do it to night, too, because if some body sees these holes they'll know in a minute what's here and they'll go for it."

"Well, I'll come around and maow to night."

"All right. Let's hide the tools in the bushes."

The boys were there that night, about the appointed time. They sat in the shadow waiting. It was a lonely place, and an hour made solemn by old traditions. Spirits whispered in the rustling leaves, ghosts lurked in the murky nooks, the deep baying of a hound floated up out of the distance, an owl answered with his sepulchral note. The boys were subdued by these solemnities, and talked little. By and by they judged that twelve had come; they marked where the shadow fell, and began to dig. Their hopes commenced to rise. Their interest grew stronger, and their industry kept pace with it. The hole deepened and still deepened, but every time their hearts jumped to hear the pick strike upon something, they only suffered a new disappointment. It was only a stone or a chunk. At last Tom said:—

"It ain't any use, Huck, we're wrong again."

"Well but we *can't* be wrong. We spotted the shadder to a dot."

"I know it, but then there's another thing."

"What's that?"

"Why we only guessed at the time. Like enough it was too late or too early."

Huck dropped his shovel.

"That's it," said he. "That's the very trouble. We got to give this one up. We can't ever tell the right time, and besides this kind of thing's too awful, here this time of night with witches and ghosts of fluttering around so. I feel as if something's behind me all the time; and I'm afeared to turn around, becuz maybe there's others in front a-waiting for a chance. I been creeping all over, ever since I got here."

"Well, I've been pretty much so, too, Huck. They most always put in a dead man when they bury a treasure under a tree, to look out for it."

"Lordy!"

"Yes, they do. I've always heard that."

"Tom I don't like to fool around much where there's dead people. A body's bound to get into trouble with 'em, sure."

"I don't like to stir 'em up, either. S'pose this one here was to stick his skull out and say something!"

"Don't, Tom! It's awful."

"Well it just is. Huck, I don't feel comfortable a bit."

"Say, Tom, let's give this place up, and try somewheres else."

"All right, I reckon we better."

"What'll it be?"

Tom considered a while; and then said—

"The ha'nted house. That's it!"

"Blame it, I don't like ha'nted houses Tom. Why they're a dern sight worse'n dead people. Dead people might talk, maybe, they they don't come sliding around in a shroud, when you ain't noticing, and peep over your shoulder all of a sudden and grit their teeth, the way a ghost does. I couldn't stand such a thing as that, Tom—nobody could."

"Yes, but Huck, ghosts don't travel around only at night. They won't hender us from digging there in the day time."

"Well that's so. But you know mighty well people don't go about that ha'nted house in the day nor the night."

"Well, that's mostly because they don't like to go where a man's been murdered, anyway—but nothing's ever been seen around that house except in the night—just some blue lights slipping by the windows—no regular ghosts."

"Well where you see one of them blue lights flickering around, Tom, you can bet there's a ghost mighty close behind it. It stands to reason. Becuz *you* know that they don't let anybody but ghosts use 'em."

"Yes, that's so. But anyway they don't come around in the daytime, so what's the use of our being afeared?"

"Well, all right. We'll tackle the ha'nted house if you say so—but I reckon it's taking chances."

They had started down the hill by this time. There in the middle of the moonlit valley below them stood the "ha'nted" house, utterly isolated, its fences gone long ago, rank weeds smothering the very doorsteps, the chimney crumbled to ruin, the window-sashes vacant, a corner of the roof caved in. The boys gazed a while, half expecting to see a blue light flit past the window; then talking in a low tone, as befitted the time and the circumstances, they struck far off to the right, to give the haunted house a wide berth, and took their way homeward through the woods that adorned the rearward side of Cardiff Hill.

CHAPTER XXVI

About noon the next day the boys arrived at the dead tree; they had come for their tools. Tom was impatient to go to the haunted house; Huck was measurably so, also—but suddenly said—

"Lookyhere, Tom, do you know what day it is?"

Tom mentally ran over the days of the week, and then quickly lifted his eyes with a startled look in them—

"My! I never once thought of it, Huck!"

"Well I didn't neither, but all at once it popped onto me that it was Friday."

"Blame it, a body can't be too careful, Huck. We might a got into an awful scrape, tackling such a thing on a Friday."

"*Might!* Better say we *would!* There's some lucky days, maybe, but Friday ain't."

"Any fool knows that. I don't reckon *you* was the first that found it out, Huck."

"Well, I never said I was, did I? And Friday ain't all, neither. I had a rotten bad dream last night—dreampt about rats."

"No! Sure sign of trouble. Did they fight?"

"No."

"Well that's good, Huck. When they don't fight it's only a sign that there's trouble around, you know. All we got to do is to look mighty sharp and keep out of it. We'll drop this thing for today, and play. Do you know Robin Hood, Huck?"

"No. Who's Robin Hood?"

"Why he was one of the greatest men that was ever in England— and the best. He was a robber."

"Cracky, I wisht I was. Who did he rob?"

"Only sheriffs and bishops and rich people and kings, and such like. But he never bothered the poor. He loved 'em. He always divided up with 'em perfectly square."

"Well, he must 'a' been a brick."

"I bet you he was, Huck. Oh, he was the noblest man that ever was. They ain't such men now, I can tell you. He could lick any man in England, with one hand tied behind him; and he could take his yew bow and plug a ten cent piece every time, a mile and a half."

"What's a *yew* bow?"

"*I* don't know. It's some kind of a bow, of course. And if he hit that dime only on the edge he would set down and cry—and curse. But we'll play Robin Hood—it's noble fun. I'll learn you."

"I'm agreed."

So they played Robin Hood all the afternoon, now and then
casting a yearning eye down upon the haunted house and passing a
remark about the morrow's prospect and possibilities there. As the
sun began to sink into the west they took their way homeward
athwart the long shadows of the trees and soon were buried from
sight in the forests of Cardiff Hill.

On Saturday, shortly after noon, the boys were at the dead tree
again. They had a smoke and a chat in the shade, and then dug a
little in their last hole, not with great hope, but merely because Tom
said there were so many cases where people had given up a treasure
after getting down within six inches of it, and then somebody else
had come along and turned it up with a single thrust of a shovel. The
thing failed this time, however, so the boys shouldered their tools
and went away feeling that they had not trifled with fortune but had
fulfilled all the requirements that belong to the business of treasure-
hunting.

When they reached the haunted house there was something so
wierd and grisly about the dead silence that reigned there under the
baking sun, and something so depressing about the loneliness and
desolation of the place, that they were afraid, for a moment, to
venture in. Then they crept to the door and took a trembling peep.
They saw a weed-grown, floorless room, unplastered, an ancient
fireplace, vacant windows, a ruinous staircase; and here, there, and
everywhere, hung ragged and abandoned cobwebs. They presently
entered, softly, with quickened pulses, talking in whispers, ears alert
to catch the slightest sound, and muscles tense and ready for instant
retreat.

In a little while familiarity modified their fears and they gave the
place a critical and interested examination, rather admiring their
own boldness, and wondering at it, too. Next they wanted to look up
stairs. This was something like cutting off retreat, but they got to
daring each other, and of course there could be but one result—they
threw their tools into a corner and made the ascent. Up there were
the same signs of decay. In one corner they found a closet that
promised mystery, but the promise was a fraud—there was nothing
in it. Their courage was up now and well in hand. They were about to
go down and begin work when—

"Sh!" said Tom.

"What is it?" whispered Huck, blanching with fright.

"Sh!.....There!.....Hear it?"

"Yes!.....O, my! Let's run!"

"Keep still! Don't you budge! They're coming right toward the
door."

The boys stretched themselves upon the floor with their eyes to
knot holes in the planking, and lay waiting, in a misery of fear.

"They've stopped.....No—coming......Here they are. Don't

whisper another word, Huck. My goodness, I wish I was out of this!"

Two men entered. Each boy said to himself: "There's the old deaf and dumb Spaniard that's been about town once or twice lately— never saw t'other man before."

"T'other" was a ragged, unkempt creature, with nothing very pleasant in his face. The Spaniard was wrapped in a *serapè;* he had bushy white whiskers; long white hair flowed from under his sombrero, and he wore green goggles. When they came in, "T'other" was talking in a low voice; they sat down on the ground, facing the door, with their backs to the wall, and the speaker continued his remarks. His manner became less guarded and his words more distinct as he proceeded:

"No," said he, "I've thought it all over, and I don't like it. It's dangerous."

"Dangerous!" grunted the "deaf and dumb" Spaniard,—to the vast surprise of the boys. "Milksop!"

This voice made the boys gasp and quake. It was Injun Joe's! There was silence for some time. Then Joe said:

"What's any more dangerous than that job up yonder—but nothing's come of it."

"That's different. Away up the river so, and not another house about. 'Twon't ever be known that we tried, anyway, long as we didn't succeed."

"Well, what's more dangerous than coming here in the day time! —anybody would suspicion us that saw us."

"*I* know that. But there warn't any other place as handy after that fool of a job. I want to quit this shanty. I wanted to yesterday, only it warn't any use trying to stir out of here, with those infernal boys playing over there on the hill right in full view."

"Those infernal boys," quaked again under the inspiration of this remark, and thought how lucky it was that they had remembered it was Friday and concluded to wait a day. They wished in their hearts they had waited a year.

The two men got out some food and made a luncheon. After a long and thoughtful silence, Injun Joe said:

"Look here, lad—you go back up the river where you belong. Wait there till you hear from me. I'll take the chances on dropping into this town just once more, for a look. We'll do that 'dangerous' job after I've spied around a little and think things look well for it. Then for Texas! We'll leg it together!"

This was satisfactory. Both men presently fell to yawning, and Injun Joe said:

"I'm dead for sleep! It's your turn to watch."

He curled down in the weeds and soon began to snore. His comrade stirred him once or twice and he became quiet. Presently the watcher began to nod; his head drooped lower and lower, both men began to snore now.

The boys drew a long, grateful breath. Tom whispered—
"Now's our chance—come!"
Huck said:
"I can't—I'd die if they was to wake."
Tom urged—Huck held back. At last Tom rose slowly and softly,
and started alone. But the first step he made wrung such a hideous
creak from the crazy floor that he sank down almost dead with
fright. He never made a second attempt. The boys lay there counting
the dragging moments till it seemed to them that time must be done
and eternity growing gray; and then they were grateful to note that
at last the sun was setting.
Now one snore ceased. Injun Joe sat up, stared around—smiled
grimly upon his comrade, whose head was drooping upon his knees
—stirred him up with his foot and said—
"Here! *You're* a watchman, ain't you! All right, though—
nothing's happened."
"My! have I been asleep?"
"Oh, partly, partly. Nearly time for us to be moving, pard. What'll
we do with what little swag we've got left?"
"I don't know—leave it here as we've always done, I reckon. No
use to take it away till we start south. Six hundred and fifty in silver's
something to carry."
"Well—all right—it won't matter to come here once more."
"No—but I'd say come in the night as we used to do—it's better."
"Yes; but look here; it may be a good while before I get the right
chance at that job; accidents might happen; 'tain't in such a very
good place; we'll just regularly bury it—and bury it deep."
"Good idea," said the comrade, who walked across the room,
knelt down, raised one of the rearward hearthstones and took out a
bag that jingled pleasantly. He subtracted from it twenty or thirty
dollars for himself and as much for Injun Joe and passed the bag to
the latter, who was on his knees in the corner, now, digging with his
bowie knife.
The boys forgot all their fears, all their miseries in an instant.
With gloating eyes they watched every movement. Luck!—the
splendor of it was beyond all imagination! Six hundred dollars was
money enough to make half a dozen boys rich! Here was treasure-
hunting under the happiest auspices—there would not be any
bothersome uncertainty as to where to dig. They nudged each other
every moment—eloquent nudges and easily understood, for they
simply meant—"O, but ain't you glad *now* we're here!"
Joe's knife struck upon something.
"Hello!" said he.
"What is it?" said his comrade.
"Half-rotten plank—no it's a box, I believe. Here—bear a hand
and we'll see what it's here for. Never mind, I've broke a hole.
He reached his hand in and drew it out—

"Man, it's money!"

The two men examined the handful of coins. They were gold. The boys above were as excited as themselves, and as delighted.

Joe's comrade said—

"We'll make quick work of this. There's an old rusty pick over amongst the weeds in the corner the other side of the fire-place—I saw it a minute ago."

He ran and brought the boys' pick and shovel. Injun Joe took the pick, looked it over critically, shook his head, muttered something to himself, and then began to use it. The box was soon unearthed. It was not very large; it was iron bound and had been very strong before the slow years had injured it. The men contemplated the treasure a while in blissful silence.

"Pard, there's thousands of dollars here," said Injun Joe.

" 'Twas always said that Murrel's gang used around here one summer," the stranger observed.

"I know it," said Injun Joe; "and this looks like it, I should say."

"*Now* you won't need to do that job."

The half-breed frowned. Said he—

"You don't know me. Least you don't know all about that thing. 'Tain't robbery altogether—it's *revenge!*" and a wicked light flamed in his eyes. "I'll need your help in it. When it's finished—then Texas. Go home to your Nance and your kids, and stand by till you hear from me."

"Well—if you say so, what'll we do with this—bury it again?"

"Yes. [Ravishing delight overhead.] *No!* by the great Sachem, no! [Profound distress overhead.] I'd nearly forgot. That pick had fresh earth on it! [The boys were sick with terror in a moment.] What business has a pick and a shovel here? What business with fresh earth on them? Who brought them here—and where are they gone? Have you heard anybody?—seen anybody? What! bury it again and leave them to come and see the ground disturbed? Not exactly—not exactly. We'll take it to my den."

"Why of course! Might have thought of that before. You mean Number One?"

"No—Number Two—under the cross. The other place is bad— too common."

"All right. It's nearly dark enough to start."

Injun Joe got up and went about from window to window cautiously peeping out. Presently he said:

"Who could have brought those tools here? Do you reckon they can be up stairs?"

The boys' breath forsook them. Injun Joe put his hand on his knife, halted a moment, undecided, and then turned toward the stairway. The boys thought of the closet, but their strength was gone. The steps came creaking up the stairs—the intolerable distress of the situation woke the stricken resolution of the lads—they were about to spring for the closet, when there was a crash of rotten timbers and Injun Joe landed on the ground amid the *débris* of the ruined stairway. He gathered himself up cursing, and his comrade said:

"Now what's the use of all that? If it's anybody, and they're up there, let them *stay* there—who cares? If they want to jump down, now, and get into trouble, who objects? It will be dark in fifteen minutes—and then let them follow us if they want to. I'm willing. In my opinion, whoever hove those things in here caught a sight of us and took us for ghosts or devils or something. I'll bet they're running yet."

Joe grumbled a while; then he agreed with his friend that what daylight was left ought to be economized in getting things ready for leaving. Shortly afterward they slipped out of the house in the deepening twilight, and moved toward the river with their precious box.

Tom and Huck rose up, weak but vastly relieved, and stared after them through the chinks between the logs of the house. Follow? Not they. They were content to reach ground again without broken necks, and take the townward track over the hill. They did not talk much. They were too much absorbed in hating themselves—hating the ill luck that made them take the spade and the pick there. But for that, Injun Joe never would have suspected. He would have hidden the silver with the gold to wait there till his "revenge" was satisfied, and then he would have had the misfortune to find that money turn up missing. Bitter, bitter luck that the tools were ever brought there!

They resolved to keep a lookout for that Spaniard when he should come to town spying out for chances to do his revengeful job, and follow him to "Number Two," wherever that might be. Then a ghastly thought occurred to Tom:

"Revenge?" What if he means *us,* Huck!"

"O, don't!" said Huck, nearly fainting.

They talked it all over, and as they entered town they agreed to believe that he might possibly mean somebody else—at least that he might at least mean nobody but Tom, since only Tom had testified.

Very, very small comfort it was to Tom to be alone in danger! Company would be a palpable improvement, he thought.

CHAPTER XXVII

The adventure of the day mightily tormented Tom's dreams that night. Four times he had his hands on that rich treasure and four times it wasted to nothingness in his fingers as sleep forsook him and wakefulness brought back the hard reality of his misfortune. As he lay in the early morning recalling the incidents of his great adventure, he noticed that they seemed curiously subdued and far away—somewhat as if they had happened in another world, or in a time long gone by. Then it occurred to him that the great adventure itself must be a dream! There was one very strong argument in favor of this idea—namely, that the quantity of coin he had seen was too vast to be real. He had never seen as much as fifty dollars in one mass before, and he was like all boys of his age and station in life, in that he imagined that all references to "hundreds" and "thousands" were mere fanciful forms of speech, and that no such sums really existed in the world. He never had supposed for a moment that so large a sum as a hundred dollars was to be found in actual money in any one's possession. If his notions of hidden treasure had been analyzed, they would have been bound to consist of a handful of real dimes and a bushel of vague, splendid, graspable dollars.

But the incidents of his adventure grew sensibly sharper and clearer under the attrition of thinking them over, and so he presently found himself leaning to the impression that the thing might not have been a dream, after all. This uncertainty must be swept away. He would snatch a hurried breakfast and go and find Huck.

Huck was sitting on the gunwale of a flatboat, listlessly dangling his feet in the water and looking very melancholy. Tom concluded to let Huck lead up to the subject. If he did not do it, then the adventure would be proved to have been only a dream.

"Hello, Huck!"

"Hello, yourself."

Silence, for a minute.

"Tom, if we'd a left the blame tools at the dead tree, we'd 'a' got the money. O, ain't it awful!"

" 'Tain't a dream, then, 'tain't a dream! Somehow I most wish it was. Dog'd if I don't, Huck."

"What ain't a dream?"

"Oh, that thing yesterday. I been half thinking it was."

"Dream! If them stairs hadn't broke down you'd 'a' seen how much dream it was! I've had dreams enough all night—with that patch-eyed Spanish devil going for me all through 'em—rot him!"

"No, not rot him. *Find* him! Track the money!"

"Tom, we'll never find him. A feller don't have only once chance for such a pile—and that one's lost. I'd feel mighty shaky if I was to see him, anyway."

"Well, so'd I; but I'd like to see him, anyway—and track him out —to his Number Two."

"Number Two—yes, that's it. I been thinking 'bout that. But I can't make nothing out of it. What do you reckon it is?"

"I dono. It's too deep. Say, Huck—maybe it's the number of a house!"

"Goody! . . . . . . No, Tom, that ain't it. If it is, it ain't in this one-horse town. They ain't no numbers here."

"Well, that's so. Lemme think a minute. Here—it's the number of a room—in a tavern, you know!"

"O, that's the trick! They ain't only two taverns. We can find out quick."

"You stay here, Huck, till I come."

Tom was off at once. He did not care to have Huck's company in public places. He was gone half an hour. He found that in the best tavern, No. 2 had been occupied by a young lawyer, and was still so occupied. In the less ostentatious house No. 2 was a mystery. The tavern-keeper's young son said it was kept locked all the time, and he never saw anybody go into or come out of it except at night; he did not know any particular reason for this state of things; had had some little curiosity, but it was rather feeble; had made the most of the mystery by entertaining himself with the idea that the room was "ha'nted;" had noticed that there was a light in there the night before.

"That's what I've found out, Huck. I reckon that's the very No. 2 we're after."

"I reckon it is, Tom. Now what you going to do?"

"Lemme think."

Tom thought a long time. Then he said:

"I'll tell you. The back door of that No. 2 is the door that comes out into that little close alley between the tavern and the old rattle-trap of a brick store. Now you get hold of all the door-keys you can find, and I'll nip all of Auntie's and the first dark night we'll go there and try 'em. And mind you keep a lookout for Injun Joe, because he said he was going to drop into town and spy around once more for a chance to get his revenge. If you see him, you just follow him; and if he don't go to that No. 2, that ain't the place."

"Lordy I don't want to foller him by myself!"

"Why it'll be night, sure. He mightn't ever see you—and if he did, maybe he'd never think anything."

"Well, if it's pretty dark I reckon I'll track him. I dono—I dono. I'll try."

"You bet I'll follow him, if it's dark, Huck. Why he might 'a' found out he couldn't get his revenge, and be going right after that money."

"It's so, Tom, it's so. I'll foller him; I will, by jingoes!"

"Now you're *talking!* Don't you ever weaken, Huck, and I won't."

CHAPTER XXVIII

That night Tom and Huck were ready for their adventure. They hung around the neighborhood of the tavern until after nine, one watching the alley at a distance and the other the tavern door. Nobody entered the alley or left it; nobody resembling the Spaniard entered or left the tavern door. The night promised to be a fair one; so Tom went home with the understanding that if a considerable degree of darkness came on, Huck was to come and "maow," whereupon he would slip out and try the keys. But the night remained clear, ahd Huck closed his watch and retired to bed in an empty sugar hogshead about twelve.

Tuesday the boys had the same ill luck. Also Wednesday. But Thursday night promised better. Tom slipped out in good season with his aunt's old tin lantern, and a large towel to blindfold it with. He hid the lantern in Huck's sugar hogshead and the watch began. An hour before midnight the tavern closed up and its lights (the only ones thereabouts) were put out. No Spaniard had been seen. Nobody had entered or left the alley. Everything was auspicious. The blackness of darkness reigned, the perfect stillness was interrupted only by occasional mutterings of distant thunder.

Tom got his lantern, lit it in the hogshead, wrapped it closely in the towel, and the two adventurers crept in the gloom toward the tavern. Huck stood sentry and Tom felt his way into the alley. Then there was a season of waiting anxiety that weighed upon Huck's spirits like a mountain. He began to wish he could see a flash from the lantern—it would frighten him, but it would at least tell him that Tom was alive yet. It seemed hours since Tom had disappeared. Surely he must have fainted; maybe he was dead; maybe his heart had burst under terror and excitement. In his uneasiness Huck found himself drawing closer and closer to the alley; fearing all sorts of dreadful things, and momentarily expecting some catastrophe to happen that would take away his breath. There was not much to take away, for he seemed only able to inhale it by thimblefuls, and his heart would soon wear itself out, the way it was beating. Suddenly there was a flash of light and Tom came tearing by him:

"Run!" said he; "run, for your life!"

He needn't have repeated it; once was enough; Huck was making thirty or forty miles an hour before the repetition was uttered. The boys never stopped till they reached the shed of a deserted slaughter-house at the lower end of the village. Just as they got within its shelter the storm burst and the rain poured down. As soon as Tom got his breath he said:

"Huck, it was awful! I tried two of the keys, just as soft as I could; but they seemed to make such a power of racket that I couldn't hardly get my breath I was so scared. They wouldn't turn in the lock, either. Well, without noticing what I was doing, I took hold of the knob, and open comes the door! It warn't locked! I hopped in, and shook off the towel, and, *great Caesar's ghost!*"

"What!—what'd you see, Tom!"

"Huck, I most stepped onto Injun Joe's hand!"

"No!"

"Yes! He was laying there, sound asleep on the floor, with his old patch on his eye and his arms spread out."

"Lordy, what did you do? Did he wake up?"

"No, never budged. Drunk, I reckon. I just grabbed that towel and started!"

"I'd never 'a' thought of the towel, I bet!"

"Well, *I* would. My aunt would make me mighty sick if I lost it."

"Say, Tom, did you see that box?"

"Huck, I didn't wait to look around. I didn't see the box, I didn't see the cross. I didn't see anything but a bottle and a tin cup on the floor by Injun Joe; yes, and I saw two barrels and lots more bottles in the room. Don't you see, now, what's the matter with that ha'nted room?"

"How?"

"Why it's ha'nted with whisky! Maybe *all* the Temperance Taverns have got a ha'nted room, hey Huck?"

"Well I reckon maybe that's so. Who'd 'a' thought such a thing? But say, Tom, now's a mighty good time to get that box, if Injun Joe's drunk."

"It is, that! You try it!"

Huck shuddered.

"Well, no—I reckon not."

"And *I* reckon not, Huck. Only one bottle alongside of Injun Joe ain't enough. If there'd been three, he'd be drunk enough and I'd do it."

There was a long pause for reflection, and then Tom said:

"Lookyhere, Huck, less not try that thing any more till we know Injun Joe's not in there. It's too scary. Now if we watch every night, we'll be dead sure to see him go out some time or other, and then we'll snatch that box quicker'n lightning."

"Well, I'm agreed. I'll watch the whole night long, and I'll do it every night, too, if you'll do the other part of the job."

"All right, I will. All you got to do is to trot up Hooper street a block and maow—and if I'm asleep, you throw some gravel at the window and that'll fetch me."

"Agreed, and good as wheat!"

"Now Huck, the storm's over, and I'll go home. It'll begin to be daylight in a couple of hours. You go back and watch that long, will you?"

"I said I would, Tom, and I will. I'll ha'nt that tavern every night for a year! I'll sleep all day and I'll stand watch all night."

"That's all right. Now where you going to sleep?"

"In Ben Rogers's hayloft. He lets me, and so does his pap's nigger man, Uncle Jake. I tote water for Uncle Jake whenever he wants me to, and any time I ask him he gives me a little something to eat if he can spare it. That's a mighty good nigger, Tom. He likes me, becuz I don't ever act as if I was above him. Sometimes I've set right down and eat *with* him. But you needn't tell that. A body's got to do things when he's awful hungry he wouldn't want to do as a steady thing."

"Well, if I don't want you in the day time, I'll let you sleep. I won't

come bothering around. Any time you see something's up, in the
night, just skip right around and maow."

CHAPTER XXIX

The first thing Tom heard on Friday morning was a glad piece of
news—Judge Thatcher's family had come back to town the night
before. Both Injun Joe and the treasure sunk into secondary
importance for a moment, and Becky took the chief place in the
boy's interest. He saw her and they had an exhausting good time
playing "hi-spy" and "gully-keeper" with a crowd of their
schoolmates. The day was completed and crowned in a peculiarly
satisfactory way: Becky teased her mother to appoint the next day
for the long-promised and long-delayed picnic, and she consented.
The child's delight was boundless; and Tom's not more moderate.
The invitations were sent out before sunset, and straightway the
young folks of the village were thrown into a fever of preparation
and pleasurable anticipation. Tom's excitement enabled him to keep
awake until a pretty late hour, and he had good hopes of hearing
Huck's "maow," and of having his treasure to astonish Becky and
the pic-nickers with, next day; but he was disappointed. No signal
came that night.

Morning came, eventually, and by ten or eleven o'clock a giddy
and rollicking company were gathered at Judge Thatcher's, and
everything was ready for a start. It was not the custom for elderly
people to mar pic-nics with their presence. The children were
considered safe enough under the wings of a few young ladies of
eighteen and a few young gentlemen of twenty-three or thereabouts.
The old steam ferry-boat was chartered for the occasion; presently
the gay throng filed up the main street laden with provision baskets.
Sid was sick and had to miss the fun; Mary remained at home to
entertain him. The last thing Mrs. Thatcher said to Becky, was—

"You'll not get back till late. Perhaps you'd better stay all night
with some of the girls that live near the ferry landing, child."

"Then I'll stay with Susy Harper, mamma."

"Very well. And mind and behave yourself and don't be any
trouble."

Presently, as they tripped along, Tom said to Becky:

"Say—I'll tell you what we'll do. 'Stead of going to Joe Harper's
we'll climb right up the hill and stop at the Widow Douglas's. She'll
have ice cream! She has it most every day—dead loads of it. And
she'll be awful glad to have us."

"O, that will be fun!"

Then Becky reflected a moment and said:

"But what will mamma say?"

"How'll she ever know?"

The girl turned the idea over in her mind, and said reluctantly:

"I reckon it's wrong—but—"

"But shucks! Your mother won't know, and so what's the harm? All she wants is that you'll be safe; and I bet you she'd 'a' said go there if she'd 'a' thought of it. I know she would!"

The widow Douglas's splendid hospitality was a tempting bait. It and Tom's persuasions presently carried the day. So it was decided to say nothing to anybody about the night's programme. Presently it occurred to Tom that maybe Huck might come this very night and give the signal. The thought took a deal of the spirit out of his anticipations. Still he could not bear to give up the fun at Widow Douglas's. And why should he give it up, he reasoned—the signal did not come the night before, so why should it be any more likely to come to-night? The sure fun of the evening outweighed the uncertain treasure; and boy like, he determined to yield to the stronger inclination and not allow himself to think of the box of money another time that day.

Three miles below town the ferry-boat stopped at the mouth of a woody hollow and tied up. The crowd swarmed ashore and soon the forest distances and craggy heights echoed far and near with shoutings and laughter. All the different ways of getting hot and tired were gone through with, and by and by the rovers straggled back to camp fortified with responsible appetites, and then the destruction of the good things began. After the feast there was a refreshing season of rest and chat in the shade of spreading oaks. By and by somebody shouted—"Who's ready for the cave?"

Everybody was. Bundles of candles were procured, and straightway there was a general scamper up the hill. The mouth of the cave was up the hillside—an opening shaped like a letter A. It's massive oaken door stook unbarred. Within was a small chamber, chilly as an ice-house and walled by Nature with solid limestone that was dewy with a cold sweat. It was romantic and mysterious to stand here in the deep gloom and look out upon the green valley shining in the sun. But the impressiveness of the situation quickly wore off, and the romping began again. The moment a candle was lighted there was a general rush upon the owner of it; a struggle and a gallant defense followed, but the candle was soon knocked down or blown out, and then there was a glad clamor of laughter and a new chase. But all things have an end. By and by the procession went filing down the steep descent of the main avenue, the flickering rank of lights dimly revealing the lofty walls of rock almost to their point of junction sixty feet overhead. This main avenue was not more than eight or ten feet wide. Every few steps other lofty and still narrower crevices branched from it on either hand—for McDougal's cave was but a vast labyrinth of crooked isles that ran into each other and out again and led nowhere. It was said that one might wander days and nights together through its intricate tangle of rifts and chasms, and never find the end of the cave; and that he might go down, and down, and still down, into the earth, and it was just the same—labyrinth underneath labyrinth, and no end to any of them. No man "knew" the cave. That was an impossible thing. Most of the young men knew a portion of it, and it was not customary to venture much beyond this known portion. Tom Sawyer knew as much of the cave as any one.

The procession moved along the main avenue some three-quarters of a mile, and then groups and couples began to slip aside into branch avenues, fly along the dismal corridors, and take each other by surprise at points where the corridors joined again. Parties were able to elude each other for the space of half an hour without going beyond the "known" ground.

By and by, one group after another came straggling back to the mouth of the cave, panting, hilarious, smeared from head to foot with tallow drippings, daubed with clay, and entirely delighted with the success of the day. Then they were astonished to find that they had been taking no note of time and that night was about at hand. The clanging bell had been calling for half an hour. However, this sort of close to the day's adventures was romantic and therefore satisfactory. When the ferry-boat with her wild freight pushed into the stream, nobody cared sixpence for the wasted time but the captain of the craft.

Huck was already upon his watch when the ferry-boat's lights went glinting past the wharf. He heard no noise on board, for the young people were as subdued and still as people usually are who are nearly tired to death. He wondered what boat it was, and why she did not stop at the wharf—and then he dropped her out of his mind and put his attention upon his business. The night was growing cloudy and dark. Ten o'clock came, and the noise of vehicles ceased, scattered lights began to wink out, all straggling foot passengers disappeared, the village betook itself to its slumbers and left the small watcher alone with the silence and the ghosts. Eleven o'clock came, and the tavern lights were put out; darkness everywhere, now. Huck waited what seemed a weary long time, but nothing happened. His faith was weakening. Was there any use? Was there really any use? Why not give it up and turn in?

A noise fell upon his ear. He was all attention in an instant. The alley door closed softly. He sprang to the corner of the brick store. The next moment two men brushed by him, and one seemed to have something under his arm. It must be that box! So they were going to remove the treasure. Why call Tom now? It would be absurd—the men would get away with the box and never be found again. No, he would stick to their wake and follow them; he would trust to the darkness for security from discovery. So communing with himself, Huck stepped out and glided along behind the men, cat-like, with bare feet, allowing them to keep just far enough ahead not to be invisible.

They moved up the river street three blocks, then turned to the left up a cross street. They went straight ahead, then, until they came to the path that led up Cardiff Hill; this they took. They passed by the old Welchman's house, half way up the hill without hesitating, and still climbed upward. Good, thought Huck, they will bury it in the old quarry. But they never stopped at the quarry. They passed on, up the summit. They plunged into the narrow path between the tall sumach bushes, and were at once hidden in the gloom. Huck closed up and shortened his distance, now, for they would never be able to see him. He trotted along a while; then slackened his pace, fearing he was gaining too fast; moved on a piece, then stopped altogether; listened; no sound; none, save that he seemed to hear the beating of his own heart. The hooting of an owl came from over the hill— ominous sound! But no footsteps. Heavens, was everything lost! He was about to spring with winged feet, when a man cleared his throat not four feet from him! Huck's heart shot into his throat, but he swallowed it again; and then he stood there shaking as if a dozen agues had taken charge of him at once, and so weak that he thought he must surely fall to the ground. He knew where he was. He knew he was within five steps of the stile leading into Widow Douglas's grounds. Very well, he thought, let them bury it there; it won't be hard to find.

Now there was a voice—a very low voice—Injun Joe's:

"Damn her, maybe she's got company—there's lights, late as it is."

"I can't see any."

This was that stranger's voice—the stranger of the haunted house. A deadly chill went to Huck's heart—this, then, was the "revenge" job! His thought was, to fly. Then he remembered that the Widow Douglas had been kind to him more than once, and maybe these men were going to murder her. He wished he dared venture to warn her; but he knew he didn't dare—they might come and catch him. He thought all this and more in the moment that elapsed between the stranger's remark and Injun Joe's next—which was—

"Because the bush is in your way. Now—this way—now you see, don't you?"

"Yes. Well there *is* company there, I reckon. Better give it up."

"Give it up, and I just leaving this country forever! Give it up and maybe never have another chance. I tell you again, as I've told you before, I don't care for her swag—you may have it. But her husband was rough on me—many times he was rough on me—and mainly he was the justice of the peace that jugged me for a vagrant. And that ain't all. It ain't a millionth part of it! He had me *horsewhipped!*— horsewhipped in front of the jail, like a nigger!—with all the town looking on! HORSEWHIPPED!—do you understand? He took advantage of me and died. But I'll take it out of *her*."

"Oh, don't kill her! Don't do that!"

"Kill? Who said anything about killing? I would kill *him* if he was here; but not her. When you want to get revenge on a woman you don't kill her—bosh! you go for her looks. You slit her nostrils— you notch her ears like a sow!"

"By God, that's—"

"Keep your opinion to yourself! It will be safest for you. I'll tie her to the bed. If she bleeds to death, is that my fault? I'll not cry, if she does. My friend, you'll help in this thing—for *my* sake— that's why you're here—I mightn't be able alone. If you flinch, I'll kill you. Do you understand that? And if I have to kill you, I'll kill her—and then I reckon nobody'll ever know much about who done this business."

"Well, if it's got to be done, let's get at it. The quicker the better— I'm all in a shiver."

"Do it *now?* And company there? Look here—I'll get suspicious of you, first thing you know. No—we'll wait till the lights are out— there's no hurry."

Huck felt that a silence was going to ensue—a thing still more awful than any amount of murderous talk; so he held his breath and stepped gingerly back; planted his foot carefully and firmly, after balancing, one-legged, in a precarious way and almost toppling over, first on one side and then on the other. He took another step back, with the same elaboration and the same risks; then another and another, and—a twig snapped under his foot! His breath stopped and he listened. There was no sound—the stillness was perfect. His gratitude was measureless. Now he turned in his tracks, between the walls of sumach bushes—turned himself as carefully as if he were a ship—and then stepped quickly but cautiously along. When he emerged at the quarry he felt secure, and so he picked up his nimble heels and flew. Down, down he sped, till he reached the Welchman's. He banged at the door, and presently the heads of the old man and his two stalwart sons were thrust from windows.

"What's the row there? Who's banging? What do you want?"

"Let me in—quick! I'll tell everything."

"Why who are you?"

"Huckleberry Finn—quick, let me in!"

"Huckleberry Finn, indeed! It ain't a name to open many doors, I judge! But let him in, lads, and let's see what's the trouble."

"Please don't ever tell *I* told you," were Huck's words when he got in "Please don't—I'd be killed, sure—but the Widow's been good friends to me sometimes, and I want to tell—I *will* tell if you'll promise you won't ever say it was me."

"By George he *has* got something to tell, or he wouldn't act so!" exclaimed the old man; "out with it and nobody here'll ever tell, lad."

Three minutes later the old man and his sons, well armed, were up the hill, and just entering the sumach path on tip-toe, their weapons in their hands. Huck accompanied them no further. He hid behind a great bowlder and fell to listening. There was a lagging, anxious silence, and then all of a sudden there was an explosion of firearms and a cry.

Huck waited for no particulars. He sprang away and sped down the hill as fast as his legs could carry him.

CHAPTER XXX

As the earliest suspicion of dawn appeared on Sunday morning, Huck came groping up the hill and rapped gently at the old Welchman's door. The inmates were asleep but it was a sleep that was set on a hair-trigger, on account of the exciting episode of the night. A call came from a window—

"Who's there!"

Huck's scared voice answered in a low tone:

"Please let me in! It's only Huck Finn!"

"It's a name that can open this door night or day, lad!—and welcome!"

These were strange words to the vagabond boy's ears, and the pleasantest he had ever heard. He could not recollect that the closing word had ever been applied in his case before. The door was quickly unlocked, and he entered. Huck was given a seat and the old man and his brace of tall sons speedily dressed themselves.

"Now my boy I hope you're good and hungry, because breakfast will be ready as soon as the sun's up, and we'll have a piping hot one, too—make yourself easy about that! I and the boys hoped you'd turn up and stop here last night."

"I was awful scared," said Huck, "and I run. I took out when the pistols went off, and I didn't stop for three mile. I've come now becuz I wanted to know about it, you know; and I came before daylight becuz I didn't want to run acrost them devils, even if they was dead."

"Well, poor chap, you do look as if you'd had a hard night of it—but there's a bed here for you when you've had your breakfast. No, they ain't dead, lad—we are sorry enough for that. You see we knew right where to put our hands on them, by your description; so we crept along on tip-toe till we got within fifteen feet of them—dark as a cellar that sumach path was—and just then I found I was going to sneeze. It was the meanest kind of luck! I tried to keep it back, but no use—'twas bound to come, and it did come! I was in the lead with my pistol raised, and when the sneeze started those scoundrels a-rustling to get out of the path, I sung out, 'Fire, boys!' and blazed away at the place where the rustling was. So did the boys. But they were off in a jiffy, those villains, and we after them, down through the woods. I judge we never touched them. They fired a shot apiece as they started, but their bullets whizzed by and didn't do us any harm. As soon as we lost the sound of their feet we quit chasing, and

went down and stirred up the constables. They got a posse together,
and went off to guard the river bank, and as soon as it is light the
sheriff and a gang are going to beat up the woods. My boys will be
with them presently. I wish we had some sort of description of those
rascals—'twould help a good deal. But you could'nt see what they
were like, in the dark, lad, I suppose?"

"O, yes, I saw them down town and follered them."

"Splendid! Describe them—describe them, my boy!"

"One's the old deaf and dumb Spaniard that's ben around here
once or twice, and t'other's a mean looking ragged—"

"That's enough, lad, we know the men! Happened on them in the
woods back of the widow's one day, and they slunk away. Off with
you, boys, and tell the sheriff—get your breakfast to-morrow
morning!"

The Welchman's sons departed at once. As they were leaving the
room Huck sprang up and exclaimed:

"Oh, please don't tell *any*body it was me that blowed on them!
Oh, please!"

"All right if you say it, Huck, but you ought to have the credit of
what you did."

"Oh, no, no! Please don't tell!"

When the young men were gone, the old Welchman said—

"They won't tell—and I won't. But why don't you want it
known?"

Huck would not explain, further than to say that he already knew
too much about one of those men and would not have the man know
that he knew anything against him for the whole world—he would be
killed for knowing it, sure.

The old man promised secrecy once more, and said:

"How did you come to follow these fellows, lad? Were they
looking suspicious?"

Huck was silent while he framed a duly cautious reply. Then he
said:

"Well, you see, I'm a kind of a hard lot,—least everybody says so,
and I don't see nothing agin it—and sometimes I can't sleep much,
on accounts of thinking about it and sort of trying to strike out a new
way of doing. That was the way of it last night. I couldn't sleep, and
so I come along up street 'bout midnight, a-turning it all over, and
when I got to that old shackly brick store by the Temperance Tavern,
I backed up agin the wall to have another think. Well, just then
along comes these two chaps slipping along close by me, with
something under their arm and I reckoned they'd stole it. One was
a-smoking, and t'other one wanted a light; so they stopped right
before me and the cigars lit up their faces and I see that the big one
was the deaf and dumb Spaniard, by his white whiskers and the
patch on his eye, and t'other one was a rusty, ragged looking devil."

"Could you see the rags by the light of the cigars?"

This staggered Huck for a moment. Then he said:

"Well, I don't know—but somehow it seems as if I did."

"Then they went on, and you—"

"Follered 'em—yes. That was it. I wanted to see what was up—they sneaked along so. I dogged 'em to the widder's stile, and stood in the dark and heard the ragged one beg for the widder, and the Spaniard swear he'd spile her looks just as I told you and your two—"

"What! The *deaf and dumb* man said all that!"

Huck had made another terrible mistake! He was trying his best to keep the old man from getting the faintest hint of who the Spaniard might be, and yet his tongue seemed determined to get him into trouble in spite of all he could do. He made several efforts to creep out of his scrape, but the old man's eye was upon him and he made blunder after blunder. Presently the Welchman said:

"My boy, don't be afraid of me. I wouldn't hurt a hair of your head for all the world. No—I'd protect you—I'd protect you. This Spaniard is not deaf and dumb; you've let that slip without intending it; you can't cover that up now. You know something about that Spaniard that you want to keep dark. Now trust me—tell me what it is, and trust me—I won't betray you."

Huck looked into the old man's honest eyes a moment, then bent over and whispered in his ear—

" 'Tain't a Spaniard—it's Injun Joe!"

The Welchman almost jumped out of his chair. In a moment he said:

"It's all plain enough, now. When you talked about notching ears and slitting noses I judged that that was your own embellishment, because white men don't take that sort of revenge. But an Injun! That's a different matter altogether."

During breakfast the talk went on, and in the course of it the old man said that the last thing which he and his sons had done, before going to bed, was to get a lantern and examine the stile and its vicinity for marks of blood. They found none, but captured a bulky bundle of—

"Of WHAT?"

If the words had been lightning they could not have leaped with a more stunning suddenness from Huck's blanched lips. His eyes were staring wide, now, and his breath suspended—waiting for the answer. The Welchman started—stared in return—three seconds—five seconds—ten—then replied—

"Of burglar's tools. Why what's the *matter* with you?"

Huck sank back, panting gently, but deeply, unutterably grateful. The Welchman eyed him gravely, curiously—and presently said—

"Yes, burglar's tools. That appears to relieve you a good deal. But what did give you that turn? What were *you* expecting we'd found?"

Huck was in a close place—the inquiring eye was upon him—he

would have given anything for material for a plausible answer—
nothing suggested itself—the inquiring eye was boring deeper and
deeper—a senseless reply offered—there was no time to weigh it, so
at a venture he uttered it—feebly:

"Sunday-school books, maybe."

Poor Huck was too distressed to smile, but the old man laughed
loud and joyously, shook up the details of his anatomy from head to
foot, and ended by saying that such a laugh was money in a man's
pocket, because it cut down the doctor's bills like everything. Then
he added:

"Poor old chap, you're white and jaded—you ain't well a bit—no
wonder you're a little flighty and off your balance. But you'll come
out of it. Rest and sleep will fetch you out all right, I hope."

Huck was irritated to think he had been such a goose and
betrayed such a suspicious excitement, for he had dropped the idea
that the parcel brought from the tavern was the treasure, as soon as
he had heard the talk at the widow's stile. He had only *thought* it was
not the treasure, however—he had not known that it wasn't—and so
the suggestion of a captured bundle was too much for his self-
possession. But on the whole he felt glad the little episode had
happened, for now he knew beyond all question that that bundle was
not *the* bundle, and so his mind was at rest and exceedingly
comfortable. In fact everything seemed to be drifting just in the right
direction, now; the treasure must be still in No. 2, the men would be
captured and jailed that day, and he and Tom could seize the gold
that night without any trouble or any fear of interruption.

Just as breakfast was completed there was a knock on the door.
Huck jumped for a hiding place, for he had no mind to be connected
even remotely with the late event. The Welchman admitted several
ladies and gentlemen, among them the widow Douglas, and noticed
that groups of citizens were climbing up the hill—to stare at the
stile. So the news had spread.

The Welchman had to tell the story of the night to the visitors. The
widow's gratitude for her preservation was outspoken.

"Don't say a word about it madam. There's another that you're
more beholden to than you are to me and my boys, maybe, but he
don't allow me to tell his name. We wouldn't have been there but for
him."

Of course this excited a curiosity so vast that it almost belittled the
main matter—but the Welchman allowed it to eat into the vitals of
his visitors, and through them be transmitted to the whole town, for
he refused to part with his secret. When all else had been learned,
the widow said:

"I went to sleep reading in bed and slept straight through all that
noise. Why didn't you come and wake me?"

"We judged it warn't worth while. Those fellows warn't likely to
come again—they hadn't any tools left to work with, and what was

the use of waking you up and scaring you to death? My three negro men stood guard at your house all the rest of the night. They've just come back."

More visitors came, and the story had to be told and re-told for a couple of hours more.

There was no Sabbath-school during day-school vacation, but everybody was early at church. The stirring event was well canvassed. News came that not a sign of the two villains had been yet discovered. When the sermon was finished, Judge Thatcher's wife dropped alongside of Mrs. Harper as she moved down the aisle with the crowd and said:

"Is my Becky going to sleep all day? I just expected she would be tired to death."

"Your Becky?"

"Yes," with a startled look,—"didn't she stay with you last night?"

"Why, no."

Mrs. Thatcher turned pale, and sank into a pew, just as Aunt Polly, talking briskly with a friend, passed by. Aunt Polly said:

"Good morning, Mrs. Thatcher. Good morning Mrs. Harper. I've got a boy that's turned up missing. I reckon my Tom staid at your house last night—one of you. And now he's afraid to come to church. I've got to settle with him."

Mrs. Thatcher shook her head feebly and turned paler than ever.

"He didn't stay with us," said Mrs. Harper, beginning to look uneasy. A marked anxiety came into Aunt Polly's face.

"Joe Harper, have you seen my Tom this morning?"

"No'm."

"When did you see him last?"

Joe tried to remember, but was not sure he could say. The people had stopped moving out of church. Whispers passed along, and a boding uneasiness took possession of every countenance. Children were anxiously questioned, and young teachers. They all said they had not noticed whether Tom and Becky were on board the ferry-boat on the homeward trip; it was dark; no one thought of inquiring if any one was missing. One young man finally blurted out his fear that they were still in the cave! Mrs. Thatcher swooned away. Aunt Polly fell to crying and wringing her hands.

The alarm swept from lip to lip, from group to group, from street to street, and within five minutes the bells were wildly clanging and the whole town was up! The Cardiff Hill episode sank into instant insignificance, the burglars were forgotten, horses were saddled, skiffs were manned, the ferry-boat ordered out, and before the horror was half an hour old, two hundred men were pouring down high-road and river toward the cave.

All the long afternoon the village seemed empty and dead. Many women visited Aunt Polly and Mrs. Thatcher and tried to comfort them. They cried with them, too, and that was still better than words. All the tedious night the town waited for news; but when the morning dawned at last, all the word that came was, "Send more candles—and send food." Mrs. Thatcher was almost crazed; and Aunt Polly also. Judge Thatcher sent messages of hope and encouragement from the cave, but they conveyed no real cheer.

The old Welchman came home toward daylight, spattered with candle grease, smeared with clay, and almost worn out. He found Huck still in the bed that had been provided for him, and delirious with fever. The physicians were all at the cave, so the Widow Douglas came and took charge of the patient. She said she would do her best by him, because, whether he was good, bad, or indifferent, he was the Lord's, and nothing that was the Lord's was a thing to be neglected. The Welchman said Huck had good spots in him, and the widow said—

"You can depend on it. That's the Lord's mark. He don't leave it off. He never does. Puts it somewhere on every creature that comes from his hands."

Early in the forenoon parties of jaded men began to straggle into the village, but the strongest of the citizens continued searching. All the news that could be gained was that remotenesses of the cavern were being ransacked that had never been visited before; that every corner and crevice was going to be thoroughly searched; that wherever one wandered through the maze of passages, lights were to be seen flitting hither and thither in the distance, and shoutings and pistol shots sent their hollow reverberations to the ear down the sombre aisles. In one place, far from the section usually traversed by tourists, the names "BECKY & TOM" had been found traced upon the rocky wall with candle smoke, and near at hand a grease-soiled bit of ribbon. Mrs. Thatcher recognized the ribbon and cried over it. She said it was the last relic she should ever have of her child; and that no other memorial of her could ever be so precious, because this one parted latest from the living body before the awful death came. Some said that now and then, in the cave, a far-away speck of light would glimmer, and then a glorious shout would burst forth and a score of men go trooping down the echoing aisle—and then a sickening disappointment always followed; the children were not there; it was only a searcher's light.

Three dreadful days and nights dragged their tedious hours along, and the village sank into a hopeless stupor. No one had heart for anything. The accidental discovery, just made, that the proprietor of the Temperance Tavern kept liquor on his premises, scarcely fluttered the public pulse, tremendous as the fact was. In a lucid interval, Huck feebly led up to the subject of taverns, and finally asked—dimly dreading the worst—if anything had been discovered at the Temperance Tavern since he had been ill?

"Yes," said the widow.

Huck started up in bed, wild-eyed:

"What! What was it?"

"Liquor!—and the place has been shut up. Lie down, child—what a turn you did give me!"

"Only tell me just one thing—only just one—please! Was it Tom Sawyer that found it?"

The widow burst into tears. "Hush, hush, child, hush! I've told you before, you must *not* talk. You are very, very sick!"

Then nothing but liquor had been found; there would have been a great pow-wow if it had been the gold. So the treasure was gone forever—gone forever! But what could she be crying about? Curious that she should cry.

These thoughts worked their dim way through Huck's mind, and under the weariness they gave him he fell asleep. The widow said to herself:

"There—he's asleep, poor wreck. Tom Sawyer find it! Pity but somebody could find Tom Sawyer! Ah, there ain't many left, now, that's got hope enough, or strength enough, either, to go on searching."

CHAPTER XXXI

Now to return to Tom and Becky's share in the pic-nic. They tripped along the murky aisles with the rest of the company, visiting the familiar wonders of the cave—wonders dubbed with rather over-descriptive names, such as "The Drawing-Room," "The Cathedral," "Aladdin's Palace," and so on. Presently the hide-and-seek frolicking began, and Tom and Becky engaged in it with zeal until the exertion began to grow a trifle wearisome; then they wandered down a sinuous avenue holding their candles aloft and reading the tangled web-work of names, dates, post-office addresses and mottoes with which the rocky walls had been frescoed (in candle smoke). Still drifting along and talking, they scarcely noticed that they were now in a part of the cave whose walls were not frescoed. They smoked their own names under an overhanging shelf and moved on. Presently they came to a place where a little stream of water, trickling over a ledge and carrying a limestone sediment with it, had, in the slow-dragging ages, formed a laced and ruffled Niagara in gleaming and imperishable stone. Tom squeezed his small body behind it in order to illuminate it for Becky's gratification. He found that it curtained a sort of steep natural stairway which was enclosed between narrow walls, and at once the ambition to be a discoverer seized him. Becky responded to his call, and they made a smokemark for future guidance, and started upon their quest. They wound this way and that, far down into the secret depths of the cave, made another mark, and

branched off in search of novelties to tell the upper world about.
In one place they found a spacious cavern, from whose ceiling
depended a multitude of shining stalactites of the length and
circumference of a man's leg; they walked all about it, wondering
and admiring, and presently left it by one of the numerous
passages that opened into it. This shortly brought them to a
bewitching spring, whose basin was encrusted with a frost work of
glittering crystals; it was in the midst of a cavern whose walls were
supported by many fantastic pillars which had been formed by the
joining of great stalactites and stalagmites together, the result
of the ceaseless water-drip of centuries. Under the roof vast knots
of bats had packed themselves together, thousands in a bunch;
the lights disturbed the creatures and they came flocking down by
hundreds, squeaking and darting furiously at the candles. Tom
knew their ways and the danger of this sort of conduct. He siezed
Becky's hand and hurried her into the first corridor that offered;
and none too soon, for a bat struck Becky's light out with its wing
while she was passing out of the cavern. The bats chased the
children a good distance; but the fugitives plunged into every new
passage that offered, and at last got rid of the perilous things. Tom
found a subterranean lake, shortly, which stretched its dim length
away until its shape was lost in the shadows. He wanted to explore
its borders, but concluded that it would be best to sit down and
rest a while, first. Now, for the first time, the deep stillness of the
place laid a clammy hand upon the spirits of the children. Becky
said—

"Why, I didn't notice, but it seems ever so long since I heard any
of the others."

"Come to think, Becky, we are away down below them—and
I don't know how far away north, or south, or east, or whichever
it is. We couldn't hear them here."

Becky grew apprehensive.

"I wonder how long we've been down here, Tom. We better
start back."

"Yes, I reckon we better. P'raps we better."

"Can you find the way, Tom? It's all a mixed-up crookedness
to me."

"I reckon I could find it—but then the bats. If they put both
our candles out it will be an awful fix. Let's try some other way,
so as not to go through there."

"Well. But I hope we won't get lost. It would be so awful!" and
the girl shuddered at the thought of the dreadful possibilities.

They started through a corridor, and traversed it in silence a long
way, glancing at each new opening, to see if there was anything
familiar about the look of it; but they were all strange. Every time
Tom made an examination, Becky would watch his face for an
encouraging sign, and he would say cheerily—

"Oh, it's all right. This ain't the one, but we'll come to it right away!"

But he felt less and less hopeful with each failure, and presently began to turn off into diverging avenues at sheer random, in desperate hope of finding the one that was wanted. He still said it was "all right," but there was such a leaden dread at his heart, that the words had lost their ring and sounded just as if he had said, "All is lost!" Becky clung to his side in an anguish of fear, and tried hard to keep back the tears, but they would come. At last she said:

"O, Tom, never mind the bats, let's go back that way! We seem to get worse and worse off all the time."

Tom stopped.

"Listen!" said he.

Profound silence; silence so deep that even their breathings were conspicuous in the hush. Tom shouted. The call went echoing down the empty aisles and died out in the distance in a faint sound that resembled a ripple of mocking laughter.

"Oh, don't do it again, Tom, it is too horrid," said Becky.

"It is horrid, but I better, Becky; they *might* hear us, you know" and he shouted again.

The "might" was even a chillier horror than the ghostly laughter, it so confessed a perishing hope. The children stood still and listened; there was no result. Tom turned upon the back track at once, and hurried his steps. It was but a little while before a certain indecision in his manner revealed another fearful fact to Becky—he could not find his way back!

"O, Tom, you didn't make any marks!"

"Becky I was such a fool! Such a fool! I never thought we might want to come back! No—I can't find the way. It's all mixed up."

"Tom, Tom, we're lost! we're lost! We never can get out of this awful place! O, why *did* we ever leave the others!"

She sank to the ground and burst into such a frenzy of crying that Tom was appalled with the idea that she might die, or lose her reason. He sat down by her and put his arms around her; she buried her face in his bosom, she clung to him, she poured out her terrors, her unavailing regrets, and the far echoes turned them all to jeering laughter. Tom begged her to pluck up hope again, and she said she could not. He fell to blaming and abusing himself for getting her into this miserable situation; this had a better effect. She said she would try to hope again, she would get up and follow wherever he might lead if only he would not talk like that any more. For he was no more to blame than she, she said.

So they moved on again—aimlessly—simply at random—all they could do was to move, keep moving. For a little while, hope made a show of reviving—not with any reason to back it, but only because it is its nature to revive when the spring has not been taken out of it by age and familiarity with failure.

By and by Tom took Becky's candle and blew it out. This economy meant so much! Words were not needed. Becky understood, and her hope died again. She knew that Tom had a whole candle and three or four pieces in his pockets—yet he must economise.

By and by, fatigue began to assert its claims; the children tried to pay no attention, for it was dreadful to think of sitting down when time was grown to be so precious; moving, in some direction, in any direction, was at least progress and might bear fruit; but to sit down was to invite death and shorten its pursuit.

At last Becky's frail limbs refused to carry her farther. She sat down. Tom rested with her, and they talked of home, and the friends there, and the comfortable beds and above all, the light! Becky cried, and Tom tried to think of some way of comforting her, but all his encouragements were grown threadbare with use, and sounded like sarcasms. Fatigue bore so heavily upon Becky that she drowsed off to sleep. Tom was grateful. He sat looking into her drawn face and saw it grow smooth and natural under the influence of pleasant dreams; and by and by a smile dawned and rested there. The peaceful face reflected somewhat of peace and healing into his own spirit, and his thoughts wandered away to by-gone times and dreamy memories. While he was deep in his musings, Becky woke up with a breezy little laugh—but it was stricken dead upon her lips, and a groan followed it.

"Oh, how *could* I sleep! I wish I never, never had waked! No! No, I don't, Tom! Don't look so! I won't say it again."

"I'm glad you've slept, Becky; you'll feel rested, now, and we'll find the way out."

"We can try, Tom; but I've seen such a beautiful country in my dream. I reckon we are going there."

"Maybe not, maybe not. Cheer up, Becky, and let's go on trying."

They rose up and wandered along, hand in hand and hopeless. They tried to estimate how long they had been in the cave, but all they knew was that it seemed days and weeks, and yet it was plain that this could not be, for their candles were not gone yet. A long time after this—they could not tell how long—Tom said they must go softly and listen for dripping water—they must find a spring. They found one presently, and Tom said it was time to rest again. Both were cruelly tired, yet Becky said she thought she could go on a little farther. She was surprised to hear Tom dissent. She could not understand it. They sat down, and Tom fastened his candle to the wall in front of them with some clay. Thought was soon busy; nothing was said for some time. Then Becky broke the silence:

"Tom, I am so hungry!"

Tom took something out of his pocket.

"Do you remember this?" said he.

Becky almost smiled.

"It's our wedding cake, Tom."

"Yes—I wish it was as big as a barrel, for it's all we've got."

"I saved it from the pic-nic for us to dream on, Tom, the way grown-up people do with wedding cake—but it'll be our—"

She dropped the sentence where it was. Tom divided the cake and Becky ate with good appetite, while Tom nibbled at his moiety. There was abundance of cold water to finish the feast with. By and by Becky suggested that they move on again. Tom was silent a moment. Then he said:

"Becky, can you bear it if I tell you something?"

Becky's face paled, but she thought she could.

"Well then, Becky, we must stay here, where there's water to drink. That little piece is our last candle!"

Becky gave loose to tears and wailings. Tom did what he could to comfort her but with little effect. At length Becky said:

"Tom!"

"Well, Becky?"

"They'll miss us and hunt for us!"

"Yes, they will! Certainly they will!"

"Maybe they're hunting for us now, Tom."

"Why I reckon maybe they are. I hope they are."

"When would they miss us, Tom?"

"When they get back to the boat, I reckon."

"Tom, it might be dark, then—would they notice we hadn't come?"

"I don't know. But anyway, your mother would miss you as soon as they got home."

A frightened look in Becky's face brought Tom to his senses and he saw that he had made a blunder. Becky was not to have gone home that night! The children became silent and thoughtful. In a moment a new burst of grief from Becky showed Tom that the thing in his mind had struck hers also—that the Sabbath morning might be half spent before Mrs. Thatcher discovered that Becky was not at Mrs. Harper's.

The children fastened their eyes upon their bit of candle and watched it melt slowly and pitilessly away; saw the half inch of wick stand alone at last; saw the feeble flame rise and fall, climb the thin column of smoke, linger at its top a moment, and then— the horror of utter darkness reigned!

How long afterward it was that Becky came to a slow consciousness that she was crying in Tom's arms, neither could tell. All that they knew was, that after what seemed a mighty stretch of time, both awoke out of a dead stupor of sleep and resumed their miseries once more. Tom said it might be Sunday, now—maybe Monday. He tried to get Becky to talk, but her sorrows were too oppressive, all her hopes were gone. Tom said that

they must have been missed long ago, and no doubt the search
was going on. He would shout and maybe some one would come.
He tried it; but in the darkness the distant echoes sounded so
hideously that he tried it no more.

The hours wasted away, and hunger came to torment the
captives again. A portion of Tom's half of the cake was left; they
divided and ate it. But they seemed hungrier than before. The poor
morsel of food only whetted desire.

By and by Tom said:

"*Sh!* Did you hear that?"

Both held their breath and listened. There was a sound like the
faintest, far-off shout. Instantly Tom answered it, and leading
Becky by the hand, started groping down the corridor in its
direction. Presently he listened again; again the sound was heard,
and apparently a little nearer.

"It's them!" said Tom; "they're coming! Come along Becky—
we're all right now!"

The joy of the prisoners was almost overwhelming. Their speed
was slow, however, because pitfalls were somewhat common, and
had to be guarded against. They shortly came to one and had to
stop. It might be three feet deep, it might be a hundred—there
was no passing it at any rate. Tom got down on his breast and
reached as far down as he could. No bottom. They must stay there
and wait until the searchers came. They listened; evidently the
distant shoutings were growing more distant! a moment or two
more and they had gone altogether. The heart-sinking misery of
it! Tom whooped until he was hoarse, but it was of no use. He
talked hopefully to Becky; but an age of anxious waiting passed
and no sounds came again.

The children groped their way back to the spring. The weary
time dragged on; they slept again, and awoke famished and
woe-stricken. Tom believed it must be Tuesday by this time.

Now an idea struck him. There were some side passages near
at hand. It would be better to explore some of these than bear the
weight of the heavy time in idleness. He took a kite-line from his
pocket, tied it to a projection, and he and Becky started, Tom in
the lead, unwinding the line as he groped along. At the end of
twenty steps the corridor ended in a "jumping-off place." Tom
got down on his knees and felt below, and then as far around the
corner as he could reach with his hands conveniently; he made
an effort to stretch yet a little further to the right, and at that
moment, not twenty yards away, a human hand, holding a candle,
appeared from behind a rock! Tom lifted up a glorious shout,
and instantly that hand was followed by the body it belonged to—
Injun Joe's! Tom was paralyzed; he could not move. He was vastly
gratified the next moment, to see the "Spaniard" take to his heels
and get himself out of sight. Tom wondered that Joe had not

recognized his voice and come over and killed him for testifying in court. But the echoes must have disguised the voice. Without doubt, that was it, he reasoned. Tom's fright weakened every muscle in his body. He said to himself that if he had strength enough to get back to the spring he would stay there, and nothing should tempt him to run the risk of meeting Injun Joe again. He was careful to keep from Becky what it was he had seen. He told her he had only shouted "for luck."

But hunger and wretchedness rise superior to fears in the long run. Another tedious wait at the spring and another long sleep brought changes. The children awoke tortured with a raging hunger. Tom believed that it must be Wednesday or Thursday or even Friday or Saturday, now, and that the search had been given over. He proposed to explore another passage. He felt willing to risk Injun Joe and all other terrors. But Becky was very weak. She had sunk into a dreary apathy and would not be roused. She said she would wait, now, where she was, and die—it would not be long. She told Tom to go with the kite-line and explore if he chose; but she implored him to come back every little while and speak to her; and she made him promise that when the awful time came, he would stay by her and hold her hand until all was over.

Tom kissed her, with a choking sensation in his throat, and made a show of being confident of finding the searchers or an escape from the cave; then he took the kite-line in his hand and went groping down one of the passages on his hands and knees, distressed with hunger and sick with bodings of coming doom.

CHAPTER XXXII

Tuesday afternoon came, and waned to the twilight. The village of St. Petersburg still mourned. The lost children had not been found. Public prayers had been offered up for them, and many and many a private prayer that had the petitioner's whole heart in it; but still no good news came from the cave. The majority of the searchers had given up the quest and gone back to their daily avocations, saying that it was plain the children could never be found. Mrs. Thatcher was very ill, and a great part of the time delirious. People said it was heartbreaking to hear her call her child, and raise her head and listen a whole minute at a time, then lay it wearily down again with a moan. Aunt Polly had drooped into a settled melancholy, and her gray hair had grown almost white. The village went to its rest on Tuesday night, sad and forlorn.

Away in the middle of the night a wild peal burst from the village bells, and in a moment the streets were swarming with frantic half-clad people, who shouted, "Turn out! turn out! they're found! they're found!" Tin pans and horns were added to the din, the population massed itself and moved toward the river, met the children coming in an open carriage drawn by shouting citizens, thronged around it, joined its homeward march, and swept magnificently up the main street roaring huzzah after huzzah!

The village was illuminated; nobody went to bed again; it was the greatest night the little town had ever seen. During the first half hour a procession of villagers filed through Judge Thatcher's house, siezed the saved ones and kissed them, squeezed Mrs. Thatcher's hand, tried to speak but couldn't—and drifted out raining tears all over the place.

Aunt Polly's happiness was complete, and Mrs. Thatcher's nearly so. It would be complete, however, as soon as the messenger dispatched with the great news to the cave should get the word to her husband. Tom lay upon a sofa with an eager auditory about him and told the history of the wonderful adventure, putting in many striking additions to adorn it withal; and closed with a description of how he left Becky and went on an exploring expedition; how he followed two avenues as far as his kite-line would reach; how he followed a third to the fullest stretch of the kite-line, and was about to turn back when he glimpsed a far-off speck that looked like daylight; dropped the line and groped toward it, pushed his head and shoulders through a small hole and saw the broad Mississippi rolling by! And if it had only happened to be night he would not have seen that speck of daylight and would not have explored that passage any more! He told how he went back for Becky and broke the good news and she told him not to fret her with such stuff, for she was tired, and knew she was going to die, and wanted to. He described how he labored with her and convinced her; and how she almost died for joy when she had groped to where she actually saw the blue speck of daylight; how he pushed his way out at the hole and then helped her out; how they sat there and cried for gladness; how some men came along in a skiff and Tom hailed them and told them their situation and their famished condition; how the men didn't believe the wild tale at first, "because," said they, "you are five miles down the river below the valley the cave is in"—then took them aboard, rowed to a house, gave them supper, made them rest till two or three hours after dark and then brought them home.

Before day-dawn, Judge Thatcher and the handful of searchers with him were tracked out, in the cave, by the twine clews they had strung behind them, and informed of the great news.

Three days and nights of toil and hunger in the cave were not to be shaken off at once, as Tom and Becky soon discovered. They were bedridden all of Wednesday and Thursday, and seemed to grow more and more tired and worn, all the time. Tom got about, a little, on Thursday, was down town Friday, and nearly as whole as ever Saturday; but Becky did not leave her room until Sunday, and then she looked as if she had passed through a wasting illness.

Tom learned of Huck's sickness and went to see him on Friday, but could not be admitted to the bedroom; neither could he on Saturday or Sunday. He was admitted daily after that, but was warned to keep still about his adventure and introduce no exciting topic. The widow Douglas staid by to see that he obeyed. At home Tom learned of the Cardiff Hill event; also that the "ragged man's" body had eventually been found in the river near the ferry landing; he had been drowned while trying to escape, perhaps.

About a fortnight after Tom's rescue from the cave, he started off to visit Huck, who had grown plenty strong enough, now, to hear exciting talk, and Tom had some that would interest him, he thought. Judge Thatcher's house was on Tom's way, and he stopped to see Becky. The Judge and some friends set Tom to talking, and some one asked him ironically if he wouldn't like to go to the cave again. Tom said he thought he wouldn't mind it. The Judge said:

"Well, there are others just like you, Tom, I've not the least doubt. But we have taken care of that. Nobody will get lost in that cave any more."

"Why?"

"Because I had its big door sheathed with boiler iron two weeks ago, and triple-locked—and I've got the keys."

Tom turned as white as a sheet.

"What's the matter, boy! Here, run, somebody! Fetch a glass of water!"

The water was brought and thrown into Tom's face.

"Ah, now you're all right. What was the matter with you, Tom?"

"Oh, Judge, Injun Joe's in the cave!"

CHAPTER XXXIII

Within a few minutes the news had spread, and a dozen skiff-loads of men were on their way to McDougal's cave, and the ferry-boat, well filled with passengers, soon followed. Tom Sawyer was in the skiff that bore Judge Thatcher.

When the cave door was unlocked, a sorrowful sight presented itself in the dim twilight of the place. Injun Joe lay stretched upon the ground, dead, with his face close to the crack of the door, as if his longing eyes had been fixed, to the latest moment, upon the light and the cheer of the free world outside. Tom was touched, for he knew by his own experience how this wretch had suffered. His pity was moved, but nevertheless he felt an abounding sense of relief and security, now, which revealed to him in a degree which he had not fully appreciated before how vast a weight of dread had been lying upon him since the day he lifted his voice against this bloody-minded outcast.

Injun Joe's bowie knife lay close by, its blade broken in two. The great foundation-beam of the door had been chipped and hacked through, with tedious labor; useless labor, too, it was, for the native rock formed a sill outside it, and upon that stubborn material the knife had wrought no effect; the only damage done was to the knife itself. But if there had been no stony obstruction there the labor would have been useless still, for if the beam had been wholly cut away Injun Joe could not have squeezed his body under the door, and he knew it. So he had only hacked that place in order to be doing something—in order to pass the weary time—in order to employ his tortured faculties. Ordinarily one could find half a dozen bits of candle stuck around in the crevices of this vestibule, left there by tourists; but there were none now. The prisoner had searched them out and eaten them. He had also contrived to catch a few bats, and these, also, he had eaten, leaving only their claws. The poor unfortunate had starved to death. In one place near at hand, a stalagmite had been slowly growing up from the ground for ages, builded by the water-drip from a stalactite overhead. The captive had broken off the stalagmite, and upon the stump had placed a stone, wherein he had scooped a shallow hollow to catch the precious drop that fell once in every three minutes with the dreary regularity of a clock-tick—a dessert spoonful once in four and twenty hours. That drop was falling when the Pyramids were new; when Troy fell; when the foundations of Rome were laid; when Christ was crucified; when the Conqueror created the British empire; when Columbus sailed; when the massacre at Lexington was "news." It is falling now; it will still be falling when all these things shall have sunk down the afternoon of history, and the twilight of tradition, and been swallowed up in the thick night of oblivion. Has everything a purpose and a mission? Did this drop fall patiently during five thousand years to be ready for this flitting human insect's need? and has it another important object to accomplish ten thousand years to come? No matter. It is many and many a year since the hapless half-breed scooped out the stone to catch the priceless drops, but to this day the tourist stares longest at that pathetic stone and that slow dropping water when he comes to see the wonders of McDougal's cave. Injun Joe's cup stands first in the list of the cavern's marvels; even "Aladdin's Palace" cannot rival it.

Injun Joe was buried near the mouth of the cave; and people flocked there in boats and wagons from the towns and from all the farms and hamlets for seven miles around; they brought their children, and all sorts of provisions, and confessed that they had had almost as satisfactory a time at the funeral as they could have had at the hanging.

This funeral stopped the further growth of one thing—the petition to the Governor for Injun Joe's pardon. The petition had been largely signed; many tearful and eloqent meetings had been

held, and a committee of sappy women been appointed to go in
deep mourning and wail around the governor, and implore him to
be a merciful ass and trample his duty under foot. Injun Joe was
believed to have killed five citizens of the village, but what of that?
If he had been Satan himself there would have been plenty of
weaklings ready to scribble their names to a pardon-petition, and
drip a tear on it from their permanently impaired and leaky
water-works.

The morning after the funeral Tom took Huck to a private
place to have an important talk. Huck had learned all about Tom's
adventure from the Welchman and the widow Douglas, by this
time, but Tom said he reckoned there was one thing they had not
told him; that thing was what he wanted to talk about now. Huck's
face saddened. He said:

"I know what it is. You got into No. 2 and never found anything
but whisky. Nobody told me it was you; but I just knowed it must
'a' ben you, soon as I heard 'bout that whisky business; and I
knowed you hadn't got the money becuz you'd 'a' got at me some
way or other and told me even if you was mum to everybody else.
Tom, something's always told me we'd never get holt of that swag."

"Why Huck, *I* never told on that tavern-keeper. *You* know his
tavern was all right the Saturday I went to the pic-nic. Don't you
remember you was to watch there that night?"

"Oh, yes! Why it seems 'bout a year ago. It was that very night
that I follered Injun Joe to the widder's."

"*You* followed him?"

"Yes—but you keep mum. I reckon Injun Joe's left friends
behind him, and I don't want 'em souring on me and doing me
mean tricks. If it hadn't ben for me he'd be down in Texas now, all
right."

Then Huck told his entire adventure in confidence to Tom, who
had only heard of the Welchmen's part of it before.

"Well," said Huck, presently, coming back to the main question,
"whoever nipped the whisky in No. 2, nipped the money too, I
reckon—anyways it's a goner for us, Tom."

"Huck, that money wasn't ever in No. 2!"

"What!" Huck searched his comrade's face keenly. "Tom, have
you got on the track of that money again?"

"Huck, it's in the cave!"

Huck's eyes blazed.

"Say it again, Tom!"

"The money's in the cave!"

"Tom,—honest injun, now—is it fun, or earnest?"

"Earnest, Huck—just as earnest as ever I was in my life. Will
you go in there with me and help get it out?"

"I bet I will! I will if it's where we can blaze our way to it and not
get lost."

"Huck, we can do that without the least little bit of trouble in
the world."

"Good as wheat! What makes you think the money's—"

"Huck, you just wait till we get in there. If we don't find it I'll
agree to give you my drum and everything I've got in the world.
I will, by jings."

"All right—it's a whiz. When do you say?"

"Right now, if you say it. Are you strong enough?"

"Is it far in the cave? I ben on my pins a little, three or four days,
now, but I can't walk more'n a mile, Tom—least I don't think I
could."

"It's about five mile into there the way anybody but me would
go, Huck, but there's a mighty short cut that they don't anybody
but me know about. Huck, I'll take you right to it in a skiff. I'll
float the skiff down there, and I'll pull it back again all by myself.
You needn't ever turn your hand over."

"Less start right off, Tom."

"All right. We want some bread and meat, and our pipes, and a
little bag or two, and two or three kite-strings, and some of these
new fangled things they call lucifer matches. I tell you many's the
time I wished I had some when I was in there before."

A trifle after noon the boys borrowed a small skiff from a citizen
who was absent, and got under way at once. When they were
several miles below "Cave Hollow," Tom said:

"Now you see this bluff here looks all alike all the way down
from the cave hollow—no houses, no wood-yards, bushes all
alike. But do you see that white place up yonder where there's been
a landslide? Well that's one of my marks. We'll get ashore, now."

They landed.

"Now Huck, where we're a-standing you could touch that hole
I got out of with a fishing-pole. See if you can find it."

Huck searched all the place about, and found nothing. Tom
proudly marched into a thick clump of sumach bushes and said—

"Here you are! Look at it, Huck; it's the snuggest hole in this
country. You just keep mum about it. All along I've been wanting
to be a robber, but I knew I'd got to have a thing like this, and
where to run across it was the bother. We've got it now, and we'll
keep it quiet, only we'll let Joe Harper and Ben Rogers in—because
of course there's got to be a Gang, or else there wouldn't be any
style about it. Tom Sawyer's Gang—it sounds splendid, don't it,
Huck?"

"Well, it just does, Tom. And who'll we rob?"

"Oh, most anybody. Waylay people—that's mostly the way."

"And kill them?"

"No—not always. Hive them in the cave till they raise a ransom."

"What's a ransom?"

"Money. You make them raise all they can, off'n their friends;

and after you've kept them a year, if it ain't raised then you kill
them. That's the general way. Only you don't kill the women. You
shut up the women, but you don't kill them. They're always
beautiful and rich, and awfully scared. You take their watches and
things, but you always take your hat off and talk polite. They ain't
anybody as polite as robbers—you'll see that in any book. Well
the women get to loving you, and after they've been in the cave a
week or two weeks they stop crying and after that you couldn't get
them to leave. If you drove them out they'd turn right around and
come back. It's so in all the books."

"Why it's real bully, Tom. I b'lieve it's better'n to be a pirate."

"Yes, it's better in some ways, because it's close to home and
circuses and all that."

By this time everything was ready and the boys entered the hole,
Tom in the lead. They toiled their way to the farther end of the
tunnel, then made their spliced kite-strings fast and moved on.
A few steps brought them to the spring and Tom felt a shudder
quiver all through him. He showed Huck the fragment of
candle-wick perched on a lump of clay against the wall, and
described how he and Becky had watched the flame struggle and
expire.

The boys began to quiet down to whispers, now, for the stillness
and gloom of the place oppressed their spirits. They went on, and
presently entered and followed Tom's other corridor until they
reached the "jumping-off place." The candles revealed the fact
that it was not really a precipice, but only a steep clay hill twenty
or thirty feet high. Tom whispered—

"Now I'll show you something, Huck."

He held his candle aloft and said—

"Look as far around the corner as you can. Do you see that?
There—on the big rock over yonder—done with candle smoke."

"Tom, its a *cross!*"

"*Now* where's your Number Two? *'Under the cross,'* hey? Right
yonder's where I saw Injun Joe poke up his candle, Huck!"

Huck stared at the mystic sign a while, and then said with a
shaky voice—

"Tom, less git out of here!"

"What! and leave the treasure?"

"Yes—leave it. Injun Joe's ghost is round about there, certain."

"No it ain't, Huck, no it ain't. It would ha'nt the place where
he died—away out at the mouth of the cave—five mile from here."

"No, Tom, it wouldn't. It would hang round the money. I know
the ways of ghosts, and so do you."

Tom began to fear that Huck was right. Misgivings gathered in
his mind. But presently an idea occurred to him—

"Looky here, Huck, what fools we're making of ourselves! Injun
Joe's ghost ain't a going to come around where there's a cross!"

The point was well taken. It had its effect.

"Tom I didn't think of that. But that's so. It's luck for us, that cross is. I reckon we'll climb down there and have a hunt for that box."

Tom went first, cutting rude steps in the clay hill as he descended. Huck followed. Four avenues opened out of the small cavern which the great rock stood in. The boys examined three of them with no result. They found a small recess in the one nearest the base of the rock, with a pallet of blankets spread down in it; also an old suspender, some bacon rhind, and the well gnawed bones of two or three fowls. But there was no money box. The lads searched and re-searched this place, but in vain. Tom said:

"He said *under* the cross. Well, this comes nearest to being under the cross. It can't be under the rock itself, because that sets solid on the ground."

They searched everywhere once more, and then sat down discouraged. Huck could suggest nothing. By and by Tom said:

"Looky here, Huck, there's foot-prints and some candle grease on the clay about one side of this rock, but not on the other sides. Now what's that for? I bet you the money *is* under the rock. I'm going to dig in the clay."

"That ain't no bad notion, Tom!" said Huck with animation.

Tom's "real Barlow" was out at once, and he had not dug four inches before he struck wood.

"Hey, Huck!—you hear that?"

Huck began to dig and scratch now. Some boards were soon uncovered and removed. They had concealed a natural chasm which led under the rock. Tom got into this and held his candle as far under the rock as he could, but said he could not see to the end of the rift. He proposed to explore. He stooped and passed under; the narrow way descended gradually. He followed its winding course, first to the right, then to the left, Huck at his heels. Tom turned a short curve, by and by, and exclaimed—

"My goodness, Huck, looky here!"

It was the treasure box, sure enough, occupying a snug little cavern, along with an empty powder keg, a couple of guns in leather cases, two or three pairs of old moccasins, a leather belt, and some other rubbish well soaked with the water-drip.

"Got it at last!" said Huck, plowing among the tarnished coins with his hand. "My, but we're rich, Tom!"

"Huck, I always reckoned we'd get it. It's just too good to believe, but we *have* got it, sure! Say—let's not fool around here. Let's snake it out. Lemme see if I can lift the box."

It weighed about fifty pounds. Tom could lift it, after an awkward fashion, but could not carry it conveniently.

"I thought so," he said; *they* carried it like it was heavy, that day at the ha'nted house. I noticed that. I reckon I was right to think of fetching the little bags along."

The money was soon in the bags and the boys took it up to the cross-rock.

"Now less fetch the guns and things," said Huck.

"No, Huck—leave them there. They're just the tricks to have when we go to robbing. We'll keep them there all the time, and we'll hold our orgies there, too. It's an awful snug place for orgies."

"What's orgies?"

"*I* dono. But robbers always have orgies, and of course we've got to have them, too. Come along, Huck, we've been in here a long time. It's getting late, I reckon. I'm hungry, too. We'll eat and smoke when we get to the skiff."

They presently emerged into the clump of sumach bushes, looked warily out, found the coast clear, and were soon lunching and smoking in the skiff. As the sun dipped toward the horizon they pushed out and got under way. Tom skimmed up the shore through the long twilight, chatting cheerily with Huck, and landed shortly after dark.

"Now Huck," said Tom, "we'll hide the money in the loft of the widow's wood-shed, and I'll come up in the morning and we'll count it and divide, and then we'll hunt up a place out in the woods for it where it will be safe. Just you lay quiet here and watch the stuff till I run and hook Benny Taylor's little wagon; I won't be gone a minute."

He disappeared, and presently returned with the wagon, put the two small sacks into it, threw some old rags on top of them, and started off, dragging his cargo behind him. When the boys reached the Welchman's house, they stopped to rest. Just as they were about to move on, the Welchman stepped out and said:

"Hallo, who's that?"

"Huck and Tom Sawyer."

"Good! Come along with me, boys, you are keeping everybody waiting. Here—hurry up, trot ahead—I'll haul the wagon for you. Why, it's not as light as it might be. Got bricks in it?—or old metal?"

"Old metal," said Tom.

"I judged so; the boys in this town will take more trouble and fool away more time, hunting up six bit's worth of old iron to sell to the foundry than they would to make twice the money at regular work. But that's human nature—hurry along, hurry along!"

The boys wanted to know what the hurry was about.

"Never mind; you'll see, when we get to the Widow Douglas's."

Huck said with some apprehension—for he was long used to being falsely accused—

"Mr. Jones, *we* haven't been doing nothing."

The Welchman laughed.

"Well, I don't know, Huck, my boy. I don't know about that.

Ain't you and the widow good friends?''

"Yes. Well, she's been good friends to me, any ways.''

"All right, then. What do you want to be afraid for?''

This question was not entirely answered in Huck's slow mind before he found himself pushed, along with Tom, into Mrs. Douglas's drawing-room. Mr. Jones left the wagon near the door and followed.

The place was grandly lighted, and everybody that was of any consequence in the village was there. The Thatchers were there, the Harpers, the Rogerses, Aunt Polly, Sid, Mary, the minister, the editor, and a great many more, and all dressed in their best. The widow received the boys as heartily as any one could well receive two such looking beings. They were covered with clay and candle grease. Aunt Polly blushed crimson with humiliation, and frowned and shook her head at Tom. Nobody suffered half as much as the two boys did, however. Mr. Jones said:

"Tom wasn't at home, yet, so I gave him up; but I stumbled on him and Huck right at my door, so I just brought them along in a hurry.''

"And you did just right," said the widow:—"Come with me, boys.''

She took them to a bed chamber and said:

"Now wash and dress yourselves. Here are two new suits of clothes—shirts, socks, everything complete. They're Huck's—no, no thanks, Huck—Mr. Jones bought one and I the other. But they'll fit both of you. Get into them. We'll wait—come down when you are slicked up enough.''

Then she left.

CHAPTER XXXIV

Huck said: "Tom, we can slope, if we can find a rope. The window ain't high from the ground.''

"Shucks, what do you want to slope for?''

"Well I ain't used to that kind of a crowd. I can't stand it. I ain't going down there, Tom.''

"O, bother! It ain't anything. I don't mind it a bit. I'll take care of you.''

Sid appeared.

"Tom," said he, "Auntie has been waiting for you all the afternoon. Mary got your Sunday clothes ready, and everybody's been fretting about you. Say—ain't this grease and clay, on your clothes?''

"Now Mr. Siddy, you jist 'tend to your own business. What's all this blow-out about, anyway?''

"It's one of the widow's parties that she's always having. This time its for the Welchman and his sons, on account of that scrape

they helped her out of the other night. And say—I can tell you
something, if you want to know."

"Well, what?"

"Why old Mr. Jones is going to try to spring something on the
people here to-night, but I overheard him tell auntie to-day about
it, as a secret, but I reckon it's not much of a secret *now*.
Everybody knows—the widow, too, for all she tries to let on she
don't. Mr. Jones was bound Huck should be here—couldn't get
along with his grand secret without Huck, you know!"

"Secret about what, Sid?"

"About Huck tracking the robbers to the widow's. I reckon Mr.
Jones was going to make a grand time over his surprise, but I bet
you it will drop pretty flat."

Sid chuckled in a very contented and satisfied way.

"Sid, was it you that told?"

"O, never mind who it was. *Somebody* told—that's enough."

"Sid, there's only one person in this town mean enough to do
that, and that's you. If you had been in Huck's place you'd 'a'
sneaked down the hill and never told anybody on the robbers.
You can't do any but mean things, and you can't bear to see
anybody praised for doing good ones. There—no thanks, as the
widow says"—and Tom cuffed Sid's ears and helped him to the
door with several kicks. "Now go and tell auntie if you dare—and
to-morrow you'll catch it!"

Some minutes later the widow's guests were at the supper table,
and a dozen children were propped up at little side tables in the
same room, after the fashion of that country and that day. At the
proper time Mr. Jones made his little speech, in which he thanked
the widow for the honor she was doing himself and his sons, but
said that there was another person whose modesty—

And so forth and so on. He sprung his secret about Huck's
share in the adventure in the finest dramatic manner he was
master of, but the surprise it occasioned was largely counterfeit
and not as clamorous and effusive as it might have been under
happier circumstances. However, the widow made a pretty fair
show of astonishment, and heaped so many compliments and so
much gratitude upon Huck that he almost forgot the nearly
intolerable discomfort of his new clothes in the entirely intolerable
discomfort of being set up as a target for everybody's gaze and
everybody's laudations.

The widow said she meant to give Huck a home under her roof
and have him educated; and that when she could spare the
money she would start him in business in a modest way. Tom's
chance was come. He said:

"Huck don't need it. Huck's rich!"

Nothing but a heavy strain upon the good manners of the
company kept back the due and proper complimentary laugh

at this pleasant joke. But the silence was a little awkward. Tom broke it—

"Huck's got money. Maybe you don't believe it, but he's got lots of it. Oh, you needn't smile—I reckon I can show you. You just wait a minute."

Tom ran out of doors. The company looked at each other with a perplexed interest—and inquiringly at Huck, who was tongue-tied.

"Sid, what ails Tom?" said Aunt Polly. "He—well, there ain't ever any making of that boy out. I never—"

Tom entered, struggling with the weight of his sacks, and Aunt Polly did not finish her sentence. Tom poured the mass of yellow coin upon the table and said—

"There—what did I tell you? Half of it's Huck's and half of it's mine!"

The spectacle took the general breath away. All gazed, nobody spoke for a moment. Then there was a unanimous call for an explanation. Tom said he could furnish it, and he did. The tale was long, but brim full of interest. There was scarcely an interruption from anyone to break the charm of its flow. When he had finished, Mr. Jones said—

"I thought I had fixed up a little surprise for this occasion, but it don't amount to anything now. This one makes it sing mighty small, I'm willing to allow."

The money was counted. The sum amounted to a little over twelve thousand dollars. It was more than any one present had ever seen at one time before, though several persons were there who were worth considerably more than that in property.

CHAPTER XXXV

The reader may rest satisfied that Tom's and Huck's windfall made a mighty stir in the poor little village of St. Petersburg. So vast a sum, all in actual cash, seemed next to incredible. It was talked about, gloated over, glorified, until the reason of many of the citizens tottered under the strain of the unhealthy excitement. Every "haunted" house in St. Petersburg and the neighboring villages was dissected, plank by plank, and its foundations dug up and ransacked for hidden treasure—and not by boys, but men—pretty grave, unromantic men, too, some of them. Wherever Tom and Huck appeared they were courted, admired, stared at. The boys were not able to remember that their remarks had possessed weight before; but now their sayings were treasured and repeated; everything they did seemed somehow to be regarded as remarkable; they had evidently lost the power of doing and saying commonplace things; moreover, their past history was raked up and discovered to bear marks of conspicuous originality. The village paper published biographical sketches of the boys.

The widow Douglas put Huck's money out at six per cent., and Judge Thatcher did the same with Tom's at Aunt Polly's request. Each lad had an income, now, that was simply prodigious—a dollar for every week-day in the year and half of the Sundays. It was just what the minister got—no, it was what he was promised—he generally couldn't collect it. A dollar and a quarter a week would board, lodge and school a boy in those old simple days—and clothe him and wash him, too, for that matter.

Judge Thatcher had conceived a great opinion of Tom. He said that no commonplace boy would ever have got his daughter out of the cave. When Becky told her father, in strict confidence, how Tom had taken her whipping at school, the Judge was visibly moved; and when she pleaded grace for the mighty lie which Tom had told in order to shift that whipping from her shoulders to his own, the Judge said with a fine outburst that it was a noble, a generous, a magnanimous lie—a lie that was worthy to hold up its head and march down through history breast to breast with George Washington's lauded Truth about the hatchet! Becky thought her father had never looked so tall and so superb as when he walked the floor and stamped his foot and said that. She went straight off and told Tom about it.

Judge Thatcher hoped to see Tom a great lawyer or a great soldier some day. He said he meant to look to it that Tom should be admitted to the National military academy and afterwards trained in the best law school in the country, in order that he might be ready for either career or both.

Huck Finn's wealth and the fact that he was now under the widow Douglas's protection, introduced him into society—no, dragged him into it, hurled him into it—and his sufferings were almost more than he could bear. The widow's servants kept him clean and neat, combed and brushed, and they bedded him nightly in unsympathetic sheets that had not one little spot or stain which he could press to his heart and know for a friend. He had to eat with knife and fork; he had to use napkin, cup and plate; he had to learn his book, he had to go to church; he had to talk so properly that speech was become insipid in his mouth; whithersoever he turned, the bars and shackles of civilization shut him in and bound him hand and foot.

He bravely bore his miseries three weeks, and then one day turned up missing. For forty-eight hours the widow hunted for him everywhere in great distress. The public were profoundly concerned; they searched high and low, they dragged the river for his body. Early the third morning Tom Sawyer wisely went poking among some old empty hogsheads down behind the

abandoned slaughter-house, and in one of them he found the refugee.
Huck had slept there; he had just breakfasted upon some stolen
odds and ends of food, and was lying off, now, in comfort with
his pipe. He was unkempt, uncombed, and clad in the same old
ruin of rags that had made him picturesque in the days when
he was free and happy. Tom routed him out, told him the
trouble he had been causing, and urged him to go home. Huck's
face lost its tranquil content, and took a melancholy cast. He said:
"Don't talk about it, Tom. I've tried it, and it don't work; it
don't work, Tom. It ain't for me; I ain't used to it. The widder's
good to me, and friendly; but I can't stand them ways. She
makes me git up just at the same time every morning; she makes
me wash, they comb me all to thunder; she won't let me sleep in
the wood-shed; I got to wear them blamed clothes that just
smothers me, Tom; they don't seem to any air git through 'em,
somehow; and they're so rotten nice that I can't set down, nor
lay down, nor roll around anywher's; I hain't slid on a cellar-door
for—well, it 'pears to be years; I got to go to church and sweat
and sweat—I hate them ornery sermons! I can't ketch a fly in
there, I can't chaw, I got to wear shoes all Sunday. The widder
eats by a bell; she goes to bed by a bell; she gits up by a bell—
everything's so awful reg'lar a body can't stand it."
"Well, everybody does that way, Huck."
"Tom, it don't make no difference. I ain't everybody, and I
can't *stand* it. It's awful to be tied up so. And grub comes too
easy—I don't take no interest in vittles, that way. I got to ask, to
go a-fishing; I got to ask, to go in a-swimming—dern'd if I hain't
got to ask to do everything. Well, I'd got to talk so nice it wasn't
no comfort—I'd got to go up in the attic and rip out a while,
every day, to git a taste in my mouth, or I'd a died, Tom. The
widder wouldn't let me smoke; she wouldn't let me yell, she
wouldn't let me gape, nor stretch, nor scratch, before folks—"
[Then with a spasm of special irritation and injury],—"And dad
fetch it, she prayed all the time! I never *see* such a woman! I *had*
to shove, Tom—I just had to. And besides, that school's going to
open, and I'd a had to go to it—well, I wouldn't stand *that,*
Tom. Lookyhere, Tom, being rich ain't what it's cracked up to
be. It's just worry and worry, and sweat and sweat, and a-wishing
you was dead all the time. Now these clothes suits me, and this
bar'l suits me, and I ain't ever going to shake 'em any more.
Tom, I wouldn't ever got into all this trouble if it hadn't 'a' been
for that money; now you just take my sheer of it, along with
your'n, and gimme a ten-center sometimes—not many times,
becuz I don't give a dern for a thing 'thout it's tollable hard to
git—and you go and beg off for me with the widder."
"Oh, Huck, you know I can't do that. 'Taint fair; and besides
if you'll try this thing just a while longer you'll come to like it."

"Like it! Yes—the way I'd like a hot stove if I was to set on it
long enough. No, Tom, I won't be rich, and I won't live in them
cussed smothery houses. I like the woods, and the river, and
hogsheads, and I'll stick to 'em, too. Blame it all! just as we'd
got guns, and a cave, and all just fixed to rob, here this dern
foolishness has got to come up and spile it all!"

Tom saw his opportunity—

"Lookyhere, Huck, being rich ain't going to keep me back
from turning robber."

"No! Oh, good-licks, are you in real dead-wood earnest, Tom?"

"Just as dead earnest as I'm a sitting here. But Huck, we can't
let you into the gang if you ain't respectable, you know."

Huck's joy was quenched.

"Can't let me in, Tom? Didn't you let me go for a pirate?"

"Yes, but that's different. A robber is more high-toned than
what a pirate is—as a general thing. In most countries they're
awful high up in the nobility—dukes and such."

"Now Tom, hain't you always ben friendly to me? You
wouldn't shet me out, would you, Tom? You wouldn't do that,
now, *would* you, Tom?"

"Huck, I wouldn't want to, and I *don't* want to—but what
would people say? Why they'd say, 'Mph! Tom Sawyer's Gang!
pretty low characters in it!' They'd mean you, Huck. You
wouldn't like that, and I wouldn't."

Huck was silent for some time, engaged in a mental struggle.
Finally he said:

"Well, I'll go back to the widder for a month and tackle it and
see if I can come to stand it, if you'll let me b'long to the gang,
Tom."

"All right, Huck, it's a whiz! Come along, old chap, and I'll
ask the widow to let up on you a little, Huck."

"Will you Tom—now will you? That's good. If she'll let up on
some of the roughest things, I'll smoke private and cuss private,
and crowd through or bust. When you going to start the gang and
turn robbers?"

"Oh, right off. We'll get the boys together and have the
initiation to-night, maybe."

"Have the which?"

"Have the initiation."

"What's that?"

"It's to swear to stand by one another, and never tell the gang's
secrets, even if you're chopped all to flinders, and kill anybody
and all his family that hurts one of the gang."

"That's gay—that's mighty gay, Tom, I tell you."

"Well I bet it is. And all that swearing's got to be done at
midnight, in the lonesomest, awfulest place you can find—a
ha'nted house is the best, but they're all ripped up now."

"Well, midnight's good, anyway, Tom."

"Yes, so it is. And you've got to swear on a coffin, and sign it with blood."

"Now that's something *like!* Why it's a million times bullier than pirating. I'll stick to the widder till I rot, Tom; and if I git to be a reg'lar ripper of a robber, and everybody talking 'bout it, I reckon she'll be proud she snaked me in out of the wet."

CONCLUSION

So endeth this chronicle. It being strictly a history of a *boy,* it must stop here; the story could not go much further without becoming the history of *a man.* When one writes a novel about grown people, he knows exactly where to stop—that is, with a marriage; but when he writes of juveniles, he must stop where he best can.

Most of the characters that perform in this book still live, and are prosperous and happy. Some day it may seem worth while to take up the story of the younger ones again and see what sort of men and women they turned out to be; therefore it will be wisest not to reveal any of that part of their lives at present.

THE ADVENTURES
OF
HUCKLEBERRY FINN

THE ADVENTURES OF HUCKLEBERRY FINN

EXPLANATORY.

In this book a number of dialects are used, to wit: the Missouri negro dialect; the extremest form of the backwoods South-Western dialect; the ordinary "Pike-County" dialect; and four modified varieties of this last. The shadings have not been done in a haphazard fashion, or by guess-work; but pains-takingly, and with the trustworthy guidance and support of personal familiarity with these several forms of speech.

I make this explanation for the reason that without it many readers would suppose that all these characters were trying to talk alike and not succeeding.

THE AUTHOR.

CHAPTER I

You don't know about me, without you have read a book by the name of "The Adventures of Tom Sawyer," but that ain't no matter. That book was made by Mr. Mark Twain, and he told the truth, mainly. There was things which he stretched, but mainly he told the truth. That is nothing. I never seen anybody but lied, one time or another, without it was Aunt Polly, or the widow, or maybe Mary. Aunt Polly—Tom's Aunt Polly, she is—and Mary, and the Widow Douglas, is all told about in that book—which is mostly a true book; with some stretchers, as I said before.

Now the way that the book winds up, is this: Tom and me found the money that the robbers hid in the cave, and it made us rich. We got six thousand dollars apiece—all gold. It was an awful sight of money when it was piled up. Well, Judge Thatcher, he took it and put it out at interest, and it fetched us a dollar a day apiece, all the year round—more than a body could tell what to do with. The Widow Douglas, she took me for her son, and allowed she would sivilize me; but it was rough living in the house all the time, considering how dismal regular and decent the widow was in all her ways; and so when I couldn't stand it no longer, I lit out. I got into my old rags, and my sugar-hogshead again, and was free and satisfied. But Tom Sawyer, he hunted me up and said he was going to start a band of robbers, and I might join if I would go back to the widow and be respectable. So I went back.

The widow she cried over me, and called me a poor lost lamb, and she called me a lot of other names, too, but she never meant no harm by it. She put me in them new clothes again, and I couldn't do nothing but sweat and sweat, and feel all cramped up. Well, then, the old thing commenced again. The widow rung a bell for supper, and you had to come to time. When you got to the table you couldn't go right to eating, but you had to wait for the widow to tuck down her head and grumble a little over the victuals, though there warn't really anything the matter with them. That is, nothing only everything was cooked by itself. In a barrel of odds and ends it is different; things get mixed up, and the juice kind of swaps around, and the things go better.

After supper she got out her book and learned me about Moses and the Bulrushers; and I was in a sweat to find out all about him; but by-and-by she let it out that Moses had been dead a considerable long time; so then I didn't care no more about him; because I don't take no stock in dead people.

Pretty soon I wanted to smoke, and asked the widow to let me. But she wouldn't. She said it was a mean practice and wasn't clean, and I must try to not do it any more. That is just the way with some people. They get down on a thing when they don't know nothing about it. Here she was a bothering about Moses, which was no kin to her, and no use to anybody, being gone, you see, yet finding a power of fault with me for doing a thing that had some good in it. And she took snuff too; of course that was all right, because she done it herself.

Her sister, Miss Watson, a tolerable slim old maid, with goggles on, had just come to live with her, and took a set at me now, with a spelling-book. She worked me middling hard for about an hour, and then the widow made her ease up. I couldn't stood it much longer. Then for an hour it was deadly dull, and I was fidgety. Miss Watson would say, "Dont put your feet up there, Huckleberry;" and "dont scrunch up like that, Huckleberry—set up straight;" and pretty soon she would say, "Don't gap and stretch like that, Huckleberry—why don't you try to behave?" Then she told me all about the bad place, and I said I wished I was there. She got mad, then, but I didn't mean no harm. All I wanted was to go somewheres; all I wanted was a change, I warn't particular. She said it was wicked to say what I said; said she wouldn't say it for the whole world; *she* was going to live so as to go to the good place. Well, I couldn't see no advantage in going where she was going, so I made up my mind I wouldn't try for it. But I never said so, because it would only make trouble, and wouldn't do no good.

Now she had got a start, and she went on and told me all about the good place. She said all a body would have to do there was to go around all day long with a harp and sing, forever and ever. So I didn't think much of it. But I never said so. I asked her if she reckoned Tom Sawyer would go there, and, she said, not by a considerable sight. I was glad about that, because I wanted him and me to be together.

Miss Watson she kept pecking at me, and it got tiresome and lonesome. By-and-by they fetched the niggers in and had prayers, and then everybody was off to bed. I went up to my room with a piece of candle and put it on the table. Then I set down in a chair by the window and tried to think of something cheerful, but it warn't no use. I felt so lonesome I most wished I was dead. The stars was shining and the leaves rustled in the woods ever so mournful; and I heard an owl, away off, who-whooing about somebody that was dead, and a whippowill and a dog crying about somebody that was going to die; and the wind was trying to whisper something to me and I couldn't make out what it was, and so it made the cold shivers run over me. Then away out in the woods I heard that kind of a sound that a ghost makes when it wants to tell about something that's on its mind and can't make itself understood, and so can't rest easy in its grave and has to go about that way every night grieving. I got so down-hearted and scared, I did wish I had some company. Pretty soon a spider went crawling up my shoulder, and I flipped it off and it lit in the candle; and before I could budge it was all shriveled up. I didn't need anybody to tell

me that that was an awful bad sign and would fetch me some bad
luck, so I was scared and most shook the clothes off of me. I got up
and turned around in my tracks three times and crossed my breast
every time; and then I tied up a little lock of my hair with a thread
to keep witches away. But I hadn't no confidence. You do that when
you've lost a horse-shoe that you've found, instead of nailing it up
over the door, but I hadn't ever heard anybody say it was any way
to keep off bad luck when you'd killed a spider.

I set down again, a shaking all over, and got out my pipe for a
smoke; for the house was all as still as death, now, and so the
widow wouldn't know. Well, after a long time I heard the clock
away off in the town go boom—boom—boom—twelve licks—and
all still again—stiller than ever. Pretty soon I heard a twig snap,
down in the dark amongst the trees—something was a stirring. I
set still and listened. Directly I could just barely hear a *"me-yow!
me-yow!"* down there. That was good! Says I, *"me-yow! me-yow!"*
as soft as I could, and then I put out the light and scrambled out
of the window onto the shed. Then I slipped down to the ground
and crawled in amongst the trees, and sure enough there was Tom
Sawyer waiting for me.

CHAPTER II

We went tip-toeing along a path amongst the trees back towards
the end of the widow's garden, stooping down so as the branches
wouldn't scrape our heads. When we was passing by the kitchen I
fell over a root and made a noise. We scrouched down and laid
still. Miss Watson's big nigger, named Jim, was setting in the
kitchen door; we could see him pretty clear, because there was a
light behind him. He got up and stretched his neck out about a
minute, listening. Then he says,

"Who dah?"

He listened some more; then he come tip-toeing down and stood
right between us; we could a touched him, nearly. Well, likely it
was minutes and minutes that there warn't a sound, and we all
there so close together. There was a place on my ankle that got to
itching; but I dasn't scratch it; and then my ear begun to itch; and
next my back, right between my shoulders. Seemed like I'd die if I
couldn't scratch. Well, I've noticed that thing plenty of times since.
If you are with the quality, or at a funeral, or trying to go to sleep
when you ain't sleepy—if you are anywheres where it won't do for
you to scratch, why you will itch all over in upwards of a thousand
places. Pretty soon Jim says:

"Say—who is you? Whar is you? Dog my cats ef I didn' hear
sumf'n. Well, I knows what I's gwyne to do. I's gwyne to set down
here and listen tell I hears it agin."

So he set down on the ground betwixt me and Tom. He leaned

his back up against a tree, and stretched his legs out till one of
them most touched one of mine. My nose begun to itch. It itched
till the tears come into my eyes. But I dasn't scratch. Then it begun
to itch on the inside. Next I got to itching underneath. I didn't
know how I was going to set still. This miserableness went on as
much as six or seven minutes; but it seemed a sight longer than that.
I was itching in eleven different places now. I reckoned I couldn't
stand it more'n a minute longer, but I set my teeth hard and got
ready to try. Just then Jim begun to breathe heavy; next he begun to
snore—and then I was pretty soon comfortable again.

Tom he made a sign to me—kind of a little noise with his
mouth—and we went creeping away on our hands and knees. When
we was ten foot off, Tom whispered to me and wanted to tie Jim to
the tree for fun; but I said no; he might wake and make a
disturbance, and then they'd find out I warn't in. Then Tom said he
hadn't got candles enough, and he would slip in the kitchen and
get some more. I didn't want him to try. I said Jim might wake up
and come. But Tom wanted to resk it; so we slid in there and got
three candles, and Tom laid five cents on the table for pay. Then
we got out, and I was in a sweat to get away; but nothing would do
Tom but he must crawl to where Jim was, on his hands and knees,
and play something on him. I waited, and it seemed a good while,
everything was so still and lonesome.

As soon as Tom was back, we cut along the path, around the
garden fence, and by-and-by fetched up on the steep top of the hill
the other side of the house. Tom said he slipped Jim's hat off of
his head and hung it on a limb right over him, and Jim stirred a
little, but he didn't wake. Afterwards Jim said the witches bewitched
him and put him in a trance, and rode him all over the State, and
then set him under the trees again and hung his hat on a limb to
show who done it. And next time Jim told it he said they rode him
down to New Orleans; and after that, every time he told it he spread
it more and more, till by-and-by he said they rode him all over the
world, and tired him most to death, and his back was all over
saddle-boils. Jim was monstrous proud about it, and he got so he
wouldn't hardly notice the other niggers. Niggers would come miles
to hear Jim tell about it, and he was more looked up to than any
nigger in that country. Strange niggers would stand with their
mouths open and look him all over, same as if he was a wonder.
Niggers is always talking about witches in the dark by the kitchen
fire; but whenever one was talking and letting on to know all about
such things, Jim would happen in and say, "Hm! What you know
'bout witches?" and that nigger was corked up and had to take a
back seat. Jim always kept that five-center piece around his neck
with a string and said it was a charm the devil give to him with his
own hands and told him he could cure anybody with it and fetch
witches whenever he wanted to, just by saying something to it; but

he never told what it was he said to it. Niggers would come from all around there and give Jim anything they had, just for a sight of that five-center piece; but they wouldn't touch it, because the devil had had his hands on it. Jim was most ruined, for a servant, because he got so stuck up on account of having seen the devil and been rode by witches.

Well, when Tom and me got to the edge of the hill-top, we looked away down into the village and could see three or four lights twinkling, where there was sick folks, may be; and the stars over us was sparkling ever so fine; and down by the village was the river, a whole mile broad, and awful still and grand. We went down the hill and found Jo Harper, and Ben Rogers, and two or three more of the boys, hid in the old tanyard. So we unhitched a skiff and pulled down the river two mile and a half, to the big scar on the hillside, and went ashore.

We went to a clump of bushes, and Tom made everybody swear to keep the secret, and then showed them a hole in the hill, right in the thickest part of the bushes. Then we lit the candles and crawled in on our hands and knees. We went about two hundred yards, and then the cave opened up. Tom poked about amongst the passages and pretty soon ducked under a wall where you wouldn't a noticed that there was a hole. We went along a narrow place and got into a kind of room, all damp and sweaty and cold, and there we stopped. Tom says:

"Now we'll start this band of robbers and call it Tom Sawyer's Gang. Everybody that wants to join has got to take an oath, and write his name in blood."

Everybody was willing. So Tom got out a sheet of paper that he had wrote the oath on, and read it. It swore every boy to stick to the band, and never tell any of the secrets; and if anybody done anything to any boy in the band, whichever boy was ordered to kill that person and his family must do it, and he mustn't eat and he mustn't sleep till he had killed them and hacked a cross in their breasts, which was the sign of the band. And nobody that didn't belong to the band could use that mark, and if he did he must be sued; and if he done it again he must be killed. And if anybody that belonged to the band told the secrets, he must have his throat cut, and then have his carcass burnt up and the ashes scattered all around, and his name blotted off of the list with blood and never mentioned again by the gang, but have a curse put on it and be forgot, forever.

Everybody said it was a real beautiful oath, and asked Tom if he got it out of his own head. He said, some of it, but the rest was out of pirate books, and robber books, and every gang that was high-toned had it.

Some thought it would be good to kill the *families* of boys that told the secrets. Tom said it was a good idea, so he took a pencil and wrote it in. Then Ben Rogers says:

"Here's Huck Finn, he hain't got no family—what you going to do 'bout him?"

"Well, hain't he got a father?" says Tom Sawyer.

"Yes, he's got a father, but you can't never find him, these days. He used to lay drunk with the hogs in the tanyard, but he hain't been seen in these parts for a year or more."

They talked it over, and they was going to rule me out, because they said every boy must have a family or somebody to kill, or else it wouldn't be fair and square for the others. Well, nobody could think of anything to do—everybody was stumped, and set still. I was most ready to cry; but all at once I thought of a way, and so I offered them Miss Watson—they could kill her. Everybody said:

"Oh, she'll do, she'll do. That's all right. Huck can come in."

Then they all stuck a pin in their fingers to get blood to sign with, and I made my mark on the paper.

"Now," says Ben Rogers, "what's the line of business of this Gang?"

"Nothing only robbery and murder," Tom said.

"But who are we going to rob? houses—or cattle—or——"

"Stuff! stealing cattle and such things ain't robbery, it's burglary," says Tom Sawyer. "We ain't burglars. That ain't no sort of style. We are highwaymen. We stop stages and carriages on the road, with masks on, and kill the people and take their watches and money."

"Must we always kill the people?"

"Oh, certainly. It's best. Some authorities think different, but mostly it's considered best to kill them. Except some that you bring to the cave here and keep them till they're ransomed."

"Ransomed? What's that?"

"I don't know. But that's what they do. I've seen it in books; and so of course that's what we've got to do."

"But how can we do it if we don't know what it is?"

"Why blame it all, we've *got* to do it. Don't I tell you it's in the books? Do you want to go to doing different from what's in the books, and get things all muddled up?"

"Oh, that's all very fine to *say,* Tom Sawyer, but how in the nation are these fellows going to be ransomed if we don't know how to do it to them? that's the thing *I* want to get at. Now what do you *reckon* it is?"

"Well I don't know. But per'aps if we keep them till they're ransomed, it means that we keep them till they're dead."

"Now, that's something *like.* That'll answer. Why couldn't you said that before? We'll keep them till they're ransomed to death— and a bothersome lot they'll be, too, eating up everything and always trying to get loose."

"How you talk, Ben Rogers. How can they get loose when there's a guard over them, ready to shoot them down if they move a peg?"

"A guard. Well, that *is* good. So somebody's got to set up all night and never get any sleep, just so as to watch them. I think that's foolishness. Why can't a body take a club and ransom them as soon as they get here?"

"Because it ain't in the books so—that's why. Now Ben Rogers, do you want to do things regular, or don't you?—that's the idea. Don't you reckon that the people that made the books knows what's the correct thing to do? Do you reckon *you* can learn 'em anything? Not by a good deal. No, sir, we'll just go on and ransom them in the regular way."

"All right. I don't mind; but I say it's a fool way, anyhow. Say— do we kill the women, too?"

"Well, Ben Rogers, if I was as ignorant as you I wouldn't let on. Kill the women? No—nobody ever saw anything in the books like that. You fetch them to the cave, and you're always as polite as pie to them; and by-and-by they fall in love with you and never want to go home any more."

"Well, if that's the way, I'm agreed, but I don't take no stock in it. Mighty soon we'll have the cave so cluttered up with women, and fellows waiting to be ransomed, that there won't be no place for the robbers. But go ahead, I ain't got nothing to say."

Little Tommy Barnes was asleep, now, and when they waked him up he was scared, and cried, and said he wanted to go home to his ma, and didn't want to be a robber any more.

So they all made fun of him, and called him cry-baby, and that made him mad, and he said he would go straight and tell all the secrets. But Tom give him five cents to keep quiet, and said we would all go home and meet next week and rob somebody and kill some people.

Ben Rogers said he couldn't get out much, only Sundays, and so he wanted to begin next Sunday; but all the boys said it would be wicked to do it on Sunday, and that settled the thing. They agreed to get together and fix a day as soon as they could, and then we elected Tom Sawyer first captain and Jo Harper second captain of the Gang, and so started home.

I clumb up the shed and crept into my window just before day was breaking. My new clothes was all greased up and clayey, and I was dog-tired.

CHAPTER III

Well, I got a good going-over in the morning, from old Miss Watson, on account of my clothes; but the widow she didn't scold, but only cleaned off the grease and clay and looked so sorry that I thought I would behave a while if I could. Then Miss Watson she took me in the closet and prayed, but nothing come of it. She told me to pray every day, and whatever I asked for I would get it. But it warn't so. I tried it. Once I got a fish-line, but no hooks. It warn't any good to me without hooks. I tried for the hooks three or four times, but somehow I couldn't make it work. By-and-by, one day, I asked Miss Watson to try for me, but she said I was a fool. She never told me why, and I couldn't make it out no way.

I set down, one time, back in the woods, and had a long think about it. I says to myself, if a body can get anything they pray for, why don't Deacon Winn get back the money he lost on pork? Why can't the widow get back her silver snuff-box that was stole? Why can't Miss Watson fat up? No, says I to myself, there ain't nothing in it. I went and told the widow about it, and she said the thing a body could get by praying for it was "spiritual gifts." This was too many for me, but she told me what she meant—I must help other people, and do everything I could for other people, and look out for them all the time, and never think about myself. This was including Miss Watson, as I took it. I went out in the woods and turned it over in my mind a long time, but I couldn't see no advantage about it—except for the other people—so at last I reckoned I wouldn't worry about it any more, but just let it go. Sometimes the widow would take me one side and talk about Providence in a way to make a body's mouth water; but maybe next day Miss Watson would take hold and knock it all down again. I judged I could see that there was two Providences, and a poor chap would stand considerable show with the widow's Providence, but if Miss Watson's got him there warn't no help for him any more. I thought it all out, and reckoned I would belong to the widow's, if he wanted me, though I couldn't make out how he was agoing to be any better off then that what he was before, seeing I was so ignorant and so kind of low-down and ornery.

Pap he hadn't been seen for more than a year, and that was comfortable for me; I didn't want to see him no more. He used to always whale me when he was sober and could get his hands on me; though I used to take to the woods most of the time when he was around. Well, about this time he was found in the river drowned, about twelve mile above town, so people said. They judged it was him, anyway; said this drowned man was just his size, and was ragged, and had uncommon long hair—which was all like pap— but they couldn't make nothing out of the face, because it had been in the water so long it warn't much like a face at all. They said he was floating on his back in the water. They took him and buried him on the bank. But I warn't comfortable long, because I happened to think of something. I knowed mighty well that a drownded man don't float on his back, but on his face. So I knowed, then, that this warn't pap, but a woman dressed up in a man's clothes. So I was uncomfortable again. I judged the old man would turn up again by-and-by, though I wished he wouldn't.

We played robber now and then about a month, and then I
resigned. All the boys did. We hadn't robbed nobody, we hadn't
killed any people, but only just pretended. We used to hop out of
the woods and go charging down on hog-drovers and women in
carts taking garden stuff to market, but we never hived any of them.
Tom Sawyer called the hogs "ingots," and he called the turnips and
stuff "julery" and we would go to the cave and pow-wow over what
we had done and how many people we had killed and marked. But
I couldn't see no profit in it. One time Tom sent a boy to run about
town with a blazing stick, which he called a slogan (which was the
sign for the Gang to get together), and then he said he had got
secret news by his spies that next day a whole parcel of Spanish
merchants and rich A-rabs was going to camp in Cave Hollow with
two hundred elephants, and six hundred camels, and over a
thousand "sumter" mules, all loaded down with di'monds, and they
didn't have only a guard of four hundred soldiers, and so we would
lay in ambuscade, as he called it, and kill the lot and scoop the
things. He said we must slick up our swords and guns, and get ready.
He never could go after even a turnip-cart but he must have the
swords and guns all scoured up for it; though they was only lath
and broom-sticks, and you might scour at them till you rotted
and then they warn't worth a mouthful of ashes more than what
they was before. I didn't believe we could lick such a crowd of
Spaniards and A-rabs, but I wanted to see the camels and elephants,
so I was on hand next day, Saturday, in the ambuscade; and when
we got the word, we rushed out of the woods and down the hill.
But there warn't no Spaniards and A-rabs, and there warn't no
camels nor no elephants. It warn't anything but a Sunday-school
picnic, and only a primer-class at that. We busted it up, and chased
the children up the hollow; but we never got anything but some
doughnuts and jam, though Ben Rogers got a rag doll, and Jo
Harper got a hymn-book and a tract; and then the teacher charged
in and made us drop everything and cut. I didn't see no di'monds,
and I told Tom Sawyer so. He said there was loads of them there,
anyway; and he said there was A-rabs there, too, and elephants
and things. I said, why couldn't we see them, then? He said if I
warn't so ignorant, but had read a book called "Don Quixote,"
I would know without asking. He said it was all done by
enchantment. He said there was hundreds of soldiers there, and
elephants and treasure, and so on, but we had enemies which he
called magicians, and they had turned the whole thing into an
infant Sunday school, just out of spite. I said, all right, then the
thing for us to do was to go for the magicians. Tom Sawyer said
I was a numskull.

"Why," says he, "a magician could call up a lot of genies, and
they would hash you up like nothing before you could say Jack
Robinson. They are as tall as a tree and as big around as a church."

"Well," I says, "s'pose we got some genies to help *us*—can't we lick the other crowd then?"

"How you going to get them?"

"I don't know. How do *they* get them?"

"Why they rub an old tin lamp or an iron ring, and then the genies come tearing in, with the thunder and lightning a-ripping around and the smoke a-rolling, and everything they're told to do they up and do it. They don't think nothing of pulling a shot tower up by the roots, and belting a Sunday-school superintendent over the head with it—or any other man."

"Who makes them tear around so?"

"Why, whoever rubs the lamp or the ring. They belong to whoever rubs the lamp or the ring, and they've got to do whatever he says. If he tells them to build a palace forty miles long, out of di'monds, and fill it full of chewing gum, or whatever you want, and fetch an emperor's daughter from China for you to marry, they've got to do it—and they've got to do it before sun-up next morning, too. And more—they've got to waltz that palace around over the country wherever you want it, you understand."

"Well," says I, "I think they are a pack of flatheads for not keeping the palace themselves 'stead of fooling them away like that. And what's more—if I was one of them I would see a man in Jericho before I would drop my business and come to him for the rubbing of an old tin lamp."

"How you talk, Huck Finn. Why, you'd *have* to come when he rubbed it, whether you wanted to or not."

"What, and I as high as a tree and as big as a church? All right, then; I *would* come; but I lay I'd make that man climb the highest tree there was in the country."

"Shucks, it ain't no use to talk to you, Huck Finn. You don't seem to know anything, somehow—perfect sap-head."

I thought all this over for two or three days, and then I reckoned I would see if there was anything in it. I got an old tin lamp and an iron ring and went out in the woods and rubbed and rubbed till I sweat like an Injun, calculating to build a palace and sell it; but it warn't no use, none of the genies come. So then I judged that all that stuff was only just one of Tom Sawyer's lies. I reckoned he believed in the A-rabs and the elephants, but as for me I think different. It had all the marks of a Sunday school.

CHAPTER IV

Well, three or four months run along, and it was well into the winter, now. I had been to school most all the time, and could spell, and read, and write just a little, and could say the multiplication table up to six times seven is thirty-five, and I don't reckon I could ever get any further than that if I was to live forever. I don't take no stock in mathematics, anyway.

At first I hated the school, but by-and-by I got so I could stand it.
Whenever I got uncommon tired I played hookey, and the hiding I
got next day done me good and cheered me up. So the longer I went
to school the easier it got to be. I was getting sort of used to the
widow's ways, too, and they warn't so raspy on me. Living in a house,
and sleeping in a bed, pulled on me pretty tight, mostly, but before
the cold weather I used to slide out and sleep in the woods,
sometimes, and so that was a rest to me. I liked the old ways best,
but I was getting so I liked the new ones, too, a little bit. The widow
said I was coming along slow but sure, and doing very satisfactory.
She said she warn't ashamed of me.

One morning I happened to turn over the salt-cellar at breakfast.
I reached for some of it as quick as I could, to throw over my left
shoulder and keep off the bad luck, but Miss Watson was in ahead
of me, and crossed me off. She says, "Take your hands away,
Huckleberry—what a mess you are always making." The widow put
in a good word for me, but that warn't going to keep off the bad
luck, I knowed that well enough. I started out, after breakfast,
feeling worried and shaky, and wondering where it was going to fall
on me, and what it was going to be. There is ways to keep off some
kinds of bad luck, but this wasn't one of them kind; so I never tried
to do anything, but just poked along low-spirited and on the
watch-out.

I went down the front garden and clumb over the stile, where you
go through the high board fence. There was an inch of new snow on
the ground, and I seen somebody's tracks. They had come up from
the quarry and stood around the stile a while, and then went on
around the garden fence. It was funny they hadn't come in, after
standing around so. I couldn't make it out. It was very curious,
somehow. I was going to follow around, but I stooped down to look
at the tracks first. I didn't notice anything at first, but next I did.
There was a cross in the left boot-heel made with big nails, to keep
off the devil.

I was up in a second and shinning down the hill. I looked over
my shoulder every now and then, but I didn't see nobody. I was at
Judge Thatcher's as quick as I could get there. He said:

"Why, my boy, you are all out of breath. Did you come for your
interest?"

"No sir," I says; "is there some for me?"

"Oh, yes, a half-yearly is in, last night. Over a hundred and
fifty dollars. Quite a fortune for you. You better let me invest it
along with your six thousand, because if you take it you'll spend it."

"No sir," I says, "I don't want to spend it. I don't want it at all—
nor the six thousand, nuther. I want you to take it; I want to give it
to you—the six thousand and all."

He looked surprised. He couldn't seem to make it out. He says:

"Why, what can you mean, my boy?"

I says, "Don't you ask me no questions about it, please. You'll take it—won't you?"

He says:

"Well I'm puzzled. Is something the matter?"

"Please take it," says I, "and don't ask me nothing—then I won't have to tell no lies."

He studied a while, and then he says:

"Oho-o. I think I see. You want to *sell* all your property to me—not give it. That's the correct idea."

Then he wrote something on a paper and read it over, and says:

"There—you see it says 'for a consideration.' That means I have bought it of you and paid you for it. Here's a dollar for you. Now, you sign it."

So I signed it, and left.

Miss Watson's nigger, Jim, had a hair-ball as big as your fist, which had been took out of the fourth stomach of an ox, and he used to do magic with it. He said there was a spirit inside of it, and it knowed everything. So I went to him that night and told him pap was here again, for I found his tracks in the snow. What I wanted to know, was, what he was going to do, and was he going to stay? Jim got out his hair-ball, and said something over it, and then he held it up and dropped it on the floor. It fell pretty solid, and only rolled about an inch. Jim tried it again, and then another time, and it acted just the same. Jim got down on his knees and put his ear against it and listened. But it warn't no use; he said it wouldn't talk. He said sometimes it wouldn't talk without money. I told him I had an old slick counterfeit quarter that warn't no good because the brass showed through the silver a little, and it wouldn't pass nohow, even if the brass didn't show, because it was so slick it felt greasy, and so that would tell on it every time. (I reckoned I wouldn't say nothing about the dollar I got from the judge.) I said it was pretty bad money, but maybe the hair-ball would take it, because maybe it wouldn't know the difference. Jim smelt it, and bit it, and rubbed it, and said he would manage so the hair-ball would think it was good. He said he would split open a raw Irish potato and stick the quarter in between and keep it there all night, and next morning you couldn't see no brass, and it wouldn't feel greasy no more, and so anybody in town would take it in a minute, let alone a hair-ball. Well, I knowed a potato would do that, before, but I had forgot it.

Jim put the quarter under the hair-ball and got down and listened again. This time he said the hair-ball was all right. He said it would tell my whole fortune if I wanted it to. I says, go on. So the hair-ball talked to Jim, and Jim told it to me. He says:

"Yo' ole father doan' know, yit, what he's a-gwyne to do.

Sometimes he spec he'll go 'way, en den agin he spec he'll stay. De bes' way is to res' easy en let de ole man take his own way. Dey's two angels hoverin' roun' 'bout him. One uv 'em is white en shiny, en 'tother one is black. De white one gits him to go right, a little while, den de black one sail in en bust it all up. A body can't tell, yit, which one gwyne to fetch him at de las'. But you is all right. You gwyne to have considable trouble in yo' life, en considable joy. Sometimes you gwyne to git hurt, en sometimes you gwyne to git sick; but every time you's gwyne to git well agin. Dey's two gals flyin' 'bout you in yo' life. One uv 'em's light en 'tother one is dark. One is rich en 'tother is po'. You's gwyne to marry de po' one fust en de rich one by-en-by. You wants to keep 'way fum de water as much as you kin, en don't run no resk, 'kase it's down in de bills dat you's gwyne to git hung."

When I lit my candle and went up to my room that night, there set pap, his own self!

CHAPTER V

I had shut the door to. Then I turned around, and there he was. I used to be scared of him all the time, he tanned me so much. I reckoned I was scared now, too; but in a minute I see I was mistaken. That is, after the first jolt, as you may say, when my breath sort of hitched—he being so unexpected; but right away after, I see I warn't scared of him worth bothering about.

He was most fifty, and he looked it. His hair was long and tangled and greasy, and hung down, and you could see his eyes shining through like he was behind vines. It was all black, no gray; so was his long, mixed-up whiskers. There warn't no color in his face, where his face showed; it was white; not like another man's white, but a white to make a body sick, a white to make a body's flesh crawl— a tree-toad white, a fish-belly white. As for his clothes—just rags, that was all. He had one ankle resting on 'tother knee; the boot on that foot was busted, and two of his toes stuck through, and he worked them now and then. His hat was laying on the floor; an old black slouch with the top caved in, like a lid.

I stood a-looking at him; he set there a-looking at me, with his chair tilted back a little. I set the candle down. I noticed the window was up; so he had clumb in by the shed. He kept a-looking me all over. By-and-by he says:

"Starchy clothes—very. You think you're a good deal of a big-bug, *don't* you?"

"Maybe I am, maybe I ain't," I says.

"Don't you give me none o' your lip," says he. "You've put on considerable many frills since I been away. I'll take you down a peg before I get done with you. You're educated, too, they say; can read and write. You think you're better'n your father, now, don't

you, because he can't? *I*'ll take it out of you. Who told you you
might meddle with such hifalut'n foolishness, hey?—who told you
you could?''

"The widow. She told me."

"The widow, hey?—and who told the widow she could put in her
shovel about a thing that ain't none of her business?''

"Nobody never told her."

"Well, I'll learn her how to meddle. And looky here—you drop
that school, you hear? I'll learn people to bring up a boy to put on
airs over his own father and let on to be better'n what *he* is. You
lemme catch you fooling around that school again, you hear? Your
mother couldn't read, and she couldn't write, nuther, before she
died. None of the family couldn't, before *they* died. *I* can't; and
here you're a-swelling yourself up like this. I ain't the man to stand
it—you hear? Say—lemme hear you read."

I took up a book and begun something about General
Washington and the wars. When I'd read about a half a minute,
he fetched the book a whack with his hand and knocked it across
the house. He says:

"It's so. You can do it. I had my doubts when you told me. Now
looky here; you stop that putting on frills. I won't have it. I'll lay
for you, my smarty; and if I catch you about that school I'll tan
you good. First you know you'll get religion, too. I never see such
a son."

He took up a little blue and yaller picture of some cows and a boy,
and says:

"What's this?"

"It's something they give me for learning my lessons good."

He tore it up, and says—

"I'll give you something better—I'll give you a cowhide."

He set there a-mumbling and a-growling a minute, and then he
says—

"*Ain't* you a sweet-scented dandy, though? A bed; and
bedclothes; and a look'n-glass; and a piece of carpet on the floor—
and your own father got to sleep with the hogs in the tanyard. I
never see such a son. I bet I'll take some o' these frills out o' you
before I'm done with you. Why there ain't no end to your airs—
they say you're rich. Hey?—how's that?"

"They lie—that's how."

"Looky here—mind how you talk to me; I'm a-standing about
all I can stand, now—so don't gimme no sass. I've been in town
two days, and I hain't heard nothing but about you being' rich. I
heard about it away down the river, too. That's why I come. You git
me that money to-morrow—I want it."

"I hain't got no money."

"It's a lie. Judge Thatcher's got it. You git it. I want it."

"I hain't got no money, I tell you. You ask Judge Thatcher; he'll tell you the same."

"All right. I'll ask him; and I'll make him pungle, too, or I'll know the reason why. Say—how much you got in your pocket? I want it."

"I hain't got only a dollar, and I want that to—"

"It don't make no difference what you want it for—you just shell it out."

He took it and bit it to see if it was good, and then he said he was going down town to get some whisky; said he hadn't had a drink all day. When he had got out on the shed, he put his head in again, and cussed me for putting on frills and trying to be better than him; and when I reckoned he was gone, he come back and put his head in again, and told me to mind about that school, because he was going to lay for me and lick me if I didn't drop that.

Next day he was drunk, and he went to Judge Thatcher's and bullyragged him and tried to make him give up the money, but he couldn't, and then he swore he'd make the law force him.

The judge and the widow went to law to get the court to take me away from him and let one of them be my guardian; but it was a new judge that had just come, and he didn't know the old man; so he said courts mustn't interfere and separate families if they could help it; said he'd druther not take a child away from its father. So Judge Thatcher and the widow had to quit on the business.

That pleased the old man till he couldn't rest. He said he'd cowhide me till I was black and blue if I didn't raise some money for him. I borrowed three dollars from Judge Thatcher, and pap took it and got drunk and went a-blowing around and cussing and whooping and carrying on; and he kept it up all over town, with a tin pan, till most midnight; then they jailed him, and next day they had him before court, and jailed him again for a week. But he said *he* was satisfied; said he was boss of his son, and he'd make it warm for *him*.

When he got out the new judge said he was agoing to make a man of him. So he took him to his own house, and dressed him up clean and nice, and had him to breakfast and dinner and supper with the family, and was just old pie to him, so to speak. And after supper he talked to him about temperance and such things till the old man cried, and said he'd been a fool, and fooled away his life; but now he was agoing to turn over a new leaf and be a man nobody wouldn't be ashamed of, and he hoped the judge would help him and not look down on him. The judge said he could hug him for them words; so *he* cried, and his wife she cried again; pap said he'd been a man that had always been misunderstood before, and the judge said he believed it. The old man said that what a man wanted that was down, was sympathy; and the judge said it was so; so they cried again. And when it was bedtime, the old man rose up and held out his hand, and says:

"Look at it gentlemen, and ladies all; take ahold of it; shake it. There's a hand that was the hand of a hog; but it ain't so no more; it's the hand of a man that's started in on a new life, and 'll die before he'll go back. You mark them words—don't forget I said them. It's a clean hand now; shake it—don't be afeard."

So they shook it, one after the other, all around, and cried. The judge's wife she kissed it. Then the old man he signed a pledge—made his mark. The judge said it was the holiest time on record, or something like that. Then they tucked the old man into a beautiful room, which was the spare room, and in the night sometime he got powerful thirsty and clumb out onto the porch-roof and slid down a stanchion and traded his new coat for a jug of forty-rod, and clumb back again and had a good old time; and towards daylight he crawled out again, drunk as a fiddler, and rolled off the porch and broke his left arm in two places and was most froze to death when somebody found him after sun-up. And when they come to look at that spare room, they had to take soundings before they could navigate it.

The judge he felt kind of sore. He said he reckoned a body could reform the ole man with a shot-gun, maybe, but he didn't know no other way.

CHAPTER VI

Well, pretty soon the old man was up and around again, and then he went for Judge Thatcher in the courts to make him give up that money, and he went for me, too, for not stopping school. He catched me a couple of times and thrashed me, but I went to school just the same, and dodged him or out-run him most of the time. I didn't want to go to school much, before, but I reckoned I'd go now to spite pap. That law trial was a slow business; appeared like they warn't ever going to get started on it; so every now and then I'd borrow two or three dollars off of the judge for him, to keep from getting a cowhiding. Every time he got money he got drunk; and every time he got drunk he raised Cain around town; and every time he raised Cain he got jailed. He was just suited—this kind of thing was right in his line.

He got to hanging around the widow's too much, and so she told him at last, that if he didn't quit using around there she would make trouble for him. Well, *wasn't* he mad? He said he would show who was Huck Finn's boss. So he watched out for me one day in the spring, and catched me, and took me up the river about three mile, in a skiff, and crossed over to the Illinois shore where it was woody and there warn't no houses but an old log hut in a place where the timber was so thick you couldn't find it if you didn't know where it was.

He kept me with him all the time, and I never got a chance to

run off. We lived in that old cabin, and he always locked the door
and put the key under his head, nights. He had a gun which he
had stole, I reckon, and we fished and hunted, and that was what
we lived on. Every little while he locked me in and went down to the
store, three miles, to the ferry, and traded fish and game for whisky
and fetched it home and got drunk and had a good time, and licked
me. The widow she found out where I was, by-and-by, and she sent
a man over to try to get hold of me, but pap drove him off with the
gun, and it warn't long after that till I was used to being where I
was, and liked it, all but the cowhide part.

It was kind of lazy and jolly, laying off comfortable all day,
smoking and fishing, and no books nor study. Two months or more
run along, and my clothes got to be all rags and dirt, and I didn't
see how I'd ever got to like it so well at the widow's, where you had
to wash, and eat on a plate, and comb up, and go to bed and get
up regular, and be forever bothering over a book and have old Miss
Watson pecking at you all the time. I didn't want to go back no
more. I had stopped cussing, because the widow didn't like it; but
now I took to it again because pap hadn't no objections. It was pretty
good times up in the woods there, take it all around.

But by-and-by pap got too handy with his hick'ry, and I couldn't
stand it. I was all over welts. He got to going away so much, too, and
locking me in. Once he locked me in and was gone three days. It
was dreadful lonesome. I judged he had got drowned and I wasn't
ever going to get out any more. I was scared. I made up my mind I
would fix up some way to leave there. I had tried to get out of that
cabin many a time, but I couldn't find no way. There warn't a
window to it big enough for a dog to get through. I couldn't get
up the chimbly, it was too narrow. The door was thick solid oak
slabs. Pap was pretty careful not to leave a knife or anything in the
cabin when he was away; I reckon I had hunted the place over as
much as a hundred times; well, I was 'most all the time at it, because
it was about the only way to put in the time. But this time I found
something at last; I found an old rusty wood-saw without any
handle; it was laid in between a rafter and the clapboards of the
roof. I greased it up and went to work. There was an old
horse-blanket nailed against the logs at the far end of the cabin
behind the table, to keep the wind from blowing through the chinks
and putting the candle out. I got under the table and raised the
blanket and went to work to saw a section of the big bottom log out,
big enough to let me through. Well, it was a good long job, but I
was getting towards the end of it when I heard pap's gun in the
woods. I got rid of the signs of my work, and dropped the blanket
and hid my saw, and pretty soon pap come in.

Pap warn't in a good humor—so he was his natural self. He said
he was down to town, and everything was going wrong. His lawyer
said he reckoned he would win his lawsuit and get the money, if

they ever got started on the trial; but then there was ways to put it off a long time, and Judge Thatcher knowed how to do it. And he said people allowed there'd be another trial to get me away from him and give me to the widow for my guardian, and they guessed it would win, this time. This shook me up considerable, because I didn't want to go back to the widow's any more and be so cramped up and sivilized, as they called it. Then the old man got to cussing, and cussed everything and everybody he could think of, and then cussed them all over again to make sure he hadn't skipped any, and after that he polished off with a kind of a general cuss all round, including a considerable parcel of people which he didn't know the names of, and so called them what's-his-name, when he got to them, and went right along with his cussing.

He said he would like to see the widow get me. He said he would watch out, and if they tried to come any such game on him he knowed of a place six or seven mile off, to stow me in, where they might hunt till they dropped and they couldn't find me. That made me pretty uneasy again, but only for a minute; I reckoned I wouldn't stay on hand till he got that chance.

The old man made me go to the skiff and fetch the things he had got. There was a fifty-pound sack of corn meal, and a side of bacon, ammunition, and a four-gallon jug of whisky, and an old book and two newspapers for wadding, besides some tow. I toted up a load, and went back and set down on the bow of the skiff to rest. I thought it all over, and I reckoned I would walk off with the gun and some lines, and take to the woods when I run away. I guessed I wouldn't stay in one place, but just tramp right across the country, mostly night times, and hunt and fish to keep alive, and so get so far away that the old man nor the widow couldn't ever find me any more. I judged I would saw out and leave that night if pap got drunk enough, and I reckoned he would. I got so full of it I didn't notice how long I was staying, till the old man hollered and asked me whether I was asleep or drownded.

I got the things all up to the cabin, and then it was about dark. While I was cooking supper the old man took a swig or two and got sort of warmed up, and went to ripping again. He had been drunk over in town, and laid in the gutter all night, and he was a sight to look at. A body would a thought he was Adam, he was just all mud. Whenever his liquor begun to work, he most always went for the govment. This time he says:

"Call this a govment! why, just look at it and see what it's like. Here's the law a-standing ready to take a man's son away from him—a man's own son, which he has had all the trouble and all the anxiety and all the expense of raising. Yes, just as that man has got that son raised at last, and ready to go to work and begin to do suthin' for *him* and give him a rest, the law up and goes for him. And they call *that* govment! That ain't all, nuther. The law backs

that old Judge Thatcher up and helps him to keep me out o' my
property. Here's what the law does. The law takes a man worth six
thousand dollars and upards, and jams him into an old trap of a
cabin like this, and lets him go round in clothes that ain't fitten
for a hog. They call that govment! A man can't get his rights in a
govment like this. Sometimes I've a mighty notion to just leave the
country for good and all. Yes, and I *told* 'em so; I told old
Thatcher so to his face. Lots of 'em heard me, and can tell what I
said. Says I, for two cents I'd leave the blamed country and never
come anear it agin. Them's the very words. I says, look at my hat—if
you call it a hat—but the lid raises up and the rest of it goes down
till it's below my chin, and then it ain't rightly a hat at all, but more
like my head was shoved up through a jint o' stove-pipe. Look at it,
says I—such a hat for me to wear—one of the wealthiest men in
this town, if I could git my rights.

"Oh, yes, this is a wonderful govment, wonderful. Why, looky
here. There was a free nigger there, from Ohio; a mulatter, most as
white as a white man. He had the whitest shirt on you ever see, too,
and the shiniest hat; and there ain't a man in that town that's got
as fine clothes as what he had; and he had a gold watch and chain,
and a silver-headed cane—the awfulest old gray-headed nabob in
the State. And what do you think? they said he was a p'fessor in a
college, and could talk all kinds of languages, and knowed
everything. And that ain't the wust. They said he could *vote,* when
he was at home. Well, that let me out. Thinks I, what is the country
a-coming to? It was 'lection day, and I was just about to go and vote,
myself, if I warn't too drunk to get there; but when they told me
there was a State in this country where they'd let that nigger vote,
I drawed out. I says I'll never vote agin. Them's the very words I
said; they all heard me; and the country may rot for all me—
I'll never vote agin as long as I live. And to see the cool way of that
nigger—why, he wouldn't a give me the road if I hadn't shoved him
out o' the way. I says to the people, why ain't this nigger put up at
auction and sold?—that's what I want to know. And what do you
reckon they said? Why, they said he couldn't be sold till he'd been
in the State six months, and he hadn't been there that long yet.
There, now—that's a specimen. They call that a govment that can't
sell a free nigger till he's been in the State six months. Here's a
govment that calls itself a govment, and lets on to be a govment,
and thinks it is a govment, and yet's got to set stock-still for six
whole months before it can take ahold of a prowling, thieving,
infernal, white-shirted free nigger, and——"

Pap was 'agoing on so, he never noticed where his old limber legs
was taking him to, so he went head over heels over the tub of salt
pork, and barked both shins, and the rest of his speech was all the
hottest kind of language—mostly hove at the nigger and the
govment, though he give the tub some, too, all along, here and

there. He hopped around the cabin considerable, first on one leg
and then on the other, holding first one shin and then the other
one, and at last he let out with his left foot all of a sudden and
fetched the tub a rattling kick. But it warn't good judgment,
because that was the boot that had a couple of his toes leaking out
of the front end of it; so now he raised a howl that fairly made a
body's hair raise, and down he went in the dirt, and rolled there,
and held his toes; and the cussing he done then laid over anything
he had ever done previous. He said so his own self, afterwards. He
had heard old Sowberry Hagan in his best days, and he said it laid
over him, too; but I reckon that was sort of piling it on, maybe.

After supper pap took the jug, and said he had enough whisky
there for two drunks and one delirium tremens. That was always
his word. I judged he would be blind drunk in about an hour, and
then I would steal the key, or saw myself out, one or 'tother. He
drank, and drank, and tumbled down on his blankets, by-and-by;
but luck didn't run my way. He didn't go sound asleep, but was
uneasy. He groaned, and moaned, and thrashed around this way
and that, for a long time. At last I got so sleepy I couldn't keep
my eyes open, all I could do, and so before I knowed what I was
about I was sound asleep, and the candle burning.

I don't know how long I was asleep, but all of a sudden there was
an awful scream and I was up. There was pap, looking wild and
skipping around every which way and yelling about snakes. He said
they was crawling up his legs; and then he would give a jump and
scream, and say one had bit him on the cheek—but I couldn't see
no snakes. He started and run round and round the cabin, hollering
"take him off! take him off! he's biting me on the neck!" I never see
a man look so wild in the eyes. Pretty soon he was all fagged out,
and fell down panting; then he rolled over and over, wonderful
fast, kicking things every which way, and striking and grabbing at
the air with his hands, and screaming, and saying there was devils
ahold of him. He wore out, by-and-by, and laid still a while,
moaning. Then he laid stiller, and didn't make a sound. I could hear
the owls and the wolves, away off in the woods, and it seemed
terrible still. He was laying over by the corner. By-and-by he raised
up, part way, and listened, with his head to one side. He says very
low:

"Tramp—tramp—tramp; that's the dead; tramp—tramp—
tramp; they're coming after me; but I won't go— Oh, they're here!
don't touch me—don't! hands off—they're cold; let go— Oh, let a
poor devil alone!"

Then he went down on all fours and crawled off begging them to
let him alone, and he rolled himself up in his blanket and wallowed
in under the old pine table, still a-begging; and then he went to
crying. I could hear him through the blanket.

By-and-by he rolled out and jumped up on his feet looking wild,

and he see me and went for me. He chased me round and round
the place, with a clasp-knife, calling me the Angel of Death and
saying he would kill me and then I couldn't come for him no more.
I begged, and told him I was only Huck, but he laughed *such* a
screechy laugh, and roared and cussed, and kept on chasing me up.
Once when I turned short and dodged under his arm he made a grab
and got me by the jacket between my shoulders, and I thought I
was gone; but I slid out of the jacket quick as lightning, and saved
myself. Pretty soon he was all tired out, and dropped down with his
back against the door, and said he would rest a minute and then
kill me. He put his knife under him, and said he would sleep and
get strong, and then he would see who was who.

So he dozed off, pretty soon. By-and-by I got the old split-bottom
chair and clumb up, as easy as I could, not to make any noise, and
got down the gun. I slipped the ramrod down it to make sure it was
loaded, and then I laid it across the turnip barrel, pointing towards
pap, and set down behind it to wait for him to stir. And how slow
and still the time did drag along.

CHAPTER VII

"Git up! what you 'bout!"

I opened my eyes and looked around, trying to make out where
I was. It was after sun-up, and I had been sound asleep. Pap was
standing over me, looking sour—and sick, too. He says—

"What you doin' with this gun?"

I judged he didn't know nothing about what he had been doing,
so I says:

"Somebody tried to get in, so I was laying for him."

"Why didn't you roust me out?"

"Well I tried to, but I couldn't; I couldn't budge you."

"Well, all right. Don't stand there palavering all day, but out with
you and see if there's a fish on the lines for breakfast. I'll be along
in a minute."

He unlocked the door and I cleared out, up the river bank. I
noticed some pieces of limbs and such things floating down, and a
sprinkling of bark; so I knowed the river had begun to rise. I
reckoned I would have great times, now, if I was over at the town.
The June rise used to be always luck for me; because as soon as
that rise begins, here comes cord-wood floating down, and pieces
of log rafts—sometimes a dozen logs together; so all you have
to do is to catch them and sell them to the wood yards and the
sawmill.

I went along up the bank with one eye out for pap and 'tother
one out for what the rise might fetch along. Well, all at once, here
comes a canoe; just a beauty, too, about thirteen or fourteen foot
long, riding high like a duck. I shot head first off of the bank, like

a frog, clothes and all on, and struck out for the canoe. I just
expected there'd be somebody laying down in it, because people
often done that to fool folks, and when a chap had pulled a skiff
out most to it they'd raise up and laugh at him. But it warn't so
this time. It was a drift-canoe, sure enough, and I clumb in and
paddled her ashore. Thinks I, the old man will be glad when he
sees this—she's worth ten dollars. But when I got to shore pap
wasn't in sight yet, and as I was running her into a little creek like
a gully, all hung over with vines and willows, I struck another idea;
I judged I'd hide her good, and then, stead of taking to the woods
when I run off, I'd go down the river about fifty mile and camp in
one place for good, and not have such a rough time tramping on
foot.

It was pretty close to the shanty, and I thought I heard the old
man coming, all the time; but I got her hid; and then I out and
looked around a bunch of willows, and there was the old man down
the path apiece just drawing a bead on a bird with his gun. So he
hadn't seen anything.

When he got along, I was hard at it taking up a "trot" line. He
abused me a little for being so slow, but I told him I fell in the river
and that was what made me so long. I knowed he would see I was
wet, and then he would be asking questions. We got five cat-fish
off of the lines and went home.

While we laid off, after breakfast, to sleep up, both of us being
about wore out, I got to thinking that if I could fix up some way to
keep pap and the widow from trying to follow me, if would be a
certainer thing than trusting to luck to get far enough off before
they missed me; you see, all kinds of things might happen. Well, I
didn't see no way for a while, but by-and-by pap raised up a minute,
to drink another barrel of water, and he says:

"Another time a man comes a-prowling round here, you roust
me out, you hear? That man warn't here for no good. I'd a shot him.
Next time, you roust me out, you hear?"

Then he dropped down and went to sleep again—but what he
had been saying give me the very idea I wanted. I says to myself,
I can fix it now so nobody won't think of following me.

About twelve o'clock we turned out and went along up the bank.
The river was coming up pretty fast, and lots of drift-wood going
by on the rise. By-and-by, along comes part of a log raft—nine logs
fast together. We went out with the skiff and towed it ashore. Then
we had dinner. Anybody but pap would a waited and seen the day
through, so as to catch more stuff; but that warn't pap's style. Nine
logs was enough for one time; he must shove right over to town and
sell. So he locked me in and took the skiff and started off towing the
raft about half-past three. I judged he wouldn't come back that
night. I waited till I reckoned he had got a good start, then I out
with my saw and went to work on that log again. Before he was

'tother side of the river I was out of the hole; him and his raft was
just a speck on the water away off yonder.

I took the sack of corn meal and took it to where the canoe was
hid, and shoved the vines and branches apart and put it in; then
I done the same with the side of bacon; then the whisky jug; I took
all the coffee and sugar there was, and all the ammunition; I took
the wadding; I took the bucket and gourd, I took a dipper and a
tin cup, and my old saw and two blankets, and the skillet and the
coffee-pot. I took fish-lines and matches and other things—
everything that was worth a cent. I cleaned out the place. I wanted
an axe, but there wasn't any, only the one out at the wood pile, and
I knowed why I was going to leave that. I fetched out the gun, and
now I was done.

I had wore the ground a good deal, crawling out of the hole and
dragging out so many things. So I fixed that as good as I could
from the outside by scattering dust on the place, which covered up
the smoothness and the sawdust. Then I fixed the piece of log back
into its place, and put two rocks under it and one against it to
hold it there,—for it was bent up at that place, and didn't quite
touch ground. If you stood four or five foot away and didn't know
it was sawed, you wouldn't ever notice it; and besides, this was the
back of the cabin and it warn't likely anybody would go fooling
around there.

It was all grass clear to the canoe; so I hadn't left a track. I
followed around to see. I stood on the bank and looked out over the
river. All safe. So I took the gun and went up a piece into the woods
and was hunting around for some birds, when I see a wild pig; hogs
soon went wild in them bottoms after they had got away from the
prairie farms. I shot this fellow and took him into camp.

I took the axe and smashed in the door—I beat it and hacked it
considerable, a-doing it. I fetched the pig in and took him back
nearly to the table and hacked into his throat with the ax, and
laid him down on the ground to bleed—I say ground, because it
was ground—hard packed, and no boards. Well, next I took an
old sack and put a lot of big rocks in it,—all I could drag—and I
started it from the pig and dragged it to the door and through the
woods down to the river and dumped it in, and down it sunk, out of
sight. You could easy see that something had been dragged over
the ground. I did wish Tom Sawyer was there, I knowed he would
take an interest in this kind of business, and throw in the fancy
touches. Nobody could spread himself like Tom Sawyer in such a
thing as that.

Well, last I pulled out some of my hair, and bloodied the ax good,
and stuck it on the back side, and slung the ax in the corner. Then
I took up the pig and held him to my breast with my jacket (so he
couldn't drip) till I got a good piece below the house and then
dumped him into the river. Now I thought of something else. So I

went and got the bag of meal and my old saw out of the canoe and
fetched them to the house. I took the bag to where it used to stand,
and ripped a hole in the bottom of it with the saw, for there warn't
no knives and forks on the place—pap done everything with his
clasp-knife, about the cooking. Then I carried the sack about a
hundred yards across the grass and through the willows east of the
house, to a shallow lake that was five mile wide and full of rushes—
and ducks too, you might say, in the season. There was a slough or
a creek leading out of it on the other side, that went miles away, I
don't know where, but it didn't go to the river. The meal sifted out
and made a little track all the way to the lake. I dropped pap's
whetstone there too, so as to look like it had been done by accident.
Then I tied up the rip in the meal sack with a string, so it wouldn't
leak no more, and took it and my saw to the canoe again.

It was about dark, now; so I dropped the canoe down the river
under some willows that hung over the bank, and waited for the
moon to rise. I made fast to a willow; then I took a bite to eat, and
by-and-by laid down in the canoe to smoke a pipe and lay out a
plan. I says to myself, they'll follow the track of that sackful of
rocks to the shore and then drag the river for me. And they'll follow
that meal track to the lake and go browsing down the creek that
leads out of it to find the robbers that killed me and took the things.
They won't ever hunt the river for anything but my dead carcass.
They'll soon get tired of that, and won't bother no more about me.
All right; I can stop anywhere I want to. Jackson's Island is good
enough for me; I know that island pretty well, and nobody ever
comes there. And then I can paddle over to town, nights, and slink
around and pick up things I want. Jackson's Island's the place.

I was pretty tired, and the first thing I knowed, I was asleep.
When I woke up I didn't know where I was, for a minute. I set up
and looked around, a little scared. Then I remembered. The river
looked miles and miles across. The moon was so bright I could a
counted the drift logs that went a slipping along, black and still,
hundred of yards out from shore. Everything was dead quiet, and
it looked late, and *smelt* late. You know what I mean—I don't
know the words to put it in.

I took a good gap and a stretch, and was just going to unhitch and
start, when I heard a sound away over the water. I listened. Pretty
soon I made it out. It was that dull kind of a regular sound that
comes from oars working in rowlocks when it's a still night. I peeped
out through the willow branches, and there it was—a skiff, away
across the water. I couldn't tell how many was in it. It kept
a-coming, and when it was abreast of me I see there warn't but
one man in it. Thinks I, maybe it's pap, though I warn't expecting
him. He dropped below me, with the current, and by-and-by he
come a-swinging up shore in the easy water, and he went by so
close I could a reached out the gun and touched him. Well, it *was*

pap, sure enough—and sober, too, by the way he laid to his oars.

I didn't lose no time. The next minute I was a-spinning down stream soft but quick in the shade of the bank. I made two mile and a half, and then struck out a quarter of a mile or more towards the middle of the river, because pretty soon I would be passing the ferry landing and people might see me and hail me. I got out amongst the drift-wood and then laid down in the bottom of the canoe and let her float. I laid there and had a good rest and a smoke out of my pipe, looking away into the sky, not a cloud in it. The sky looks ever so deep when you lay down on your back in the moonshine; I never knowed it before. And how far a body can hear on the water such nights! I heard people talking at the ferry landing. I heard what they said, too, every word of it. One man said it was getting towards the long days and the short nights, now. 'Tother one said *this* warn't one of the short ones, he reckoned— and then they laughed, and he said it over again and they laughed again; then they waked up another fellow and told him, and laughed, but he didn't laugh; he ripped out something brisk and said let him alone. The first fellow said he 'lowed to tell it to his old woman—she would think it was pretty good; but he said that warn't nothing to some things he had said in his time. I heard one man say it was nearly three o'clock, and he hoped daylight wouldn't wait more than about a week longer. After that, the talk got further and further away, and I couldn't make out the words any more, but I could hear the mumble; and now and then a laugh, too, but it seemed a long ways off.

I was away below the ferry now. I rose up and there was Jackson's Island, about two mile and a half down stream, heavy-timbered and standing up out of the middle of the river, big and dark and solid, like a steamboat without any lights. There warn't any signs of the bar at the head—it was all under water, now.

It didn't take me long to get there. I shot past the head at a ripping rate, the current was so swift, and then I got into the dead water and landed on the side towards the Illinois shore. I run the canoe into a deep dent in the bank that I knowed about; I had to part the willow branches to get in; and when I made fast nobody could a seen the canoe from the outside.

I went up and set down on a log at the head of the island and looked out on the big river and the black driftwood, and away over to the town, three mile away, where there was three or four lights twinkling. A monstrous big lumber raft was about a mile up stream, coming along down, with a lantern in the middle of it. I watched it come creeping down, and when it was most abreast of where I stood I heard a man say, "Stern oars, there! heave her head to stabboard!" I heard that just as plain as if the man was by my side.

There was a little gray in the sky, now; so I stepped into the woods and laid down for a nap before breakfast.

CHAPTER VIII

The sun was up so high when I waked, that I judged it was after eight o'clock. I laid there in the grass and the cool shade, thinking about things and feeling rested and ruther comfortable and satisfied. I could see the sun out at one or two holes, but mostly it was big trees all about, and gloomy in there amongst them. There was freckled places on the ground where the light sifted down through the leaves, and the freckled places swapped about a little, showing there was a little breeze up there. A couple of squirrels set on a limb and jabbered at me very friendly.

I was powerful lazy and comfortable—didn't want to get up and cook breakfast. Well, I was dozing off again, when I thinks I hears a deep sound of "boom!" away up the river. I rouses up and rests on my elbow and listens; pretty soon I hears it again. I hopped up and went and looked out at a hole in the leaves, and I see a bunch of smoke laying on the water a long ways up—about abreast the ferry. And there was the ferry-boat full of people, floating along down. I knowed what was the matter, now. "Boom!" I see the white smoke squirt out of the ferry-boat's side. You see, they was firing cannon over the water, trying to make my carcass come to the top.

I was pretty hungry, but it warn't going to do for me to start a fire, because they might see the smoke. So I set there and watched the cannon-smoke and listened to the boom. The river was a mile wide, there, and it always looks pretty on a summer morning—so I was having a good enough time seeing them hunt for my remainders, if I only had a bite to eat. Well, then I happened to think how they always put quicksilver in loaves of bread and float them off because they always go right to the drownded carcass and stop there. So says I, I'll keep a lookout, and if any of them's floating around after me, I'll give them a show. I changed to the Illinois edge of the island to see what luck I could have, and I warn't disappointed. A big double loaf come along, and I most got it, with a long stick, but my foot slipped and she floated out further. Of course I was where the current set in the closest to the shore—I knowed enough for that. But by-and-by along comes another one, and this time I won. I took out the plug and shook out the little dab of quicksilver, and set my teeth in. It was "baker's bread"— what the quality eat—none of your low-down corn-pone.

I got a good place amongst the leaves, and set there on a log, munching the bread and watching the ferry-boat, and very well satisfied. And then something struck me. I says, now I reckon the widow or the parson or somebody prayed that this bread would find me, and here it has gone and done it. So there ain't no doubt but there is something in that thing. That is, there's something in it when a body like the widow or the parson prays, but it don't work for me, and I reckon it don't work for only just the right kind.

I lit a pipe and had a good long smoke and went on watching.
The ferry-boat was floating with the current, and I allowed I'd have
a chance to see who was aboard when she come along, because she
would come in close, where the bread did. When she'd got pretty
well along down towards me, I put out my pipe and went to where
I fished out the bread, and laid down behind a log on the bank in
a little open place. Where the log forked I could peep through.

By-and-by she come along, and she drifted in so close that they
could a run out a plank and walked ashore. Most everybody was
on the boat. Pap, and Judge Thatcher, and Bessie Thatcher, and Jo
Jo Harper, and Tom Sawyer, and his old Aunt Polly, and Sid and
Mary, and plenty more. Everybody was talking about the murder,
but the captain broke in and says:

"Look sharp, now; the current sets in the closest here, and maybe
he's washed ashore and got tangled amongst the brush at the water's
edge. I hope so, anyway."

I didn't hope so. They all crowded up and leaned over the rails,
nearly in my face, and kept still, watching with all their might. I
could see them first-rate, but they couldn't see me. Then the captain
sung out:

"Stand away!" and the cannon let off such a blast right before me
that it made me deef with the noise and pretty near blind with the
smoke, and I judged I was gone. If they'd a had some bullets in, I
reckon they'd a got the corpse they was after. Well, I see I warn't
hurt, thanks to goodness. The boat floated on and went out of sight
around the shoulder of the island. I could hear the booming, now
and then, further and further off, and by-and-by after an hour,
I didn't hear it no more. The island was three mile long. I judged
they had got to the foot, and was giving it up. But they didn't yet
a while. They turned around the foot of the island and started up
the channel on the Missouri side, under steam, and booming once
in a while as they went. I crossed over to that side and watched them.
When they got abreast the head of the island they quit shooting and
dropped over to the Missouri shore and went home to the town.

I knowed I was all right now. Nobody else would come a-hunting
after me. I got my traps out of the canoe and made me a nice camp
in the thick woods. I made a kind of a tent out of my blankets to
put my things under so the rain couldn't get at them. I catched a
cat-fish and haggled him open with my saw, and towards sundown
I started my camp fire and had supper. Then I set out a line to catch
some fish for breakfast.

When it was dark I set by my camp fire smoking, and feeling
pretty satisfied; but by-and-by it got sort of lonesome, and so I went
and set on the bank and listened to the currents washing along, and
counted the stars and drift-logs and rafts that come down, and then
went to bed; there ain't no better way to put in time when you are
lonesome; you can't stay so, you soon get over it.

And so for three days and nights. No difference—just the same thing. But the next day I went exploring around down through the island. I was boss of it; it all belonged to me, so to say, and I wanted to know all about it; but mainly I wanted to put in the time. I found plenty strawberries, ripe and prime; and green summer-grapes, and green razberries; and the green blackberries was just beginning to show. They would all come handy by-and-by, I judged.

Well, I went fooling along in the deep woods till I judged I warn't far from the foot of the island. I had my gun along, but I hadn't shot nothing; it was for protection; thought I would kill some game nigh home. About this time I mighty near stepped on a good sized snake, and it went sliding off through the grass and flowers, and I after it, trying to get a shot at it. I clipped along, and all of a sudden I bounded right on to the ashes of a camp fire that was still smoking.

My heart jumped up amongst my lungs. I never waited for to look further, but uncocked my gun and went sneaking back on my tip-toes as fast as ever I could. Every now and then I stopped a second, amongst the thick leaves, and listened; but my breath come so hard I couldn't hear nothing else. I slunk along another piece further, then listened again; and so on, and so on; if I see a stump, I took it for a man; if I trod on a stick and broke it, it made me feel like a person had cut one of my breaths in two and I only got half, and the short half, too.

When I got to camp I warn't feeling very brash, there warn't much sand in my craw; but I says, this ain't no time to be fooling around. So I got all my traps into my canoe again so as to have them out of sight, and I put out the fire and scattered the ashes around to look like an old last year's camp, and then clumb a tree.

I reckon I was up in the tree two hours; but I didn't see nothing, I didn't hear nothing—I only *thought* I heard and seen as much as a thousand things. Well, I couldn't stay up there forever; so at last I got down, but I kept in the thick woods and on the lookout all the time. All I could get to eat was berries and what was left over from breakfast.

By the time it was night I was pretty hungry. So when it was good and dark, I slid out from shore before moonrise and paddled over to the Illinois bank—about a quarter of a mile. I went out in the woods and cooked a supper, and I had about made up my mind I would stay there all night, when I hear a *plunkety-plunk, plunkety-plunk,* and says to myself, horses coming; and next I hear people's voices. I got everything into the canoe as quick as I could, and then went creeping through the woods to see what I could find out. I hadn't got far when I hear a man say:

"We better camp here, if we can find a good place; the horses is about beat out. Let's look around."

I didn't wait, but shoved out and paddled away easy. I tied up in the old place, and reckoned I would sleep in the canoe.

I didn't sleep much. I couldn't, somehow, for thinking. And every time I waked up I thought somebody had me by the neck. So the sleep didn't do me no good. By-and-by I says to myself, I can't live this way; I'm agoing to find out who it is that's here on the island with me; I'll find it out or bust. Well, I felt better, right off.

So I took my paddle and slid out from shore just a step or two, and then let the canoe drop along down amongst the shadows. The moon was shining, and outside of the shadows it made it most as light as day. I poked along well onto an hour, everything still as rocks and sound asleep. Well by this time I was most down to the foot of the island. A little ripply, cool breeze begun to blow, and that was as good as saying the night was about done. I give her a turn with the paddle and brung her nose to shore; then I got my gun and slipped out and into the edge of the woods. I set down there on a log and looked out through the leaves. I see the moon go off watch and the darkness begin to blanket the river. But in a little while I see a pale streak over the tree-tops, and knowed the day was coming. So I took my gun and slipped off towards where I had run across that camp fire, stopping every minute or two to listen. But I hadn't no luck, somehow; I couldn't seem to find the place. But by-and-by, sure enough, I catched a glimpse of fire, away through the trees. I went for it, cautious and slow. By-and-by I was close enough to have a look, and there laid a man on the ground. It most give me the fan-tods. He had a blanket around his head, and his head was nearly in the fire. I set there behind a clump of bushes, in about six foot of him, and kept my eyes on him steady. It was getting gray daylight, now. Pretty soon he gapped, and stretched himself, and hove off the blanket, and it was Miss Watson's Jim! I bet I was glad to see him. I says:

"Hello, Jim!" and skipped out.

He bounced up and stared at me wild. Then he drops down on his knees, and puts his hands together and says:

"Doan' hurt me—don't! I hain't ever done no harm to a ghos'. I awluz liked dead people, en done all I could for 'em. You go en git in de river agin, whah you b'longs, en doan' do nuffin to Ole Jim, 'at 'uz awluz yo' fren'."

Well, I warn't long making him understand I warn't dead. I was ever so glad to see Jim. I warn't lonesome, now. I told him I warn't afraid of *him* telling the people where I was. I talked along, but he only set there and looked at me; never said nothing. Then I says:

"It's good daylight. Le's get breakfast. Make up your camp fire good."

"What's de use er makin' up de camp fire to cook strawbries en sich truck? But you got a gun, hain't you? Den we kin git sumfn better den strawbries."

"Strawberries and such truck," I says. "Is that what you live on?"

"I couldn't git nuffn else," he says.

"Why, how long you been on the island, Jim?"

"I come heah de night arter you's killed."

"What, all that time?"

"Yes-indeedy."

"And ain't you had nothing but that kind of rubbage to eat?"

"No, sah—nuffn else."

"Well, you must be most starved, ain't you?"

"I reck'n I could eat a hoss. I think I could. How long you ben on de islan'?"

"Since the night I got killed."

"No! W'y, what has you lived on? But you got a gun. Oh, yes, you got a gun. Dat's good. Now you kill sumfn en I'll make up de fire."

So we went over to where the canoe was, and while he built a fire in a grassy open place amongst the trees, I fetched meal and bacon and coffee, and coffee-pot and frying-pan, and sugar and tin cups, and the nigger was set back considerable, because he reckoned it was all done with witchcraft. I catched a good big cat-fish, too, and Jim cleaned him with his knife, and fried him.

When breakfast was ready, we lolled on the grass and eat it smoking hot. Jim laid it in with all his might, for he was most about starved. Then when we had got pretty well stuffed, we laid off and lazied.

By-and-by Jim says:

"But looky here, Huck, who wuz it dat 'uz killed in dat shanty, ef it warn't you?"

Then I told him the whole thing, and he said it was smart. He said Tom Sawyer couldn't get up no better plan than what I had. Then I says:

"How do you come to be here, Jim, and how'd you get here?"

He looked pretty uneasy, and didn't say nothing for a minute. Then he says:

"Maybe I better not tell."

"Why, Jim?"

"Well, dey's reasons. But you wouldn' tell on me ef I 'uz to tell you, would you, Huck?"

"Blamed if I would, Jim."

"Well, I b'lieve you, Huck. I—I *run off.*"

"Jim!"

"But mind, you said you wouldn't tell—you know you said you wouldn't tell, Huck."

"Well, I did. I said I wouldn't, and I'll stick to it. Honest *injun* I will. People would call me a low down Ablitionist and despise me for keeping mum—but that don't make no difference. I ain't agoing to tell, and I ain't agoing back there anyways. So now, le's know all about it."

"Well, you see, it 'uz dis way. Ole Missus—dat's Miss Watson—

she pecks on me all de time, en treats me pooty rough, but she awluz
said she wouldn' sell me down to Orleans. But I noticed dey wuz a
nigger trader roun' de place considable, lately, en I begin to git
oneasy. Well, one night I creeps to de do', pooty late, en de do'
warn't quite shet, en I hear ole missus tell de widder she gwyne to
sell me down to Orelans, but she didn' want to, but she could git
eight hund'd dollars for me, en it 'uz sich a big stack o' money she
couldn' resis'. De widder she try to git her to say she wouldn't do it,
but I never waited to hear de res'. I lit out mighty quick, I tell you.

"I tuck out en shin down de hill en 'spec to steal a skift 'long de
sho' som'ers 'bove de town, but dey wuz people a-stirrin' yit, so I
hid in de ole tumble-down cooper shop on de bank to wait for
everybody to go 'way. Well, I wuz dah all night. Dey wuz somebody
roun' all de time. 'Long 'bout six in de mawnin', skifts begin to go
by, en 'bout eight er nine every skift dat went 'long wuz talkin'
'bout how yo' pap come over to de town en say you's killed. Dese las'
skifts wuz full o' ladies en genlmen agoin' over for to see de place.
Sometimes dey'd pull up at de sho' en take a res' b'fo' dey started
acrost, so by de talk I got to know all 'bout de killin'. I 'uz powerful
sorry you's killed, Huck, but I ain't no mo', now.

"I laid dah under de shavins all day. I' uz hungry, but I warn't
afeared; bekase I knowed ole missus en de widder wuz goin' to start
to de camp-meetn' right arter breakfas' en be gone all day, en dey
knows I goes off wid de cattle 'bout daylight, so dey wouldn' 'spec
to see me roun' de place, en so dey wouldn' miss me tell arter dark
in de evenin'. De yuther servants wouldn' miss me, kase dey'd shin
out en take holiday, soon as de ole folks 'uz out'n de way.

"Well, when it come dark I tuck out up de river road, en went
'bout two mile er more to whah dey warn't no houses. I'd made up
my mine 'bout what I's agwyne to do. You see ef I kep' on tryin'
to git away afoot, de dogs 'ud track me; ef I stole a skift to cross
over, dey'd miss dat skift, you see, en dey'd know 'bout whah I'd
lan' on de yuther side en whah to pick up my track. So I says, a raff'
if what I's arter; it doan' *make* no track.

"I see a light a-comin' roun' de p'int, bymeby, so I wade' in en
shove' a log ahead of' me, en swum more'n half-way acrost de river,
en got in 'mongst de drift-wood, en kep' my head down low, en
kinder swum agin de current tell de raff come along. Den I swum to
de stern uv it, en tuck aholt. It clouded up en 'uz pooty dark for a
little while. So I clumb up en laid down on de planks. De men 'uz
all 'way yonder in de middle, whah de lantern wuz. De river wuz
arisin' en dey wuz a good current; so I reck'n'd 'at by fo' in de
mawnin' I'd be twenty-five mile down de river, en den I'd slip in,
jis' b'fo' daylight, en swim asho' en take to de woods on de Illinoi
side.

"But I didn' have no luck. When we 'uz mos' down to de head er
de islan', a man begin to come aft wid de lantern. I see it warn't

no use fer to wait, so I slid overboard, en struck out fer de islan'. Well,
I had a notion I could lan' mos' anywhers, but I couldn't—bank
too bluff. I 'uz mos' to de foot er de islan' b'fo' I foun' a good place.
I went into de woods en judged I wouldn' fool wid raffs no mo',
long as dey move de lantern roun' so. I had my pipe en a plug er dog-
leg, en some matches in my cap, en dey warn't wet, so I 'uz all right."

"And so you ain't had no meat nor bread to eat all this time?
Why didn't you get mud-turkles?"

"How you gwyne to git'm? You can't slip up on um en grab um;
it in de night? en I warn't gwyne to show mysef on de bank in de
daytime."

"Well, that's so. You've had to keep in the woods all the time, of
course. Did you hear 'em shooting the cannon?"

"Oh, yes. I knowed dey was arter you. I see um go by heah;
watched um thoo de bushes."

Some young birds come along, flying a yard or two at a time and
lighting. Jim said it was a sign it was going to rain. He said it was a
sign when young chickens flew that way, and so he reckoned it was
the same way when young birds done it. I was going to catch some
of them, but Jim wouldn't let me. He said it was death. He said his
father laid mighty sick once, and some of them catched a bird, and
his old granny said his father would die, and he did.

And Jim said you musn't count the things you are going to cook
for dinner, because that would bring bad luck. The same if you
shook the table-cloth after sundown. And he said if a man owned
a bee-hive, and that man died, the bees must be told about it
before sun-up next morning, or else the bees would all weaken down
and quit work and die. Jim said bees wouldn't sting idiots; but I
didn't believe that, because I had tried them lots of times myself,
and they wouldn't sting me.

I had heard about some of these things before, but not all of them.
Jim knowed all kinds of signs. He said he knowed most everything.
I said it looked to me like all the signs was about bad luck, and so
I asked him if there warn't any good-luck signs. He says:

"Mighty few—an' *dey* ain' no use to a body. What you want to
know when good luck's a-comin' for? want to keep it off?" And
he said: "Ef you's got hairy arms en a hairy breas', it's a sign dat
you's agwyne to be rich. Well, dey's some use in a sign like dat,
'kase it's so fur ahead. You see, maybe you's got to be po' a long time
fust, en so you might git discourage' en kill yo'sef 'f you did n' know
by de sign dat you gwyne to be rich bymeby."

"Have you got hairy arms and a hairy breast, Jim?"

"What's de use to ax dat question? don' you see I has?"

"Well, are you rich?"

"No, but I ben rich wunst, and gwyne to be rich agin. Wunst I
had foteen dollars, but I tuck to specalat'n', en got busted out."

"What did you speculate in, Jim?"

"Well, fust I tackled stock."

"What kind of stock?"

"Why, live stock. Cattle, you know. I put ten dollars in a cow. But I ain' gwyne to resk no mo' money in stock. De cow up 'n' died on my han's."

"So you lost the ten dollars."

"No, I didn' lose it all. I on'y los' 'bout nine of it. I sole de hide en taller for a dollar en ten cents."

"You had five dollars and ten cents left. Did you speculate any more?"

"Yes. You know dat one-laigged nigger dat b'longs to old Misto Bradish? well, he sot up a bank, en say anybody dat put in a dollar would git fo' dollars mo' at de en' er de year. Well, all de niggers went in, but dey didn' have much. I wuz de on'y one dat had much. So I stuck out for mo' dan fo' dollars, en I said 'f I didn' git it I'd start a bank mysef. Well o' course dat nigger want' to keep me out er de business, bekase he say dey warn't business 'nough for two banks, so he say I could put in my five dollars en he pay me thirty-five at de en' er de year.

"So I done it. Den I reck'n'd I'd inves' de thirty-five dollars right off en keep things a-movin'. Dey wuz a nigger name' Bob, dat had ketched a wood-flat, en his marster didn' know it; en I bought it off'n him en told him to take de thirty-five dollars when de en' er de year come; but somebody stole de wood-flat dat night, en nex' day de one-laigged nigger say de bank's busted. So dey didn' none uv us git no money."

"What did you do with the ten cents, Jim?"

"Well, I 'uz gwyne to spen' it, but I had a dream, en de dream tole me to give it to a nigger name' Balum—Balum's Ass dey call him for short, he's one er dem chuckle-heads, you know. But he's lucky, dey say, en I see I warn't lucky. De dream say let Balum inves' de ten cents en he'd make a raise for me. Well, Balum he tuck de money, en when he wuz in church he hear de preacher say dat whoever give to de po' len' to de Lord, en boun' to git his money back a hund'd times. So Balum he tuck en give de ten cents to de po,' en laid low to see what wuz gwyne to come of it."

"Well, what did come of it, Jim?"

"Nuffn' never come of it. I couldn' manage to k'leck dat money no way; en Balum he couldn'. I ain' gwyne to len' no mo' money 'dout I see de security. Boun' to git yo' money back a hund'd times, de preacher says! Ef I could git de ten *cents* back, I'd call it squah, en be glad er de chanst."

"Well, it's all right, anyway, Jim, long as you're going to be rich again some time or other."

"Yes—en I's rich now, come to look at it. I owns mysef, en I's wuth eight hund'd dollars. I wisht I had de money, I wouldn' want no mo'."

CHAPTER IX

I wanted to go and look at a place right about the middle of the island, that I'd found when I was exploring; so we started, and soon got to it, because the island was only three miles long and a quarter of a mile wide.

This place was a tolerable long steep hill or ridge, about forty foot high. We had a rough time getting to the top, the sides was so steep and the bushes so thick. We tramped and clumb around all over it, and by-and-by found a good big cavern in the rock, most up to the top on the side towards Illinois. The cavern was as big as two or three rooms bunched together, and Jim could stand up straight in it. It was cool in there. Jim was for putting our traps in there, right away, but I said we didn't want to be climbing up and down there all the time.

Jim said if we had the canoe hid in a good place, and had all the traps in the cavern, we could rush there if anybody was to come to the island, and they would never find us without dogs. And besides, he said them little birds had said it was going to rain, and did I want the things to get wet?

So we went back and got the canoe and paddled up abreast the cavern, and lugged all the traps up there. Then we hunted up a place close by to hide the canoe in, amongst the thick willows. We took some fish off of the lines and set them again, and begun to get ready for dinner.

The door of the cavern was big enough to roll a hogshead in, and on one side of the door the floor stuck out a little bit and was flat and a good place to build a fire on. So we built it there and cooked dinner.

We spread the blankets inside for a carpet, and eat our dinner in there. We put all the other things handy at the back of the cavern. Pretty soon it darkened up and begun to thunder and lighten; so the birds was right about it. Directly it begun to rain, and it rained like all fury, too, and I never see the wind blow so. It was one of these regular summer storms. It would get so dark that it looked all blue-black outside, and lovely; and the rain would thrash along by so thick that the trees off a little ways looked dim and spider-webby; and here would come a blast of wind that would bend the trees down and turn up the pale underside of the leaves; and then a perfect ripper of a gust would follow along and set the branches to tossing their arms as if they was just wild; and next, when it was just about the bluest and blackest—*fst!* it was as bright as glory and you'd have a little glimpse of tree-tops a-plunging about, away off yonder in the storm, hundreds of yards further than you could see before; dark as sin again in a second, and now you'd hear the thunder let go with an awful crash and then go rumbling, grumbling, tumbling down the sky towards the under side of the world, like rolling empty barrels down stairs, where it's long stairs and they bounce a good deal, you know.

"Jim, this is nice," I says. "I wouldn't want to be nowhere else but here. Pass me along another hunk of fish and some hot corn-bread."

"Well, you wouldn't a ben here, 'f it hadn't a ben for Jim. You'd a ben down dah in de woods widout any dinner, en gittn' mos' drownded, too, dat you would, honey. Chickens knows when its gwyne to rain, en so do de birds, chile."

The river went on raising and raising for ten or twelve days, till at last it was over the banks. The water was three or four foot deep on the island in the low places and on the Illinois bottom. On that side it was a good many miles wide; but on the Missouri side it was the same old distance across—a half a mile—because the Missouri shore was just a wall of high bluffs.

Daytimes we paddled all over the island in the canoe. It was mighty cool and shady in the deep woods even if the sun was blazing outside. We went winding in and out amongst the trees; and sometimes the vines hung so thick we had to back away and go some other way. Well, on every old broken-down tree, you could see rabbits, and snakes, and such things; and when the island had been overflowed a day or two, they got so tame, on account of being hungry, that you could paddle right up and put your hand on them if you wanted to; but not the snakes and turtles—they would slide off in the water. The ridge our cavern was in, was full of them. We could a had pets enough if we'd wanted them.

One night we catched a little section of a lumber raft—nice pine planks. It was twelve foot wide and fifteen or sixteen foot long, and the top stood above water six or seven inches, a solid level floor. We could see saw-logs go by in the daylight, sometimes, but we let them go; we didn't show ourselves in daylight.

Another night, when we was up at the head of the island, just before daylight, here comes a frame house down, on the west side. She was a two-story, and tilted over, considerable. We paddled out and got aboard—clumb in at an up-stairs window. But it was too dark to see yet, so we made the canoe fast and set in her to wait for daylight.

The light begun to come before we got to the foot of the island. Then we looked in at the window. We could make out a bed, and a table, and two old chairs, and lots of things around about on the floor; and there was clothes hanging against the wall. There was something laying on the floor in the far corner that looked like a man. So Jim says:

"Hello, you!"

But it didn't budge. So I hollered again, and then Jim says:

"De man ain't asleep—he's dead. You hold still—I'll go en see."

He went and bent down and looked, and says:

"It's a dead man. Yes, indeedy; naked, too. He's ben shot in de back. I reck'n he's ben dead two er three days. Come in, Huck, but doan' look at his face—it's too gashly."

I didn't look at him at all. Jim threw some old rags over him, but he needn't done it; I didn't want to see him. There was heaps of old greasy cards scattered around over the floor, and old whisky bottles, and a couple of masks made out of black cloth; and all over the walls was the ignorantest kind of words and pictures, made with charcoal. There was two old dirty calico dresses, and a sun-bonnet, and some women's under-clothes, hanging against the wall, and some men's clothing, too. We put the lot into the canoe; it might come good. There was a boy's old speckled straw hat on the floor; I took that too. And there was a bottle that had had milk in it; and it had a rag stopper for a baby to suck. We would a took the bottle, but it was broke. There was a seedy old chest, and an old hair trunk with the hinges broke. They stood open, but there warn't nothing left in them that was any account. They stood open, but there warn't nothing left in them that was any account. The way things was scattered about, we reckoned the people left in a hurry and warn't fixed so as to carry off most of their stuff.

We got an old tin lantern, and a butcher knife without any handle, and a bran-new Barlow knife worth two bits in any store, and a lot of tallow candles, and a tin candlestick, and a gourd, and a tin cup, and a ratty old bed-quilt off the bed, and a reticule with needles and pins and beeswax and buttons and thread and all such truck in it, and a hatchet and some nails, and a fish-line as thick as my little finger, with some monstrous hooks on it, and a roll of buckskin, and a leather dog-collar, and a horse-shoe, and some vials of medicine that didn't have no label on them; and just as we was leaving I found a tolerable good curry-comb, and Jim he found a ratty old fiddle-bow, and a wooden leg. The straps was broke off of it, but barring that, it was a good enough leg, though it was too long for me and not long enough for Jim, and we couldn't find the other one, though we hunted all around.

And so, take it all around, we made a good haul. When we was ready to shove off, we was a quarter of a mile below the island, and it was pretty broad day; so I made Jim lay down in the canoe and cover up with the quilt, because if he set up, people could tell he was a nigger a good ways off. I paddled over to the Illinois shore, and drifted down most a half a mile doing it. I crept up the dead water under the bank and hadn't no accidents and didn't see nobody. We got home all safe.

CHAPTER X

After breakfast I wanted to talk about the dead man and guess out how he come to be killed, but Jim didn't want to. He said it would fetch bad luck; and besides, he said, he might come and ha'nt us; he said a man that warn't buried was more likely to go a-ha'nting around than one that was planted and comfortable. That sounded pretty reasonable, so I didn't say no more; but I couldn't keep from studying over it and wishing I knowed who shot the man, and what they done it for.

We rummaged the clothes we'd got, and found eight dollars in silver sewed up in the lining of an old blanket overcoat. Jim said he reckoned the people in that house stole the coat, because if they'd a knowed the money was there they wouldn't a left it. I said I reckoned they killed him, too; but Jim didn't want to talk about that. I says:

"Now you think it's bad luck; but what did you say when I fetched in the snake-skin that I found on the top of the ridge day before yesterday? You said it was the worst bad luck in the world to touch a snake-skin with my hands. Well, here's your bad luck! We've raked in all this truck and eight dollars besides. I wish we could have some bad luck like this every day, Jim."

"Never you mind, honey, never you mind. Don't you git too peart. It's a-comin'. Mind I tell you, it's a-comin'."

It did come, too. It was a Tuesday that we had that talk. Well, after dinner Friday, we was laying around in the grass at the upper end of the ridge, and got out of tobacco. I went to the cavern to get some, and found a rattlesnake in there. I killed him, and curled him up on the foot of Jim's blanket, ever so natural, thinking there'd be some fun when Jim found him there. Well, by night I forgot all about the snake, and when Jim flung himself down on the blanket while I struck a light, the snake's mate was there, and bit him.

He jumped up yelling, and the first thing the light showed was the varmit curled up and ready for another spring. I laid him out in a second with a stick, and Jim grabbed pap's whisky jug and begun to pour it down.

He was barefooted, and the snake bit him right on the heel. That all comes of my being such a fool as to not remember that wherever you leave a dead snake its mate always comes there and curls around it. Jim told me to chop off the snake's head and throw it away, and then skin the body and roast a piece of it. I done it, and he eat it and said it would help cure him. He made me take off the rattles and tie them around his wrist, too. He said that that would help. Then I slid out quiet and throwed the snakes clear away amongst the bushes; for I warn't going to let Jim find out it was all my fault, not if I could help it.

Jim sucked and sucked at the jug, and now and then he got out of his head and pitched around and yelled; but every time he come to to himself he went to sucking at the jug again. His foot swelled up pretty big, and so did his leg; but by-and-by the drunk begun to come, and so I judged he was all right; but I'd druther been bit with a snake than pap's whisky.

Jim was laid up for four days and nights. Then the swelling was all gone and he was around again. I made up my mind I wouldn't ever take aholt of a snake-skin again with my hands, now that I see what had come of it. Jim said he reckoned I would believe him next time. And he said that handling a snake-skin was such awful bad luck that maybe we hadn't got to the end of it yet. He said he druther see the new moon over his left shoulder as much as a thousand times than take up a snake-skin in his hand. Well, I was getting to feel that way myself, though I've always reckoned that looking at the new moon over your left shoulder is one of the carelessest and foolishest things a body can do. Old Hank Bunker done it once, and bragged about it; and in less than two years he got drunk and fell off of the shot tower and spread himself out so that he was just a kind of a layer, as you may say; and they slid him edgeways between two barn doors for a coffin, and buried him so, so they say, but I didn't see it. Pap told me. But anyway, it all come of looking at the moon that way, like a fool.

Well, the days went along, and the river went down between its banks again; and about the first thing we done was to bait one of the big hooks with a skinned rabbit and set it and catch a cat-fish that was as big as a man, being six foot two inches long, and weighed over two hundred pounds. We couldn't handle him, of course; he would a flung us into Illinois. We just set there and watched him rip and tear around till he drownded. We found a brass button in his stomach, and a round ball, and lots of rubbage. We split the ball open with the hatchet, and there was a spool in it. Jim said he'd had it there a long time, to coat it over so and make a ball of it. It was as big a fish as was ever catched in the Mississippi, I reckon. Jim said he hadn't ever seen a bigger one. He would a been worth a good deal over at the village. They peddle out such a fish as that by the pound in the market house there; everybody buys some of him; his meat's as white as snow and makes a good fry.

Next morning I said it was getting slow and dull, and I wanted to get a stirring up, some way. I said I reckoned I would slip over the river and find out what was going on. Jim liked that notion; but he said I must go in the dark and look sharp. Then he studied it over and said, couldn't I put on some of them old things and dress up like a girl? That was a good notion, too. So we shortened up one of the calico gowns and I turned up my trowser-legs to my knees and got into it. Jim hitched it behind with the hooks, and it was a fair fit. I put on the sun-bonnet and tied it under my chin, and then for a body to look in and see my face was like looking down a joint of stove-pipe. Jim said nobody would know me, even in the daytime,

hardly. I practiced around all day to get the hang of the things, and
by-and-by I could do pretty well in them, only Jim said I didn't walk
like a girl; and he said I must quit pulling up my gown to get at my
britches pocket. I took notice, and done better.

I started up the Illinois shore in the canoe just after dark.

I started across to the town from a little below the ferry landing,
and the drift of the current fetched me in at the bottom of the town.
I tied up and started along the bank. There was a light burning in a
little shanty that hadn't been lived in for a long time, and I wondered
who had took up quarters there. I slipped up and peeped in at the
window. There was a woman about forty year old in there, knitting
by a candle that was on a pine table. I didn't know her face; she was
a stranger, for you couldn't start a face in that town that I didn't
know. Now this was lucky, because I was weakening; I was getting
afraid I had come; people might know my voice and find me out. But
if this woman had been in such a little town two days she could tell
me all I wanted to know; so I knocked at the door, and made up my
mind I wouldn't forget I was a girl.

CHAPTER XI

"Come in," says the woman, and I did. She says:

"Take a cheer."

I done it. She looked me all over with her little shiny eyes, and
says:

"What might your name be?"

"Sarah Williams."

"Where 'bouts do you live? In this neighborhood?"

"No'm. In Hookerville, seven miles below. I've walked all the way
and I'm all tired out."

"Hungry, too, I reckon. I'll find you something."

"No'm, I ain't hungry. I was so hungry I had to stop two mile
below here at a farm; so I ain't hungry no more. It's what makes me
so late. My mother's down sick, and out of money and everything,
and I come to tell my uncle Abner Moore. He lives at the upper end
of the town, she says. I hain't ever been here before. Do you know
him?"

"No; but I don't know everybody yet. I haven't lived here quite
two weeks. It's a considerable ways to the upper end of the town.
You better stay here all night. Take off your bonnet."

"No," I says, "I'll rest a while, I reckon, and go on. I ain't afeared
of the dark."

She said she wouldn't let me go by myself, but her husband would
be in by-and-by, maybe in a hour and a half, and she'd send him
along with me. Then she got to talking about her husband, and
about her relations up the river, and her relations down the river,
and about how much better off they used to was, and how they didn't

know but they'd made a mistake coming to our town, instead of
letting well alone—and so on and so on, till I was afeard *I* had made
a mistake coming to her to find out what was going on in the town;
but by-and-by she dropped onto pap and the murder, and then I was
pretty willing to let her clatter right along. She told about me and
Tom Sawyer finding the six thousand dollars (only she got it ten) and
all about pap and what a hard lot he was, and what a hard lot I was,
and at last she got down to where I was murdered. I says:

"Who done it? We've heard considerable about these goings on,
down in Hookerville, but we don't know who 'twas that killed Huck
Finn."

"Well, I reckon there's a right smart chance of people *here* that'd
like to know who killed him. Some thinks old Finn done it himself."

"No—is that so?"

"Most everybody thought it at first. He'll never know how nigh he
come to getting lynched. But before night they changed around and
judged it was done by a runaway nigger named Jim."

"Why *he*—"

I stopped. I reckoned I better keep still. She run on, and never
noticed I had put in at all.

"The nigger run off the very night Huck Finn was killed. So
there's a reward out for him—three hundred dollars. And there's
a reward out for old Finn too—two hundred dollars. You see, he
come to town the morning after the murder, and told about it, and
was out with 'em on the ferry-boat hunt, and right away after he up
and left. Before night they wanted to lynch him, but he was gone,
you see. Well, next day they found out the nigger was gone; they
found out he hadn't ben seen sence ten o'clock the night the murder
was done. So then they put it on him, you see, and while they was
full of it, next day back comes old Finn and went boo-hooing to
Judge Thatcher to get money to hunt for the nigger all over Illinois
with. The judge give him some, and that evening he got drunk and
was around till after midnight with a couple of mighty hard looking
strangers, and then went off with them. Well, he hain't come back
sence, and they ain't looking for him back till this thing blows over a
little, for people thinks now that he killed his boy and fixed things so
folks would think robbers done it, and then he'd get Huck's money
without having to bother a long time with a lawsuit. People do say
he warn't any too good to do it. Oh, he's sly, I reckon. If he don't
come back for a year, he'll be all right. You can't prove anything on
him, you know; everything will be quieted down then, and he'll walk
into Huck's money as easy as nothing."

"Yes, I reckon so, 'm. I don't see nothing in the way of it. Has
everybody quit thinking the nigger done it?"

"Oh, no, not everybody. A good many thinks he done it. But
they'll get the nigger pretty soon, now, and maybe they can scare it
out of him."

"Why, are they after him yet?"

"Well, you're innocent, ain't you! Does three hundred dollars lay round every day for people to pick up? Some folks thinks the nigger ain't far from here. I'm one of them—but I hain't talked it around. A few days ago I was talking with an old couple that lives next door in the log shanty, and they happened to say hardly anybody ever goes to that island over yonder that they call Jackson's Island. Don't anybody live there? says I. No, nobody, says they. I didn't say any more, but I done some thinking. I was pretty near certain I'd seen smoke over there, about the head of the island, a day or two before that, so I says to myself, like as not that nigger's hiding over there; anyway, says I, it's worth the trouble to give the place a hunt. I hain't seen any smoke sence, so I reckon maybe he's gone, if it was him; but husband's going over to see—him and another man. He was gone up the river; but he got back to-day and I told him as soon as he got here two hours ago."

I had got so uneasy I couldn't set still. I had to do something with my hands; so I took up a needle off of the table and went to threading it. My hands shook, and I was making a bad job of it. When the woman stopped talking, I looked up, and she was looking at me pretty curious, and smiling a little. I put down the needle and thread and let on to be interested—and I was, too—and says:

"Three hundred dollars is a power of money. I wish my mother could get it. Is your husband going over there to-night?"

"Oh, yes. He went up town with the man I was telling you of, to get a boat and see if they could borrow another gun. They'll go over after midnight."

"Couldn't they see better if they was to wait till daytime?"

"Yes. And couldn't the nigger see better, too? After midnight he'll likely be asleep, and they can slip around through the woods and hunt up his camp fire all the better for the dark, if he's got one."

"I didn't think of that."

The woman kept looking at me pretty curious, and I didn't feel a bit comfortable. Pretty soon she says:

"What did you say your name was, honey?"

"M—Mary Williams."

Somehow it didn't seem to me that I said it was Mary before, so I didn't look up; seemed to me I said it was Sarah; so I felt sort of cornered, and was afeared maybe I was looking it, too. I wished the woman would say something more; the longer she set still, the uneasier I was. But now she says:

"Honey, I thought you said it was Sarah when you first come in?"

"Oh, yes'm, I did. Sarah Mary Williams. Sarah's my first name. Some calls me Sarah, some calls me Mary."

"Oh, that's the way of it?"

"Yes'm."

I was feeling better, then, but I wished I was out of there, anyway.

I couldn't look up yet.

Well, the woman fell to talking about how hard times was, and how poor they had to live, and how the rats was as free as if they owned the place, and so forth, and so on, and then I got easy again. She was right about the rats. You'd see one stick his nose out of a hole in the corner every little while. She said she had to have things handy to throw at them when she was alone, or they wouldn't give her no peace. She showed me a bar of lead, twisted up into a knot, and said she was a good shot with it generly, but she'd wrenched her arm a day or two ago, and didn't know whether she could throw true, now. But she watched for a chance, and directly she banged away at a rat, but she missed him wide, and said "Ouch!" it hurt her arm so. Then she told me to try for the next one. I wanted to be getting away before the old man got back, but of course I didn't let on. I got the thing, and the first rat that showed his nose I let drive, and if he'd a stayed where he was he'd a been a tolerable sick rat. She said that that was first-rate, and she reckoned I would hive the next one. She went and got the lump of lead and fetched it back and brought along a hank of yarn, which she wanted me to help her with. I held up my two hands and she put the hank over them and went on talking about her and her husband's matters. But she broke off to say:

"Keep your eye on the rats. You better have the lead in your lap, handy."

So she dropped the lump into my lap, just at that moment, and I clapped my legs together on it and she went on talking. But only about a minute. Then she took off the hank and looked me straight in the face, but very pleasant, and says:

"Come, now—what's your real name?"

"Wh-what, mum?"

"What's your real name? Is it Bill, or Tom, or Bob?—or what is it?"

I reckon I shook like a leaf, and I didn't know hardly what to do. But I says:

"Please to don't poke fun at a poor girl like me, mum. If I'm in the way, here, I'll—"

"No, you won't. Set down and stay where you are. I ain't going to hurt you, and I ain't going to tell on you, nuther. You just tell me your secret, and trust me. I'll keep it; and what's more, I'll help you. So'll my old man, if you want him to. You see, you're a runaway 'prentice—that's all. It ain't anything. There ain't any harm in it. You've been treated bad, and you made up your mind to cut. Bless you, child, I wouldn't tell on you. Tell me all about it, now—that's a good boy."

So I said it wouldn't be no use to try to play it any longer, and I would just make a clean breast and tell her everything, but she mustn't go back on her promise. Then I told her my father and

mother was dead, and the law had bound me out to a mean old
farmer in the country thirty mile back from the river, and he treated
me so bad I couldn't stand it no longer; he went away to be gone a
couple of days, and so I took my chance and stole some of his
daughter's old clothes, and cleared out, and I had been three nights
coming the thirty miles; I traveled nights, and hid day-times and
slept, and the bag of bread and meat I carried from home lasted me
all the way and I had a plenty. I said I believed my uncle Abner
Moore would take care of me, and so that was why I struck out for
this town of Goshen."

"Goshen, child? This ain't Goshen. This is St. Petersburg.
Goshen's ten mile further up the river. Who told you this was
Goshen?"

"Why, a man I met at day-break this morning, just as I was going
to turn into the woods for my regular sleep. He told me when the
roads forked I must take the right hand, and five mile would fetch
me to Goshen."

"He was drunk I reckon. He told you just exactly wrong."

"Well, he did act like he was drunk, but it ain't no matter now. I
got to be moving along. I'll fetch Goshen before day-light."

"Hold on a minute. I'll put you up a snack to eat. You might want
it."

So she put me up a snack, and says:

"Say—when a cow's laying down, which end of her gets up first?
Answer up prompt, now—don't stop to study over it. Which end
gets up first?"

"The hind end, mum."

"Well, then, a horse?"

"The for'rard end, mum."

"Which side of a tree does the most moss grow on?"

"North side."

"If fifteen cows is browsing on a hillside, how many of them eats
with their heads pointed the same direction?"

"The whole fifteen, mum."

"Well, I reckon you *have* lived in the country. I thought maybe
you was trying to hocus me again. What's your real name, now?"

"George Peters, mum."

"Well, try to remember it, George. Don't forget and tell me it's
Elexander before you go, and then get out by saying it's George-
Elexander when I catch you. And don't go about women in that old
calico. You do a girl tolerable poor, but you might fool men, maybe.
Bless you, child, when you set out to thread a needle, don't hold the
thread still and fetch the needle up to it; hold the needle still and
poke the thread at it—that's the way a woman most always does;
but a man always does 'tother way. And when you throw at a rat or
anything, hitch yourself up a tip-toe, and fetch your hand up over
your head as awkard as you can, and miss your rat about six or

seven foot. Throw stiff-armed from the shoulder, like there was a
pivot there for it to turn on—like a girl; not from the wrist and
elbow, with your arm out to one side, like a boy. And mind you,
when a girl tries to catch anything in her lap, she throws her knees
apart; she don't clap them together, the way you did when you
catched you catched the lump of lead. Why, I spotted you for a boy
when you was threading the needle; and I contrived the other things
just to make certain. Now trot along to your uncle, Sarah Mary
Williams George Elexander Peters, and if you get into trouble you
send word to Mrs. Judith Loftus, which is me, and I'll do what I can
to get you out of it. Keep the river road, all the way, and next time
you tramp, take shoes and socks with you. The river road's a rocky
one, and your feet 'll be in a condition when you get to Goshen, I
reckon."

I went up the bank about fifty yards, and then I doubled on my
tracks and slipped back to where my canoe was, a good piece below
the house. I jumped in and was off in a hurry. I went up stream far
enough to make the head of the island, and then started across.
I took off the sun-bonnet, for I didn't want no blinders on, then.
When I was about the middle, I hear the clock begin to strike; so
I stops and listens; the sound come faint over the water, but clear—
eleven. When I struck the head of the island I never waited to blow,
though I was most winded, but I shoved right into the timber where
my old camp used to be, and started a good fire there on a high-and-
dry spot.

Then I jumped in the canoe and dug out for our place a mile and a
half below, as hard as I could go. I landed, and slopped through the
timber and up the ridge and into the cavern. There Jim laid, sound
asleep on the ground. I roused him out and says:

"Git up and hump yourself, Jim! There ain't a minute to lose.
They're after us!"

Jim never asked no questions, he never said a word; but the way he
worked for the next half an hour showed about how he was scared.
By that time everything we had in the world was on our raft and she
was ready to be shoved out from the willow cove where she was hid.
We put out the camp fire at the cavern the first thing, and didn't
show a candle outside after that.

I took the canoe out from shore a little piece and took a look, but
if there was a boat around I couldn't see it, for stars and shadows
ain't good to see by. Then we got out the raft and slipped along down
in the shade, past the foot of the island dead still, never saying a
word.

CHAPTER XII

It must a been close onto one o'clock when we got below the
island at last, and the raft did seem to go mighty slow. If a boat

was to come along, we was going to take to the canoe and break for
the Illinois shore; and it was well a boat didn't come, for we hadn't
ever thought to put the gun into the canoe, or a fishing-line or
anything to eat. We was in ruther too much of a sweat to think of so
many things. It warn't good judgment to put *everything* on the raft.

If the men went to the island, I just expect they found the camp
fire I built, and watched it all night for Jim to come. Anyways, they
stayed away from us, and if my building the fire never fooled them
it warn't no fault of mine. I played it as low-down on them as I could.

When the first streak of day begun to show, we tied up to a
tow-head in a big bend on the Illinois side, and hacked off cotton-
wood branches with the hatchet and covered up the raft with them
so she looked like there had been a cave-in in the bank there. A
tow-head is a sand-bar that has cotton-woods on it as thick as
harrow-teeth.

We had mountains on the Missouri shore and heavy timber on
the Illinois side, and the channel was down the Missouri shore at
that place, so we warn't afraid of anybody running across us. We
laid there all day and watched the rafts and steamboats spin down
the Missouri shore, and up-bound steamboats fight the big river
in the middle. I told Jim all about the time I had jabbering with that
woman; and Jim said she was a smart one, and if she was to start
after us herself *she* wouldn't set down and watch a camp fire—no,
sir, she'd fetch a dog. Well, then, I said, why couldn't she tell her
husband to fetch a dog? Jim said he bet she did think of it by the
time the men was ready to start, and he believed they must a gone
up town to get a dog and so they lost all that time, or else we
wouldn't be here on a tow-head sixteen or seventeen mile below the
village—no, indeedy, we would be in that same old town again. So
I said I didn't care what was the reason they didn't get us, as long as
they didn't.

When it was beginning to come on dark, we poked our heads
out of the cottonwood thicket and looked up, and down, and across;
nothing in sight; so Jim took up some of the top planks of the raft
and built a snug wigwam to get under in blazing weather and rainy,
and to keep the things dry. Jim made a floor for the wigwam, and
raised it a foot or more above the level of the raft, so now the
blankets and all the traps was out of the reach of steamboat waves.
Right in the middle of the wigwam we made a layer of dirt about
five or six inches deep with a frame around it for to hold it to its
place; this was to build a fire on in sloppy weather or chilly; the
wigwam would keep it from being seen. We made an extra steering
oar, too, because one of the others might get broke, on a snag or
something. We fixed up a short forked stick to hang the old lantern
on; because we must always light the lantern whenever we see a
steamboat coming down stream, to keep from getting run over;
but we wouldn't have to light it for upstream boats unless we see

we was in what they call a "crossing;" for the river was pretty high
yet, very low banks being still a little under water; so up-bound
boats didn't always run the channel, but hunted easy water.

This second night we run between seven and eight hours, with a
current that was making over four mile an hour. We catched fish,
and talked, and we took a swim now and then to keep off sleepiness.
It was kind of solemn, drifting down the big still river, laying on our
backs looking up at the stars, and we didn't ever feel like talking
loud, and it warn't often that we laughed, only a little kind of low
chuckle. We had mighty good weather, as a general thing, and
nothing ever happened to us at all, that night, nor the next, nor the
next.

Every night we passed towns, some of them away up on black
hillsides, nothing but just a shiny bed of lights, not a house could
you see. The fifth night we passed St. Louis, and it was like the
whole world lit up. In St. Petersburg they used to say there was
twenty or thirty thousand people in St. Louis, but I never believed
it till I see that wonderful spread of lights at two o'clock that still
night. There warn't a sound there; everybody was asleep.

Every night, now, I used to slip ashore, towards ten o'clock, at
some little village, and buy ten or fifteen cents' worth of meal or
bacon or other stuff to eat; and sometimes I lifted a chicken that
warn't roosting comfortable, and took him along. Pap always said,
take a chicken when you get a chance, because if you don't want
him yourself you can easy find somebody that does, and a good deed
ain't ever forgot. I never see pap when he didn't want the chicken
himself, but that is what he used to say, anyway.

Mornings, before daylight, I slipped into corn fields and borrowed
a watermelon, or a mush-melon, or a punkin, or some new corn, or
things of that kind. Pap always said it warn't no harm to borrow
things, if you was meaning to pay them back, sometime; but the
widow said it warn't anything but a soft name for stealing, and no
decent body would do it. Jim said he reckoned the widow was partly
right and pap was partly right; so the best way would be for us to
pick out two or three things from the list and say we wouldn't borrow
them anymore—then he reckoned it wouldn't be no harm to borrow
the others. So we talked it over all one night, drifting along down the
river, trying to make up our minds whether to drop the watermelons,
or the cantelopes, or the mushmelons, or what. But towards daylight
we got it all settled satisfactory, and concluded to drop crabapples
and p'simmons. We warn't feeling just right, before that, but it was
all comfortable now. I was glad the way it come out, too, because
crabapples ain't ever good, and the p'simmons wouldn't be ripe for
two or three months yet.

We shot a water-fowl, now and then, that got up too early in the
morning or didn't go to bed early enough in the evening. Take it
all around, we lived pretty high.

The fifth night below St. Louis we had a big storm after midnight,
with a power of thunder and lightning, and the rain poured down
in a solid sheet. We stayed in the wigwam and let the raft take care
of itself. When the lightning glared out we could see a big straight
river ahead, and high rocky bluffs on both sides. By-and-by says I,
"Hel-*lo,* Jim, looky yonder!" It was a steamboat that had killed
herself on a rock. We was drifting straight down for her. The
lightning showed her very distinct. She was leaning over, with part
of her upper deck above water, and you could see every little
chimbly-guy clean and clear, and a chair by the big bell, with an old
slouch hat hanging on the back of it when the flashes come.

Well, it being away in the night, and stormy, and all so
mysterious-like, I felt just the way any other boy would a felt when
I see that wreck laying there so mournful and lonesome in the
middle of the river. I wanted to get aboard of her and slink around a
little, and see what there was there. So I says:

"Le's land on her, Jim."

But Jim was dead against it, at first. He says:

"I doan' want to go fool'n 'long er no wrack. We's doin' blame'
well, en we better let blame' well alone, as de good book says. Like
as not dey's a watchman on dat wrack.'

"Watchman your grandmother," I says; "there ain't nothing to
watch but the texas and the pilot-house; and do you reckon
anybody's going to resk his life for a texas and a pilot-house such
a night as this, when it's likely to break up and wash off down the
river any minute?" Jim couldn't say nothing to that, so he didn't
try. "And besides," I says, "we might borrow something worth
having, out of the captain's stateroom. Seegars, *I* bet you—and cost
five cents apiece, solid cash. Steamboat captains is always rich, and
get sixty dollars a month, and *they* don't care a cent what a thing
costs, you know, long as they want it. Stick a candle in your pocket;
I can't rest, Jim, till we give her a rummaging. Do you reckon Tom
Sawyer would ever go by this thing? Not for pie, he wouldn't.
He'd call it an adventure—that's what he'd call it; and he'd land on
that wreck if it was his last act. And wouldn't he throw style into
it?—wouldn't he spread himself, nor nothing? Why, you'd think
it was Christopher C'lumbus discovering Kingdom-Come. I wish
Tom Sawyer *was* here."

Jim he grumbled a little, but give in. He said we mustn't talk any
more than we could help, and then talk mighty low. The lightning
showed us the wreck again, just in time, and we fetched the
starboard derrick, and made fast there.

The deck was high out, here. We went sneaking down the slope
of it to labboard, in the dark, towards the texas, feeling our way slow
with our feet, and spreading our hands out to fend off the guys,
for it was so dark we couldn't see no sign of them. Pretty soon we
struck the forward end of the skylight, and clumb onto it; and the

next step fetched us in front of the captain's door, which was open, and by Jimminy, away down through the texas-hall we see a light! and all in the same second we seem to hear low voices in yonder!

Jim whispered and said he was feeling powerful sick, and told me to come along. I says, all right; and was going to start for the raft; but just then I heard a voice wail out and say:

"Oh, please don't, boys; I swear I won't ever tell!"

Another voice said, pretty loud:

"It's a lie, Jim Turner. You've acted this way before. You always want more'n your share of the truck, and you've always got it, too, because you've swore 't if you didn't you'd tell. But this time you've said it jest one time too many. You're the meanest, treacherousest hound in this country."

By this time Jim was gone for the raft. I was just a-biling with curiosity; and I says to myself, Tom Sawyer wouldn't back out now, and so I won't either; I'm agoing to see what's going on here. So I dropped on my hands and knees, in the little passage, and crept aft in the dark, till there warn't but about one stateroom betwixt me and the cross-hall of the texas. Then, in there I see a man stretched on the floor and tied hand and foot, and two men standing over him, and one of them had a dim lantern in his hand, and the other one had a pistol. This one kept pointing the pistol at the man's head on the floor and saying—

"I'd *like* to! And I orter, too, a mean skunk!"

The man on the floor would shrivel up, and say: "Oh, please don't, Bill—I hain't ever goin' to tell."

And every time he said that, the man with the lantern would laugh, and say:

" 'Deed you *ain't!* You never said no truer thing 'n that, you bet you." And once he said: "Hear him beg! and yit if we hadn't got the best of him and tied him, he'd a killed us both. And what *for?* Jist for noth'n. Jist because we stood on our *rights*—that's what for. But I lay you ain't agoin' to threaten nobody any more, Jim Turner. Put *up* that pistol, Bill."

Bill says:

"I don't want to, Jake Packard. I'm for killin' him—and didn't he kill old Hatfield jist the same way—and don't he deserve it?"

"But I don't *want* him killed, and I've got my reasons for it."

"Bless yo' heart for them words, Jake Packard! I'll never forgit you, long's I live!" says the man on the floor, sort of blubbering.

Packard didn't take no notice of that, but hung up his lantern on a nail, and started towards where I was, there in the dark, and motioned Bill to come. I crawfished as fast as I could, about two yards, but the boat slanted so that I couldn't make very good time; so to keep from getting run over and catched I crawled into a stateroom on the upper side. The man came a-pawing along in the dark, and when Packard got to my stateroom, he says:

"Here—come in here."

And in he come, and Bill after him. But before they got in, I was
up in the upper berth, cornered, and sorry I come. Then they stood
there, with their hands on the ledge of the berth, and talked. I
couldn't see them, but I could tell where they was, by the whisky
they'd been having. I was glad I didn't drink whisky; but it wouldn't
made much difference, anyway, because most of the time they
couldn't a treed me because I didn't breathe. I was too scared.
And besides, a body *couldn't* breathe, and hear such talk. They
talked low and earnest. Bill wanted to kill Turner. He says:

"He's said he'll tell, and he will. If we was to give both our shares
to him *now,* it wouldn't make no difference after the row, and the
way we've served him. Shore's you're born, he'll turn State's
evidence; now you hear *me.* I'm for putting him out of his troubles."

"So'm I," says Packard, very quiet.

"Blame it, I'd sorter begun to think you wasn't. Well, then, that's
all right. Les' go and do it."

"Hold on a minute; I hain't had my say yit. You listen to me.
Shooting's good, but there's quieter ways if the thing's *got* to be
done. But what *I* say, is this; it ain't good sense to go court'n around
after a halter, if you can git at what you're up to in some way that's
jist as good and at the same time don't bring you into no resks.
Ain't that so?"

"You bet it is. But how you goin' to manage it this time?"

"Well, my idea is this: we'll rustle around and gether up whatever
pickins we've overlooked in the staterooms, and shove for shore
and hide the truck. Then we'll wait. Now I say it ain't agoin' to
be more'n two hours befo' this wrack breaks up and washes off
down the river. See? He'll be drownded, and won't have nobody to
blame for it but his own self. I reckon that's a considerble sight
better'n killin' of him. I'm unfavorable to killin' a man as long as
you can git around it; it ain't good sense, it ain't good morals. Ain't
I right?"

"Yes—I reck'n you are. But s'pose she *don't* break up and wash
off?"

"Well, we can wait the two hours, anyway, and see, can't we?"

"All right, then; come along."

So they started, and I lit out, all in a cold sweat, and scrambled
forward. It was dark as pitch there; but I said in a kind of a coarse
whisper, "Jim!" and he answered up, right at my elbow, with a sort
of a moan, and I says:

"Quick, Jim, it ain't no time for fooling around and moaning;
there's a gang of murderers in yonder, and if we don't hunt up their
boat and set her drifting down the river so these fellows can't get
away from the wreck, there's one of 'em going to be in a bad fix.
But if we find their boat we can put *all* of 'em in a bad fix—for the
Sheriff'll get 'em. Quick—hurry! I'll hunt the labboard side, you

hunt the stabboard. You start at the raft, and—"

"Oh, my lordy, lordy! *Raf*? Dey ain' no raf' no mo', she done broke loose en gone!—'en here we is!"

CHAPTER XIII

Well, I catched my breath and most fainted. Shut up on a wreck with such a gang as that! But it warn't no time to be sentimentering. We'd *got* to find that boat, now—had to have it for ourselves. So we went a-quaking and shaking down the stabboard side, and slow work it was, too—seemed a week before we got to the stern. No sign of a boat. Jim said he didn't believe he could go any further—so scared he hadn't hardly any strength left, he said. But I said come on, if we get left on this wreck, we are in a fix, sure. So on we prowled, again. We struck for the stern of the texas, and found it, and then scrabbled along forwards on the skylight, hanging on from shutter to shutter, for the edge of the skylight was in the water. When we got pretty close to the cross-hall door, there was the skiff, sure enough! I could just barely see her. I felt ever so thankful. In another second I would a been aboard of her; but just then the door opened. One of the men stuck his head out, only about a couple of foot from me, and I thought I was gone; but he jerked it in again, and says:

"Heave that blame lantern out o' sight, Bill!"

He flung a bag of something into the boat, and then got in himself, and set down. It was Packard. Then Bill *he* come out and got in. Packard says, in a low voice:

"All ready—shove off!"

I couldn't hardly hang onto the shutters, I was so weak. But Bill says:

"Hold on—'d you go through him?"

"No. Didn't you?"

"No. So he's got his share o' the cash, yet."

"Well, then, come along—no use to take truck and leave money."

"Say—won't he suspicion what we're up to?"

"Maybe he won't. But we got to have it anyway. Come along."

So they got out and went in.

The door slammed to, because it was on the careened side; and in a half second I was in the boat, and Jim come a tumbling after me. I out with my knife and cut the rope, and away we went!

We didn't touch an oar, and we didn't speak nor whisper, nor hardly even breathe. We went gliding swift along, dead silent, past the tip of the paddlebox, and past the stern; then in a second or two more we was a hundred yards below the wreck, and the darkness soaked her up, every last sign of her, and we was safe, and knowed it.

When we was three or four hundred yards down stream, we see

the lantern show like a little spark at the texas door, for a second,
and we knowed by that that the rascals had missed their boat, and
was beginning to understand that they was in just as much trouble,
now, as Jim Turner was.

Then Jim manned the oars, and we took out after our raft. Now
was the first time that I begun to worry about the men—I reckon
I hadn't had time to before. I begun to think how dreadful it was,
even for murderers, to be in such a fix. I says to myself, there ain't
no telling but I might come to be a murderer myself, yet, and then
how would *I* like it? So says I to Jim:

"The first light we see, we'll land a hundred yards below it or
above it, in a place where it's a good hiding-place for you and the
skiff, and then I'll go and fix up some kind of a yarn, and get
somebody to go for that gang and get them out of their scrape, so
they can be hung when their time comes."

But that idea was a failure; for pretty soon it begun to storm
again, and this time worse than ever. The rain poured down, and
never a light showed; everybody in bed, I reckon. We boomed along
down the river, watching for lights and watching for our raft. After
a long time the rain let up, but the clouds staid, and the lightning
kept whimpering, and by-and-by a flash showed us a black thing
ahead, floating, and we made for it.

It was the raft, and mighty glad was we to get aboard of it again.
We seen a light, now, away down to the right, on shore. So I said
I would go for it. The skiff was half full of plunder which that gang
had stole, there on the wreck. We hustled it onto the raft in a pile,
and I told Jim to float along down, and show a light when he judged
he had gone about two mile, and keep it burning till I come; then I
manned my oars and shoved for the light. As I got down towards
it, three or four more showed—up on a hillside. It was a village. I
closed in above the shore-light, and laid on my oars and floated.
As I went by, I see it was a lantern hanging on the jackstaff of a
double-hull ferry-boat. I skimmed around for the watchman,
a-wondering whereabouts he slept; and by-and-by I found him
roosting on the bitts, forward, with his head down between his
knees. I give his shoulder two or three little shoves, and begun to cry.

He stirred up, in a kind of a startlish way; but when he see it was
only me, he took a good gap and stretch, and then he says:

"Hello, what's up? Don't cry, bub. What's the trouble?"

I says:

"Pap, and mam, and sis, and—"

Then I broke down. He says:

"Oh, dang it, now, *don't* take on so, we all has to have our
troubles and this'n 'll come out all right. What's the matter with
'em?"

"They're—they're—are you the watchman of the boat?"

"Yes," he says, kind of pretty-well-satisfied like. "I'm the captain and the owner, and the mate, and the pilot, and watchman, and head deck-hand; and sometimes I'm the freight and passengers. I ain't as rich as old Jim Hornback, and I can't be so blame' generous and good to Tom, Dick and Harry as what he is, and slam around money the way he does; but I've told him a many a time 't I wouldn't trade places with him; for, says I, a sailor's life's the life for me, and I'm derned if *I'd* live two mile out o' town, where there ain't nothing ever goin' on, not for all his spondulicks and as much more on top of it. Says I—"

I broke in and says:

"They're in an awful peck of trouble, and——"

"*Who* is?"

"Why, pap, and mam, and sis, and Miss Hooker; and if you'd take your ferry-boat and go up there——"

"Up where? Where are they?"

"On the wreck."

"What wreck?"

"Why, there ain't but one."

"What, you don't mean the *Walter Scott?*"

"Yes."

"Good land! what are they doin' *there,* for gracious sakes?"

"Well, they didn't go there a-purpose."

"I bet they didn't! Why, great goodness, there ain't no chance for 'em if they don't git off mighty quick! Why, how in the nation did they ever git into such a scrape?"

"Easy enough. Miss Hooker was a-visiting, up there to the town——"

"Yes, Booth's Landing—go on."

"She was a-visiting, there at Booth's Landing, and just in the edge of the evening she started over with her nigger woman in the horse-ferry, to stay all night at her friend's house, Miss What-you-may-call-her, I disremember her name, and they lost their steering-oar, and swung around and went a-floating down, stern-first, about two mile, and saddle-baggsed on the wreck, and the ferry man and the nigger woman and the horses was all lost, but Miss Hooker she made a grab and got aboard the wreck. Well, about an hour after dark, we come along down in our trading-scow, and it was so dark we didn't notice the wreck till we was right on it; and so *we* saddle-baggsed; but all of us was saved but Bill Whipple—and oh, he *was* the best cretur!—I most wish't it had been me, I do."

"My George! It's the beatenest thing I ever struck. And *then* what did you all do."

"Well, we hollered and took on, but it's so wide there, we couldn't make nobody hear. So pap said somebody got to get ashore and get help somehow. I was the only one that could swim, so I made a dash for it, and Miss Hooker she said if I didn't strike help sooner, come here and hunt up her uncle, and he'd fix the thing. I made the land

about a mile below, and been fooling along ever since, trying to get
people to do something, but they said, 'What, in such a night and
such a current? there ain't no sense in it; go for the steam-ferry.'
Now if you'll go, and——"

"By Jackson, I'd *like* to, and blame it I don't know but I will;
but who is the dingnation's agoin' to *pay* for it? Do you reckon your
pap——"

"Why *that's* all right. Miss Hooker she told me, *particular,*
that her uncle Hornback——"

"Great guns! is *he* her uncle? Looky here, you break for that
light over yonder-way, and turn out west when you git there, and
about a quarter of a mile out you'll come to the tavern; tell 'em to
dart you out to Jim Hornback's and he'll foot the bill. And don't
you fool around any, because he'll want to know the news. Tell him
I'll have his niece all safe before he can get to town. Hump yourself,
now; I'm agoing up around the corner here, to roust out my
engineer."

I struck for the light, but as soon as he turned the corner I went
back and got into my skiff and bailed her out and then pulled up
shore in the easy water about six hundred yards, and tucked myself
in among some woodboats; for I couldn't rest easy till I could see the
ferry-boat start. But take it all around, I was feeling ruther
comfortable on accounts of taking all this trouble for that gang,
for not many would a done it. I wished the widow knowed about
it. I judged she would be proud of me for helping these rapscallions,
because rapscallions and dead beats is the kind the widow and
good people takes the most interest in.

Well, before long, here comes the wreck, dim and dusky, sliding
along down! A kind of cold shiver went through me, and then I
struck out for her. She was very deep, and I see in a minute there
warn't much chance for anybody being alive in her. I pulled all
around her and hollered a little, but there wasn't any answer; all
dead still. I felt a little bit heavy-hearted about the gang, but not
much, for I reckoned if they could stand it, I could.

Then here comes the ferry-boat; so I shoved for the middle of the
river on a long down-stream slant; and when I judged I was out of
eye-reach, I laid on my oars, and looked back and see her go and
smell around the wreck for Miss Hooker's remainders, because the
captain would know her uncle Hornback would want them; and
then pretty soon the ferry-boat give it up and went for shore, and I
laid into my work and went a-booming down the river.

It did seem a powerful long time before Jim's light showed up;
and when it did show, it looked like it was a thousand mile off. By
the time I got there the sky was beginning to get a little gray in the
east; so we struck for an island, and hid the raft, and sunk the skiff,
and turned in and slept like dead people.

CHAPTER XIV

By-and-by, when we got up, we turned over the truck the gang had stole off of the wreck, and found boots, and blankets, and clothes, and all sorts of other things, and a lot of books, and a spyglass, and three boxes of seegars. We hadn't ever been this rich before, in neither of our lives. The seegars was prime. We laid off all the afternoon in the woods talking, and me reading the books, and having a general good time. I told Jim all about what happened inside the wreck, and at the ferry-boat; and I said these kinds of things was adventures; but he said he didn't want no more adventures. He said that when I went in the texas and he crawled back to get on the raft and found her gone, he nearly died; because he judged it was all up with *him,* anyway it could be fixed; for if he didn't get saved he would get drownded; and if he did get saved, whoever saved him would send him back home so as to get the reward, and then Miss Watson would sell him South, sure. Well, he was right; he was most always right; he had an uncommon level head, for a nigger.

I read considerable to Jim about kings, and dukes, and earls, and such, and how gaudy they dressed, and how much style they put on, and called each other your majesty, and your grace, and your lordship, and so on, 'stead of mister; and Jim's eyes bugged out, and he was interested. He says:

"I didn' know dey was so many un um. I hain't hearn 'bout none un um, skasely, but ole King Sollermun, onless you counts dem kings dat's in a pack er k'yards. How much do a king git?'

"Get?" I says; "why, they get a thousand dollars a month if they want it; they can have just as much as they want; everything belongs to them."

"*Ain'* dat gay? En what dey got to do, Huck?"

"*They* don't do nothing! Why how you talk. They just set around."

"No—is dat so?"

"Of course it is. They just set around. Except maybe when there's a war; then they go to the war. But other times they just lazy around; or go hawking—just hawking and sp— Sh!—d'you hear a noise?"

We skipped out and looked; but it warn't nothing but the flutter of a steamboat's wheel, away down coming around the point; so we come back.

"Yes," says I, "and other times, when things is dull, they fuss with the parlyment; and if everybody don't go just so he whacks their heads off. But mostly they hang round the harem."

"Roun' de which?"

"Harem."

"What's de harem?"

"The place where he keep his wives. Don't you know about the harem? Solomon had one; he had about a million wives."

"Why, yes, dat's so; I—I'd done forgot it. A harem's a bo'd'n-house, I reck'n. Mos' likely dey has rackety times in de nussery. En I reck'n de wives quarrels considable; en dat 'crease de racket. Yit dey say Sollermun de wises' man dat ever live'. I doan' take no stock in dat. Bekase why: would a wise man want to live in de mids' er sich a blimblammin' all de time? No—'deed he wouldn't. A wise man 'ud take en buil' a biler-factry; en den he could shet *down* de biler-factry when he want to res'."

"Well, but he *was* the wisest man, anyway; because the widow she told me so, her own self."

"I doan k'yer what de widder say, he *warn't* no wise man, nuther. He had some er de dad-fetchedes' ways I ever see. Does you know 'bout dat chile dat he 'uz gwyne to chop in two?"

"Yes, the widow told me all about it."

"*Well*, den! Warn' dat de beatenes' notion in de worl'? You jes' take en look at it a minute. Dah's de stump, dah—dat's one er de women; heah's you—dat's de yuther one; I's Sollermun; en dish-yer dollar bill's de chile. Bofe un you claims it. What does I do? Does I shin aroun' mongs' de neighbors en fine out which un you de bill *do* b'long to, en han' it over to de right one, all safe en soun', de way dat anybody dat had any gumption would? No—I take en whack de bill in *two*, en give half un it to you, en de yuther half to de yuther woman. Dat's de way Sollermun was gwyne to do wid de chile. Now I want to ast you: what's de use er dat half a bill?—can't buy noth'n wid it. En what use is a half a chile? I would'n give a dern for a million un um."

"But hang it, Jim, you've clean missed the point—blame it, you've missed it a thousand mile."

"Who? Me? Go 'long. Doan' talk to *me* 'bout yo' pints. I reck'n I knows sense when I sees it; en dey ain' no sense in sich doin's as dat. De 'spute warn't 'bout a half a chile, de 'spute was 'bout a whole chile; en de man dat think he kin settle a 'spute 'bout a whole chile wid a half a chile, doan' know enough to come in out'n de rain. Doan' talk to me 'bout Sollermun, Huck, I knows him by de back."

"But I tell you you don't get the point."

"Blame de pint! I reck'n I knows what I knows. En mine you, de *real* pint is down furder—it's down deeper. It lays in de way Sollermun was raised. You take a man dat's got on'y one er two chillen; is dat man gwyne to be waseful o' chillen? No, he ain't; he can't 'ford it. *He* know how to value 'em. But you take a man dat's got 'bout five million chillen runnin' roun' de house, en it's diffunt. *He* as soon chop a chile in two as a cat. Dey's plenty mo'. A chile er two, mo' er less, warn't no consekens to Sollermun, dad fetch him!"

I never see such a nigger. If he got a notion in his head once, there warn't no getting it out again. He was the most down on Solomon of

any nigger I ever see. So I went to talking about other kings, and let
Solomon slide. I told about Louis Sixteenth that got his head cut off
in France long time age; and about his little boy the dolphin, that
would a been a king, but they took and shut him up in jail, and some
say he died there.

"Po' little chap."

"But some says he got out and got away, and come to America."

"Dat's good! But he'll be pooty lonesome—dey ain' no kings
here, is dey, Huck?"

"No."

"Den he cain't git no situation. What he gwyne to do?"

"Well, I don't know. Some of them gets on the police, and some
of them learns people how to talk French."

"Why, Huck, doan' de French people talk de same way we does?"

"*No*, Jim; you couldn't understand a word they said—not a
single word."

"Well, now, I be ding-busted! How do dat come?"

"*I* don't know; but it's so. I got some of their jabber out of a book.
Spose a man was to come to you and say *Polly-voo-franzy*—what
would you think?"

"I wouldn' think nuff'n; I'd take en bust him over de head. Dat
is, if he warn't white. I wouldn't 'low no nigger to call me dat."

"Shucks, it ain't calling you anything. It's only saying do you
know how to talk French."

"Well, den, why couldn't he *say* it?"

"Why, he *is* a-saying it. That's a Frenchman's *way* of saying it."

"Well, it's a blame' ridicklous way, en I doan' want to hear no
mo' 'bout it. Dey ain' no sense in it."

"Looky here, Jim; does a cat talk like we do?"

"No, a cat don't."

"Well, does a cow?"

"No, a cow don't, nuther."

"Does a cat talk like a cow, or a cow talk like a cat?"

"No, dey don't."

"It's natural and right for 'em to talk different from each other,
ain't it?"

"Course."

"And ain't it natural and right for a cat and a cow to talk
different from *us?*"

"Why, mos' sholy it is."

"Well, then, why ain't it natural and right for a *Frenchman*
to talk different from us? You answer me that."

"Is a cat a man, Huck?"

"No."

"Well, den, dey ain't no sense in a cat talkin' like a man. Is a
cow a man?—er is a cow a cat?"

"No, she ain't either of them."

"Well, den, she ain' got no business to talk like either one er the yuther of 'em. Is a Frenchman a man?"

"Yes."

"*Well,* den! Dad blame it, why doan' he *talk* like a man? You answer me *dat!*"

I see it warn't no use wasting words—you can't learn a nigger to argue. So I quit.

CHAPTER XV

We judged that three nights more would fetch us to Cairo, at the bottom of Illinois, where the Ohio River comes in, and that was what we was after. We would sell the raft and get on a steamboat and go way up the Ohio amongst the free States, and then be out of trouble.

Well, the second night a fog begun to come on, and we made for a tow-head to tie to, for it wouldn't do to try to run in fog; but when I paddled ahead in the canoe, with the line, to make fast, there warn't anything but little saplings to tie to. I passed the line around one of them right on the edge of the cut bank, but there was a stiff current, and the raft come booming down so lively she tore it out by the roots and away she went. I see the fog closing down, and it made me so sick and scared I couldn't budge for most a half a minute it seemed to me—and then there warn't no raft in sight; you couldn't see twenty yards. I jumped into the canoe and run back to the stern and grabbed the paddle and set her back a stroke. But she didn't come. I was in such a hurry I hadn't untied her. I got up and tried to untie her, but I was so excited my hands shook so I couldn't hardly do anything with them.

As soon as I got started I took out after the raft, hot and heavy, right down the tow-head. That was all right as far as it went, but the tow-head warn't sixty yards long, and the minute I flew by the foot of it I shot out into the solid white fog, and hadn't no more idea which way I was going than a dead man.

Thinks I, it won't do to paddle; first I know I'll run into the bank or a tow-head or something; I got to set still and float, and yet it's mighty fidgety business to have to hold your hands still at such a time. I whooped and listened. Away down there, somewheres, I hears a small whoop, and up comes my spirits. I went tearing after it, listening sharp to hear it again. The next time it come, I see I warn't heading for it but heading away to the right of it. And the next time, I was heading away to the left of it—and not gaining on it much, either, for I was flying around, this way and that and 'tother, but it was going straight ahead all the time.

I did wish the fool would think to beat a tin pan, and beat it all the time, but he never did, and it was the still places between the whoops that was making the trouble for me. Well, I fought along, and directly I hears the whoop *behind* me. I was tangled good, now. That was somebody else's whoop, or else I was turned around.

I throwed the paddle down. I heard the whoop again; it was behind me yet, but in a different place; it kept coming, and kept changing its place, and I kept answering, till by-and-by it was in front of me again and I knowed the current had swung the canoe's head down stream and I was all right, if that was Jim and not some other raftsman hollering. I couldn't tell nothing about voices in a fog; for nothing don't look natural nor sound natural in a fog.

The whooping went on, and in about a minute I come a booming down on a cut bank with smoky ghosts of big trees on it, and the current throwed me off to the left and shot by, amongst a lot of snags that fairly roared, the current was tearing by them so swift.

In another second or two it was solid white and still again. I set perfectly still, then, listening to my heart thump, and I reckon I didn't draw a breath while it thumped a hundred.

I just give up, then. I knowed what the matter was. That cut bank was an island, and Jim had gone down 'tother side of it. It warn't no tow-head, that you could float by in ten minutes. It had the big timber of a regular island; it might be five or six mile long and more than a half a mile wide.

I kept quiet, with my ears cocked, about fifteen minutes, I reckon. I was floating along, of course, four or five mile an hour; but you don't ever think of that. No, you *feel* like you are laying dead still on the water; and if a little glimpse of a snag slips by, you don't think to yourself how fast *you're* going, but you catch your breath and think, my! how that snag's tearing along. If you think it ain't dismal and lonesome out in a fog that way, by yourself, in the night, you try it once—you'll see.

Next, for about a half an hour, I whoops now and then; at last I hears the answer a long ways off, and tries to follow it, but I couldn't do it, and directly I judged I'd got into a nest of tow-heads, for I had little dim glimpses of them on both sides of me, sometimes just a narrow channel between; and some that I couldn't see, I knowed was there, because I'd hear the wash of the current against the old dead brush and trash that hung over the banks. Well, I warn't long losing the whoops, down amongst the tow-heads; and I only tried to chase them a little while, anyway, because it was worse than chasing a Jack-o-lantern. You never knowed a sound dodge around so, and swap places so quick and so much.

I had to claw away from the bank pretty lively, four or five times, to keep from knocking the islands out of the river; and so I judged the raft must be butting into the bank every now and then, or else it would get further ahead and clear out of hearing—it was floating a little faster than what I was.

Well, I seemed to be in the open river again, by-and-by, but I couldn't hear no sign of a whoop nowheres. I reckoned Jim had

fetched up on a snag, maybe, and it was all up with him. I was good
and tired, so I laid down in the canoe and said I wouldn't bother
no more. I didn't want to go to sleep, of course; but I was so sleepy
I couldn't help it; so I thought I would take just one little cat-nap.

But I reckon it was more than a cat-nap, for when I waked up the
stars was shining bright, the fog was all gone, and I was spinning
down a big bend stern first. First I didn't know where I was; I
thought I was dreaming; and when things begun to come back to
me, they seemed to come up dim out of last week.

It was a monstrous big river here, with the tallest and the
thickest kind of timber on both banks; just a solid wall, as well as
I could see, by the stars. I looked away down stream, and seen a
black speck on the water. I took out after it; but when I got to it
it warn't nothing but a couple of saw-logs made fast together. Then
I see another speck, and chased that; then another, and this time
I was right. It was the raft.

When I got to it Jim was setting there with his head down between
his knees, asleep, with his right arm hanging over the steering oar.
The other oar was smashed off, and the raft was littered up with
leaves and branches and dirt. So she'd had a rough time.

I made fast and laid down under Jim's nose on the raft, and
begun to gap, and stretch my fists out against Jim, and says:

"Hello, Jim, have I been asleep? Why didn't you stir me up?"

"Goodness gracious, is dat you, Huck? En you ain' dead—you
ain' drownded—you's back agin? It's too good for true, honey, it's
too good for true. Lemme look at you, chile, lemme feel o' you. No,
you ain' dead! you's back agin,' live en soun', jis de same old Huck—
de same ole Huck, thanks to goodness!"

"What's the matter with you, Jim? You been a drinking?"

"Drinkin'? Has I ben a drinkin'? Has I had a chance to be a
drinkin'?"

"Well, then, what makes you talk so wild?"

"How does I talk wild?"

"*How?* why, hain't you been talking about my coming back, and
all that stuff, as if I'd been gone away?"

"Huck—Huck Finn, you look me in de eye; look me in de eye.
Hain't you ben gone away?"

"Gone away? Why, what in the nation do you mean? *I* hain't
been gone anywheres. Where would I go to?"

"Well, looky here, boss, dey's sumf'n wrong, dey is. Is I *me,* or
who *is* I? Is I heah, or whah *is* I? Now dat's what I wants to know?"

"Well, I think you're here, plain enough, but I think you're a
tangle-headed old fool, Jim."

"I is, is I? Well you answer me dis. Didn't you tote out de line in
de canoe, fer to make fas' to de tow-head?"

"No, I didn't. What tow-head? I hain't seen no tow-head."

"You hain't seen no tow-head? Looky here—didn't de line pull

loose en de raf' go a hummin' down de river, en leave you en de
canoe behine in de fog?"

"What fog?"

"Why *de* fog. De fog dat's ben aroun' all night. En didn't you
whoop, en didn't I whoop, tell we got mix' up in de islands en one un
us got los' en 'tother one was jis' as good as los', 'kase he didn'
know whah he wuz? En didn't I bust up agin a lot er dem islands
en have a turrible time en mos' git drownded? Now ain' dat so,
boss—ain't it so? You answer me dat."

"Well, this is too many for me, Jim. I hain't seen no fog, nor no
islands, nor no troubles, nor nothing. I been setting here talking
with you all night till you went to sleep about ten minutes ago, and
I reckon I done the same. You couldn't a got drunk in that time,
so of course you've been dreaming."

"Dad fetch it, how is I gwyne to dream all dat in ten minutes?"

"Well, hang it all, you did dream it, because there didn't any
of it happen."

"But Huck, it's all jis' as plain to me as——"

"It don't make no difference how plain it is, there ain't nothing
in it. I know, because I've been here all the time."

Jim didn't say nothing for about five minutes, but set there
studying over it. Then he says:

"Well, den, I reck'n I did dream it, Huck; but dog my cats ef
it ain't de powerfullest dream I ever see. En I hain't ever had no
dream b'fo' dat's tired me like dis one."

"Oh, well, that's all right, because a dream does tire a body like
everything, sometimes. But this one was a staving dream—tell me
all about it, Jim."

So Jim went to work and told me the whole thing right through,
just as it happened, only he painted it up considerable. Then he said
he must start in and " 'terpret" it, because it was sent for a warning.
He said the first tow-head stood for a man that would try to do
us some good, but the current was another man that would get us
away from him. The whoops was warnings that would come to us
every now and then, and if we didn't try hard to make out to
understand them they'd just take us into bad luck, 'stead of keeping
us out of it. The lot of tow-heads was troubles we was going to get
into with quarrelsome people and all kinds of mean folks, but if
we minded our business and didn't talk back and aggravate them,
we would pull through and get out of the fog and into the big clear
river, which was the free States, and wouldn't have no more trouble.

It had clouded up pretty dark just after I got onto the raft, but it
was clearing up again, now.

"Oh, well, that's all interpreted well enough, as far as it goes,
Jim," I says; "but what does *these* things stand for?"

It was the leaves and rubbish on the raft, and the smashed oar.
You could see them first rate, now.

Jim looked at the trash, and then looked at me, and back at the trash again. He had got the dream fixed so strong in his head that he couldn't seem to shake it loose and get the facts back into its place again, right away. But when he did get the thing straightened around, he looked at me steady, without ever smiling, and says:

"What do dey stan' for? I's gwyne to tell you. When I got all wore out wid work, en wid de callin' for you, en went to sleep, my heart wuz mos' broke bekase you wuz los', en I didn' k'yer no mo' what become er me en de raf'. En when I wake up en fine you back agin', all safe en soun', de tears come en I could a got down on my knees en kiss' yo' foot I's so thankful. En all you wuz thinkin 'bout wuz how you could make a fool uv old Jim wid a lie. Dat truck dah is *trash;* en trash is what people is dat puts dirt on de head er dey fren's en makes 'em ashamed."

Then he got up slow, and walked to the wigwam, and went in there, without saying anything but that. But that was enough. It made me feel so mean I could almost kissed *his* foot to get him to take it back.

It was fifteen minutes before I could work myself up to go and humble myself to a nigger—but I done it, and I warn't ever sorry for it afterwards, neither. I didn't do him no more mean tricks, and I wouldn't done that one if I'd a knowed it would make him feel that way.

CHAPTER XVI

We slept most all day, and started out at night, a little ways behind a monstrous long raft that was as long going by as a procession. She had four long sweeps at each end, so we judged she carried as many as thirty men, likely. She had five big wig-wams aboard, wide apart, and an open camp fire in the middle, and a tall flag-pole at each end. There was a power of style about her. It *amounted* to something being a raftsman on such a craft as that.

We went drifting down into a big bend, and the night clouded up and got hot. The river was very wide, and was walled with solid timber on both sides; you couldn't see a break in it hardly ever, or a light. We talked about Cairo, and wondered whether we would know it when we got to it. I said likely we wouldn't, because I had heard say there warn't but about a dozen houses there, and if they didn't happen to have them lit up, how was we going to know we was passing a town? Jim said if the two big rivers joined together there, that would show. But I said maybe we might think we was passing the foot of an island and coming into the same old river again. That disturbed Jim—and me too. So the question was, what to do? I said, paddle ashore the first time a light showed, and tell them pap was behind, coming along with a trading-scow, and was a green hand at the business, and wanted to know how far it was to

Cairo. Jim thought it was a good idea, so we took a smoke on it and waited.

There warn't nothing to do, now, but to look out sharp for the town, and not pass it without seeing it. He said he'd be mighty sure to see it, because he'd be a free man the minute he seen it, but if he missed it he'd be in the slave country again and no more show for freedom. Every little while he jumps up and says:

"Dah she is!"

But it warn't. It was Jack-o-lanterns, or lightning-bugs; so he set down again, and went to watching, same as before. Jim said it made him all over trembly and feverish to be so close to freedom. Well, I can tell you it made me all over trembly and feverish, too, to hear him, because I begun to get it through my head that he *was* most free—and who was to blame for it? Why, *me*. I couldn't get that out of my conscience, no how nor no way. It got to troubling me so I couldn't rest; I couldn't stay still in one place. It hadn't ever come home to me before, what this thing was that I was doing. But now it did; and it staid with me, and scorched me more and more. I tried to make out to myself that *I* warn't to blame, because *I* didn't run Jim off from his rightful owner; but it warn't no use, conscience up and says, every time, "But you knowed he was running for his freedom, and you could a paddled ashore and told somebody." That was so—I couldn't get around that, noway. That was where it pinched. Conscience says to me, "What had poor Miss Watson done to you, that you could see her nigger go off right under your eyes and never say one single word? What did that poor old woman do to you, that you could treat her so mean? Why, she tried to learn you your book, she tried to learn you your manners, she tried to be good to you every way she knowed how. *That's* what she done."

I got to feeling so mean and so miserable I most wished I was dead. I fidgeted up and down the raft, abusing myself to myself, and Jim was fidgeting up and down past me. We neither of us could keep still. Every time he danced around and says, "Dah's Cairo!" it went through me like a shot, and I thought if it *was* Cairo I reckoned I would die of miserableness.

Jim talked out loud all the time while I was talking to myself. He was saying how the first thing he would do when he got to a free State he would go to saving up money and never spend a single cent, and when he got enough he would buy his wife, which was owned on a farm close to where Miss Watson lived; and then they would both work to buy the two children, and if their master wouldn't sell them, they'd get an Ab'litionist to go and steal them.

It most froze me to hear such talk. He wouldn't ever dared to talk such talk in his life before. Just see what a difference it made in him the minute he judged he was about free. It was according to the old saying, "give a nigger an inch and he'll take an ell." Thinks I, this is what comes of my not thinking. Here was this nigger which I had

as good as helped to run away, coming right out flat-footed and
saying he would steal his children—children that belonged to a man
I didn't even know; a man that hadn't ever done me no harm.

I was sorry to hear Jim say that, it was such a lowering of him.
My conscience got to stirring me up hotter than ever, until at last
I says to it, "Let up on me—it ain't too late, yet—I'll paddle ashore
at the first light, and tell." I felt easy, and happy, and light as a
feather, right off. All my troubles was gone. I went to looking out
sharp for a light, and sort of singing to myself. By-and-by one
showed. Jim sings out:

"We's safe, Huck, we's safe! Jump up and crack yo' heels, dat's
de good ole Cairo at las', I jis knows it!"

I says:

"I'll take the canoe and go see, Jim. It mightn't be, you know."

He jumped and got the canoe ready, and put his old coat in the
bottom for me to set on, and give me the paddle; and as I shoved
off, he says:

"Pooty soon I'll be a-shout'n for joy, en I'll say, it's all on accounts
o' Huck; I's a free man, en I couldn't ever ben free ef it hadn' ben
for Huck; Huck done it. Jim won't ever forget you, Huck; you's
de bes' fren' Jim's ever had; en you's de *only* fren' ole Jim's got
now."

I was paddling off, all in a sweat to tell on him; but when he says
this, it seemed to kind of take the tuck all out of me. I went along
slow then, and I warn't right down certain whether I was glad I
started or whether I warn't. When I was fifty yards off, Jim says:

"Dah you goes, de ole true Huck; de on'y white genlman dat
ever kep' his promise to ole Jim."

Well, I just felt sick. But I says, I *got* to do it—I can't get *out*
of it. Right then, along comes a skiff with two men in it, with guns,
and they stopped and I stopped. One of them says:

"What's that, yonder?"

"A piece of a raft," I says.

"Do you belong on it?"

"Yes, sir."

"Any men on it?"

"Only one, sir."

"Well, there's five niggers run off to-night, up yonder above the
head of the bend. Is your man white or black?"

I didn't answer up prompt. I tried to, but the words wouldn't
come. I tried, for a second or two, to brace up and out with it, but I
warn't man enough—hadn't the spunk of a rabbit. I see I was
weakening; so I just give up trying, and up and says—

"He's white."

"I reckon we'll go and see for ourselves."

"I wish you would," says I, "because it's pap that's there, and
maybe you'd help me tow the raft ashore where the light is. He's

sick—and so is mam and Mary Ann."

"Oh, the devil! we're in a hurry, boy. But I s'pose we've got to.
Come—buckle to you paddle, and let's get along."

I buckled to my paddle and they laid to their oars. When we had
made a stroke or two, I says:

"Pap'll be mighty much obleeged to you, I can tell you. Everybody
goes away when I want them to help me tow the raft ashore, and I
can't do it by myself."

"Well, that's infernal mean. Odd, too. Say, boy, what's the matter
with your father?"

"It's the—a—the—well, it ain't anything, much."

They stopped pulling. It warn't but a mighty little ways to the raft
now. One says:

"Boy, that's a lie. What *is* the matter with your pap? Answer up
square now, and it'll be the better for you."

"I will, sir, I will, honest—but don't leave us, please. It's the—
the—gentlemen, if you'll only pull ahead, and let me heave you the
head-line, you won't have to come a-near the raft—please do."

"Set her back, John, set her back!" says one. They backed water.
"Keep away, boy—keep to looard. Confound it, I just expect the
wind has blowed it to us. Your pap's got the small-pox, and you
know it precious well. Why didn't you come out and say so? Do you
want to spread it all over?"

"Well," says I, a-blubbering, "I've told everybody before, and
then they just went away and left us."

"Poor devil, there's something in that. We are right down sorry
for you, but we—well, hang it, we don't want the small-pox, you see.
Look here, I'll tell you what to do. Don't you try to land by yourself,
or you'll smash everything to pieces. You float along down about
twenty miles and you'll come to a town on the left-hand side of the
river. It will be long after sun-up, then, and when you ask for help,
you tell them your folks are all down with chills and fever. Don't
be a fool again, and let people guess what is the matter. Now we're
trying to do you a kindness; so you just put twenty miles between us,
that's a good boy. It wouldn't do any good to land yonder where
the light is—it's only a wood-yard. Say—I reckon your father's
poor, and I'm bound to say he's in pretty hard luck. Here—I'll put
a twenty dollar gold piece on this board, and you get it when it
floats by. I feel mighty mean to leave you, but my kingdom! it won't
do to fool with small-pox, don't you see?"

"Hold on, Parker," says the other man, "here's a twenty to put
on the board for me. Good-bye, boy, you do as Mr. Parker told you,
and you'll be all right."

"That's so, my boy—good-bye, good-bye. If you see any runaway
niggers, you get help and nab them, and you can make some money
by it."

"Good-bye, sir," says I, "I won't let no runaway niggers get by me if I can help it."

They went off, and I got aboard the raft, feeling bad and low,
because I knowed very well I had done wrong, and I see it warn't
no use for me to try to learn to do right; a body that don't get *started*
right when he's little, ain't got no show—when the pinch comes
there ain't nothing to back him up and keep him to his work, and so
he gets beat. Then I thought a minute, and says to myself, hold on,—
s'pose you'd a done right and give Jim up; would you felt better than
what you do now? No, says I, I'd feel bad—I'd feel just the same
way I do now. Well, then, says I, what's the use you learning to do
right, when it's troublesome to do right and ain't no trouble to do
wrong, and the wages is just the same? I was stuck. I couldn't
answer that. So I reckoned I wouldn't bother no more about it, but
after this always do whichever come handiest at the time.

I went into the wigwam; Jim warn't there. I looked all around;
he warn't anywhere. I says:

"Jim!"

"Here I is, Huck. Is dey out o' sight yit? Don't talk loud."

He was in the river, under the stern oar, with just his nose out.
I told him they was out of sight, so he come aboard. He says:

"I was a-listenin' to all de talk, en I slips into de river en was
gwyne to shove for sho' if dey come aboard. Den I was gwyne to
swim to de raf' agin when dey was gone. But lawsy, how you did
fool 'em, Huck! Dat *wuz* de smartes' dodge! I tell you, chile, I
'speck it save' ole Jim—ole Jim ain't gwyne to forgit you for dat,
honey."

Then we talked about the money. It was a pretty good raise,
twenty dollars apiece. Jim said we could take deck passage on a
steamboat now, and the money would last us as far as we wanted
to go in the free States. He said twenty mile more warn't far for the
raft to go, but he wished we was already there.

Towards daybreak we tied up, and Jim was mighty particular
about hiding the raft good. Then he worked all day fixing things
in bundles, and getting all ready to quit rafting.

That night about ten we hove in sight of the lights of a town away
down in a left-hand bend.

I went off in the canoe, to ask about it. Pretty soon I found a
man out in the river with a skiff, setting a trot-line. I ranged up and
says:

"Mister, is that town Cairo?"

"Cairo? no. You must be a blame' fool."

"What town is it, mister?"

"If you want to know, go and find out. If you stay here botherin'
around me for about a half a minute longer, you'll get something you
won't want."

I paddled to the raft. Jim was awful disappointed, but I said
never mind, Cairo would be the next place, I reckoned.

We passed another town before daylight, and I was going out
again; but it was high ground, so I didn't go. No high ground about
Cairo, Jim said. I had forgot it. We laid up for the day, on a
tow-head tolerable close to the left-hand bank. I begun to
suspicion something. So did Jim. I says:

"Maybe we went by Cairo in the fog that night."

He says:

"Doan' less' talk about it, Huck. Po' niggers can't have no luck.
I awluz 'spected dat rattle-snake skin warn't done wid it's work."

"I wish I'd never seen that snake-skin, Jim—I do wish I'd never
laid eyes on it."

"It ain't yo' fault, Huck; you didn' know. Don't you blame
yo'self 'bout it."

When it was daylight, here was the clear Ohio water in shore, sure
enough, and outside was the old regular Muddy! So it was all up
with Cairo.

We talked it all over. It wouldn't do to take to the shore; we
couldn't take the raft up the stream, of course. There warn't no way
but to wait for dark, and start back in the canoe and take the
chances. So we slept all day amongst the cotton-wood thicket, so
as to be fresh for the work, and when we went back to the raft
about dark the canoe was gone!

We didn't say a word for a good while. There warn't anything to
say. We both knowed well enough it was some more work of the
rattle-snake skin; so what was the use to talk about it? It would only
look like we was finding fault, and that would be bound to fetch
more bad luck—and keep on fetching it, too, till we knowed enough
to keep still.

By-and-by we talked about what we better do, and found there
warn't no way but just to go along down with the raft till we got a
chance to buy a canoe to go back in. We warn't going to borrow
it when there warn't anybody around, the way pap would do, for that
might set people after us.

So we shoved out, after dark, on the raft.

Anybody that don't believe yet, that it's foolishness to handle a
snake-skin, after all that snake-skin done for us, will believe it now,
if they read on and see what more it done for us.

The place to buy canoes is off of rafts laying up at shore. But we
didn't see no rafts laying up; so we went along during three hours
and more. Well, the night got gray, and ruther thick, which is the
next meanest thing to fog. You can't tell the shape of the river, and
you can't see no distance. It got to be very late and still, and then
along comes a steamboat up the river. We lit the lantern, and
judged she would see it. Up-stream boats didn't generly come close
to us; they go out and follow the bars and hunt for easy water under
the reefs; but nights like this they bull right up the channel against
the whole river.

We could hear her pounding along, but we didn't see her good till she was close. She aimed right for us. Often they do that and try to see how close they can come without touching; sometimes the wheel bites off a sweep, and then the pilot sticks his head out and laughs, and thinks he's mighty smart. Well, here she comes, and we said she was goi g to try to shave us; but she didn't seem to be sheering off a bit She was a big one, and she was coming in a hurry, too, looking like a black cloud with rows of glow-worms around it; but all of a sudden she bulged out, big and scary, with a long row of wide-open furnace doors shining like red-hot teeth, and her monstrous bows and guards hanging right over us. There was a yell at us, and a jingling of bells to stop the engines, a pow-wow of cussing, and whistling of steam—and as Jim went overboard on one side and I on the other, she come smashing straight through the raft.

I dived—and I aimed to find the bottom, too, for a thirty-foot wheel had got to go over me, and I wanted it to have plenty of room. I could always stay under water a minute; this time I reckon I staid under water a minute and a half. Then I bounced for the top in a hurry, for I was nearly busting. I popped out to my arm-pits and blowed the water out of my nose, and puffed a bit. Of course there was a booming current; and of course that boat started her engines again ten seconds after she stopped them, for they never cared much for raftsmen; so now whe was churning along up the river, out of sight in the thick weather, though I could hear her.

I sung out for Jim about a dozen times, but I didn't get any answer; so I grabbed a plank that touched me while I was "treadin water," and struck out for shore, shoving it ahead of me. But I made out to see that the drift of the current was towards the left-hand shore, which meant that I was in a crossing; so I changed off and went that way.

It was one of these long, slanting, two-mile crossings; so I was a good long time in getting over. I made a safe landing, and clum up the bank. I couldn't see but a little ways, but I went poking along over rough ground for a quarter of a mile or more, and then I run across a big old-fashioned double log house before I noticed it. I was going to rush by and get away, but a lot of dogs jumped out and went to howling and barking at me, and I knowed better than to move another peg.

CHAPTER XVII

In about half a minute somebody spoke out of a window, without putting his head out, and says:

"Be done, boys! Who's there?"

I says:

"It's me."

"Who's me?"

"George Jackson, sir."

"What do you want?"

"I don't want nothing, sir. I only want to go along by, but the dogs won't let me."

"What are you prowling around here this time of night, for—hey?"

"I warn't prowling around, sir; I fell overboard off of the steamboat."

"Oh, you did, did you? Strike a light there, somebody. What did you say your name was?"

"George Jackson, sir. I'm only a boy."

"Look here; if you're telling the truth, you needn't be afraid—nobody'll hurt you. But don't try to budge; stand right where you are. Rouse out Bob and Tom, some of you, and fetch the guns. George Jackson, is there anybody with you?"

"No, sir, nobody."

I heard the people stirring around in the house, now, and see a light. The man sung out:

"Snatch that light away, Betsy, you old fool—ain't you got any sense? Put it on the floor behind the front door. Bob, if you and Tom are ready, take your places."

"All ready."

"Now, George Jackson, do you know the Shepherdsons?"

"No, sir—I never heard of them."

"Well, that may be so, and it mayn't. Now, all ready. Step forward, George Jackson. And mind, don't you hurry—come mighty slow. If there's anybody with you, let him keep back—if the shows himself he'll be shot. Come along, now. Come slow; push the door open, yourself—just enough to squeeze in, d' you hear?"

I didn't hurry, I couldn't if I'd a wanted to. I took one slow step at a time, and there warn't a sound, only I thought I could hear my heart. The dogs were as still as the humans, but they followed a little behind me. When I got to the three log door-steps, I heard them unlocking and unbarring and unbolting. I put my hand on the door and pushed it a little and a little more, till somebody said, "There, that's enough—put your head in." I done.it, but I judged they would take it off.

The candle was on the floor, and there they all was, looking at me, and me at them, for about a quarter of a minute. Three big men with guns pointed at me, which made me wince, I tell you; the oldest, gray and about sixty, the other two thirty or more—all of them fine and handsome—and the sweetest old gray-headed lady, and back of her two young women which I couldn't see right well. The old gentleman says:

"There—I reckon it's all right. Come in."

As soon as I was in, the old gentleman he locked the door and barred it and bolted it, and told the young men to come in with

their guns, and they all went in a big parlor that had a new rag
carpet on the floor, and got together in a corner that was out of
range of the front windows—there warn't none on the side. They
held the candle, and took a good look at me, and all said, "Why
he ain't a Shepherdson—no, there ain't any Shepherdson about
him." Then the old man said he hoped I wouldn't mind being
searched for arms, because he didn't mean no harm by it—it was
only to make sure. So he didn't pry into my pockets, but only felt
outside with his hands, and said it was all right. He told me to
make myself easy and at home, and tell all about myself; but the
old lady says:

"Why bless you, Saul, the poor thing's as wet as he can be; and
don't you reckon it may be he's hungry?"

"True for you, Rachel—I forgot."

So the old lady says:

"Betsy" (this was a nigger woman), "you fly around and get him
something to eat, as quick as you can, poor thing; and one of you
girls go and wake up Buck and tell him— Oh, here he is himself.
Buck, take this little stranger and get the wet clothes off from him
and dress him up in some of yours that's dry."

Buck looked about as old as me—thirteen or fourteen or along
there, though he was a little bigger than me. He hadn't on anything
but a shirt, and he was very frowsy-headed. He come in gaping and
digging one fist into his eyes, and he was dragging a gun along
with the other one. He says:

"Ain't they no Shepherdsons around?"

They said, no, 'twas a false alarm.

"Well," he says, "if they'd a ben some, I reckon I'd a got one."

They all laughed, and Bob says:

"Why, Buck, they might have scalped us all, you've been so slow
in coming."

"Well, nobody come after me, and it ain't right. I'm always kep'
down; I don't get no show."

"Never mind, Buck, my boy," says the old man, "you'll have
show enough, all in good time, don't you fret about that. Go 'long
with you now, and do as your mother told you."

When we got up stairs to his room, he got me a coarse shirt and
a round-about and pants of his, and I put them on. While I was at
it he asked me what my name was, but before I could tell him, he
started to telling me about a blue jay and a young rabbit he had
catched in the woods day before yesterday, and he asked me where
Moses was when the candle went out. I said I didn't know; I hadn't
heard about it before, no way.

"Well, guess," he says.

"How'm I going to guess," says I, "when I never heard tell about
it before?"

"But you can guess, can't you? It's just as easy."

"*Which* candle?" I says.

"Why, any candle," he says.

"I don't know where he was," says I; "where was he?"

"Why he was in the *dark!* That's where he was!"

"Well, if you knowed where he was, what did you ask me for?"

"Why, blame it, it's a riddle, don't you see? Say, how long are you going to stay here? You got to stay always. We can just have booming times—they don't have no school now. Do you own a dog? I've got a dog—and he'll go in the river and bring out chips that you throw in. Do you like to comb up, Sundays, and all that kind of foolishness? You bet I don't, but ma she makes me. Confound these ole britches, I reckon I'd better put 'em on, but I'd ruther not, it's so warm. Are you all ready? All right—come along, old hoss."

Cold corn-pone, cold corn-beef, butter and butter-milk—that is what they had for me down there, and there ain't nothing better that ever I've come across yet. Buck and his ma and all of them smoked cob pipes, except the nigger woman, which was gone, and the two young women. They all smoked and talked, and I eat and talked. The young women had quilts around them, and their hair down their backs. They all asked me questions, and I told them how pap and me and all the family was living on a little farm down at the bottom of Arkansaw, and my sister Mary Ann run off and got married and never was heard of no more, and Bill went to hunt them and he warn't heard of no more, and Tom and Mort died, and then there warn't nobody but just me and pap left, and he was just trimmed down to nothing, on account of his troubles; so when he died I took what there was left, because the farm didn't belong to us, and started up the river, deck passage, and fell overboard; and that was how I come to be here. So they said I could have a home there as long as I wanted it. Then it was most daylight, and everybody went to bed, and I went to bed with Buck, and when I waked up in the morning, drat it all, I had forgot what my name was. So I laid there about an hour trying to think, and when Buck waked up, I says:

"Can you spell, Buck?"

"Yes," he says.

"I bet you can't spell my name," says I.

"I bet you what you dare I can," says he.

"All right," says I, "go ahead."

"G-o-r-g-e J-a-x-o-n—there now," he says.

"Well," says I, "you done it, but I didn't think you could. It ain't no slouch of a name to spell—right off without studying."

I set it down, private, because somebody might want *me* to spell it, next, and so I wanted to be handy with it and rattle it off like I was used to it.

It was a mighty nice family, and a mighty nice house, too. I hadn't seen no house out in the country before that was so nice and had so much style. It didn't have an iron latch on the front door, nor a wooden one with a buckskin string, but a brass knob to turn, the same as houses in a town. There warn't no bed in the parlor, not a sign of a bed; but heaps of parlors in towns has beds in them. There was a big fireplace that was bricked on the bottom, and the bricks was kept clean and red by pouring water on them and scrubbing them with another brick; sometimes they washed them over with red water-paint that they call Spanish-brown, same as they do in town. They had big brass dog-irons that could hold up a saw-log. There was a clock on the middle of the mantel-piece, with a picture of a town painted on the bottom half of the glass front, and a round place in the middle of it for the sun, and you could see the pendulum swing behind it. It was beautiful to hear that clock tick; and sometimes when one of these peddlers had been along and scoured her up and got her in good shape, she would start in and strike a hundred and fifty before she got tuckered out. They wouldn't took any money for her.

Well, there was a big outlandish parrot on each side of the clock, made out of something like chalk, and painted up gaudy. By one of the parrots was a cat made of crockery, and a crockery dog by the other; and when you pressed down on them they squeaked, but didn't open their mouths nor look different nor interested. They squeaked through underneath. There was a couple of big wild-turkey-wing fans spread out behind those things. On a table in the middle of the room was a kind of a lovely crockery basket that had apples and oranges and peaches and grapes piled up in it which was much redder and yellower and prettier than real ones is, but they warn't real because you could see where pieces had got chipped off and showed the white chalk or whatever it was, underneath.

This table had a cover made out of beautiful oil-cloth, with a red and blue spread-eagle painted on it, and a painted border all around. It come all the way from Philadelphia, they said. There was some books too, piled up perfectly exact, on each corner of the table. One was a big family Bible, full of pictures. One was "Pilgrim's Progress," about a man that left his family it didn't say why. I read considerable in it now and then. The statements was interesting, but tough. Another was "Friendship's Offering," full of beautiful stuff and poetry; but I didn't read the poetry. Another was Henry Clay's Speeches, and another was Dr. Gunn's Family Medicine, which told you all about what to do if a body was sick or dead. There was a Hymn Book, and a lot of other books. And there was nice split-bottom chairs, and perfectly sound, too—not bagged down in the middle and busted, like an old basket.

They had pictures hung on the walls—mainly Washingtons and Lafayettes, and battles, and Highland Marys, and one called "Signing the Declaration." There was some that they called crayons, which one of the daughters which was dead made her own self when she was only fifteen years old. They was different from any pictures I ever see before; blacker, mostly, than is common. One was a woman in a slim black dress, belted small under the arm-pits, with bulges like a cabbage in the middle of the sleeves, and a large black scoop-shovel bonnet with a black veil, and white slim ankles crossed about with black tape, and very wee black slippers, like a chisel, and she was leaning pensive on a tombstone on her right elbow, under a weeping willow, and her other hand hanging down her side holding a white handkerchief and a reticule, and underneath the picture it said "Shall I Never See Thee More Alas." Another one was a young lady with her hair all combed up straight to the top of her head, and knotted there in front of a comb like a chair-back, and she was crying into a handerchief and had a dead bird laying on its back in her other hand with its heels up, and underneath the picture it said "I Shall Never Hear Thy Sweet Chirrup More Alas." There was one where a young lady was at a window looking up at the moon, and tears running down her cheeks; and she had an open letter in one hand with black sealing-wax showing on one edge of it, and she was mashing a locket with a chain to it against her mouth, and underneath the picture it said "And Art Thou Gone Yes Thou Art Gone Alas." These was all nice pictures, I reckon, but I didn't somehow seem to take to them, because if ever I was down a little, they always give me the fan-tods. Everybody was sorry she died, because she had laid out a lot more of these pictures to do, and a body could see by what she had done what they had lost. But I reckoned, that with her disposition, she was having a better time in the graveyard. She was at work on what they said was her greatest picture when she took sick, and every day and every night it was her prayer to be allowed to live till she got it done, but she never got the chance. It was a picture of a young woman in a long white gown, standing on the rail of a bridge all ready to jump off, with her hair all down her back, and looking up to the moon, with the tears running down her face, and she had two arms folded across her breast, and two arms stretched out in front, and two more reaching up towards the moon—and the idea was, to see which pair would look best and then scratch out all the other arms; but, as I was saying, she died before she got her mind made up, and now they kept this picture over the head of the bed in her room, and every time her birthday come they hung flowers on it. Other times it was hid with a little curtain. The young woman in the picture had a kind of a nice sweet face, but there was so many arms it made her look too spidery, seemed to me.

This young girl kept a scrap-book when she was alive, and used to paste obituaries and accidents and cases of patient suffering in it out of the *Presbyterian Observer,* and write poetry. This is what she wrote about a boy by the name of Stephen Dowling Bots that fell down a well and was drownded:

ODE TO STEPHEN DOWLING BOTS, DEC'D.

And did young Stephen sicken,
  And did young Stephen die?
And did the sad hearts thicken,
  And did the mourners cry?

No; such was not the fate of
  Young Stephen Dowling Bots;
Though sad hearts round him thickened,
  'Twas not from sickness' shots.

No whooping-cough did rack his frame,
  Nor measles drear, with spots;
Not these impaired the sacred name
  Of Stephen Dowling Bots.

Despised love struck not with woe
  That head of curly knots,
Nor stomach troubles laid him low.
  Young Stephen Dowling Bots.

O no. Then list with tearful eye,
  Whilst I his fate do tell.
His soul did from this cold world fly,
  By falling down a well.

They got him out and emptied him;
  Alas it was too late;
His spirit was gone for to sport aloft
  In the realms of the good and great.

If Emmeline Grangerford could make poetry like that before she was fourteen, there ain't no telling what she could a done by-and-by. Buck said she could rattle off poetry like nothing. She didn't ever have to stop to think. He said she would slap down a line, and if she couldn't find anything to rhyme with it she would just scratch it out and slap down another one, and go ahead. She warn't particular, she could write about anything you choose to give her to write about, just so it was sadful. Every time a man died, or a woman died, or a child died, she would be on hand with her "tribute" before he was cold. She called them tributes. The neighbors said it was the doctor first, then Emmeline, then the undertaker—the undertaker never got in ahead of Emmeline but once, and then she hung fire on a rhyme for the dead person's name, which was Whistler. She warn't ever the same, after that; she never complained, but she kind of pined away and did not live long. Poor thing, many's the time I made myself go up to the little room that used to be hers and get out her poor old scrap-book and read in it when her pictures had been aggravating me and I had soured on

her a little. I liked all that family, dead ones and all, and warn't
going to let anything come between us. Poor Emmeline made poetry
about all the dead people when she was alive, and it didn't seem
right that there warn't nobody to make some about her, now she was
gone; so I tried to sweat out a verse or two myself, but I couldn't
seem to make it go, somehow. They kept Emmeline's room trim and
nice and all the things fixed in it just the way she liked to have them
when she was alive, and nobody ever slept there. The old lady took
care of the room herself, though there was plenty of niggers, and she
sewed there a good deal and read her Bible there, mostly.

Well, as I was saying about the parlor, there was beautiful
curtains on the windows; white, with pictures painted on them, of
castles with vines all down the walls, and cattle coming down to
drink. There was a little old piano, too, that had tin pans in it, I
reckon, and nothing was ever so lovely as to hear the young ladies
sing, "The Last Link is Broken" and play "The Battle of Prague"
on it. The walls of all the rooms was plastered, and most had
carpets on 'he floors, and the whole house was whitewashed on the
outside.

It was a double house, and the big open place betwixt them was
roofed and floored; and sometimes the table was set there in the
middle of the day, and it was a cool, comfortable place. Nothing
couldn't be better. And warn't the cooking good, and just bushels
of it too!

CHAPTER XVIII

Col. Grangerford was a gentleman, you see. He was a gentleman
all over; and so was his family. He was well born, as the saying is,
and that's worth as much in a man as it is in a horse, so the Widow
Douglass said, and nobody ever denied that she was of the first
aristocracy in our town; and pap he always said it, too, though he
warn't no more quality than a mud-cat, himself. Col. Grangerford
was very tall and very slim, and had a darkish-paly complexion,
not a sign of red in it anywheres; he was cleanshaved every morning,
all over his thin face, and he had the thinnest kind of lips, and the
thinnest kind of nostrils, and a high nose, and heavy eyebrows, and
the blackest kind of eyes, sunk so deep back that they seemed like
they was looking out of caverns at you, as you may say. His forehead
was high, and his hair was black and straight, and hung to his
shoulders. His hands was long and thin, and every day of his life he
put on a clean shirt and a full suit from head to foot made out of
linen so white it hurt your eyes to look at it; and on Sundays he wore
a blue tail-coat with brass buttons on it. He carried a mahogany
cane with a silver head to it. There warn't no frivolishness about
him, not a bit, and he warn't ever loud. He was as kind as he could
be—you could feel that, you know, and so you had confidence.

Sometimes he smiled, and it was good to see; but when he straightened himself up like a liberty-pole, and the lightning begun to flicker out from under his eyebrows you wanted to climb a tree first, and find out what the matter was afterwards. He didn't ever have to tell anybody to mind their manners—everybody was always good mannered where he was. Everybody loved to have him around, too; he was sunshine most always—I mean he made it seem like good weather. When he turned into a cloud-bank it was awful dark for a half a minute and that was enough; there wouldn't nothing go wrong again for a week.

When him and the old lady come down in the morning, all the family got up out of their chairs and give them good-day, and didn't set down again till they had set down. Then Tom and Bob went to the sideboard where the decanters was, and mixed a glass of bitters and handed it to him, and he held it in his hand and waited till Tom's and Bob's was mixed, and then they bowed and said "Our duty to you, sir, and madam;" and *they* bowed the least bit in the world and said thank you, and so they drank, all three, and Bob and Tom poured a spoonful of water on the sugar and the mite of whisky or apple brandy in the bottom of their tumblers, and give it to me and Buck, and we drank to the old people too.

Bob was the oldest, and Tom next. Tall, beautiful men with very broad shoulders and brown faces, and long black hair and black eyes. They dressed in white linen from head to foot, like the old gentleman, and wore broad Panama hats.

Then there was Miss Charlotte, she was twenty-five, and tall and proud and grand, but as good as she could be, when she warn't stirred up; but when she was, she had a look that would make you wilt in your tracks, like her father. She was beautiful.

So was her sister, Miss Sophia, but it was a different kind. She was gentle and sweet, like a dove, and she was only twenty.

Each person had their own nigger to wait on them—Buck, too. My nigger had a monstrous easy time, because I warn't used to having anybody do anything for me, but Buck's was on the jump most of the time.

This was all there was of the family, now; but there used to be more—three sons; they got killed; and Emmeline that died.

The old gentleman owned a lot of farms, and over a hundred niggers. Sometimes a stack of people would come there, horseback, from ten or fifteen mile around, and stay five or six days, and have such junketings round about and on the river, and dances and picnics in the woods, day-times, and balls at the house, nights. These people was mostly kin-folks of the family. The men brought their guns with them. It was a handsome lot of quality, I tell you.

There was another clan of aristocracy around there—five or six families—mostly of the name of Shepherdson. They was as high-toned, and well born, and rich and grand, as the tribe of

Grangerfords. The Shepherdsons and the Grangerfords used the same steamboat landing, which was about two mile above our house; so sometimes when I went up there with a lot of our folks I used to see a lot of the Shepherdsons there, on their fine horses.

One day Buck and me was away out in the woods, hunting, and heard a horse coming. We was crossing the road. Buck says:

"Quick! Jump for the woods!"

We done it, and then peeped down the woods through the leaves. Pretty soon a splendid young man come galloping down the road, setting his horse easy and looking like a soldier. He had his gun across his pommel. I had seen him before. It was young Harney Shepherdson. I heard Buck's gun go off at my ear, and Harney's hat tumbled off from his head. He grabbed his gun and rode straight to the place where we was hid. But we didn't wait. We started through the woods on a run. The woods warn't thick, so I looked over my shoulder, to dodge the bullet, and twice I seen Harney cover Buck with his gun; and then he rode away the way he come— to get his hat, I reckon, but I couldn't see. We never stopped running till we got home. The old gentleman's eyes blazed a minute—'twas pleasure, mainly, I judged—then his face sort of smoothed down, and he says, kind of gentle:

"I don't like that shooting from behind a bush. Why didn't you step into the road, my boy?"

"The Shepherdsons don't, father. They always take advantage."

Miss Charlotte she held her head up like a queen while Buck was telling his tale, and her nostrils spread and her eyes snapped. The two young men looked dark, but never said nothing. Miss Sophia she turned pale, but the color come back when she found the man warn't hurt.

Soon as I could get Buck down by the corn-cribs under the trees by ourselves, I says:

"Did you want to kill him, Buck?"

"Well, I bet I did."

"What did he do to you?"

"Him? He never done nothing to me."

"Well, then, what did you want to kill him for?"

"Why nothing—only it's on account of the feud."

"What's a feud?"

"Why, where was you raised? Don't you know what a feud is?"

"Never heard of it before—tell me about it."

"Well," says Buck, "a feud is this way. A man has a quarrel with another man, and kills him; then that other man's brother kills *him*; then the other brothers, on both sides, goes for one another; then the *cousins* chip in—and by-and-by everybody's killed off, and there ain't no more feud. But it's kind of slow, and takes a long time."

"Has this one been going on long, Buck?"

"Well I should *reckon!* it started thirty year ago, or som'ers along
there. There was trouble 'bout something and then a lawsuit to
settle it; and the suit went agin one of the men, and so he up and
shot the man that won the suit—which he would naturally do, of
course. Anybody would."

"What was the trouble about, Buck?—land?"

"I reckon maybe—I don't know."

"Well, who done the shooting?—was it a Grangerford or a
Shepherdson?"

"Laws, how do *I* know? it was so long ago."

"Don't anybody know?"

"Oh, yes, pa knows, I reckon, and some of the other old folks;
but they don't know, now, what the row was about in the first place."

"Has there been many killed, Buck?"

"Yes—right smart chance of funerals. But they don't always
kill. Pa's got a few buck-shot in him; but he don't mind it 'cuz he
don't weigh much anyway. Bob's been carved up some with a bowie,
and Tom's been hurt once or twice."

"Has anybody been killed this year, Buck?"

"Yes, we got one and they got one. 'Bout three months ago, my
cousin Bud, fourteen year old, was riding through the woods, on
t'other side of the river, and didn't have no weapon with him, which
was blame' foolishness, and in a lonesome place he hears a horse
a-coming behind him, and sees old Baldy Shepherdson a-linkin'
after him with his gun in his hand and his white hair a-flying in the
wind; and 'stead of jumping off and taking to the brush, Bud 'lowed
he could outrun him; so they had it, nip and tuck, for five mile or
more, the old man a-gaining all the time; so at last Bud seen it
warn't any use, so he stopped and faced around so as to have the
bullet holes in front, you know, and the old man he rode up and
shot him down. But he didn't git much chance to enjoy his luck,
for inside of a week our folks laid *him* out."

"I reckon that old man was a coward, Buck."

"I reckon he *warn't* a coward. Not by a blame' sight. There ain't
a coward amongst them Shepherdsons—not a one. And there ain't
no cowards amongst the Grangerfords, either. Why, that old man
kep' up his end in a fight one day, for a half an hour, against three
Grangerfords, and come out winner. They was all a-horseback;
he lit off of his horse and got behind a little wood-pile, and kep'
his horse before him to stop the bullets; but the Grangerfords staid
on their horses and capered around the old man, and peppered
away at him, and he peppered away at them. Him and his horse
both went home pretty leaky and crippled, but the Grangerfords
had to be *fetched* home—and one of 'em was dead, and another
died the next day. No, sir, if a body's out hunting for cowards, he
don't want to fool away any time amongst them Shepherdsons,
becuz they don't breed any of that *kind.*"

Next Sunday we all went to church, about three mile, everybody a-horseback. The men took their guns along, so did Buck, and kept them between their knees or stood them handy against the wall. The Shepherdsons done the same. It was pretty ornery preaching— all about brotherly love, and such-like tiresomeness; but everybody said it was a good sermon, and they all talked it over going home, and had such a powerful lot to say about faith, and good works and free grace, and preforeordestination, and I don't know what all, that it did seem to me to be one of the roughest Sundays I had run across yet.

About an hour after dinner everybody was dozing around, some in their chairs and some in their rooms, and it got to be pretty dull. Buck and a dog was stretched out on the grass in the sun, sound asleep. I went up to our room, and judged I would take a nap myself. I found that sweet Miss Sophia standing in her door, which was next to ours, and she took me in her room and shut the door very soft, and asked me if I liked her, and I said I did; and she asked me if I would do something for her and not tell anybody, and I said I would. Then she said she'd forgot her Testament, and left it in the seat at church, between two other books and would I slip out quiet and go there and fetch it to her, and not say nothing to nobody. I said I would. So I slid out and slipped off up the road, and there warn't anybody at the church, except maybe a hog or two, for there warn't any lock on the door, and hogs likes a puncheon floor in summer-time because it's cool. If you notice, most folks don't go to church only when they've got to; but a hog is different.

Says I to myself something's up—it ain't natural for a girl to be in such a sweat about a Testament; so I give it a shake, and out drops a little piece of paper with *"Half-past two"* wrote on it with a pencil. I ransacked it, but couldn't find anything else. I couldn't make anything out of that, so I put the paper in the book again, and when I got home and up stairs, there was Miss Sophia in her door waiting for me. She pulled me in and shut the door; then she looked in the Testament till she found the paper, and as soon as she read it she looked glad; and before a body could think, she grabbed me· and give me a squeeze, and said I was the best boy in the world, and not to tell anybody. She was mighty red in the face, for a minute, and her eyes lighted up and it made her powerful pretty. I was a good deal astonished, but when I got my breath I asked her what the paper was about, and she asked me if I had read it, and I said no, and she asked me if I could read writing, and I told her "no, only coarse-hand," and then she said the paper warn't anything but a book-mark to keep her place, and I might go and play now.

I went off down to the river, studying over this thing, and pretty soon I notice that my nigger was following along behind. When we was out of sight of the house, he looked back and around a second, and then comes a-running and says:

"Mars Jawge, if you'll come down into de swamp, I'll show you a whole stack o' water-moccasins."

Thinks I, that's mighty curious; he said that yesterday. He oughter know a body don't love water-moccasins enough to go around hunting for them. What is he up to anyway? So I says—

"All right, trot ahead."

I followed a half a mile, then he struck out over the swamp and waded ankle deep as much as another half mile. We come to a little flat piece of land which was dry and very thick with trees and bushes and vines, and he says—

"You shove right in dah, jist a few steps, Mars Jawge, dah's whah dey is. I's seed 'm befo', I don't k'yer to see 'em no mo'."

Then he slopped right along and went away, and pretty soon the trees hid him. I poked into the place a-ways, and come to a little open patch as big as a bedroom, all hung around with vines, and found a man laying there asleep—and by jings it was my old Jim!

I waked him up, and I reckoned it was going to be a grand surprise to him to see me again, but it warn't. He nearly cried, he was so glad, but he warn't surprised. Said he swum along behind me, that night, and heard me yell every time, but dasn't answer, because he didn't want nobody to pick *him* up, and take him into slavery again. Says he—

"I got hurt a little, en couldn't swim fas', so I wuz a considable ways behine you, towards de las'; when you landed I reck'ned I could ketch up wid you on de lan' 'dout havin' to shout at you, but when I see dat house I begin to go slow. I 'uz off too fur to hear what dey say to you—I wuz 'fraid o' de dogs—but when it 'uz all quiet agin, I knowed you's in de house, so I struck out for de woods to wait for day. Early in de mawnin' some er de niggers come along, gwyne to de fields, en dey tuck me en showed me dis place, whah de dogs can't track me on accounts o' de water, en dey brings me truck to eat every night, en tells me how you's a gitt'n along."

"Why didn't you tell my Jack to fetch me here sooner, Jim?"

"Well, 'twarn't no use to 'sturb you, Huck, tell we could do sumfn—but we's all right, now. I ben a-buyin' pots en pans en vittles, as I got a chanst, en a patchin' up de raf', nights, when——"

"*What* raft, Jim?"

"Our ole raf'."

"You mean to say our old raft warn't smashed all to flinders?"

"No, she warn't. She was tore up a good deal—one en' of her was—but dey warn't no great harm done, on'y our traps was mos' all los'. Ef we hadn' dive' so deep en swum so fur under water, en de night hadn' ben so dark, en we warn't so sk'yerd, en ben sich punkin-heads, as de sayin' is, we'd a seed de raf'. But it's jis' as well we didn't, 'kase now she's all fixed up agin mos' as good as new, en we's got a new lot o' stuff, too, in de place o' what 'uz los'."

"Why, how did you get hold of the raft again, Jim—did you catch her?"

"How I gwyne to ketch her, en I out in de woods? No, some er de niggers foun' her ketched on a snag, along heah in de ben', en dey hid her in a crick, 'mongst de willows, en dey wuz so much jawin' 'bout which un 'um she b'long to de mos', dat I come to heah 'bout it pooty soon, so I ups en settles de trouble by tellin' 'um she don't b'long to none uv um, but to you en me; en I ast'm if dey gwyne to grab a young white genlman's propaty, en git a hid'n for it? Den I gin 'm ten cents apiece, en dey 'uz mighty well satisfied, en wisht some mo' raf's 'ud come along en make 'm rich agin. Dey's mighty good to me, dese niggers is, en whatever I wants 'm to do fur me, I doan' have to ast 'm twice, honey. Dat Jack's a good nigger, en pooty smart."

"Yes, he is. He ain't ever told me you was here; told me to come, and he'd show me a lot of water-moccasins. If anything happens, *he* ain't mixed up in it. He can say he never seen us together, and it'll be the truth."

I don't want to talk much about the next day. I reckon I'll cut it pretty short. I waked up about dawn, and was agoing to turn over and go to sleep again, when I noticed how still it was—didn't seem to be anybody stirring. That warn't usual. Next I notice that Buck was up and gone. Well, I gets up, a-wondering, and goes down stairs—nobody around; everything as still as a mouse. Just the same outside; thinks I, what does it mean? Down by the wood-pile I comes across my Jack, and says:

"What's it all about?"

Says he:

"Don't you know, Mars Jawge?"

"No," says I, "I don't."

"Well, den, Miss Sophia's run off! 'deed she has. She run off in de night, sometime—nobody don't know jis' when—run off to git married to dat young Harney Shepherdson, you know—leastways, so dey 'spec. De fambly foun' it out, 'bout half an hour ago—maybe a little mo'—en I *tell* you dey warn't no time los'. Sich another hurryin' up guns en hosses *you* never see! De women folks has gone for to stir up de relations, en ole Mars Saul en de boys tuck dey guns en rode up de river road for to try to ketch dat young man en kill him 'fo' he kin git acrost de river wid Miss Sophia. I reck'n dey's gwyne to be mighty rough times."

"Buck went off 'thout waking me up."

"Well I reck'n he *did!* Dey warn't gwyne to mix you up in it. Mars Buck he loaded up his gun en 'lowed he's gwyne to fetch home a Shepherdson or bust. Well, dey'll be plenty un 'm dah, I reck'n, en you bet you he'll fetch one if he gits a chanst."

I took up the river road as hard as I could put. By-and-by I begin to hear guns a good ways off. When I come in sight of the log store and the wood-pile where the steamboats lands, I worked along

under the trees and brush till I got to a good place, and then I clumb
up into the forks of a cotton-wood that was out of reach, and
watched. There was a wood-rank four foot high, a little ways in
front of the tree, and first I was going to hide behind that; but
maybe it was luckier I didn't.

There was four or five men cavorting around on their horses in
the open place before the log store, cussing and yelling, and trying
to get at a couple of young chaps that was behind the wood-rank
alongside of the steamboat landing—but they couldn't come it.
Every time one of them showed himself on the river side of the
wood-pile he got shot at. The two boys was squatting back to back
behind the pile, so they could watch both ways.

By-and-by the men stopped cavorting around and yelling. They
started riding towards the store; then up gets one of the boys, draws
a steady bead over the wood-rank, and drops one of them out of his
saddle. All the men jumped off of their horses and grabbed the
hurt one and started to carry him to the store; and that minute the
two boys started on the run. They got half-way to the tree I was in
before the men noticed. Then the men see them, and jumped on
their horses and took out after them. They gained on the boys, but
it didn't do no good, the boys had too good a start; they got to the
wood-pile that was in front of my tree, and slipped in behind it, and
so they had the bulge on the men again. One of the boys was Buck,
and the other was a slim young chap about nineteen years old.

The men ripped around awhile, and then rode away. As soon as
they was out of sight, I sung out to Buck and told him. He didn't
know what to make of my voice coming out of the tree, at first. He
was awful surprised. He told me to watch out sharp and let him
know when the men come in sight again; said they was up to some
devilment or other—wouldn't be gone long. I wished I was out of
that tree, but I dasn't come down. Buck begun to cry and rip, and
'lowed that him and his cousin Joe (that was the other young chap)
would make up for this day, yet. He said his father and his two
brothers was killed, and two or three of the enemy. Said the
Shepherdsons laid for them, in ambush. Buck said his father and
brothers ought to waited for their relations—the Shepherdsons
was too strong for them. I asked him what was become of young
Harney and Miss Sophia. He said they'd got across the river and
was safe. I was glad of that; but the way Buck did take on because
he didn't manage to kill Harney that day he shot at him—I hain't
ever heard anything like it.

All of a sudden, bang! bang! bang! goes three or four guns—the
men had slipped around through the woods and come in from
behind without their horses! The boys jumped for the river—both of
them hurt—and as they swum down the current the men run along
the bank shooting at them and singing out, "Kill them, kill them!"
It made me so sick I most fell out of the tree. I ain't agoing to tell

all that happened—it would make me sick again if I was to do that.
I wished I hadn't ever come ashore that night, to see such things.
I ain't ever going to get shut of them—lots of times I dream about
them.

I staid in the tree till it begun to get dark, afraid to come down.
Sometimes I heard guns away off in the woods; and twice I seen
little gangs of men gallop past the log store with guns; so I reckoned
the trouble was still agoing on. I was mighty down-hearted; so I
made up my mind I wouldn't ever go anear that house again,
because I reckoned I was to blame, somehow. I judged that that
piece of paper meant that Miss Sophia was to meet Harney
somewheres at half-past two and run off; and I judged I ought to
told her father about the paper and the curious way she acted, and
then maybe he would a locked her up and this awful mess wouldn't
ever happened.

When I got down out of the tree, I crept along down the river
bank a piece, and found the two bodies laying in the edge of the
water, and tugged at them till I got them ashore; then I covered
up their faces, and got away as quick as I could. I cried a little when
I was covering up Buck's face, for he was mighty good to me.

It was just dark, now. I never went near the house, but struck
through the woods and made for the swamp. Jim warn't on his
island, so I tramped off in a hurry for the crick, and crowded
through the willows, red-hot to jump aboard and get out of that
awful country—the raft was gone! My souls, but I was scared! I
couldn't get my breath for most a minute. Then I raised a yell. A
voice not twenty-five foot from me, says—

"Good lan'! is dat you, honey? Doan' make no noise."

It was Jim's voice—nothing ever sounded so good before. I run
along the bank a piece and got aboard, and Jim he grabbed me and
hugged me, he was so glad to see me. He says—

"Laws bless you, chile, I 'uz right down sho' you's dead agin.
Jack's been heah, he say he reck'n you's ben shot, kase you didn'
come home no mo'; so I's jes' dis minute a startin' de raf' down
towards de mouf er de crick, so's to be all ready for to shove out en
leave soon as Jack comes agin en tells me for certain you *is* dead.
Lawsy, I's mighty glad to git you back agin, honey."

I says—

"All right—that's mighty good; they won't find me, and they'll
think I've been killed, and floated down the river—there's
something up there that'll help them to think so—so don't you lose
no time, Jim, but just shove off for the big water as fast as ever you
can."

I never felt easy till the raft was two mile below there and out
in the middle of the Mississippi. Then we hung up our signal
lantern, and judged that we was free and safe once more. I hadn't
had a bite to eat since yesterday; so Jim he got out some

corn-dodgers and buttermilk, and pork and cabbage, and greens—
there ain't nothing in the world so good, when it's cooked right—
and whilst I eat my supper we talked, and had a good time. I was
powerful glad to get away from the feuds, and so was Jim to get
away from the swamp. We said there warn't no home like a raft,
after all. Other places do seem so cramped up and smothery, but a
raft don't. You feel mighty free and easy and comfortable on a raft.

CHAPTER XIX

Two or three days and nights went by; I reckon I might say they
swum by, they slid along so quiet and smooth and lovely. Here is
the way we put in the time. It was a monstrous big river down
there—sometimes a mile and a half wide; we run nights, and laid
up and hid day-times; soon as night was most gone, we stopped
navigating and tied up—nearly always in the dead water under a
tow-head; and then cut young cottonwoods and willows and hid the
raft with them. Then we set out the lines. Next we slid into the river
and had a swim, so as to freshen up and cool off; then we set down
on the sandy bottom where the water was about knee deep, and
watched the daylight come. Not a sound, anywheres—perfectly
still—just like the whole world was asleep, only sometimes the
bull frogs a-cluttering, maybe. The first thing to see, looking away
over the water, was a kind of dull line—that was the woods on
t'other side—you couldn't make nothing else out; then a pale place
in the sky; then more paleness, spreading around; then the river
softened up, away off, and warn't black any more, but gray; you
could see little dark spots drifting along, ever so far away—trading
scows, and such things; and long black streaks—rafts; sometimes
you could hear a sweep screaking; or jumbled up voices, it was so
still, and sounds come so far; and by-and-by you could see a streak
on the water which you know by the look of the streak that there's
a snag there in a swift current which breaks on it and makes that
streak look that way; and you see the mist curl up off of the water,
and the east reddens up, and the river, and you make out a log
cabin in the edge of the woods, away on the bank on t'other side of
the river, being a wood-yard, likely, and piled by them cheats so you
can throw a dog through it anywheres; then the nice breeze springs
up and comes fanning you from over there, so cool and fresh, and
sweet to smell, on account of the woods and the flowers; but
sometimes not that way, because they've left dead fish laying
around, gars, and such, and they do get pretty rank; and next
you've got the full day, and everything smiling in the sun, and the
song-birds just going it!

A little smoke couldn't be noticed, now, so we would take some
fish off of the lines, and cook up a hot breakfast. And afterwards
we would watch the lonesomeness of the river, and kind of lazy

along, and by-and-by lazy off to sleep. Wake up, by-and-by, and
look to see what done it, and maybe see a steamboat, coughing along
up stream, so far off towards the other side you couldn't tell nothing
about her only whether she was stern-wheel or side-wheel,
then for about an hour there wouldn't be nothing to hear nor
nothing to see—just solid lonesomeness. Next you'd see a raft sliding
by, away off yonder, and maybe a galoot on it chopping, because
they're most always doing it on a raft; you'd see the ax flash, ane
come down—you don't hear nothing; you see that ax go up again,
and by the time it's above the man's head, then you hear the
k'chunk!—it had took all that time to come over the water. So we
would put in the day, lazying around, listening to the stillness.
Once there was a thick fog, and the rafts and things that went by
was beating tin pans so the steamboats wouldn't run over them.
A scow or a raft went by so close we could hear them talking and
cussing and laughing—heard them plain; but we couldn't see no
sign of them; it made you feel crawly, it was like spirits carrying on
that way in the air. Jim said he believed it was spirits; but I says:
   "No, spirits wouldn't say, 'dern the dern fog.' "
   Soon as it was night, out we shoved; when we got her out to about
the middle, we let her alone, and let her float wherever the current
wanted her to; then we lit the pipes, and dangled our legs in the
water and talked about all kinds of things—we was always naked,
day and night, whenever the mosquitoes would let us—the new
clothes Buck's folks made for me was too good to be comfortable,
and besides I didn't go much on clothes, nohow.
   Sometimes we'd have that whole river all to ourselves for the
longest time. Yonder was the banks and the islands, across the
water; and maybe a spark—which was a candle in a cabin window—
and sometimes on the water you could see a spark or two—on a raft
or a scow, you know; and maybe you could hear a fiddle or a song
coming over from one of them crafts. It's lovely to live on a raft.
We had the sky, up there, all speckled with stars, and we used to lay
on our backs and look up at them, and discuss about whether they
was made, or only just happened—Jim he allowed they was made,
but I allowed they happened; I judged it would have took too long
to *make* so many. Jim said the moon could a *laid* them; well, that
looked kind of reasonable, so I didn't say nothing against it,
because I've seen a frog lay most as many, so of course it could
be done. We used to watch the stars that fell, too, and see them
streak down. Jim allowed they'd got spoiled and was hove out of the
nest.
   Once or twice of a night we would see a steamboat slipping along
in the dark, and now and then she would belch a whole world of
sparks up out of her chimbleys, and they would rain down in the
river and look awful pretty; then she would turn a corner and her
lights would wink out and her pow-wow shut off and leave the

river still again; and by-and-by her waves would get to us, a long
time after she was gone, and joggle the raft a bit, and after that you
wouldn't hear nothing for you couldn't tell how long, except maybe
frogs or something.

After midnight the people on shore went to bed, and then for two
or three hours the shores was black—no more sparks in the cabin
windows. These sparks was our clock—the first one that showed
again meant morning was coming, so we hunted a place to hide and
tie up, right away.

One morning about day-break, I found a canoe and crossed over
a chute to the main shore—it was only two hundred yards—and
paddled about a mile up a crick amongst the cypress woods, to see
if I couldn't get some berries. Just as I was passing a place where a
kind of a cow-path crossed the crick, here comes a couple of men
tearing up the path as tight as they could foot it. I thought I was a
goner, for whenever anybody was after anybody I judged it was
me—or maybe Jim. I was about to dig out from there in a hurry,
but they was pretty close to me then, and sung out and begged me
to save their lives—said they hadn't been doing nothing, and was
being chased for it—said there was men and dogs a-coming. They
wanted to jump right in, but I says—

"Don't you do it. I don't hear the dogs and horses yet; you've
got time to crowd through the brush and get up the crick a little
ways; then you take to the water and wade down to me and get in—
that'll throw the dogs off the scent."

They done it, and soon as they was aboard I lit out for our
tow-head, and in about five or ten minutes we heard the dogs and
the men away off, shouting. We heard them come along towards
the crick, but couldn't see them; they seemed to stop and fool
around a while; then, as we got further and further away all the
time, we couldn't hardly hear them at all; by the time we had left a
mile of woods behind us and struck the river, everything was quiet,
and we paddled over to the tow-head and hid in the cotton-woods
and was safe.

One of these fellows was about seventy, or upwards, and had a
bald head and very gray whiskers. He had an old battered-up slouch
hat on, and a greasy blue woolen shirt, and ragged old blue jeans
britches stuffed into his boot tops, and home-knit galluses—no,
he only had one. He had an old long-tailed blue jeans coat with
slick brass buttons, flung over his arm, and both of them had big fat
ratty-looking carpet-bags.

The other fellow was about thirty and dressed about as ornery.
After breakfast we all laid off and talked, and the first thing that
come out was that these chaps didn't know one another.

"What got you into trouble?" says the baldhead to t'other chap.

"Well, I'd been selling an article to take the tartar off the teeth—
and it does take it off, too, and generly the enamel along with it—

but I staid about one night longer than I ought to, and was just in
the act of sliding out when I ran across you on the trail this side
of town, and you told me they were coming, and begged me to help
you to get off. So I told you I was expecting trouble myself and
would scatter out *with* you. That's the whole yarn—what's yourn?''

"Well, I'd ben a-runnin' a little temperance revival thar, 'bout
a week, and was the pet of the women-folks, big and little, for I
was makin' it mighty warm for the rummies, I *tell* you, and takin'
as much as five or six dollars a night—ten cents a head, children
and niggers free—and business a growin' all the time; when
somehow or another a little report got around, last night, that I
had a way of puttin' in my time with a private jug, on the sly. A
nigger rousted me out this mornin', and told me the people was
getherin' on the quiet, with their dogs and horses, and they'd be
along pretty soon and give me 'bout half an hour's start, and then
run me down, if they could; and if they got me they'd tar and feather
me and ride me on a rail, sure. I·didn't wait for no breakfast—I
warn't hungry.''

"Old man,'' says the young one, "I reckon we might double-team
it together; what do you think?''

"I ain't undisposed. What's your line—mainly?''

"Jour printer, by trade; do a little in patent medicines;
theatre-actor—tragedy, you know; take a turn at mesmerism and
phrenology when there's a chance; teach singing-geography school
for a change; sling a lecture, sometimes—oh, I do lots of things—
most anything that comes handy, so it ain't work. What's your lay?''

"I've done considerble in the doctoring way in my time. Layin'
on o' hands is my best holt—for cancer, and paralysis, and sich
things; and I k'n tell a fortune pretty good, when I've got somebody
along to find out the facts for me. Preachin's my line, too; and
workin' camp-meetin's; and missionaryin' around.''

Nobody never said anything for a while; then the young man
hove a sigh and says—

"Alas!''

"What're you alassin' about?'' says the baldhead.

"To think I should have lived to be leading such a life, and be
degraded down into such company.'' And he begun to wipe the
corner of his eye with a rag.

"Dern your skin, ain't the company good enough for you?'' says
the baldhead, pretty pert and uppish.

"Yes, it *is* good enough for me; it's as good as I deserve; for who
fetched me so low, when I was so high? *I* did myself. I don't blame
you, gentlemen—far from it; I don't blame anybody. I deserve it
all. Let the cold world do its worst; one thing I know—there's a
grave somewhere for me. The world may go on just as its always
done, and take everything from me—loved ones, property,
everything—but it can't take that. Some day I'll lie down in it and

forget it all, and my poor broken heart will be at rest." He went on a-wiping.

"Drot your pore broken heart," says the baldhead; "what are you heaving your pore broken heart at *us* f'r? *We* hain't done nothing."

"No, I know you haven't. I ain't blaming you, gentlemen. I brought myself down—yes, I did it myself. It's right I should suffer—perfectly right—I don't make any moan."

"Brought you down from whar? Whar was you brought down from?"

"Ah, you would not believe me; the world never believes—let it pass—'tis no matter. The secret of my birth——"

"The secret of your birth? Do you mean to say——"

"Gentlemen," says the young man, very solemn, "I will reveal it to you, for I feel I may have confidence in you. By rights I am a duke!"

Jim's eyes bugged out when he heard that; and I reckon mine did, too. Then the baldhead says: "No! you can't mean it?"

"Yes. My great-grandfather, eldest son of the Duke of Bridgewater, fled to this country about the end of the last century, to breathe the pure air of freedom; married here, and died, leaving a son, his own father dying about the same time. The second son of the late duke seized the title and estates—the infant real duke was ignored. I am the lineal descendant of that infant—I am the rightful Duke of Bridgewater; and here am I, forlorn, torn from my high estate, hunted of men, despised by the cold world, ragged, worn, heart-broken, and degraded to the companionship of felons on a raft!"

Jim pitied him ever so much, and so did I. We tried to comfort him, but he said it warn't much use, he couldn't be much comforted; said if we was a mind to acknowledge him, that would do him more good than most anything else; so we said we would, if he would tell us how. He said we ought to bow, when we spoke to him, and say "Your Grace," or "My Lord," or "Your Lordship"— and he wouldn't mind it if we called him plain "Bridgewater," which he said was a title, anyway, and not a name; and one of us ought to wait on him at dinner, and do any little thing for him he wanted done.

Well, that was all easy, so we done it. All through dinner Jim stood around and waited on him, and says, "Will yo' Grace have some o' dis, or some o' dat?" and so on, and a body could see it was mighty pleasing to him.

But the old man got pretty silent, by-and-by—didn't have much to say and didn't look pretty comfortable over all that petting that was going on around that duke. He seemed to have something on his mind. So, along in the afternoon, he says:

"Looky here, Bilgewater," he says, "I'm nation sorry for you, but you ain't the only person that's had troubles like that."

"No?"

"No, you ain't. You ain't the only person that's ben snaked down wrongfully out'n a high place."

"Alas!"

"No, you ain't the only person that's had a secret of his birth." And by jings, *he* begins to cry.

"Hold! What do you mean?"

"Bilgewater, kin I trust you?" says the old man, still sort of sobbing.

"To the bitter death!" He took the old man by the hand and squeezed it, and says, "The secret of your being: speak!"

"Bilgewater, I am the late Dauphin!"

You bet you Jim and me stared, this time. Then the duke says: "You are what?"

"Yes, my friend, it is too true—your eyes is lookin' at this very moment on the pore disappeared Dauphin, Looy the Seventeen, son of Looy the Sixteen and Marry Antonette."

"You! At your age! No! You mean you're the late Charlemagne; you must be six or seven hundred years old, at the very least."

"Trouble has done it, Bilgewater, trouble has done it; trouble has brung these gray hairs and this premature balditude. Yes, gentlemen, you see before you, in blue jeans and misery, the wanderin', exiled, trampled-on and sufferin' rightful King of France."

Well, he cried and took on so, that me and Jim didn't know hardly what to do, we was so sorry—and so glad and proud we'd got him with us, too. So we set in, like we done before with the duke, and tried to comfort *him.* But he said it warn't no use, nothing but to be dead and done with it all could do him any good; though he said it often made him feel easier and better for a while if people treated him according to his rights, and got down on one knee to speak to him, and always called him "Your Majesty," and waited on him first at meals, and didn't set down in his presence till he asked them. So Jim and me set to majestying him, and doing this and that and t'other for him, and standing up till he told us we might set down. This done him heaps of good, and so he got cheerful and comfortable. But the duke kind of soured on him, and didn't look a bit satisfied with the way things was going; still, the king acted real friendly towards him, and said the duke's great-grandfather and all the other Dukes of Bilgewater was a good deal thought of by *his* father and was allowed to come to the palace considerable; but the duke staid huffy a good while, till by-and-by the king says:

"Like as not we got to be together a blamed long time, on this h-yer raft, Bilgewater, and so what's the use o' your bein' sour? It'll only make things oncomfortable. It ain't my fault I warn't born

a duke, it ain't your fault you warn't born a king—so what's the use
to worry? Make the best o' things the way you find 'em, says I—
that's my motto. This ain't no bad thing that we've struck here—
plenty grub and an easy life—come, give us your hand, Duke, and
less all be friends."

The duke done it, and Jim and me was pretty glad to see it. It took
away all the uncomfortableness, and we felt mighty good over it,
because it would a been a miserable business to have any
unfriendliness on the raft; for what you want, above all things, on a
raft, is for everybody to be satisfied, and feel right and kind towards
the others.

It didn't take me long to make up my mind that these liars warn't
no kings nor dukes, at all, but just low-down humbugs and frauds.
But I never said nothing, never let on; kept it to myself; it's the best
way; then you don't have no quarrels, and don't get into no trouble.
If they wanted us to call them kings and dukes, I hadn't no
objections, 'long as it would keep peace in the family; and it warn't
no use to tell Jim, so I didn't tell him. If I never learnt nothing else
out of pap, I learnt that the best way to get along with his kind of
people is to let them have their own way.

CHAPTER XX

They asked us considerable many questions; wanted to know what
we covered up the raft that way for, and laid by in the day-time
instead of running—was Jim a runaway nigger? Says I—

"Goodness sakes, would a runaway nigger run *south?*"

No, they allowed he wouldn't. I had to account for things some
way, so I says:

"My folks was living in Pike County, in Missouri, where I was
born, and they all died off but me and pa and my brother Ike. Pa,
he 'lowed he'd break up and go down and live with Uncle Ben, who's
got a little one-horse place on the river, forty-four mile below
Orleans. Pa was pretty poor, and had some debts; so when he'd
squared up there warn't nothing left but sixteen dollars and our
nigger, Jim. That warn't enough to take us fourteen hundred mile,
deck passage nor no other way. Well, when the river rose, pa had
a streak of luck one day; he ketched this piece of a raft; so we
reckoned we'd go down to Orleans on it. Pa's luck didn't hold out;
a steamboat run over the forrard corner of the raft, one night, and
we all went overboard and dove under the wheel; Jim and me come
up, all right, but pa was drunk, and Ike was only four years old, so
they never come up no more. Well, for the next day or two we had
considerable trouble, because people was always coming out in
skiffs and trying to take Jim away from me, saying they believed he
was a runaway nigger. We don't run day-times no more, now;
nights they don't bother us."

The duke says—

"Leave me alone to cipher out a way so we can run in the day-time if we want to. I'll think the thing over—I'll invent a plan that'll fix it. We'll let it alone for to-day, because of course we don't want to go by that town yonder in daylight—it mightn't be healthy."

Towards night it begun to darken up and look like rain; the heat lightning was squirting around, low down in the sky, and the leaves was beginning to shiver—it was going to be pretty ugly, it was easy to see that. So the duke and the king went to overhauling our wigwam, to see what the beds was like. My bed was a straw tick—better than Jim's, which was a corn-shuck tick; there's always cobs around about in a shuck tick, and they poke into you and hurt; and when you roll over, the dry shucks sound like you was rolling over in a pile of dead leaves; it makes such a rustling that you wake up. Well, the duke allowed he would take my bed; but the king allowed he wouldn't. He says—

"I should a reckoned the difference in rank would a sejested to you that a corn-shuck bed warn't just fitten for me to sleep on. Your Grace'll take the shuck bed yourself."

Jim and me was in a sweat again, for a minute, being afraid there was going to be some more trouble amongst them; so we was pretty glad when the duke says—

" 'Tis my fate to be always ground into the mire under the iron heel of oppression. Misfortune has broken my once haughty spirit; I yield, I submit; 'tis my fate. I am alone in the world—let me suffer; I can bear it."

We got away as soon as it was good and dark. The king told us to stand well out towards the middle of the river, and not show a light till we got a long ways below the town. We come in sight of the little bunch of lights by-and-by—that was the town, you know—and slid by, about a half a mile out, all right. When we was three-quarters of a mile below, we hoisted up our signal lantern; and about ten o'clock it come on to rain and blow and thunder and lighten like everything; so the king told us to both stay on watch till the weather got better; then him and the duke crawled into the wigwam and turned in for the night. It was my watch below, till twelve, but I wouldn't a turned in, anyway, if I'd had a bed; because a body don't see such a storm as that every day in the week, not by a long sight. My souls, how the wind did scream along! And every second or two there'd come a glare that lit up the white-caps for a half a mile around, and you'd see the islands looking dusty through the rain, and the trees thrashing around in the wind; then comes a *h-wack!*—bum! bum! bumble-umble-um-bum-bum-bum-bum—and the thunder would go rumbling and grumbling away, and quit—and then *rip* comes another flash and another sockdolager. The waves most washed me off the raft, sometimes, but I hadn't any clothes on, and didn't mind. We didn't have no trouble about snags; the lightning was glaring and flittering around so constant that we could see them plenty soon enough to throw her head this way or that and miss them.

I had the middle watch, you know, but I was pretty sleepy by that time, so Jim he said he would stand the first half of it for me; he was always mighty good, that way, Jim was. I crawled into the wigwam, but the king and the duke had their legs sprawled around so there warn't no show for me; so I laid outside—I didn't mind the rain, because it was warm, and the waves warn't running so high, now. About two they come up again, though, and Jim was going to call me, but he changed his mind because he reckoned they warn't high enough yet to do any harm; but he was mistaken about that, for pretty soon all of a sudden along comes a regular ripper, and washed me overboard. It most killed Jim a-laughing. He was the easiest nigger to laugh that ever was, anyway.

I took the watch, and Jim he laid down and snored away; and by-and-by the storm let up for good and all; and the first cabin-light that showed, I rousted him out and we slid the raft into hiding-quarters for the day.

The king got out an old ratty deck of cards, after breakfast, and him and the duke played seven-up a while, five cents a game. Then they got tired of it, and allowed they would "lay out a campaign," as they called it. The duke went down into his carpet-bag and fetched up a lot of little printed bills, and read them out loud. One bill said "The celebrated Dr. Armand de Montalban of Paris," would "lecture on the Science of Phrenology" at such and such a place, on the blank day of blank, at ten cents admission, and "furnish charts of character at twenty-five cents apiece." The duke said that was *him.* In another bill he was the "world renowned Shaksperean tragedian, Garrick the Younger, of Drury Lane, London." In other bills he had a lot of other names and done other wonderful things, like finding water and gold with a "divining rod," "dissipating witch-spells," and so on. By-and-by he says—

"But the histrionic muse is the darling. Have you ever trod the boards, Royalty?"

"No," says the king.

"You shall, then, before you're three days older, Fallen Grandeur," says the duke. "The first good town we come to, we'll hire a hall and do the sword-fight in Richard III. and the balcony scene in Romeo and Juliet. How does that strike you?"

"I'm in, up to the hub, for anything that will pay, Bilgewater, but you see I don't know nothing about play-actn', and hain't ever seen much of it. I was too small when pap used to have 'em at the palace. Do you reckon you can learn me?"

"Easy!"

"All right. I'm jist a-freezn' for something fresh, anyway. Less commence, right away."

So the duke he told him all about who Romeo was, and who Juliet was, and said he was used to being Romeo, so the king could be Juliet.

"But if Juliet's such a young gal, Duke, my peeled head and my white whiskers is goin' to look oncommon odd on her, maybe."

"No, don't you worry—these country jakes won't ever think of that. Besides, you know, you'll be in costume, and that makes all the difference in the world; Juliet's in a balcony, enjoying the moonlight before she goes to bed, and she's got on her night-gown and her ruffled night-cap. Here are the costumes for the parts."

He got out two or three curtain-calico suits, which he said was meedyevil armor for Richard III. and t'other chap, and a long white cotton night-shirt and a ruffled night-cap to match. The king was satisfied; so the duke got out his book and read the parts over in the most splendid spread-eagle way, prancing around and acting at the same time, to show how it had got to be done; then he give the book to the king and told him to get his part by heart.

There was a little one-horse town about three mile down the bend, and after dinner the duke said he had ciphered out his idea about how to run in daylight without it being dangersome for Jim; so he allowed he would go down to the town and fix that thing. The king allowed he would go too, and see if he couldn't strike something. We was out of coffee, so Jim said I better go along with them in the canoe and get some.

When we got there, there warn't nobody stirring; streets empty, and perfectly dead and still, like Sunday. We found a sick nigger sunning himself in a back yard, and he said everybody that warn't too young or too sick or too old, was gone to camp-meeting, about two mile back in the woods. The king got the directions, and allowed he'd go and work that camp-meeting for all it was worth, and I might go, too.

The duke said what he was after was a printing office. We found it; a little bit of a concern, up over a carpenter shop—carpenters and printers all gone to the meeting, and no doors locked. It was a dirty, littered-up place, and had ink marks, and handbills with pictures of horses and runaway niggers on them, all over the walls. The duke shed his coat and said he was all right, now. So me and the king lit out for the camp-meeting.

We got there in about a half an hour, fairly dripping, for it was a most awful hot day. There was as much as a thousand people there, from twenty mile around. The woods was full of teams and wagons, hitched everywheres, feeding out of the wagon troughs and stomping to keep off the flies. There was sheds made of poles and roofed over with branches, where they had lemonade and gingerbread to sell, and piles of watermelons and green corn and such-like truck.

The preaching was going on under the same kinds of sheds, only

they was bigger and held crowds of people. The benches was made
out of outside slabs of logs, with holes bored in the round side to
drive sticks into for legs. They didn't have no backs. The preachers
had high platforms to stand on, at one end of the sheds. The women
had on sun-bonnets; and some had linsey-woolsey frocks, some
gingham ones, and a few of the young ones had on calico. Some of
the young men was barefooted, and some of the children didn't
have on any clothes but just a tow-linen shirt. Some of the old
women was knitting, and some of the young folks was courting on
the sly.

The first shed we come to, the preacher was lining out a hymn.
He lined out two lines, everybody sung it, and it was kind of grand
to hear it, there was so many of them and they done it in such a
rousing way; then he lined out two more for them to sing—and so
on. The people woke up more and more, and sung louder and
louder; and towards the end, some begun to groan, and some begun
to shout. Then the preacher begun to preach; and begun in earnest,
too; and went weaving first to one side of the platform and then the
other, and then a leaning down over the front of it, with his arms
and his body going all the time, and shouting his words out with
all his might; and every now and then he would hold up his Bible
and spread it open, and kind of pass it around this way and that,
shouting, "It's the brazen serpent in the wilderness! Look upon
it and live!" And people would shout out, "Glory!—A-a-*men!*"
And so he went on, and the people groaning and crying and saying
amen:

"Oh, come to the mourners' bench! come, black with sin! (*amen!*)
come, sick and sore! (*amen!*) come, lame and halt, and blind!
(*amen!*) come, pore and needy, sunk in shame! (*a-a-men!*) come all
that's worn, and soiled, and suffering!—come with a broken spirit!
come with a contrite heart! come in your rags and sin and dirt!
the waters that cleanse is free, the door of heaven stands open—oh,
enter in and be at rest!" (*a-a-men! glory, glory hallelujah!*)

And so on. You couldn't make out what the preacher said, any
more, on account of the shouting and crying. Folks got up,
everywheres in the crowd, and worked their way, just by main
strength, to the mourners' bench, with the tears running down their
faces; and when all the mourners had got up there to the front
benches in a crowd, they sung, and shouted, and flung themselves
down on the straw, just crazy and wild.

Well, the first I knowed, the king got agoing; and you could hear
him over everybody; and next he went a-charging up on to the
platform and the preacher he begged him to speak to the people,
and he done it. He told them he was a pirate—been a pirate for
thirty years, out in the Indian Ocean, and his crew was thinned out
considerable, last spring, in a fight, and he was home now, to take
out some fresh men, and thanks to goodness he'd been robbed last

night, and put ashore off of a steamboat without a cent, and he was
glad of it, it was the blessedest thing that ever happened to him,
because he was a changed man now, and happy for the first time in
his life; and poor as he was, he was going to start right off and work
his way back to the Indian Ocean and put in the rest of his life
trying to turn the pirates into the true path; for he could do it better
than anybody else, being acquainted with all the pirate crews in
that ocean; and though it would take him a long time to get there,
without money, he would get there anyway, and every time he
convinced a pirate he would say to him, "Don't you thank me, don't
you give me no credit, it all belongs to them dear people in Pokeville
camp-meeting, natural brothers and benefactors of the race—and
that dear preacher there, the truest friend a pirate ever had!"

And then he busted into tears, and so did everybody. Then
somebody sings out, "Take up a collection for him, take up a
collection!" Well, a half a dozen made a jump to do it, but
somebody sings out, "Let *him* pass the hat around!" Then
everybody said it, the preacher too.

So the king went all through the crowd with his hat, swabbing his
eyes, and blessing the people and praising them and thanking them
for being so good to the poor pirates away off there; and every little
while the prettiest kind of girls with the tears running down their
cheeks, would up and ask him would he let them kiss him, for to
remember him by; and he always done it; and some of them he
hugged and kissed as many as five or six times—and he was invited
to stay a week; and everybody wanted him to live in their houses,
and said they'd think it was an honor; but he said as this was the last
day of the camp-meeting he couldn't do no good, and besides he was
in a sweat to get to the Indian Ocean right off and go to work on the
pirates.

When we got back to the raft and he come to count up, he found
he had collected eighty-seven dollars and seventy-five cents. And
then he had fetched away a three-gallon jug of whisky, too, that
he found under a wagon when we was starting home through the
woods. The king said, take it all around, it laid over any day he'd
ever put in in the missionarying line. He said it warn't no use talking,
heathens don't amount to shucks, alongside of pirates, to work a
camp-meeting with.

The duke was thinking *he'd* been doing pretty well, till the king
come to show up, but after that he didn't think so so much. He
had set up and printed off two little jobs for farmers, in that printing
office—horse bills—and took the money, four dollars. And he
had got in ten dollars worth of advertisements for the paper, which
he said he would put in for four dollars if they would pay in
advance—so they done it. The price of the paper was two dollars
a year, but he took in three subscriptions for half a dollar apiece
on condition of them paying him in advance; they were going to pay

in cord-wood and onions, as usual, but he said he had just bought
the concern and knocked down the price as low as he could afford it,
and was going to run it for cash. He set up a little piece of poetry,
which he made, himself, out of his own head—three verses—kind
of sweet and saddish—the name of it was, "Yes, crush, cold world,
this breaking heart"—and he left that all set up and ready to print
in the paper and didn't charge nothing for it. Well, he took in nine
dollars and a half, and said he'd done a pretty square day's work
for it.

Then he showed us another little job he'd printed and hadn't
charged for, because it was for us. It had a picture of a runaway
nigger, with a bundle on a stick, over his shoulder, and "$200
reward" under it. The reading was all about Jim, and just described
him to a dot. It said he run away from St. Jacques' plantation, forty
mile below New Orleans, last winter, and likely went north, and
whoever would catch him and send him back, he could have the
reward and expenses.

"Now," says the duke, "after to-night we can run in the daytime
if we want to. Whenever we see anybody coming, we can tie Jim
hand and foot with a rope, and lay him in the wigwam and show this
handbill and say we captured him up the river, and were too poor
to travel on a steamboat, so we got this little raft on credit from
our friends and are going down to get the reward. Handcuffs and
chains would look still better on Jim, but it wouldn't go well with the
story of us being so poor. Too much like jewelry. Ropes are the
correct thing—we must preserve the unities, as we say on the
boards."

We all said the duke was pretty smart, and there couldn't be no
trouble about running daytimes. We judged we could make miles
enough that night to get out of the reach of the pow-wow we
reckoned the duke's work in the printing office was going to make
in that little town—then we could boom right along, if we wanted
to.

We laid low and kept still, and never shoved out till nearly ten
o'clock; then we slid by, pretty wide away from the town, and didn't
hoist our lantern till we was clear out of sight of it.

When Jim called me to take the watch at four in the morning, he
says—

"Huck, does you rek'n we gwyne to run acrost any mo' kings
on dis trip?"

"No," I says, "I reckon not."

"Well," says he, "dat's all right, den. I doan' mine one er two
kings, but dat's enough. Dis one's powerful drunk, en de duke ain'
much better."

I found Jim had been trying to get him to talk French, so he could
hear what it was like; but he said he had been in this country so long,
and had so much trouble, he'd forgot it.

CHAPTER XXI

It was after sun-up, now, but we went right on, and didn't tie up. The king and the duke turned out, by-and-by, looking pretty rusty; but after they'd jumped overboard and took a swim, it chippered them up a good deal. After breakfast the king he took a seat on a corner of the raft, and pulled off his boots and rolled up his britches, and let his legs dangle in the water, so as to be comfortable, and lit his pipe, and went to getting his Romeo and Juliet by heart. When he had got it pretty good, him and the duke begun to practice it together. The duke had to learn him over and over again, how to say every speech; and he made him sigh, and put his hand on his heart, and after while he said he done it pretty well; "only," he says, "you mustn't bellow out *Romeo!* that way, like a bull—you must say it soft, and sick, and languishy, so—R-o-o-meo! that is the idea; for Juliet's a dear sweet mere child of a girl, you know, and she don't bray like a jackass."

Well, next they got a couple of long swords that the duke made out of oak laths, and begun to practice the sword-fight—the duke called himself Richard III.; and the way they laid on, and pranced around the raft was grand to see. But by-and-by the king tripped and fell overboard, and after that they took a rest, and had a talk about all kinds of adventures they'd had in other times along the river.

After dinner, the duke says:

"Well, Capet, we'll want to make this a first-class show, you know, so I guess we'll add a little more to it. We want a little something to answer encores with, anyway."

"What's onkores, Bilgewater?"

The duke told him, and then says:

"I'll answer by doing the Highland fling or the sailor's hornpipe; and you—well, let me see—oh, I've got it—you can do Hamlet's soliloquy."

"Hamlet's which?"

"Hamlet's soliloquy, you know; the most celebrated thing in Shakespeare. Ah, it's sublime, sublime! Always fetches the house. I haven't got it in the book—I've only got one volume—but I reckon I can piece it out from memory. I'll just walk up and down a minute, and see if I can call it back from recollection's vaults."

So he went to marching up and down, thinking, and frowning horrible every now and then; then he would hoist up his eyebrows; next he would squeeze his hand on his forehead and stagger back and kind of moan; next he would sigh, and next he'd let on to drop a tear. It was beautiful to see him. By-and-by he got it. He told us to give attention. Then he strikes a most noble attitude, with one leg shoved forwards, and his arms stretched away up, and his head

tilted back, looking up at the sky; and then he begins to rip and
rave and grit his teeth; and after that, all through his speech he
howled, and spread around, and swelled up his chest, and just
knocked the spots out of any acting ever *I* see before. This is the
speech—I learned it, easy enough, while he was learning it to the
king:

> To be, or not to be; that is the bare bodkin
> That makes calamity of so long life;
> For who would fardels bear, till Birnam Wood do come to Dunsinane,
> But that the fear of something after death
> Murders the innocent sleep,
> Great nature's second course,
> And makes us rather sling the arrows of outrageous fortune
> Than fly to others that we know not of.
> There's the respect must give us pause:
> Wake Duncan with thy knocking! I would thou couldst:
> For who would bear the whips and scorns of time,
> The oppressor's wrong, the proud man's contumely,
> The law's delay, and the quietus which his pangs might take,
> In the dead waste and middle of the night, when churchyards yawn
> In customary suits of solemn black,
> But that the undiscovered country from whose bourne no
>   traveler returns,
> Breathes forth contagion on the world,
> And thus the native hue of resolution, like the poor cat i' the adage,
> Is sicklied o'er with care,
> And all the clouds that lowered o'er our housetops,
> With this regard their currents turn awry,
> And lose the name of action.
> 'Tis a consummation devoutly to be wished. But soft you, the
>   fair Ophelia;
> Ope not they ponderous and marble jaws,
> But get thee to a nunnery—go!

Well, the old man he liked that speech, and he mighty soon got it
so he could do it first rate. It seemed like he was just born for it; and
when he had his hand in and was excited, it was perfectly lovely the
way he would rip and tear and rair up behind when he was getting
it off.

The first chance we got, the duke he had some show bills printed;
and after that, for two or three days, as we floated along, the raft
was a most uncommon lively place, for there warn't nothing but
sword-fighting and rehearsing—as the duke called it—going on all
the time. One morning, when we was pretty well down the State of
Arkansaw, we come in sight of a little one-horse town in a big bend;
so we tied up about three-quarters of a mile above it, in the mouth
of a crick which was shut in like a tunnel by the cypress trees, and
all of us but Jim took the canoe and went down there to see if there
was any chance in that place for our show.

We struck it mighty lucky; there was going to be a circus there that afternoon, and the country people was already beginning to come in, in all kinds of old shackly wagons, and on horses. The circus would leave before night, so our show would have a pretty good chance. The duke he hired the court house, and we went around and stuck up our bills. They read like this:

Shaksperean Revival! ! !
Wonderful Attraction!
For One Night Only!
The world renowned tragedians,
David Garrick the younger, of Drury Lane Theatre, London,
and
Edmund Kean the elder, of the Royal Haymarket Theatre, White-
chapel, Pudding Lane, Piccadilly, London, and the
Royal Continental Theatres, in their sublime
Shaksperean Spectacle entitled
The Balcony Scene
in
Romeo and Juliet! ! !

Romeo . . . . Mr. Garrick
Juliet . . . . Mr. Kean

Assisted by the whole strength of the company!
New costumes, new scenery, new appointments!
Also:
The thrilling, masterly, and blood-curdling
Broad-sword conflict
In Richard III. ! ! !

Richard III . . . . Mr. Garrick.
Richmond . . . . Mr. Kean.

also:
(by special request,)
Hamlet's Immortal Soliloquy! !
By the Illustrious Kean!
Done by him 300 consecutive nights in Paris!
For One Night Only,
On account of imperative European engagements!
Admission 25 cents; children and servants, 10 cents.

Then we went loafing around the town. The stores and houses was most all old shackly dried-up frame concerns that hadn't ever been painted; they was set up three or four foot above ground on stilts, so as to be out of reach of the water when the river was overflowed. The houses had little gardens around them, but they didn't seem to raise hardly anything in them but jimpson weeds, and sunflowers, and ash-piles, and old curled-up boots and shoes, and pieces of bottles, and rags, and played-out tin-ware. The fences was made of different kinds of boards, nailed on at different times; and they leaned every which-way, and had gates that didn't generly

have but one hinge—a leather one. Some of the fences had been
whitewashed, some time or another, but the duke said it was in
Clumbus's time, like enough. There was generly hogs in the garden,
and people driving them out.

All the stores was along one street. They had white-domestic
awnings in front, and the country people hitched their horses to the
awning-posts. There was empty dry-goods boxes under the awnings,
and loafers roosting on them all day long, whittling them with their
Barlow knives; and chawing tobacco, and gaping and yawning and
stretching—a mighty ornery lot. They generly had on yellow straw
hats most as wide as an umbrella, but didn't wear no coats nor
waistcoats; they called one another Bill, and Buck, and Hank, and
Joe, and Andy, and talked lazy and drawly, and used considerable
many cuss-words. There was as many as one loafer leaning up
against every awning-post, and he most always had his hands in his
britches pockets, except when he fetched them out to lend a chaw
of tobacco or scratch. What a body was hearing amongst them, all
the time was—

"Gimme a chaw 'v tobacker, Hank."

"Cain't—I hain't got but one chaw left. Ask Bill."

Maybe Bill he gives him a chaw; maybe he lies and says he ain't
got none. Some of them kinds of loafers never has a cent in the
world, nor a chaw of tobacco of their own. They get all their
chawing by borrowing—they say to a fellow, "I wisht you'd len' me
a chaw, Jack, I just this minute give Ben Thompson the last chaw I
had"—which is a lie, pretty much every time; it don't fool nobody
but a stranger; but Jack ain't no stranger, so he says—

"*You* give him a chaw, did you? so did your sister's cat's
grandmother. You pay me back the chaws you've awready borry'd
off'n me, Lafe Buckner, then I'll loan you one or two ton of it, and
won't charge you no back intrust, nuther."

"Well, I *did* pay you back some of it wunst."

"Yes, you did—'bout six chaws. You borry'd store tobacker and
paid back nigger-head."

Store tobacco is flat black plug, but these fellows mostly chaws
the natural leaf twisted. When they borrow a chaw, they don't
generly cut it off with a knife, but they set the plug in between their
teeth, and gnaw with their teeth and tug at the plug with their
hands till they get it in two—then sometimes the one that owns the
tobacco looks mournful at it when it's handed back, and says,
sarcastic—

"Here, gimme the *chaw*, and you take the *plug*."

All the streets and lanes was just mud, they warn't nothing else
but mud—mud as black as tar, and nigh about a foot deep in some
places; and two or three inches deep in *all* the places. The hogs
loafed and grunted around, everywheres. You'd see a muddy sow
and a litter of pigs come lazying along the street and whollop

herself right down in the way, where folks had to walk around her, and she'd stretch out, and shut her eyes and wave her ears, whilst the pigs was milking her, and look as happy as if she was on salary. And pretty soon you'd hear a loafer sing out, "Hi! *so* boy! sick him, Tige!" and away the sow would go, squealing most horrible, with a dog or two swinging to each ear, and three or four dozen more a-coming; and then you would see all the loafers get up and watch the thing out of sight, and laugh at the fun and look grateful for the noise. Then they'd settle back again till there was a dog-fight. There couldn't anything wake them up all over, and make them happy all over, like a dog-fight—unless it might be putting turpentine on a stray dog and setting fire to him, or tying a tin pan to his tail and see him run himself to death.

On the river front some of the houses was sticking out over the bank, and they was bowed and bent, and about ready to tumble in. The people had moved out of them. The bank was caved away under one corner of some others, and that corner was hanging over. People lived in them yet, but it was dangersome, because sometimes a strip of land as wide as a house caves in at a time. Sometimes a belt of land a quarter of a mile deep will start in and cave along and cave along till it all caves into the river one summer. Such a town as that has to be always moving back, and back, and back, because the river's always gnawing at it.

The nearer it got to noon that day, the thicker and thicker was the wagons and horses in the streets, and more coming all the time. Families fetched their dinners with them, from the country, and eat them in the wagons. There was considerable whiskey drinking going on, and I seen three fights. By-and-by somebody sings out—

"Here comes old Boggs!—in from the country for his little old monthly drunk—here he comes, boys!"

All the loafers looked glad—I reckoned they was used to having fun out of Boggs. One of them says—

"Wonder who he's a gwyne to chaw up this time. If he'd a chawed up all the men he's ben a gwyne to chaw up in the last twenty year, he'd have considerble ruputation, now."

Another one says, "I wisht old Boggs'd threaten me, 'cuz then I'd know I warn't gwyne to die for a thousan' year."

Boggs comes a-tearing along on his horse, whooping and yelling like an Injun, and singing out—

"Cler the track, thar. I'm on the waw-path, and the price uv coffins is a gwyne to raise."

He was drunk, and weaving about in his saddle; he was over fifty year old, and had a very red face. Everybody yelled at him, and laughed at him, and sassed him, and he sassed back, and said he'd attend to them and lay them out in their regular turns, but he couldn't wait now, because he'd come to town to kill old Colonel Sherburn, and his motto was, "meat first, and spoon vittles to top off on.''

He sees me, and rode up and says—

"Whar'd you come f'm, boy? You prepared to die?"

Then he rode on. I was scared; but a man says—

"He don't mean nothing; he's always a carryin' on like that,
when he's drunk. He's the best-naturedest old fool in Arkansaw—
never hurt nobody, drunk nor sober.''

Boggs rode up before the biggest store in town and bent his head
down so he could see under the curtain of the awning, and yells—

"Come out here, Sherburn! Come out and meet the man you've
swindled. You're the houn' I'm after, and I'm a gwyne to have you,
too!''

And so he went on, calling Sherburn everything he could lay his
tongue to, and the whole street packed with people listening and
laughing and going on. By-and-by a proud-looking man about
fifty-five—and he was a heap the best dressed man in that town,
too—steps out of the store, and the crowd drops back on each side
to let him come. He says to Boggs, mighty ca'm and slow—he says:

"I'm tired of this; but I'll endure it till one o'clock. Till one
o'clock, mind—no longer. If you open you mouth against me only
once, after that time, you can't travel so far but I will find you.''

Then he turns and goes in. The crowd looked mighty sober;
nobody stirred, and there warn't no more laughing. Boggs rode off
blackguarding Sherburn as loud as he could yell, all down the
street; and pretty soon back he comes and stops before the store,
still keeping it up. Some men crowded around him and tried to get
him to shut up, but he wouldn't; they told him it would be one
o'clock in about fifteen minutes, and so he *must* go home—he must
go right away. But it didn't do no good. He cussed away, with all his
might, and throwed his hat down in the mud and rode over it, and
pretty soon away he went a-raging down the street again, with his
gray hair a-flying. Everybody that could get a chance at him tried
their best to coax him off of his horse so they could lock him up
and get him sober; but it warn't no use—up the street he would
tear again, and give Sherburn another cussing. By-and-by
somebody says—

"Go for his daughter!—quick, go for his daughter; sometimes
he'll listen to her. If anybody can persuade him, she can.''

So somebody started on a run. I walked down street a ways, and
stopped. In above five or ten minutes, here comes Boggs again—
but not on his horse. He was a-reeling across the street towards me,
bareheaded, with a friend on both sides of him aholt of his arms
and hurrying him along. He was quiet, and looked uneasy; and he
warn't hanging back any, but was doing some of the hurrying
himself. Somebody sings out—

"Boggs!''

I looked over there to see who said it, and it was that Colonel

Sherburn. He was standing perfectly still, in the street, and had a
pistol raised in his right hand—not aiming it, but holding it out
with the barrel tilted up towards the sky, The same second I see a
young girl coming on the run, and two men with her. Boggs and the
men turned round to see who called him, and when they see the
pistol the men jumped to one side, and the pistol barrel come down
slow and steady to a level—both barrels cocked. Boggs throws up
both of his hands, and says, "O Lord, don't shoot!" Bang! goes the
first shot, and he staggers back clawing at the air—bang! goes the
second one, and he tumbles backwards onto the ground, heavy and
solid, with his arms spread out. That young girl screamed out, and
comes rushing, and down she throws herself on her father, crying,
and saying, "Oh, he's killed him, he's killed him!" The crowd
closed up around them, and shouldered and jammed one another,
with their necks stretched, trying to see, and people on the inside
trying to shove them back, and shouting, "Back, back! give him air,
give him air!"

Colonel Sherburn he tossed his pistol onto the ground, and
turned around on his heels and walked off.

They took Boggs to a little drug store, the crowd pressing around,
just the same, and the whole town following, and I rushed and got a
good place at the window, where I was close to him and could see
in. They laid him on the floor, and put one large Bible under his
head, and opened another one and spread it on his breast—but
they tore open his shirt first, and I seen where one of the bullets
went in. He made about a dozen long gasps, his breast lifting the
Bible up when he drawed in his breath, and letting it down again
when he breathed it out—and after that he laid still; he was dead.
Then they pulled his daughter away from him, screaming and
crying, and took her off. She was about sixteen, and very sweet and
gentle-looking, but awful pale and scared.

Well, pretty soon the whole town was there, squirming and
scrouging and pushing and shoving to get at the window and have
a look, but people that had the places wouldn't give them up, and
folks behind them was saying all the time, "Say, now, you've looked
enough, you fellows; 'taint right and 'taint fair, for you to stay thar
all the time, and never give nobody a chance; other folks has their
rights as well as you."

There was considerable jawing back, so I slid out, thinking
maybe there was going to be trouble. The streets was full, and
everybody was excited. Everybody that seen the shooting was telling
how it happened, and there was a big crowd packed around each
one of these fellows, stretching their necks and listening. One long
lanky man, with long hair and a big white fur stove-pipe hat on the
back of his head, and a crooked-handled cane, marked out the
places on the ground where Boggs stood, and where Sherburn stood,
and the people following him around from one place to t'other and

watching everything he done, and bobbing their heads to show they understood, and stooping a little and resting their hands on their thighs to watch him mark the places on the ground with his cane; and then he stood up straight and stiff where Sherburn had stood, frowning and having his hat-brim down over his eyes, and sung out, "Boggs!" and then fetched his cane down slow to a level, and says "Bang!" staggered backwards, says "Bang!" again, and fell down flat on his back. The people that had seen the thing said he done it perfect; said it was just exactly the way it all happened. Then as much as a dozen people got out their bottles and treated him.

Well, by-and-by somebody said Sherburn ought to be lynched. In about a minute everybody was saying it; so away they went, mad and yelling, and snatching down every clothes-line they come to, to do the hanging with.

CHAPTER XXII

They swarmed up the street towards Sherburn's house, a-whooping and yelling and raging like Injuns, and everything had to clear the way or get run over and tromped to mush, and it was awful to see. Children was heeling it ahead of the mob, screaming and trying to get out of the way; and every window along the road was full of women's heads, and there was nigger boys in every tree, and bucks and wenches looking over every fence; and as soon as the mob would get nearly to them they would break and skaddle back out of reach. Lots of the women and girls was crying and taking on, scared most to death.

They swarmed up in front of Sherburn's palings as thick as they could jam together, and you couldn't hear yourself think for the noise. It was a little twenty-foot yard. Some sung out "Tear down the fence! tear down the fence!" Then there was a racket of rippings and tearing and smashing, and down she goes, and the front wall of the crowd begins to roll in like a wave.

Just then Sherburn steps out on to the roof of his little front porch, with a double-barrel gun in his hand, and takes his stand, perfectly ca'm and deliberage, not saying a word. The racket stoppped, and the wave sucked back.

Sherburn never said a word—just stood there, looking down. The stillness was awful creepy and uncomfortable. Sherburn run his eye slow along the crowd; and wherever it struck, the people tried a little to outgaze him, but they couldn't; they dropped their eyes and looked sneaky. Then pretty soon Sherburn sort of laughed; not the pleasant kind, but the kind that makes you feel like when you are eating bread that's got sand in it.

Then he says, slow and scornful:

"The idea of *you* lynching anybody! It's amusing. The idea of you thinking you had pluck enough to lynch a *man!* Because you're

brave enough to tar and feather poor friendless cast-out women
that come along here, did that make you think you had grit
enough to lay your hands on a *man?* Why, a *man's* safe in the
hands of ten thousand of your kind—as long as it's day-time and
you're not behind him.

"Do I know you? I know you clear through. I was born and
raised in the South, and I've lived in the North; so I know the
average all around. The average man's a coward. In the North he
lets anybody walk over him that wants to, and goes home and prays
for a humble spirit to bear it. In the South one man, all by himself,
has stopped a stage full of men, in the day-time, and robbed the
lot. Your newspapers call you a brave people so much that you
think you *are* braver than any other people—whereas you're just *as*
brave, and no braver. Why don't your juries hang murderers?
Because they're afraid the man's friends will shoot them in the
back, in the dark—and it's just what they *would* do.

"So they always acquit; and then a *man* goes in the night, with a
hundred masked cowards at his back, and lynches the rascal. Your
mistake is, that you didn't bring a man with you; that's one
mistake, and the other is that you didn't come in the dark, and
fetch your masks. You brought *part* of a man—Buck Harkness,
there—and if you hadn't had him to start you, you'd a taken it out
in blowing.

"You didn't want to come. The average man don't like trouble
and danger. *You* don't like trouble and danger. But if only *half* a
man—like Buck Harkness, there—shouts 'Lynch him, lynch him!'
you're afraid to back down—afraid you'll be found out to be what
you are—*cowards*—and so you raise a yell, and hang yourselves
onto that half-a-man's coat tail, and come raging up here, swearing
what big things you're going to do. The pitifulest thing out is a
mob; that's what an army is—a mob; they don't fight with courage
that's born in them, but with courage that's borrowed from their
mass, and from their officers. But a mob without any *man* at the
head of it, is *beneath* pitifulness. Now the thing for *you* to do, is to
droop your tails and go home and crawl in a hole. If any real
lynching's going to be done, it will be done in the dark, Southern
fashion; and when they come they'll bring their masks, and fetch a
man along. Now *leave*—and take your half-a-man with you"—
tossing his gun up across his left arm and cocking it, when he says
this.

The crowd washed back sudden, and then broke all apart and
went tearing off every which way, and Buck Harkness he heeled it
after them, looking tolerable cheap. I could a staid, if I'd a wanted
to, but I didn't want to.

I went to the circus, and loafed around the back side till the
watchman went by, and then dived in under the tent. I had my
twenty-dollar gold piece and some other money, but I reckoned I

better save it, because there ain't no telling how soon you are going
to need it, away from home and amongst strangers, that way. You
can't be too careful. I ain't opposed to spending money on circuses,
when there ain't no other way, but there ain't no use in *wasting* it
on them.

It was a real bully circus. It was the splendidest sight that ever
was, when they all come riding in, two and two, a gentleman and
lady, side by side, the men just in their drawers and under-shirts,
and no shoes nor stirrups, and resting their hands on their thighs,
easy and comfortable—there must a' been twenty of them—and
every lady with a lovely complexion, and perfectly beautiful, and
looking just like a gang of real sure-enough queens, and dressed in
clothes that cost millions of dollars, and just littered with
diamonds. It was a powerful fine sight; I never see anything so
lovely. And then one by one they got up and stood, and went
a-weaving around the ring so gentle and wavy and graceful, the
men looking ever so tall and airy and straight, with their heads
bobbing and skimming along, away up there under the tent-roof,
and every lady's rose-leafy dress flapping soft and silky around her
hips, and she looking like the most loveliest parasol.

And then faster and faster they went, all of them dancing, first
one foot stuck out in the air and then the other, the horses leaning
more and more, and the ring-master going round and round the
centre-pole, cracking his whip and shouting "hi!—hi!" and the
clown cracking jokes behind him; and by-and-by all hands dropped
the reins, and every lady put her knuckles on her hips and every
gentleman folded his arms, and then how the horses did lean over
and hump themselves! And so, one after the other they all skipped
off into the ring and made the sweetest bow I ever see, and then
scampered out, and everybody clapped their hands and went just
about wild.

Well, all through the circus they done the most astonishing
things; and all the time that clown carried on so it most killed the
people. The ring-master couldn't ever say a word to him but he was
back at him quick as a wink with the funniest thing a body ever
said; and how he ever *could* think of so many of them, and so
sudden and so pat, was what I couldn't noway understand. Why, I
couldn't a thought of them in a year. And by-and-by a drunk man
tried to get into the ring—said he wanted to ride; said he could ride
as well as anybody that ever was. They argued and tried to keep
him out, but he wouldn't listen, and the whole show come to a
standstill. Then the people begun to holler at him and make fun of
him, and that made him mad, and he begun to rip and tear; so
that stirred up the poeple, and a lot of men begun to pile down off
of the benches and swarm towards the ring, saying, "Knock him
down! throw him out!" and one or two women begun to scream. So,
then, the ring-master he made a little speech, and said he hoped

there wouldn't be no disturbance, and if the man would promise he
wouldn't make no more trouble, he would let him ride, if he
thought he could stay on the horse. So everybody laughed and said
all right, and the man got on. The minute he was on, the horse
begun to rip and tear and jump and cavort around, with two circus
men hanging onto his bridle trying to hold him, and the drunk man
hanging onto his neck, and his heels flying in the air every jump,
and the whole crowd of people standing up shouting and laughing
till the tears rolled down. And at last, sure enough, all the circus
men could do, the horse broke loose, and away he went like the
very nation, round and round the ring, with that sot laying down on
him and hanging to his neck, with first one leg hanging most to the
ground on the side, and then t'other one on t'other side, and the
people just crazy. It warn't funny to me, though; I was all of a
tremble to see his danger. But pretty soon he struggled up astraddle
and grabbed the bridle, a-reeling this way and that; and the next
minute he sprung up and dropped the bridle and stood! and the
horse agoing like a house afire too. He just stood there, a-sailing
around as easy and comfortable as if he warn't ever drunk in his
life—and then he begun to pull off his clothes and sling them. He
shed them so thick they kind of clogged up the air, and altogether
he shed seventeen suits. And then, there he was, slim and
handsome, and dressed the gaudiest and prettiest you ever saw, and
he lit into that horse with his whip and made him fairly hum—and
finally skipped off, and made his bow and danced off to the
dressing-room, and everybody just a-howling with pleasure and
astonishment.

Then the ring-master he see how he had been fooled, and he *was*
the sickest ring-master you ever see, I reckon. Why, it was one of
his own men! He had got up that joke all out of his own head, and
never let on to nobody. Well, I felt sheepish enough, to be took in
so, but I wouldn't a been in that ring-master's place, not for a
thousand dollars. I don't know; there may be bullier circuses than
what that one was, but I never struck them yet. Anyways it was
plenty good enough for *me;* and wherever I run across it, it can
have all of my custom, every time.

Well, that night we had *our* show; but there warn't only about
twelve people there; just enough to pay expenses. And they laughed
all the time, and that made the duke mad; and everybody left,
anyway, before the show was over, but one boy which was asleep. So
the duke said these Arkansaw lunkheads couldn't come up to
Shakspeare; what they wanted was low comedy—and may be
something ruther worse than low comedy, he reckoned. He said he
could size their style. So next morning he got some big sheets of
wrapping-paper and some black paint, and drawed off some
handbills and stuck them up all over the village. The bills said:

AT THE COURT HOUSE!
FOR 3 NIGHTS ONLY!
The World-Renowned Tragedians
DAVID GARRICK THE YOUNGER!
AND
EDMUND KEAN THE ELDER!
*Of the London and Continental
Theatres,*
In their Thrilling Tragedy of
THE KING'S CAMELOPARD
OR
THE ROYAL NONESUCH!!!
Admission 50 cents.

Then at the bottom was the biggest line of all—which said:

LADIES AND CHILDREN NOT ADMITTED.

"There," says he, "if that line don't fetch them, I don't know Arkansaw!"

CHAPTER XXIII

Well, all day him and the king was hard at it, rigging up a stage, and a curtain, and a row of candles for footlights; and that night the house was jam full of men in no time. When the place couldn't hold no more, the duke he quit tending door and went around the back way and come onto the stage and stood up before the curtain, and made a little speech, and praised up this tragedy, and said it was the most thrillingest one that ever was; and so he went on a-bragging about the tragedy and about Edmund Kean the Elder, which was to play the main principal part in it; and at last when he'd got everybody's expectations up high enough, he rolled up the curtain, and the next minute the king come a-prancing out on all fours, naked; and he was painted all over, ring-streaked-and-striped, all sorts of colors, as splendid as a rainbow. And—but never mind the rest of his outfit, it was just wild, but it was awful funny. The people most killed themselves laughing; and when the king got done capering, and capered off behind the scenes, they roared and clapped and stormed and haw-hawed till he come back and done it over again; and after that, they made him do it another time. Well, it would a made a cow laugh to see the shines that old idiot cut.

Then the duke he lets the curtain down, and bows to the people, and says the great tragedy will be performed only two nights more, on accounts of pressing London engagements, where the seats is all sold aready for it in Drury Lane; and then he makes them another bow, and says if he has succeeded in pleasing and instructing them, he will be deeply obleeged if they will mention it to their friends and get them to come and see it.

Twenty people sings out:

"What, is it over? Is that *All?*"

The duke says yes. Then there was a fine time. Everybody sings out "sold," and rose up mad, and was agoing for that stage and them tragedians. But a big fine-looking man jumps up on a bench, and shouts:

"Hold on! Just a word, gentlemen." They stopped to listen. "We are sold—mighty badly sold. But we don't want to be the laughing-stock of this whole town, I reckon, and never hear the last of this thing as long as we live. *No.* What we want, is to get out of here quiet, and talk this show up, and sell the *rest* of the town. Then we'll all be in the same boat. Ain't that sensible?" ("You bet it is!—the jedge is right!" everybody sings out.) "All right, then—not a word about any sell. Go along home, and advise everybody to come and see the tragedy."

Next day you couldn't hear nothing around that town but how splendid that show was. House was jammed again, that night, and we sold this crowd the same way. When me and king and the duke got home to the raft, we all had a super; and by-and-by, about midnight, they made Jim and me back her out and float her down the middle of the river and fetch her in and hide her about two miles below town.

The third night the house was crammed again—and they warn't new-comers, this time, but people that was at the show the other two nights. I stood by the duke at the door, and I see that every man that went in had his pockets bulging, or something muffled up under his coat—and I see it warn't no perfumery neither, not by a long sight. I smelt sickly eggs by the barrel, and rotten cabbages, and such things; and if I know the signs of a dead cat being around, and I bet I do, there was sixty-four of them went in. I shoved in there for a minute, but it was too various for me, I couldn't stand it. Well, when the place couldn't hold no more people, the duke he give a fellow a quarter and told him to tend door for him a minute, and then he started around for the stage door, I after him; but the minute we turned the corner and was in the dark, he says:

"Walk fast, now, till you get away from the houses, and then shin for the raft like the dickens was after you!"

I done it, and he done the same. We struck the raft at the same time, and less than two seconds we was gliding down steam, all dark and still, and edging towards the middle of the river, nobody saying a word. I reckoned the poor king was in for a gaudy time of it with the audience; but nothing of the sort; pretty soon he crawls out from under the wigwam, and says:

"Well, how'd the old thing pan out this time, Duke?"

He hadn't been up town at all.

We never showed a light till we was about ten mile below that
village. Then we lit up and had a supper and the king and the
duke fairly laughed their bones loose over the way they'd served
them people. The duke says:

"Greenhorns, flatheads! *I* knew the first house would keep mum
and let the rest of the town get roped in; and I knew they'd lay for
us the third night, and consider it was *their* turn now. Well, it *is*
their turn, and I'd give something to know how much they'd take
for it. I *would* just like to know how they're putting in their
opportunity. They can turn it into a picnic, if they want to—they
brought plenty provisions."

Them rapscallions took in four hundred and sixty-five dollars in
that three nights. I never see money hauled in by the wagon-load
like that, before.

By-and-by, when they was asleep and snoring, Jim says:

"Don't it 'sprise you, de way dem kings carries on, Huck?"

"No," I says, "it don't."

"Why don't it, Huck?"

"Well, it don't, because it's in the breed. I reckon they're all
alike."

"But, Huck, dese kings o' ourn is regular rapscallions; dat's jist
what dey is; dey's regular rapscallions."

"Well, that's what I'm a-saying; all kings is mostly rapscallions,
as fur as I can make out."

"Is dat so?"

"You read about them once—you'll see. Look at Henry the
Eight; this'n 's a Sunday-School Superintendent to *him*. And look
at Charles Second, and Louis Fourteen, and Louis Fifteen, and
James Second, and Edward Second, and Richard Third, and forty
more; besides all them Saxon heptarchies that used to rip around
so in old times and raise Cain. My, you ought to seen old Henry the
Eight when he was in bloom. He *was* a blossom. He used to marry
a new wife every day, and chop off her head next morning. And he
would do it just as indifferent as if he was ordering up eggs. 'Fetch
up Nell Gwynn," he says. They fetch her up. Next morning, 'Chop
off her head!' And they chop it off. 'Fetch up Jane Shore,' he says;
and up she comes. Next morning 'Chop off her head'—and they
chop it off. 'Ring up Fair Rosamun.' Fair Rosamun answers the
bell. Next morning, 'Chop off her head.' And he made every one of
them tell him a tale every night; and he put them all in a book, and
called it Domesday Book—which was a good name and stated the
case. You don't know kings, Jim, but I know them; and this old rip
of ourn is one of the cleanest I've struck in history. Well, Henry he
takes a notion he wants to get up some trouble with this country.
How does he go at it—give notice?—give the country a show? No.
All of a sudden he heaves all the tea in Boston Harbor overboard,
and whacks out a declaration of independence, and dares them to

come on. That was *his* style—he never give anybody a chance. He
had suspicions of his father, the Duke of Wellington. Well, what
did he do?—ask him to show up? No—drownded him in a butt of
mamsey, like a cat. Spose people left money laying around where
he was—what did he do? He collared it. Spose he contracted to do
a thing; and you paid him, and didn't set down there and see that
he done it—what did he do? He always done the other thing. Spose
he opened his mouth—what then? If he didn't shut it up powerful
quick, he'd lose a lie, every time. That's the kind of a bug Henry
was; and if we'd a had him along 'stead of our kings, he'd a fooled
that town a heap worse than ourn done. I don't say that ourn is
lambs, because they ain't, when you come right down to the cold
facts; but they ain't nothing to *that* old ram, anyway. All I say is,
kings is kings, and you got to make allowances. Take them all
around, they're a mighty ornery lot. It's the way they're raised."

"But dis one do *smell* so like de nation, Huck."

"Well, they all do, Jim. *We* can't help the way a king smells;
history don't tell no way."

"Now de duke, he's a tolerable likely man, in some ways."

"Yes, a duke's different. But not very different. This one's a
middling hard lot, for a duke, When he's drunk, there ain't no
near-sighted man could tell him from a king."

"Well, anyways, I doan' hanker for no mo' un um, Huck. Dese is
all I kin stan'."

"It's the way I feel, too, Jim. But we've got them on our hands,
and we got to remember what they are, and make allowances.
Sometimes I wish we could hear of a country that's out of kings."

What was the use to tell Jim these warn't real kings and dukes?
It wouldn't a done no good; and besides, it was just as I said; you
couldn't tell them from the real kind.

I went to sleep, and Jim didn't call me when it was my turn. He
often done that. When I waked up, just at day-break, he was setting
there with his head down betwixt his knees, moaning and mourning
to himself. I didn't take notice, nor let on. I knowed what it was
about. He was thinking about his wife and his children, away up
yonder, and he was low and homesick; because he hadn't ever been
away from home before in his life; and I do believe he cared just
as much for his people as white folks does for their'n. It don't seem
natural, but I reckon it's so. He was often moaning and mourning
that way, nights, when he judged I was asleep, and saying, "Po'
little 'Lizabeth! po' little Johnny! its mighty hard; I spec' I ain't
ever gwyne to see you no mo', no mo'!" He was a mighty good nigger,
Jim was.

But this time I somehow got to talking to him about his wife and
young ones; and by-and-by he says:

"What makes me feel so bad dis time, 'uz bekase I hear sumpn
over yonder on de bank like a whack, er a slam, while ago, en it

mine me er de time I treat my little 'Lizabeth so ornery. She warn't
on'y 'bout fo' year ole, en she tuck de sk'yarlet-fever, en had a
powful rough spell; but she got well, en one day she was a-stannin'
around', en I says to her, I says:

"Shet de do'.'

"She never done it; jis' stood dah, kiner smilin' up at me. It
make me mad; en I says agin, mighty loud, I says:

" 'Doan' you hear me?—shet de do'!'

"She jis' stood de same way, kiner smilin' up. I was a-bilin'!
I says:

" 'I lay I *make* you mine!'

"En wid dat I fetch' her a slap side de head dat sont her
a-sprawlin'. Den I went into de yuther room, en 'uz gone 'bout ten
minutes; en when I come back, dah was dat do' a-stanning' open
yit, en dat chile stannin' mos' right in it, a-lookin' down and
mournin', en de tears runnin' down. My, but I *wuz* mad, I was
agwyne for de chile, but jis' den—it was a do' dat open innerds—
jis' den, 'long come de wind en slam it to, behine de chile,
ker-*blam!*—en my lan', de chile never move'! My breff mos' hop
outer me; en I feel so—so—I don't know *how* I feel. I crope out, all
a-tremblin', en crope aroun' en open de do' easy en slow, en poke
my head in behind de chile, sof' en still, en all uv a sudden, I says
pow! just' as loud as I could yell. *She never budge!* Oh, Huck, I
bust out a-cryin' en grab her up in my arms, en say, 'Oh, de po'
little thing! de Lord God Amighty fogive po' ole Jim, kaze he never
gwyne to fogive hisself as long's he live!' Oh, she was plumb deef en
dumb, Huck, plumb deef en dumb—en I'd been a-treat'n her so!''

CHAPTER XXIV

Next day, towards night, we laid up under a little willow tow-
head out in the middle, where there was a village on each side of
the river, and the duke and the king begun to lay out a plan for
working them towns. Jim he spoke to the duke, and said he hoped
it wouldn't take but a few hours, because it got mighty heavy and
tiresome to him when he had to lay all day in the wigwam tied with
the rope. You see, when we left him all alone we had to tie him,
because if anybody happened on him all by himself and not tied, it
wouldn't look much like he was a runaway nigger, you know. So the
duke said it *was* kind of hard to have to lay roped all day, and he'd
cipher out some way to get around it.

He was uncommon bright, the duke was, and he soon struck it.
He dressed Jim up in King Lear's outfit—it was a long curtain-
calico gown, and a white horse-hair wig and whiskers; and then he
took his theatre-paint and painted Jim's face and hands and ears
and neck all over a dead dull solid blue, like a man that's been
drownded nine days. Blamed if he warn't the horriblest looking

outrage I ever see. Then the duke took and wrote out a sign on a shingle so—

Sick Arab—but harmless when not out of his head.

And he nailed that shingle to a lath, and stood the lath up four or five foot in front of the wigwam. Jim was satisfied. He said it was a sight better than laying tied a couple of years every day and trembling all over every time there was a sound. The duke told him to make himself free and easy, and if anybody ever come meddling around, he must hop out of the wigwam, and carry on a little, and fetch a howl or two like a wild beast, and he reckoned they would light out and leave him alone. Which was sound enough judgment; but you take the average man, and he wouldn't wait for him to howl. Why, he didn't only look like he was dead, he looked considerable more than that.

These rapscallions wanted to try the Nonesuch again, because there was so much money in it, but they judged it wouldn't be safe, because maybe the news might a worked along down by this time. They couldn't hit no project that suited, exactly; so at last the duke said he reckoned he'd lay off and work his brains an hour or two and see if he couldn't put up something on the Arkansaw village; and the king he allowed he would drop over to t'other village, without any plan, but just trust in Providence to lead him the profitable way—meaning the devil, I reckon. We had all bought store clothes where we stopped last; and now the king put his'n on, and he did look real swell and starchy. I never knowed how clothes could change a body before. Why, before, he looked like the orneriest old rip that ever was; but now, when he'd take off his new white beaver and make a bow and do a smile, he looked that grand and good and pious that you'd say he had walked right out of the ark, and maybe was old Leviticus himself. Jim cleaned up the canoe, and I got my paddle ready. There was a big steamboat laying at the shore away up under the point, about three mile above town—been there a couple of hours, taking on freight. Says the king:

"Seein' how I'm dressed, I reckon maybe I better arrive down from St. Louis or Cincinnati, or some other big place. Go for the steamboat, Huckleberry; we'll come down to the village on her."

I didn't have to be ordered twice, to go and take a steamboat ride. I fetched the shore a half a mile above the village, and then went scooting along the bluff bank in the easy water. Pretty soon we come to a nice innocent-looking young country jake setting on a log swabbing the sweat off of his face, for it was powerful warm weather; and he had a couple of big carpet-bags by him.

"Run her nose in shore," says the king. I done it. "Wher' you bound for, young man?"

"For the steamboat; going to Orleans."

"Git aboard," says the king. "Hold on a minute, my servant 'll

he'p you with them bags. Jump out and he'p the gentleman,
Adolphus"—meaning me, I see.

I done so, and then we all three started on again. The young
chap was mighty thankful; said it was tough work toting his
baggage such weather. He asked the king where he was going, and
the king told him he'd come down the river and landed at the other
village this morning, and now he was going up a few mile to see an
old friend on a farm up there. The young fellow says:

"When I first see you, I says to myself, 'It's Mr. Wilks, sure, and
he come mighty near getting here in time.' But then I says again,
'No, I reckon it ain't him, or else he wouldn't be paddling up the
river.' You *ain't* him, are you?"

"No, my name's Blodgett—Elexander Blodgett—*Reverend*
Elexander Blodgett, I spose I must say, as I'm one o' the Lord's
poor servants. But still I'm jist as able to be sorry for Mr. Wilks for
not arriving in time, all the same, if he's missed anything by it—
which I hope he hasn't."

"Well, he don't miss any property by it, because he'll get that all
right; but he's missed seeing his brother Peter die—which he
mayn't mind, nobody can tell as to that—but his brother would a
give anything in this world to see *him* before he died; never talked
about nothing else all these three weeks; hadn't seen him since they
was boys together—and hadn't ever seen his brother William at all
—that's the deef and dumb one—William ain't more than thirty or
thirty-five. Peter and George was the only ones that come out here;
George was the married brother; him and his wife both died last
year. Harvey and William's the only ones that's left now; and, as I
was saying, they haven't got here in time."

"Did anybody send 'em word?"

"Oh, yes; a month or two ago, when Peter was first took; because
Peter said then that he sorter felt like he warn't going to get well
this time. You see, he was pretty old, and George's g'yirls was too
young to be much company for him, except Mary Jane the red-
headed one; and so he was kinder lonesome after George and his
wife died, and didn't seem to care much to live. He most
desperately wanted to see Harvey—and William too, for that matter
—because he was one of them kind that can't bear to make a will.
He left a letter behind for Harvey, and said he'd told in it where
his money was hid, and how he wanted the rest of the property
divided up so George's g'yirls would be all right—for George didn't
leave nothing. And that letter was all they could get him to put a
pen to."

"Why do you reckon Harvey don't come? Wher' does he live?"

"Oh, he lives in England—Sheffield—preaches there—hasn't
ever been in this country. He hasn't had any too much time—and
beside he mightn't a got the letter at all, you know."

"Too bad, too bad he couldn't a lived to see his brothers, poor soul. You going to Orleans, you say?"

"Yes, but that ain't only a part of it. I'm going in a ship,
next Wednesday, for Ryo Janeero, where my uncle lives."

"It's a pretty long journey. But it'll be lovely; I wisht I was
agoing. Is Mary Jane the oldest? How old is the others?"

"Mary Jane's nineteen, Susan's fifteen, and Joanna's about
fourteen—that's the one that gives herself to good works and has a
hare-lip."

"Poor things! to be left alone in the cold world so."

"Well, they could be worse off. Old Peter had friends, and they
ain't going to let them come to no harm. There's Hobson, the
Babtis' preacher; and Deacon Lot Hovey, and Ben Rucker, and
Abner Shackleford, and Levi Bell, the lawyer; and Dr. Robinson,
and their wives, and the widow Bartley, and—well, there's a lot of
them; but these are the ones that Peter was thickest with, and used
to write about sometimes, when he wrote home; so Harvey'll know
where to look for friends when he get's here."

Well, the old man he went on asking questions till he just fairly
emptied that young fellow. Blamed if he didn't inquire about
everybody and everything in that blessed town, and all about all the
Wilkses; and about Peter's business—which was a tanner; and
about George's—which was a carpenter; and about Harvey's—
which was a dissentering minister; and so on, and so on. Then he
says:

"What did you want to walk all the way up to the steamboat
for?"

"Because she's a big Orleans boat, and I was afeard she mightn't
stop there. When they're deep they won't stop for a hail. A
Cincinnati boat will, but this is a St. Louis one."

"Was Peter Wilks well off?"

"Oh, yes, pretty well off. He had houses and land, and it's
reckoned he left three or four thousand in cash hid up som'ers."

"When did you say he died?"

"I didn't say, but it was last night."

"Funeral to-morrow, likely?"

"Yes, 'bout the middle of the day."

"Well, it's all terrible sad; but we've all got to go, one time or
another. So what we want to do is to be prepared; then we're all
right."

"Yes, sir, it's the best way. Ma used to always say that."

When we struck the boat, she was about done loading, and pretty
soon she got off. The king never said nothing about going aboard,
so I lost my ride, after all. When the boat was gone, the king made
me paddle up another mile to a lonesome place, and then he got
ashore, and says:

"Now hustle back, right off, and fetch the duke up here, and the
new carpet-bags. And if he's gone over to t'other side, go over there

and git him. And tell him to git himself up regardless. Shove along,
now.''

I see what *he* was up to; but I never said nothing, of course.
When I got back with the duke, we hid the canoe and then they set
down on a log, and the king told him everything, just like the young
fellow had said it—every last word of it. And all the time he was a
doing it, he tried to talk like an Englishman; and he done it pretty
well too, for a slouch. I can't imitate him, and so I ain't agoing to
try to; but he really done it pretty good. Then he says:

"How are you on the deef and dumb, Bilgewater?''

The duke said, leave him alone for that; said he had played a
deef and dumb person on the histrionic boards. So then they waited
for a steamboat.

About the middle of the afternoon a couple of little boats come
along, but they didn't come from high enough up the river; but at
last there was a big one, and they hailed her. She sent out her yawl,
and we went aboard, and she was from Cincinnati; and when they
found we only wanted to go four or five mile, they was booming
mad, and give us a cussing, and said they wouldn't land us. But the
king was ca'm. He says:

"If gentlemen kin afford to pay a dollar a mile apiece, to be took
on and put off in a yawl, a steamboat kin afford to carry 'em, can't
it?''

So they softened down and said it was all right; and when we got
to the village, they yawled us ashore. About two dozen men flocked
down, when they see the yawl a coming; and when the king says—

"Kin any of you gentlemen tell me wher' Mr. Peter Wilks lives?''
they give a glance at one another, and nodded their heads, as much
as to say, "What d' I tell you?'' Then one of them says, kind of soft
and gentle:

"I'm sorry, sir, but the best we can do is to tell you where he *did*
live yesterday evening.''

Sudden as winking, the ornery old cretur went all to smash, and
fell up against the man, and put his chin on his shoulder, and cried
down his back, and says:

"Alas, alas, our poor brother—gone, and we never got to see
him; oh, it's too, *too* hard!''

Then he turns around, blubbering, and makes a lot of idiotic
signs to the duke on his hands, and blamed if *he* didn't drop a
carpet-bag and bust out a-crying. If they warn't the beatenest lot,
them two frauds, that ever I struck.

Well, the men gethered around, and sympathized with them, and
said all sorts of kind things to them, and carried their carpet-bags
up the hill for them, and let them lean on them and cry, and told
the king all about his brother's last moments and the king he told
it all over again on his hands to the duke, and both of them took
on about that dead tanner like they'd lost the twelve disciples. Well,

if ever I struck anything like it, I'm a nigger. It was enough to make
a body ashamed of the human race.

CHAPTER XXV

The news was all over town in two minutes, and you could see the
people tearing down on the run, from every which way, some of
them putting on their coats as they come. Pretty soon we was in the
middle of a crowd, and the noise of the tramping was like a soldier-
march. The windows and door-yards was full; and every minute
somebody would say, over a fence:

"Is it *them?*"

And somebody trotting along with the gang would answer back
and say,

"You bet it is."

When we got to the house, the street in front of it was packed,
and the three girls was standing in the door. Mary Jane *was* red-
headed, but that don't make no difference, she was most awful
beautiful, and her face and her eyes was all lit up like glory, she was
so glad her uncles was come. The king he spread his arms, and
Mary Jane she jumped for them, and the hare-lip jumped for the
duke, and there they *had* it! Everybody most, leastways women,
cried for joy to see them meet again at last and have such good
times.

Then the king he hunched the duke, private—I see him do it—
and then he looked around and see the coffin, over in the corner on
two chairs; so then, him and the duke, with a hand across each
other's shoulder, and t'other hand to their eyes, walked slow and
solemn over there, everybody dropping back to give them room,
and all the talk and noise stopping, people saying "Sh!" and all
the men taking their hats off and drooping their heads, so you could
a heard a pin fall. And when they got there, they bent over and
looked in the coffin, and took one sight, and then they bust out a
crying so you could a heard them to Orleans, most; and then they
put their arms around each other's necks, and hung their chins
over each other's shoulders; and then for three minutes, or maybe
four, I never see two men leak the way they done. And mind you,
everybody was doing the same; and the place was that damp I never
see anything like it. Then one of them got on one side of the coffin,
and t'other on t'other side, and they kneeled down and rested their
foreheads on the coffin, and let on to pray all to theirselves. Well,
when it come to that, it worked the crowd like you never see anything like it, and so everybody broke down and went to sobbing
right out loud—the poor girls, too; and every woman, nearly, went
up to the girls, without saying a word, and kissed them, solemn, on
the forehead, and then put their hand on their head, and looked up
towards the sky, with the tears running down, and then busted out

and went off sobbing and swabbing, and give the next woman a
show. I never see anything so disgusting.

Well, by-and-by the king he gets up and comes forward a little,
and works himself up and slobbers out a speech, all full of tears
and flapdoodle about its being a sore trial for him and his poor
brother to lose the diseased, and to miss seeing diseased alive, after
the long journey of four thousand mile, but its a trial that's
sweetened and sanctified to us by this dear sympathy and these holy
tears, and so he thanks them out of his heart and out of his brother's
heart, because out of their mouths they can't, words being too weak
and cold, and all that kind of rot and slush, till it was just
sickening; and then he blubbers out a pious goody-goody Amen,
and turns himself loose and goes to crying fit to bust.

And the minute the words was out of his mouth somebody over
in the crowd struck up the doxolojer, and everybody joined in with
all their might, and it just warmed you up and made you feel as
good as church letting out. Music *is* a good thing; and after all that
soul-butter and hogwash, I never see it freshen up things so, and
sound so honest and bully.

Then the king begins to work his jaw again, and says how him
and his nieces would be glad if a few of the main principal friends
of the family would take supper here with them this evening, and
help set up with the ashes of the diseased; and says if his poor
brother laying yonder could speak, he knows who he would name,
for they was names that was very dear to him and mentioned often
in his letters; so he will name the same, to-wit, as follows, vizz:—
Rev. Mr. Hobson, and Deacon Lot Hovey, and Mr. Ben Rucker, and
Abner Shackleford, and Levi Bell, and Dr. Robinson, and their
wives, and the widow Bartley.

Rev. Hobson and Dr. Robinson was down to the end of the town,
a-hunting together; that is, I mean the doctor was shipping a sick
man to t'other world, and the preacher was pinting him right.
Lawyer Bell was away up to Louisville on some business. But the
rest was on hand, and so they all come and shook hands with the
king and thanked him and talked to him; and then they shook
hands with the duke, and didn't say nothing but just kept a-smiling
and bobbing their heads like a passel of sapheads whilst he made
all sorts of signs with his hands and said "Goo-goo—goo-goo-goo,"
all the time, like a baby that can't talk.

So the king he blatted along, and managed to inquire about pretty
much everybody and dog in town, by his name, and mentioned all
sorts of little things that happened one time or another in the town,
or to George's family, or to Peter; and he always let on that Peter
wrote him the things, but that was a lie, he got every blessed one of
them out of that young flathead that we canoed up to the
steamboat.

Then Mary Jane she fetched the letter her father left behind, and

the king he read it out loud and cried over it. It give the dwelling-
house and three thousand dollars, gold, to the girls; and it give the
tanyard (which was doing a good business), along with some other
houses and land (worth about seven thousand), and three thousand
dollars in gold to Harvey and William, and told where the six
thousand cash was hid, down cellar. So these two frauds said they'd
go and fetch it up, and have everything square and above-board;
and told me to come with a candle. We shut the cellar door behind
us, and when they found the bag they spilt it out on the floor, and it
was a lovely sight, all them yaller-boys. My, the way the king's eyes
did shine! He slaps the duke on the shoulder, and says:

"Oh, *this* ain't bully, nor noth'n! Oh, no, I reckon not! Why,
Biljy, it beats the Nonesuch, *don't* it!"

The duke allowed it did. They pawed the yaller-boys, and sifted
them through their fingers and let them jingle down on the floor;
and the king says:

"It ain't no use talkin'; being' brothers to a rich dead man, and
representatives of furrin heirs that's got left, is the line for you and
me, Bilge. Thish-yer comes of trust'n to Providence. It's the best
way, in the long run. I've tried 'em all, and ther' ain't no better
way."

Most everybody would a been satisfied with the pile, and took it
on trust; but no, they must count it. So they counts it, and it comes
out four hundred and fifteen dollars short. Says the king:

"Dern him, I wonder what he done with that four hundred and
fifteen dollars?"

They worried over that a while, and ransacked all around for it.
Then the duke says:

"Well, he was a pretty sick man, and likely he made a mistake—
I reckon that's the way of it. The best way's to let it go, and keep
still about it. We can spare it."

"Oh, shucks, yes, we can *spare* it. I don't k'yer noth'n 'bout that
—it's the *count* I'm thinkin' about. We want to be awful square
and open and above-board, here, you know. We want to lug this
h-yer money up stairs and count it before everybody—then ther'
ain't noth'n suspicious. But when the dead man says ther's six
thous'n dollars, you know, we don't want to—"

"Hold on," says the duke. "Less make up the deffisit"—and he
begun to haul out yaller-boys out of his pocket.

"It's a most amaz'n' good idea, duke—you *have* got a rattlin'
clever head on you," says the king. "Blest if the old Nonesuch ain't
a heppin' us out agin"—and *he* begun to haul out yaller-jackets
and stack them up.

It most busted them, but they made up the six thousand clean
and clear.

"Say," says the duke, "I got another idea. Le's go up stairs and
count this money, and then take and *give it to the girls.*"

"Good land, duke, lemme hug you! It's the most dazzling idea 'at ever a man struck. You have cert'nly got the most astonishin' head I ever see. Oh, this is the boss dodge, ther' ain't no mistake 'bout it. Let 'em fetch along their suspicions now, if they want to—this'll lay 'em out."

When we got up stairs, everybody gethered around the table, and the king he counted it and stacked it up, three hundred dollars in a pile—twenty elegant little piles. Everybody looked hungry at it, and licked their chops. Then they raked it into the bag again, and I see the king begin to swell himself up for another speech. He says:

"Friends all, my poor brother that lays yonder, has done generous by them that's left behind in the vale of sorrers. He has done generous by these-yer poor little lambs that he loved and sheltered, and that's left fatherless and motherless. Yes, and we that knowed him, knows that he would a done *more* generous by 'em if he hadn't ben afeard o' woundin' his dear William and me. Now, *wouldn't* he? Ther' ain't no question 'bout it, in *my* mind. Well, then—what kind o' brothers would it be, that'd stand in his way at sech a time? And what kind o' uncles would it be that'd rob—yes, *rob*—sech poor sweet lambs as these 'at he loved so, at sech a time? If I know William—and I *think* I do—he—well, I'll jest ask him." He turns around and begins to make a lot of signs to the duke with his hands; and the duke he looks at him stupid and leather-headed a while, then all of a sudden he seems to catch his meaning, and jumps for the king, goo-gooing with all his might for joy, and hugs him about fifteen times before he lets up. Then the king says, "I knowed it; I reckon *that* 'll convince anybody the way *he* feels about it. Here, Mary Jane, Susan, Joanner, take the money—take it *all*. It's the gift of him that lays yonder, cold but joyful."

Mary Jane she went for him, Susan and the hare-lip went for the duke, and then such another hugging and kissing I never see yet. And everybody crowded up with the tears in their eyes, and most shook the hands off of them frauds, saying all the time:

"You *dear* good souls?—how *lovely!*—how *could* you!"

Well, then, pretty soon all hands got to talking about the diseased again, and how good he was, and what a loss he was, and all that; and before long a big iron-jawed man worked himself in there from outside, and stood a listening and looking, and not saying anything; and nobody saying anything to him either, because the king was talking and they was all busy listening. The king was saying—in the middle of something he'd started in on—

"—they bein' partickler friends o' the diseased. That's why they're invited here this evenin'; but to-morrow we want *all* to come—everybody; for he respected everybody, he liked everybody, and so it's fitten that his funeral orgiess h'd be public."

And so he went a-mooning on and on, liking to hear himself talk, and every little while he fetched in his funeral orgies again, till the

duke he couldn't stand it no more; so he writes on a little scrap of
paper, *"obsequies,* you old fool," and folds it up and goes to goo-
gooing and reaching it over people's heads to him. The king he
reads it, and puts it in his pocket, and says:

"Poor William, afflicted as he is, his *heart's* aluz right. Asks me
to invite everybody to come to the funeral—wants me to make 'em
all welcome. But he needn't a worried—it was jest what I was at."

Then he weaves along again, perfectly ca'm, and goes to
dropping in his funeral orgies again every now and then, just like
he done before. And when he done it the third time, he says:

"I say orgies, not because it's the common term, because it ain't
—obsequies bein' the common term—but because orgies is the
right term. Obsequies ain't used in England no more, now—it's
gone out. We say orgies now, in England. Orgies is better, because
it means the thing you're after, more exact. It's a word that's made
up out'n the Greek *orgo,* outside, open, abroad; and the Hebrew
jeesum, to plant, cover up; hence in*ter.* So, you see, funeral orgies
is an open er public funeral."

He was the *worst* I ever struck. Well, the iron-jawed man he
laughed right in his face. Everybody was shocked. Everybody says,
"Why *doctor!*" and Abner Shackleford says:

"Why, Robinson, hain't you heard the news? This is Harvey
Wilks."

The king he smiled eager, and shoved out his flapper, and says:

"Is it my poor brother's dear good friend and physician? I—"

"Keep your hands off of me!" says the doctor. *"You* talk like an
Englishman—*don't* you? It's the worse imitation I ever heard. *You*
Peter Wilks's brother. You're a fraud, that's what you are!"

Well, how they all took on! They crowded around the doctor, and
tried to quiet him down, and tried to explain to him, and tell him
how Harvey'd showed in forty ways that he *was* Harvey, and
knowed everybody by name, and the names of the very dogs, and
begged and *begged* him not to hurt Harvey's feelings and the poor
girls' feelings, and all that; but it warn't no use, he stormed right
along, and said any man that pretended to be an Englishman and
couldn't imitate the lingo no better than what he did, was a fraud
and a liar. The poor girls was hanging to the king and crying; and
all of a sudden the doctor ups and turns on *them.* He says:

"I was your father's friend, and I'm your friend; and I warn you
as a friend, and an honest one, that wants to protect you and keep
you out of harm and trouble, to turn your backs on that scoundrel,
and have nothing to do with him, the ignorant tramp, with his
idiotic Greek and Hebrew as he calls it. He is the thinnest kind of
an impostor—has come here with a lot of empty names and facts
which he has picked up somewheres, and you take them for *proofs,*
and are helped to fool yourselves by these foolish friends here, who
ought to know better. Mary Jane Wilks, you know me for your

friend, and for your unselfish friend, too. Now listen to me; turn this pitiful rascal out—I *beg* you to do it. Will you?"

Mary Jane straightened herself up, and my, but she was handsome! She says:

"*Here* is my answer." She hove up the bag of money and put it in the king's hands, and says, "Take this six thousand dollars, and invest for me and my sisters any way you want to, and don't give us no receipt for it."

Then she put her arm around the king on one side, and Susan and the hare-lip done the same on the other. Everybody clapped their hands and stomped on the floor like a perfect storm, whilst the king held up his head and smiled proud. The doctor says:

"All right, I wash *my* hands of the matter. But I warn you all that a time's coming when you're going to feel sick whenever you think of this day"—and away he went.

"All right, doctor," says the king, kinder mocking him, "we'll try and get 'em to send for you"—which made them all laugh, and they said it was a prime good hit.

CHAPTER XXVI

Well when they was all gone, the king he asks Mary Jane how they was off for spare rooms, and she said she had one spare room, which would do for Uncle William, and she'd give her own room to Uncle Harvey, which was a little bigger, and she would turn into the room with her sisters and sleep on a cot; and up garret was a little cubby, with a pallet in it. The king said the cubby would do for his valley—meaning me.

So Mary Jane took us up, and she showed them their rooms, which was plain but nice. She said she'd have her frocks and a lot of other traps took out of her room if they was in Uncle Harvey's way, but he said they warn't. The frocks was hung along the wall, and before them was a curtain made out of calico that hung down to the floor. There was an old hair trunk in one corner, and a guitar box in another, and all sorts of little knickknacks and jimcracks around, like girls brisken up a room with. The king said it was all the more homely and more pleasanter for these fixings, and so don't disturb them. The duke's room was pretty small, but plenty good enough, and so was my cubby.

That night they had a big supper, and all them men and women was there, and I stood behind the king and the duke's chairs and waited on them, and the niggers waited on the rest. Mary Jane she set at the head of the table, with Susan along side of her, and said how bad the biscuits was, and how mean the preserves was, and how ornery and tough the fried chickens was—and all that kind of rot, the way women always do for to force out compliments; and the people all knowed everything was tip-top, and said so—said

"How *do* you get biscuits to brown so nice?" and "Where, for the land's sake *did* you get these amaz'n pickles?" and all that kind of humbug talky-talk, just the way people always does at a supper, you know.

And when it was all done, me and the hare-lip had supper in the kitchen off of the leavings, whilst the others was helping the niggers clean up the things. The hare-lip she got to pumping me about England, and blest if I didn't think the ice was getting mighty thin, sometimes. She says:

"Did you ever see the king?"

"Who? William Fourth? Well, I bet I have—he goes to our church." I knowed he was dead years ago, but I never let on. So when I says he goes to our church, she says:

"What—regular?"

"Yes—regular. His pew's right over opposite ourn—on 'tother side the pulpit."

"I thought he lived in London?"

"Well, he does. Where *would* he live?"

"But I thought *you* lived in Sheffield?"

I see I was up a stump. I had to let on to get choked with a chicken bone, so as to get time to think how to get down again. Then I says:

"I mean he goes to our church regular when he's in Sheffield. That's only in the summer-time, when he comes there to take the sea baths."

"Why, how you talk—Sheffield ain't on the sea."

"Well, who said it was?"

"Why, you did."

"I *didn't*, nuther."

"You did!"

"I didn't."

"You did."

"I never said nothing of the kind."

"Well, what *did* you say, then?"

"Said he come to take the sea *baths*—that's what I said."

"Well, then! how's he going to take the sea baths if it ain't on the sea?"

"Looky here," I says; "did you ever see any Congress water?"

"Yes."

"Well, did you have to go to Congress to get it?"

"Why, no."

"Well, neither does William Fourth have to go to the sea to get a sea bath."

"How does he get it, then?"

"Gets it the way people down here gets Congress-water—in barrels. There in the palace at Sheffield they've got furnaces, and he wants his water hot. They can't bile that amount of water away off there at the sea. They haven't got no conveniences for it."

"Oh, I see, now. You might a said that in the first place and saved time."

When she said that, I see I was out of the woods again, and so I was comfortable and glad. Next, she says:

"Do you go to church, too?"

"Yes—regular."

"Where do you set?"

"Why, in our pew."

"*Whose* pew?"

"Why, *ourn*—your Uncle Harvey's."

"His'n? What does *he* want with a pew?"

"Wants it to set in. What did you *reckon* he wanted with it?"

"Why, I thought he'd be in the pulpit."

Rot him, I forgot he was a preacher. I see I was up a stump again, so I played another chicken bone and got another think. Then I says:

"Blame it, do you suppose there ain't but one preacher to a church?"

"Why, what do they want with more?"

"What!—to preach before a king? I never see such a girl as you. They don't have no less than seventeen."

"Seventeen! My land! Why, I wouldn't set out such a string as that, not if I *never* got to glory. It must take 'em a week."

"Shucks, they don't *all* of 'em preach the same day—only *one* of 'em."

"Well, then, what does the rest of 'em do?"

"Oh, nothing much. Loll around, pass the plate—and one thing or another. But mainly they don't do nothing."

"Well, then, what are they *for?*"

"Why, they're for *style.* Don't you know nothing?"

"Well, I don't *want* to know no such foolishness as that. How is servants treated in England? Do they treat 'em better 'n we treat our niggers?"

"*No!* A servant ain't nobody there. They treat them worse than dogs."

"Don't they give 'em holidays, the way we do, Christmas and New Year's week, and Fourth of July?"

"Oh, just listen! A body could tell *you* hain't ever been to England, by that. Why, Hare-l—why, Joanna, they never see a holiday from year's end to year's end; never got to the circus, nor theatre, nor nigger shows, nor nowheres."

"Nor church?"

"Nor church."

"But *you* always went to church."

Well, I was gone up again. I forgot I was the old man's servant. But next minute I whirled in on a kind of an explanation how a valley was different from a common servant, and *had* to go to church whether he wanted to or not, and set with the family, on account of it's being the law. But I didn't do it pretty good, and when I got done I see she warn't satisfied. She says:

"Honest injun, now, hain't you been telling me a lot of lies?"

"Honest injun," says I.

"None of it at all?"

"None of it at all. Not a lie in it," says I.

"Lay your hand on this book and say it."

I see it warn't nothing but a dictionary, so I laid my hand on it and said it. So then she looked a little better satisfied, and says:

"Well, then, I'll believe some of it; but I hope to gracious if I'll believe the rest."

"What is it you won't believe, Joe?" says Mary Jane, stepping in with Susan behind her. "It ain't right nor kind for you to talk so to him, and him a stranger and so far from his people. How would you like to be treated so?"

"That's always your way, Maim—always sailing in to help somebody before they're hurt. I hain't done nothing to him. He's told some stretchers, I reckon; and I said I wouldn't swallow it all; and that's every bit and grain I *did* say. I reckon he can stand a little thing like that, can't he?"

"I don't care whether 'twas little or whether 'twas big, he's here in our house and a stranger, and it wasn't good of you to say it. If you was in his place, it would make you feel ashamed; and so you oughtn't to say a thing to another person that will make *them* feel ashamed."

"Why, Maim, he said——"

"It don't make no difference what he *said*—that ain't the thing. The thing is for you to treat him *kind,* and not be saying things to make him remember he ain't in his own country and amongst his own folks."

I says to myself, *this* is a girl that I'm letting that old reptle rob her of her money!

Then Susan *she* waltzed in; and if you'll believe me, she did give Hare-lip hark from the tomb!

Says I to myself, And this is *another* one that I'm letting him rob her of her money!

Then Mary Jane she took another inning, and went in sweet and lovely again—which was her way—but when she got done there warn't hardly anything left o' poor Hare-lip. So she hollered.

"All right, then," says the other girls, "you just ask his pardon."

She done it, too. And she done it beautiful. She done it so beautiful it was good to hear; and I wished I could tell her a thousand lies, so she could do it again.

I says to myself, this is *another* one that I'm letting him rob her of her money. And when she got through, they all jest laid

theirselves out to make me feel at home and know I was amongst
friends. I felt so ornery and low down and mean, that I says to
myself, My mind's made up; I'll hive that money for them or bust.

So then I lit out—for bed, I said, meaning some time or another.
When I got by myself, I went to thinking the thing over. I says to
myself, shall I go to that doctor, private, and blow on these frauds?
No—that won't do. He might tell who told him; then the king and
the duke would make it warm for me. Shall I go, private, and tell
Mary Jane? No—I dasn't do it. Her face would give them a hint,
sure; they've got the money, and they'd slide right out and get away
with it. If she was to fetch in help, I'd get mixed up in the business,
before it was done with, I judge. No, there ain't no good way but
one. I got to steal that money, somehow; and I got to steal it some
way that they won't suspicion that I done it. They've got a good
thing, here; and they ain't agoing to leave till they've played this
family and this town for all they're worth, so I'll find a chance time
enough. I'll steal it, and hide it; and by-and-by, when I'm away
down the river, I'll write a letter and tell Mary Jane where it's hid.
But I better hive it to-night, if I can, because the doctor maybe
hasn't let up as much as he lets on he has; he might scare them
out of here, yet.

So, thinks I, I'll go and search them rooms. Up stairs the hall
was dark, but I found the duke's room, and started to paw around
it with my hands; but I recollected it wouldn't be much like the king
to let anybody else take care of that money but his own self; so
then I went to his room and begun to paw around there. But I see
I couldn't do nothing without a candle, and I dasn't light one, of
course. So I judged I'd got to do the other thing—lay for them,
and eavesdrop. About that time, I hears their footsteps coming, and
was going to skip under the bed; I reached for it, but it wasn't
where I thought it would be; but I touched the curtain that hid
Mary Jane's frocks, so I jumped in behind that and snuggled in
amongst the gowns, and stood there perfectly still.

They come in and shut the door; and the first thing the duke done
was to get down and look under the bed. Then I was glad I hadn't
found the bed when I wanted it. And yet, you know, it's kind of
natural to hide under the bed when you are up to anything private.
They sets down, then, and the king says:

"Well, what is it? and cut it middlin' short, because it's better
for us to be down there a whoopin'-up the mournin', than up here
givin' em a chance to talk us over."

"Well, this is it, Capet. I ain't easy; I ain't comfortable. That
doctor lays on my mind. I wanted to know your plans. I've got a
notion, and I think it's a sound one."

"What is it, duke?"

"That we better glide out of this, before three in the morning, and
clip it down the river with what we've got. Specially, seeing we got

it so easy—*given* back to us, flung at our heads, as you may say, when of course we allowed to have to steal it back. I'm for knocking off and lighting out.''

That made me feel pretty bad. About an hour or two ago, it would a been a little different, but now it made me feel bad and disappointed. The king rips out and says:

''What! And not sell out the rest o' the property? March off like a passel o' fools and leave eight or nine thous'n dollars' worth o' property layin' around jest sufferin' to be scooped in?—and all good salable stuff, too.''

The duke he grumbled; said the bag of gold was enough, and he didn't want to go no deeper—didn't want to rob a lot of orphans of *everything* they had.

''Why, how you talk!'' says the king. ''We shan't rob 'em of nothing at all but jest this money. The people that *buys* the property is the suff'rers; because as soon's it's found out 'at we didn't own it—which won't be long after we've slid—the sale won't be valid, and it'll all go back to the estate. These-yer orphans'll git their house back agin, and that's enough for *them;* they're young and spry, and k'n easy earn a livin'. *They* ain't agoing to suffer. Why, jest think—there's thous'n's and thous'n's that ain't nigh so well off. Bless you, *they* ain't got noth'n to complain of.''

Well, the king he talked him blind; so at last he give in, and said all right, but said he believed it was blame foolishness to stay, and that doctor hanging over them. But the king says:

''Cuss the doctor! What do we k'yer for *him?* Hain't we got all the fools in town on our side? and ain't that a big enough majority in any town?''

So they got ready to go down stairs again. The duke says:

''I don't think we put that money in a good place.''

That cheered me up. I'd begun to think I warn't going to get a hint of no kind to help me. The king says:

''Why?''

''Because Mary Jane'll be in mourning from this out; and first you know the nigger that does up the rooms will get an order to box these duds up and put 'em away; and do you reckon a nigger can run across money and not borrow some of it?''

''Your head's level, agin, duke,'' says the king; and he come a fumbling under the curtain two or three foot from where I was. I stuck tight to the wall, and kept mighty still, though quivery; and I wondered what them fellows would say to me if they catched me; and I tried to think what I'd better do if they did catch me. But the king he got the bag before I could think more than about a half a thought, and he never suspicioned I was around. They took and shoved the bag through a rip in the straw tick that was under the feather bed, and crammed it in a foot or two amongst the straw and said it was all right, now, because a nigger only makes up the feather bed, and don't turn over the straw tick only about twice a year, and so it warn't in no danger of getting stole, now.

But I knowed better. I had it out of there before they was half-way down stairs. I groped along up to my cubby, and hid it there till I could get a chance to do better. I judged I better hide it outside of the house somewheres, because if they missed it they would give the house a good ransacking. I knowed that very well. Then I turned in, with my clothes all on; but I couldn't a gone to sleep, if I'd a wanted to, I was in such a sweat to get through with the business. By-and-by I heard the king and the duke come up; so I rolled off of my pallet and laid with my chin at the top of my ladder and waited to see if anything was going to happen. But nothing did.

So I held on till all the late sounds had quit and the early ones hadn't begun, yet; and then I slipped down the ladder.

CHAPTER XXVII

I crept to their doors and listened; they was snoring, so I tip-toed along, and got down stairs all right. There warn't a sound anywheres. I peeped through a crack of the dining-room door, and see the men that was watching the corpse all sound asleep on their chairs. The door was open into the parlor, where the corpse was laying, and there was a candle in both rooms. I passed along, and the parlor door was open; but I see there warn't nobody in there but the remainders of Peter; so I shoved on by; but the front door was locked, and the key wasn't there. Just then I heard somebody coming down the stairs, back behind me. I run in the parlor, and took a swift look around, and the only place I see to hide the bag was in the coffin. The lid was shoved along about a foot, showing the dead man's face down in there, with a wet cloth over it, and his shroud on. I tucked the money-bag in under the lid, just down beyond where his hands was crossed, which made me creep, they was so cold, and then I run back across the room and in behind the door.

The person coming was Mary Jane. She went to the coffin, very soft, and kneeled down and looked in; then she put up her handkerchief and I see she begun to cry, though I couldn't hear her, and her back was to me. I slid out, and as I passed the dining-room I thought I'd make sure them watchers hadn't seen me; so I looked through the crack and everything was all right. They hadn't stirred.

I slipped up to bed, feeling ruther blue, on accounts of the thing playing out that way after I had took so much trouble and run so much resk about it. Says I, if it could stay where it is, all right; because when we get down the river a hundred mile or two, I could write back to Mary Jane, and she could dig him up again and get it; but that ain't the thing that's going to happen; the thing that's

going to happen is, the money'll be found when they come to screw
on the lid. Then the king'll get it again, and it'll be a long day
before he gives anybody another chance to smouch it from him. Of
course I *wanted* to slide down and get it out of there, but I dasn't
try it. Every minute it was getting earlier, now, and pretty soon some
of them watchers would begin to stir, and I might get catched—
catched with six thousand dollars in my hands that nobody hadn't
hired me to take care of. I don't wish to be mixed up in no such
business as that, I says to myself.

When I got down stairs in the morning, the parlor was shut up,
and the watchers was gone. There warn't nobody around but the
family and the widow Bartley and our tribe. I watched their faces
to see if anything had been happening, but I couldn't tell.
Towards the middle of the day the undertaker come, with his
man, and they set the coffin in the middle of the room on a couple of
chairs, and then set all our chairs in rows, and borrowed more from
the neighbors till the hall and the parlor and the dining-room was
full. I see the coffin lid was the way it was before, but I dasn't go to
look in under it, with folks around.

Then the people begun to flock in, and the beats and the girls
took seats in the front row at the head of the coffin, and for a half
an hour the people filed around slow, in single rank, and looked
down at the dead man's face a minute, and some dropped in a tear,
and it was all very still and solemn, only the girls and the beats
holding handkerchiefs to their eyes and keeping their heads bent,
and sobbing a little. There warn't no other sound but the scraping
of the feet on the floor, and blowing noses—because people always
blows them more at a funeral than they do at other places except
church.

When the place was packed full, the undertaker he slid around
in his black gloves with his softy soothering ways, putting on the
last touches, and getting people and things all shipshape and
comfortable, and making no more sound than a cat. He never spoke;
he moved people around, he squeezed in late ones, he opened up
passage-ways, and done it all with nods, and signs with his hands.
Then he took his place over against the wall. He was the softest,
glidingest, stealthiest man I ever see; and there warn't no more
smile to him than there is to a ham.

They had borrowed a melodeum—a sick one; and when
everything was ready, a young woman set down and worked it, and
it was pretty skreeky and colicky, and everybody joined in and sung,
and Peter was the only one that had a good thing, according to my
notion. Then the Reverend Hobson opened up, slow and solemn,
and begun to talk; and straight off the most outrageous row busted
out in the cellar a body ever heard; it was only one dog, but he made
a most powerful racket, and he kept it up, right along; the parson
he had to stand there, over the coffin, and wait—you couldn't hear

yourself think. It was right down awkward, and nobody didn't
seem to know what to do. But pretty soon they see that long-legged
undertaker make a sign to the preacher as much as to say, "Don't
you worry—just depend on me." Then he stooped down and begun
to glide along the wall, just his shoulders showing over the people's
heads. So he glided along, and the pow-wow and racket getting
more and more outrageous all the time; and at last, when he had
gone around two sides of the room, he disappears down cellar. Then,
in about two seconds we heard a whack, and the dog he finished up
with a most amazing howl or two, and then everything was dead
still, and the parson begun his solemn talk where he left off. In a
minute or two here comes this undertaker's back and shoulders
gliding along the wall again; and so he glided, and glided, around
three sides of the room, and then rose up, and shaded his mouth
with his hands, and stretched his neck out towards the preacher,
over the people's heads, and says, in a kind of a coarse whisper,
"He had a rat!" Then he drooped down and glided along the wall
again to his place. You could see it was a great satisfaction to the
people, because naturally they wanted to know. A little thing like
that don't cost nothing, and it's just the little things that makes
a man to be looked up to and liked. There warn't no more popular
man in town than what that undertaker was.

Well, the funeral sermon was very good, but pison long and
tiresome; and then the king he shoved in and got off some of his
usual rubbage, and at last the job was through, and the undertaker
begun to sneak up on the coffin with his screw-driver. I was in a
sweat then, and watched him pretty keen. But he never meddled at
all; just slid the lid along, as soft as mush, and screwed it down
tight and fast. So there I was! I didn't know whether the money was
in there, or not. So, says I, spose somebody has hogged that bag on
the sly?—now how do *I* know whether to write to Mary Jane or not?
'Spose she dug him up and didn't find nothing—what would she
think of me? Blame it, I says, I might get hunted up and jailed;
I'd better lay low and keep dark, and not write at all; the thing's
awful mixed, now; trying to better it, I've worsened it a hundred
times, and I wish to goodness I'd just let it alone, dad fetch the whole
business!

They buried him, and we come back home, and I went to
watching faces again—I couldn't help it, and I couldn't rest easy.
But nothing come of it; the faces didn't tell me nothing.

The king he visited around, in the evening, and sweetened every
body up, and made himself ever so friendly; and he give out the
idea that his congregation over in England would be in a sweat
about him, so he must hurry and settle up the estate right away, and
leave for home. He was very sorry he was so pushed, and so was
everybody; they wished he could stay longer, but they said they
could see it couldn't be done. And he said of course him and

William would take the girls home with them; and that pleased everybody too, because then the girls would be well fixed, and amongst their own relations; and it pleased the girls, too—tickled them so they clean forgot they ever had a trouble in the world; and told him to sell out as quick as he wanted to, they would be ready. Them poor things was that glad and happy it made my heart ache to see them getting fooled and lied to so, but I didn't see no safe way for me to chip in and change the general tune.

Well, blamed if the king didn't bill the house and the niggers and all the property for auction straight off—sale two days after the funeral; but anybody could buy private beforehand if they wanted to.

So the next day after the funeral, along about noontime, the girls' joy got the first jolt; a couple of nigger traders come along, and the king sold them the niggers reasonable, for three-day drafts as they called it, and away they went, the two sons up the river to Memphis, and their mother down the river to Orleans. I thought them poor girls and them niggers would break their hearts for grief; they cried around each other, and took on so it most made me down sick to see it. The girls said they hadn't ever dreamed of seeing the family separated or sold away from the town. I can't ever get it out of my memory, the sight of them poor miserable girls and niggers hanging around each other's necks and crying; and I reckon I couldn't a stood it all but would a had to bust out and tell on our gang if I hadn't knowed the sale warn't no account and the niggers would be back home in a week or two.

The thing made a big stir in the town, too, and a good many come out flat-footed and said it was scandalous to separate the mother and the children that way. It injured the frauds some; but the old fool he bulled right along, spite of all the duke could say or do, and I tell you the duke was powerful uneasy.

Next day was auction day. About broad-day in the morning, the king and the duke come up in the garret and woke me up, and I see by their look that there was trouble. The king says:

"Was you in my room night before last?"

"No, your majesty"—which was the way I always called him when nobody but our gang warn't around.

"Was you in there yesterday er last night?"

"No, your majesty."

"Honor bright, now—no lies."

"Honor bright, your majesty, I'm telling you the truth. I hain't been anear your room since Miss Mary Jane took you and the duke and showed it to you."

The duke says:

"Have you seen anybody else go in there?"

"No, your grace, not as I remember, I believe."

"Stop and think."

I studied a while, and see my chance, then I says:

"Well, I see the niggers go in there several times."

Both of them give a little jump; and looked like they hadn't ever expected it, and then like they *had*. Then the duke says:

"What, *all* of them?"

"No—leastways not all at once. That is, I don't think I ever see them all come *out* at once but just one time."

"Hello—when was that?"

"It was the day we had the funeral. In the morning. It warn't early, because I overslept. I was just starting down the ladder, and I see them."

"Well, go on, *go* on—what did they do? How'd they act?"

"They didn't do nothing. And they didn't act anyway, much, as fur as I see. They tip-toed away; so I seen, easy enough, that they'd shoved in there to do up your majesty's room, or something, sposing you was up; and found you *warn't* up, and so they was hoping to slide out of the way of trouble without waking you up, if they hadn't already waked you up."

"Great guns, *this* is a go!" says the king; and both of them looked pretty sick, and tolerable silly. They stood there a thinking and scratching their heads, a minute, and then the duke he bust into a kind of a little raspy chuckle, and says:

"It does beat all, how neat the niggers played their hand. They let on to be *sorry* they was going out of this region! and I believed they *was* sorry. And so did you, and so did everybody. Don't ever tell *me* any more that a nigger ain't got any histrionic talent. Why, the way they played that thing, it would fool *anybody*. In my opinion there's a fortune in 'em. If I had capital and a theatre, I wouldn't want a better lay out than that—and here we've gone and sold 'em for a song. Yes, and ain't privileged to sing the song, yet. Say, where *is* that song?—that draft."

"In the bank for to be collected. Where *would* it be?"

"Well, *that's* all right then, thank goodness."

Says I, kind of timid-like:

"Is something gone wrong?"

The king whirls on me and rips out:

"None o' your business! You keep your head shet, and mind y'r own affairs—if you got any. Long as you're in this town, don't you forget *that,* you hear?" Then he says to the duke, "We got to jest swaller it, and say noth'n: mum's the word for *us.* "

As they was starting down the ladder, the duke he chuckles again, and says:

"Quick sales *and* small profits! It's a good business—yes."

The king snarls around on him and says,

"I was trying to do for the best, in sellin' 'm out so quick. If the profits has turned out to be none, lackin' considable, and none to carry, is it my fault any more'n it's yourn?"

"Well, *they'd* be in this house yet, and we *wouldn't* if I could a got my advice listened to."

The king sassed back, as much as was safe for him, and then swapped around and lit into *me* again. He give me down the banks for not coming and *telling* him I see the niggers come out of his room acting that way—said any fool would a *knowed* something was up. And then waltzed in and cussed *himself* a while; and said it all come of him not laying late and taking his natural rest that morning, and he'd be blamed if he'd ever do it again. So they went off a jawing; and I felt dreadful glad I'd worked it all off onto the niggers and yet hadn't done the niggers no harm by it.

CHAPTER XXVIII

By-and-by it was getting-up time; so I come down the ladder and started for down stairs, but as I come to the girls' room, the door was open, and I see Mary Jane setting by her old hair trunk, which was open and she'd been packing things in it—getting ready to go to England. But she had stopped now, with a folded gown in her lap, and had her face in her hands, crying. I felt awful bad to see it; of course anybody would. I went in there, and says:

"Miss Mary Jane, you can't abear to see people in trouble, and *I* can't—most always. Tell me about it."

So she done it. And it was the niggers—I just expected it. She said the beautiful trip to Englaịd was most about spoiled for her; she didn't know *how* she was ever going to be happy there, knowing the mother and the children warn't ever going to see each other no more—and then busted out bitterer than ever, and flung up her hands, and says:

"Oh, dear, dear, to think they ain't *ever* going to see each other any more!"

"But they *will*—and inside of two weeks—and I *know* it!" says I.

Laws it was out before I could think!—and before I could budge, she throws her arms around my neck, and told me to say it *again*, say it *again*, say it *again!*

I see I had spoke too sudden, and said too much, and was in a close place. I asked her to let me think a minute; and she set there, very impatient and excited, and handsome, but looking kind of happy and eased-up, like a person that's had a tooth pulled out. So I went to studying it out. I says to myself, I reckon a body that ups and tells the truth when he is in a tight place, is taking considerable many resks, though I ain't had no experience, and can't say for certain; but it looks so to me, anyway; and yet here's a case where I'm blest if it don't look to me like the truth is better, and actuly *safer,* than a lie. I must lay it by in my mind, and think it over some time or other, it's so kind of strange and unregular. I never see nothing like it. Well, I says to myself at last, I'm agoing to chance it;

I'll up and tell the truth this time, though it does seem most like
setting down on a kag of powder and touching it off just to see
where you'll go to. Then I says:

"Miss Mary Jane, is there any place out of town a little ways,
where you could go and stay three or four days?"

"Yes—Mr. Lothrop's. Why?"

"Never mind why, yet. If I'll tell you how I know the niggers will
see each other again—inside of two weeks—here in this house—and
prove how I know it—will you go to Mr. Lothrop's and stay four
days?"

"Four days!" she says; "I'll stay a year!"

"All right," I says, "I don't want nothing more out of *you* than
just your word—I druther have it than another man's kiss-the-
Bible." She smiled, and reddened up very sweet, and I says, "If you
don't mind it, I'll shut the door—and bolt it."

Then I come back and set down again, and says:

"Don't you holler. Just set still, and take it like a man. I got to
tell the truth, and you want to brace up, Miss Mary, because it's
a bad kind, and going to be hard to take, but there ain't no help
for it. These uncles of yourn ain't no uncles at all—they're a
couples of frauds—regular dead-beats. There, now we're over the
worst of it—you can stand the rest middling easy."

It jolted her up like everything, of course; but I was over the
shoal water now, so I went right along, her eyes a blazing higher
and higher all the time, and told her every blame thing, from where
we first struck that young fool going up to the steamboat, clear
through to where she flung herself onto the king's breast at the front
door and he kissed her sixteen or seventeen times—and then up she
jumps, with her face afire like sunset, and says:

"The brute! Come—don't waste a minute—not a *second*—we'll
have them tarred and feathered, and flung in the river!"

Says I:

"Cert'nly. But do you mean, *before* you go to Mr. Lothrop's,
or——"

"Oh," she says, "what am I *thinking* about!" she says, and set
right down again. "Don't mind what I said—please don't—you
won't now, *will* you?" Laying her silky hand on mine in that kind
of a way that I said I would die first. "I never thought. I was so
stirred up," she says; "now go on, and I won't do so any more. You
tell me what to do, and whatever you say, I'll do it."

"Well," I says, "it's a rough gang, them two frauds, and I'm fixed
so I got to travel with them a while longer, whether I want to or
not—I druther not tell you why—and if you was to blow on them this
town would get me out of their claws, and *I'd* be all right, but there'd
be another person that you don't know about who'd be in big
trouble. Well, we got to save *him,* hain't we? Of course. Well, then,
we won't blow on them."

Saying them words put a good idea in my head. I see how maybe
I could get me and Jim rid of the frauds; get them jailed here, and
then leave. But I didn't want to run the raft in day-time, without
anybody aboard to answer questions but me; so I didn't want the
plan to begin working till pretty late to-night. I says:

"Miss Mary Jane, I'll tell you what we'll do—and you won't have
to stay at Mr. Lothrop's so long, nuther. How fur is it?"

"A little short of four miles—right out in the country, back here."

"Well, that'll answer. Now you go along out there, and lay low till
nine or half-past, to-night, and then get them to fetch you home
again—tell them you've thought of something. If you get here before
eleven, put a candle in this window, and if I don't turn up, wait
till eleven, and *then* if I don't turn up it means I'm gone, and out of
the way, and safe. Then you come out and spread the news around,
and get these beats jailed."

"Good," she says, "I'll do it."

"And if it just happens so that I don't get away, but get took up
along with them, you must up and say I told you the whole thing
beforehand, and you must stand by me all you can."

"Stand by you, indeed I will. They sha'n't touch a hair of your
head!" she says, and I see her nostrils spread and her eyes snap when
she said it, too.

"If I get away, I sha'n't be here," I says, "to prove these
rapscallions ain't your uncles, and I couldn't do it if I *was* here. I
could swear they was beats and bummers, that's all; though that's
worth something. Well, there's others can do that better than what
I can—and they're people that ain't going to be doubted as quick
as I'd be. I'll tell you how to find them. Gimme a pencil and a
piece of paper. There—'*Royal Nonesuch, Bricksville.*' Put it away,
and don't lose it. When the court wants to find out something
about these two, let them send up to Bricksville and say they've
got the men that played the Royal Nonesuch, and ask for some
witnesses—why, you'll have that entire town down here before you
can hardly wink, Miss Mary. And they'll come a-biling, too."

I judged we had got everything fixed about right now. So I says:

"Just let the auction go right along, and don't worry. Nobody
don't have to pay for the things they buy till a whole day after the
auction, on accounts of the short notice, and they ain't going out of
this till they get that money—and the way we've fixed it the sale
ain't going to count, and they ain't going to *get* no money. It's just
like the way it was with the niggers—it warn't no sale, and the
niggers will be back before long. Why, they can't collect the money
for the *niggers,* yet—they're in the worst kind of a fix, Miss Mary."

"Well," she says, "I'll run down to breakfast now, and then
I'll start straight for Mr. Lothrop's."

" 'Deed, *that* ain't the ticket, Miss Mary Jane," I says, "by no
manner of means; go *before* breakfast."

"Why?"

"What did you reckon I wanted you to go at all for, Miss Mary?"

"Well, I never thought—and come to think, I don't know. What was it?"

"Why, it's because you ain't one of these leather-face people. I don't want no better book that what your face is. A body can set down and read it off like coarse print. Do you reckon you can go and face your uncles, when they come to kiss you good-morning, and never——"

"There, there, don't! Yes, I'll go before breakfast—I'll be glad to. And leave my sisters with them?"

"Yes—never mind about them. They've got to stand it yet a while. They might suspicion something if all of you was to go. I don't want you to see them, nor your sisters, nor nobody in this town—if a neighbor was to ask how is your uncles this morning, your face would tell something. No, you go right along, Miss Mary Jane, and I'll fix it with all of them. I'll tell Miss Susan to give your love to your uncles and say you've went away for a few hours for to get a little rest and change, or to see a friend, and you'll be back to-night or early in the morning."

"Gone to see a friend is all right, but I won't have my love given to them."

"Well, then, it sha'n't be." It was well enough to tell *her* so—no harm in it. It was only a little thing to do, and no trouble; and it's the little things that smoothes people's roads the most, down here below; it would make Mary Jane comfortable, and it wouldn't cost nothing. Then I says: "There's one more thing—that bag of money."

"Well, they've got that; and it makes me feel pretty silly to think *how* they got it."

"No, you're out, there. They hain't got it."

"Why, who's got it?"

"I wish I knowed, but I don't. I *had* it, because I stole it from them: and I stole it to give to you; and I know where I hid it, but I'm afraid it ain't there no more. I'm awful sorry, Miss Mary Jane, I'm just as sorry as I can be; but I done the best I could; I did, honest. I come nigh getting caught, and I had to shove it into the first place I come to, and run—and it warn't a good place."

"Oh, stop blaming yourself—it's too bad to do it, and I won't allow it—you couldn't help it; it wasn't your fault. Where did you hide it?"

I didn't want to set her to thinking about her troubles again; and I couldn't seem to get my mouth to tell her what would make her see that corpse laying in the coffin with that bag of money on his stomach. So for a minute I didn't say nothing—then I says:

"I'd ruther not *tell* you where I put it, Miss Mary Jane, if you don't mind letting me off; but I'll write it for you on a piece of paper, and you can read it along the road to Mr. Lothrop's, if you want to. Do you reckon that'll do?"

"Oh, yes."

So I wrote: "I put it in the coffin. It was in there when you was crying there, away in the night. I was behind the door, and I was mighty sorry for you, Miss Mary Jane."

It made my eyes water a little, to remember her crying there all by herself in the night, and them devils laying there right under her own roof, shaming her and robbing her; and when I folded it up and give it to her, I see the water come into her eyes, too; and she shook me by the hand, hard, and says:

"*Good*-bye—I'm going to do everything just as you've told me; and if I don't ever see you again, I sha'n't ever forget you, and I'll think of you a many and a many a time, and I'll *pray* for you, too!"—and she was gone.

Pray for me! I reckoned if she knowed me she'd take a job that was more nearer her size. But I bet she done it, just the same—she was just that kind. She had the grit to pray for Judus if she took the notion—there warn't no backdown to her, I judge. You may say what you want to, but in my opinion she had more sand in her than any girl I ever see; in my opinion she was just full of sand. It sounds like flattery, but it ain't no flattery. And when it comes to beauty—and goodness too—she lays over them all. I hain't ever seen her since that time that I see her go out of that door; no, I hain't ever seen her since, but I reckon I've thought of her a many and a many a million times, and of her saying she would pray for me; and if ever I'd a thought it would do any good for me to pray for *her,* blamed if I wouldn't a done it or bust.

Well, Mary Jane she lit out the back way, I reckon; because nobody see her go. When I struck Susan and the hare-lip, I says:

"What's the name of them people over on t'other side of the river that you all goes to see sometimes?"

They says:

"There's several; but it's the Proctors, mainly."

"That's the name," I says; "I most forgot it. Well, Miss Mary Jane she told me to tell you she's gone over there in a dreadful hurry—one of them's sick."

"Which one?"

"I don't know; leastways I kinder forget; but I think it's——"

"Sakes alive, I hope it ain't *Hanner?*"

"I'm sorry to say it," I says, "but Hanner's the very one."

"My goodness—and she so well only last week! Is she took bad?"

"It ain't no name for it. They set up with her all night, Miss Mary Jane said, and they don't think she'll last many hours."

"Only think of that, now! What's the matter with her!"

I couldn't think of anything reasonable, right off that way, so I says:

"Mumps."

"Mumps your granny! They don't set up with people that's got the mumps."

HANNER WITH THE MUMPS.

"They don't, don't they? You better bet they do with *these* mumps. These mumps is different. It's a new kind, Miss Mary Jane said."

"How's it a new kind?"

"Because it's mixed up with other things."

"What other things?"

"Well, measles, and whooping-cough, and erysiplas, and consumption, and yaller jandees, and brain fever, and I don't know what all."

"My land! And they call it the *mumps?*"

"That's what Miss Mary Jane said."

"Well, what in the nation do they call it the *mumps* for?"

"Why, because it *is* the mumps. That's what it starts with."

"Well, ther' ain't no sense in it. A body might stump his toe, and take pison, and fall down the well, and break his neck, and bust his brains out, and somebody come along and ask what killed him, and some numskull up and say, 'Why he stumped his *toe*.' Would ther' be any sense in that? *No.* And thar' ain't no sense in *this,* nuther. Is it ketching?"

"Is it *ketching?* Why, how you talk. Is a *harrow* catching?—in the dark? If you don't hitch onto one tooth, you're bound to on another, ain't you? And you can't get away with that tooth without fetching the whole harrow along, can you? Well, these kind of mumps is a kind of a harrow, as you may say— and it ain't no slouch of a harrow, nuther, you come to get it hitched on good."

"Well, it's awful, *I* think," says the hare-lip. "I'll go to Uncle Harvey and——"

"Oh, yes," I says, "I *would.* Of *course* I would. I wouldn't lose no time."

"Well, why wouldn't you?"

"Just look at it a minute, and maybe you can see. Hain't your uncles obleeged to get along home to England as fast as they can? And do you reckon they'd be mean enough to go off and leave you to go all that journey by yourselves? *You* know they'll wait for you. So fur, so good. Your uncle Harvey's a preacher, ain't he? Very well, then; is a *preacher* going to deceive a steamboat clerk? Is he going to deceive a *ship clerk?*—so as to get them to let Miss Mary Jane go aboard? Now *you* know he ain't. What *will* he do, then? Why, he'll say, 'It's a great pity, but my church matters has got to get along the best way they can; for my niece has been exposed to the dreadful pluribus-unum mumps, and so it's my bounden duty to set down here and wait the three months it takes to show on her if she's got it.' But never mind, if you think it's best to tell your uncle Harvey——"

"Shucks, and stay fooling around here when we could all be having good times in England whilst we was waiting to find out whether Mary Jane's got it or not? Why, you talk like a muggins."

"Well, anyway, maybe you better tell some of the neighbors."

"Listen at that, now. You do beat all, for natural stupidness. Can't you *see* that *they'd* go and tell? Ther' ain't no way but just to not tell anybody at *all*."

"Well, maybe you're right—yes, I judge you *are* right."

"But I reckon we ought to tell Uncle Harvey she's gone out a while, anyway, so he won't be uneasy about her?"

"Yes, Miss Mary Jane she wanted you to do that. She says, 'Tell them to give Uncle Harvey and William my love and a kiss, and say I've run over the river to see Mr.—Mr.—what *is* the name of that rich family your uncle Peter used to think so much of?—I mean the one that——"

"Why, you must mean the Apthorps, ain't it?"

"Of course; bother them kind of names, a body can't ever seem to

remember them, half the time, somehow. Yes, she said, say she has
run over for to ask the Apthorps to be sure and come to the auction
and buy this house, because she allowed her uncle Peter would
ruther they had it than anybody else; and she's going to stick to them
till they say they'll come, and then, if she ain't too tired, she's coming
home; and if she is, she'll be home in the morning anyway. She said,
don't say nothing about the Proctors, but only about the Apthorps—
which'll be perfectly true, because she *is* going there to speak about
their buying the house; I know it, because she told me so, herself.''

"All right," they said, and cleared out to lay for their uncles, and
give them the love and the kisses, and tell them the message.

Everything was all right now. The girls wouldn't say nothing
because they wanted to go to England; and the king and the duke
would ruther Mary Jane was off working for the auction than around
in reach of Doctor Robinson. I felt very good; I judged I had done it
pretty neat—I reckoned Tom Sawyer couldn't a done it no neater
himself. Of course, he would a throwed more style into it, but I can't
do that very handy, not being brung up to it.

Well, they held the auction in the public square, along towards the
end of the afternoon, and it strung along, and strung along, and the
old man he was on hand and looking his level pisonest, up there
longside of the auctioneer, and chipping in a little Scripture, now
and then, or a little goody-goody saying, of some kind, and the duke
he was around goo-gooing for sympathy all he knowed how, and
just spreading himself generly.

But by-and-by the thing dragged through, and everything was
sold. Everything but a little old trifling lot in the graveyard. So
they'd got to work *that* off—I never see such a girafft as the king was
for wanting to swallow *everything*. Well, whilst they was at it, a
steamboat landed, and in about two minutes up comes a crowd a
whooping and yelling and laughing and carrying on, and singing
out:

"*Here's* your opposition line! here's your two sets o' heirs to old
Peter Wilks—and you pays your money and you takes your choice!"

CHAPTER XXIX

They was fetching a very nice looking old gentleman along, and a
nice looking younger one, with his right arm in a sling. And my souls,
how the people yelled, and laughed, and kept it up. But I didn't see
no joke about it, and I judged it would strain the duke and the king
some to see any. I reckoned they'd turn pale. But no, nary a pale
did *they* turn. The duke he never let on he suspicioned what was
up, but just went a goo-gooing around, happy and satisfied, like a
jug that's googling out buttermilk; and as for the king, he just
gazed and gazed down sorrowful on them newcomers like it give
him the stomach-ache in his very heart to think there could be such

frauds and rascals in the world. Oh, he done it admirable. Lots of
the principal people gethered around the king, to let him see they
was on his side. That old gentleman that had just come looked all
puzzled to death. Pretty soon he begun to speak, and I see, straight
off, he pronounced *like* an Englishman, not the king's way, though
the king's *was* pretty good, for an imitation. I can't give the old
gent's words, nor I can't imitate him; but he turned around to the
crowd, and says, about like this:

"This is a surprise to me which I wasn't looking for; and I'll
acknowledge, candid and frank, I ain't very well fixed to meet it
and answer it; for my brother and me has had misfortunes, he's
broke his arm, and our baggage got put off at a town above here,
last night in the night by a mistake. I am Peter Wilks's brother
Harvey. and this is his brother William, which can't hear nor speak
—and can't even make signs to amount to much; now 't he's only
got one hand to work them with. We are who we say we are; and in
a day or two, when I get the baggage, I can prove it. But, up till
then, I won't say nothing more, but go to the hotel and wait."

So him and the new dummy started off; and the king he laughs,
and blethers out:

"Broke his arm—*very* likely *ain't* it?—and very convenient, too,
for a fraud that's got to make signs, and hain't learnt how. Lost
their baggage! That's *mighty* good!—and mighty ingenious—under
the *circumstances!*"

So he laughed again; and so did everybody else, except three or
four, or maybe half a dozen. One of these was that doctor; another
one was a sharp looking gentleman, with a carpet-bag of the old-
fashioned kind made out of carpet-stuff, that had just come off of
the steamboat and was talking to him in a low voice, and glancing
towards the king now and then and nodding their heads—it was
Levi Bell, the lawyer that was gone up to Louisville; and another
one was a big rough husky that come along and listened to all the
old gentleman said, and was listening to the king now. And when
the king got done, this husky up and says:

"Say, looky here; if you are Harvey Wilks, when'd you come to
this town?"

"The day before the funeral, friend," said the king.

"But what time o' day?"

"In the evenin'—'bout an hour er two before sundown."

"*How'd* you come?"

"I come down on the *Susan Powell,* from Cincinnati."

"Well, then, how'd you come to be up at the Pint in the *mornin'*
—in a canoe?"

"I warn't up at the Pint in the mornin'."

"It's a lie."

Several of them jumped for him and begged him not to talk that
way to an old man and a preacher.

"Preacher be hanged, he's a fraud and a liar. He was up at the
Pint that mornin'. I live up there, don't I? Well, I was up there, and
he was up there. I *see* him there. He come in a canoe, along with
Tim Collins and a boy."

The doctor he up and says:

"Would you know the boy again if you was to see him, Hines?"

"I reckon I would, but I don't know. Why, yonder he is, now. I
know him perfectly easy."

It was me he pointed at. The doctor says:

"Neighbors, I don't know whether the new couple is frauds or
not; but if *these* two ain't frauds, I am an idiot, that's all. I think
it's our duty to see that they don't get away from here till we've
looked into this thing. Come along, Hines; come along, the rest of
you. We'll take these fellows to the tavern and affront them with
t'other couple, and I reckon we'll find out *something* before we get
through."

It was nuts for the crowd, though maybe not for the king's
friends; so we all started. It was about sundown. The doctor he led
me along by the hand, and was plenty kind enough, but he never
let *go* my hand.

We all got in a big room in the hotel, and lit up some candles,
and fetched in the new couple. First, the doctor says:

"I don't wish to be too hard on these two men, but *I* think
they're frauds, and they may have complices that we don't know
nothing about. If they have, won't the complices get away with that
bag of gold Peter Wilks left? It ain't unlikely. If these men ain't
frauds, they won't object to sending for that money and letting us
keep it till they prove they're all right—ain't that so?"

Everybody agreed to that. So I judged they had our gang in a
pretty tight place, right at the outstart. But the king he only looked
sorrowful, and says:

"Gentlemen, I wish the money was there, for I ain't got no
disposition to throw anything in the way of a fair, open, out-and-
out investigation o' this misable business; but alas, the money ain't
there; you k'n send and see, if you want to."

"Where is it, then?"

"Well, when my niece give it to me to keep for her, I took and
hid it inside o' the straw tick o' my bed, not wishin' to bank it for
the next few days we'd be here, and considerin' the bed a safe
place, we not bein' used to niggers, and suppos'n' 'em honest, like
servants in England. The niggers stole it the very next mornin' after
I had went down stairs; and when I sold 'em, I hadn't missed the
money yit, so they got clean away with it. My servant here k'n tell
you 'bout it gentlemen."

The doctor and several said "Shucks!" and I see nobody didn't
altogether believe him. One man asked me if I see the niggers steal
it. I said no, but I see them sneaking out of the room and hustling

away, and I never thought nothing, only I reckoned they was afraid they had waked up my master and was trying to get away before he made trouble with them. That was all they asked me. Then the doctor whirls on me and says:

"Are *you* English too?"

I says yes; and him and some others laughed, and said, "Stuff!"

Well, then they sailed in on the general investigation, and there we had it, up and down, hour in, hour out, and nobody said a word about supper, nor ever seemed to think about it—and so they kept it up, and kept it up; and it *was* the worst mixed-up thing you ever see. They made the king tell his yarn, and they made the old gentleman tell his'n; and anybody but a lot of prejudiced chuckleheads would a *seen* that the old gentleman was spinning truth and t'other one lies. And by-and-by they had me up to tell what I knowed. The king he give me a left handed look out of the corner of his eye, and so I knowed enough to talk on the right side. I begun to tell about Sheffield, and how we lived there, and all about the English Wilkses, and so on; but I didn't get pretty fur till the doctor begun to laugh; and Levi Bell, the lawyer, says:

"Set down, my boy, I wouldn't strain myself, if I was you. I reckon you ain't used to lying, it don't seem to come handy; what you want is practice. You do it pretty awkward."

I didn't care nothing for the compliment, but I was glad to be let off, anyway.

The doctor he started to say something, and turns and says:

"If you'd been in town at first, Levi Bell—"

The king broke in and reached out his hand, and says:

"Why, is this my poor dead brother's old friend that he's wrote so often about?"

The lawyer and him shook hands, and the lawyer smiled and looked pleased, and they talked right along a while, and then got to one side and talked low; and at last the lawyer speaks up and says:

"That'll fix it. I'll take the order and send it, along with your brother's, and then they'll know it's all right."

So they got some paper and a pen, and the king he set down and twisted his head to one side, and chawed his tongue, and scrawled off something; and then they give the pen to the duke—and then for the first time, the duke looked sick. But he took the pen and wrote. So then the lawyer turns to the new old gentleman and says:

"You and your brother please write a line or two and sign your names."

The old gentleman wrote, but nobody couldn't read it. The lawyer looked powerful astonished, and says:

"Well, it beats *me*"—and snaked a lot of old letters out of his pocket, and examined them, and then examined the old man's writing, and then *them* again; and then says: "These old letters is from Harvey Wilks; and here's *these* two's handwritings, and anybody can see *they* didn't write them" (the king and the duke looked sold and foolish, I tell you, to see how the lawyer had took them in), "and here's *this* old gentleman's handwriting, and anybody can tell, easy enough, *he* didn't write them—fact is, the scratches he makes ain't properly *writing,* at all. Now here's some letters from—"

The new old gentleman says—

"If you please, let me explain. Nobody can read my hand but my brother there—so he copies for me. It's *his* hand you've got there, not mine."

"*Well!*" says the lawyer, "this *is* a state of things. I've got some of Williams's letters too; so if you'll get him to write a line or so we can com—"

"He *can't* write with his left hand," says the old gentleman. "If he could use his right hand, you would see that he wrote his own letters and mine too. Look at both, please—they're by the same hand."

The lawyer done it, and says:

"I believe it's so—and if it ain't so, there's a heap stronger resemblance than I'd noticed before, anyway. Well, well, well! I thought we was right on the track of a slution, but it's gone to grass, partly. But anyway, *one* thing is proved—*these* two ain't either of 'em Wilkses"—and he wagged his head towards the king and the duke.

Well, what do you think?—that muleheaded old fool wouldn't give in *then!* Indeed he wouldn't. Said it warn't no fair test. Said his brother William was the cussedest joker in the world, and hadn't *tried* to write—*he* see William was going to play one of his jokes the minute he put the pen to paper. And so he warmed up and went warbling and warbling right along, till he was actuly beginning to believe what he was saying, *himself*—but pretty soon the new old gentleman broke in, and says:

"I've thought of something. Is there anybody here that helped to lay out my br—helped to lay out the late Peter Wilks for burying?"

"Yes," says somebody, "me and Ab Turner done it. We're both here."

Then the old man turns towards the king, and says:

"Perhaps this gentleman can tell me what was tatooed on his breast?"

Blamed if the king didn't have to brace up mighty quick, or he'd a squshed down like a bluff bank that the river has cut under, it took him so sudden—and mind you, it was a thing that was calculated to make most *anybody* sqush to get fetched such a solid one as that without any notice—because how was *he* going to know what was tatooed on the man? He whitened a little; he couldn't help it; and it was mighty still in there, and everybody bending a little forwards and gazing at him. Says I to myself, *Now* he'll throw

up the sponge—there ain't no more use. Well, did he? A body can't
hardly believe it, but he didn't. I reckon he thought he'd keep the
thing up till he tired them people out, so they'd thin out, and him
and the duke could break loose and get away. Anyway, he set there,
and pretty soon he begun to smile, and says:

"Mf! It's a *very* tough question, *ain't* it! *Yes,* sir, I k'n tell you
what's tatooed on his breast. It's jest a small, thin, blue arrow—
that's what it is; and if you don't look clost, you can't see it. *Now*
what do you say—hey?"

Well, *I* never see anything like that old blister for clean out-and-
out cheek.

The new old gentleman turns brisk towards Ab Turner and his
pard, and his eye lights up like he judged he'd got the king *this*
time, and says:

"There—you've heard what he said! Was there any such mark
on Peter Wilks's breast?"

Both of them spoke up and says:

"We didn't see no such mark."

"Good!" says the old gentleman. "Now, what you *did* see on his
breast was a small dim P, and a B (which is an initial he dropped
when he was young), and a W, with dashes between them, so:
P-B-W"—and he marked them that way on a piece of paper.
"Come—ain't that what you saw?"

Both of them spoke up again, and says:

"No, we *didn't.* We never seen any marks at all."

Well, everybody *was* in a state of mind, now; and they sings out:

"The whole *bilin'* of 'm's frauds! Le's duck 'em! le's drown 'em!
le's ride 'em on a rail!" and everybody was whooping at once, and
there was a rattling pow-wow. But the lawyer he jumps on the table
and yells, and says:

"Gentlemen—*gentlemen!* Hear me just a word—just a *single*
word—if you PLEASE! There's one way yet—let's go and dig up
the corpse and look."

That took them.

"Horray!" they all shouted, and was starting right off; but the
lawyer and the doctor sung out:

"Hold on, hold on! Collar all these four men and the boy, and
fetch *them* along, too!"

"We'll do it!" they all shouted: "and if we don't find them marks
we'll lynch the whole gang!"

I *was* scared, now, I tell you. But there warn't no getting away,
you know. They gripped us all, and marched us right along,
straight for the graveyard, which was a mile and a half down the
river, and the whole town at our heels, for we made noise enough,
and it was only nine in the evening.

As we went by our house I wished I hadn't sent Mary Jane out of
town; because now if I could tip her the wink, she'd light out and

save me, and blow on our dead-beats.

Well, we swarmed along down the river road, just carrying on
like wild-cats; and to make it more scary, the sky was darking up,
and the lightning beginning to wink and flitter, and the wind to
shiver amongst the leaves. This was the most awful trouble and
most dangersome I ever was in; and I was kinder stunned;
everything was going so different from what I had allowed for;
stead of being fixed so I could take my own time, if I wanted to,
and see all the fun, and have Mary Jane at my back to save me and
set me free when the close-fit come, here was nothing in the world
betwixt me and sudden death but just them tatoo-marks. If they
didn't find them—

I couldn't bear to think about it; and yet, somehow, I couldn't
think about nothing else. It got darker and darker, and it was a
beautiful time to give the crowd a slip; but that big husky had me
by the wrist—Hines—and a body might as well try to give Goliar
the slip. He dragged me right along, he was so excited; and I had
to run to keep up.

When they got there they swarmed into the graveyard and
washed over it like an overflow. And when they got to the grave,
they found they had about a hundred times as many shovels as they
wanted, but nobody hadn't thought to fetch a lantern. But they
sailed into digging, anyway, by the flicker of the lightning, and sent
a man to the nearest house a half a mile off, to borrow one.

So they dug and dug, like everything; and it got awful dark, and
the rain started, and the wind swished and swushed along, and the
lightning come brisker and brisker, and the thunder boomed; but
them people never took no notice of it, they was so full of this
business; and one minute you could see everything and every face
in that big crowd, and the shovelfuls of dirt sailing up out of the
grave, and the next second the dark wiped it all out, and you
couldn't see nothing at all.

At last they got out the coffin, and begun to unscrew the lid, and
then such another crowding, and shouldering, and shoving as there
was, to scrouge in and get a sight, you never see; and in the dark,
that way, it was awful. Hines he hurt my wrist dreadful, pulling
and tugging so, and I reckon he clean forgot I was in the world, he
was so excited and panting.

All of a sudden the lightning let go a perfect sluice of white glare,
and somebody sings out:

"By the living jingo, here's the bag of gold on his breast!"

Hines lets out a whoop, like everybody else, and dropped my
wrist and give a big surge to bust his way in and get a look, and
the way I lit out and shinned for the road in the dark, there ain't
nobody can tell.

I had the road all to myself, and I fairly flew—leastways I had it
all to myself except the solid dark, and the now-and-then glares,

and the buzzing of the rain, and the thrashing of the wind, and the splitting of the thunder; and sure as you are born I did clip it along!

When I struck the town, I see there warn't nobody out in the storm, so I never hunted for no back streets, but humped it straight through the main one; and when I begun to get towards our house I aimed my eye and set it. No light there; the house all dark—which made me feel sorry and disappointed, I didn't know why. But at last, just as I was sailing by, *flash* comes the light in Mary Jane's window! and my heart swelled up sudden, like to bust; and the same second the house and all was behind me in the dark, and wasn't ever going to be before me no more in this world. She *was* the best girl I ever see, and had the most sand.

The minute I was far enough above the town to see I could make the towhead, I begun to look sharp for a boat to borrow; and the first time the lightning showed me one that wasn't chained, I snatched it and shoved. It was a canoe, and warn't fastened with nothing but a rope. The towhead was a rattling big distance off, away out there in the middle of the river, but I didn't lose no time; and when I struck the raft at last, I was so fagged I would a just laid down to blow and gasp if I could afforded it. But I didn't. As I sprung aboard I sung out:

"Out with you Jim, and set her loose! Glory be to goodness, we're shut of them!"

Jim lit out, and was a coming for me with both arms spread, he was so full of joy; but when I glimpsed him in the lightning, my heart shot up in my mouth, and I went overboard backwards; for I forgot he was old King Lear and a drownded A-rab all in one, and it most scared the livers and lights out of me. But Jim fished me out, and was going to hug me and bless me, and so on, he was so glad I was back and we was shut of the king and the duke, but I says:

"Not now—have it for breakfast, have it for breakfast! Cut loose and let her slide!"

So, in two seconds, away we went, a sliding down the river, and it *did* seem so good to be free again and all by ourselves on the big river and nobody to bother us. I had to skip around a bit, and jump up and crack my heels a few times, I couldn't help it; but about the third crack, I noticed a sound that I knowed mighty well—and held my breath and listened and waited—and sure enough, when the next flash busted out over the water, here they come!—and just a laying to their oars and making their skiff hum! It was the king and the duke.

So I wilted right down onto the planks, then, and give up; and it was all I could do to keep from crying.

CHAPTER XXX

When they got aboard, the king went for me, and shook me by the collar, and says:

"Tryin' to give us the slip, was ye, you pup! Tired of our company—hey?"

I says:

"No, your majesty, we warn't—*please* don't, your majesty!"

"Quick, then, and tell us what *was* your idea, or I'll shake the insides out o' you!"

"Honest, I'll tell you everything, just as it happened, your majesty. The man that had aholt of me was very good to me, and kept saying he had a boy about as big as me that died last year, and he was sorry to see a boy in such a dangerous fix; and when they was all took by surprise by finding the gold, and made a rush for the coffin, he lets go of me and whispers, 'Heel it, now, or they'll hang ye, sure!' and I lit out. It didn't seem no good for *me* to stay —*I* couldn't do nothing, and I didn't want to be hung if I could get away. So I never stopped running till I found the canoe; and when I got here I told Jim to hurry, or they'd catch me and hang me yet, and said I was afeard you and the duke wasn't alive, now, and I was awful sorry, and so was Jim, and was awful glad when we see you coming, you may ask Jim if I didn't."

Jim said it was so; and the king told him to shut up, and said, "Oh, yes, it's *mighty* likely!" and shook me up again, and said he reckoned he'd drownd me. But the duke says:

"Leggo the boy, you old idiot! Would *you* a done any different? Did you inquire around for *him,* when you got loose? I don't remember it."

So the king let go of me, and begun to cuss that town and everybody in it. But the duke says:

"You better a blame sight give *yourself* a good cussing, for you're the one that's entitled to it most. You hain't done a thing, from the start, that had any sense in it, except coming out so cool and cheeky with that imaginary blue-arrow mark. That *was* bright—it was right down bully; and it was the thing that saved us. For if it hadn't been for that, they'd a jailed us till them Englishmen's baggage come—and then—the penitentiary, you bet! But that trick took 'em to the graveyard, and the gold done us a still bigger kindness; for if the excited fools hadn't let go all holts and made that rush to get a look, we'd a slept in our cravats to-night—cravats warranted to *wear,* too—longer than *we'd* need 'em."

They was still a minute—thinking—then the king says, kind of absent-minded like:

"Mf! And we reckoned the *niggers* stole it!"

That made me squirm!

"Yes," says the duke, kinder slow, and deliberate, and sarcastic,

"*We* did."

After about a half a minute, the king drawls out:

"Leastways—*I* did."

The duke says, pretty brisk:

"On the contrary—*I* did."

The king kind of ruffles up, and says:

"Looky here, Bilgewater, what'r you referrin' to?"

The duke says, pretty brish:

"When it comes to that, maybe you'll let me ask, what was *you* referring to?"

"Shucks!" says the king, very sarcastic; "but *I* don't know— maybe you was asleep, and didn't know what you was about."

The duke bristles right up, now, and says:

"Oh, let *up* on this cussed nonsense—do you take me for a blame' fool? Don't you reckon *I* know who hid that money in that coffin?"

"*Yes,* sir! I know you *do* know—because you done it yourself!"

"It's a lie!"—and the duke went for him. The king sings out:

"Take y'r hands off!—leggo my throat!—I take it all back!"

The duke says:

"Well, you just own up, first, that you *did* hide that money there, intending to give me the slip one of these days, and come back and dig it up, and have it all to yourself."

"Wait jest a minute, duke—answer me this one question, honest and fair; if you didn't put the money there, say it, and I'll b'lieve you, and take back everything I said."

"You old scoundrel, I didn't, and you know I didn't. There, now!"

"Well, then, I b'lieve you. But answer me only jest this one more —now *don't* git mad; didn't you have it in your *mind* to hook the money and hide it?"

The duke never said nothing for a little bit; then he says:

"Well—I don't care if I *did,* I didn't *do* it, anyway. But you not only had it in mind to do it, but you *done* it."

"I wisht I may never die if I done it, duke, and that's honest. I won't say I warn't *goin'* to do it, because I *was;* but you—I mean somebody—got in ahead o' me."

"It's a lie! You done it, and you got to *say* you done it, or—"

The king begun to gurgle, and then he gasps out:

" 'Nough!—*I own up!*"

I was very glad to hear him say that, it made me feel much more easier than what I was feeling before. So the duke took his hands off, and says:

"If you ever deny it again, I'll drown you. It's *well* for you to set there and blubber like a baby—it's fitten for you, after the way you've acted. I never see such an old ostrich for wanting to gobble everything—and I a trusting you all the time, like you was my own

father. You ought to been ashamed of yourself to stand by and hear
it saddled onto a lot of poor niggers and you never say a word for
'em. It makes me feel ridiculous to think I was soft enough to
believe that rubbage. Cuss you, I can see, now, why you was so
anxious to make up the deffesit—you wanted to get what money
I'd got out of the Nonesuch and one thing or another, and scoop
it *all!*"

The king says, timid, and still a snuffling:

"Why, duke, it was you that said make up the deffersit, it
warn't me."

"Dry up! I don't want to hear no more *out* of you!" says the
duke. "And *now* you see what you *got* by it. They've got all their
own money back, and all of *ourn* but a shekel or two, *besides.*
G'long to bed—and don't you deffersit *me* no more deffersits, long
's *you* live!"

So the king sneaked into the wigwam, and took to his bottle for
comfort; and before long the duke tackled *his* bottle; and so in
about a half an hour they was as thick as thieves again, and the
tighter they got, the lovinger they got; and went off a snoring in
each other's arms. They both got powerful mellow, but I noticed the
king didn't get mellow enough to forget to remember to not deny
about hiding the money-bag again. That made me feel easy and
satisfied. Of course when they got to snoring, we had a long gabble,
and I told Jim everything.

CHAPTER XXXI

We dasn't stop again at any town, for days and days; kept right
along down the river. We was down south in the warm weather,
now, and a mighty long ways from home. We begun to come to
trees with Spanish moss on them, hanging down from the limbs like
long gray beards. It was the first I ever see it growing, and it made
the woods look solemn and dismal. So now the frauds reckoned
they was out of danger, and they begun to work the villages again.

First they done a lecture on temperance; but they didn't make
enough for them both to get drunk on. Then in another village they
started a dancing school; but they didn't know no more how to
dance than a kangaroo does; so the first prance they made, the
general public jumped in and pranced them out of town. Another
time they tried to go at yellocution; but they didn't yellocute long
till the audience got up and give them a solid good cussing and
made them skip out. They tackled missionarying, and
mesmerizering, and doctoring, and telling fortunes, and a little of
everything; but they couldn't seem to have no luck. So at last they
got just about dead broke, and laid around the raft, as she floated
along, thinking, and thinking, and never saying nothing, by the half
a day at a time, and dreadful blue and desperate.

And at last they took a change, and begun to lay their heads together in the wigwam and talk low and confidential two or three hours at a time. Jim and me got uneasy. We didn't like the look of it. We judged they was studying up some kind of worse deviltry than ever. We turned it over and over, and at last we made up our minds they was going to break into somebody's house or store, or was going into the counterfeit-money business, or something. So then we was pretty scared, and made up an agreement that we wouldn't have nothing in the world to do with such actions, and if we ever got the least show we would give them the cold shake, and clear out and leave them behind. Well, early one morning we hid the raft in a good safe place about two mile below a little bit of a shabby village, named Pikesville, and the king he went ashore, and told us all to stay hid whilst he went up to town and smelt around to see if anybody had got any wind of the Royal Nonesuch there yet. ("House to rob, you *mean*," says I to myself, "and when you get through robbing it you'll come back here and wonder what's become of me and Jim and the raft—and you'll have to take it out in wondering.") And he said if he warn't back by midday, the duke and me would know it was all right, and we was to come along.

So we staid where we was. The duke he fretted and sweated around, and was in a mighty sour way. He scolded us for everything, and we couldn't seem to do nothing right; he found fault with every little thing. Something was a-brewing, sure. I was good and glad when midday come and no king; we could have a change, anyway—and maybe a chance for *the* change, on top of it. So me and the duke went up to the village, and hunted around there for the king, and by-and-by we found him in the back room of a little low doggery, very tight, and a lot of loafers bullyragging him for sport, and he a cussing and threatening with all his might, and so tight he couldn't walk, and couldn't do nothing to them. The duke he begun to abuse him for an old fool, and the king begun to sass back; and the minute they was fairly at it, I lit out, and shook the reefs out of my hind legs, and spun down the river road like a deer—for I see our chance; and I made up my mind that it would be a long day before they ever see me and Jim again. I got down there all out of breath but loaded up with joy, and sung out—

"Set her loose, Jim, we're all right, now!"

But there warn't no answer, and nobody come out of the wigwam. Jim was gone! I set up a shout—and then another—and then another one; and run this way and that in the woods, whooping and screeching; but it warn't no use—old Jim was gone. Then I set down and cried; I couldn't help it. But I couldn't set still long. Pretty soon I went out on the road, trying to think what I better do, and I run across a boy walking, and asked him if he'd seen a strange nigger, dressed so and so, and he says:

"Yes."

"Whereabouts?" says I.

"Down to Silas Phelps's place, two mile below here. He's a runaway nigger, and they've got him. Was you looking for him?"

"You bet I ain't! I run across him in the woods about an hour or two ago, and he said if I hollered he'd cut my livers out—and told me to lay down and stay where I was; and I done it. Been there ever since; afeard to come out."

"Well," he says, "you needn't be afeard no more, becuz they've got him. He run off f'm down South, som'ers."

"It's a good job they got him."

"Well, I *reckon!* There's two hundred dollars reward on him. It's like picking up money out'n the road."

"Yes, it is—and *I* could a had it if I'd been big enough; I see him *first.* Who nailed him?"

"It was an old fellow—a stranger—and he sold out his chance in him for forty dollars becuz he's got to go up the river and can't wait. Think o' that, now! You bet *I'd* wait, if it was seven year."

"That's me, every time," says I. "But maybe his chance ain't worth no more than that, if he'll sell it so cheap. Maybe there's something ain't straight about it."

"But it *is,* though—straight as a string. I see the handbill myself. It tells all about him, to a dot—paints him like a picture, and tells the plantation he's frum, below New*rleans.* No-sirree-*bob,* they ain't no trouble 'bout *that* speculation, you bet you. Say, gimme a chaw tobacker, won't ye?"

I didn't have none, so he left. I went to the raft, and set down in the wigwam to thing. But I couldn't come to nothing. I thought till I wore my head sore, but I couldn't see no way out of the trouble. After all this long journey, and after all we'd done for them scoundrels, here was it all come to nothing, everything all busted up and ruined, because they could have the heart to serve Jim such a trick as that, and make him a slave again all his life, and amongst strangers, too, for forty dirty dollars.

Once I said to myself it would be a thousand times better for Jim to be a slave at home where his family was, as long as he'd *got* to be a slave, and so I'd better write a letter to Tom Sawyer and tell him to tell Miss Watson where he was. But I soon give up that notion, for tow things: she'd be made and disgusted at his rascality and ungratefulness for leaving her, and so she'd sell him straight down the river again; and if she didn't, everybody naturally despises an ungrateful nigger, and they'd make Jim feel it all the time, and so he'd feel ornery and disgraced. And then think of *me!* It would get all around, the Huck Finn helped a nigger to get his freedom; and if I was to ever see anybody from that town again, I'd be ready to get down and lick his boots for shame. That's just the way: a person does a low-down thing, and then he don't want to

take no consequences of it. Thinks as long as he can hide it, ain't
no disgrace. That was my fix exactly. The more I studied about
this, the more my conscience went to grinding me, and the more
wicked and low-down and ornery I got to feeling. And at last, when
it hit me all of a sudden that here was the plain hand of Providence
slapping me in the face and letting me know my wickedness was
being watched all the time from up there in heaven, whilst I was
stealing a poor old woman's nigger that hadn't ever done me no
harm, and now was showing me there's One that's always on the
lookout, and ain't agoing to allow no such miserable doings to go
only just so fur and no further, I most dropped in my tracks I was
so scared. Well, I tried the best I could to kinder soften it up
somehow for myself, by saying I was brung up wicked, and so I
warn't so much to blame; but something inside of me kept saying,
"There was the Sunday school, you could a gone to it; and if you'd
a done it they'd a learnt you, there, that people that acts as I'd been
acting about that nigger goes to everlasting fire."

It made me shiver. And I about made up my mind to pray; and see
if I couldn't try to quit being the kind of a boy I was, and be better.
So I kneeled down. But the words wouldn't come. Why wouldn't
they? It warn't no use to try and hide it from Him. Nor from *me*,
neither. I knowed very well why they wouldn't come. It was because
my heart warn't right; it was because I warn't square; it was because
I was playing double. I was letting *on* to give up sin, but away inside
of me I was holding on to the biggest one of all. I was trying to make
my mouth *say* I would do the right thing and the clean thing, and go
and write to that nigger's owner and tell where he was; but deep
down in me I knowed it was a lie—and He knowed it. You can't pray
a lie—I found that out.

So I was full of trouble, full as I could be; and didn't know what to
do. At last I had an idea; and I says, I'll go and write the letter—and
then see if I can pray. Why, it was astonishing, the way I felt as light
as a feather, right straight off, and my troubles all gone. So I got a
piece of paper and a pencil, all glad and excited, and set down
and wrote:

> Miss Watson your runaway nigger Jim is down here two mile below
> Pikesville and Mr. Phelps has got him and he will give him up for the
> reward if you send.   HUCK FINN.

I felt good and all washed clean of sin for the first time I had ever
felt so in my life, and I knowed I could pray now. But I didn't do it
straight off, but laid the paper down and set there thinking—
thinking how good it was all this happened so, and how near I come
to being lost and going to hell. And went on thinking. And got to
thinking over our trip down the river; and I see Jim before me, all the
time, in the day, and in the nighttime, sometimes moonlight,

sometimes storms, and we a floating along, talking, and singing, and
laughing. But somehow I couldn't seem to strike no places to harden
me against him, but only the other kind. I'd see him standing my
watch on top of his'n, stead of calling me, so I could go on sleeping;
and see him how glad he was when I come back out of the fog; and
when I come to him again in the swamp, up there where the feud
was; and such-like times; and would always call me honey, and pet
me, and do everything he could think of for me, and how good he
always was; and at last I struck the time I saved him by telling the
men we had small-pox aboard, and he was so grateful, and said I was
the best friend old Jim ever had in the world, and the *only* one he's
got now; and then I happened to look around, and see that paper.

It was a close place. I took it up, and held it in my hand. I was a
trembling, because I'd got to decide, forever, betwixt two things, and
I knowed it. I studied a minute, sort of holding my breath, and then
says to myself:

"All right, then, I'll *go* to hell"—and tore it up.

It was awful thoughts, and awful words, but they was said. And I
let them stay said; and never thought no more about reforming. I
shoved the whole thing out of my head; and said I would take up
wickedness again, which was in my line, being brung up to it, and
the other warn't. And for a starter, I would go to work and steal Jim
out of slavery again; and if I could think up anything worse, I would
do that, too; because as long as I was in, and in for good, I might as
well go the whole hog.

Then I set to thinking over how to get at it, and turned over
considerable many ways in my mind; and at last fixed up a plan that
suited me. So then I took the bearings of a woody island that was
down the river a piece, and as soon as it was fairly dark I crept out
with my raft and went for it, and hid it there, and then turned in.
I slept the night through, and got up before it was light, and had my
breakfast, and put on my store clothes, and tied up some others and
one thing or another in a bundle, and took the canoe and cleared for
shore. I landed below where I judged was Phelps's place, and hid my
bundle in the woods, and then filled up the canoe with water, and
loaded rocks into her and sunk her where I could find her again
when I wanted her, about a quarter of a mile below a little steam
sawmill that was on the bank.

Then I struck up the road, and when I passed the mill I see a sign
on it, "Phelps's Sawmill," and when I come to the farm-houses,
two or three hundred yards further along, I kept my eyes peeled, but
didn't see nobody around, though it was good daylight, now. But
I didn't mind, because I didn't want to see nobody just yet—I only
wanted to get the lay of the land. According to my plan, I was going
to turn up there from the village, not from below. So I just took a
look, and shoved along, straight for town. Well, the very first man
I see, when I got there, was the duke. He was sticking up a bill for

the Royal Nonesuch—three-night performance—like that other
time. *They* had the cheek, them frauds! I was right on him, before
I could shirk. He looked astonished, and says:

"Hel-*lo!* Where'd *you* come from?" Then he says, kind of glad
and eager, "Where's the raft?—got her in a good place?"

I says:

"Why, that's just what I was agoing to ask your grace."

Then he didn't look so joyful—and says:

"What was your idea for asking *me?*" he says.

"Well," I says, "when I see the king in that doggery yesterday,
I says to myself, we can't get him home for hours, till he's soberer;
so I went a loafing around town to put in the time, and wait. A man
up and offered me ten cents to help him pull a skiff over the river
and back to fetch a sheep, and so I went along; but when we was
dragging him to the boat, and the man left me aholt of the rope and
went behind him to shove him along, he was too strong for me, and
jerked loose and run, and we after him. We didn't have no dog, and
so we had to chase him all over the country till we tired him out.
We never got him till dark, then we fetched him over, and I started
down for the raft. When I got there and see it was gone, I says to
myself, 'they've got into trouble and had to leave; and they've took
my nigger, which is the only nigger I've got in the world, and now
I'm in a strange country, and ain't got no property no more, nor
nothing, and no way to make my living;' so I set down and cried.
I slept in the woods all night. But what *did* become of the raft
then?—and Jim, poor Jim!"

"Blamed if *I* know—that is, what's become of the raft. That old
fool had made a trade and got forty dollars, and when we found him
in the doggery the loafers had matched half dollars with him and
got every cent but what he'd spent for whisky; and when I got him
home late last night and found the raft gone, we said, 'That little
rascal has stole our raft and shook us, and run off down the river.' "

"I wouldn't shake my *nigger,* would I?—the only nigger I had in
the world, and the only property."

"We never thought of that. Fact is, I reckon we'd come to
consider him our nigger; yes, we did consider him so—goodness
knows we had trouble enough for him. So when we see the raft was
gone, and we flat broke, there warn't anything for it but to try the
Royal Nonesuch another shake. And I've pegged along ever since,
dry as a powderhorn. Where's that ten cents? Give it here."

I had considerable money, so I give him ten cents, but begged him
to spend it for something to eat, and give me some, because it was
all the money I had, and I hadn't had nothing to eat since yesterday.
He never said nothing. The next minute he whirls on me and says:

"Do you reckon that nigger would blow on us? We'd skin him
if he done that!"

"How can he blow? Hain't he run off?"

"No! That old fool sold him, and never divided with me, and the money's gone."

"*Sold* him?" I says, and begun to cry; "why, he was *my* nigger, and that was my money. Where is he?—I want my nigger."

"Well, you can't *get* your nigger, that's all—so dry up your blubbering. Looky here—do you think *you'd* venture to blow on us? Blamed if I think I'd trust you. Why, if you *was* to blow on us—"

He stopped, but I never see the duke look so ugly out of his eyes before. I went on a-whimpering, and says:

"I don't want to blow on nobody; and I ain't got no time to blow, nohow. I got to turn out and find my nigger."

He looked kinder bothered, and stood there with his bills fluttering on his arm, thinking, and wrinkling up his forehead. At last he says:

"I'll tell you something. We got to be here three days. If you'll promise you won't blow, and won't let the nigger blow, I'll tell you where to find him."

So I promised, and he says:

"A farmer by the name of Silas Ph—" and then he stopped. You see he started to tell me the truth; but when he stopped, that way, and begun to study and think again, I reckoned he was changing his mind. And so he was. He wouldn't trust me; he wanted to make sure of having me out of the way the whole three days. So pretty soon he says: "The man that bought him is named Abram Foster—Abram G. Foster—and he lives forty mile back here in the country, on the road to Lafayette."

"All right," I says, "I can walk it in three days. And I'll start this very afternoon."

"No you won't, you'll start *now;* and don't you lose any time about it, neither, nor do any gabbling by the way. Just keep a tight tongue in your head and move right along, and then you won't get into trouble with *us,* d'ye hear?"

That was the order I wanted, and that was the one I played for. I wanted to be left free to work my plans.

"So clear out," he says; "and you can tell Mr. Foster whatever you want to. Maybe you can get him to believe that Jim *is* your nigger—some idiots don't require documents—leastways I've heard there's such down South here. And when you tell him the handbill and the reward's bogus, maybe he'll believe you when you explain to him what the idea was for getting 'em out. Go 'long, now, and tell him anything you want to; but mind you don't work your jaw any *between* here and there."

So I left, and struck for the back country. I didn't look around, but I kinder felt like he was watching me. But I knowed I could tire him out at that. I want straight out in the country as much as a mile, before I stopped; then I doubled back through the woods towards Phelps's. I reckoned I better start in on my plan straight off, without

fooling around, because I wanted to stop Jim's mouth till these
fellows could get away. I didn't want no trouble with their kind. I'd
seen all I wanted to of them, and wanted to get entirely shut
of them.

CHAPTER XXXII

When I got there it was all still and Sunday-like, and hot and
sunshiny—the hands was gone to the fields; and there was them
kind of faint dronings of bugs and flies in the air that makes it seem
so lonesome and like everybody's dead and gone; and if a breeze
fans along and quivers the leaves, it makes you feel mournful,
because you feel like it's spirits whispering—spirits that's been
dead ever so many years—and you always think they're talking
about *you*. As a general thing it makes a body wish *he* was dead, too,
and done with it all.

Phelps's was one of these little one-horse cotton plantations;
and they all look alike. A rail fence round a two-acre yard; a stile,
made out of logs sawed off and up-ended, in steps, like barrels of
a different length, to climb over the fence with, and for the women
to stand on when they are going to jump onto a horse; some sickly
grass-patches in the big yard, but mostly it was bare and smooth,
like an old hat with the nap rubbed off; big double log house for the
white folks—hewed logs, with the chinks stopped up with mud or
mortar, and these mud-stripes been whitewashed some time or
another; round-log kitchen, with a big broad, open but roofed
passage joining it to the house; log smoke-house back of the kitchen;
three little log nigger-cabins in a row t'other side the smokehouse;
one little hut all by itself away down against the back fence, and
some out-buildings down a piece the other side; ash-hopper, and big
kettle to bile soap in, by the little hut; bench by the kitchen door,
with bucket of water and a gourd; hound asleep there, in the sun;
more hounds asleep, round about; about three shade-trees away
off in a corner; some currant bushes and gooseberry bushes in one
place by the fence; outside of the fence a garden and a water-melon
patch; then the cotton fields begins; and after the fields, the woods.

I went around and clumb over the back stile by the ash-hopper,
and started for the kitchen. When I got a little ways, I heard the dim
hum of a spinning-wheel wailing along up and sinking along down
again; and then I knowed for certain I wished I was dead—for that
is the lonesomest sound in the whole world.

I went right along, not fixing up any particular plan, but just
trusting to Providence to put the right words in my mouth when the
time come; for I'd noticed that Providence always did put the right
words in my mouth, if I left it alone.

When I got half-way, first one hound and then another got up and
went for me, and of course I stopped and faced them, and kept

still. And such another pow-wow as they made! In a quarter of a
minute I was a kind of a hub of a wheel, as you may say—spokes
made out of dogs—circle of fifteen of them packed together around
me, with their necks and noses stretched up towards me, a barking
and howling; and more a coming; you could see them sailing over
fences and around corners from everywheres.

A nigger woman come tearing out of the kitchen with a rolling-
pin in her hand, singing out, "Begone! *you* Tige! you Spot! begone,
sah!" and she fetched first one and then another of them a clip and
sent him howling, and then the rest followed; and the next second,
half of them come back, wagging their tails around me and
making friends with me. There ain't no harm in a hound, nohow.

And behind the woman comes a little nigger girl and two little
nigger boys, without anything on but tow-linen shirts, and they
hung onto their mother's gown, and peeped out from behind her
at me, bashful, the way they always do. And here comes the white
woman running from the house, about forty-five or fifty year old,
bareheaded, and her spinning-stick in her hand; and behind her
comes her little white children, acting the same way the little
niggers was doing. She was smiling all over so she could hardly
stand—and says:

"It's *you,* at last!—*ain't* it?"

I out with a "Yes'm," before I thought.

She grabbed me and hugged me tight; and then gripped me by
both hands and shook and shook; and the tears come in her eyes,
and run down over; and she couldn't seem to hug and shake enough,
and kept saying, "You don't look as much like your mother as I
reckoned you would, but law sakes, I don't care for that, I'm *so*
glad to see you! Dear, dear, it does seem like I could eat you up!
Children, it's your cousin Tom!—tell him howdy."

But they ducked their heads, and put their fingers in their
mouths, and hid behind her. So she run on:

"Lize, hurry up and get him a hot breakfast, right away—or did
you get your breakfast on the boat?"

I said I had got it on the boat. So then she started for the house,
leading me by the hand, and the children tagging after. When we
got there, she set me down in a split-bottomed chair, and set
herself down on a little low stool in front of me, holding both of my
hands, and says:

"Now I can have a *good* look at you; and laws-a-me, I've been
hungry for it a many and a many a time, all these long years, and it's
come at last! We been expecting you a couple of days and more.
What's kep' you?—boat get aground?"

"Yes'm—she——"

"Don't say yes'm—say Aunt Sally. Where'd she get aground?"

I didn't rightly know what to say, because I didn't know
whether the boat would be coming up the river or down. But I go

a good deal on instinct; and my instinct said she would be coming
up—from down towards Orleans. That did'nt help me much,
though; for I didn't know the names of bars down that way. I see
I'd got to invent a bar, or forget the name of the one we got aground
on—or— Now I struck an idea, and fetched it out:

"It warn't the grounding—that didn't keep us back but a little.
We blowed out a cylinder-head."

"Good gracious! anybody hurt?"

"No'm. Killed a nigger."

"Well, it's lucky; because sometimes people do get hurt. Two
years ago last Christmas, your uncle Silas was coming up from
Newrleans on the old *Lally Rook,* and she blowed out a cylinder-
head and crippled a man. And I think he died afterwards. He was
a Babtist. Your uncle Silas knowed a family in Baton Rouge that
knowed his people very well. Yes, I remember, now he *did* die.
Mortification set in, and they had to amputate him. But it didn't
save him. Yes, it was mortification—that was it. He turned blue all
over, and died in the hope of a glorious resurrection. They say he
was a sight to look at. Your uncle's been up to the town every day to
fetch you. And he's gone again, not more'n an hour ago; he'll be
back any minute, now. You must a met him on the road, didn't
you?—oldish man, with a—"

"No, I didn't see nobody, Aunt Sally. The boat landed just at
daylight, and I left my baggage on the wharf-boat and went looking
around the town and out a piece in the country, to put in the time
and not get here too soon; and so I come down the back way."

"Who'd you give the baggage to?"

"Nobody."

"Why, child, it'll be stole!"

"Not where *I* hid it I reckon it won't," I says.

"How'd you get your breakfast so early on the boat?"

It was kinder thin ice, but I says:

"The captain see me standing around, and told me I better have
something to eat before I went ashore; so he took me in the texas
to the officers' lunch, and give me all I wanted."

I was getting so uneasy I couldn't listen good. I had my mind on
the children all the time; I wanted to get them out to one side, and
pump them a little, and find out who I was. But I couldn't get no
show, Mrs. Phelps kept it up and run on so. Pretty soon she made
the cold chills streak all down my back, because she says:

"But here we're a running on this way, and you hain't told me a
word about Sis, nor any of them. Now I'll rest my works a little, and
you start up yourn; just tell me *everything*—tell me all about 'm
all—every one of 'm; and how they are, and what they're doing,
and what they told you to tell me; and every last thing you can
think of."

Well, I see I was up a stump—and up it good. Providence had

stood by me this far, all right, but I was hard and tight aground,
now. I see it warn't a bit of use to try to go ahead—I'd *got* to throw
up my hand. So I says to myself, here's another place where I got to
resk the truth. I opened my mouth to begin; but she grabbed me and
hustled me in behind the bed, and says:

"Here he comes! stick your head down lower—there, that'll do;
you can't be seen, now. Don't you let on you're here. I'll play a joke
on him. Children, don't you say a word."

I see I was in a fix, now. But it warn't no use to worry; there warn't
nothing to do but just hold still, and try and be ready to stand from
under when the lightning struck.

I had just one little glimpse of the old gentleman when he come in,
then the bed hid him. Mrs. Phelps she jumps for him and says:

"Has he come?"

"No," says her husband.

"Good-*ness* gracious!" she says, "what in the world *can* have
become of him?"

"I can't imagine," says the old gentleman; "and I must say, it
makes me dreadful uneasy."

"Uneasy!" she says, "I'm ready to go distracted! He *must* a come;
and you've missed him along the road. I *know* it's so—something
tells me so."

"Why Sally, I *couldn't* miss him along the road—*you* know that."

"But oh, dear, dear, what *will* Sis say! He must a come! You
must a missed him. He——"

"Oh, don't distress me any more'n I'm already distressed. I don't
know what in the world to make of it. I'm at my wit's end, and I
don't mind acknowledging 't I'm right down scared. But there's
no hope that he's come; for he *couldn't* come and me miss him.
Sally, it's terrible—just terrible—something's happened to the
boat, sure!"

"Why, Silas! Look yonder!—up the road!—ain't that somebody
coming?"

He sprung to the window at the head of the bed, and that give
Mrs. Phelps the chance she wanted. She stooped down quick, at the
foot of the bed, and give me a pull, and out I come; and when he
turned back from the window, there she stood, a-beaming and
a-smiling like a house afire, and I standing pretty meek and sweaty
alongside. The old gentleman stared, and says:

"Why, who's that?"

"Who do you reckon 't is?"

"I haint no idea. Who *is* it?"

"It's *Tom Sawyer!*"

By jings, I most slumped through the floor. But there warn't no
time to swap knives; the old man grabbed me by the hand and
shook, and kept on shaking; and all the time, how the woman did
dance around and laugh and cry; and then how they both did fire off

questions about Sid, and Mary, and the rest of the tribe.

But if they was joyful, it warn't nothing to what I was; for it was like being born again, I was so glad to find out who I was. Well, they froze to me for two hours; and at last when my chin was so tired it couldn't hardly go, any more, I had told them more about my family—I mean the Sawyer family—than ever happened to any six Sawyer families. And I explained all about how we blowed out a cylinder-head at the mouth of White River and it took us three days to fix it. Which was all right, and worked first rate; because *they* didn't know but what it would take three days to fix it. If I'd a called it a bolt-head it would a done just as well.

Now I was feeling pretty comfortable all down one side, and pretty uncomfortable all up the other. Being Tom Sawyer was easy and comfortable; and it stayed easy and comfortable till by-and-by I hear a steamboat coughing along down the river—then I says to myself, spose Tom Sawyer come down on that boat?—and spose he steps in here, any minute, and sings out my name before I can throw him a wink to keep quiet? Well, I couldn't *have* it that way—it wouldn't do at all. I must go up the road and waylay him. So I told the folks I reckoned I would go up to the town and fetch down my baggage. The old gentleman was for going along with me, but I said no, I could drive the horse myself, and I druther he wouldn't take no trouble about me.

CHAPTER XXXIII

So I started for town, in the wagon, and when I was half-way I see a wagon coming, and sure enough it was Tom Sawyer, and I stopped and waited till he come along. I says "Hold on!" and it stopped alongside, and his mouth opened up like a trunk, and staid so; and he swallowed two or three times like a person that's got a dry throat, and then says:

"I hain't ever done you no harm. You know that. So then, what you want to come back and ha'nt *me* for?"

I says:

"I hain't come back—I hain't been *gone*."

When he heard my voice, it righted him up some, but he warn't quite satisfied yet. He says:

"Don't you play nothing on me, because I wouldn't on you. Honest injun, now, you ain't a ghost?"

"Honest injun, I ain't," I says.

"Well—I—I—well, that ought to settle it, of course; but I can't somehow seem to understand it, no way. Looky here, warn't you ever murdered *at all?*"

"No. I warn't ever murdered at all—I played it on them. You come in here and feel of me if you don't believe me."

So he done it; and it satisfied him; and he was that glad to see

me again, he didn't know what to do. And he wanted to know all
about it right off; because it was a grand adventure, and mysterious,
and so it hit him where he lived. But I said, leave it alone till by-and-
by; and told his driver to wait, and we drove off a little piece, and I
told him the kind of a fix I was in, and what did he reckon we better
do? He said, let him alone a minute, and don't disturb him. So he
thought and thought, and pretty soon he says:

"It's all right, I've got it. Take my trunk in your wagon, and let
on it's your'n; and you turn back and fool along slow, so as to get
to the house about the time you ought to; and I'll go towards town
a piece, and take a fresh start, and get there a quarter or a half an
hour after you; and you needn't let on to know me, at first."

I says:

"All right; but wait a minute. There's one more thing—a thing
that *nobody* don't know but me. And that is, there's a nigger here
that I'm a trying to steal out of slavery—and his name is *Jim*—old
Miss Watson's Jim."

He says:

"What! Why Jim is——"

He stopped and went to studying. I says:

"*I* know what you'll say. You'll say it's dirty low-down business;
but what if it is?—*I'*m low down; and I'm agoing to steal him, and I
want you to keep mum and not let on. Will you?"

His eye lit up, and he says:

"I'll *help* you steal him!"

Well, I let go all holts then, like I was shot. It was the most
astonishing speech I ever heard—and I'm bound to say Tom Sawyer
fell, considerable, in my estimation. Only I couldn't believe it. Tom
Sawyer a *nigger stealer!*

"Oh, shucks," I says, "you're joking."

"I ain't joking, either."

"Well, then," I says, "joking or no joking, if you hear anything
said about a runaway nigger, don't forget to remember that *you*
don't know nothing about him, and *I* don't know nothing about
him."

Then we took the trunk and put it in my wagon, and he drove off
his way, and I drove mine. But of course I forgot all about driving
slow, on accounts of being glad and full of thinking; so I got home a
heap too quick for that length of a trip. The old gentleman was at
the door, and he says:

"Why, this is wonderful. Who ever would a thought it was in that
mare to do it. I wish we'd a timed her. And she hain't sweated a
hair—not a hair. It's wonderful. Why, I wouldn't take a hundred
dollars for that horse now; I wouldn't honest; and yet I'd a sold her
for fifteen before, and thought 'twas all she was worth."

That's all he said. He was the innocentest, best old soul I ever
see. But it warn't surprising; because he warn't only just a farmer,

he was a preacher, too, and had a little one-horse log church down back of the plantation, which he built it himself at his own expense, for a church and school-house, and never charged nothing for his preaching, and it was worth it, too. There was plenty other farmer-preachers like that, and done the same way, down South.

In about half an hour Tom's wagon drove up to the front stile, and Aunt Sally she see it through the window because it was only about fifty yards, and says:

"Why, there's somebody come! I wonder who 'tis? Why, I do believe it's a stranger. Jimmy" (that's one of the children), "run and tell Lize to put on another plate for dinner."

Everybody made a rush for the front door, because, of course, a stranger don't come *every* year, and so he lays over the yaller fever, for interest, when he does come. Tom was over the stile and starting for the house; the wagon was spinning up the road for the village, and we was all bunched in the front door. Tom had his store clothes on, and an audience—and that was always nuts for Tom Sawyer. In them circumstances it warn't no trouble to him to throw in an amount of style that was suitable. He warn't a boy to meeky along up that yard like a sheep; no, he come ca'm and important, like the ram. When he got afront of us, he lifts his hat ever so gracious and dainty, like it was the lid of a box that had butterflies asleep in it and he didn't want to disturb them, and says:

"Mr. Archibald Nichols, I presume?"

"No, my boy," says the old gentleman, "I'm sorry to say 't your driver has deceived you; Nichols's place is down a matter of three mile more. Come in, come in."

Tom he took a look back over his shoulder, and says, "Too late—he's out of sight."

"Yes, he's gone, my son, and you must come in and eat your dinner with us; and then we'll hitch up and take you down to Nichols's."

"Oh, I *can't* make you so much trouble; I couldn't think of it. I'll walk—I don't mind the distance."

"But we won't *let* you walk—it wouldn't be Southern hospitality to do it. Come right in."

"Oh, *do,*" says Aunt Sally; "it ain't a bit of trouble to us, not a bit in the world. You *must* stay. It's a long, dusty three mile, and we *can't* let you walk. And besides, I've already told 'em to put on another plate, when I see you coming; so you mustn't disappoint us. Come right in, and make yourself at home."

So Tom he thanked them very hearty and handsome, and let himself be persuaded, and come in; and when he was in, he said he was a stranger from Hicksville, Ohio, and his name was William Thompson—and he made another bow.

Well, he run on, and on, and on, making up stuff about Hicksville and everybody in it he could invent, and I getting a little nervous,

and wondering how this was going to help me out of my scrape;
and at last, still talking along, he reached over and kissed Aunt
Sally right on the mouth, and then settled back again in his chair,
comfortable, and was going on talking; but she jumped up and
wiped it off with the back of her hand, and says:

"You owdacious puppy!"

He looked kind of hurt, and says:

"I'm surprised at you, m'am."

"You're s'rp— Why, what do you reckon *I* am? I've a good notion
to take and—say, what do you mean by kissing me?"

He looked kind of humble, and says:

"I didn't mean nothing, m'am. I didn't mean no harm. I—I—
thought you'd like it."

"Why, you born fool!" She took up the spining-stick, and it
looked like it was all she could do to keep from giving him a crack
with it. "What made you think I'd like it?"

"Well, I don't know. Only, they—they—told me you would."

"*They* told you I would. Whoever told you's *another* lunatic. I
never heard the beat of it. Who's *they?*"

"Why—everybody. They all said so, m'am."

It was all she could do to hold in; and her eyes snapped, and her
fingers worked like she wanted to scratch him; and she says:

"Who's 'everybody?' Out with their names—or ther'll be an idiot
short."

He got up and looked distressed, and fumbled his hat, and says:

"I'm sorry, and I warn't expecting it. They told me to. They all
told me to. They all said kiss her; and said she'll like it. They all
said it—every one of them. But I'm sorry, m'am, and I won't do it
no more—I won't, honest."

"You won't, won't you? Well, I sh'd *reckon* you won't!"

"No'm, I'm honest about it; I won't ever do it again. Till you ask
me."

"Till I *ask* you! Well, I never see the beat of it in my born days!
I lay you'll be the Methusalem-numskull of creation before ever *I*
ask you—or the likes of you."

"Well," he says, "it does surprise me so. I can't make it out,
somehow. They said you would, and I thought you would. But—"
He stopped and looked around slow, like he wished he could run
across a friendly eye, somewhere's; and fetched up on the old
gentleman's, and says, "Didn't *you* think she'd like me to kiss her,
sir?"

"Why, no, I—I—well, no, I b'lieve I didn't."

Then he looks on around, the same way, to me—and says:

"Tom, didn't *you* think Aunt Sally'd open out her arms and say,
'Sid Sawyer——' "

"My land!" she says, breaking in and jumping for him, "you
impudent young rascal, to fool a body so—" and was going to hug

him, but he fended her off, and says:

"No, not till you've asked me, first."

So she didn't lose no time, but asked him; and hugged him and kissed him, over and over again, and then turned him over to the old man, and he took what was left. And after they got a little quiet again, she says:

"Why, dear me, I never see such a surprise. We warn't looking for *you,* at all, but only Tom. Sis never wrote to me about anybody coming but him."

"It's because it warn't *intended* for any of us to come but Tom," he says; "but I begged and begged, and at the last minute she let me come, too; so, coming down the river, me and Tom thought it would be a first-rate surprise for him to come here to the house first, and for me to by-and-by tag along and drop in and let on to be a stranger. But it was a mistake, Aunt Sally. This ain't no healthy place for a stranger to come."

"No—not impudent whelps, Sid. You ought to had your jaws boxed; I hain't been so put out since I don't know when. But I don't care, I don't mind the terms—I'd be willing to stand a thousand such jokes to have you here. Well, to think of that performance! I don't deny it, I was most putrified with astonishment when you give me that smack."

We had dinner out in that broad open passage betwixt the house and the kitchen; and there was things enough on that table for seven families—and all hot, too; none of your flabby tough meat that's laid in a cupboard in a damp cellar all night and tastes like a hunk of old cold cannibal in the morning. Uncle Silas he asked a pretty long blessing over it, but it was worth it; and it didn't cool it a bit, neither, the way I've seen them kind of interruptions do, lots of times.

There was a considerable good deal of talk, all the afternoon, and me and Tom was on the lookout all the time, but it warn't no use, they didn't happen to say nothing about my runaway nigger, and we was afraid to try to work up to it. But at supper, at night, one of the little boys says:

"Pa, mayn't Tom and Sid and me go to the show?"

"No," says the old man, "I reckon there ain't going to be any; and you couldn't go if there was; because the runaway nigger told Burton and me all about that scandalous show, and Burton said he would tell the people; so I reckon they've drove the owdacious loafers out of town before this time."

So there it was!—but *I* couldn't help it. Tom and me was to sleep in the same room and bed; so, being tired, we bid good-night and went up to bed, right after supper, and clumb out of the window and down the lightning-rod, and shoved for the town; for I didn't believe anybody was going to give the king and the duke a hint, and so, if I didn't hurry up and give them one they'd get into trouble sure.

On the road Tom he told me all about how it was reckoned I was murdered, and how pap disappeared, pretty soon, and didn't come back no more, and what a stir there was when Jim run away; and I told Tom all about our Royal Nonesuch rapscallions, and as much of the raft-voyage as I had time to; and as we struck into the town and up through the middle of it—it was as much as half after eight, then—here comes a raging rush of people, with torches, and an awful whooping and yelling, and banging tin pans and blowing horns; and we jumped to one side to let them go by; and as they went by, I see they had the king and the duke astraddle of a rail—that is, I knowed it *was* the king and the duke, though they was all over tar and feathers, and didn't look like nothing in the world that was human—just looked like a couple of monstrous big soldier-plumes. Well, it made me sick to see it; and I was sorry for them poor pitiful rascals, it seemed like I couldn't ever feel any hardness against them any more in the world. It was a dreadful thing to see. Human beings *can* be awful cruel to one another.

We see we was too late—couldn't do no good. We asked some stragglers about it, and they said everybody went to the show looking very innocent; and laid low and kept dark till the poor old king was in the middle of his cavortings on the stage; then somebody give a signal, and the house rose up and went for them.

So we poked along back home, and I warn't feeling so brash as I was before, but kind of ornery, and humble, and to blame, somehow—though *I* hadn't done nothing. But that's always the way; it don't make no difference whether you do right or wrong, a person's conscience ain't got no sense, and just goes for him *anyway*. If I had a yaller dog that didn't know no more than a person's conscience does, I would pison him. It takes up more room than all the rest of a person's insides, and yet ain't no good, nohow. Tom Sawyer he says the same.

CHAPTER XXXIV

We stopped talking, and got to thinking.

By-and-by Tom says:

"Looky here, Huck, what fools we are, to not think of it before! I bet I know where Jim is."

"No! Where?"

"In that hut down by the ash-hopper. Why, looky here. When we was at dinner, didn't you see a nigger man go in there with some vittles?"

"Yes."

"What did you think the vittles was for?"

"For a dog."

"So'd I. Well, it wasn't for a dog."

"Why?"

"Because part of it was watermelon."

"So it was—I noticed it. Well, it does beat all, that I never thought about a dog not eating watermelon. It shows how a body can see and don't see at the same time."

"Well, the nigger unlocked the padlock when he went in, and he locked it again when he come out. He fetched uncle a key, about the time we got up from table—same key, I bet. Watermelon shows man, lock shows prisoner; and it ain't likely there's two prisoners on such a little plantation, and where the people's all so kind and good. Jim's the prisoner. All right—I'm glad we found it out detective fashion; I wouldn't give shucks for any other way. Now you work your mind and study out a plan to steal Jim, and I will study out one, too; and we'll take the one we like the best."

What a head for just a boy to have! If I had Tom Sawyer's head, I wouldn't trade it off to be a duke, nor mate of a steamboat, nor clown in a circus, nor nothing I can think of. I went to thinking out a plan, but only just to be doing something; I knowed very well where the right plan was going to come from. Pretty soon, Tom says:

"Ready?"

"Yes," I says.

"All right—bring it out."

"My plan is this," I says. "We can easy find out if it's Jim in there. Then get up my canoe to-morrow night, and fetch my raft over from the island. Then the first dark night that comes, steal the key out of the old man's britches, after he goes to bed, and shove off down the river on the raft, with Jim, hiding daytimes and running nights, the way me and Jim used to do before. Wouldn't that plan work?"

"*Work?* Why cert'nly, it would work, like rats a fighting. But it's too blame' simple; there ain't nothing *to* it. What's the good of a plan that ain't no more trouble than that? It's as mild as goose-milk. Why, Huck, it wouldn't make no more talk than breaking into a soap factory."

I never said nothing, because I warn't expecting nothing different; but I knowed mighty well that whenever he got *his* plan ready it wouldn't have none of them objections to it.

And it didn't. He told me what it was, and I see in a minute it was worth fifteen of mine, for style, and would make Jim just as free a man as mine would, and maybe get us all killed besides. So I was satisfied, and said we would waltz in on it. I needn't tell what it was, here, because I knowed it wouldn't stay the way it was. I knowed he would be changing it around, every which way, as we went along, and heaving in new bullinesses wherever he got a chance. And that is what he done.

Well, one thing was dead sure; and that was, that Tom Sawyer was in earnest and was actuly going to help steal that nigger out of slavery. That was the thing that was too many for me. Here was

a boy that was respectable, and well brung up; and had a character
to lose; and folks at home that had characters; and he was bright
and not leather-headed; and knowing and not ignorant; and not
mean, but kind; and yet here he was, without any more pride, or
rightness, or feeling, than to stoop to this business, and make
himself a shame, and his family a shame, before everybody. I
couldn't understand it, no way at all. It was outrageous, and I
knowed I ought to just up and tell him so; and so be his true friend,
and let him quit the thing right where he was, and save himself.
And I *did* start to tell him; but he shut me up, and says:

"Don't you reckon I know what I'm about? Don't I generly
know what I'm about?"

"Yes."

"Didn't I *say* I was going to help steal the nigger?"

"Yes."

"*Well* then."

That's all he said, and that's all I said. It warn't no use to say any
more; because when he said he'd do a thing, he always done it. But
I couldn't make out how he was willing to go into this thing; so I
just let it go, and never bothered no more about it. If he was bound
to have it so, *I* couldn't help it.

When we got home, the house was all dark and still; so we went
on down to the hut by the ash-hopper, for to examine it. We went
through the yard, so as to see what the hounds would do. They
knowed us, and didn't make no more noise than country dogs is
always doing when anything comes by in the night. When we got to
the cabin, we took a look at the front and the two sides; and on the
side I warn't acquainted with—which was the north side—we found
a square window-hole, up tolerable high, with just one stout board
nailed across it. I says:

"Here's the ticket. This hole's big enough for Jim to get through,
if we wrench off the board."

Tom says:

"It's as simple as tit-tat-toe, three-in-a-row, and as easy as playing
hooky. I should *hope* we can find a way that's a little more
complicated than *that*, Huck Finn."

"Well then," I says, "how'll it do to saw him out, the way I done
before I was murdered, that time?"

"That's more *like*," he says. "It's real mysterious, and
troublesome, and good," he says; "but I bet we can find a way that's
twice as long. There ain't no hurry; le's keep on looking around."

Betwixt the hut and the fence, on the back side, was a lean-to,
that joined the hut at the eaves, and was made out of plank. It
was as long as the hut, but narrow—only about six foot wide. The
door to it was at the south end, and was padlocked. Tom he went to
the soap kettle, and searched around and fetched back the iron
thing they lift the lid with; so he took it and prized out one of the

staples. The chain fell down, and we opened the door and went in,
and shut it, and struck a match, and see the shed was only built
against the cabin and hadn't no connection with it; and there warn't
no floor to the shed, nor nothing in it but some old rusty played-out
hoes, and spades, and picks, and a crippled plow. The match
went out, and so did we, and shoved in the staple again, and the
door was locked as good as ever. Tom was joyful. He says:

"Now we're all right. We'll *dig* him out. It'll take about a week!"

Then we started for the house, and I went in the back door—you
only have to pull a buckskin latch-string, they don't fasten the
doors—but that warn't romantical enough for Tom Sawyer: no
way would do him but he must climb up the lightning-rod. But
after he got up half-way about three times, and missed fire and fell
every time, and the last time most busted his brains out, he thought
he'd got to give it up; but after he was rested, he allowed he would
give her one more turn for luck, and this time he made the trip.

In the morning we was up at break of day, and down to the nigger
cabins to pet the dogs and make friends with the nigger that fed
Jim—if it *was* Jim that was being fed. The niggers was just getting
through breakfast and starting for the fields; and Jim's nigger was
piling up a tin pan with bread and meat and things; and whilst
the others was leaving, the key come from the house.

This nigger had a good-natured, chuckle-headed face, and his
wool was all tied up in little bunches with thread. That was to keep
witches off. He said the witches was pestering him awful, these
nights, and making him see all kinds of strange things, and hear
all kinds of strange words and noises, and he didn't believe he was
ever witched so long, before, in his life. He got so worked up, and
got to running on so about his troubles, he forgot all about what
he'd been agoing to do. So Tom says:

"What's the vittles for? Going to feed the dogs?"

The nigger kind of smiled around graduly over his face, like when
you heave a brickbat in a mud puddle, and he says:

"Yes, Mars Sid, a dog. Cur'us dog, too. Does you want to go en
look at 'im?"

"Yes."

I hunched Tom, and whispers:

"You going, right here in the day-break? *That* warn't the plan."

"No, it warn't—but it's the plan *now.*"

So, drat him, we went along, but I didn't like it much. When we
got in, we couldn't hardly see anything, it was so dark; but Jim was
there, sure enough, and could see us; and he sings out:

"Why, *Huck!* En good *lan'!* ain' dat Misto Tom?"

I just knowed how it would be; I just expected it. *I* didn't know
nothing to do; and if I had, I couldn't a done it; because that nigger
busted in and says:

"Why, de gracious sakes! do he know you genlmen?"

We could see pretty well, now. Tom he looked at the nigger, steady and kind of wondering, and says:

"Does *who* know us?"

"Why, dish-yer runaway nigger."

"I don't reckon he does; but what put that into your head?"

"What *put* it dar? Didn' he jis' dis minute sing out like he knowed you?"

Tom says, in a puzzled-up kind of way:

"Well, that's mighty curious. *Who* sung out? *When* did he sing out? *What* did he sing out?" And turns to me, perfectly c'am, and says, "Did *you* hear anybody sing out?"

Of course there warn't nothing to be said but the one thing; so I says:

"No; *I* ain't heard nobody say nothing."

Then he turns to Jim, and looks him over like he never see him before; and says:

"Did you sing out?"

"No, sah," says Jim; "*I* hain't said nothing, sah."

"Not a word?"

"No, sah, I hain't said a word."

"Did you ever see us before?"

"No, sah; not as *I* knows on."

So Tom turns to the nigger, which was looking wild and distressed, and says, kind of severe:

"What do you reckon's the matter with you, anyway? What made you think somebody sung out?"

"Oh, it's de dad-blame' witches, sah, en I wisht I was dead, I do. Dey's awluz at it, sah, en dey do mos' kill me, dey sk'yers me so. Please to don't tell nobody 'bout it sah, er ole Mars Silas he'll scole me; 'kase he say dey *ain't* no witches. I jis' wish to goodness he was heah now—*den* what would he say! I jis' bet he couldn' fine no way to git aroun' it *dis* time. But it's awluz jis' so; people dat's *sot*, stays sot; dey won't look into nothn' en fine it out f'r deyselves, en when *you* fine it out en tell um 'bout it, dey doan' b'lieve you."

Tom give him a dime, and said we wouldn't tell nobody; and told him to buy some more thread to tie up his wool with; and then looks at Jim, and says:

"I wonder if Uncle Silas is going to hang this nigger. If I was to catch a nigger that was ungrateful enough to run away, *I* wouldn't give him up, I'd hang him." And whilst the nigger stepped to the door to look at the dime and bite it to see if it was good, he whispers to Jim, and says:

"Don't ever let on to know us. And if you hear any digging going on nights, it's us: we're going to set you free."

Jim only had time to grab us by the hand and squeeze it, then the nigger come back, and we said we'd come again some time if the nigger wanted us to; and he said he would, more particular if it was dark, because the witches went for him mostly in the dark, and it was good to have folks around then.

CHAPTER XXXV

It would be most an hour, yet, till breakfast, so we left, and struck down into the woods; because Tom said we got to have *some* light to see how to dig by, and a lantern makes too much, and might get us into trouble; what we must have was a lot of them rotten chunks that's called fox-fire and just makes a soft kind of a glow when you lay them in a dark place. We fetched an armful and hid it in the weeds, and set down to rest, and Tom says, kind of dissatisfied:

"Blame it, this whole thing is just as easy and awkard as it can be. And so it makes it so rotten difficult to get up a difficult plan. There ain't no watchman to be drugged—now there *ought* to be a watchman. There ain't even a dog to give a sleeping-mixture to. And there's Jim chained by one leg, with a ten-foot chain, to the leg of his bed: why, all you got to do is to lift up the bedstead and slip off the chain. And Uncle Silas he trusts everybody; sends the key to the punkin-headed nigger, and don't send nobody to watch the nigger. Jim could a got out of that window hole before this, only there wouldn't be no use trying to travel with a ten-foot chain on his leg. Why, drat it, Huck, it's the stupidest arrangement I ever see. You got to invent *all* the difficulties. Well, we can't help it, we got to do the best we can with the materials we've got. Anyhow, there's one thing—there's more honor in getting him out through a lot of difficulties and dangers, where there warn't one of them furnished to you by the people who it was their duty to furnish them, and you had to contrive them all out of your own head. Now look at just that one thing of the lantern. When you come down to the cold facts, we simply got to *let on* that a lantern's resky. Why, we could work with a torchlight procession if we wanted to, *I* believe. Now, whilst I think of it, we got to hunt up something to make a saw out of, the first chance we get."

"What do we want of a saw?"

"What do we *want* of it? Hain't we got to saw the leg of Jim's bed off, so as to get the chain loose?"

"Why, you just said a body could lift up the bedstead and slip the chain off."

"Well, if that ain't just like you, Huck Finn. You *can* get up the infant-schooliest ways of going at a thing. Why, hain't you ever read any books at all?—Baron Trenck, nor Casanova, nor Benvenuto Chelleeny, nor Henri IV., nor none of them heroes? Whoever heard of getting a prisoner loose in such an old-maidy was as that? No; the way all the best authorities does, is to saw the bed-leg in two, and leave it just so, and swallow the sawdust, so it can't be found, and put some dirt and grease around the sawed place so the very

keenest seneskal can't see no sign of it's being sawed, and thinks
the bed-leg is perfectly sound. Then, the night you're ready, fetch
the leg a kick, down she goes; slip off your chain, and there you are.
Nothing to do but hitch your rope-ladder to the battlements, shin
down it, break your leg in the moat—because a rope-ladder is
nineteen foot too short, you know—and there's your horses and your
trusty vassles, and they scoop you up and fling you across a saddle
and away you go, to your native Langudoc, or Navarre, or wherever
it is. It's gaudy, Huck. I wish there was a moat to this cabin. If we
get time, the night of the escape, we'll dig one."

I says:

"What do we want of a moat, when we're going to snake him out
from under the cabin?"

But he never heard me. He had forgot me and everything else. He
had his chin in his hand, thinking. Pretty soon, he sighs, and shakes
his head; then sighs again, and says:

"No, it wouldn't do—there ain't necessity enough for it."

"For what?" I says.

"Why, to saw Jim's leg off," he says.

"Good land!" I says, "why, there ain't *no* necessity for it. And
what would you want to saw his leg off for, anyway?"

"Well, some of the best authorities has done it. They couldn't
get the chain off, so they just cut their hand off, and shoved. And a
leg would be better still. But we got to let that go. There ain't
necessity enough in this case; and besides, Jim's a nigger and
wouldn't understand the reasons for it, and how it's the custom in
Europe; so we'll let it go. But there's one thing—he can have a
rope-ladder; we can tear up our sheets and make him a rope-ladder
easy enough. And we can send it to him in a pie; it's mostly done
that way. And I've et worse pies."

"Why, Tom Sawyer, how you talk," I says; "Jim ain't got no use
for a rope ladder."

"He *has* got use for it. How *you* talk, you better say; you don't
know nothing about it. He's *got* to have a rope ladder; they all do."

"What in the nation can he *do* with it?"

"Do with it? He can hide it in his bed, can't he? That's what they
all do; and *he's* got to, too. Huck, you don't ever seem to want to do
anything that's regular; you want to be starting something fresh all
the time. Spose he *don't* do nothing with it? ain't it there in his bed,
for a clew, after he's gone? and don't you reckon they'll want clews?
Of course they will. And you wouldn't leave them any? That would
be a *pretty* howdy-do, *wouldn't* it! I never heard of such a thing."

"Well," I says, "if it's in the regulations, and he's got to have it,
all right, let him have it; because I don't wish to go back on no
regulations; but there's one thing, Tom Sawyer—if we go to tearing
up our sheets to make Jim a rope-ladder, we're going to get into
trouble with Aunt Sally, just as sure as you're born. Now, the way I

look at it, a hickry-bark ladder don't cost nothing, and don't waste nothing, and is just as good to load up a pie with, and hide in a straw tick, as any rag ladder you can start; and as for Jim, he ain't had no experience, and so *he* don't care what kind of a——"

"Oh, shucks, Huck Finn, if I was as ignorant as you, I'd keep still—that's what *I'd* do. Who ever heard of a state prisoner escaping by a hickry-bark ladder? Why, it's perfectly ridiculous."

"Well, all right, Tom, fix it your own way; but if you'll take my advice, you'll let me borrow a sheet off of the clothes-line."

He said that would do. And that give him another idea, and he says:

"Borrow a shirt, too."

"What do we want of a shirt, Tom?"

"Want it for Jim to keep a journal on."

"Journal your granny—*Jim* can't write."

"Spose he *can't* write—he can make marks on the shirt, can't he, if we make him a pen out of an old pewter spoon or a piece of an old iron barrel-hoop?"

"Why, Tom, we can pull a feather out of a goose and make him a better one; and quicker, too."

"*Prisoners* don't have geese running around the donjon-keep to pull pens out of, you muggins. They *always* make their pens out of the hardest, toughest, troublesomest piece of old brass candlestick or something like that they can get their hands on; and it takes them weeks and weeks, and months and months to file it out, too, because they've got to do it by rubbing it on the wall. *They* wouldn't use a goose-quill if they had it. It ain't regular."

"Well, then, what'll we make him the ink out of?"

"Many makes it out of iron-rust and tears; but that's the common sort and women; the best authorities uses their own blood. Jim can do that; and when he wants to send any little common ordinary mysterious message to let the world know where he's captivated, he can write it on the bottom of a tin plate with a fork and throw it out of the window. The Iron Mask always done that, and it's a blame' good way, too."

"Jim ain't got no tin plates. They feed him in a pan."

"That ain't anything; we can get him some."

"Can't nobody *read* his plates."

"That ain't got nothing to *do* with it, Huck Finn. All *he's* got to do is to write on the plate and throw it out. You don't *have* to be able to read it. Why, half the time you can't read anything a prisoner writes on a tin plate, or anywhere else."

"Well, then, what's the sense in wasting the plates?"

"But it's *somebody's* plates, ain't it?"

"Well, spos'n it is? What does the *prisoner* care whose——"

"Why, blame it all, it ain't the *prisoner's* plates."

He broke off there, because we heard the breakfast-horn blowing.

So we cleared out for the house.

Along during that morning I borrowed a sheet and a white shirt off of the clothes-line; and I found an old sack and put them in it, and we went down and got the fox-fire, and put that in too. I called it borrowing, because that was what pap always called it; but Tom said it warn't borrowing, it was stealing. He said we was representing prisoners; and prisoners don't care how they get a thing so they get it, and nobody don't blame them for it, either. It ain't no crime in a prisoner to steal the thing he needs to get away with, Tom said; it's his right; and so, as long as we was representing a prisoner, we had a perfect right to steal anything on this place we had the least use for, to get ourselves out of prison with. He said if we warn't prisoners it would be a very different thing, and nobody but a mean ornery person would steal when he warn't a prisoner. So we allowed we would steal everything there was that come handy. And yet he made a mighty fuss, one day, after that, when I stole a watermelon out of the nigger patch and eat it; and he made me go and give the niggers a dime, without telling them what it was for. Tom said that what he meant was, we could steal anything we *needed*. Well, I says, I needed the watermelon. But he said I didn't need it to get out of prison with, there's where the difference was. He said if I'd a wanted it to hide a knife in, and smuggle it to Jim to kill the seneskal with, it would a been all right. So I let it go at that, though I couldn't see no advantage in my representing a prisoner, if I got to set down and chaw over a lot of gold-leaf distinctions like that, every time I see a chance to hog a watermelon.

Well, as I was saying, we waited that morning till everybody was settled down to business, and nobody in sight around the yard; then Tom he carried the sack into the lean-to whilst I stood off a piece to keep watch. By-and-by he come out, and we went and set down on the wood-pile, to talk. He says:

"Everything's all right, now, except tools: and that's easy fixed."

"Tools?" I says.

"Yes."

"Tools for what?"

"Why, to dig with. We ain't agoing to *gnaw* him out, are we?"

"Ain't them old crippled picks and things in there good enough to dig a nigger out with?" I says.

He turns on me looking pitying enough to make a body cry, and says:

"Huck Finn, did you *ever* hear of a prisoner having picks and shovels, and all the modern conveniences in his wardrobe to dig himself out with? Now I want to ask you—if you got any reasonableness in you at all—what kind of a show would *that* give him to be a hero? Why, they might as well lend him the key, and done with it. Picks and shovels—why they wouldn't furnish 'em to a king."

"Well, then," I says, "if we don't want the picks and shovels, what do we want?"

"A couple of case-knives."

"To dig the foundations out from under that cabin with?"

"Yes."

"Confound it, it's foolish, Tom."

"It don't make no difference how foolish it is, it's the *right* way— and it's the regular way. And there ain't no *other* way, that ever *I* heard of, and I've read all the books that gives any information about these things. They always dig out with a case-knife—and not through dirt, mind you; generly it's through solid rock. And it takes them weeks and weeks and weeks, and for ever and ever. Why, look at one of them prisoners in the bottom dungeon of the Castle Deef, in the harbor of Marseilles, that dug himself out that way; how long was *he* at it, you reckon?"

"I don't know."

"Well, guess."

"I don't know. A month and a half?"

"*Thirty-seven year*—and he come out in China. *That's* the kind. I wish the bottom of *this* fortress was solid rock."

"*Jim* don't know nobody in China."

"What's *that* got to do with it? Neither did that other fellow. But you're always a-wandering off on a side issue. Why can't you stick to the main point?"

"All right—*I* don't care where he comes out, so he *comes* out; and Jim don't, either, I reckon. But there's one thing, anyway—Jim's too old to be dug out with a case-knife. He won't last."

"Yes he will *last*, too. You don't reckon it's going to take thirty-seven years to dig out through a *dirt* foundation, do you?"

"How long will it take, Tom?"

"Well, we can't resk being as long as we ought to, because it mayn't take very long for Uncle Silas to hear from down there by New Orleans. He'll hear Jim ain't from there. Then his next move will be to advertise Jim, or something like that. So we can't resk being as long digging him out as we ought to. By rights I reckon we ought to be a couple of years; but we can't. Things being so uncertain, what I recommend is this: that we really dig right in, as quick as we can; and after that, we can *let on*, to ourselves, that we was at it thirty-seven years. Then we can snatch him out and rush him away the first time there's an alarm. Yes, I reckon that'll be the best way."

"Now, there's *sense* in that," I says. "Letting on don't cost nothing; letting on ain't no trouble; and if it's any object, I don't mind letting on we was at it a hundred and fifty year. It wouldn't strain me none, after I got my hand in. So I'll mosey along now, and smouch a couple of case-knives."

"Smouch three," he says; "we want one to make a saw out of."

"Tom, if it ain't unregular and irreligious to sejest it," I says, "there's an old rusty saw-blade around yonder sticking under the weatherboarding behind the smoke-house."

He looked kind of weary and discouraged-like, and says:

"It ain't no use to try to learn you nothing, Huck. Run along and smouch the knives—three of them." So I done it.

CHAPTER XXXVI

As soon as we reckoned everybody was asleep, that night, we went down the lightning-rod, and shut ourselves up in the lean-to, and got out our pile of fox-fire, and went to work. We cleared everything out of the way, about four or five foot along the middle of the bottom log. Tom said he was right behind Jim's bed now, and we'd dig in right under it, and when we got through there couldn't nobody in the cabin ever know there was any hole there, because Jim's counterpin hung down most to the ground, and you'd have to raise it up and look under to see the hole. So we dug and dug, with the case-knives, till most midnight; and then we was dog-tired, and our hands was blistered, and yet you couldn't see we'd done anything, hardly. At last I says:

"This ain't no thirty-seven year job, this is a thirty-eight year job, Tom Sawyer."

He never said nothing. But he sighed, and pretty soon he stopped digging, and then for a good little while I knowed he was thinking. Then he says:

"It ain't no use, Huck, it ain't agoing to work. If we was prisoners it would, because then we'd have as many years as we wanted, and no hurry; and we wouldn't get but a few minutes to dig, every day, while they was changing watches, and so our hands wouldn't get blistered, and we could keep it up right along, year in and year out, and do it right, and the way it ought to be done. But *we* can't fool along, we got to rush; we ain't got no time to spare. If we was to put in another night this way, we'd have to knock off for a week to let our hands get well—couldn't touch a case-knife with them sooner."

"Well, then, what we going to do, Tom?"

"I'll tell you. It ain't right, and it ain't moral, and I wouldn't like it to get out—but there ain't only just the one way; we got to dig him out with the picks, and *let on* it's case-knives."

"Now you're *talking!"* I says; "your head gets leveler and leveler all the time, Tom Sawyer," I says. "Picks is the thing, moral or no moral; and as for me, I don't care shucks for the morality of it, nohow. When I start in to steal a nigger, or a watermelon, or a Sunday-school book, I ain't no ways particular how it's done so it's done. What I want is my nigger; or what I want is my

watermelon; or what I want is my Sunday-school book; and if a
pick's the handiest thing, that's the thing I'm agoing to dig that
nigger or that watermelon or that Sunday-school book out with;
and I don't give a dead rat what the authorities thinks about it
nuther."

"Well," he says, "there's excuse for picks and letting-on in a
case like this; if it warn't so, I wouldn't approve of it, nor I wouldn't
stand by and see the rules broke—because right is right, and wrong
is wrong, and a body ain't got no business doing wrong when he
ain't ignorant and knows better. It might answer for *you* to dig
Jim out with a pick, *without* any letting-on, because you don't know
no better; but it wouldn't for me, because I do know better. Gimme
a case-knife."

He had his own by him, but I handed him mine. He flung it
down, and says:

"Gimme a *case-knife.*"

I didn't know just what to do—but then I thought. I scratched
around amongst the old tools, and got a pick-ax and give it to him,
and he took it and went to work, and never said a word.

He was always just that particular. Full of principle.

So then I got a shovel, and then we picked and shoveled, turn
about, and made the fur fly. We stuck to it about a half an hour,
which was as long as we could stand up; but we had a good deal
of a hole to show for it. When I got up stairs, I looked out at the
window and see Tom doing his level best with the lightning-rod,
but he couldn't come it, his hands was so sore. At last he says:

"It ain't no use, it can't be done. What you reckon I better do?
Can't you think up no way?"

"Yes," I says, "but I reckon it ain't regular. Come up the stairs,
and let on it's a lightning-rod."

So he done it.

Next day Tom stole a pewter spoon and a brass candlestick in
the house, for to make some pens for Jim out of, and six tallow
candles; and I hung around the nigger cabins, and laid for a chance,
and stole three tin plates. Tom said it wasn't enough; but I said
nobody wouldn't ever see the plates that Jim throwed out, because
they'd fall in the dog-fennel and jimpson weeds under the
window-hole—then we could tote them back and he could use them
over again. So Tom was satisfied. Then he says:

"Now, the thing to study out is, how to get the things to Jim."

"Take them in through the hole," I says, "when we get it done."

He only just looked scornful, and said something about nobody
ever heard of such an idiotic idea, and then he went to studying.
By-and-by he said he had ciphered out two or three ways, but there
warn't no need to decide on any of them yet. Said we'd got to post
Jim first.

That night we went down the lightning-rod a little after ten, and took one of the candles along, and listened under the window-hole, and heard Jim snoring; so we pitched it in, and it didn't wake him. Then we whirled in with the pick and shovel, and in about two hours and a half the job was done. We crept in under Jim's bed and into the cabin, and pawed around and found the candle and lit it, and stood over Jim a while, and found him looking hearty and healthy, and then we woke him up gentle and gradual. He was so glad to see us he most cried; and called us honey, and all the pet names he could think of; and was for having us hunt up a cold chisel to cut the chain off of his leg with, right away, and clearing out without losing any time. But Tom he showed him how unregular it would be, and set down and told him all about our plans, and how we could alter them in a minute any time there was an alarm; and not to be the least afraid, because we would see he got away, *sure.*

So Jim he said it was all right, and we set there and talked over old times a while, and then Tom asked a lot of questions, and when Jim told him Uncle Silas come in every day or two to pray with him, and Aunt Sally come in to see if he was comfortable and had plenty to eat, and both of them was kind as they could be, Tom says:

"Now I know how to fix it. We'll send you some things by them."

I said, "Don't do nothing of the kind; it's one of the most jackass ideas I ever struck;" but he never paid no attention to me; went right on. It was his way when he'd got his plans set.

So he told Jim how we'd have to smuggle in the rope-ladder pie, and the other large things, by Nat, the nigger that fed him, and he must be on the lookout, and not be surprised, and not let Nat see him open them; and we would put small things in uncle's coat pockets and he must steal them out; and we would tie things to aunt's apron strings or put them in her apron pocket, if we got a chance; and told him what they would be and what they was for. And told him how to keep a journal on the shirt with his blood, and all that. He told him everything. Jim he couldn't see no sense in the most of it, but he allowed we was white folks and knowed better than him; so he was satisfied, and said he would do it all just as Tom said.

Jim had plenty corn-cob pipes and tobacco; so we had a right down good sociable time; then we crawled out through the hole, and so home to bed, with hands that looked like they'd been chawed. Tom was in high spirits. He said it was the best fun he ever had in his life, and the most intellectural; and said if he only could see his way to it we would keep it up all the rest of our lives and leave Jim to our children to get out; for he believed Jim would come to like it better and better the more he got used to it. He said that in that way it could be strung out to as much as eighty year, and would be the best time on record. And he said it would make us all celebrated that had a hand in it.

In the morning we went out to the wood-pile and chopped up the

brass candlestick into handy sizes, and Tom put them and the
pewter spoon in his pocket. Then we went to the nigger cabins,
and while I got Nat's notice off, Tom shoved a piece of candlestick
into the middle of a corn-pone that was in Jim's pan, and we went
along with Nat to see how it would work, and it just worked noble;
when Jim bit into it it most mashed all his teeth out; and there
warn't ever anything could a worked better. Tom said so himself.
Jim he never let on but what it was only just a piece of rock or
something like that that's always getting into bread, you know;
but after that he never bit into nothing but what he jabbed his fork
into it three or four places, first.

And whilst we was a standing there in the dimmish light, here
comes a couple of the hounds bulging in, from under Jim's bed;
and they kept on piling in till there was eleven of them, and there
warn't hardly room in there to get your breath. By jings, we forgot
to fasten that lean-to door. The nigger Nat he only just hollered
"witches!" once, and keeled over onto the floor amongst the dogs,
and begun to groan like he was dying. Tom jerked the door open
and flung out a slab of Jim's meat, and the dogs went for it, and in
two seconds he was out himself and back again and shut the door,
and I knowed he'd fixed the other door too. Then he went to work
on the nigger, coaxing him and petting him, and asking him if he'd
been imagining he saw something again. He raised up, and blinked
his eyes around, and says:

"Mars Sid, you'll say I's a fool, but if I didn't b'lieve I see most
a million dogs, er devils, er some'n, I wisht I may die right heah in
dese tracks. I did, mos' sholy. Mars Sid, I *felt* um—I *felt* um, sah;
dey was all over me. Dad fetch it, I jus' wisht I could git my han's
on one er dem witches jis' wunst —on'y jis' wunst—it's all *I*'d ast.
But mos'ly I wisht dey'd lemme 'lone, I does."

Tom says:

"Well, I tell you what *I* think. What makes them come here
just at this runaway nigger's breakfast-time? It's because they're
hungry; that's the reason. You make them a witch pie; that's the
thing for *you* to do."

"But my lan', Mars Sid, how's *I* gwyne to make 'm a witch pie?
I doan' know how to make it. I hain't ever hearn er sich a thing
b'fo.' "

"Well, then, I'll have to make it myself."

"Will you do it, honey?—will you? I'll wusshup de groun' und'
yo' foot, I will!"

"All right, I'll do it, seeing it's you, and you've been good to us
and showed us the runaway nigger. But you got to be mighty
careful. When we come around, you turn your back; and then
whatever we've put in the pan, don't you let on you see it at all. And
don't you look, when Jim unloads the pan—something might
happen, I don't know what. And above all, don't you *handle* the

witch-things.''

"Hannel 'm Mars Sid? What *is* you a talkin' 'bout? I wouldn'
lay de weight er my finger on um, not f'r ten hund'd thous'n' billion
dollars, I wouldn't.''

CHAPTER XXXVII

That was all fixed. So then we went away and went to the
rubbage-pile in the back yard where they keep the old boots, and
rags, and pieces of bottles, and wore-out tin things, and all such
truck, and scratched around and found an old tin washpan and
stopped up the holes as well as we could, to bake the pie in, and
took it down cellar and stole it full of flour, and started for
breakfast and found a couple of shingle-nails that Tom said would
be handy for a prisoner to scrabble his name and sorrows on the
dungeon walls with, and dropped one of them in Aunt Sally's apron
pocket which was hanging on a chair, and t'other we stuck in the
band of Uncle Silas's hat, which was on the bureau, because we
heard the children say their pa and ma was going to the runaway
nigger's house this morning, and then went to breakfast, and Tom
dropped the pewter spoon in Uncle Silas's coat pocket, and Aunt
Sally wasn't come yet, so we had to wait a little while.

And when she come she was hot, and red, and cross, and couldn't
hardly wait for the blessing; and then she went to sluicing out
coffee with one hand and cracking the handiest child's head with
her thimble with the other, and says:

"I've hunted high, and I've hunted low, and it does beat all, what
has become of your other shirt."

My heart fell down amongst my lungs and livers and things, and
a hard piece of corn-crust started down my throat after it and got
met on the road with a cough and was shot across the table and took
one of the children in the eye and curled him up like a fishing-worm,
and let a cry out of him the size of a war-whoop, and Tom he turned
kinder blue around the gills, and it all amounted to a considerable
state of things for about a quarter of a minute or as much as that,
and I would a sold out for half price if there was a bidder. But after
that we was all right again—it was the sudden surprise of it that
knocked us all so kind of cold. Uncle Silas he says:

"It's most uncommon curious, I can't understand it. I know
perfectly well I took it *off,* because——"

"Because you hain't got but one *on.* Just *listen* at the man! *I*
know you took it off, and know it by a better way than your
wool-gathering memory, too, because it was on the clo'es-line
yesterday—I see it there myself. But it's gone—that's the long and
the short of it, and you'll just have to change to a red flann'l one
till I can get time to make a new one. And it'll be the third I've made
in two years; it just keeps a body on the jump to keep you in shirts;

and whatever you do manage to *do* with 'm all, is more'n *I* can make
out. A body'd think you *would* learn to take some sort of care of
'em, at your time of life.''

"I know it, Sally, and I do try all I can. But it oughtn't to be
altogether my fault, because you know I don't see them nor have
nothing to do with them except when they're on me; and I don't
believe I've ever lost one of them *off* of me.''

"Well, it ain't *your* fault if you haven't, Silas—you'd a done it
if you could, I reckon. And the shirt ain't all that's gone, nuther.
Ther's a spoon gone; and *that* ain't all. There was ten, and now
ther's only nine. The calf got the shirt I reckon, but the calf never
took the spoon, *that's* certain.''

"Why, what else is gone, Sally?''

"Ther's six *candles* gone—that's what. The rats could a got the
candles, and I reckon they did; I wonder they don't walk off with
the whole place, the way you're always going to stop their holes
and don't do it; and if they warn't fools they'd sleep in your hair,
Silas—*you'd* never find it out; but you can't lay the *spoon* on the
rats, and that I *know*.''

"Well, Sally, I'm in fault, and I acknowledge it; I've been remiss;
but I won't let to-morrow go by without stopping up them holes.''

"Oh, I wouldn't hurry, next year'll do. Matilda Angelina
Araminta *Phelps!*''

Whack comes the thimble, and the child snatches her claws out
of the sugar-bowl without fooling around any. Just then, the
nigger woman steps onto the passage, and says:

"Missus, dey's a sheet gone.''

"A *sheet* gone! Well, for the land's sake!''

"I'll stop up them holes *to-day*," says Uncle Silas, looking
sorrowful.

"Oh, *do* shet up!—spose the rats took the *sheet? Where's* it gone,
Lize?''

"Clah to goodness I hain't no notion, Miss Sally. She wuz on de
clo's-line yistiddy, but she done gone; she ain' dah no mo,' now.''

"I reckon the world *is* coming to an end. I *never* see the beat of
it, in all my born days. A shirt, and a sheet, and a spoon, and six
can——''

"Missus," comes a young yaller wench, "dey's a brass
cannelstick miss'n.''

"Cler out from here, you hussy, er I'll take a skillet to ye!''

Well, she was just a biling. I begun to lay for a chance; I reckoned
I would sneak out and go for the woods till the weather moderated.
She kept a raging right along, running her insurrection all by
herself, and everybody else mighty meek and quiet; and at last
Uncle Silas, looking kind of foolish, fishes up that spoon out of
his pocket. She stopped, with her mouth open and her hands up;
and as for me, I wished I was in Jerusalem or somewheres. But not

long; because she says:

"It's *just* as I expected. So you had it in your pocket all the time; and like as not you've got the other things there, too. How'd it get there?"

"I reely don't know, Sally," he says, kind of apologizing, "or you know I would tell. I was a-studying over my text in Acts Seventeen, before breakfast, and I reckon I put it in there, not noticing, meaning to put my Testament in, and it must be so, because my Testament ain't in, but I'll go and see, and if the Testament is where I had it, I'll know I didn't put it in, and that will show that I laid the Testament down and took up the spoon, and——"

"Oh, for the land's sake! Give a body a rest! Go 'long now, the whole kit and biling of ye; and don't come nigh me again till I've got back my peace of mind."

I'd a heard her, if she'd a said it to herself, let alone speaking it out; and I'd a got up and obeyed her, if I'd a been dead. As we was passing through the setting-room, the old man he took up his hat, and the shingle-nail fell out on the floor, and he just merely picked it up and laid it on the mantel-shelf, and never said nothing, and went out. Tom see him do it, and remembered about the spoon, and says:

"Well, it ain't no use to send things by *him* no more, he ain't reliable." Then he says: "But he done us a good turn with the spoon anyway, without knowing it, and so we'll go and do him one without *him* knowing it—stop up his rat-holes."

There was a noble good lot of them, down cellar, and it took us a whole hour, but we done the job tight and good, and ship-shape. Then we heard steps on the stairs, and blowed out our light, and hid; and here comes the old man, with a candle in one hand and a bundle of stuff in t'other, looking as absent-minded as year before last. He went a mooning around, first to one rat-hole and then another, till he'd been to them all. Then he stood about five minutes, picking tallow-drip off of his candle and thinking. Then he turns off slow and dreamy towards the stairs, saying:

"Well, for the life of me I can't remember when I done it. I could show her now that I warn't to blame on account of the rats. But never mind—let it go. I reckon it wouldn't do no good."

And so he went on a mumbling up stairs, and then we left. He was a mighty nice old man. And always is.

Tom was a good deal bothered about what to do for a spoon, but he said we'd got to have it; so he took a think. When he had ciphered it out, he told me how we was to do; then we went and waited around the spoon-basket till we see Aunt Sally coming, and then Tom went to counting the spoons and laying them out to one side, and I slid one of them up my sleeve, and Tom says:

"Why, Aunt Sally, there ain't but nine spoons, *yet.*"

She says:

"Go 'long to your play, and don't bother me. I know better, I counted 'm myself."

"Well, I've counted them twice, Aunty, and *I* can't make but nine."

She looked out of all patience, but of course she come to count—anybody would.

"I declare to gracious ther' *ain't* but nine!" she says. "Why, what in the world—plague *take* the things, I'll count 'm again."

So I slipped back the one I had, and when she got done counting, she says:

"Hang the troublesome rubbage, there's *ten,* now!" and she looked huffy and bothered both. But Tom says:

"Why, Aunty, *I* don't think there's ten."

"You numskull, didn't you see me *count* 'm?"

"I know, but——"

"Well, I'll count 'm *again.*"

So I smouched one, and they come out nine same as the other time. Well, she *was* in a tearing way—just a trembling all over, she was so mad. But she counted and counted, till she got that addled she'd start to count-in the *basket* for a spoon, sometimes; and so, three times they come out right, and three times they come out wrong. Then she grabbed up the basket and slammed it across the house and knocked the cat galley-west; and she said cle'r out and let her have some peace, and if we come bothering around her again betwixt that and dinner, she'd skin us. So we had the odd spoon; and dropped it in her apron pocket whilst she was a giving us our sailing-orders, and Jim got it all right, along with her shingle-nail, before noon. We was very well satisfied with this business, and Tom allowed it was worth twice the trouble it took, because he said *now* she couldn't ever count them spoons twice alike again to save her life; and wouldn't believe she'd counted them right, if she *did;* and said that after she'd about counted her head off, for the next three days, he judged she'd give it up and offer to kill anybody that wanted her to ever count them any more.

So we put the sheet back on the line, that night, and stole one out of her closet; and kept on putting it back and stealing it again, for a couple of days, till she didn't know how many sheets she had, any more, and said she didn't *care,* and warn't agoing to bullyrag the rest of her soul out about it, and wouldn't count them again not to save her life, she druther die first.

So we was all right now, as to the shirt and the sheet and the spoon and the candles, by the help of the calf and the rats and the mixed-up counting; and as to the candlestick, it warn't no consequence, it would blow over by-and-by.

But that pie was a job; we had no end of trouble with that pie. We fixed it up away down in the woods, and cooked it there; and

we got it done at last, and very satisfactory, too; but not all in one
day; and we had to use up three wash-pans full of flour, before we
got through, and we got burnt pretty much all over, in places, and
eyes put out with the smoke, because, you see, we didn't want
nothing but a crust, and we couldn't prop it up right, and she would
always cave in. But of course we thought of the right way at last;
which was to cook the ladder, too, in the pie. So then we laid in with
Jim, the second night, and tore up the sheet all in little strings, and
twisted them together, and long before daylight we had a lovely
rope, that you could a hung a person with. We let on it took nine
months to make it.

And in the forenoon we took it down to the woods, but it
wouldn't go in the pie. Being made of a whole sheet, that way, there
was rope enough for forty pies, if we'd a wanted them, and plenty
left over for soup, or sausage, or anything you choose. We could
a had a whole dinner.

But we didn't need it. All we needed was just enough for the pie,
and so we throwed the rest away. We didn't cook none of the pies
in the washpan, afraid the solder would melt; but Uncle Silas he
had a noble brass warming-pan which he thought considerable
of, because it belonged to one of his ancestors with a long wooden
handle that come over from England with William the Conqueror
in the *Mayflower* or one of them early ships and was hid away up
garret with a lot of other old pots and things that was valuable,
not on account of being any account because they warn't, but
on account of them being relicts, you know, and we snaked her
out, private, and took her down there, but she failed on the first
pies, because we didn't know how, but she come up smiling on the
last one. We took and lined her with dough, and set her in the coals,
and loaded her up with rag-rope, and put on a dough roof, and shut
down the lid, and put hot embers on top, and stood off five foot, with
the long handle, cool and comfortable, and in fifteen minutes she
turned out a pie that was a satisfaction to look at. But the person
that et it would want to fetch a couple of kags of toothpicks along,
for if that rope-ladder wouldn't cramp him down to business, I
don't know nothing what I'm talking about, and lay him in enough
stomach-ache to last him till next time, too.

Nat didn't look, when we put the witch-pie in Jim's pan; and we
put the three tin plates in the bottom of the pan under the vittles;
and so Jim got everything all right, and as soon as he was by himself
he busted into the pie and hid the rope-ladder inside of his straw
tick, and scratched some marks on a tin plate and throwed it out
of the window-hole.

CHAPTER XXXVIII

Making them pens was a distressid-tough job, and so was the saw; and Jim allowed the inscription was going to be the toughest of all. That's the one which the prisoner has to scrabble on the wall. But we had to have it; Tom said we'd *got* to; there warn't no case of a state prisoner not scrabbling his inscription to leave behind, and his coat of arms.

"Look at Lady Jane Grey," he says; "look at Gilford Dudley; look at old Northumberland! Why, Huck, spose it *is* considerble trouble?—what you going to do?—how you going to get around it? Jim's *got* to do his inscription and coat of arms. They all do."

Jim says:

"Why, Mars Tom, I hain't got no coat o' arms; I hain't got nuffn but dish-yer old shirt, en you knows I got to keep de journal on dat."

"Oh, you don't understand, Jim; a coat of arms is very different."

"Well," I says, "Jim's right, anyway, when he says he hain't got no coat of arms, because he hain't."

"I reckon *I* knowed that," Tom says, "but you bet he'll have one before he goes out of this—because he's going out *right,* and there ain't going to be no flaws in his record."

So whilst me and Jim filed away at the pens on a brickbat apiece, Jim a making his'n out of the brass and I making mine out of the spoon, Tom set to work to think out the coat of arms. By-and-by he said he'd struck so many good ones he didn't hardly know which to take, but there was one which he reckoned he'd decide on. He says:

"On the scutcheon we'll have a bend *or* in the dexter base, a saltire *murrey* in the fess, with a dog, couchant, for common charge, and under his foot a chain enbattled, for slavery, with a chevron *vert* in a chief engrailed, and three invected lines on a field *azure,* with the nombril points rampant on a dancette indented; crest, a runaway nigger, *sable,* with his bundle over his shoulder on a bar sinister: and a couple of gules for supporters, which is you and me; motto, *Maggiore fretta, minore atto.* Got it out of a book—means, the more haste, the less speed."

"Geewhillikins," I says, "but what does the rest of it mean?"

"We ain't got no time to bother over that," he says, "we got to dig in like all git-out."

"Well, anyway," I says, "what's *some* of it? What's a fess?"

"A fess—a fess is—*you* don't need to know what a fess is. I'll show him how to make it when he gets to it."

"Shucks, Tom," I says, "I think you might tell a person. What's a bar sinister?"

"Oh, *I* don't know. But he's got to have it. All the nobility does."

That was just his way. If it didn't suit him to explain a thing to you, he wouldn't do it. You might pump at him a week, it wouldn't make no difference.

He'd got all that coat of arms business fixed, so now he started in to finish up the rest of that part of the work, which was to plan out a mournful inscription—said Jim got to have one, like they all done. He made up a lot, and wrote them out on a paper, and read them off, so:

1. *Here a captive heart busted.*
2. *Here a poor prisoner, forsook by the world and friends, fretted out his sorrowful life.*
3. *Here a lonely heart broke, and a worn spirit went to its rest, after thirty-seven years of solitary captivity.*
4. *Here, homeless and friendless, after thirty-seven years of bitter captivity, perished a noble stranger, natural son of Louis XIV.*

Tom's voice trembled, whilst he was reading them, and he most broke down. When he got done, he couldn't no way make up his mind which one for Jim to scrabble onto the wall, they was all so good; but at last he allowed he would let him scrabble them all on. Jim said it would take him a year to scrabble such a lot of truck onto the logs with a nail, and he didn't know how to make letters, besides; but Tom said he would block them out for him, and then he wouldn't have nothing to do but just follow the lines. Then pretty soon he says:

"Come to think, the logs ain't agoing to do; they don't have log walls in a dungeon: we got to dig the inscriptions into a rock. We'll fetch a rock."

Jim said the rock was worse than the logs; he said it would take him such a pison long time to dig them into a rock, he wouldn't ever get out. But Tom said he would let me help him do it. Then he took a look to see how me and Jim was getting along with the pens. It was most pesky tedious hard work and slow, and didn't give my hands no show to get well of the sores, and we didn't seem to make no headway, hardly. So Tom says:

"I know how to fix it. We got to have a rock for the coat of arms and mournful inscriptions, and we can kill two birds with that same rock. There's a gaudy big grindstone down at the mill, and we'll smouch it, and carve the things on it, and file out the pens and the saw on it, too."

It warn't no slouch of an idea; and it warn't no slouch of a grindstone nuther; but we allowed we'd tackle it. It warn't quite midnight, yet, so we cleared out for the mill, leaving Jim at work. We smouched the grindstone, and set out to roll her home, but it was a most nation tough job. Sometimes, do what we could, we couldn't keep her from falling over, and she come mighty near mashing us, every time. Tom said she was going to get one of us, sure, before we got through. We got her half way; and then we was plumb played out, and most drownded with sweat. We see it

warn't no use, we got to go and fetch Jim. So he raised up his bed
and slid the chain off of the bed-leg, and wrapt it round his neck,
and we crawled out through our hole and down there, and Jim and
me laid into that grindstone and walked her along like nothing;
and Tom superintended. He could out-superintend any boy I ever
see. He knowed how to do everything.

Our hole was pretty big, but it warn't big enough to get the
grindstone through; but Jim he took the pick and soon made it big
enough. Then Tom marked out them things on it with the nail,
and set Jim to work on them, with the nail for a chisel and an iron
bolt from the rubbage in the lean-to for a hammer, and told him to
work till the rest of his candle quit on him, and then he could go to
bed, and hide the grindstone under his straw tick and sleep on
it. Then we helped him fix his chain back on the bed-leg, and was
ready for bed ourselves. But Tom thought of something, and says:

"You got any spiders in here, Jim?"

"No, sah, thanks to goodness I hain't, Mars Tom."

"All right, we'll get you some."

"But bless you, honey, I doan' *want* none. I's afeard un um. I
jis' 's soon have rattlesnakes aroun'."

Tom thought a minute or two, and says:

"It's a good idea. And I reckon it's been done. It *must* a been
done; it stands to reason. Yes, it's a prime good idea. Where could
you keep it?"

"Keep what, Mars Tom?"

"Why, a rattlesnake."

"De goodness gracious alive, Mars Tom! Why, if dey was a
rattlesnake to come in heah, I'd take en bust right out thoo dat
log wall, I would, wid my head."

"Why, Jim, you woulnd't be afraid of it, after a little. You could
tame it."

"*Tame* it!"

"Yes—easy enough. Every animal is grateful for kindness and
petting, and they wouldn't *think* of hurting a person that pets them.
Any book will tell you that. You try—that's all I ask; just try for two
or three days. Why, you can get him so, in a little while, that he'll
love you; and sleep with you; and won't stay away from you a
minute; and will let you wrap him round your neck and put his head
in your mouth."

"*Please,* Mars Tom—*doan'* talk so! I can't *stan'* it! He'd *let*
me shove his head in my mouf—fer a favor, hain't it? I lay he'd wait
a pow'ful long time 'fo' I *ast* him. En mo' en dat, I doan *want* him
to sleep wid me."

"Jim, don't act so foolish. A prisoner's *got* to have some kind of
a dumb pet, and if a rattlesnake hain't ever been tried, why, there's
more glory to be gained in your being the first to ever try it than
any other way you could ever think of to save your life."

"Why, Mars Tom, I doan' *want* no sich glory. Snake take 'n bite Jim's chin off, den *whah* is de glory? No, sah, I doan' want no sich doin's."

"Blame it, can't you *try?* I only *want* you to try—you needn't keep it up if it don't work."

"But de trouble all *done,* ef de snake bite me while I's a tryin' him. Mars Tom, I's willin' to tackle mos' anything 'at ain't onreasonable, but ef you en Huck fetches a rattlesnake in heah for me to tame, I's gwyne to *leave,* dat's *shore.*"

"Well, then, let it go, let it go, if you're so bullheaded about it. We can get you some garter-snakes and you can tie some buttons on their tails, and let on they're rattlesnakes, and I reckon that'll have to do."

"I k'n stan' *dem,* Mars Tom, but blame' 'f I couldn' get along widout um, I tell you dat. I never knowed b'fo', 't was so much bother and trouble to be a prisoner."

"Well, it *always* is, when it's done right. You got any rats around here?"

"No, sah, I hain't seed none."

"Well, we'll get you some rats."

"Why, Mars Tom, I doan' *want* no rats. Dey's de dad-blamedest creturs to sturb a body, en rustle roun' over 'im, en bite his feet, when he's tryin' to sleep, I ever see. No, sah, gimme g'yarter-snakes, 'f I's got to have 'm, but doan' gimme no rats, I ain' got no use f'r um, skasely."

"But Jim, you *got* to have 'em—they all do. So don't make no more fuss about it. Prisoners ain't ever without rats. There ain't no instance of it. And they train them, and pet them, and learn them tricks, and they get to be as sociable as flies. But you got to play music to them. You got anything to play music on?"

"I ain' got nuffn but a coase comb en a piece o' paper, en a juice-harp; but I reck'n dey wouldn' take no stock in a juice-harp."

"Yes they would. *They* don't care what kind of music 'tis. A jews-harp's plenty good enough for a rat. All animals likes music—in a prison they dote on it. Specially, painful music; and you can't get no other kind out of a jews-harp. It always interest them; they come out to see what's the matter with you. Yes, you're all right; you're fixed very well. You want to set on your bed, nights, before you go to sleep, and early in the mornings, and play your jews-harp; play The Last Link is Broken—that's the thing that'll scoop a rat, quicker'n anything else: and when you've played about two minutes, you'll see all the rats, and the snakes, and spiders, and things begin to feel worried about you, and come. And they'll just fairly swarm over you, and have a noble good time."

"Yes, *dey* will, I reck'n, Mars Tom, but what kine er time is *Jim* havin'? Blest if I kin see de pint. But I'll do it ef I got to. I reck'n I better keep de animals satisfied, en not have no trouble in de house."

Tom waited to think over, and see if there wasn't nothing else; and pretty soon he says:

"Oh—there's one thing I forgot. Could you raise a flower here, do you reckon?"

"I doan' know but maybe I could, Mars Tom; but it's tolable dark in heah, en I ain' got no use f'r no flower, nohow, en she'd be a pow'ful sight o' trouble."

"Well, you try it, anyway. Some other prisoners has done it."

"One er dem big cat-tail-lookin' mullen-stalks would grow in heah, Mars Tom, I reck'n, but she wouldn' be wuth half de trouble she'd coss."

"Don't you believe it. We'll fetch you a little one, and you plant it in the corner, over there, and raise it. And don't call it mullen. call it Pitchiola—that's its right name, when it's in a prison. And you want to water it with your tears."

"Why, I got plenty spring water, Mars Tom."

"You don't *want* spring water; you want to water it with your tears. It's the way they always do."

"Why, Mars Tom, I lay I kin raise one er dem mullen-stalks twyste wid spring water whiles another man's a *start'n* one wid tears."

"That ain't the idea. You *got* to do it with tears."

"She'll die on my han's, Mars Tom, she sholy will; kase I doan' skasely ever cry."

So Tom was stumped. But he studied it over, and then said Jim would have to worry along the best he could with an onion. He promised he would go to the nigger cabins and drop one, private, in Jim's coffee-pot, in the morning. Jim said he would "jis' 's soon have tobacker in his coffee;" and found so much fault with it, and with the work and bother of raising the mullen, and jews-harping the rats, and petting and flattering up the snakes and spiders and things, on top of all the other work he had to do on pens, and inscriptions, and journals, and things, which made it more trouble and worry and responsibility to be a prisoner than anything he ever undertook, that Tom most lost all patience with him; and said he was just loadened down with more gaudier chances than a prisoner ever had in the world to make a name for himself, and yet he didn't know enough to appreciate them, and they was just about wasted on him. So Jim he was sorry, and said he wouldn't behave so no more, and then me and Tom shoved for bed.

CHAPTER XXXIX

In the morning we went up to the village and bought a wire rat trap and fetched it down, and unstopped the best rat hole, and in about an hour we had fifteen of the bulliest kind of ones; and then we took it and put it in a safe place under Aunt Sally's bed. But while we was gone for spiders, little Thomas Franklin Benjamin Jefferson Elexander Phelps found it there, and opened the door of it to see if the rats would come out, and they did; and Aunt Sally she come in, and when we got back she was a standing on top of the bed raising Cain, and the rats was doing what they could to keep off the dull times for her. So she took and dusted us both with the hickry, and we was as much as two hours catching another fifteen or sixteen, drat that meddlesome cub, and they warn't the likeliest, nuther, because the first haul was the pick of the flock. I never see a likelier lot of rats than what that first haul was.

We got a splendid stock of sorted spiders, and bugs, and frogs, and caterpillars, and one thing or another; and we like-to got a hornet's nest, but we didn't. The family was at home. We didn't give it right up, but staid with them as long as we could; because we allowed we'd tired them out or they'd got to tire us out, and they done it. Then we got allycumpain and rubbed on the places, and was pretty near all right again, but couldn't set down convenient. And so we went for the snakes, and grabbed a couple of dozen garters and house-snakes, and put them in a bag, and put it in our room, and by that time it was supper time, and a rattling good honest day's work; and hungry?—oh, no, I reckon not! And there warn't a blessed snake up there, when we went back—we didn't half tie the sack, and they worked out, somehow, and left. But it didn't matter much, because they was still on the premises somewheres. So we judged we could get some of them again. No, there warn't no real scarcity of snakes about the house for a considerble spell. You'd see them dripping from the rafters and places, every now and then; and they generly landed in your plate, or down the back of your neck, and most of the time where you didn't want them. Well, they was handsome, and striped, and there warn't no harm in a million of them; but that never made no difference to Aunt Sally, she despised snakes, be the breed what they might, and she couldn't stand them no way you could fix it; and every time one of them flopped down on her, it didn't make no difference what she was doing, she would just lay that work down and light out. I never see such a woman. And you could hear her whoop to Jericho. You couldn't get her to take aholt of one of them with the tongs. And if she turned over and found one in bed, she would scramble out and lift a howl that you would think the house was afire. She disturbed the old man so, that he said he could most wish there hadn't ever been no snakes created. Why, after every last snake had been gone clear out of the house for

as much as a week, Aunt Sally warn't over it yet; she warn't near
over it; when she was setting thinking about something, you could
touch her on the back of her neck with a feather and she would jump
right out of her stockings. It was very curious. But Tom said all
women was just so. He said they was made that way; for some reason
or other.

We got a licking every time one of our snakes come in her way;
and she allowed these lickings warn't nothing to what she would do
if we ever loaded up the place again with them. I didn't mind the
lickings, because they didn't amount to nothing; but I minded the
trouble we had, to lay in another lot. But we got them laid in, and all
the other things; and you never see a cabin as blithesome as Jim's
was when they'd all swarm out for music and go for him. Jim didn't
like the spiders, and the spiders didn't like Jim; and so they'd lay
for him and make it mighty warm for him. And he said that between
the rats, and the snakes, and the grindstone, there warn't no room
in bed for him, skasely; and when there was, a body couldn't sleep,
it was so lively, and it was always lively, he said, because *they* never
all slept at one time, but took turn about, so when the snakes was
asleep the rats was on deck, and when the rats turned in the snakes
come on watch, so he always had one gang under him, in his way,
and t'other gang having a circus over him, and if he got up to hunt
a new place, the spiders would take a chance at him as he crossed
over. He said if he ever got out, this time, he wouldn't ever be a
prisoner again, not for a salary.

Well, by the end of three weeks, everything was in pretty good
shape. the shirt was sent in early, in a pie, and every time a rat bit
Jim he would get up and write a little in his journal whilst the ink
was fresh; the pens was made, the inscriptions and so on was all
carved on the grindstone; the bed-leg was sawed in two, and we had
et up the sawdust, and it give us a most amazing stomach-ache.
We reckoned we was all going to die, but didn't. It was the most
undigestible sawdust I ever see; and Tom said the same. But as I
was saying, we'd got all the work done, now, as last; and we was
all pretty much fagged out, too, but mainly Jim. The old man had
wrote a couple of times to the plantation below Orleans to come and
get their runaway nigger, but hadn't got no answer, because there
warn't no such plantation; so he allowed he would advertise Jim in
the St. Louis and New Orleans papers; and when he mentioned the
St. Louis ones, it give me the cold shivers, and I see we hadn't no
time to lose. So Tom said, now for the nonnamous letters.

"What's them?" I says.

"Warnings to the people that something is up. Sometimes it's
done one way, sometimes another. But there's always somebody
spying around, that gives notice to the governor of the castle. When
Louis XVI. was going to light out of the Tooleries, a servant girl done
it. It's a very good way, and so is the nonnamous letters. We'll use

them both. And it's usual for the prisoner's mother to change clothes
with him, and she stays in, and he slides out in her clothes. We'll
do that too."

"But looky here, Tom, what do we want to *warn* anybody for, that
something's up? Let them find it out for themselves—it's their
lookout."

"Yes, I know; but you can't depend on them. It's the way
they've acted from the very start—left us to do *everything*. They're
so confiding and mullet-headed they don't take notice of nothing at
all. So if we don't *give* them notice, there won't be nobody nor
nothing to interfere with us, and so after all our hard work and
trouble this escape 'll go off perfectly flat: won't amount to
nothing—won't be nothing *to* it."

"Well, as for me, Tom, that's the way I'd like."

"Shucks," he says, and looked disgusted. So I says:

"But I ain't going to make no complaint. Anyway that suits me.
What you going to do about the servant-girl?"

"You'll be her. You slide in, in the middle of the night, and hook
that yaller girl's frock."

"Why, Tom, that'll make trouble next morning; because of course
she prob'bly hain't got any but that one."

"I know; but you don't want it but fifteen minutes, to carry the
nonnamous letter and shove it under the front door."

"All right, then, I'll do it; but I could carry it just as handy in my
own togs."

"You wouldn't look like a servant-girl *then*, would you?"

"No, but there won't be nobody to see what I look like, *anyway*."

"That ain't got nothing to do with it. The thing for us to do, is
just to do our *duty*, and not worry about whether anybody *sees* us
do it or not. Hain't you got no principle at all?"

"All right, I ain't saying nothing; I'm the servant-girl. Who's
Jim's mother?"

"I'm his mother. I'll hook a gown from Aunt Sally."

"Well, then, you'll have to stay in the cabin when me and Jim
leaves."

"Not much. I'll stuff Jim's clothes full of straw and lay it on his
bed to represent his mother in disguise, and Jim 'll take the nigger
woman's gown off of me and wear it, and we'll all evade together.
When a prisoner of style escapes, it's called an evasion. It's always
called so when a king escapes, f'rinstance. And the same with a
king's son; it don't make no difference whether he's a natural one or
an unnatural one."

So Tom he wrote the nonnamous letter, and I smouched the yaller
wench's frock, that night, and put it on, and shoved it under the
front door, the way Tom told me to. It said:

Beware. Trouble is brewing. Keep a sharp lookout.   UNKNOWN FRIEND.

Next night we stuck a picture which Tom drawed in blood, of a skull and crossbones, on the front door; and next night another one of a coffin, on the back door. I never see a family in such a sweat. They couldn't been worse scared if the place had a been full of ghosts laying for them behind everything and under the beds and shivering through the air. If a door banged, Aunt Sally she jumped, and said "ouch!" if anything fell, she jumped and said "ouch!" if you happened to touch her, when she warn't noticing, she done the same; she couldn't face noway and be satisfied, because she allowed there was something behind her every time—so she was always a whirling around, sudden, and saying "ouch," and before she'd get two-thirds around, she'd whirl back again, and say it again; and she was afraid to go to bed, but she dasn't set up. So the thing was working very well, Tom said; he said he never see a thing work more satisfactory. He said it showed it was done right.

So he said, now for the grand bulge! So the very next morning at the streak of dawn we got another letter ready, and was wondering what we better do with it, because we heard them say at supper they was going to have a nigger on watch at both doors all night. Tom he went down the lightning-rod to spy around; and the nigger at the back door was asleep, and he stuck it in the back of his neck and come back. This letter said:

> *Don't betray me, I wish to be your friend. There is a desprate gang of cutthroats from over in the Ingean Territory going to steal your runaway nigger to-night, and they have been trying to scare you so as you will stay in the house and not bother them. I am one of the gang, but have got religgion and wish to quit it and lead a honest life again, and will betray the helish design. They will sneak down from northards, along the fence at midnight exact, with a false key, and go in the nigger's cabin to get him. I am to be off a piece and blow a tin horn if I see any danger; but stead of that, I will ba like a sheep soon as they get in and not blow at all, then whilst they are getting his chains loose, you slip there and lock them in, and can kill them at your leasure. Don't do anything but just the way I am telling you, if you do they will suspicion something and raise whoopjamboreehoo. I do not wish any reward but to know I have done the right thing.*
>
> UNKNOWN FRIEND.

CHAPTER XL

We was feeling pretty good, after breakfast, and took my canoe and went over the river a fishing, with a lunch, and had a good time, and took a look at the raft and found her all right, and got home late to supper, and found them in such a sweat and worry they didn't know which end they was standing on, and made us go right off to bed the minute we was done supper, and wouldn't tell us what the trouble was, and never let on a word about the new letter, but didn't need to, because we knowed as much about it as anybody did, and

348 MARK TWAIN

as soon as we was half up stairs and her back was turned, we slid for
the cellar cubboard and loaded up a good lunch and took it up to
our room and went to bed, and got up about half-past eleven, and
Tom put on Aunt Sally's dress that he stole and was going to start
with the lunch, but says:

"Where's the butter?"

"I laid out a hunk of it," I says, "on a piece of a corn-pone."

"Well, you *left* it laid out, then—it ain't here."

"We can get along without it," I says.

"We can get along *with* it, too," he says; "just you slide down
cellar and fetch it. And then mosey right down the lightning-rod and
come along. I'll go and stuff the straw into Jim's clothes to represent
his mother in disguise, and be ready to *ba* like a sheep and shove
soon as you get there."

So out he went, and down cellar went I. The hunk of butter, big as
a person's fist, was where I had left it, so I took up the slab of corn-
pone with it on, and blowed out my light, and started up stairs, very
stealthy, and got up to the main floor all right, but here comes Aunt
Sally with a candle, and I clapped the truck in my hat, and clapped
my hat on my head, and the next second she see me; and she says:

"You been down cellar?"

"Yes'm."

"What you been doing down there?"

"Noth'n."

"*Noth'n!*"

"No'm."

"Well, then, what possessed you to go down there, this time of
night?"

"I don't know'm."

"You don't *know*? Don't answer me that way, Tom, I want to
know what you been *doing* down there?"

"I hain't been doing a single thing, Aunt Sally, I hope to gracious
if I have."

I reckoned she'd let me go, now, and as a generl thing she would;
but I spose there was so many strange things going on she was just
in a sweat about every little thing that warn't yard-stick straight; so
she says, very decided:

"You just march into that setting-room and stay there till I come.
You been up to something you no business to, and I lay I'll find out
what it is before *I'm* done with you."

So she went away as I opened the door and walked into the
setting-room. My, but there was a crowd there! Fifteen farmers, and
every one of them had a gun. I was most powerful sick, and slunk to
a chair and set down. They was setting around, some of them talking
a little, in a low voice, and all of them fidgety and uneasy, but trying
to look like they warn't; but I knowed they was, because they was
always taking off their hats, and putting them on, and scratching

their heads, and changing their seats, and fumbling with their buttons. I warn't easy myself, but I didn't take my hat off, all the same.

I did wish Aunt Sally would come, and get done with me, and lick me, if she wanted to, and let me get away and tell Tom how we'd overdone this thing, and what a thundering hornet's nest we'd got ourselves into, so we could stop fooling around, straight off, and clear out with Jim before these rips got out of patience and come for us.

At last she come, and begun to ask me questions, but I *couldn't* answer them straight, I didn't know which end of me was up; because these men was in such a fidget now, that some was wanting to start right *now* and lay for them desperadoes, and saying it warn't but a few minutes to midnight; and others was trying to get them to hold on and wait for the sheep-signal; and here was aunty pegging away at the questions, and me a shaking all over and ready to sink down in my tracks I was that scared; and the place getting hotter and hotter, and the butter beginning to melt and run down my neck and behind my ears: and pretty soon, when one of them says, "*I'm* for going and getting in the cabin *first*, and right *now*, and catching them when they come," I most dropped; and a streak of butter come a trickling down my forehead, and Aunt Sally she see it, and turns white as a sheet, and says:

"For the land's sake what *is* the matter with the child!—he's got the brain fever as shore as you're born, and they're oozing out!"

And everybody runs to see, and she snatches off my hat, and out comes the bread, and what was left of the butter, and she grabbed me, and hugged me, and says:

"Oh, what a turn you did give me! and how glad and grateful I am it ain't no worse; for luck's against us, and it never rains but it pours, and when I see that truck I thought we'd lost you, for I knowed by the color and all, it was just like your brains would be if— Dear, dear, whyd'nt you *tell* me that was what you'd been down there for, *I* wouldn't a cared. Now cler out to bed, and don't lemme see no more of you till morning!"

I was up stairs in a second, and down the lightning-rod in another one, and shinning through the dark for the lean-to. I couldn't hardly get my words out, I was so anxious; but I told Tom as quick as I could, we must jump for it, now, and not a minute to lose—the house full of men, yonder, with guns!

His eyes just blazed; and he says:

"No!—is that so? *Ain't* it bully! Why, Huck, if it was to do over again, I bet I could fetch two hundred! If we could put it off till—"

"Hurry! *hurry!*" I says. "Where's Jim?"

"Right at your elbow; if you reach out your arm you can touch him. He's dressed and everything's ready. Now we'll slide out and give the sheep-signal."

But then we heard the tramp of men, coming to the door, and
heard them begin to fumble with the padlock; and heard a man say:

"I *told* you we'd be too soon; they haven't come—the door is
locked. Here I'll lock some of you into the cabin and you lay for 'em
in the dark and kill 'em when they come; and the rest scatter around
a piece, and listen if you can hear 'em coming."

So in they come, but couldn't see us in the dark, and most trod on
us whilst we was hustling to get under the bed. But we got under all
right, and out through the hole, swift but soft—Jim first, me next,
and Tom last, which was according to Tom's orders. Now we was in
the lean-to, and heard trampings close by outside. So we crept to
the door, and Tom stopped us there and put his eye to the crack, but
couldn't make out nothing, it was so dark; and whispered and said
he would listen for the steps to get further, and when he nudged us
Jim must glide out first, and him last. So he set his ear to the crack
and listened, and listened, and listened, and the steps a scraping
around, out there, all the time; and at last he nudged us, and we slid
out, and stooped down, not breathing, and not making the least
noise, and slipped stealthy towards the fence, in Injun file, and got
to it, all right, and me and Jim over it; but Tom's britches catched
fast on a splinter on the top rail, and then he hear the steps coming,
so he had to pull loose, which snapped the splinter and made a
noise; and as he dropped in our tracks and started, somebody sings
out:

"Who's that? Answer, or I'll shoot!"

But we didn't answer; we just unfurled our heels and shoved.
Then there was a rush, and a *bang, bang, bang!* and the bullets
fairly whizzed around us! We heard them sing out:

"Here they are! They've broke for the river! after 'em, boys! And
turn loose the dogs!"

So here they come, full tilt. We could hear them, because they
wore boots, and yelled, but we didn't wear no boots, and didn't yell.
We was in the path to the mill; and when they got pretty close onto
us, we dodged into the bush and let them go by, and then dropped
in behind them. They'd had all the dogs shut up, so they wouldn't
scare off the robbers; but by this time somebody had let them
loose, and here they come, making pow-wow enough for a million;
but they was our dogs; so we stopped in our tracks till they catched
up; and when they see it warn't nobody but us, and no excitement
to offer them, they only just said howdy, and tore right ahead
towards the shouting and clattering; and then we up steam again
and whizzed along after them till we was nearly to the mill, and
then struck up through the bush to where my canoe was tied, and
hopped in and pulled for dear life towards the middle of the river,
but didn't make no more noise than we was obleeged to. Then we
struck out, easy and comfortable, for the island where my raft was;
and we could hear them yelling and barking at each other all up

and down the bank, till we was so far away the sounds got dim and
died out. And when we stepped onto the raft, I says:

"*Now*, old Jim, you're a free man *again*, and I bet you won't ever
be a slave no more."

"En a mighty good job it wuz, too, Huck. It 'uz planned
beautiful, en it 'uz *done* beautiful; en dey ain't *nobody* kin git up a
plan dat's mo' mixed-up en splendid den what dat one wuz."

We was all as glad as we could be, but Tom was the gladdest of
all, because he had a bullet in the calf of his leg.

When me and Jim heard that, we didn't feel so brash as what we
did before. It was hurting him considerble, and bleeding; so we
laid him in the wigwam and tore up one of the duke's shirts for to
bandage him, but he says:

"Gimme the rags, I can do it myself. Don't stop, now; don't fool
around here, and the evasion booming along so handsome; man
the sweeps, and set her loose! Boys, we done it elegant!—'deed we
did. I wish *we'd* a had the handling of Louis XVI., there wouldn't
a been no 'Son of Saint Louis, ascend to heaven!' wrote down in
his biography: no, sir, we'd a whooped him over the *border*—that's
what we'd a done with *him*—and done it just as slick as nothing at
all, too. Man the sweeps—man the sweeps!"

But me and Jim was consulting—and thinking. And after we'd
thought a minute, I says:

"Say it, Jim."

So he says:

"Well, den, dis is de way it look to me, Huck. Ef it wuz *him* dat
'uz bein' sot free, en one er de boys wuz to git shot, would he say,
'Go on en save me, nemmine 'bout a doctor f'r to save dis one? Is
dat like Mars Tom Sawyer? Would he say dat? You *bet* he
wouldn't! *Well,* den, is *Jim* gwyne to say it? No, sah—I doan'
budge a step out'n dis place, 'dout a *doctor;* not it it's forty year!"

I knowed he was white inside, and I reckoned he'd say what he
did say—so it was all right, now, and I told Tom I was agoing for a
doctor. He raised considerble row about it, but me and Jim stuck
to it and wouldn't budge; so he was for crawling out and setting the
raft loose himself; but we wouldn't let him. Then he give us a piece
of his mind—but it didn't do no good.

So when he see me getting the canoe ready, he says:

"Well, then, if you're bound to go, I'll tell you the way to do,
when you get to the village. Shut the door, and blindfold the doctor
tight and fast, and make him swear to be silent as the grave, and
put a purse full of gold in his hand, and then take and lead him all
around the back alleys and everywheres, in the dark, and then
fetch him here in the canoe, in a roundabout way amongst the
islands and search him and take his chalk away from him, and
don't give it back to him till you get him back to the village, or else
he will chalk this raft so he can find it again. It's the way they all do."

So I said I would, and left, and Jim was to hide in the woods
when he see the doctor coming, till he was gone again.

CHAPTER XLI

The doctor was an old man; a very nice, kind-looking old man,
when I got him up. I told him me and my brother was over on
Spanish Island hunting, yesterday afternoon, and camped on a
piece of a raft we found, and about midnight he must a kicked his
gun in his dreams, for it went off and shot him in the leg, and we
wanted him to go over there and fix it and not say nothing about it,
nor let anybody know, because we wanted to come home this
evening, and surprise the folks.

"Who is your folks?" he says.

"The Phelpses, down yonder."

"Oh," he says. And after a minute, he says: "How'd you say he
got shot?"

"He had a dream," I says, "and it shot him."

"Singular dream," he says.

So he lit up his lantern, and got his saddle-bags, and we started.
But when he see the canoe, he didn't like the look of her—said she
was big enough for one, but didn't look pretty safe for two. I says:

"Oh, you needn't be afeard, sir, she carried the three of us, easy
enough."

"What three?"

"Why, me and Sid, and—and—and *the guns;* that's what I
mean."

"Oh," he says.

But he put his foot on the gunnel, and rocked her; and shook his
head, and said he reckoned he'd look around for a bigger one. But
they was all locked and chained; so he took my canoe, and said for
me to wait till he come back, or I could hunt around further, or
maybe I better go down home and get them ready for the surprise,
if I wanted to. But I said I didn't; so I told him just how to find the
raft, and then he started.

I struck an idea, pretty soon. I says to myself, spos'n he can't fix
that leg just in three shakes of a sheep's tail, as the saying is?
spos'n it takes him three or four days? What are we going to do?—
lay around there till he lets the cat out of the bag? No, sir, I know
what *I'll* do. I'll wait, and when he comes back, if he says he's got
to go any more, I'll get down there, too, if I swim; and we'll take
and tie him, and keep him, and shove out down the river; and
when Tom's done with him, we'll give him what it's worth, or all
we got, and then let him get shore.

So then I crept into a lumber pile to get some sleep; and next
time I waked up the sun was away up over my head! I shot out and

went for the doctor's house, but they told me he'd gone away in
the night, some time or other, and warn't back yet. Well, thinks I,
that looks powerful bad for Tom, and I'll dig out for the island,
right off. So away I shoved, and turned the corner, and nearly
rammed my head into Uncle Silas's stomach! He says:

"Why, *Tom!* Where you been, all this time, you rascal?"

"*I* hain't been nowheres," I says, "only just hunting for the
runaway nigger—me and Sid."

"Why, where ever did you go?" he says. "Your aunt's been
mighty uneasy."

"She needn't," I says, "because we was all right. We followed
the men and the dogs, but they out-run us, and we lost them; but
we thought we heard them on the water, so we got a canoe and
took out after them, and crossed over but couldn't find nothing of
them; so we cruised along up-shore till we got kind of tired and
beat out; and tied up the canoe and went to sleep, and never
waked up till about an hour ago, then we paddled over here to hear
the news, and Sid's at the post-office to see what he can hear, and
I'm a branching out to get something to eat for us, and then we're
going home."

So then we went to the post-office to get "Sid"; but just as I
suspicioned, he warn't there; so the old man he got a letter out of
the office, and we waited a while longer but Sid didn't come; so
the old man said come along, let Sid foot it home, or canoe-it,
when he got done fooling around—but we would ride. I couldn't
get him to let me stay and wait for Sid; and he said there warn't no
use in it, and I must come along, and let Aunt Sally see we was
all right.

When we got home, Aunt Sally was that glad to see me she
laughed and cried both, and hugged me, and give me one of them
lickings of hern that don't amount to shucks, and said she'd serve
Sid the same when he come.

And the place was plumb full of farmers and farmers' wives, to
dinner; and such another clack a body never heard. Old Mrs.
Hotchkiss was the worst; her tongue was agoing all the time. She
says:

"Well, Sister Phelps, I've ransacked that-air cabin over an' I
b'lieve the nigger was crazy. I says so to Sister Damrell—didn't I,
Sister Damrell?—s'I, he's crazy, s'I—them's the very words I said.
You all hearn me: He's crazy, s'I; everything shows it, s'I. Look at
that-air grindstone, s'I; want to tell *me*'t any cretur 'tis in his right
mind's agoin' to scrabble all them crazy things onto a grindstone,
s'I? Here sich 'n' sich a person busted his heart; 'n' here so 'n' so
pegged along for thirty-seven year, 'n' all that—natcherl son o'
Louis somebody, 'n' sich everlast'n rubbage. He's plumb crazy, s'I;
it's what I says in the fust place, it's what I says in the middle, 'n'
it's what I says last 'n' all the time—the nigger's crazy—crazy's

Nebokoodneezer, s'I."

"An' look at that-air ladder made out'n rags, Sister Hotchkiss,"
says old Mrs. Damrell, "what in the name o' goodness *could* he
every want of—"

"The very words I was a-sayin' no longer ago th'n this minute to
Sister Utterback, 'n' she'll tell you so herself. Sh-she, look at that-
air rag ladder, sh-she; 'n' s'I, yes, *look* at it, s'I. Sh-she, Sister
Hotchkiss, sh-she—"

"But how in the nation'd they ever *git* that grindstone *in* there,
any-way? 'n' who dug that-air *hole?* 'n' who—"

"My very *words*, Brer Penrod! I was a-sayin'—pass that-air
sasser o' m'lasses, won't ye?—I was a-sayin' to Sister Dunlap, jist
this minute, how *did* they git that grindstone in there, s'I. Without
help, mind you—'thout *help! Thar's* wher' 'tis. Don't tell *me*, s'I;
there *wuz* help, s'I; 'n' ther' wuz a *plenty* help, too, s'I; ther's ben
a *dozen* a-helpin' that nigger, 'n' I lay I'd skin every last nigger on
this place, but *I'd* find out who done it, s'I; 'n' moreover, s'I—"

"A *dozen* says you!—*forty* couldn't a done everything that's
been done. Look at them case-knife saws and things, how tedious
they've been made; look at that bed-leg sawed off with 'm, a week's
work for six men; look at that nigger made out'n straw on the bed;
and look at——"

"You may *well* say it, Brer Hightower! It's jist as I was a-sayin'
to Brer Phelps, his own self. S'e, what do *you* think of it, Sister
Hotchkiss, s'e? think o' what, Brer Phelps, s'I? think o' that bed-
leg sawed off that a way, s'e? *think* of it, s'I? I lay it never sawed
itself off, s'I—somebody *sawed* it, s'I; that's my opinion, take it or
leave it, it mayn't be no 'count, s'I, but sich as 't is, it's my opinion,
s'I, 'n' if anybody k'n start a better one, s'I, let him *do* it, s'I, that's
all. I says to Sister Dunlap, s'I——"

"Why, dog my cats, they must a ben a house-full o' niggers in
there every night for four weeks, to a done all that work, Sister
Phelps. Look at that shirt—every last inch of it kivered over with
secret African writ'n done with blood! Must a ben a raft uv 'm at
it right along, all the time, amost. Why, I'd give two dollars to have
it read to me; 'n' as for the niggers that wrote it, I 'low I'd take 'n'
lash 'm t'll——"

"People to *help* him, Brother Marples! Well, I reckon you'd
think so, if you'd a been in this house for a while back. Why,
they've stole everything they could lay their hands on—and we a
watching, all the time, mind you. They stole that shirt right off o'
the line! and as for that sheet they made the rag ladder out of
ther' ain't no telling how many times they *didn't* steal that; and
flour, and candles, and candlesticks, and spoons, and the old
warming-pan, and most a thousand things that I disremember,
now, and my new calico dress; and me, and Silas, and my Sid and
Tom on the constant watch day *and* night, as I was a telling you,

and not a one of us could catch hide nor hair, nor sight nor sound of them; and here at the last minute, lo and behold you, they slides right in under our noses, and fools us, and not only fools *us* but the Injun Territory robbers too, and actuly gets *away* with that nigger, safe and sound, and that with sixteen men and twenty-two dogs right on their very heels at that very time! I tell you, it just bangs anything i ever *heard* of. Why, *sperits* couldn't a done better, and been no smarter. And I reckon they must a *been* sperits—because, *you* know our dogs, and ther' ain't no better; well, them dogs never even got on the *track* of 'm, once! You explain *that* to me, if you can!—*any* of you!"

"Well, it does beat——"
"Laws alive, I never——"
"So help me, I wouldn't a be——"
"*House*-thieves as well as——"
"Goodnessgracioussakes, I'd a ben afeard to *live* in sich a——"

" 'Fraid to *live!*—why, I was that scared I das'nt hardly go to bed, or get up, or lay down, or *set* down, Sister Ridgeway. Why, they'd steal the very—why, goodness sakes, you can guess what kind of a fluster *I* was in by the time midnight come, last night. I hope to gracious if I warn't afraid they'd steal some o' the family! I was just to that pass, I didn't have no reasoning faculties no more. It looks foolish enough, *now*, in the day-time; but I says to myself, there's my two poor boys asleep, 'way up stairs in that lonesome room, and I declare to goodness I was that uneasy 't I crep' up there and locked 'em in! I *did*. And anybody would. Because, you know, when you get scared, that way, and it keeps running on, and getting worse and worse, all the time, and your wits gets to addling, and you get to doing all sorts o' wild things, and by-and-by you think to yourself, spos'n *I* was a boy, and was away up there, and the door ain't locked, and you——" She stopped, looking kind of wondering, and then she turned her head around slow, and when her eye lit on me—I got up and took a walk.

Says I to myself, I can explain better how we come to not be in that room this morning, if I go out to one side and study over it a little. So I done it. But I dasn't go fur, or she'd a sent for me. And when it was late in the day, the people all went, and then I come in and told her the noise and shooting waked up me and "Sid," and the door was locked, and we wanted to see the fun, so we went down the lightning-rod, and both of us got hurt a little, and we didn't never want to try *that* no more. And then I went on and told her all what I told Uncle Silas before; and then she said she'd forgive us, and maybe it was all right enough anyway, and about what a body might expect of boys, for all boys was a pretty harum-scarum lot, as fur as she could see; and so, as long as no harm hadn't come of it, she judged she better put in her time being

grateful we was alive and well and she had us still, stead of fretting
over what was past and done. So then she kissed me, and patted
me on the head, and dropped into a kind of a brown study; and
pretty soon jumps up, and says:

"Why, lawsamercy, it's most night, and Sid not come yet! What
has become of that boy?"

I see my chance; so I skips up and says:

"I'll run right up to town and get him," I says.

"No you won't," she says. "You'll stay right wher' you are; *one's*
enough to be lost at a time. If he ain't here to supper, your uncle'll
go."

Well, he warn't there to supper; so right after supper uncle went.

He come back about ten, a little bit uneasy; hadn't run across
Tom's track. Aunt Sally was a good *deal* uneasy; but Uncle Silas
he said there warn't no occasion to be—boys will be boys, he said,
and you'll see this one turn up in the morning, all sound and right.
So she had to be satisfied. But she said she'd set up for him a
while, anyway, and keep a light burning, so he could see it.

And then when I went up to bed she come up with me and
fetched her candle, and tucked me in, and mothered me so good I
felt mean, and like I couldn't look her in the face; and she set
down on the bed and talked with me a long time, and said what a
splendid boy Sid was, and didn't seem to want to ever stop talking
about him; and kept asking me every now and then, if I reckoned
he could a got lost, or hurt, or maybe drownded, and might be
laying at this minute, somewheres, suffering or dead, and she not
by him to help him, and so the tears would drip down, silent, and
I would tell her that Sid was all right, and would be home in the
morning, sure; and she would squeeze my hand, or maybe kiss me,
and tell me to say it again, and keep on saying it, because it done
her good, and she was in so much trouble. And when she was going
away, she looked down in my eyes, so steady and gentle, and says:

"The door ain't going to be locked, Tom; and there's the window
and the rod; but you'll be good, *won't* you? And you won't go? For
my sake."

Laws knows I *wanted* to go, bad enough, to see about Tom, and
was all intending to go; but after that, I wouldn't a went, not for
kingdoms.

But she was on my mind, and Tom was on my mind; so I slept
very restless. And twice I went down the rod, away in the night, and
slipped around front, and see her setting there by her candle in the
window with her eyes towards the road and the tears in them; and
I wished I could do something for her, but I couldn't, only to swear
that I wouldn't never do nothing to grieve her any more. And the
third time, I waked up at dawn, and slid down, and she was there
yet, and her candle was most out, and her old gray head was
resting on her hand, and she was asleep.

CHAPTER XLII

The old man was up town again, before breakfast, but couldn't get no track of Tom; and both of them set at the table, thinking, and not saying nothing, and looking mournful, and their coffee getting cold, and not eating anything. And by-and-by the old man says:

"Did I give you the letter?"

"What letter?"

"The one I got yesterday out of the post-office."

"No, you didn't give me no letter."

"Well, I must a forgot it."

So he rummaged his pockets, and then went off somewheres where he had laid it down, and fetched it, and give it to her. She says:

"Why, it's from St. Petersburg—it's from Sis."

I allowed another walk would do me good; but I couldn't stir. But before she could break it open, she dropped it and run—for she see something. And so did I. It was Tom Sawyer on a mattress; and that old doctor; and Jim, in *her* calico dress, with his hands tied behind him; and a lot of people. I hid the letter behind the first thing that come handy, and rushed. She flung herself at Tom, crying, and says:

"Oh, he's dead, he's dead, I know he's dead!"

And Tom he turned his head a little, and muttered something or other, which showed he warn't in his right mind; then she flung up her hands, and says:

"He's alive, thank God! And that's enough!" and she snatched a kiss of him, and flew for the house to get the bed ready, and scattering orders right and left at the niggers and everybody else, as fast as her tongue could go, every jump of the way.

I followed the men to see what they was going to do with Jim; and the old doctor and Uncle Silas followed after Tom into the house. The men was very huffy, and some of them wanted to hang Jim, for an example to all the other niggers around there, so they wouldn't be trying to run away, like Jim done, and making such a raft of trouble, and keeping a whole family scared most to death for days and nights. But the others said, don't do it, it wouldn't answer at all, he ain't our nigger, and his owner would turn up and make us pay for him, sure. So that cooled them down a little, because the people that's always the most anxious for to hang a nigger that hain't done just right, is always the very ones that ain't the most anxious to pay for him when they've got their satisfaction out of him.

They cussed Jim considerble, though, and give him a cuff or two, side the head, once in a while, but Jim never said nothing, and he never let on to know me, and they took him to the same cabin, and

put his own clothes on him, and chained him again, and not to
no bed-leg, this time, but to a big staple drove into the bottom log,
and chained his hands, too, and both legs, and said he warn't to
have nothing but bread and water to eat, after this, till his owner
come or he was sold at auction, because he didn't come in a certain
length of time, and filled up our hole, and said a couple of farmers
with guns must stand watch around about the cabin every night,
and a bull-dog tied to the door in the day-time; and about this
time they was through with the job and was tapering off with a
kind of generl good-bye cussing, and then the old doctor comes and
takes a look, and says:

"Don't be no rougher on him than you're obleeged to, because
he ain't a bad nigger. When I got to where I found the boy, I see
I couldn't cut the bullet out without some help, and he warn't in
no condition for me to leave, to go and get help; and he got a little
worse and a little worse, and after a long time he went out of his
head, and wouldn't let me come anigh him, any more, and said if
I chalked his raft he'd kill me, and no end of wild foolishness like
that, and I see I couldn't do anything at all with him; so I says, I
got to have *help,* somehow; and the minute I says it, out crawls this
nigger from somewhere, and says he'll help, and he done it, too,
and done it very well. Of course I judged he must be a runaway
nigger, and there I *was!* and there I had to stick, right straight
along all the rest of the day, and all night. It was a fix, I tell you!
I had a couple of patients with the chills, and of course I'd of liked
to run up to town and see them, but I dasn't, because the nigger
might get away, and then I'd be to blame; and yet never a skiff
come close enough for me to hail. So there I had to stick, plumb till
daylight this morning; and I never see a nigger that was a better
nuss or faithfuller, and yet he was resking his freedom to do it, and
was all tired out, too, and I see plain enough he'd been worked
main hard, lately. I liked the nigger for that; I tell you, gentlemen,
a nigger like that is worth a thousand dollars—and kind treatment,
too. I had everything I needed, and the boy was doing as well there
as he would a done at home—better, maybe, because it was so
quiet; but there I *was,* with both of 'm on my hands; and there I
had to stick, till about dawn this morning; then some men in a
skiff come by, and as good luck would have it, the nigger was
setting by the pallet with his head propped on his knees, sound
asleep; so I motioned them in, quiet, and they slipped up on him
and grabbed him and tied him before he knowed what he was
about, and we never had no trouble. And the boy being in a kind of
a flighty sleep, too, we muffled the oars and hitched the raft on,
and towed her over very nice and quiet, and the nigger never made
the least row nor said a word, from the start. He ain't no bad
nigger, gentlemen; that's what I think about him."

Somebody says:

"Well, it sounds very good, doctor, I'm obleeged to say."

Then the others softened up a little, too, and I was mighty
thankful to that old doctor for doing Jim that good turn; and I
was glad it was according to my judgment of him, too; because I
thought he had a good heart in him and was a good man, the first
time I see him. Then they all agreed that Jim had acted very well,
and was deserving to have some notice took of it, and reward. So
every one of them promised, right out and hearty, that they
wouldn't cuss him no more.

Then they come out and locked him up. I hoped they was going
to say he could have one or two of the chains took off, because they
was rotten heavy, or could have meat and greens with his bread
and water, but they didn't think of it, and I reckoned it warn't best
for me to mix in, but I judged I'd get the doctor's yarn to Aunt
Sally, somehow or other, as soon as I'd got through the breakers
that was laying just ahead of me. Explanations, I mean, of how I
forgot to mention about Sid being shot, when I was telling how him
and me put in that dratted night paddling around hunting the
runaway nigger.

But I had plenty time. Aunt Sally she stuck to the sick-room all
day and all night; and every time I see Uncle Silas mooning
around, I dodged him.

Next morning I heard Tom was a good deal better, and they said
Aunt Sally was gone to get a nap. So I slips to the sick-room, and
if I found him awake I reckoned we could put up a yarn for the
family that would wash. But he was sleeping, and sleeping very
peaceful, too; and pale, not fire-faced the way he was when he
come. So I set down and laid for him to wake. In about a half an
hour, Aunt Sally comes gliding in, and there I was, up a stump
again! She motioned me to be still, and set down by me, and begun
to whisper, and said we could all be joyful now, because all the
symptoms was first rate, and he'd been sleeping like that for ever
so long, and looking better and peacefuller all the time, and ten to
one he'd wake up in his right mind.

So we set there watching, and by-and-by he stirs a bit, and
opened his eyes very natural, and takes a look, and says:

"Hello, why I'm at *home!* How's that? Where's the raft?"

"It's all right," I says.

"And *Jim?*"

"The same," I says, but couldn't say it pretty brash. But he
never noticed, but says:

"Good! Splendid! *Now* we're all right and safe! Did you tell
Aunty?"

I was going to say yes; but she chipped in and says:

"About what, Sid?"

"Why, about the way the whole thing was done."

"What whole thing?"

"Why, *the* whole thing. There ain't but one; how we set the runaway nigger free—me and Tom."

"Good land! Set the run— What *is* the child talking about! Dear, dear, out of his head again!"

"*No,* I ain't out of my HEAD; I know all what I'm talking about. We *did* set him free—me and Tom. We laid out to do it, and we *done* it. And we done it elegant, too." He'd got a start, and she never checked him up, just set and stared and stared, and let him clip along, and I see it warn't no use for *me* to put in. "Why, Aunty, it cost us a power of work—weeks of it—hours and hours, every night, whilst you was all asleep. And we had to steal candles, and the sheet, and the shirt, and your dress, and spoons, and tin plates, and case-knives, and the warming-pan, and the grindstone, and flour, and just no end of things, and you can't think what work it was to make the saws, and pens, and inscriptions, and one thing or another, and you can't think *half* the fun it was. And we had to make up the pictures of coffins and things, and nonnamous letters from the robbers, and get up and down the lighting-rod, and dig the hole into the cabin, and make the rope-ladder and send it in cooked up in a pie, and send in spoons and things to work with, in your apron pocket"——

"Mercy sakes!"

——"and load up the cabin with rats and snakes and so on, for company for Jim; and then you kept Tom here so long with the butter in his hat that you come near spiling the whole business, because the men come before we was out of the cabin, and we had to rush, and they heard us and let drive at us, and I got my share, and we dodged out of the path and let them go by, and when the dogs come they warn't interested in us, but went for the most noise, and we got our canoe, and made for the raft, and was all safe, and Jim was a free man, and we done it all by ourselves, and *wasn't* it bully, Aunty!"

"Well, I never heard the likes of it in all my born days! So it was *you,* you little rapscallions, that's been making all this trouble, and turned everybody's wits clean inside out and scared us all most to death. I've as good a notion as ever I had in my life, to take it out o' you this very minute. To think, here I've been, night after night, a—*you* just get well once, you young scamp, and I lay I'll tan the Old Harry out o' both o' ye!"

But Tom, he *was* so proud and joyful, he just *couldn't* hold in, and his tongue just *went* it—she a-chipping in, and spitting fire all along, and both of them going it at once, like a cat-convention; and she says:

"*Well,* you get all the enjoyment you can out of it *now,* for mind I tell you if I catch you meddling with him again——"

"Meddling with *who?*" Tom says, dropping his smile and looking surprised.

"With *who?* Why, the runaway nigger, of course. Who'd you reckon?"

Tom looks at me very grave, and says:

"Tom, didn't you just tell me he was all right? Hasn't he got away?"

"*Him?*" says Aunt Sally; "the runaway nigger? 'Deed he hasn't. They've got him back, safe and sound, and he's in that cabin again, on bread and water, and loaded down with chains, till he's claimed or sold!"

Tom rose square up in bed, with his eye hot, and his nostrils opening and shutting like gills, and sings out to me:

"They hain't no *right* to shut him up! *Shove!*—and don't you lose a minute. Turn him loose! he ain't no slave; he's as free as any cretur that walks this earth!"

"What *does* the child mean?"

"I mean every word I *say,* Aunt Sally, and if somebody don't go, *I*'ll go. I've knowed him all his life, and so has Tom, there. Old Miss Watson died two months ago, and she was ashamed she ever was going to sell him down the river, and *said* so; and she let him free in her will."

"Then what on earth did *you* want to set him free for, seeing he was already free?"

"Well, that *is* a question, I must say; and *just* like women! Why, I wanted the *adventure* of it; and I'd a waded neck-deep in blood to—goodness alive, AUNT POLLY!"

If she warn't standing right there, just inside the door, looking as sweet and contented as an angel half-full of pie, I wish I may never!

Aunt Sally jumped for her, and most hugged the head off of her, and cried over her, and I found a good enough place for me under the bed, for it was getting pretty sultry for *us,* seemed to me. And I peeped out, and in a little while Tom's Aunt Polly shook herself loose and stood there looking across at Tom over her spectacles—kind of grinding him into the earth, you know. And then she says:

"Yes, you *better* turn y'r head away—I would if I was you, Tom."

"Oh, deary me!" says Aunt Sally; "*is* he changed so? Why, that ain't *Tom* it's Sid; Tom's—Tom's—why, where is Tom? He was here a minute ago."

"You mean where's Huck *Finn*—that's what you mean! I reckon I hain't raised such a scamp as my Tom all these years, not to know him when I *see* him. That *would* be a pretty howdy-do. Come out from under that bed, Huck Finn."

So I done it. But not feeling brash.

Aunt Sally she was one of the mixed-upest looking persons I ever see; except one, and that was Uncle Silas, when he come in, and they told it all to him. It kind of made him drunk, as you may say, and he didn't know nothing at all the rest of the day, and preached a prayer-meeting sermon that night that give him a rattling reputation, because the oldest man in the world couldn't a understood it. So Tom's Aunt Polly, she told all about who I was, and what; and I had to up and tell how I was in such a tight place that when Mrs. Phelps took me for Tom Sawyer—she chipped in and says, "Oh, go on and call me Aunt Sally, I'm used to it, now, and 'taint no need to change"—that when Aunt Sally took me for Tom Sawyer, I had to stand it—there warn't no other way, and I knowed he wouldn't mind, because it would be nuts for him, being a mystery, and he'd make an adventure out of it and be perfectly satisfied. And so it turned out, and he let on to be Sid, and made things as soft as he could for me.

And his Aunt Polly she said Tom was right about old Miss Watson setting Jim free in her will; and so, sure enough, Tom Sawyer had gone and took all that trouble and bother to set a free nigger free! and I couldn't ever understand, before, until that minute and that talk, how he *could* help a body set a nigger free, with his bringing-up.

Well, Aunt Polly she said that when Aunt Sally wrote to her that Tom and *Sid* had come, all right and safe, she says to herself:

"Look at that, now! I might have expected it, letting him go off that way without anybody to watch him. So now I got to go and trapse all the way down the river, eleven hundred mile, and find out what that creetur's up to, *this* time; as long as I couldn't seem to get any answer out of you about it."

"Why, I never heard nothing from you," says Aunt Sally.

"Well, I wonder! Why, I wrote to you twice, to ask you what you could mean by Sid being here."

"Well, I never got 'em, Sis."

Aunt Polly, she turns around slow and severe, and says:

"You, Tom!"

"Well—*what?*" he says, kind of pettish.

"Don't you what *me,* you impudent thing—hand out them letters."

"What letters?"

"*Them* letters. I be bound, if I have to take aholt of you I'll——"

"They're in the trunk. There, now. And they're just the same as they was when I got them out of the office. I hain't looked into them, I hain't touched them. But I knowed they'd make trouble, and I thought if you warn't in no hurry, I'd——"

"Well, you *do* need skinning, there ain't no mistake about it. And I wrote another one to tell you I was coming; and I spose he——"

"No, it come yesterday; I hain't read it yet, but *it's* all right, I've got that one."

I wanted to offer to bet two dollars she hadn't, but I reckoned maybe it was just as safe to not to. So I never said nothing.

CHAPTER THE LAST

The first time I catched Tom, private, I asked him what was his idea, time of the evasion?—what it was he'd planned to do if the evasion worked all right and he managed to set a nigger free that was already free before? And he said, what he had planned in his head, from the start, if we got Jim out all safe, was for us to run him down the river, on the raft, and have adventures plumb to the mouth of the river, and then tell him about his being free, and take him back up home on a steamboat, in style, and pay him for his lost time, and write word ahead and get out all the niggers around, and have them waltz him into town with a torchlight procession and a brass band, and then he would be a hero, and so would we. But I reckened it was about as well the way it was.

We had Jim out of the chains in no time, and when Aunt Polly and Uncle Silas and Aunt Sally found out how good he helped the doctor nurse Tom, they made a heap of fuss over him, and fixed him up prime, and give him all he wanted to eat, and a good time, and nothing to do. And we had him up to the sick-room; and had a high talk; and Tom give Jim forty dollars for being prisoner for us so patient, and doing it up so good, and Jim was pleased most to death, and busted out, and says:

"*Dah*, now, Huck, what I tell you?—what I tell you up dah on Jackson islan'? I *tole* you I got a hairy breas', en what's de sign un it; en I *tole* you I ben rich wunst, en gwineter to be rich *again;* en it's come true; en heah she *is! Dah,* now! doan' talk to *me—* signs is *signs,* mine I tell you; en I knowed jis' 's well 'at I 'uz gwineter be rich agin as I's a stannin' heah dis minute!"

And then Tom he talked along, and talked along, and says, le's all three slide out of here, one of these nights, and get an outfit, an go for howling adventures amongst the Injuns, over in the Territory, for a couple of weeks or two; and I says, all right, that suits me, but I aint got no money for to buy the outfit, and I reckon I couldn't get none from home, because it's likely pap's been back before now, and got it all away from Judge Thatcher and drunk it up.

"No he hain't," Tom says; "it's all there, yet—six thousand dollars and more; and your pap hain't ever been back since. Hadn't when I come away, anyhow."

Jim says, kind of solemn:

"He ain't a comin' back no mo', Huck."

I says:

"Why, Jim?"

"Nemmine why, Huck—but he ain't comin' back no mo'."

But I kept at him; so at last he says:

"Doan' you 'member de house dat was float'n down de river, en dey wuz a man in dah, kivered up, en I went in en unkivered him

and didn' let you come in? Well, den, you k'n git yo' money when
you wants it: kase dat wuz him."

Tom's most well, now, and got his bullet around his neck on a
watch-guard for a watch, and is always seeing what time it is, and
so there ain't nothing more to write about, and I am rotten glad of
it, because if I'd a knowed what a trouble it was to make a book I
wouldn't a tackled it and aint't agoing to no more. But I reckon I
got to light out for the Territory ahead of the rest, because Aunt
Sally she's going to adopt me and sivilize me and I can't stand it.
I been there before.

THE END. YOURS TRULY, HUCK FINN

THE PRINCE
AND
THE PAUPER

THE PRINCE AND THE PAUPER

I will set down a tale as it was told to me by one who had it of his father, which latter had it of *his* father, this last having in like manner had it of *his* father—and so on, back and still back, three hundred years and more, the fathers transmitting it to the sons and so preserving it. It may be history, it may be only a legend, a tradition. It may have happened, it may not have happened: but it *could* have happened. It may be that the wise and the learned believed it in the old days; it may be that only the unlearned and the simple loved it and credited it.

HUGH LATIMER, *Bishop of Worcester, to* LORD CROMWELL, *on the birth of the* PRINCE OF WALES (*afterward* EDWARD VI.).

FROM THE NATIONAL MANUSCRIPTS PRESERVED BY THE BRITISH GOVERNMENT.

HUGH LATIMER, *Bishop of Worcester, to* LORD CROMWELL, *on the birth of the* PRINCE OF WALES (*afterward* EDWARD VI.).

FROM THE NATIONAL MANUSCRIPTS PRESERVED BY THE BRITISH GOVERNMENT.

Ryght honorable, *Salutem in Christo Jesu,* and Syr here ys no lesse joynge and rejossynge in thes partees for the byrth of our prynce, hoom we hungurde for so longe, then ther was (I trow), *inter vicinos* att the byrth of S. I. Baptyste, as thys berer, Master Erance, can telle you. Gode gyffe us alle grace, to yelde dew thankes to our Lorde Gode, Gode of Inglonde, for verely He hathe shoyd Hym selff Gode of Inglonde, or rather an Inglyssh Gode, yf we consydyr and pondyr welle alle Hys procedynges with us from tyme to tyme. He hath overcumme allè our yllnesse with Hys excedynge goodnesse, so that we ar now moor then compellyd to serve Hym, seke Hys glory, promott Hys wurde, yf the Devylle of alle Devylles be natt in us. We have now the stooppe of vayne trustes ande the stey of vayne expectations; lett us alle pray for hys preservatione. And I for my partt wylle wyssh that hys Grace allways have, and evyn now from the begynynge, Governares, Instructores and offyceres of ryght judgmente, *ne optimum ingenium non optima educatione depravetur.*

Butt whatt a grett fowlle am I! So, whatt devotione shoyth many tymys but lytelle dyscretione! Ande thus the Gode of Inglonde be ever with you in alle your procedynges.

The 19 of October.

Youres, H. L. B. of Wurcestere, now att Hartlebury.

Yf you wolde excytt thys berere to be moore hartye ayen the abuse of ymagry or mor forwarde to promotte the veryte, ytt myght doo goode. Natt that ytt came of me, butt of your selffe, &c.

(Addressed) To the Ryght Honorable Loorde P. Sealle hys synguler gode Lorde.

CHAPTER I

THE BIRTH OF THE PRINCE AND THE PAUPER

In the ancient city of London, on a certain autumn day in the second quarter of the sixteenth century, a boy was born to a poor family of the name of Canty, who did not want him. On the same day another English child was born to a rich family of the name of Tudor, who did want him. All England wanted him too. England had so longed for him, and hoped for him, and prayed God for him, that, now that he was really come, the people went nearly mad for joy. Mere acquaintances hugged and kissed each other and cried. Everybody took a holiday, and high and low, rich and poor, feasted and danced and sang, and got very mellow; and they kept this up for days and nights together. By day, London was a sight to see, with gay banners waving from every balcony and house-top, and splendid pageants marching along. By night, it was again a sight to see, with its great bonfires at every corner, and its troops of revelers making merry around them. There was no talk in all England but of the new baby, Edward Tudor, Prince of Wales, who lay lapped in silks and satins, unconscious of all this fuss, and not knowing that great lords and ladies were tending him and watching over him—and not caring, either. But there was no talk about the other baby, Tom Canty, lapped in his poor rags, except among the family of paupers whom he had just come to trouble with his presence.

CHAPTER II

TOM'S EARLY LIFE

Let us skip a number of years.

London was fifteen hundred years old, and was a great town—for that day. It had a hundred thousand inhabitants—some think double as many. The streets were very narrow, and crooked, and dirty, especially in the part where Tom Canty lived, which was not far from London Bridge. The houses were of wood, with the second story projecting over the first, and the third sticking its elbows out beyond the second. The higher the houses grew, the broader they grew. They were skeletons of strong criss-cross beams, with solid material between, coated with plaster. The beams were painted red or blue or black, according to the owner's taste, and this gave the houses a very picturesque look. The windows were small, glazed with little diamond-shaped panes, and they opened outward, on hinges, like doors.

The house which Tom's father lived in was up a foul little pocket called Offal Court, out of Pudding Lane. It was small, decayed, and rickety, but it was packed full of wretchedly poor families. Canty's tribe occupied a room on the third floor. The mother and father had a sort of bedstead in the corner; but Tom, his grandmother, and his two sisters, Bet and Nan, were not restricted—they had all the floor to themselves, and might sleep where they chose. There were the remains of a blanket or two, and some bundles of ancient and dirty straw, but these could not rightly be called beds, for they were not organized; they were kicked into a general pile, mornings, and selections made from the mass at night, for service.

Bet and Nan were fifteen years old—twins. They were good-hearted girls, unclean, clothed in rags, and profoundly ignorant. Their mother was like them. But the father and the grandmother were a couple of fiends. They got drunk whenever they could; then they fought each other or anybody else who came in the way; they cursed and swore always, drunk or sober; John Canty was a thief, and his mother a beggar. They made beggars of the children, but failed to make thieves of them. Among, but not of, the dreadful rabble that inhabited the house, was a good old priest whom the King had turned out of house and home with a pension of a few farthings, and he used to get the children aside and teach them right ways secretly. Father Andrew also taught Tom a little Latin, and how to read and write; and would have done the same with the girls, but they were afraid of the jeers of their friends, who could not have endured such a queer accomplishment in them.

All Offal Court was just such another hive as Canty's house. Drunkenness, riot, and brawling were the order, there, every night and nearly all night long. Broken heads were as common as hunger in that place. Yet little Tom was not unhappy. He had a hard time of it, but did not know it. It was the sort of time that all the Offal Court boys had, therefore he supposed it was the correct and comfortable thing. When he came home empty handed at night, he knew his father would curse him and thrash him first, and that when he was done the awful grandmother would do it all over again and improve on it; and that away in the night his starving mother would slip to him stealthily with any miserable scrap or crust she had been able to save for him by going hungry herself, notwithstanding she was often caught in that sort of treason and soundly beaten for it by her husband.

No, Tom's life went along well enough, especially in summer. He only begged just enough to save himself, for the laws against mendicancy were stringent, and the penalties heavy; so he put in a good deal of his time listening to good Father Andrew's charming old tales and legends about giants and fairies, dwarfs and genii, and enchanted castles, and gorgeous kings and princes. His head grew to be full of these wonderful things, and many a night as he lay in the dark on his scant and offensive straw, tired, hungry, and smarting from a thrashing, he unleashed his imagination and soon forgot his aches and pains in delicious picturings to himself of the charmed life of a petted prince in a regal palace. One desire came

in time to haunt him day and night: it was to see a real prince, with
his own eyes. He spoke of it once to some of his Offal Court
comrades; but they jeered him and scoffed him so unmercifully
that he was glad to keep his dream to himself after that.

He often read the priest's old books and got him to explain and
enlarge upon them. His dreamings and readings worked certain
changes in him, by and by. His dream-people were so fine that he
grew to lament his shabby clothing and his dirt, and to wish to be
clean and better clad. He went on playing in the mud just the
same, and enjoying it, too; but instead of splashing around in the
Thames solely for the fun of it, he began to find an added value in
it because of the washings and cleansings it afforded.

Tom could always find something going on around the Maypole
in Cheapside, and at the fairs; and now and then he and the rest
of London had a chance to see a military parade when some famous
unfortunate was carried prisoner to the Tower, by land or boat.
One summer's day he saw poor Anne Askew and three men burned
at the stake in Smithfield, and heard an ex-Bishop preach a sermon
to them which did not interest him. Yes, Tom's life was varied and
pleasant enough, on the whole.

By and by Tom's reading and dreaming about princely life
wrought such a strong effect upon him that he began to *act* the
prince, unconsciously. His speech and manners became curiously
ceremonious and courtly, to the vast admiration and amusement
of his intimates. But Tom's influence among these young people
began to grow, now, day by day; and in time he came to be looked
up to, by them, with a sort of wondering awe, as a superior being.
He seemed to know so much! and he could do and say such
marvellous things! and withal, he was so deep and wise! Tom's
remarks, and Tom's performances, were reported by the boys to
their elders; and these, also, presently began to discuss Tom Canty,
and to regard him as a most gifted and extraordinary creature.
Full grown people brought their perplexities to Tom for solution,
and were often astonished at the wit and wisdom of his decisions.
In fact he was become a hero to all who knew him except his own
family—these, only, saw nothing in him.

Privately, after a while, Tom organized a royal court! He was
the prince; his special comrades were guards, chamberlains,
equerries, lords and ladies in waiting, and the royal family. Daily
the mock prince was received with elaborate ceremonials borrowed
by Tom from his romantic readings; daily the great affairs of the
mimic kingdom were discussed in the royal council, and daily his
mimic highness issued decrees to his imaginary armies, navies,
and viceroyalties.

After which, he would go forth in his rags and beg a few
farthings, eat his poor crust, take his customary cuffs and abuse,
and then stretch himself upon his handful of foul straw, and resume

his empty grandeurs in his dreams.

And still his desire to look just once upon a real prince, in the flesh, grew upon him, day by day, and week by week, until at last it absorbed all other desires, and became the one passion of his life.

One January day, on his usual begging tour, he tramped despondently up and down the region round about Mincing Lane and Little East Cheap, hour after hour, bare-footed and cold, looking in at cook-shop windows and longing for the dreadful pork-pies and other deadly inventions displayed there—for to him these were dainties fit for the angels; that is, judging by the smell, they were—for it had never been his good luck to own and eat one. There was a cold drizzle of rain; the atmosphere was murky; it was a melancholy day. At night Tom reached home so wet and tired and hungry that it was not possible for his father and grandmother to observe his forlorn condition and not be moved—after their fashion; wherefore they gave him a brisk cuffing at once and sent him to bed. For a long time his pain and hunger, and the swearing and fighting going on in the building, kept him awake; but at last his thoughts drifted away to far, romantic lands, and he fell asleep in the company of jewelled and gilded princelings who lived in vast palaces, and had servants salaaming before them or flying to execute their orders. And then, as usual, he dreamed that *he* was a princeling himself.

All night long the glories of his royal estate shone upon him; he moved among great lords and ladies, in a blaze of light, breathing perfumes, drinking in delicious music, and answering the reverent obeisances of the glittering throng as it parted to make way for him, with here a smile, and there a nod of his princely head.

And when he awoke in the morning and looked upon the wretchedness about him, his dream had had its usual effect—it had intensified the sordidness of his surroundings a thousand fold. Then came bitterness, and heart-break, and tears.

CHAPTER III

TOM'S MEETING WITH THE PRINCE

Tom got up hungry, and sauntered hungry away, but with his thoughts busy with the shadowy splendors of his night's dreams. He wandered here and there in the city, hardly noticing where he was going, or what was happening around him. People jostled him and some gave him rough speech; but it was all lost on the musing boy. By and by he found himself at Temple Bar, the farthest from home he had ever travelled in that direction. He stopped and considered a moment, then fell into his imaginings again, and passed on outside the walls of London. The Strand had ceased to be a country-road then, and regarded itself as a street, but by a strained construction;

for, though there was a tolerably compact row of houses on one side
of it, there were only some scattering great buildings on the other,
these being palaces of rich nobles, with ample and beautiful grounds
stretching to the river,—grounds that are now closely packed with
grim acres of brick and stone.

Tom discovered Charing Village presently, and rested himself
at the beautiful cross built there by a bereaved king of earlier days;
then idled down a quiet, lovely road, past the great cardinal's
stately palace, toward a far more mighty and majestic palace
beyond,—Westminster. Tom stared in glad wonder at the vast
pile of masonry, the wide-spreading wings, the frowning bastions
and turrets, the huge stone gateway, with its gilded bars and its
magnificent array of colossal granite lions, and the other signs and
symbols of English royalty. Was the desire of his soul to be
satisfied at last? Here, indeed, was a king's palace. Might he not
hope to see a prince now,—a prince of flesh and blood, if Heaven
were willing?

At each side of the gilded gate stood a living statue, that is to say,
an erect and stately and motionless man-at-arms, clad from head
to heel in shining steel armor. At a respectful distance were many
country folk, and people from the city, waiting for any chance
glimpse of royalty that might offer. Splendid carriages, with
splendid people in them and splendid servants outside, were
arriving and departing by several other noble gateways that pierced
the royal enclosure.

Poor little Tom, in his rags, approached, and was moving slowly
and timidly past the sentinels, with a beating heart and a rising
hope, when all at once he caught sight through the golden bars of
a spectacle that almost made him shout for joy. Within was a
comely boy, tanned and brown with sturdy out-door sports and
exercises, whose clothing was all of lovely silks and satins, shining
with jewels; at his hip a little jewelled sword and dagger; dainty
buskins on his feet, with red heels; and on his head a jaunty crimson
cap, with drooping plumes fastened with a great sparkling gem.
Several gorgeous gentlemen stood near,—his servants, without
a doubt. Oh! he was a prince—a prince, a living prince, a real
prince—without the shadow of a question; and the prayer of the
pauper-boy's heart was answered at last.

Tom's breath came quick and short with excitement, and his
eyes grew big with wonder and delight. Every thing gave way in his
mind instantly to one desire: that was to get close to the prince,
and have a good, devouring look at him. Before he knew what he
was about, he had his face against the gate-bars. The next instant
one of the soldiers snatched him rudely away, and sent him spinning
among the gaping crowd of country gawks and London idlers.
The soldier said,—

"Mind thy manners, thou young beggar!"

The crowd jeered and laughed; but the young prince sprang
to the gate with his face flushed, and his eyes flashing with
indignation, and cried out,—

"How dar'st thou use a poor lad like that! How dar'st thou use
the King my father's meanest subject so! Open the gates, and let
him in!"

You should have seen that fickle crowd snatch off their hats then.
You should have heard them cheer, and shout, "Long live the
Prince of Wales!"

The soldiers presented arms with their halberds, opened the
gates, and presented again as the little Prince of Poverty passed in,
in his fluttering rags, to join hands with the Prince of Limitless
Plenty.

Edward Tudor said,—

"Thou lookest tired and hungry: thou'st been treated ill. Come
with me."

Half a dozen attendants sprang forward to—I don't know what;
interfere, no doubt. But they were waved aside with a right royal
gesture, and they stopped stock still where they were, like so many
statues. Edward took Tom to a rich apartment in the palace, which
he called his cabinet. By his command a repast was brought such as
Tom had never encountered before except in books. The prince,
with princely delicacy and breeding, sent away the servants, so that
his humble guest might not be embarrassed by their critical
presence; then he sat near by, and asked questions while Tom ate.

"What is thy name, lad?"

"Tom Canty, an' it please thee, sir."

" 'Tis an odd one. Where dost live?"

"In the city, please thee, sir. Offal Court, out of Pudding Lane."

"Offal Court! Truly 'tis another odd one. Hast parents?"

"Parents have I, sir, and a grand-dam likewise that is but
indifferently precious to me, God forgive me if it be offence to say
it—also twin sisters, Nan and Bet."

"Then is thy grand-dam not over kind to thee, I take it."

"Neither to any other is she, so please your Worship. She hath a
wicked heart, and worketh evil all her days."

"Doth she mistreat thee?"

"There be times that she stayeth her hand, being asleep or
overcome with drink; but when she hath her judgment clear again,
she maketh it up to me with goodly beatings."

A fierce look came into the little prince's eyes, and he cried out,—

"What! Beatings?"

"Oh, indeed, yes, please you, sir."

"*Beatings!*—and thou so frail and little. Hark ye: before the
night come, she shall hie her to the Tower. The King my father"—

"In sooth, you forget, sir, her low degree. The Tower is for the
great alone."

"True, indeed. I had not thought of that. I will consider of her punishment. Is thy father kind to thee?"

"Not more than Gammer Canty, sir."

"Fathers be alike, mayhap. Mine hath not a doll's temper. He smiteth with a heavy hand, yet spareth me: he spareth me not always with his tongue, though, sooth to say. How doth thy mother use thee?"

"She is good, sir, and giveth me neither sorrow nor pain of any sort. And Nan and Bet are like to her in this."

"How old be these?"

"Fifteen, an' it please you, sir."

"The Lady Elizabeth, my sister, is fourteen, and the Lady Jane Grey, my cousin, is of mine own age, and comely and gracious withal; but my sister the Lady Mary, with her gloomy mien and— Look you: do thy sisters forbid their servants to smile, lest the sin destroy their souls?"

"They? Oh, dost think, sir, that *they* have servants?"

The little prince contemplated the little pauper gravely a moment, then said,—

"And prithee, why not? Who helpeth them undress at night? who attireth them when they rise?"

"None, sir. Wouldst have them take off their garment, and sleep without,—like the beasts?"

"Their garment! Have they but one?"

"Ah, good your worship, what would they do with more? Truly they have not two bodies each."

"It is a quaint and marvellous thought! Thy pardon, I had not meant to laugh. But thy good Nan and thy Bet shall have raiment and lackeys enow, and that soon, too: my cofferer shall look to it. No, thank me not; 'tis nothing. Thou speakest well; thou hast an easy grace in it. Art learned?"

"I know not if I am or not, sir. The good priest that is called Father Andrew taught me, of his kindness, from his books."

"Know'st thou the Latin?"

"But scantly, sir, I doubt."

"Learn it, lad: 'tis hard only at first. The Greek is harder; but neither these nor any tongues else, I think, are hard to the Lady Elizabeth and my cousin. Thou shouldst hear those damsels at it! But tell me of thy Offal Court. Hast thou a pleasant life there?"

"In truth, yes, so please you, sir, save when one is hungry. There be Punch-and-Judy shows, and monkeys,—oh, such antic creatures! and so bravely dressed!—and there be plays wherein they that play do shout and fight till all are slain, and 'tis so fine to see, and costeth but a farthing—albeit 'tis main hard to get the farthing, please your worship."

"Tell me more."

"We lads of Offal Court do strive against each other with the cudgel, like to the fashion of the 'prentices, sometimes.''

The prince's eyes flashed. Said he,—

"Marry, that would I not mislike. Tell me more.''

"We strive in races, sir, to see who of us shall be fleetest."

"That would I like also. Speak on."

"In summer, sir, we wade and swim in the canals and in the river, and each doth duck his neighbor, and spatter him with water, and dive and shout and tumble and"—

" 'Twould be worth my father's kingdom but to enjoy it once! Prithee go on."

"We dance and sing about the Maypole in Cheapside; we play in the sand, each covering his neighbor up; and times we make mud pastry—oh, the lovely mud, it hath not its like for delightfulness in all the world!—we do fairly wallow in the mud, sir, saving your worship's presence."

"Oh, prithee, say no more, 'tis glorious! If that I could but clothe me in raiment like to thine, and strip my feet, and revel in the mud once, just once, with none to rebuke me or forbid, meseemeth I could forego the crown!"

"And if that I could clothe me once, sweet sir, as thou art clad— just once"—

"Oho, wouldst like it? Then so shall it be. Doff thy rags, and don these splendors, lad! It is a brief happiness, but will be not less keen for that. We will have it while we may, and change again before any come to molest."

A few minutes later the little Prince of Wales was garlanded with Tom's fluttering odds and ends, and the little Prince of Pauperdom was tricked out in the gaudy plumage of royalty. The two went and stood side by side before a great mirror, and lo, a miracle: there did not seem to have been any change made! They stared at each other, then at the glass, then at each other again. At last the puzzled princeling said,—

"What dost thou make of this?"

"Ah, good your worship, require me not to answer. It is not meet that one of my degree should utter the thing."

"Then will I utter it. Thou hast the same hair, the same eyes, the same voice and manner, the same form and stature, the same face and countenance, that I bear. Fared we forth naked, there is none could say which was you, and which the Prince of Wales. And, now that I am clothed as thou wert clothed, it seemeth I should be able the more nearly to feel as thou didst when the brute soldier— Hark ye, is not this a bruise upon your hand?"

"Yes; but it is a slight thing, and your worship knoweth that the poor man-at-arms"—

"Peace! It was a shameful thing and a cruel!" cried the little prince, stamping his bare foot. "If the King—Stir not a step till I come again! It is a command!"

In a moment he had snatched up and put away an article of
national importance that lay upon a table, and was out at the door
and flying through the palace grounds in his bannered rags, with a
hotface and glowing eyes. As soon as he reached the great gate, he
seized the bars, and tried to shake them, shouting,—

"Open! Unbar the gates!"

The soldier that had maltreated Tom obeyed promptly; and as
the prince burst through the portal, half-smothered with royal
wrath, the soldier fetched him a sounding box on the ear that sent
him whirling to the roadway, and said,—

"Take that, thou beggar's spawn, for what thou got'st me from
his Highness!"

The crowd roared with laughter. The prince picked himself out
of the mud, and made fiercely at the sentry, shouting,—

"I am the Prince of Wales, my person is sacred; and thou shalt
hang for laying thy hand upon me!"

The soldier brought his halberd to a present-arms and said
mockingly,—

"I salute your gracious Highness." Then angrily, "Be off, thou
crazy rubbish!"

Here the jeering crowd closed around the poor little prince, and
hustled him far down the road, hooting him, and shouting, "Way
for his royal Highness! way for the Prince of Wales!"

CHAPTER IV

THE PRINCE'S TROUBLES BEGIN

After hours of persistent pursuit and persecution, the little prince
was at last deserted by the rabble and left to himself. As long as he
had been able to rage against the mob, and threaten it royally, and
royally utter commands that were good stuff to laugh at, he was
very entertaining; but when weariness finally forced him to be silent,
he was no longer of use to his tormentors, and they sought
amusement elsewhere. He looked about him, now, but could not
recognize the locality. He was with the city of London—that was
all he knew. He moved on, aimlessly, and in a little while the houses
thinned, and the passers-by were infrequent. He bathed his bleeding
feet in the brook which flowed then where Farringdon Street now is;
rested a few moments, then passed on, and presently came upon a
great space with only a few scattered houses in it, and a prodigious
church. He recognized this church. Scaffoldings were about,
everywhere, and swarms of workmen; for it was undergoing
elaborate repairs. The prince took heart at once—he felt that his
troubles were at an end, now. He said to himself, "It is the ancient
Grey Friars' church, which the king my father hath taken from the
monks and given for a home forever for poor and forsaken children,

and new-named it Christ's Church. Right gladly will they serve the
son of him who hath done so generously by them—and the more
that that son is himself as poor and as forlorn as any that be
sheltered here this day, or ever shall be."

He was soon in the midst of a crowd of boys who were running,
jumping, playing at ball and leap-frog and otherwise disporting
themselves, and right noisily, too. They were all dressed alike, and
in the fashion which in that day prevailed among serving-men and
'prentices*—that is to say, each had on the crown of his head a flat
black cap about the size of a saucer, which was not useful as a
covering, it being of such scanty dimensions, neither was it
ornamental; from beneath it the hair fell, unparted, to the middle
of the forehead, and was cropped straight around; a clerical band
at the neck; a blue gown that fitted closely and hung as low as the
knees or lower; full sleeves, a broad red belt; bright yellow stockings,
gartered above the knees; low shoes with large metal buckles. It
was a sufficiently ugly costume.

The boys stopped their play and flocked about the prince, who
said with native dignity—

"Good lads, say to your master that Edward Prince of Wales
desireth speech with him."

A great shout went up, at this, and one rude fellow said—

"Marry, art thou his grace's messenger, beggar?"

The prince's face flushed with anger, and his ready hand flew to
his hip, but there was nothing there. There was a storm of laughter,
and one boy said—

"Didst mark that? He fancied he had a sword—belike he is the
prince himself."

This sally brought more laughter. Poor Edward drew himself up
proudly and said—

"I am the prince; and it ill beseemeth you that feed upon the
king my father's bounty to use me so."

This was vastly enjoyed, as the laughter testified. The youth who
had first spoken, shouted to his comrades—

"Ho, swine, slaves, pensioners of his grace's princely father,
where be your manners? Down on your marrow bones, all of ye,
and do reverence to his kingly port and royal rags!"

With boisterous mirth they dropped upon their knees in a body
and did mock homage to their prey. The prince spurned the nearest
boy with his foot, and said fiercely—

"Take thou that, till the morrow come and I build thee a gibbet!"

Ah, but this was not a joke—this was going beyond fun. The
laughter ceased on the instant, and fury took its place. A dozen
shouted—

"Hale him forth! To the horse-pond, to the horse-pond! Where
be the dogs? Ho, there, Lion! ho, Fangs!"

Then followed such a thing as England had never seen before—

*See Note 1, at end of the volume.

the sacred person of the heir to the throne rudely buffeted by
plebeian hands, and set upon and torn by dogs.

As night drew to a close that day, the prince found himself far
down in the close-built portion of the city. His body was bruised, his
hands were bleeding, and his rags were all besmirched with mud.
He wandered on and on, and grew more and more bewildered, and
so tired and faint he could hardly drag one foot after the other. He
had ceased to ask questions of any one, since they brought him only
insult instead of information. He kept muttering to himself, "Offal
Court—that is the name; if I can but find it before my strength is
wholly spent and I drop, then am I saved—for his people will take
me to the palace and prove that I am none of theirs, but the true
prince, and I shall have mine own again." And now and then his
mind reverted to his treatment by those rude Christ's Hospital boys,
and he said, "When I am king, they shall not have bread and
shelter only, but also teachings out of books; for a full belly is little
worth where the mind is starved, and the heart. I will keep this
diligently in my remembrance, that this day's lesson be not lost
upon me, and my people suffer thereby; for learning softeneth the
heart and breedeth gentleness and charity."*

The lights began to twinkle, it came on to rain, the wind rose,
and a raw and gusty night set in. The houseless prince, the homeless
heir to the throne of England, still moved on, drifting deeper into the
maze of squalid alleys where the swarming hives of poverty and
misery were massed together.

Suddenly a great drunken ruffian collared him and said—

"Out to this time of night again, and hast not brought a farthing
home, I warrant me! If it be so, an' I do not break all the bones
in thy lean body, then am I not John Canty, but some other."

The prince twisted himself loose, unconsciously brushed his
profaned shoulder, and eagerly said—

"O, art *his* father, truly? Sweet heaven grant it be so—then wilt
thou fetch him away and restore me!"

"*His* father? I know not what thou mean'st; I but know I am *thy*
father, as thou shalt soon have cause to"—

"O, jest not, palter not, delay not!—I am worn, I am wounded, I
can bear no more. Take me to the king my father, and he will make
thee rich beyond thy wildest dreams. Believe me, man, believe me!—
I speak no lie, but only the truth!—put forth thy hand and save me!
I am indeed the Prince of Wales!"

The man stared down, stupefied, upon the lad, then shook his
head and muttered—

"Gone stark mad as any Tom o' Bedlam!"—then collared him
once more, and said with a coarse laugh and an oath, "But mad or
no mad, I and thy Gammer Canty will soon find where the soft
places in thy bones lie, or I'm no true man!"

With this he dragged the frantic and struggling prince away, and

*See Note 2, at end of the volume.

disappeared up a front court followed by a delighted and noisy swarm of human vermin.

CHAPTER V

TOM AS A PATRICIAN

Tom Canty, left alone in the prince's cabinet, made good use of his opportunity. He turned himself this way and that before the great mirror, admiring his finery; then walked away, imitating the prince's high-bred carriage, and still observing results in the glass. Next he drew the beautiful sword, and bowed, kissing the blade, and laying it across his breast, as he had seen a noble knight do, by way of salute to the lieutenant of the Tower, five or six weeks before, when delivering the great lords of Norfolk and Surrey into his hands for captivity. Tom played with the jewelled dagger that hung upon his thigh; he examined the costly and exquisite ornaments of the room; he tried each of the sumptuous chairs, and thought how proud he would be if the Offal Court herd could only peep in and see him in his grandeur. He wondered if they would believe the marvellous tale he should tell when he got home, or if they would shake their heads, and say his overtaxed imagination had at last upset his reason.

At the end of half an hour it suddenly occurred to him that the prince was gone a long time; then right away he began to feel lonely; very soon he fell to listening and longing, and ceased to toy with the pretty things about him; he grew uneasy, then restless, then distressed. Suppose some one should come, and catch him in the prince's clothes, and the prince not there to explain. Might they not hang him at once, and inquire into his case afterward? He had heard that the great were prompt about small matters. His fears rose higher and higher; and trembling he softly opened the door to the antechamber, resolved to fly and seek the prince, and, through him, protection and release. Six gorgeous gentlemen-servants and two young pages of high degree, clothed like butterflies, sprung to their feet, and bowed low before him. He stepped quickly back, and shut the door. He said,—

"Oh, they mock at me! They will go and tell. Oh! why came I here to cast away my life?"

He walked up and down the floor, filled with nameless fears, listening, starting at every trifling sound. Presently the door swung open, and a silken page said,—

"The Lady Jane Grey."

The door closed, and a sweet young girl, richly clad, bounded towards him. But she stopped suddenly, and said in a distressed voice,—

"Oh, what aileth thee, my lord?"

Tom's breath was nearly failing him; but he made shift to
stammer out,—

"Ah, be merciful, thou! In sooth I am no lord, but only poor Tom
Canty of Offal Court in the city. Prithee let me see the prince, and
he will of his grace restore to me my rags, and let me hence unhurt.
Oh, be thou merciful, and save me!"

By this time the boy was on his knees, and supplicating with his
eyes and uplifted hands as well as with his tongue. The young girl
seemed horror-stricken. She cried out—

"O my lord, on thy knees?—and to *me!*"

Then she fled away in fright; and Tom, smitten with despair,
sank down, murmuring—

"There is no help, there is no hope. Now will they come and
take me."

Whilst he lay there benumbed with terror, dreadful tidings were
speeding through the palace. The whisper, for it was whispered
always, flew from menial to menial, from lord to lady, down all the
long corridors, from story to story, from saloon to saloon, "The
prince hath gone mad, the prince hath gone mad!" Soon every
saloon, every marble hall, had its groups of glittering lords and
ladies, and other groups of dazzling lesser folk, talking earnestly
together in whispers, and every face had in it dismay. Presently a
splendid official came marching by these groups, making solemn
proclamation,—

"In the Name of the King.

Let none list to his false and foolish matter, upon pain of death,
nor discuss the same, nor carry it abroad. In the name of the King!"

The whisperings ceased as suddenly as if the whisperers had been
stricken dumb.

Soon there was a general buzz along the corridors, of "The prince!
See, the prince comes!"

Poor Tom came slowly walking past the low-bowing groups, trying
to bow in return, and meekly gazing upon his strange surroundings
with bewildered and pathetic eyes. Great nobles walked upon each
side of him, making him lean upon them, and so steady his steps.
Behind him followed the court-physicians and some servants.

Presently Tom found himself in a noble apartment of the
palace, and heard the door close behind him. Around him stood
those who had come with him.

Before him, at a little distance, reclined a very large and very fat
man, with a wide, pulpy face, and a stern expression. His large
head was very gray; and his whiskers, which he wore only around
his face, like a frame, were gray also. His clothing was of rich stuff
but old, and slightly frayed in places. One of his swollen legs had a
pillow under it, and was wrapped in bandages. There was silence

now; and there was no head there but was bent in reverence, except this man's. This stern-countenanced invalid was the dread Henry VIII. He said,—and his face grew gentle as he began to speak,—

"How now, my lord Edward, my prince? Hast been minded to cozen me, the good King thy father, who loveth thee, and kindly useth thee, with a sorry jest?"

Poor Tom was listening, as well as his dazed faculties would let him, to the beginning of this speech; but when the words "me the good King" fell upon his ear, his face blanched, and he dropped as instantly upon his knees as if a shot had brought him there. Lifting up his hands, he exclaimed,—

"Thou the *King?* Then am I undone indeed!"

This speech seemed to stun the King. His eyes wandered from face to face aimlessly, then rested, bewildered, upon the boy before him. Then he said in a tone of deep disappointment,—

"Alack, I had believed the rumor disproportioned to the truth; but I fear me 'tis not so." He breathed a heavy sigh, and said in a gentle voice, "Come to thy father, child: thou art not well."

Tom was assisted to his feet, and approached the Majesty of England, humble and trembling. The King took the frightened face between his hands, and gazed earnestly and lovingly into it awhile, as if seeking some grateful sign of returning reason there, then pressed the curly head against his breast, and patted it tenderly. Presently he said,—

"Dost thou know thy father, child? Break not mine old heart; say thou know'st me. Thou *dost* know me, dost thou not?"

"Yea: thou art my dread lord the King, whom God preserve!"

"True, true—that is well—be comforted, tremble not so; there is none here who would hurt thee; there is none here but loves thee. Thou art better now; thy ill dream passeth—is't not so? And thou knowest thyself now also—is't not so? Thou wilt not miscall thyself again, as they say thou didst a little while agone?"

"I pray thee of thy grace believe me, I did but speak the truth, most dread lord; for I am the meanest among thy subjects, being a pauper born, and 'tis by a sore mischance and accident I am here, albeit I was therein nothing blameful. I am but young to die, and thou canst save me with one little word. Oh speak it, sir!"

"Die? Talk not so, sweet prince—peace, peace, to thy troubled heart—thou shalt not die!"

Tom dropped upon his knees with a glad cry,—

"God requite thy mercy, oh my King, and save thee long to bless thy land!" Then springing up, he turned a joyful face toward the two lords in waiting, and exclaimed, "Thou heard'st it! I am not to die: the King hath said it!" There was no movement, save that all bowed with grave respect; but no one spoke. He hesitated, a little confused, then turned timidly toward the King, saying, "I may go now?"

"Go? Surely, if thou desirest. But why not tarry yet a little? Whither wouldst go?"

Tom dropped his eyes, and answered humbly,—

"Peradventure I mistook; but I did think me free, and so was I moved to seek again the kennel where I was born and bred to misery, yet which harboreth my mother and my sisters, and so is home to me; whereas these pomps and splendors where unto I am not used— oh, please you, sir, to let me go!"

The King was silent and thoughtful a while, and his face betrayed a growing distress and uneasiness. Presently he said, with something of hope in his voice,—

"Perchance he is but mad upon this one strain, and hath his wits unmarred as toucheth other matter. God send it may be so! We will make trial."

Then he asked Tom a question in Latin, and Tom answered him lamely in the same tongue. The King was delighted, and showed it. The lords and doctors manifested their gratification also. The King said,—

" 'Twas not according to his schooling and ability, but sheweth that his mind is but diseased, not stricken fatally. How say you, sir?"

The physician addressed bowed low, and replied,—

"It jumpeth with mine own conviction, sir, that thou hast divined aright."

The King looked pleased with this encouragement, coming as it did from so excellent authority, and continued with good heart,—

"Now mark ye all: we will try him further."

He put a question to Tom in French. Tom stood silent a moment, embarrassed by having so many eyes centred upon him, then said diffidently,—

"I have no knowledge of this tongue, so please your majesty."

The king fell back upon his couch. The attendants flew to his assistance; but he put them aside, and said,—

"Trouble me not— it is nothing but a scurvy faintness. Raise me! there, 'tis sufficient. Come hither, child; there, rest thy poor troubled head upon thy father's heart, and be at peace. Thou'lt soon be well; 'tis but a passing fantasy. Fear thou not; thou'lt soon be well."

Then he turned toward the company: his gentle manner changed, and baleful lightnings began to play from his eyes. He said,—

"List ye all! This my son is mad; but it is not permanent. Over-study hath done this, and somewhat too much of confinement. Away with his books and teachers! see ye to it. Pleasure him with sports, beguile him in wholesome ways, so that his health come again." He raised himself higher still, and went on with energy.

He raised himself higher still, and went on with energy.

"He is mad; but he is my son, and England's heir; and, mad or sane, still shall he reign! And hear ye further, and proclaim it: whoso speaketh of this his distemper worketh against the peace and order

of these realms, and shall to the gallows!... Give me to drink—I
burn: This sorrow sappeth my strength.... There, take away the
cup.... Support me. There, that is well. Mad, is he? Were he a
thousand times mad, yet is he Prince of Wales, and I the King will
confirm it. This very morrow shall he be installed in his princely
dignity in due and ancient form. Take instant order for it, my lord
Hertford."

"The King's majesty knoweth that the Hereditary Great Marshal
of England lieth attainted in the Tower. It were not meet that one
attainted"—

"Peace! Insult not mine ears with his hated name. Is this man
to live forever? Am I to be balked of my will? Is the prince to tarry
uninstalled, because, forsooth, the realm lacketh an earl marshal
free of treasonable taint to invest him with his honors? No, by the
splendor of God! Warn my parliament to bring me Norfolk's doom
before the sun rise again, else shall they answer for it grievously!"*

Lord Hertford said,—

"The King's will is law;" and, rising, returned to his former
place.

Gradually the wrath faded out of the old King's face, and he
said,—

"Kiss me, my prince. There ... what fearest thou? Am I not thy
loving father?"

"Thou art good to me that am unworthy, O mighty and gracious
lord: that in truth I know. But—but—it grieveth me to think of
him that is to die, and"—

"Ah, 'tis like thee, 'tis like thee! I know thy heart is still the same,
even though thy mind hath suffered hurt, for thou wert ever of a
gentle spirit. But this duke standeth between thee and thine honors:
I will have another in his stead that shall bring no taint to his great
office. Comfort thee, my prince: trouble not thy poor head with this
matter."

"But is it not I that speed him hence, my liege? How long might
he not live, but for me?"

"Take no thought of him, my prince: he is not worthy. Kiss me
once again, and go to thy trifles and amusements; for my malady
distresseth me. I am aweary, and would rest. Go with thine uncle
Hertford and thy people, and come again when my body is
refreshed."

Tom, heavy-hearted, was conducted from the presence, for this
last sentence was a death-blow to the hope he had cherished that
now he would be set free. Once more he heard the buzz of low voices
exclaiming, "The prince, the prince comes!"

His spirits sank lower and lower as he moved between the
glittering files of bowing courtiers; for he recognized that he was
indeed a captive now, and might remain forever shut up in this
gilded cage, a forlorn and friendless prince, except God in his

*See Note 3, at end of the volume.

mercy take pity on him and set him free.

And, turn where he would, he seemed to see floating in the air the severed head and the remembered face of the great Duke of Norfolk, the eyes fixed on him reproachfully.

His old dreams had been so pleasant; but this reality was so dreary!

CHAPTER VI

TOM RECEIVES INSTRUCTIONS

Tom was conducted to the principal apartment of a noble suite, and made to sit down—a thing which he was loath to do, since there were elderly men and men of high degree about him. He begged them to be seated, also, but they only bowed their thanks or murmured them, and remained standing. He would have insisted, but his "uncle" the earl of Hertford whispered in his ear—

"Prithee, insist not, my lord; it is not meet that they sit in thy presence."

The lord St. John was announced, and after making obeisance to Tom, he said—

"I come upon the king's errand, concerning a matter which requireth privacy. Will it please your royal highness to dismiss all that attend you here, save my lord the earl of Hertford?"

Observing that Tom did not seem to know how to proceed, Hertford whispered him to make a sign with his hand and not trouble himself to speak unless he chose. When the waiting gentlemen had retired, lord St. John said—

"His majesty commandeth, that for due and weighty reasons of state, the prince's grace shall hide his infirmity in all ways that be within his power, till it be passed and he be as he was before. To wit, that he shall deny to none that he is the true prince, and heir to England's greatness; that he shall uphold his princely dignity, and shall receive, without word or sign of protest, that reverence and observance which unto it do appertain of right and ancient usage; that he shall cease to speak to any of that lowly birth and life his malady hath conjured out of the unwholesome imaginings of o'erwrought fancy; that he shall strive with diligence to bring unto his memory again those faces which he was wont to know—and where he faileth he shall hold his peace, neither betraying by semblance of surprise, or other sign, that he hath forgot; that upon occasions of state, whensoever any matter shall perplex him as to the thing he should do or the utterance he should make, he shall show nought of unrest to the curious that look on, but take advice in that matter of the lord Hertford, or my humble self, which are commanded of the king to be upon this service and close at call, till this commandment be dissolved. Thus saith the king's majesty,.

who sendeth greeting to your royal highness and prayeth that God will of His mercy quickly heal you and have you now and ever in his holy keeping."

The lord St. John made reverence and stood aside. Tom replied, resignedly—

"The king hath said it. None may palter with the king's command, or fit it to his ease, where it doth chafe, with deft evasions. The king shall be obeyed."

Lord Hertford said—

"Touching the king's majesty's ordainment concerning books and such like serious matters, it may peradventure please your highness to ease your time with lightsome entertainment, lest you go wearied to the banquet and suffer harm thereby."

Tom's face showed enquiring surprise; and a blush followed when he saw lord St. John's eyes bent sorrowfully upon him. His lordship said—

"Thy memory still wrongeth thee, and thou hast shown surprise— but suffer it not to trouble thee, for 'tis a matter that will not bide, but depart with thy mending malady. My lord of Hertford speaketh of the city's banquet which the king's majesty did promise two months flown, your highness should attend. Thou recallest it now?"

"It grieves me to confess it had indeed escaped me," said Tom, in a hesitating voice; and blushed again.

At that moment the lady Elizabeth and the lady Jane Grey were announced. The two lords exchanged significant glances, and Hertford stepped quickly toward the door. As the young girls passed him, he said in a low voice—

"I pray ye, ladies, seem not to observe his humors, nor show surprise when his memory doth lapse—it will grieve you to note how it doth stick at every trifle."

Meanwhile lord St. John was saying in Tom's ear—

"Please you sir, keep diligently in mind his majesty's desire. Remember all thou canst—*Seem* to remember all else. Let them not perceive that thou art much changed from thy wont, for thou knowest how tenderly thy old play-fellows bear thee in their hearts and how 'twould grieve them. Art willing, sir, that I remain?— and thine uncle?"

Tom signified assent with a gesture and a murmured word, for he was already learning, and in his simple heart was resolved to acquit himself as best he might, according to the king's command.

In spite of every precaution, the conversation among the young people became a little embarrassing, at times. More than once, in truth, Tom was near to breaking down and confessing himself unequal to his tremendous part; but the tact of the princess Elizabeth saved him, or a word from one or the other of the vigilant lords, thrown in apparently by chance, had the same happy effect. Once the little lady Jane turned to Tom and dismayed him with this question—

"Hast paid thy duty to the queen's majesty today, my lord?"

Tom hesitated, looked distressed, and was about to stammer out something at hazard, when lord St. John took the word and answered for him with the easy grace of a courtier accustomed to encounter delicate difficulties and to be ready for them—

"He hath indeed, madam, and she did greatly hearten him, as touching his majesty's condition; is it not so, your highness?"

Tom mumbled something that stood for assent, but felt that he was getting upon dangerous ground. Somewhat later it was mentioned that Tom was to study no more at present, whereupon her little ladyship exclaimed—

" 'Tis a pity, 'tis such a pity! Thou wert proceeding bravely. But bide thy time in patience; it will not be for long. Thou'lt yet be graced with learning like thy father, and make thy tongue master of as many languages as his, good my prince."

"My father!" cried Tom, off his guard for the moment. "I trow he cannot speak his own so that any but the swine that wallow in the styes may tell his meaning; and as for learning of any sort so-ever"—

He looked up and encountered a solemn warning in my lord St. John's eyes.

He stopped, blushed, then continued low and sadly: "Ah, my malady persecuteth me again, and my mind wandereth. I meant the king's grace no irreverence."

"We know it, sir," said the princess Elizabeth, taking her "brother's" hand between her two palms, respectfully but caressingly; "trouble not thyself as to that. The fault is none of thine, but thy distemper's."

"Thou'rt a gentle comforter, sweet lady," said Tom, gratefully, "and my heart moveth me to thank thee for't, an' I may be so bold."

Once the giddy little lady Jane fired a simple Greek phrase at Tom. The princess Elizabeth's quick eye saw by the serene blankness of the target's front that the shaft was overshot; so she tranquilly delivered a return volley of sounding Greek on Tom's behalf, and then straightway changed the talk to other matters.

Time wore on pleasantly, and likewise smoothly, on the whole. Snags and sandbars grew less and less frequent, and Tom grew more and more at his ease, seeing that all were so lovingly bent upon helping him and overlooking his mistakes. When it came out that the little ladies were to accompany him to the Lord Mayor's banquet in the evening, his heart gave a bound of relief and delight, for he felt that he should not be friendless, now, among that multitude of strangers, whereas, an hour earlier, the idea of their going with him would have been an insupportable terror to him.

Tom's guardian angels, the two lords, had had less comfort in the interview than the other parties to it. They felt much as if they were piloting a great ship through a dangerous channel; they were on the

alert constantly, and found their office no child's play. Wherefore,
at last, when the ladies' visit was drawing to a close and the lord
Guilford Dudley was announced, they not only felt that their charge
had been sufficiently taxed for the present, but also that they
themselves were not in the best condition to take their ship back and
make their anxious voyage all over again. So they respectfully
advised Tom to excuse himself, which he was very glad to do,
although a slight shade of disappointment might have been observed
upon my lady Jane's face when she heard the splendid stripling
denied admittance.

There was a pause, now, a sort of waiting silence which Tom could
not understand. He glanced at lord Hertford, who gave him a sign—
but he failed to understand that, also. The ready Elizabeth came to
the rescue with her usual easy grace. She made reverence and said,—

"Have we leave of the prince's grace my brother to go?"

Tom said—

"Indeed your ladyships can have whatsoever of me they will, for
the asking; yet would I rather give them any other thing that in my
poor power lieth, than leave to take the light and blessing of their
presence hence. Give ye good den, and God be with ye!" Then he
smiled inwardly at the thought, " 'tis not for nought I have dwelt
but among princes in my reading, and taught my tongue some
slight trick of their broidered and gracious speech withal!"

When the illustrious maidens were gone, Tom turned wearily to
his keepers and said—

"May it please your lordships to grant me leave to go into some
corner and rest me!"

Lord Hertford said—

"So please your highness, it is for you to command, it is for us to
obey. That thou shouldst rest, is indeed a needful thing, since thou
must journey to the city presently."

He touched a bell, and a page appeared, who was ordered to
desire the presence of Sir William Herbert. This gentleman came
straightway, and conducted Tom to an inner apartment. Tom's
first movement, there, was to reach for a cup of water; but a
silk-and-velvet servitor seized it, dropped upon one knee, and
offered it to him on a golden salver.

Next, the tired captive sat down and was going to take off his
bushkins, timidly asking leave with his eye, but another silk-
and-velvet discomforter went down upon his knees and took the
office from him. He made two or three further efforts to help
himself, but being promptly forestalled each time, he finally gave
up, with a sigh of resignation and a murmured "Beshrew me but I
marvel they do not require to breathe for me also!" Slippered, and
wrapped in a sumptuous robe, he laid himself down at last to rest,
but not to sleep, for his head was too full of thoughts and the room
too full of people. He could not dismiss the former, so they staid;

he did not know enough to dismiss the latter, so they staid also, to his vast regret,—and theirs.

Tom's departure had left his two noble guardians alone. They mused a while, with much headshaking and walking the floor, then lord St. John said—

"Plainly, what dost thou think?"

"Plainly, then, this. The king is near his end, my nephew is mad, mad will mount the throne, and mad remain. God protect England, since she will need it!"

"Verily it promiseth so, indeed. But . . . have you no misgivings as to . . . as to" . . .

The speaker hesitated, and finally stopped. He evidently felt that he was upon delicate ground. Lord Hertford stopped before him, looked into his face with a clear, frank eye, and said—

"Speak on—there is none to hear but me. Misgivings as to what?"

"I am full loath to word the thing that is in my mind, and thou so near to him in blood, my lord. But craving pardon if I do offend, seemeth it not strange that madness could so change his port and manner!—not but that his port and speech are princely still, but that they *differ* in one unweighty trifle or another, from what his custom was aforetime. Seemeth it not strange that madness should filch from his memory his father's very lineaments; the customs and observances that are his due from such as be about him; and, leaving him his Latin, strip him of his Greek and French? My lord, be not offended, but ease my mind of its disquiet and receive my grateful thanks. It haunteth me, his saying he was not the prince, and so"—

"Peace, my lord, thou utterest treason! Hast forgot the king's command? Remember I am party to thy crime, if I but listen."

St. John paled, and hastened to say—

"I was in fault, I do confess it. Betray me not, grant me this grace out of thy courtesy, and I will neither think nor speak of this thing more. Deal not hardly with me, sir, else am I ruined."

"I am content, my lord. So thou offend not again, here or in the ears of others, it shall be as though thou hadst not spoken. But thou needst not have misgivings. He is my sister's son; are not his voice, his face, his form, familiar to me from his cradle? Madness can do all the odd conflicting things thou seest in him, and more. Dost not recall how that the old Baron Marley, being mad, forgot the favor of his own countenance that he had known for sixty years, and held it was another's; nay, even claimed he was the son of Mary Magdalene, and that his head was made of Spanish glass; and sooth to say, he suffered none to touch it, lest by mischance some heedless hand might shiver it. Give thy misgivings easement, good my lord. This is the very prince, I know him well—and soon will be thy king; it may advantage thee to bear this in mind and more dwell upon it than the other."

After some further talk, in which the lord St. John covered up his mistake as well as he could by repeated protests that his faith was thoroughly grounded, now, and could not be assailed by doubts again, the lord Hertford relieved his fellow keeper, and sat down to keep watch and ward alone. He was soon deep in meditation. And evidently the longer he thought, the more he was bothered. By and by he began to pace the floor and mutter.

"Tush, he *must* be the prince! Will any he in all the land maintain there can be two, not of one blood and birth, so marvellously twinned? And even were it so, 'twere yet a stranger miracle that chance should cast the one into the other's place. Nay, 'tis folly, folly, folly!"

Presently he said—

"Now were he impostor and called himself prince, look you *that* would be natural; that would be reasonable. But lived ever an impostor yet, who, being called prince by the king, prince by the court, prince by all, *denied* his dignity and pleaded against his exaltation? *No!* By the soul of St. Swithin, no! This is the true prince, gone mad!"

CHAPTER VII

TOM'S FIRST ROYAL DINNER

Somewhat after one in the afternoon, Tom resignedly underwent the ordeal of being dressed for dinner. He found himself as finely clothed as before, but every thing different, every thing changed, from his ruff to his stockings. He was presently conducted with much state to a spacious and ornate apartment, where a table was already set for one. Its furniture was all of massy gold, and beautifued with designs which well-nigh made it priceless, since they were the work of Benvenuto. The room was half filled with noble servitors. A chaplain said grace, and Tom was about to fall to, for hunger had long been constitutional with him, but was interrupted by my lord the Earl of Berkeley, who fastened a napkin about his neck; for the great post of Diaperers to the Princes of Wales was hereditary in this nobleman's family. Tom's cupbearer was present, and forestalled all his attempts to help himself to wine. The Taster to his highness the Prince of Wales was there also, prepared to taste any suspicious dish upon requirement, and run the risk of being poisoned.

He was only an ornamental appendage at this time, and was seldom called to exercise his function; but there had been times, not many generations past, when the office of taster had its perils, and was not a grandeur to be desired. Why they did not use a dog or a plumber seems strange; but all the ways of royalty are strange. My lord d'Arcy, First Groom of the Chamber, was there, to do goodness knows what; but there he was—let that suffice. The Lord Chief

Butler was there, and stood behind Tom's chair, overseeing the
solemnities, under command of the Lord Great Steward and the
Lord Head Cook, who stood near. Tom had three hundred and
eighty-four servants beside these; but they were not all in that room,
of course, nor the quarter of them; neither was Tom aware yet that
they existed.

All those that were present had been well drilled within the
hour to remember that the prince was temporarily out of his head,
and to be careful to show no surprise at his vagaries. These
"vagaries" were soon on exhibition before them; but they only
moved their compassion and their sorrow, not their mirth. It was a
heavy affliction to them to see the beloved prince so stricken.

Poor Tom ate with his fingers mainly; but no one smiled at it, or
even seemed to observe it. He inspected his napkin curiously, and
with deep interest, for it was of a very dainty and beautiful fabric,
then said with simplicity,—

"Prithee take it away, lest in mine unheedfulness it be soiled."

The Hereditary Diaperer took it away with reverent manner, and
without word or protest of any sort.

Tom examined the turnips and the lettuce with interest, and
asked what they were, and if they were to be eaten; for it was only
recently that men had begun to raise these things in England in
place of importing them as luxuries from Holland.* His question
was answered with grave respect, and no surprise manifested. When
he had finished his dessert, he filled his pockets with nuts; but
nobody appeared to be aware of it, or disturbed by it. But the next
moment he was himself disturbed by it, and showed discomposure;
for this was the only service he had been permitted to do with his
own hands during the meal, and he did not doubt that he had done
a most improper and unprincely thing. At that moment the muscles
of his nose began to twitch, and the end of that organ to lift and
wrinkle. This continued, and Tom began to evince a growing
distress. He looked appealingly, first at one and then another of the
lords about him, and tears came into his eyes. They sprang forward
with dismay in their faces, and begged to know his trouble. Tom
said with genuine anguish,—

"I crave your indulgence: my nose itcheth cruelly. What is the
custom and usage in this emergence? Prithee speed, for 'tis but a
little time that I can bear it."

None smiled; but all were sore perplexed, and looked one to the
other in deep tribulation for counsel. But behold, here was a dead
wall, and nothing in English history to tell how to get over it.
The Master of Ceremonies was not present: there was no one who
felt safe to venture upon this uncharted sea, or risk the attempt to
solve this solemn problem. Alas! there was no Hereditary Scratcher.
Meantime the tears had overflowed their banks, and begun to
trickle down Tom's cheeks. His twitching nose was pleading more

*See Note 4, at end of volume.

urgently than ever for relief. At last nature broke down the barriers of etiquette: Tom lifted up an inward prayer for pardon if he was doing wrong, and brought relief to the burdened hearts of his court by scratching his nose himself.

His meal being ended, a lord came and held before him a broad, shallow, golden dish with fragrant rose-water in it, to cleanse his mouth and fingers with; and my lord the Hereditary Diaperer stood a napkin for his use. Tom gazed at the dish a puzzled moment or two, then raised it to his lips, and gravely took a draught. Then he returned it to the waiting lord, and said,—

"Nay, it likes me not, my lord: it hath a pretty flavor, but it wanteth strength."

This new eccentricity of the prince's ruined mind made all the hearts about him ache; but the sad sight moved none to merriment.

Tom's next unconscious blunder was to get up and leave the table just when the chaplain had taken his stand behind his chair and with uplifted hands, and closed, uplifted eyes, was in the act of beginning the blessing. Still nobody seemed to perceive that the prince had done a thing unusual.

By his own request, our small friend was now conducted to his private cabinet, and left there alone to his own devices. Hanging upon hooks in the oaken wainscoting were the several pieces of a suit of shining steel armor, covered all over with beautiful designs exquisitely inlaid in gold. This martial panoply belonged to the true prince,—a recent present from Madam Parr the Queen. Tom put on the greaves, the gauntlets, the plumed helmet, and such other pieces as he could don without assistance, and for a while was minded to call for help and complete the matter, but bethought him of the nuts he had brought away from dinner, and the joy it would be to eat them with no crowd to eye him, and no Grand Hereditaries to pester him with undesired services; so he restored the pretty things to their several places, and soon was cracking nuts, and feeling almost naturally happy for the first time since God for his sins had made him a prince. When the nuts were all gone, he stumbled upon some inviting books in a closet, among them one about the etiquette of the English court. This was a prize. He lay down upon a sumptuous divan, and proceeded to instruct himself with honest zeal. Let us leave him there for the present.

CHAPTER VIII

THE QUESTION OF THE SEAL

About five o'clock Henry VIII. awoke out of an unrefreshing nap, and muttered to himself, "Troublous dreams, troublous dreams! Mine end is now at hand: so say these warnings, and my failing pulses do confirm it." Presently a wicked light flamed up in his eye, and he muttered, "Yet will not I die till *he* go before."

His attendants perceiving that he was awake, one of them asked his pleasure concerning the Lord Chancellor, who was waiting without.

"Admit him, admit him!" exclaimed the King eagerly.

The Lord Chancellor entered, and knelt by the King's couch, saying,—

"I have given order, and, according to the King's command, the peers of the realm, in their robes, do now stand at the bar of the House, where, having comfirmed the Duke of Norfolk's doom, they humbly wait his majesty's further pleasure in the matter."

The King's face lit up with a fierce joy. Said he,—

"Lift me up! In mine own person will I go before my Parliament, and with mine own hand will I seal the warrant that rids me of"—

His voice failed; an ashen pallor swept the flush from his cheeks; and the attendants eased him back upon his pillows, and hurriedly assisted him with restoratives. Presently he said sorrowfully,—

"Alack, how have I longed for this sweet hour! and lo, too late it cometh, and I am robbed of this so coveted chance. But speed ye, speed ye! let others do this happy office sith 'tis denied to me. I put my great seal in commission: choose thou the lords that shall compose it, and get ye to your work. Speed ye, man! Before the sun shall rise and set again, bring me his head that I may see it."

"According to the King's command, so shall it be. Will 't please your majesty to order that the Seal be now restored to me, so that I may forth upon the business?"

"The seal! Who keepeth the Seal but thou?"

"Please your majesty, you did take it from me two days since, saying it should no more do its office till your own royal hand should use it upon the Duke of Norfolk's warrant."

"Why, so in sooth I did: I do remember it. . . . What did I with it? . . . I am very feeble. . . . So oft these days doth my memory play the traitor with me. . . . 'Tis strange, strange"—

The King dropped into inarticulate mumblings, shaking his gray head weakly from time to time, and gropingly trying to recollect what he had done with the Seal. At last my lord Hertford ventured to kneel and offer information,—

"Sire, if that I may be so bold, here be several that do remember with me how that you gave the Great Seal into the hands of his highness the Prince of Wales to keep against the day that"—

"True, most true!" interrupted the King. "Fetch it! Go: time flieth!"

Lord Hertford flew to Tom, but returned to the King before very long, troubled and empty-handed. He delivered himself to this effect,—

"It grieveth me, my lord the King, to bear so heavy and unwelcome tidings; but it is the will of God that the prince's affliction abideth still, and he cannot recall to mind that he received the Seal. So came I quickly to report, thinking it were waste of precious time, and little worth withal, that any should attempt to search the long array of chambers and saloons that belong unto his royal high"—

A groan from the King interrupted my lord at this point. After a little while his majesty said, with a deep sadness in his tone,—

"Trouble him no more, poor child. The hand of God lieth heavy upon him, and my heart goeth out in loving compassion for him, and sorrow that I may not bear his burden on mine own old trouble-weighted shoulders, and so bring him peace."

He closed his eyes, fell to mumbling, and presently was silent. After a time he opened his eyes again, and gazed vacantly around until his glance rested upon the kneeling Lord Chancellor. Instantly his face flushed with wrath,—

"What, thou here yet! By the glory of God, an' thou gettest not about that traitor's business, thy mitre shall have holiday the morrow for lack of a head to grace withal!"

The trembling Chancellor answered,—

"Good your majesty, I cry you mercy! I but waited for the Seal."

"Man, hast lost thy wits? The small Seal which aforetime I was wont to take with me abroad lieth in my treasury. And, since the Great Seal hath flown away, shall not it suffice? Hast lost thy wits? Begone! And hark ye,—come no more till thou do bring his head."

The poor Chancellor was not long in removing himself from this dangerous vicinity; nor did the commission waste time in giving the royal assent to the work of the slavish Parliament, and appointing the morrow for the beheading of the premier peer of England, the luckless Duke of Norfolk.*

CHAPTER IX

THE RIVER PAGEANT

At nine in the evening the whole vast riverfront of the palace was blazing with light. The river itself, as far as the eye could reach citywards, was so thickly covered with watermen's boats and with pleasure-barges, all fringed with colored lanterns, and gently agitated by the waves, that it resembled a glowing and limitless garden of flowers stirred to soft motion by summer winds. The grand terrace of stone steps leading down to the water, spacious enough to mass the army of a German principality upon, was a picture to see, with its ranks of royal halberdiers in polished armor, and its troops of brilliantly costumed servitors flitting up and down, and to and fro, in the hurry of preparation.

Presently a command was given, and immediately all living creatures vanished from the steps. Now the air was heavy with the

*See Note 5, at end of volume.

hush of suspense and expectancy. As far as one's vision could carry,
he might see the myriads of people in the boats rise up, and shade
their eyes from the glare of lanterns and torches, and gaze toward
the palace.

A file of forty or fifty state barges drew up to the steps. They were
richly gilt, and their lofty prows and sterns were elaborately carved.
Some of them were decorated with banners and streamers; some
with cloth-of-gold and arras embroidered with coats-of-arms; others
with silken flags that had numberless little silver bells fastened to
them, which shook out tiny showers of joyous music whenever the
breezes fluttered them; others of yet higher pretensions, since they
belonged to nobles in the prince's immediate service, had their sides
picturesquely fenced with shields gorgeously emblazoned with
armorial bearings. Each state barge was towed by a tender. Besides
the rowers, these tenders carried each a number of men-at-arms in
glossy helmet and breastplate, and a company of musicians.

The advance-guard of the expected procession now appeared in
the great gateway, a troop of halberdiers. "They were dressed in
striped hose of black and tawny, velvet caps graced at the sides with
silver roses, and doublets of murrey and blue cloth, embroidered on
the front and back with the three feathers, the prince's blazon,
woven in gold. Their halberd staves were covered with crimson
velvet, fastened with gilt nails, and ornamented with gold tassels.
Filing off on the right and left, they formed two long lines, extending
from the gateway of the palace to the water's edge. A thick, rayed
cloth or carpet was then unfolded, and laid down between them by
attendants in the gold-and-crimson liveries of the prince. This done,
a flourish of trumpets resounded from within. A lively prelude arose
from the musicians on the water; and two ushers with white wands
marched with a slow and stately pace from the portal. They were
followed by an officer bearing the civic mace, after whom came
another carrying the city's sword; then several sergeants of the city
guard, in their full accoutrements, and with badges on their sleeves;
then the garter king-at-arms, in his tabard; then several knights of
the bath, each with a white lace on his sleeve; then their esquires;
then the judges, in their robes of scarlet and coifs; then the lord high
chancellor of England, in a robe of scarlet, open before, and purfled
with minever; then a deputation of aldermen, in their scarlet cloaks;
and then the heads of the different civic companies, in their robes of
state. Now came twelve French gentlemen, in splendid habiliments,
consisting of pourpoints of white damask barred with gold, short
mantles of crimson velvet lined with violet taffeta, and carnation-
colored *hauts-de-chausses,* and took their way down the steps. They
were of the suite of the French ambassador, and were followed by
twelve cavaliers of the suite of the Spanish ambassador, clothed in
black velvet, unrelieved by any ornament. Following these came
several great English nobles with their attendants."

There was a flourish of trumpets within; and the prince's uncle, the future great Duke of Somerset, emerged from the gateway, arrayed in a "doublet of black cloth-of-gold, and a cloak of crimson satin flowered with gold, and ribanded with nets of silver." He turned, doffed his plumed cap, bent his body in a low reverence, and began to step backward, bowing at each step. A prolonged trumpet-blast followed, and a proclamation, "Way for the high and mighty, the Lord Edward, Prince of Wales!" High aloft on the palace walls a long line of red tongues of flame leaped forth with a thunder-crash: the massed world on the river burst into a mighty roar of welcome; and Tom Canty, the cause and hero of it all, stepped into view, and slightly bowed his princely head.

He was "magnificently habited in a doublet of white satin, with a front-piece of purple cloth-of-tissue, powdered with diamonds, and edged with ermine. Over this he wore a mantle of white cloth-of-gold, pounced with the triple-feather crest, lined with blue satin, set with pearls and precious stones, and fastened with a clasp of brilliants. About his neck hung the order of the Garter, and several princely foreign orders;" and wherever light fell upon him jewels responded with a blinding flash. O Tom Canty, born in a hovel, bred in the gutters of London, familiar with rags and dirt and misery, what a spectacle is this!

CHAPTER X

THE PRINCE IN THE TOILS

We left John Canty dragging the rightful prince into Offal Court, with a noisy and delighted mob at his heels. There was but one person in it who offered a pleading word for the captive, and he was not heeded: he was hardly even heard, so great was the turmoil. The prince continued to struggle for freedom, and to rage against the treatment he was suffering, until John Canty lost what little patience was left in him, and raised his oaken cudgel in a sudden fury over the prince's head. The single pleader for the lad sprang to stop the man's arm, and the blow descended upon his own wrist. Canty roared out,—

"Thou'lt meddle, wilt thou? Then have thy reward."

His cudgel crashed down upon the meddler's head: there was a groan, a dim form sank to the ground among the feet of the crowd, and the next moment it lay there in the dark alone. The mob pressed on, their enjoyment nothing disturbed by this episode.

Presently the prince found himself in John Canty's abode, with the door closed against the outsiders. By the vague light of a tallow candle which was thrust into a bottle, he made out the main features of the loathsome den, and also the occupants of it. Two frowsy girls and a middle-aged woman cowered against the wall in one corner,

with the aspect of animals habituated to harsh usage, and expecting
and dreading it now. From another corner stole a withered hag with
streaming gray hair and malignant eyes. John Canty said to this
one,—

"Tarry! There's fine mummeries here. Mar them not till thou'st
enjoyed them; then let thy hand be heavy as thou wilt. Stand forth,
lad. Now say thy foolery again, an' thou'st not forgot it. Name thy
name. Who art thou?"

The insulted blood mounted to the little prince's cheek once
more, and he lifted a steady and indignant gaze to the man's face,
and said,—

"'Tis but ill-breeding in such as thou to command me to speak.
I tell thee now, as I told thee before, I am Edward, Prince of
Wales, and none other."

The stunning surprise of this reply nailed the hag's feet to the
floor where she stood, and almost took her breath. She stared at
the prince in stupid amazement, which so amused her ruffianly
son, that he burst into a roar of laughter. But the effect upon Tom
Canty's mother and sisters was different. Their dread of bodily
injury gave way at once to distress of a different sort. They ran
forward with woe and dismay in their faces, exclaiming,—

"O poor Tom, poor lad!"

The mother fell on her knees before the prince, put her hands
upon his shoulders, and gazed yearningly into his face through her
rising tears. Then she said,—

"O my poor boy! thy foolish reading hath wrought its woful work
at last, and ta'en thy wit away. Ah! why didst thou cleave to it when
I so warned thee 'gainst it? Thou'st broke thy mother's heart."

The prince looked into her face, and said gently,—

"Thy son is well, and hath not lost his wits, good dame. Comfort
thee: let me to the palace where he is, and straightway will the
King my father restore him to thee."

"The King thy father! O my child! unsay these words that be
freighted with death for thee, and ruin for all that be near to thee.
Shake off this grewsome dream. Call back thy poor wandering
memory. Look upon me. Am not I thy mother that bore thee, and
loveth thee?"

The prince shook his head, and reluctantly said,—

"God knoweth I am loath to grieve thy heart; but truly have I
never looked upon thy face before."

The woman sank back to a sitting posture on the fllor, and,
covering her eyes with her hands, gave way to heart-broken sobs
and wailings.

"Let the show go on!" shouted Canty. "What, Nan! what, Bet!
Mannerless wenches! will ye stand in the prince's presence? Upon
your knees, ye pauper scum, and do him reverence!"

He followed this with another horse-laugh. The girls began to plead timidly for their brother; and Nan said,—

"An' thou wilt but let him to bed, father, rest and sleep will heal his madness: prithee, do."

"Do, father," said Bet: "he is more worn than is his wont. To-morrow will he be himself again, and will beg with diligence, and come not empty home again."

This remark sobered the father's joviality, and brought his mind to business. He turned angrily upon the prince, and said,—

"The morrow must we pay two pennies to him that owns this hole; two pennies, mark ye,—all this money for a half-year's rent, else out of this we go. Show what thou'st gathered with thy lazy begging."

The prince said,—

"Offend me not with thy sordid matters. I tell thee again I am the King's son."

A sounding blow upon the prince's shoulder from Canty's broad palm sent him staggering into goodwife Canty's arms, who clasped him to her breast, and sheltered him from a pelting rain of cuffs and slaps by interposing her own person.

The frightened girls retreated to their corner; but the grandmother stepped eagerly forward to assist her son. The prince sprang away from Mrs. Canty, exclaiming,—

"Thou shalt not suffer for me, madam. Let these swine do their will upon me alone."

This speech infuriated the swine to such a degree that they set about their work without waste of time. Between them they belabored the boy right soundly, and then gave the girls and their mother a beating for showing sympathy for the victim.

"Now," said Canty, "to bed, all of ye. The entertainment has tired me."

The light was put out, and the family retired. As soon as the snorings of the head of the house and his mother showed that they were asleep, the young girls crept to where the prince lay, and covered him tenderly from the cold with straw and rags; and their mother crept to him also, and stroked his hair, and cried over him, whispering broken words of comfort and compassion in his ear the while. She had saved a morsel for him to eat, also; but the boy's pains had swept away all appetite,—at least for black and tasteless crusts. He was touched by her brave and costly defence of him, and by her commiseration; and he thanked her in very noble and princely words, and begged her to go to her sleep and try to forget her sorrows. And he added that the King his father would not let her loyal kindness and devotion go unrewarded. This return to his "madness" broke her heart anew, and she strained him to her breast again and again and then went back, drowned in tears, to her bed.

As she lay thinking and mourning, the suggestion began to creep

into her mind that there was an undefinable something about this
boy that was lacking in Tom Canty, mad or sane. She could not
describe it, she could not tell just what it was, and yet her sharp
mother-instinct seemed to detect it and perceive it. What if the boy
were really not her son, after all? O, absurd! She almost smiled at
the idea, spite of her griefs and troubles. No matter, she found that
it was an idea that would not "down," but persisted in haunting her.
It pursued her, it harassed her, it clung to her, and refused to be put
away or ignored. At last she perceived that there was not going to
be any peace for her until she should devise a test that should prove,
clearly and without question, whether this lad was her son or not,
and so banish these wearing and worrying doubts. Ah yes, this was
plainly the right way out of the difficulty; therefore she set her wits
to work at once to contrive that test. But it was an easier thing to
propose than to accomplish. She turned over in her mind one
promising test after another, but was obliged to relinquish them
all—none of them were absolutely sure, absolutely perfect; and an
imperfect one could not satisfy her. Evidently she was racking her
head in vain—it seemed manifest that she must give the matter up.
While this depressing thought was passing through her mind, her
ear caught the regular breathing of the boy, and she knew he had
fallen asleep. And while she listened, the measured breathing was
broken by a soft, startled cry, such as one utters in a troubled dream.
This chance occurrence furnished her instantly with a plan worth
all her labored tests combined. She at once set herself feverishly,
but noiselessly, to work, to relight her candle, muttering to herself,
"Had I but seen him *then,* I should have known! Since that day,
when he was little, that the powder burst in his face, he hath never
been startled of a sudden out of his dreams or out of his thinkings,
but he hath cast his hand before his eyes, even as he did that day,
and not as others would do it, with the palm inward, but always with
the palm turned outward—I have seen it a hundred times, and it
hath never varied nor ever failed. Yes, I shall soon know, now!"

By this time she had crept to the slumbering boy's side, with the
candle, shaded, in her hand. She bent heedfully and warily over him,
scarcely breathing, in her suppressed excitement, and suddenly
flashed the light in his face and struck the floor by his ear with her
knuckles. The sleeper's eyes sprung wide open, and he cast a startled
stare about him—but he made no special movement with his hands.

The poor woman was smitten almost helpless with surprise and
grief; but she contrived to hide her emotions, and to soothe the boy
to sleep again; then she crept apart and communed miserably with
herself upon the disastrous result of her experiment. She tried to
believe that her Tom's madness had banished this habitual gesture
of his; but she could not do it. "No," she said, "his *hands* are not
mad, they could not unlearn so old a habit in so brief a time.
O, this is a heavy day for me!"

Still, hope was as stubborn, now, as doubt had been before; she could not bring herself to accept the verdict of the test; she must try the thing again—the failure must have been only an accident; so she startled the boy out of his sleep a second and a third time, at intervals—with the same result which had marked the first test—then she dragged herself to bed, and fell sorrowfully asleep, saying, "But I cannot give him up—O, no, I cannot, I cannot—he *must* be my boy!"

The poor mother's interruptions having ceased, and the prince's pains having gradually lost their power to disturb him, utter weariness at last sealed his eyes in a profound and restful sleep. Hour after hour slipped away, and still he slept like the dead. Thus four or five hours passed. Then his stupor began to lighten. Presently while half asleep and half awake, he murmured—

"Sir William!"

After a moment—

"Ho, Sir William Herbert! Hie thee hither, and list to the strangest dream that ever. . .Sir William! Dost hear? Man, I did think me changed to a pauper, and. . .Ho there! Guards! Sir William! What! is there no groom of the chamber in waiting? Alack it shall go hard with"—

"What aileth thee?" asked a whisper near him. "Who art thou calling?"

"Sir William Herbert. Who art thou?"

"I? Who should I be, but thy sister Nan? O, Tom, I had forgot! Thou'rt mad yet—poor lad thou'rt mad yet, would I had never woke to know it again! But prithee master thy tongue, lest we be all beaten till we die!"

The startled prince sprang partly up, but a sharp reminder from his stiffened bruises brought him to himself, and he sunk back among his foul straw with a moan and the ejaculation—

"Alas, it was no dream, then!"

In a moment all the heavy sorrow and misery which sleep had banished were upon him again, and he realized that he was no longer a petted prince in a palace, with the adoring eyes of a nation upon him, but a pauper, an outcast, clothed in rags, prisoner in a den fit only for beasts, and consorting with beggars and thieves.

In the midst of his grief he began to be conscious of hilarious noises and shoutings, apparently but a block or two away. The next moment there were several sharp raps at the door; John Canty ceased from snoring and said—

"Who knocketh? What wilt thou?"

A voice answered—

"Know'st thou who it was thou laid thy cudgel on?"

"No. Neither know I, nor care."

"Belike thou'lt change thy note eftsoons. An' thou would save thy neck, nothing but flight may stead thee. The man is this moment delivering up the ghost. 'Tis the priest, Father Andrew!''

"God-a-mercy!'' exclaimed Canty. He roused his family, and
hoarsely commanded, "Up with ye all and fly—or bide where ye are
and perish!''

Scarcely five minutes later the Canty household were in the street
and flying for their lives. John Canty held the prince by the wrist,
and hurried him along the dark way, giving him this caution in a
low voice—

"Mind thy tongue, thou mad fool, and speak not our name. I will
choose me a new name, speedily, to throw the law's dogs off the
scent. Mind thy tongue, I tell thee!''

He growled these words to the rest of the family—

"If it so chance that we be separated, let each make for London
bridge; whoso findeth himself as far as the last linen-draper's shop
on the bridge, let him tarry there till the others be come, then will we
flee into Southwark together.''

At this moment the party burst suddenly out of darkness into
light; and not only into light, but into the midst of a multitude of
singing, dancing, and shouting people, massed together on the river
frontage. There was a line of bonfires stretching as far as one could
see, up and down the Thames; London bridge was illuminated;
Southwark bridge likewise; the entire river was aglow with the flash
and sheen of colored lights; and constant explosions of fireworks
filled the skies with an intricate commingling of shooting splendors
and a thick rain of dazzling sparks that almost turned night into
day; everywhere were crowds of revellers; all London seemed to be
at large.

John Canty delivered himself of a furious curse and commanded
a retreat; but it was too late. He and his tribe were swallowed up in
that swarming hive of humanity, and hopelessly separated from each
other in an instant. We are not considering that the prince was one
of his tribe; Canty still kept his grip upon him. The prince's heart
was beating high with hopes of escape, now. A burly waterman,
considerably exalted with liquor, found himself rudely shoved, by
Canty, in his efforts to plough through the crowd; he laid his great
hand on Canty's shoulder and said—

"Nay, wither so fast, friend? Dost canker thy soul with sordid
business when all that be leal men and true make holiday?''

"Mine affairs are mine own, they concern thee not," answered
Canty, roughly; "take away thy hand and let me pass.''

"Sith that is thy humor, thou'lt *not* pass, till thou'st drunk to the
Prince of Wales, I tell thee that," said the waterman, barring the
way resolutely.

"Give me the cup, then, and make speed, make speed!''

Other revellers were interested by this time. They cried out—

"The loving-cup, the loving-cup! make the sour knave drink the
loving-cup, else will we feed him to the fishes.''

So a huge loving-cup was brought; the waterman, grasping it by one of its handles, and with his other hand bearing up the end of an imaginary napkin, presented it in due and ancient form to Canty, who had to grasp the opposite handle with one of his hands and take off the lid with the other, according to ancient custom.* This left the prince hand-free for a second, of course. He wasted no time, but dived among the forest of legs about him and disappeared. In another moment he could not have been harder to find, under that tossing sea of life, if its billows had been the Atlantic's and he a lost sixpence.

He very soon realized this fact, and straightway busied himself about his own affairs without further thought of John Canty. He quickly realized another thing, too. To wit, that a spurious Prince of Wales was being feasted by the city in his stead. He easily concluded that the pauper lad, Tom Canty, had deliberatley taken advantage of his stupendous opportunity and become a usurper.

Therefore there was but one course to pursue—find his way to the Guildhall, make himself known, and denounce the impostor. He also made up his mind that Tom should be allowed a reasonable time for spiritual preparation, and then be hanged, drawn and quartered, according to the law and usage of the day, in cases of high treason.

CHAPTER XI

AT GUILDHALL

The royal barge, attended by its gorgeous fleet, took its stately way down the Thames through the wilderness of illuminated boats. The air was laden with music; the river banks were beruffled with joy-flames; the distant city lay in a soft luminous glow from its countless invisible bonfires; above it rose many a slender spire into the sky, incrusted with sparkling lights, wherefore in their remoteness they seemed like jeweled lances thrust aloft; as the fleet swept along, it was greeted from the banks with a continuous hoarse roar of cheers and the ceaseless flash and boom of artillery.

To Tom Canty, half buried in his silken cushions, these sounds and this spectacle were a wonder unspeakably sublime and astonishing. To his little friends at his side, the princess Elizabeth and the lady Jane Grey, they were nothing.

Arrived at the Dowgate, the fleet was towed up the limpid Walbrook (whose channel has now been for two centuries buried out of sight under acres of buildings,) to Bucklersbury, past houses and under bridges populous with merry-makers and brilliantly lighted, and at last came to a halt in a basin where now is Barge Yard, in the centre of the ancient city of London. Tom disembarked, and he and his gallant procession crossed Cheapside and made a

*See Note 6, at end of volume.

short march through the Old Jewry and Basinghall Street to the
Guildhall.

Tom and his little ladies were received with due ceremony by the
Lord Mayor and the Fathers of the City, in their gold chains and
scarlet robes of state, and conducted to a rich canopy of state at the
head of the great hall, preceded by heralds making proclamation,
and by the Mace and the City Sword. The lords and ladies who were
to attend upon Tom and his two small friends took their places
behind their chairs.

At a lower table the court grandees and other guests of noble
degree were seated, with the magnates of the city; the commoners
took places at a multitude of tables on the main floor of the hall.
From their lofty vantage-ground, the giants Gog and Magog, the
ancient guardians of the city, contemplated the spectacle below
them with eyes grown familiar to it in forgotten generations. There
was a bugle-blast and a proclamation, and a fat butler appeared in
a high perch in the leftward wall, followed by his servitors bearing
with impressive solemnity a royal Baron of Beef, smoking hot and
ready for the knife.

After grace, Tom, (being instructed) rose—and the whole house
with him—and drank from a portly golden loving-cup with the
princess Elizabeth; from her it passed to the lady Jane, and then
traversed the general assemblage. So the banquet began.

By midnight the revelry was at its height. Now came one of those
picturesque spectacles so admired in that old day. A description of it
is still extant in the quaint wording of a chronicler who witnessed it:

"Space being made, presently entered a baron and an earl
appareled after the Turkish fashion in long robes of bawdkin
powdered with gold; hats on their heads of crimson velvet, with great
rolls of gold, girded with two swords, called scimitars, hanging by
great bawdricks of gold. Next came yet another baron and another
earl, in two long gowns of yellow satin, traversed with white satin,
and in every bend of white was a bend of crimson satin, after the
fashion of Russia, with furred hats of gray on their heads; either of
them having an hatchet in their hands, and boots with *pykes*"
(points a foot long), "turned up. And after them came a knight,
then the Lord High Admiral, and with him five nobles, in doublets
of crimson velvet, voyded low on the back and before to the
cannellbone, laced on the breasts with chains of silver; and, over
that, short cloaks of crimson satin, and on their heads hats after
the dancers' fashion, with pheasants' feathers in them. These were
appareled after the fashion of Prussia. The torch-bearers, which
were about an hundred, were appareled in crimson satin and green,
like Moors, their faces black. Next came in a *mommarye*. Then the
minstrels, which were disguised, danced; and the lords and ladies
did wildly dance also, that it was a pleasure to behold."

And while Tom, in his high seat, was gazing upon this "wild" dancing, lost in admiration of the dazzling commingling of kaleidoscopic colors which the whirling turmoil of gaudy figures below him presented, the ragged but real little prince of Wales was proclaiming his rights and his wrongs, denouncing the impostor, and clamoring for admission at the gates of Guildhall! The crowd enjoyed this episode prodigiously, and pressed forward and craned their necks to see the small rioter. Presently they began to taunt him and mock at him, purposely to goad him into a higher and still more entertaining fury. Tears of mortification sprung to his eyes, but he stood his ground and defied the mob right royally. Other taunts followed, added mockings stung him, and he exclaimed,—

"I tell ye again, you pack of unmannerly curs, I am the prince of Wales! And all forlorn and friendless as I be, with none to give me word of grace or help me in my need, yet will not I be driven from my ground, but will maintain it!"

"Though thou be prince or no prince, 'tis all one, thou be'st a gallant lad, and not friendless neither! Here stand I by thy side to prove it; and mind I tell thee thou might'st have a worser friend than Miles Hendon and yet not tire thy legs with seeking. Rest thy small jaw, my child, I talk the language of these base kennel-rats like to a very native."

The speaker was a sort of Don Caesar de Bazan in dress, aspect, and bearing. He was tall, trim-built, muscular. His doublet and trunks were of rich material, but faded and threadbare, and their goldlace adornments were sadly tarnished; his ruff was rumpled and damaged; the plume in his slouched hat was broken and had a bedraggled and disreputable look; at his side he wore a long rapier in a rusty iron sheath; his swaggering carriage marked him at once as a ruffler of the camp. The speech of this fantastic figure was received with an explosion of jeers and laughter. Some cried, " 'Tis another prince in disguise!" " 'Ware thy tongue, friend, belike he is dangerous!" "Marry, he looketh it—mark his eye!" "Pluck the lad from him—to the horse-pond wi' the cub!"

Instantly a hand was laid upon the prince, under the impulse of this happy thought; as instantly the stranger's long sword was out and the meddler went to the earth under a sounding thump with the flat of it. The next moment a score of voices shouted "Kill the dog! kill him! kill him!" and the mob closed in on the warrior, who backed himself against a wall and began to lay about him with his long weapon like a madman. His victims sprawled this way and that, but the mob-tide poured over their prostrate forms and dashed itself against the champion with undiminished fury. His moments seemed numbered, his destruction certain, when suddenly a trumpet-blast sounded, a voice shouted, "Way for the king's messenger!" and a troop of horsemen came charging down upon the mob, who fled out of harm's reach as fast as their legs could carry them. The bold

stranger caught up the prince in his arms, and was soon far away
from danger and the multitude.

Return we within the Guildhall. Suddenly, high above the jubilant
roar and thunder of the revel, broke the clear peal of a bugle-note.
There was instant silence,—a deep hush; then a single voice rose—
that of the messenger from the palace—and began to pipe forth a
proclamation, the whole multitude standing, listening. The closing
words, solemnly pronounced, were—

"The king is dead!"

The great assemblage bent their heads upon their breasts with
one accord; remained so, in profound silence, a few moments; then
all sunk upon their knees in a body, stretched out their hands
toward Tom, and a mighty shout burst forth that seemed to shake
the building—

"Long live the king!"

Poor Tom's dazed eyes wandered abroad over this stupefying
spectacle, and finally rested dreamily upon the kneeling princesses
beside him, a moment, then upon the earl of Hertford. A sudden
purpose dawned in his face. He said, in a low tone, at lord
Hertford's ear—

"Answer me truly, on thy faith and honor! Uttered I here a
command, the which none but a king might hold privilege and
prerogative to utter, would such commandment be obeyed, and
none rise up to say me nay?"

"None, my liege, in all these realms. In thy person bides the
majesty of England. Thou art the king—thy word is law."

Tom responded, in a strong, earnest voice, and with great
animation—

"Then shall the king's law be law of mercy, from this day, and
never more be law of blood! Up from thy knees and away! To the
Tower and say the king decrees the duke of Norfolk shall not die!"*

The words were caught up and carried eagerly from lip to lip
far and wide over the hall, and as Hertford hurried from the
presence, another prodigious shout burst forth—

"The reign of blood is ended! Long live Edward, king of
England!"

CHAPTER XII

THE PRINCE'S TROUBLES BEGIN

As soon as Miles Hendon and the little prince were clear of the
mob, they struck down through back lanes and alleys toward the
river. Their way was unobstructed until they approached London
Bridge; then they ploughed into the multitude again, Hendon
keeping a fast grip upon the prince's—no, the king's—wrist. The
tremendous news was already abroad, and the boy learned it from a

*See Note 7, at end of volume.

thousand voices at once—"The king is dead!" The tidings struck a
chill to the heart of the poor little waif, and sent a shudder through
his frame. He realized the greatness of his loss, and was filled with a
bitter grief; for the grim tyrant who had been such a terror to others
had always been gentle with him. The tears sprung to his eyes and
blurred all objects. For an instant he felt himself the most forlorn,
outcast, and forsaken of God's creatures—then another cry shook
the night with its far-reaching thunders: "Long live King Edward
the Sixth!" and this made his eyes kindle, and thrilled him with
pride to his fingers' ends. "Ah," he thought, "how grand and
strange it seems—I AM KING!"

Our friends threaded their way slowly through the throngs upon
the Bridge. This structure, which had stood for six hundred years,
and had been a noisy and populous thoroughfare all that time,
was a curious affair, for a closely packed rank of stores and shops,
with family quarters overhead, stretched along both sides of it,
from one bank of the river to the other. The Bridge was a sort of
town to itself; it had its inn, its beer houses, its bakeries, its
haberdasheries, its food markets, its manufacturing industries, and
even its church. It looked upon the two neighbors which it linked
together—London and Southwark—as being well enough, as
suburbs, but not otherwise particularly important. It was a close
corporation, so to speak; it was a narrow town, of a single street a
fifth of a mile long, its population was but a village population, and
everybody in it knew all his fellow townsmen intimately, and had
known their fathers and mothers before them—and all their little
family affairs into the bargain. It had its aristocracy, of course—
its fine old families of butchers, and bakers, and what-not, who
had occupied the same old premises for five or six hundred years,
and knew the great history of the Bridge from beginning to end,
and all its strange legends; and who always talked bridgy talk, and
thought bridgy thoughts, and lied in a long, level, direct, substantial
bridgy way. It was just the sort of population to be narrow and
ignorant and self-conceited. Children were born on the Bridge,
were reared there, grew to old age and finally died without ever
having set a foot upon any part of the world but London Bridge
alone. Such people would naturally imagine that the mighty and
interminable procession which moved through its street night and
day, with its confused roar of shouts and cries, its neighings and
bellowings and bleatings and its muffled thunder-tramp, was the
one great thing in this world, and themselves somehow the
proprietors of it. And so they were in effect—at least they could
exhibit it from their windows, and did—for a consideration—
whenever a returning king or hero gave it a fleeting splendor, for
there was no place like it for affording a long, straight,
uninterrupted view of marching columns.

Men born and reared upon the Bridge found life unendurably

dull and inane, elsewhere. History tells of one of these who left the
Bridge at the age of seventy-one and retired to the country. But he
could only fret and toss in his bed; he could not go to sleep, the deep
stillness was so painful, so awful, so oppressive. When he was worn
out with it, at last, he fled back to his old home, a lean and haggard
spectre, and fell peacefully to rest and pleasant dreams under the
lulling music of the lashing waters and the boom and crash and
thunder of London Bridge.

In the times of which we are writing, the Bridge furnished "object
lessons" in English history, for its children—namely, the livid and
decaying heads of renowned men impaled upon iron spikes atop of
its gateways. But we digress.

Hendon's lodgings were in the little inn on the Bridge. As he
neared the door with his small friend, a rough voice said—

"So, thou'rt come at last! Thou'lt not escape again, I warrant
thee; and if pounding thy bones to a pudding can teach thee
somewhat, thou'lt not keep us waiting another time, mayhap"—
and John Canty put out his hand to seize the boy.

Miles Hendon stepped in the way, and said—
"Not too fast, friend. Thou art needlessly rough, methinks. What
is the lad to thee?"

"If it be any business of thine to make and meddle in others'
affairs, he is my son."

" 'Tis a lie!" cried the little king, hotly.

"Boldly said, and I believe thee, whether thy small head-piece be
sound or cracked, my boy. But whether this scurvy ruffian be thy
father or no, 'tis all one, he shall not have thee to beat thee and
abuse, according to his threat, so thou prefer to abide with me."

"I do, I do—I know him not, I loathe him, and will die before I
will go with him."

"Then 'tis settled, and there is nought more to say."

"We will see, as to that!" exclaimed John Canty, striding past
Hendon to get at the boy; "by force shall he"—

"If thou do but touch him, thou animated offal, I will spit thee
like a goose!" said Hendon, barring the way and laying his hand
upon his sword hilt. Canty drew back. "Now mark ye," continued
Hendon, "I took this lad under my protection when a mob of such
as thou would have mishandled him, mayhap killed him; dost
imagine I will desert him now to a worser fate?—for whether thou
art his father or no,—and sooth to say, I think it is a lie—a decent
swift death were better for such a lad than life in such brute hands
as thine. So go thy ways, and set quick about it, for I like not much
bandying of words, being not overpatient in my nature."

John Canty moved off, muttering threats and curses, and was
swallowed from sight in the crowd. Hendon ascended three flights
of stairs to his room, with his charge, after ordering a meal to be
sent thither. It was a poor apartment, with a shabby bed and some

odds and ends of old furniture in it, and was vaguely lighted by a
couple of sickly candles. The little king dragged himself to the bed
and lay down upon it, almost exhausted with hunger and fatigue.
He had been on his feet a good part of a day and a night, for it was
now two or three o'clock in the morning, and had eaten nothing
meantime. He murmured drowsily—

"Prithee call me when the table is spread," and sunk into a deep
sleep immediately.

A smile twinkled in Hendon's eye, and he said to himself—

"By the mass, the little beggar takes to one's quarters and usurps
one's bed with as natural and easy a grace as if he owned them—
with never a by-your-leave or so-please-it-you, or anything of the
sort. In his diseased ravings he called himself the prince of Wales,
and bravely doth he keep up the character. Poor little friendless rat,
doubtless his mind has been disordered with ill usage. Well, I will
be his friend; I have saved him, and it draweth me strongly to him;
already I love the bold-tongued little rascal. How soldier-like he
faced the smutty rabble and flung back his high defiance! And what
a comely, sweet and gentle face he hath, now that sleep hath
conjured away its troubles and its griefs. I will teach him, I will cure
his malady; yea, I will be his elder brother, and care for him and
watch over him; and whoso would shame him or do him hurt, may
order his shroud, for though I be burnt for it he shall need it!"

He bent over the boy and contemplated him with kind and pitying
interest, tapping the young cheek tenderly and smoothing back the
tangled curls with his great brown hand. A slight shiver passed over
the boy's form. Hendon muttered—

"See, now, how like a man it was to let him lie here uncovered
and fill his body with deadly rheums. Now what shall I do? 'twill
wake him to take him up and put him within the bed, and he sorely
needeth sleep."

He looked about for extra covering, but finding none, doffed his
doublet and wrapped the lad in it, saying, "I am used to nipping air
and scant apparel, 'tis little I shall mind the cold"—then walked
up and down the room to keep his blood in motion, soliloquizing,
as before.

"His injured mind persuades him he is prince of Wales; 'twill
be odd to have a prince of Wales still with us, now that he that *was*
the prince is prince no more, but king,—for this poor mind is set
upon the one fantasy, and will not reason out that now it should
cast by the prince and call itself the king. . . . If my father liveth
still, after these seven years that I have heard naught from home in
my foreign dungeon, he will welcome the poor lad and give him
generous shelter for my sake; so will my good elder brother, Arthur;
my other brother, Hugh—but I will crack his crown, an *he* interfere,
the fox-hearted, ill-conditioned animal! Yes, thither will we fare—
and straightway, too."

A servant entered with a smoking meal, disposed it upon a small
deal table, placed the chairs, and took his departure, leaving such
cheap lodgers as these to wait upon themselves. The door slammed
after him, and the noise woke the boy, who sprung to a sitting
posture, and shot a glad glance about him; then a grieved look came
into his face and he murmured, to himself, with a deep sigh, "Alack,
it was but a dream, woe is me." Next he noticed Miles Hendon's
doublet—glanced from that to Hendon, comprehended the sacrifice
that had been made for him, and said, gently—

"Thou art good to me, yes, thou art very good to me. Take it and
put it on—I shall not need it more."

Then he got up and walked to the washstand in the corner, and
stood there, waiting. Hendon said in a cheery voice—

"We'll have a right hearty sup and bite, now, for every thing
is savory and smoking hot, and that and thy nap together will make
thee a little man again, never fear!"

The boy made no answer, but bent a steady look, that was filled
with grave surprise, and also somewhat touched with impatience,
upon the tall knight of the sword. Hendon was puzzled, and said—

"What's amiss?"

"Good sir, I would wash me."

"O, is that all! Ask no permission of Miles Hendon for aught thou
cravest. Make thyself perfectly free here, and welcome, with all
that are his belongings."

Still the boy stood, and moved not; more, he tapped the floor
once or twice with his small impatient foot. Hendon was wholly
perplexed. Said he—

"Bless us, what is it?"

"Prithee pour the water, and make not so many words!"

Hendon, suppressing a horse-laugh, and saying to himself, "By
all the saints, but this is admirable!" stepped briskly forward and
did the small insolent's bidding; then stood by, in a sort of
stupefaction, until the command, "Come—the towel!" woke
sharply up. He took up a towel, from under the boy's nose, and
handed it to him, without comment. He now proceeded to comfort
his own face with a wash, and while he was at it his adopted child
seated himself at the table and prepared to fall to. Hendon
despatched his ablutions with alacrity, then drew back the other
chair and was about to place himself at table, when the boy said,
indignantly—

"Forbear! Wouldst sit in the presence of the king?"

This blow staggered Hendon to his foundations. He muttered to
himself, "Lo, the poor thing's madness is up with the time! it hath
changed with the great change that is come to the realm, and now
in fancy is he *king!* Good lack, I must humor the conceit, too—there
is no other way—faith, he would order me to the Tower, else!"

And pleased with this jest, he removed the chair from the table,

took his stand behind the king, and proceeded to wait upon him in
the courtliest way he was capable of.

When the king ate, the rigor of his royal dignity relaxed a little,
and with his growing contentment came a desire to talk. He said—

"I think thou callest thyself Miles Hendon, if I heard thee
aright?"

"Yes, sire," Miles replied; then observed to himself, "If I *must*
humor the poor lad's madness, I must sire him, I must majesty him,
I must not go by halves, I must stick at nothing that belongeth to
the part I play, else shall I play it ill and work evil to this charitable
and kindly cause."

The king warmed his heart with a second glass of wine, and said—
"I would know thee—tell me thy story. Thou hast a gallant way with
thee, a noble—art nobly born?"

"We are of the tail of the nobility, good your majesty. My father
is a baronet—one of the smaller lords, by knight service*—Sir
Richard Hendon, of Hendon Hall, by Monk's Holm in Kent."

"The name has escaped my memory. Go on—tell me thy story."

"'Tis not much, your majesty, yet perchance it may beguile a
short half hour for want of a better. My father, Sir Richard, is very
rich, and of a most generous nature. My mother died whilst I was
yet a boy. I have two brothers: Arthur, my elder, with a soul like to
his father's; and Hugh, younger than I, a mean spirit, covetous,
treacherous, vicious, underhanded—a reptile. Such was he from the
cradle; such was he ten years past, when I last saw him—a ripe
rascal at nineteen, I being twenty, then, and Arthur twenty-two.
There is none other of us but the lady Edith, my cousin—she was
sixteen, then—beautiful, gentle, good, the daughter of an earl, the
last of her race, heiress of a great fortune and a lapsed title. My
father was her guardian. I loved her and she loved me; but she was
betrothed to Arthur from the cradle, and Sir Richard would not
suffer the contract to be broken. Arthur loved another maid, and
bade us be of good cheer and hold fast to the hope that delay and
luck together would some day give success to our several causes.
Hugh loved the lady Edith's fortune, though in truth he said it was
herself he loved—but then 'twas his way, alway, to say one thing and
mean the other. But he lost his arts upon the girl: he could deceive
my father, but none else. My father loved him best of us all, and
trusted and believed him; for he was the youngest child and others
hated him—these qualities being in all ages sufficient to win a
parent's dearest love; and he had a smooth persuasive tongue, with
an admirable gift of lying—and these be qualities which do mightily
assist a blind affection to cozen itself. I was wild—in troth I might
go yet farther and say *very* wild, though 'twas a wildness of an
innocent sort, since it hurt none but me, brought shame to none,
nor loss, nor had in it any taint of crime or baseness, or what might

*He refers to the order of baronets, or baronettes,—the *barones minores*, as distinct from
the parliamentary barons:—not, it need hardly be said, the baronets of later creation.

not beseem mine honorable degree.

"Yet did my brother Hugh turn these faults to good account—he seeing that our brother Arthur's health was but indifferent, and hoping the worst might work him profit were I swept out of the path—so,—but 'twere a long tale, good my liege, and little worth the telling. Briefly, then, this brother did deftly magnify my faults and make them crimes; ending his base work with finding a silken ladder in mine apartments—conveyed thither by his own means—and did convince my father by this, and suborned evidence of servants and other lying knaves, that I was minded to carry off my Edith and marry with her, in rank defiance of his will.

"Three years of banishment from home and England might make a soldier and a man of me, my father said, and teach me some degree of wisdom. I fought out my long probation in the continental wars, tasting sumptuously of hard knocks, privation and adventure; but in my last battle I was taken captive, and during the seven years that have waxed and waned since then, a foreign dungeon hath harbored me. Through wit and courage I won to the free air at last, and fled hither straight; and am but just arrived, right poor in purse and raiment, and poorer still in knowledge of what these dull seven years have wrought at Hendon Hall, its people and belongings. So please you, sir, my meagre tale is told."

"Thou hast been shamefully abused!" said the little king, with a flashing eye. "But I will right thee—by the cross will I! The king hath said it."

Then, fired by the story of Miles's wrongs, he loosed his tongue and poured the history of his own recent misfortunes into the ears of his astonished listener. When he had finished, Miles said to himself—

"Lo, what an imagination he hath! Verily this is no common mind; else, crazed or sane, it could not weave so straight and gaudy a tale as this out of the airy nothings wherewith it hath wrought this curious romaunt. Poor ruined little head, it shall not lack friend or shelter whilst I bide with the living. He shall never leave my side; he shall be my pet, my little comrade. And he shall be cured!— aye, made whole and sound—then will he make himself a name—and proud shall I be to say, 'Yes, he is mine—I took him, a homeless little ragamuffin, but I saw what was in him, and I said his name would be heard someday—behold him, observe him—was I right?' "

The king spoke—in a thoughtful, measured voice—

"Thou didst save me injury and shame, perchance my life, and so my crown. Such service demandeth rich reward. Name thy desire, and so it be within the compass of my royal power, it is thine."

This fantastic suggestion startled Hendon out of his revery. He was about to thank the king and put the matter aside with saying he had only done his duty and desired no reward, but a wiser thought came into his head, and he asked leave to be silent a few moments and consider the gracious offer—an idea which the king gravely approved, remarking that it was best to be not too hasty with a thing of such great import.

Miles reflected during some moments, then said to himself, "Yes, that is the thing to do—by any other means it were impossible to get at it—and certes, this hour's experience has taught me 'twould be most wearing and inconvenient to continue it as it is. Yes, I will propose it; 'twas a happy accident that I did not throw the chance away." Then he dropped upon one knee and said—

"My poor service went not beyond the limit of a subject's simple duty, and therefore hath no merit; but since your majesty is pleased to hold it worthy some reward, I take heart of grace to make petition to this effect. Near four hundred years ago, as your grace knoweth, there being ill blood betwixt John, King of England, and the King of France, it was decreed that two champions should fight together in the lists, and so settle the dispute by what is called the arbitrament of God. These two kings, and the Spanish king, being assembled to witness and judge the conflict, the French champion appeared; but so redoubtable was he, that our English knights refused to measure weapons with him. So the matter, which was a weighty one, was like to go against the English monarch by default. Now in the Tower lay the lord de Courcy, the mightiest arm in England, stripped of his honors and possessions, and wasting with long captivity. Appeal was made to him; he gave assent, and came forth arrayed for battle; but no sooner did the Frenchman glimpse his huge frame and hear his famous name but he fled away, and the French king's cause was lost. King John restored de Courcy's titles and possessions, and said, 'Name thy wish and thou shalt have it, though it cost me half my kingdom;' whereat de Courcy, kneeling, as I do now, made answer, 'This, then, I ask, my liege; that I and my successors may have and hold the privilege of remaining covered in the presence of the kings of England, henceforth while the throne shall last.' The boon was granted, as your majesty knoweth; and there hath been no time, these four hundred years, that that line has failed of an heir; and so, even unto this day, the head of that ancient house still weareth his hat or helm before the king's majesty, without let or hindrance, and this none other may do.* Invoking this precedent in aid of my prayer, I beseech the king to grant to me but this once grace and privilege—to my more than sufficient reward—and none other, to wit: that I and my heirs, forever, may *sit* in the presence of the majesty of England!"

"Rise, Sir Miles Hendon, Knight," said the king, gravely—giving the accolade with Hendon's sword—"rise, and seat thyself. Thy petition is granted. Whilst England remains, and the crown continues, the privilege shall not lapse."

His majesty walked apart, musing, and Hendon dropped into a chair at table, observing to himself, " 'Twas a brave thought, and

*The lords of Kingsale, descendants of de Courcy, still enjoy this curious privilege.

hath wrought me a mighty deliverance; my legs are grievously
wearied. An' I had not thought of that, I must have had to stand for
weeks, till my poor lad's wits are cured." After a little, he went on,
"And so I become a knight of the Kingdom of Dreams and
Shadows! A most odd and strange position, truly, for one so
matter-of-fact as I. I will not laugh—no, God forbid, for this thing
which is so substanceless to me is *real* to him. And to me, also, in
one way, it is not a falsity, for it reflects with truth the sweet and
generous spirit that is in him." After a pause: "Ah, what if he should
call me by my fine title before folk!—there'd be a merry contrast
betwixt my glory and my raiment! But no matter: let him call me
what he will, so it please him; I shall be content."

CHAPTER XIII

THE DISAPPEARANCE OF THE PRINCE

A heavy drowsiness presently fell upon the two comrades. The
king said—
"Remove these rags"—meaning his clothing.
Hendon disappareled the boy without dissent or remark, tucked
him up in bed, then glanced about the room, saying to himself,
ruefully, "He hath taken my bed again, as before—marry, what
shall *I* do?" The little king observed his perplexity, and dissipated it
with a word. He said, sleepily—
"Thou wilt sleep athwart the door, and guard it." In a moment
more he was out of his troubles, in a deep slumber.
"Dear heart, he should have been born a king!" muttered
Hendon, admiringly; "he playeth the part to a marvel."
Then he stretched himself across the door, on the floor, saying
contentedly—
"I have lodged worse for seven years; 'twould be but ill gratitude
to Him above to find fault with this."
He dropped asleep as the dawn appeared. Toward noon he rose,
uncovered his unconscious ward—a section at a time—and took
his measure with a string. The king awoke, just as he had completed
his work, complained of the cold, and asked what he was doing.
" 'Tis done, now, my liege," said Hendon; "I have a bit of
business outside, but will presently return; sleep thou again—thou
needest it. There—let me cover thy head also—thou'lt be warm the
sooner."
The king was back in dreamland before this speech was ended.
Miles slipped softly out, and slipped as softly in again, in the course
of thirty or forty minutes, with a complete second-hand suit of
boy's clothing, of cheap material, and showing signs of wear; but
tidy, and suited to the season of the year. He seated himself, and

began to overhaul his purchase, mumbling to himself—

"A longer purse would have got a better sort, but when one has
not the long purse one must be content with what a short one
may do—

> " 'There was a woman in our town,
>   In our town did dwell'—

"He stirred, methinks—I must sing in a less thunderous key;
'tis not good to mar his sleep, with this journey before him and he
so wearied out, poor chap. . . . This garment—'tis well enough—a
stitch here and another one there will set it aright. This other is
better, albeit a stitch or two will not come amiss in it, likewise. . . .
These be very good and sound, and will keep his small feet warm and
dry—an odd new thing to him, belike, since he has doubtless been
used to foot it bare, winters and summers the same. . . . Would
thread were bread, seeing one getteth a year's sufficiency for a
farthing, and such a brave big needle without cost, for mere love.
Now shall I have the demon's own time to thread it!"

And so he had. He did as men have always done, and probably
always will do, to the end of time—held the needle still, and tried to
thrust the thread through the eye, which is the opposite of a
woman's way. Time and time again the thread missed the mark,
going sometimes on one side of the needle, sometimes on the other,
sometimes doubling up against the shaft; but he was patient, having
been through these experiences before, when he was soldiering. He
succeeded at last, and took up the garment that had lain waiting,
meantime, across his lap, and began his work.

"The inn is paid—the breakfast that is to come, included—and
there is wherewithal left to buy a couple of donkeys and meet our
little costs for the two or three days betwixt this and the plenty that
awaits us at Hendon Hall—

> " 'She loved her hus'—

"Boby o' me! I have driven the needle under my nail! . . . It
matters little—'tis not a novelty—yet 'tis not a convenience,
neither. . . . We shall be merry there, little one, never doubt it!
Thy troubles will vanish, there, and likewise thy sad distemper—

> " 'She loved her husband dearilee,
>   But another man'—

"These be noble large stitches!"—holding the garment up and
viewing it admiringly—"they have a grandeur and a majesty that
do cause these small stingy ones of the tailor-man to look mighty
paltry and plebeian—

> " 'She loved her husband dearilee,
>   But another man he loved she,'—

"Mary, 'tis done—a goodly piece of work, too, and wrought with expedition. Now will I wake him, apparel him, pour for him, feed him, and then will we hie us to the mart by the Tabard inn in Southwark and—be pleased to rise, my liege!—he answereth not— what ho, my liege!—of a truth must I profane his sacred person with a touch, sith his slumber is deaf to speech. What!"

He threw back the covers—the boy was gone!

He stared about him in speechless astonishment for a moment; noticed for the first time that his ward's ragged raiment was also missing, then he began to rage and storm, and shout for the innkeeper.—At that moment a servant entered with the breakfast.

"Explain, thou limb of Satan, or thy time is come!" roared the man of war, and made so savage a spring toward the waiter that this latter could not find his tongue, for the instant, for fright and surprise. "Where is the boy?"

In disjointed and trembling syllables the man gave the information desired.

"You were hardly gone from the place, your worship, when a youth came running and said it was your worship's will that the boy come to you straight, at the bridge-end on the Southwark side. I brought him hither; and when he woke the lad and gave his message, the lad did grumble some little for being distrubed 'so early,' as he called it, but straightway trussed on his rags and went with the youth, only saying it had been better manners that your worship came yourself, not sent a stranger—and so"—

"And so thou'rt a fool!—a fool, and easily cozened—hang all thy breed! Yet mayhap no hurt is done. Possibly no harm is meant the boy. I will go fetch him. Make the table ready. Stay! the coverings of the bed were disposed as if one lay beneath them— happened that by accident?"

"I know not, good your worship. I saw the youth meddle with them—he that came for the boy."

"Thousand deaths! 'twas done to deceive me— 'tis plain 'twas done to gain time. Hark ye! Was that youth alone?"

"All alone, your worship."

"Art sure?"

"Sure, your worship."

"Collect thy scattered wits—bethink thee—take time, man."

After a moment's thought, the servant said—

"When he came, none came with him; but now I remember me that as the two stepped into the throng of the Bridge, a ruffian- looking man plumged out from some near place; and just as he was joining them"—

"What *then?*—out with it!" thundered the impatient Hendon, interrupting.

"Just then the crowd lapped them up and closed them in, and I saw no more, being called by my master, who was in a rage because

a joint that the scrivener had ordered was forgot, though I take all
the saints to witness that to blame *me* for that miscarriage were
like holding the unborn babe to judgment for sins com"—

"Out of my sight, idiot! Thy prating drives me mad! Hold!
whither art flying? Canst not bide still an instant? Went they toward
Southwark?"

"Even so, your worship—for, as I said before, as to that detestable
joint, the babe unborn is no whit more blameless than"—

"Art here *yet!* And prating still? Vanish, lest I throttle thee!"
The servitor vanished. Hendon followed after him, passed him,
and plunged down the stairs two steps at a stride, muttering,
" 'Tis that scurvy villain that claimed he was his son. I have lost thee,
my poor little mad master—it is a bitter thought—and I had come
to love thee so! No! by book and bell, *not* lost! Not lost, for I will
ransack the land till I find thee again. Poor child, yonder is his
breakfast—and mine, but I have no hunger now—so, let the rats
have it—speed, speed! that is the word!" As he wormed his swift
way through the noisy multitudes upon the Bridge, he several times
said to himself—clinging to the thought as if it were a particularly
pleasing one—"He grumbled, but he *went*—he went, yes, because
he thought Miles Hendon asked it, sweet lad—he would ne'er have
done it for another, I know it well!"

CHAPTER XIV

"LE ROI EST MORT—VIVE LE ROI"

Toward daylight of the same morning, Tom Canty stirred out of
a heavy sleep and opened his eyes in the dark. He lay silent a few
moments, trying to analyze his confused thoughts and impressions,
and get some sort of meaning out of them, then suddenly he burst
out in a rapturous but guarded voice—

"I see it all, I see it all! Now God be thanked, I am indeed awake
at last! Come, joy! vanish, sorrow! Ho, Nan! Bet! kick off your straw
and hie ye hither to my side, till I do pour into your unbelieving ears
the wildest madcap dream that ever the spirits of night did conjure
up to astonish the soul of man withal!...Ho, Nan, I say! Bet!"...

A dim form appeared at his side, and a voice said—

"Wilt deign to deliver thy commands!"

"Commands?...O, woe is me, I know thy voice! Speak, thou—
who am I?"

"Thou? In sooth, yesternight wert thou the prince of Wales, to-
day art thou my most gracious liege, Edward, King of England."

Tom buried his head among his pillows, murmuring plaintively—

"Alack, it was no dream! Go to thy rest, sweet sir—leave me to
my sorrows."

Tom slept again, and after a time he had this pleasant dream. He thought it was summer and he was playing, all alone, in the fair meadow called Goodman's Fields, when a dwarf only a foot high, with long red whiskers and a humped back appeared to him suddenly and said, "Dig, by that stump." He did so, and found twelve bright new pennies—wonderful riches! Yet this was not the best of it; for the dwarf said—

"I know thee. Thou art a good lad and deserving; thy distresses shall end, for the day of thy reward is come. Dig here every seventh day, and thou shalt find always the same treasure, twelve bright new pennies. Tell none—keep the secret."

Then the dwarf vanished, and Tom flew to Offal Court with his prize, saying to himself, "Every night will I give my father a penny; he will think I begged it, it will glad his heart, and I shall no more be beaten. One penny every week the good priest that teacheth me shall have; mother, Nan and Bet the other four. We be done with hunger and rags, now, done with fears and frets and savage usage."

In his dream he reached his sordid home all out of breath, but with eyes dancing with grateful enthusiasm; cast four of his pennies into his mother's lap and cried out—

"They are for thee!—all of them, every one!—for thee and Nan and Bet—and honestly come by, not begged nor stolen!"

The happy and astonished mother strained him to her breast and exclaimed—

"It waxeth late—may it please your majesty to rise?"

Ah, that was not the answer he was expecting. The dream had snapped asunder—he was awake.

He opened his eyes—the richly clad First Lord of the Bedchamber was kneeling by his couch. The gladness of the lying dream faded away—the poor boy recognized that he was still a captive and a king. The room was filled with courtiers clothed in purple mantles—the mourning color—and with noble servants of the monarch. Tom sat up in bed and gazed out from the heavy silken curtains upon this fine company.

The weighty business of dressing began, and one courtier after another knelt and paid his court and offered to the little King his condolences upon his heavy loss, whilst the dressing proceeded. In the beginning, a shirt was taken up by the Chief Equerry in Waiting, who passed it to the First Lord of the Buckhounds, who passed it to the Second Gentleman of the Bedchamber, who passed it to the Head Ranger of Windsor Forest, who passed it to the Third Groom of the Stole, who passed it to the Chancellor Royal of the Duchy of Lancaster, who passed it to the Master of the Wardrobe, who passed it to Norroy King-at-Arms, who passed it to the Constable of the Tower, who passed it to the Chief Steward of the Household, who passed it to the Hereditary Grand Diaperer, who passed it to the Lord High Admiral of England, who passed it to the Archbishop of

Canterbury, who passed it to the First Lord of the Bedchamber,
who took what was left of it and put it on Tom. Poor little wondering
chap, it reminded him of passing buckets at a fire.

Each garment in its turn had to go through this slow and solemn
process; consequently Tom grew very weary of the ceremony; so
weary that he felt an almost gushing gratefulness when he at last saw
his long silken hose begin the journey down the line and knew that
the end of the matter was drawing near. But he exulted too soon.
The first Lord of the Bedchamber received the hose and was about
to encase Tom's legs in them, when a sudden flush invaded his face
and he hurriedly hustled the things back into the hands of the
Archbishop of Canterbury with an astounded look and a whispered,
"See, my lord!"—pointing to a something connected with the hose.
The Archbishop paled, then flushed, and passed the hose to the
Lord High Admiral, whispering, "See, my lord!" The Admiral
passed ths hose to the Hereditary Grand Diaperer, and had hardly
breath enough in his body to ejaculate, "See, my lord!" The hose
drifted backward along the line, to the Chief Steward of the
Household, the Constable of the Tower, Norroy King-at-Arms,
the Master of the Wardrobe, the Chancellor Royal of the Duchy of
Lancaster, the Third Groom of the Stole, the Head Ranger of
Windsor Forest, the Second Gentleman of the Bedchamber, the
First Lord of the Buckhounds,—accompanied always with that
amazed and frightened "See! see!"—till they finally reached the
hands of the Chief Equerry in Waiting, who gazed a moment, with
a pallid face, upon what had caused all this dismay, then hoarsely
whispered, "Body of my life, a tag gone from a truss point!—to the
Tower with the Head Keeper of the King's Hose!"—after which he
leaned upon the shoulder of the First Lord of the Buckhounds to
regather his vanished strength whilst fresh hose, without any
damaged strings to them, were brought.

But all things must have an end, and so in time Tom Canty was in
a condition to get out of bed. The proper official poured water, the
proper official engineered the washing, the proper official stood by
with a towel, and by and by Tom got safely through the purifying
stage and was ready for the services of the Hairdresser-royal. When
he at length emerged from this master's hands, he was a gracious
figure and as pretty as a girl, in his mantle and trunks of purple
satin, and purple-plumed cap. He now moved in state toward his
breakfast room, through the midst of the courtly assemblage; and
as he passed, these fell back, leaving his way free, and dropped upon
their knees.

After breakfast he was conducted, with regal ceremony, attended
by his great officers and his guard of fifty Gentlemen Pensioners
bearing gilt battle-axes, to the throne-room, where he proceeded
to transact business of state. His "uncle," lord Hertford, took his
stand by the throne, to assist the royal mind with wise counsel.

The body of illustrious men named by the late king as his executors, appeared, to ask Tom's approval of certain acts of theirs— rather a form, and yet not wholly a form, since there was no Protector as yet. The Archbishop of Canterbury made report of the decree of the Council of Executors concerning the obsequies of his late most illustrious majesty, and finished by reading the signatures of the Executors, to wit: the Archbishop of Canterbury; the Lord Chancellor of England; William Lord St. John; John Lord Russell; Edward Earl of Hertford; John Viscount Lisle; Cuthbert Bishop of Durham—

Tom was not listening—an earlier clause of the document was puzzling him. At this point he turned and whispered to lord Hertford—

"What day did he say the burial hath been appointed for?"

"The 16th of the coming month, my liege."

" 'Tis a strange folly. Will he keep?"

Poor chap, he was still new to the customs of royalty; he was used to seeing the forlorn dead of Offal Court hustled out of the way with a very different sort of expedition. However, the lord Hertford set his mind at rest with a word or two.

A secretary of state presented an order of the Council appointing the morrow at eleven for the reception of the foreign ambassadors, and desired the king's assent.

Tom turned an inquiring look toward Hertford, who whispered—

"Your majesty will signify consent. They come to testify their royal masters' sense of the heavy calamity which hath visited your grace and the realm of England."

Tom did as he was bidden. Another secretary began to read a preamble concerning the expenses of the late king's household, which had amounted to £28,000 during the preceding six months— a sum so vast that it made Tom Canty gasp; he gasped again when the fact appeared that £20,000 of this money was still owing and unpaid;* and once more when it appeared that the king's coffers were about empty, and his twelve hundred servants much embarrassed for lack of the wages due them. Tom spoke out, with lively apprehension.

"We be going to the dogs, 'tis plain. 'Tis meet and necessary that we take a smaller house and set the servants at large, sith they be of no value but to make delay, and trouble one with offices that harass the spirit and shame the soul, they misbecoming any but a doll, that hath nor brains nor hands to help itself withal. I remember me of a small house that standeth over against the fish-market, by Billingsgate"—

A sharp pressure upon Tom's arm stopped his foolish tongue and sent a blush to his face; but no countenance there betrayed any sign that this strange speech had been remarked or given concern.

A secretary made report that forasmuch as the late king had

*Hume.

provided in his will for conferring the ducal degree upon the earl of
Hertford and raising his brother, Sir Thomas Seymour, to the
peerage, and likewise Hertford's son to an earldom, together with
similar aggrandizements to other great servants of the crown, the
Council had resolved to hold a sitting on the 16th of February for the
delivering and confirming of these honors; and that meantime, the
late king not having granted, in writing, estates suitable to the
support of these dignities, the Council, knowing his private wishes
in that regard, had thought proper to grant to Seymour " £ 500
lands," and to Hertford's son "800 pound lands, and 300 pound of
the next bishop's lands which should fall vacant,"—his present
majesty being willing.*

Tom was about to blurt out something about the propriety of
paying the late King's debts first, before squandering all this money;
but a timely touch upon his arm, from the thoughtful Hertford,
saved him this indiscretion; wherefore he gave the royal assent,
without spoken comment, but with much inward discomfort. While
he sat reflecting, a moment, over the ease with which he was doing
strange and glittering miracles, a happy thought shot into his mind:
why not make his mother Duchess of Offal Court and give her an
estate? But a sorrowful thought swept it instantly away: he was only
a king in name, these grave veterans and great nobles were his
masters; to them his mother was only the creature of a diseased
mind; they would simply listen to his project with unbelieving ears,
then send for the doctor.

The dull work went tediously on. Petitions were read, and
proclamations, patents, and all manner of wordy, repetitious and
wearisome papers relating to the public business; and at last Tom
sighed pathetically and murmured to himself, "In what have I
offended, that the good God should take me away from the fields
and the free air and the sunshine, to shut me up here and make me
a king and afflict me so?" Then his poor muddled head nodded a
while, and presently dropped to his shoulder; and the business of
the empire came to a stand-still for want of that august factor, the
ratifying power. Silence ensued, around the slumbering child, and
the sages of the realm ceased from their deliberations.

During the forenoon, Tom had an enjoyable hour, by permission
of his keepers, Hertford and St. John, with the lady Elizabeth and
the little lady Jane Grey; though the spirits of the princesses were
rather subdued by the mighty stroke that had fallen upon the royal
house; and at the end of the visit his "elder sister"—afterwards the
"Bloody Mary" of history—chilled him with a solemn interview
which had but one merit in his eyes, its brevity. He had a few
moments to himself, and then a slim lad of about twelve years of
age was admitted to his presence, whose clothing, except his snowy
ruff and the laces about his wrists, was of black,—doublet, hose and
all. He bore no badge of mourning but a knot of purple ribbon on his

* Hume.

shoulder. He advanced hesitatingly, with head bowed and bare, and
dropped upon one knee in front of Tom. Tom sat still and
contemplated him soberly for a moment. Then he said—

"Rise, lad. Who art thou? What wouldst have?"

The boy rose, and stood at graceful ease, but with an aspect of
concern in his face. He said—

"Of a surety thou must remember me, my lord. I am thy
whipping-boy."

"My *whipping*-boy?"

"The same, your grace. I am Humphrey—Humphrey Marlow."

Tom perceived that here was some one whom his keepers ought to
have posted him about. The situation was delicate. What should he
do?—pretend that he knew this lad, and then betray by his every
utterance, that he had never heard of him before? No, that would
not do. An idea came to his relief: accidents like this might be likely
to happen with some frequency, now that business urgencies would
often call Hertford and St. John from his side, they being members
of the council of executors; therefore perhaps it would be well to
strike out a plan himself to meet the requirements of such
emergencies. Yes, that would be a wise course—he would practise on
this boy, and see what sort of success he might achieve. So he stroked
his brow, perplexedly, a moment or two, and presently said—

"Now I seem to remember thee somewhat—but my wit is clogged
and dim with suffering"—

"Alack, my poor master!" ejaculated the whipping-boy, with
feeling; adding, to himself, "In truth 'tis as they said—his mind is
gone—alas, poor soul! But misfortune catch me, how am I
forgetting! they said one might not seem to observe that aught is
wrong with him."

"'Tis strange how my memory doth wanton with me these days,"
said Tom. "But mind it not—I mend apace—a little clew doth often
serve to bring me back again the things and names which had
escaped me. [And not they, only, forsooth, but e'en such as I ne'er
heard before—as this lad shall see.] Give thy business speech."

"'Tis matter of small weight, my liege, yet will I touch upon it
an' it please your grace. Two days gone by, when your majesty
faulted thrice in your Greek—in the morning lessons,—dost
remember it?"

"Y-e-s—methinks I do. [It is not much of a lie—an' I had meddled
with the Greek at all, I had not faulted simply thrice, but forty
times.] Yes, I do recall it, now—go on."

—"The master, being wroth with what he termed such slovenly
and doltish work, did promise that he would soundly whip me for it
—and"—

"Whip *thee!*" said Tom, astonished out of his presence of mind.
"Why should he whip *thee* for faults of mine?"

"Ah, your grace forgetteth again. He always scourgeth me, when thou dost fail in thy lessons."

"True, true—I had forgot. Thou teachest me in private—then if I fail, he argueth that thy office was lamely done, and"—

"O, my liege, what words are these? I, the humblest of thy servants, presume to teach *thee?*"

"Then where is thy blame? What riddle is this? Am I in truth gone mad, or is it thou? Explain—speak out."

"But good your majesty, there's nought that needeth simplifying. —None may visit the sacred person of the prince of Wales with blows; wherefore when he faulteth, 'tis I that take them; and meet it is and right, for that it is mine office and my livelihood."*

Tom stared at the tranquil boy, observing to himself, "Lo, it is a wonderful thing,—a most strange and curious trade; I marvel they have not hired a boy to take my combings and my dressings for me— would heaven they would!—an' they will do this thing, I will take my lashings in mine own person, giving God thanks for the change." Then he said aloud—

"And hast thou been beaten, poor friend, according to the promise?"

"No, good your majesty, my punishment was appointed for this day, and peradventure it may be annulled, as unbefitting the season of mourning that is come upon us; I know not, and so have made bold to come hither and remind your grace about your gracious promise to intercede in my behalf"—

"With the master? To save thee thy whipping?"

"Ah thou dost remember!"

"My memory mendeth, thou seest. Set thy mind at ease—thy back shall go unscathed—I will see to it."

"O, thanks, my good lord!" cried the boy, dropping upon his knee again. "Mayhap I have ventured far enow; and yet" . . .

Seeing Master Humphrey hesitate, Tom encouraged him to go on, saying he was "in the granting mood."

"Then will I speak it out, for it lieth near my heart. Sith thou art no more prince of Wales but King, thou canst order matters as thou wilt, with none to say thee nay; wherefore it is not in reason that thou wilt longer vex thyself with dreary studies, but wilt burn thy books and turn thy mind to things less irksome. Then am I ruined, and mine orphan sisters with me!"

"Ruined? Prithee how?"

"My back is my bread, O my gracious liege! if it go idle, I starve. An' thou cease from study, mine office is gone, thou'lt need no whipping-boy. Do not turn me away!"

Tom was touched with this pathetic distress. He said, with a right royal burst of generosity—

"Discomfort thyself no further, lad. Thine office shall be permanent in thee and thy line, forever." Then he struck the boy a light blow on the shoulder with the flat of his sword, exclaiming,

*See Note 8, at end of volume.

"Rise, Humphrey Marlow, Hereditary Grand Whipping-Boy to the
royal house of England! Banish sorrow—I will betake me to my
books again, and study so ill that they must in justice treble thy
wage, so mightily shall the business of thine office be augmented."

The grateful Humphrey responded fervidly—

"Thanks, O most noble master, this princely lavishness doth far
surpass my most distempered dreams of fortune. Now shall I be
happy all my days, and all the house of Marlow after me."

Tom had wit enough to perceive that here was a lad who could be
useful to him. He encouraged Humphrey to talk, and he was nothing
loath. He was delighted to believe that he was helping in Tom's
"cure"; for always, as soon as he had finished calling back to Tom's
diseased mind the various particulars of his experiences and
adventures in the royal school-room and elsewhere about the palace,
he noticed that Tom was then able to "recall" the circumstances
quite clearly. At the end of an hour Tom found himself well freighted
with very valuable information concerning personages and matters
pertaining to the Court; so he resolved to draw instruction from this
source daily; and to this end he would give order to admit Humphrey
to the royal closet whenever he might come, provided the majesty of
England was not engaged with other people. Humphrey had hardly
been dismissed when my lord Hertford arrived with more trouble
for Tom.

He said that the lords of the Council, fearing that some
overwrought report of the king's damaged health might have leaked
out and got abroad, they deemed it wise and best that his majesty
should begin to dine in public after a day or two—his wholesome
complexion and vigorous step, assisted by a carefully guarded repose
of manner and ease and grace of demeanor, would more surely quiet
the general pulse—in case any evil rumors *had* gone about—than
any other scheme that could be devised.

Then the earl proceeded, very delicately, to instruct Tom as to the
observances proper to the stately occasion, under the rather thin
disguise of "reminding" him concerning things already known to
him; but to his vast gratification it turned out that Tom needed very
little help in this line—he had been making use of Humphrey in that
direction, for Humphrey had mentioned that within a few days he
was to begin to dine in public; having gathered it from the swift-
winged gossip of the Court. Tom kept these facts to himself however.

Seeing the royal memory so improved, the earl ventured to apply
a few tests to it, in an apparently casual way, to find out how far its
amendment had progressed. The results were happy, here and there,
in spots—spots where Humphrey's tracks remained—and on the
whole my lord was greatly pleased and encouraged. So encouraged
was he, indeed, that he spoke up and said in a quite hopeful voice—

"Now am I persuaded that if your majesty will but tax your
memory yet a little further, it will resolve the puzzle of the Great Seal

—a loss which was of moment yesterday, although of none to-day, since its term of service ended with our late lord's life. May it please your grace to make the trial?"

Tom was at sea—a Great Seal was a something which he was totally unacquainted with. After a moment's hesitation, he looked up innocently and asked—

"What was it like, my Lord?"

The earl started, almost imperceptibly, muttering to himself, "Alack, his wits are flown again!—it was ill wisdom to lead him on to strain them"—then he deftly turned the talk to other matters, with the purpose of sweeping the unlucky Seal out of Tom's thoughts —a purpose which easily succeeded.

CHAPTER XV

TOM AS KING

The next day the foreign ambassadors came, with their gorgeous trains; and Tom, throned in awful state, received them. The splendors of the scene delighted his eye and fired his imagination, at first, but the audience was long and dreary, and so were most of the addresses—wherefore, what began as a pleasure, grew into weariness and homesickness by and by. Tom said the words which Hertford put into his mouth from time to time, and tried hard to acquit himself satisfactorily, but he was too new to such things, and too ill at ease to accomplish more than a tolerable success. He looked sufficiently like a king, but he was ill able to feel like one. He was cordially glad when the ceremony was ended.

The larger part of his day was "wasted"—as he termed it, in his own mind—in labors pertaining to his royal office. Even the two hours devoted to certain princely pastimes and recreations were rather a burden to him, than otherwise, they were so fettered by restrictions and ceremonious observances. However he had a private hour with his whipping-boy which he counted clear gain, since he got both entertainment and needful information out of it.

The third day of Tom Canty's Kingship came and went much as the others had done, but there was a lifting of his cloud in one way— he felt less uncomfortable than at first; he was getting a little used to his circumstances and surroundings; his chains still galled, but not all the time; he found that the presence and homage of the great afflicted and embarrassed him less and less sharply with every hour that drifted over his head.

But for one single dread, he could have seen the fourth day approach without serious distress—the dining in public; it was to begin that day. There were greater matters in the programme—for on that day he would have to preside at a Council which would take his views and commands concerning the policy to be pursued toward various foreign nations scattered far and near over the great globe; on that day, too, Hertford would be formally chosen to the grand office of Lord Protector; other things of note were appointed for that fourth day, also, but to Tom they were all insignificant compared with the ordeal of dining all by himself with a multitude of curious eyes fastened upon him and a multitude of mouths whispering comments upon his performance,—and upon his mistakes, if he should be so unlucky as to make any.

Still, nothing could stop that fourth day, and so it came. It found poor Tom low-spirited and absent-minded, and this mood continued; he could not shake it off. The ordinary duties of the morning dragged upon his hands, and wearied him. Once more he felt the sense of captivity heavy upon him.

Late in the forenoon he was in a large audience chamber, conversing with the earl of Hertford and dully awaiting the striking of the hour appointed for a visit of ceremony from a considerable number of great officials and courtiers.

After a little while, Tom, who had wandered to a window and become interested in the life and movement of the great highway beyond the palace gates—and not idly interested, but longing with all his heart to take part in person in its stir and freedom—saw the van of a hooting and shouting mob of disorderly men, women and children of the lowest and poorest degree approaching from up the road.

"I would I knew what 'tis about!" he exclaimed, with all a boy's curiosity in such happenings.

"Thou art the king!" solemnly responded the earl, with a reverence. "Have I your grace's leave to act?"

"O blithely, yes! O gladly, yes!" exclaimed Tom, excitedly, adding to himself with a lively sense of satisfaction, "In truth, being a king is not all dreariness—it hath its compensations and conveniences."

The earl called a page, and sent him to the captain of the guard with the order—

"Let the mob be halted, and inquiry made concerning the occasion of its movement. By the king's command!"

A few seconds later a long rank of the royal guards, cased in flashing steel, filed out at the gates and formed across the highway in front of the multitude. A messenger returned, to report that the crowd was following a man, a woman, and a young girl to execution for crimes committed against the peace and dignity of the realm.

Death—and a violent death—for these poor unfortunates! The thought wrung Tom's heartstrings. The spirit of compassion took control of him, to the exclusion of all other considerations; he never thought of the offended laws, or of the grief or loss which these three criminals had inflicted upon their victims, he could think of nothing but the scaffold and the grisly fate hanging over the heads of the

condemned. His concern made him even forget, for the moment, that
he was but the false shadow of a king, not the substance; and before
he knew it he had blurted out the command—

"Bring them here!"

Then he blushed scarlet, and a sort of apology sprung to his lips;
but observing that his order had wrought no sort of surprise in the
earl or the waiting page, he suppressed the words he was about to
utter. The page, in the most matter-of-course way, made a profound
obeisance and retired backward out of the room to deliver the
command. Tom experienced a glow of pride and a renewed sense of
the compensating advantages of the kingly office. He said to himself,
"Truly it is like what I used to feel when I read the old priest's tales,
and did imagine mine own self a prince, giving law and command to
all, saying, 'Do this, do that,' whilst none durst offer let or hindrance
to my will."

Now the doors swung open; one high-sounding title after another
was announced, the personages owning them followed, and the place
was quickly half filled with noble folk and finery. But Tom was
hardly conscious of the presence of these people, so wrought up was
he and so intensely absorbed in that other and more interesting
matter. He seated himself, absently, in his chair of state, and turned
his eyes upon the door with manifestations of impatient expectancy;
seeing which, the company forbore to trouble him, and fell to
chatting a mixture of public business and court gossip one with
another.

In a little while the measured tread of military men was heard
approaching, and the culprits entered the presence in charge of an
under-sheriff and escorted by a detail of the king's guard. The civil
officer knelt before Tom, then stood aside; the three doomed persons
knelt, also, and remained so; the guard took position behind Tom's
chair. Tom scanned the prisoners curiously. Something about the
dress or appearance of the man had stirred a vague memory in him.
"Methinks I have seen this man ere now . . . but the when or the
where fail me"—such was Tom's thought. Just then the man glanced
quickly up, and quickly dropped his face again, not being able to
endure the awful port of sovereignty; but the one full glimpse of the
face, which Tom got, was sufficient. He said to himself: "Now is the
matter clear; this is the stranger that plucked Giles Witt out of the
Thames, and saved his life, that windy, bitter first day of the New
Year—a brave, good deed—pity he hath been doing baser ones and
got himself in this sad case . . . . I have not forgot the day, neither the
hour; by reason that an hour after, upon the stroke of eleven, I did
get a hiding by the hand of Gammer Canty which was of so goodly
and admired severity that all that went before or followed after it
were but fondlings and caresses by comparison."

Tom now ordered that the woman and the girl be removed from
the presence for a little time; then addressed himself to the under-

sheriff, saying—

"Good sir, what is this man's offence?"

The officer knelt, and answered—

"So please your majesty, he hath taken the life of a subject by poison."

Tom's compassion for the prisoner, and admiration of him as the daring rescuer of a drowning boy, experienced a most damaging shock.

"The thing was proven upon him?" he asked.

"Most clearly, sire."

Tom sighed, and said—

"Take him away—he hath earned his death. 'Tis a pity, for he was a brave heart—na—na, I mean he hath the *look* of it!"

The prisoner clasped his hands together with sudden energy, and wrung them despairingly, at the same time appealing imploringly to the "King" in broken and terrified phrases—

"O my lord the king, an' thou canst pity the lost, have pity upon me! I am innocent—neither hath that wherewith I am charged been more than but lamely proved—yet I speak not of that; the judgment is gone forth against me and may not suffer alteration; yet in mine extremity I beg a boon, for my doom is more than I can bear. A grace, a grace, my lord the king! in thy royal compassion grant my prayer—give commandment that I be hanged!"

Tom was amazed. This was not the outcome he had looked for.

"Odds my life, a strange *boon!* Was it not the fate intended thee?"

"O good my liege, not so! It is ordered that I be *boiled alive!*"

The hideous surprise of these words almost made Tom spring from his chair. As soon as he could recover his wits he cried out—

"Have thy wish, poor soul! an' thou had poisoned a hundred men thou shouldst not suffer so miserable a death."

The prisoner bowed his face to the ground and burst into passionate expressions of gratitude—ending with—

"If ever thou shouldst know misfortune—which God forbid!—may thy goodness to me this day be remembered and requited!"

Tom turned to the earl of Hertford, and said—

"My lord, is it believable that there was warrant for this man's ferocious doom?"

"It is the law, your grace—for poisoners. In Germany coiners be boiled to death in *oil*—not cast in of a sudden, but by a rope let down into the oil by degrees, and slowly; first the feet, then the legs, then"—

"O prithee no more, my lord, I cannot bear it!" cried Tom, covering his eyes with his hands to shut out the picture. "I beseech your good lordship that order be taken to change this law—O, let no more poor creatures be visited with its tortures."

The earl's face showed profound gratification, for he was a man of merciful and generous impulses—a thing not very common with his class in that fierce age. He said—

"These your grace's noble words have sealed its doom. History will remember it to the honor of your royal house."

The under-sheriff was about to remove his prisoner; Tom gave him a sign to wait; then he said—

"Good sir, I would look into this matter further. The man has said his deed was but lamely proved. Tell me what thou knowest."

"If the king's grace please, it did appear upon the trial, that this man entered into a house in the hamlet of Islington where one lay sick—three witnesses say it was at ten of the clock in the morning and two say it was some minutes later—the sick man being alone at the time, and sleeping—and presently the man came forth again, and went his way. The sick man died within the hour, being torn with spasms and retchings."

"Did any see the poison given? Was poison found?"

"Marry, no, my liege."

"Then how doth one know there was poison given at all?"

"Please your majesty, the doctors testified that none die with such symptoms but by poison."

Weighty evidence, this—in that simple age. Tom recognized its formidable nature, and said—

"The doctor knoweth his trade—belike they were right. The matter hath an ill look for this poor man."

"Yet was not this all, your majesty; there is more and worse. Many testified that a witch, since gone from the village, none know whither, did foretell, and speak it privately in their ears, that the sick man *would die by poison*—and more, that a stranger would give it—a stranger with brown hair and clothed in a worn and common garb; and surely this prisoner doth answer woundily to the bill. Please your majesty to give the circumstance that solemn weight which is its due, seeing it was *foretold.*"

This was an argument of tremendous force, in that superstitious day. Tom felt that the thing was settled; if evidence was worth anything, this poor fellow's guilt was proved. Still he offered the prisoner a chance, saying—

"If thou canst say aught in thy behalf, speak."

"Nought that will avail, my king. I am innocent, yet cannot I make it appear. I have no friends, else might I show that I was not in Islington that day; so also might I show that at that hour they name I was above a league away, seeing I was at Wapping Old Stairs; yea more, my King, for I could show, that whilst they say I was *taking* life, I was *saving* it. A drowning boy"—

"Peace! Sheriff, name the day the deed was done!"

"At ten in the morning, or some minutes later, the first day of the new year, most illustrious"—

"Let the prisoner go free—it is the king's will!"

Another blush followed this unregal outburst, and he covered his indecorum as well as he could by adding—

"It enrageth me that a man should be hanged upon such idle, hare-brained evidence!"

A low buzz of admiration swept through the assemblage. It was not admiration of the decree that had been delivered by Tom, for the propriety or expediency of pardoning a convicted poisoner was a thing which few there would have felt justified in either admitting or admiring—no, the admiration was for the intelligence and spirit which Tom had displayed. Some of the low-voiced remarks were to this effect—

"This is no mad king—he hath his wits sound."

"How sanely he put his questions—how like his former natural self was this abrupt, imperious disposal of the matter!"

"God be thanked his infirmity is spent! This is no weakling, but a king. He hath borne himself like to his own father."

The air being filled with applause, Tom's ear necessarily caught a little of it. The effect which this had upon him was to put him greatly at his ease, and also to charge his system with very gratifying sensations.

However, his juvenile curiosity soon rose superior to these pleasant thoughts and feelings; he was eager to know what sort of deadly mischief the woman and the little girl could have been about; so, by his command the two terrified and sobbing creatures were brought before him.

"What is it that these have done?" he inquired of the sheriff.

"Please your majesty, a black crime is charged upon them, and clearly proven: wherefore the judges have decreed, according to the law, that they be hanged. They sold themselves to the devil—such is their crime."

Tom shuddered. He had been taught to abhor people who did this wicked thing. Still, he was not going to deny himself the pleasure of feeding his curiosity, for all that; so he asked—

"Where was this done?—and when?"

"On a midnight, in December—in a ruined church, your majesty."

Tom shuddered again.

"Who was there present?"

"Only these two, your grace—and *that other.*"

"Have these confessed?"

"Nay, not so, sire—they do deny it."

"Then prithee, how was it known?"

"Certain witnesses did see them wending thither, good your majesty; this bred the suspicion, and dire effects have since confirmed and justified it. In particular, it is in evidence that through the wicked power so obtained, they did invoke and bring about a storm that wasted all the region round about. Above forty witnesses have proved the storm; and sooth one might have had a thousand, for all had reason to remember it, sith all had suffered by it."

"Certes this is a serious matter." Tom turned this dark piece of scoundrelism over in his mind a while, then asked—

"Suffered the woman, also, by the storm?"

Several old heads among the assemblage nodded their recognition of the wisdom of this question. The sheriff, however, saw nothing consequential in the inquiry; he answered, with simple directness—

"Indeed, did she, your majesty, and most righteously, as all aver. Her habitation was swept away, and herself and child left shelterless."

"Methinks the power to do herself so ill a turn was dearly bought. She had been cheated, had she paid for a farthing for it; that she paid her soul, and her child's, argueth that she is mad; if she is mad she knoweth not what she doth, therefore sinneth not."

The elderly heads nodded recognition of Tom's wisdom once more, and one individual murmured, "An' the king be mad himself, according to report, then is it a madness of a sort that would improve the sanity of some I wot of, if by the gentle providence of God they could but catch it."

"What age hath the child?" asked Tom.

"Nine years, please your majesty."

"By the law of England may a child enter into covenant and sell itself, my lord?" asked Tom, turning to a learned judge.

"The law doth not permit a child to make or meddle in any weighty matter, good my liege, holding that its callow wit unfitteth it to cope with the riper wit and evil schemings of them that are its elders. The *devil* may buy a child, if he so choose, and the child agree thereto, but not an Englishman—in this latter case the contract would be null and void."

"It seemeth a rude unchristian thing, and ill contrived, that English law denieth privileges to Englishmen, to waste them on the devil!" cried Tom, with honest heat.

This novel view of the matter excited many smiles, and was stored away in many heads to be repeated about the court as evidence of Tom's originality as well as progress toward mental health.

The elder culprit had ceased from sobbing, and was hanging upon Tom's words with an excited interest and a growing hope. Tom noticed this, and it strongly inclined his sympathies toward her in her perilous and unfriended situation. Presently he asked—

"How wrought they, to bring the storm?"

"*By pulling off their stockings,* sire."

This astonished Tom, and also fired his curiosity to fever heat. He said, eagerly—

"It is wonderful! Hath it always this dread effect?"

"Always, my liege—at least if the woman desire it, and utter the needful words, either in her mind or with her tongue."

Tom turned to the woman, and said with impetuous zeal—
"Exert thy power—I would see a storm!"

There was a sudden paling of cheeks in the superstitious
assemblage, and a general, though unexpressed, desire to get out of
the place—all of which was lost upon Tom, who was dead to
everything but the proposed cataclysm. Seeing a puzzled and
astonished look in the woman's face, he added, excitedly—

"Never fear—thou shalt be blameless. More—thou shalt go free—
none shall touch thee. Exert thy power."

"O, my lord the king, I have it not—I have been falsely accused."

"Thy fears stay thee. Be of good heart, thou shalt suffer no harm.
Make a storm—it mattereth not how small a one—I require nought
great or harmful, but indeed prefer the opposite—do this and thy life
is spared—thou shalt go out free, with thy child, bearing the king's
pardon, and safe from hurt or malice from any in the realm."

The woman prostrated herself, and protested, with tears, that she
had no power to do the miracle, else she would gladly win her child's
life, alone, and be content to lose her own, if by obedience to the
king's command so precious a grace might be acquired.

Tom urged—the woman still adhered to her declarations. Finally
he said—

"I think the woman hath said true. An' *my* mother were in her
place and gifted with the devil's functions, she had not stayed a
moment to call her storms and lay the whole land in ruins, if the
saving of my forfeit life were the price she got! It is argument that
other mothers are made in like mould. Thou art free, good wife—
thou and thy child—for I do think thee innocent. *Now* thou'st
nought to fear, being pardoned—pull off thy stockings!—an' thou
canst make me a storm, thou shalt be rich!"

The redeemed creature was loud in her gratitude, and proceeded
to obey, whilst Tom looked on with eager expectancy, a little marred
by apprehension; the courtiers at the same time manifesting decided
discomfort and uneasiness. The woman stripped her own feet and
her little girl's also, and plainly did her best to reward the king's
generosity with an earthquake, but it was all a failure and a
disappointment. Tom sighed, and said—

"There, good soul, trouble thyself no further, thy power is
departed out of there. Go thy way in peace; and if it return to thee
at any time, forget me not, but fetch me a storm."*

* See Notes to Chapter 15 at the end of the volume.

CHAPTER XVI

THE STATE DINNER

The dinner hour drew near—yet strangely enough, the thought brought but slight discomfort to Tom, and hardly any terror. The morning's experiences had wonderfully built up his confidence; the poor little ash-cat was already more wonted to his strange garret, after four days' habit, than a mature person could have become in a full month. A child's facility in accommodating itself to circumstances was never more strikingly illustrated.

Let us privileged ones hurry to the great banqueting room and have a glance at matters there whilst Tom is being made ready for the imposing occasion. It is a spacious apartment, with gilded pillars and pilasters, and pictured walls and ceilings. At the door stand tall guards, as rigid as statues, dressed in rich and picturesque costumes, and bearing halberds. In a high gallery which runs all around the place is a band of musicians and a packed company of citizens of both sexes, in brilliant attire. In the centre of the room, upon a raised platform, is Tom's table. Now let the ancient chronicler speak:

"A gentleman enters the room bearing a rod, and along with him another bearing a table-cloth, which, after they have both kneeled three times with the utmost veneration, he spreads upon the table, and after kneeling again they both retire; then come two others, one with the rod again, the other with a salt-cellar, a plate, and bread; when they have kneeled as the others had done, and placed what was brought upon the table, they too retire with the same ceremonies performed by the first; at last come two nobles, richly clothed, one bearing a tasting-knife, who, after prostrating themselves in the most graceful manner, approach and rub the table with bread and salt, with as much awe as if the king had been present."*

So end the solemn preliminaries. Now, far down the echoing corridors we hear the bugle-blast, and the indistinct cry, "Place for the king! way for the king's most excellent majesty!" These sounds are momently repeated—they grow nearer and nearer—and presently, almost in our faces, the martial note peals and the cry rings out, "Way for the king!" At this instant the shining pageant appears, and files in at the door, with a measured march. Let the chronicler speak again:

"First come Gentlemen, Barons, Earls, Knights of the Garter, all richly dressed and bareheaded; next comes the Chancellor, between two, one of which carries the royal sceptre, the other the Sword of State in a red scabbard, studded with golden fleurs-de-lis, the point upwards; next comes the King himself—whom, upon his appearing, twelve trumpets and many drums salute with a great burst of welcome, whilst all in the galleries rise in their places, crying "God

*Leigh Hunt's "The Town," p. 408, quotation from an early tourist.

save the King!" After him come nobles attached to his person, and on his right and left march his guard of honor, his fifty Gentlemen Pensioners, with gilt battle-axes."

This was all fine and pleasant. Tom's pulse beat high and a glad light was in his eye. He bore himself right gracefully, and all the more so because he was not thinking of how he was doing it, his mind being charmed and occupied with the blithe sights and sounds about him—and besides, nobody can be very ungraceful in nicely-fitting beautiful clothes after he has grown a little used to them—especially if he is for the moment unconscious of them. Tom remembered his instructions, and acknowledged his greeting with a slight inclination of his plumed head, and a courteous "I thank ye, my good people."

He seated himself at table, without removing his cap; and did it without the least embarrassment; for to eat with one's cap on was the one solitary royal custom upon which the kings and the Cantys met upon common ground, neither party having any advantage over the other in the matter of old familiarity with it. The pageant broke up and grouped itself picturesquely, and remained bareheaded.

Now, to the sound of gay music, the Yeomen of the Guard entered, —"the tallest and mightiest men in England, they being selected in this regard"—but we will let the chronicler tell about it:

"The Yeomen of the Guard entered, bareheaded, clothed in scarlet, with golden roses upon their backs; and these went and came, bringing in each turn a course of dishes, served in plate. These dishes were received by a gentleman in the same order they were brought, and placed upon the table, while the taster gave to each guard a mouthful to eat of the particular dish he had brought, for fear of any poison."

Tom made a good dinner, notwithstanding he was conscious that hundreds of eyes followed each morsel to his mouth and watched him eat it with an interest which could not have been more intense if it had been a deadly explosive and was expected to blow him up and scatter him all over the place. He was careful not to hurry, and equally careful not to do any thing whatever for himself, but wait till the proper official knelt down and did it for him. He got through without a mistake—flawless and precious triumph.

When the meal was over at last and he marched away in the midst of his bright pageant, with the happy noises in his ears of blaring bugles, rolling drums and thundering acclamations, he felt that if he had seen the worst of dining in public, it was an ordeal which he would be glad to endure several times a day if by that means he could but buy himself free from some of the more formidable requirements of his royal office.

CHAPTER XVII

FOO-FOO THE FIRST

Miles Hendon hurried along toward the Southwark end of the bridge, keeping a sharp lookout for the persons he sought, and hoping and expecting to overtake them presently. He was disappointed in this, however. By asking questions, he was enabled to track them part of the way through Southwark; then all traces ceased, and he was perplexed as to how to proceed. Still, he continued his efforts as best he could during the rest of the day. Nightfall found him leg-weary, half famished, and his desire as far from accomplishment as ever; so he supped at the Tabard inn and went to bed, resolved to make an early start in the morning, and give the town an exhaustive search. As he lay thinking and planning, he presently began to reason thus: The boy would escape from the ruffian, his reputed father, if possible; would he go back to London and seek his former haunts? no, he would not do that, he would avoid recapture. What, then, would he do? Never having had a friend in the world, or a protector, until he met Miles Hendon, he would naturally try to find that friend again, provided the effort did not require him to go toward London and danger. He would strike for Hendon Hall, that is what he would do, for he knew Hendon was homeward bound and there he might expect to find him. Yes, the case was plain to Hendon—he must lose no more time in Southwark, but move at once through Kent, toward Monk's Holm, searching the wood and inquiring as he went. Let us return to the vanished little king, now.

The ruffian whom the waiter at the inn on the bridge saw "about to join" the youth and the king, did not exactly join them, but fell in close behind them and followed their steps. He said nothing. His left arm was in a sling, and he wore a large green patch over his left eye; he limped slightly, and used an oaken staff as a support. The youth led the king a crooked course through Southwark, and by and by struck into the high road beyond. The king was irritated, now, and said he would stop here—it was Hendon's place to come to him, not his to go to Hendon. He would not endure such insolence; he would stop where he was. The youth said—

"Thou'lt tarry here, and thy friend lying wounded in the wood yonder? So be it, then."

The king's manner changed at once. He cried out—

"Wounded? And who hath dared to do it? But that is apart; lead on, lead on! Faster, sirrah! art shod with lead? Wounded, is he? Now though the doer of it be a duke's son, he shall rue it!"

It was some distance to the wood, but the space was speedily traversed. The youth looked about him, discovered a bough sticking

in the ground, with a small bit of rag tied to it, then led the way into
the forest, watching for similar boughs and finding them at intervals:
they were evidently guides to the point he was aiming at. By and by
an open place was reached, where were the charred remains of a
farm-house, and near them a barn which was falling to ruin and
decay. There was no sign of life anywhere, and utter silence
prevailed. The youth entered the barn, the king following eagerly
upon his heels. No one there! The king shot a surprised and
suspicious glance at the youth, and asked—

"Where is he?"

A mocking laugh was his answer. The king was in a rage in a
moment; he seized a billet of wood and was in the act of charging
upon the youth when another mocking laugh fell upon his ear. It was
from the lame ruffian, who had been following at a distance. The
king turned and said angrily—

"Who art thou? What is thy business here?"

"Leave thy foolery," said the man, "and quiet thyself. My disguise
is none so good that thou canst pretend thou knowest not thy father
through it."

"Thou art not my father. I knew thee not. I am the king. If thou
hast hid my servant, find him for me, or thou shalt sup sorrow for
what thou hast done."

John Canty replied, in a stern and measured voice—

"It is plain thou art mad, and I am loth to punish thee; but if thou
provoke me, I must. Thy prating doth no harm here, where there are
no ears that need to mind thy follies, yet is it well to practice thy
tongue to wary speech, that it may do no hurt when our quarters
change. I have done a murder, and may not tarry at home—neither
shalt thou, seeing I need thy service. My name is changed, for wise
reasons; it is Hobbs—John Hobbs; thine is Jack—charge thy
memory accordingly. Now, then, speak. Where is thy mother? where
are thy sisters? They came not to the place appointed—knowest thou
whither they went?"

The king answered, sullenly—

"Trouble me not with these riddles. My mother is dead; my sisters
are in the palace."

The youth near by burst into a derisive laugh, and the king would
have assaulted him, but Canty—or Hobbs, as he now called himself
—prevented him, and said—

"Peace, Hugo, vex him not; his mind is astray, and thy ways fret
him. Sit thee down, Jack, and quiet thyself; thou shalt have a morsel
to eat, anon."

Hobbs and Hugo fell to talking together, in low voices, and the
king removed himself as far as he could from their disagreeable
company. He withdrew into the twilight of the farther end of the
barn, where he found the earthen floor bedded a foot deep with
straw. He lay down here, drew straw over himself in lieu of blankets,

and was soon absorbed in thinking. He had many griefs, but the
minor ones were swept almost into forgetfulness by the supreme one,
the loss of his father. To the rest of the world the name of Henry
VIII. brought a shiver, and suggested an ogre whose nostrils
breathed destruction and whose hand dealt scourgings and death;
but to this boy the name brought only sensations of pleasure, the
figure it invoked wore a countenance that was all gentleness and
affection. He called to mind a long succession of loving passages
between his father and himself, and dwelt fondly upon them, his
unstinted tears attesting how deep and real was the grief that
possessed his heart. As the afternoon wasted away, the lad, wearied
with his troubles, sunk gradually into a tranquil and healing
slumber.

After a considerable time—he could not tell how long—his senses
struggled to a half-consciousness, and as he lay with closed eyes
vaguely wondering where he was and what had been happening, he
noted a murmurous sound, the sullen beating of rain upon the roof.
A snug sense of comfort stole over him, which was rudely broken, the
next moment, by a chorus of piping cackles and coarse laughter. It
startled him disagreeably, and he unmuffled his head to see whence
this interruption proceeded. A grim and unsightly picture met his
eye. A bright fire was burning in the middle of the floor, at the other
end of the barn; and around it, and lit weirdly up by the red glare,
lolled and sprawled the motliest company of tattered gutterscum and
ruffians, of both sexes, he had ever read or dreamed of. There were
huge, stalwart men, brown with exposure, long-haired, and clothed
in fantastic rags; there were middle-sized youths, of truculent
countenance, and similarly clad; there were blind mendicants, with
patched or bandaged eyes; crippled ones, with wooden legs and
crutches; there was a villain-looking peddler with his pack; a knife-
grinder, a tinker, and a barber-surgeon, with the implements of their
trades; some of the females were hardly-grown girls, some were at
prime, some were old and wrinkled hags, and all were loud, brazen,
foul-mouthed; and all soiled and slatternly; there were three sore-
faced babies; there were a couple of starveling curs, with strings
about their necks, whose office was to lead the blind.

The night was come, the gang had just finished feasting, an orgy
was beginning, the can of liquor was passing from mouth to mouth.
A general cry broke forth—

"A song! a song from the Bat and Dick Dot-and-go-One!"

One of the blind men got up, and made ready by casting aside the
patches that sheltered his excellent eyes, and the pathetic placard
which recited the cause of his calamity. Dot-and-go-One
disencumbered himself of his timber leg and took his place, upon
sound and healthy limbs, beside his fellow-rascal; then they roared
out a rollicking ditty, and were re-enforced by the whole crew, at the
end of each stanza, in a rousing chorus. By the time the last stanza

was reached, the half-drunken enthusiasm had risen to such a pitch, that everybody joined in and sang it clear through from the beginning, producing a volume of villainous sound that made the rafters quake. These were the inspiring words:

> "Bien Darkmans then, Bouse Mort and Ken,
>   The bien Coves bings awast,
>   On Chates to trine by Rome Coves dine
>   For his long lib at last.
>   Bing'd out bien Morts and toure, and toure,
>   Bing out of the Rome vile bine,
>   And toure the Cove that cloy'd your duds,
>   Upon the Chates to trine."*

Conversation followed; not in the thieves' dialect of the song, for that was only used in talk when unfriendly ears might be listening. In the course of it it appeared that "John Hobbs" was not altogether a new recruit, but had trained in the gang at some former time. His later history was called for, and when he said he had "accidentally" killed a man, considerable satisfaction was expressed; when he added that the man was a priest, he was roundly applauded, and had to take a drink with everybody. Old acquaintances welcomed him joyously, and new ones were proud to shake him by the hand. He was asked why he had "tarried away so many months." He answered—

"London is better than the country, and safer these late years, the laws be so bitter and so diligently enforced. An' I had not had that accident, I had staid there. I had resolved to stay, and never more venture country-wards—but the accident has ended that."

He inquired how many persons the gang numbered now. The "Ruffler," or chief, answered—

"Five and twenty sturdy budges, bulks, files, clapperdogeons and maunders, counting the dells and doxies and other morts.† Most are here, the rest are wandering eastward, along the winter lay. We follow at dawn."

"I do not see the Wen among the honest folk about me. Where may he be?"

"Poor lad, his diet is brimstone, now, and over hot for a delicate taste. He was killed in a brawl, somewhere about midsummer."

"I sorrow to hear that; the Wen was a capable man, and brave."

"That was he, truly. Black Bess, his dell, is of us yet, but absent on the eastward tramp; a fine lass, of nice ways and orderly conduct, none ever seeing her drunk above four days in the seven."

"She was ever strict—I remember it well—a goodly wench and worthy all commendation. Her mother was more free and less particular; a troublesome and ugly tempered beldame, but furnished with a wit above the common."

*From "The English Rogue:" London. 1665.

†Canting terms for various kinds of thieves, beggars and vagabonds, and their female companions.

"We lost her through it. Her gift of palmistry and other sorts of fortune-telling begot for her at last a witch's name and fame. The law roasted her to death at a slow fire. It did touch me to a sort of tenderness to see the gallant way she met her lot—cursing and reviling all the crowd that gaped and gazed around her, whilst the flames licked upward toward her face and catched her thin locks and crackled about her old gray head—cursing them, said I?—cursing them! why an' thou shouldst live a thousand years thou'dst never hear so masterful a cursing. Alack, her art died with her. There be base and weakling imitations left, but no true blasphemy."

The Ruffler sighed; the listeners sighed in sympathy; a general depression fell upon the company for a moment, for even hardened outcasts like these are not wholly dead to sentiment, but are able to feel a fleeting sense of loss and affliction at wide intervals and under peculiarly favoring circumstances—as in cases like to this, for instance, when genius and culture depart and leave no heir. However, a deep drink all round soon restored the spirits of the mourners.

"Have any others of our friends fared hardly?" asked Hobbs.

"Some—yes. Particularly new comers—such as small husbandmen turned shiftless and hungry upon the world because their farms were taken from them to be changed to sheep ranges. They begged, and were whipped at the cart's tail, naked from the girdle up, till the blood ran; then set in the stocks to be pelted; they begged again, were whipped again, and deprived of an ear; they begged a third time—poor devils, what else could they do?—and were branded on the cheek with a red hot iron, then sold for slaves; they ran away, were hunted down, and hanged. 'Tis a brief tale, and quickly told. Others of us have fared less hardly. Stand forth, Yokel, Burns, and Hodge—show your adornments!"

These stood up and stripped away some of their rags, exposing their backs, criss-crossed with ropy old welts left by the lash; one turned up his hair and showed the place where a left ear had once been; another showed a brand upon his shoulder—the letter V— and a mutilated ear; the third said:

"I am Yokel, once a farmer and prosperous, with loving wife and kids—now am I somewhat different in estate and calling; and the wife and kids are gone; mayhap they are in heaven, maybe in—in the other place—but the kindly God be thanked, they bide no more in *England!* My good old blameless mother strove to earn bread by nursing the sick; one of these died, the doctors knew not how, so my mother was burnt for a witch, whilst my babes looked on and wailed. English law!—up, all, with your cups!—now altogether and with a cheer!—drink to the merciful English law that delivered *her* from the English hell! Thank you, mates, one and all. I begged, from house to house—I and the wife—bearing with us the hungry kids— but it was crime to be hungry in England—so they stripped us and lashed us through three towns!—for its lash drank deep of my

Mary's blood and its blessed deliverance came quick. She lies there,
in the potter's field, safe from all harms. And the kids—well, whilst
the law lashed me from town to town, they starved. Drink lads—only
a drop—a drop to the poor kids, that never did any creature harm. I
begged again—begged for a crust, and got the stocks and lost an
ear—see, here bides the stump; I begged again, and here is the
stump of the other to keep me minded of it. And still I begged again,
and was sold for a slave—here on my cheek under this stain, if I
washed it off, ye might see the red S the branding-iron left there!
A Slave! Do ye understand that word! An English Slave!—that is he
that stands before ye. I have run from my master, and when I am
found—the heavy curse of heaven fall on the law of the land
that hath commanded it!—I shall hang!"*

A ringing voice came through the murky air—

"Thou shalt *not!*—and this day the end of that law is come!"

All turned, and saw the fantastic figure of the little king
approaching hurriedly; as it emerged into the light and was clearly
revealed, a general explosion of inquiries broke out:

"Who is it? *What* is it? Who art thou, manikin?"

The boy stood confused in the midst of all those surprised and
questioning eyes, and answered with princely dignity—

"I am Edward, king of England."

A wild burst of laughter followed, partly of derision and partly of
delight in the excellence of the joke. The king was stung. He said
sharply—

"Ye mannerless vagrants, is this your recognition of the royal
boon I have promised?"

He said more, with angry voice and excited gesture, but it was lost
in a whirlwind of laughter and mocking exclamations. "John
Hobbs" made several attempts to make himself heard above the din,
and at last succeeded—saying—

"Mates, he is my son, a dreamer, a fool, and stark mad—mind
him not—he thinketh he *is* the king."

"I *am* the king," said Edward, turning toward him, "as thou shalt
know to thy cost, in good time. Thou hast confessed a murder—thou
shalt swing for it."

"*Thou'lt* betray me!—*thou?* An' I get my hand upon thee"—

"Tut-tut!" said the burly Ruffler, interposing in time to save the
king, and emphasizing this service by knocking Hobbs down with
his fist, "hast respect for neither Kings *nor* Rufflers? An' thou insult
my presence so again, I'll hang thee up myself." Then he said to his
majesty, "Thou must make no threats against thy mates, lad; and
thou must guard thy tongue from saying evil of them elsewhere.
Be king, if it please thy mad humor, but be not harmful in it. Sink
the title thou hast uttered,—'tis treason; we be bad men, in some few
trifling ways, but none among us is so base as to be traitor to his
king; we be loving and loyal hearts, in that regard. Note if I speak

* See Note 10, at end of volume.

truth. Now—all together: 'Long live Edward, king of England!' "

"LONG LIVE EDWARD, KING OF ENGLAND!"

The response came with such a thundergust from the motley crew
that the crazy building vibrated to the sound. The little king's face
lighted with pleasure for an instant, and he slightly inclined his head
and said with grave simplicity—

"I thank you, my good people."

This unexpected result threw the company into convulsions of
merriment. When something like quiet was presently come again,
the Ruffler said, firmly, but with an accent of good nature—

"Drop it, boy, 'tis not wise, nor well. Humor thy fancy, if thou
must, but choose some other title."

A tinker shrieked out a suggestion—

"Foo-foo the First, King of the Mooncalves!"

The title "took," at once, every throat responded, and a roaring
shout went up, of—

"Long live Foo-foo the First, King of the Mooncalves!" followed
by hootings, cat-calls, and peals of laughter.

"Hale him forth, and crown him!"

"Robe him!"

"Sceptre him!"

"Throne him!"

These and twenty other cries broke out at once; and almost before
the poor little victim could draw a breath he was crowned with a tin
basin, robed in a tattered blanket, throned upon a barrel, and
sceptred with the tinker's soldering-iron. Then all flung themselves
upon their knees about him and sent up a chorus of ironical
wailings, and mocking supplications, whilst they swabbed their eyes
with their soiled and ragged sleeves and aprons—

"Be gracious to us, O, sweet king!"

"Trample not upon thy beseeching worms, O noble majesty!"

"Pity thy slaves, and comfort them with a royal kick!"

"Cheer us and warm us with they gracious rays, O flaming sun of
sovereignty!"

"Sanctify the ground with the touch of thy foot, that we may eat
the dirt and be ennobled!"

"Deign to spit upon us, O sire, that our children's children may
tell of thy princely condescension, and be proud and happy forever!"

But the humorous tinker made the "hit" of the evening and
carried off the honors. Kneeling, he pretended to kiss the king's
foot, and was indignantly spurned; whereupon he went about
begging for a rag to paste over the place upon his face which had
been touched by the foot, saying it must be preserved from contact
with the vulgar air, and that he should make his fortune by going on
the highway and exposing it to view at the rate of a hundred shillings
a sight. He made himself so killingly funny that he was the envy and
admiration of the whole mangy rabble.

Tears of shame and indignation stood in the little monarch's
eyes; and the thought in his heart was, "Had I offered them a deep
wrong they could not be more cruel—yet have I proffered nought but
to do them a kindness—and it is thus they use me for it!"

CHAPTER XVIII

THE PRINCE WITH THE TRAMPS

The troop of vagabonds turned out at early dawn, and set forward
on their march. There was a lowering sky overhead, sloppy ground
under foot, and a winter chill in the air. All gayety was gone from
the company; some were sullen and silent, some were irritable and
petulant, none were gentle-humored, all were thirsty.

The Ruffler put "Jack" in Hugo's charge, with some brief
instructions, and commanded John Canty to keep away from him
and let him alone; he also warned Hugo not to be too rough with
the lad.

After a while the weather grew milder, and the clouds lifted
somewhat. The troop ceased to shiver, and their spirits began to
improve. They grew more and more cheerful, and finally began to
chaff each other and insult passengers along the highway. This
showed that they were awaking to an appreciation of life and its
joys once more. The dread in which their sort was held was apparent
in the fact that everybody gave them the road, and took their ribald
insolences meekly, without venturing to talk back. They snatched
linen from the hedges, occasionally, in full view of the owners, who
made no protest, but only seemed grateful that they did not take the
hedges, too.

By and by they invaded a small farm house and made themselves
at home while the trembling farmer and his people swept the larder
clean to furnish a breakfast for them. They chucked the housewife
and her daughters under the chin whilst receiving the food from
their hands, and made coarse jests about them, accompanied with
insulting epithets and bursts of horse-laughter. They threw bones
and vegetables at the farmer and his sons, kept them dodging all
the time, and applauded uproariously when a good hit was made.
They ended by buttering the head of one of the daughters who
resented some of their familiarities. When they took their leave
they threatened to come back and burn the house over the heads of
the family if any report of their doings got to the ears of the
authorities.

About noon, after a long and weary tramp, the gang came to a
halt behind a hedge on the outskirts of a considerable village. An
hour was allowed for rest, then the crew scattered themselves
abroad to enter the village at different points to ply their various
trades.—"Jack" was sent with Hugo. They wandered hither and

thither for some time, Hugo watching for opportunities to do a
stroke of business but finding none—so he finally said—

"I see nought to steal; it is a paltry place. Wherefore we will beg."

"*We*, forsooth! Follow thy trade—it befits thee. But *I* will not
beg."

"Thou'lt not beg!" exclaimed Hugo, eying the king with surprise.
"Prithee, since when hast thou reformed?"

"What dost thou mean?"

"Mean? Hast thou not begged the streets of London all thy life?"

"I? Thou idiot!"

"Spare thy compliments—thy stock will last the longer. Thy
father says thou hast begged all thy days. Mayhap he lied.
Peradventure you will even make so bold as to *say* he lied," scoffed
Hugo.

"Him *you* call my father? Yes, he lied."

"Come, play not thy merry game of madman so far, mate; use it
for thy amusement, not thy hurt. An' I tell him this, he will scorch
thee finely for it."

"Save thyself the trouble. I will tell him."

"I like thy spirit, I do in truth; but I do not admire thy judgment.
Bone-rackings and bastings be plenty enow in this life, without
going out of one's way to invite them. But a truce to these matters;
I believe your father. I doubt not he can lie; I doubt not he *doth*
lie, upon occasion, for the best of us do that; but there is no occasion
here. A wise man does not waste so good a commodity as lying for
nought. But come; sith it is thy humor to give over begging,
wherewithal shall we busy ourselves? With robbing kitchens?"

The king said, impatiently—

"Have done with this folly—you weary me!"

Hugo replied, with temper—

"Now harkee, mate; you will not beg, you will not rob; so be it.
But I will tell you what you *will* do. You will play decoy whilst *I* beg.
Refuse, an' you think you may venture!"

The king was about to reply contemptuously, when Hugo said,
interrupting—

"Peace! Here comes one with a kindly face. Now will I fall down
in a fit. When the stranger runs to me, set you up a wail, and fall
upon your knees, seeming to weep; then cry out as if all the devils
of misery were in your belly, and say, 'O, sir, it is my poor afflicted
brother, and we be friendless; o' God's name cast through your
merciful eyes one pitiful look upon a sick, forsaken and most
miserable wretch; bestow one little penny out of thy riches upon
one smitten of God and ready to perish!'—and mind you, keep you
on wailing, and abate not till we bilk him of his penny, else shall
you rue it."

Then immediately Hugo began to moan, and groan, and roll his
eyes, and reel and totter about; and when the stranger was close at

hand, down he sprawled before him, with a shriek, and began to
writhe and wallow in the dirt, in seeming agony.

"O dear, O dear!" cried the benevolent stranger. "O poor soul,
poor soul, how he doth suffer! There—let me help thee up."

"O, noble sir, forbear, and God love you for a princely
gentleman—but it giveth me cruel pain to touch me when I am
taken so. My brother there will tell your worship how I am racked
with anguish when these fits be upon me. A penny, dear sir, a penny,
to buy a little food; then leave me to my sorrows."

"A penny! thou shalt have three, thou hapless creature"—and he
fumbled in his pocket with nervous haste and got them out. "There,
poor lad, take them, and most welcome. Now come hither, my boy,
and help me carry thy stricken brother to yon house, where"—

"I am not his brother," said the king, interrupting.

"What! not his brother?"

"O hear him!" groaned Hugo, then privately ground his teeth.
"He denies his own brother—and he with one foot in the grave!"

"Boy, thou art indeed hard of heart, if this is thy brother. For
shame!—and he scarce able to move hand or foot. If he is not thy
brother, who is he, then?"

"A beggar and a thief! He has got your money and has picked
your pocket likewise. An' thou wouldst do a healing miracle, lay
thy staff over his shoulders and trust Providence for the rest."

But Hugo did not tarry for the miracle. In a moment he was up
and off like the wind, the gentleman following after and raising the
hue and cry lustily as he went. The king, breathing deep gratitude
to Heaven for his own release, fled in the opposite direction and did
not slacken his pace until he was out of harm's reach. He took the
first road that offered, and soon put the village behind him. He
hurried along, as briskly as he could, during several hours, keeping
a nervous watch over his shoulder for pursuit; but his fears left him
at last, and a grateful sense of security took their place. He
recognized, now, that he was hungry; and also very tired. So he
halted at a farm house; but when he was about to speak, he was cut
short and driven rudely away. His clothes were against him.
He wandered on, wounded and indignant, and was resolved to
put himself in the way of light treatment no more. But hunger is
pride's master; so as the evening drew near, he made an attempt
at another farm house; but here he fared worse than before; for he
was called hard names and was promised arrest as a vagrant except
he moved on promptly.

The night came on, chilly and overcast; and still the footsore
monarch labored slowly on. He was obliged to keep moving, for
every time he sat down to rest he was soon penetrated to the bone
with the cold. All his sensations and experiences, as he moved
through the solemn gloom and the empty vastness of the night,
were new and strange to him. At intervals he heard voices approach,

pass by, and fade into silence; and as he saw nothing more of the
bodies they belonged to than a sort of formless drifting blur, there
was something spectral and uncanny about it all that made him
shudder. Occasionally he caught the twinkle of a light—always
far away, apparently—almost in another world; if he heard the
tinkle of a sheep's bell, it was vague, distant, indistinct; the muffled
lowing of the herds floated to him on the night wind in vanishing
cadences, a mournful sound; now and then came the complaining
howl of a dog over viewless expanses of field and forest; all sounds
were remote; they made the little king feel that all life and activity
were far removed from him, and that he stood solitary,
companionless, in the centre of a measureless solitude.

He stumbled along, through the grewsome fascinations of this
new experience, startled occasionally by the soft rustling of the dry
leaves overhead, so like human whispers they seemed to sound; and
by and by he came suddenly upon the freckled light of a tin lantern
near at hand. He stepped back into the shadows and waited. The
lantern stood by the open door of a barn. The king waited some
time—there was no sound, and nobody stirring. He got so cold,
standing still, and the hospitable barn looked so enticing, that at
last he resolved to risk everything and enter. He started swiftly and
stealthily, and just as he was crossing the threshold he heard voices
behind him. He darted behind a cask, within the barn, and stooped
down. Two farm laborers came in, bringing the lantern with them,
and fell to work, talking meanwhile. Whilst they moved about with
the light, the king made good use of his eyes and took the bearings
of what seemed to be a good sized stall at the further end of the
place, purposing to grope his way to it when he should be left to
himself. He also noted the position of a pile of horse blankets,
midway of the route, with the intent to levy upon them for the
service of the crown of England for one night.

By and by the men finished and went away, fastening the door
behind them and taking the lantern with them. The shivering king
made for the blankets, with as good speed as the darkness would
allow; gathered them up and then groped his way safely to the
stall. Of two of the blankets he made a bed, then covered himself
with the remaining two. He was a glad monarch, now, though the
blankets were old and thin, and not quite warm enough; and
besides gave out a pungent horsy odor that was almost suffocatingly
powerful.

Although the king was hungry and chilly, he was also so tired and
so drowsy that these latter influences soon began to get the
advantage of the former, and he presently dozed off into a state of
semi-consciousness. Then, just as he was on the point of losing
himself wholly, he distinctly felt something touch him! He was
broad awake in a moment, and gasping for breath. The cold horror
of that mysterious touch in the dark almost made his heart stand

still. He lay motionless, and listened, scarcely breathing. But nothing
stirred, and there was no sound. He continued to listen, and wait,
during what seemed a long time, but still nothing stirred, and there
was no sound. So he began to drop into a drowse once more, at last;
and all at once he felt that mysterious touch again! It was a grisly
thing, this light touch from this noiseless and invisible presence; it
made the boy sick with ghostly fears. What should he do? That was
the question; but he did not know how to answer it. Should he leave
these reasonably comfortable quarters and fly from this inscrutable
horror? But fly whither? He could not get out of the barn; and the
idea of scurrying blindly hither and thither in the dark, within the
captivity of the four walls, with this phantom gliding after him, and
visiting him with that soft hideous touch upon cheek or shoulder at
every turn, was intolerable. But to stay where he was, and endure
this living death all night?—was that better? No. What, then, was
there left to do? Ah, there was but one course; he knew it well—he
must put out his hand and find that thing!

It was easy to think this; but it was hard to brace himself up to
try it. Three times he stretched his hand a little way out into the
dark, gingerly; and snatched it suddenly back, with a gasp—not
because it had encountered any thing, but because he had felt so
sure it was just *going* to. But the fourth time, he groped a little
further, and his hand lightly swept against something soft and
warm. This petrified him, nearly, with fright—his mind was in such
a state that he could imagine the thing to be nothing else than a
corpse, newly dead and still warm. He thought he would rather die
than touch it again. But he thought this false thought because he
did not know the immortal strength of human curiosity. In no long
time his hand was tremblingly groping again—against his judgment,
and without his consent—but groping persistently on, just the same.
It encountered a bunch of long hair; he shuddered, but followed up
the hair and found what seemed to be a warm rope; followed up the
rope and found an innocent calf!—for the rope was not a rope at all,
but the calf's tail.

The king was cordially ashamed of himself for having gotten all
that fright and misery out of so paltry a matter as a slumbering calf;
but he need not have felt so about it, for it was not the calf that
frightened him but a dreadful non-existent something which the
calf stood for; and any other boy, in those old superstitious times,
would have acted and suffered just as he had done.

The king was not only delighted to find that the creature was only
a calf, but delighted to have the calf's company; for he had been
feeling so lonesome and friendless that the company and
comradeship of even this humble animal was welcome. And he had
been so buffeted, so rudely entreated by his own kind, that it was
a real comfort to him to feel that he was at last in the society of a
fellow creature that had at least a soft heart and a gentle spirit,

whatever loftier attributes might be lacking. So he resolved to waive
rank and make friends with the calf.

While stroking its sleek warm back—for it lay near him and
within easy reach—it occurred to him that this calf might be utilized
in more ways than one. Whereupon he re-arranged his bed,
spreading it down close to the calf; then he cuddled himself up to
the calf's back, drew the covers up over himself and his friend, and
in a minute or two was as warm and comfortable as he had ever been
in the downy couches of the regal palace of Westminster.

Pleasant thoughts came, at once; life took on a cheerfuller
seeming. He was free of the bonds of servitude and crime, free of
the companionship of base and brutal outlaws; he was warm, he was
sheltered; in a word, he was happy. The night wind was rising; it
swept by in fitful gusts that made the old barn quake and rattle,
then its forces died down at intervals, and went moaning and wailing
around corners and projections—but it was all music to the king,
now that he was snug and comfortable: let it blow and rage, let it
batter and bang, let it moan and wail, he minded it not, he only
enjoyed it. He merely snuggled the closer to his friend, in a luxury of
warm contentment, and drifted blissfully out of consciousness into
a deep and dreamless sleep that was full of serenity and peace. The
distant dogs howled, the melancholy kine complained, and the
winds went on raging, whilst furious sheets of rain drove along the
roof; but the majesty of England slept on, undisturbed, and the
calf did the same, it being a simple creature and not easily troubled
by storms or embarrassed by sleeping with a king.

CHAPTER XIX

THE PRINCE WITH THE PEASANTS

When the king awoke in the early morning, he found that a wet
but thoughtful rat had crept into the place during the night and
made a cosey bed for itself in his bosom. Being disturbed, now, it
scampered away. The boy smiled, and said, "Poor fool, why so
fearful? I am as forlorn as thou. 'Twould be a shame in me to hurt
the helpless, who am myself so helpless. Moreover, I owe you thanks
for a good omen; for when a king has fallen so low that the very
rats do make a bed of him, it surely meaneth that his fortunes be
upon the turn, since it is plain he can no lower go."

He got up and stepped out of the stall, and just then he heard the
sound of children's voices. The barn door opened and a couple of
little girls came in. As soon as they saw him their talking and
laughing ceased, and they stopped and stood still, gazing at him with
strong curiosity; they presently began to whisper together, then they
approached nearer, and stopped again to gaze and whisper. By and

by they gathered courage and began to discuss him aloud. One
said—

"He hath a comely face."

The other added—

"And pretty hair."

"But is ill clothed enow."

"And how starved he looketh."

They came still nearer, sidling shyly around and about him,
examining him minutely from all points, as if he were some strange
new kind of animal; but warily and watchfully, the while, as if they
half feared he might be a sort of animal that would bite, upon
occasion. Finally they halted before him, holding each other's
hands, for protection, and took a good satisfying stare with their
innocent eyes; then one of them plucked up all her courage and
inquired with honest directness—

"Who art thou, boy?"

"I am the king," was the grave answer.

The children gave a little start, and their eyes spread themselves
wide open and remained so during a speechless half minute. Then
curiosity broke the silence—

"The *king?* What king?"

"The king of England."

The children looked at each other—then at him—then at each
other again—wonderingly, perplexedly—then one said—

"Didst hear him, Margery?—he saith he is the king. Can that be
true?"

"How can it be else but true, Prissy? Would he say a lie? For look
you, Prissy, an' it were not true, it *would* be a lie. It surely would be.
Now think on't. For all things that be not true, be lies—thou canst
make nought else out of it."

It was a good tight argument, without a leak in it anywhere; and
it left Prissy's half-doubts not a leg to stand on. She considered a
moment, then put the king upon his honor with the simple remark—

"If thou art truly the king, then I believe thee."

"I am truly the king."

This settled the matter. His majesty's royalty was accepted
without further question or discussion, and the two little girls began
at once to inquire into how he came to be where he was, and how he
came to be so unroyally clad, and whither he was bound, and all
about his affairs. It was a mighty relief to him to pour out his
troubles where they would not be scoffed at or doubted; so he told
his tale with feeling, forgetting even his hunger for the time; and it
was received with the deepest and tenderest sympathy by the gentle
little maids. But when he got down to his latest experiences and
they learned how long he had been without food, they cut him short
and hurried him away to the farm-house to find a breakfast for him.

The king was cheerful and happy, now, and said to himself,

"When I am come to mine own again, I will always honor little children, remembering how that these trusted me and believed in me in my time of trouble; whilst they that were older, and thought themselves wiser, mocked at me and held me for a liar."

The children's mother received the king kindly, and was full of pity; for his forlorn condition and apparently crazed intellect touched her womanly heart. She was a widow, and rather poor; consequently she had seen trouble enough to enable her to feel for the unfortunate. She imagined that the demented boy had wandered away from his friends or keepers; so she tried to find out whence he had come, in order that she might take measures to return him; but all her references to neighboring towns and villages, and all her inquiries in the same line, went for nothing—the boy's face, and his answers, too, showed that the things she was talking of were not familiar to him. He spoke earnestly and simply about court matters; and broke down, more than once, when speaking of the late king "his father;" but whenever the conversation changed to baser topics, he lost interest and became silent.

The woman was mightily puzzled; but she did not give up. As she proceeded with her cooking, she set herself to contriving devices to surprise the boy into betraying his real secret. She talked about cattle—he showed no concern; then about sheep—the same result— so her guess that he had been a shepherd boy was an error; she talked about mills; and about weavers, tinkers, smiths, trades and tradesmen of all sorts; and about Bedlam, and jails, and charitable retreats; but no matter, she was baffled at all points. Not altogether, either; for she argued that she had narrowed the thing down to domestic service. Yes, she was sure she was on the right track, now— he must have been a house servant. So she led up to that. But the result was discouraging. The subject of sweeping appeared to weary him; fire-building failed to stir him; scrubbing and scouring awoke no enthusiasm. Then the goodwife touched, with a perishing hope, and rather as a matter of form, upon the subject of cooking. To her surprise, and her vast delight, the king's face lighted at once! Ah, she had hunted him down at last, she thought; and she was right proud too, of the devious shrewdness and tact which had accomplished it.

Her tired tongue got a chance to rest, now; for the king's, inspired by gnawing hunger and the fragrant smells that came from the sputtering pots and pans, turned itself loose and delivered itself up to such an eloquent dissertation upon certain toothsome dishes, that within three minutes the woman said to herself, "Of a truth I was right—he hath holpen in a kitchen!" Then he broadened his bill of fare, and discussed it with such appreciation and animation, that the goodwife said to herself, "Good lack! how can he know so many dishes, and so fine ones withal? For these belong only upon the tables of the rich and great. Ah, now I see! ragged outcast as he

is, he must have served in the palace before his reason went astray;
yes, he must have helped in the very kitchen of the king himself!
I will test him."

Full of eagerness to prove her sagacity, she told the king to mind
the cooking a moment—hinting that he might manufacture and add
a dish or two, if he chose—then she went out of the room and gave
her children a sign to follow after. The king muttered—

"Another English king had a commission like to this, in a bygone
time—it is nothing against my dignity to undertake an office which
the great Alfred stooped to assume. But I will try to better serve my
trust than he; for he let the cakes burn."

The intent was good, but the performance was not answerable to
it; for this king, like the other one, soon fell into deep thinkings
concerning his vast affairs, and the same calamity resulted—the
cookery got burned. The woman returned in time to save the
breakfast from entire destruction; and she promptly brought the
king out of his dreams with a brisk and cordial tongue-lashing.
Then, seeing how troubled he was, over his violated trust, she
softened at once and was all goodness and gentleness toward him.

The boy made a hearty and satisfying meal, and was greatly
refreshed and gladdened by it. It was a meal which was distinguished
by this curious feature, that rank was waived on both sides; yet
neither recipient of the favor was aware that it had been extended.
The goodwife had intended to feed this young tramp with broken
victuals in a corner, like any other tramp, or like a dog; but she was
so remorseful for the scolding she had given him, that she did what
she could to atone for it by allowing him to sit at the family table and
eat with his betters, on ostensible terms of equality with them; and
the king, on his side, was so remorseful for having broken his trust,
after the family had been so kind to him, that he forced himself to
atone for it by humbling himself to the family level, instead of
requiring the woman and her children to stand and wait upon him
while he occupied their table in the solitary state due his birth and
dignity. It does us all good to unbend sometimes. This good woman
was made happy all the day long by the applauses she got out of
herself for her magnanimous condescension to a tramp; and the
king was just as self-complacent over his gracious humility toward
a humble peasant woman.

When breakfast was over, the housewife told the king to wash up
the dishes. This command was a staggerer, for a moment, and the
king came near rebelling: but then he said to himself, "Alfred the
Great watched the cakes; doubtless he would have washed the
dishes, too—therefore will I essay it."

He made a sufficiently poor job of it; and to his surprise, too, for
the cleaning of wooden spoons and trenchers had seemed an easy
thing to do. It was a tedious and troublesome piece of work, but he
finished it at last. He was becoming impatient to get away on his

journey now; however, he was not to lose this thrifty dame's society
so easily. She furnished him some little odds and ends of
employment, which he got through with after a fair fashion and with
some credit. Then she set him and the little girls to paring some
winter apples; but he was so awkward at this service, that she retired
him from it and gave him a butcher knife to grind. Afterward she
kept him carding wool until he began to think he had laid the good
King Alfred about far enough in the shade for the present, in the
matter of showy menial heroisms that would read picturesquely in
story-books and histories, and so he was half minded to resign. And
when, just after the noonday dinner, the goodwife gave him a basket
of kittens to drown, he did resign. At least he was just going to
resign—for he felt that he must draw the line somewhere, and it
seemed to him that to draw it at kitten-drowning was about the right
thing—when there was an interruption. The interruption was John
Canty—with a peddler's pack on his back—and Hugo!

The King discovered these rascals approaching the front gate
before they had had a chance to see him; so he said nothing about
drawing the line, but took up his basket of kittens and stepped
quietly out the back way, without a word. He left the creatures in an
outhouse, and hurried on, into a narrow lane at the rear.

CHAPTER XX

THE PRINCE AND THE HERMIT

The high hedge hid him from the house, now; and so, under the
impulse of a deadly fright, he let out all his forces and sped toward a
wood in the distance. He never looked back until he had almost
gained the shelter of the forest; then he turned and descried two
figures in the distance. That was sufficient; he did not wait to scan
them critically, but hurried on, and never abated his pace till he was
far within the twilight depths of the wood. Then he stopped; being
persuaded that he was now tolerably safe. He listened intently, but
the stillness was profound and solemn—awful, even, and depressing
to the spirits. At wide intervals his straining ear did detect sounds,
but they were so remote, and hollow, and mysterious, that they
seemed not to be real sounds, but only the moaning and complaining
ghosts of departed ones. So the sounds were yet more dreary than the
silence which they interrupted.

It was his purpose, in the beginning, to stay where he was, the rest
of the day; but a chill soon invaded his perspiring body, and he was
at last obliged to resume movement in order to get warm. He struck
straight through the forest, hoping to pierce to a road presently,
but he was disappointed in this. He travelled on and on; but the
farther he went, the denser the wood became, apparently. The gloom
began to thicken, by and by, and the king realized that the night

was coming on. It made him shudder to think of spending it in such
an uncanny place; so he tried to hurry faster, but he only made the
less speed, for he could not now see well enough to choose his steps
judiciously; consequently he kept tripping over roots and tangling
himself in vines and briers.

And how glad he was when at last he caught the glimmer of a
light! He approached it warily, stopping often to look about him and
listen. It came from an unglazed window-opening in a little hut.
He heard a voice, now, and felt a disposition to run and hide; but he
changed his mind at once, for this voice was praying, evidently. He
glided to the one window of the hut, raised himself on tiptoe, and
stole a glance within. The room was small; its floor was the natural
earth, beaten hard by use; in a corner was a bed of rushes and a
ragged blanket or two; near it was a pail, a cup, a basin, and two or
three pots and pans; there was a short bench and a three-legged
stool; on the hearth the remains of a fagot fire were smouldering;
before a shrine, which was lighted by a single candle, knelt an aged
man, and on an old wooden box at his side, lay an open book and a
human skull. The man was of large, bony frame; his hair and
whiskers were very long and snowy white; he was clothed in a robe of
sheepskins which reached from his neck to his heels.

"A holy hermit!" said the king to himself; "now am I indeed
fortunate."

The hermit rose from his knees; the king knocked. A deep voice
responded—

"Enter!—but leave sin behind, for the ground whereon thou shalt
stand is holy!"

The king entered, and paused. The hermit turned a pair of
gleaming, unrestful eyes upon him, and said—

"Who art thou?"

"I am the king," came the answer, with placid simplicity.

"Welcome, king!" cried the hermit, with enthusiasm. Then,
bustling about with feverish activity, and constantly saying
"Welcome, welcome," he arranged his bench, seated the king on it,
by the hearth, threw some fagots on the fire, and finally fell to pacing
the floor, with a nervous stride.

"Welcome! Many have sought sanctuary here, but they were not
worthy, and were turned away. But a king who casts his crown away,
and despises the vain splendors of his office, and clothes his body in
rags, to devote his life to holiness and the mortification of the flesh—
he is worthy, he is welcome!—here shall he abide all his days till
death come." The king hastened to interrupt and explain, but the
hermit paid no attention to him—did not even hear him, apparently,
but went right on with his talk, with a raised voice and a growing
energy. "And thou shalt be at peace here. None shall find out thy
refuge to disquiet thee with supplications to return to that empty
and foolish life which God hath moved thee to abandon. Thou shalt

pray, here; thou shalt study the Book; thou shalt meditate upon the follies and delusions of this world, and upon the sublimities of the world to come; thou shalt feed upon crusts and herbs, and scourge thy body with whips, daily, to the purifying of thy soul. Thou shalt wear a hair shirt next thy skin; thou shalt drink water, only; and thou shalt be at peace; yes, wholly at peace; for whoso comes to seek thee shall go his way again, baffled; he shall not find thee, he shall not molest thee."

The old man, still pacing back and forth, ceased to speak aloud, and began to mutter. The king seized this opportunity to state his case; and he did it with an eloquence inspired by uneasiness and apprehension. But the hermit went on muttering, and gave no heed. And still muttering, he approached the king and said, impressively—

" 'Sh! I will tell you a secret!" He bent down to impart it, but checked himself, and assumed a listening attitude. After a moment or two he went on tiptoe to the window-opening, put his head out and peered around in the gloaming, then came tip-toeing back again, put his face close down to the king's, and whispered—

"I am an archangel!"

The king started violently, and said to himself, "Would God I were with the outlaws again; for lo, now am I the prisoner of a madman!" His apprehensions were heightened, and they showed plainly in his face. In a low, excited voice, the hermit continued—

"I see you feel my atmosphere! There's awe in your face! None may be in this atmosphere and not be thus affected; for it is the very atmosphere of heaven. I go thither and return, in the twinkling of an eye. I was made an archangel on this very spot, it is five years ago, by angels sent from heaven to confer that awful dignity. Their presence filled this place with an intolerable brightness. And they knelt to me, king! yes, they knelt to me! for I was greater than they. I have walked in the courts of heaven, and held speech with the patriarch. Touch my hand—be not afraid—touch it. There—now thou has touched a hand which has been clasped by Abraham and Isaac and Jacob! For I have walked in the golden courts, I have seen the Deity face to face!" He paused, to give this speech effect; then his face suddenly changed, and he started to his feet again, saying, with angry energy, "Yes, I am an archangel; *a mere archangel!*— I that might have been pope! It is verily true. I was told it from heaven in a dream, twenty years ago; ah, yes I was to be pope!—and I *should* have been pope, for Heaven had said it—but the king dissolved my religious house, and I, poor obscure unfriended monk, was cast homeless upon the world, robbed of my mighty destiny!" Here he began to mumble again, and beat his forehead in futile rage, with his fist; now and then articulating a venomous curse, and now and then a pathetic "Wherefore I am nought but an archangel— I that should have been pope!"

So he went on, for an hour, whilst the poor little king sat and

suffered. Then all at once the old man's frenzy departed, and he
became all gentleness. His voice softened, he came down out of his
clouds, and fell to prattling along so simply and so humanely, that
he soon won the king's heart completely. The old devotee moved
the boy nearer to the fire and made him comfortable; doctored his
small bruises and abrasions with a deft and tender hand; and then
set about preparing and cooking a supper—chatting pleasantly all
the time, and occasionally stroking the lad's cheek or patting his
head, in such a gently caressing way that in a little while all the
fear and repulsion inspired by the archangel were changed to
reverence and affection for the man.

This happy state of things continued while the two ate the
supper; then, after a prayer before the shrine, the hermit put the
boy to bed, in a small adjoining room, tucking him in as snugly
and lovingly as a mother might; and so, with a parting caress, left
him and sat down by the fire, and began to poke the brands about
in an absent and aimless way. Presently he paused; then tapped his
forehead several times with his fingers, as if trying to recall some
thought which had escaped from his mind. Apparently he was
unsuccessful. Now he started quickly up, and entered his guest's
room, and said—

"Thou art king?"

"Yes," was the response, drowsily uttered.

"What king?"

"Of England."

"Of England! Then Henry is gone!"

"Alack, it is so. I am his son."

A black frown settled down upon the hermit's face, and he
clenched his bony hands with a vindictive energy. He stood a few
moments, breathing fast and swallowing repeatedly, then said in a
husky voice—

"Dost know it was he that turned us out into the world houseless
and homeless?"

There was no response. The old man bent down and scanned the
boy's reposeful face and listened to his placid breathing. "He sleeps
—sleeps soundly;" and the frown vanished away and gave place to
an expression of evil satisfaction. A smile flitted across the
dreaming boy's features. The hermit muttered, "So—his heart is
happy;" and he turned away. He went stealthily about the place,
seeking here and there for something; now and then halting to
listen, now and then jerking his head around and casting a quick
glance toward the bed; and always muttering, always mumbling to
himself. At last he found what he seemed to want—a rusty old
butcher knife and a whetstone. Then he crept to his place by the
fire, sat himself down, and began to whet the knife softly on the
stone, still muttering, mumbling, ejaculating. The winds sighed
around the lonely place, the mysterious voices of the night floated

by out of the distances. The shining eyes of venturesome mice and rats peered out at the old man from cracks and coverts, but he went on with his work, rapt absorbed, and noted none of these things.

At long intervals he drew his thumb along the edge of his knife, and nodded his head with satisfaction. "It grows sharper," he said; "yes, it grows sharper."

He took no note of the flight of time, but worked tranquilly on, entertaining himself with his thoughts, which broke out occasionally in articulate speech:

"His father wrought us evil, he destroyed us—and is gone down into the eternal fires! Yes, down into the eternal fires! He escaped us—but it was God's will, yes it was God's will, we must not repine. But he hath not escaped the fires! no, he hath not escaped the fires, the consuming, unpitying, remoreseless fires—and *they* are everlasting!"

And so he wrought; and still wrought; mumbling—chuckling a low rasping chuckle, at times—and at times breaking again into words:

"It was his father that did it all. I am but an archangel—but for him, I should be pope!"

The king stirred. The hermit sprang noiselessly to the bedside, and went down upon his knees, bending over the prostrate form with his knife uplifted. The boy stirred again; his eyes came open for an instant, but there was no speculation in them, they saw nothing; the next moment his tranquil breathing showed that his sleep was sound once more.

The hermit watched and listened, for a time, keeping his position and scarcely breathing; then he slowly lowered his arm, and presently crept away, saying,—

"It is long past midnight—it is not best that he should cry out, lest by accident some one be passing."

He glided about his hovel, gathering a rag here, a thong there, and another one yonder; then he returned, and by careful and gentle handling, he managed to tie the king's ankles together without waking him. Next he essayed to tie the wrists; he made several attempts to cross them, but the boy always drew one hand or the other away, just as the cord was ready to be applied; but at last, when the archangel was almost ready to despair, the boy crossed his hands himself, and the next moment they were bound. Now a bandage was passed under the sleeper's chin and brought up over his head and tied fast—and so softly, so gradually, and so deftly were the knots drawn together and compacted, that the boy slept peacefully through it all without stirring.

CHAPTER XXI

HENDON TO THE RESCUE

The old man glided away, stooping, stealthily, cat-like, and brought the low bench. He seated himself upon it, half his body in the dim and flickering light, and the other half in shadow; and so, with his craving eyes bent upon the slumbering boy, he kept his patient vigil there, heedless of the drift of time, and softly whetted his knife, and mumbled and chuckled; and in aspect and attitude he resembled nothing so much as a grizzly, monstrous spider, gloating over some hapless insect that lay bound and helpless in his web.

After a long while, the old man, who was still gazing,—yet not seeing, his mind having settled into a dreamy abstraction,— observed on a sudden, that the boy's eyes were open—wide open and staring!—staring up in frozen horror at the knife. The smile of a gratified devil crept over the old man's face, and he said, without changing his attitude or occupation—

"Son of Henry the Eighth, hast thou prayed?"

The boy struggled helplessly in his bonds; and at the same time forced a smothered sound through his closed jaws, which the hermit chose to interpret as an affirmative answer to his question.

"Then pray again. Pray the prayer for the dying!"

A shudder shook the boy's frame, and his face blenched. Then he struggled again to free himself—turning and twisting himself this way and that; tugging frantically, fiercely, desperately—but uselessly—to burst his fetters: and all the while the old ogre smiled down upon him, and nodded his head, and placidly whetted his knife; mumbling, from time to time. "The moments are precious, they are few and precious—pray the prayer for the dying!"

The boy uttered a despairing groan, and ceased from his struggles, panting. The tears came, then, and trickled, one after the other, down his face; but this piteous sight wrought no softening effect upon the savage old man.

The dawn was coming, now; the hermit observed it, and spoke up sharply, with a touch of nervous apprehension in his voice:

"I may not indulge this ecstasy longer! The night is already gone. It seems but a moment—only a moment; would it had endured a year! Seed of the Church's spoiler, close thy perishing eyes, an' thou fearest to look upon" ...

The rest was lost in inarticulate mutterings. The old man sunk upon his knees, his knife in his hand, and bent himself over the moaning boy—

Hark! There was a sound of voices near the cabin—the knife dropped from the hermit's hand; he cast a sheepskin over the boy and started up, trembling. The sounds increased, and presently the voices became rough and angry; then came blows, and cries for help; then a clatter of swift footsteps, retreating. Immediately came a succession of thundering knocks upon the cabin door, followed by—

"Hullo-o-o! Open! And despatch, in the name of all the devils!"

O, this was the blessedest sound that had ever made music in the king's ears; for it was Miles Hendon's voice!

The hermit, grinding his teeth in impotent rage, moved swiftly out of the bedchamber, closing the door behind him; and straightway the king heard a talk, to this effect, proceeding from the "chapel:"

"Homage and greeting, reverend sir! Where is the boy—*my* boy?"

"What boy, friend?"

"What boy! Lie me no lies, sir priest, play me no deceptions!—I am not in the humor for it. Near to this place I caught the scoundrels who I judged did steal him from me, and I made them confess; they said he was at large again, and they had tracked him to your door. They showed me his very footprints. Now palter no more; for look you, holy sir, an' thou produce him not— Where is the boy?"

"O, good sir, peradventure you mean the ragged regal vagrant that tarried here the night. If such as you take interest in such as he, know, then, that I have sent him of an errand. He will be back anon."

"How soon? How soon? Come, waste not the time—cannot I overtake him? How soon will he be back?"

"Thou needst not stir; he will return quickly."

"So be it then. I will try to wait. But stop!—*you* sent him of an errand?—you! Verily, this is a lie—he would not go. He would pull thy old beard, an' thou didst offer him such an insolence. Thou hast lied, friend; thou hast surely lied! He would not go for thee nor for any man."

"For any *man*—no; haply not. But I am not a man."

"*What!* Now o' God's name what art thou, then?"

"It is a secret—mark thou reveal it not. I am an archangel!"

There was a tremendous ejaculation from Miles Hendon—not altogether unprofane—followed by—

"This doth well and truly account for his complaisance! Right well I knew he would budge nor hand nor foot in the menial service of any mortal; but lord, even a king must obey when an archangel gives the word o' command! Let me—'sh! What noise was that?"

All this while the king had been yonder, alternately quaking with terror and trembling with hope; and all the while, too, he had thrown all the strength he could into his anguished moanings, constantly expecting them to reach Hendon's ear, but always realizing, with bitterness, that they failed, or at least made no

MARK TWAIN

impression. So this last remark of his servant came as comes a reviving breath from fresh fields to the dying; and he exerted himself once more, and with all his energy, just as the hermit was saying—

"Noise? I heard only the wind."

"Mayhap it was. Yes, doubtless that was it. I have been hearing it faintly all the—there it is again! It is not the wind! What an odd sound! Come, we will hunt it out!"

Now the king's joy was nearly insupportable. His tired lungs did their utmost—and hopefully, too—but the sealed jaws and the muffling sheepskin sadly crippled the effort. Then the poor fellow's heart sank, to hear the hermit say—

"Ah, it came from without—I think from the copse yonder. Come, I will lead the way."

The king heard the two pass out, talking; heard their footsteps die quickly away—then he was alone with a boding, brooding, awful silence.

It seemed an age till he heard the steps and voices approaching again—and this time he heard an added sound—the trampling of hoofs, apparently. Then he heard Hendon say—

"I will not wait longer. I *cannot* wait longer. He has lost his way in this thick wood. Which direction took he? Quick—point it out to me."

"He—but wait; I will go with thee."

"Good—good! Why, truly thou art better than thy looks. Marry I do think there's not another archangel with so right a heart as thine. Wilt ride? Wilt take the wee donkey that's for my boy, or wilt thou fork thy holy legs over this ill-conditioned slave of a mule that I have provided for myself?—and had been cheated in, too, had he cost but the indifferent sum of a month's usury on a brass farthing let to a tinker out of work."

"No—ride thy mule, and lead thine ass; I am surer on mine own feet, and will walk."

"Then prithee mind the little beast for me while I take my life in my hands and make what success I may toward mounting the big one."

Then followed a confusion of kicks, cuffs, tramplings and plungings, accompanied by a thunderous intermingling of volleyed curses, and finally a bitter apostrophe to the mule, which must have broken its spirit, for hostilities seemed to cease from that moment.

With unutterable misery the fettered little king heard the voices and footsteps fade away and die out. All hope forsook him, now, for the moment, and a dull despair settled down upon his heart. "My only friend is deceived and got rid of," he said; "the hermit will return and"—He finished with a gasp; and at once fell to struggling so frantically with his bonds again, that he shook off the smothering sheepskin.

And now he heard the door open! The sound chilled him to the marrow—already he seemed to feel the knife at his throat. Horror made him close his eyes; horror made him open them again—and before him stood John Canty and Hugo!

He would have said "Thank God!" if his jaws had been free.

A moment or two later his limbs were at liberty, and his captors each gripping him by an arm, were hurrying him with all speed through the forest.

CHAPTER XXII

A VICTIM OF TREACHERY

Once more "King Foo-Foo the First" was roving with the tramps and outlaws, a butt for their coarse jests and dull-witted railleries, and sometimes the victim of small spitefulnesses at the hands of Canty and Hugo when the Ruffler's back was turned. None but Canty and Hugo really disliked him. Some of the others liked him, and all admired his pluck and spirit. During two or three days, Hugo, in whose ward and charge the king was, did what he covertly could to make the boy uncomfortable; and at night, during the customary orgies, he amused the company by putting small indignities upon him—always as if by accident. Twice he stepped upon the king's toes—accidentally—and the king, as became his royalty, was contemptuously unconscious of it and indifferent to it; but the third time Hugo entertained himself in that way, the king felled him to the ground with a cudgel, to the prodigious delight of the tribe. Hugo, consumed with anger and shame, sprang up, seized a cudgel, and came at his small adversary in a fury. Instantly a ring was formed around the gladiators, and the betting and cheering began. But poor Hugo stood no chance whatsoever. His frantic and lubberly 'prentice-work found but a poor market for itself when pitted against an arm which had been trained by the first masters of Europe in single-stick, quarter-staff, and every art and trick of swordsmanship. The little king stood, alert but at graceful ease, and caught and turned aside the thick rain of blows with a facility and precision which set the motley on-lookers wild with admiration; and every now and then, when his practised eye detected an opening, and a lightning-swift rap upon Hugo's head followed as a result, the storm of cheers and laughter that swept the place was something wonderful to hear. At the end of fifteen minutes, Hugo, all battered, bruised, and the target for a pitiless bombardment of ridicule, slunk from the field; and the unscathed hero of the fight was seized and borne aloft upon the shoulders of the joyous rabble to the place of honor beside the Ruffler, where with vast ceremony he was crowned King of the Game-Cocks; his

meaner title being at the same time solemnly cancelled and
annulled, and a decree of banishment from the gang pronounced
against any who should henceforth utter it.

All attempts to make the king serviceable to the troop had failed.
He had stubbornly refused to act; moreover he was always trying to
escape. He had been thrust into an unwatched kitchen, the first day
of his return; he not only came forth empty handed, but tried to
rouse the housemates. He was sent out with a tinker to help him at
his work; he would not work; moreover he threatened the tinker
with his own soldering-iron; and finally both Hugo and the tinker
found their hands full with the mere matter of keeping him from
getting away. He delivered the thunders of his royalty upon the
heads of all who hampered his liberties or tried to force him to
service. He was sent out, in Hugo's charge, in company with a
slatternly woman and a diseased baby, to beg; but the result was
not encouraging—he declined to plead for the mendicants, or be a
party to their cause in any way.

Thus several days went by; and the miseries of this tramping life,
and the weariness and sordidness and meanness and vulgarity of it,
became gradually and steadily so intolerable to the captive that he
began at last to feel that his release from the hermit's knife must
prove only a temporary respite from death, at best.

But at night, in his dreams, these things were forgotten, and he
was on his throne, and master again. This, of course, intensified
the sufferings of the awakening—so the mortifications of each
succeeding morning of the few that passed between his return to
bondage and the combat with Hugo, grew bitterer and bitterer, and
harder and harder to bear.

The morning after that combat, Hugo got up with a heart filled
with vengeful purposes against the king. He had two plans, in
particular. One was to inflict upon the lad what would be, to his
proud spirit and "imagined" royalty, a peculiar humiliation; and if
he failed to accomplish this, his other plan was to put a crime of
some kind upon the king and then betray him into the implacable
clutches of the law.

In pursuance of the first plan, he proposed to put a "clime"
upon the king's leg; rightly judging that that would mortify him to
the last and perfect degree; and as soon as the clime should
operate, he meant to get Canty's help, and *force* the king to expose
his leg in the highway and beg for alms. "Clime" was the cant term
for a sore, artificially created. To make a clime, the operator made
a paste or poultice of unslaked lime, soap, and the rust of old iron,
and spread it upon a piece of leather, which was then bound tightly
upon the leg. This would presently fret off the skin, and make the
flesh raw and angry-looking; blood was then rubbed upon the limb,
which, being fully dried, took on a dark and repulsive color. Then a
bandage of soiled rags was put on in a cleverly careless way which

would allow the hideous ulcer to be seen and move the compassion of the passer-by.*

Hugo got the help of the tinker whom the king had cowed with the soldering-iron; they took the boy out on a tinkering tramp, and as soon as they were out of sight of the camp they threw him down and the tinker held him while Hugo bound the poultice tight and fast upon his leg.

The king raged and stormed, and promised to hang the two the moment the sceptre was in his hand again; but they kept a firm grip upon him and enjoyed his impotent struggling and jeered at his threats. This continued until the poultice began to bite; and in no long time its work would have been perfected, if there had been no interruption. But there was; for about this time the "slave" who had made the speech denouncing England's laws, appeared on the scene and put an end to the enterprise, and stripped off the poultice and bandage.

The King wanted to borrow his deliverer's cudgel and warm the jackets of the two rascals on the spot; but the man said no, it would bring trouble—leave the matter till night; the whole tribe being together, then, the outside world would not venture to interfere or interrupt. He marched the party back to camp and reported the affair to the Ruffler, who listened, pondered, and then decided that the king should not be again detailed to beg, since it was plain he was worthy of something higher and better— wherefore, on the spot he promoted him from the mendicant rank and appointed him to steal!

Hugo was overjoyed. He had already tried to make the king steal, and failed; but there would be no more trouble of that sort, now, for of course the king would not dream of defying a distinct command delivered directly from headquarters. So he planned a raid for that very afternoon, purposing to get the king in the law's grip in the course of it; and to do it, too, with such ingenious strategy, that it should seem to be accidental and unintentional; for the King of the Game-Cocks was popular, now, and the gang might not deal over-gently with an unpopular member who played so serious a treachery upon him as the delivering him over to the common enemy, the law.

Very well. All in good time Hugo strolled off to a neighboring village with his prey; and the two drifted slowly up and down one street after another, the one watching sharply for a sure chance to achieve his evil purpose, and the other watching as sharply for a chance to dart away and get free of his infamous captivity forever.

Both threw away some tolerably fair-looking opportunities; for both, in their secret hearts, were resolved to make absolutely sure work this time, and neither meant to allow his fevered desires to seduce him into any venture that had much uncertainty about it.

Hugo's chance came first. For at last a woman approached who

*From "The English Rogue;" London, 1665.

carried a fat package of some sort in a basket. Hugo's eyes sparkled
with sinful pleasure as he said to himself, "Breath o' my life, an' I
can but put *that* upon him, 'tis good-den and God keep thee, King
of the Game-Cocks!" He waited and watched—outwardly patient,
but inwardly consuming with excitement—till the woman had
passed by, and the time was ripe; then said, in a low voice—"Tarry
here till I come again," and darted stealthily after the prey.

The king's heart was filled with joy—he could make his escape,
now, if Hugo's quest only carried him far enough away.

But he was to have no such luck. Hugo crept behind the woman,
snatched the package, and came running back, wrapping it in an
old piece of blanket which he carried on his arm. The hue and cry
was raised in a moment, by the woman, who knew her loss by the
lightening of her burden, although she had not seen the pilfering
done. Hugo thrust the bundle into the king's hands without halting,
saying,—

"Now speed ye after me with the rest, and cry 'Stop thief!' but
mind ye lead them astray!"

The next moment Hugo turned a corner and darted down a
crooked alley,—and in another moment or two he lounged into view
again, looking innocent and indifferent, and took up a position
behind a post to watch results.

The insulted king threw the bundle on the ground; and the
blanket fell away from it just as the woman arrived, with an
augmenting crowd at her heels; she seized the king's wrist with one
hand, snatched up her bundle with the other, and began to pour
out a tirade of abuse upon the boy while he struggled, without
success, to free himself from her grip.

Hugo had seen enough—his enemy was captured and the law
would get him, now—so he slipped away, jubilant and chuckling,
and wended campwards, framing a judicious version of the matter
to give to the Ruffler's crew as he strode along.

The king continued to struggle in the woman's grasp, and now
and then cried out, in vexation—

"Unhand me, thou foolish creature; it was not I that bereaved
thee of thy paltry goods."

The crowd closed around, threatening the king and calling him
names; a brawny blacksmith in leather apron, and sleeves rolled to
his elbows, made a reach for him, saying he would trounce him
well, for a lesson; but just then a long sword flashed in the air and
fell with convincing force upon the man's arm, flat-side down, the
fantastic owner of it remarking pleasantly at the same time—

"Marry, good souls, let us proceed gently, not with ill blood and
uncharitable words. This is matter for the law's consideration, not
private and unofficial handling. Loose thy hold from the boy, goodwife."

The blacksmith averaged the stalwart soldier with a glance, then went muttering away, rubbing his arm; the woman released the boy's wrist reluctantly; the crowd eyed the stranger unlovingly, but prudently closed their mouths. The king sprang to his deliverer's side, with flushed cheeks and sparkling eyes, exclaiming—

"Thou has lagged sorely, but thou comest in good season, now'. Sir Miles; carve me this rabble to rags!"

CHAPTER XXIII

THE PRINCE A PRISONER

Hendon forced back a smile, and bent down and whispered in the king's ear—

"Softly, softly, my prince, wag thy tongue warily—nay, suffer it not to wag at all. Trust in me—all shall go well in the end." Then he added, to himself: "*Sir* Miles! Bless me, I had totally forgot I was a knight! Lord how marvellous a thing it is, the grip his memory doth take upon his quaint and crazy fancies! ... An empty and foolish title is mine, and yet it is something to have deserved it, for I think it is more honor to be held worthy to be a spectre-knight in his Kingdom of Dreams and Shadows, than to be held base enough to be an earl in some of the *real* kingdoms of this world."

The crowd fell apart to admit a constable, who approached and was about to lay his hand upon the king's shoulder, when Hendon said—

"Gently, good friend, withhold your hand—he shall go peaceably; I am responsible for that. Lead on, we will follow."

The officer led, with the woman and her bundle; Miles and the king followed after, with the crowd at their heels. The King was inclined to rebel; but Hendon said to him in a low voice—

"Reflect, sire—your laws are the wholesome breath of your own royalty; shall their source resist them, yet require the branches to respect them? Apparently one of these laws has been broken; when the king is on his throne again, can it ever grieve him to remember that when he was seemingly a private person he loyally sunk the king in the citizen and submitted to its authority?"

"Thou art right; say no more; thou shalt see that whatsoever the king of England requires a subject to suffer under the law, he will himself suffer while he holdeth the station of a subject."

When the woman was called upon to testify before the justice of the peace, she swore that the small prisoner at the bar was the person who had committed the theft; there was none able to show the contrary, so the king stood convicted. The bundle was now unrolled, and when the contents proved to be a plump little dressed pig, the judge looked troubled, whilst Hendon turned pale, and his body was thrilled with an electric shiver of dismay; but the king remained unmoved, protected by his ignorance. The judge

meditated, during an ominous pause, then turned to the woman,
with the question—

"What dost thou hold this property to be worth?"

The woman courtesied and replied—

"Three shillings and eightpence, your worship—I could not abate
a penny and set forth the value honestly."

The justice glanced around uncomfortably upon the crowd, then
nodded to the constable and said—

"Clear the court and close the doors."

It was done. None remained but the two officials, the accused,
the accuser, and Miles Hendon. This latter was rigid and colorless,
and on his forehead big drops of cold sweat gathered, broke and
blended together, and trickled down his face. The judge turned to
the woman again, and said, in a compassionate voice—

" 'Tis a poor ignorant lad, and mayhaps was driven hard by
hunger, for these be grievous times for the unfortunate; mark you,
he hath not an evil face—but when hunger driveth— Good woman!
dost know that when one steals a thing above the value of thirteen
pence ha'penny the law saith he shall *hang* for it?"

The little king started, wide-eyed with consternation, but
controlled himself and held his peace; but not so the woman. She
sprang to her feet, shaking with fright, and cried out—

"O, good lack, what have I done! God-a-mercy, I would not
hang the poor thing for the whole world! Ah, save me from this,
your worship—what shall I do, what *can* I do?"

The justice maintained his judicial composure, and simply said—

"Doubtless it is allowable to revise the value, since it is not yet
writ upon the record."

"Then in God's name call the pig eightpence, and heaven bless
the day that freed my conscience of this awesome thing!"

Miles Hendon forgot all decorum in his delight; and surprised
the king and wounded his dignity, by throwing his arms around
him and hugging him. The woman made her grateful adieux and
started away with her pig; and when the constable opened the door
for her, he followed her out into the narrow hall. The justice
proceeded to write in his record book. Hendon, always alert,
thought he would like to know why the officer followed the woman
out; so he slipped softly into the dusky hall and listened. He heard
a conversation to this effect—

"It is a fat pig, and promises good eating; I will buy it of thee;
here is the eightpence."

"Eightpence, indeed! Thou'lt do no such thing. It cost me three
shillings and eightpence, good honest coin of the last reign, that old
Harry that's just dead ne'er touched nor tampered with. A fig for
thy eightpence!"

"Stands the wind in that quarter? Thou wast under oath, and so
swore falsely when thou saidst the value was but eightpence. Come

straightway back with me before his worship, and answer for the crime!—and then the lad will hang."

"There, there, dear heart, say no more, I am content. Give me the eightpence, and hold thy peace about the matter."

The woman went off crying; Hendon slipped back into the court room, and the constable presently followed, after hiding his prize in some convenient place. The justice wrote a while longer, then read the king a wise and kindly lecture, and sentenced him to a short imprisonment in the common jail, to be followed by a public flogging. The astounded king opened his mouth and was probably going to order the good judge to be beheaded on the spot; but he caught a warning sign from Hendon, and succeeded in closing his mouth again before he lost any thing out of it. Hendon took him by the hand, now made reverence to the justice, and the two departed in the wake of the constable toward the jail. The moment the street was reached, the inflamed monarch halted, snatched away his hand, and exclaimed—

"Idiot, dost imagine I will enter a common jail *alive?*"

Hendon bent down and said, somewhat sharply—

"*Will* you trust in me? Peace! and forbear to worsen our chances with dangerous speech. What God wills, will happen; thou canst not hurry it, thou canst not alter it; therefore wait, and be patient—'twill be time enow to rail or rejoice when what is to happen has happened."*

CHAPTER XXIV

THE ESCAPE

The short winter day was nearly ended. The streets were deserted, save for a few random stragglers, and these hurried straight along, with the intent look of people who were only anxious to accomplish their errands as quickly as possible and then snugly house themselves from the rising wind and the gathering twilight. They looked neither to the right nor to the left; they paid no attention to our party, they did not even seem to see them. Edward the Sixth wondered if the spectacle of a king on his way to jail had ever encountered such marvellous indifference before. By and by the constable arrived at a deserted market-square and proceeded to cross it. When he had reached the middle of it, Hendon laid his hand upon his arm, and said in a low voice—

"Bide a moment, good sir, there is none in hearing, and I would say a word to thee."

"My duty forbids it, sir; prithee hinder me not, the night comes on."

"Stay, nevertheless, for the matter concerns thee nearly. Turn thy back a moment and seem not to see; *let this poor lad escape.*"

*Notes to Chapter 23, at end of volume.

"This to me, sir! I arrest thee in"—

"Nay, be not too hasty. See thou be careful and commit no foolish error"—then he shut his voice down to a whisper, and said in the man's ear—"the pig thou hast purchased for eightpence may cost thee thy neck, man!"

The poor constable, taken by surprise, was speechless, at first, then found his tongue and fell to blustering and threatening; but Hendon was tranquil, and waited with patience till his breath was spent; then said—

"I have a liking to thee, friend, and would not willingly see thee come to harm. Observe, I heard it all—every word. I will prove it to thee." Then he repeated the conversation which the officer and the woman had had together in the hall, word for word, and ended with—

"There—have I set it forth correctly? Should not I be able to set it forth correctly before the judge, if occasion required?"

The man was dumb with fear and distress, for a moment; then he rallied and said with forced lightness—

" 'Tis making a mighty matter indeed, out of a jest; I but plagued the woman for mine amusement."

"Kept you the woman's pig for amusement?"

The man answered sharply—

"Nought else, good sir—I tell thee 'twas but a jest."

"I do begin to believe thee," said Hendon, with a perplexing mixture of mockery and half-conviction in his tone; "but tarry thou here a moment whilst I run and ask his worship—for nathless, he being a man experienced in law, in jests, in"—

He was moving away, still talking; the constable hesitated, fidgeted, spat out an oath or two, then cried out—

"Hold, hold, good sir—prithee wait a little—the judge! why man, he hath no more sympathy with a jest than hath a dead corpse!—come, and we will speak further. Ods body! I seem to be in evil case—and all for an innocent and thoughtless pleasantry. I am a man of family; and my wife and little ones— List to reason, good your worship; what wouldst thou of me?"

"Only that thou be blind and dumb and paralytic whilst one may count a hundred thousand—counting slowly," said Hendon, with the expression of a man who asks but a reasonable favor, and that a very little one.

"It is my destruction!" said the constable despairingly. "Ah, be reasonable, good sir; only look at this matter, on all its sides, and see how mere a jest it is—how manifestly and how plainly it is so. And even if one granted it were not a jest, it is a fault so small that e'en the grimmest penalty it could call forth would be but a rebuke and warning from the judge's lips."

Hendon replied with a solemnity which chilled the air about him—

"This jest of thine hath a name, in law,—wot you what it is?"

"I knew it not! Peradventure I have been unwise. I never dreamed it had a name—ah, sweet heaven, I thought it was original."

"Yes, it hath a name. In the law this crime is called *Non compos mentis lex talionis sic transit gloria Mundi.*"

"Ah, my God!"

"And the penalty is death!"

"God be merciful to me, a sinner!"

"By advantage taken of one in fault, in dire peril, and at thy mercy, thou hast seized goods worth above thirteen pence ha'penny, paying but a trifle for the same; and this, in the eye of the law, is constructive barratry, misprision of treason, malfeasance in office, *ad hominem expurgatis in statu quo*—and the penalty is death by the halter, without ransom, commutation, or benefit of clergy."

"Bear me up, bear me up, sweet sir, my legs do fail me! Be thou merciful—spare me this doom, and I will turn my back and see nought that shall happen."

"Good! now thou'rt wise and reasonable. And thou'll restore the pig?"

"I will, I will indeed—nor ever touch another, though heaven send it and an archangel fetch it. Go—I am blind for thy sake—I see nothing. I will say thou didst break in and wrest the prisoner from my hands by force. It is but a crazy, ancient door—I will batter it down myself betwixt midnight and the morning."

"Do it, good soul, no harm will come of it; the judge hath a loving charity for this poor lad, and will shed no tears and break no jailer's bones for his escape."

CHAPTER XXV

HENDON HALL

As soon as Hendon and the king were out of sight of the constable, his majesty was instructed to hurry to a certain place outside the town, and wait there, whilst Hendon should go to the inn and settle his account. Half an hour later the two friends were blithely jobbing eastward on Hendon's sorry steeds. The king was warm and comfortable, now, for he had cast his rags and clothed himself in the second-hand suit which Hendon had bought on London Bridge.

Hendon wished to guard against over-fatiguing the boy; he judged that hard journeys, irregular meals, and illiberal measures of sleep would be bad for his crazed mind; whilst rest, regularity, and moderate exercise would be pretty sure to hasten its cure; he longed to see the stricken intellect made well again and its diseased

visions driven out of the tormented little head; therefore he
resolved to move by easy stages toward the home whence he had so
long been banished, instead of obeying the impulse of his
impatience and hurrying along night and day.

When he and the king had journeyed about ten miles, they
reached a considerable village, and halted there for the night, at a
good inn. The former relations were resumed; Hendon stood
behind the king's chair, while he dined, and waited upon him;
undressed him when he was ready for bed; then took the floor for
his own quarters, and slept athwart the door, rolled up in a
blanket.

The next day, and the next day after, they jogged lazily along
talking over the adventures they had met since their separation, and
mightily enjoying each other's narratives. Hendon detailed all his
wide wanderings in search of the king, and described how the
archangel had led him a fool's journey all over the forest, and taken
him back to the hut, finally, when he found he could not get rid of
him. Then—he said—the old man went into the bedchamber and
came staggering back looking broken-hearted, and saying he had
expected to find that the boy had returned and lain down in there to
rest, but it was not so. Hendon had waited at the hut all day; hope
of the king's return died out, then, and he departed upon the
quest again.

"And old Sanctum Sanctorum *was* truly sorry your highness came
not back," said Hendon; "I saw it in his face."

"Marry I will never doubt *that!*" said the king—and then told his
own story; after which, Hendon was sorry he had not destroyed the
archangel.

During the last day of the trip, Hendon's spirits were soaring. His
tongue ran constantly. He talked about his old father, and his
brother Arthur, and told of many things which illustrated their high
and generous characters; he went into loving frenzies over his Edith,
and was so gladhearted that he was even able to say some gentle
and brotherly things about Hugh. He dwelt a deal on the coming
meeting at Hendon Hall; what a surprise it would be to everybody,
and what an outburst of thanksgiving and delight there would be.

It was a fair region, dotted with cottages and orchards, and the
road led through broad pasture lands whose receding expanses,
marked with gentle elevations and depressions, suggested the
swelling and subsiding undulations of the sea. In the afternoon the
returning prodigal made constant deflections from his course to see
if by ascending some hillock he might not pierce the distance and
catch a glimpse of his home. At last he was successful, and cried
out excitedly—

"There is the village, my prince, and there is the Hall close by!
You may see the towers from here; and that wood there—that is my
father's park. Ah, *now* thou'lt know what state and grandeur be! A

house with seventy rooms—think of that!and seven and twenty
servants! A brave lodging for such as we, is it not so? Come, let us
speed—my impatience will not brook further delay.''

All possible hurry was made; still, it was after three o'clock before
the village was reached. The travellers scampered through it,
Hendon's tongue going all the time. "Here is the church—covered
with the same ivy—none gone, none added." "Yonder is the inn, the
old Red Lion,—and yonder is the marketplace." "Here is the
Maypole, and here the pump—nothing is altered; nothing but the
people at any rate; ten years make a change in people; some of these
I seem to know, but none know me." So his chat ran on. The end of
the village was soon reached; then the travelers struck into a
crooked, narrow road, walled in with tall hedges, and hurried briskly
along it for a half mile, then passed into a vast flower garden
through an imposing gateway whose huge stone pillars bore
sculptured armorial devices. A noble mansion was before them.

"Welcome to Hendon Hall, my king!" exclaimed Miles. "Ah, 'tis
a great day! My father and my brother, and the lady Edith will be
so mad with joy that they will have eyes and tongue for none but me
in the first transports of the meeting, and so thou'lt seem but coldly
welcomed—but mind it not; 'twill soon seem otherwise; for when I
say thou art my ward, and tell them how costly is my love for thee,
thou'lt see them take thee to their breasts for Miles Hendon's sake,
and make their house and hearts thy home forever after!"

The next moment Hendon sprang to the ground before the great
door, helped the king down, then took him by the hand and rushed
within. A few steps brought him to a spacious apartment; he
entered, seated the king with more hurry than ceremony, then ran
toward a young man who sat at a writing-table in front of a generous
fire of logs.

"Embrace me, Hugh," he cried, "and say thou'rt glad I am come
again! and call our father, for home is not home till I shall touch his
hand, and see his face, and hear his voice once more!"

But Hugh only drew back, after betraying a momentary surprise,
and bent a grave stare upon the intruder—a stare which indicated
somewhat of offended dignity, at first, then changed, in response to
some inward thought or purpose, to an expression of marvelling
curiosity, mixed with a real or assumed compassion. Presently he
said, in a mild voice—

"Thy wits seem touched, poor stranger; doubtless thou hast
suffered privations and rude buffetings at the world's hands; thy
looks and dress betoken it. Whom dost thou take me to be?"

"Take thee? Prithee for whom else than whom thou art? I take
thee to be Hugh Hendon," said Miles, sharply.

The other continued, in the same soft tone—

"And whom dost thou imagine thyself to be?"

"Imagination hath nought to do with it! Dost thou pretend thou knowest me not for thy brother Miles Hendon?"

An expression of pleased surprise flitted across Hugh's face, and he exclaimed—

"What! thou art not jesting? can the dead come to life? God be praised if it be so! Our poor lost boy restored to our arms after all these cruel years! Ah, it seems too good to be true, it *is* too good to be true—I charge thee, have pity, do not trifle with me! Quick—come to the light—let me scan thee well!"

He seized Miles by the arm, dragged him to the window, and began to devour him from head to foot with his eyes, turning him this way and that, and stepping briskly around him and about him to prove him from all points of view; whilst the returned prodigal, all aglow with gladness, smiled, laughed, and kept nodding his head and saying—

"Go on, brother, go on, and fear not; thou'lt find nor limb nor feature that cannot bide the test. Scour and scan me to thy content, my dear old Hugh—I am indeed thy old Miles, thy same old Miles, thy lost brother, is't not so? Ah, 'tis a great day—I *said* 'twas a great day! Give me thy hand, give me thy cheek—lord, I am like to die of very joy!"

He was about to throw himself upon his brother; but Hugh put up his hand in dissent, then dropped his chin mournfully upon his breast, saying with emotion—

"Ah, God of his mercy give me strength to bear this grievous disappointment!"

Miles, amazed, could not speak, for a moment; then he found his tongue, and cried out—

"*What* disappointment? Am I not thy brother?"

Hugh shook his head sadly, and said—

"I pray heaven it may prove so, and that other eyes may find the resemblances that are hid from mine. Alack, I fear me the letter spoke but too truly."

"What letter?"

"One that came from over sea, some six or seven years ago. It said my brother died in battle."

"It was a lie! Call thy father—he will know me."

"One may not call the dead."

"Dead?" Miles's voice was subdued, and his lips trembled. "My father dead!—O, this is heavy news. Half my new joy is withered now. Prithee let me see my brother Arthur—he will know me; he will know me and console me."

"He, also, is dead."

"God be merciful to me, a stricken man! Gone,—both gone—the worthy taken and the worthless spared, in me! Ah! I crave your mercy!—do not say the lady Edith"—

"Is dead? No, she lives."

"Then, God be praised, my joy is whole again! Speed thee,

brother—let her come to me! An' *she* say I am not myself,—but she will not; no, no, *she* will know me, I were a fool to doubt it. Bring her—bring the old servants; they, too, will know me."

"All are gone but five—Peter, Halsey, David, Bernard and Margaret."

So saying, Hugh left the room. Miles stood musing, a while, then began to walk the floor, muttering—

"The five arch villains have survived the two-and-twenty leal and honest—'tis an odd thing."

He continued walking back and forth, muttering to himself; he had forgotten the king entirely. By and by his majesty said gravely, and with a touch of genuine compassion, though the words themselves were capable of being interpreted ironically—

"Mind not thy mischance, good man; there be others in the world whose identity is denied, and whose claims are derided. Thou hast company."

"Ah, my king," cried Hendon, coloring slightly, "do not thou condemn me—wait, and thou shalt see. I am no impostor—she will say it; you shall hear it from the sweetest lips in England. I an impostor? Why I know this old hall, these pictures of my ancestors, and all these things that are about us, as a child knoweth its own nursery. Here was I born and bred, my lord; I speak the truth; I would not deceive thee; and should none else believe, I pray thee do not *thou* doubt me—I could not bear it."

"I do not doubt thee," said the king, with a childlike simplicity and faith.

"I thank thee out of my heart!" exclaimed Hendon, with a fervency which showed that he was touched. The king added, with the same gentle simplicity—

"Dost thou doubt *me?*"

A guilty confusion seized upon Hendon, and he was grateful that the door opened to admit Hugh, at that moment, and saved him the necessity of replying.

A beautiful lady, richly clothed, followed Hugh, and after her came several liveried servants. The lady walked slowly, with her head bowed and her eyes fixed upon the floor. The face was unspeakably sad. Miles Hendon sprang forward, crying out—

"O, my Edith, my darling"—

But Hugh waved him back, gravely, and said to the lady—

"Look upon him. Do you know him?"

At the sound of Miles's voice the woman had started, slightly, and her cheeks had flushed; she was trembling, now. She stood still, during an impressive pause of several moments; then slowly lifted up her head and looked into Hendon's eyes with a stony and frightened gaze; the blood sank out of her face, drop by drop, till nothing remained but the gray pallor of death; then she said, in a voice as dead as the face, "I know him not!" and turned, with a moan and a stifled sob, and tottered out of the room.

Miles Hendon sank into a chair and covered his face with his hands. After a pause, his brother said to the servants—

"You have observed him. Do you know him?"

They shook their heads; then the master said—

"The servants know you not, sir. I fear there is some mistake. You have seen that my wife knew you not."

"Thy *wife!*" In an instant Hugh was pinned to the wall, with an iron grip about his throat. "O, thou fox-hearted slave, I see it all! Thou'st writ the lying letter thyself, and my stolen bride and goods are its fruit. There—now get thee gone, lest I shame mine honorable soldiership with the slaying of so pitiful a manikin!"

Hugh, red-faced, and almost suffocated, reeled to the nearest chair, and commanded the servants to seize and bind the murderous stranger. They hesitated, and one of them said—

"He is armed, Sir Hugh, and we are weaponless."

"Armed? What of it, and ye so many? Upon him, I say!"

But Miles warned them to be careful what they did, and added—

"Ye know me of old—I have not changed; come on, an' it like you."

This reminder did not hearten the servants much; they still held back.

"Then go, ye paltry cowards, and arm yourselves and guard the doors, whilst I send one to fetch the watch;" said Hugh. He turned, at the threshold, and said to Miles, "You'll find it to your advantage to offend not with useless endeavors at escape."

"Escape? Spare thyself discomfort, an' that is all that troubles thee. For Miles Hendon is master of Hendon Hall and all its belongings. He will remain—doubt it not."

CHAPTER XXVI

DISOWNED

The king sat musing a few moments, then looked up and said—

" 'Tis strange—most strange. I cannot account for it."

"No, it is not strange, my liege. I know him, and this conduct is but natural. He was a rascal from his birth."

"O, I spake not of *him,* Sir Miles."

"Not of him? Then of what? What is it that is strange?"

"That the king is not missed."

"How? Which? I doubt I do not understand."

"Indeed! Doth it not strike you as being passing strange that the land is not filled with couriers and proclamations describing my person and making search for me? Is it no matter for commotion and distress that the head of the State is gone?—that I am vanished away and lost?"

"Most true, my king, I had forgot." Then Hendon sighed, and muttered to himself, "Poor ruined mind—still busy with its pathetic dream."

"But I have a plan that shall right us both. I will write a paper, in three tongues—Latin, Greek and English—and thou shalt haste away with it to London in the morning. Give it to none but my uncle, the lord Hertford; when he shall see it, he will know and say I wrote it. Then he will send for me."

"Might it not be best, my prince, that we wait, here, until I prove myself and make my rights secure to my domains? I should be so much the better able then to"—

The king interrupted him imperiously—

"Peace! What are thy paltry domains, thy trivial interests, contrasted with matters which concern the weal of a nation and the integrity of a throne!" Then he added, in a gentle voice, as if he were sorry for his severity, "Obey and have no fear; I will right thee, I will make thee whole—yes, more than whole. I shall remember, and requite."

So saying, he took the pen, and set himself to work. Hendon contemplated him lovingly, a while, then said to himself—

"An' it were dark, I should think it *was* a king that spoke; there's no denying it, when the humor's upon him he doth thunder and lighten like your true king—now where got he that trick? See him scribble and scratch away contentedly at his meaningless pot-hooks, fancying them to be Latin and Greek—and except my wit shall serve me with a lucky device for diverting him from his purpose, I shall be forced to pretend to post away to-morrow on this wild errand he hath invented for me."

The next moment Sir Miles's thoughts had gone back to the recent episode. So absorbed was he in his musings, that when the king presently handed him the paper which he had been writing, he received it and pocketed it without being conscious of the act. "How marvellous strange she acted," he muttered. "I think she knew me—and I think she did *not* know me. These opinions do conflict, I perceive it plainly; I cannot reconcile them, neither can I, by argument, dismiss either of the two, or even persuade one to outweigh the other. The matter standeth simply thus: she *must* have known my face, my figure, my voice, for how could it be otherwise? yet she *said* she knew me not, and that is proof perfect, for she cannot lie. But stop—I think I begin to see. Peradventure he hath influenced her—commanded her—compelled her, to lie. That is the solution! The riddle is unriddled. She seemed dead with fear—yes, she was under his compulsion. I will seek her; I will find her; now that he is away, she will speak her true mind. She will remember the old times when we were little playfellows together, and this will soften her heart, and she will no more betray me, but will confess me. There is no treacherous blood in her—no, she was always honest and true. She has loved me in those old days—this is my security; for whom one has loved, one cannot betray."

He stepped eagerly toward the door; at that moment it opened, and the lady Edith entered. She was very pale, but she walked with a firm step, and her carriage was full of grace and gentle dignity. Her face was as sad as before.

Miles sprang forward, with a happy confidence, to meet her, but she checked him with a hardly perceptible gesture, and he stopped where he was. She seated herself, and asked him to do likewise. Thus simply did she take the sense of old-comradeship out of him, and transform him into a stranger and a guest. The surprise of it, the bewildering unexpectedness of it, made him begin to question, for a moment, if he *was* the person he was pretending to be, after all. The lady Edith said—

"Sir, I have come to warn you. The mad cannot be persuaded out of their delusions, perchance; but doubtless they may be persuaded to avoid perils. I think this dream of yours hath the seeming of honest truth to you, and therefore is not criminal—but do not tarry here with it; for here it is dangerous." She looked steadily into Miles's face, a moment, then added, impressively, "It is the more dangerous for that you *are* much like what our lost lad must have grown to be, if he had lived."

"Heavens, madame, but I *am* he!"

"I truly think you think it, sir. I question not your honesty in that—I but warn you, that is all. My husband is master in this region; his power hath hardly any limit; the people prosper or starve, as he wills. If you resembled not the man whom you profess to be, my husband might bid you pleasure yourself with your dream in peace; but trust me, I know him well, I know what he will do; he will say to all, that you are but a mad impostor, and straightway all will echo him." She bent upon Miles that same steady look once more, and added: "If you *were* Miles Hendon, and he knew it and all the region knew it—consider what I am saying, weigh it well—you would stand in the same peril, your punishment would be no less sure; he would deny you and denounce you, and none would be bold enough to give you countenance."

"Most truly I believe it," said Miles, bitterly.

"The power that can command one life-long friend to betray and disown another, and be obeyed, may well look to be obeyed in quarters where bread and life are on the stake and no cobweb ties of loyalty and honor are concerned."

A faint tinge appeared for a moment in the lady's cheek, and she dropped her eyes to the floor; but her voice betrayed no emotion when she proceeded—

"I have warned you, I must still warn you, to go hence. This man will destroy you, else. He is a tyrant who knows no pity. I, who am

his fettered slave, know this. Poor Miles, and Arthur, and my dear
guardian, Sir Richard, are free of him, and at rest—better that
you were with them than that you bide here in the clutches of this
miscreant. Your pretensions are a menace to his title and
possessions; you have assaulted him in his own house—you are
ruined if you stay. Go—do not hesitate. If you lack money, take this
purse, I beg of you, and bribe the servants to let you pass. O be
warned, poor soul, and escape while you may."

Miles declined the purse with a gesture, and rose up and stood
before her.

"Grant me one thing," he said. "Let your eyes rest upon mine, so
that I may see if they be steady. There—now answer me. Am I
Miles Hendon?"

"No. I know you not."

"Swear it!"

The answer was low, but distinct—

"I swear."

"O, this passes belief!"

"Fly! Why will you waste the precious time? Fly and save
yourself."

At that moment the officers burst into the room and a violent
struggle began; but Hendon was soon overpowered and dragged
away. The king was taken, also, and both were bound, and led to
prison.

CHAPTER XXVII

IN PRISON

The cells were all crowded; so the two friends were chained in
a large room where persons charged with trifling offenses were
commonly kept. They had company, for there were some twenty
manacled or fettered prisoners here, of both sexes and of varying
ages,—an obscene and noisy gang. The king chafed bitterly over the
stupendous indignity thus put upon his royalty, but Hendon was
moody and taciturn. He was pretty thoroughly bewildered. He had
come home, a jubilant prodigal, expecting to find everybody wild
with joy over his return; and instead had got the cold shoulder and
a jail. The promise and the fulfilment differed so widely, that the
effect was stunning; he could not decide whether it was most tragic
or most grotesque. He felt much as a man might who had danced
blithely out to enjoy a rainbow, and got struck by lightning.

But gradually his confused and tormenting thoughts settled down
into some sort of order, and then his mind centred itself upon
Edith. He turned her conduct over, and examined it in all lights,
but he could not make any thing satisfactory out of it. Did she know
him?—or didn't she know him? It was a perplexing puzzle, and

occupied him a long time: but he ended, finally, with the conviction
that she did know him, and had repudiated him for interested
reasons. He wanted to load her name with curses now; but this name
had so long been sacred to him that he found he could not bring
his tongue to profane it.

Wrapped in prison blankets of a soiled and tattered condition,
Hendon and the king passed a troubled night. For a bribe the jailer
had furnished liquor to some of the prisoners; singing of ribald
songs, fighting, shouting, and carousing, was the natural
consequence. At last, a while after midnight, a man attacked a
woman and nearly killed her by beating her over the head with his
manacles before the jailer could come to the rescue. The jailer
restored peace by giving the man a sound clubbing about the head
and shoulders—then the carousing ceased; and after that, all had an
opportunity to sleep who did not mind the annoyance of the
moanings and groanings of the two wounded people.

During the ensuing week, the days and nights were of a
monotonous sameness, as to events; men whose faces Hendon
remembered more or less distinctly, came, by day, to gaze at the
"impostor" and repudiate and insult him; and by night the
carousing and brawling went on, with symmetrical regularity.
However, there was a change of incident at last. The jailer brought
in an old man, and said to him—

"The villain is in this room—cast thy old eyes about and see if
thou canst say which is he."

Hendon glanced up, and experienced a pleasant sensation for
the first time since he had been in the jail. He said to himself,
"This is Blake Andrews, a servant all his life in my father's family—
a good honest soul, with a right heart in his breast. That is, formerly.
But none are true, now; all are liars. This man will know me—and
will deny me, too, like the rest."

The old man gazed around the room, glanced at each face in turn,
and finally said—

"I see none here but paltry knaves, scum o' the streets. Which is
he?"

The jailer laughed.

"Here," he said; "scan this big animal, and grant me an opinion."

The old man approached, and looked Hendon over, long and
earnestly, then shook his head and said—

"Marry, *this* is no Hendon—nor ever was!"

"Right! Thy old eyes are sound yet. An' I were Sir Hugh, I would
take the shabby carle and"—

The jailer finished by lifting himself a-tip-toe with an imaginary
halter, at the same time making a gurgling noise in his throat
suggestive of suffocation. The old man said, vindictively—

"Let him bless God an' he fare no worse. An' *I* had the handling
o' the villain, he should roast, or I am no true man!"

The jailer laughed a pleasant hyena laugh, and said—

"Give him a piece of thy mind, old man—they all do it. Thou'lt find it good diversion."

Then he sauntered toward his ante-room and disappeared. The old man dropped upon his knees and whispered—

"God be thanked, thou'rt come again, my master! I believed thou wert dead these seven years, and lo, here thou art alive! I knew thee the moment I saw thee; and main hard work it was to keep a stony countenance and seem to see none here but tuppeny knaves and rubbish o' the streets. I am old and poor, Sir Miles; but say the word and I will go forth and proclaim the truth though I be strangled for it."

"No," said Hendon, "thou shalt not. It would ruin thee, and yet help but little in my cause. But I thank thee; for thou hast given me back somewhat of my lost faith in my kind."

The old servant became very valuable to Hendon and the king; for he dropped in several times a day to "abuse" the former, and always smuggled in a few delicacies to help out the prison bill of fare; he also furnished the current news. Hendon reserved the dainties for the king; without them his majesty might not have survived, for he was not able to eat the coarse and wretched food provided by the jailer. Andrews was obliged to confine himself to brief visits, in order to avoid suspicion; but he managed to impart a fair degree of information each time—information delivered in a low voice, for Hendon's benefit, and interlarded with insulting epithets delivered in a louder voice, for the benefit of other hearers.

So, little by little, the story of the family came out. Arthur had been dead six years. This loss, with the absence of news from Hendon, impaired the father's health; he believed he was going to die, and he wished to see Hugh and Edith settled in life before he passed away; but Edith begged hard for delay, hoping for Miles's return; then the letter came which brought the news of Miles's death; the shock prostrated Sir Richard; he believed his end was very near, and he and Hugh insisted upon the marriage; Edith begged for and obtained a month's respite; then another, and finally a third; the marriage then took place, by the death-bed of Sir Richard. It had not proved a happy one. It was whispered about the country that shortly after the nuptials the bride found among her husband's papers several rough and incomplete drafts of the fatal letter, and had accused him of precipitating the marriage— and Sir Richard's death, too—by a wicked forgery. Tales of cruelty to the lady Edith and the servants were to be heard on all hands; and since the father's death Sir Hugh had thrown off all soft disguises and become a pitiless master toward all who in any way depended upon him and his domains for bread.

There was a bit of Andrews's gossip which the king listened to with a lively interest—

"There is rumor that the king is mad. But in charity forbear to say *I* mentioned it, for 'tis death to speak of it, they say."

His majesty glared at the old man and said—

"The king is *not* mad, good man—and thou'lt find it to thy advantage to busy thyself with matters that nearer concern thee than this seditious prattle."

"What doth the lad mean?" said Andrews, surprised at this brisk assault from such an unexpected quarter. Hendon gave him a sign, and he did not pursue his question, but went on with his budget—

"The late king is to be buried at Windsor in a day or two—the 16th of the month,—and the new king will be crowned at Westminster the 20th."

"Methinks they must needs find him first," muttered his majesty; then added, confidently, "but they will look to that—and so also shall I."

"In the name of"—

But the old man got no further—a warning sign from Hendon checked his remark. He resumed the thread of his gossip—

"Sir Hugh goeth to the coronation—and with grand hopes. He confidently looketh to come back a peer, for he is high in favor with the Lord Protector."

"What Lord Protector?" asked his majesty.

"His grace the Duke of Somerset."

"What Duke of Somerset?"

"Marry, there is but one—Seymour, Earl of Hertford."

The king asked, sharply—

"Since when is *he* a duke, and Lord Protector?"

"Since the last day of January."

"And prithee who made him so?"

"Himself and the great Council—with help of the king."

His majesty started violently. "The *king!*" he cried. "*What* king, good sir?"

"What king, indeed! (God-a-mercy, what aileth the boy?) Sith we have but one, 'tis not difficult to answer—his most sacred majesty King Edward the Sixth—whom God preserve! Yea, and a dear and gracious little urchin is he, too; and whether he be mad or no—and they say he mendeth daily—his praises are on all men's lips; and all bless him, likewise, and offer prayers that he may be spared to reign long in England; for he began humanely, with saving the old duke of Norfolk's life, and now is he bent on destroying the cruelest of the laws that harry and oppress the people."

This news struck his majesty dumb with amazement, and plunged him into so deep and dismal a revery that he heard no more of the old man's gossip. He wondered if the "little urchin" was the beggar-boy whom he left dressed in his own garments in the palace. It did not seem possible that this could be, for surely his manners

and speech would betray him if he pretended to be the prince of
Wales—then he would be driven out, and search made for the true
prince. Could it be that the Court had set up some sprig of the
nobility in his place? No, for his uncle would not allow that—he
was all-powerful and could and would crush such a movement, of
course. The boy's musings profited him nothing; the more he tried
to unriddle the mystery the more perplexed he became, the more his
head ached, and the worse he slept. His impatience to get to London
grew hourly, and his captivity became almost unendurable.

Hendon's arts all failed with the king—he could not be comforted,
but a couple of women who were chained near him, succeeded
better. Under their gentle ministrations he found peace and learned
a degree of patience. He was very grateful, and came to love them
dearly and to delight in the sweet and soothing influence of their
presence. He asked them why they were in prison, and when they
said they were Baptists, he smiled, and inquired—

"Is that a crime to be shut up for, in a prison? Now I grieve, for
I shall lose ye—they will not keep ye long for such a little thing."

They did not answer; and something in their faces made him
uneasy. He said, eagerly—

"You do not speak—be good to me, and tell me—there will be no
other punishment? Prithee tell me there is no fear of that."

They tried to change the topic, but his fears were aroused, and
he pursued it—

"Will they scourge thee? No, no, they would not be so cruel!
Say they would not. Come, they *will* not, will they?"

The women betrayed confusion and distress, but there was no
avoiding an answer, so one of them said, in a voice choked with
emotion—

"O, thou'lt break our hearts, thou gentle spirit! God will help
us to bear our"—

"It is a confession!" the king broke in. "Then they *will* scourge
thee, the stonyhearted wretches! But O, thou must not weep, I
cannot bear it. Keep up thy courage—I shall come to my own in time
to save thee from this bitter thing, and I will do it!"

When the king awoke in the morning, the women were gone.

"They are saved!" he said, joyfully; then added, despondently,
"but woe is me!—for they were my comforters."

Each of them had left a shred of ribbon pinned to his clothing,
in token of remembrance. He said he would keep these things
always; and that soon he would seek out these dear good friends of
his and take them under his protection.

Just then the jailer came in with some subordinates and
commanded that the prisoners be conducted to the jail-yard. The
king was overjoyed—it would be a blessed thing to see the blue sky
and breathe the fresh air once more. He fretted and chafed at the
slowness of the officers, but his turn came at last and he was

released from his staple and ordered to follow the other prisoners, with Hendon.

The court or quadrangle, was stone-paved, and open to the sky. The prisoners entered it through a massive archway of masonry, and were placed in file, standing, with their backs against the wall. A rope was stretched in front of them, and they were also guarded by their officers. It was a chill and lowering morning, and a light snow which had fallen during the night whitened the great empty space and added to the general dismalness of its aspect. Now and then a wintry wind shivered through the place and sent the snow eddying hither and thither.

In the centre of the court stood two women, chained to posts. A glance showed the king that these were his good friends. He shuddered, and said to himself, "Alack, they are not gone free, as I had thought. To think that such as these should know the lash!— in England! Ay there's the shame of it—not in Heathenesse, but Christian England! They will be scourged; and I, whom they have comforted and kindly entreated, must look on and see the great wrong done; it is strange, so strange! that I, the very source of power in this broad realm, am helpless to protect them. But let these miscreants look well to themselves, for there is a day coming when I will require of them a heavy reckoning for this work. For every blow they strike now, they shall feel a hundred, then."

A great gate swung open and a crowd of citizens poured in. They flocked around the two women, and hid them from the king's view. A clergyman entered and passed through the crowd, and he also was hidden. The king now heard talking, back and forth, as if questions were being asked and answered, but he could not make out what was said. Next there was a deal of bustle and preparation, and much passing and repassing of officials through that part of the crowd that stood on the further side of the women; and whilst this proceeded a deep hush gradually fell upon the people.

Now, by command, the masses parted and fell aside, and the king saw a spectacle that froze the marrow in his bones. Fagots had been piled about the two women, and a kneeling man was lighting them!

The women bowed their heads, and covered their faces with their hands; the yellow flames began to climb upward among the snapping and crackling fagots, and wreaths of blue smoke to stream away on the wind; the clergyman lifted his hands and began a prayer—just then two young girls came flying through the great gate, uttering piercing screams, and threw themselves upon the women at the stake. Instantly they were torn away by the officers, and one of them was kept in a tight grip, but the other broke loose, saying she would die with her mother; and before she could be stopped she had flung her arms about her mother's neck again. She was torn away once more, and with her gown on fire. Two or

three men held her, and the burning portion of her gown was
snatched off and thrown flaming aside, she struggling all the
while to free herself, and saying she would be alone in the world,
now, and begging to be allowed to die with her mother. Both the
girls screamed continually, and fought for freedom; but suddenly
this tumult was drowned under a volley of heart-piercing shrieks
of mortal agony,—the king glanced from the frantic girls to the
stake, then turned away and leaned his ashen face against the wall,
and looked no more. He said, "That which I have seen, in that one
little moment, will never go out from my memory, but will abide
there; and I shall see it all the days, and dream of it all the nights,
till I die. Would God I had been blind!"

Hendon was watching the king. He said to himself, with
satisfaction, "His disorder mendeth; he hath changed, and groweth
gentler. If he had followed his wont, he would have stormed at these
varlets, and said he was king, and commanded that the women be
turned loose unscathed. Soon his delusion will pass away and be
forgotten, and his poor mind will be whole again. God speed the
day!"

That same day several prisoners were brought in to remain over
night, who were being conveyed, under guard, to various places in
the kingdom, to undergo punishment for crimes committed. The
king conversed with these,—he had made it a point, from the
beginning, to instruct himself for the kingly office by questioning
prisoners whenever the opportunity offered—and the tale of their
woes wrung his heart. One of them was a poor half-witted woman
who had stolen a yard or two of cloth from a weaver—she was to
be hanged for it. Another was a man who had been accused of
stealing a horse; he said the proof had failed, and he had imagined
that he was safe from the halter; but no—he was hardly free before
he was arraigned for killing a deer in the king's park; this was
proved against him, and now he was on his way to the gallows. There
was a tradesman's apprentice whose case particularly distressed the
king; this youth said he found a hawk, one evening, that had
escaped from its owner, and he took it home with him, imagining
himself entitled to it; but the court convicted him of stealing it, and
sentenced him to death.

The king was furious over these inhumanities, and wanted
Hendon to break jail and fly with him to Westminster, so that he
could mount his throne and hold out his sceptre in mercy over these
unfortunate people and save their lives. "Poor child," sighed
Hendon, "these woful tales have brought his malady upon him
again—alack, but for his evil hap, he would have been well in a little
time."

Among these prisoners was an old lawyer—a man with a strong
face and a dauntless mien. Three years past, he had written a
pamphlet against the Lord Chancellor, accusing him of injustice,

and had been punished for it by the loss of his ears in the pillory,
and degradation from the bar, and in addition had been fined
£3000 and sentenced to imprisonment for life. Lately he had
repeated his offence; and in consequence was now under sentence
to lose *what remained of his ears*, pay a fine of £5000, be branded
on both cheeks, and remain in prison for life.

"These be honorable scars," he said, and turned back his gray
hair and showed the mutilated stubs of what had once been his ears.

The king's eye burned with passion. He said—

"None believe in me—neither wilt thou. But no matter—within
the compass of a month thou shalt be free; and more, the laws that
have dishonored thee, and shamed the English name, shall be swept
from the statute books. The world is made wrong, kings should
go to school to their own laws, at times, and so learn mercy."*

CHAPTER XXVIII

THE SACRIFICE

Meantime Miles was growing sufficiently tired of confinement and
inaction. But now his trial came on, to his great gratification, and he
thought he could welcome any sentence provided a further
imprisonment should not be a part of it. But he was mistaken about
that. He was in a fine fury when he found himself described as a
"sturdy vagabond" and sentenced to sit two hours in the pillory for
bearing that character and for assaulting the master of Hendon
Hall. His pretensions as to brothership with his prosecutor, and
rightful heirship to the Hendon honors and estates, were left
contemptuously unnoticed, as being not even worth examination.

He raged and threatened, on his way to punishment, but it did no
good; he was snatched roughly along, by the officers, and got an
occasional cuff, besides, for his unreverent conduct.

The king could not pierce through the rabble that swarmed
behind; so he was obliged to follow in the rear, remote from his good
friend and servant. The king had been nearly condemned to the
stocks, himself, for being in such bad company, but had been let off
with a lecture and a warning, in consideration of his youth. When
the crowd at last had left, he flitted feverishly from point to point
around the outer rim, hunting a place to get through; and at last,
after a deal of difficulty and delay, succeeded. There sat his poor
henchman in the degrading stocks, the sport and butt of a dirty
mob—he, the body servant of the king of England! Edward had
heard the sentence pronounced, but he had not realized the half that
it meant. His anger began to rise as the sense of this new indignity
which had been put upon him sank home; it jumped to summer
heat, the next moment, when he saw an egg sail through the air and
crush itself against Hendon's cheek, and heard the crowd roar its

*See Notes to Chapter 27, at end of volume.

enjoyment of the episode. He sprang across the open circle and confronted the officer in charge, crying—

"For shame! This is my servant—set him free! I am the—"

"O, peace!" exclaimed Hendon, in a panic, "thou'lt destroy thyself. Mind him not, officer, he is mad."

"Give thyself no trouble as to the matter of minding him, good man, I have small mind to mind him; but as to teaching him somewhat, to that I am well inclined." He turned to a subordinate and said, "Give the little fool a taste or two of the lash, to mend his manners."

"Half a dozen will better serve his turn," suggested Sir Hugh, who had ridden up, a moment before, to take a passing glance at the proceedings.

The king was seized. He did not even struggle, so paralyzed was he with the mere thought of the monstrous outrage that was proposed to be inflicted upon his sacred person. History was already defiled with the record of the scourging of an English king with whips—it was an intolerable reflection that he must furnish a duplicate of that shameful page. He was in the toils, there was no help for him: he must either take his punishment or beg for its remission. Hard conditions; he would take the stripes—a king might do that, but a king could not beg.

But meantime, Miles Hendon was resolving the difficulty. "Let the child go," said he; "ye heartless dogs, do ye not see how young and frail he is? Let him go—I will take his lashes."

"Marry, a good thought,—and thanks for it," said Sir Hugh, his face lighting with a sardonic satisfaction. "Let the little beggar go, and give this fellow a dozen in his place—an honest dozen, well laid on." The king was in the act of entering a fierce protest, but Sir Hugh silenced him with the potent remark, "Yes, speak up, do, and free thy mind—only, mark ye, that for each word you utter he shall get six strokes the more."

Hendon was removed from the stocks, and his back laid bare; and whilst the lash was applied the poor little king turned away his face and allowed unroyal tears to channel his cheeks unchecked. "Ah, brave good heart," he said to himself, "this loyal deed shall never perish out of my memory. I will not forget it—and neither shall *they!*" he added, with passion. Whilst he mused, his appreciation of Hendon's magnanimous conduct grew to greater and still greater dimensions in his mind, and so also did his gratefulness for it. Presently he said to himself, "Who saves his prince from wounds and possible death—and this he did for me—performs high service; but it is little—it is nothing!—O, less than nothing!—when 'tis weighed against the act of him who saves his prince from SHAME!"

Hendon made no outcry, under the scourge, but bore the heavy blows with soldierly fortitude. This, together with his redeeming the boy by taking his stripes for him, compelled the respect of even that

forlorn and degraded mob that was gathered there; and its gibes and
hootings died away, and no sound remained but the sound of the
falling blows. The stillness that pervaded the place, when Hendon
found himself once more in the stocks, was in strong contrast with
the insulting clamor which had prevailed there so little a while
before. The king came softly to Hendon's side, and whispered in
his ear—

"Kings cannot ennoble thee, thou good, great soul, for One who is
higher than kings hath done that for thee; but a king can confirm
thy nobility to men." He picked up the scourge from the ground,
touched Hendon's bleeding shoulders lightly with it, and whispered,
"Edward of England dubs thee earl!"

Hendon was touched. The water welled to his eyes, yet at the same
time the grisly humor of the situation and circumstances so
undermined his gravity that it was all he could do to keep some sign
of his inward mirth from showing outside. To be suddenly hoisted,
naked and gory, from the common stocks to the Alpine altitude and
splendor of an Earldom, seemed to him the last possibility in the line
of the grotesque. He said to himself, "Now am I finely tinselled,
indeed! The spectre-knight of the Kingdom of Dreams and Shadows
is become a spectre-earl!—a dizzy flight for a callow wing! An' this
go on, I shall presently be hung like a very may-pole with fantastic
gauds and make-believe honors. But I shall value them, all valueless
as they are, for the love that doth bestow them. Better these poor
mock dignities of mine, that come unasked, from a clean hand and
a right spirit, than real ones bought by servility from grudging and
interested power."

The dreaded Sir Hugh wheeled his horse about, and as he spurred
away, the living wall divided silently to let him pass, and as silently
closed together again. And so remained; nobody went so far as to
venture a remark in favor of the prisoner, or in compliment to him;
but no matter, the absence of abuse was a sufficient homage in itself.
A late comer who was not posted as to the present circumstances,
and who delivered a sneer at the "impostor" and was in the act of
following it with a dead cat, was promptly knocked down and kicked
out, without any words, and then the deep quiet resumed sway
once more.

CHAPTER XXIX

TO LONDON

When Hendon's term of service in the stocks was finished, he was
released and ordered to quit the region and come back no more. His
sword was restored to him, and also his mule and his donkey. He
mounted and rode off, followed by the king, the crowd opening with
quiet respectfulness to let them pass, and then dispersing when they

were gone.

Hendon was soon absorbed in thought. There were questions of high import to be answered. What should he do? Whither should he go? Powerful help must be found, somewhere, or he must relinquish his inheritance and remain under the imputation of being an impostor besides. Where could he hope to find this powerful help? Where, indeed! It was a knotty question. By and by a thought occurred to him which pointed to a possibility—the slenderest of slender possibilities, certainly, but still worth considering, for lack of any other that promised any thing at all. He remembered what old Andrews had said about the young king's goodness and his generous championship of the wronged and unfortunate. Why not go and try to get speech of him and beg for justice? Ah, yes, but could so fantastic a pauper get admission to the august presence of a monarch? Never mind—let that matter take care of itself; it was a bridge that would not need to be crossed till he should come to it. He was an old campaigner, and used to inventing shifts and expedients; no doubt he would be able to find a way. Yes, he would strike for the capital. Maybe his father's old friend Sir Humphrey Marlow would help him—"good old Sir Humphrey, Head Lieutenant of the late king's kitchen, or stables, or something"—Miles could not remember just what or which. Now that he had something to turn his energies to, a distinctly defined object to accomplish, the fog of humiliation and depression which had settled down upon his spirits lifted and blew away, and he raised his head and looked about him. He was surprised to see how far he had come; the village was away behind him. The king was jogging along in his wake, with his head bowed; for he, too, was deep in plans and thinkings. A sorrowful misgiving clouded Hendon's new-born cheerfulness: would the boy be willing to go again to a city where, during all his brief life, he had never known any thing but ill usage and pinching want? But the question must be asked; it could not be avoided; so Hendon reined up, and called out—

"I had forgotten to inquire whither we are bound. Thy commands, my liege?"

"To London!"

Hendon moved on again, mightily contented with the answer—but astounded at it, too.

The whole journey was made without an adventure of importance. But it ended with one. About ten o'clock on the night of the 19th of February, they stepped upon London Bridge, in the midst of a writhing, struggling jam of howling and hurrahing people, whose beer-jolly faces stood out strongly in the glare from manifold torches—and at that instant the decaying head of some former duke or other grandee tumbled down between them, striking Hendon on the elbow and then bounding off among the hurrying confusion of feet. So evanescent and unstable are men's works, in this world!—

the late good king is but three weeks dead and three days in his grave, and already the adornments which he took such pains to select from prominent people for his noble bridge are falling. A citizen stumbled over that head, and drove his own head into the back of somebody in front of him, who turned and knocked down the person that came handy, and was promptly laid out himself by that person's friend. It was the right ripe time for a free fight, for the festivities of the morrow—Coronation Day—were already beginning; everybody was full of strong drink and patriotism; within five minutes the free fight was occupying a good deal of ground; within ten or twelve it covered an acre or so, and was become a riot. By this time Hendon and the king were hopelessly separated from each other and lost in the rush and turmoil of the roaring masses of humanity. And so we leave them.

CHAPTER XXX

TOM'S PROGRESS

Whilst the true King wandered about the land poorly clad, poorly fed, cuffed and derided by tramps one while, herding with thieves and murderers in a jail another, and called idiot and impostor by all impartially, the mock King Tom Canty enjoyed a quite different experience.

When we saw him last, royalty was just beginning to have a bright side for him. This bright side went on brightening more and more every day: in a very little while it was become almost all sunshine and delightfulness. He lost his fears; his misgivings faded out and died; his embarrassments departed, and gave place to an easy and confident bearing. He worked the whipping-boy mine to ever-increasing profit.

He ordered my Lady Elizabeth and my Lady Jane Grey into his presence when he wanted to play or talk, and dismissed them when he was done with them, with the air of one familiarly accustomed to such performances. It no longer confused him to have these lofty personages kiss his hand at parting.

He came to enjoy being conducted to bed in state at night, and dressed with intricate and solemn ceremony in the morning. It came to be a proud pleasure to march to dinner attended by a glittering procession of officers of state and gentlemen-at-arms; insomuch, indeed, that he doubled his guard of gentlemen-at-arms, and made them a hundred. He liked to hear the bugles sounding down the long corridors, and the distant voices responding, "Way for the King!"

He even learned to enjoy sitting in throned state in council, and seeming to be something more than the Lord Protector's mouth-piece. He liked to receive great ambassadors and their gorgeous trains, and listen to the affectionate messages they brought from

illustrious monarchs who called him "brother." O happy Tom
Canty, late of Offal Court!

He enjoyed his splendid clothes, and ordered more: he found his
four hundred servants too few for his proper grandeur, and trebled
them. The adulation of salaaming courtiers came to be sweet music
to his ears. He remained kind and gentle, and a sturdy and
determined champion of all that were oppressed, and he made
tireless war upon unjust laws: yet upon occasion, being offended, he
could turn upon an earl, or even a duke, and give him a look that
would make him tremble. Once, when his royal "sister," the grimly,
holy Lady Mary, set herself to reason with him against the wisdom of
his course in pardoning so many people who would otherwise be
jailed, or hanged, or burned, and reminded him that their august
late father's prisons had sometimes contained as high as sixty
thousand convicts at one time, and that during his admirable reign
he had delivered seventy-two thousand thieves and robbers over to
death by the executioner,* the boy was filled with generous
indignation, and commanded her to go to her closet, and beseech
God to take away the stone that was in her breast, and give her a
human heart.

Did Tom Canty never feel troubled about the poor little rightful
prince who had treated him so kindly, and flown out with such hot
zeal to avenge him upon the insolent sentinel at the palace-gate?
Yes; his first royal days and nights were pretty well sprinkled with
painful thoughts about the lost prince, and with sincere longings
for his return, and happy restoration to his native rights and
splendors. But as time wore on, and the prince did not come, Tom's
mind became more and more occupied with his new and enchanting
experiences, and by little and little the vanished monarch faded
almost out of his thoughts; and finally, when he did intrude upon
them at intervals, he was become an unwelcome spectre, for he made
Tom feel guilty and ashamed.

Tom's poor mother and sisters travelled the same road out of his
mind. At first he pined for them, sorrowed for them, longed to see
them, but later, the thought of their coming some day in their rags
and dirt, and betraying him with their kisses, and pulling him down
from his lofty place, and dragging him back to penury and
degradation and the slums, made him shudder. At last they ceased
to trouble his thoughts almost wholly. And he was content, even
glad; for, whenever their mournful and accusing faces did rise
before him now, they made him feel more despicable than the
worms that crawl.

At midnight of the 19th of February, Tom Canty was sinking to
sleep in his rich bed in the palace, guarded by his loyal vassals, and
surrounded by the pomps of royalty, a happy boy; for to-morrow
was the day appointed for his solemn crowning as King of England.
At that same hour, Edward, the true king, hungry and thirsty, soiled

*Hume's England.

and draggled, worn with travel, and clothed in rags and shreds,—
his share of the results of the riot,—was wedged in among a crowd
of people who were watching with deep interest certain hurrying
gangs of workmen who streamed in and out of Westminster Abbey,
busy as ants: they were making the last preparation for the royal
coronation.

CHAPTER XXXI

THE RECOGNITION PROCESSION

When Tom Canty awoke the next morning, the air was heavy with
a thunderous murmur: all the distances were charged with it. It was
music to him; for it meant that the English world was out in its
strength to give loyal welcome to the great day.

Presently Tom found himself once more the chief figure in a
wonderful floating pageant on the Thames; for by ancient custom
the "recognition procession" through London must start from the
Tower, and he was bound thither.

When he arrived there, the sides of the venerable fortress seemed
suddenly rent in a thousand places, and from every rent leaped a
red tongue of flame and a white gush of smoke; a deafening
explosion followed, which drowned the shoutings of the multitude,
and made the ground tremble; the flame-jets, the smoke, and the
explosions, were repeated over and over again with marvellous
celerity, so that in a few moments the old Tower disappeared in the
vast fog of its own smoke, all but the very top of the tall pile called
the White Tower: this, with its banners, stood out above the dense
bank of vapor as a mountain-peak projects above a cloud-rack.
as a mountain-peak projects above a cloud-rack.

Tom Canty, splendidly arrayed, mounted a prancing war-steed,
whose rich trappings almost reached to the ground; his "uncle,"
the Lord Protector Somerset, similarly mounted, took place in his
rear; the King's Guard formed in single ranks on either side, clad
in burnished armor; after the protector followed a seemingly
interminable procession of resplendent nobles attended by their
vassals; after these came the lord mayor and the aldermanic body,
in crimson velvet robes, and with their gold chains across their
breasts; and after these the officers and members of all the guilds
of London, in rich raiment, and bearing the showy banners of the
several corporations. Also in the procession, as a special guard of
honor through the city, was the Ancient and Honorable Artillery
Company,—an organization already three hundred years old at that
time, and the only military body in England possessing the privilege
(which it still possesses in our day) of holding itself independent
of the commands of Parliament. It was a brilliant spectacle, and was
hailed with acclamations all along the line, as it took its stately way

through the packed multitudes of citizens. The chronicler says, "The King, as he entered the city, was received by the people with prayers, welcomings, cries, and tender words, and all signs which argue an earnest love of subjects toward their sovereign; and the King, by holding up his glad countenance to such as stood afar off, and most tender language to those that stood nigh his Grace, showed himself no less thankful to receive the people's good will than they to offer it. To all that wished him well, he gave thanks. To such as bade 'God save his Grace,' he said in return, 'God save you all!' and added that 'he thanked them with all his heart.' Wonderfully transported were the people with the loving answers and gestures of their King."

In Fenchurch Street a "fair child, in costly apparel," stood on a stage to welcome his Majesty to the city. The last verse of his greeting was in these words:

"Welcome, O King! as much as hearts can think;
  Welcome again, as much as tongue can tell,—
Welcome to joyous tongues, and hearts that will not shrink:
  God thee preserve, we pray, and wish thee ever well."

The people burst forth in a glad shout, repeating with one voice what the child had said. Tom Canty gazed abroad over the surging sea of eager faces, and his heart swelled with exultation; and he felt that the one thing worth living for in this world was to be a king, and a nation's idol. Presently he caught sight, at a distance, of a couple of his ragged Offal Court comrades,—one of them the lord high admiral in his late mimic court, the other the first lord of the bedchamber in the same pretentious fiction; and his pride swelled higher than ever. Oh, if they could only recognize him now! What unspeakable glory it would be, if they could recognize him, and realize that the derided mock king of the slums and back alleys was become a real king, with illustrious dukes and princes for his humble menials, and the English world at his feet! But he had to deny himself, and choke down his desire, for such a recognition might cost more than it would come to: so he turned away his head, and left the two soiled lads to go on with their shoutings and glad adulations, unsuspicious of whom it was they were lavishing them upon.

Every now and then rose the cry, "A largess! a largess!" and Tom responded by scattering a handful of bright new coins abroad for the multitude to scramble for.

The chronicler says, "At the upper end of Gracechurch Street, before the sign of the Eagle, the city had erected a gorgeous arch, beneath which was a stage, which stretched from one side of the street to the other. This was a historical pageant, representing the King's immediate progenitors. There sat Elizabeth of York in the

midst of an immense white rose, whose petals formed elaborate
furbelows around her; by her side was Henry VII., issuing out of a
vast red rose, disposed in the same manner: the hands of the royal
pair were locked together, and the wedding-ring ostentatiously
displayed. From the red and white roses proceeded a stem, which
reached up to a second stage, occupied by Henry VIII., issuing from
a red-and-white rose, with the effigy of the new king's mother, Jane
Seymour, represented by his side. One branch sprang from this pair,
which mounted to a third stage, where sat the effigy of Edward VI.
himself, enthroned in royal majesty; and the whole pageant was
framed with wreaths of roses, red and white.''

This quaint and gaudy spectacle so wrought upon the rejoicing
people, that their acclamations utterly smothered the small voice
of the child whose business it was to explain the thing in eulogistic
rhymes. But Tom Canty was not sorry; for this loyal uproar was
sweeter music to him than any poetry, no matter what its quality
might be. Whithersoever Tom turned his happy young face, the
people recognized the exactness of his effigy's likeness to himself,
the flesh and blood counterpart; and new whirlwinds of applause
burst forth.

The great pageant moved on, and still on, under one triumphal
arch after another, and past a bewildering succession of spectacular
and symbolical tableaux, each of which typified and exalted some
virtue, or talent, or merit, of the little king's. ''Throughout the whole
of Cheapside, from every penthouse and window, hung banners
and streamers; and the richest carpets, stuffs, and cloth-of-gold
tapestried the streets,—specimens of the great wealth of the stores
within; and the splendor of this thoroughfare was equalled in the
other streets, and in some even surpassed.''

''And all these wonders and these marvels are to welcome
me—me!'' murmured Tom Canty.

The mock king's cheeks were flushed with excitement, his eyes
were flashing, his senses swam in a delirium of pleasure. At this
point, just as he was raising his hand to fling another rich largess,
he caught sight of a pale, astounded face which was strained forward
out of the second rank of the crowd, its intense eyes riveted upon
him. A sickening consternation struck through him; he recognized
his mother! and up flew his hand, palm outward, before his eyes,—
that old involuntary gesture, born of a forgotten episode, and
perpetuated by habit. In an instant more she had torn her way out
of the press, and past the guards, and was at his side. She embraced
his leg, she covered it with kisses, she cried, ''O my child, my
darling!'' lifting toward him a face that was transfigured with joy
and love. The same instant an officer of the King's Guard snatched
her away with a curse, and sent her reeling back whence she came
with a vigorous impulse from his strong arm. The words ''I do not
know you, woman!'' were falling from Tom Canty's lips when this

piteous thing occurred; but it smote him to the heart to see her
treated so; and as she turned for a last glimpse of him, whilst the
crowd was swallowing her from his sight, she seemed so wounded, so
broken-hearted, that a shame fell upon him which consumed his
pride to ashes and withered his stolen royalty. His grandeurs were
striken valueless: they seemed to fall away from him like rotten rags.

The procession moved on, and still on, through ever augmenting
splendors and ever augmenting tempests of welcome; but to Tom
Canty they were as if they had not been. He neither saw nor heard.
Royalty had lost its grace and sweetness; its pomps were become a
reproach. Remorse was eating his heart out. He said, "Would God I
were free of my captivity!"

He had unconsciously dropped back into the phraseology of the
first days of his compulsory greatness.

The shining pageant still went winding like a radiant and
interminable serpent down the crooked lanes of the quaint old
city, and through the huzzaing hosts; but still the King rode with
bowed head and vacant eyes, seeing only his mother's face and that
wounded look in it.

"Largess, largess!" The cry fell upon an unheeding ear.

"Long live Edward of England!" It seemed as if the earth shook
with the explosion; but there was no response from the King. He
heard it only as one hears the thunder of the surf when it is blown
to the ear out of a great distance, for it was smothered under another
sound which was still nearer, in his own breast, in his accusing
conscience,—a voice which kept repeating those shameful words,
"I do not know you, woman!"

The words smote upon the King's soul as the strokes of a funeral
bell smite upon the soul of a surviving friend when they remind him
of secret treacheries suffered at his hands by him that is gone.

New glories were unfolded at every turning; new wonders, new
marvels, sprung into view; the pent clamors of waiting batteries
were released; new raptures poured from the throats of the waiting
multitudes: but the King gave no sign, and the accusing voice that
went moaning through his comfortless breast was all the sound he
heard.

By and by the gladness in the faces of the populace changed a
little, and became touched with a something like solicitude or
anxiety: an abatement in the volume of applause was observable too.
The lord protector was quick to notice these things: he was as quick
to detect the cause. He spurred to the King's side, bent low in his
saddle, uncovered, and said,—

"My liege, it is an ill time for dreaming. The people observe thy
downcast head, thy clouded mien, and they take it for an omen.
Be advised: unveil the sun of royalty, and let it shine upon these
boding vapors, and disperse them. Lift up they face, and smile upon
the people."

So saying, the duke scattered a handful of coins to right and left, then retired to his place. The mock king did mechanically as he had been bidden. His smile had no heart in it, but few eyes were near enough or sharp enough to detect that. The noddings of his plumed head as he saluted his subjects were full of grace and graciousness; the largess which he delivered from his hand was royally liberal: so the people's anxiety vanished, and the acclamations burst forth again in as mighty a volume as before.

Still once more, a little before the progress was ended, the duke was obliged to ride forward, and make remonstrance. He whispered,—

"O dread sovereign! shake off these fatal humors: the eyes of the world are upon thee." Then he added with sharp annoyance, "Perdition catch that crazy pauper! 'twas she that hath disturbed your Highness."

The gorgeous figure turned a lustreless eye upon the duke, and said in a dead voice,—

"She was my mother!"

"My God!" groaned the protector as he reined his horse backward to his post, "the omen was pregnant with prophecy. He is gone mad again!"

CHAPTER XXXII

CORONATION DAY

Let us go backward a few hours, and place ourselves in Westminster Abbey, at four o'clock in the morning of this memorable Coronation Day. We are not without company; for although it is still night, we find the torch-lighted galleries already filling up with people who are well content to sit still and wait seven or eight hours till the time shall come for them to see what they may not hope to see twice in their lives—the coronation of a king. Yes, London and Westminster have been astir ever since the warning guns boomed at three o'clock, and already crowds of untitled rich folk who have bought the privilege of trying to find sitting-room in the galleries are flocking in at the entrances reserved for their sort.

The hours drag along, tediously enough. All stir has ceased for some time, for every gallery has long ago been packed. We may sit, now, and look and think at our leisure. We have glimpses, here and there and yonder, through the dim cathedral twilight, of portions of many galleries and balconies, wedged full with people, the other portions of these galleries and balconies being cut off from sight by intervening pillars and architectural projections. We have in view the whole of the great north transept—empty, and waiting for England's privileged ones. We see also the ample area or platform, carpeted with rich stuffs, whereon the throne stands. The

throne occupies the centre of the platform, and is raised above it
upon an elevation of four steps. Within the seat of the throne is
enclosed a rough flat rock—the stone of Scone—which many
generations of Scottish kings sat on to be crowned, and so it in time
became holy enough to answer a like purpose for English monarchs.
Both the throne and its footstool are covered with cloth of gold.

Stillness reigns, the torches blink dully, the time drags heavily.
But at last the lagging daylight asserts itself, the torches are
extinguished, and a mellow radiance suffuses the great spaces. All
features of the noble building are distinct, now, but soft and
dreamy, for the sun is lightly veiled with clouds.

At seven o'clock the first break in the drowsy monotony occurs;
for on the stroke of this hour the first peeress enters the transept,
clothed like Solomon for splendor, and is conducted to her
appointed place by an official clad in satins and velvets, whilst
a duplicate of him gathers up the lady's long train, follows after,
and, when the lady is seated, arranges the train across her lap for
her. He then places her footstool according to her desire, after
which he puts her coronet where it will be convenient to her hand
when the time for the simultaneous coronetting of the nobles shall
arrive.

By this time the peeresses are flowing in in a glittering stream,
and satin-clad officials are flitting and glinting everywhere, seating
them and making them comfortable. The scene is animated enough,
now. There is stir and life, and shifting color everywhere. After a
time, quiet reigns again; for the peeresses are all come, and are all
in their places—a solid acre, or such a matter, of human flowers,
resplendent in variegated colors, and frosted like a Milky Way with
diamonds. There are all ages, here: brown, wrinkled, whitehaired
dowagers who are able to go back, and still back, down the stream
of time, and recall the crowning of Richard III. and the troublous
days of that old forgotten age; and there are handsome middle-aged
dames; and lovely and gracious young matrons; and gentle and
beautiful young girls, with beaming eyes and fresh complexions,
who may possibly put on their jewelled coronets awkwardly when the
great time comes; for the matter will be new to them, and their
excitement will be a sore hindrance. Still this may not happen, for
the hair of all these ladies has been arranged with a special view to
the swift and successful lodging of the crown in its place when
the signal comes.

We have seen that this massed array of peeresses is sown thick
with diamonds, and we also see that it is a marvellous spectacle—but
now we are about to be astonished in earnest. About nine, the clouds
suddenly break away and a shaft of sunshine cleaves the mellow
atmosphere, and drifts slowly along the ranks of ladies; and every
rank it touches flames into a dazzling splendor of many-colored
fires, and we tingle to our finger-tips with the electric thrill that is

shot through us by the surprise and the beauty of the spectacle!
Presently a special envoy from some distant corner of the Orient,
marching with the general body of foreign ambassadors, crosses
this bar of sunshine, and we catch our breath, the glory that streams
and flashes and palpitates about him is so overpowering; for he is
crusted from head to heels with gems, and his slightest movement
showers a dancing radiance all around him.

Let us change the tense for convenience. The time drifted along,—
one hour—two hours—two hours and a half; then the deep booming
of artillery told that the king and his grand procession had arrived
at last; so the waiting multitude rejoiced. All knew that a further
delay must follow, for the king must be prepared and robed for the
solemn ceremony; but this delay would be pleasantly occupied by the
assembling of the peers of the realm in their stately robes. These
were conducted ceremoniously to their seats, and their coronets
placed conveniently at hand; and meanwhile the multitude in the
galleries were alive with interest, for most of them were beholding
for the first time, dukes, earls and barons, whose names had been
historical for five hundred years. When all were finally seated, the
spectacle from the galleries and all coigns of vantage was complete;
a gorgeous one to look upon and to remember.

Now the robed and mitred great heads of the church, and their
attendants, filed in upon the platform and took their appointed
places; these were followed by the Lord Protector and other great
officials, and these again by a steel-clad detachment of the Guard.

There was a waiting pause; then, at a signal, a triumphant peal
of music burst forth, and Tom Canty, clothed in a long robe of cloth
of gold, appeared at a door, and stepped upon the platform. The
entire multitude rose, and the ceremony of the Recognition ensued.

Then a noble anthem swept the Abbey with its rich waves of
sound; and thus heralded and welcomed, Tom Canty was conducted
to the throne. The ancient ceremonies went on, with impressive
solemnity, whilst the audience gazed; and as they drew nearer and
nearer to completion, Tom Canty grew pale, and still paler, and a
deep and steadily deepening woe and despondency settled down
upon his spirits and upon his remorseful heart.

At last the final act was at hand. The Archbishop of Canterbury
lifted up the crown of England from its cushion and held it out
over the trembling mock-king's head. In the same instant a
rainbow-radiance flashed along the spacious transept; for with one
impulse every individual in the great concourse of nobles lifted a
coronet and poised it over his or her head,—and paused in that
attitude.

A deep hush pervaded the Abbey. At this impressive moment, a
startling apparition intruded upon the scene—an apparition
observed by none in the absorbed multitude, until it suddenly
appeared, moving up the great central aisle. It was a boy,

bare-headed, ill shod, and clothed in coarse plebeian garments
that were falling to rags. He raised his hand with a solemnity which
ill comported with his soiled and sorry aspect, and delivered this
note of warning—

"I forbid you to set the crown of England upon that forfeited
head. *I* am the king!"

In an instant several indignant hands were laid upon the boy; but
in the same instant Tom Canty, in his regal vestments, made a
swift step forward and cried out in a ringing voice—

"Loose him and forbear! He *is* the king!"

A sort of panic of astonishment swept the assemblage, and they
partly rose in their places and started in a bewildered way at one
another and at the chief figures in this scene, like persons who
wondered whether they were awake and in their senses, or asleep
and dreaming. The Lord Protector was as amazed as the rest, but
quickly recovered himself and exclaimed in a voice of authority—

"Mind not his Majesty, his malady is upon him again—seize the
vagabond!"

He would have been obeyed, but the mock-king stamped his foot
and cried out—

"On your peril! Touch him not, he is the king!"

The hands were withheld; a paralysis fell upon the house; no one
moved, no one spoke; indeed no one knew how to act or what to say,
in so strange and surprising an emergency. While all minds were
struggling to right themselves, the boy still moved steadily forward,
with high port and confident mien; he had never halted from the
beginning; and while the tangled minds still floundered helplessly,
he stepped upon the platform, and the mock-king ran with a glad
face to meet him; and fell on his knees before him and said—

"O, my lord the king, let poor Tom Canty be first to swear fealty
to thee, and say 'Put on thy crown and enter into thine own
again!' "

The Lord Protector's eye fell sternly upon the new-comer's face;
but straightway the sternness vanished away, and gave place to an
expression of wondering surprise. This thing happened also to the
other great officers. They glanced at each other, and retreated a
step by a common and unconscious impulse. The thought in each
mind was the same: "What a strange resemblance!"

The Lord Protector reflected a moment or two, in perplexity, then
he said, with grave respectfulness—

"By your favor, sir, I desire to ask certain questions which'"—

"I will answer them, my lord."

The duke asked him many questions about the court, the late
king, the prince, the princesses,—the boy answered them correctly
and without hesitating. He described the rooms of state in the
palace, the late king's apartments, and those of the Prince of Wales.

It was strange; it was wonderful; yes, it was unaccountable—so all said that heard it. The tide was beginning to turn, and Tom Canty's hopes to run high, when the Lord Protector shook his head and said—

"It is true it is most wonderful—but it is no more than our lord the king likewise can do." This remark, and this reference to himself as still the king, saddened Tom Canty, and he felt his hopes crumbling from under him. "These are not *proofs,*" added the Protector.

The tide was turning very fast, now, very fast indeed—but in the wrong direction; it was leaving poor Tom Canty stranded on the throne, and sweeping the other out to sea. The Lord Protector communed with himself—shook his head—the thought forced itself upon him, "It is perilous to the State and to us all, to entertain so fateful a riddle as this; it could divide the nation and undermine the throne." He turned and said—

"Sir Thomas, arrest this—no, hold!" His face lighted, and he confronted the ragged candidate with this question—

"Where lieth the Great Seal? Answer me this truly, and the riddle is unriddled; for only he that was Prince of Wales *can* so answer! On so trivial a thing hang a throne and a dynasty!"

It was a lucky thought, a happy thought. That it was so considered by the great officials was manifested by the silent applause that shot from eye to eye around their circle in the form of bright approving glances. Yes, none but the true prince could dissolve the stubborn mystery of the vanished Great Seal—this forlorn little impostor had been taught his lesson well, but here his teachings must fail, for his teacher himself could not answer *that* question—ah, very good, very good indeed; now we shall be rid of this troublesome and perilous business in short order! And so they nodded invisibly and smiled inwardly with satisfaction, and looked to see this foolish lad stricken with a palsy of guilty confusion. How surprised they were, then, to see nothing of the sort happen—how they marvelled to hear him answer up promptly, in a confident and untroubled voice, and say—

"There is nought in this riddle that is difficult." Then, without so much as a by-your-leave to anybody, he turned and gave this command, with the easy manner of one accustomed to doing such things: "My lord St. John, go you to my private cabinet in the palace—for none knoweth the place better than you—and, close down the door that opens from the ante-chamber, you shall find in the wall a brazen nail-head; press upon it and a little jewel-closet will fly open which not even you do know of—no, nor any soul else, in all the world but me and the trusty artisan that did contrive it for me. The first thing that falleth under your eye will be the Great Seal—fetch it hither."

All the company wondered at this speech, and wondered still more to see the little mendicant pick out this peer without hesitancy or apparent fear of mistake, and call him by name with such a placidly convincing air of having known him all his life. The peer was almost surprised into obeying. He even made a movement as if to go, but quickly recovered his tranquil attitude and confessed his blunder with a blush. Tom Canty turned upon him and said, sharply—

"Why dost thou hesitate? Hast not heard the king's command? Go!"

The lord St. John made a deep obeisance—and it was observed that it was a significantly cautious and non-committal one, it not being delivered at either of the kings, but at the neutral ground about half way between the two—and took his leave.

Now began a movement of the gorgeous particles of that official group which was slow, scarcely perceptible, and yet steady and persistent—a movement such as is observed in a kaleidoscope that is turned slowly, whereby the components of one splendid cluster fall away and join themselves to another—a movement which little by little, in the present case, dissolved the glittering crowd that stood about Tom Canty and clustered it together again in the neighborhood of the new-comer. Tom Canty stood almost alone. Now ensued a brief season of deep suspense and waiting—during which even the few faint-hearts still remaining near Tom Canty gradually scraped together courage enough to glide, one by one, over to the majority. So at last Tom Canty, in his royal robes and jewels, stood wholly alone and isolated from the world, a conspicuous figure, occupying an eloquent vacancy.

Now the lord St. John was seen returning. As he advanced up the mid-aisle the interest was so intense that the low murmur of conversation in the great assemblage died out and was succeeded by a profound hush, a breathless stillness, through which his footfalls pulsed with a dull and distant sound. Every eye was fastened upon him as he moved along. He reached the platform, paused a moment, then moved toward Tom Canty with a deep obeisance, and said—

"Sire, the Seal is not there!"

A mob does not melt away from the presence of a plague-patient with more haste than the band of pallid and terrified courtiers melted away from the presence of the shabby little claimant of the Crown. In a moment he stood all alone, without friend or supporter, a target upon which was concentrated a bitter fire of scornful and angry looks. The Lord Protector called out fiercely—

"Cast the beggar into the street, and scourge him through the town—the paltry knave is worth no more consideration!"

Officers of the guard sprang forward to obey, but Tom Canty waved them off and said—

"Back! Whoso touches him perils his life!"

The Lord Protector was perplexed, in the last degree. He said to the lord St. John—

"Searched you well?—but it boots not to ask that. It doth seem passing strange. Little things, trifles, slip out of one's ken, and one does not think it matter for surprise; but how a so bulky thing as the Seal of England can vanish away and no man be able to get track of it again—a massy golden disk"—

Tom Canty, with beaming eyes, sprang forward and shouted—

"Hold, that is enough! Was it round?—and thick? and had it letters and devices graved upon it?—Yes? O, *now* I know what this Great Seal is that there's been such worry and bother about! An' ye had described it to me, ye could have had it three weeks ago. Right well I know where it lies; but it was not I that put it there—first."

"Who, then, my liege?" asked the Lord Protector.

"He that stands there—the rightful king of England. And he shall tell you himself where it lies—then you will believe he knew it of his own knowledge. Bethink thee, my king—spur thy memory—it was the last, the very *last* thing thou didst that day before thou didst rush forth from the palace, clothed in my rags, to punish the soldier that insulted me."

A silence ensued, undisturbed by a movement or a whisper, and all eyes were fixed upon the new-comer, who stood, with bent head and corrugated brow, groping in his memory among a thronging multitude of valueless recollections for one single little elusive fact, which, found, would seat him upon a throne—unfound, would leave him as he was, for good and all—a pauper and an outcast. Moment after moment passed—still the boy struggled silently on, and gave no sign. But at last he heaved a sigh, shook his head slowly, and said, with a trembling lip and in a despondent voice—

"I call the scene back—all of it—but the Seal hath no place in it." He paused, then looked up, and said with gentle dignity, "My lords and gentlemen, if ye will rob your rightful sovereign of his own for lack of this evidence which he is not able to furnish, I may not stay ye, being powerless. But"—

"O, folly, O, madness, my king!" cried Tom Canty, in a panic, "wait!—think! Do not give up!—the cause is not lost! Nor *shall* be, neither! List to what I say—follow every word—I am going to bring that morning back again, every hap just as it happened. We talked—I told you of my sisters, Nan and Bet—ah, yes, you remember that; and about mine old grandam—and the rough games of the lads of Offal Court—yes, you remember these things also; very well, follow me still, you shall recall every thing. You gave me food and drink, and did with princely courtesy send away the servants, so that my low breeding might not shame me before them—ah, yes, this also you remember."

As Tom checked off his details, and the other boy nodded his head in recognition of them, the great audience and the officials stared in puzzled wonderment; the tale sounded like true history, yet how could this impossible conjunction between a prince and a beggar boy have come about? Never was a company of people so perplexed, so interested, and so stupefied, before.

"For a jest, my prince, we did exchange garments. Then we stood before a mirror; and so alike were we that both said it seemed as if there had been no change made—yes, you remember that. Then you noticed that the soldier had hurt my hand—look! here it is, I cannot yet even write with it, the fingers are so stiff. At this your Highness sprang up, vowing vengeance upon that soldier, and ran toward the door—you passed a table—that thing you call the Seal lay on that table—you snatched it up and looked eagerly about, as if for a place to hide it—your eye caught sight of"—

"There, 'tis sufficient!—and the dear God be thanked!" exclaimed the ragged claimant, in a mighty excitement. "Go, my good St. John,—in an arm-piece of the Milanese armor that hangs on the wall, thou'lt find the Seal!"

"Right, my king! right!" cried Tom Canty; "*now* the sceptre of England is thine own; and it was better for him that would dispute it that he had been born dumb! Go, my lord St. John, give thy feet wings!"

The whole assemblage was on its feet, now, and well nigh out of its mind with uneasiness, apprehension, and consuming excitement. On the floor and on the platform a deafening buzz of frantic conversation burst forth, and for some time nobody knew any thing or heard any thing or was interested in any thing but what his neighbor was shouting into his ear, or he was shouting into his neighbor's ear. Time—nobody knew how much of it—swept by unheeded and unnoted.—At last a sudden hush fell upon the house, and in the same moment St. John appeared upon the platform and held the Great Seal aloft in his hand. Then such a shout went up!

"Long live the true King!"

For five minutes the air quaked with shouts and the crash of musical instruments, and was white with a storm of waving handkerchiefs; and through it all a ragged lad, the most conspicuous figure in England, stood, flushed and happy and proud, in the centre of the spacious platform, with the great vassals of the kingdom kneeling around him.

Then all rose, and Tom Canty cried out—

"Now, O, my king, take these regal garments back, and give poor Tom, thy servant, his shreds and remnants again."

The Lord Protector spoke up—

"Let the small varlet be stripped and flung into the Tower."

But the new king, the true king, said—

"I will not have it so. But for him I had not got my crown again—none shall lay a hand upon him to harm him. And as for thee, my good uncle, my Lord Protector, this conduct of thine is not grateful toward this poor lad, for I hear he hath made thee a duke"—the Protector blushed—"yet he was not a king; wherefore, what is thy fine title worth, now? To-morrow you shall sue to me, *through him,* for its confirmation, else no duke, but a simple earl, shalt thou remain."

Under this rebuke, his grace the duke of Somerset retired a little from the front for the moment. The king turned to Tom, and said, kindly—

"My poor boy, how was it that you could remember where I hid the Seal when I could not remember it myself?"

"Ah, my king, that was easy, since I used it divers days."

"Used it,—yet could not explain where it was?"

"I did not know it was *that* they wanted. They did not describe it, your majesty."

"Then how used you it?"

The red blood began to steal up into Tom's cheeks, and he dropped his eyes and was silent.

"Speak up, good lad, and fear nothing," said the king. "How used you the Great Seal of England?"

Tom stammered a moment, in a pathetic confusion, then got it out—

"To crack nuts with!"

Poor child, the avalanche of laughter that greeted this, nearly swept him off his feet. But if a doubt remained in any mind that Tom Canty was not the king of England and familiar with the august appurtenances of royalty, this reply disposed of it utterly.

Meantime the sumptuous robe of state had been removed from Tom's shoulders to the king's, whose rags were effectually hidden from sight under it. Then the coronation ceremonies were resumed; the true king was anointed and the crown set upon his head, whilst cannon thundered the news to the city, and all London seemed to rock with applause.

CHAPTER XXXIII

EDWARD AS KING

Miles Hendon was picturesque enough before he got into the riot on London Bridge—he was more so when he got out of it. He had but little money when he got in, none at all when he got out. The pickpockets had stripped him of his last farthing.

But no matter, so he found his boy. Being a soldier, he did not go at his task in a random way, but set to work, first of all, to arrange his campaign.

What would the boy naturally do? Where would he naturally go? Well—argued Miles—he would naturally go to his former haunts, for that is the instinct of unsound minds, when homeless and forsaken, as well as of sound ones. Whereabouts were his former haunts? His rags, taken together with the low villain who seemed to know him and who even claimed to be his father, indicated that his home was in one or another of the poorest and meanest districts of London. Would the search for him be difficult, or long? No, it was likely to be easy and brief. He would not hunt for the boy, he would hunt for a crowd; in the centre of a big crowd or a little one, sooner or later, he should find his poor little friend, sure; and the mangy mob would be entertaining itself with pestering and aggravating the boy, who would be proclaiming himself king, as usual. Then Miles Hendon would cripple some of those people, and carry off his little ward, and comfort and cheer him with loving words, and the two would never be separated any more.

So Miles started on his quest. Hour after hour he tramped through back alleys and squalid streets, seeking groups and crowds, and finding no end of them, but never any sign of the boy. This greatly surprised him, but did not discourage him. To his notion, there was nothing the matter with his plan of campaign; the only miscalculation about it was that the campaign was becoming a lengthy one, whereas he had expected it to be short.

When daylight arrived, at last, he had made many a mile, and canvassed many a crowd, but the only result was that he was tolerably tired, rather hungry, and very sleepy. He wanted some breakfast, but there was no way to get it. To beg for it did not occur to him; as to pawning his sword, he would as soon have thought of parting with his honor; he could spare some of his clothes—yes, but one could as easily find a customer for a disease as for such clothes.

At noon he was still tramping—among the rabble which followed after the royal procession, now; for he argued that this regal display would attract his little lunatic powerfully. He followed the pageant through all its devious windings about London, and all the way to Westminster and the Abbey. He drifted here and there amongst the multitudes that were massed in the vicinity for a weary long time, baffled and perplexed, and finally wandered off, thinking, and trying to contrive some way to better his plan of campaign. By and by, when he came to himself out of his musings, he discovered that the town was far behind him and that the day was growing old. He was near the river, and in the country; it was a region of fine rural seats—not the sort of district to welcome clothes like his.

It was not at all cold; so he stretched himself on the ground in the lee of a hedge to rest and think. Drowsiness presently began to settle upon his senses; the faint and far-off boom of cannon was wafted to his ear, and he said to himself "The new king is crowned," and straightway fell asleep. He had not slept or rested, before, for more than thirty hours. He did not wake again until near the middle of the next morning.

He got up, lame, stiff, and half famished, washed himself in the river, stayed his stomach with a pint or two of water, and trudged off toward Westminster grumbling at himself for having wasted so much time. Hunger helped him to a new plan, now; he would try to get speech with old Sir Humphrey Marlow and borrow a few marks, and—but that was enough of a plan for the present; it would be time enough to enlarge it when this first stage should be accomplished.

Toward eleven o'clock he approached the palace; and although a host of showy people were about him, moving in the same direction, he was not inconspicuous—his costume took care of that. He watched these people's faces narrowly, hoping to find a charitable one whose possessor might be willing to carry his name to the old lieutenant—as to trying to get into the palace himself, that was simply out of the question.

Presently our whipping-boy passed him, then wheeled about and scanned his figure well, saying to himself, "An' that is not the very vagabond his majesty is in such a worry about, then am I an ass— though belike I was that before. He answereth that description to a rag—that God should make two such, would be to cheapen miracles, by wasteful repetition. I would I could contrive an excuse to speak with him."

Miles Hendon saved him the trouble; for he turned about, then, as a man generally will when somebody mesmerizes him by gazing hard at him from behind; and observing a strong interest in the boy's eyes, he stepped toward him and said—

"You have just come out from the palace; do you belong there?"

"Yes, your worship."

"Know you Sir Humphrey Marlow?"

The boy started, and said to himself, "Lord! mine old departed father!" Then he answered, aloud, "Right well, your worship."

"Good—is he within?"

"Yes," said the boy; and added, to himself, "within his grave."

"Might I crave your favor to carry my name to him, and say I beg to say a word in his ear?"

"I will despatch the business right willingly, fair sir."

"Then say Miles Hendon, son of Sir Richard, is here without— I shall be greatly bounden to you, my good lad."

The boy looked disappointed—"the king did not name him so," he said to himself—"but it mattereth not, this is his twin brother, and can give his majesty news of 'tother Sir-Odds-and-Ends, I warrant." So he said to Miles, "Step in there a moment, good sir, and wait till I bring you word."

Hendon retired to the place indicated—it was a recess sunk in the palace wall, with a stone bench in it—a shelter for sentinels in bad weather. He had hardly seated himself when some halberdiers, in charge of an officer, passed by. The officer saw him, halted his men, and commanded Hendon to come forth. He obeyed, and was promptly arrested as a suspicious character prowling within the precincts of the palace. Things began to look ugly. Poor Miles was going to explain, but the officer roughly silenced him, and ordered his men to disarm him and search him.

"God of his mercy grant that they find somewhat," said poor Miles; "I have searched enow, and failed, yet is my need greater than theirs."

Nothing was found but a document. The officer tore it open, and Hendon smiled when he recognized the "pot-hooks" made by his lost little friend that black day at Hendon Hall. The officer's face grew dark as he read the English paragraph, and Miles blenched to the opposite color as he listened.

"Another new claimant of the crown!" cried the officer. "Verily they breed like rabbits, to-day. Seize the rascal, men, and see ye keep him fast whilst I convey this precious paper within and send it to the king."

He hurried away, leaving the prisoner in the grip of the halberdiers.

"Now is my evil luck ended at last," muttered Hendon, "for I shall dangle at a rope's end for a certainty, by reason of that bit of writing. And what will become of my poor lad!—ah, only the good God knoweth."

By and by he saw the officer coming again, in a great hurry; so he plucked his courage together, purposing to meet his trouble as became a man. The officer ordered the men to loose the prisoner and return his sword to him; then bowed respectfully, and said—

"Please you sir, to follow me."

Hendon followed, saying to himself, "An' I were not travelling to death and judgment, and so must needs economize in sin, I would throttle this knave for his mock courtesy."

The two traversed a populous court, and arrived at the grand entrance of the palace, where the officer, with another bow, delivered Hendon into the hands of a gorgeous official, who received him with profound respect and led him forward through a great hall, lined on both sides with rows of splendid flunkies (who made reverential obeisance as the two passed along, but fell into death-throes of silent laughter at our stately scare-crow the moment his back was turned), and up a broad staircase, among flocks of fine folk, and finally conducted him into a vast room, clove a passage for him through the assembled nobility of England, then made a bow, reminded him to take his hat off, and left him standing in the middle of the room, a mark for all eyes, for plenty of indignant frowns, and for a sufficiency of amused and derisive smiles.

Miles Hendon was entirely bewildered. There sat the young king, under a canopy of state, five steps away, with his head bent down

and aside, speaking with a sort of human bird of paradise—a duke,
maybe; Hendon observed to himself that it was hard enough to be
sentenced to death in the full vigor of life, without having this
peculiarly public humiliation added. He wished the king would
hurry about it—some of the gaudy people near by were becoming
pretty offensive. At this moment the king raised his head slightly
and Hendon caught a good view of his face. The sight nearly took
his breath away!—He stood gazing at the fair young face like one
transfixed; then presently ejaculated—

"Lo, the lord of the Kingdom of Dreams and Shadows on his
throne!"

He muttered some broken sentences, still gazing and marvelling;
then turned his eyes around and about, scanning the gorgeous
throng and the splendid saloon, murmuring "But these are *real*—
verily these are *real*—surely it is not a dream."

He stared at the king again—and thought, "*Is* it a dream?... or
is he the veritable sovereign of England, and not the friendless poor
Tom o' Bedlam I took him for—who shall solve me this riddle?"

A sudden idea flashed in his eye, and he strode to the wall,
gathered up a chair, brought it back, planted it on the floor, and
sat down in it!

A buzz of indignation broke out, a rough hand was laid upon
him, and a voice exclaimed,—

"Up, thou mannerless clown!—wouldst sit in the presence of
the king?"

The disturbance attracted his majesty's attention, who stretched
forth his hand and cried out—

"Touch him not, it is his right!"

The throng fell back, stupefied. The king went on—

"Learn ye all, ladies, lords and gentlemen, that this is my trusty
and well-beloved servant, Miles Hendon, who interposed his good
sword and saved his prince from bodily harm and possible death—
and for this he is a knight, by the king's voice. Also learn, that for
a higher service, in that he saved his sovereigh stripes and shame,
taking these upon himself, he is a peer of England, Earl of Kent,
and shall have gold and lands meet for the dignity. More—the
privilege which he hath just exercised is his by royal grant; for we
have ordained that the chiefs of his line shall have and hold the
right to sit in the presence of the majesty of England henceforth,
age after age, so long as the crown shall endure. Molest him not."

Two persons, who, through delay, had only arrived from the
country during this morning, and had now been in this room only
five minutes, stood listening to these words and looking at the king,
then at the scare-crow, then at the king again, in a sort of torpid
bewilderment. These were Sir Hugh and the Lady Edith. But the
new Earl did not see them. He was still staring at the monarch, in a
dazed way, and muttering—

"O, body o' me! *This* my pauper! This my lunatic! This is he whom *I* would show what grandeur was, in my house of seventy rooms and seven and twenty servants! This is he who had never known aught but rags for raiment, kicks for comfort, and offal for diet! This is he whom *I* adopted and would make respectable! Would God I had a bag to hide my head in!"

Then his manners suddenly came back to him, and he dropped upon his knees, with his hands between the king's, and swore allegiance and did homage for his lands and titles. Then he rose and stood respectfully aside, a mark still for all eyes—and much envy, too.

Now the king discovered Sir Hugh, and spoke out, with wrathful voice and kindling eye—

"Strip this robber of his false show and stolen estates, and put him under lock and key till I have need of him."

The late Sir Hugh was led away.

There was a stir at the other end of the room, now; the assemblage fell apart, and Tom Canty, quaintly but richly clothed, marched down, between these living walls, preceded by an usher. He knelt before the king, who said—

"I have learned the story of these past few weeks, and am well pleased with thee. Thou hast governed the realm with right royal gentleness and mercy. Thou hast found thy mother and thy sisters again? Good; they shall be cared for—and thy father shall hang, if thou desire it and the law consent. Know, all ye that hear my voice, that from this day, they that abide in the shelter of Christ's Hospital and share the king's bounty, shall have their minds and hearts fed, as well as their baser parts; and this boy shall dwell there, and hold the chief place in its honorable body of governors, during life. And for that he hath been a king, it is meet that other than common observance shall be his due; wherefore, note this his dress of state, for by it he shall be known, and none shall copy it; and wheresoever he shall come, it shall remind the people that he hath been royal, in his time, and none shall deny him his due of reverence or fail to give him salutation. He hath the throne's protection, he hath the crown's support, he shall be known and called by the honorable title of the King's Ward."

The proud and happy Tom Canty rose and kissed the king's hand, and was conducted from the presence. He did not waste any time, but flew to his mother, to tell her and Nan and Bet all about it and get them to help him enjoy the great news.*

*See Notes to Chapter 33 at end of the volume.

CONCLUSION

JUSTICE AND RETRIBUTION

When the mysteries were all cleared up, it came out, by confession of Hugh Hendon, that his wife had repudiated Miles by his command, that day at Hendon Hall—a command assisted and supported by the perfectly trustworthy promise that if she did not deny that he was Miles Hendon, and stand firmly to it, he would have her life; whereupon she said take it, she did not value it—and she would not repudiate Miles; then the husband said he would spare her life but have Miles assassinated! This was a different matter; so she gave her word and kept it.

Hugh was not prosecuted for his threats or for stealing his brother's estates and title, because the wife and brother would not testify against him—and the former would not have been allowed to do it, even if she had wanted to. Hugh deserted his wife and went over to the continent, where he presently died; and by and by the earl of Kent married his relict. There were grand times and rejoicings at Hendon village when the couple paid their first visit to the Hall.

Tom Canty's father was never heard of again.

The king sought out the farmer who had been branded and sold as a slave, and reclaimed him from his evil life with the Ruffler's gang, and put him in the way of a comfortable livelihood.

He also took that old lawyer out of prison and remitted his fine. He provided good homes for the daughters of the two Baptist women whom he saw burned at the stake, and roundly punished the official who laid the undeserved stripes upon Miles Hendon's back.

He saved from the gallows the boy who had captured the stray falcon, and also the woman who had stolen a remnant of cloth from a weaver; but he was too late to save the man who had been convicted of killing a deer in the royal forest.

He showed favor to the justice who had pitied him when he was supposed to have stolen a pig, and he had the gratification of seeing him grow in the public esteem and become a great and honored man.

As long as the king lived he was fond of telling the story of his adventures, all through, from the hour that the sentinel cuffed him away from the palace gate till the final midnight when he deftly mixed himself into a gang of hurrying workmen and so slipped into the Abbey and climbed up and hid himself in the Confessor's tomb, and then slept so long, next day, that he came within one of missing the Coronation altogether. He said that the frequent rehearsing of the precious lesson kept him strong in his purpose to make its teachings yield benefits to his people; and so, whilst his life was spared he should continue to tell the story, and thus keep its sorrowful spectacles fresh in his memory and the springs of pity replenished in his heart.

Miles Hendon and Tom Canty were favorites of the king, all through his brief reign, and his sincere mourners when he died. The good earl of Kent had too much good sense to abuse his peculiar privilege but he exercised it twice after the instance we have seen of it before he was called from the world; once at the accession of Queen Mary, and once at the accession of Queen Elizabeth. A descendant of his exercised it at the accession of James I. Before this one's son chose to use the privilege, near a quarter of a century had elapsed, and the "privilege of the Kents" had faded out of most people's memories; so, when the Kent of that day appeared before Charles I. and his court and sat down in the sovereign's presence to assert and perpetuate the right of his house, there was a fine stir, indeed! But the matter was soon explained and the right confirmed. The last earl of the line fell in the wars of the Commonwealth fighting for the king, and the odd privilege ended with him.

Tom Canty lived to be a very old man, a handsome, white-haired old fellow, of grave and benignant aspect. As long as he lasted he was honored; and he was also reverenced, for his striking and peculiar costume kept the people reminded that "in his time he had been royal;" so, wherever he appeared the crowd fell apart, making way for him, and whispering, one to another, "Doff thy had, it is the King's Ward!"—and so they saluted, and got his kindly smile in return—and they valued it, too, for his was an honorable history.

Yes, King Edward VI. lived only a few years, poor boy, but he lived them worthily. More than once, when some great dignitary, some gilded vassal of the crown, made argument against his leniency, and urged that some law which he was bent upon amending was gentle enough for its purpose, and wrought no suffering or oppression which any one need mightily mind, the young king turned the mournful eloquence of his great compassionate eyes upon him and answered—

"What dost *thou* know of suffering and oppression? I and my people know, but not thou."

The reign of Edward VI. was a singularly merciful one for those harsh times. Now that we are taking leave of him let us try to keep this in our minds, to his credit.

NOTES

NOTE 1.—Page 605.

Christ's Hospital Costume.

It is most reasonable to regard the dress as copied from the costume of the citizens of London of that period, when long blue coats were the common habit of apprentices and serving-men, and yellow stockings were generally worn; the coat fits closely to the body, but has loose sleeves, and beneath is worn a sleeveless yellow under-coat; around the waist is a red leathern girdle; a clerical band around the neck, and a small flat black cap, about the size of a saucer, completes the costume.—*Timbs' "Curiosities of London."*

NOTE 2.—Page 606.

It appears that Christ's Hospital was not originally founded as a *school;* its object was to rescu. children from the streets, to shelter, feed, clothe them, etc.—*Timbs' "Curiosities of London."*

NOTE 3.—Page 611.

The Duke of Norfolk's Condemnation Commanded.

The King was now approaching fast towards his end; and fearing lest Norfolk should escape him, he sent a message to the Commons, by which he desired them to hasten the bill, on pretence that Norfolk enjoyed the dignity of earl marshal, and it was necessary to appoint another, who might officiate at the ensuing ceremony of installing his son Prince of Wales.—*Hume,* vol. iii. p. 307.

NOTE 4.—Page 618

It was not till the end of this reign [Henry VIII] that any salads, carrots, turnips, or other edible roots were produced in England. The little of these vegetables that was used, was formerly imported from Holland and Flanders. Queen Catherine, when she wanted a salad, was obliged to despatch a messenger thither on purpose.—*Hume's History of England,* vol. iii. p. 314.

NOTE 5.—Page 621.

Attainder of Norfolk.

The house of peers, without examining the prisoner, without trial or evidence, passed a bill of attainder against him and sent it down to the commons.... The obsequious commons obeyed his [the King's] directions; and the King, having affixed the royal assent to the bill by commissioners, issued orders for the execution of Norfolk on the morning of the twenty-ninth of January, [the next day.]—*Hume's England,* vol. iii. p. 306.

NOTE 6.—Page 629.

The Loving-Cup.

The loving-cup, and the peculiar ceremonies observed in drinking from it, are older than English history. It is thought that both are Danish importations. As far back as knowledge goes, the loving-cup has always been drunk at English banquets. Tradition explains the ceremonies in this way: in the rude ancient times it was deemed a wise precaution to have both hands of both drinkers employed, lest while the pledger pledged his love and fidelity to the pledgee the pledgee take that opportunity to slip a dirk into him!

NOTE 7.—Page 632.

The Duke of Norfolk's Narrow Escape.

Had Henry VIII survived a few hours longer, his order for the duke's execution would have been carried into effect. "But news being carried to the Tower that the King himself had expired that night, the lieutenant deferred obeying the warrant; and it was not thought advisable by the Council to begin a new reign by the death of the greatest nobleman in the Kingdom, who had been condemned by a sentence so unjust and tyrannical."—*Hume's England*, vol. iii. p. 307.

NOTE 8.—Page 649.

The Whipping-Boy

James I and Charles II had whipping-boys when they were little fellows, to take their punishment for them when they fell short in their lessons; so I have ventured to furnish my small prince with one, for my own purposes.

NOTES TO CHAPTER XV.—Page 658.

Character of Hertford.

The young king discovered an extreme attachment to his uncle, who was, in the main, a man of moderation and probity.—*Hume's England*, vol. iii. p. 324.

But if he [the Protector] gave offence by assuming too much state, he deserves great praise on account of the laws passed this session, by which the rigor of former statutes was much mitigated, and some security given to the freedom of the constitution. All laws were repealed which extended the crime of treason beyond the statute of the twenty-fifth of Edward III; all laws enacted during the late reign extending the crime of felony; all the former laws against Lollardy or heresy, together with the statute of the Six Articles. None were to be accused for words, but within a month after they were spoken. By these repeals several of the most rigorous laws that ever had passed in England were annulled; and some dawn, both of civil and religious liberty, began to appear to the people. A repeal also passed of that law, the destruction of all laws, by which the king's proclamation was made of equal force with a statute.—*Ibid.*, vol. iii. p. 339.

Boiling to Death.

In the reign of Henry VIII, poisoners were, by act of parliament, condemned to be *boiled to death.* This act was repealed in the following reign.

In Germany, even in the 17th century, this horrible punishment was inflicted on coiners and counterfeiters. Taylor, the Water Poet, describes an execution he witnessed in Hamburg, in 1616. The judgment pronounced against a coiner of false money was that he should "be *boiled to death in oil:* not thrown into the vessel at once, but with a pulley or rope to be hanged under the armpits, and then let down into the oil *by degrees;* first the feet, and next the legs, and so to boil his flesh from his bones alive."—*Dr. J. Hammond Trumbull's "Blue Laws, True and False,"* p. 13.

The Famous Stocking Case.

A woman and her daughter, *nine years old,* were hanged in Huntingdon for selling their souls to the devil, and raising a storm by pulling off their stockings!—*Ibid.,* p. 20.

NOTE 10.—Page 666.
Enslaving.

So young a king, and so ignorant a peasant were likely to make mistakes—and this is an instance in point. This peasant was suffering from this law *by anticipation;* the king was venting his indignation against a law which was not yet in existence: for this hideous statute was to have birth in this little king's own reign. However, we know, from the humanity of his character, that it could never have been suggested by him.

NOTES TO CHAPTER XXIII.—Page 691.
Death for Trifling Larcenies.

When Connecticut and New Haven were framing their first codes, larceny above the value of twelve pence was a capital crime in England—as it had been since the time of Henry I.—*Dr. J. Hammond Trumbull's "Blue Laws, True and False,"* p. 17.

The curious old book called "The English Rogue" makes the limit thirteen pence ha'penny; death being the portion of any who steal a thing "above the value of thirteen pence ha'penny."

NOTES TO CHAPTER XXVII.—Page 708.

From many descriptions of larceny, the law expressly took away the benefit of clergy; to steal a horse, or a *hawk,* or woolen cloth from the weaver, was a hanging matter. So it was, to kill a deer from the king's forest, or to export sheep from the Kingdom.—*Dr. J. Hammond Trumbull's "Blue Laws, True and False,"* p. 13.

William Prynne, a learned barrister, was sentenced—[long after Edward the Sixth's time]—to lose both his ears in the pillory; to degradation from the bar; a fine of £3,000, and imprisonment for life. Three years afterwards, he gave new offence to Laud, by publishing a pamphlet against the hierarchy. He was again prosecuted, and was sentenced to lose *what remained of his ears;* to pay a fine of £5,000; to be *branded on both cheeks* with the letters S. L. (for Seditious Libeller,) and to remain in prison for life. The severity of this sentence was equalled by the savage rigor of its execution.— *Ibid.,* p. 12.

NOTES TO CHAPTER XXXII.—Page 731.

Christ's Hospital, or Blue Coat School, "the Noblest Institution in the World."

The ground on which the Priory of the Grey Friars stood was conferred by Henry the Eighth on the Corporation of London, [who caused the institution there of a home for poor boys and girls.] Subsequently, Edward the Sixth caused the old priory to be properly repaired, and founded within it that noble establishment called the Blue Coat School, or Christ's Hospital, for the *education* and maintenance of orphans and the children of indigent persons. . . . . Edward would not let him [Bishop Ridley] depart till the letter was written, [to the Lord Mayor,] and then charged him to deliver it himself, and signify his special request and commandment that no time might be lost in proposing what was convenient, and apprising him of the proceedings. The work was zealously undertaken, Ridley himself engaging in it; and the result was, the founding of Christ's Hospital for the Education of Poor Children. [The king endowed several other charities at the same time.] "Lord God," said he, "I yield thee most hearty thanks that thou hast given me life thus long, to finish this work to the glory of thy name!" That innocent and most exemplary life was drawing rapidly to its close, and in a few days he rendered up his spirit to his Creator, praying God to defend the realm from Papistry.—*J. Heneage Jesse's "London, its Celebrated Characters and Places."*

In the Great Hall hangs a large picture of King Edward VI seated on his throne, in a scarlet and ermined robe, holding the sceptre in his left hand, and presenting with the other the Charter to the kneeling Lord Mayor. By his side stands the Chancellor, holding the seals, and next to him are other officers of state. Bishop Ridley kneels before him with uplifted hands, as if supplicating a blessing on the event; whilst the Aldermen, etc., with the Lord Mayor, kneel on both sides, occupying the middle ground of the picture; and lastly, in front, are a double row of boys on one side, and girls on the other, from the master and matron down to the boy and girl who have stepped forward from their respective rows, and kneel with raised hands before the king.—*Timbs' "Curiosities of London,"* p. 98.

Christ's Hospital, by ancient custom, possesses the privilege of addressing the Sovereign on the occasion of his or her coming into the City to partake of the hospitality of the Corporation of London. —*Ibid.*

The Dining-Hall, with its lobby and organ-gallery, occupies the entire story, which is 187 feet long, 51 feet wide, and 47 feet high; it is lit by nine large windows, filled with stained glass on the south side; and is, next to Westminster Hall, the noblest room in the metropolis. Here the boys, now about 800 in number, dine; and here are held the "Suppings in Public," to which visitors are admitted by tickets, issued by the Treasurer and by the Governors of Christ's Hospital. The tables are laid with cheese in wooden bowls; beer in wooden piggins, poured from leathern jacks; and bread brought in large baskets. The official company enter; the Lord Mayor, or President, takes his seat in a state chair, made of oak from St. Catherine's Church by the Tower; a hymn is sung, accompanied by the organ; a "Grecian," or head boy, reads the prayers from the pulpit, silence being enforced by three drops of a wooden hammer. After prayer the supper commences, and the visitors walk between the tables. At its close, the "tradeboys" take up the baskets, bowls, jacks, piggins, and candlesticks, and pass in procession, the bowing to the Governors being curiously formal. This spectacle was witnessed by Queen Victoria and Prince Albert in 1845.

Among the more eminent Blue Coat boys are Joshua Barnes, editor of Anacreon and Euripides; Jeremiah Markland, the eminent critic, particularly in Greek literature; Camden, the antiquary; Bishop Stillingfleet; Samuel Richardson, the novelist; Thomas Mitchell, the translator of Aristophanes; Thomas Barnes, many years editor of the London *Times;* Coleridge, Charles Lamb, and Leigh Hunt.

No boy is admitted before he is seven years old, or after he is nine; and no boy can remain in the school after he is fifteen, King's boys and "Grecians" alone excepted. There are about 500 Governors, at the head of whom are the Sovereign and the Prince of Wales. The qualification for a Governor is payment of £500.— *Ibid.*

GENERAL NOTE

ONE *hears much about the "hideous Blue-Laws of Connecticut," and is accustomed to shudder piously when they are mentioned. There are people in America—and even in England!—who imagine that they were a very monument of malignity, pitilessness, and inhumanity; whereas, in reality they were about the first* SWEEPING DEPARTURE FROM JUDICIAL ATROCITY *which the "civilized" world had seen. This humane and kindly Blue-Law code, of two hundred and forty years ago, stands all by itself, with ages of bloody law on the further side of it, and a century and three-quarters of bloody English law on* THIS *side of it.*

There has never been a time—under the Blue-Laws or any other—when above FOURTEEN *crimes were punishable by death in Connecticut. But in England, within the memory of men who are still hale in body and mind,* TWO HUNDRED AND TWENTY-THREE *crimes were punishable by death!* These facts are worth knowing—and worth thinking about, too.*

*See Dr. J. Hammond Trumbull's "Blue Laws, True and False," p. 11.

A
CONNECTICUT
YANKEE
IN
KING ARTHUR'S
COURT

A CONNECTICUT YANKEE IN KING ARTHUR'S COURT

PREFACE

The ungentle laws and customs touched upon in this tale are historical, and the episodes which are used to illustrate them are also historical. It is not pretended that these laws and customs existed in England in the sixth century; no, it is only pretended that inasmuch as they existed in the English and other civilizations of far later times, it is safe to consider that it is no libel upon the sixth century to suppose them to have been in practice in that day also. One is quite justified in inferring that whatever one of these laws or customs was lacking in that remote time, its place was competently filled by a worse one.

The question as to whether there is such a thing as divine right of kings is not settled in this book. It was found too difficult. That the executive head of a nation should be a person of lofty character and extraordinary ability, was manifest and indisputable; that none but the Deity could select that head unerringly, was also manifest and indisputable; that the Deity ought to make that selection, then, was likewise manifest and indisputable; consequently, that He does make it, as claimed, was an unavoidable deduction. I mean, until the author of this book encountered the Pompadour, and Lady Castlemaine and some other executive heads of that kind; these were found so difficult to work into the scheme, that it was judged better to take the other tack in this book, (which must be issued this fall,) and then go into training and settle the question in another book. It is of course a thing which ought to be settled, and I am not going to have anything particular to do next winter anyway.

MARK TWAIN.

A WORD OF EXPLANATION

It was in Warwick Castle that I came across the curious stranger whom I am going to talk about. He attracted me by three things: his candid simplicity, his marvelous familiarity with ancient armor, and the restfulness of his company—for he did all the talking. We fell together, as modest people will, in the tail of the herd that was being shown through, and he at once began to say things which interested me. As he talked along, softly, pleasantly, flowingly, he seemed to drift away imperceptibly out of this world and time, and into some remote era and old forgotten country; and so he gradually wove such a spell about me that I seemed to move among the spectres and shadows and dust and mold of a gray antiquity, holding speech with a relic of it! Exactly as I would speak of my nearest personal friends or enemies, or my most familiar neighbors, he spoke of Sir Bedivere, Sir Bors de Ganis, Sir Launcelot of the Lake, Sir Galahad, and all the other great names of the Table Round—and how old, old, unspeakably old and faded and dry and musty and ancient he came to look as he went on! Presently he turned to me and said, just as one might speak of the weather, or any other common matter—

"You know about transmigration of souls; do you know about transposition of epochs—and bodies?"

I said I had not heard of it. He was so little interested—just as when people speak of the weather—that he did not notice whether I made him any answer or not. There was half a moment of silence, immediately interrupted by the droning voice of the salaried cicerone:

"Ancient hauberk, date of the sixth century, time of King Arthur and the Round Table; said to have belonged to the knight Sir Sagramor le Desirous; observe the round hole through the chain-mail in the left breast; can't be accounted for; supposed to have been done with a bullet since invention of firearms—perhaps maliciously by Cromwell's soldiers."

My acquaintance smiled—not a modern smile, but one that must have gone out of general use many, many centuries ago—and muttered apparently to himself:

"Wit ye well, *I saw it done*." Then, after a pause, added: "I did it myself."

By the time I had recovered from the electric surprise of this remark, he was gone.

All that evening I sat by my fire at the Warwick Arms, steeped in a dream of the olden time, while the rain beat upon the windows, and the wind roared about the eaves and corners. From time to time I dipped into old Sir Thomas Malory's enchanting book, and fed at its rich feast of prodigies and adventures, breathed in the fragrance of its obsolete names, and dreamed again. Midnight being come at

length, I read another tale, for a night-cap—this which here follows,
to wit:

HOW SIR LAUNCELOT SLEW TWO GIANTS, AND MADE A CASTLE FREE

Anon withal came there upon him two great giants, well armed, all save
the heads, with two horrible clubs in their hands. Sir Launcelot put his
shield afore him, and put the stroke away of the one giant, and with his
sword he clave his head asunder. When his fellow saw that, he ran away
as he were wood,* for fear of the horrible strokes, and Sir Launcelot after
him with all his might, and smote him on the shoulder, and clave him to
the middle. Then Sir Launcelot went into the hall, and there came afore
him three score ladies and damsels, and all kneeled unto him, and thanked
God and him of their deliverance. For, sir, said they, the most part of us
have been here this seven year their prisoners, and we have worked all
manner of silk works for our meat, and we are all great gentlewomen born,
and blessed be the time, knight, that ever thou wert born; for thou hast
done the most worship that ever did knight in the world, that will we bear
record, and we all pray you to tell us your name, that we may tell our
friends who delivered us out of prison. Fair damsels, he said, my name is
Sir Launcelot du Lake. And so he departed from them and betaught them
unto God. And then he mounted upon his horse, and rode into many
strange and wild countries, and through many waters and valleys, and evil
was he lodged. And at the last by fortune him happened against a night to
come to a fair courtilage, and therein he found an old gentlewoman that
lodged him with a good-will, and there he had good cheer for him and his
horse. And when time was, his host brought him into a fair garret over
the gate to his bed. There Sir Launcelot unarmed him, and set his harness
by him, and went to bed, and anon he fell on sleep. So, soon after there
came one on horseback, and knocked at the gate in great haste. And when
Sir Launcelot heard this he rose up, and looked out at the window, and
saw by the moonlight three knights come riding after that one man, and
all three lashed on him at once with swords, and that one knight turned on
them knightly again and defended him. Truly, said Sir Launcelot, yonder
one knight shall I help, for it were shame for me to see three knights on one,
and if he be slain I am partner of his death. And therewith he took his
harness and went out at a window by a sheet down to the four knights, and
then Sir Launcelot said on high, Turn you knights unto me, and leave your
fighting with that knight. And then they all three left Sir Kay, and turned
unto Sir Launcelot, and there began great battle, for they alight all three,
and strake many strokes at Sir Launcelot, and assailed him on every side.
Then Sir Kay dressed him for to have holpen Sir Launcelot. Nay, sir, said
he, I will none of your help, therefore as ye will have my help let me alone
with them. Sir Kay for the pleasure of the knight suffered him for to do his
will, and so stood aside. And then anon within six strokes Sir Launcelot
had stricken them to the earth.
And then they all three cried, Sir knight, we yield us unto you as man of
might matchless. As to that, said Sir Launcelot, I will not take your yielding
unto me, but so that ye yield you unto Sir Kay the seneschal, on that
covenant I will save your lives and else not. Fair knight, said they, that

*Demented.

were we loath to do; for as for Sir Kay we chased him hither, and had overcome him had ye not been; therefore, to yield us unto him it were no reason. Well, as to that, said Sir Launcelot, advise you will, for ye may choose whether ye will die or live, for an ye be yielden, it shall be unto Sir Kay. Fair knight, then they said, in saving our lives we will do as thou commandest us. Then shall ye, said Sir Launcelot, on Whitsunday next coming go unto the court of King Arthur, and there shall ye yield you unto Queen Guenever, and put you all three in her grace and mercy, and say that Sir Kay sent you thither to be her prisoners. On the morn Sir Launcelot arose early, and left Sir Kay sleeping: and Sir Launcelot took Sir Kay's armor and his shield and armed him, and so he went to the stable and took his horse, and took his leave of his host, and so he departed. Then soon after arose Sir Kay and missed Sir Launcelot: and then he espied that he had his armor and his horse. Now by my faith I know well that he will grieve some of the court of King Arthur: for on him knights will be bold, and deem that it is I, and that will beguile them; and because of his armor and shield I am sure I shall ride in peace. And then soon after departed Sir Kay, and thanked his host.

As I laid the book down there was a knock at the door, and my stranger came in. I gave him a pipe and a chair, and made him welcome. I also comforted him with a hot Scotch whiskey; gave him another one; then still another—hoping always for his story. After a fourth persuader, he drifted into it himself, in a quite simple and natural way:

THE STRANGER'S HISTORY

I am an American. I was born and reared in Hartford, in the State of Connecticut—anyway, just over the river, in the country. So I am a Yankee of the Yankees—and practical; yes, and nearly barren of sentiment, I suppose—or poetry, in other words. My father was a blacksmith, my uncle was a horse doctor, and I was both, along at first. Then I went over to the great arms factory and learned my real trade; learned all there was to it; learned to make everything: guns, revolvers, cannon, boilers, engines, all sorts of labor-saving machinery. Why, I could make anything a body wanted—anything in the world, it didn't make any difference what; and if there wasn't any quick new-fangled way to make a thing, I could invent one— and do it as easy as rolling off a log. I became head superintendent; had a couple of thousand men under me.

Well, a man like that is a man that is full of fight—that goes without saying. With a couple of thousand rough men under one, one has plenty of that sort of amusement. I had, anyway. At last I met my match, and I got my dose. It was during a misunderstanding conducted with crowbars with a fellow we used to call Hercules. He laid me out with a crusher alongside the head that made everything crack, and seemed to spring every joint in my skull and made it overlap its neighbor. Then the world went out in darkness, and I didn't feel anything more, and didn't know anything at all—at least for a while.

When I came to again, I was sitting under an oak tree, on the grass, with a whole beautiful and broad country landscape all to myself—nearly. Not entirely; for there was a fellow on a horse, looking down at me—a fellow fresh out of a picture-book. He was in oldtime iron armor from head to heel, with a helmet on his head the shape of a nail-keg with slits in it; and he had a shield, and a sword, and a prodigious spear; and his horse had armor on, too, and a steel horn projecting from his forehead, and gorgeous red and green silk trappings that hung down all around him like a bed-quilt, nearly to the ground.

"Fair sir, will ye just?" said this fellow.

"Will I which?"

"Will ye try a passage of arms for land or lady or for—"

"What are you giving me?" I said. "Get along back to your circus, or I'll report you."

Now what does this man do but fall back a couple of hundred yards and then come rushing at me as hard as he could tear, with his nail-keg bent down nearly to his horse's neck and his long spear pointed straight ahead. I saw he meant business, so I was up the tree when he arrived.

He allowed that I was his property, the captive of his spear. There was argument on his side—and the bulk of the advantage—so I judged it best to humor him. We fixed up an agreement whereby I was to go with him and he was not to hurt me. I came down, and we started away, I walking by the side of his horse. We marched comfortably along, through glades and over brooks which I could not remember to have seen before—which puzzled me and made me wonder—and yet we did not come to any circus or sign of a circus. So I gave up the idea of a circus, and concluded he was from an asylum. But we never came to an asylum—so I was up a stump, as you may say. I asked him how far we were from Hartford. He said he had never heard of the place; which I took to be a lie, but allowed it to go at that. At the end of an hour we saw a far-away town sleeping in a valley by a winding river; and beyond it on a hill, a vast gray fortress, with towers and turrets, the first I had ever seen out of a picture.

"Bridgeport?" said I, pointing.

"Camelot," said he.

My stranger had been showing signs of sleepiness. He caught himself nodding, now, and smiled one of those pathetic, obsolete smiles of his, and said:

"I find I can't go on; but come with me, I've got it all written out, and you can read it if you like."

In his chamber, he said: "First, I kept a journal; then by-and-by, after years, I took the journal and turned it into a book. How long ago that was!"

"Begin here—I've already told you what goes before." He was steeped in drowsiness by this time. As I went out at his door I heard him murmur sleepily: "Give you good den, fair sir."

I sat down by my fire and examined my treasure. The first part of it—the great bulk of it—was parchment, and yellow with age. I scanned a leaf particularly and saw that it was a palimpsest. Under the old dim writing of the Yankee historian appeared traces of a penmanship which was older and dimmer still—Latin words and sentences: fragments from old monkish legends, evidently. I turned to the place indicated by my stranger and began to read—as follows:

THE TALE OF THE LOST LAND

CHAPTER I

CAMELOT

"Camelot—Camelot," said I to myself. "I don't seem to remember hearing of it before. Name of the asylum, likely."

It was a soft, reposeful summer landscape, as lovely as a dream, and as lonesome as Sunday. The air was full of the smell of flowers, and the buzzing of insects, and the twittering of birds, and there were no people, no wagons, there was no stir of life, nothing going on. The road was mainly a winding path with hoof-prints in it, and now and then a faint trace of wheels on either side in the grass— wheels that apparently had a tire as broad as one's hand.

Presently a fair slip of a girl, about ten years old, with a cataract of golden hair streaming down over her shoulders, came along. Around her head she wore a hoop of flame-red poppies. It was as sweet an outfit as ever I saw, what there was of it. She walked indolently along, with a mind at rest, its peace reflected in her innocent face. The circus man paid no attention to her; didn't even seem to see her. And she—she was no more startled at his fantastic make-up than if she was used to his like every day of her life. She was going by as indifferently as she might have gone by a couple of cows; but when she happened to notice me, *then* there was a change! Up went her hands, and she was turned to stone; her mouth dropped open, her eyes stared wide and timorously, she was the picture of astonished curiosity touched with fear. And there she stood gazing, in a sort of stupefied fascination, till we turned a corner of the wood and were lost to her view. That she should be startled at me instead of at the other man, was too many for me; I couldn't make head or tail of it. And that she should seem to consider me a spectacle, and totally overlook her own merits in that respect, was another puzzling thing, and a display of magnanimity, too, that was surprising in one so young. There was food for thought here. I moved along as one in a dream.

As we approached the town, signs of life began to appear. At intervals we passed a wretched cabin, with a thatched roof, and about it small fields and garden patches in an indifferent state of cultivation. There were people, too; brawny men, with long, coarse, uncombed hair that hung down over their faces and made them look like animals. They and the women, as a rule, wore a coarse tow-linen robe that came well below the knee, and a rude sort of sandals, and many wore an iron collar. The small boys and girls were always naked; but nobody seemed to know it. All of these people stared at me, talked about me, ran into the huts and fetched out their families to gape at me; but nobody ever noticed that other fellow, except to make him humble salutation and get no response for their pains.

In the town were some substantial windowless houses of stone scattered among a wilderness of thatched cabins; the streets were mere crooked alleys, and unpaved; troops of dogs and nude children played in the sun and made life and noise; hogs roamed and rooted contentedly about, and one of them lay in a reeking wallow in the middle of the main thoroughfare and suckled her family. Presently there was a distant blare of military music; it came nearer, still nearer, and soon a noble cavalcade wound into view, glorious with plumed helmets and flashing mail and flaunting banners and rich doublets and horse-cloths and gilded spear heads; and through the muck and swine, and naked brats, and joyous dogs, and shabby huts it took its gallant way, and in its wake we followed. Followed through one winding alley and then another,—and climbing, always climbing—till at last we gained the breezy height where the huge castle stood. There was an exchange of bugle blasts; then a parley from the walls, where men-at-arms, in hauberk and morion marched back and forth with halberd at shoulder under flapping banners with the rude figure of a dragon displayed upon them; and then the great gates were flung open, the drawbridge was lowered, and the head of the cavalcade swept forward under the frowning arches; and we, following, soon found ourselves in a great paved court, with towers and turrets stretching up into the blue air on all the four sides; and all about us the dismount was going on, and much greeting and ceremony, and running to and fro, and a gay display of moving and intermingling colors, and an altogether pleasant stir and noise and confusion.

CHAPTER II

KING ARTHUR'S COURT

The moment I got a chance I slipped aside privately and touched an ancient common looking man on the shoulder and said, in an insinuating, confidential way—

"Friend, do me a kindness. Do you belong to the asylum, or are you just here on a visit or something like that?"

He looked me over stupidly, and said—

"Marry, fair sir, me seemeth—"

"That will do," I said; "I reckon you are a patient."

I moved away, cogitating, and at the same time keeping an eye out for any chance passenger in his right mind that might come along and give me some light. I judged I had found one, presently; so I drew him aside and said in his ear—

"If I could see the head keeper a minute—only just a minute—"

"Prithee do not let me."

"Let you *what?*"

"*Hinder* me, then, if the word please thee better." Then he went on to say he was an under-cook and could not stop to gossip, though he would like it another time; for it would comfort his very liver to know where I got my clothes. As he started away he pointed and said yonder was one who was idle enough for my purpose, and was seeking me besides, no doubt. This was an airy slim boy in shrimp-colored tights that made him look like a forked carrot; the rest of his gear was blue silk and dainty laces and ruffles; and he had long yellow curls, and wore a plumed pink satin cap tilted complacently over his ear. By his look, he was good-natured; by his gait, he was satisfied with himself. He was pretty enough to frame. He arrived, looked me over with a smiling and impudent curiosity; said he had come for me, and informed me that he was a page.

"Go 'long," I said; "you ain't more than a paragraph."

It was pretty severe, but I was nettled. However, it never phazed him; he didn't appear to know he was hurt. He began to talk and laugh, in happy, thoughtless, boyish fashion, as we walked along, and made himself old friends with me at once; asked me all sorts of questions about myself and about my clothes, but never waited for an answer—always chattered straight ahead, as if he didn't know he had asked a question and wasn't expecting any reply, until at last he happened to mention that he was born in the beginning of the year 513.

It made the cold chills creep over me! I stopped, and said, a little faintly:

"Maybe I didn't hear you just right. Say it again—and say it slow. What year was it?"

"513."

"513! You don't look it! Come, my boy, I am a stranger and friendless; be honest and honorable with me. Are you in your right mind?"

He said he was.

"Are these other people in their right minds?"

He said they were.

"And this isn't an asylum? I mean, it isn't a place where they cure crazy people?"

He said it wasn't.

"Well, then," I said, "either I am a lunatic, or something just as awful has happened. Now tell me, honest and true, where am I?"

"IN KING ARTHUR'S COURT."

I waited a minute, to let that idea shudder its way home, and then said:

"And according to your notions, what year is it now?"

"528—nineteenth of June."

I felt a mournful sinking at the heart, and muttered: "I shall never see my friends again—never, never again. They will not be born for more than thirteen hundred years yet."

I seemed to believe the boy, I didn't know why. *Something* in me seemed to believe him—my consciousness, as you may say; but my reason didn't. My reason straightway began to clamor; that was natural. I didn't know how to go about satisfying it, because I knew that the testimony of men wouldn't serve—my reason would say they were lunatics, and throw out their evidence. But all of a sudden I stumbled on the very thing, just by luck. I knew that the only total eclipse of the sun in the first half of the sixth century occurred on the 21st of June, A.D. 528, O.S., and began at 3 minutes after 12 noon. I also knew that no total eclipse of the sun was due in what to *me* was the present year—*i. e.,* 1879. So, if I could keep my anxiety and curiosity from eating the heart out of me for forty-eight hours, I should then find out for certain whether this boy was telling me the truth or not.

Wherefore, being a practical Connecticut man, I now shoved this whole problem clear out of my mind till its appointed day and hour should come, in order that I might turn all my attention to the circumstances of the present moment, and be alert and ready to make the most out of them that could be made. One thing at a time, is my motto—and just play that thing for all it is worth, even if it's only two pair and a jack. I made up my mind to two things; if it was still the nineteenth century and I was among lunatics and couldn't get away, I would presently boss that asylum or know the reason why; and if on the other hand it was really the sixth century, all right, I didn't want any softer thing: I would boss the whole country inside of three months; for I judged I would have the start of the best-educated man in the kingdom by a matter of thirteen hundred years and upwards. I'm not a man to waste time after my mind's made up and there's work on hand; so I said to the page—

"Now, Clarence, my boy—if that might happen to be your name— I'll get you to post me up a little if you don't mind. What is the name of that apparition that brought me here?"

"My master and thine? That is the good knight and great lord Sir Kay the Seneschal, foster brother to our liege the king."

"Very good; go on, tell me everything."

He made a long story of it; but the part that had immediate
interest for me was this. He said I was Sir Kay's prisoner, and that
in the due course of custom I would be flung into a dungeon and left
there on scant commons until my friends ransomed me—unless I
chanced to rot, first. I saw that the last chance had the best show,
but I didn't waste any bother about that; time was too precious. The
page said, further, that dinner was about ended in the great hall
by this time, and that as soon as the sociability and the heavy
drinking should begin, Sir Kay would have me in and exhibit me
before King Arthur and his illustrious knights seated at the Table
Round, and would brag about his exploit in capturing me, and
would probably exaggerate the facts a little, but it wouldn't be good
form for me to correct him, and not over safe, either; and when I
was done being exhibited, then ho for the dungeon; but he,
Clarence, would find a way to come and see me every now and then,
and cheer me up, and help me get word to my friends.

Get word to my friends! I thanked him; I couldn't do less; and
about this time a lackey came to say I was wanted; so Clarence led
me in and took me off to one side and sat down by me.

Well, it was a curious kind of spectacle, and interesting. It was an
immense place, and rather naked—yes, and full of loud contrasts.
It was very, very lofty; so lofty that the banners descending from the
arched beams and girders away up there floated in a sort of twilight;
there was a stone-railed gallery at each end, high up, with musicians
in the one, and women, clothed in stunning colors, in the other. The
floor was of big stone flags laid in black and white squares, rather
battered by age and use, and needing repair. As to ornament, there
wasn't any, strictly speaking; though on the walls hung some huge
tapestries which were probably taxed as works of art; battle-pieces,
they were, with horses shaped like those which children cut out of
paper or create in gingerbread; with men on them in scale armor
whose scales are represented by round holes—so that the man's
coat looks as if it had been done with a biscuit-punch. There was a
fireplace big enough to camp in; and its projecting sides and hood,
of carved and pillared stone-work, had the look of a cathedral door.
Along the walls stood men-at-arms, in breastplate and morion,
with halberds for their only weapon—rigid as statues; and that is
what they looked like.

In the middle of this groined and vaulted public square was an
oaken table which they called the Table Round. It was as large as a
circus ring; and around it sat a great company of men dressed in
such various and splendid colors that it hurt one's eyes to look at
them. They wore their plumed hats, right along, except that
whenever one addressed himself directly to the king, he lifted his hat
a trifle just as he was beginning his remark.

Mainly they were drinking—from entire ox horns; but a few were
still munching bread or gnawing beef bones. There was about an

average of two dogs to one man; and these sat in expectant attitudes
till a spent bone was flung to them, and then they went for it by
brigades and divisions, with a rush, and there ensued a fight which
filled the prospect with a tumultuous chaos of plunging heads and
bodies and flashing tails, and the storm of howlings and barkings
deafened all speech for the time; but that was no matter, for the
dog-fight was always a bigger interest anyway; the men rose,
sometimes, to observe it the better and bet on it, and the ladies and
the musicians stretched themselves out over their balusters with the
same object; and all broke into delighted ejaculations from time
to time. In the end, the winning dog stretched himself out
comfortably with his bone between his paws, and proceeded to
growl over it, and gnaw it, and grease the floor with it, just as fifty
others were already doing; and the rest of the court resumed
their previous industries and entertainments.

As a rule the speech and behavior of these people were gracious
and courtly; and I noticed that they were good and serious listeners
when anybody was telling anything—I mean in a dog-fightless
interval. And plainly, too, they were a childlike and innocent lot;
telling lies of the stateliest pattern with a most gentle and winning
naivety, and ready and willing to listen to anybody else's lie, and
believe it, too. It was hard to associate them with anything cruel
or dreadful; and yet they dealt in tales of blood and suffering with a
guileless relish that made me almost forget to shudder.

I was not the only prisoner present. There were twenty or more.
Poor devils, many of them were maimed, hacked, carved, in a
frightful way: and their hair, their faces, their clothing, were caked
with black and stiffened drenchings of blood. They were suffering
sharp physical pain, of course; and weariness, and hunger and
thirst, no doubt; and at least none had given them the comfort of
a wash, or even the poor charity of a lotion for their wounds; yet
you never heard them utter a moan or a groan, or saw them show
any sign of restlessness, or any disposition to complain. The thought
was forced upon me: "The rascals—*they* have served other people
so in their day; it being their own turn, now, they were not expecting
any better treatment than this; so their philosophical bearing is not
an outcome of mental training, intellectual fortitude, reasoning;
it is mere animal training; they are white Indians."

CHAPTER III

KNIGHTS OF THE TABLE ROUND

Mainly the Round Table talk was monologues—narrative
accounts of the adventures in which these prisoners were captured
and their friends and backers killed and stripped of their steeds and
armor. As a general thing—as far as I could make out—these

murderous adventures were not forays undertaken to avenge injuries, nor to settle old disputes or sudden fallings out; no, as a rule they were simply duels between strangers—duels between people who had never even been introduced to each other, and between whom existed no cause of offence whatever. Many a time I had seen a couple of boys, strangers, meet by chance, and say simultaneously, "I can lick you," and go at it on the spot; but I had always imagined until now that that sort of thing belonged to children only, and was a sign and mark of childhood; but here were these big boobies sticking to it and taking pride in it clear up into full age and beyond. Yet there was something very engaging about these great simple-hearted creatures, something attractive and lovable. There did not seem to be brains enough in the entire nursery, so to speak, to bait a fish-hook with; but you didn't seem to mind that, after a little, because you soon saw that brains were not needed in a society like that, and, indeed would have marred it, hindered it, spoiled its symmetry—perhaps rendered its existence impossible.

There was a fine manliness observable in almost every face; and in some a certain loftiness and sweetness that rebuked your belittling criticisms and stilled them. A most noble benignity and purity reposed in the countenance of him they called Sir Galahad, and likewise in the king's also; and there was majesty and greatness in the giant frame and high bearing of Sir Launcelot of the Lake.

There was presently an incident which centred the general interest upon this Sir Launcelot. At a sign from a sort of master of ceremonies, six or eight of the prisoners rose and came forward in a body and knelt on the floor and lifted up their hands toward the ladies' gallery and begged the grace of a word with the queen. The most conspicuously situated lady in that massed flower-bed of feminine show and finery inclined her head by way of assent, and then the spokesman of the prisoners delivered himself and his fellows into her hands for free pardon, ransom, captivity or death, as she in her good pleasure might elect; and this, as he said, he was doing by command of Sir Kay the Seneschal, whose prisoners they were, he having vanquished them by his single might and prowess in sturdy conflict in the field.

Surprise and astonishment flashed from face to face all over the house; the queen's gratified smile faded out at the name of Sir Kay, and she looked disappointed; and the page whispered in my ear with an accent and manner expressive of extravagant derision—

"Sir *Kay,* forsooth! Oh, call me pet names, dearest, call me a marine! In twice a thousand years shall the unholy invention of man labor at odds to beget the fellow to this majestic lie!"

Every eye was fastened with severe inquiry upon Sir Kay. But he was equal to the occasion. He got up and played his hand like a major—and took every trick. He said he would state the case, exactly according to the facts; he would tell the simple straight-forward tale, without comment of his own; "and then," said he, "if ye find glory and honor due, ye will give it unto him who is the mightiest man of his hands that ever bare shield or strake with sword in the ranks of Christian battle—even him that sitteth there!" and he pointed to Sir Launcelot. Ah, he fetched them; it was a rattling good stroke. Then he went on and told how Sir Launcelot, seeking adventures, some brief time gone by, killed seven giants at one sweep of his sword, and set a hundred and forty-two captive maidens free; and then went further, still seeking adventures, and found him (Sir Kay) fighting a desperate fight against nine foreign knights, and straightway took the battle solely into his own hands, and conquered the nine; and that night Sir Launcelot rose quietly, and dressed him in Sir Kay's armor and took Sir Kay's horse and gat him away into distant lands, and vanquished sixteen knights in one pitched battle and thirty-four in another; and all these and the former nine he made to swear that about Whitsuntide they would ride to Arthur's court and yield them to Queen Guenever's hands as captives of Sir Kay the Seneschal, spoil of his knightly prowess; and now here were these half-dozen, and the rest would be along as long as they might be healed of their desperate wounds.

Well, it was touching to see the queen blush and smile, and look embarrassed and happy, and fling furtive glances at Sir Launcelot that would have got him shot in Arkansas, to a dead certainty.

Everybody praised the valor and magnanimity of Sir Launcelot; and as for me, I was perfectly amazed, that one man, all by himself, should have been able to beat down and capture such battalions of practised fighters. I said as much to Clarence; but this mocking featherhead only said—

"An Sir Kay had had time to get another skin of sour wine into him, ye had seen the accompt doubled."

I looked at the boy in sorrow; and as I looked I saw the cloud of a deep despondency settle upon his countenance. I followed the direction of his eye, and saw that a very old and white-bearded man, clothed in a flowing black gown, had risen and was standing at the table upon unsteady legs, and feebly swaying his ancient head and surveying the company with his watery and wandering eye. The same suffering look that was in the page's face was observable in all the faces around—the look of dumb creatures who know that they must endure and make no moan.

"Marry, we shall have it again," sighed the boy; "that same old weary tale that he hath told a thousand times in the same words, and that he *will* tell till he dieth, every time he hath gotten his barrel full and feeleth his exaggeration-mill a-working. Would God I had died or I saw this day!"

"Who is it?"

"Merlin, the mighty liar and magician, perdition singe him for
the weariness he worketh with his one tale! But that men fear him
for that he hath the storms and the lightnings and all the devils
that be in hell at his beck and call, they would have dug his entrails
out these many years ago to get at that tale and squelch it. He
telleth it always in the third person, making believe he is too
modest to glorify himself—maledictions light upon him, misfortune
be his dole! Good friend, prithee call me for evensong."

The boy nestled himself upon my shoulder and pretended to go
to sleep. The old man began his tale; and presently the lad was
asleep in reality; so also were the dogs, and the court, the lackeys,
and the files of men-at-arms. The droning voice droned on; a soft
snoring arose on all sides and supported it like a deep and subdued
accompaniment of wind instruments. Some heads were bowed
upon folded arms, some lay back with open mouths that issued
unconscious music; the flies buzzed and bit, unmolested, the rats
swarmed softly out from a hundred holes, and pattered about, and
made themselves at home everywhere; and one of them sat up like
a squirrel on the king's head and held a bit of cheese in its hands
and nibbled it, and dribbled the crumbs in the king's face with
naive and impudent irreverence. It was a tranquil scene, and restful
to the weary eye and the jaded spirit.

This was the old man's tale. He said:

"Right so the king and Merlin departed, and went until an
hermit that was a good man and a great leech. So the hermit
searched all his wounds and gave him good salves; so the king was
there three days, and then were his wounds well amended that he
might ride and go, and so departed. And as they rode, Arthur said,
I have no sword. No force,* said Merlin, hereby is a sword that
shall be yours and I may. So they rode till they came to a lake, the
which was a fair water and broad, and in the midst of the lake
Arthur was ware of an arm clothed in white samite, that held a fair
sword in that hand. Lo, said Merlin, yonder is that sword that I
spake of. With that they saw a damsel going upon the lake. What
damsel is that? said Arthur. That is the Lady of the lake, said
Merlin; and within that lake is a rock, and therein is as fair a place
as any on earth, and richly beseen, and this damsel will come to
you anon, and then speak ye fair to her that she will give you that
sword. Anon withal came the damsel unto Arthur and saluted him,
and he her again. Damsel, said Arthur, what sword is that, that
yonder the arm holdeth above the water? I would it were mine, for
I have no sword. Sir Arthur King, said the damsel, that sword is
mine, and if ye will give me a gift when I ask it you, ye shall have it.
By my faith, said Arthur, I will give you what gift ye will ask. Well,
said the damsel, go ye into yonder barge and row yourself to the
sword, and take it and the scabbard with you, and I will ask my
gift when I see my time. So Sir Arthur and Merlin alight, and tied

*No matter.

their horses to two trees, and so they went into the ship, and when
they came to the sword that the hand held, Sir Arthur took it up by
the handles, and took it with him. And the arm and the hand went
under the water; and so they came unto the land and rode forth.
And then Sir Arthur saw a rich pavilion. What signifieth yonder
pavilion? It is the knight's pavilion, said Merlin, that ye fought
with last, Sir Pellinore, but he is out, he is not there; he hath ado
with a knight of yours, that hight Egglame, and they have fought
and he hath chased him even to Carlion, and we shall meet with
him anon in the highway. That is well said, said Arthur, now have
I a sword, now will I wage battle with him, and be avenged on him.
Sir, ye shall not so, said Merlin, for the knight is weary of fighting
and chasing, so that ye shall have no worship to have ado with him;
also, he will not lightly be matched of one knight living; and
therefore it is my counsel, let him pass, for he shall do you good
service in short time, and his sons, after his days. Also ye shall see
that day in short space ye shall be right glad to give him your sister
to wed. When I see him, I will do as ye advise me, said Arthur.
Then Sir Arthur looked on the sword, and liked it passing well.
Whether liketh you better, said Merlin, the sword or the scabbard?
Me liketh better the sword, said Arthur. Ye are more unwise, said
Merlin, for the scabbard is worth ten of the sword, for while ye
have the scabbard upon you ye shall never lose no blood, be ye
never so sore wounded; therefore, keep well the scabbard always
with you. So they rode unto Carlion, and by the way they met with
Sir Pellinore; but Merlin had done such a craft that Pellinore saw
not Arthur, and he passed by without any words. I marvel, said
Arthur, that the knight would not speak. Sir, said Merlin, he saw
you not; for and he had seen you ye had not lightly departed. So
they came unto Carlion, whereof his knights were passing glad.
And when they heard of his adventures they marvelled that he
would jeopard his person so alone. But all men of worship said it
was merry to be under such a chieftain that would put his person in
adventure as other poor knights did."

CHAPTER IV

SIR DINADAN THE HUMORIST

It seemed to me that this quaint lie was most simply and
beautifully told; but then I had heard it only once, and that makes
a difference; it was pleasant to the others when it was fresh, no
doubt.

Sir Dinadan the Humorist was the first to awake, and he soon
roused the rest with a practical joke of a sufficiently poor quality.
He tied some metal mugs to a dog's tail and turned him loose, and

he tore around and around the place in a frenzy of fright, with all
the other dogs bellowing after him and battering and crashing
against everything that came in their way and making altogether a
chaos of confusion and a most deafening din and turmoil; at which
every man and woman of the multitude laughed till the tears
flowed, and some fell out of their chairs and wallowed on the floor
in ecstasy. It was just like so many children. Sir Dinadan was so
proud of his exploit that he could not keep from telling over and
over again, to weariness, how the immortal idea happened to occur
to him; and as is the way with humorists of his breed, he was still
laughing at it after everybody else had got through. He was so set
up that he concluded to make a speech—of course a humorous
speech. I think I never heard so many old played-out jokes strung
together in my life. He was worse than the minstrels, worse than
the clown in the circus. It seemed peculiarly sad to sit here, thirteen
hundred years before I was born and listen again to poor, flat,
worm-eaten jokes that had given me the dry gripes when I was a
boy thirteen hundred years afterwards. It about convinced me that
there isn't any such thing as a new joke possible. Everybody
laughed at these antiquities—but then they always do; I had
noticed that, centuries later. However, of course the scoffer didn't
laugh—I mean the boy. No, he scoffed; there wasn't anything he
wouldn't scoff at. He said the most of Sir Dinadan's jokes were
rotten and the rest were petrified. I said "petrified" was good; as I
believed, myself, that the only right way to classify the majestic
ages of some of those jokes was by geologic periods. But that neat
idea hit the boy in a blank place, for geology hadn't been invented
yet. However, I made a note of the remark, and calculated to
educate the commonwealth up to it if I pulled through. It is no use
to throw a good thing away merely because the market isn't ripe
yet.

   Now Sir Kay arose and began to fire up on his history-mill with
me for fuel. It was time for me to feel serious, and I did. Sir Kay
told how he had encountered me in a far land of barbarians, who
all wore the same ridiculous garb that I did—a garb that was a
work of enchantment, and intended to make the wearer secure
from hurt by human hands. However, he had nullified the force of
the enchantment by prayer, and had killed my thirteen knights in
a three-hours' battle, and taken me prisoner, sparing my life in
order that so strange a curiosity as I was might be exhibited to the
wonder and admiration of the king and the court. He spoke of me
all the time, in the blandest way, as "this prodigious giant," and
"this horrible sky-towering monster," and "this tusked and taloned
man-devouring ogre;" and everybody took in all this bosh in the
naivest way, and never smiled or seemed to notice that there was
any discrepancy between these watered statistics and me. He said
that in trying to escape from him I sprang into the top of a tree two

hundred cubits high at a single bound, but he dislodged me with a stone the size of a cow, which "all-to brast" the most of my bones, and then swore me to appear at Arthur's court for sentence. He ended by condemning me to die at noon on the 21st; and was so little concerned about it that he stopped to yawn before he named the date.

I was in a dismal state by this time; indeed, I was hardly enough in my right mind to keep the run of a dispute that sprung up as to how I had better be killed, the possibility of the killing being doubted by some, because of the enchantment in my clothes. And yet it was nothing but an ordinary suit of fifteen-dollar slop-shops. Still, I was sane enough to notice this detail, to wit: many of the terms used in the most matter-of-fact way by this great assemblage of the first ladies and gentlemen in the land would have made a Comanche blush. Indelicacy is too mild a term to convey the idea. However, I had read "Tom Jones," and "Roderick Random," and other books of that kind, and knew that the highest and first ladies and gentlemen in England had remained little or no cleaner in their talk, and in the morals and conduct which such talk implies, clear up to a hundred years ago; in fact clear into our own nineteenth century—in which century, broadly speaking, the earliest samples of the real lady and real gentleman discoverable in English history—or in European history, for that matter—may be said to have made their appearance. Suppose the mouths of his characters, had allowed the characters to speak for themselves? We should have had talk from Rachel and Ivanhoe and the soft lady Rowena which would embarrass a tramp in our day. However, to the unconsciously indelicate all things are delicate. King Arthur's people were not aware that they were indecent, and I had presence of mind enough not to mention it.

They were so troubled about my enchanted clothes that they were mightily relieved, at last, when old Merlin swept the difficulty away for them with a common-sense hint. He asked them why they were so dull—why didn't it occur to them to strip me. In half a minute I was as naked as a pair of tongs! And dear, dear, to think of it: I was the only embarrassed person there. Everybody discussed me; and did it as unconcernedly as if I had been a cabbage. Queen Guenever was as naively interested as the rest, and said she had never seen anybody with legs just like mine before. It was the only compliment I got—if it was a compliment.

Finally, I was carried off in one direction, and my perilous clothes in another. I was shoved into a dark and narrow cell in a dungeon, with some scant remnants for dinner, some mouldy straw for a bed, and no end of rats for company.

CHAPTER V

AN INSPIRATION

I was so tired that even my fears were not able to keep me awake long.

When I next came to myself, I seemed to have been asleep a very long time. My first thought was, "Well, what an astonishing dream I've had! I reckon I've waked only just in time to keep from being hanged or drowned or burned, or something.... I'll nap again till the whistle blows, and then I'll go down to the arms factory and have it out with Hercules."

But just then I heard the harsh music of rusty chains and bolts, a light flashed in my eyes, and that butterfly, Clarence, stood before me! I gasped with surprise; my breath almost got away from me.

"What!" I said, "you here yet? Go along with the rest of the dream! scatter!"

But he only laughed, in his light-hearted way, and fell to making fun of my sorry plight.

"All right," I said resignedly, "let the dream go on; I'm in no hurry."

"Prithee what dream?"

"What dream? Why, the dream that I am in Arthur's court—a person who never existed; and that I am talking to you, who are nothing but a work of the imagination."

"Oh, la, indeed! and is it a dream that you're to be burned to-morrow? Ho-ho—answer me that!"

The shock that went through me was distressing. I now began to reason that my situation was in the last degree serious, dream or no dream; for I knew by past experience of the life-like intensity of dreams, that to be burned to death, even in a dream, would be very far from being a jest, and was a thing to be avoided, by any means, fair or foul, that I could contrive. So I said beseechingly:

"Ah, Clarence, good boy, only friend I've got,—for you *are* my friend, aren't you?—don't fail me; help me to devise some way of escaping from this place!"

"Now do but hear thyself! Escape? Why, man, the corridors are in guard and keep of men-at-arms."

"No doubt, no doubt. But how many, Clarence? Not many, I hope?"

"Full a score. One may not hope to escape." After a pause— hesitatingly: "and there be other reasons—and weightier."

"Other ones? What are they?"

"Well, they say—oh, but I daren't, indeed I daren't!"

"Why, poor lad, what is the matter? Why do you blench? Why do you tremble so?"

"Oh, in sooth, there is need! I do want to tell you, but—"

"Come, come, be brave, be a man—speak out, there's a good lad!"

He hesitated, pulled one way by desire, the other way by fear; then he stole to the door and peeped out, listening; and finally crept close to me and put his mouth to my ear and told me his fearful news in a whisper, and with all the cowering apprehension of one who was venturing upon awful ground and speaking of things whose very mention might be freighted with death.

"Merlin, in his malice, has woven a spell about this dungeon, and there bides not the man in these kingdoms that would be desperate enough to essay to cross its lines with you! Now God pity me, I have told it! Ah, be kind to me, be merciful to a poor boy who means thee well; for an thou betray me I am lost!"

I laughed the only really refreshing laugh I had had for some time; and shouted—

"Merlin has wrought a spell! *Merlin,* forsooth! That cheap old humbug, that maundering old ass? Bosh, pure bosh, the silliest bosh in the world! Why, it does seem to me that of all the childish, idiotic, chuckle-headed, chicken-livered superstitions that ev— oh, damn Merlin!"

But Clarence had slumped to his knees before I had half finished, and he was like to go out of his mind with fright.

"Oh, beware! These are awful words! Any moment these walls may crumble upon us if you say such things. Oh call them back before it is too late!"

Now this strange exhibition gave me a good idea and set me to thinking. If everybody about here was so honestly and sincerely afraid of Merlin's pretended magic as Clarence was, certainly a superior man like me ought to be shrewd enough to contrive some way to take advantage of such a state of things. I went on thinking, and worked out a plan. Then I said:

"Get up. Pull yourself together; look me in the eye. Do you know why I laughed?"

"No—but for our blessed Lady's sake, do it no more."

"Well, I'll tell you why I laughed. Because I'm a magician myself."

"Thou!" The boy recoiled a step, and caught his breath, for the thing hit him rather sudden; but the aspect which he took on was very, very respectful, I took quick note of that; it indicated that a humbug didn't need to have a reputation in this asylum; people stood ready to take him at his word, without that. I resumed:

"I've known Merlin seven hundred years, and he—"

"Seven hun—"

"Don't interrupt me. He has died and come alive again thirteen times, and travelled under a new name every time: Smith, Jones, Robinson, Jackson, Peters, Haskins, Merlin—a new alias every time

he turns up. I knew him in Egypt three hundred years ago; I knew
him in India five hundred years ago—he is always blethering
around in my way, everywhere I go; he makes me tired. He don't
amount to shucks, as a magician; knows some of the old common
tricks, but has never got beyond the rudiments, and never will. He
is well enough for the provinces—one-night stands and that sort of
thing, you know—but dear me, *he* oughtn't to set up for an
expert—anyway not where there's a real artist. Now look here,
Clarence, I am going to stand your friend, right along, and in
return you must be mine. I want you to do me a favor. I want you
to get word to the king that I am a magician myself—and the
Supreme Grand High-yu-Muck-amuck and head of the tribe, at
that; and I want him to be made to understand that I am just
quietly arranging a little calamity here that will make the fur fly in
these realms if Sir Kay's project is carried out and any harm comes
to me. Will you get that to the king for me?"

The poor boy was in such a state that he could hardly answer
me. It was pitiful to see a creature so terrified, so unnerved, so
demoralized. But he promised everything; and on my side he made
me promise over and over again that I would remain his friend,
and never turn against him or cast any enchantments upon him.
Then he worked his way out, staying himself with his hand along
the wall, like a sick person.

Presently this thought occurred to me: how heedless I have been!
When the boy gets calm, he will wonder why a great magician like
me should have begged a boy like him to help me get out of this
place; he will put this and that together, and will see that I am a
humbug.

I worried over that heedless blunder for an hour, and called
myself a great many hard names, meantime. But finally it occurred
to me all of a sudden that these animals didn't reason; that *they*
never put this and that together; that all their talk showed that
they didn't know a discrepancy when they saw it. I was at
rest, then.

But as soon as one is at rest, in this world, off he goes on
something else to worry about. It occurred to me that I had made
another blunder: I had sent the boy off to alarm his betters with a
threat—I intending to invent a calamity at my leisure; now the
people who are the readiest and eagerest and willingest to swallow
miracles are the very ones who are hungriest to see you perform
them; suppose I should be called on for a sample? Suppose I
should be asked to name my calamity? Yes, I had made a blunder;
I ought to have invented my calamity first. "What shall I do? what
can I say, to gain a little time?" I was in trouble again; in the
deepest kind of trouble: . . . "There's a footstep!—they're coming.
If I had only just a moment to think. . . . Hoof, I've got it. I'm
all right."

You see, it was the eclipse. It came into my mind, in the nick of time, how Columbus, or Cortez, or one of those people, played an eclipse as a saving trump once, on some savages, and I saw my chance. I could play it myself, now; and it wouldn't be any plagiarism, either, because I should get it in nearly a thousand years ahead of those parties.

Clarence came in, subdued, distressed, and said:

"I hasted the message to our liege the king, and straightway he had me to his presence. He was frighted even to the marrow, and was minded to give order for your instant enlargement, and that you be clothed in fine raiment and lodged as befitted one so great; but then came Merlin and spoiled all; for he persuaded the king that you are mad, and know not whereof you speak; and said your threat is but foolishness and idle vaporing. They disputed long, but in the end, Merlin, scoffing, said, 'Wherefore hath he not *named* his brave calamity? Verily it is because he cannot.' This thrust did in a most sudden sort close the king's mouth, and he could offer naught to turn the argument; and so, reluctant, and full loth to do you the discourtesy, he yet prayeth you to consider his perplexed case, as noting how the matter stands, and name the calamity—if so be you have determined the nature of it and the time of its coming. Oh, prithee delay not; to delay at such a time were to double and treble the perils that already compass thee about. Oh, be thou wise—name the calamity!"

I allowed silence to accumulate while I got my impressiveness together, and then said:

"How long have I been shut up in this hole?"

"Ye were shut up when yesterday was well spent. It is 9 of the morning now."

"No! Then I have slept well, sure enough. Nine in the morning now! And yet it is the very complexion of midnight, to a shade. This is the 20th, then?"

"The 20th—yes."

"And I am to be burned alive to-morrow." The boy shuddered.

"At high noon."

"Now then, I will tell you what to say." I paused, and stood over that cowering lad a whole minute in awful silence; then, in a voice deep, measured, charged with doom, I began, and rose by dramatically graded stages to my colossal climax, which I delivered in as sublime and noble a way as ever I did such a thing in my life: "Go back and tell the king that at that hour I will smother the whole world in the dead blackness of midnight; I will blot out the sun, and he shall never shine again; the fruits of the earth shall rot for lack of light and warmth, and the peoples of the earth shall famish and die, to the last man!"

I had to carry the boy out myself, he sunk into such a collapse. I handed him over to the soldiers, and went back.

CHAPTER VI

THE ECLIPSE

In the stillness and the darkness, realization soon began to supplement knowledge. The mere knowledge of a fact is pale; but when you come to *realize* your fact, it takes on color. It is all the difference between hearing of a man being stabbed to the heart, and seeing it done. In the stillness and the darkness, the knowledge that I was in deadly danger took to itself deeper and deeper meaning all the time; a something which was realization crept inch by inch through my veins and turned me cold.

But it is a blessed provision of nature that at times like these, as soon as a man's mercury has got down to a certain point there comes a revulsion, and he rallies. Hope springs up, and cheerfulness along with it, and then he is in good shape to do something for himself, if anything can be done. When my rally came, it came with a bound. I said to myself that my eclipse would be sure to save me, and make me the greatest man in the kingdom besides; and straightway my mercury went up to the top of the tube, and my solicitudes all vanished. I was as happy a man as there was in the world. I was even impatient for to-morrow to come, I so wanted to gather-in that great triumph and be the centre of all the nation's wonder and reverence. Besides, in a business way it would be the making of me; I knew that.

Meantime there was one thing which had got pushed into the background of my mind. That was the half-conviction that when the nature of my proposed calamity should be reported to those superstitious people, it would have such an effect that they would want to compromise. So, by-and-by when I heard footsteps coming, that thought was recalled to me, and I said to myself, "As sure as anything, it's the compromise. Well, if it is good, all right, I will accept; but if it isn't, I mean to stand my ground and play my hand for all it is worth."

"The stake is ready. Come!"

The stake! The strength went out of me, and I almost fell down. It is hard to get one's breath at such a time, such lumps come into one's throat and such gaspings; but as soon as I could speak, I said:

"But this is a mistake—the execution is to-morrow."

"Order changed; been set forward a day. Haste thee!"

I was lost. There was no help for me. I was dazed, stupefied; I had no command over myself; I only wandered purposelessly about like one out of his mind; so the soldiers took hold of me, and pulled me along with them, out of the cell and along the maze of underground corridors, and finally into the fierce glare of daylight and the upper world. As we stepped into the vast enclosed court of the castle I got a shock; for the first thing I saw was the stake, standing in the centre, and near it the piled fagots and a monk. On all four sides of the court the seated multitudes rose rank above rank, forming sloping terraces that were rich with color. The king and the queen sat in their thrones, the most conspicuous figures there, of course.

To note all this, occupied but a second. The next second Clarence had slipped from some place of concealment and was pouring news into my ear, his eyes beaming with triumph and gladness. He said:

" 'Tis through *me* the change was wrought! And main hard have I worked to do it, too. But when I revealed to them the calamity in store, and saw how mighty was the terror it did engender, then saw I also that this was the time to strike! Wherefore I diligently pretended, unto this and that and the other one, that your power against the sun could not reach its full until the morrow; and so if any would save the sun and the world, you must be slain to-day, whilst your enchantments are but in the weaving and lack potency. Odsbodikins, it was but a dull lie, a most indifferent invention, but you should have seen them seize it and swallow it, in the frenzy of their fright, as it were salvation sent from heaven; and all the while was I laughing in my sleeve the one moment, to see them so cheaply deceived, and glorifying God the next, that He was content to let the meanest of His creatures be His instrument to the saving of thy life. Ah, how happy has the matter sped! You will not need to do the sun a *real* hurt—ah, forget not that, on your soul forget it not! Only make a little darkness—only the littlest little darkness, mind, and cease with that. It will be sufficient. They will see that I spoke falsely,—being ignorant, as they will fancy—and with the falling of the first shadow of that darkness you shall see them go mad with fear; and they will set you free and make you great! Go to thy triumph, now! But remember—ah, good friend, I implore thee remember my supplication, and do the blessed sun no hurt. For *my* sake, thy true friend."

I choked out some words through my grief and misery; as much as to say I would spare the sun; for which the lad's eyes paid me back with such deep and loving gratitude that I had not the heart to tell him his good-hearted foolishness had ruined me and sent me to my death.

As the soldiers assisted me across the court the stillness was so profound that if I had been blindfold I should have supposed I was in a solitude instead of walled in by four thousand people. There was not a movement perceptible in those masses of humanity; they were as rigid as stone images, and as pale; and dread sat upon every countenance. This hush continued while I was being chained to the stake; it still continued while the fagots were carefully and tediously piled about my ankles, my knees, my thighs,

my body. Then there was a pause, and a deeper hush, if possible,
and a man knelt down at my feet with a glazing torch; the
multitude strained forward, gazing, and parting slightly from their
seats without knowing it; the monk raised his hands above my
head, and his eyes toward the blue sky, and began some words in
Latin; in this attitude he droned on and on, a little while, and then
stopped. I waited two or three moments; then looked up; he was
standing there petrified. With a common impulse the multitude
rose slowly up and stared into the sky. I followed their eyes; as sure
as guns, there was my eclipse beginning! The life went boiling
through my veins; I was a new man! The rim of black spread
slowly into the sun's disk, my heart beat higher and higher, and
still the assemblage and the priest stared into the sky, motionless.
I knew that this gaze would be turned upon me, next. When it
was, I was ready. I was in one of the most grand attitudes I ever
struck, with my arm stretched up pointing to the sun. It was a
noble effect. You could *see* the shudder sweep the mass like a wave.
Two shouts rang out, one close upon the heels of the other:

"Apply the torch!"

"I forbid it!"

The one was from Merlin, the other from the king. Merlin
started from his place—to apply the torch himself, I judged. I said:

"Stay where you are. If any man moves—even the king—before
I give him leave, I will blast him with thunder, I will consume him
with lightnings!"

The multitude sank meekly into their seats, and I was just
expecting they would. Merlin hesitated a moment or two, and I was
on pins and needles during that little while. Then he sat down, and
I took a good breath; for I knew I was master of the situation now.
The king said:

"Be merciful, fair sir, and essay no further in this perilous
matter, lest disaster follow. It was reported to us that your powers
could not attain unto their full strength until the morrow; but—"

"Your Majesty thinks the report may have been a lie? It *was*
a lie."

That made an immense effect; up went appealing hands
everywhere, and the king was assailed with a storm of supplications
that I might be bought off at any price, and the calamity stayed.
The king was eager to comply. He said:

"Name any terms, reverend sir, even to the halving of my
kingdom; but banish this calamity, spare the sun!"

My fortune was made. I would have taken him up in a minute,
but *I* couldn't stop an eclipse; the thing was out of the question. So
I asked time to consider. The king said—

"How long—ah, how long, good sir? Be merciful; look, it
groweth darker, moment by moment. Prithee how long?"

"Not long. Half an hour—maybe an hour."

There were a thousand pathetic protests, but I couldn't shorten
up any, for I couldn't remember how long a total eclipse lasts. I
was in a puzzled condition, anyway, and wanted to think.
Something was wrong about that eclipse, and the fact was very
unsettling. If this wasn't the one I was after, how was I to tell
whether this was the sixth century, or nothing but a dream? Dear
me, if I could only prove it was the latter! Here was a glad new
hope. If the boy was right about the date, and this was surely the
20th, it *wasn't* the sixth century. I reached for the monk's sleeve, in
considerable excitement, and asked him what day of the month
it was.

Hang him, he said it was the *twenty-first!* It made me turn cold
to hear him. I begged him not to make any mistake about it; but
he was sure; he knew it was the 21st. So, that feather-headed boy
had botched things again! The time of the day was right for the
eclipse; I had seen that for myself, in the beginning, by the dial
that was near by. Yes, I *was* in King Arthur's court, and I might as
well make the most out of it I could.

The darkness was steadily growing, the people becoming more
and more distressed. I now said:

"I have reflected, Sir King. For a lesson, I will let this darkness
proceed, and spread night in the world; but whether I blot out the
sun for good, or restore it, shall rest with you. These are the terms,
to wit: You shall remain king over all your dominions, and receive
all the glories and honors that belong to the kingship; but you shall
appoint me your perpetual minister and executive, and give me for
my services one per cent. of such actual increase of revenue over
and above its present amount as I may succeed in creating for the
state. If I can't live on that, I sha'n't ask anybody to give me a lift.
Is it satisfactory?"

There was a prodigious roar of applause, and out of the midst of
it the king's voice rose, saying:

"Away with his bonds, and set him free! and do him homage,
high and low, rich and poor, for he is become the king's right hand,
is clothed with power and authority, and his seat is upon the
highest step of the throne! Now sweep away his creeping night, and
bring the light and cheer again, that all the world may bless thee."

But I said:

"That a common man should be shamed before the world, is
nothing; but it were dishonor to the *king* if any that saw his
minister naked should not also see him delivered from his shame.
If I might ask that my clothes be brought again—"

"They are not meet," the king broke in. "Fetch raiment of
another sort; clothe him like a prince!"

My idea worked. I wanted to keep things as they were till the
eclipse was total, otherwise they would be trying again to get me to
dismiss the darkness, and of course I couldn't do it. Sending for

the clothes gained some delay, but not enough. So I had to make
another excuse. I said it would be but natural if the king should
change his mind and repent to some extent of what he had done
under excitement; therefore I would let the darkness grow a while,
and if at the end of a reasonable time the king had kept his mind
the same, the darkness should be dismissed. Neither the king nor
anybody else was satisfied with that arrangement, but I had to stick
to my point.

It grew darker and darker and blacker and blacker, while I
struggled with those awkward sixth-century clothes. It got to be
pitch dark, at last, and the multitude groaned with horror to feel
the cold uncanny night breezes fan through the place and see the
stars come out and twinkle in the sky. At last the eclipse was total,
and I was very glad of it, but everybody else was in misery; which
was quite natural. I said:

"The king, by his silence, still stands to the terms." Then I lifted
up my hands—stood just so a moment—then I said, with the most
awful solemnity: "Let the enchantment dissolve and pass harmless
away!"

There was no response, for a moment, in that deep darkness and
that graveyard hush. But when the silver rim of the sun pushed
itself out, a moment or two later, the assemblage broke loose with
a vast shout and came pouring down like a deluge to smother me
with blessings and gratitude; and Clarence was not the last of the
wash, be sure.

CHAPTER VII

MERLIN'S TOWER

Inasmuch as I was now the second personage in the Kingdom, as
far as political power and authority were concerned, much was
made of me. My raiment was of silks and velvets and cloth of gold,
and by consequence was very showy, also uncomfortable. But
habit would soon reconcile me to my clothes; I was aware of that. I
was given the choicest suite of apartments in the castle, after the
king's. They were aglow with loud-colored silken hangings, but the
stone floors had nothing but rushes on them for a carpet, and they
misfit rushes at that, being not all of one breed. As for
conveniences properly speaking, there weren't any. I mean *little*
conveniences; it is the little conveniences that make the real
comfort of life. The big oaken chairs, graced with rude carvings,
were well enough, but that was the stopping-place. There was no
soap, no matches, no looking-glass—except a metal one, about as
powerful as a pail of water. And not a chromo. I had been used to
chromos for years, and I saw now that without my suspecting it a
passion for art had got worked into the fabric of my being, and was

become a part of me. It made me homesick to look around over
this proud and gaudy but heartless barrenness and remember that
in our house in East Hartford, all unpretending as it was, you
couldn't go into a room but you would find an insurance-chromo,
or at least a three-color God-Bless-Our-Home over the door; and in
the parlor we had nine. But here, even in my grand room of state,
there wasn't anything in the nature of a picture except a thing the
size of a bed-quilt, which was either woven or knitted, (it had
darned places in it,) and nothing in it was the right color or the
right shape; and as for proportions, even Raphael himself couldn't
have botched them more formidably, after all his practice on those
nightmares they call his "celebrated Hampton court cartoons."
Raphael was a bird. We had several of his chromos; one was his
"Miraculous Draught of Fishes," where he puts in a miracle of his
own—puts three men into a canoe which wouldn't have held a dog
without upsetting. I always admired to study R.'s art, it was so
fresh and unconventional.

There wasn't even a bell or a speaking-tube in the castle. I had a
great many servants, and those that were on duty lolled in the
anteroom; and when I wanted one of them I had to go and call for
him. There was no gas, there were no candles; a bronze dish half
full of boarding-house butter with a blazing rag floating in it was
the thing that produced what was regarded as light. A lot of these
hung along the walls and modified the dark, just toned it down
enough to make it dismal. If you went out at night, your servants
carried torches. There were no books, pens, paper, or ink, and no
glass in the openings they believed to be windows. It is a little
thing—glass is—until it is absent, then it becomes a big thing. But
perhaps the worst of all was, that there wasn't any sugar, coffee,
tea or tobacco. I saw that I was just another Robinson Crusoe cast
away on an uninhabited island, with no society but some more or
less tame animals, and if I wanted to make life bearable I must do
as he did—invent, contrive, create, reorganize things; set brain and
hand to work, and keep them busy. Well, that was in my line.

One thing troubled me along at first—the immense interest
which people took in me. Apparently the whole nation wanted a
look at me. It soon transpired that the eclipse had scared the
British world almost to death: that while it lasted the whole
country, from one end to the other, was in a pitiable state of panic,
and the churches, hermitages, and monkeries overflowed with
praying and weeping poor creatures who thought the end of the
world was come. Then had followed the news that the producer of
this awful event was a stranger, a mighty magician at Arthur's
court; that he could have blown out the sun like a candle, and was
just going to do it when his mercy was purchased, and he then
dissolved his enchantments, and was now recognized and honored
as the man who had by his unaided might saved the globe from

destruction and its peoples from extinction. Now if you consider
that everybody believed that, and not only believed it but never
even dreamed of doubting it, you will easily understand that there
was not a person in all Britain that would not have walked fifty
miles to get a sight of me. Of course I was all the talk—all other
subjects were dropped; even the king became suddenly a person of
minor interest and notoriety. Within twenty-four hours the
delegations began to arrive, and from that time onward for a
fortnight they kept coming. The village was crowded, and all the
countryside. I had to go out a dozen times a day and show myself
to these reverent and awe-stricken multitudes. It came to be a great
burden, as to time and trouble, but of course it was at the same
time compensatingly agreeable to be so celebrated and such a
centre of homage. It turned Brer Merlin green with envy and spite,
which was a great satisfaction to me. But there was one thing I
couldn't understand; nobody had asked for an autograph. I spoke
to Clarence about it. By George, I had to explain to him what it
was. Then he said nobody in the country could read or write but a
few dozen priests. Land! think of that.

There was another thing that troubled me a little. Those
multitudes presently began to agitate for another miracle. That was
natural. To be able to carry back to their far homes the boast that
they had seen the man who could command the sun, riding in the
heavens, and be obeyed, would make them great in the eyes of their
neighbors, and envied by them all; but to be able to also say they
had seen him work a miracle themselves—why, people would come
a distance to see *them.* The pressure got to be pretty strong. There
was going to be an eclipse of the moon, and I knew the date and
hour, but it was too far away. Two years. I would have given a good
deal for license to hurry it up and use it now when there was a big
market for it. It seemed a great pity to have it wasted, so, and come
lagging along at a time when a body wouldn't have any use for it as
like as not. If it had been booked for only a month away, I could
have sold it short; but as matters stood, I couldn't seem to cipher
out any way to make it do me any good, so I gave up trying. Next,
Clarence found that old Merlin was making himself busy on the sly
among those people. He was spreading a report that I was a
humbug, and that the reason I didn't accommodate the people
with a miracle was because I couldn't. I saw that I must do
something. I presently thought out a plan.

By my authority as executive I threw Merlin into prison—the
same cell I had occupied myself. Then I gave public notice by
herald trumpet that I should be busy with affairs of state for a
fortnight, but about the end of that time I would take a moment's
leisure and blow up Merlin's stone tower by fires from heaven; in
the meantime, whoso listened to evil reports about me, let him
beware. Furthermore, I would perform but this one miracle at this

time, and no more; if it failed to satisfy and any murmured, I would turn the murmurers into horses, and make them useful. Quiet ensued.

I took Clarence into my confidence, to a certain degree, and we went to work privately. I told him that this was a sort of miracle that required a trifle of preparation, and that it would be sudden death to ever talk about these preparations to anybody. That made his mouth safe enough. Clandestinely we made a few bushels of first-rate blasting-powder, and I superintended my armorers while they constructed a lightning-rod and some wires. This old stone tower was very massive—and rather ruinous, too, for it was Roman, and four hundred years old. Yes, and handsome, after a rude fashion, and clothed with ivy from base to summit, as with a shirt of scale mail. It stood on a lonely eminence, in good view from the castle, and about half a mile away.

Working by night, we stowed the powder in the tower—dug stones out, on the inside, and buried the powder in the walls themselves, which were fifteen feet thick at the base. We put in a peck at a time, in a dozen places. We could have blown up the Tower of London with these charges. When the thirteenth night was come we put up our lightning-rod, bedded it in one of the batches of powder, and ran wires from it to the other batches. Everybody had shunned that locality from the day of my proclamation, but on the morning of the fourteenth I thought best to warn the people, through the heralds, to keep clear away—a quarter of a mile away. Then added, by command, that at some time during the twenty-four hours I would consummate the miracle, but would first give a brief notice; by flags on the castle towers, if in the daytime, by torch-baskets in the same places if at night.

Thunder-showers had been tolerably frequent of late, and I was not much afraid of a failure; still, I shouldn't have cared for a delay of a day or two; I should have explained that I was busy with affairs of state, yet, and the people must wait.

Of course we had a blazing sunny day—almost the first one without a cloud for three weeks; things always happen so. I kept secluded, and watched the weather. Clarence dropped in from time to time and said the public excitement was growing and growing all the time, and the whole country filling up with human masses as far as one could see from the battlements. At last the wind sprang up and a cloud appeared—in the right quarter, too, and just at nightfall. For a little while I watched that distant cloud spread and blacken, then I judged it was time for me to appear. I ordered the torch-baskets to be lit, and Merlin liberated and sent to me. A quarter of an hour later I ascended the parapet and there found the king and the court assembled and gazing off in the darkness toward Merlin's Tower. Already the darkness was so heavy that one

could not see far; these people, and the old turrets, being partly in
deep shadow and partly in the red glow from the great torch-
baskets overhead, made a good deal of a picture.

Merlin arrived in a gloomy mood. I said:

"You wanted to burn me alive when I had not done you any
harm, and latterly you have been trying to injure my professional
reputation. Therefore I am going to call down fire and blow up
your tower, but it is only fair to give you a chance; now if you think
you can break my enchantments and ward off the fires, step to the
bat, it's your innings."

"I can, fair sir, and I will. Doubt it not."

He drew an imaginary circle on the stones of the roof, and burnt
a pinch of powder in it which sent up a small cloud of aromatic
smoke, whereat everybody fell back, and began to cross themselves
and get uncomfortable. Then he began to mutter and make passes
in the air with his hands. He worked himself up slowly and
gradually into a sort of frenzy, and got to thrashing around with his
arms like the sails of a windmill. By this time the storm had about
reached us; the gusts of wind were flaring the torches and making
the shadows swash about, the first heavy drops of rain were falling,
the world abroad was black as pitch, the lightning began to wink
fitfully. Of course my rod would be loading itself now. In fact,
things were imminent. So I said:

"You have had time enough. I have given you every advantage,
and not interfered. It is plain your magic is weak. It is only fair that
I begin now."

I made about three passes in the air, and then there was an awful
crash and that old tower leaped into the sky in chunks, along with
a vast volcanic fountain of fire that turned night to noonday, and
showed a thousand acres of human beings grovelling on the ground
in a general collapse of consternation. Well, it rained mortar and
masonry the rest of the week. This was the report; but probably the
facts would have modified it.

It was an effective miracle. The great bothersome temporary
population vanished. There were a good many thousand tracks in
the mud the next morning, but they were all outward bound. If I
had advertised another miracle I couldn't have raised an audience
with a sheriff.

Merlin's stock was flat. The king wanted to stop his wages; he
even wanted to banish him, but I interfered. I said he would be
useful to work the weather, and attend to small matters like that,
and I would give him a lift now and then when his poor little
parlor-magic soured on him. There wasn't a rag of his tower left,
but I had the government rebuild it for him, and advised him to
take boarders; but he was too high-toned for that. And as for being
grateful, he never even said thank-you. He was a rather hard lot,
take him how you might; but then you couldn't fairly expect a man
to be sweet that had been set back so.

CHAPTER VIII

THE BOSS

To be vested with enormous authority is a fine thing; but to have the on-looking world consent to it is a finer. The tower episode solidified my power, and made it impregnable. If any were perchance disposed to be jealous and critical before that, they experienced a change of heart, now. There was not any one in the kingdom who would have considered it good judgment to meddle with my matters.

I was fast getting adjusted to my situation and circumstances. For a time, I used to wake up, mornings, and smile at my "dream," and listen for the Colt's factory whistle; but that sort of thing played itself out, gradually, and at last I was fully able to realize that I was actually living in the sixth century, and in Arthur's court, not a lunatic asylum. After that, I was just as much at home in that century as I could have been in any other; and as for preference, I wouldn't have traded it for the twentieth. Look at the opportunities here for a man of knowledge, brains, pluck and enterprise to sail in and grow up with the country. The grandest field that ever was; and all my own; not a competitor; not a man who wasn't a baby to me in acquirements and capacities; whereas, what would I amount to in the twentieth century? I should be foreman of a factory, that is about all; and could drag a seine down-street any day and catch a hundred better men than myself.

What a jump I had made! I couldn't keep from thinking about it, and contemplating it, just as one does who has struck oil. There was nothing back of me that could approach it, unless it might be Joseph's case; and Joseph's only approached it, it didn't equal it, quite. For it stands to reason that as Joseph's splendid financial ingenuities advantaged nobody but the king, the general public must have regarded him with a good deal of disfavor, whereas I had done my entire public a kindness in sparing the sun, and was popular by reason of it.

I was no shadow of a king; I was the substance; the king himself was the shadow. My power was colossal; and it was not a mere name, as such things have generally been, it was the genuine article. I stood here, at the very spring and source of the second great period of the world's history; and could see the trickling stream of that history gather, and deepen and broaden, and roll its mighty tides down the far centuries; and I could note the upspringing of adventurers like myself in the shelter of its long array of thrones: De Montforts, Gavestons, Mortimers, Villierses; the war-making, campaign-directing wantons of France, and

Charles the Second's sceptre-wielding drabs; but nowhere in the procession was my full-sized fellow visible. I was a Unique; and glad to know that that fact could not be dislodged or challenged for thirteen centuries and a half, for sure.

Yes, in power I was equal to the king. At the same time there was another power that was a trifle stronger than both of us put together. That was the Church. I do not wish to disguise that fact. I couldn't, if I wanted to. But never mind about that, now; it will show up, in its proper place, later on. It didn't cause me any trouble in the beginning—at least any of consequence.

Well, it was a curious country, and full of interest. And the people! They were the quaintest and simplest and trustingest race; why, they were nothing but rabbits. It was pitiful for a person born in a wholesome free atmosphere to listen to their humble and hearty outpourings of loyalty toward their king and Church and nobility; as if they had any more occasion to love and honor king and Church and noble than a slave has to love and honor the lash, or a dog has to love and honor the stranger that kicks him! Why, dear me, *any* kind of royalty, howsoever modified, *any* kind of aristocracy, howsoever pruned, is rightly an insult; but if you are born and brought up under that sort of arrangment you probably never find it out for yourself, and don't believe it when somebody else tells you. It is enough to make a body ashamed of his race to think of the sort of froth that has always occupied its thrones without shadow of right or reason, and the seventh-rate people that have always figured as its aristocracies—a company of monarchs and nobles who, as a rule, would have achieved only poverty and obscurity if left, like their betters, to their own exertions.

The most of King Arthur's British nation were slaves, pure and simple, and bore that name, and wore the iron collar on their necks; and the rest were slaves in fact, but without the name; they imagined themselves men and freemen, and called themselves so. The truth was, the nation as a body was in the world for one object, and one only: to grovel before king and Church and noble; to slave for them, sweat blood for them, starve that they might be fed, work that they might play, drink misery to the dregs that they might be happy, go naked that they might wear silks and jewels, pay taxes that they might be spared from paying them, be familiar all their lives with the degrading language and postures of adulation that they might walk in pride and think themselves the gods of this world. And for all this, the thanks they got were cuffs and contempt; and so poor-spirited were they that they took even this sort of attention as an honor.

Inherited ideas are a curious thing, and interesting to observe and examine. I had mine, the king and his people had theirs. In both cases they flowed in ruts worn deep by time and habit, and the man who should have proposed to divert them by reason and argument

would have had a long contract on his hands. For instance, those
people had inherited the idea that all men without title and a long
pedigree, whether they had great natural gifts and acquirements
or hadn't, were creatures of no more consideration than so many
animals, bugs, insects; whereas I had inherited the idea that human
daws who can consent to masquerade in the peacock-shams of
inherited dignities and unearned titles, are of no good but to be
laughed at. The way I was looked upon was odd, but it was natural.
You know how the keeper and the public regard the elephant in the
menagerie: well, that is the idea. They are full of admiration of his
vast bulk and his prodigious strength; they speak with pride of the
fact that he can do a hundred marvels which are far and away
beyond their own powers; and they speak with the same pride of the
fact that in his wrath he is able to drive a thousand men before him.
But does that make him one of *them?* No; the raggedest tramp in
the pit would smile at the idea. He couldn't comprehend it; couldn't
take it in; couldn't in any remote way conceive of it. Well, to the
king, the nobles, and all the nation, down to the very slaves and
tramps, I was just that kind of an elephant, and nothing more. I was
admired, also feared; but it was as an animal is admired and
feared. The animal is not reverenced, neither was I; I was not even
respected. I had no pedigree, no inherited title; so in the king's and
nobles' eyes I was mere dirt; the people regarded me with wonder
and awe, but there was no reverence mixed with it; through the
fore of inherited ideas they were not able to conceive of anything
being entitled to that except pedigree and lordship. There you see
the hand of that awful power, the Roman Catholic Church. In two
or three little centuries it had converted a nation of men to a nation
of worms. Before the day of the Church's supremacy in the world,
men were men, and held their heads up, and had a man's pride and
spirit and independence; and what of greatness and position a
person got, he got mainly by achievement, not by birth. But then the
Church came to the front, with an axe to grind; and she was wise,
subtle, and knew more than one way to skin a cat—or a nation; she
invented "divine right of kings," and propped it all around, brick
by brick, with the Beatitudes—wrenching them from their good
purpose to make them fortify an evil one; she preached (to the
commoner,) humility, obedience to superiors, the beauty of
self-sacrifice; she preached (to the commoner,) meekness under
insult; preached (still to the commoner, always to the commoner,)
patience, meanness of spirit, non-resistance under oppression; and
she introduced heritable ranks and aristocracies, and taught all the
Christian populations of the earth to bow down to them and worship
them. Even down to my birth-century that poison was still in the
blood of Christendom, and the best of English commoners was still
content to see his inferiors impudently continuing to hold a number
of positions, such as lordships and the throne, to which the

grotesque laws of his country did not allow him to aspire; in fact he
was not merely contented with this strange condition of things, he
was even able to persuade himself that he was proud of it. It seems
to show that there isn't anything you can't stand, if you are only born
and bred to it. Of course that taint, that reverence for rank and title,
had been in our American blood, too—I know that; but when I left
America it had disappeared—at least to all intents and purposes.
The remnant of it was restricted to the dudes and dudesses. When
a disease has worked its way down to that level, it may fairly be said
to be out of the system.

But to return to my anomalous position in King Arthur's
kingdom. Here I was, a giant among pigmies, a man among
children, a master intelligence among intellectual moles: by all
rational measurement the one and only actually great man in that
whole British world; and yet there and then, just as in the remote
England of my birth-time, the sheep-witted earl who could claim
long descent from a king's leman, acquired at second-hand from the
slums of London, was a better man than I was. Such a personage
was fawned upon in Arthur's realm and reverently looked up to by
everybody, even though his dispositions were as mean as his
intelligence, and his morals as base as his lineage. There were times
when *he* could sit down in the king's presence, but I couldn't. I could
have got a title easily enough, and that would have raised me a
large step in everybody's eyes; even in the king's, the giver of it. But
I didn't ask for it; and I declined it when it was offered. I couldn't
have enjoyed such a thing with my notions; and it wouldn't have
been fair, anyway, because as far back as I could go, our tribe had
always been short of the bar sinister. I couldn't have felt really and
satisfactorily fine and proud and set-up over any title except one that
should come from the nation itself, the only legitimate source; and
such an one I hoped to win; and in the course of years of honest and
honorable endeavor, I did win it and did wear it with a high and
clean pride. This title fell casually from the lips of a blacksmith,
one day, in a village, was caught up as a happy thought and tossed
from mouth to mouth with a laugh and an affirmative vote; in ten
days it had swept the kingdom, and was become as familiar as the
king's name. I was never known by any other designation
afterwards, whether in the nation's talk or in grave debate upon
matters of state at the council-board of the sovereign. This title,
translated into modern speech, would be THE BOSS. Elected by the
nation. That suited me. And it was a pretty high title. There were
very few THE'S, and I was one of them. If you spoke of the duke, or
the earl, or the bishop, how could anybody tell which one you
meant? But if you spoke of The King or The Queen or The Boss,
it was different.

Well, I liked the king, and *as* king I respected him—respected
the office; at least respected it as much as I was capable of

respecting any unearned supremacy; but as *men* I looked down upon him and his nobles—privately. And he and they liked me, and respected my office; but as an animal, without birth or sham title, they looked down upon me—and were not particularly private about it, either. I didn't charge for my opinion about them, and they didn't charge for their opinion about me: the account was square, the books balanced, everybody was satisfied.

CHAPTER IX

THE TOURNAMENT

They were always having grand tournaments there at Camelot; and very stirring and picturesque and ridiculous human bull-fights they were, too, but just a little wearisome to the practical mind. However, I was generally on hand—for two reasons: a man must not hold himself aloof from the things which his friends and his community have at heart if he would be liked—especially as a statesman; and both as businessman and statesman I wanted to study the tournament and see if I couldn't invent an improvement on it. That reminds me to remark, in passing, that the very first official thing I did, in my administration—and it was on the very first day of it, too—was to start a patent office, for I knew that a country without a patent office and good patent laws was just a crab, and couldn't travel any way but sideways or backwards.

Things ran along, a tournament nearly every week; and now and then the boys used to want me to take a hand—I mean Sir Launcelot and the rest—but I said I would by-and-by; no hurry yet, and too much government machinery to oil up and set to rights and start a-going.

We had one tournament which was continued from day to day during more than a week, and as many as five hundred knights took part in it, from first to last. They were weeks gathering. They came on horseback from everywhere; from the very ends of the country, and even from beyond the sea; and many brought ladies and all brought squires, and troops of servants. It was a most gaudy and gorgeous crowd, as to costumery, and very characteristic of the country and the time, in the way of high animal spirits, innocent indecencies of language, and happy-hearted indifference to morals. It was fight or look on, all day and every day; and sing, gamble, dance, carouse half the night every night. They had a most noble good time. You never saw such people. Those banks of beautiful ladies, shining in their barbaric splendors, would see a knight sprawl from his horse in the lists with a lance-shaft the thickness of your ankle clean through him and the blood spouting, and instead of fainting they would clap their hands and crowd each other for a better view; only sometimes one would dive into her handkerchief, and look ostentatiously broken-hearted, and then you could lay two to one that there was a scandal there somewhere and she was afraid the public hadn't found it out.

The noise at night would have been annoying to me ordinarily, but I didn't mind it in the present circumstances, because it kept me from hearing the quacks detaching legs and arms from the day's cripples. They ruined an uncommon good old cross-cut saw for me, and broke the saw-buck, too, but I let it pass. And as for my axe— well, I made up my mind that the next time I lent an axe to a surgeon I would pick my century.

I not only watched this tournament from day to day, but detailed an intelligent priest from my Department of Public Morals and Agriculture, and ordered him to report it; for it was my purpose by-and-by, when I should have gotten the people along far enough, to start a newspaper. The first thing you want in a new country, is a patent office; then work up your school system; and after that, out with your paper. A newspaper has its faults, and plenty of them, but no matter, it's hark from the tomb for a dead nation, and don't you forget it. You can't resurrect a dead nation without it; there isn't any way. So I wanted to sample things, and be finding out what sort of reporter-material I might be able to rake together out of the sixth century when I should come to need it.

Well, the priest did very well, considering. He got in all the details, and that is a good thing in a local item: you see he had kept books for the undertaker-department of his church when he was younger, and there, you know, the money's in the details; the more details, the more swag: bearers, mutes, candles, prayers,— everything counts; and if the bereaved don't buy prayers enough you mark up your candles with a forked pencil, and your bill shows up all right. And he had a good knack at getting in the complimentary thing here and there about a knight that was likely to advertise—no, I mean a knight that had influence; and he also had a neat gift of exaggeration, for in his time he had kept door for a pious hermit who lived in a sty and worked miracles.

Of course his novice's report lacked whoop and crash and lurid description, and therefore wanted the true ring; but its antique wording was quaint and sweet and simple, and full of the fragrances and flavors of the time, and these little merits made up in a measure for its more important lacks. Here is an extract from it:

Then Sir Brian de les Isles and Grummore Grummorsum, knights of the castle, encountered with Sir Aglovale and Sir Tor, and Sir Tor smote down Sir Grummore Grummorsum to the earth. Then came in Sir Carados of the dolorous tower, and Sir Turquine, knights of the castle, and there encountered with them Sir Percivale de Galis and Sir Lamorak de Galis, that were two brethren, and then encountered Sir Percivale with Sir Carados, and either brake their spears unto their hands, and then Sir

Turquine with Sir Lamorak, and either of them smote down other, horse
and all, to the earth, and either parties rescued other and horsed them
again. And Sir Arnold, and Sir Gauter, knights of the castle, encountered
with Sir Brandiles and Sir Kay, and these four knights encountered
mightily, and brake their spears to their hands. Then came Sir Pertolope
from the castle, and there encountered with him Sir Lionel, and there Sir
Pertolope the green knight smote down Sir Lionel, brother to Sir Launcelot.
All this was marked by noble heralds, who bare him best, and their names.
Then Sir Bleobaris brake his spear upon Sir Gareth, but of that stroke Sir
Bleobaris fell to the earth. When Sir Galihodin saw that, he bad Sir Gareth
keep him, and Sir Gareth smote him to the earth. Then Sir Galihud gat a
spear to avenge his brother, and in the same wise Sir Gareth served him,
and Sir Dinadan and his brother La Cote Male Taile, and Sir Sagramore le
Desirous, and Sir Dodinas le Savage; all these he bare down with one spear.
When King Agwisance of Ireland saw Sir Gareth fare so he marvelled what
he might be, that one time seemed green, and another time, at his again
coming, he seemed blue. And thus at every course that he rode to and fro he
changed his color, so that there might neither king nor knight have ready
cognizance of him. Then Sir Agwisance the King of Ireland encountered
with Sir Gareth, and there Sir Gareth smote him from his horse, saddle
and all. And then came King Carados of Scotland, and Sir Gareth smote
him down horse and man. And in the same wise he served King Uriens of
the land of Gore. And then there came in Sir Bagdemagus, and Sir Gareth
smote him down horse and man to the earth. And Bagdemagus's son
Meliganus brake a spear upon Sir Gareth mightily and knightly. And then
Sir Galahault the noble prince cried on high, Knight with the many colors,
well hast thou justed; now make thee ready that I may just with thee. Sir
Gareth heard him, and he gat a great spear, and so they encountered
together, and there the prince brake his spear; but Sir Gareth smote him
upon the left side of the helm, that he reeled here and there, and he had
fallen down had not his men recovered him. Truly said King Arthur, that
knight with the many colors is a good knight. Wherefore the king called
unto him Sir Launcelot, and prayed him to encounter with that knight.
Sir, said Launcelot, I may as well find in my heart for to forbear him at this
time, for he hath had travail enough this day, and when a good knight doth
so well upon some day, it is no good knight's part to let him of his worship,
and, namely, when he seeth a knight hath done so great labour: for
peradventure, said Sir Launcelot, his quarrel is here this day, and
peradventure he is best beloved with this lady of all that be here, for I see
well he paineth himself and enforceth him to do great deeds, and therefore,
said Sir Launcelot, as for me, this day he shall have the honour: though it
lay in my power to put him from it, I would not.

There was an unpleasant little episode that day, which for reasons
of state I struck out of my priest's report. You will have noticed that
Garry was doing some great fighting in the engagement. When I say
Garry I mean Sir Gareth. Garry was my private pet name for him;
it suggests that I had a deep affection for him, and that was the
case. But is was a private pet name only, and never spoken aloud to
any one, much less to him; being a noble, he would not have endured
a familiarity like that from me. Well, to proceed: I sat in the private

box set apart for me as the king's minister. While Sir Dinadan was
waiting for his turn to enter the lists, he came in there and sat down
and began to talk; for he was always making up to me, because I
was a stranger and he liked to have a fresh market for his jokes, the
most of them having reached that stage of wear where the teller has
to do the laughing himself while the other person looks sick. I had
always responded to his efforts as well as I could, and felt a very deep
and real kindness for him, too, for the reason that if by malice of
fate he knew the one particular anecdote which I had heard oftenest
and had most hated and most loathed all my life, he had at least
spared it me. It was one which I had heard attributed to every
humorous person who had ever stood on American soil, from
Columbus down to Artemus Ward. It was about a humorous
lecturer who flooded an ignorant audience with the killingest jokes
for an hour and never got a laugh; and then when he was leaving,
some gray simpletons wrung him gratefully by the hand and said it
had been the funniest thing they had ever heard, and "it was all they
could do to keep from laughin' right out in meetin'." That anecdote
never saw the day that it was worth the telling; and yet I had sat
under the telling of it hundreds and thousands and millions and
billions of times, and cried and cursed all the way through. Then
who can hope to know what my feelings were, to hear this armor-
plated ass start in on it again, in the murky twilight of tradition,
before the dawn of history, while even Lactantius might be referred
to as "the late Lactantius," and the Crusades wouldn't be born for
five hundred years yet? Just as he finished, the call-boy came; so,
haw-hawing like a demon, he went rattling and clanking out like a
crate of loose castings, and I knew nothing more. It was some
minutes before I came to, and then I opened my eyes just in time to
see Sir Gareth fetch him an awful welt, and I unconsciously out with
the prayer, "I hope to gracious he's killed!" But by ill-luck, before I
had got half through with the words, Sir Gareth crashed into Sir
Sagramor le Desirous and sent him thundering over his horse's
crupper, and Sir Sagramor caught my remark and thought I meant
it for *him*.

Well, whenever one of those people got a thing into his head,
there was no getting it out again. I knew that, so I saved my breath,
and offered no explanations. As soon as Sir Sagramor got well, he
notified me that there was a little account to settle between us, and
he named a day three or four years in the future; place of settlement,
the lists where the offence had been given. I said I would be ready
when he got back. You see, he was going for the Holy Grail. The
boys all took a flier at the Holy Grail now and then. It was a several
years' cruise. They always put in the long absence snooping around,
in the most conscientious way, though none of them had any idea
where the Holy Grail really was, and I don't think any of them
actually expected to find it, or would have known what to do with

it if he *had* run across it. You see, it was just the Northwest Passage
of that day, as you may say; that was all. Every year expeditions
went out holy grailing, and next year relief expeditions went out to
hunt for *them*. There was worlds of reputation in it, but no money.
Why, they actually wanted *me* to put in! Well, I should smile.

CHAPTER X

BEGINNINGS OF CIVILIZATION

The Round Table soon heard of the challenge, and of course it
was a good deal discussed, for such things interested the boys. The
king thought I ought now to set forth in quest of adventures, so that
I might gain renown and be the more worthy to meet Sir Sagramor
when the several years should have rolled away. I excused myself
for the present; I said it would take me three or four years yet to get
things well fixed up and going smoothly; then I should be ready;
all the chances were that at the end of that time Sir Sagramor would
still be out grailing, so no valuable time would be lost by the
postponement; I should then have been in office six or seven years,
and I believed my system and machinery would be so well developed
that I could take a holiday without its working any harm.

I was pretty well satisfied with what I had already accomplished.
In various quiet nooks and corners I had the beginnings of all sorts
of industries under way—nuclei of future vast factories, the iron and
steel missionaries of my future civilization. In these were gathered
together the brightest young minds I could find, and I kept agents
out raking the country for more, all the time. I was training a crowd
of ignorant folk into experts—experts in every sort of handiwork
and scientific calling. These nurseries of mine went smoothly and
privately along undisturbed in their obscure country retreats, for
nobody was allowed to come into their precincts without a special
permit—for I was afraid of the Church.

I had started a teacher-factory and a lot of Sunday-schools the
first thing; as a result, I now had an admirable system of graded
schools in full blast in those places, and also a complete variety of
Protestant congregations all in a prosperous and growing condition.
Everybody could be any kind of a Christian he wanted to; there
was perfect freedom in that matter. But I confined public religious
teaching to the churches and the Sunday-schools, permitting
nothing of it in my other educational buildings. I could have given
my own sect the preference and made everybody a Presbyterian
without any trouble, but that would have been to affront a law of
human nature: spiritual wants and instincts are as various in the
human family as are physical appetites, complexions, and features,
and a man is only at his best, morally, when he is equipped with the

religious garment whose color and shape and size most nicely
accommodate themselves to the spiritual complexion, angularities,
and stature of the individual who wears it; and besides I was afraid
of a united Church; it makes a mighty power, the mightiest
conceivable, and then when it by-and-by gets into selfish hands, as
it is always bound to do, it means death to human liberty, and
paralysis to human thought.

All mines were royal property, and there were a good many of
them. They had formerly been worked as savages always work
mines—holes grubbed in the earth and the mineral brought up in
sacks of hide by hand, at the rate of a ton a day; but I had begun to
put the mining on a scientific basis as early as I could.

Yes, I had made pretty handsome progress when Sir Sagramor's
challenge struck me.

Four years rolled by—and then! Well, you would never imagine
it in the world. Unlimited power *is* the ideal thing when it is in safe
hands. The despotism of heaven is the one absolutely perfect
government. An earthly despotism would be the absolutely perfect
earthly government, if the conditions were the same, namely, the
despot the perfectest individual of the human race, and his lease of
life perpetual. But as a perishable perfect man must die, and leave
his despotism in the hands of an imperfect successor, an earthly
despotism is not merely a bad form of government, it is the worst
form that is possible.

My works showed what a despot could do with the resources of a
kingdom at his command. Unsuspected by this dark land, I had the
civilization of the nineteenth century booming under its very nose!
It was fenced away from the public view, but there it was, a gigantic
and unassailable fact—and to be heard from, yet, if I lived and had
luck. There it was, as sure a fact, and as substantial a fact as any
serene volcano, standing innocent with its smokeless summit in the
blue sky and giving no sign of the rising hell in its bowels. My schools
and churches were children four years before; they were grown-up,
now; my shops of that day were vast factories, now; where I had a
dozen trained men then, I had a thousand, now; where I had one
brilliant expert then, I had fifty now. I stood with my hand on the
cock, so to speak, ready to turn it on and flood the midnight world
with light at any moment. But I was not going to do the thing in that
sudden way. It was not my policy. The people could not have stood
it; and moreover I should have had the Established Roman Catholic
Church on my back in a minute.

No, I had been going cautiously all the while. I had had
confidential agents trickling through the country some time, whose
office was to undermine knighthood by imperceptible degrees, and
to gnaw a little at this and that and the other superstition, and so
prepare the way gradually for a better order of things. I was turning
on my light one-candle-power at a time, and meant to continue to
do so.

I had scattered some branch schools secretly about the kingdom, and they were doing very well. I meant to work this racket more and more, as time wore on, if nothing occurred to frighten me. One of my deepest secrets was my West Point—my military academy. I kept that most jealously out of sight; and I did the same with my naval academy which I had established at a remote seaport. Both were prospering to my satisfaction.

Clarence was twenty-two now, and was my head executive, my right hand. He was a darling; he was equal to anything; there wasn't anything he couldn't turn his hand to. Of late I had been training him for journalism, for the time seemed about right for a start in the newspaper line; nothing big, but just a small weekly for experimental circulation in my civilization-nurseries. He took to it like a duck; there was an editor concealed in him, sure. Already he had doubled himself in one way; he talked sixth century and wrote nineteenth. His journalistic style was climbing, steadily; it was already up to the back settlement Alabama mark, and couldn't be told from the editorial output of that region either by matter or flavor.

We had another large departure on hand, too. This was a telegraph and a telephone; our first venture in this line. These wires were for private service only, as yet, and must be kept private until a riper day should come. We had a gang of men on the road, working mainly by night. They were stringing ground wires; we were afraid to put up poles, for they would attract too much inquiry. Ground wires were good enough, in both instances, for my wires were protected by an insulation of my own invention which was perfect. My men had orders to strike across country, avoiding roads, and establishing connection with any considerable towns whose lights betrayed their presence, and leaving experts in charge. Nobody could tell you how to find any place in the kingdom, for nobody ever went intentionally to any place, but only struck it by accident in his wanderings, and then generally left it without thinking to inquire what its name was. At one time and another we had sent out topographical expeditions to survey and map the kingdom, but the priests had always interfered and raised trouble. So we had given the thing up, for the present; it would be poor wisdom to antagonize the Church.

As for the general condition of the country, it was as it had been when I arrived in it, to all intents and purposes. I had made changes, but they were necessarily slight, and they were not noticeable. Thus far, I had not even meddled with taxation, outside of the taxes which provided the royal revenues. I had systematized those, and put the service on an effective and righteous basis. As a result, these revenues were already quadrupled, and yet the burden was so much more equably distributed than before, that all the kingdom felt a sense of relief, and the praises of my administration were hearty and general.

Personally, I struck an interruption, now, but I did not mind it,
it could not have happened at a better time. Earlier it could have
annoyed me, but now everything was in good hands and swimming
right along. The king had reminded me several times, of late, that
the postponement I had asked for, four years before, had about run
out, now. It was a hint that I ought to be starting out to seek
adventures and get up a reputation of a size to make me worthy of
the honor of breaking a lance with Sir Sagramor, who was still out
grailing, but was being hunted for by various relief expeditions,
and might be found any year, now. So you see I was expecting this
interruption; it did not take me by surprise.

CHAPTER XI

THE YANKEE IN SEARCH OF ADVENTURES

There never was such a country for wandering liars; and they
were of both sexes. Hardly a month went by without one of these
tramps arriving; and generally loaded with a tale about some
princess or other wanting help to get her out of some far-away castle
where she was held in captivity by a lawless scoundrel, usually a
giant. Now you would think that the first thing the king would do
after listening to such a novelette from an entire stranger, would
be to ask for credentials—yes, and a pointer or two as to locality of
castle, best route to it, and so on. But nobody ever thought of so
simple and common-sense a thing as that. No, everybody swallowed
these people's lies whole, and never asked a question of any sort or
about anything. Well, one day when I was not around, one of these
people came along—it was a she one, this time—and told a tale of
the usual pattern. Her mistress was a captive in a vast and gloomy
castle, along with forty-four other young and beautiful girls, pretty
much all of them princesses; they had been languishing in that
cruel captivity for twenty-six years; the masters of the castle were
three stupendous brothers, each with four arms and one eye—the
eye in the centre of the forehead, and as big as a fruit. Sort of fruit
not mentioned; their usual slovenliness in statistics.

Would you believe it? The king and the whole Round Table were
in raptures over this preposterous opportunity for adventure. Every
knight of the Table jumped for the chance, and begged for it; but to
their vexation and chagrin the king conferred it upon me, who had
not asked for it at all.

By an effort, I contained my joy when Clarence brought me the
news. But he—he could not contain his. His mouth gushed delight
and gratitude in a steady discharge—delight in my good fortune,
gratitude to the king for this splendid mark of his favor for me. He
could keep neither his legs nor his body still, but pirouetted about
the place in an airy ecstasy of happiness.

On my side, I could have cursed the kindness that conferred upon me this benefaction, but I kept my vexation under the surface for policy's sake, and did what I could to let on to be glad. Indeed, I *said* I was glad. And in a way it was true; I was as glad as a person is when he is scalped.

Well, one must make the best of things, and not waste time with useless fretting, but get down to business and see what can be done. In all lies there is wheat among the chaff; I must get at the wheat in this case: so I sent for the girl and she came. She was a comely enough creature, and soft and modest, but if signs went for anything, she didn't know as much as a lady's watch. I said—

"My dear, have you been questioned as to particulars?"

She said she hadn't.

"Well, I didn't expect you had, but I thought I would ask to make sure; it's the way I've been raised. Now you mustn't take it unkindly if I remind you that as we don't know you, we must go a little slow. You may be all right, of course, and we'll hope that you are; but to take it for granted isn't business. *You* understand that. I'm obliged to ask you a few questions; just answer up fair and square, and don't be afraid. Where do you live, when you are at home?"

"In the land of Moder, fair sir."

"Land of Moder. I don't remember hearing of it before. Parents living?"

"As to that, I know not if they be yet on live, sith it is many years that I have lain shut up in the castle."

"Your name, please?"

"I hight the Demoiselle Alisande la Carteloise, an it please you."

"Do you know anybody here who can identify you?"

"That were not likely, fair lord, I being come hither now for the first time."

"Have you brought any letters—any documents—any proofs that you are trustworthy and truthful?"

"Of a surety, no; and wherefore should I? Have I not a tongue, and cannot I say all that myself?"

"But *your* saying it, you know, and somebody else's saying it, is different."

"Different? How might that be? I fear me I do not understand."

"Don't *understand?* Land of—why, you see—you see—why, great Scott, can't you understand a little thing like that? Can't you understand the difference between your—*why* do you look so innocent and idiotic!"

"I? In truth I know not, but an it were the will of God."

"Yes, yes, I reckon that's about the size of it. Don't mind my seeming excited; I'm not. Let us change the subject. Now as to this castle, with forty-five princesses in it, and three ogres at the head of it, tell me—where is this harem?"

"Harem?"

"The *castle*, you understand; where is the castle?"

"Oh, as to that, it is great, and strong, and well beseen, and lieth in a far country. Yes, it is many leagues."

"*How* many?"

"Ah, fair sir, it were woundily hard to tell, they are so many, and do so lap the one upon the other, and being made all in the same image and tincted with the same color, one may not know the one league from its fellow, nor how to count them except they be taken apart, and ye wit well it were God's work to do that, being not within man's capacity; for ye will note—"

"Hold on, hold on, never mind about the distance; *whereabouts* does the castle lie? What's the direction from here?"

"Ah, please you sir, it hath no direction from here; by reason that the road lieth not straight, but turneth evermore; wherefore the direction of its place abideth not, but is sometime under the one sky and anon under another, whereso if ye be minded that it is in the east, and wend thitherward, ye shall observe that the way of the road doth yet again turn upon itself by the space of half a circle, and this marvel happing again and yet again and still again, it will grieve you that you had thought by vanities of the mind to thwart and bring to naught the will of Him that giveth not a castle a direction from a place except it pleaseth Him, and if it please Him not, will the rather that even all castles and all directions thereunto vanish out of the earth, leaving the places wherein they tarried desolate and vacant, so warning His creatures that where He will He will, and where He will not He—"

"Oh, that's all right, that's all right, give us a rest; never mind about the direction, *hang* the direction—I beg pardon, I beg a thousand pardons, I am not well to-day; pay no attention when I soliloquize, it is an old habit, an old, bad habit, and hard to get rid of when one's digestion is all disordered with eating food that was raised forever and ever before he was born; good land! a man can't keep his functions regular on spring chickens thirteen hundred years old. But come—never mind about that; let's—have you got such a thing as a map of that region about you? Now a good map—"

"Is it peradventure that manner of thing which of late the unbelievers have brought from over the great seas, which, being boiled in oil, and an onion and salt added thereto, doth—"

"What, a map? What are you talking about? Don't you know what a map is? There, there, never mind, don't explain, I hate explanations; they fog a thing up so that you can't tell anything about it. Run along, dear; good-day; show her the way, Clarence."

Oh, well, it was reasonably plain, now, why these donkeys didn't prospect these liars for details. It may be that this girl had a fact in her somewhere, but I don't believe you could have sluiced it out with a hydraulic; nor got it with the earlier forms of blasting, even; it was a case for dynamite. Why, she was a perfect ass; and yet the

king and his knights had listened to her as if she had been a leaf out
of the gospel. It kind of sizes up the whole party. And think of the
simple ways of this court: this wandering wench hadn't any more
trouble to get access to the king in his palace than she would have
had to get into the poor-house in my day and country. In fact he
was glad to see her, glad to hear her tale; with that adventure of
hers to offer, she was as welcome as a corpse is to a coroner.

Just as I was ending-up these reflections, Clarence came back.
I remarked upon the barren result of my efforts with the girl; hadn't
got hold of a single point that could help me to find the castle. The
youth looked a little surprised, or puzzled, or something, and
intimated that he had been wondering to himself what I had wanted
to ask the girl all those questions for.

"Why, great guns," I said, "don't I want to find the castle? And
how else would I go about it?"

"La, sweet your worship, one may lightly answer that, I ween.
She will go with thee. They always do. She will ride with thee."

"Ride with me? Nonsense!"

"But of a truth she will. She will ride with thee. Thou shalt see."

"What? She browse around the hills and scour the woods with
me—alone—and I as good as engaged to be married? Why, it's
scandalous. Think how it would look."

My, the dear face that rose before me! The boy was eager to know
all about this tender matter. I swore him to secrecy and then
whispered her name—"Puss Flanagan." He looked disappointed,
and said he didn't remember the countess. How natural it was for
the little courtier to give her a rank. He asked me where she lived.

"In East Har—" I came to myself and stopped, a little confused;
then I said, "Never mind, now; I'll tell you sometime."

And might he see her? Would I let him see her some day?

It was but a little thing to promise—thirteen hundred years or
so—and he so eager, so I said Yes. But I sighed; I couldn't help it.
And yet there was no sense in sighing, for she wasn't born yet. But
that is the way we are made: we don't reason, where we feel; we just
feel.

My expedition was all the talk that day and that night, and the
boys were very good to me, and made much of me, and seemed to
have forgotten their vexation and disappointment, and come to be
as anxious for me to hive those ogres and set those ripe old virgins
loose as if it were themselves that had the contract. Well, they *were*
good children—but just children, that is all. And they gave me no
end of points about how to scout for giants, and how to scoop them
in; and they told me all sorts of charms against enchantments, and
gave me salves and other rubbish to put on my wounds. But it never
occurred to one of them to reflect that if I was such a wonderful
necromancer as I was pretending to be, I ought not to need salves or
instructions, or charms against enchantments, and least of all, arms

and armor, on a foray of any kind—even against fire-spouting
dragons, and devils hot from perdition, let alone such poor
adversaries as these I was after, these commonplace ogres of the
back settlements.

I was to have an early breakfast, and start at dawn, for that was
the usual way; but I had the demon's own time with my armor, and
this delayed me a little. It is troublesome to get into, and there is so
much detail. First you wrap a layer or two of blanket around your
body, for a sort of cushion and to keep off the cold iron; then you put
on your sleeves and shirt of chain-mail—these are made of small
steel links woven together, and they form a fabric so flexible that if
you toss your shirt onto the floor, it slumps into a pile like a peck of
wet fish-net; it is very heavy and is nearly the uncomfortablest
material in the world for a night-shirt, yet plenty used it for that—
tax collectors, and reformers, and one-horse kings with a defective
title, and those sorts of people; then you put on your shoes—flat-
boats roofed over with interleaving bands of steel—and screw your
clumsy spurs into the heels. Next you buckle your greaves on your
legs, and your cuisses on your thighs; then come your backplate and
your breastplate, and you begin to feel crowded; then you hitch onto
the breastplate the half-petticoat of broad overlapping bands of steel
which hangs down in front but is scolloped out behind so you can sit
down, and isn't any real improvement on an inverted coal scuttle,
either for looks or for wear, or to wipe your hands on; next you belt
on your sword; then you put your stove-pipe joints onto your arms,
your iron gauntlets onto your hands, your iron rat-trap onto your
head, with a rag of steel web hitched onto it to hang over the back of
your neck—and there you are, snug as a candle in a candle-mould.
This is no time to dance. Well, a man that is packed away like that,
is a nut that isn't worth the cracking, there is so little of the meat,
when you get down to it, by comparison with the shell.

The boys helped me, or I never could have got in. Just as we
finished, Sir Bedivere happened in, and I saw that as like as not I
hadn't chosen the most convenient outfit for a long trip. How stately
he looked; and tall and broad and grand. He had on his head a
conical steel casque that only came down to his ears, and for visor
had only a narrow steel bar that extended down to his upper lip and
protected his nose; and all the rest of him, from neck to heel, was
flexible chain-mail, trousers and all. But pretty much all of him was
hidden under his outside garment, which of course was of chain-
mail, as I said, and hung straight from his shoulders to his ankles;
and from his middle to the bottom, both before and behind, was
divided, so that he could ride and let the skirts hang down on each
side. He was going grailing, and it was just the outfit for it, too. I
would have given a good deal for that ulster, but it was too late now
to be fooling around. The sun was just up, the king and the court
were all on hand to see me off and wish me luck; so it wouldn't be

etiquette for me to tarry. You don't get on your horse yourself; no, if you tried it you would get disappointed. They carry you out, just as they carry a sun-struck man to the drug store, and put you on, and help get you to rights, and fix your feet in the stirrups; and all the while you do feel so strange and stuffy and like somebody else— like somebody that has been married on a sudden, or struck by lightning, or something like that, and hasn't quite fetched around, yet, and is sort of numb, and can't just get his bearings. Then they stood up the mast they called a spear, in its socket by my left foot, and I gripped it with my hand; lastly they hung my shield around my neck, and I was all complete and ready to up anchor and get to sea. Everybody was as good to me as they could be, and a maid of honor gave me the stirrup-cup her own self. There was nothing more to do, now, but for that damsel to get up behind me on a pillion, which she did, and put an arm or so around me to hold on.

And so we started; and everybody gave us a goodbye and waved their handkerchiefs or helmets. And everybody we met, going down the hill and through the village was respectful to us, except some shabby little boys on the outskirts. They said—

"Oh, what a guy!" And hove clods at us.

In my experience boys are the same in all ages. They don't respect anything, they don't care for anything or anybody. They say "Go up, baldhead" to the prophet going his unoffending way in the gray of antiquity; they sass me in the holy gloom of the Middle Ages; and I had seen them act the same way in Buchanan's administration; I remember, because I was there and helped. The prophet had his bears and settled with his boys; and I wanted to get down and settle with mine, but it wouldn't answer, because I couldn't have got up again. I hate a country without a derrick.

CHAPTER XII

SLOW TORTURE

Straight off, we were in the country. It was most lovely and pleasant in those sylvan solitudes in the early cool morning in the first freshness of autumn. From hill-tops we saw fair green valleys lying spread out below, with streams winding through them, and island-groves of trees here and there, and huge lonely oaks scattered about and casting black blots of shade; and beyond the valleys we saw the ranges of hills, blue with haze, stretching away in billowy perspective to the horizon, with at wide intervals a dim fleck of white or gray on a wave-summit, which we knew was a castle. We crossed broad natural lawns sparkling with dew, and we moved like spirits, the cushioned turf giving out no sound of foot-fall; we dreamed along through glades in a mist of green light that got its tint from the

sun-drenched roof of leaves over-head, and by our feet the clearest
and coldest of runlets went frisking and gossiping over its reefs and
making a sort of whispering music comfortable to hear; and at times
we left the world behind and entered into the solemn great deeps
and rich gloom of the forest, where furtive wild things whisked and
scurried by and were gone before you could even get your eye on the
place where the noise was; and where only the earliest birds were
turning out and getting to business with a song here and a quarrel
yonder and a mysterious far-off hammering and drumming for
worms on a tree-trunk away somewhere in the impenetrable
remotenesses of the woods. And by-and-by out we would swing
again into the glare.

About the third or fourth or fifth time that we swung out into the
glare—it was along there somewhere, a couple of hours or so after
sun-up—it wasn't as pleasant as it had been. It was beginning to
get hot. This was quite noticeable. We had a very long pull, after
that, without any shade. Now it is curious how progressively little
frets grow and multiply after they once get a start. Things which I
didn't mind at all, at first, I began to mind now—and more and
more, too, all the time. The first ten or fifteen times I wanted my
handkerchief I didn't seem to care; I got along, and said never mind,
it isn't any matter, and dropped it out of my mind. But now it was
different; I wanted it all the time; it was nag, nag, nag, right along,
and no rest; I couldn't get it out of my mind; and so at last I lost my
temper and said hang a man that would make a suit of armor
without any pockets in it. You see I had my handkerchief in my
helmet; and some other things; but it was that kind of a helmet that
you can't take off by yourself. That hadn't occurred to me when I
put it there; and in fact I didn't know it. I supposed it would be
particularly convenient there. And so now, the thought of its being
there, so handy and close by, and yet not get-at-able, made it all the
worse and the harder to bear. Yes, the thing that you can't get is
the thing that you want, mainly; every one has noticed that. Well,
it took my mind off from everything else; took it clear off, and
centred it in my helmet; and mile after mile, there it stayed,
imagining the handkerchief, picturing the handkerchief; and it was
bitter and aggravating to have the salt sweat keep trickling down
into my eyes, and I couldn't get at it. It seems like a little thing, on
paper, but it was not a little thing at all; it was the most real kind of
misery. I would not say it if it was not so. I made up my mind that I
would carry along a reticule next time, let it look how it might, and
people say what they would. Of course these irons dudes of the
Round Table would think it was scandalous, and maybe raise Sheol
about it, but as for me, give me comfort first, and style afterwards.
So we jogged along, and now and then we struck a stretch of dust,
and it would tumble up in clouds and get into my nose and make me
sneeze and cry; and of course I said things I oughtn't to have said,

I don't deny that. I am not better than others. We couldn't seem to meet anybody in this lonesome Britain, not even an ogre; and in the mood I was in then, it was well for the ogre; that is, an ogre with a handkerchief. Most knights would have thought of nothing but getting his armor; but so I got his bandanna, he could keep his hardware, for all me.

Meantime it was getting hotter and hotter in there. You see, the sun was beating down and warming up the iron more and more all the time. Well, when you are hot, that way, every little thing irritates you. When I trotted, I rattled like a crate of dishes, and that annoyed me; and moreover I couldn't seem to stand that shield slatting and banging, now about my breast, now around my back; and if I dropped into a walk my joints creaked and screeched in that wearisome way that a wheelbarrow does, and as we didn't create any breeze at that gait, I was like to get fried in that stove; and besides, the quieter you went the heavier the iron settled down on you and the more and more tons you seemed to weigh every minute. And you had to be always changing hands, and passing your spear over to the other foot, it got so irksome for one hand to hold it long at a time.

Well, you know, when you perspire that way, in rivers, there comes a time when you—when you—well, when you itch. You are inside, your hands are outside; so there you are; nothing but iron between. It is not a light thing, let it sound as it may. First it is one place; then another; then some more; and it goes on spreading and spreading, and at last the territory is all occupied, and nobody can imagine what you feel like, nor how unpleasant it is. And when it had got to the worst, and it seemed to me that I could not stand anything more, a fly got in through the bars and settled on my nose, and the bars were stuck and wouldn't work, and I couldn't get the visor up; and I could only shake my head, which was baking hot by this time, and the fly—well, you know how a fly acts when he has got a certainty—he only minded the shaking enough to change from nose to lip, and lip to ear, and buzz and buzz all around in there, and keep on lighting and biting, in a way that a person already so distressed as I was, simply could not stand. So I gave in, and got Alisande to unship the helmet and relieve me of it. Then she emptied the conveniences out of it and fetched it full of water, and I drank and then stood up and she poured the rest down inside the armor. One cannot think how refreshing it was. She continued to fetch and pour until I was well soaked and thoroughly comfortable.

It was good to have a rest—and peace. But nothing is quite perfect in this life, at any time. I had made a pipe a while back, and also some pretty fair tobacco; not the real thing, but what some of the Indians use: the inside bark of the willow, dried. These comforts had been in the helmet, and now I had them again, but no matches.

Gradually, as the time wore along, one annoying fact was borne

in upon my understanding—that we were weather-bound. An armed
novice cannot mount his horse without help and plenty of it. Sandy
was not enough; not enough for me, anyway. We had to wait until
somebody should come along. Waiting, in silence, would have been
agreeable enough, for I was full of matter for reflection, and wanted
to give it a chance to work. I wanted to try and think out how it was
that rational or even half-rational men could ever have learned to
wear armor, considering its inconveniences; and how they had
managed to keep up such a fashion for generations when it was
plain that what I had suffered to-day they had had to suffer all the
days of their lives. I wanted to think that out; and moreover I wanted
to think out some way to reform this evil and persuade the people
to let the foolish fashion die out; but thinking was out of the
question in the circumstances. You couldn't think, where Sandy
was. She was a quite biddable creature and good-hearted, but she
had a flow of talk that was as steady as a mill, and made your head
sore like the drays and wagons in a city. If she had had a cork she
would have been a comfort. But you can't cork that kind; they
would die. Her clack was going all day, and you would think
something would surely happen to her works, by-and-by; but no,
they never got out of order; and she never had to slack up for
words. She could grind, and pump, and churn and buzz by the
week, and never stop to oil up or blow out. And yet the result
was just nothing but wind. She never had any ideas, any more
than a fog has. She was a perfect blatherskite; I mean for jaw, jaw,
jaw, talk, talk, talk, jabber, jabber, jabber; but just as good as she
could be. I hadn't minded her mill that morning, on account of
having that hornet's nest of other troubles; but more than once in
the afternoon I had to say—

"Take a rest, child; the way you are using up all the domestic
air, the kingdom will have to go to importing it by to-morrow, and
it's a low enough treasury without that."

CHAPTER XIII

FREEMEN!

Yes, it is strange how little a while at a time a person can be
contented. Only a little while back, when I was riding and suffering,
what a heaven this peace, this rest, this sweet serenity in this
secluded shady nook by this purling stream would have seemed,
where I could keep perfectly comfortable all the time by pouring a
dipper of water into my armor now and then; yet already I was
getting dissatisfied; partly because I could not light my pipe—for
although I had long ago started a match factory, I had forgotten to
bring matches with me—and partly because we had nothing to eat.

Here was another illustration of the childlike improvidence of this age and people. A man in armor always trusted to chance for his food on a journey, and would have been scandalized at the idea of hanging a basket of sandwiches on his spear. There was probably not a knight of all the Round Table combination who would not rather have died than been caught carrying such a thing as that on his flagstaff. And yet there could not be anything more sensible. It had been my intention to smuggle a couple of sandwiches into my helmet, but I was interrupted in the act, and had to make an excuse and lay them aside, and a dog got them.

Night approached, and with it a storm. The darkness came on fast. We must camp, of course. I found a good shelter for the demoiselle under a rock, and went off and found another for myself. But I was obliged to remain in my armor, because I could not get it off by myself and yet could not allow Alisande to help, because it would have seemed so like undressing before folk. It would not have amounted to that in reality, because I had clothes on underneath; but the prejudices of one's breeding are not gotten rid of just at a jump, and I knew that when it came to stripping off that bob-tailed iron petticoat I should be embarrassed.

With the storm came a change of weather; and the stronger the wind blew, and the wilder the rain lashed around, the colder and colder it got. Pretty soon, various kinds of bugs and ants and worms and things began to flock in out of the wet and crawl down inside my armor to get warm; and while some of them behaved well enough, and smuggled up amongst my clothes and got quiet, the majority were of a restless, uncomfortable sort, and never stayed still, but went on prowling and hunting for they did not know what; especially the ants, which went tickling along in wearisome procession from one end of me to the other by the hour, and are a kind of creatures which I never wish to sleep with again. It would be my advice to persons situated in this way, to not roll or thrash around, because this excites the interest of all the different sorts of animals and makes every last one of them want to turn out and see what is going on, and this makes things worse than they were before, and of course makes you objurgate harder, too, if you can. Still, if one did not roll and thrash around he would die; so perhaps it is as well to do one way as the other, there is no real choice. Even after I was frozen solid I could still distinguish that tickling, just as a corpse does when he is taking electric treatment. I said I would never wear armor after this trip.

All those trying hours whilst I was frozen and yet was in a living fire, as you may say, on account of that swarm of crawlers, that same unaswerable question kept circling and circling through my tired head: How do people stand this miserable armor? How have they managed to stand it all these generations? How can they sleep at night for dreading the tortures of next day?

When the morning came at last, I was in a bad enough plight:
seedy, drowsy, fagged, from want of sleep; weary from thrashing
around, famished from long fasting; pining for a bath, and to get
rid of the animals; and crippled with rheumatism. And how had it
fared with the nobly born, the titled aristocrat, the Demoiselle
Alisande la Carteloise? Why, she was as fresh as a squirrel; she had
slept like the dead; and as for a bath, probably neither she nor any
other noble in the land had ever had one, and so she was not missing
it. Measured by modern standards, they were merely modified
savages, those people. This noble lady showed no impatience to get
to breakfast—and that smacks of the savage, too. On their journeys
those Britons were used to long fasts, and knew how to bear them;
and also how to freight up against probable fasts before starting,
after the style of the Indian and the anaconda. As like as not, Sandy
was loaded for a three-day stretch.

We were off before sunrise, Sandy riding and I limping along
behind. In half an hour we came upon a group of ragged poor
creatures who had assembled to mend the thing which was regarded
as a road. They were as humble as animals to me; and when I
proposed to breakfast with them, they were so flattered, so
overwhelmed by this extraordinary condescension of mine that at
first they were not able to believe that I was in earnest. My lady put
up her scornful lip and withdrew to one side; she said in their
hearing that she would as soon think of eating with the other cattle
—a remark which embarrassed these poor devils merely because
it referred to them, and not because it insulted or offended them,
for it didn't. And yet they were not slaves, not chattels. By a
sarcasm of law and phrase they were freemen. Seven-tenths of the
free population of the country were of just their class and degree:
small "independent" farmers, artisans, etc.; which is to say, they
were the nation, the actual Nation; they were about all of it that was
useful, or worth saving, or really respectworthy; and to subtract
them would have been to subtract the Nation and leave behind some
dregs, some refuse, in the shape of a king, nobility and gentry, idle,
unproductive, acquainted mainly with the arts of wasting and
destroying, and of no sort of use or value in any rationally
constructed world. And yet, by ingenious contrivance, this gilded
minority, instead of being in the tail of the procession where it
belonged, was marching head up and banners flying, at the other
end of it; had elected itself to be the Nation, and these innumerable
clams had permitted it so long that they had come at last to accept
it as a truth; and not only that, but to believe it right and as it should
be. The priests had told their fathers and themselves that this
ironical state of things was ordained of God; and so, not reflecting
upon how unlike God it would be to amuse himself with sarcasms,
and especially such poor transparent ones as this, they had dropped
the matter there and become respectfully quiet.

The talk of these meek people had a strange enough sound in a formerly American ear. They were freemen, but they could not leave the estates of their lord or their bishop without his permission; they could not prepare their own bread, but must have their corn ground and their bread baked at his mill and his bakery, and pay roundly for the same; they could not sell a piece of their own property without paying him a handsome percentage of the proceeds, nor buy a piece of somebody else's without remembering him in cash for the privilege; they had to harvest his grain for him gratis, and be ready to come at a moment's notice, leaving their own crop to destruction by the threatened storm; they had to let him plant fruit trees in their fields, and then keep their indignation to themselves when his heedless fruit gatherers trampled the grain around the trees; they had to smother their anger when his hunting parties galloped through their fields laying waste the result of their patient toil; they were not allowed to keep doves themselves, and when the swarms from my lord's dovecote settled on their crops they must not lose their temper and kill a bird, for awful would the penalty be; when the harvest was at last gathered, then came the procession of robbers to levy their blackmail upon it: first the Church carted off its fat tenth, then the king's commissioner took his twentieth, then my lord's people made a mighty inroad upon the remainder; after which, the skinned freeman had liberty to bestow the remnant in his barn, in case it was worth the trouble; there were taxes, and taxes, and taxes, and more taxes, and taxes again, and yet other taxes—upon this free and independent pauper, but none upon his lord the baron or the bishop, none upon the wasteful nobility or the all-devouring Church; if the baron would sleep unvexed, the freeman must sit up all night after his day's work and whip the ponds to keep the frogs quiet; if the freeman's daughter— but no, that last infamy of monarchical government is unprintable; and finally, if the freeman, grown desperate with his tortures, found his life unendurable under such conditions, and sacrificed it and fled to death for mercy and refuge, the gentle Church condemned him to eternal fire, the gentle law buried him at midnight at the cross-roads with a stake through his back, and his master the baron or the bishop confiscated all his property and turned his widow and his orphans out of doors.

And here were these freemen assembled in the early morning to work on their lord the bishop's road three days each—gratis; every head of a family, and every son of a family, three days each, gratis, and a day or so added for their servants. Why, it was like reading about France and the French, before the ever-memorable and blessed Revolution, which swept a thousand years of such villany away in one swift tidal-wave of blood—one: a settlement of that hoary debt in the proportion of half a drop of blood for each hogshead of it that had been pressed by slow tortures out of that

people in the weary stretch of ten centuries of wrong and shame
and misery the like of which was not to be mated but in hell. There
were two "Reigns of Terror," if we would but remember it and
consider it; the one wrought murder in hot passion, the other in
heartless cold blood; the one lasted mere months, the other had
lasted a thousand years; the one inflicted death upon ten thousand
persons, the other upon a hundred millions; but our shudders are
all for the "horrors" of the minor Terror, the momentary Terror,
so to speak; whereas, what is the horror of swift death by the axe,
compared with life-long death from hunger, cold, insult, cruelty
and heart-break? What is swift death by lightning compared with
death by slow fire at the stake? A city cemetery could contain the
coffins filled by that brief Terror which we have all been so diligently
taught to shiver at and mourn over; but all France could hardly
contain the coffins filled by that older and real Terror—that
unspeakably bitter and awful Terror which none of us has been
taught to see in its vastness or pity as it deserves.

These poor ostensible freemen who were sharing their breakfast
and their talk with me, were as full of humble reverence for their
king and Church and nobility as their worst enemy could desire.
There was something pitifully ludicrous about it. I asked them if
they supposed a nation of people ever existed, who, with a free vote
in every man's hand, would elect that a single family and its
descendants should reign over it forever, whether gifted or boobies,
to the exclusion of all other families—including the voter's; and
would also elect that a certain hundred families should be raised
to dizzy summits of rank, and clothed-on with offensive
transmissible glories and privileges to the exclusion of the rest of the
nations's families—*including his own*.

They all looked unhit, and said they didn't know; that they had
never thought about it before, and it hadn't ever occurred to them
that a nation could be so situated that every man *could* have a say
in the government. I said I had seen one—and that it would last
until it had an Established Church. Again they were all unhit—at
first. But presently one man looked up and asked me to state that
proposition again; and state it slowly, so it could soak into his
understanding. I did it; and after a little he had the idea, and he
brought his fist down and said *he* didn't believe a nation where every
man had a vote would voluntarily get down in the mud and dirt in
any such way; and that to steal from a nation its will and preference
must be a crime and the first of all crimes.

I said to myself:

"This one's a man. If I were backed by enough of his sort, I would
make a strike for the welfare of this country, and try to prove myself
its loyalest citizen by making a wholesome change in its system of
government."

You see my kind of loyalty was loyalty to one's country, not to its
institutions or its office-holders. The country is the real thing, the

substantial thing, the eternal thing; it is the thing to watch over, and care for, and be loyal to; institutions are extraneous, they are its mere clothing, and clothing can wear out, become ragged, cease to be comfortable, cease to protect the body from winter, disease, and death. To be loyal to rags, to shout for rags, to worship rags, to die for rags—that is a loyalty of unreason, it is pure animal; it belongs to monarchy, was invented by monarchy; let monarchy keep it. I was from Connecticut, whose Constitution declares "that all political power is inherent in the people, and all free governments are founded on their authority and instituted for their benefit; and that they have *at all times* an undeniable and indefeasible right to *alter their form of government* in such a manner as they may think expedient."

Under that gospel, the citizen who thinks he sees that the commonwealth's political clothes are worn out, and yet holds his peace and does not agitate for a new suit, is disloyal; he is a traitor. That he may be the only one who thinks he sees this decay, does not excuse him; it is his duty to agitate anyway, and it is the duty of the others to vote him down if they do not see the matter as he does.

And now here I was, in a country where a right to say how the country should be governed was restricted to six persons in each thousand of its population. For the nine hundred and ninety-four to express dissatisfaction with the regnant system and propose to change it, would have made the whole six shudder as one man, it would have been so disloyal, so dishonorable, such putrid black treason. So to speak, I was become a stockholder in a corporation where nine hundred and ninety-four of the members furnished all the money and did all the work, and the other six elected themselves a permanent board of direction and took all the dividends. It seemed to me that what the nine hundred and ninety-four dupes needed was a new deal. The thing that would have best suited the circus side of my nature would have been to resign the Boss-ship and get up an insurrection and turn it into a revolution; but I knew that the Jack Cade or the Wat Tyler who tried such a thing without first educating his materials up to revolution-grade is almost absolutely certain to get left. I had never been accustomed to getting left, even if I do say it myself. Wherefore, the "deal" which had been for some time working into shape in my mind was of a quite different pattern from the Cade-Tyler sort.

So I did not talk blood and insurrection to that man there who sat munching black bread with that abused and mistaught herd of human sheep, but took him aside and talked matter of another sort to him. After I had finished, I got him to lend me a little ink from his veins; and with this and a sliver I wrote on a piece of bark—

Put him in the Man-Factory—

and gave it to him, and said—
"Take it to the palace at Camelot and give it into the hands of

Amyas le Poulet, whom I call Clarence, and he will understand."

"He is a priest, then," said the man, and some of the enthusiasm
went out of his face.

"How—a priest? Didn't I tell you that no chattel of the Church,
no bond-slave of pope or bishop can enter my Man-Factory? Didn't
I tell you that *you* couldn't enter unless your religion, whatever it
might be, was your own free property?"

"Marry, it is so, and for that I was glad; wherefore it liked me not,
and bred in me a cold doubt, to hear of this priest being there."

"But he isn't a priest, I tell you."

The man looked far from satisfied. He said:

"He is not a priest, and yet can read?"

"He is not a priest and yet can read—yes, and write, too, for that
matter. I taught him myself." The man's face cleared. "And it is
the first thing that you yourself will be taught in that Factory—"

"I? I would give blood out of my heart to know that art. Why, I
will be your slave, your—"

"No you won't, you won't be anybody's slave. Take your family
and go along. Your lord the bishop will confiscate your small
property, but no matter, Clarence will fix you all right."

CHAPTER XIV

"DEFEND THEE, LORD!"

I paid three pennies for my breakfast, and a most extravagant
price it was, too, seeing that one could have breakfasted a dozen
persons for that money; but I was feeling good by this time, and I
had always been a kind of spendthrift anyway; and then these
people had wanted to give me the food for nothing, scant as their
provision was, and so it was a grateful pleasure to emphasize my
appreciation and sincere thankfulness with a good big financial
lift where the money would do so much more good than it would
in my helmet, where, these pennies being made of iron and not
stinted in weight, my half-dollar's worth was a good deal of a burden
to me. I spent money rather too freely in those days, it is true; but
one reason for it was that I hadn't got the proportions of things
entirely adjusted, even yet, after so long a sojourn in Britain—
hadn't got along to where I was able to absolutely realize that a
penny in Arthur's land and a couple of dollars in Connecticut were
about one and the same thing: just twins, as you may say, in
purchasing power. If my start from Camelot could have been
delayed a very few days I could have paid these people in beautiful
new coins from our own mint, and that would have pleased me;
and them, too, not less. I had adopted the American values
exclusively. In a week or two now, cents, nickels, dimes, quarters

and half-dollars, and also a trifle of gold, would be trickling in thin but steady streams all through the commercial veins of the kingdom, and I looked to see this new blood freshen up its life.

The farmers were bound to throw in something, to sort of offset my liberality, whether I would or no; so I let them give me a flint and steel; and as soon as they had comfortably bestowed Sandy and me on our horse, I lit my pipe. When the first blast of smoke shot out through the bars of my helmet, all those people broke for the woods, and Sandy went over backwards and struck the ground with a dull thud. They thought I was one of those fire-belching dragons they had heard so much about from knights and other professional liars. I had infinite trouble to persuade those people to venture back within explaining distance. Then I told them that this was only a bit of enchantment which would work harm to none but my enemies. And I promised, with my hand on my heart, that if all who felt no enmity toward me would come forward and pass before me they should see that only those who remained behind would be struck dead. The procession moved with a good deal of promptness. There were no casualties to report, for nobody had curiosity enough to remain behind to see what would happen.

I lost some time, now, for these big children, their fears gone, became so ravished with wonder over my awe-compelling fireworks that I had to stay there and smoke a couple of pipes out before they would let me go. Still the delay was not wholly unproductive, for it took all that time to get Sandy thoroughly wonted to the new thing, she being so close to it, you know. It plugged up her conversation-mill, too, for a considerable while, and that was a gain. But above all other benefits accruing, I had learned something. I was ready for any giant or any ogre that might come along, now.

We tarried with a holy hermit, that night, and my opportunity came about the middle of the next afternoon. We were crossing a vast meadow by way of short-cut, and I was musing absently, hearing nothing, seeing nothing, when Sandy suddenly interrupted a remark which she had begun that morning, with the cry—

"Defend thee, lord!—peril of life is toward!"

And she slipped down from the horse and ran a little way and stood. I looked up and saw, far off in the shade of a tree, half a dozen armed knights and their squires; and straightway there was bustle among them and tightening of saddle-girths for the mount. My pipe was ready and would have been lit, if I had not been lost in thinking about how to banish oppression from this land and restore to all its people their stolen rights and manhood without disobliging anybody. I lit up at once, and by the time I had got a good head of reserved steam on, here they came. All together, too; none of those chivalrous magnanimities which one reads so much about—one courtly rascal at a time, and the rest standing by to see fair play. No, they came in a body, they came with a whirr and a

rush, they came like a volley from a battery; came with heads low
down, plumes streaming out behind, lances advanced at a level. It
was a handsome sight, a beautiful sight—for a man up a tree. I
laid my lance in rest and waited, with my heart beating, till the
iron wave was just ready to break over me, then spouted a column
of white smoke through the bars of my helmet. You should have
seen the wave go to pieces and scatter! This was a finer sight than the
other one.

But these people stopped, two or three hundred yards away, and
this troubled me. My satisfaction collapsed, and fear came; I judged
I was a lost man. But Sandy was radiant; and was going to be
eloquent, but I stopped her, and told her my magic had miscarried,
somehow or other, and she must mount, with all despatch, and we
must ride for life. No, she wouldn't. She said that my enchantment
had disabled those knights; they were not riding on, because they
couldn't; wait, they would drop out of their saddles presently, and
we would get their horses and harness. I could not deceive such
trusting simplicity, so I said it was a mistake; that when my
fireworks killed at all, they killed instantly; no, the men would not
die, there was something wrong about my apparatus, I couldn't
tell what; but we must hurry and get away, for those people would
attack us again, in a minute. Sandy laughed and said—

"Lack-a-day, sir, they be not of that breed! Sir Launcelot will
give battle to dragons, and will abide by them, and will assail them
again, and yet again, and still again, until he do conquer and
destroy them; and so likewise will Sir Pellinore and Sir Aglovale
and Sir Carados, and mayhap others, but there be none else that will
venture it, let the idle say what the idle will. And, la, as to yonder
base rufflers, think ye they have not their fill, but yet desire more?"

"Well, then, what are they waiting, for? Why don't they leave?
Nobody's hindering. Good land, I'm willing to let by-gones be
by-gones, I'm sure."

"Leave, is it? Oh, give thyself easement as to that. They dream not
of it, no, not they. They wait to yield them."

"Come—really, is that 'sooth'—as you people say? If they want to,
why don't they?"

"It would like them much; but an ye wot how dragons are
esteemed, ye would not hold them blamable. They fear to come."

"Well, then, suppose I go to them instead, and—"

"Ah, wit ye well they would not abide your coming. I will go."

And she did. She was a handy person to have along on a raid. I
would have considered this a doubtful errand, myself. I presently
saw the knights riding away, and Sandy coming back. That was a
relief. I judged she had somehow failed to get the first innings—I
mean in the conversation; otherwise the interview wouldn't have
been so short. But it turned out that she had managed the business
well; in fact admirably. She said that when she told those people

I was The Boss, it hit them where they lived; "smote them sore with fear and dread" was her word; and then they were ready to put up with anything she might require. So she swore them to appear at Arthur's court within two days and yield them, with horse and harness, and be my knights henceforth, and subject to my command. How much better she managed that thing than I should have done it myself! She was a daisy.

CHAPTER XV

SANDY'S TALE

"And so I'm proprietor of some knights," said I, as we rode off. "Who would ever have supposed that I should live to list up assets of that sort. I shan't know what to do with them; unless I raffle them off. How many of them are there, Sandy?"

"Seven, please you, sir, and their squires."

"It is a good haul. Who are they? Where do they hang out?"

"Where do they hang out?"

"Yes, where do they live?"

"Ah, I understood thee not. That will I tell eftsoons." Then she said musingly, and softly, turning the words daintily over her tongue: "Hang they out —hang they out—where hang—where do they hang out; eh, right so; where do they hang out. Of a truth the phrase hath a fair and winsome grace, and is prettily worded withal. I will repeat it anon and anon in mine idlesse, whereby I may peradventure learn it. Where do they hang out. Even so! already it falleth trippingly from my tongue, and forasmuch as—"

"Don't forget the cow-boys, Sandy."

"Cow-boys?"

"Yes; the knights, you know: You were going to tell me about them. A while back, you remember. Figuratively speaking, game's called."

"Game—"

"Yes, yes, yes! Go to the bat. I mean, get to work on your statistics, and don't burn so much kindling getting your fire started. Tell me about the knights."

"I will well, and lightly will begin. So they two departed and rode into a great forest. And—"

"Great Scott!"

You see, I recognized my mistake at once. I had set her works a-going; it was my own fault; she would be thirty days getting down to those facts. And she generally began without a preface and finished without a result. If you interrupted her she would either go right along without noticing, or answer with a couple of words, and go back and say the sentence over again. So, interruptions only

did harm; and yet I had to interrupt, and interrupt pretty frequently,
too, in order to save my life; a person would die if he let her
monotony drip on him right along all day.

"Great Scott!" I said in my distress. She went right back and
began over again:

"So they two departed and rode into a great forest. And—"

"Which two?"

"Sir Gawaine and Sir Uwaine. And so they came to an abbey of
monks, and there were well lodged. So on the morn they heard their
masses in the abbey, and so they rode forth till they came to a great
forest; then was Sir Gawaine ware in a valley by a turret, of twelve
fair damsels, and two knights armed on great horses, and the
damsels went to and fro by a tree. And then was Sir Gawaine ware
how there hung a white shield on that tree, and ever as the damsels
came by it they spit upon it, and some threw mire upon the shield—"

"Now, if I hadn't seen the like myself in this country, Sandy, I
wouldn't believe it. But I've seen it, and I can just see those creatures
now, parading before that shield and acting like that. The women
here do certainly act like all possessed. Yes, and I mean your best,
too, society's very choicest brands. The humblest hello-girl along
ten thousand miles of wire could teach gentleness, patience,
modesty, manners, to the highest duchess in Arthur's land."

"Hello-girl?"

"Yes, but don't you ask me to explain; it's a new kind of girl;
they don't have them here; one often speaks sharply to them when
they are not the least in fault, and he can't get over feeling sorry for
it and ashamed of himself in thirteen hundred years, it's such
shabby mean conduct and so unprovoked; the fact is, no gentlemen
ever does it—though I—well, I myself, if I've got to confess—"

"Peradventure she—"

"Never mind her; never mind her; I tell you I couldn't ever
explain her so you would understand."

"Even so be it, sith ye are so minded. Then Sir Gawaine and Sir
Uwaine went and saluted them, and asked them why they did that
despite to the shield. Sirs, said the damsels, we shall tell you. There
is a knight in this country that owneth this white shield, and he is
a passing good man of his hands, but he hateth all ladies and
gentlewomen, and therefore we do all this despite to the shield. I
will say you, said Sir Gawaine, it beseemeth evil a good knight to
despise all ladies and gentlewomen, and peradventure though he
hate you he hath some cause, and peradventure he loveth in some
other places ladies and gentlewomen, and to be loved again, and he
such a man of prowess as ye speak of—"

"Man of prowess—yes, that is the man to please them, Sandy.
Man of brains—that is a thing they never think of. Tom Sayers—
John Heenan—John L. Sullivan—pity but you could be here. You
would have your legs under the Round Table and a 'Sir' in front of

your names within the twenty-four hours; and you could bring about
a new distribution of the married princesses and duchesses of the
Court in another twenty-four. The fact is, it is just a sort of
polished-up court of Comanches, and there isn't a squaw in it who
doesn't stand ready at the dropping of a hat to desert to the buck
with the biggest string of scalps at his belt."

"—and he be such a man of prowess as ye speak of, said Sir
Gawaine. Now what is his name? Sir, said they, his name is Marhaus
the king's son of Ireland."

"Son of the king of Ireland, you mean; the other form doesn't
mean anything. And look out and hold on tight now, we must jump
this gully. . . . There, we are all right now. This horse belongs in
the circus; he is born before his time."

"I know him well, said Sir Uwaine, he is a passing good knight as
any is on live."

"*On live.* If you've got a fault in the world, Sandy, it is that you
are a shade too archaic. But it isn't any matter."

"—for I saw him once proved at a justs where many knights were
gathered, and that time there might no man withstand him. Ah,
said Sir Gawaine, damsels, methinketh ye are to blame, for it is to
suppose he that hung that shield there will not be long therefrom,
and then may those knights match him on horseback, and that is
more your worship than thus; for I will abide no longer to see a
knight's shield dishonored. And therewith Sir Uwaine and Sir
Gawaine departed a little from them, and then were they ware where
Sir Marhaus came riding on a great horse straight toward them.
And when the twelve damsels saw Sir Marhaus they fled into the
turret as they were wild, so that some of them fell by the way. Then
the one of the knights of the tower dressed his shield, and said on
high, Sir Marhaus defend thee. And so they ran together that the
knight brake his spear on Marhaus, and Sir Marhaus smote him
so hard that he brake his neck and the horse's back—"

"Well, that is just the trouble about this state of things, it ruins
so many horses."

"That saw the other knight of the turret, and dressed him toward
Marhaus, and they went so eagerly together, that the knight of the
turret was soon smitten down, horse and man, stark dead—"

"*Another* horse gone; I tell you it is a custom that ought to be
broken up. I don't see how people with any feeling can applaud and
support it."

*   *   *   *   *   *

"So these two knights came together with great random—"

I saw that I had been asleep and missed a chapter, but I didn't
say anything. I judged that the Irish knight was in trouble with the
visitors by this time, and this turned out to be the case.

"—that Sir Uwaine smote Sir Marhaus that his spear brast in pieces on the shield, and Sir Marhaus smote him so sore that horse and man he bare to the earth, and hurt Sir Uwaine on the left side—"

"The truth is, Alisande, these archaics are a little *too* simple; the vocabulary is too limited, and so, by consequence, descriptions suffer in the matter of variety; they run too much to level Saharas of fact, and not enough to picturesque detail; this throws about them a certain air of the monotonous; in fact the fights are all alike; a couple of people come together with great random—random is a good word, and so is exegesis, for that matter, and so is holocaust, and defalcation, and usufruct and a hundred others, but land! a body ought to discriminate—they come together with great random, and a spear is brast, and one party break his shield and the other one goes down, horse and man, over his horse-tail and brake his neck, and then the next candidate comes randoming in, and brast *his* spear, and the other man brast his shield, and down *he* goes, horse and man, over his horse-tail, and brake *his* neck, and then there's another elected, and another and another and still another, till the material is all used up; and when you come to figure up results, you can't tell one fight from another, nor who whipped; and as a *picture*, of living, raging, roaring battle, sho! why, it's pale and noiseless—just ghosts scuffling in a fog. Dear me, what would this barren vocabulary get out of the mightiest spectacle?—the burning of Rome in Nero's time, for instance? Why, it would merely say, 'Town burned down; no insurance; boy brast a window, fireman brake his neck!' Why, *that* ain't a picture!"

It was a good deal of a lecture, I thought, but it didn't disturb Sandy, didn't turn a feather; her steam soared steadily up again, the minute I took off the lid:

"Then Sir Marhaus turned his horse and rode toward Gawaine with his spear. And when Sir Gawaine saw that, he dressed his shield, and they aventred their spears, and they came together with all the might of their horses, that either knight smote other so hard in the midst of their shields, but Sir Gawaine's spear brake—"

"I knew it would."

—"but Sir Marhaus's spear held; and therewith Sir Gawaine and his horse rushed down to the earth—"

"Just so—and brake his back."

—"and lightly Sir Gawaine rose upon his feet and pulled out his sword, and dressed him toward Sir Marhaus on foot, and therewith either came unto other eagerly, and smote together with their swords, that their shields flew in cantels, and they bruised their helms and their hauberks, and wounded either other. But Sir Gawaine, fro it passed nine of the clock, waxed by the space of three hours ever stronger and stronger, and thrice his might was increased. All this espied Sir Marhaus, and had great wonder how

his might increased, and so they wounded other passing sore; and
then when it was come noon—"

The pelting sing-song of it carried me forward to scenes and
sounds of my boyhood days:

"N-e-e-ew Haven! ten minutes for refreshments—knductr 'll
strike the gong-bell two minutes before train leaves—passengers
for the Shore-line please take seats in the rear k'yar, this k'yar
don't go no furder—*ahh*-pls, *aw*-rnjz, b'*nan*ners, *s-a-n-d*'ches.
p——*op*-corn!"

——"and waxed past noon and drew toward evensong. Sir
Gawaine's strength feebled and waxed passing faint, that unnethes
he might dure any longer, and Sir Marhaus was then bigger and
bigger—"

"Which strained his armor, of course; and yet little would one of
these people mind a small thing like that."

—"and so, Sir Knight, said Sir Marhaus, I have well felt that ye
are a passing good knight, and a marvellous man of might as ever
I felt any, while it lasteth, and our quarrels are not great, and
therefore it were a pity to do you hurt, for I feel you are passing
feeble. Ah, said Sir Gawaine, gentle knight, ye say the word that I
should say. And therewith they took off their helms and either kissed
other, and there they swore together either to love other as brethren—"

But I lost the thread there, and dozed off to slumber, thinking
about what a pity it was that men with such superb strength—
strength enabling them to stand up cased in cruelly burdensome
iron and drenched with perspiration, and hack and batter and
bang each other for six hours on a stretch—should not have been
born at a time when they could put it to some useful purpose. Take
a jackass, for instance: a jackass has that kind of strength, and puts
it to a useful purpose, and is valuable to this world because he *is*
a jackass; but a nobleman is not valuable because he is a jackass.
It is a mixture that is always ineffectual, and should never have been
attempted in the first place. And yet, once you start a mistake, the
trouble is done and you never know what is going to come of it.

When I came to myself again and began to listen, I perceived that
I had lost another chapter, and that Alisande had wandered a long
way off with her people.

"And so they rode and came into a deep valley full of stones,
and thereby they saw a fair stream of water; above thereby was the
head of the stream, a fair fountain, and three damsels sitting
thereby. In this country, said Sir Marhaus, came never knight since
it was christened, but he found strange adventures—"

"This is not good form, Alisande. Sir Marhaus the king's son
of Ireland talks like all the rest; you ought to give him a brogue, or
at least a characteristic expletive; by this means one would recognize
him as soon as he spoke, without his ever being named. It is a
common literary device with the great authors. You should make

him say, 'In this country, be jabers, came never knight since it was
christened, but he found strange adventures, be jabers.' You see
how much better that sounds."

—"came never knight but he found strange adventures, be jabers.
Of a truth it doth indeed, fair lord, albeit 'tis passing hard to say,
though peradventure that will not tarry but better speed with usage.
And then they rode to the damsels, and either saluted other, and the
eldest had a garland of gold about her head, and she was
threescore winter of age or more—"

"The *damsel* was?"

"Even so, dear lord—and her hair was white under the garland—"

"Celluloid teeth, nine dollars a set, as like as not—the loose-fit
kind, that go up and down like a portcullis when you eat, and fall
out when you laugh."

"The second damsel was of thirty winter of age, with a circlet of
gold about her head. The third damsel was but fifteen year of age—"

Billows of thought came rolling over my soul, and the voice faded
out of my hearing!

Fifteen! Break—my heart! oh, my lost darling! Just her age who
was so gentle, and lovely, and all the world to me, and whom I shall
never see again! How the thought of her carries me back over wide
seas of memory to a vague dim time, a happy time, so many, many
centuries hence, when I used to wake in the soft summer mornings,
out of sweet dreams of her, and say "Hello, Central!" just to hear
her dear voice come melting back to me with a "Hello, Hank!"
that was music of the spheres to my enchanted ear. She got three
dollars a week, but she was worth it.

I could not follow Alisande's further explanation of who our
captured knights were, now—I mean in case she should ever get to
explaining who they were. My interest was gone, my thoughts were
far away, and sad. By fitful glimpses of the drifting tale, caught
here and there and now and then, I merely noted in a vague way that
each of these three knights took one of these three damsels up
behind him on his horse, and one rode north, another east, the other
south, to seek adventures, and meet again and lie, after year and
day. Year and day—and without baggage. It was of a piece with the
general simplicity of the country.

The sun was now setting. It was about three in the afternoon when
Alisande had begun to tell me who the cowboys were; so she had
made pretty good progress with it—for her. She would arrive some
time or other, no doubt, but she was not a person who could be
hurried.

We were approaching a castle which stood on high ground; a
huge, strong, venerable structure, whose gray towers and
battlements were charmingly draped with ivy, and whose whole
majestic mass was drenched with splendors flung from the sinking

sun. It was the largest castle we had seen, and so I thought it might
be the one we were after, but Sandy said no. She did not know who
owned it; she said she had passed it without calling, when she went
down to Camelot.

CHAPTER XVI

MORGAN LE FAY

If knights errant were to be believed, not all castles were desirable
places to seek hospitality in. As a matter of fact, knights errant were
not persons to be believed—that is, measured by modern standards
of veracity; yet, measured by the standards of their own time, and
scaled accordingly, you got the truth. It was very simple: you
discounted a statement ninety-seven per cent.; the rest was fact.
Now after making this allowance, the truth remained that if I could
find out something about a castle before ringing the door-bell—I
mean hailing the warders—it was the sensible thing to do. So I was
pleased when I saw in the distance a horseman making the bottom
turn of the road that wound down from this castle.

As we approached each other, I saw that he wore a plumed
helmet, and seemed to be otherwise clothed in steel, but bore a
curious addition also—a stiff square garment like a herald's
tabard. However, I had to smile at my own forgetfulness when I
got nearer and read this sign on his tabard:

"Persimmons's Soap—All the Prime-Donne Use It."

That was a little idea of my own, and had several wholesome
purposes in view toward the civilizing and uplifting of this nation.
In the first place, it was a furtive, underhand blow at this nonsense
of knight errantry, though nobody suspected that but me. I had
started a number of these people out—the bravest knights I could
get—each sandwiched between bulletin-boards bearing one device
or another, and I judged that by-and-by when they got to be
numerous enough they would begin to look ridiculous; and then,
even the steel-clad ass that *hadn't* any board would himself begin
to look ridiculous because he was out of the fashion.

Secondly, these missionaries would gradually, and without
creating suspicion or exciting alarm, introduce a rudimentary
cleanliness among the nobility, and from them it would work down
to the people, if the priests could be kept quiet. This would
undermine the Church. I mean would be a step toward that. Next,
education—next, freedom—and then she would begin to crumble.
It being my conviction that any Established Church is an established

crime, and established slave-pen, I had no scruples, but was willing
to assail it in any way or with any weapon that promised to hurt it.
Why, in my own former day—in remote centuries not yet stirring in
the womb of time—there were old Englishmen who imagined that
they had been born in a free country: a "free" country with the
Corporation Act and the Test still in force in it—timbers propped
against men's liberties and dishonored consciences to shore up an
Established Anachronism with.

My missionaries were taught to spell out the gilt signs on their
tabards—the showy gilding was a neat idea, I could have got the
king to wear a bulletin-board for the sake of that barbaric
splendor—they were to spell out these signs and then explain to the
lords and ladies what soap was; and if the lords and ladies were
afraid of it, get them to try it on a dog. The missionary's next move
was to get the family together and try it on himself; he was to stop
at no experiment, however desperate, that could convince the
nobility that soap was harmless; if any final doubt remained, he
must catch a hermit—the woods were full of them; saints they called
themselves, and saints they were believed to be. They were
unspeakably holy, and worked miracles, and everybody stood in
awe of them. If a hermit could survive a wash, and that failed to
convince a duke, give him up, let him alone.

Whenever my missionaries overcame a knight errant on the
road they washed him, and when he got well they swore him to go
and get a bulletin-board and disseminate soap and civilization
the rest of his days. As a consequence the workers in the field were
increasing by degrees, and the reform was steadily spreading. My
soap factory felt the strain early. At first I had only two hands;
but before I had left home I was already employing fifteen, and
running night and day; and the atmospheric result was getting so
pronounced that the king went sort of fainting and gasping around
and said he did not believe he could stand it much longer, and Sir
Launcelot got so that he did hardly anything but walk up and down
the roof and swear, although I told him it was worse up there than
anywhere else, but he said he wanted plenty of air; and he was
always complaining that a palace was no place for a soap factory,
anyway, and said if a man was to start one in his house he would
be damned if he wouldn't strangle him. There were ladies present,
too, but much these people ever cared for that; they would swear
before children, if the wind was their way when the factory was
going.

This missionary knight's name was La Cote Male Taile, and he
said that this castle was the abode of Morgan le Fay, sister of King
Arthur, and wife of King Uriens, monarch of a realm about as big
as the District of Columbia—you could stand in the middle of it
and throw bricks into the next kingdom. "Kings" and "Kingdoms"
were as thick in Britain as they had been in little Palestine in

Joshua's time, when people had to sleep with their knees pulled up
because they couldn't stretch out without a passport.

La Cote was much depressed, for he had scored here the worst
failure of his campaign. He had not worked off a cake; yet he had
tried all the tricks of the trade, even to the washing of a hermit;
but the hermit died. This was indeed a bad failure, for this animal
would now be dubbed a martyr, and would take his place among
the saints of the Roman calendar. Thus made he his moan, this poor
Sir La Cote Male Taile, and sorrowed passing sore. And so my
heart bled for him, and I was moved to comfort and stay him.
Wherefore I said—

"Forbear to grieve, fair knight, for this is not a defeat. We have
brains, you and I; and for such as have brains there are no defeats,
but only victories. Observe how we will turn this seeming disaster
into an advertisement; an advertisement for our soap; and the
biggest one, to draw, that was ever thought of; an advertisement
that will transform that Mount Washington defeat into a
Matterhorn victory. We will put on your bulletin-board, 'Patronized
by the Elect.' How does that strike you?"

"Verily, it is wonderly bethought!"

"Well, a body is bound to admit that for just a modest little
one-line ad, it's a corker."

So the poor colporteur's griefs vanished away. He was a brave
fellow, and had done mighty feats of arms in his time. His chief
celebrity rested upon the events of an excursion like this one of mine,
which he had once made with a damsel named Maledisant, who
was as handy with her tongue as was Sandy, though in a different
way, for her tongue churned forth only railings and insult, whereas
Sandy's music was of a kindlier sort. I knew his story well, and so
I knew how to interpret the compassion that was in his face when he
bade me farewell. He supposed I was having a bitter hard time of it.

Sandy and I discussed his story, as we rode along, and she said
that La Cote's bad luck had begun with the very beginning of that
trip; for the king's fool had overthrown him on the first day, and in
such cases it was customary for the girl to desert to the conqueror,
but Maledisant didn't do it; and also persisted afterward in sticking
to him, after all his defeats. But, said I, suppose the victor should
decline to accept his spoil? She said that that wouldn't answer—he
must. He couldn't decline; it wouldn't be regular. I made a note of
that. If Sandy's music got to be too burdensome, some time, I would
let a knight defeat me, on the chance that she would desert to him.

In due time we were challenged by the warders, from the castle
walls, and after a parley admitted. I have nothing pleasant to tell
about that visit. But it was not a disappointment, for I knew Mrs.
le Fay by reputation, and was not expecting anything pleasant. She
was held in awe by the whole realm, for she had made everybody
believe she was a great sorceress. All her ways were wicked, all her

instincts devilish. She was loaded to the eye-lids with cold malice.
All her history was black with crime; and among her crimes murder
was common. I was most curious to see her; as curious as I could
have been to see Satan. To my surprise she was beautiful; black
thoughts had failed to make her expression repulsive, age had
failed to wrinkle her satin skin or mar its bloomy freshness. She
could have passed for old Urien's grand-daughter, she could have
been mistaken for sister to her own son.

As soon as we were fairly within the castle gates we were ordered
into her presence. King Uriens was there, a kind-faced old man with
a subdued look; and also the son, Sir Uwaine le Blanchemains, in
whom I was of course interested on account of the tradition that he
had once done battle with thirty knights, and also on account of
his trip with Sir Gawaine and Sir Marhaus, which Sandy had
been aging me with. But Morgan was the main attraction, the
conspicuous personality here; she was head chief of this household,
that was plain. She caused us to be seated, and then she began
with all manner of pretty graces and graciousnesses, to ask me
questions. Dear me, it was like a bird or a flute, or something,
talking. I felt persuaded that this woman must have been
misrepresented, lied about. She trilled along, and trilled along, and
presently a handsome young page, clothed like the rainbow, and
as easy and undulatory of movement as a wave, came with something
on a golden salver, and kneeling to present it to her, overdid his
graces and lost his balance, and so fell lightly against her knee.
She slipped a dirk into him in as matter-of-course a way as another
person would have harpooned a rat!

Poor child, he slumped to the floor, twisted his silken limbs in
one great straining contortion of pain, and was dead. Out of the old
king was wrung an involuntary "O-h!" of compassion. The look he
got, made him cut it suddenly short and not put any more hyphens
in it. Sir Uwaine, at a sign from his mother, went to the ante-room
and called some servants, and meanwhile madame went rippling
sweetly along with her talk.

I saw that she was a good housekeeper, for while she talked she
kept a corner of her eye on the servants to see that they made no
balks in handling the body and getting it out; when they came with
fresh clean towels, she sent back for the other kind; and when they
had finished wiping the floor and were going, she indicated a
crimson fleck the size of a tear which their duller eyes had
overlooked. It was plain to me that La Cote Male Taile had failed
to see the mistress of the house. Often, how louder and clearer than
any tongue, does dumb circumstantial evidence speak.

Morgan le Fay rippled along as musically as ever. Marvellous
woman. And what a glance she had: when it fell in reproof upon
those servants, they shrank and quailed as timid people do when
the lightning flashes out of a cloud. I could have got the habit

myself. It was the same with that poor old Brer Uriens; he was always on the ragged edge of apprehension; she could not even turn toward him but he winced.

In the midst of the talk I let drop a complimentary word about King Arthur, forgetting for the moment how this woman hated her brother. That one little compliment was enough. She clouded up like a storm; she called for her guards, and said—

"Hale me these varlets to the dungeons."

That struck cold on my ears, for her dungeons had a reputation. Nothing occurred to me to say—or do. But not so with Sandy. As the guard laid a hand upon me, she piped up with the tranquilest confidence, and said—

"God's wownds, dost thou covet destruction, thou maniac? It is The Boss!"

Now what a happy idea that was!—and so simple; yet it would never have occurred to me. I was born modest; not all over, but in spots; and this was one of the spots.

The effect upon madame was electrical. It cleared her countenance and brought back her smiles and all her persuasive graces and blandishments; but nevertheless she was not able to entirely cover up with them the fact that she was in a ghastly fright. She said:

"La, but do list to thine handmaid! as if one gifted with powers like to mine might say the thing which I have said unto one who has vanquished Merlin, and not be jesting. By mine enchantments I foresaw your coming, and by them I knew you when you entered here. I did but play this little jest with hope to surprise you into some display of your art, as not doubting you would blast the guards with occult fires, consuming them to ashes on the spot, a marvel much beyond mine own ability, yet one which I have long been childishly curious to see."

The guards were less curious, and got out as soon as they got permission.

CHAPTER XVII

A ROYAL BANQUET

Madame seeing me pacific and unresentful, no doubt judged that I was deceived by her excuse; for her fright dissolved away, and she was soon so importunate to have me give an exhibition and kill somebody, that the thing grew to be embarrassing. However, to my relief she was presently interrupted by the call to prayers. I will say this much for the nobility: that, tyrannical, murderous, rapacious and morally rotten as they were, they were deeply and enthusiastically religious. Nothing could divert them from the

regular and faithful performance of the pieties enjoined by the
Church. More than once I had seen a noble who had gotten his
enemy at a disadvantage, stop to pray before cutting his throat;
more than once I had seen a noble, after ambushing and
despatching his enemy, retire to the nearest wayside shrine and
humbly give thanks, without ever waiting to rob the body. There
was to be nothing finer or sweeter in the life of even Benvenuto
Cellini, that rough-hewn saint, ten centuries later. All of the nobles
of Britain, with their families, attended divine service morning and
night daily, in their private chapels, and even the worst of them had
family worship five or six times a day besides. The credit of this
belonged entirely to the Church. Although I was no friend to that
Catholic Church, I was obliged to admit this. And often, in spite of
me, I found myself saying. "What would this country be without
the Church?"

After prayers we had dinner in a great banqueting hall which was
lighted by hundreds of grease-jets, and everything was as fine and
lavish and rudely splendid as might become the royal degree of the
hosts. At the head of the hall, on a dais, was the table of the king,
queen, and their son, Prince Uwaine. Stretching down the hall from
this, was the general table, on the floor. At this, above the salt, sat
the visiting nobles and the grown members of their families, of both
sexes,—the resident Court, in effect—sixty-one persons; below the
salt sat minor officers of the household, with their principal
subordinates: altogether a hundred and eighteen persons sitting,
and about as many liveried servants standing behind their chairs, or
serving in one capacity or another. It was a very fine show. In a
gallery a band with cymbals, horns, harps and other horrors, opened
the proceedings with what seemed to be the crude first-draft or
original agony of the wail known to later centuries as "In the Sweet
Bye and Bye." It was new, and ought to have been rehearsed a little
more. For some reason or other the queen had the composer hanged,
after dinner.

After this music, the priest who stood behind the royal table said a
noble long grace in ostensible Latin. Then the battalion of waiters
broke away from their posts, and darted, rushed, flew, fetched and
carried, and the mighty feeding began; no words anywhere, but
absorbing attention to business. The rows of chops opened and shut
in vast unison, and the sound of it was like to the muffled burr of
subterranean machinery.

The havoc continued an hour and a half, and unimaginable was
the destruction of substantials. Of the chief feature of the feast—the
huge wild boar that lay stretched out so portly and imposing at the
start—nothing was left but the semblance of a hoop-skirt; and he
was but the type and symbol of what had happened to all the
other dishes.

With the pastries and so-on, the heavy drinking began—and the talk. Gallon after gallon of wine and mead disappeared, and everybody got comfortable, then happy, then sparklingly joyous—both sexes,—and by-and-by pretty noisy. Men told anecdotes that were terrific to hear, but nobody blushed; and when the nub was sprung, the assemblage let go with a horse-laugh that shook the fortress. Ladies answered back with historiettes that would almost have made Queen Margaret of Navarre or even the great Elizabeth of England hide behind a handkerchief, but nobody hid here, but only laughed—howled, you may say. In pretty much all of these dreadful stories, ecclesiastics were the hardy heroes, but that didn't worry the chaplain any, he had his laugh with the rest; more than that, upon invitation he roared out a song which was of as daring a sort as any that was sung that night.

By midnight everybody was fagged out, and sore with laughing; and as a rule, drunk: some weepingly, some affectionately, some hilariously, some quarrelsomely, some dead and under the table. Of the ladies, the worst spectacle was a lovely young duchess, whose wedding-eve this was; and indeed she was a spectacle, sure enough. Just as she was she could have sat in advance for the portrait of the young daughter of the Regent d'Orleans, at the famous dinner whence she was carried, foul-mouthed, intoxicated and helpless, to her bed, in the lost and lamented days of the Ancient Regime.

Suddenly, even while the priest was lifting his hands, and all conscious heads were bowed in reverent expectation of the coming blessing, there appeared under the arch of the far-off door at the bottom of the hall, an old and bent and white-haired lady, leaning upon a crutch-stick; and she lifted the stick and pointed it toward the queen and cried out—

"The wrath and curse of God fall upon you, woman without pity, who have slain mine innocent grandchild and made desolate this old heart that had nor chick nor friend nor stay nor comfort in all this world but him!"

Everybody crossed himself in a grisly fright, for a curse was an awful thing to those people; but the queen rose up majestic, with the death-light in her eye, and flung back this ruthless command:

"Lay hands on her! To the stake with her!"

The guards left their posts to obey. It was a shame; it was a cruel thing to see. What could be done? Sandy gave me a look; I knew she had another inspiration. I said—

"Do what you choose."

She was up and facing toward the queen in a moment. She indicated me, and said:

"Madame, *he* saith this may not be. Recall the commandment, or he will dissolve the castle and it shall vanish away like the instable fabric of a dream!"

Confound it, what a crazy contract to pledge a person to! What if the queen—

But my consternation subsided there, and my panic passed off; for
the queen, all in a collapse, made no show of resistance but gave a
countermanding sign and sunk into her seat. When she reached it
she was sober. So were many of the others. The assemblage rose,
whiffed ceremony to the winds, and rushed for the door like a mob;
overturning chairs, smashing crockery, tugging, struggling,
shouldering, crowding—anything to get out before I should change
my mind and puff the castle into the measureless dim vacancies of
space. Well, well, well, they *were* a superstitious lot. It is all a body
can do to conceive of it.

The poor queen was so scared and humbled that she was even
afraid to hang the composer without first consulting me. I was very
sorry for her—indeed any one would have been, for she was really
suffering; so I was willing to do anything that was reasonable, and
had no desire to carry things to wanton extremities. I therefore
considered the matter thoughtfully, and ended by having the
musicians ordered into our presence to play that Sweet Bye and Bye
again, which they did. Then I saw that she was right, and gave her
permission to hang the whole band. This little relaxation of
sternness had a good effect upon the queen. A statesman gains little
by the arbitrary exercise of iron-clad authority upon all occasions
that offer, for this wounds the just pride of his subordinates, and
thus tends to undermine his strength. A little concession, now and
then, where it can do no harm, is the wiser policy.

Now that the queen was at ease in her mind once more, and
measurably happy, her wine naturally began to assert itself again,
and it got a little the start of her. I mean it set her music going—her
silver bell of a tongue. Dear me, she was a master talker. It would not
become me to suggest that it was pretty late and that I was a tired
man and very sleepy. I wished I had gone off to bed when I had the
chance. Now I must stick it out; there was no other way. So she
tinkled along and along, in the otherwise profound and ghostly hush
of the sleeping castle, until by-and-by there came, as if from deep
down under us, a faraway sound, as of a muffled shriek—with an
expression of agony about it that made my flesh crawl. The queen
stopped, and her eyes lighted with pleasure; she tilted her graceful
head as a bird does when it listens. The sound bored its way up
through the stillness again.

"What is it?" I said.

"It is a truly a stubborn soul, and endureth long. It is many
hours now."

"Endureth what?"

"The rack. Come—ye shall see a blithe sight. An he yield not his
secret now, ye shall see him torn asunder."

What a silky smooth hellion she was; and so composed and
serene, when the cords all down my legs were hurting in sympathy
with that man's pain. Conducted by mailed guards bearing flaring

torches, we tramped along echoing corridors, and down stone
stairways dank and dripping, and smelling of mould and ages of
imprisoned night—a chill, uncanny journey and a long one, and not
made the shorter or the cheerier by the sorceress's talk, which was
about this sufferer and his crime. He had been accused by an
anonymous informer, of having killed a stag in the royal preserves.
I said—

"Anonymous testimony isn't just the right thing, your Highness.
It were fairer to confront the accused with the accuser."

"I had not thought of that, it being but of small consequence.
But an I would, I could not, for that the accuser came masked by
night, and told the forester, and straightway got him hence again,
and so the forester knoweth him not."

"Then is this Unknown the only person who saw the stag killed?"

"Marry, *no* man *saw* the killing, but this Unknown saw this hardy
wretch near to the spot where the stag lay, and came with right loyal
zeal and betrayed him to the forester."

"So the Unknown was near the dead stag, too? Isn't it just
possible that he did the killing himself? His loyal zeal—in a mask—
looks just a shade suspicious. But what is your Highness's idea for
racking the prisoner? Where is the profit?"

"He will not confess, else; and then were his soul lost. For his
crime his life is forfeited by the law—and of a surety will I see that he
payeth it!—but it were peril to my own soul to let him die
unconfessed and unabsolved. Nay, I were a fool to fling me into hell
for *his* accommodation."

"But, your Highness, suppose he has nothing to confess?"

"As to that, we shall see, anon. An I rack him to death and he
confess not, it will peradventure show that he had indeed naught to
confess—ye will grant that that is sooth? Then shall I not be damned
for an unconfessed man that had naught to confess—wherefore,
I shall be safe."

It was the stubborn unreasoning of the time. It was useless to
argue with her. Arguments have no chance against petrified
training; they wear it as little as the waves wear a cliff. And her
training was everybody's. The brightest intellect in the land would
not have been able to see that her position was defective.

As we entered the rack-cell I caught a picture that will not go from
me; I wish it would. A native young giant of thirty or thereabouts,
lay stretched upon the frame on his back, with his wrists and ankles
tied to ropes which led over windlasses at either end. There was no
color in him; his features were contorted and set, and sweat-drops
stood upon his forehead. A priest bent over him on each side; the
executioner stood by; guards were on duty; smoking torches stood in
sockets along the walls; in a corner crouched a poor young creature,
her face drawn with anguish, a half-wild and hunted look in her
eyes, and in her lap lay a little child asleep. Just as we stepped across

the threshold the executioner gave his machine a slight turn, which
wrung a cry from both the prisoner and the woman; but I shouted
and the executioner released the strain without waiting to see who
spoke. I could not let this horror go on; it would have killed me to see
it. I asked the queen to let me clear the place and speak to the
prisoner privately; and when she was going to object I spoke in a
low voice and said I did not want to make a scene before her
servants, but I must have my way; for I was King Arthur's
representative, and was speaking in his name. She saw she had to
yield. I asked her to indorse me to these people, and then leave me.
It was not pleasant for her, but she took the pill; and even went
further than I was meaning to require. I only wanted the backing of
her own authority; but she said—

"Ye will do in all things as this lord shall command. It is
The Boss."

It was certainly a good word to conjure with: you could see it by
the squirming of these rats. The queen's guards fell into line, and
she and they marched away, with their torch-bearers, and woke the
echoes of the cavernous tunnels with the measured beat of their
retreating foot-falls. I had the prisoner taken from the rack and
placed upon his bed, and medicaments applied to his hurts, and
wine given him to drink. The woman crept near and looked on,
eagerly, lovingly, but timorously,—like one who fears a repulse;
indeed, she tried furtively to touch the man's forehead, and jumped
back, the picture of fright, when I turned unconsciously toward her.
It was pitiful to see.

"Lord," I said, "stroke him, lass, if you want to. Do anything
you're a mind to; don't mind me."

Why, her eyes were as grateful as an animal's, when you do it a
kindness that it understands. The baby was out of her way and she
had her cheek against the man's in a minute, and her hands
fondling his hair, and her happy tears running down. The man
revived, and caressed his wife with his eyes, which was all he could
do. I judged I might clear the den, now, and I did; cleared it of all
but the family and myself. Then I said—

"Now my friend, tell me your side of this matter; I know the
other side."

The man moved his head in sign of refusal. But the woman looked
pleased—as it seemed to me—pleased with my suggestion. I went
on:

"You know of me?"

"Yes. All do, in Arthur's realms."

"If my reputation has come to you right and straight, you should
not be afraid to speak."

The woman broke in, eagerly:

"Ah, fair my lord, do thou persuade him! Thou canst an thou

wilt. Ah, he suffereth so; and it is for me—for *me!* And how can I
bear it? I would I might see him die—a sweet, swift death; oh, my
Hugo, I cannot bear this one!"

And she fell to sobbing and grovelling about my feet, and still
imploring. Imploring what? The man's death? I could not quite get
the bearings of the thing. But Hugo interrupted her and said—

"Peace! Ye wit not what ye ask. Shall I starve whom I love, to win
a gentle death? I wend thou knewest me better."

"Well," I said, "I can't quite make this out. It is a puzzle. Now—"

"Ah, dear my lord, an ye will but persuade him! Consider how
these his tortures wound me! Oh, and he will not speak!—whereas,
the healing, the solace that lie in a blessed swift death—"

"What *are* you maundering about? He's going out from here a
free man and whole—he's not going to die."

The man's white face lit up, and the woman flung herself at me in
a most surprising explosion of joy, and cried out—

"He is saved!—for it is the king's word by the mouth of the king's
servant—Arthur, the king whose word is gold!"

"Well, then you do believe I can be trusted, after all. Why didn't
you before?"

"Who doubted? Not I, indeed; and not she."

"Well, why wouldn't you tell me your story, then?"

"Ye had made no promise; else had it been otherwise."

"I see, I see. . . . And yet I believe I don't quite see, after all.
You stood the torture and refused to confess; which shows plain
enough to even the dullest understanding that you had nothing
to confess—"

"*I,* my lord? How so? It was I that killed the deer!"

"You *did?* Oh, dear, this is the most mixed-up business
that ever—"

"Dear lord, I begged him on my knees to confess, but—"

"You *did!* It gets thicker and thicker. What did you want him to
do that for?"

"Sith it would bring him a quick death and save him all this
cruel pain."

"Well—yes, there is reason in that. But *he* didn't want the
quick death."

"He? Why, of surety he *did*."

"Well, then, why in the world *didn't* he confess?"

"Ah, sweet sir, and leave my wife and chick without bread
and shelter?"

"Oh, heart of gold, now I see it! The bitter law takes the convicted
man's estate and beggars his widow and his orphans. They could
torture you to death, but without conviction or confession they could
not rob your wife and baby. You stood by them like a man; and
you—true wife and true woman that you are—you would have

brought him release from torture at cost to yourself of slow
starvation and death—well, it humbles a body to think what your sex
can do when it comes to self-sacrifice. I'll book you both for my
colony; you'll like it there; it's a Factory where I'm going to turn
groping and grubbing automata into *men.*"

CHAPTER XVIII

IN THE QUEEN'S DUNGEONS

Well, I arranged all that; and I had the man sent to his home. I
had a great desire to rack the executioner; not because he was a
good, pains-taking and pain-giving official,—for surely it was not to
his discredit that he performed his functions well—but to pay him
back for wantonly cuffing and otherwise distressing that young
woman. The priests told me about this, and were generously hot to
have him punished. Something of this disagreeable sort was turning
up every now and then. I mean, episodes that showed that not all
priests were frauds and self-seekers, but that many, even the great
majority, of these that were down on the ground among the common
people, were sincere and right-hearted, and devoted to the
alleviation of human troubles and sufferings. Well, it was a thing
which could not be helped, so I seldom fretted about it, and never
many minutes at a time; it has never been my way to bother much
about things which you can't cure. But I did not like it, for it
was just the sort of thing to keep people reconciled to an Established
Church. We *must* have a religion—it goes without saying—but my
idea is, to have it cut up into forty free sects, so that they will police
each other, as had been the case in the United States in my time.
Concentration of power in a political machine is bad; and an
Established Church is only a political machine; it was invented for
that; it is nursed, cradled, preserved for that; it is an enemy to
human liberty, and does no good which it could not better do in a
split-up and scattered condition. That wasn't law; it wasn't gospel:
it was only an opinion—my opinion, and I was only a man, one
man: so it wasn't worth any more than the pope's—or any less, for
that matter.

Well, I couldn't rack the executioner, neither would I overlook the
just complaint of the priests. The man must be punished somehow
or other, so I degraded him from his office and made him leader of
the band—the new one that was to be started. He begged hard, and
said he couldn't play—a plausible excuse, but too thin; there wasn't
a musician in the country that could.

The queen was a good deal outraged, next morning, when she
found she was going to have neither Hugo's life nor his property.
But I told her she must bear this cross; that while by law and custom

she certainly was entitled to both the man's life and his property, there were extenuating circumstances, and so in Arthur the king's name I had pardoned him. The deer was ravaging the man's fields, and he had killed it in sudden passion, and not for gain; and he had carried it into the royal forest in the hope that that might make detection of the misdoer impossible. Confound her, I couldn't make her see that sudden passion is an extenuating circumstance in the killing of venison—or of a person—so I gave it up and let her sulk it out. I *did* think I was going to make her see it by remarking that her own sudden passion in the case of the page modified that crime.

"Crime!" she exclaimed. "How thou talkest! Crime, forsooth! Man, I am going to *pay* for him!"

Oh, it was no use to waste sense on her. Training—training is everything; training is all there is *to* a person. We speak of nature; it is folly; there is no such thing as nature; what we call by that misleading name is merely heredity and training. We have no thoughts of our own, no opinions of our own; they are transmitted to us, trained into us. All that is original in us, and therefore fairly creditable or discreditable to us, can be covered up and hidden by the point of a cambric needle, all the rest being atoms contributed by, and inherited from, a procession of ancestors that stretches back a billion years to the Adam-clam or grasshopper or monkey from whom our race has been so tediously and ostentatiously and unprofitably developed. And as for me, all that I think about in this plodding sad pilgrimage, this pathetic drift between the eternities, is to look out and humbly live a pure and high and blameless life, and save that one microscopic atom in me that is truly *me:* the rest may land in Sheol and welcome for all I care.

No, confound her, her intellect was good, she had brains enough, but her training made her an ass—that is, from a many-centuries-later point of view. To kill the page was no crime—it was her right; and upon her right she stood, serenely and unconscious of offence. She was a result of generations of training in the unexamined and unassailed belief that the law which permitted her to kill a subject when she chose was a perfectly right and righteous one.

Well, we must give even Satan his due. She deserved a compliment for one thing; and I tried to pay it, but the words stuck in my throat. She had a right to kill the boy, but she was in no wise obliged to pay for him. That was law for some other people, but not for her. She knew quite well that she was doing a large and generous thing to pay for that lad, and that I ought in common fairness to come out with something handsome about it, but I couldn't—my mouth refused. I couldn't help seeing, in my fancy, that poor old grandma with the broken heart, and that fair young creature lying butchered, his little silken pomps and vanities laced with his golden blood. How could she *pay* for him! *Whom* could she pay? And so, well knowing that this woman, trained as she had been, deserved praise, even

adulation, I was yet not able to utter it, trained as *I* had been. The
best I could do was to fish up a compliment from outside, so to
speak—and the pity of it was, that it was true:

"Madame, your people will adore you for this."

Quite true, but I meant to hang her for it some day, if I lived.
Some of those laws were too bad, altogether too bad. A master
might kill his slave for nothing: for mere spite, malice, or to pass the
time—just as we have seen that the crowned head could do it with
his slave, that is to say, anybody. A gentleman could kill a free
commoner, and pay for him—cash or garden-truck. A noble could
kill a noble without expense, as far as the law was concerned, but
reprisals in kind were to be expected. *Any*body could kill *some*body,
except the commoner and the slave; these had no privileges. If they
killed, it was murder, and the law wouldn't stand murder. It made
short work of the experimenter—and of his family too, if he
murdered somebody who belonged up among the ornamental ranks.
If a commoner gave a noble even so much as a Damiens-scratch
which didn't kill or even hurt, he got Damiens's dose for it just the
same; they pulled him to rags and tatters with horses, and all the
world came to see the show, and crack jokes, and have a good time;
and some of the performances of the best people present were as
tough, and as properly unprintable, as any that have been printed by
the pleasant Casanova in his chapter about the dismemberment of
Louis X V.'s poor awkward enemy.

I had had enough of this grisly place by this time, and wanted to
leave, but I couldn't, because I had something on my mind that
my conscience kept prodding me about, and wouldn't let me forget.
If I had the remaking of man, he wouldn't have any conscience. It
is one of the most disagreeable things connected with a person;
and although it certainly does a great deal of good, it cannot be
said to pay, in the long run; it would be much better to have less
good and more comfort. Still, this is only my opinion, and I am only
one man; others, with less experience, may think differently. They
have a right to their view. I only stand to this: I have noticed my
conscience for many years, and I know it is more trouble and bother
to me than anything else I started with. I suppose that in the
beginning I prized it, because we prize anything that is ours; and
yet how foolish it was to think so. If we look at it in another way,
we see how absurd it is: if I had an anvil in me would I prize
it? Of course not. And yet when you come to think, there is no real
difference between a conscience and an anvil—I mean for comfort.
I have noticed it a thousand times. And you could dissolve an anvil
with acids, when you couldn't stand it any longer; but there isn't
any way that you can work off a conscience—at least so it will stay
worked off; not that I know of, anyway.

There was something I wanted to do before leaving, but it was a
disagreeable matter, and I hated to go at it. Well, it bothered me all

the morning. I could have mentioned it to the old king, but what would be the use?—he was but an extinct volcano; he had been active in his time, but his fire was out, this good while, he was only a stately ash-pile, now; gentle enough, and kindly enough for my purpose, without doubt, but not usable. He was nothing, this so-called king: the queen was the only power there. And she was a Vesuvius. As a favor, she might consent to warm a flock of sparrows for you, but then she might take that very opportunity to turn herself loose and bury a city. However, I reflected that as often as any other way, when you are expecting the worst, you get something that is not so bad, after all.

So I braced up and placed my matter before her royal Highness. I said I had been having a general jail-delivery at Camelot and among neighboring castles, and with her permission I would like to examine her collection, her bric-a-brac—that is to say, her prisoners. She resisted; but I was expecting that. But she finally consented. I was expecting that, too, but not so soon. That about ended my discomfort. She called her guards and torches, and we went down into the dungeons. These were down under the castle's foundations, and mainly were small cells hollowed out of the living rock. Some of these cells had no light at all. In one of them was a woman, in foul rags, who sat on the ground, and would not answer a question, or speak a word, but only looked up at us once or twice, through a cobweb of tangled hair, as if to see what casual thing it might be that was disturbing with sound and light the meaningless dull dream that was become her life; after that, she sat bowed, with her dirt-caked fingers idly interlocked in her lap, and gave no further sign. This poor rack of bones was a woman of middle age, apparently; but only apparently; she had been there nine years, and was eighteen when she entered. She was a commoner, and had been sent here on her bridal night by Sir Breuse Sance Pité, a neighboring lord whose vassal her father was, and to which said lord she had refused what has since been called *le droit du seigneur;* and moreover, had opposed violence to violence and spilt half a gill of his almost sacred blood. The young husband had interfered at that point, believing the bride's life in danger, and had flung the noble out into the midst of the humble and trembling wedding guests, in the parlor, and left him there astonished at this strange treatment, and implacably embittered against both bride and groom. The said lord being cramped for dungeon-room had asked the queen to accommodate his two criminals, and here in her bastile they had been ever since; hither indeed, they had come before their crime was an hour old, and had never seen each other since. Here they were, kernelled like toads in the same rock; they had passed nine pitch dark years within fifty feet of each other, yet neither knew whether the other was alive or not. All the first years, their only question had been—asked with beseechings and tears that might have moved

stones, in time, perhaps, but hearts are not stones: "Is he alive?"
"Is she alive?" But they had never got an answer; and at last that
question was not asked any more—or any other.

I wanted to see the man, after hearing all this. He was thirty-four
years old, and looked sixty. He sat upon a squared block of stone,
with his head bent down, his forearms resting on his knees, his long
hair hanging like a fringe before his face, and he was muttering to
himself. He raised his chin and looked us slowly over, in a listless
dull way, blinking with the distress of the torchlight, then dropped
his head and fell to muttering again and took no further notice of us.
There were some pathetically suggestive dumb witnesses present.
On his wrists and ankles were cicatrices, old smooth scars, and
fastened to the stone on which he sat was a chain with manacles and
fetters attached; but this apparatus lay idle on the ground, and was
thick with rust. Chains cease to be needed after the spirit has gone
out of a prisoner.

I could not rouse the man; so I said we would take him to her,
and see—to the bride who was the fairest thing in the earth to him,
once—roses, pearls and dew made flesh, for him; a wonder-work,
the master-work of nature: with eyes like no other eyes, and voice
like no other voice, and a freshness, and lithe young grace, and
beauty, that belonged properly to the creatures of dreams—as he
thought—and to no other. The sight of her would set his stagnant
blood leaping; the sight of her—

But it was a disappointment. They sat together on the ground
and looked dimly wondering into each other's faces a while, with
a sort of weak animal curiosity; then forgot each other's presence,
and dropped their eyes, and you saw that they were away again and
wandering in some far land of dreams and shadows that we know
nothing about.

I had them taken out and sent to their friends. The queen did not
like it much. Not that she felt any personal interest in the matter,
but she thought it disrespectful to Sir Breuse Sance Pité. However, I
assured her that if he found he couldn't stand it I would fix him so
that he could.

I set forty-seven prisoners loose out of those awful rat-holes, and
left only one in captivity. He was a lord, and had killed another lord,
a sort of kinsman of the queen. That other lord had ambushed him
to assassinate him, but this fellow had got the best of him and cut
his throat. However, it was not for that that I left him jailed, but for
maliciously destroying the only public well in one of his wretched
villages. The queen was bound to hang him for killing her kinsman,
but I would not allow it: it was no crime to kill an assassin. But I
said I was willing to let her hang him for destroying the well; so she
concluded to put up with that, as it was better than nothing.

Dear me, for what trifling offences the most of those forty-seven
men and women were shut up there! Indeed, some were there for no

distinct offence at all, but only to gratify somebody's spite; and not
always the queen's by any means, but a friend's. The newest
prisoner's crime was a mere remark which he had made. He said he
believed that men were about all alike, and one man as good as
another, barring clothes. He said he believed that if you were to
strip the nation naked and send a stranger through the crowd, he
couldn't tell the king from a quack doctor, nor a duke from a hotel
clerk. Apparently here was a man whose brains had not been
reduced to an ineffectual mush by idiotic training. I set him loose
and sent him to the Factory.

Some of the cells carved in the living rock were just behind the
face of the precipice, and in each of these an arrow-slit had been
pierced outward to the daylight, and so the captive had a thin ray
from the blessed sun for his comfort. The case of one of these poor
fellows was particularly hard. From his dusky swallow's hole high up
in that vast wall of native rock he could peer out through the
arrow-slit and see his own home off yonder in the valley; and for
twenty-two years he had watched it, with heart-ache and longing,
through that crack. He could see the lights shine there at night, and
in the daytime he could see figures go in and come out—his wife and
children, some of them, no doubt, though he could not make out, at
that distance. In the course of years he noted festivities there, and
tried to rejoice, and wondered if they were weddings or what they
might be. And he noted funerals; and they wrung his heart. He could
make out the coffin, but he could not determine its size, and so could
not tell whether it was wife or child. He could see the procession
form, with priests and mourners, and move solemnly away, bearing
the secret with them. He had left behind him five children and a
wife; and in nineteen years he had seen five funerals issue, and none
of them humble enough in pomp to denote a servant. So he had lost
five of his treasures; there must still be one remaining—one now
infinitely, unspeakably precious,—but *which* one? wife, or child?
That was the question that tortured him, by night and by day, asleep
and awake. Well, to have an interest, of some sort, and half a ray of
light, when you are in a dungeon, is a great support to the body and
preserver of the intellect. This man was in pretty good condition
yet. By the time he had finished telling me his distressful tale,
I was in the same state of mind that you would have been in yourself,
if you have got average human curiosity: that is to say, I was as
burning up as he was to find out which member of the family it was
that was left. So I took him over home myself; and an amazing kind
of a surprise party it was, too—typhoons and cyclones of frantic
joy, and whole Niagaras of happy tears; and by George we found the
aforetime young matron graying toward the imminent verge of her
half century, and the babies all men and women, and some of them
married and experimenting familywise themselves—for not a soul
of the tribe was dead! Conceive of the ingenious devilishness of that

queen: she had a special hatred for this prisoner, and she had *invented* all those funerals herself, to scorch his heart with; and the sublimest stroke of genius of the whole thing was leaving the family-invoice a funeral *short,* so as to let him wear his poor old soul out guessing.

But for me, he never would have got out. Morgan le Fay hated him with her whole heart, and she never would have softened toward him. And yet his crime was committed more in thoughtlessness than deliberate depravity. He had said she had red hair. Well, she had; but that was no way to speak of it. When red-headed people are above a certain social grade their hair is auburn.

Consider it: among these forty-seven captives there were five whose names, offences, and dates of incarceration were no longer known! One woman and four men—all bent, and wrinkled, and mind-extinguished patriarchs. They themselves had long ago forgotten these details; at any rate they had mere vague theories about them, nothing definite and nothing that they repeated twice in the same way. The succession of priests whose office it had been to pray daily with the captives and remind them that God had put them there, for some wise purpose or other, and teach them that patience, humbleness, and submission to oppression was what He loved to see in parties of a subordinate rank, had traditions about these poor old human ruins, but nothing more. These traditions went but little way, for they concerned the length of the incarceration only, and not the names of the offences. And even by the help of tradition the only thing that could be proven was that none of the five had seen daylight for thirty-five years: how much longer this privation had lasted was not guessable. The king and the queen knew nothing about these poor creatures, except that they were heirlooms, assets inherited, along with the throne, from the former firm. Nothing of their history had been transmitted with their persons, and so the inheriting owners had considered them of no value, and had felt no interest in them. I said to the queen—

"Then why in the world didn't you set them free?"

The question was a puzzler. She didn't know *why* she hadn't; the thing had never come up in her mind. So here she was, forecasting the veritable history of future prisoners of the Castle d'If, without knowing it. It seemed plain to me now, that with her training, those inherited prisoners were merely property—nothing more, nothing less. Well, when we inherit property, it does not occur to us to throw it away, even when we do not value it.

When I brought my procession of human bats up into the open world and the glare of the afternoon sun—previously blind-folding them, in charity for eyes so long untortured by light—they were a spectacle to look at. Skeletons, scarecrows, goblins, pathetic frights, every one: legitimatest possible children of Monarchy by the Grace of God and the Established Church. I muttered absently—

"I *wish* I could photograph them!"

You have seen that kind of people who will never let on that they don't know the meaning of a new big word. The more ignorant they are, the more pitifully certain they are to pretend you haven't shot over their heads. The queen was just one of that sort, and was always making the stupidest blunders by reason of it. She hesitated a moment; then her face brightened up with sudden comprehension, and she said she would do it for me.

I thought to myself: She? why what can she know about photography? But it was a poor time to be thinking. When I looked around, she was moving on the procession with an axe!

Well, she certainly was a curious one, was Morgan le Fay. I have seen a good many kinds of women in my time, but she laid over them all, for variety. And how sharply characteristic of her this episode was. She had no more idea than a horse, of how to photograph a procession; but being in doubt, it was just like her to try to do it with an axe.

CHAPTER XIX

KNIGHT ERRANTRY AS A TRADE

Sandy and I were on the road again, next morning, bright and early. It was *so* good to open up one's lungs and take in whole luscious barrels-full of the blessed God's untainted, dew-freshened, woodland-scented air once more, after suffocating body and mind for two days and nights in the moral and physical stenches of that intolerable old buzzard-roost! I mean, for me: of course the place was all right and agreeable enough for Sandy, for she had been used to high life all her days.

Poor girl, her jaws had had a wearisome rest, now for a while, and I was expecting to get the consequences. I was right; but she had stood by me most helpfully in the castle, and had mightily supported and reinforced me with gigantic foolishnesses which were worth more for the occasion than wisdoms double their size; so I thought she had earned a right to work her mill for a while, if she wanted to, and I felt not a pang when she started it up:

"Now turn we unto Sir Marhaus that rode with the damsel of thirty winter of age southward—"

"Are you going to see if you can work up another half-stretch on the trail of the cowboys, Sandy?"

"Even so, fair my lord."

"Go ahead, then. I won't interrupt this time, if I can help it. Begin over again; start fair, and shake out all your reefs, and I will load my pipe and give good attention."

"Now turn we unto Sir Marhaus that rode with the damsel of

thirty winter of age southward. And so they came into a deep forest,
and by fortune they were nighted, and rode along in a deep way,
and at the last they came into a courtelage where abode the duke of
South Marches, and there they asked harbour. And on the morn the
duke sent unto Sir Marhaus, and bad him make him ready. And so
Sir Marhaus arose and armed him, and there was a mass sung
afore him, and he brake his fast, and so mounted on horseback
in the court of the castle, there they should do the battle. So there
was the duke already on horseback, clean armed, and his six
sons by him, and every each had a spear in his hand, and so they
encountered, whereas the duke and his two sons brake their spears
upon him, but Sir Marhaus held up his spear and touched none of
them. Then came the four sons by couples, and two of them brake
their spears, and so did the other two. And all this while Sir
Marhaus touched them not. Then Sir Marhaus ran to the duke, and
smote him with his spear that horse and man fell to the earth. And
so he served his sons. And then Sir Marhaus alight down, and bad
the duke yield him or else he would slay him. And then some of his
sons recovered, and would have set upon Sir Marhaus. Then Sir
Marhaus said to the duke, Cease thy sons, or else I will do the
uttermost to you all. When the duke saw he might not escape the
death, he cried to his sons, and charged them to yield them to Sir
Marhaus. And they kneeled all down and put the pommels of their
swords to the knight, and so he received them. And then they holp
up their father, and so by their common assent promised unto Sir
Marhaus never to be foes unto King Arthur, and thereupon at
Whitsuntide after, to come he and his sons, and put them in the
king's grace.*

"Even so standeth the history, fair Sir Boss. Now ye shall wit that
that very duke and his six sons are they whom but few days past
you also did overcome and send to Arthur's court!"

"Why, Sandy, you can't mean it!"

"An I speak not sooth, let it be the worse for me."

"Well, well, well,—now who would ever have thought it? One
whole duke and six dukelets; why, Sandy, it was an elegant haul.
Knight-errantry is a most chuckle-headed trade, and it is tedious
hard work, too, but I begin to see that there *is* money in it, after all,
if you have luck. Not that I would ever engage in it as a business;
for I wouldn't. No sound and legitimate business can be established
on a basis of speculation. A successful whirl in the knight-errantry
line—now what is it when you blow away the nonsense and come
down to the cold facts? It's just a corner in pork, that's all and
you can't make anything else out of it. You're rich—yes,—suddenly
rich—for about a day, maybe a week: then somebody corners the
market on *you*, and down goes your bucket-shop; ain't that so,
Sandy?"

*The story is borrowed, language and all, from the *Morte d'Arthur.* —M.T.

"Whethersoever it be that my mind miscarrieth, bewraying simple language in such sort that the words do seem to come endlong and overthwart—"

"There's no use in beating about the bush and trying to get around it that way, Sandy, it's *so*, just as I say, I *know* it's so. And, moreover, when you come right down to the bed-rock, knight-errantry is *worse* than pork; for whatever happens, the pork's left, and so somebody's benefited, anyway; but when the market breaks, in a knight-errantry whirl, and every knight in the pool passes in his checks, what have you got for assets? Just a rubbish-pile of battered corpses and a barrel or two of busted hardware. Can you call *those* assets? Give me pork, every time. Am I right?"

"Ah, peradventure my head being distraught by the manifold matters whereunto the confusions of these but late adventured haps and fortunings whereby not I alone nor you alone, but every each of us, meseemeth—"

"No, it's not your head, Sandy. Your head's all right, as far as it goes, but you don't know business; that's where the trouble is. It unfits you to argue about business, and you're wrong to be always trying. However, that aside, it was a good haul, anyway, and will breed a handsome crop of reputation in Arthur's court. And speaking of the cowboys, what a curious country this is for women and men that never get old. Now there's Morgan le Fay, as fresh and young as a Vassar pullet, to all appearances, and here is this old duke of the South Marches still slashing away with sword and lance at his time of life, after raising such a family as he has raised. As I understand it, Sir Gawaine killed seven of his sons, and still he had six left for Sir Marhaus and me to take into camp. And then there was that damsel of sixty winter of age still excursioning around in her frosty bloom— How old are you, Sandy?"

It was the first time I ever struck a still place in her. The mill had shut down for repairs, or something.

CHAPTER XX

THE OGRE'S CASTLE

Between six and nine we made ten miles, which was plenty for a horse carrying triple—man, woman, and armor; then we stopped for a long nooning, under some trees by a limpid brook.

Right so came by-and-by a knight riding; and as he drew near he made dolorous moan, and by the words of it I perceived that he was cursing and swearing; yet nevertheless was I glad of his coming, for that I saw he bore a bulletin-board whereon in letters all of shining gold was writ—

"USE PETERSON'S PROPHYLACTIC TOOTH-BRUSH
—ALL THE GO."

I was glad of his coming, for even by this token I knew him for
knight of mine. It was Sir Madok de la Montaine, a burly great
fellow whose chief distinction was that he had come within an ace of
sending Sir Launcelot down over his horse-tail once. He was never
long in a stranger's presence without finding some pretext or other
to let out that great fact. But there was another fact of nearly the
same size, which he never pushed upon anybody unasked, and yet
never withheld when asked: that was, that the reason he didn't
quite succeed was, that he was interrupted and sent down over
horse-tail himself. This innocent vast lubber did not see any
particular difference between the two facts. I liked him, for he was
earnest in his work, and very valuable. And he was so fine to look at,
with his broad mailed shoulders, and the grand leonine set of his
plumed head, and his big shield with its quaint device of a
gauntleted hand clutching a prophylactic tooth-brush, with motto:
"Try Noyoudont." This was a tooth-wash that I was introducing.

He was aweary, he said, and indeed he looked it; but he would not
alight. He said he was after the stove-polish man; and with this he
broke out cursing and swearing anew. The bulletin-boarder referred
to was Sir Ossaise of Surluse, a brave knight, and of considerable
celebrity on account of his having tried conclusions in a tournament,
once, with no less a Mogul than Sir Gaheris himself—although not
successfully. He was of a light and laughing disposition, and to him
nothing in this world was serious. It was for this reason that I had
chosen him to work up a stove-polish sentiment. There were no
stoves yet, and so there could be nothing serious about stove-polish.
All that the agent needed to do was to deftly and by degrees prepare
the public for the great change, and have them established in
predilections toward neatness against the time when the stove should
appear upon the stage.

Sir Madok was very bitter, and brake out anew with cursings.
He said he had cursed his soul to rage; and yet he would not get
down from his horse, neither would he take any rest, or listen to
any comfort, until he should have found Sir Ossaise and settled this
account. It appeared, by what I could piece together of the
unprofane fragments of his statement, that he had chanced upon
Sir Ossaise at dawn of the morning, and been told that if he would
make a short cut across the fields and swamps and broken hills and
glades, he could head off a company of travellers who would be
rare customers for prophylactics and tooth-wash. With
characteristic zeal Sir Madok had plunged away at once upon this
quest, and after three hours of awful crosslot riding had overhauled
his game. And behold, it was the five patriarchs that had been
released from the dungeons the evening before! Poor old creatures,

it was all of twenty years since any one of them had known what it was to be equipped with any remaining snag or remnant of a tooth.

"Blank-blank-blank him," said Sir Madok, "an I do not stove-polish him an I may find him, leave it to me; for never no knight that hight Ossaise or aught else may do me this disservice and bide on live, an I may find him, the which I have thereunto sworn a great oath this day."

And with these words, and others, he lightly took his spear and gat him thence. In the middle of the afternoon we came upon one of those very patriarchs ourselves, in the edge of a poor village. He was basking in the love of relatives and friends whom he had not seen for fifty years; and about him and caressing him were also descendants of his own body whom he had never seen at all till now; but to him these were all strangers, his memory was gone, his mind was stagnant. It seemed incredible that a man could outlast half a century shut up in a dark hole like a rat, but here were his old wife and some old comrades to testify to it. They could remember him as he was in the freshness and strength of his young manhood, when he kissed his child and delivered it to its mother's hands and went away into that long oblivion. The people at the castle could not tell within half a generation the length of time the man had been shut up there for his unrecorded and forgotten offence; but this old wife knew; and so did her old child, who stood there among her married sons and daughters trying to realize a father who had been to her a name, a thought, a formless image, a tradition, all her life, and now was suddenly concreted into actual flesh and blood and set before her face.

It was a curious situation; yet it is not on that account that I have made room for it here, but on account of a thing which seemed to me still more curious. To wit, that this dreadful matter brought from these drown-trodden people no outburst of rage against these oppressors. They had been heritors and subjects of cruelty and outrage so long that nothing could have startled them but a kindness. Yes, here was a curious revelation indeed, of the depth to which people had been sunk in slavery. Their entire being was reduced to a monotonous dead level of patience, resignation, dumb uncomplaining acceptance of whatever might befall them in this life. Their very imagination was dead. When you can say that of a man, he has struck bottom, I reckon; there is no lower deep for him.

I rather wished I had gone some other road. This was not the sort of experience for a statesman to encounter who was planning out a peaceful revolution in his mind. For it could not help bringing up the un-get-aroundable fact that, all gentle cant and philosophizing to the contrary notwithstanding, no people in the world ever did achieve their freedom by goody-goody talk and moral suasion: it being immutable law that all revolutions that will succeed, must *begin* in blood, whatever may answer afterward. If history teaches

anything, it teaches that. What this folk needed, then, was a Reign
of Terror and a guillotine, and I was the wrong man for them.

Two days later, toward noon, Sandy began to show signs of
excitement and feverish expectancy. She said we were approaching
the ogre's castle. I was surprised into an uncomfortable shock. The
object of our quest had gradually dropped out of my mind; this
sudden resurrection of it made it seem quite a real and startling
thing, for a moment, and roused up in me a smart interest. Sandy's
excitement increased every moment; and so did mine, for that sort
of thing is catching. My heart got to thumping. You can't reason
with your heart; it has its own laws, and thumps about things which
the intellect scorns. Presently, when Sandy slid from the horse,
motioned me to stop, and went creeping stealthily, with her head
bent nearly to her knees, toward a row of bushes that bordered a
declivity, the thumpings grew stronger and quicker. And they kept
it up while she was gaining her ambush and getting her glimpse
over the declivity; and also while I was creeping to her side on my
knees. Her eyes were burning, now, as she pointed with her finger,
and said in a panting whisper—

"The castle! The castle! Lo, where it looms!"

What a welcome disappointment I experienced! I said—

"Castle? It is nothing but a pig-sty; a pig-sty with a wattled fence
around it."

She looked surprised and distressed. The animation faded out of
her face; and during many moments she was lost in thought and
silent. Then—

"It was not enchanted aforetime," she said in a musing fashion,
as if to herself. "And how strange is this marvel, and how awful—
that to the one perception it is enchanted and dight in a base and
shameful aspect; yet to the perception of the other it is not
enchanted, hath suffered no change, but stands firm and stately
still, girt with its moat and waving its banners in the blue air from its
towers. And God shield us, how it pricks the heart to see again these
captives, and the sorrow deepened in their sweet faces! We have
tarried along, and are to blame."

I saw my cue. The castle was enchanted to *me*, not to her. It would
be wasted time to try to argue her out of her delusion, it couldn't be
done; I must just humor it. So I said—

"This is a common case—the enchanting of a thing to one eye and
leaving it in its proper form to another. You have heard of it before,
Sandy, though you haven't happened to experience it. But no harm
is done. In fact it is lucky the way it is. If these ladies were hogs to
everybody and to themselves, it would be necessary to break the
enchantment, and that might be impossible if one failed to find out
the particular process of the enchantment. And hazardous, too; for
in attempting a disenchantment without the true key, you are liable
to err, and turn your hogs into dogs, and the dogs into cats, the cats

into rats, and so on, and end by reducing your materials to nothing,
finally, or to an odorless gas which you can't follow—which of course
amounts to the same thing. But here, by good-luck, no one's eyes but
mine are under the enchantment, and so it is of no consequence to
dissolve it. These ladies remain ladies to you, and to themselves,
and to everybody else; and at the same time they will suffer in no way
from my delusion, for when I know that an ostensible hog is a lady,
that is enough for me, I know how to treat her."

"Thanks, oh sweet my lord, thou talkest like an angel. And I
know that thou wilt deliver them, for that thou art minded to great
deeds and art as strong a knight of your hands and as brave to will
and to do, as any that is on life."

"I will not leave a princess in the sty, Sandy. Are those three
yonder that to my disordered eyes are starveling swine-herds—"

"The ogres? Are *they* changed also? It is most wonderful. Now am
I fearful; for how canst thou strike with sure aim when five of their
nine cubits of stature are to thee invisible? Ah, go warily, fair sir;
this is a mightier emprise than I wend."

"You be easy, Sandy. All I need to know is, how *much* of an ogre is
invisible; then I know how to locate his vitals. Don't you be afraid,
I will make short work of these bunco-steerers. Stay where you are."

I left Sandy kneeling there, corpse-faced but plucky and hopeful,
and rode down to the pig-sty, and struck up a trade with the
swine-herds. I won their gratitude by buying out all the hogs at the
lump sum of sixteen pennies, which was rather above latest
quotations. I was just in time; for the Church, the lord of the manor,
and the rest of the tax gatherers would have been along next day and
swept off pretty much all the stock, leaving the swine-herds very
short of hogs and Sandy out of princesses. But now the tax people
could be paid in cash, and there would be a stake left besides. One
of the men had ten children; and he said that last year when a priest
came and of his ten pigs took the fattest one for tithes, the wife burst
out upon him, and offered him a child and said—

"Thou beast without bowels of mercy, why leave me my child, yet
rob me of the wherewithal to feed it?"

How curious. The same thing had happened in the Wales of my
day, under this same old Established Church, which was supposed
by many to have changed its nature when it changed its disguise.

I sent the three men away, and then opened the sty gate and
beckoned Sandy to come—which she did; and not leisurely, but
with the rush of a prairie-fire. And when I saw her fling herself
upon those hogs, with tears of joy running down her cheeks, and
strain them to her heart, and kiss them, and caress them, and call
them reverently by grand princely names, I was ashamed of her,
ashamed of the human race.

We had to drive those hogs home—ten miles; and no ladies were
ever more fickle-minded or contrary. They would stay in no road,

no path; they broke out through the brush on all sides, and flowed away in all directions, over rocks, and hills, and the roughest places they could find. And they must not be struck, or roughly accosted; Sandy could not bear to see them treated in ways unbecoming their rank. The troublesomest old sow of the lot had to be called my Lady, and your Highness, like the rest. It is annoying and difficult to scour around after hogs, in armor. There was one small countess, with an iron ring in her snout and hardly any hair on her back, that was the devil for perversity. She gave me a race of an hour, over all sorts of country, and then we were right where we had started from, having made not a rod of real progress. I seized her at last by the tail, and brought her along, squealing. When I overtook Sandy, she was horrified, and said it was in the last degree indelicate to drag a countess by her train.

We got the hogs home just at dark—most of them. The princess Nerovens de Morganore was missing, and two of her ladies in waiting: namely, Miss Angela Bohun, and the Demoiselle Elaine Courtemains, the former of these two being a young black sow with a white star in her forehead, and the latter a brown one with thin legs and a slight limp in the forward shank on the starboard side—a couple of the tryingest blisters to drive, that I ever saw. Also among the missing were several mere baronesses—and I wanted them to stay missing; but no, all that sausage-meat had to be found; so servants were sent out with torches to scour the woods and hills to that end.

Of course the whole drove was housed in the house, and great guns!—well, I never saw anything like it. Nor ever heard anything like it. And never smelt anything like it. It was like an insurrection in a gasometer.

CHAPTER XXI

THE PILGRIMS

When I did get to bed at last I was unspeakably tired; the stretching out, and the relaxing of the long-tense muscles, how luxurious, how delicious! but that was as far as I could get—sleep was out of the question, for the present. The ripping and tearing and squealing of the nobility up and down the halls and corridors was pandemonium come again, and kept me broad awake. Being awake, my thoughts were busy of course; and mainly they busied themselves with Sandy's curious delusion. Here she was, as sane a person as the kingdom could produce; and yet, from my point of view she was acting like a crazy woman. My land, the power of training! of influence! of education! It can bring a body up to believe anything. I had to put myself in Sandy's place to realize that she was not a lunatic. Yes, and put her in mine, to demonstrate how easy it

is to seem a lunatic to a person who has not been taught as you have
been taught. If I had told Sandy I had seen a wagon, uninfluenced
by enchantment, spin along fifty miles an hour; had seen a man,
unequipped with magic powers, get into a basket and soar out of
sight among the clouds; and had listened, without any
necromancer's help, to the conversation of a person who was several
hundred miles away, Sandy would not merely have supposed me to
be crazy, she would have thought she knew it. Everybody around her
believed in enchantments; nobody had any doubts; to doubt that a
castle could be turned into a sty, and its occupants into hogs, would
have been the same as my doubting, among Connecticut people, the
actuality of the telephone and its wonders,—and in both cases
would be absolute proof of a diseased mind, an unsettled reason.
Yes, Sandy was sane; that must be admitted. If I also would be
sane—to Sandy—I must keep my superstitions about unenchanted
and unmiraculous locomotives, balloons and telephones, to myself.
Also, I believed that the world was not flat, and hadn't pillars under
it to support it, nor a canopy over it to turn off a universe of water
that occupied all space above: but as I was the only person in the
kingdom afflicted with such impious and criminal opinions, I
recognized that it would be good wisdom to keep quiet about this
matter, too, if I did not wish to be suddenly shunned and forsaken
by everybody as a madman.

The next morning Sandy assembled the swine in the dining-room
and gave them their breakfast, waiting upon them personally and
manifesting in every way the deep reverence which the natives of her
island, ancient and modern, have always felt for rank, let its outward
casket and the mental and moral contents be what they may. I could
have eaten with the hogs if I had had birth approaching my lofty
official rank; but I hadn't, and so accepted the unavoidable slight
and made no complaint. Sandy and I had our breakfast at the
second table. The family were not at home. I said:

"How many are in the family, Sandy, and where do they keep
themselves?"

"Family?"

"Yes."

"Which family, good my lord?"

"Why, this family; your own family."

"Sooth to say, I understand you not. I have no family."

"No family? Why, Sandy, isn't this your home?"

"Now how indeed might that be? I have no home."

"Well, then, whose house is this?"

"Ah, wit you well I would tell you an I knew myself."

"Well, then, whose house is this?"

"Ah, wit you well I would tell you an I knew myself."

"Come—you don't even know these people? Then who invited us
here?"

"None invited us. We but came; that is all."

"Why, woman, this is a most extraordinary performance. The effrontery of it is beyond admiration. We blandly march into a man's house, and cram it full of the only really valuable nobility the sun has yet discovered in the earth, and then it turns out that we don't even know the man's name. How did you ever venture to take this extravagant liberty? I supposed, of course, it was your home. What will the man say?"

"What will he say? Forsooth what can he say but give thanks?"

"Thanks for what?"

Her face was filled with a puzzled surprise:

"Verily, thou troublest mine understanding with strange words. Do ye dream that one of his estate is like to have the honor twice in his life to entertain company such as we have brought to grace his house withal?"

"Well, no—when you come to that. No, it's an even bet that this is the first time he has had a treat like this."

"Then let him be thankful, and manifest the same by grateful speech and due humility; he were a dog, else, and the heir and ancestor of dogs."

To my mind, the situation was uncomfortable. It might become more so. It might be a good idea to muster the hogs and move on. So I said:

"The day is wasting, Sandy. It is time to get the nobility together and be moving."

"Wherefore, fair sir and Boss?"

"We want to take them to their home, don't we?"

"La, but list to him! They be of all the regions of the earth! Each must hie to her own home; wend you we might do all these journeys in one so brief life as He hath appointed that created life, and thereto death likewise with help of Adam, who by sin done through persuasion of his helpmeet, she being wrought upon and bewrayed by the beguilements of the great enemy of man, that serpent hight Satan, aforetime consecrated and set apart unto that evil work by overmastering spite and envy begotten in his heart through fell ambitions that did blight and mildew a nature erst so white and pure whenso it hove with the shining multidudes its brethren-born in glade and shade of that fair heaven wherein all such as native be to that rich estate and—"

"Great Scott!"

"My lord?"

"Well, you know we haven't got time for this sort of thing. Don't you see, we could distribute these people around the earth in less time than it is going to take you to explain that we can't. We mustn't talk now, we must act. You want to be careful; you mustn't let your mill get the start of you that way, at a time like this. To business, now—and sharp's the word. Who is to take the aristocracy home?"

"Even their friends. These will come for them from the far parts of the earth."

This was lightning from a clear sky, for unexpectedness; and the relief of it was like pardon to a prisoner. She would remain to deliver the goods, of course.

"Well, then, Sandy, as our enterprise is handsomely and successfully ended, I will go home and report; and if ever another one—"

"I also am ready; I will go with thee."

This was recalling the pardon.

"How? You will go with me? Why should you?"

"Will I be traitor to my knight, dost think? That were dishonor. I may not part from thee until in knightly encounter in the field some overmatching champion shall fairly win and fairly wear me. I were to blame an I thought that that might ever hap."

"Elected for the long term," I sighed to myself. "I may as well make the best of it." So then I spoke up and said:

"All right; let us make a start."

While she was gone to cry her farewells over the pork, I gave that whole peerage away to the servants. And I asked them to take a duster and dust around a little where the nobilities had mainly lodged and promenaded, but they considered that that would be hardly worth while, and would moreover be a rather grave departure from custom, and therefore likely to make talk. A departure from custom—that settled it; it was a nation capable of committing any crime but that. The servants said they would follow the fashion, a fashion grown sacred through immemorial observance: they would scatter fresh rushes in all the rooms and halls, and then the evidence of the aristocratic visitation would be no longer visible. It was a kind of satire on Nature; it deposited the history of the family in a stratified record; and the antiquary could dig through it and tell by the remains of each period what changes of diet the family had introduced successively for a hundred years.

The first thing we struck that day was a procession of pilgrims. It was not going our way, but we joined it nevertheless; for it was hourly being borne in upon me, now, that if I would govern this country wisely, I must be posted in the details of its life, and not at second hand but by personal observation and scrutiny.

This company of pilgrims resembled Chaucer's in this: that it had in it a sample of about all the upper occupations and professions the country could show, and a corresponding variety of costume. There were young men and old men, young women and old women, lively folk and grave folk. They rode upon mules and horses, and there was not a side-saddle in the party; for this specialty was to remain unknown in England for nine hundred years yet.

It was a pleasant, friendly, sociable herd; pious, happy, merry, and full of unconscious coarsenesses and innocent indecencies.

What they regarded as the merry tale went the continual round and
caused no more embarrassment than it would have caused in the
best English society twelve centuries later. Practical jokes worthy of
the English wits of the first quarter of the far-off nineteenth
century were sprung here and there and yonder along the line, and
compelled the delightedest applause; and sometimes when a bright
remark was made at one end of the procession and started on its
travels toward the other, you could note its progress all the way by
the sparkling spray of laughter it threw off from its bows as it plowed
along; and also by the blushes of the mules in its wake.

Sandy knew the goal and purpose of this pilgrimage and she
posted me. She said:

"They journey to the Valley of Holiness, for to be blessed of the
godly hermits and drink of the miraculous waters and be cleansed
from sin."

"Where is this watering place?"

"It lieth a two day journey hence, by the borders of the land that
hight the Cuckoo Kingdom."

"Tell me about it. Is it a celebrated place?"

"Oh, of a truth, yes. There be none more so. Of old time there
lived there an abbot and his monks. Belike were none in the world
more holy than these; for they gave themselves to study of pious
books, and spoke not the one to the other, or indeed to any, and ate
decayed herbs and naught thereto, and slept hard, and prayed
much, and washed never; also they wore the same garment until it
fell from their bodies through age and decay. Right so came they to
be known of all the world by reason of these holy austerities, and
visited by rich and poor, and reverenced."

"Proceed."

"But always there was lack of water there. Whereas, upon a time,
the holy abbot prayed, and for answer a great stream of clear water
burst forth by miracle in a desert place. Now were the fickle monks
tempted of the Fiend, and they wrought with their abbot unceasingly
by beggings and beseechings that he would construct a bath; and
when he was become aweary and might not resist more, he said have
ye your will, then, and granted that they asked. Now mark thou
what 'tis to forsake the ways of purity the which He loveth, and
wanton with such as be worldly and an offence. These monks did
enter into the bath and come thence washed as white as snow; and
lo, in that moment His sign appeared, in miraculous rebuke! for His
insulted waters ceased to flow, and utterly vanished away."

"They fared mildly, Sandy, considering how that kind of crime
is regarded in this country."

"Belike; but it was their first sin; and they had been of perfect
life for long, and differing in naught from the angels. Prayers, tears,
torturings of the flesh, all was vain to beguile that water to flow
again. Even processions; even burnt-offerings; even votive candles

to the Virgin, did fail every each of them; and all in the land
did marvel."

"How odd to find that even this industry has its financial panics,
and at times sees its assignats and greenbacks languish to zero, and
everything come to a standstill. Go on, Sandy."

"And so upon a time, after year and day, the good abbot made
humble surrender and destroyed the bath. And behold, His anger
was in that moment appeased, and the waters gushed richly forth
again, and even unto this day they have not ceased to flow in that
generous measure."

"Then I take it nobody has washed since."

"He that would essay it could have his halter free; yea, and swiftly
would he need it, too."

"The community has prospered since?"

"Even from that very day. The fame of the miracle went abroad
into all lands. From every land came monks to join; they came even
as the fishes come, in shoals; and the monastery added building to
building, and yet others to these, and so spread wide its arms and
took them in. And nuns came, also; and more again, and yet more;
and built over against the monastery on the yon side of the vale,
and added building to building, until mighty was that nunnery.
And these were friendly unto those, and they joined their loving
labors together, and together they built a fair great foundling asylum
midway of the valley between."

"You spoke of some hermits, Sandy."

"These have gathered there from the ends of the earth. A hermit
thriveth best where there be multitudes of pilgrims. Ye shall not find
no hermit of no sort wanting. If any shall mention a hermit of a
kind he thinketh new and not to be found but in some far strange
land, let him but scratch among the holes and caves and swamps
that line that Valley of Holiness, and whatsoever be his breed, it
skills not, he shall find a sample of it there."

I closed up alongside of a burly fellow with a fat good-humored
face, purposing to make myself agreeable and pick up some further
crumbs of fact; but I had hardly more than scraped acquaintance
with him when he began eagerly and awkwardly to lead up, in the
immemorial way, to that same old anecdote—the one Sir Dinadan
told me, what time I got into trouble with Sir Sagramor and was
challenged of him on account of it. I excused myself and dropped to
the rear of the procession, sad at heart, willing to go hence from
this troubled life, this vale of tears, this brief day of broken rest, of
cloud and storm, of weary struggle and monotonous defeat; and yet
shrinking from the change, as remembering how long eternity is,
and how many have wended thither who know that anecdote.

Early in the afternoon we overtook another procession of pilgrims;
but in this one was no merriment, no jokes, no laughter, no playful
ways, nor any happy giddiness, whether of youth or age. Yet both

were here, both age and youth; gray old men and women, strong
men and women of middle age, young husbands, young wives, little
boys and girls, and three babies at the breast. Even the children
were smileless; there was not a face among all these half a hundred
people but was cast down, and bore that set expression of
hopelessness which is bred of long and hard trials and old
acquaintance with despair. They were slaves. Chains led from their
fettered feet and their manacled hands to a sole-leather belt about
their waists; and all except the children were also linked together in
a file, six feet apart, by a single chain which led from collar to collar
all down the line. They were on foot, and had tramped three
hundred miles in eighteen days, upon the cheapest odds and ends of
food, and stingy rations of that. They had slept in these chains every
night, bundled together like swine. They had upon their bodies
some poor rags, but they could not be said to be clothed. Their irons
had chafed the skin from their ankles and made sores which were
ulcerated and wormy. Their naked feet were torn, and none walked
without a limp. Originally there had been a hundred of these
unfortunates, but about half had been sold on the trip. The trader
in charge of them rode a horse and carried a whip with a short
handle and a long heavy lash divided into several knotted tails at the
end. With this whip he cut the shoulders of any that tottered from
weariness and pain, and straitened them up. He did not speak;
the whip conveyed his desire without that. None of these poor
creatures looked up as we rode along by; they showed no
consciousness of our presence. And they made no sound but one;
that was the dull and awful clank of their chains from end to end of
the long file, as forty-three burdened feet rose and fell in unison.
The file moved in a cloud of its own making.

All these faces were gray with a coating of dust. One has seen the
like of this coating upon furniture in unoccupied houses, and has
written his idle thought in it with his finger. I was reminded of this
when I noticed the faces of some of those women, young mothers
carrying babes that were near to death and freedom, how a
something in their hearts was written in the dust upon their faces,
plain to see, and lord how plain to read! for it was the track of tears.
One of these young mothers was but a girl, and it hurt me to the
heart to read that writing, and reflect that it was come up out of the
breast of such a child, a breast that ought not to know trouble yet,
but only the gladness of the morning of life; and no doubt—

She reeled just then, giddy with fatigue, and down came the lash
and flicked a flake of skin from her naked shoulder. It stung me as
if I had been hit instead. The master halted the file and jumped from
his horse. He stormed and swore at this girl, and said she had made
annoyance enough with her laziness, and as this was the last chance
he should have, he would settle the account now. She dropped on her
knees and put up her hands and began to beg and cry and implore,

in a passion of terror, but the master gave no attention. He snatched the child from her, and then made the men-slaves who were chained before and behind her throw her on the ground and hold her there and expose her body; and then he laid on with the lash like a madman till her back was flayed, she strieking and struggling the while, piteously. One of the men who was holding her turned away his face, and for this humanity he was reviled and flogged.

All our pilgrims looked on and commented—on the expert way in which the whip was handled. They were too much hardened by lifelong every-day familiarity with slavery to notice that there was anything else in the exhibition that invited comment. This was what slavery could do, in the way of ossifying what one may call the superior lobe of human feeling; for these pilgrims were kind-hearted people, and they would not have allowed that man to treat a horse like that.

I wanted to stop the whole thing and set the slave free, but that would not do. I must not interfere too much and get myself a name for riding over the country's laws and the citizen's rights roughshod. If I lived and prospered I would be the death of slavery, that I was resolved upon; but I would try to fix it so that when I became its executioner it should be by command of the nation.

Just here was the wayside shop of a smith; and now arrived a landed proprietor who had bought this girl a few miles back, deliverable here where her irons could be taken off. They were removed; then there was a squabble between the gentleman and the dealer as to which should pay the blacksmith. The moment the girl was delivered from her irons, she flung herself, all tears and frantic sobbings, into the arms of the slave who had turned away his face when she was whipped. He strained her to his breast, and smothered her face and the child's with kisses, and washed them with the rain of his tears. I suspected. I inquired. Yes, I was right: it was husband and wife. They had to be torn apart by force; the girl had to be dragged away, and she struggled and fought and shrieked like one gone mad till a turn of the road hid her from sight; and even after that, we could still make out the fading plaint of those receding shrieks. And the husband and father, with his wife and child gone, never to be seen by him again in life?—well, the look of him one might not bear at all, and so I turned away; but I knew I should never get his picture out of my mind again, and there it is to this day, to wring my heartstrings whenever I think about it.

We put up at the inn in a village just at nightfall, and when I rose next morning and looked abroad, I was ware where a knight came riding in the golden glory of the new day, and recognized him for knight of mine—Sir Ozana le Cure Hardy. He was in the gentlemen's furnishing line, and his missionarying specialty was plug hats. He was clothed all in steel, in the beautifulest armor of the time—up to where his helmet ought to have been; but he hadn't

any helmet, he wore a shiny stove-pipe hat, and was as ridiculous a
spectacle as one might want to see. It was another of my
surreptitious schemes for extinguishing knighthood by making it
grotesque and absurd. Sir Ozana's saddle was hung about with
hat-boxes, and every time he overcame a wandering knight he swore
him into my service and fitted him with a plug and made him wear
it. I dressed and ran down to welcome Sir Ozana and get his news.

"How is trade?" I asked.

"Ye will note that I have but these four left; yet were they sixteen
whenas I got me from Camelot."

"Why, you have certainly done nobly, Sir Ozana. Where have you
been foraging of late?"

"I am but now come from the Valley of Holiness, please you sir."

"I am pointed for that place myself. Is there anything stirring in
the monkery, more than common?"

"By the mass ye may not question it! . . . Give him good feed, boy,
and stint it not, an thou valuest thy crown; so get ye lightly to the
stable and do even as I bid......Sir, it is parlous news I bring,
and—be these pilgrims? Then ye may not do better, good folk,
than gather and hear the tale I have to tell, sith it concerneth you,
forasmuch as ye go to find that ye will not find, and seek that ye will
seek in vain, my life being hostage for my word, and my word and
message being these, namely: That a hap has happened whereof the
like has not been seen no more but once this two hundred years,
which was the first and last time that that said misfortune strake the
holy valley in that form by commandment of the Most High
whereto by reasons just and causes thereunto contributing, wherein
the matter—"

"The miraculous fount hath ceased to flow!" This shout burst
from twenty pilgrim mouths at once.

"Ye say well, good people. I was verging to it, even when ye
spake."

"Has somebody been washing again?"

"Nay, it is suspected, but none believe it. It is thought to be some
other sin, but none wit what."

"How are they feeling about the calamity?"

"None may describe it in words. The fount is these nine days dry.
The prayers that did begin then, and the lamentations in sackcloth
and ashes, and the holy processions, none of these have ceased nor
night nor day; and so the monks and the huns and the foundlings
be all exhausted, and do hang up prayers writ upon parchment,
sith that no strength is left in man to lift up voice. And at last they
sent for thee, Sir Boss, to try magic and enchantment; and if you
could not come, then was the messenger to fetch Merlin, and he is
there these three days now, and saith he will fetch that water though
he burst the globe and wreck its kingdoms to accomplish it; and
right bravely doth he work his magic and call upon his hellions to hie

them hither and help, but not a whiff of moisture hath he started
yet, even so much as might qualify as mist upon a copper mirror
an ye count not the barrel of sweat he sweateth betwixt sun and sun
over the dire labors of his task; and if ye—"

Breakfast was ready. As soon as it was over I showed to Sir Ozana
these words which I had written on the inside of his hat: "*Chemical
Department, Laboratory extension, Section G. Pxxp. Send two of
first size, two of No. 3, and six of No. 4, together with the proper
complementary details—and two of my trained assistants.*" And
I said:

"Now get you to Camelot as fast as you can fly, brave knight, and
show the writing to Clarence, and tell him to have these required
matters in the Valley of Holiness with all possible despatch."

"I will well, Sir Boss," and he was off.

CHAPTER XXII

THE HOLY FOUNTAIN

The pilgrims were human beings. Otherwise they would have
acted differently. They had come a long and difficult journey, and
now when the journey was nearly finished, and they learned that the
main thing they had come for had ceased to exist, they didn't do as
horses or cats or angle-worms would probably have done—turn
back and get at something profitable—no, anxious as they had
before been to see the miraculous fountain, they were as much as
forty times as anxious now to see the place where it had used to be.
There is no accounting for human beings.

We made good time; and a couple of hours before sunset we stood
upon the high confines of the Valley of Holiness, and our eyes swept
it from end to end and noted its features. That is, its large features.
These were the three masses of buildings. They were distant and
isolated temporalities shrunken to toy constructions in the lonely
waste of what seemed a desert—and was. Such a scene is always
mournful, it is so impressively still, and looks so steeped in death.
But there was a sound here which interrupted the stillness only to
add to its mournfulness; this was the faint far sound of tolling bells
which floated fitfully to us on the passing breeze, and so faintly,
so softly, that we hardly knew whether we heard it with our ears or
with our spirits.

We reached the monastery before dark, and there the males were
given lodging, but the women were sent over to the nunnery. The
bells were close at hand, now, and their solemn booming smote upon
the ear like a message of doom. A superstitious despair possessed
the heart of every monk and published itself in his ghastly face.
Everywhere, these black-robed, soft-sandled, tallow-visaged spectres

appeared, flitted about and disappeared, noiseless as the creatures
of a troubled dream, and as uncanny.

The old abbot's joy to see me was pathetic. Even to tears; but he
did the shedding himself. He said:

"Delay not, son, but get to thy saving work. An we bring not the
water back again, and soon, we are ruined, and the good work of
two hundred years must end. And see thou do it with enchantments
that be holy, for the Church will not endure that work in her cause be
done by devil's magic."

"When I work, Father, be sure there will be no devil's work
connected with it. I shall use no arts that come of the devil, and no
elements not created by the hand of God. But is Merlin working
strictly on pious lines?"

"Ah, he said he would, my son, he said he would, and took oath
to make his promise good."

"Well, in that case, let him proceed."

"But surely you will not sit idle by, but help?"

"It will not answer to mix methods, Father; neither would it be
professional courtesy. Two of a trade must not underbid each other.
We might as well cut rates and be done with it; it would arrive at
that in the end. Merlin has the contract; no other magician can
touch it till he throws it up."

"But I will take it from him; it is a terrible emergency and the act
is thereby justified. And if it were not so, who will give law to the
Church? The Church giveth law to all; and what she wills to do, that
she may do, hurt whom it may. I will take it from him; you shall
begin upon the moment."

"It may not be, Father. No doubt, as you say, where power is
supreme, one can do as one likes and suffer no injury; but we poor
magicians are not so situated. Merlin is a very good magician in a
small way, and has quite a neat provincial reputation. He is
struggling along, doing the best he can, and it would not be etiquette
for me to take his job until he himself abandons it."

The abbot's face lighted.

"Ah, that is simple. There are ways to persuade him to
abandon it."

"No-no, Father, it skills not, as these people say. If he were
persuaded against his will, he would load that well with a malicious
enchantment which would balk me until I found out its secret.
It might take a month. I could set up a little enchantment of mine
which I call the telephone, and he could not find out its secret in a
hundred years. Yes, you perceive, he might block me for a month.
Would you like to risk a month in a dry time like this?"

"A month! The mere thought of it maketh me to shudder. Have
it thy way, my son. But my heart is heavy with this disappointment.
Leave me, and let me wear my spirit with weariness and waiting,
even as I have done these ten long days, counterfeiting thus the

thing that is called rest, the prone body making outward sign of
repose where inwardly is none."

Of course it would have been best, all round, for Merlin to waive
etiquette and quit and call it half a day, since he would never be able
to start that water, for he was a true magician of the time: which is
to say, the big miracles, the ones that gave him his reputation, always
had the luck to be performed when nobody but Merlin was present;
he couldn't start this well with all this crowd around to see; a crowd
was as bad for a magician's miracle in that day as it was for a
spiritualist's miracle in mine: there was sure to be some skeptic
on hand to turn up the gas at the crucial moment and spoil
everything. But I did not want Merlin to retire from the job until I
was ready to take hold of it effectively myself; and I could not do that
until I got my things from Camelot, and that would take two or
three days.

My presence gave the monks hope, and cheered them up a good
deal; insomuch that they ate a square meal that night for the first
time in ten days. As soon as their stomachs had been properly
reinforced with food, their spirits began to rise fast; when the mead
began to go round they rose faster. By the time everybody was
half-seas over, the holy community was in good shape to make a
night of it; so we stayed by the board and put it through on that line.
Matters got to be very jolly. Good old questionable stories were told
that made the tears run down and cavernous mouths stand wide and
the round bellies shake with laughter; and questionable songs were
bellowed out in a mighty chorus that drowned the boom of the
tolling bells.

At last I ventured a story myself; and vast was the success of it.
Not right off, of course, for the native of those islands does not as a
rule dissolve upon the early applications of a humorous thing; but
the fifth time I told it, they began to crack, in places; the eighth
time I told it, they began to crumble; at the twelfth repetition they
fell apart in chunks; and at the fifteenth they disintegrated, and I
got a broom and swept them up. This language is figurative. Those
islanders—well, they are slow pay, at first, in the matter of return for
your investment of effort, but in the end they make the pay of all
other nations poor and small by contrast.

I was at the well next day betimes. Merlin was there, enchanting
away like a beaver, but not raising the moisture. He was not in a
pleasant humor; and every time I hinted that perhaps this contract
was a shade too hefty for a novice he unlimbered his tongue and
cursed like a bishop—French bishop of the Regency days, I mean.

Matters were about as I expected to find them. The "fountain"
was an ordinary well, it had been dug in the ordinary way, and
stoned up in the ordinary way. There was no miracle about it. Even
the lie that had created its reputation was not miraculous; I could
have told it myself, with one hand tied behind me. The well was in

a dark chamber which stood in the centre of a cut-stone chapel,
whose walls were hung with pious pictures of a workmanship that
would have made a chromo feel good; pictures historically
commemorative of curative miracles which had been achieved by
the waters when nobody was looking. That is, nobody but angels:
they are always on deck when there is a miracle to the fore—so as
to get put in the picture, perhaps. Angels are as fond of that as a
fire-company; look at the old masters.

The well-chamber was dimly lighted by lamps; the water was
drawn with a windlass and chain, by monks, and poured into
troughs which delivered it into stone reservoirs outside, in the
chapel—when there was water to draw, I mean—and none but
monks could enter the well-chamber. I entered it, for I had
temporary authority to do so, by courtesy of my professional brother
and subordinate. But he hadn't entered it himself. He did everything
by incantations; he never worked his intellect. If he had stepped in
there and used his eyes, instead of his disordered mind, he could
have cured the well by natural means, and then turned it into a
miracle in the customary way; but no, he was an old numskull,
a magician who believed in his own magic; and no magician can
thrive who is handicapped with a superstition like that.

I had an idea that the well had sprung a leak; that some of the
wall stones near the bottom had fallen and exposed fissures that
allowed the water to escape. I measured the chain—98 feet. Then I
called in a couple of monks, locked the door, took a candle, and
made them lower me in the bucket. When the chain was all paid
out, the candle confirmed my suspicion; a considerable section of
the wall was gone, exposing a good big fissure.

I almost regretted that my theory about the well's trouble was
correct, because I had another one that had a showy point or two
about it for a miracle. I remembered that in America, many
centuries later, when an oil well ceased to flow, they used to blast it
out with a dynamite torpedo. If I should find this well dry, and no
explanation of it, I could astonish these people most nobly by having
a person of no especial value drop a dynamite bomb into it. It was
my idea to appoint Merlin. However, it was plain that there was no
occasion for the bomb. One cannot have everything the way he
would like it. A man has no business to be depressed by a
disappointment, anyway; he ought to make up his mind to get even.
That is what I did. I said to myself, I am in no hurry, I can wait;
that bomb will come good, yet. And it did, too.

When I was above ground again, I turned out the monks, and let
down a fish-line: the well was a hundred and fifty feet deep, and
there was forty-one feet of water in it! I called in a monk and asked:

"How deep is the well?"

"That, sir, I wit not, having never been told."

"How does the water usually stand in it?"

"Near the top, these two centuries, as the testimony goeth, brought down to us through our predecessors."

It was true—as to recent times at least—for there was witness to it, and better witness than a monk: only about twenty or thirty feet of chain showed wear and use, the rest of it was unworn and rusty. What had happened when the well gave out that other time? Without doubt some practical person had come along and mended the leak, and then had come up and told the abbot he had discovered by divination that if the sinful bath were destroyed the well would flow again. The leak had befallen again, now, and these children would have prayed, and processioned, and tolled their bells for heavenly succor till they all dried up and blew away, and no innocent of them all would ever have thought to drop a fish-line into the well or go down in it and find out what was really the matter. Old habit of mind is one of the toughest things to get away from in the world. It transmits itself like physical form and feature; and for a man, in those days, to have had an idea that his ancestors hadn't had, would have brought him under suspicion of being illegitimate. I said to the monk:

"It is a difficult miracle to restore water in a dry well, but we will try, if my brother Merlin fails. Brother Merlin is a very passable artist, but only in the parlor-magic line, and he may not succeed; in fact is not likely to succeed. But that should be nothing to his discredit; the man that can do *this* kind of miracle knows enough to keep hotel."

"Hotel? I mind not to have heard—"

"Of hotel? It's what you call hostel. The man that can do this miracle can keep hostel. I can do this miracle; I shall do this miracle; yet I do not try to conceal from you that it is a miracle to tax the occult powers to the last strain."

"None knoweth that truth better than the brotherhood, indeed; for it is of record that aforetime it was parlous difficult and took a year. Natheless, God send you good success, and to that end will we pray."

As a matter of business it was a good idea to get the notion around that the thing was difficult. Many a small thing has been made large by the right kind of advertising. That monk was filled up with the difficulty of this enterprise; he would fill up the others. In two days the solicitude would be booming.

On my way home at noon, I met Sandy. She had been sampling the hermits. I said:

"I would like to do that, myself. This is Wednesday. Is there a matinée?"

"A which, please you sir?"

"Matinée. Do they keep open afternoons?"

"Who?"

"The hermits, of course."

"Keep open?"

"Yes, keep open. Isn't that plain enough? Do they knock off
at noon?"

"Knock off?"

"Knock off?—yes, knock off. What is the matter with knock off?
I never saw such a dunderhead; can't you understand anything at
all? In plain terms, do they shut up shop, draw the game, bank
the fires—"

"Shut up shop, draw—"

"There, never mind, let it go; you make me tired. You can't seem
to understand the simplest thing."

"I would I might please thee, sir, and it is to me dole and sorrow
that I fail, albeit sith I am but a simple damsel and taught of none,
being from the cradle unbaptized in those deep waters of learning
that do anoint with a sovereignty him that partaketh of that most
noble sacrament, investing him with reverend state to the mental eye
of the humble mortal who, by bar and lack of that great consecration
seeth in his own unlearned estate but a symbol of that other sort of
lack and loss which men do publish to the pitying eye with sackcloth
trappings whereon the ashes of grief do lie bepowdered and
bestrewn, and so, when such shall in the darkness of his mind
encounter these golden phrases of high mystery, these shut-up-
shops, and draw-the-game, and bank-the-fires, it is but by the grace
of God that he burst not for envy of the mind that can beget, and
tongue that can deliver so great and mellow-sounding miracles of
speech, and if there do ensue confusion in that humbler mind, and
failure to divine the meanings of these wonders, then if so be this
miscomprehension is not vain but sooth and true, wit ye well it is
the very substance of worshipful dear homage and may not lightly
be misprized, nor had been, an ye had noted this complexion of my
mood and mind and understood that that I would I could not, and
that I could not I might not, nor yet nor might *nor* could, nor
might-not nor could-not, might be by advantage turned to the
desired *would*, and so I pray you mercy of my fault, and that ye
will of your kindness and your charity forgive it, good my master and
most dear lord."

I couldn't make it all out—that is, the details—but I got the
general idea; and enough of it, too, to be ashamed. It was not fair to
spring those nineteenth century technicalities upon the untutored
infant of the sixth and then rail at her because she couldn't get their
drift; and when she was making the honest best drive at it she could,
too, and no fault of hers that she couldn't fetch the home-plate;
and I apologized. Then we meandered pleasantly away toward the
hermit-holes in sociable converse together, and better friends
than ever.

I was gradually coming to have a mysterious and shuddery
reverence for this girl; for now-a-days whenever she pulled out from

the station and got her train fairly started on one of those horizonless transcontinental sentences of hers, it was borne in upon me that I was standing in the awful presence of the Mother of the German Language. I was so impressed with this, that sometimes when she began to empty one of these sentences on me I unconsciously took the very attitude of reverence, and stood uncovered; and if words had been water, I had been drowned, sure. She had exactly the German way: whatever was in her mind to be delivered, whether a mere remark, or a sermon, or a cyclopedia, or the history of a war, she would get it into a single sentence or die. Whenever the literary German dives into a sentence, that is the last you are going to see of him till he emerges on the other side of his Atlantic with his verb in his mouth.

We drifted from hermit to hermit all the afternoon. It was a most strange menagerie. The chief emulation among them seemed to be, to see which could manage to be the uncleanest and most prosperous with vermin. Their manner and attitudes were the last expression of complacent self-righteousness. It was one anchorite's pride to lie naked in the mud and let the insects bite him and blister him unmolested; it was another's to lean against a rock, all day long, conspicuous to the admiration of the throng of pilgrims, and pray; it was another's to go naked, and crawl around on all fours; it was another's to drag about with him, year in and year out, eighty pounds of iron; it was another's to never lie down when he slept, but to stand among the thorn-bushes and snore when there were pilgrims around to look; a woman, who had the white hair of age, and no other apparel, was black from crown to heel with forty-seven years of holy abstinence from water. Groups of gazing pilgrims stood around all and every of these strange objects, lost in reverent wonder, and envious of the fleckless sanctity which these pious austerities had won for them from an exacting heaven.

By-and-by we went to see one of the supremely great ones. He was a mighty celebrity; his fame had penetrated all Christendom; the noble and the renowned journeyed from the remotest lands on the globe to pay him reverence. His stand was in the centre of the widest part of the valley; and it took all that space to hold his crowds.

His stand was a pillar sixty feet high, with a broad platform on the top of it. He was now doing what he had been doing every day for twenty years up there—bowing his body ceaselessly and rapidly almost to his feet. It was his way of praying. I timed him with a stop-watch, and he made 1244 revolutions in 24 minutes and 46 seconds. It seemed a pity to have all this power going to waste. It was one of the most useful motions in mechanics, the pedal-movement; so I made a note in my memorandum-book, purposing some day to apply a system of elastic cords to him and run a sewing-machine with it. I afterwards carried out that scheme, and got five years' good service out of him; in which time he turned

out upwards of eighteen thousand first-rate tow-linen shirts, which
was ten a day. I worked him Sundays and all; he was going, Sundays,
the same as weekdays, and it was no use to waste the power. These
shirts cost me nothing but just the mere trifle for the materials—
I furnished those myself, it would not have been right to make him
do that—and they sold like smoke to pilgrims at a dollar and a half
apiece, which was the price of fifty cows or a blooded race-horse in
Arthurdom. They were regarded as a perfect protection against sin,
and advertised as such by my knights everywhere, with the paint-pot
and stencil-plate; insomuch that there was not a cliff or a bowlder
or a dead-wall in England but you could read on it at a mile
distance:

*"Buy the only genuine St. Stylite; patronized by the Nobility.
Patent applied for."*

There was more money in the business than one knew what to do
with. As it extended, I brought out a line of goods suitable for kings,
and a nobby thing for duchesses and that sort, with ruffles down the
fore-hatch and the running-gear clewed up with a feather-stitch to
leeward and then hauled aft with a back-stay and triced up with a
half-turn in the standing rigging forward of the weather-gaskets.
Yes, it was a daisy.

But about that time I noticed that the motive power had taken to
standing on one leg, and I found that there was something the
matter with the other one; so I stocked the business and unloaded,
taking Sir Bors de Ganis into camp financially along with certain of
his friends: for the works stopped within a year, and the good saint
got him to his rest. But he had earned it. I can say that for him.

When I saw him that first time—however, his personal condition
will not quite bear description here. You can read it in the Lives
of the Saints.*

CHAPTER XXIII

RESTORATION OF THE FOUNTAIN

Saturday noon I went to the well and looked on a while. Merlin
was still burning smoke-powders, and pawing the air, and muttering
gibberish as hard as ever, but looking pretty down-hearted, for of
course he had not started even a perspiration in that well yet.
Finally I said:

"How does the thing promise by this time, partner?"

"Behold, I am even now busied with trial of the powerfulest
enchantment known to the princes of the occult arts in the lands

*All the details concerning the hermits, in this chapter, are from Lecky—
but greatly modified. This book not being a history but only a tale, the
majority of the historian's frank details were too strong for reproduction
in it.—EDITOR.

of the East; an it fail me, naught can avail. Peace, until I finish."

He raised a smoke this time that darkened all the region, and must have made matters uncomfortable for the hermits, for the wind was their way, and it rolled down over their dens in a dense and billowy fog. He poured out volumes of speech to match, and contorted his body and sawed the air with his hands in a most extraordinary way. At the end of twenty minutes he dropped down panting, and about exhausted. Now arrived the abbot and several hundred monks and nuns, and behind them a multitude of pilgrims and a couple of acres of foundlings, all drawn by the prodigious smoke, and all in a grand state of excitement. The abbot inquired anxiously for results. Merlin said:

"If any labor of mortal might break the spell that binds these waters, this which I have but just essayed had done it. It has failed; whereby I do now know that that which I had feared is a truth established: the sign of this failure is, that the most potent spirit known to the magicians of the East, and whose name none may utter and live, has laid his spell upon this well. The mortal does not breathe, nor ever will, who can penetrate the secret of that spell, and without that secret none can break it. The water will flow no more forever, good Father. I have done what man could. Suffer me to go."

Of course this threw the abbot into a good deal of a consternation. He turned to me with the signs of it in his face, and said:

"Ye have heard from him. Is it true?"

"Part of it is."

"Not all, then, not all! What part is true?"

"That that spirit with the Russian name has put his spell upon the well."

"God's wownds, then are we ruined!"

"Possibly."

"But not certainly? Ye mean, not certainly?"

"That is it."

"Wherefore, ye also mean that when he saith none can break the spell—"

"Yes, when he says that, he says what isn't necessarily true. There are conditions under which an effort to break it may have some chance—that is, some small, some trifling chance—of success."

"The conditions—"

"Oh, they are nothing difficult. Only these: I want the well and the surroundings for the space of half a mile, entirely to myself from sunset to-day until I remove the ban—and nobody allowed to cross the ground but by my authority."

"Are these all?"

"Yes."

"And you have no fear to try?"

"Oh, none. One may fail, of course; and one may also succeed.

One can try, and I am ready to chance it. I have my conditions?"

"These and all others ye may name. I will issue commandment to that effect."

"Wait," said Merlin, with an evil smile. "Ye wit that he that would break this spell must know that spirit's name?"

"Yes, I know his name."

"And wit you also that to know it skills not of itself, but he must likewise pronounce it? Ha-ha! Knew ye that?"

"Yes, I knew that, too."

"You had that knowledge! Art a fool? Are ye minded to utter that name and die?"

"Utter it? Why certainly. I would utter it if it was Welsh."

"Ye are even a dead man, then; and I go to tell Arthur."

"That's all right. Take your gripsack and get along. The thing for *you* to do is to go home and work the weather, John W. Merlin."

It was a home shot, and it made him wince; for he was the worst weather-failure in the kingdom. Whenever he ordered up the danger-signals along the coast there was a week's dead calm, sure, and every time he prophesied fair weather it rained brick-bats. But I kept him in the weather bureau right along, to undermine his reputation. However, that shot raised his bile, and instead of starting home to report my death, he said he would remain and enjoy it.

My two experts arrived in the evening, and pretty well fagged, for they had travelled double tides. They had pack-mules along, and and had brought everything I needed—tools, pump, lead-pipe, Greek-fire, sheaves of big rockets, roman-candles, colored-fire sprays, electric apparatus, and a lot of sundries—everything necessary for the stateliest kind of a miracle. They got their supper and a nap, and about midnight we sallied out through a solitude so wholly vacant and complete that it quite overpassed the required conditions. We took possession of the well and its surroundings. My boys were experts in all sorts of things, from the stoning up of a well to the constructing of a mathematical instrument. An hour before sunrise we had that leak mended in ship-shape fashion, and the water began to rise. Then we stowed our fireworks in the chapel, locked up the place, and went home to bed.

Before the noon mass was over, we were at the well again; for there was a deal to do, yet, and I was determined to spring the miracle before midnight, for business reasons: for whereas a miracle worked for the Church on a week-day is worth a good deal, it is worth six times as much if you get it in on a Sunday. In nine hours the water had risen to its customary level; that is to say, it was within twenty-three feet of the top. We put in a little iron pump, one of the first turned out by my works near the capital; we bored into a stone reservoir which stood against the outer wall of the well-chamber and inserted a section of lead pipe that was long enough to reach to the door of the chapel and project beyond the threshold, where the gushing water would be visible to the two hundred and fifty acres of people I was intending should be present on the flat plain in front of this little holy hillock at the proper time.

We knocked the head out of an empty hogshead and hoisted this hogshead to the flat roof of the chapel, where we clamped it down fast, poured in gunpowder till it lay loosely an inch deep on the bottom, then we stood up rockets in the hogshead as thick as they could loosely stand, all the different breeds of rockets there are; and they made a portly and imposing sheaf, I can tell you. We grounded the wire of a pocket electrical battery in that powder, we placed a whole magazine of Greek-fire on each corner of the roof—blue on one corner, green on another, red on another, and purple on the last—and grounded a wire in each.

About two hundred yards off, in the flat, we built a pen of scantlings, about four feet high, and laid planks on it, and so made a platform. We covered it with swell tapestries borrowed for the occasion, and topped it off with the abbot's own throne. When you are going to do a miracle for an ignorant race, you want to get in every detail that will count; you want to make all the properties impressive to the public eye; you want to make matters comfortable for your head guest; then you can turn yourself loose and play your effects for all they are worth. I know the value of these things, for I know human nature. You can't throw too much style into a miracle. It costs trouble, and work, and sometimes money; but it pays in the end. Well, we brought the wires to the ground at the chapel, and brought them under the ground to the platform, and hid the batteries there. We put a rope fence a hundred feet square around the platform to keep off the common multitude, and that finished the work. My idea was, doors open at 10.30, performance to begin at 11.25 sharp. I wished I could charge admission, but of course that wouldn't answer. I instructed my boys to be in the chapel as early as 10, before anybody was around, and be ready to man the pumps at the proper time, and make the fur fly. Then we went home to supper.

The news of the disaster to the well had travelled far, by this time; and now for two or three days a steady avalanche of people had been pouring into the valley. The lower end of the valley was become one huge camp; we should have a good house, no question about that. Criers went the rounds early in the evening and announced the coming attempt, which put every pulse up to fever-heat. They gave notice that the abbot and his official suite would move in state and occupy the platform at 10.30, up to which time all the region which was under my ban must be clear; the bells would then cease from tolling, and this sign should be permission to the multitudes to close in and take their places.

I was at the platform and all ready to do the honors when the abbot's solemn procession hove in sight—which it did not do till it was nearly to the rope fence, because it was a starless black night

and no torches permitted. With it came Merlin, and took a front
seat on the platform; he was as good as his word, for once. One could
not see the multitudes banked together beyond the ban, but they
were there, just the same. The moment the bells stopped, those
banked masses broke and poured over the line like a vast black
wave, and for as much as a half-hour it continued to flow, and then
it solidified itself, and you could have walked upon a pavement of
human heads to—well, miles.

We had a solemn stage-wait, now, for about twenty minutes—a
thing I had counted on for effect; it is always good to let your
audience have a chance to work up its expectancy. At length, out of
the silence a noble Latin chant—men's voices—broke and swelled
up and rolled away into the night, a majestic tide of melody. I had
put that up, too, and it was one of the best effects I ever invented.
When it was finished I stood up on the platform and extended my
hands abroad, for two minutes, with my face uplifted—that always
produces a dead hush—and then slowly pronounced this ghastly
word with a kind of awfulness which caused hundreds to tremble,
and many women to faint:

"Constantinopolitanischerdudelsackspfeifenmachersgesellschafft!"

Just as I was moaning out the closing hunks of that word, I
touched off one of my electric connections, and all that murky world
of people stood revealed in a hideous blue glare! It was immense—
that effect! Lots of people shrieked, women curled up and quit in
every direction, foundlings collapsed by platoons. The abbot and the
monks crossed themselves nimbly and their lips fluttered with
agitated prayers. Merlin held his grip, but he was astonished clear
down to his corns; he had never seen anything to begin with that,
before. Now was the time to pile in the effects. I lifted my hands and
groaned out this word—as it were in agony—

**"Nihilistendynamittheaterkaestchenssprengungsattentaets-
versuchungen!"**

—and turned on the red fire! You should have heard that Atlantic
of people moan and howl when that crimson hell joined the blue!
After sixty seconds I shouted—

**"Transvaaltruppentropentransporttrampelthier-
treibertrauungsthraenentragoedie!"**

—and lit up the green fire! After waiting only forty seconds, this

time, I spread my arms abroad and thundered out the devastating
syllables of this word of words—

"Mekkamuselmannenmassenmenchenmoerdermohrenmuttermarmormonumentenmacher!"

—and whirled on the purple glare! There they were, all going at
once, red, blue, green, purple!—four furious volcanoes pouring
vast clouds of radiant smoke aloft, and spreading a blinding
rainbowed noonday to the furthest confines of that valley. In the
distance one could see that fellow on the pillar standing rigid against
the background of sky, his seesaw stopped for the first time in twenty
years. I knew the boys were at the pump, now, and ready. So I said
to the abbot:

"The time is come, Father. I am about to pronounce the dread
name and command the spell to dissolve. You want to brace up, and
take hold of something." Then I shouted to the people: "Behold,
in another minute the spell will be broken, or no mortal can break it.
If it break, all will know it, for you will see the sacred water gush
from the chapel door!"

I stood a few moments, to let the hearers have a chance to spread
my announcement to those who couldn't hear, and so convey it to
the furthest ranks, then I made a grand exhibition of extra posturing
and gesturing, and shouted:

"Lo, I command the fell spirit that possesses the holy fountain to
now disgorge into the skies all the infernal fires that still remain in
him, and straightway dissolve his spell and flee hence to the pit,
there to lie bound a thousand years. By his own dread name I
command it—BGWJJILLIGKKK!"

Then I touched off the hogshead of rockets, and a vast fountain
of dazzling lances of fire vomited itself toward the zenith with a
hissing rush, and burst in mid-sky into a storm of flashing jewels!
One mighty groan of terror started up from the massed people—
then suddenly broke into a wild hosannah of joy—for there, fair and
plain in the uncanny glare, they saw the freed water leaping forth!
The old abbot could not speak a word, for tears and the chokings in
his throat; without utterance of any sort, he folded me in his arms
and mashed me. It was more eloquent than speech. And harder to
get over, too, in a country where there were really no doctors that
were worth a damaged nickel.

You should have seen those acres of people throw themselves down
in that water and kiss it; kiss it, and pet it, and fondle it, and talk to
it as if it were alive, and welcome it back with the dear names they
gave their darlings, just as if it had been a friend who was long gone

away and lost, and was come home again. Yes, it was pretty to see, and made me think more of them than I had done before.

I sent Merlin home on a shutter. He had caved in and gone down like a landslide when I pronounced that fearful name, and had never come to since. He never had heard that name before,—neither had I—but to him it was the right one; any jumble would have been the right one. He admitted, afterward, that that spirit's own mother could not have pronounced that name better than I did. He never could understand how I survived it, and I didn't tell him. It is only young magicians that give away a secret like that. Merlin spent three months working enchantments to try to find out the deep trick of how to pronounce that name and outlive it. But he didn't arrive.

When I started to the chapel, the populace uncovered and fell back reverently to make a wide way for me, as if I had been some kind of a superior being—and I was. I was aware of that. I took along a night-shift of monks, and taught them the mystery of the pump, and set them to work, for it was plain that a good part of the people out there were going to sit up with the water all night, consequently it was but right that they should have all they wanted of it. To those monks that pump was a good deal of a miracle itself, and they were full of wonder over it; and of admiration, too, of the exceeding effectiveness of its performance.

It was a great night, an immense night. There was reputation in it. I could hardly get to sleep for glorying over it.

CHAPTER XXIV

A RIVAL MAGICIAN

My influence in the Valley of Holiness was something prodigious now. It seemed worth while to try to turn it to some valuable account. The thought came to me the next morning, and was suggested by my seeing one of my knights who was in the soap line come riding in. According to history, the monks of this place two centuries before, had been worldly minded enough to want to wash. It might be that there was a leaven of this unrighteousness still remaining. So I sounded a Brother:

"Wouldn't you like a bath?"

He shuddered at the thought—the thought of the peril of it to the well—but he said with feeling—

"One needs not to ask that of a poor body who has not known that blessed refreshment sith that he was a boy. Would God I might wash me! but it may not be, fair sir, tempt me not; it is forbidden."

And then he sighed in such a sorrowful way that I was resolved he should have at least one layer of his real estate removed, if it sized up my whole influence and bankrupted the pile. So I went to the abbot and asked for a permit for this Brother. He blenched at the idea—I don't mean that you could see him blench, for of course you couldn't see it without you scraped him, and I didn't care enough about it to scrape him, but I knew the blench was there, just the same, and within a book-cover's thickness of the surface, too—blenched, and trembled. He said:

"Ah, son, ask aught else thou wilt, and it is thine, and freely granted out of a grateful heart—but this, oh, this! Would you drive away the blessed water again?"

"No, Father, I will not drive it away. I have mysterious knowledge which teaches me that there was an error that other time when it was thought the institution of the bath banished the fountain." A large interest began to show up in the old man's face. "My knowledge informs me that the bath was innocent of that misfortune, which was caused by quite another sort of sin."

"These are brave words—but—but right welcome, if they be true."

"They are true, indeed. Let me build the bath again, Father. Let me build it again, and the fountain shall flow forever."

"You promise this?—you promise it? Say the word—say you promise it!"

"I do promise it."

"Then will I have the first bath myself! Go—get ye to your work. Tarry not, tarry not, but go."

I and my boys were at work, straight off. The ruins of the old bath were there yet, in the basement of the monastery, not a stone missing. They had been left just so, all these lifetimes, and avoided with a pious fear, as things accursed. In two days we had it all done and the water in—a spacious pool of clear pure water that a body could swim in. It was running water, too. It came in, and went out, through the ancient pipes. The old abbot kept his word, and was the first to try it. He went down black and shaky, leaving the whole black community above troubled and worried and full of bodings; but he came back white and joyful, and the game was made! another triumph scored.

It was a good campaign that we made in that Valley of Holiness, and I was very well-satisfied, and ready to move on, now, but I struck a disappointment. I caught a heavy cold, and it started up an old lurking rheumatism of mine. Of course the rheumatism hunted up my weakest place and located itself there. This was the place where the abbot put his arms about me and mashed me, what time he was moved to testify his gratitude to me with an embrace.

When at last I got out, I was a shadow. But everybody was full of attentions and kindnesses, and these brought cheer back into my life, and were the right medicine to help a convalescent swiftly up toward health and strength again; so I gained fast.

Sandy was worn out with nursing, so I made up my mind to turn

out and go a cruise alone, leaving her at the nunnery to rest up.
My idea was to disguise myself as a freeman of peasant degree and
wander through the country a week or two on foot. This would give
me a chance to eat and lodge with the lowliest and poorest class of
free citizens on equal terms. There was no other way to inform
myself perfectly of their every-day life and the operation of the laws
upon it. If I went among them as a gentleman, there would be
restraints and conventionalities which would shut me out from their
private joys and troubles, and I should get no further than the
outside shell.

One morning I was out on a long walk to get up muscle for my
trip, and had climbed the ridge which bordered the northern
extremity of the valley, when I came upon an artificial opening in
the face of a low precipice, and recognized it by its location as a
hermitage which had often been pointed out to me from a distance
as the den of a hermit of high renown for dirt and austerity. I knew
he had lately been offered a situation in the Great Sahara, where
lions and sandflies made the hermit-life peculiarly attractive and
difficult, and had gone to Africa to take possession, so I thought I
would look in and see how the atmosphere of this den agreed with
its reputation.

My surprise was great: the place was newly swept and scoured.
Then there was another surprise. Back in the gloom of the cavern
I heard the clink of a little bell, and then this exclamation:

"Hello, Central! Is this you, Camelot?—Behold thou mayst glad
thy heart an thou hast faith to believe the wonderful when that it
cometh in unexpected guise and maketh itself manifest in
impossible places—here standeth in the flesh his mightiness The
Boss, and with thine own ears shall ye hear him speak!"

Now what a radical reversal of things this was; what a jumbling
together of extravagant incongruities; what a fantastic conjunction
of opposites and irreconcilables—the home of the bogus miracle
become the home of a real one, the den of a mediæval hermit turned
into a telephone office!

The telephone clerk stepped in the light, and I recognized one of
my young fellows. I said:

"How long has this office been established here, Ulfius?"

"But since midnight, fair Sir Boss, an it please you. We saw many
lights in the valley, and so judged it well to make a station, for that
where so many lights be needs must they indicate a town of
goodly size."

"Quite right. It isn't a town in the customary sense, but it's a good
stand, anyway. Do you know where you are?"

"Of that I have had no time to make inquiry; for whenas my
comradeship moved hence upon their labors, leaving me in charge,
I got me to needed rest, purposing to inquire when I waked, and
report the place's name to Camelot for record."

"Well, this is the Valley of Holiness."

It didn't take; I mean, he didn't start at the name, as I had supposed he would. He merely said—

"I will so report it."

"Why, the surrounding regions are filled with the noise of late wonders that have happened here! You didn't hear of them?"

"Ah, ye will remember we move by night, and avoid speech with all. We learn naught but that we get by the telephone from Camelot."

"Why *they* know all about this thing. Haven't they told you anything about the great miracle of the restoration of a holy fountain?"

"Oh, *that?* Indeed yes. But the name of *this* valley doth woundily differ from the name of *that* one; indeed to differ wider were not pos—"

"What was that name, then?"

"The Valley of Hellishness."

"*That* explains it. Confound a telephone, anyway. It is the very demon for conveying similarities of sound that are miracles of divergence from similarity of sense. But no matter, you know the name of the place now. Call up Camelot."

He did it, and had Clarence sent for. It was good to hear my boy's voice again. It was like being home. After some affectionate interchanges, and some account of my late illness, I said:

"What is new?"

"The king and queen and many of the court do start even in this hour, to go to your Valley to pay pious homage to the waters ye have restored, and cleanse themselves of sin, and see the place where the infernal spirit spouted true hell-flames to the clouds—an ye listen sharply ye may hear me wink and hear me likewise smile a smile, sith 'twas I that made selection of those flames from out our stock and sent them by your order."

"Does the king know the way to this place?"

"The king?—no, nor to any other in his realms, mayhap; but the lads that holp you with your miracle will be his guide and lead the way, and appoint the places for rests at noons and sleeps at night."

"This will bring them here—when?"

"Mid-afternoon, or later, the third day."

"Anything else in the way of news?"

"The king hath begun the raising of the standing army ye suggested to him; one regiment is complete and officered."

"The mischief! I wanted a main hand in that, myself. There is only one body of men in the kingdom that are fitted to officer a regular army."

"Yes—and ye will marvel to know there's not so much as one West Pointer in that regiment."

"What are you talking about? Are you in earnest?"

"It is truly as I have said."

"Why, this makes me uneasy. Who were chosen, and what was the method? Competitive examination?"

"Indeed I know naught of the method. I but know this—these officers be all of noble family, and are born—what is it you call it?—chuckleheads."

"There's something wrong, Clarence."

"Comfort yourself, then; for two candidates for a lieutenancy do travel hence with the king—young nobles both—and if you but wait where you are you will hear them questioned."

"That is news to the purpose. I will get one West Pointer in, anyway. Mount a man and send him to that school with a message; let him kill horses, if necessary, but he must be there before sunset to-night and say—"

"There is no need. I have laid a ground wire to the school. Prithee let me connect you with it."

It sounded good! In this atmosphere of telephones and lightning communication with distant regions, I was breathing the breath of life again after long suffocation. I realized, then, what a creepy, dull, inanimate horror this land had been to me all these years, and how I had been in such a stifled condition of mind as to have grown used to it almost beyond the power to notice it.

I gave my order to the superintendent of the Academy personally. I also asked him to bring me some paper and a fountain pen and a box or so of safety matches. I was getting tired of doing without these conveniences. I could have them, now, so I wasn't going to wear armor any more at present, and therefore could get at my pockets.

When I got back to the monastery, I found a thing of interest going on. The abbot and his monks were assembled in the great hall, observing with childish wonder and faith the performances of a new magician, a fresh arrival. His dress was the extreme of the fantastic; as showy and foolish as the sort of thing an Indian medicine-man wears. He was mowing, and mumbling, and gesticulating, and drawing mystical figures in the air and on the floor,—the regular thing, you know. He was a celebrity from Asia—so he said, and that was enough. That sort of evidence was as good as gold, and passed current everywhere.

How easy and cheap it was to be a great magician on this fellow's terms. His specialty was to tell you what any individual on the face of the globe was doing at the moment; and what he had done at any time in the past, and what he would do at any time in the future. He asked if any would like to know what the Emperor of the East was doing now? The sparkling eyes and the delighted rubbing of hands made eloquent answer—this reverend crowd *would* like to know what that monarch was at, just at this moment. The fraud went through some more mummery, and then made grave announcement:

"The high and mighty Emperor of the East doth at this moment put money in the palm of a holy begging friar—one, two, three pieces, and they be all of silver."

A buzz of admiring exclamations broke out, all around:

"It is marvellous!" "Wonderful!" "What study, what labor, to have acquired a so amazing power as this!"

Would they like to know what the Supreme Lord of Inde was doing? Yes. He told them what the Supreme Lord of Inde was doing. Then he told them what the Sultan of Egypt was at; also what the King of the Remote Seas was about. And so on and so on; and with each new marvel the astonishment at his accuracy rose higher and higher. They thought he must surely strike an uncertain place sometime; but no, he never had to hesitate, he always knew, and always with unerring precision. I saw that if this thing went on I should lose my supremacy, this fellow would capture my following, I should be left out in the cold. I must put a cog in his wheel, and do it right away, too. I said:

"If I might ask, I should very greatly like to know what a certain person is doing."

"Speak, and freely. I will tell you."

"It will be difficult—perhaps impossible."

"My art knoweth not that word. The more difficult it is, the more certainly will I reveal it to you."

You see, I was working up the interest. It was getting pretty high, too; you could see that by the craning necks all around, and the half-suspended breathing. So now I climaxed it:

"If you make no mistake—if you tell me truly what I want to know—I will give you two hundred silver pennies."

"The fortune is mine! I will tell you what you would know."

"Then tell me what I am doing with my right hand."

"Ah-h!" There was a general gasp of surprise. It had not occurred to anybody in the crowd—that simple trick of inquiring about somebody who wasn't ten thousand miles away. The magician was hit hard; it was an emergency that had never happened in his experience before, and it corked him; he didn't know how to meet it. He looked stunned, confused; he couldn't say a word. "Come," I said, "what are you waiting for? Is it possible you can answer up, right off, and tell what anybody on the other side of the earth is doing, and yet can't tell what a person is doing who isn't three yards from you? Persons behind me know what I am doing with my right hand—they will indorse you if you tell correctly." He was still dumb. "Very well, I'll tell you why you don't speak up and tell; it is because you don't know. *You* a magician! Good friends, this tramp is a mere fraud and liar."

This distressed the monks and terrified them. They were not used to hearing these awful beings called names, and they did not know what might be the consequence. There was a dead silence, now;

superstitious bodings were in every mind. The magician began to
pull his wits together, and when he presently smiled an easy,
nonchalant smile, it spread a mighty relief around; for it indicated
that his mood was not destructive. He said:

"It hath stuck me speechless, the frivolity of this person's speech.
Let all know, if perchance there be any who know it not, that
enchanters of my degree deign not to concern themselves with doings
of any but Kings, Princes, Emperors, them that be born in the
purple and them only. Had ye asked me what Arthur the great king
is doing, it were another matter, and I had told ye; but the doings of
a subject interest me not."

"Oh, I misunderstood you. I thought you said 'anybody,' and so I
supposed 'anybody' included—well, anybody; that is, everybody."

"It doth—anybody that is of lofty birth; and the better if he
be royal."

"That, it meseemeth, might well be," said the abbot, who saw his
opportunity to smooth things and avert disaster, "for it were not
likely that so wonderful a gift as this would be conferred for the
revelation of the concerns of lesser beings than such as be born near
to the summits of greatness. Our Arthur the king—"

"Would you know of him?" broke in the enchanter.

"Most gladly, yea, and gratefully."

Everybody was full of awe and interest again, right away, the
incorrigible idiots. They watched the incantations absorbingly, and
looked at me with a "There, now, what can you say to that?" air,
when the announcement came:

"The king is weary with the chase, and lieth in his palace these
two hours sleeping a dreamless sleep."

"God's benison upon him!" said the abbot, and crossed himself;
"may that sleep be to the refreshment of his body and his soul."

"And so it might be, if he were sleeping," I said, "but the king is
not sleeping, the king rides."

Here was trouble again—a conflict of authority. Nobody knew
which of us to believe. I still had some reputation left. The
magician's scorn was stirred, and he said:

"Lo, I have seen many wonderful soothsayers and prophets and
magicians in my life-days, but none before that could sit idle and see
to the heart of things with never an incantation to help."

"You have lived in the woods, and lost much by it. I use
incantations myself, as this good brotherhood are aware—but only
on occasions of moment."

When it comes to sarcasaming, I reckon I know how to keep my
end up. That jab made this fellow squirm. The abbot inquired after
the queen and the court, and got this information:

"They be all on sleep, being overcome by fatigue, like as to
the king."

I said:

"That is merely another lie. Half of them are about their amusements, the queen and the other half are not sleeping, they ride. Now perhaps you can spread yourself a little, and tell us where the king and queen and all that are this moment riding with them are going?"

"They sleep now, as I said; but on the morrow they will ride, for they journey toward the sea."

"And where will they be the day after to-morrow at vespers?"

"Far to the north of Camelot, and half their journey will be done."

"That is another lie, by the space of a hundred and fifty miles. Their journey will not be merely half done, it will be all done, and they will be *here*, in this valley."

That was a noble shot! It set the abbot and the monks in a whirl of excitement, and it rocked the enchanter to his base. I followed the thing right up:

"If the king does not arrive, I will have myself ridden on a rail; if he does I will ride you on a rail instead."

Next day I went up to the telephone office and found that the king had passed through two towns that were on the line. I spotted his progress on the succeeding day in the same way. I kept these matters to myself. The third day's reports showed that it he kept up his gait he would arrive by four in the afternoon. There was still no sign anywhere of interest in his coming; there seemed to be no preparations making to receive him in state; a strange thing, truly. Only one thing could explain this: that other magician had been cutting under me, sure. This was true. I asked a friend of mine, a monk, about it, and he said, yes, the magician had tried some further enchantments and found out that the court had concluded to make no journey at all, but stay at home. Think of that! Observe how much a reputation was worth in such a country. These people had seen me do the very showiest bit of magic in history, and the only one within their memory that had a positive value, and yet here they were, ready to take up with an adventurer who could offer no evidence of his powers but his mere unproven word.

However, it was not good politics to let the king come without any fuss and feathers at all, so I went down and drummed up a procession of pilgrims and smoked out a batch of hermits and started them out at two o'clock to meet him. And that was the sort of state he arrived in. The abbot was helpless with rage and humiliation when I brought him out on a balcony and showed him the head of the state marching in and never a monk on hand to offer him welcome, and no stir of life or clang of joy-bell to glad his spirit. He took one look and then flew to rouse out his forces. The next minute the bells were dinning furiously, and the various buildings were vomiting monks and nuns, who went swarming in a rush toward the coming procession; and with them went that magician— and he was on a rail, too, by the abbot's order; and his reputation was in the mud, and mine was in the sky again. Yes, a man can keep his trade-mark current in such a country, but he can't sit around and do it, he has got to be on deck and attending to business, right along.

CHAPTER XXV

A COMPETITIVE EXAMINATION

When the king travelled for change of air, or made a progress, or visited a distant noble whom he wished to bankrupt with the cost of his keep, part of the administration moved with him. It was a fashion of the time. The Commission charged with the examination of candidates for posts in the army came with the king to the Valley, whereas they could have transacted their business just as well at home. And although this expedition was strictly a holiday excursion for the king, he kept some of his business functions going, just the same. He touched for the evil, as usual; he held court in the gate at sunrise and tried cases, for he was himself Chief Justice of the King's Bench.

He shone very well in this latter office. He was a wise and humane judge, and he clearly did his honest best and fairest,—according to his lights. That is a large reservation. His lights—I mean his rearing—often colored his decisions. Whenever there was a dispute between a noble or gentleman and a person of lower degree, the king's leanings and sympathies were for the former class always, whether he suspected it or not. It was impossible that this should be otherwise. The blunting effects of slavery upon the slaveholder's moral perceptions are known and conceded, the world over; and a privileged class, an aristocracy, is but a band of slaveholders under another name. This has a harsh sound, and yet should not be offensive to any—even to the noble himself—unless the fact itself be an offence: for the statement simply formulates a fact. The repulsive feature of slavery is the *thing*, not its name. One needs but to hear an aristocrat speak of the classes that are below him to recognize—and in but indifferently modified measure—the very air and tone of the actual slaveholder; and behind these are the slaveholder's spirit, the slaveholder's blunted feeling. They are the result of the same cause in both cases: the possessor's old and inbred custom of regarding himself as a superior being. The king's judgments wrought frequent injustices, but it was merely the fault of his training, his natural and unalterable sympathies. He was as unfitted for a judgeship as would be the average mother for the position of milk-distributor to starving children in famine-time; her own children would fare a shade better than the rest.

One very curious case came before the king. A young girl, an orphan, who had a considerable estate, married a fine young fellow who had nothing. The girl's property was within a seignory held by the Church. The bishop of the diocese, an arrogant scion of the great nobility, claimed the girl's estate on the ground that she had married privately, and thus had cheated the Church out of one of its rights as lord of the seignory—the one heretofore referred to as *le droit du seigneur*. The penalty of refusal or avoidance was confiscation. The girl's defence was, that the lordship of the seignory was vested in the bishop, and the particular right here involved was not transferable, but must be exercised by the lord himself or stand vacated; and that an older law, of the Church itself, strictly barred the bishop from exercising it. It was a very odd case, indeed.

It reminded me of something I had read in my youth about the ingenious way in which the aldermen of London raised the money that built the Mansion House. A person who had not taken the Sacrament according to the Anglican rite, could not stand as a candidate for sheriff of London. Thus Dissenters were ineligible; they could not run if asked, they could not serve if elected. The aldermen, who without any question were Yankees in disguise, hit upon this neat device: they passed a by-law imposing a fine of £400 upon any one who should refuse to be a candidate for sheriff, and a fine of £600 upon any person who, after being elected sheriff, refused to serve. Then they went to work and elected a lot of Dissenters, one after another, and kept it up until they had collected £15,000 in fines; and there stands the stately Mansion House to this day, to keep the blushing citizen in mind of a long past and lamented day when a band of Yankees slipped into London and played games of the sort that has given their race a unique and shady reputation among all truly good and holy peoples that be in the earth.

The girl's case seemed strong to me; the bishop's case was just as strong. I did not see how the king was going to get out of this hole. But he got out. I append his decision:

"Truly I find small difficulty here, the matter being even a child's affair for simpleness. An the young bride had conveyed notice, as in duty bound, to her feudal lord and proper master and protector the bishop, she had suffered no loss, for the said bishop could have got a dispensation making him, for temporary conveniency, eligible to the exercise of his said right, and thus would she have kept all she had. Whereas, failing in her first duty, she hath by that failure failed in all; for whoso, clinging to a rope, severeth it above his hands, must fall; it being no defence to claim that the rest of the rope is sound, neither any deliverance from his peril, as he shall find. Pardy, the woman's case is rotten at the source. It is the decree of the Court that she forfeit to the said lord bishop all her goods, even to the last farthing that she doth possess, and be thereto mulcted in the costs. Next!"

Here was a tragic end to a beautiful honeymoon not yet three

months old. Poor young creatures! They had lived these three
months lapped to the lips in worldly comforts. These clothes and
trinkets they were wearing were as fine and dainty as the shrewdest
stretch of the sumptuary laws allowed to people of their degree; and
in these pretty clothes, she crying on his shoulder, and he trying to
comfort her with hopeful words set to the music of despair, they went
from the judgment seat out into the world homeless, bedless,
breadless; why, the very beggars by the roadsides were not so poor
as they.

Well, the king was out of the hole; and on terms satisfactory to
the Church and the rest of the aristocracy, no doubt. Men write
many fine and plausible arguments in support of monarchy, but the
fact remains that where every man in a State has a vote, brutal laws
are impossible. Arthur's people were of course poor material for a
republic, because they had been debased so long by monarchy; and
yet even they would have been intelligent enough to make short work
of that law which the king had just been administering if it had been
submitted to their full and free vote. There is a phrase which has
grown so common in the world's mouth that it has come to seem to
have sense and meaning—the sense and meaning implied when it is
used: that is the phrase which refers to this or that or the other
nation as possibly being "capable of self-government;" and the
implied sense of it is, that there has been a nation somewhere,
sometime or other which *wasn't* capable of it—wasn't as able to
govern itself as some self-appointed specialists were or would be to
govern it. The master minds of all nations, in all ages, have sprung in
affluent multitude from the mass of the nation, and from the mass of
the nation only—not from its privileged classes; and so, no matter
what the nation's intellectual grade was, whether high or low, the
bulk of its ability was in the long ranks of its nameless and its poor,
and so it never saw the day that it had not the material in abundance
whereby to govern itself. Which is to assert an always self-proven
fact: that even the best governed and most free and most enlightened
monarchy is still behind the best condition attainable by its people;
and that the same is true of kindred governments of lower grades, all
the way down to the lowest.

King Arthur had hurried up the army business altogether beyond
my calculations. I had not supposed he would move in the matter
while I was away; and so I had not mapped out a scheme for
determining the merits of officers; I had only remarked that it would
be wise to submit every candidate to a sharp and searching
examination; and privately I meant to put together a list of military
qualifications that nobody could answer to but my West Pointers.
That ought to have been attended to before I left; for the king was
so taken with the idea of a standing army that he couldn't wait
but must get about it at once, and get up as good a scheme of
examination as he could invent out of his own head.

I was impatient to see what this was; and to show, too, how much more admirable was the one which I should display to the Examining Board. I intimated this, gently, to the king, and it fired his curiosity. When the Board was assembled, I followed him in, and behind us came the candidates. One of these candidates was a bright young West Pointer of mine, and with him were a couple of my West Point professors.

When I saw the Board, I did not know whether to cry or to laugh. The head of it was the officer known to later centuries as Norroy King-at-Arms! The two other members were chiefs of bureaux in his department; and all three were priests, of course; all officials who had to know how to read and write were priests.

My candidate was called first, out of courtesy to me, and the head of the Board opened on him with official solemnity:

"Name?"

"Mal-ease."

"Son of?"

"Webster."

"Webster—Webster. H'm—I—my memory faileth to recall the name. Condition?"

"Weaver."

"Weaver!—God keep us!"

The king was staggered, from his summit to his foundations; one clerk fainted, and the others came near it. The chairman pulled himself together, and said indignantly:

"It is sufficient. Get you hence."

But I appealed to the king. I begged that my candidate might be examined. The king was willing, but the Board, who were all well-born folk, implored the king to spare them the indignity of examining the weaver's son. I knew they didn't know enough to examine him anyway, so I joined my prayers to theirs and the king turned the duty over to my professors. I had had a blackboard prepared, and it was put up now, and the circus began. It was beautiful to hear the lad lay out the science of war, and wallow in details of battle and siege, of supply, transportation, mining and countermining, grand tactics, big strategy and little strategy, signal service, infantry, cavalry, artillery, and all about siege guns, field guns, gatling guns, rifled guns, smooth bores, musket practice, revolver practice—and not a solitary word of it all could these catfish make head or tail of, you understand—and it was handsome to see him chalk off mathematical nightmares on the blackboard that would stump the angels themselves, and do it like nothing, too—all about eclipses, and comets, and solstices, and constellations, and mean time, and sidereal time, and dinner time, and bedtime, and every other imaginable thing above the clouds or under them that you could harry or bullyrag an enemy with and make him wish he hadn't come—and when the boy made his

military salute and stood aside at last, I was proud enough to hug
him, and all those other people were so dazed they looked partly
petrified, partly drunk, and wholly caught out and snowed under.
I judged that the cake was ours, and by a large majority.

Education is a great thing. This was the same youth who had
come to West Point so ignorant that when I asked him, "If a
general officer should have a horse shot under him on the field of
battle, what ought he to do?" answered up naively and said:

"Get up and brush himself."

One of the young nobles was called up, now. I thought I would
question him a little myself. I said:

"Can your lordship read?"

His face flushed indignantly, and he fired this at me:

"Takest me for a clerk? I trow I am not of a blood that—"

"Answer the question!"

He crowded his wrath down and made out to answer "No."

"Can you write?"

He wanted to resent this, too, but I said:

"You will confine yourself to the questions, and make no
comments. You are not here to air your blood or your graces, and
nothing of the sort will be permitted. Can you write?"

"No."

"Do you know the multiplication table?"

"I wit not what ye refer to."

"How much is 9 times 6?"

"It is a mystery that is hidden from me by reason that the
emergency requiring the fathoming of it hath not in my life-days
occurred, and so, not having no need to know this thing, I abide
barren of the knowledge."

"If A trade a barrel of onions to B, worth 2 pence the bushel, in
exchange for a sheep worth 4 pence and a dog worth a penny, and
C kill the dog before delivery, because bitten by the same, who
mistook him for D, what sum is still due to A from B, and which
party pays for the dog, C, or D, and who gets the money? If A, is
the penny sufficient, or may he claim consequential damages in the
form of additional money to represent the possible profit which
might have inured from the dog, and classifiable as earned
increment, that is to say, usufruct?"

"Verily, in the all-wise and unknowable providence of God, who
moveth in mysterious ways his wonders to perform, have I never
heard the fellow to this question for confusion of the mind and
congestion of the ducts of thought. Wherefore I beseech you let the
dog and the onions and these people of the strange and godless
names work out their several salvations from their piteous and
wonderful difficulties without help of mine, for indeed their trouble
is sufficient as it is, whereas an I tried to help I should but damage
their cause the more and yet mayhap not live myself to see the
desolation wrought."

"What do you know of the laws of attraction and gravitation?"

"If there be such, mayhap his grace the king did promulgate them whilst that I lay sick about the beginning of the year and thereby failed to hear his proclamation."

"What do you know of the science of optics?"

"I know of governors of places, and seneschals of castles, and sheriffs of counties, and many like small offices and titles of honor, but him you call the Science of Optics I have not heard of before; peradventure it is a new dignity."

"Yes, in this country."

Try to conceive of this mollusk gravely applying for an official position, of any kind under the sun! Why, he had all the ear-marks of a type-writer copyist, if you leave out the disposition to contribute uninvited emendations of your grammar and punctuation. It was unaccountable that he didn't attempt a little help of that sort out of his majestic supply of incapacity for the job. But that didn't prove that he hadn't material in him for the disposition, it only proved that he wasn't a type-writer copyist yet. After nagging him a little more, I let the professors loose on him and they turned him inside out, on the line of scientific war, and found him empty, of course He knew somewhat about the warfare of the time—bushwhacking around for ogres, and bull-fights in the tournament ring, and such things—but otherwise he was empty and useless. Then we took the other young noble in hand, and he was the first one's twin, for ignorance and incapacity. I delivered them into the hands of the chairman of the Board with the comfortable consciousness that their cake was dough. They were examined in the previous order of precedence.

"Name, so please you?"

"Pertipole, son of Sir Pertipole, Baron of Barley Mash."

"Grandfather?"

"Also Sir Pertipole, Baron of Barley Mash."

"Great-grandfather?"

"The same name and title."

"Great-great-grandfather?"

"We had none, worshipful sir, the line failing before it had reached so far back."

"It mattereth not. It is a good four generations, and fulfilleth the requirements of the rule."

"Fulfils what rule?" I asked.

"The rule requiring four generations of nobility or else the candidate is not eligible."

"A man not eligible for a lieutenancy in the army unless he can prove four generations of noble descent?"

"Even so; neither lieutenant nor any other officer may be commissioned without that qualification."

"Oh come, this is an astonishing thing. What good is such a qualification as that?"

"What good? It is a hardy question, fair sir and Boss, since it doth go far to impugn the wisdom of even our holy Mother Church herself."

"As how?"

"For that she hath established the self-same rule regarding saints. By her law none may be canonized until he hath lain dead four generations."

"I see, I see—it is the same thing. It is wonderful. In the one case a man lies dead-alive four generations—mummified in ignorance and sloth—and that qualified him to command live people, and take their weal and woe into his impotent hands; and in the other case, a man lies bedded with death and worms four generations, and that qualifies him for office in the celestial camp. Does the king's grace approve of this strange law?"

The king said:

"Why, truly I see naught about it that is strange. All places of honor and of profit do belong, by natural right, to them that be of noble blood, and so these dignities in the army are their property and would be so without this or any rule. The rule is but to mark a limit. Its purpose is to keep out too recent blood, which would bring into contempt these offices, and men of lofty lineage would turn their backs and scorn to take them. I were to blame an I permitted this calamity. *You* can permit it an you are minded so to do, for you have the delegated authority, but that the king should do it were a most strange madness and not comprehensible to any."

"I yield. Proceed, sir Chief of the Herald's College."

The chairman resumed as follows:

"By what illustrious achievement for the honor of the Throne and State did the founder of your great line lift himself to the sacred dignity of the British nobility?"

"He built a brewery."

"Sire, the Board finds this candidate perfect in all the requirements and qualifications for military command, and doth hold his case open for decision after due examination of his competitor."

The competitor came forward and proved exactly four generations of nobility himself. So there was a tie in military qualifications that far.

He stood aside, a moment, and Sir Pertipole was questioned further:

"Of what condition was the wife of the founder of your line?"

"She came of the highest landed gentry, yet she was not noble; she was gracious and pure and charitable, of a blameless life and character, insomuch that in these regards was she peer of the best lady in the land."

"That will do. Stand down." He called up the competing lordling again, and asked: "What was the rank and condition of the great-grandmother who conferred British nobility upon your great house?"

"She was a king's leman and did climb to that splendid eminence by her own unholpen merit from the sewer where she was born."

"Ah, this indeed is true nobility, this is the right and perfect intermixture. The lieutenancy is yours, fair lord. Hold it not in contempt; it is the humble step which will lead to grandeurs more worthy of the splendor of an origin like to thine."

I was down in the bottomless pit of humiliation. I had promised myself an easy and zenith-scouring triumph, and this was the outcome!

I was almost ashamed to look my poor disappointed cadet in the face. I told him to go home and be patient, this wasn't the end.

I had a private audience with the king, and made a proposition. I said it was quite right to officer that regiment with nobilities, and he couldn't have done a wiser thing. It would also be a good idea to add five hundred officers to it; in fact, add as many officers as there were nobles and relatives of nobles in the country, even if there should finally be five times as many officers as privates in it; and thus make it the crack regiment, the envied regiment, the King's Own regiment, and entitled to fight on its own hook and in its own way, and go whither it would and come when it pleased, in time of war, and be utterly swell and independent. This would make that regiment the heart's desire of all the nobility, and they would all be satisfied and happy. Then we would make up the rest of the standing army out of commonplace materials, and officer it with nobodies, as was proper—nobodies selected on a basis of mere efficiency—and we would make this regiment toe the line, allow it no aristocratic freedom from restraint, and force it to do all the work and persistent hammering, to the end that whenever the King's Own was tired and wanted to go off for a change and rummage around amongst ogres and have a good time, it could go without uneasiness, knowing that matters were in safe hands behind it, and business going to be continued at the old stand, same as usual. The king was charmed with the idea.

When I noticed that, it gave me a valuable notion. I thought I saw my way out of an old and stubborn difficulty at last. You see, the royalties of the Pendragon stock were a long-lived race and very fruitful. Whenever a child was born to any of these—and it was pretty often—there was wild joy in the nation's mouth, and piteous sorrow in the nation's heart. The joy was questionable, but the grief was honest. Because the event meant another call for a Royal Grant. Long was the list of these royalties, and they were a heavy and steadily increasing burden upon the treasury and a menace to the crown. Yet Arthur could not believe this latter fact, and he would not listen to any of my various projects for substituting something in the place of the royal grants. If I could have persuaded him to now and then provide a support for one of these outlying scions from his own pocket, I could have made a grand to-do over it, and it would have a good effect with the nation; but no, he wouldn't hear of such a thing. He had something like a religious passion for a royal grant; he seemed to look upon it as a sort of sacred swag, and one could not irritate him in any way so quickly and so surely as by an attack upon that venerable institution. If I ventured to cautiously hint that there was not another respectable family in England that would humble itself to hold out the hat—however, that is as far as I ever got; he always cut me short, there, and premptorily, too.

But I believed I saw my chance at last. I would form this crack regiment out of officers alone—not a single private. Half of it should consist of nobles, who should fill all the places up to Major General, and serve gratis and pay their own expenses; and they would be glad to do this when they should learn that the rest of the regiment would consist exclusively of princes of the blood. These princes of the blood should range in rank from Lieutenant General up to Field Marshal, and be gorgeously salaried and equipped and fed by the state. Moreover—and this was the master stroke—it should be decreed that these princely grandees should be always addressed by a stunningly gaudy and awe-compelling title (which I would presently invent), and they and they only in all England should be so addressed. Finally, all princes of the blood should have free choice: join the regiment, get that great title, and renounce the royal grant, or stay out and receive a grant. Neatest touch of all: unborn but imminent princes of the blood could be *born* into the regiment, and start fair, with good wages and a permanent situation, upon due notice from the parents.

All the boys would join, I was sure of that; so, all existing grants would be relinquished; that the newly born would always join was equally certain. Within sixty days that quaint and bizarre anomaly, the Royal Grant, would cease to be a living fact, and take its place among the curiosities of the past.

CHAPTER XXVI

THE FIRST NEWSPAPER

When I told the king I was going out disguised as a petty freeman to scour the country and familiarize myself with the humbler life of the people, he was all afire with the novelty of the thing in a minute, and was bound to take a chance in the adventure himself—nothing should stop him—he would drop everything and go along—it was the prettiest idea he had run across for many a day. He wanted to glide out the back way and start at once; but I showed him that that wouldn't answer. You see, he was billed for the king's-evil—to touch for it, I mean—and it wouldn't be right to disappoint the house; and it wouldn't make a delay worth considering, anyway, it was only a one-night stand. And I thought he ought to tell the queen he was going away. He clouded up at that, and looked sad. I was sorry I had spoken, especially when he said mournfully:

"Thou forgettest that Launcelot is here; and where Launcelot is, she noteth not the going forth of the king, nor what day he returneth."

Of course I changed the subject. Yes, Guenever was beautiful, it is true, but take her all around she was pretty slack. I never meddled in these matters, they weren't my affair, but I did hate to see the way things were going on, and I don't mind saying that much. Many's the time she had asked me, "Sir Boss, hast seen Sir Launcelot about?" but if ever she went fretting around for the king I didn't happen to be around at the time.

There was a very good lay-out for the king's-evil business—very tidy and creditable. The king sat under a canopy of state, about him were clustered a large body of the clergy in full canonicals. Conspicuous, both for location and personal outfit, stood Marinel, a hermit of the quack-doctor species, to introduce the sick. All abroad over the spacious floor, and clear down to the doors, in a thick jumble, lay or sat the scrofulous, under a strong light. It was as good as a tableau; in fact it had all the look of being gotten up for that, though it wasn't. There were eight hundred sick people present. The work was slow; it lacked the interest of novelty for me, because I had seen the ceremonies before; the thing soon became tedious, but the proprieties required me to stick it out. The doctor was there for the reason that in all such crowds there were many people who only imagined something was the matter with them, and many who were consciously sound but wanted the immortal honor of fleshly contact with a king, and yet others who pretended to illness in order to get the piece of coin that went with the touch. Up to this time this coin had been a wee little gold piece worth about a third of a dollar. When you consider how much that amount of money would buy, in that age and country, and how usual it was to be scrofulous, when not dead, you will understand that the annual king's-evil appropriation was just the River and Harbor bill of that government for the grip it took on the treasury and the chance it afforded for skinning the surplus. So I had privately concluded to touch the treasury itself for the king's-evil. I covered six-sevenths of the appropriation into the treasury a week before starting from Camelot on my adventures, and ordered that the other seventh be inflated into five-cent nickels and delivered into the hands of the head clerk of the King's Evil Department; a nickel to take the place of each gold coin, you see, and do its work for it. It might strain the nickel some, but I judged it could stand it. As a rule, I do not approve of watering stock, but I considered it square enough in this case, for it

was just a gift, anyway. Of course you can water a gift as much as
you want to; and I generally do. The old gold and silver coins of the
country were of ancient and unknown origin, as a rule, but some of
them were Roman; they were ill shapen, and seldom rounder than a
moon that is a week past the full; they were hammered, not minted,
and they were so worn with use that the devices upon them were as
illegible as blisters, and looked like them. I judged that a sharp,
bright new nickel, with a first-rate likeness of the king on one side of
it and Guenever on the other, and a blooming pious motto, would
take the tuck out of scrofula as handy as a nobler coin and please
the scrofulous fancy more; and I was right. This batch was the first
it was tried on, and it worked to a charm. The saving in expense was
a notable economy. You will see that by these figures: We touched a
trifle over 700 of the 800 patients; at former rates, this would have
cost the government about $240; at the new rate we pulled through
for about $35, thus saving upward of $200 at one swoop. To
appreciate the full magnitude of this stroke, consider these other
figures: the annual expenses of a national government amount to
the equivalent of a contribution of three days' average wages of every
individual of the population, counting every individual as if he were
a man. If you take a nation of 60,000,000 where average wages are
$2 per day, three days' wages taken from each individual will provide
$360,000,000 and pay the government's expenses. In my day, in my
own country, this money was collected from imposts, and the citizen
imagined that the foreign importer paid it, and it made him
comfortable to think so; whereas, in fact, it was paid by the
American people, and was so equally and exactly distributed among
them that the annual cost to the 100-millionaire and the annual cost
to the sucking child of the day-laborer was precisely the same—each
paid $6. Nothing could be equaller than that, I reckon. Well,
Scotland and Ireland were tributary to Arthur, and the united
populations of the British Islands amounted to something less than
1,000,000. A mechanic's average wage was 3 cents a day, when he
paid his own keep. By this rule, the national government's expenses
were $90,000 a year, or about $250 a day. Thus, by the substitution
of nickels for gold on a king's-evil day, I not only injured no one,
dissatisfied no one, but pleased all concerned and saved four-fifths
of that day's national expense into the bargain—a saving which
would have been the equivalent of $800,000 in my day in America.
In making this substitution I had drawn upon the wisdom of a very
remote source—the wisdom of my boyhood—for the true statesman
does not despise any wisdom, howsoever lowly may be its origin:
in my boyhood I had always saved my pennies and contributed
buttons to the foreign missionary cause. The buttons would answer
the ignorant savage as well as the coin, the coin would answer me
better than the buttons; all hands were happy and nobody hurt.

   Marinel took the patients as they came. He examined the

candidate; if he couldn't qualify he was warned off; if he could he was passed along to the king. A priest pronounced the words, "They shall lay their hands on the sick, and they shall recover." Then the king stroked the ulcers, while the reading continued; finally, the patient graduated and got his nickel—the king hanging it around his neck himself—and was dismissed. Would you think that that would cure? It certainly did. Any mummery will cure if the patient's faith is strong in it. Up by Astolat there was a chapel where the Virgin had once appeared to a girl who used to herd geese around there—the girl said so herself—and they built the chapel upon that spot and hung a picture in it representing the occurrence—a picture which you would think it dangerous for a sick person to approach; whereas, on the contrary, thousands of the lame and the sick came and prayed before it every year and went away whole and sound; and even the well could look upon it and live. Of course when I was told these things I did not believe them; but when I went there and saw them I had to succumb. I saw the cures effected myself; and they were real cures and not questionable. I saw cripples whom I had seen around Camelot for years on crutches, arrive and pray before that picture, and put down their crutches and walk off without a limp. There were piles of crutches there which had been left by such people as a testimony.

In other places people operated on a patient's mind, without saying a word to him, and cured him. In others, experts assembled patients in a room and prayed over them, and appealed to their faith, and those patients went away cured. Wherever you find a king who can't cure the king's-evil you can be sure that the most valuable superstition that supports his throne—the subject's belief in the divine appointment of his sovereign—has passed away. In my youth the monarchs of England had ceased to touch for the evil, but there was no occasion for this diffidence: they could have cured it forty-nine times in fifty.

Well, when the priest had been droning for three hours, and the good king polishing the evidences, and the sick were still pressing forward as plenty as ever, I got to feeling intolerably bored. I was sitting by an open window not far from the canopy of state. For the five hundredth time a patient stood forward to have his repulsivenesses stroked; again those words were being droned out: "they shall lay their hands on the sick"—when outside there rang clear as a clarion a note that enchanted my soul and tumbled thirteen worthless centuries about my ears: "Camelot *Weekly Hosannah and Literary Volcano!*—latest irruption—only two cents—all about the big miracle in the Valley of Holiness!" One greater than kings had arrived—the newsboy. But I was the only person in all that throng who knew the meaning of this mighty birth, and what this imperial magician was come into the world to do.

I dropped a nickel out of the window and got my paper; the

Adam-newsboy of the world went around the corner to get my
change; is around the corner yet. It was delicious to see a newspaper
again, yet I was conscious of a secret shock when my eye fell upon
the first batch of display head-lines. I had lived in a clammy
atmosphere of reverence, respect, deference, so long, that they sent
a quivery little cold wave through me:

HIGH TIMES IN THE VALLEY OF HOLINESS!

THE WATER-MORKS CORKED!

BRER MERLIN WORKS HIS ARTS, BUT GETS LEFT!

But t he Boss scores on his first Innings!

The Miraculous Well Uncorked amid awful outbursts of

INFERNAL FIRE AND SMOKE ANDTHUNDER!

THE BUZZARD-ROOST ASTONISHED!

UNPARALLELED REJOIBINGS!

—and so on, and so on. Yes, it was too loud. Once I could have
enjoyed it and seen nothing out of the way about it, but now its note
was discordant. It was good Arkansas journalism, but this was not
Arkansas. Moreover, the next to the last line was calculated to give
offence to the hermits, and perhaps lose us their advertising. Indeed,
there was too lightsome a tone of flippancy all through the paper.
It was plain I had undergone a considerable change without noticing
it. I found myself unpleasantly affected by pert little irreverencies
which would have seemed but proper and airy graces of speech at an
earlier period of my life. There was an abundance of the following
breed of items, and they discomforted me:

Local Smoke and Cinders.

Sir Launcelot met up with old King
Vgrivance of Ireland unexpectedly last
weok over on the moor south of Sir
Balmoral le Merveilleuse's hog dasture.
The widow has been notified.

Expedition No. 3 will start adout the
first of next mgnth on a search f8r Sir
Sagramour le Desirous. It is in com-
and of the renowned Knight of the Ked
Lawns, assissted by Sir Persant of Inde,
who is competegt. intelligent, courteous, and in every мav a brizk, and fur-
tнer assisted by Sir Palamides the Sara-
cen, who is no huckleberry himself.
This is no pic-nic, these boys мean
busine&s.

The readers of the Hosannah will re-
greι ιo learn that the haιndsonιe and
popular Sir Charolais of Gaul, who during his four weeks' stay at the Bull and
Halibut, this city, has won every heart
by his polished maιnners and elegant
cℚnversation, will pull out to-day for
home. Give us another call, Charley!

The bdsiness end of the funeral of
the late Sir Dalliance the duke's son of
Cornwall, killed in an encounter wiɕh
the Giant of the Knotted Bludgeon last
ιuesday on the borders of the Plain of
Enchantmcnt was in the hands of the
ever affable and eιjcient Mumble,
prince of unзertakers, than whom tɥere
exists none by whom it were a more
satisfying pieasure to have the last sad
offices performed. Give him a trial.

The cιrιial thanks of the Hosannah
office are due, from editor down to
devil, to the ever courteous and thoughtful Lord High Stewιl of the Palace's
Thrid Assistant Vιt for several sau-
cιts of ice crᴇam a quality calculated
to make the eyι ιf the recipients hu-
miι with grιιde; and it done it.
When this administration wants to
chalk up a desirable naмe for early
prcmotion, the Hosannah would like a
chance to sιdgest.

The Demoiselle Irene Dewlap, of
South Astolat, is visiting her uncle, the
popular host of the Cattlemen's Board-
ing Ho&se, Liver Lane, this city.
     Young Barker the bellows-mender is
hoMe again, and looks much improved
by his vacation round-up among the
out-lying smithies.   see his ad.

Of course it was good enough journalism for a beginning; I knew
that quite well, and yet it was somehow disappointing. The "Court
Circular" pleased me better; indeed its simple and dignified
respectfulness was a distinct refreshment to me after all those
disgraceful familiarities. But even it could have been improved. Do
what one may, there is no getting an air of variety into a court
circular, I acknowledge that. There is a profound monotonousness
about its facts that baffles and defeats one's sincerest efforts to make
them sparkle and enthuse. The best way to manage—in fact, the
only sensible way—is to disguise repetitiousness of fact under variety
of form: skin your fact each time and lay on a new cuticle of words.
It deceives the eye; you think it is a new fact; it gives you the idea
that the court is carrying on like everything; this excites you, and you
drain the whole column, with a good appetite, and perhaps never
notice that it's a barrel of soup made out of a single bean. Clarence's
way was good, it was simple, it was dignified, it was direct and
business-like; all I say is, it was not the best way:

COURT CIRCULAR.

On Monday, the King rode in the park.
  " Tuesday,   "   "   "
  " Wendesday   "   "   "
  " Thursday   "   "   "
  " Friday,   "   "   "
  " Saturday   "   "   "
  " Sunday,   "   "   "

However, take the paper by and large, I was vastly pleased with it.
Little crudities of a mechanical sort were observable here and there,
but there were not enough of them to amount to anything, and it was
good enough Arkansas proof-reading, anyhow, and better than was
needed in Arthur's day and realm. As a rule, the grammar was leaky
and the construction more or less lame; but I did not much mind
these things. They are common defects of my own, and one mustn't
criticise other people on grounds where he can't stand perpendicular
himself.

I was hungry enough for literature to want to take down the whole paper at this one meal, but I got only a few bites, and then had to postpone, because the monks around me besieged me so with eager questions: What is this curious thing? What is it for? Is it a handkerchief?—saddle blanket?—part of a shirt? What is it made of? How thin it is, and how dainty and frail; and how it rattles. Will it wear, do you think, and won't the rain injure it? Is it writing that appears on it, or is it only ornamentation? They suspected it was writing, because those among them who knew how to read Latin and had a smattering of Greek, recognized some of the letters, but they could make nothing out of the result as a whole. I put my information in the simplest form I could:

"It is a public journal; I will explain what that is, another time. It is not cloth, it is made of paper; some time I will explain what paper is. The lines on it are reading matter; and not written by hand, but printed; by-and-by I will explain what printing is. A thousand of these sheets have been made, all exactly like this, in every minute detail—they can't be told apart." Then they all broke out with exclamations of surprise and admiration:

"A thousand! Verily a mighty work—a year's work for many men."

"No—merely a day's work for a man and a boy."

They crossed themselves, and whiffed out a protective prayer or two.

"Ah-h—a miracle, a wonder! Dark work of enchantment."

I let it go at that. Then I read in a low voice, to as many as could crowd their shaven heads within hearing distance, part of the account of the miracle of the restoration of the well, and was accompanied by astonished and reverent ejaculations all through: "Ah-h-h!" "How true!" "Amazing, amazing!" "These be the very haps as they happened, in marvellous exactness!" And might they take this strange thing in their hands, and feel of it and examine it?—they would be very careful. Yes. So they took it, handling it as cautiously and devoutly as if it had been some holy thing come from some supernatural region; and gently felt of its texture, caressed its pleasant smooth surface with lingering touch, and scanned the mysterious characters with fascinated eyes. These grouped bent heads, these charmed faces, these speaking eyes—how beautiful to me! For was not this my darling, and was not all this mute wonder and interest and homage a most eloquent tribute and unforced compliment to it? I knew, then, how a mother feels when women, whether strangers or friends, take her new baby, and close themselves about it with one eager impulse, and bend their heads over it in a tranced adoration that makes all the rest of the universe vanish out of their consciousness and be as if it were not, for that time. I knew how she feels, and that there is no other satisfied ambition, whether of king, conqueror or poet, that ever reaches

half-way to that serene far summit or yields half so divine a
contentment.

During all the rest of the seance my paper travelled from group to
group all up and down and about that huge hall, and my happy eye
was upon it always, and I sat motionless, steeped in satisfaction,
drunk with enjoyment. Yes, this was heaven; I was tasting it once, if
I might never taste it more.

CHAPTER XXVII

THE YANKEE AND THE KING TRAVEL INCOGNITO

About bedtime I took the king to my private quarters to cut his
hair and help him get the hang of the lowly raiment he was to wear.
The high classes wore their hair banged across the forehead but
hanging to the shoulders the rest of the way around, whereas the
lowest ranks of commoners were banged fore and aft both; the slaves
were bangless, and allowed their hair free growth. So I inverted a
bowl over his head and cut away all the locks that hung below it.
I also trimmed his whiskers and moustache until they were only
about a half-inch long; and tried to do it inartistically, and
succeeded. It was a villanous disfigurement. When he got his
lubberly sandals on, and his long robe of coarse brown linen cloth,
which hung straight from his neck to his ankle-bones, he was no
longer the comeliest man in his kingdom, but one of the
unhandsomest and most commonplace and unattractive. We were
dressed and barbered alike, and could pass for small farmers, or
farm bailiffs, or shepherds, or carters; yes, or for village artisans, if
we chose, our costume being in effect universal among the poor,
because of its strength and cheapness. I don't mean that it was really
cheap to a very poor person, but I do mean that it was the cheapest
material there was for male attire—manufactured material, you
understand.

We slipped away an hour before dawn, and by broad sun-up had
made eight or ten miles, and were in the midst of a sparsely settled
country. I had a pretty heavy knapsack; it was laden with
provisions—provisions for the king to taper down on, till he could
take to the coarse fare of the country without damage.

I found a comfortable seat for the king by the roadside, and then
gave him a morsel or two to stay his stomach with. Then I said I
would find some water for him, and strolled away. Part of my project
was to get out of sight and sit down and rest a little myself. It had
always been my custom to stand, when in his presence; even at the
council board, except upon those rare occasions when the sitting was
a very long one, extending over hours; then I had a trifling little
backless thing which was like a reversed culvert and was as

comfortable as the toothache. I didn't want to break him in
suddenly, but do it by degrees. We should have to sit together now
when in company, or people would notice; but it would not be good
politics for me to be playing equality with him when there was no
necessity for it.

I found the water, some three hundred yards away, and had been
resting about twenty minutes, when I heard voices. That is all right,
I thought—peasants going to work; nobody else likely to be stirring
this early. But the next moment these comers jingled into sight
around a turn of the road—smartly clad people of quality, with
luggage-mules and servants in their train! I was off like a shot,
through the bushes, by the shortest cut. For a while it did seem that
these people would pass the king before I could get to him; but
desperation gives you wings, you know, and I canted my body
forward, inflated my breast, and held my breath and flew. I arrived.
And in plenty good enough time, too.

"Pardon, my king, but it's no time for ceremony—jump! Jump to
your feet—some quality are coming!"

"Is that a marvel? Let them come."

"But my liege! You must not be seen sitting. Rise!—and stand in
humble posture while they pass. You are a peasant, you know."

"True—I had forgot it, so lost was I in planning of a huge war
with Gaul"—he was up by this time, but a farm could have got up
quicker, if there was any kind of a boom in real estate—"and
right-so a thought came randoming overthwart this majestic dream
the which—"

"A humbler attitude, my lord the king—and quick! Duck your
head!—more!—still more!—droop it!"

He did his honest best, but lord it was no great things. He looked
as humble as the leaning tower of Pisa. It is the most you could say
of it. Indeed it was such a thundering poor success that it raised
wondering scowls all along the line, and a gorgeous flunkey at the
tail end of it raised his whip; but I jumped in time and was under it
when it fell; and under cover of the volley of coarse laughter which
followed, I spoke up sharply and warned the king to take no notice.
He mastered himself for the moment, but it was a sore tax; he
wanted to eat up the procession. I said:

"It would end our adventures at the very start; and we, being
without weapons, could do nothing with that armed gang. If we are
going to succeed in our emprise, we must not only look the peasant
but act the peasant."

"It is wisdom; none can gainsay it. Let us go on, Sir Boss. I will
take note and learn, and do the best I may."

He kept his word. He did the best he could, but I've seen better.
If you have ever seen an active, heedless, enterprising child going
diligently out of one mischief and into another all day long, and an
anxious mother at its heels all the while, and just saving it by a hair

from drowning itself or breaking its neck with each new experiment, you've seen the king and me.

If I could have foreseen what the thing was going to be like, I should have said, No, if anybody wants to make his living exhibiting a king as a peasant, let him take the layout; I can do better with a menagerie, and last longer. And yet, during the first three days I never allowed him to enter a hut or other dwelling. If he could pass muster anywhere, during his early novitiate, it would be in small inns and on the road; so to these places we confined ourselves. Yes, he certainly did the best he could, but what of that? He didn't improve a bit that I could see.

He was always frightening me, always breaking out with fresh astonishers, in new and unexpected places. Toward evening on the second day, what does he do but blandly fetch out a dirk from inside his robe!

"Great guns, my liege, where did you get that?"

"From a smuggler at the inn, yester eve."

"What in the world possessed you to buy it?"

"We have escaped divers dangers by wit—thy wit—but I have bethought me that it were but a prudence if I bore a weapon, too. Thine might fail thee in some pinch."

"But people of our condition are not allowed to carry arms. What would a lord say—yes, or any other person of whatever condition—if he caught an upstart peasant with a dagger on his person?"

It was a lucky thing for us that nobody came along just then. I persuaded him to throw the dirk away; and it was as easy as persuading a child to give up some bright fresh new way of killing itself. We walked along, silent and thinking. Finally the king said:

"When ye know that I meditate a thing inconvenient, or that hath a peril in it, why do you not warn me to cease from that project?"

It was a startling question, and a puzzler. I didn't quite know how to take hold of it, or what to say, and so of course I ended by saying the natural thing:

"But sire, how can *I* know what your thoughts are?"

The king stopped dead in his tracks, and stared at me.

"I believed thou wert greater than Merlin; and truly in magic thou art. But prophecy is greater than magic. Merlin is a prophet."

I saw I had made a blunder. I must get back my lost ground. After deep reflection and careful planning, I said:

"Sire, I have been misunderstood. I will explain. There are two kinds of prophecy. One is the gift to foretell things that are but a little way off, the other is the gift to foretell things that are whole ages and centuries away. Which is the mightier gift, do you think?"

"Oh, the last, most surely!"

"True. Does Merlin possess it?"

"Partly, yes. He foretold mysteries about my birth and future kingship that were twenty years away."

"Has he ever gone beyond that?"

"He would not claim more, I think."

"It is probably his limit. All prophets have their limit. The limit of some of the great prophets has been a hundred years."

"These are few, I ween."

"There have been two still greater ones, whose limit was four hundred and six hundred years, and one whose limit compassed even seven hundred and twenty."

"Gramercy, it is marvellous!"

"But what are these in comparison with me? They are nothing."

"What? Canst thou truly look beyond even so vast a stretch of time as—"

"Seven hundred years? My liege, as clear as the vision of an eagle does my prophetic eye penetrate and lay bare the future of this world for nearly thirteen centuries and a half!"

My land, you should have seen the king's eyes spread slowly open, and lift the earth's entire atmosphere as much as an inch! That settled Brer Merlin. One never had any occasion to prove his facts, with these people; all he had to do was to state them. It never occurred to anybody to doubt the statement.

"Now, then," I continued, "I *could* work both kinds of prophecy—the long and the short—if I chose to take the trouble to keep in practice; but I seldom exercise any but the long kind, because the other is beneath my dignity. It is properer to Merlin's sort—stump-tail prophets, as we call them in the profession. Of course I whet up now and then and flirt out a minor prophecy, but not often—hardly ever, in fact. You will remember that there was great talk, when you reached the Valley of Holiness, about my having prophesied your coming and the very hour of your arrival, two or three days beforehand."

"Indeed, yes, I mind it now."

"Well, I could have done it as much as forty times easier, and piled on a thousand times more detail into the bargain, if it had been five hundred years away instead of two or three days."

"How amazing that it should be so!"

"Yes, a genuine expert can always foretell a thing that is five hundred years away easier than he can a thing that's only five hundred seconds off."

"And yet in reason it should clearly be the other way; it should be five hundred times as easy to foretell the last as the first, for indeed it is so close by that one uninspired might almost see it. In truth the law of prophecy doth contradict the likelihoods, most strangely making the difficult easy, and the easy difficult."

It was a wise head. A peasant's cap was no safe disguise for it; you could know it for a king's, under a diving-bell, if you could hear it work its intellect.

I had a new trade, now, and plenty of business in it. The king was as hungry to find out everything that was going to happen during the next thirteen centuries as if he were expecting to live in them. From that time out, I prophesied myself bald-headed trying to supply the demand. I have done some indiscreet things in my day, but this thing of playing myself for a prophet was the worst. Still, it had its ameliorations. A prophet doesn't have to have any brains. They are good to have, of course, for the ordinary exigencies of life, but they are no use in professional work. It is the restfulest vocation there is. When the spirit of prophecy comes upon you, you merely cake your intellect and lay it off in a cool place for a rest, and unship your jaw and leave it alone; it will work itself: the result is prophecy.

Every day a knight-errant or so came along, and the sight of them fired the king's martial spirit every time. He would have forgotten himself, sure, and said something to them in a style a suspicious shade or so above his ostensible degree, and so I always got him well out of the road in time. Then he would stand, and look with all his eyes; and a proud light would flash from them, and his nostrils would inflate like a war-horse's, and I knew he was longing for a brush with them. But about noon of the third day I had stopped in the road to take a precaution which had been suggested by the whip-stroke that had fallen to my share two days before; a precaution which I had afterward decided to leave untaken. I was so loath to institute it; but now I had just had a fresh reminder: while striding heedlessly along, with jaw spread and intellect at rest, for I was prophesying, I stubbed my toe and fell sprawling. I was so pale I couldn't think, for a moment; then I got softly and carefully up and unstrapped my knapsack. I had that dynamite bomb in it, done up in wool, in a box. It was a good thing to have along; the time would come when I could do a valuable miracle with it, maybe, but it was a nervous thing to have about me, and I didn't like to ask the king to carry it. Yet I must either throw it away or think up some safe way to get along with its society. I got it out and slipped it into my scrip, and just then, here come a couple of knights. The king stood, stately as a statue, gazing toward them—had forgotten himself again, of course—and before I could get a word of warning out, it was time for him to skip, and well that he did it, too. He supposed they would turn aside. Turn aside to avoid trampling peasant dirt under foot? When had he ever turned aside himself—or ever had the chance to do it, if a peasant saw him or any other noble knight in time to judiciously save him the trouble? The knights paid no attention to the king at all; it was his place to look out himself, and if he hadn't skipped he would have been placidly ridden down, and laughed at besides.

The king was in a flaming fury, and launched out his challenge and epithets with a most royal vigor. The knights were some little distance by, now. They halted, greatly surprised, and turned in their saddles and looked back, as if wondering if it might be worth while to bother with such scum as we. Then they wheeled and started for

us. Not a moment must be lost. I started for *them*. I passed them at a
rattling gait, and as I went by I flung out a hair-lifting
soul-scorching thirteen-jointed insult which made the king's effort
poor and cheap by comparison. I got it out of the nineteenth century
where they know how. They had such headway that they were nearly
to the king before they could check up; then, frantic with rage, they
stood up their horses on their hind hoofs and whirled them around,
and the next moment here they came, breast to breast. I was seventy
yards off, then, and scrambling up a great bowlder at the road-side.
When they were within thirty yards of me they let their long lances
droop to a level, depressed their mailed heads, and so, with their
horse-hair plumes streaming straight out behind, most gallant to
see, this lightning express came tearing for me! When they were
within fifteen yards, I sent that bomb with a sure aim, and it struck
the ground just under the horses' noses.

Yes, it was a neat thing, very neat and pretty to see. It resembled
a steamboat explosion on the Mississippi; and during the next
fifteen minutes we stood under a steady drizzle of microscopic
fragments of knights and hardware and horse-flesh. I say we, for the
king joined the audience, of course, as soon as he had got his breath
again. There was a hole there which would afford steady work for all
the people in that region for some years to come—in trying to
explain it, I mean; as for filling it up, that service would be
comparatively prompt, and would fall to the lot of a select few—
peasants of that seignory; and they wouldn't get anything for it,
either.

But I explained it to the king myself. I said it was done with a
dynamite bomb. This information did him no damage, because it
left him as intelligent as he was before. However, it was a noble
miracle, in his eyes, and was another settler for Merlin. I thought it
well enough to explain that this was a miracle of so rare a sort that it
couldn't be done except when the atmospheric conditions were just
right. Otherwise he would be encoring it every time we had a good
subject, and that would be inconvenient, because I hadn't any
more bombs along.

CHAPTER XXVIII

DRILLING THE KING

On the morning of the fourth day, when it was just sunrise, and we
had been tramping an hour in the chill dawn, I came to a resolution:
the king *must* be drilled; things could not go on so, he must be taken
in hand and deliberately and conscientiously drilled, or we couldn't
ever venture to enter a dwelling; the very cats would know this

masquerader for a humbug and no peasant. So I called a halt
and said:

"Sire, as between clothes and countenance, you are all right,
there is no discrepancy; but as between your clothes and your
bearing, you are all wrong, there is a most noticeable discrepancy.
Your soldierly stride, your lordly port—these will not do. You stand
too straight, your looks are too high, too confident. The cares of a
kingdom do not stoop the shoulders, they do not droop the chin,
they do not depress the high level of the eye-glance, they do not put
doubt and fear in the heart and hang out the signs of them in
slouching body and unsure step. It is the sordid cares of the lowly
born that do these things. You must learn the trick; you must imitate
the trade-marks of poverty, misery, oppression, insult, and the other
several and common inhumanities that sap the manliness out of a
man and make him a loyal and proper and approved subject and a
satisfaction to his masters, or the very infants will know you for
better than your disguise, and we shall go to pieces at the first hut we
stop at. Pray try to walk like this."

The king took careful note, and then tried an imitation.

"Pretty fair—pretty fair. Chin a little lower, please—there, very
good. Eyes too high; pray don't look at the horizon, look at the
ground, ten steps in front of you. Ah—that is better, that is very
good. Wait, please; you betray too much vigor, too much decision;
you want more of a shamble. Look at me, please—this is what I
mean. . . . . . Now you are getting it; that is the idea—at least, it
sort of approaches it. . . . . . Yes, that is pretty fair. *But!* There is a
great big something wanting, I don't quite know what it is. Please
walk thirty yards, so that I can get a perspective on the thing.
. . . . Now, then—your head's right, speed's right, shoulders right,
eyes right, chin right, gait, carriage, general style right—everything's
right! And yet the fact remains, the aggregrate's wrong. The account
don't balance. Do it again, please . . . . *now* I think I begin to see
what it is. Yes, I've struck it. You see, the genuine spiritlessness is
wanting; that's what's the trouble. It's all *amateur*—mechanical
details all right, almost to a hair; everything about the delusion
perfect, except that it don't delude."

"What then, must one do, to prevail?"

"Let me think . . . . . I can't seem to quite get at it. In fact there
isn't anything that can right the matter but practice. This is a good
place for it: roots and stony ground to break up your stately gait,
a region not liable to interruption, only one field and one hut in
sight, and they so far away that nobody could see us from there. It
will be well to move a little off the road and put in the whole day
drilling you, sire."

After the drill had gone on a little while, I said:

"Now, sire, imagine that we are at the door of the hut yonder, and
the family are before us. Proceed, please—accost the head of
the house."

The king unconsciously straightened up like a monument, and said, with frozen austerity:

"Varlet, bring a seat; and serve to me what cheer ye have."

"Ah, your grace, that is not well done."

"In what lacketh it?"

"These people do not call *each other* varlets."

"Nay, is that true?"

"Yes; only those above them call them so."

"Then must I try again. I will call him villein."

"No-no; for he may be a freeman."

"Ah—so. Then peradventure I should call him goodman."

"That would answer, your grace, but it would be still better if you said friend, or brother."

"Brother!—to dirt like that?"

"Ah, but *we* are pretending to be dirt like that, too."

"It is even true. I will say it. Brother, bring a seat, and thereto what cheer ye have, withal. *Now* 'tis right."

"Not quite, not wholly right. You have asked for one, not *us*—for one, not both; food for one, a seat for one."

The king looked puzzled—he wasn't a very heavy weight, intellectually. His head was an hour-glass; it could stow an idea, but it had to do it a grain at a time, not the whole idea at once.

"Would *you* have a seat also—and sit?"

"If I did not sit, the man would perceive that we were only pretending to be equals—and playing the deception pretty poorly, too."

"It is well and truly said! How wonderful is truth, come it in whatsoever unexpected form it may! Yes, he must bring out seats and food for both, and in serving us present not ewer and napkin with more show of respect to the one than to the other."

"And there is even yet a detail that needs correcting. He must bring nothing outside;—we will go in—in among the dirt, and possibly other repulsive things,—and take the food with the household, and after the fashion of the house, and all on equal terms, except the man be of the serf class; and finally, there will be no ewer and no napkin, whether he be serf or free. Please walk again, my liege. There—it is better—it is the best yet; but not perfect. The shoulders have known no ignobler burden than iron mail, and they will not stoop."

"Give me, then, the bag. I will learn the spirit that goeth with burdens that have not honor. It is the spirit that stoopeth the shoulders, I ween, and not the weight; for armor is heavy, yet it is a proud burden, and a man standeth straight in it. . . . . . Nay, but me no buts, offer me no objections. I will have the thing. Strap it upon my back."

He was complete, now, with that knapsack on, and looked as little like a king as any man I had ever seen. But it was an obstinate pair of shoulders; they could not seem to learn the trick of stooping with any sort of deceptive naturalness. The drill went on, I prompting and correcting:

"Now, make believe you are in debt, and eaten up by relentless creditors; you are out of work—which is horse-shoeing, let us say—and can get none; and your wife is sick, your children are crying because they are hungry—"

And so on, and so on. I drilled him as representing in turn all sorts of people out of luck and suffering dire privations and misfortunes. But lord it was only just words—they meant nothing in the world to him, I might just as well have whistled. Words realize nothing, vivify nothing to you, unless you have suffered in your own person the thing which the words try to describe. There are wise people who talk ever so knowingly and complacently about "the working classes," and satisfy themselves that a day's hard intellectual work is very much harder than a day's hard manual toil, and is righteously entitled to much bigger pay. Why, they really think that, you know, because they know all about the one, but haven't tried the other. But I know all about both; and so far as I am concerned, there isn't money enough in the universe to hire me to swing a pick-axe thirty days, but I will do the hardest kind of intellectual work for just as near nothing as you can cipher it down—and I will be satisfied, too.

Intellectual "work" is misnamed; it is a pleasure, a dissipation, and is its own highest reward. The poorest paid architect, engineer, general, author, sculptor, painter, lecturer, advocate, legislator, actor, preacher, singer, is constructively in heaven when he is at work; and as for the musician with the fiddlebow in his hand who sits in the midst of a great orchestra with the ebbing and flowing tides of divine sound washing over him—why, certainly, he is at work, if you wish to call it that, but lord, it's a sarcasm just the same. The law of work does seem utterly unfair—but there it is, and nothing can change it: the higher the pay in enjoyment the worker gets out of it, the higher shall be his pay in cash, also. And it's also the very law of those transparent swindles, transmissible nobility and kingship.

CHAPTER XXIX

THE SMALL-POX HUT

When we arrived at that hut at mid-afternoon, we saw no signs of life about it. The field near by had been denuded of its crop some time before, and had a skinned look, so exhaustively had it been harvested and gleaned. Fences, sheds, everything had a ruined look, and were eloquent of poverty. No animal was around anywhere, no living thing in sight. The stillness was awful, it was like the stillness of death. The cabin was a one-story one, whose thatch was black with age, and ragged from lack of repair.

The door stood a trifle ajar. We approached it stealthily—on tiptoe and at half-breath—for that is the way one's feeling makes him do, at such a time. The king knocked. We waited. No answer. Knocked again. No answer. I pushed the door softly open and looked in. I made out some dim forms, and a woman started up from the ground and stared at me, as one does who is wakened from sleep. Presently she found her voice—

"Have mercy!" she pleaded. "All is taken, nothing is left."

"I have not come to take anything, poor woman."

"You are not a priest?"

"No."

"Nor come not from the lord of the manor?"

"No, I am a stranger."

"Oh, then, for the fear of God, who visits with misery and death such as be harmless, tarry not here, but fly! This place is under his curse—and his Church's."

"Let me come in and help you—you are sick and in trouble."

I was better used to the dim light, now. I could see her hollow eyes fixed upon me. I could see how emaciated she was.

"I tell you the place is under the Church's ban. Save yourself—and go, before some straggler see thee here, and report it."

"Give yourself no trouble about me; I don't care anything for the Church's curse. Let me help you."

"Now all good spirits—if there be any such—bless thee for that word. Would God I had a sup of water!—but hold, hold, forget I said it, and fly; for there is that here that even he that feareth not the Church must fear; this disease whereof we die. Leave us, thou brave, good stranger, and take with thee such whole and sincere blessing as them that be accursed can give."

But before this I had picked up a wooden bowl and was rushing past the king on my way to the brook. It was ten yards away. When I got back and entered, the king was within, and was opening the shutter that closed the window-hole, to let in air and light. The place was full of a foul stench. I put the bowl to the woman's lips, and as she gripped it with her eager talons the shutter came open and a strong light flooded her face. Small-pox!

I sprang to the king, and said in his ear:

"Out of the door on the instant, sire! the woman is dying of that disease that wasted the skirts of Camelot two years ago."

He did not budge.

"Of a truth I shall remain—and likewise help."

I whispered again:

"King, it must not be. You must go."

"Ye mean well, and ye speak not unwisely. But it were shame that a king should know fear, and shame that belted knight should

withhold his hand where be such as need succor. Peace, I will not go.
It is you who must go. The Church's ban is not upon me, but it
forbiddeth you to be here, and she will deal with you with a heavy
hand an word come to her of your trespass."

It was a desperate place for him to be in, and might cost him his
life, but it was no use to argue with him. If he considered his
knightly honor at stake here, that was the end of argument; he
would stay, and nothing could prevent it; I was aware of that. And so
I dropped the subject. The woman spoke:

"Fair sir, of your kindness will ye climb the ladder there, and
bring me news of what ye find? Be not afraid to report, for times can
come when even a mother's heart is past breaking—being already
broke."

"Abide," said the king, "and give the woman to eat. I will go."
And he put down the knapsack.

I turned to start but the king had already started. He halted, and
looked down upon a man who lay in a dim light, and had not noticed
us, thus far, or spoken.

"Is it your husband?" the king asked.

"Yes."

"Is he asleep?"

"God be thanked for that one charity, yes—these three hours.
Where shall I pay to the full, my gratitude! for my heart is bursting
with it for that sleep he sleepeth now."

I said:

"We will be careful. We will not wake him."

"Ah, no, that ye will not, for he is dead."

"Dead?"

"Yes, what triumph it is to know it! None can harm him, none
insult him more. He is in heaven, now, and happy; or if not there, he
bides in hell and is content; for in that place he will find neither
abbot nor yet bishop. We were boy and girl together; we were man
and wife these five and twenty years, and never separated till this
day. Think how long that is, to love and suffer together. This
morning was he out of his mind, and in his fancy we were boy and
girl again and wandering in the happy fields; and so in that innocent
glad converse wandered he far and farther, still lightly gossiping,
and entered into those other fields we know not of, and was shut
away from mortal sight. And so there was no parting, for in his fancy
I went with him; he knew not but I went with him, my hand in his—
my young soft hand, not this withered claw. Ah, yes, to go, and know
it not; to separate and know it not; how could one go peacefuller
than that? It was his reward for a cruel life patiently borne."

There was a slight noise from the direction of the dim corner
where the ladder was. It was the king, descending. I could see that he
was bearing something in one arm, and assisting himself with the
other. He came forward into the light; upon his breast lay a slender

girl of fifteen. She was but half conscious; she was dying of
small-pox. Here was heroism at its last and loftiest possibility, its
utmost summit; this was challenging death in the open field
unarmed, with all the odds against the challenger, no reward set
upon the contest, and no admiring world in silks and cloth of gold to
gaze and applaud; and yet the king's bearing was as serenely brave
as it had always been in those cheaper contests where knight meets
knight in equal fight and clothed in protecting steel. He was great,
now; sublimely great. The rude statues of his ancestors in his palace
should have an addition—I would see to that; and it would not be a
mailed king killing a giant or a dragon, like the rest, it would be a
king in commoner's garb bearing death in his arms that a peasant
mother might look her last upon her child and be comforted.

He laid the girl down by her mother, who poured out endearments
and caresses from an overflowing heart, and one could detect a
flickering faint light of response in the child's eyes, but that was all.
The mother hung over her, kissing her, petting her, and imploring
her to speak, but the lips only moved and no sound came. I snatched
my liquor flask from my knapsack, but the woman forbade me,
and said:

"No—she does not suffer; it is better so. It might bring her back
to life. None that be so good and kind as ye are would do her that
cruel hurt. For look you: what is left to live for? Her brothers are
gone, her father is gone, her mother goeth, the Church's curse is
upon her and none may shelter or befriend her even though she lay
perishing in the road. She is desolate. I have not asked you, good
heart, if her sister be still on live, here overhead; I had no need; ye
had gone back, else, and not left the poor thing forsaken—"

"She lieth at peace," interrupted the king, in a subdued voice.

"I would not change it. How rich is this day in happiness! Ah, my
Annis, thou shalt join thy sister soon—thou'rt on the way, and these
be merciful friends, that will not hinder."

And so she fell to murmuring and cooing over the girl again, and
softly stroking her face and hair, and kissing her and calling her by
endearing names; but there was scarcely sign of response, now, in
the glazing eyes. I saw tears well from the king's eyes, and trickle
down his face. The woman noticed them, too, and said:

"Ah, I know that sign: thou'st a wife at home, poor soul, and you
and she have gone hungry to bed, many's the time, that the little
ones might have your crust; you know what poverty is, and the daily
insults of your betters, and the heavy hand of the Church and the
king."

The king winced under this accidental home-shot, but kept still;
he was learning his part; and he was playing it well, too, for a pretty
dull beginner. I struck up a diversion. I offered the woman food and
liquor, but she refused both. She would allow nothing to come
between her and the release of death. Then I slipped away and

brought the dead child from aloft, and laid it by her. This broke her down again, and there was another scene that was full of heartbreak. By-and-by I made another diversion, and beguiled her to sketch her story.

"Ye know it well, yourselves, having suffered it—for truly none of our condition in Britain escape it. It is the old, weary tale. We fought and struggled and succeeded; meaning by success, that we lived and did not die; more than that is not to be claimed. No troubles came that we could not outlive, till this year brought them; then came they all at once, as one might say, and overwhelmed us. Years ago the lord of the manor planted certain fruit trees on our farm; in the best part of it, too—a grievous wrong and shame—"

"But it was his right," interrupted the king.

"None denieth that, indeed; an the law mean anything, what is the lord's is his, and what is mine is his also. Our farm was ours by lease, therefore 'twas likewise his, to do with it as he would. Some little time ago, three of those trees were found hewn down. Our three grown sons ran frightened to report the crime. Well, in his lordship's dungeon there they lie, who saith there shall they lie and rot till they confess. They have naught to confess, being innocent, wherefore there will they remain until they die. Ye know that right well, I ween. Think how this left us; a man, a woman and two children, to gather a crop that was planted by so much greater force, yes, and protect it night and day from pigeons and prowling animals that be sacred and must not be hurt by any of our sort. When my lord's crop was nearly ready for the harvest, so also was ours; when his bell rang to call us to his fields to harvest his crops for nothing, he would not allow that I and my two girls should count for our three captive sons, but for only two of them; so, for the lacking one were we daily fined. All this time our own crop was perishing through neglect; and so both the priest and his lordship fined us because their shares of it were suffering through damage. In the end the fines ate up our crop—and they took it all; they took it all and made us harvest it for them, without pay or food, and we starving. Then the worst came when I, being out of my mind with hunger and loss of my boys, and grief to see my husband and my little maids in rags and misery and despair, uttered a deep blasphemy—oh! a thousand of them!— against the Church and the Church's ways. It was ten days ago. I had fallen sick with this disease, and it was to the priest I said the words, for he was come to chide me for lack of due humility under the chastening hand of God. He carried my trespass to his betters; I was stubborn; wherefore, presently upon my head and upon all heads that were dear to me, fell the curse of Rome.

"Since that day, we are avoided, shunned with horror. None has come near this hut to know whether we live or not. The rest of us were taken down. Then I roused me and got up, as wife and mother will. It was little they could have eaten in any case; it was less than little they had to eat. But there was water, and I gave them that.

How they craved it! and how they blessed it! But the end came yesterday; my strength broke down. Yesterday was the last time I ever saw my husband and this youngest child alive. I have lain here all these hours—these ages, ye may say— listening, listening, for any sound up there that—"

She gave a sharp quick glance at her eldest daughter, then cried out, "Oh, my darling!" and feebly gathered the stiffening form to her sheltering arms. She had recognized the death-rattle.

CHAPTER XXX

THE TRAGEDY OF THE MANOR-HOUSE

At midnight all was over, and we sat in the presence of four corpses. We covered them with such rags as we could find, and started away, fastening the door behind us. Their home must be these people's grave, for they could not have Christian burial, or be admitted to consecrated ground. They were as dogs, wild beasts, lepers, and no soul that valued its hope of eternal life would throw it away by meddling in any sort with these rebuked and smitten outcasts.

We had not moved four steps when I caught a sound as of footsteps upon gravel. My heart flew to my throat. We must not be seen coming from that house. I plucked at the king's robe and we drew back and took shelter behind the corner of the cabin.

"Now we are safe," I said, "but it was a close call—so to speak. If the night had been lighter he might have seen us, no doubt, he seemed to be so near."

"Mayhap it is but a beast and not a man at all."

"True. But man or beast, it will be wise to stay here a minute and let it get by and out of the way."

"Hark! It cometh hither."

True again. The step was coming toward us—straight toward the hut. It must be a beast, then, and we might as well have saved our trepidation. I was going to step out, but the king laid his hand upon my arm. There was a moment of silence, then we heard a soft knock on the cabin door. It made me shiver. Presently the knock was repeated, and then we heard these words in a guarded voice:

"Mother! Father! Open—we have got free, and we bring news to pale your cheeks but glad your hearts; and we may not tarry, but must fly! And—but they answer not. Mother! Father!—"

I drew the king toward the other end of the hut and whispered:

"Come—now we can get to the road."

The king hesitated, was going to demur; but just then we heard the door give way, and knew that those desolate men were in the presence of their dead.

"Come, my liege! in a moment they will strike a light, and then will follow that which it would break your heart to hear."

He did not hesitate this time. The moment we were in the road, I ran; and after a moment he threw dignity aside and followed. I did not want to think of what was happening in the hut—I couldn't bear it; I wanted to drive it out of my mind; so I struck into the first subject that lay under that one in my mind:

"I have had the disease those people died of, and so have nothing to fear; but if you have not had it also—"

He broke in upon me to say he was in trouble, and it was his conscience that was troubling him:

"These young men have got free, they say—but *how?* It is not likely that their lord hath set them free."

"Oh, no, I make no doubt they escaped."

"That is my trouble; I have a fear that this is so, and your suspicion doth confirm it, you having the same fear."

"I should not call it by that name though. I do suspect that they escaped, but if they did, I am not sorry, certainly."

"I am not sorry, I *think*—but—"

"What is it? What is there for one to be troubled about?"

"*If* they did escape, then are we bound in duty to lay hands upon them and deliver them again to their lord; for it is not seemly that one of his quality should suffer a so insolent and high-handed outrage from persons of their base degree."

There it was, again. He could see only one side of it. He was born so, educated so, his veins were full of ancestral blood that was rotten with this sort of unconscious brutality, brought down by inheritance from a long procession of hearts that had each done its share toward poisoning the stream. To imprison these men without proof, and starve their kindred, was no harm, for they were merely peasants and subject to the will and pleasure of their lord, no matter what fearful form it might take; but for these men to break out of unjust captivity was insult and outrage, and a thing not to be countenanced by any conscientious person who knew his duty to his sacred caste.

I worked more than half an hour before I got him to change the subject—and even then an outside matter did it for me. This was a something which caught our eyes as we struck the summit of a small hill—a red glow, a good way off.

"That's a fire," said I.

Fires interested me considerably, because I was getting a good deal of an insurance business started; and was also training some horses and building some steam fire-engines, with an eye to a paid fire department by-and-by. The priests opposed both my fire and life insurance, on the ground that it was an insolent attempt to hinder the decrees of God; and if you pointed out that they did not hinder the decrees in the least, but only modified the hard consequences of them if you took out policies and had luck, they retorted that that

was gambling against the decrees of God, and was just as bad. So
they managed to damage those industries more or less, but I got even
on my Accident business. As a rule, a knight is a lummox, and
sometimes even a labrick, and hence open to pretty poor arguments
when they come glibly from a superstition-monger, but even *he*
could see the practical side of a thing once in a while; and so of late
you couldn't clean up a tournament and pile the result without
finding one of my accident-tickets in every helmet.

We stood there awhile, in the thick darkness and stillness,
looking toward the red blur in the distance, and trying to make
out the meaning of a far-away murmur that rose and fell fitfully
on the night. Sometimes it swelled up and for a moment seemed
less remote; but when we were hopefully expecting it to betray
its cause and nature, it dulled and sank again, carrying its
mystery with it. We started down the hill in its direction, and the
winding road plunged us at once into almost solid darkness—
darkness that was packed and crammed in between two tall
forest walls. We groped along down for half a mile, perhaps, that
murmur growing more and more distinct all the time, the coming
storm threatening more and more, with now and then a little
shiver of wind, a faint show of lightning, and dull grumblings of
distant thunder. I was in the lead. I ran against something—a
soft heavy something which gave, slightly, to the impulse of my
weight; at the same moment the lightning glared out, and within
a foot of my face was the writhing face of a man who was hanging
from the limb of a tree! That is, it seemed to be writhing, but it
was not. It was a grewsome sight. Straightway there was an
earsplitting explosion of thunder, and the bottom of heaven fell
out; the rain poured down in a deluge. No matter, we must try to
cut this man down, on the chance that there might be life in him
yet, mustn't we? The lightning came quick and sharp, now, and
the place was alternately noonday and midnight. One moment
the man would be hanging before me in an intense light, and the
next he was blotted out again in the darkness. I told the king we
must cut him down. The king at once objected.

"If he hanged himself, he was willing to lose his property to his
lord; so let him be. If others hanged him, belike they had the
right—let him hang."

"But—"

"But me no buts, but even leave him as he is. And for yet
another reason. When the lightning cometh again—there, look
abroad."

Two others hanging, within fifty yards of us!

"It is not weather meet for doing useless courtesies unto dead
folk. They are past thanking you. Come—it is unprofitable to
tarry here."

There was reason in what he said, so we moved on. Within the

next mile we counted six more hanging forms by the blaze of the
lightning, and altogether it was a grisly excursion. That murmur
was a murmur no longer, it was a roar; a roar of men's voices. A
man came flying by, now, dimly through the darkness, and other
men chasing him. They disappeared. Presently another case of
the kind occurred, and then another and another. Then a sudden
turn of the road brought us in sight of that fire—it was a large
manor-house, and little or nothing was left of it—and everywhere
men were flying and other men raging after them in pursuit.

I warned the king that this was not a safe place for strangers.
We would better get away from the light, until matters should
improve. We stepped back a little, and hid in the edge of the
wood. From this hiding-place we saw both men and women
hunted by the mob. The fearful work went on until nearly dawn.
Then, the fire being out and the storm spent, the voices and flying
footsteps presently ceased, and darkness and stillness reigned
again.

We ventured out, and hurried cautiously away; and although
we were worn out and sleepy, we kept on until we had put this
place some miles behind us. Then we asked hospitality at the hut
of a charcoal burner, and got what was to be had. A woman was
up and about, but the man was still asleep, on a straw
shake-down, on the clay floor. The woman seemed uneasy until
I explained that we were travellers and had lost our way and
been wandering in the woods all night. She became talkative,
then, and asked if we had heard of the terrible goings-on at the
manor-house of Abblasoure. Yes, we had heard of them, but what
we wanted now, was rest and sleep. The king broke in:

"Sell us the house and take yourselves away, for we be perilous
company, being late come from people that died of the Spotted
Death."

It was good of him, but unnecessary. One of the commonest
decorations of the nation was the waffle-iron face. I had early
noticed that the woman and her husband were both so decorated.
She made us entirely welcome, and had no fears; and plainly she
was immensely impressed by the king's proposition; for of course
it was a good deal of an event in her life to run across a person of
the king's humble appearance who was ready to buy a man's
house for the sake of a night's lodging. It gave her a large respect
for us, and she strained the lean possibilities of her hovel to the
utmost to make us comfortable.

We slept till far into the afternoon, and then got up hungry
enough to make cotter fare quite palatable to the king, the more
particularly as it was scant in quantity. And also in variety; it
consisted solely of onions, salt, and the national black
bread—made out of horse-feed. The woman told us about the
affair of the evening before. At ten or eleven at night, when

everybody was in bed, the manor-house burst into flames. The
country-side swarmed to the rescue, and the family were saved,
with one exception, the master. He did not appear. Everybody
was frantic over this loss, and two brave yeomen sacrificed their
lives in ransacking the burning house seeking that valuable
personage. But after a while he was found—what was left of
him—which was his corpse. It was in a copse three hundred
yards away, bound, gagged, stabbed in a dozen places.

Who had done this? Suspicion fell upon a humble family in the
neighborhood who had been lately treated with peculiar harshness
by the baron; and from these people the suspicion easily extended
itself to their relatives and familiars. A suspicion was enough; my
lord's liveried retainers proclaimed an instant crusade against these
people, and were promptly joined by the community in general.
The woman's husband had been active with the mob, and had not
returned home until nearly dawn. He was gone, now, to find out what
the general result had been. While we were still talking, he came
back from his quest. His report was revolting enough. Eighteen
persons hanged or butchered, and two yeomen and thirteen
prisoners lost in the fire.

"And how many prisoners were there altogether, in the vaults?"

"Thirteen."

"Then every one of them was lost?"

"Yes, all."

"But the people arrived in time to save the family; how is it they
could save none of the prisoners?"

The man looked puzzled, and said:

"Would one unlock the vaults at such a time? Marry, some would
have escaped."

"Then you mean that nobody *did* unlock them?"

"None went near them, either to lock or unlock. It standeth to
reason that the bolts were fast; wherefore it was only needful to
establish a watch, so that if any broke the bonds he might not
escape, but be taken. None were taken."

"Natheless, three did escape," said the king, "and ye will do well
to publish it and set justice upon their track, for these murthered the
baron and fired the house."

I was just expecting he would come out with that. For a moment
the man and his wife showed an eager interest in this news and an
impatience to go out and spread it; then a sudden something else
betrayed itself in their faces, and they began to ask questions. I
answered the questions myself, and narrowly watched the effects
produced. I was soon satisfied that the knowledge of who these three
prisoners were, had somehow changed the atmosphere; that our
hosts' continued eagerness to go and spread the news was now only
pretended and not real. The king did not notice the change, and I
was glad of that. I worked the conversation around toward other

details of the night's proceedings, and noted that these people were relieved to have it take that direction.

The painful thing observable about all this business was, the alacrity with which this oppressed community had turned their cruel hands against their own class in the interest of the common oppressor. This man and woman seemed to feel that in a quarrel between a person of their own class and his lord, it was the natural and proper and rightful thing for that poor devil's whole caste to side with the master and fight his battle for him, without ever stopping to inquire into the rights or wrongs of the matter. This man had been out helping to hang his neighbors, and had done his work with zeal, and yet was aware that there was nothing against them but a mere suspicion, with nothing back of it describable as evidence, still neither he nor his wife seemed to see anything horrible about it.

This was depressing—to a man with the dream of a republic in his head. It reminded me of a time thirteen centuries away, when the "poor whites" of our South who were always despised and frequently insulted by the slave-lords around them, and who owed their base condition simply to the presence of slavery in their midst, were yet pusillanimously ready to side with the slave-lords in all political moves for the upholding and perpetuating of slavery, and did also finally shoulder their muskets and pour out their lives in an effort to prevent the destruction of that very institution which degraded them. And there was only one redeeming feature connected with that pitiful piece of history; and that was, that secretly the "poor white" did detest the slave-lord, and did feel his own shame. That feeling was not brought to the surface, but the fact that it was there and could have been brought out, under favoring circumstances, was something—in fact it was enough; for it showed that a man is at bottom a man, after all, even if it doesn't show on the outside.

Well, as it turned out, this charcoal burner was just the twin of the Southern "poor white" of the far future. The king presently showed impatience, and said:

"An ye prattle here all the day, justice will miscarry. Think ye the criminals will abide in their father's house? They are fleeing, they are not waiting. You should look to it that a party of horse be set upon their track."

The woman paled slightly, but quite perceptibly, and the man looked flustered and irresolute. I said:

"Come, friend, I will walk a little way with you, and explain which direction I think they would try to take. If they were merely resisters of the gabelle or some kindred absurdity I would try to protect them from capture; but when men murder a person of high degree and likewise burn his house, that is another matter."

The last remark was for the king—to quiet him. On the road the man pulled his resolution together, and began the march with a steady gait, but there was no eagerness in it. By-and-by I said:

"What relation were these men to you—cousins?"

He turned as white as his layer of charcoal would let him, and stopped, trembling.

"Ah, my God, how knew you that?"

"I didn't know it; it was a chance guess."

"Poor lads, they are lost. And good lads they were, too."

"Were you actually going yonder to tell on them?"

He didn't quite know how to take that; but he said, hesitatingly: "Ye-s."

"Then I think you are a damned scoundrel!"

It made him as glad as if I had called him an angel.

"Say the good words again, brother! for surely ye mean that ye would not betray me an I failed of my duty."

"Duty? There is no duty in the matter, except the duty to keep still and let those men get away. They've done a righteous deed."

He looked pleased; pleased, and touched with apprehension at the same time. He looked up and down the road to see that no one was coming, and then said in a cautious voice:

"From what land come you, brother, that you speak such perilous words, and seem not to be afraid?"

"They are not perilous words when spoken to one of my own caste, I take it. You would not tell anybody I said them?"

"I? I would be drawn asunder by wild horses first."

"Well, then, let me say my say. I have no fears of your repeating it. I think devil's work has been done last night upon those innocent poor people. That old baron got only what he deserved. If I had my way, all his kind should have the same luck."

Fear and depression vanished from the man's manner, and gratefulness and a brave animation took their place:

"Even though you be a spy, and your words a trap for my undoing, yet are they such refreshment that to hear them again and others like to them, I would go to the gallows happy, as having had one good feast at least in a starved life. And I will say my say, now, and ye may report it if ye be so minded. I helped to hang my neighbors for that it were peril to my own life to show lack of zeal in the master's cause; the others helped for none other reason. All rejoice to-day that he is dead, but all do go about seemingly sorrowing, and shedding the hypocrite's tear, for in that lies safety. I have said the words, I have said the words! the only ones that have ever tasted good in my mouth, and the reward of that taste is sufficient. Lead on, an ye will, be it even to the scaffold, for I am ready."

There it was, you see. A man *is* a man, at bottom. Whole ages of abuse and oppression cannot crush the manhood clear out of him. Whoever thinks it a mistake, is himself mistaken. Yes, there is plenty good enough material for a republic in the most degraded people that ever existed—even the Russians; plenty of manhood in them—

even in the Germans—if one could but force it out of its timid and
suspicious privacy, to overthrow and trample in the mud any throne
that ever was set up and any nobility that ever supported it. We
should see certain things yet, let us hope and believe. First, a
modified monarchy, till Arthur's days were done, then the
destruction of the throne, nobility abolished, every member of it
bound out to some useful trade, universal suffrage instituted, and
the whole government placed in the hands of the men and women of
the nation there to remain. Yes, there was no occasion to give up my
dream yet a while.

CHAPTER XXXI

MARCO

We strolled along in a sufficiently indolent fashion, now, and
talked. We must dispose of about the amount of time it ought to
take to go to the little hamlet of Abblasoure and put justice on
the track of those murderers and get back home again. And
meantime I had an auxiliary interest which had never paled yet,
never lost its novelty for me, since I had been in Arthur's
kingdom: the behavior—born of nice and exact subdivisions of
caste—of chance passers-by toward each other. Toward the
shaven monk who trudged along with his cowl tilted back and
the sweat washing down his fat jowls, the coal burner was
deeply reverent; to the gentleman he was abject; with the small
farmer and the free mechanic he was cordial and gossipy; and
when a slave passed by with a countenance respectfully lowered,
this chap's nose was in the air—he couldn't even see him. Well,
there are times when one would like to hang the whole human
race and finish the farce.

Presently we struck an incident. A small mob of half-naked boys
and girls came tearing out of the woods, scared and shrieking. The
eldest among them were not more than twelve or fourteen years
old. They implored help, but they were so beside themselves that we
couldn't make out what the matter was. However, we plunged into
the wood, they skurrying in the lead, and the trouble was quickly
revealed: they had hanged a little fellow with a bark rope, and he
was kicking and struggling, in the process of choking to death. We
rescued him, and fetched him around. It was some more human
nature; the admiring little folk imitating their elders; they were
playing mob, and had achieved a success which promised to be a
good deal more serious than they had bargained for.
serious than they had bargained for.

It was not a dull excursion for me. I managed to put in the
time very well. I made various acquaintanceships, and in my

quality of stranger was able to ask as many questions as I wanted
to. A thing which naturally interested me, as a statesman, was the
matter of wages. I picked up what I could under that head during
the afternoon. A man who hasn't had much experience, and
doesn't think, is apt to measure a nation's prosperity or lack of
prosperity by the mere size of the prevailing wages: if the wages
be high, the nation is prosperous; if low, it isn't. Which is an
error. It isn't what sum you get, it's how much you can buy with it
that's the important thing; and it's that that tells whether your
wages are high in fact or only high in name. I could remember
how it was in the time of our great civil war in the nineteenth
century. In the North a carpenter got three dollars a day, gold
valuation; in the South he got fifty—payable in Confederate
shinplasters worth a dollar a bushel. In the North a suit of overalls
cost three dollars—a day's wages; in the South it cost
seventy-five—which was two day's wages. Other things were in
proportion. Consequently, wages were twice as high in the North
as they were in the South, because the one wage had that much
more purchasing power than the other had.

Yes, I made various acquaintances in the hamlet, and a thing
that gratified me a good deal was to find our new coins in
circulation—lots of milrays, lots of mills, lots of cents, a good
many nickels, and some silver; all this among the artisans and
commonalty generally; yes, and even some gold—but that was at
the bank, that is to say, the goldsmith's. I dropped in there while
Marco the son of Marco was haggling with a shopkeeper over a
quarter of a pound of salt, and asked for change for a twenty
dollar gold piece. They furnished it—that is, after they had
chewed the piece, and rung it on the counter, and tried acid on it,
and asked me where I got it, and who I was, and where I was from,
and where I was going to, and when I expected to get there, and
perhaps a couple of hundred more questions; and when they got
aground, I went right on and furnished them a lot of information
voluntarily: told them I owned a dog, and his name was Watch,
and my first wife was a Free Will Baptist, and her grandfather
was a Prohibitionist, and I used to know a man who had two
thumbs on each hand and a wart on the inside of his upper lip,
and died in the hope of a glorious resurrection, and so-on, and
so-on, and so-on, till even that hungry village questioner began to
look satisfied, and also a shade put out; but he had to respect a
man of my financial strength, and so he didn't give me any lip,
but I noticed he took it out of his underlings, which was a
perfectly natural thing to do. Yes, they changed my twenty,
but I judged it strained the bank a little, which was a thing to be
expected, for it was the same as walking into a paltry village
store in the nineteenth century and requiring the boss of it to
change a two-thousand-dollar bill for you all of a sudden. He

could do it, maybe; but at the same time he would wonder how a
small farmer happened to be carrying so much money around in
his pocket; which was probably this goldsmith's thought, too; for he
followed me to the door and stood there gazing after me with
reverent admiration.

Our new money was not only handsomely circulating, but its
language was already glibly in use; that is to say, people had
dropped the names of the former moneys, and spoke of things as
being worth so many dollars or cents or mills or milrays, now. It
was very gratifying. We were progressing, that was sure.

I got to know several master mechanics, but about the most
interesting fellow among them was the blacksmith, Dowley. He
was a live man and a brisk talker, and had two journeymen and
three apprentices, and was doing a raging business. In fact, he
was getting rich, hand over fist, and was vastly respected. Marco
was very proud of having such a man for a friend. He had taken
me there ostensibly to let me see the big establishment which
bought so much of his charcoal, but really to let me see what easy
and almost familiar terms he was on with this great man. Dowley
and I fraternized at once; I had had just such picked men,
splendid fellows, under me in the Colt Arms Factory. I was bound
to see more of him, so I invited him to come out to Marco's,
Sunday, and dine with us. Marco was appalled, and held his
breath; and when the grandee accepted, he was so grateful that
he almost forgot to be astonished at the condescension.

Marco's joy was exuberant—but only for a moment; then he
grew thoughtful, then sad; and when he heard me tell Dowley I
should have Dickon the boss mason, and Smug the boss
wheelwright out there, too, the coal-dust on his face turned to
chalk, and he lost his grip. But I knew what was the matter with
him; it was the expense. He saw ruin before him; he judged that
his financial days were numbered. However, on our way to invite
the others, I said:

"You must allow me to have these friends come; and you must
also allow me to pay the costs."

His face cleared, and he said with spirit:

"But not all of it, not all of it. Ye cannot well bear a burden like
this alone."

I stopped him, and said:

"Now let's understand each other on the spot, old friend. I am
only a farm bailiff, it is true; but I am not poor, nevertheless. I
have been very fortunate this year—you would be astonished to
know how I have thriven. I tell you the honest truth when I say I
could squander away as many as a dozen feasts like this and
never care *that* for the expense!" and I snapped my fingers. I
could see myself rise a foot at a time in Marco's estimation, and
when I fetched out those last words I was become a very tower,

for style and altitude. "So you see, you must let me have my way.
You can't contribute a cent to this orgy, that's *settled.*"

"It's grand and good of you—"

"No, it isn't. You've opened your house to Jones and me in the
most generous way; Jones was remarking upon it to-day, just
before you came back from the village; for although he wouldn't
be likely to say such a thing to you,—because Jones isn't a talker,
and is diffident in society—he has a good heart and a grateful,
and knows how to appreciate it when he is well treated; yes, you
and your wife have been very hospitable toward us—"

"Ah, brother, 'tis nothing—*such* hospitality!"

"But it *is* something; the best a man has, freely given, is always
something, and is as good as a prince can do, and ranks right
along beside it—for even a prince can but do his best. And so
we'll shop around and get up this layout, now, and don't you
worry about the expense. I'm one of the worst spendthrifts that
ever was born. Why, do you know, sometimes in a single week I
spend—but never mind about that—you'd never believe it
anyway."

And so we went gadding along, dropping in here and there,
pricing things, and gossiping with the shopkeepers about the riot,
and now and then running across pathetic reminders of it, in the
persons of shunned and tearful and houseless remnants of
families whose homes had been taken from them and their
butchered or hanged. The raiment of Marco and his wife was of
coarse tow-linen and linsey-woolsey respectively, and resembled
township maps, it being made up pretty exclusively of patches
which had been added, township by township, in the course of
five or six years, until hardly a hand's-breadth of the original
garments was surviving and present. Now I wanted to fit these
people out with new suits, on account of that swell company, and
I didn't know just how to get at it with delicacy, until at last it
struck me that as I had already been liberal in inventing wordy
inventing wordy gratitude for the king, it would be just the thing
to back it up with evidence of a substantial sort; so I said:

"And Marco, there's another thing which you must permit—out
of kindness for Jones—because you wouldn't want to offend him.
He was very anxious to testify his appreciation in some way, but
he is so diffident he couldn't venture it himself, and so he begged
me to buy some little things and give them to you and Dame
Phyllis and let him pay for them without your ever knowing they
came from him—you know how a delicate person feels about that
sort of thing—and so I said I would, and we would keep mum.
Well, his idea was, a new outfit of clothes for you both—"

"Oh, it is wastefulness! It may not be, brother, it may not be.
Consider the vastness of the sum—"

"Hang the vastness of the sum! Try to keep quiet for a moment,

and see how it would seem; a body can't get in a word edgeways,
you talk so much. You ought to cure that, Marco; it isn't good
form, you know, and it will grow on you if you don't check it. Yes,
we'll step in here, now, and price this man's stuff—and don't
forget to remember to not let on to Jones that you know he had
anything to do with it. You can't think how curiously sensitive
and proud he is. He's a farmer—pretty fairly well-to-do farmer
—and I'm his bailiff; *but*—the imagination of that man! Why,
sometimes when he forgets himself and gets to blowing off, you'd
think he was one of the swells of the earth; and you might listen
to him a hundred years and never take him for a farmer—
especially if he talked agriculture. He *thinks* he's a Sheol of a
farmer; thinks he's old Grayback from Wayback; but between
you and me privately he don't know as much about farming as he
does about running a kingdom—still, whatever he talks about,
you want to drop your underjaw and listen, the same as if you had
never heard such incredible wisdom in all your life before, and
were afraid you might die before you got enough of it. That will
please Jones."

It tickled Marco to the marrow to hear about such an odd
character; but it also prepared him for accidents; and in my
experience when you travel with a king who is letting on to be
something else and can't remember it more than about half the
time, you can't take too many precautions.

This was the best store we had come across yet; it had
everything in it, in small quantities, from anvils and dry goods all
the way down to fish and pinchbeck jewelry. I concluded I would
bunch my whole invoice right here, and not go pricing around
any more. So I got rid of Marco, by sending him off to invite the
mason and the wheelwright, which left the field free to me. For I
never care to do a thing in a quiet way; it's got to be theatrical or
I don't take any interest in it. I showed up money enough, in a
careless way, to corral the shopkeeper's respect, and then I wrote
down a list of the things I wanted, and handed it to him to see if
he could read it. He could, and was proud to show that he could.
He said he had been educated by a priest, and could both read
and write. He ran it through, and remarked with satisfaction that
it was a pretty heavy bill. Well, and so it was, for a little concern
like that. I was not only providing a swell dinner, but some odds
and ends of extras. I ordered that the things be carted out and
delivered at the dwelling of Marco the son of Marco by Saturday
evening, and send me the bill at dinner-time Sunday. He said I
could depend upon his promptness and exactitude, it was the
rule of the house. He also observed that he would throw in a
couple of miller-guns for the Marcos gratis—that everybody was
using them now. He had a mighty opinion of that clever device.
I said:

"And please fill them up to the middle mark, too; and add that to the bill."

He would, with pleasure. He filled them, and I took them with me. I couldn't venture to tell him that the miller-gun was a little invention of my own, and that I had officially ordered that every shopkeeper in the kingdom keep them on hand and sell them at government price—which was the merest trifle, and the shopkeeper got that, not the government. We furnished them for nothing.

The king had hardly missed us when we got back at nightfall. He had early dropped again into his dream of a grand invasion of Gaul with the whole strength of his kingdom at his back, and the afternoon had slipped away without his ever coming to himself again.

CHAPTER XXXII

DOWLEY'S HUMILIATION

Well, when that cargo arrived, toward sunset, Saturday afternoon, I had my hands full to keep the Marcos from fainting. They were sure Jones and I were ruined past help, and they blamed themselves as accessories to this bankruptcy. You see, in addition to the dinner-materials, which called for a sufficiently round sum, I had bought a lot of extras for the future comfort of the family: for instance, a big lot of wheat, a delicacy as rare to the tables of their class as was ice-cream to a hermit's; also a sizeable deal dinnertable; also two entire pounds of salt, which was another piece of extravagance in those people's eyes; also crockery, stools, the clothes, a small cask of beer, and so on. I instructed the Marcos to keep quiet about this sumptuousness, so as to give me a chance to surprise the guests and show off a little. Concerning the new clothes, the simple couple were like children: they were up and down, all night, to see if it wasn't nearly daylight, so that they could put them on, and they were into them at last as much as an hour before dawn was due. Then their pleasure—not to say delirium—was so fresh and novel and inspiring that the sight of it paid me well for the interruptions which my sleep had suffered. The king had slept just as usual—like the dead. The Marcos could not thank him for their clothes, that being forbidden; but they tried every way they could think of to make him see how grateful they were. Which all went for nothing: he didn't notice any change.

It turned out to be one of those rich and rare fall days which is just a June day toned down to a degree where it is heaven to be out of doors. Toward noon the guests arrived and we assembled under a great tree and were soon as sociable as old acquaintances. Even the king's reserve melted a little, though it

was some little trouble to him to adjust himself to the name of
Jones along at first. I had asked him to try to not forget that he
was a farmer; but I had also considered it prudent to ask him to
let the thing stand at that, and not elaborate it any. Because he
was just the kind of person you could depend on to spoil a little
thing like that if you didn't warn him, his tongue was so handy,
and his spirit so willing, and his information so uncertain.

Dowley was in fine feather, and I early got him started, and
then adroitly worked him around onto his own history for a text
and himself for a hero, and then it was good to sit there and hear
him hum. Self-made man, you know. They know how to talk. They
do deserve more credit than any other breed of men, yes, that is
true; and they are among the very first to find it out, too. He told
how he had begun life an orphan lad without money and without
friends able to help him; how he had lived as the slaves of the
meanest master lived; how his day's work was from sixteen to
eighteen hours long, and yielded him only enough black bread to
keep him in a half-fed condition; how his faithful endeavors
finally attracted the attention of a good blacksmith, who came
near knocking him dead with kindness by suddenly offering,
when he was totally unprepared, to take him as his bound
apprentice for nine years and give him board and clothes and
teach him the trade—or "mystery" as Dowley called it. That was
his first great rise, his first gorgeous stroke of fortune; and
you saw that he couldn't yet speak of it without a sort of eloquent
wonder and delight that such a gilded promotion should have
fallen to the lot of a common human being. He got no new
clothing during his apprenticeship, but on his graduation day his
master tricked him out in spang-new tow-linens and made him
feel unspeakably rich and fine.

"I remember me of that day!" the wheelwright sang out, with
enthusiasm.

"And I likewise!" cried the mason. "I would not believe they
were thine own; in faith I could not."

"Nor others!" shouted Dowley, with sparkling eyes. "I was like to
lose my character, the neighbors wending I had mayhap been
stealing. It was a great day, a great day; one forgetteth not days like
that."

Yes, and his master was a fine man, and prosperous, and always
had a great feast of meat twice in the year, and with it white bread,
true wheaten bread; in fact, lived like a lord, so to speak. And in
time Dowley succeeded to the business and married the daughter.

"And now consider what is come to pass," said he, impressively.
"Two times in every month there is fresh meat upon my table." He
made a pause here, to let that fact sink home, then added—"and
eight times, salt meat."

"It is even true," said the wheelwright, with bated breath.

"I know it of mine own knowledge," said the mason, in the same reverent fashion.

"On my table appeareth white bread every Sunday in the year," added the master smith, with solemnity. "I leave it to your own consciences, friends, if this is not also true?"

"By my head, yes!" cried the mason.

"I can testify it—and I do," said the wheelwright.

"And as to furniture, ye shall say yourselves what mine equipment is." He waved his hand in fine gesture of granting frank and unhampered freedom of speech, and added: "Speak as ye are moved; speak as ye would speak an I were not here."

"Ye have five stools, and of the sweetest workmanship at that, albeit your family is but three," said the wheelwright, with deep respect.

"And six wooden goblets, and six platters of wood and two of pewter to eat and drink from withal," said the mason, impressively. "And I say it as knowing God is my judge, and we tarry not here alway, but must answer at the last day for the things said in the body, be they false or be they sooth."

"Now ye know what manner of man I am, brother Jones," said the smith, with a fine and friendly condescension, "and doubtless ye would look to find me a man jealous of his due of respect and but sparing of outgo to strangers till their rating and quality be assured, but trouble yourself not, as concerning that; wit ye well ye shall find me a man that regardeth not these matters but is willing to receive any he as his fellow and equal that carrieth a right heart in his body, be his worldly estate howsoever modest. And in token of it, here is my hand; and I say with my own mouth we are equals—equals"— and he smiled around on the company with the satisfaction of a god who is doing the handsome and gracious thing and is quite well aware of it.

The king took the hand with a poorly disguised reluctance, and let go of it as willingly as a lady lets go of a fish; all of which had a good effect, for it was mistaken for an embarrassment natural to one who was being beamed upon by greatness.

The dame brought out the table, now, and set it under the tree. It caused a visible stir of surprise, it being brand new and a sumptuous article of deal. But the surprise rose higher still, when the dame, with a body oozing easy indifference at every pore, but eyes that gave it all away by absolutely flaming with vanity, slowly unfolded an actual simon-pure tablecloth and spread it. That was a notch above even the blacksmith's domestic grandeurs, and it hit him hard; you could see it. But Marco was in Paradise; you could see that, too. Then the dame brought two fine new stools—whew! that was a sensation; it was visible in the eyes of every guest. Then she brought two more— as calmly as she could. Sensation again—with awed murmurs. Again she brought two—walking on air, she was so proud. The guests were petrified, and the mason muttered:

"There is that about earthly pomps which doth ever move to reverence."

As the dame turned away, Marco couldn't help slapping on the climax while the thing was hot; so he said with what was meant for a languid composure but was a poor imitation of it:

"These suffice; leave the rest."

So there were more yet! It was a fine effect. I couldn't have played the hand better myself.

From this out, the madam piled up the surprises with a rush that fired the general astonishment up to a hundred and fifty in the shade, and at the same time paralyzed expression of it down to gasped "Oh's" and "Ah's," and mute upliftings of hands and eyes. She fetched crockery—new, and plenty of it; new wooden goblets and other table furniture; and beer, fish, chicken, a goose, eggs, roast beef, roast mutton, a ham, a small roast pig, and a wealth of genuine white wheaten bread. Take it by and large, that spread laid everything far and away in the shade that ever that crowd had seen before. And while they sat there just simply stupefied with wonder and awe, I sort of waved my hand as if by accident, and the store-keeper's son emerged from space and said he had come to collect.

"That's all right," I said, indifferently. "What is the amount? give us the items."

Then he read off this bill, while those three amazed men listened, and serene waves of satisfaction rolled over my soul and alternate waves of terror and admiration surged over Marco's:

2 pounds salt	200
8 dozen pints beer, in the wood	800
3 bushels wheat	2,700
2 pounds fish	100
3 hens	400
1 goose	400
3 dozen eggs	150
1 roast of beef	450
1 " " mutton	400
1 ham	800
1 sucking pig	500
2 crockery dinner sets	6,000
2 men's suits and underwear	2,800
1 stuff and 1 linsey-woolsey gown and underwear	1,6000
8 wooden goblets	800
Various table furniture	10,000
1 deal table	3,000
8 stools	4,000
2 miller-guns, loaded	3,000

He ceased. There was a pale and awful silence. Not a limb stirred. Not a nostril betrayed the passage of breath.

"Is that all?" I asked, in a voice of the most perfect calmness.

"All, fair sir, save that certain matters of light moment are placed together under a head hight sundries. If it would like you, I will sepa—"

"It is of no consequence," I said, accompanying the words with a gesture of the most utter indifference; "give me the grand total, please."

The clerk leaned against the tree to stay himself, and said:

"Thirty-nine thousand one hundred and fifty milrays!"

The wheelwright fell off his stool, the others grabbed the table to save themselves, and there was a deep and general ejaculation of—

"God be with us in the day of disaster!"

The clerk hastened to say:

"My father chargeth me to say he cannot honorably require you to pay it all at this time, and therefore only prayeth you—"

I paid no more heed than if it were the idle breeze, but with an air of indifference amounting almost to weariness, got out my money and tossed four dollars onto the table. Ah, you should have seen them stare!

The clerk was astonished and charmed. He asked me to retain one of the dollars as security, until he could go to town and— I interrupted:

"What, and fetch back nine cents? Nonsense. Take the whole. Keep the change."

There was an amazed murmur to this effect:

"Verily this being is *made* of money! He throweth it away even as it were dirt."

The blacksmith was a crushed man.

The clerk took his money and reeled away drunk with fortune. I said to Marco and his wife:

"Good folk, here is a little trifle for you"—handing the miller-guns as if it were a matter of no consequence though each of them contained fifteeen cents in solid cash; and while the poor creatures went to pieces with astonishment and gratitude, I turned to the others and said as calmly as one would ask the time of day:

"Well, if we are all ready, I judge the dinner is. Come, fall to."

Ah, well, it was immense; yes, it was a daisy. I don't know that I ever put a situation together better, or got happier spectacular effects out of the materials available. The blacksmith—well, he was simply mashed. Land! I wouldn't have felt what that man was feeling, for anything in the world. Here he had been blowing and bragging about his grand meat-feast twice a year, and his fresh meat twice a month, and his salt meat twice a week, and his white bread every Sunday the year round—all for a family of three; the entire cost for the year not above 69.2.6 (sixty-nine cents, two mills

and six milrays,) and all of a sudden here comes along a man who
slashes out nearly four dollars on a single blow-out; and not only
that, but acts as if it made him tired to handle such small sums.
Yes, Dowley was a good deal wilted, and shrunk-up and collapsed;
he had the aspect of a bladder-balloon that's been stepped on by a
cow.

CHAPTER XXXIII

SIXTH CENTURY POLITICAL ECONOMY

However, I made a dead set at him, and before the first third of
the dinner was reached, I had him happy again. It was easy to do—
in a country of ranks and castes. You see, in a country where they
have ranks and castes, a man isn't ever a man, he is only part of a
man, he can't ever get his full growth. You prove your superiority
over him in station, or rank, or fortune, and that's the end of it—
he knuckles down. You can't insult him after that. No, I don't
mean quite that; of course you *can* insult him, I only mean it's
difficult; and so, unless you've got a lot of useless time on your hands
it doesn't pay to try. I had the smith's reverence, now, because I
was apparently immensely prosperous and rich; I could have had
his adoration if I had had some little gimcrack title of nobility. And
not only his, but any commoner's in the land, though he were the
mightiest production of all the ages, in intellect, worth, and
character, and I bankrupt in all three. This was to remain so, as long
as England should exist in the earth. With the spirit of prophecy
upon me, I could look into the future and see her erect statues
and monuments to her unspeakable Georges and other royal
and noble clothes-horses, and leave unhonored the creators of
this world—after God—Gutenburg, Watt, Arkwright, Whitney,
Morse, Stephenson, Bell.

The king got his cargo aboard, and then the talk not turning
upon battle, conquest, or iron-clad duel, he dulled down to
drowsiness and went off to take a nap. Mrs. Marco cleared the
table, placed the beerkeg handy, and went away to eat her
dinner of leavings in humble privacy, and the rest of us soon drifted
into matters near and dear to the hearts of our sort—business and
wages, of course. At a first glance, things appeared to be exceeding
prosperous in this little tributary kingdom—whose lord was King
Bagdemagus—as compared with the state of things in my own
region. They had the "protection" system in full force here, whereas
we were working along down towards free-trade, by easy stages,
and were now about halfway. Before long, Dowley and I were doing
all the talking, the others hungrily listening. Dowley warmed to his
work, snuffed an advantage in the air, and began to put questions

which he considered pretty awkward ones for me, and they did have something of that look:

"In your country, brother, what is the wage of a master bailiff, master hind, carter, shepherd, swineherd?"

"Twenty-five milrays a day; that is to say, a quarter of a cent."

The smith's face beamed with joy. He said:

"With us they are allowed the double of it! And what may a mechanic get—carpenter, dauber, mason, painter, blacksmith, wheelwright and the like?"

"On the average, fifty milrays; half a cent a day."

"Ho-ho! With us they are allowed a hundred! With us any good mechanic is allowed a cent a day! I count out the tailor, but not the others—they are all allowed a cent a day, and in driving times they get more—yes, up to a hundred and ten and even fifteen milrays a day. I've paid a hundred and fifteen myself, within the week. 'Rah for protection—to Sheol with free-trade!"

And his face shone upon the company like a sunburst. But I didn't scare at all. I rigged up my pile-driver, and allowed myself fifteen minutes to drive him into the earth—drive him *all* in— drive him in till not even the curve of his skull should show above ground. Here is the way I started in on him. I asked:

"What do you pay a pound for salt?"

"A hundred milrays."

"We pay forty. What do you pay for beef and mutton—when you buy it?" That was a neat hit; it made the color come.

"It varieth somewhat, but not much; one may say 75 milrays the pound."

"*We* pay 33. What do you pay for eggs?"

"Fifty milrays the dozen."

"We pay 20. What do you pay for beer?"

"It costeth us 8½ milrays the pint."

"We get it for 4; 25 bottles for a cent. What do you pay for wheat?"

"At the rate of 900 milrays the bushel."

"We pay 400. What do you pay for a man's tow-linen suit?"

"Thirteen cents."

"We pay 6. What do you pay for a stuff gown for the wife of the laborer or the mechanic?"

"We pay 8.4.0."

"Well, observe the difference: you pay eight cents and four mills, we pay only four cents." I prepared, now, to sock it to him. I said: "Look here, dear friend, *what's become of your high wages you were bragging so about, a few minutes ago?*"—and I looked around on the company with placid satisfaction, for I had slipped up on him gradually and tied him hand and foot, you see, without his ever noticing that he was being tied at all. "What's become of those noble high wages of yours?—I seem to have knocked the stuffing all out of them, it appears to me."

But if you will believe me, he merely looked surprised, that is all!
he didn't grasp the situation at all, didn't know he had walked into
a trap, didn't discover that he was *in* a trap. I could have shot him,
from sheer vexation. With cloudy eye and a struggling intellect,
he fetched this out:

"Marry, I seem not to understand. It is *proved* that our wages
be double thine; how then may it be that thou'st knocked therefrom
the stuffing?—an I miscall not the wonderly word, this being the
first time under grace and providence of God it hath been granted
me to hear it."

Well, I was stunned; partly with this unlooked-for stupidity on
his part, and partly because his fellows so manifestly sided with
him and were of his mind—if you might call it mind. My position
was simple enough, plain enough, how could it ever be simplified
more? However, I must try:

"Why, look here, brother Dowley, don't you see? Your wages
are merely higher than ours in *name,* not in *fact.*"

"Hear him! They are the *double*—ye have confessed it yourself."

"Yes-yes, I don't deny that at all. But that's got nothing to do
with it; the *amount* of the wages in mere coins, with meaningless
names attached to them to know them by, has got nothing to do with
it. The thing is, how much can you *buy* with your wages?—that's
the idea. While it is true that with you a good mechanic is allowed
about three dollars and a half a year, and with us only about a
dollar and seventy-five—"

"There—ye're confessing it again, ye're confessing it again!"

"Confound it, I've never denied it I tell you! What I say is this.
With us *half* a dollar buys more than a *dollar* buys with you—and
therefore it stands to reason and the commonest kind of common-
sense, that our wages are *higher* than yours."

He looked dazed, and said, despairingly:

"Verily, I cannot make it out. Ye've just *said* ours are the higher,
and with the same breath ye take it back."

"Oh, great Scott, isn't it possible to get such a simple thing
through your head? Now look here—let me illustrate. We pay four
cents for a woman's stuff gown, you pay 8.4.0, which is four mills
more than *double.* What do you allow a laboring woman who works
on a farm?"

"Two mills a day."

"Very good; we allow but half as much; we pay her only a tenth
of a cent a day; and—"

"Again ye're conf—"

"Wait! Now, you see, the thing is very simple; this time you'll
understand it. For instance, it takes your woman 42 days to earn her
gown, at 2 mills a day—7 weeks' work; but ours earns hers in forty
days —two days *short* of 7 weeks. Your woman has a gown, and her
whole seven weeks' wages are gone; ours has a gown, and two days'

wages left, to buy something else with. There—*now* you understand it!"

He looked—well, he merely looked dubious, it's the most I can say; so did the others. I waited—to let the thing work. Dowley spoke at last—and betrayed the fact that he actually hadn't gotten away from his rooted and grounded superstitions yet. He said, with a trifle of hesitancy:

"But—but—ye cannot fail to grant that two mills a day is better than one."

Shucks! Well, of course I hated to give it up. So I chanced another flyer:

"Let us suppose a case. Suppose one of your journeymen goes out and buys the following articles:

        "1 pound of salt;
        1 dozen eggs;
        1 dozen pints of beer;
        1 bushel of wheat;
        1 tow-linen suit;
        5 pounds of beef;
        5 pounds of mutton.

"The lot will cost him 32 cents. It takes him 32 working days to earn the money—5 weeks and 2 days. Let him come to us and work 32 days at *half* the wages; he can buy all those things for a shade under 14½ cents; they will cost him a shade under 29 days' work, and he will have about half a week's wages over. Carry it through the year; he would save nearly a week's wages every two months, *your* man nothing; thus saving five or six weeks' wages in a year. *Now* I reckon you understand that 'high wages' and 'low wages' are phrases that don't mean anything in the world until you find out which of them will *buy* the most!"

It was a crusher.

But alas, it didn't crush. No, I had to give it up. What those people valued was *high wages;* it didn't seem to be a matter of any consequence to them whether the high wages would buy anything or not. They stood for "protection," and swore by it, which was reasonable enough, because interested parties had gulled them into the notion that it was protection which had created their high wages. I proved to them that in a quarter of a century their wages had advanced but 30 per cent., while the cost of living had gone up 100; and that with us, in a shorter time, wages had advanced 40 per cent. while the cost of living had gone steadily down. But it didn't do any good. Nothing could unseat their strange beliefs.

Well, I was smarting under a sense of defeat. Undeserved defeat, but what of that? That didn't soften the smart any. And to think of the circumstances! the first statesman of the age, the capablest man, the best-informed man in the entire world, the loftiest uncrowned head that had moved through the clouds of any

political firmament for centuries, sitting here apparently defeated
in argument by an ignorant country blacksmith! And I could see
that those others were sorry for me!—which made me blush till I
could smell my whiskers scorching. Put yourself in my place; feel
as mean as I did, as ashamed as I felt—wouldn't *you* have struck
below the belt to get even? Yes, you would; it is simply human
nature. Well, that is what I did. I am not trying to justify it; I'm
only saying that I was mad, and *anybody* would have done it.

Well, when I make up my mind to hit a man, I don't plan out a
love-tap; no, that isn't my way; as long as I'm going to hit him at
all, I'm going to hit him a lifter. And I don't jump at him all of a
sudden, and risk making a blundering half-way business of it;
no, I get away off yonder to one side, and work up on him gradually,
so that he never suspects that I'm going to hit him at all; and by-
and-by, all in a flash, he's flat of his back, and he can't tell for the
life of him how it all happened. That is the way I went for brother
Dowley. I started to talking lazy and comfortable, as if I was just
talking to pass the time; and the oldest man in the world couldn't
have taken the bearings of my starting place and guessed where I
was going to fetch up:

"Boys, there's a good many curious things about law, and custom,
and usage, and all that sort of thing, when you come to look at it;
yes, and about the drift and progress of human opinion and
movement, too. There are written laws—they perish; but there are
also unwritten laws—*they* are eternal. Take the unwritten law of
wages: it says they've got to advance, little by little, straight through
the centuries. And notice how it works. We know what wages are
now, here and there and yonder; we strike an average, and say that's
the wages of to-day. We know what the wages were a hundred years
ago, and what they were two hundred years ago; that's as far back
as we can get, but it suffices to give us the law of progress, the
measure and rate of the periodical augmentation; and so, without
a document to help us, we can come pretty close to determining what
the wages were three and four and five hundred years ago. Good, so
far. Do we stop there? No. We stop looking backward; we face
around and apply the law to the future. My friends, I can tell you
what people's wages are going to be at any date in the future you
want to know, for hundreds and hundreds of years."

"What, goodman, what!"

"Yes. In seven hundred years wages will have risen to six times
what they are now, here in your region, and farm hands will be
allowed 3 cents a day, and mechanics 6."

"I would I might die now and live then!" interrupted Smug the
wheelwright, with a fine avaricious glow in his eye.

"And that isn't all; they'll get their board besides—such as it is:
it won't bloat them. Two hundred and fifty years later—pay
attention, now—a mechanic's wages will be—mind you, this is law,

not guesswork; a mechanic's wages will then be *twenty* cents a day!"

There was a general gasp of awed astonishment. Dickon the mason murmured, with raised eyes and hands:

"More than three weeks' pay for one day's work!"

"Riches!—of a truth, yes, riches!" muttered Marco, his breath coming quick and short, with excitement.

"Wages will keep on rising, little by little, little by little, as steadily as a tree grows, and at the end of three hundred and forty years more there'll be at least *one* country where the mechanic's average wage will be *two hundred* cents a day!"

It knocked them absolutely dumb! Not a man of them could get his breath for upwards of two minutes. Then the coal burner said prayerfully:

"Might I but live to see it!"

"It is the income of an earl!" said Smug.

"An earl, say ye?" said Dowley; "ye could say more than that and speak no lie; there's no earl in the realm of Bagdemagus that hath an income like to that. Income of an earl—mf! it's the income of an angel!"

"Now then, that is what is going to happen as regards wages. In that remote day, that man will earn with *one* week's work, that bill of goods which it takes you upwards of *fifty* weeks to earn now. Some other pretty surprising things are going to happen, too. Brother Dowley, who is it that determines, every spring, what the particular wage of each kind of mechanic, laborer, and servant shall be for that year?"

"Sometimes the courts, sometimes the town council; but most of all, the magistrate. Ye may say, in general terms, it is the magistrate that fixes the wages."

"Doesn't ask any of those poor devils to *help* him fix their wages for them, does he?"

"Hm! That *were* an idea! The master that's to pay him the money is the one that's rightly concerned in that matter, ye will notice."

"Yes—but I thought the other man might have some little trifle at stake in it, too; and even his wife and children, poor creatures. The masters are these: nobles, rich men, the prosperous generally. These few, who do no work, determine what pay the vast hive shall have who *do* work. You see? They're a 'combine'—a trade union, to coin a new phrase—who band themselves together to force their lowly brother to take what they choose to give. Thirteen hundred years hence—so says the unwritten law—the 'combine' will be the other way, and then how these fine people's posterity will fume and fret and grit their teeth over the insolent tyranny of trade unions! Yes indeed! the magistrate will tranquilly arrange the wages from now clear away down into the nineteenth century; and then all of a sudden the wage-earner will consider that a couple of thousand

years or so is enough of this one-sided sort of thing; and he will
rise up and take a hand in fixing his wages himself. Ah, he will have
a long and bitter account of wrong and humiliation to settle."

"Do ye believe—"

"That he actually will help to fix his own wages? Yes, indeed.
And he will be strong and able, then."

"Brave times, brave times, of a truth!" sneered the prosperous
smith.

"Oh,—and there's another detail. In that day, a master may hire
a man for only just one day, or one week, or one month at a time, if
he wants to."

"What?"

"It's true. Morever, a magistrate won't be able to force a man to
work for a master a whole year on a stretch whether the man wants
to or not."

"Will there be *no* law or sense in that day?"

"Both of them, Dowley. In that day a man will be his own
property, not the property of magistrate and master. And he can
leave town whenever he wants to, if the wages don't suit him!—and
they can't put him in the pillory for it."

"Perdition catch such an age!" shouted Dowley, in strong
indignation. "An age of dogs, an age barren of reverence for
superiors and respect for authority! The pillory—"

"Oh, wait, brother; say no good word for that institution. *I* think
the pillory ought to be abolished."

"A most strange idea. Why?"

"Well, I'll tell you why. Is a man ever put in the pillory for a
capital crime?"

"No."

"Is it right to condemn a man to a slight punishment for a small
offence and then kill him?"

There was no answer. I had scored my first point! For the first
time, the smith wasn't up and ready. The company noticed it. Good
effect.

"You don't answer, brother. You were about to glorify the pillory
a while ago, and shed some pity on a future age that isn't going to
use it. *I* think the pillory ought to be abolished. What usually
happens when a poor fellow is put in the pillory for some little
offence that didn't amount to anything in the world? The mob try
to have some fun with him, don't they?"

"Yes."

"They begin by clodding him; and they laugh themselves to pieces
to see him try to dodge one clod and get hit with another?"

"Yes."

"Then they throw dead cats at him, don't they?"

"Yes."

"Well, then, suppose he has a few personal enemies in that mob—and here and there a man or a woman with a secret grudge against him—and suppose especially that he is unpopular in the community, for his pride, or his prosperity, or one thing or another—stones and bricks take the place of clods and cats presently, don't they?"

"There is no doubt of it."

"As a rule he is crippled for life, isn't he?—jaws broken, teeth smashed out?—or legs mutilated, gangrened, presently cut off?—or an eye knocked out, maybe both eyes?"

"It is true, God knoweth it."

"And if he is unpopular he can depend on *dying*, right there in the stocks, can't he?"

"He surely can! One may not deny it."

"I take it none of *you* are unpopular—by reason of pride or insolence, or conspicuous prosperity, or any of those things that excite envy and malice among the base scum of a village? *You* wouldn't think it much of a risk to take a chance in the stocks?"

Dowley winced, visibly. I judged he was hit. But he didn't betray it by any spoken word. As for the others, they spoke out plainly, and with strong feeling. They said they had seen enough of the stocks to know what a man's chance in them was, and they would never consent to enter them if they could compromise on a quick death by hanging.

"Well, to change the subject—for I think I've established my point that the stocks ought to be abolished. I think some of our laws are pretty unfair. For instance, if I do a thing which ought to deliver me to the stocks, and you know I did it and yet keep still and don't report me, *you* will get the stocks if anybody informs on you."

"Ah, but that would serve you but right," said Dowley, "for you *must* inform. So saith the law."

The others coincided.

"Well, all right, let it go, since you vote me down. But there's one thing which certainly isn't fair. The magistrate fixes a mechanic's wage at 1 cent a day, for instance. The law says that if any master shall venture even under utmost press of business, to pay anything *over* that cent a day, even for a single day, he shall be both fined and pilloried for it; and whoever knows he did it and doesn't inform, they also shall be fined and pilloried. Now it seems to me unfair, Dowley, and a deadly peril to all of us, that because you thoughtlessly confessed, a while ago, that within a week you have paid a cent and fifteen mil—"

Oh, I tell *you* it was a smasher! You ought to have seen them go to pieces, the whole gang. I had just slipped up on poor smiling and complacent Dowley so nice and easy and softly, that he never suspected anything was going to happen till the blow came crashing down and knocked him all to rags.

A fine effect. In fact as fine as any I ever produced, with so little time to work it up in.

But I saw in a moment that I had overdone the thing a little. I was expecting to scare them, but I wasn't expecting to scare them to death. They were mighty near it, though. You see they had been a whole lifetime learning to appreciate the pillory; and to have that thing staring them in the face, and every one of them distinctly at the mercy of me, a stranger, if I chose to go and report—well, it was awful, and they couldn't seem to recover from the shock, they couldn't seem to pull themselves together. Pale, shaky, dumb, pitiful? Why, they weren't any better than so many dead men. It was very uncomfortable. Of course I thought they would appeal to me to keep mum, and then we would shake hands, and take a drink all round, and laugh it off, and there an end. But no; you see I was an unknown person, among a cruelly oppressed and suspicious people, a people always accustomed to having advantage taken of their helplessness, and never expecting just or kind treatment from any but their own families and very closest intimates. Appeal to *me* to be gentle, to be fair, to be generous? Of course they wanted to, but they couldn't dare.

CHAPTER XXXIV

THE YANKEE AND THE KING SOLD AS SLAVES

Well, what had I better do? Nothing in a hurry, sure. I must get up a diversion; anything to employ me while I could think, and while these poor fellows could have a chance to come to life again. There sat Marco, petrified in the act of trying to get the hang of his miller-gun—turned to stone, just in the attitude he was in when my pile-driver fell, the toy still gripped in his unconscious fingers. So I took it from him and proposed to explain its mystery. Mystery! a simple little thing like that; and yet it was mysterious enough, for that race and that age.

I never saw such an awkward people, with machinery; you see, they were totally unused to it. The miller-gun was a little double-barrelled tube of toughened glass, with a neat little trick of a spring to it, which upon pressure would let a shot excape. But the shot wouldn't hurt anybody, it would only drop into your hand. In the gun were two sizes—wee mustard-seed shot, and another sort that were several times larger. They were money. The mustard-seed shot represented milrays, the larger ones mills. So the gun was a purse; and very handy, too; you could pay out money in the dark with it, with accuracy; and you could carry it in your mouth; or in your vest pocket, if you had one. I made them of several sizes—one size so large that it would carry the equivalent of a dollar. Using shot for money was a good thing for the government; the metal cost nothing, and the money couldn't be counterfeited, for I was the only person in the kingdom who knew how to manage a shot tower. "Paying the shot" soon came to be a common phrase. Yes, and I knew it would still be passing men's lips, away down in the nineteenth century, yet none would suspect how and when it originated.

The king joined us, about this time, mightily refreshed by his nap, and feeling good. Anything could make me nervous now, I was so uneasy—for our lives were in danger; and so it worried me to detect a complacent something in the king's eye which seemed to indicate that he had been loading himself up for a performance of some kind or other; confound it, why must he go and choose such a time as this?

I was right. He began, straight off, in the most innocently artful, and transparent, and lubberly way, to lead up to the subject of agriculture. The cold sweat broke out all over me. I wanted to whisper in his ear, "Man, we are in awful danger! every moment is worth a principality till we get back these men's confidence; *don't* waste any of this golden time." But of course I couldn't do it. Whisper to him? It would look as if we were conspiring. So I had to sit there and look calm and pleasant while the king stood over that dynamite mine and mooned along about his damned onions and things. At first the tumult of my own thoughts, summoned by the danger-signal and swarming to the rescue from every quarter of my skull, kept up such a hurrah and confusion and fifing and drumming that I couldn't take in a word; but presently when my mob of gathering plans began to crystallize and fall into position and form line of battle, a sort of order and quiet ensued and I caught the boom of the king's batteries, as if out of remote distance:

"—were not the best way, methinks, albeit it is not to be denied that authorities differ as concerning this point, some contending that the onion is but an unwholesome berry when stricken early from the tree—"

The audience showed signs of life, and sought each other's eyes in a surprised and troubled way.

"—whileas others do yet maintain, with much show of reason, that this is not of necessity the case, instancing that plums and other like cereals do be always dug in the unripe state—"

The audience exhibited distinct distress; yes, and also fear.

"—yet are they clearly wholesome, the more especially when one doth assuage the asperities of their nature by admixture of the tranquillizing juice of the wayward cabbage—"

The wild light of terror began to glow in these men's eyes, and one of them muttered, "These be errors, every one—God hath surely smitten the mind of this farmer." I was in miserable apprehension; I sat upon thorns.

"—and further instancing the known truth that in the case of animals, the young, which may be called the green fruit of the creature, is the better, all confessing that when a goat is ripe, his fur doth heat and sore engame his flesh, the which defect, taken in connection with his several rancid habits, and fulsome appetites, and godless attitudes of mind, and bilious quality of morals—"

They rose and went for him! With a fierce shout, "The one would betray us, the other is mad! Kill them! Kill them!" they flung themselves upon us. What joy flamed up in the king's eye! He might be lame in agriculture, but this kind of thing was just in his line. He had been fasting long, he was hungry for a fight. He hit the blacksmith a crack under the jaw that lifted him clear off his feet and stretched him flat of his back. "St. George for Britain!" and he downed the wheelwright. The mason was big, but I laid him out like nothing. The three gathered themselves up and came again; went down again; came again; and kept on repeating this, with native British pluck, until they were battered to jelly, reeling with exhaustion, and so blind that they couldn't tell us from each other; and yet they kept right on, hammering away with what might was left in them. Hammering each other—for we stepped aside and looked on while they rolled, and struggled, and gouged, and pounded, and bit, with the strict and wordless attention to business of so many bulldogs. We looked on without apprehension, for they were fast getting past ability to go for help against us, and the arena was far enough from the public road to be safe from intrusion.

Well, while they were gradually playing out, it suddenly occurred to me to wonder what had become of Marco. I looked around; he was nowhere to be seen. Oh, but this was ominous! I pulled the king's sleeve, and we glided away and rushed for the hut. No Marco there, no Phyllis there! They had gone to the road for help, sure. I told the king to give his heels wings, and I would explain later. We made good time across the open ground, and as we darted into the shelter of the wood I glanced back and saw a mob of excited peasants swarm into view, with Marco and his wife at their head. They were making a world of noise, but that couldn't hurt anybody; the wood was dense, and as soon as we were well into its depths we would take to a tree and let them whistle. Ah, but then came another sound—dogs! Yes, that was quite another matter. It magnified our contract—we must find running water.

We tore along at a good gait, and soon left the sounds far behind and modified to a murmur. We struck a stream and darted into it. We waded swiftly down it, in the dim forest light, for as much as three hundred yards, and then came across an oak with a great bough sticking out over the water. We climbed up on this bough, and began to work our way along it to the body of the tree; now we began to hear those sounds more plainly; so the mob had struck our trail. For a while the sounds approached pretty fast. And then for another while they didn't. No doubt the dogs had found the place where we had entered the stream, and were now waltzing up and down the shores trying to pick up the trail again.

When we were snugly lodged in the tree and curtained with foliage, the king was satisfied, but I was doubtful. I believed we could crawl along a branch and get into the next tree, and I judged it worth while to try. We tried it, and made a success of it, though the king slipped, at the junction, and came near failing to connect. We got comfortable lodgement and satisfactory concealment among the foliage, and then we had nothing to do but listen to the hunt.

Presently we heard it coming—and coming on the jump, too; yes, and down both sides of the stream. Louder—louder—next minute it swelled swiftly up into a roar of shoutings, barkings, tramplings, and swept by like a cyclone.

"I was afraid that the overhanging branch would suggest something to them," said I, "but I don't mind the disappointment. Come, my liege, it were well that we make good use of our time. We've flanked them. Dark is coming on, presently. If we can cross the stream and get a good start, and borrow a couple of horses from somebody's pasture to use for a few hours, we shall be safe enough."

We started down, and got nearly to the lowest limb, when we seemed to hear the hunt returning. We stopped to listen.

"Yes," said I, "they're baffled, they've given it up, they're on their way home. We will climb back to our roost again, and let them go by."

So we climbed back. The king listened a moment and said:

"They still search—I wit the sign. We did best to abide."

He was right. He knew more about hunting than I did. The noise approached steadily, but not with a rush. The king said:

"They reason that we were advantaged by no parlous start of them, and being on foot are as yet no mighty way from where we took the water."

"Yes, sire, that is about it, I am afraid, though I was hoping better things."

The noise drew nearer and nearer, and soon the van was drifting

under us, on both sides of the water. A voice called a halt from the
other bank, and said:

"An they were so minded, they could get to yon tree by this
branch that overhangs, and yet not touch ground. Ye will do well
to send a man up it."

"Marry, that will we do!"

I was obliged to admire my cuteness in foreseeing this very thing
and swapping trees to beat it. But don't you know, there are some
things that can beat smartness and foresight? Awkwardness and
stupidity can. The best swordsman in the world doesn't need to
fear the second best swordsman in the world; no, the person for
him to be afraid of is some ignorant antagonist who has never had
a sword in his hand before; he doesn't do the thing he ought to do,
and so the expert isn't prepared for him; he does the thing he
ought not to do: and often it catches the expert out and ends him
on the spot. Well, how could I, with all my gifts, make any valuable
preparation against a near-sighted, cross-eyed, pudding-headed
clown who would aim himself at the wrong tree and hit the right
one? And that is what he did. He went for the wrong tree, which was
of course the right one by mistake, and up he started.

Matters were serious, now. We remained still, and awaited
developments. The peasant toiled his difficult way up. The king
raised himself up and stood; he made a leg ready, and when the
comer's head arrived in reach of it there was a dull thud, and down
went the man floundering to the ground. There was a wild outbreak
of anger, below, and the mob swarmed in from all around, and there
we were treed, and prisoners. Another man started up; the bridging
bough was detected, and a volunteer started up the tree that
furnished the bridge. The king ordered me to play Horatius and
keep the bridge. For a while the enemy came thick and fast; but no
matter, the head man of each procession always got a buffet that
dislodged him as soon as he came in reach. The king's spirits rose,
his joy was limitless. He said that if nothing occurred to mar the
prospect we should have a beautiful night, for on this line of tactics
we could hold the tree against the whole country-side.

However, the mob soon came to that conclusion themselves;
wherefore they called off the assault and began to debate other
plans. They had no weapons, but there were plenty of stones, and
stones might answer. We had no objections. A stone might possibly
penetrate to us once in a while, but it wasn't very likely; we were
well protected by boughs and foliage, and were not visible from any
good aiming-point. If they would but waste half an hour in
stone-throwing, the dark would come to our help. We were feeling
very well satisfied. We could smile; almost laugh.

But we didn't; which was just as well, for we should have been
interrupted. Before the stones had been raging through the leaves
and bouncing from the boughs fifteen minutes, we began to notice a

smell. A couple of sniffs of it was enough of an explanation: it was smoke! Our game was up at last. We recognized that. When smoke invites you, you have to come. They raised their pile of dry brush and damp weeds higher and higher, and when they saw the thick cloud begin to roll up and smother the tree, they broke out in a storm of joy-clamors. I got enough breath to say:

"Proceed, my liege; after you is manners."

The king gasped:

"Follow me down, and then back thyself against one side of the trunk, and leave me the other. Then will we fight. Let each pile his dead according to his own fashion and taste."

Then he descended barking and coughing, and I followed. I struck the ground an instant after him; we sprang to our appointed places, and began to give and take with all our might. The pow-wow and racket were prodigious; it was a tempest of riot and confusion and thick-falling blows. Suddenly some horsemen tore into the midst of the crowd, and a voice shouted:

"Hold—or ye are dead men!"

How good it sounded! The owner of the voice bore all the marks of a gentleman: picturesque and costly raiment, the aspect of command, a hard countenance, with complexion and features marred by dissipation. The mob fell humbly back, like so many spaniels. The gentleman inspected us critically, then said sharply to the peasants:

"What are ye doing to these people?"

"They be madmen, worshipful sir, that have come wandering we know not whence, and—"

"Ye know not whence? Do ye pretend ye know them not?"

"Most honored sir, we speak but the truth. They are strangers and unknown to any in this region; and they be the most violent and bloodthirsty madmen that ever—"

"Peace! Ye know not what ye say. They are not mad. Who are ye? And whence are ye? Explain."

"We are but peaceful strangers, sir," I said, "and travelling upon our own concerns. We are from a far country, and unacquainted here. We have purposed no harm; and yet but for your brave interference and protection these people would have killed us. As you have divined, sir, we are not mad; neither are we violent or bloodthirsty."

The gentleman turned to his retinue and said calmly:

"Lash me these animals to their kennels!"

The mob vanished in an instant; and after them plunged the horsemen, laying about them with their whips and pitilessly riding down such as were witless enough to keep the road instead of taking to the bush. The shrieks and supplications presently died away in the distance, and soon the horsemen began to straggle back. Meantime the gentleman had been questioning us more closely,

but had dug no particulars out of us. We were lavish of recognition
of the service he was doing us, but we revealed nothing more than
that we were friendless strangers from a far country. When the
escort were all returned, the gentleman said to one of his servants:

"Bring the led-horses and mount these people."

"Yes, my lord."

We were placed toward the rear, among the servants. We travelled
pretty fast, and finally drew rein some time after dark at a road-side
inn some ten or twelve miles from the scene of our troubles. My lord
went immediately to his room, after ordering his supper, and we
saw no more of him. At dawn in the morning we breakfasted and
made ready to start.

My lord's chief attendant sauntered forward at that moment with
indolent grace, and said:

"Ye have said ye should continue upon this road, which is our
direction likewise; wherefore my lord, the earl Grip, hath given
commandment that ye retain the horses and ride, and that certain of
us ride with ye a twenty mile to a fair town that hight Cambenet,
whenso ye shall be out of peril."

We could do nothing less than express our thanks and accept the
offer. We jogged along, six in the party, at a moderate and
comfortable gait, and in conversation learned that my lord Grip
was a very great personage in his own region, which lay a day's
journey beyond Cambenet. We loitered to such a degree that it was
near the middle of the forenoon when we entered the market square
of the town. We dismounted and left our thanks once more for my
lord, and then approached a crowd assembled in the centre of the
square, to see what might be the object of interest. It was the
remnant of that old peregrinating band of slaves! So they had been
dragging their chains about, all this weary time. That poor husband
was gone, and also many others; and some few purchases had been
added to the gang. The king was not interested, and wanted to move
along, but I was absorbed, and full of pity. I could not take my eyes
away from these worn and wasted wrecks of humanity. There they
sat, grouped upon the ground, silent, uncomplaining, with bowed
heads, a pathetic sight. And by hideous contrast, a redundant orator
was making a speech to another gathering not thirty steps away, in
fulsome laudation of "our glorious British liberties!"

I was boiling. I had forgotten I was a plebeian, I was remembering
I was a man. Cost what it might, I would mount that rostrum and—

Click! the king and I were handcuffed together! Our companions,
those servants, had done it; my lord Grip stood looking on. The king
burst out in a fury, and said:

"What meaneth this ill-mannered jest?"

My lord merely said to his head miscreant, coolly:

"Put up the slaves and sell them!"

Slaves! The word had a new sound—and how unspeakably awful!

The king lifted his manacles and brought them down with a deadly force; but my lord was out of the way when they arrived. A dozen of the rascal's servants sprang forward, and in a moment we were helpless, with our hands bound behind us. We so loudly and so earnestly proclaimed ourselves freemen, that we got the interested attention of that liberty-mounting orator and his patriotic crowd, and they gathered about us and assumed a very determined attitude. The orator said:

"If indeed ye are freemen, ye have nought to fear—the God-given liberties of Britain are about ye for your shield and shelter! (Applause.) Ye shall soon see. Bring forth your proofs."

"What proofs?"

"Proof that ye are freemen."

Ah—I remembered! I came to myself; I said nothing. But the king stormed out:

"Thou'rt insane, man. It were better, and more in reason, that this thief and scoundrel here prove that we are *not* freemen."

You see, he knew his own laws just as other people so often know the laws: by words, not by effects. They take a *meaning*, and get to be very vivid, when you come to apply them to yourself.

All hands shook their heads and looked disappointed; some turned away, no longer interested. The orator said—and this time in the tones of business, not of sentiment:

"An ye do not know your country's laws, it were time ye learned them. Ye are strangers to us; ye will not deny that. Ye may be freemen, we do not deny that; but also ye may be slaves. The law is clear: it doth not require the claimant to prove ye are slaves, it requireth you to prove ye are *not*."

I said:

"Dear sir, give us only time to send to Astolat; or give us only time to send to the Valley of Holiness—"

"Peace, good man, these are extraordinary requests, and you may not hope to have them granted. It would cost much time, and would unwarrantably inconvenience your master—"

"*Master*, idiot!" stormed the king. "I have no master, I myself am the m—"

"Silence, for God's sake!"

I got the words out in time to stop the king. We were in trouble enough already; it could not help us any to give these people the notion that we were lunatics.

There is no use in stringing out the details. The earl put us up and sold us at auction. This same infernal law had existed in our own South in my own time, more than thirteen hundred years later, and under it hundreds of freemen who could not prove that they were freemen had been sold into life-long slavery without the circumstance making any particular impression upon me; but the minute law and the auction block came into my personal experience,

a thing which had been merely improper before became suddenly
hellish. Well, that's the way we are made.

Yes, we were sold at auction, like swine. In a big town and an
active market we should have brought a good price; but this place
was utterly stagnant and so we sold at a figure which makes me
ashamed, every time I think of it. The King of England brought
seven dollars, and his prime minister nine; whereas the king was
easily worth twelve dollars and I as easily worth fifteen. But that is
the way things always go; if you force a sale on a dull market, I don't
care what the property is, you are going to make a poor business of
it, and you can make up your mind to it. If the earl had had wit
enough to—

However, there is no occasion for my working my sympathies up
on his account. Let him go, for the present: I took his number, so to
speak.

The slave dealer bought us both, and hitched us onto that long
chain of his, and we constituted the rear of his procession. We took
up our line of march and passed out of Cambenet at noon; and it
seemed to me unaccountably strange and odd that the King of
England and his chief minister, marching manacled and fettered
and yoked, in a slave convoy, could move by all manner of idle men
and women, and under windows where sat the sweet and the lovely,
and yet never attract a curious eye, never provoke a single remark.
Dear, dear, it only shows that there is nothing diviner about a king
than there is about a tramp, after all. He is just a cheap and hollow
artificiality when you don't know he is a king. But reveal his quality,
and dear me it takes your very breath away to look at him. I reckon
we are all fools. Born so, no doubt.

CHAPTER XXXV

A PITIFUL INCIDENT

It's a world of surprises. The king brooded; this was natural.
What would he brood about, should you say? Why, about the
prodigious nature of his fall, of course—from the loftiest place in the
world to the lowest; from the most illustrious station in the world to
the obscurest; from the grandest vocation among men to the basest.
No, I take my oath that the thing that gravelled him most, to start
with, was not this, but the price he had fetched! He couldn't seem to
get over that seven dollars. Well, it stunned me so, when I first found
it out, that I couldn't believe it; it didn't seem natural. But as soon
as my mental sight cleared and I got a right focus on it, I saw I was
mistaken: it *was* natural. For this reason: a king is a mere
artificiality, and so a king's feelings, like the impulses of an
automatic doll, are mere artificialities; but as a man, he is a reality,

and his feelings, as a man, are real, not phantoms. It shames the average man to be valued below his own estimate of his worth; and the king certainly wasn't anything more than an average man, if he was up that high.

Confound him, he wearied me with arguments to show that in anything like a fair market he would have fetched twenty-five dollars, sure—a thing which was plainly nonsense, and full of the baldest conceit; I wasn't worth it myself. But it was tender ground for me to argue on. In fact I had to simply shirk argument and do the diplomatic instead. I had to throw conscience aside, and brazenly concede that he ought to have brought twenty-five dollars; whereas I was quite well aware that in all the ages, the world had never seen a king that was worth half the money, and during the next thirteen centuries wouldn't see one that was worth the fourth of it. Yes, he tired me. If he began to talk about the crops; or about the recent weather; or about the condition of politics, or about dogs, or cats, or morals, or theology—no matter what—I sighed, for I knew what was coming: he was going to get out of it a palliation of that tiresome seven-dollar sale. Wherever we halted, where there was a crowd, he would give me a look which said, plainly: "if that thing could be tried over again, now, with this kind of folk, you would see a different result." Well, when he was first sold, it secretly tickled me to see him go for seven dollars; but before he was done with his sweating and worrying I wished he had fetched a hundred. The thing never got a chance to die, for every day, at one place or another, possible purchasers looked us over, and as often as any other way, their comment on the king was something like this:

"Here's a two-dollar-and-a-half chump with a thirty-dollar style. Pity but style was marketable."

At last this sort of remark produced an evil result. Our owner was a practical person and he perceived that this defect must be mended if he hoped to find a purchaser for the king. So he went to work to take the style out of his sacred majesty. I could have given the man some valuable advice, but I didn't; you mustn't volunteer advice to a slave-driver unless you want to damage the cause you are arguing for. I had found it a sufficiently difficult job to reduce the king's style to a peasant's style, even when he was a willing and anxious pupil; now then, to undertake to reduce the king's style to a slave's style—and by force—go to! it was a stately contract. Never mind the details—it will save me trouble to let you imagine them. I will only remark that at the end of a week there was plenty of evidence that lash and club and fist had done their work well; the king's body was a sight to see—and to weep over; but his spirit?—why, it wasn't even phased. Even that dull clod of a slave-driver was able to see that there can be such a thing as a slave who will remain a man till he dies; whose bones you can break, but whose manhood you can't. This man found that from his first effort down to his latest, he

couldn't ever come within reach of the king but the king was ready to
plunge for him, and did it. So he gave up, at last, and left the king in
possession of his style unimpaired. The fact is, the king was a good
deal more than a king, he was a man; and when a man is a man,
you can't knock it out of him.

We had a rough time for a month, tramping to and fro in the
earth, and suffering. And what Englishman was the most interested
in the slavery question by that time? His grace the king! Yes; from
being the most indifferent, he was become the most interested. He
was become the bitterest hater of the institution I had ever heard
talk. And so I ventured to ask once more a question which I had
asked years before and had gotten such a sharp answer that I had
not thought it prudent to meddle in the matter further. Would he
abolish slavery?

His answer was as sharp as before, but it was music this time;
I shouldn't ever wish to hear pleasanter, though the profanity was
not good, being awkwardly put together, and with the crash-word
almost in the middle instead of at the end, where of course it ought
to have been.

I was ready and willing to get free, now; I hadn't wanted to get
free any sooner. No, I cannot quite say that. I had wanted to, but I
had not been willing to take desperate chances, and had always
dissuaded the king from them. But now—ah, it was a new
atmosphere! Liberty would be worth any cost that might be put upon
it now. I set about a plan, and was straightway charmed with it. It
would require time, yes, and patience, too, a great deal of both. One
could invent quicker ways, and fully as sure ones; but none that
would be as picturesque as this; none that could be made so
dramatic. And so I was not going to give this one up. It might delay
us months, but no matter, I would carry it out or break something.

Now and then we had an adventure. One night we were overtaken
by a snow-storm while still a mile from the village we were making
for. Almost instantly we were shut up as in a fog, the driving snow
was so thick. You couldn't see a thing, and we were soon lost. The
slave-driver lashed us desperately, for he saw ruin before him, but
his lashings only made matters worse, for they drove us further from
the road and from likelihood of succor. So we had to stop, at last,
and slump down in the snow where we were. The storm continued
until toward midnight, then ceased. By this time two of our feebler
men and three of our women were dead, and others past moving and
threatened with death. Our master was nearly beside himself. He
stirred up the living, and made us stand, jump, slap ourselves, to
restore our circulation, and he helped as well as he could with his
whip.

Now came a diversion. We heard shrieks and yells, and soon a
woman came running, and crying; and seeing our group, she flung
herself into our midst and begged for protection. A mob of people

came tearing after her, some with torches, and they said she was a witch who had caused several cows to die by a strange disease, and practised her arts by help of a devil in the form of a black cat. This poor woman had been stoned until she hardly looked human, she was so battered and bloody. The mob wanted to burn her.

Well, now, what do you suppose our master did? When we closed around this poor creature to shelter her, he saw his chance. He said, burn her here, or they shouldn't have her at all. Imagine that! They were willing. They fastened her to a post; they brought wood and piled it about her; they applied the torch while she shrieked and pleaded and strained her two young daughters to her breast; and our brute, with a heart solely for business, lashed us into position about the stake and warmed us into life and commercial value by the same fire which took away the innocent life of that poor harmless mother. That was the sort of master we had. I took *his* number. That snow-storm cost him nine of his flock; and he was more brutal to us than ever, after that, for many days together, he was so enraged over his loss.

We had adventures, all along. One day we ran into a procession. And such a procession! All the riffraff of the kingdom seemed to be comprehended in it; and all drunk at that. In the van was a cart with a coffin in it, and on the coffin sat a comely young girl of about eighteen suckling a baby, which she squeezed to her breast in a passion of love every little while, and every little while wiped from its face the tears which her eyes rained down upon it; and always the foolish little thing smiled up at her, happy and content, kneading her breast with its dimpled fat hand, which she patted and fondled right over her breaking heart.

Men and women, boys and girls, trotted along beside or after the cart, hooting, shouting profane and ribald remarks, singing snatches of foul song, skipping, dancing—a very holiday of hellions, a sickening sight. We had struck a suburb of London, outside the walls, and this was a sample of one sort of London society. Our master secured a good place for us near the gallows. A priest was in attendance, and he helped the girl climb up, and said comforting words to her, and made the under-sheriff provide a stool for her. Then he stood there by her on the gallows, and for a moment looked down upon the mass of upturned faces at his feet, then out over the solid pavement of heads that stretched away on every side occupying the vacancies far and near, and then began to tell the story of the case. And there was pity in his voice—how seldom a sound that was in that ignorant and savage land! I remember every detail of what he said, except the words he said it in; and so I change it into my own words:

"Law is intended to mete out justice. Sometimes it fails. This cannot be helped. We can only grieve, and be resigned, and pray for the soul of him who falls unfairly by the arm of the law, and that his

fellows may be few. A law sends this poor young thing to death—and
it is right. But another law had placed her where she must commit
her crime or starve, with her child—and before God that law is
responsible for both her crime and her ignominious death!

"A little while ago this young thing, this child of eighteen years,
was as happy a wife and mother as any in England; and her lips were
blithe with song, which is the native speech of glad and innocent
hearts. Her young husband was as happy as she; for he was doing
his whole duty, he worked early and late at his handicraft, his bread
was honest bread well and fairly earned, he was prospering, he was
furnishing shelter and sustenance to his family, he was adding his
mite to the wealth of the nation. By consent of a treacherous law,
instant destruction fell upon this holy home and swept it away!
That young husband was waylaid and impressed, and sent to sea.
The wife knew nothing of it. She sought him everywhere, she moved
the hardest hearts with the supplications of her tears, the broken
eloquence of her despair. Weeks dragged by, she watching, waiting,
hoping, her mind going slowly to wreck under the burden of her
misery. Little by little all her small possessions went for food. When
she could no longer pay her rent, they turned her out of doors. She
begged, while she had strength; when she was starving, at last, and
her milk failing, she stole a piece of linen cloth of the value of a
fourth part of a cent, thinking to sell it and save her child. But she
was seen by the owner of the cloth. She was put in jail and brought
to trial. The man testified to the facts. A plea was made for her, and
her sorrowful story was told in her behalf. She spoke, too, by
permission, and said she did steal the cloth, but that her mind was
so disordered of late, by trouble, that when she was overborne with
hunger all acts, criminal or other, swam meaningless through her
and she knew nothing rightly, except that she was *so* hungry! For a
moment all were touched, and there was disposition to deal
mercifully with her, seeing that she was so young and friendless, and
her case so piteous, and the law that robbed her of her support to
blame as being the first and only cause of her transgression; but the
prosecuting officer replied that whereas these things were all true,
and most pitiful as well, still there was much small theft in these
days, and mistimed mercy here would be a danger to property—Oh,
my God, is there no property in ruined homes, and orphaned babes,
and broken hearts that British law holds precious!—and so he must
require sentence.

"When the judge put on his black cap, the owner of the stolen
linen rose trembling up, his lip quivering, his face as gray as ashes;
and when the awful words came, he cried out, 'Oh, poor child,
poor child, I did not know it was death!' and fell as a tree falls.
When they lifted him up his reason was gone; before the sun was
set, he had taken his own life. A kindly man; a man whose heart was
right, at bottom; add his murder to this that is to be now done here;

and charge them both where they belong—to the rulers and the bitter laws of Britain.. The time is come, my child; let me pray over thee—not *for* thee, dear abused poor heart and innocent, but for them that be guilty of thy ruin and death, who need it more."

After his prayer they put the noose around the young girl's neck, and they had great trouble to adjust the knot under her ear, because she was devouring the baby all the time, wildly kissing it, and snatching it to her face and her breast, and drenching it with tears, and half moaning half shrieking all the while, and the baby crowing, and laughing, and kicking its feet with delight over what it took for romp and play. Even the hangman couldn't stand it, but turned away. When all was ready the priest gently pulled and tugged and forced the child out of the mother's arms, and stepped quickly out of her reach; but she clasped her hands, and made a wild spring toward him, with a shriek; but the rope—and the under-sheriff—held her short. Then she went on her knees and stretched out her hands and cried:

"One more kiss—Oh, my God, one more, one more,—it is the dying that begs it!"

She got it; she almost smothered the little thing. And when they got it away again, she cried out:

"Oh, my child, my darling, it will die! It has no home, it has no father, no friend, no mother—"

"It has them all!" said that good priest. "All these will I be to it till I die."

You should have seen her face then! Gratitude? Lord, what do you want with words to express that? Words are only painted fire; a look is the fire itself. She gave that look, and carried it away to the treasury of heaven, where all things that are divine belong.

CHAPTER XXXVI

AN ENCOUNTER IN THE DARK

London—to a slave—was a sufficiently interesting place. It was merely a great big village; and mainly mud and thatch. The streets were muddy, crooked, unpaved. The populace was an ever flocking and drifting swarm of rags, and splendors, of nodding plumes and shining armor. The king had a palace there; he saw the outside of it. It made him sigh; yes, and swear a little, in a poor juvenile sixth century way. We saw knights and grandees whom we knew, but they didn't know us in our rags and dirt and raw welts and bruises, and wouldn't have recognized us if we had hailed them, nor stopped to answer, either, it being unlawful to speak with slaves on a chain. Sandy passed within ten yards of me on a mule—hunting for me, I imagined. But the thing which clean broke my heart was

something which happened in front of our old barrack in a square,
while we were enduring the spectacle of a man being boiled to death
in oil for counterfeiting pennies. It was the sight of a newsboy—and
I couldn't get at him! Still, I had one comfort; here was proof that
Clarence was still alive and banging away. I meant to be with him
before long; the thought was full of cheer.

I had one little glimpse of another thing, one day, which gave me a
great uplift. It was a wire stretching from housetop to housetop.
Telegraph or telephone, sure. I did very much wish I had a little
piece of it. It was just what I needed, in order to carry out my
project of escape. My idea was, to get loose some night, along with
the king, then gag and bind our master, change clothes with him,
batter him into the aspect of a stranger, hitch him to the slave-chain,
assume possession of the property, march to Camelot, and—

But you get my idea; you see what a stunning dramatic surprise I
would wind up with at the palace. It was all feasible, if I could only
get hold of a slender piece of iron which I could shape into a
lock-pick. I could then undo the lumbering padlocks with which our
chains were fastened, whenever I might choose. But I never had any
luck; no such thing ever happened to fall in my way. However, my
chance came at last. A gentleman who had come twice before to
dicker for me, without result, or indeed any approach to a result,
came again. I was far from expecting ever to belong to him, for the
price asked for me from the time I was first enslaved was exorbitant,
and always provoked either anger or derision, yet my master stuck
stubbornly to it—twenty-two dollars. He wouldn't bate a cent. The
king was greatly admired, because of his grand physique, but his
kingly style was against him, and he wasn't salable; nobody wanted
that kind of a slave. I considered myself safe from parting from him
because of my extravagant price. No, I was not expecting to ever
belong to this gentleman whom I have spoken of, but he had
something which I expected would belong to me eventually, if he
would but visit us often enough. It was a steel thing with a long pin
to it, with which his long cloth outside garment was fastened
together in front. There were three of them. He had disappointed me
twice, because he did not come quite close enough to me to make my
project entirely safe; but this time I succeeded; I captured the lower
clasp of the three, and when he missed it he thought he had lost it on
the way.

I had a chance to be glad about a minute, then straightway a
chance to be sad again. For when the purchase was about to fail, as
usual, the master suddenly spoke up and said what would be worded
thus—in modern English:

"I'll tell you what I'll do. I'm tired supporting these two for no
good. Give me twenty-two dollars for this one, and I'll throw the
other one in."

The king couldn't get his breath, he was in such a fury. He began to choke and gag, and meantime the master and the gentleman moved away, discussing.

"An ye will keep the offer open—"

" 'Tis open till the morrow at this hour."

"Then will I answer you at that time," said the gentleman, and disappeared, the master following him.

I had a time of it to cool the king down, but I managed it. I whispered in his ear, to this effect:

"Your grace *will* go for nothing, but after another fashion. And so shall I. To-night we shall both be free."

"Ah! How is that?"

"With this thing which I have stolen, I will unlock these locks and cast off these chains to-night. When he comes about nine thirty to inspect us for the night, we will seize him, gag him, batter him, and early in the morning we will march out of this town, proprietors of this caravan of slaves."

That was as far as I went, but the king was charmed and satisfied. That evening we waited patiently for our fellow-slaves to get to sleep and signify it by the usual sign, for you must not take many chances on those poor fellows if you can avoid it. It is best to keep your own secrets. No doubt they fidgeted only about as usual, but it didn't seem so to me. It seemed to me that they were going to be forever getting down to their regular snoring. As the time dragged on I got nervously afraid we shouldn't have enough of it left for our needs; so I made several premature attempts, and merely delayed things by it; for I couldn't seem to touch a padlock, there in the dark, without starting a rattle out of it which interrupted somebody's sleep and made him turn over and wake some more of the gang.

But finally I did get my last iron off, and was a free man once more. I took a good breath of relief, and reached for the king's irons. Too late! in comes the master, with a light in one hand and his heavy walking-staff in the other. I snuggled close among the wallow of snorers, to conceal as nearly as possible that I was naked of irons; and I kept a sharp lookout and prepared to spring for my man the moment he should bend over me.

But he didn't approach. He stopped, gazed absently toward our dusky mass a minute, evidently thinking about something else; then set down his light, moved musingly toward the door, and before a body could imagine what he was going to do, he was out of the door and had closed it behind him.

"Quick!" said the king. "Fetch him back!"

Of course it was the thing to do, and I was up and out in a moment. But dear me, there were no lamps in those days, and it was a dark night. But I glimpsed a dim figure a few steps away. I darted for it, threw myself upon it, and then there was a state of things and lively! We fought and scuffled and struggled, and drew a crowd in no time. They took an immense interest in the fight and encouraged us

all they could, and in fact couldn't have been pleasanter or more
cordial if it had been their own fight. Then a tremendous row broke
out behind us, and as much as half of our audience left us, with a
rush, to invest some sympathy in that. Lanterns began to swing in all
directions; it was the watch, gathering from far and near. Presently a
halberd fell across my back, as a reminder, and I knew what it
meant. I was in custody. So was my adversary. We were marched off
toward prison, one on each side of the watchman. Here was disaster,
here was a fine scheme gone to sudden destruction! I tried to
imagine what would happen when the master should discover that it
was I who had been fighting him; and what would happen if they
jailed us together in the general apartment for brawlers and petty
law-breakers, as was the custom; and what might—

Just then my antagonist turned his face around in my direction,
the freckled light from the watchman's tin lantern fell on it, and by
George he was the wrong man!

CHAPTER XXXVII

AN AWFUL PREDICAMENT

Sleep? It was impossible. It would naturally have been impossible
in that noisome cavern of a jail, with its mangy crowd of drunken,
quarrelsome and song-singing rapscallions. But the thing that made
sleep all the more a thing not to be dreamed of, was my racking
impatience to get out of this place and find out the whole size of
what might have happened yonder in the slave-quarters in
consequence of that intolerable miscarriage of mine.

It was a long night, but the morning got around at last. I made a
full and frank explanation to the court. I said I was a slave, the
property of the great Earl Grip, who had arrived just after dark at
the Tabard inn in the village on the other side of the water, and had
stopped there over night, by compulsion, he being taken deadly
sick with a strange and sudden disorder. I had been ordered to cross
to the city in all haste and bring the best physician; I was doing my
best; naturally I was running with all my might; the night was dark,
I ran against this common person here, who seized me by the throat
and began to pummel me, although I told him my errand, and
implored him, for the sake of the great earl my master's mortal
peril—

The common person interrupted and said it was a lie; and was
going to explain how I rushed upon him and attacked him without a
a word—

"Silence, sirrah!" from the court. "Take him hence and give him
a few stripes whereby to teach him how to treat the servant of a
nobleman after a different fashion another time. Go!"

Then the court begged my pardon, and hoped I would not fail to tell his lordship it was in no wise the court's fault that this high-handed thing had happened. I said I would make it all right, and so took my leave. Took it just in time, too; he was starting to ask me why I didn't fetch out these facts the moment I was arrested. I said I would if I had thought of it—which was true—but that I was so battered by that man that all my wit was knocked out of me—and so forth and so on, and got myself away, still mumbling.

I didn't wait for breakfast. No grass grew under my feet. I was soon at the slave quarters. Empty—everybody gone! That is, everybody except one body—the slave-master's. It lay there all battered to pulp; and all about were the evidences of a terrific fight. There was a rude board coffin on a cart at the door, and workmen, assisted by the police, were thinning a road through the gaping crowd in order that they might bring it in.

I picked out a man humble enough in life to condescend to talk with one so shabby as I, and got his account of the matter.

"There were sixteen slaves here. They rose against their master in the night, and thou seest how it ended."

"Yes. How did it begin?"

"There was no witness but the slaves. They said the slave that was most valuable got free of his bonds and escaped in some strange way—by magic arts 'twas thought, by reason that he had no key, and the locks were neither broke nor in any wise injured. When the master discovered his loss, he was mad with despair, and threw himself upon his people with his heavy stick, who resisted and brake his back and in other and divers ways did give him hurts that brought him swiftly to his end."

"This is dreadful. It will go hard with the slaves, no doubt, upon the trial."

"Marry, the trial is over."

"Over!"

"Would they be a week, think you—and the matter so simple? They were not the half of a quarter of an hour at it."

"Why, I don't see how they could determine which were the guilty ones in so short a time."

"*Which* ones? Indeed they considered not particulars like to that. They condemned them in a body. Wit ye not the law?—which men say the Romans left behind them here when they went—that if one slave killeth his master all the slaves of that man must die for it."

"True. I had forgotten. And when will these die?"

"Belike within a four and twenty hours; albeit some say they will wait a pair of days more, if peradventure they may find the missing one meantime."

The missing one! It made me feel uncomfortable.

"Is it likely they will find him?"

"Before the day is spent—yes. They seek him everywhere. They

stand at the gates of the town, with certain of the slaves who will
discover him to them if he cometh, and none can pass out but he will
be first examined."

"Might one see the place where the rest are confined?"

"The outside of it—yes. The inside of it—but ye will not want to
see that."

I took the address of that prison, for future reference, and then
sauntered off. At the first second-hand clothing shop I came to, up a
back street, I got a rough rig suitable for a common seaman who
might be going on a cold voyage, and bound up my face with a
liberal bandage, saying I had a toothache. This concealed my worst
bruises. It was a transformation. I no longer resembled my former
self. Then I struck out for that wire, found it and followed it to its
den. It was a little room over a butcher's shop—which meant that
business wasn't very brisk in the telegraphic line. The young chap in
charge was drowsing at his table. I locked the door and put the vast
key in my bosom. This alarmed the young fellow, and he was going
to make a noise; but I said:

"Save your wind; if you open your mouth you are dead, sure.
Tackle your instrument. Lively, now! Call Camelot."

"This doth amaze me! How should such as you know aught of
such matters as—"

"Call Camelot! I am a desperate man. Call Camelot, or get away
from the instrument and I will do it myself."

"What—you?"

"Yes—certainly. Stop gabbling. Call the palace." He made the
call.

"Now then, call Clarence."

"Clarence *who?*"

"Never mind Clarence who. Say you want Clarence; you'll get an
answer."

He did so. We waited five nerve-straining minutes—ten minutes—
how long it did seem!—and then came a click that was as familiar to
me as a human voice; for Clarence had been my own pupil.

"Now, my lad, vacate! They would have known *my* touch, maybe,
and so your call was surest; but I'm all right, now."

He vacated the place and cocked his ear to listen—but it didn't
win. I used a cipher. I didn't waste any time in sociabilities with
Clarence, but squared away for business, straight-off—thus:

"The king is here and in danger. We were captured and brought
here as slaves. We should not be able to prove our identity—and the
fact is, I am not in a position to try. Send a telegram for the palace
here which will carry conviction with it."

His answer came straight back:

"They don't know anything about the telegraph; they haven't
had any experience yet, the line to London is so new. Better not
venture that. They might hang you. Think up something else."

Might hang us! Little he knew how closely he was crowding the facts. I couldn't think up anything for the moment. Then an idea struck me, and I started it along:

"Send five hundred picked knights with Launcelot in the lead; and send them on the jump. Let them enter by the southwest gate, and look out for the man with a white cloth around his right arm."

The answer was prompt:

"They shall start in half an hour."

"All right, Clarence; now tell this lad here that I'm a friend of yours and a dead-head; and that he must be discreet and say nothing about this visit of mine."

The instrument began to talk to the youth and I hurried away. I fell to ciphering. In half an hour it would be nine o'clock. Knights and horses in heavy armor couldn't travel very fast. These would make the best time they could, and now that the ground was in good condition, and no snow or mud, they would probably make a seven-mile gait; they would have to change horses a couple of times; they would arrive about six, or a little after; it would still be plenty light enough; they would see the white cloth which I should tie around my right arm, and I would take command. We would surround that prison and have the king out in no time. It would be showy and picturesque enough, all things considered, though I would have preferred noonday, on account of the more theatrical aspect the thing would have.

Now then, in order to increase the strings to my bow, I thought I would look up some of those people whom I had formerly recognized, and make myself known. That would help us out of our scrape, without the knights. But I must proceed cautiously, for it was a risky business. I must get into sumptuous raiment, and it wouldn't do to run and jump into it. No, I must work up to it by degrees, buying suit after suit of clothes, in shops wide apart, and getting a little finer article with each change, until I should finally reach silk and velvet, and be ready for my project. So I started.

But the scheme fell through like scat! The first corner I turned, I came plump upon one of our slaves, snooping around with a watchman. I coughed, at the moment, and he gave me a sudden look that bit right into my marrow. I judge he thought he had heard that cough before. I turned immediately into a shop and worked along down the counter, pricing things and watching out of the corner of my eye. Those people had stopped, and were talking together and looking in at the door. I made up my mind to get out the back way, if there was a back way, and I asked the shopwoman if I could step out there and look for the escaped slave, who was believed to be in hiding back there somewhere, and said I was an officer in disguise, and my pard was yonder at the door with one of the murderers in charge, and would she be good enough to step there and tell him he needn't wait, but had better go at once to the further end of the back alley and be ready to head him off when I rousted him out.

She was blazing with eagerness to see one of those already celebrated murderers, and she started on the errand at once. I slipped out the back way, locked the door behind me, put the key in my pocket and started off, chuckling to myself and comfortable.

Well, I had gone and spoiled it again, made another mistake. A double one, in fact. There were plenty of ways to get rid of that officer by some simple and plausible device, but no, I must pick out a picturesque one; it is the crying defect of my character. And then, I had ordered my procedure upon what the officer, being human, would *naturally* do; whereas when you are least expecting it, a man will now and then go and do the very thing which it's *not* natural for him to do. The natural thing for the officer to do, in this case, was to follow straight on my heels; he would find a stout oaken door, securely locked, between him and me; before he could break it down, I should be far away and engaged in slipping into a succession of baffling disguises which would soon get me into a sort of raiment which was a surer protection from meddling law-dogs in Britain than any amount of mere innocence and purity of character. But instead of doing the natural thing, the officer took me at my word, and followed my instructions. And so, as I came trotting out of that cul de sac, full of satisfaction with my own cleverness, he turned the corner and I walked right into his handcuffs. If I had known it was a cul de sac—however, there isn't any excusing a blunder like that, let it go. Charge it up to profit and loss.

Of course I was indignant, and swore I had just come ashore from a long voyage, and all that sort of thing—just to see, you know, if it woud deceive that slave. But it didn't. He knew me. Then I reproached him for betraying me. He was more surprised than hurt. He stretched his eyes wide, and said:

"What, wouldst have me let thee, of all men, escape and not hang with us, when thou'rt the very *cause* of our hanging? Go to!"

"Go to" was their way of saying "I should smile!" or "I like that!" Queer talkers, those people.

Well, there was a sort of bastard justice in his view of the case, and so I dropped the matter. When you can't cure a disaster by argument, what is the use to argue? It isn't my way. So I only said:

"You're not going to be hanged. None of us are."

Both men laughed, and the slave said:

"Ye have not ranked as a fool—before. You might better keep your reputation, seeing the strain would not be for long."

"It will stand it, I reckon. Before to-morrow we shall be out of prison, and free to go where we will, besides."

The witty officer lifted at his left ear with his thumb, made a rasping noise in his throat, and said:

"Out of prison—yes—ye say true. And free likewise to go where ye will, so ye wander not out of his grace the Devil's sultry realm."

I kept my temper, and said, indifferently:

"Now I suppose you really think we are going to hang within a day or two."

"I thought it not many minutes ago, for so the thing was decided and proclaimed."

"Ah, then you've changed your mind, is that it?"

"Even that. I only *thought*, then; I *know*, now."

I felt sarcastical, so I said:

"Oh, sapient servant of the law, condescend to tell us, then, what you *know*.

"That ye will all be hanged *to-day*, at mid-afternoon! Oho! that shot hit home! Lean upon me."

The fact is I did need to lean upon somebody. My knights couldn't arrive in time. They would be as much as three hours too late. Nothing in the world could save the King of England; nor me, which was more important. More important, not merely to me, but to the nation—the only nation on earth standing ready to blossom into civilization. I was sick. I said no more, there wasn't anything to say. I knew what the man meant; that if the missing slave was found, the postponement would be revoked, the execution take place to-day. Well, the missing slave was found.

CHAPTER XXXVIII

SIR LAUNCELOT AND KNIGHTS TO THE RESCUE

Nearing four in the afternoon. The scene was just outside the walls of London. A cool, comfortable, superb day, with a brilliant sun; the kind of day to make one want to live, not die. The multitude was prodigious and far reaching; and yet we fifteen poor devils hadn't a friend in it. There was something painful in that thought, look at it how you might. There we sat, on our tall scaffold, the butt of the hate and mockery of all those enemies. We were being made a holiday spectacle. They had built a sort of grand stand for the nobility and gentry, and these were there in full force, with their ladies. We recognized a good many of them.

The crowd got a brief and unexpected dash of diversion out of the king. The moment we were freed of our bonds he sprang up, in his fantastic rags, with face bruised out of all recognition, and proclaimed himself Arthur, King of Britain, and denounced the awful penalties of treason upon every soul there present if hair of his sacred head were touched. It startled and surprised him to hear them break into a vast roar of laughter. It wounded his dignity, and he locked himself up in silence, then, although the crowd begged him to go on, and tried to provoke him to it by cat-calls, jeers, and

shouts of "Let him speak! The king! The king! his humble subjects
hunger and thirst for words of wisdom out of the mouth of their
master his Serene and Sacred Raggedness!"

But it went for nothing. He put on all his majesty and sat under
this rain of contempt and insult unmoved. He certainly was great in
his way. Absently, I had taken off my white bandage and wound it
about my right arm. When the crowd noticed this, they began upon
me. They said:

"Doubtless this sailor-man is his minister—observe his costly
badge of office!"

I let them go on until they got tired, and then I said:

"Yes, I am his minister, The Boss; and to-morrow you will hear
that from Camelot which—"

I got no further. They drowned me out with joyous derision. But
presently there was silence; for the sheriffs of London, in their
official robes, with their subordinates, began to make a stir which
indicated that business was about to begin. In the hush which
followed, our crime was recited, the death warrant read, then
everybody uncovered while a priest uttered a prayer.

Then a slave was blindfolded, the hangman unslung his rope.
There lay the smooth road below us, we upon one side of it, the
banked multitude walling its other side—a good clear road, and
kept free by the police—how good it would be to see my five hundred
horsemen come tearing down it! But, no, it was out of the
possibilities. I followed its receding thread out into the distance—
not a horseman on it, or sign of one.

There was a jerk, and the slave hung dangling; dangling and
hideously squirming, for his limbs were not tied.

A second rope was unslung, in a moment another slave was
dangling.

In a minute a third slave was struggling in the air. It was dreadful.
I turned away my head a moment, and when I turned back I missed
the king! They were blindfolding him! I was paralyzed; I couldn't
move, I was choking, my tongue was petrified. They finished
blindfolding him, they led him under the rope. I couldn't shake off
that clinging impotence. But when I saw them put the noose around
his neck, then everything let go in me and I made a spring to the
rescue—and as I made it I shot one more glance abroad—by
George, here they came, a-tilting!—five hundred mailed and belted
knights on bicycles!

The grandest sight that ever was seen. Lord, how the plumes
streamed, how the sun flamed and flashed from the endless
procession of webby wheels!

I waved my right arm as Launcelot swept in—he recognized my
rag—I tore away noose and bandage, and shouted:

"On your knees, every rascal of you, and salute the king! Who
fails shall sup in hell to-night!"

I always use that high style when I'm climaxing an effect. Well, it
was noble to see Launcelot and the boys swarm up onto that
scaffold and heave sheriffs and such overboard. And it was fine to
see that astonished multitude go down on their knees and beg their
lives of the king they had just been deriding and insulting. And as he
stood apart, there, receiving this homage in his rags, I thought to
myself, well really there *is* something peculiarly grand about the gait
and bearing of a king, after all.

I was immensely satisfied. Take the whole situation all around, it
was one of the gaudiest effects I ever instigated.

And presently up comes Clarence, his own self! and winks, and
says, very modernly:

"Good deal of a surprise, wasn't it? I knew you'd like it. I've had
the boys practising, this long time, privately; and just hungry for a
chance to show off."

CHAPTER XXXIX

THE YANKEE'S FIGHT WITH THE KNIGHTS

Home again, at Camelot. A morning or two later I found the
paper, damp from the press, by my plate at the breakfast table.
I turned to the advertising columns, knowing I should find
something of personal interest to me there. It was this:

DE PAR LE ROI.

Know that the great lord and illustrious kni8ht, SIR SAGRAMOR LE
DESIROUS naving condescended to
meet the King's Minister, Hank Morgan, the which is surnamed The Boss,
for satisfgction of offence anciently given,
these will engage in the lists by
Camelot about the fourth hour of the
morning on the sixteenth day of this
next succeeding month. The battle
wiil be à l'outrance, sith the said offence
was of a deadly sort, admitting of no
comPosition.

DE PAR LE ROI

Clarence's editorial reference to this affair was to this effect:

thdrew. woak maintained there since, soon listic have witq oked interest upon the e∧an- ve been m d oy the ar .s, ent out ch y by 'terian B , and some y g men of eur undei the i guidance of tha or aii in a known te great enterprise ot ...aking pure ; esent novement haa its **origin in preven**- has ever been a sions in our on of Wis- **other** one ospel, by- e Tne .he same co reoresent ized thirty of needs and hear- ∮hich, years ago ! onesgn was osgan- ng, the missions, so that both had 'o withdraw' and much to their grief,

It will be observed, by a gl7nce at our advertising columns, that the community is to be favore l with a treat of unusual interest in the tournament line. The names of the artists are warrant of good entertainment. The box-office will be open at noon of the 13th; admission 3 cents, reserved seats 5; proceeds to go to the hospital fund The royal pan and all the Court will be present. With these exceptions, and the press and the clergy, tne free list is strictly sus¶ended. Parties are hereby warned against buying tickets of speculators; they will not be good at the door. Everybody knows and likes The Boss, everybody knows ana likes Sir Sag.; come, let us give tne iads a good sendoff. ReMember, tne proceeds go to a great and free charity, and one whose broad begevolence stretcnes out its helping hand, warm with the blood of a loving heai t, to all that suIer, regardless of race, creed, condition or colou—the only charity yet established in the earth which has no politico-religious stopcock on its compassion, but says Here flows the stream, let *all* come and drink! Turn out, al' hands! fetch along your doughnuts and your gum-arops and have a good time.   Pie for sale on the grounds, and rocks to crack it with; also ciRcus-lemonade—three drops of lime juice to a barrel of water.

N. B.   *This is the first tournamen* *under the new law, whidh allows each* *combatant to use any weapon he may pre-* *fer.*   You want to make a note of that.

our disappointn. dromptly and - two of their felo erlain, and ot ers have alread.. spoken, yor ' furnisned fc their use, n make and the kind letters oj introd duction whi they are und ing friends to us ried, and leave the thot kind words enc which you, m) joy- hind ; and it is a home matter -' b it is our durp direct them tc now under the e g fields as ar Tnese young me are warm-hearte azirl, regions bei not to "build u ond,', and the der instructi ons of our another mau founhati's on., ociety, whlch They go un say tqat " inr ionaries to mon say sanding mis

Up to the day set, there was no talk in all Britain of anything but this combat. All other topics sank into insignificance and passed out of men's thoughts and interest. It was not because a tournament was a great matter; it was not because Sir Sagramor had found the Holy Grail, for he had not, but had failed; it was not because the second (official) personage in the kingdom was one of the duellists; no, all these features were commonplace. Yet there was abundant reason for the extraordinary interest which this coming fight was creating. It was born of the fact that all the nation knew that was not to be a duel between mere men, so to speak, but a duel between two mighty magicians; a duel not of muscle but of mind, not of human skill but of superhuman art and craft; a final struggle for supremacy between the two master enchanters of the age. It was realized that the most prodigious achievements of the most renowned knights could not be worthy of comparison with a spectacle like this; they could be but child's play, contrasted with this mysterious and awful battle of the gods. Yes, all the world knew it was going to be in reality a duel between Merlin and me, a measuring of his magic powers against mine. It was known that Merlin had been busy whole days and nights together, imbuing Sir Sagramor's arms and armor with supernal powers of offence and defence, and that he had procured for him from the spirits of the air a fleecy veil which would render the wearer invisible to his antagonist while still visible to other men. Against Sir Sagramor, so weaponed and protected, a thousand knights could accomplish nothing; against him no known enchantments could prevail. These facts were sure; regarding them there was no doubt, no reason for doubt. There was but one question: might there be still other enchantments, *unknown* to Merlin, which could render Sir Sagramor's veil transparent to me, and make his enchanted mail vulnerable to my weapons? This was the one thing to be decided in the lists. Until then the world must remain in suspense.

So the world thought there was a vast matter at stake here, and the world was right, but it was not the one they had in their minds. No, a far vaster one was upon the cast of this die: *the life of knight-errantry.* I was a champion, it was true, but not the champion of the frivolous black arts, I was the champion of hard unsentimental common-sense and reason. I was entering the lists to either destroy knight-errantry or be its victim.

Vast as the show-grounds were, there were no vacant spaces in them outside of the lists, at ten o'clock on the morning of the 16th. The mammoth grand-stand was clothed in flags, streamers, and rich tapestries, and packed with several acres of small-fry tributary kings, their suites, and the British aristocracy; with our own royal gang in the chief place, and each and every individual a flashing prism of gaudy silks and velvets—well, I never saw anything to begin with it but a fight between an Upper Mississippi sunset and the aurora borealis. The huge camp of beflagged and gay-colored tents at one end of the lists, with a stiff-standing sentinel at every door and a shining shield hanging by him for challenge, was another fine sight. You see, every knight was there who had any ambition or any caste feeling; for my feeling toward their order was not much of a secret, and so here was their chance. If I won my fight with Sir Sagramor, others would have the right to call me out as long as I might be willing to respond.

Down at our end there were but two tents; one for me, and

another for my servants. At the appointed hour the king made a
sign, and the heralds, in their tabards, appeared and made
proclamation, naming the combatants and stating the cause of
quarrel. There was a pause, then a ringing bugle-blast, which was
the signal for us to come forth. All the multitude caught their
breath, and an eager curiosity flashed into every face.

Out from his tent rode great Sir Sagramor, an imposing tower of
iron, stately and rigid, his huge spear standing upright in its socket
and grasped in his strong hand, his grand horse's face and breast
cased in steel, his body clothed in rich trappings that almost dragged
the ground—oh, a most noble picture. A great shout went up, of
welcome and admiration.

And then out I came. But I didn't get any shout. There was a
wondering and eloquent silence, for a moment, then a great wave of
laughter began to sweep along that human sea, but a warning
bugle-blast cut its career short. I was in the simplest and
comfortablest of gymnast costumes—flesh-colored tights from neck
to heel, with blue silk puffings about my loins, and bareheaded. My
horse was not above medium size, but he was alert, slender-limbed,
muscled with watch-springs, and just a greyhound to go. He was a
beauty, glossy as silk, and naked as he was when he was born, except
for bridle and ranger-saddle.

The iron tower and the gorgeous bed-quilt came cumbrously but
gracefully pirouetting down the lists, and we tripped lightly up to
meet them. We halted; the tower saluted, I responded; then we
wheeled and rode side by side to the grand-stand and faced our king
and queen, to whom we made obeisance. The queen exclaimed:

"Alack, Sir Boss, wilt fight naked, and without lance or sword
or—"

But the king checked her and made her understand, with a polite
phrase or two, that this was none of her business. The bugles rang
again; and we separated and rode to the ends of the lists, and took
position. Now old Merlin stepped into view and cast a dainty web of
gossamer threads over Sir Sagramor which turned him into Hamlet's
ghost; the king made a sign, the bugles blew, Sir Sagramor laid his
great lance in rest, and the next moment here he came thundering
down the course with his veil flying out behind, and I went whistling
through the air like an arrow to meet him—cocking my ear, the
while, as if noting the invisible knight's position and progress by
hearing, not sight. A chorus of encouraging shouts burst out for him,
and one brave voice flung out a heartening word for me—said:

"Go it, slim Jim!"

It was an even bet that Clarence had procured that favor for
me—and furnished the language, too. When that formidable
lance-point was within a yard and a half of my breast I twitched my
horse aside without an effort and the big knight swept by, scoring
a blank. I got plenty of applause that time. We turned, braced up,

and down we came again. Another blank for the knight, a roar of applause for me. This same thing was repeated once more; and it fetched such a whirlwind of applause that Sir Sagramor lost his temper, and at once changed his tactics and set himself the task of chasing me down. Why, he hadn't any show in the world at that; it was a game of tag, with all the advantage on my side; I whirled out of his path with ease whenever I chose, and once I slapped him on the back as I went to the rear. Finally I took the chase into my own hands; and after that, turn, or twist, or do what he would, he was never able to get behind me again; he found himself always in front, at the end of his manoeuvre. So he gave up that business and retired to his end of the lists. His temper was clear gone, now, and he forgot himself and flung an insult at me which disposed of mine. I slipped my lasso from the horn of my saddle, and grasped the coil in my right hand. This time you should have seen him come!—it was a business trip, sure; by his gait there was blood in his eye. I was sitting my horse at ease, and swinging the great loop of my lasso in wide circles about my head; the moment he was under way, I started for him; when the space between us had narrowed to forty feet, I sent the snaky spirals of the rope a-cleaving through the air, then darted aside and faced about and brought my trained animal to a halt with all his feet braced under him for a surge. The next moment the rope sprang taut and yanked Sir Sagramor out of the saddle! Great Scott, but there was a sensation!

Unquestionably the popular thing in this world is novelty. These people had never seen anything of that cowboy business before, and it carried them clear off their feet with delight. From all around and everywhere, the shout went up—

"Encore! encore!"

I wondered where they got the word, but there was no time to cipher on philological matters, because the whole knight-errantry hive was just humming, now, and my prospect for trade couldn't have been better. The moment my lasso was released and Sir Sagramor had been assisted to his tent, I hauled in the slack, took my station and began to swing my loop around my head again. I was sure to have use for it as soon as they could elect a successor for Sir Sagramor, and that couldn't take long where there were so many hungry candidates. Indeed, they elected one straight off—Sir Hervis de Revel.

Bzz! Here he came, like a house afire; I dodged; he passed like a flash, with my horse-hair coils settling around his neck; a second or so later, *fst!* his saddle was empty.

I got another encore; and another, and another, and still another. When I had snaked five men out, things began to look serious to the iron-clads, and they stopped and consulted together. As a result, they decided that it was time to waive etiquette and send their greatest and best against me. To the astonishment of that little world, I lassoed Sir Lamorak de Galis, and after him Sir Galahad. So you see there was simply nothing to be done, now, but play their right bower—bring out the superbest of the superb, the mightiest of the mighty, the great Sir Launcelot himself!

A proud moment for me? I should think so. Yonder was Arthur, King of Britain; yonder was Guenever; yes, and whole tribes of little provincial kings and kinglets; and in the tented camp yonder, renowned knights from many lands; and likewise the selectest body known to chivalry, the Knights of the Table Round, the most illustrious in Christendom; and biggest fact of all, the very sun of their shining system was yonder couching his lance, the focal point of forty thousand adoring eyes; and all by myself, here was I laying for him. Across my mind flitted the dear image of a certain hello-girl of West Hartford, and I wished she could see me now. In that moment, down came the Invincible, with the rush of a whirlwind— the courtly world rose to its feet and bent forward—the fateful coils went circling through the air, and before you could wink I was towing Sir Launcelot across the field on his back, and kissing my hand to the storm of waving kerchiefs and the thundercrash of applause that greeted me!

Said I to myself, as I coiled my lariat and hung it on my saddle-horn, and sat there drunk with glory, "The victory is perfect—no other will venture against me—knight-errantry is dead." Now imagine my astonishment—and everybody else's too—to hear the peculiar bugle-call which announces that another competitor is about to enter the lists! There was a mystery here; I couldn't account for this thing. Next, I noticed Merlin gliding away from me; and then I noticed that my lasso was gone! The old sleight-of-hand expert had stolen it, sure, and slipped it under his robe.

The bugle blew again. I looked, and down came Sagramor riding again, with his dust brushed off and his veil nicely re-arranged. I trotted up to meet him, and pretended to find him by the sound of his horse's hoofs. He said:

"Thou'rt quick of ear, but it will not save thee from this!" and he touched the hilt of his great sword. "An ye are not able to see it, because of the influence of the veil, know that it is no cumbrous lance, but a sword—and I ween ye will not be able to avoid it."

His visor was up; there was death in his smile. I should never be able to dodge his sword, that was plain. Somebody was going to die, this time. If he got the drop on me, I could name the corpse. We rode forward together, and saluted the royalties. This time the king was disturbed. He said:

"Where is thy strange weapon?"

"It is stolen, sire."

"Hast another at hand?"

"No, sire, I brought only the one."

Then Merlin mixed in:

"He brought but the one because there was but the one to bring. There exists none other but that one. It belongeth to the king of the Demons of the Sea. This man is a pretender, and ignorant; else he had known that that weapon can be used in but eight bouts only, and then it vanisheth away to its home under the sea."

"Then is he weaponless," said the king. "Sir Sagramor, ye will grant him leave to borrow."

"And I will lend!" said Sir Launcelot, limping up. "He is as brave a knight of his hands as any that be on live, and he shall have mine."

He put his hand on his sword to draw it, but Sir Sagramor said:

"Stay, it may not be. He shall fight with his own weapons; it was his privilege to choose them and bring them. If he has erred, on his head be it."

"Knight!" said the king. "Thou'rt overwrought with passion; it disorders thy mind. Wouldst kill a naked man?"

"An he do it, he shall answer it to me," said Sir Launcelot.

"I will answer it to any he that desireth!" retorted Sir Sagramor hotly.

Merlin broke in, rubbing his hands and smiling his lowdownest smile of malicious gratification:

" 'Tis well said, right well said! And 'tis enough of parleying, let my lord the king deliver the battle signal."

The king had to yield. The bugle made proclamation, and we turned apart and rode to our stations. There we stood, a hundred yards apart, facing each other, rigid and motionless, like horsed statues. And so we remained, in a soundless hush, as much as a full minute, everybody gazing, nobody stirring. It seemed as if the king could not take heart to give the signal. But at last he lifted his hand, the clear note of the bugle followed, Sir Sagramor's long blade described a flashing curve in the air, and it was superb to see him come. I sat still. On he came. I did not move. People got so excited that they shouted to me:

"Fly, fly! Save thyself! This is murther!"

I never budged so much as an inch, till that thundering apparition had got within fifteen paces of me; then I snatched a dragoon revolver out of my holster, there was a flash and a roar, and the revolver was back in the holster before anybody could tell what had happened.

Here was a riderless horse plunging by, and yonder lay Sir Sagramor, stone dead.

The people that ran to him were stricken dumb to find that the life was actually gone out of the man and no reason for it visible, no hurt upon his body, nothing like a wound. There was a hole through the breast of his chain-mail, but they attached no importance to a little thing like that; and as a bullet-wound there produces but little blood, none came in sight because of the clothing and swaddlings under the armor. The body was dragged over to let the king and the swells look down upon it. They were stupefied with astonishment, naturally. I was requested to come and explain the miracle. But I remained in my tracks, like a statue, and said:

"If it is a command, I will come, but my lord the king knows that I am where the laws of combat require me to remain while any desire to come against me."

I waited. Nobody challenged. Then I said:

"If there are any who doubt that this field is well and fairly won, I do not wait for them to challenge me, I challenge them."

"It is a gallant offer," said the king, "and well beseems you. Whom will you name, first?"

"I name none, I challenge all! Here I stand, and dare the chivalry of England to come against me—not by individuals, but in mass!"

"What!" shouted a score of knights.

"You have heard the challenge. Take it, or I proclaim you recreant knights and vanquished, every one!"

It was a "bluff" you know. At such a time it is sound judgment to put on a bold face and play your hand for a hundred times what it is worth; forty-nine times out of fifty nobody dares to "call," and you rake in the chips. But just this once—well, things looked squally! In just no time, five hundred knights were scrambling into their saddles, and before you could wink a widely scattering drove were under way and clattering down upon me. I snatched both revolvers from the holsters and began to measure distances and calculate chances.

Bang! One saddle empty. Bang! another one. Bang—bang! and I bagged two. Well it was nip and tuck with us, and I knew it. If I spent the eleventh shot without convincing these people, the twelfth man would kill me, sure. And so I never did feel so happy as I did when my ninth downed its man and I detected the wavering in the crowd which is premonitory of panic. An instant lost now, could knock out my last chance. But I didn't lose it. I raised both revolvers and pointed them—the halted host stood their ground just about one good square moment, then broke and fled.

The day was mine. Knight-errantry was a doomed institution. The march of civilization was begun. How did I feel? Ah you never could imagine it.

And Brer Merlin? His stock was flat again. Somehow, every time the magic of fol-de-rol tried conclusions with the magic of science, the magic of fol-de-rol got left.

CHAPTER XL

THREE YEARS LATER

When I broke the back of knight-errantry that time, I no longer
felt obliged to work in secret. So, the very next day I exposed my
hidden schools, my mines, and my vast system of clandestine
factories and work-shops to an astonished world. That is to say, I
exposed the nineteenth century to the inspection of the sixth.

Well it is always a good plan to follow up an advantage promptly.
The knights were temporarily down, but if I would keep them so I
must just simply paralyze them—nothing short of that would
answer. You see, I was "bluffing" that last time, in the field; it
would be natural for them to work around to that conclusion, if I
gave them a chance. So I must not give them time: and I didn't.

I renewed my challenge, engraved it on brass, posted it up where
any priest could read it to them, and also kept it standing, in the
advertising columns of the paper.

I not only renewed it, but added to its proportions. I said, name
the day, and I would take fifty assistants and stand up *against the
masses chivalry of the whole earth and destroy it.*

I was not bluffing this time. I meant what I said; I could do what
I promised. There wasn't any way to misunderstand the language
of that challenge. Even the dullest of the chivalry perceived that this
was a plain case of "put up, or shut up." They were wise and did
the latter. In all the next three years they gave me no trouble worth
mentioning.

Consider the three years sped. Now look around on England. A
happy and prosperous country, and strangely altered. Schools
everywhere, and several colleges; a number of pretty good
newspapers. Even authorship was taking a start; Sir Dinadan the
Humorist was first in the field, with a volume of gray-headed jokes
which I had been familiar with during thirteen centuries. If he had
left out that old rancid one about the lecturer I wouldn't have said
anything; but I couldn't stand that one. I suppressed the book and
hanged the author.

Slavery was dead and gone; all men were equal before the law;
taxation had been equalized. The telegraph, the telephone, the
phonograph, the typewriter, the sewing-machine, and all the
thousand willing and handy servants of steam and electricity were
working their way into favor. We had a steamboat or two on the
Thames, we had steam war-ships, and the beginnings of a steam
commercial marine; I was getting ready to send out an expedition
to discover America.

We were building several lines of railway, and our line from
Camelot to London was already finished and in operation. I was
shrewd enough to make all offices connected with the passenger

service places of high and distinguished honor. My idea was to
attract the chivalry and nobility, and make them useful and keep
them out of mischief. The plan worked very well, the competition
for the places was hot. The conductor of the 4.33 express was a duke,
there wasn't a passenger conductor on the line below the degree of
earl. They were good men, every one, but they had two defects which
I couldn't cure, and so had to wink at: they wouldn't lay aside their
armor, and they would "knock down" fares—I mean rob the
company.

There was hardly a knight in all the land who wasn't in some
useful employment. They were going from end to end of the country
in all manner of useful missionary capacities; their penchant for
wandering, and their experience in it, made them altogether the
most effective spreaders of civilization we had. They went clothed
in steel and equipped with sword and lance and battle-axe, and if
they couldn't persuade a person to try a sewing-machine on the
instalment plan, or a melodeon, or a barbed-wire fence, or a
prohibition journal, or any of the other thousand and one things
they canvassed for, they removed him and passed on.

I was very happy. Things were working steadily towards a secretly
longed-for point. You see, I had two schemes in my head which were
the vastest of all my projects. The one was, to overthrow the Catholic
Church and set up the Protestant faith on its ruins—not as an
Established Church, but a-go-as-you-please one; and the other
project was, to get a decree issued by-and-by, commanding that
upon Arthur's death unlimited suffrage should be introduced, and
given to men and women alike—at any rate to all men, wise or
unwise, and to all mothers who at middle age should be found to
know nearly as much as their sons at twenty-one. Arthur was good
for thirty years yet, he being about my own age—that is to say,
forty—and I believed that in that time I could easily have the active
part of the population of that day ready and eager for an event
which should be the first of its kind in the history of the world—a
rounded and complete governmental revolution without bloodshed.
The result to be a republic. Well, I may as well confess, though I do
feel ashamed when I think of it: I was beginning to have a base
hankering to be its first president myself. Yes, there was more or less
human nature in me; I found that out.

Clarence was with me as concerned the revolution, but in a
modified way. His idea was a republic, without privileged orders
but with a hereditary royal family at the head of it instead of an
elective chief magistrate. He believed that no nation that had ever
known the joy of worshipping a royal family could ever be robbed
of it and not fade away and die of melancholy. I urged that kings
were dangerous. He said, then have cats. He was sure that a royal
family of cats would answer every purpose. They would be as useful
as any other royal family, they would know as much, they would

have the same virtues and the same treacheries, the same disposition
to get up shindies with other royal cats, they would be laughably
vain and absurd and never know it, they would be wholly
inexpensive; finally, they would have as sound a divine right as any
other royal house, and "Tom VII., or Tom XI., or Tom XIV. by the
grace of God King," would sound as well as it would when applied
to the ordinary royal tomcat with tights on. "And as a rule," said he,
in his neat modern English, "the character of these cats would be
considerably above the character of the average king, and this would
be an immense moral advantage to the nation, for the reason that a
nation always models its morals after its monarch's. The worship
of royalty being founded in unreason, these graceful and harmless
cats would easily become as sacred as any other royalties, and indeed
more so, because it would presently be noticed that they hanged
nobody, beheaded nobody, imprisoned nobody, inflicted no cruelties
or injustices of any sort, and so must be worthy of a deeper love and
reverence than the customary human king, and would certainly get
it. The eyes of the whole harried world would soon be fixed upon this
humane and gentle system, and royal butchers would presently
begin to disappear; their subjects would fill the vacancies with
catlings from our own royal house; we should become a factory;
we should supply the thrones of the world; within forty years all
Europe would be governed by cats, and we should furnish the cats.
The reign of universal peace would begin then, to end no more
forever . . . . . . *Me-e-e-yow-ow-ow-ow—fzt!—wow!*"

Hang him, I supposed he was in earnest, and was beginning to be
persuaded by him, until he exploded that cat-howl and startled me
almost out of my clothes. But he never could be in earnest. He didn't
know what it was. He had pictured a distinct and perfectly rational
and feasible improvement upon constitutional monarchy, but he
was too feather-headed to know it, or care anything about it, either.
I was going to give him a scolding, but Sandy came flying in at that
moment, wild with terror, and so choked with sobs that for a minute
she could not get her voice. I ran and took her in my arms, and
lavished caresses upon her and said, beseechingly:

"Speak, darling, speak! What is it?"

Her head fell limp upon my bosom, and she gasped, almost
inaudibly:

"HELLO, CENTRAL!"

"Quick!" I shouted to Clarence; "telephone the king's homeopath
to come!"

In two minutes I was kneeling by the child's crib, and Sandy was
dispatching servants here, there and everywhere, all over the palace.
I took in the situation almost at a glance—membraneous croup!
I bent down and whispered:

"Wake up, sweetheart! Hello-Central!"

She opened her soft eyes languidly, and made out to say—

"Papa."

That was a comfort. She was far from dead, yet. I sent for
preparations of sulphur. I rousted out the croup-kettle myself;
for I don't sit down and wait for doctors when Sandy or the child
is sick. I knew how to nurse both of them, and had had experience.
This little chap had lived in my arms a good part of its small life,
and often I could soothe away its troubles and get it to laugh through
the tear-dews on its eye-lashes when even its mother couldn't.

Sir Launcelot, in his richest armor, came striding along the great
hall, now, on his way to the stock-board; he was president of the
stock-board, and occupied the Siege Perilous, which he had bought
of Sir Galahad; for the stock-board consisted of the Knights of the
Round Table, and they used the Round Table for business purposes,
now. Seats at it were worth—well, you would never believe the figure,
so it is no use to state it. Sir Launcelot was a bear, and he had put
up a corner in one of the new lines, and was just getting ready to
squeeze the shorts to-day; but what of that? He was the same old
Launcelot, and when he glanced in as he was passing the door and
found out that his pet was sick, that was enough for him; bulls and
bears might fight it out their own way for all him, he would come
right in here and stand by little Hello-Central for all he was worth.
And that was what he did. He shied his helmet into the corner, and
in half a minute he had a new wick in the alcohol lamp and was
firing up on the croup-kettle. By this time Sandy had built a blanket
canopy over the crib, and everything was ready.

Sir Launcelot got up steam, he and I loaded up the kettle with
unslaked lime and carbolic acid, with a touch of lactic acid added
thereto, then filled the thing up with water and inserted the
steam-spout under the canopy. Everything was ship-shape, now, and
we sat down on either side of the crib to stand our watch. Sandy was
so grateful and so comforted that she charged a couple of church-
wardens with willow-bark and sumach-tobacco for us, and told us
to smoke as much as we pleased, it couldn't get under the canopy,
and she was used to smoke, being the first lady in the land who had
ever seen a cloud blown. Well, there couldn't be a more contented
or comfortable sight than Sir Launcelot in his noble armor sitting
in gracious serenity at the end of a yard of snowy church-warden.
He was a beautiful man, a lovely man, and was just intended to
make a wife and children happy. But of course, Guenever—however,
it's no use to cry over what's done and can't be helped.

Well, he stood watch-and-watch with me, right straight through,
for three days and nights, till the child was out of danger; then he
took her up in his great arms and kissed her, with his plumes falling
about her golden head, then laid her softly in Sandy's lap again
and took his stately way down the vast hall, between the ranks of
admiring men-at-arms and menials, and so disappeared. And no
instinct warned me that I should never look upon him again in this

world! Lord, what a world of heart-break it is.

The doctors said we must take the child away, if we would coax her back to health and strength again. And she must have sea-air. So we took a man-of-war, and a suite of two hundred and sixty persons, and went cruising about, and after a fortnight of this we stepped ashore on the French coast, and the doctors thought it would be a good idea to make something of a stay there. The little king of that region offered us his hospitalities, and we were glad to accept. If he had had as many conveniences as he lacked, we should have been plenty comfortable enough; even as it was, we made out very well, in his queer old castle, by the help of comforts and luxuries from the ship.

At the end of a month I sent the vessel home for fresh supplies, and for news. We expected her back in three or four days. She would bring me, along with other news, the result of a certain experiment which I had been starting. It was a project of mine to replace the tournament with something which might furnish an escape for the extra steam of the chivalry, keep those bucks entertained and out of mischief, and at the same time preserve the best thing in them, which was their hardy spirit of emulation. I had had a choice band of them in private training for some time, and the date was now arriving for their first public effort.

This experiment was base-ball. In order to give the thing vogue from the start, and place it out of the reach of criticism, I chose my nines by rank, not capacity. There wasn't a knight in either team who wasn't a sceptred sovereign. As for material of this sort, there was a glut of it, always, around Arthur. You couldn't throw a brick in any direction and not cripple a king. Of course I couldn't get these people to leave off their armor; they wouldn't do that when they bathed. They consented to differentiate the armor so that a body could tell one team from the other, but that was the most they would do. So, one of the teams wore chain-mail ulsters, and the other wore plate-armor made of my new Bessemer steel. Their practice in the field was the most fantastic thing I ever saw. Being ball-proof, they never skipped out of the way, but stood still and took the result; when a Bessemer was at the bat and a ball hit him, it would bound a hundred and fifty yards, sometimes. And when a man was running, and threw himself on his stomach to slide to his base, it was like an iron-clad coming into port. At first I appointed men of no rank to act as umpires, but I had to discontinue that. These people were no easier to please than other nines. The umpire's first decision was usually his last; they broke him in two with a bat, and his friends toted him home on a shutter. When it was noticed that no umpire ever survived a game, umpiring got to be unpopular. So I was obliged to appoint somebody whose rank and lofty position under the government would protect him.

Here are the names of the nines:

BESSEMERS	ULSTERS
KING ARTHUR.	EMPEROR LUCIUS.
KING LOT OF LOTHIAN.	KING LOGRIS
KING OF NORTHGALIS.	KING MARHALT OF IRELAND.
KING MARSIL.	KING MORGANORE.
KING OF LITTLE BRITAIN.	KING MARK OF CORNWALL.
KING LABOR.	KING NENTRES OF GARLOT.
KING PELLAM OF LISTENGESE.	KING MELIODAS OF LIONES.
KING BAGDEMAGUS.	KING OF THE LAKE.
KING TOLLEME LA FEINTES.	THE SOWDAN OF SYRIA.

Umpire—CLARENCE

The first public game would certainly draw fifty thousand people; and for solid fun would be worth going around the world to see. Everything would be favorable; it was balmy and beautiful spring weather, now, and Nature was all tailored out in her new clothes.

CHAPTER XLI

THE INTERDICT

However, my attention was suddenly snatched from such matters; our child began to lose ground again, and we had to go to sitting up with her, her case became so serious. We couldn't bear to allow anybody to help, in this service, so we two stood watch-and-watch, day in and day out. Ah, Sandy, what a right heart she had, how simple, and genuine, and good she was! She was a flawless wife and mother; and yet I had married her for no other particular reason, except that by the customs of chivalry she was my property until some knight should win her from me in the field. She had hunted Britain over for me; had found me at the hanging-bout outside of London, and had straightway resumed her old place at my side in the placidest way and as of right. I was a New Englander, and in my opinion this sort of partnership would compromise her, sooner or later. She couldn't see how, but I cut argument short and we had a wedding.

Now I didn't know I was drawing a prize, yet that was what I did draw. Within the twelvemonth I became her worshipper; and ours was the dearest and perfectest comradeship that ever was. People talk about beautiful friendships between two persons of the same sex. What is the best of that sort, as compared with the friendship of man and wife, where the best impulses and highest ideals of both are the same? There is no place for comparison between the two friendships; the one is earthly, the other divine.

In my dreams, along at first, I still wandered thirteen centuries away, and my unsatisfied spirit went calling and harking all up and

down the unreplying vacancies of a vanished world. Many a time
Sandy heard that imploring cry come from my lips in my sleep.
With a grand magnanimity she saddled that cry of mine upon our
child, conceiving it to be the name of some lost darling of mine. It
touched me to tears, and it also nearly knocked me off my feet, too,
when she smiled up in my face for an earned reward, and played her
quaint and pretty surprise upon me:

"The name of one who was dear to thee is here preserved, here
made holy, and the music of it will abide alway in our ears. Now
thou'lt kiss me, as knowing the name I have given the child."

But I didn't know it, all the same. I hadn't an idea in the world,
but it would have been cruel to confess it and spoil her pretty game;
so I never let on, but said:

"Yes, I know, sweetheart—how dear and good it is of you, too!
But I want to hear these lips of yours, which are also mine, utter it
first—then its music will be perfect."

Pleased to the marrow, she murmured—

"HELLO-CENTRAL!"

I didn't laugh—I am always thankful for that—but the strain
ruptured every cartilage in me, and for weeks afterward I could hear
my bones clack when I walked. She never found out her mistake.
The first time she heard that form of salute used at the telephone
she was surprised, and not pleased; but I told her I had given order
for it: that henceforth and forever the telephone must always be
invoked with that reverent formality, in perpetual honor and
remembrance of my lost friend and her small namesake. This was
not true. But it answered.

Well, during two weeks and a half we watched by the crib, and in
our deep solicitude we were unconscious of any world outside of that
sick-room. Then our reward came: the centre of the universe turned
the corner and began to mend. Grateful? It isn't the term. There
isn't any term for it. You know that, yourself, if you've ever watched
your child through the Valley of the Shadow and seen it come back
to life and sweep night out of the earth with one all-illuminating
smile that you could cover with your hand.

Why, we were back in this world in one instant! Then we looked
the same startled thought into each other's eyes at the same
moment: more than two weeks gone, and that ship not back yet!

In another minute I appeared in the presence of my train. They
had been steeped in troubled bodings all this time—their faces
showed it. I called an escort and we galloped five miles to a hill-top
overlooking the sea. Where was my great commerce that so lately
had made these glistening expanses populous and beautiful with
its white-winged flocks? Vanished, every one! Not a sail, from verge
to verge, not a smoke-bank—just a dead and empty solitude, in
place of all that brisk and breezy life.

I went swiftly back, saying not a word to anybody. I told Sandy this ghastly news. We could imagine no explanation that would begin to explain. Had there been an invasion? an earthquake? a pestilence? Had the nation been swept out of existence? But guessing was profitless. I must go—at once. I borrowed the king's navy—a "ship" no bigger than a steam launch—and was soon ready.

The parting—ah, yes, that was hard. As I was devouring the child with last kisses, it brisked up and jabbered out its vocabulary!—the first time in more than two weeks, and it made fools of us for joy. The darling mispronunciations of childhood!—dear me, there's no music that can touch it; and how one grieves when it wastes away and dissolves into correctness, knowing it will never visit his bereaved ear again. Well, how good it was to be able to carry that gracious memory away with me!

I approached England the next morning, with the wide highway of salt water all to myself. There were ships in the harbor, at Dover, but they were naked as to sails, and there was no sign of life about them. It was Sunday; yet at Canterbury the streets were empty; strangest of all, there was not even a priest in sight, and no stroke of a bell fell upon my ear. The mournfulness of death was everywhere. I couldn't understand it. At last, in the further edge of that town I saw a small funeral procession—just a family and a few friends following a coffin—no priest; a funeral without bell, book or candle; there was a church there, close at hand, but they passed it by, weeping, and did not enter it; I glanced up at the belfry, and there hung the bell, shrouded in black, and its tongue tied back. Now I knew! Now I understood the stupendous calamity that had overtaken England. Invasion? Invasion is a triviality to it. It was the INTERDICT!

I asked no questions. I didn't need to ask any. The Church had struck; the thing for me to do was to get into a disguise, and go warily. One of my servants gave me a suit of his clothes, and when we were safe beyond the town I put them on, and from that time I travelled alone; I could not risk the embarrassment of company.

A miserable journey. A desolate silence everywhere. Even in London itself. Traffic had ceased; men did not talk or laugh, or go in groups, or even in couples; they moved aimlessly about, each man by himself, with his head down, and woe and terror at his heart. The Tower showed recent war-scars. Verily, much had been happening.

Of course I meant to take the train for Camelot. Train! Why, the station was as vacant as a cavern. I moved on. The journey to Camelot was a repetition of what I had already seen. The Monday and the Tuesday differed in no way from the Sunday. I arrived, far in the night. From being the best electric-lighted town in the kingdom and the most like a recumbent sun of anything you ever saw, it was become simply a blot—a blot upon darkness—that is to

say, it was darker and solider than the rest of the darkness, and
so you could see it a little better; it made me feel as if maybe it was
symbolical—a sort of sign that the Church was going to *keep* the
upper hand, now, and snuff out all my beautiful civilization just like
that. I found no life stirring in the sombre streets. I groped my way
with a heavy heart. The vast castle loomed black upon the hill-top,
not a spark visible about it. The drawbridge was down, the great
gate stood wide. I entered without challenge, my own heels making
the only sound I heard—and it was sepulchral enough, in those huge
vacant courts.

CHAPTER XLII

WAR!

I found Clarence, alone in his quarters, drowned in melancholy;
and in place of the electric light, he had reinstituted the ancient
rag-lamp, and sat there in a grisly twilight with all curtains drawn
tight. He sprang up and rushed for me eagerly, saying:

"Oh, it's worth a billion milrays to look upon a live person again!"

He knew me as easily as if I hadn't been disguised at all. Which
frightened me; one may easily believe that.

"Quick, now, tell me the meaning of this fearful disaster," I said.
"How did it come about?"

"Well, if there hadn't been any Queen Guenever, it wouldn't
have come so early; but it would have come, anyway. It would have
come on your own account, by-and-by; by luck, it happened to come
on the queen's."

"*And* Sir Launcelot's?"

"Just so."

"Give me the details."

"I reckon you will grant that during some years there has been
only one pair of eyes in these kingdoms that has not been looking
steadily askance at the queen and Sir Launcelot—"

"Yes, King Arthur's."

"—and only one heart that was without suspicion—"

"Yes—the king's; a heart that isn't capable of thinking evil of a
friend."

"Well, the king might have gone on, still happy and unsuspecting,
to the end of his days, but for one of your modern improvements—
the stock-board. When you left, three miles of the London,
Canterbury and Dover were ready for the rails, and also ready and
ripe for manipulation in the stock-market. It was wild-cat, and
everybody knew it. The stock was for sale at a give-away. What does
Sir Launcelot do, but—"

"Yes, I know; he quietly picked up nearly all of it, for a song;
then he bought about twice as much more, deliverable upon call;

and he was about to call when I left."

"Very well, he did call. The boys couldn't deliver. Oh, he had
them—and he just settled his grip and squeezed them. They were
laughing in their sleeves over their smartness in selling stock to him
at 15 and 16 and along there, that wasn't worth 10. Well, when they
had laughed long enough on that side of their mouths, they
rested-up that side by shifting the laugh to the other side. That was
when they compromised with the Invincible at 283!"

"Good land!"

"He skinned them alive, and they deserved it—anyway, the whole
kingdom rejoiced. Well, among the flayed were Sir Agravaine and
Sir Mordred, nephews to the king. End of the first act. Act second,
scene first, an apartment in Carlisle castle, where the court had gone
for a few day's hunting. Persons present, the whole tribe of the king's
nephews. Mordred and Agravaine propose to call the guileless
Arthur's attention to Guenever and Sir Launcelot. Sir Gawaine, Sir
Gareth, and Sir Gaheris will have nothing to do with it. A dispute
ensues, with loud talk; in the midst of it, enter the king. Mordred
and Agravaine spring their devastating tale upon him. *Tableau*.
A trap is laid for Launcelot, by the king's command, and Sir
Launcelot walks into it. He made it sufficiently uncomfortable for
the ambushed witnesses—to-wit, Mordred, Agravaine, and twelve
knights of lesser rank, for he killed every one them but Mordred;
but of course that couldn't straighten matters between Launcelot
and the king, and didn't."

"Oh, dear, only one thing could result—I see that. War, and the
knights of the realm divided into a king's party and a Sir
Launcelot's party."

"Yes—that was the way of it. The king sent the queen to the stake,
proposing to purify her with fire. Launcelot and his knights
rescued her, and in doing it slew certain good old friends of yours
and mine—in fact, some of the best we ever had; to-wit, Sir Belias
le Orgulous, Sir Segwarides, Sir Griflet le Fils de Dieu, Sir
Brandiles, Sir Aglovale—"

"Oh, you tear out my heartstrings."

"—wait, I'm not done yet—Sir Tor, Sir Gauter, Sir Gillimer—"

"The very best man in my subordinate nine. What a handy right-
fielder he was!"

"—Sir Reynold's three brothers, Sir Damus, Sir Priamus, Sir
Kay the Stranger—"

"My peerless short-stop! I've seen him catch a daisy-cutter in his
teeth. Come, I can't stand this!"

"—Sir Driant, Sir Lambegus, Sir Herminde, Sir Pertilope, Sir
Perimones, and—whom do you think?"

"Rush! Go on."

"Sir Gaheris, and Sir Gareth—both!"

"Oh, incredible! Their love for Launcelot was indestructible."

"Well, it was an accident. They were simply on-lookers; they were unarmed, and were merely there to witness the queen's punishment. Sir Launcelot smote down whoever came in the way of his blind fury, and he killed these without noticing who they were. Here is an instantaneous photograph one of our boys got of the battle; it's for sale on every news stand. There—the figures nearest the queen are Sir Launcelot with his sword up, and Sir Gareth gasping his latest breath. You can catch the agony in the queen's face through the curling smoke. It's a rattling battle-picture."

"Indeed it is. We must take good care of it; its historical value is incalculable. Go on."

"Well, the rest of the tale is just war, pure and simple. Launcelot retreated to his town and castle of Joyous Gard, and gathered there a great following of knights. The king, with a great host, went there, and there was desperate fighting during several days, and as a result, all the plain around was paved with corpses and cast iron. Then the Church patched up a peace between Arthur and Launcelot and the queen and everybody—everybody but Sir Gawaine. He was bitter about the slaying of his brothers, Gareth and Gaheris, and would not be appeased. He notified Launcelot to get him thence, and make swift preparation, and look to be soon attacked. So Launcelot sailed to his Duchy of Guienne, with his following, and Gawaine soon followed, with an army, and he beguiled Arthur to go with him. Arthur left the kingdom in Sir Mordred's hands until you should return—"

"Ah—a king's customary wisdom!"

"Yes. Sir Mordred set himself at once to work to make his kingship permanent. He was going to marry Guenever, as a first move; but she fled and shut herself up in the Tower of London. Mordred attacked; the Bishop of Canterbury dropped down on him with the Interdict. The king returned; Mordred fought him at Dover, at Canterbury, and again at Barham Down. Then there was talk of peace and a composition. Terms, Mordred to have Cornwall and Kent during Arthur's life, and the whole kingdom afterward."

"Well, upon my word! My dream of a republic to *be* a dream, and so remain."

"Yes. The two armies lay near Salisbury. Gawaine—Gawaine's head is at Dover Castle, he fell in the fight there—Gawaine appeared to Arthur in a dream, at least his ghost did, and warned him to refrain from conflict for a month, let the delay cost what it might. But battle was precipitated by an accident. Arthur had given order that if a sword was raised during the consultation over the proposed treaty with Mordred, sound the trumpet and fall on! for he had no confidence in Mordred. Mordred had given a similar order to *his* people. Well, by-and-by an adder bit a knight's heel; the knight forgot all about the order, and made a slash at the adder with his sword. Inside of half a minute those two prodigious hosts came

together with a crash! They butchered away all day. Then the king—
however, we have started something fresh since you left—our
paper has."

"No? What is that?"

"War correspondence!"

"Why, that's good."

"Yes, the paper was booming right along, for the Interdict made
no impression, got no grip, while the war lasted. I had war
correspondents with both armies. I will finish that battle by reading
you what one of the boys says:

Then the king looked about him, and then was he ware of all his host and
of all his good knights were left no more on live but two knights, that was
Sir Lucan de Butlere, and his brother Sir Bedivere; and they were full sore
wounded. Jesu mercy, said the king, where are all my noble knights
becomen? Alas that ever I should see this doleful day. For now, said Arthur,
I am come to mine end. But would to God that I wist where were that traitor
Sir Mordred, that hath caused all this mischief. Then was King Arthur ware
where Sir Mordred leaned upon his sword among a great heap of dead men.
Now give me my spear, said Arthur unto Sir Lucan, for yonder I have espied
the traitor that all this woe hath wrought. Sir, let him be, said Sir Lucan, for
he is unhappy; and if ye pass this unhappy day, ye shall be right well
revenged upon him. Good lord, remember ye of your night's dream, and
what the spirit of Sir Gawaine told you this night, yet God of his great
goodness hath preserved you hitherto. Therefore, for God's sake, my lord,
leave off by this. For blessed be God ye have won the field: for here we be
three on live, and with Sir Mordred is none on live. And if ye leave off now,
this wicked day of destiny is past. Tide me death, betide me life, saith the
king, now I see him yonder alone, he shall never escape mine hands, for at
a better avail shall I never have him. God speed you well, said Sir Bedivere.
Then the king gat his spear in both his hands, and ran toward Sir Mordred,
crying, Traitor, now is thy death day come. And when Sir Mordred heard
Sir Arthur, he ran until him with his sword drawn in his hand. And then
King Arthur smote Sir Mordred under the shield, with a foin of his spear
throughout the body more than a fathom. And when Sir Mordred felt that
he had his death's wound, he thrust himself, with the might that he had, up
to the but of King Arthur's spear. And right so he smote his father Arthur
with his sword holden in both his hands, on the side of the head, that the
sword pierced the helmet and the brain-pan, and therewithal Sir Mordred
fell stark dead to the earth. And the noble Arthur fell in a swoon to the
earth, and there he swooned oft-times.

"That is a good piece of war correspondence, Clarence; you are
a first-rate newspaper man. Well—is the king all right? Did he get
well?"

"Poor soul, no. He is dead."

I was utterly stunned; it had not seemed to me that any wound
could be mortal to him.

"And the queen, Clarence?"

"She is a nun, in Almesbury."

"What changes! and in such a short while. It is inconceivable. What next, I wonder?"

"I can tell you what next."

"Well?"

"Stake our lives and stand by them!"

"What do you mean by that?"

"The Church is master, now. The Interdict included you with Mordred; it is not to be removed while you remain alive. The clans are gathering. The Church has gathered all the knights that are left alive, and as soon as you are discovered we shall have business on our hands."

"Stuff! With our deadly scientific war-material; with our hosts of trained—"

"Save your breath—we haven't sixty faithful left!"

"What are you saying? Our schools, our colleges, our vast workshops, our—"

"When those knights come, those establishments will empty themselves and go over to the enemy. Did you think you had educated the superstition out of those people?"

"I certainly did think it."

"Well, then, you may unthink it. They stood every strain easily—until the Interdict. Since then, they merely put on a bold outside—at heart they are quaking. Make up your mind to it—when the armies come, the mask will fall."

"It's hard news. We are lost. They will turn our own science against us."

"No they won't."

"Why?"

"Because I and a handful of the faithful have blocked that game. I'll tell you what I've done, and what moved me to it. Smart as you are, the Church was smarter. It was the Church that sent you cruising—through her servants the doctors."

"Clarence!"

"It is the truth. I know it. Every officer of your ship was the Church's picked servant, and so was every man of the crew."

"Oh, come!"

"It is just as I tell you. I did not find out these things at once, but I found them out finally. Did you send me verbal information, by the commander of the ship, to the effect that upon his return to you, with supplies, you were going to leave Cadiz—"

"Cadiz! I haven't been at Cadiz at all!"

"—going to leave Cadiz and cruise in distant seas indefinitely, for the health of your family? Did you send me that word?"

"Of course not. I would have written, wouldn't I?"

"Naturally. I was troubled and suspicious. When the commander sailed again I managed to ship a spy with him. I have never heard of vessel or spy since. I gave myself two weeks to hear from you in. Then

I resolved to send a ship to Cadiz. There was a reason why I didn't."

"What was that?"

"Our navy had suddenly and mysteriously disappeared! Also as suddenly and as mysteriously, the railway and telegraph and telephone service ceased, the men all deserted, poles were cut down, the Church laid a ban upon the electric light! I had to be up and doing—and straight off. Your life was safe—nobody in these kingdoms but Merlin would venture to touch such a magician as you without ten thousand men at his back—I had nothing to think of but how to put preparations in the best trim against your coming. I felt safe myself—nobody would be anxious to touch a pet of yours. So this is what I did. From our various works I selected all the men— boys I mean—whose faithfulness under whatsoever pressure I could swear to, and I called them together secretly and gave them their instructions. There are fifty-two of them; none younger than fourteen, and none above seventeen years old."

"Why did you select boys?"

"Because all the others were born in an atmosphere of superstition and reared in it. It is in their blood and bones. We imagined we had educated it out of them; they thought so, too; the Interdict woke them up like a thunderclap! It revealed them to themselves, and it revealed them to me, too. With boys it was different. Such as have been under our training from seven to ten years have had no acquaintance with the Church's terrors, and it was among these that I found my fifty-two. As a next move, I paid a private visit to that old cave of Merlin's—not the small one—the big one—"

"Yes, the one where we secretly established our first great electric plant when I was projecting a miracle."

"Just so. And as that miracle hadn't become necessary then, I thought it might be a good idea to utilize the plant now. I've provisioned the cave for a siege—"

"A good idea, a first-rate idea."

"I think so. I placed four of my boys there as a guard—inside, and out of sight. Nobody was to be hurt—while outside; but any attempt to enter—well, we said just let anybody try it! Then I went out into the hills and uncovered and cut the secret wires which connected your bedroom with the wires that go to the dynamite deposits under all our vast factories, mills, workshops, magazines, etc., and about midnight I and my boys turned out and connected that wire with the cave, and nobody but you and I suspects where the other end of it goes to. We laid it under ground, of course, and it was all finished in a couple of hours or so. We sha'n't have to leave our fortress, now, when we want to blow up our civilization."

"It was the right move—and the natural one; a military necessity, in the changed condition ot things. Well, what changes *have* come! We expected to be besieged in the palace some time or other, but—

however, go on."

"Next, we built a wire fence."

"Wire fence?"

"Yes. You dropped the hint of it yourself, two or three years ago."

"Oh, I remember—the time the Church tried her strength against us the first time, and presently thought it wise to wait for a hopefuler season. Well, how have you arranged the fence?"

"I start twelve immensely strong wires—naked, not insulated— from a big dynamo in the cave—dynamo with no brushes except a positive and a negative one—"

"Yes, that's right."

"The wires go out from the cave and fence in a circle of level ground a hundred yards in diameter; they make twelve independent fences, ten feet apart—that is to say, twelve circles within circles— and their ends come into the cave again."

"Right; go on."

"The fences are fastened to heavy oaken posts only three feet apart, and these posts are sunk five feet in the ground."

"That is good and strong."

"Yes. The wires have no ground-connection outside of the cave. They go out from the positive brush of the dynamo; there is a ground-connection through the negative brush; the other ends of the wire return to the cave, and each is grounded independently."

"No-no, that won't do!"

"Why?"

"It's too expensive—uses up force for nothing. You don't want any ground-connection except the one through the negative brush. The other end of every wire must be brought back into the cave and fastened independently, and *without* any ground-connection. Now, then, observe the economy of it. A cavalry charge hurls itself against the fence; you are using no power, you are spending no money, for there is only one ground-connection till those horses come against the wire; the moment they touch it they form a connection with the negative brush *through the ground,* and drop dead. Don't you see?—you are using no energy until it is needed; your lightning is there, and ready, like a load in a gun; but it isn't costing you a cent till you touch it off. Oh, yes, the single ground-connection—"

"Of course! I don't know how I overlooked that. It's not only cheaper, but it's more effectual than the other way, for if wires break or get tangled, no harm is done."

"No, especially if we have a tell-tale in the cave and disconnect the broken wire. Well, go on. The gatlings?"

"Yes—that's arranged. In the centre of the inner circle, on a spacious platform six feet high, I've grouped a battery of thirteen gatling guns, and provided plenty of ammunition."

"That's it. They command every approach, and when the Church's knights arrive, there's going to be music. The brow of the precipice over the cave—"

"I've got a wire fence there, and a gatling. They won't drop any rocks down on us."

"Well, and the glass-cylinder dynamite torpedoes?"

"That's attended to. It's the prettiest garden that was ever planted. It's a belt forty feet wide, and goes around the other fence—distance between it and the fence one hundred yards—kind of neutral ground, that space is. There isn't a single square yard of that whole belt but is equipped with a torpedo. We laid them on the surface of the ground, and sprinkled a layer of sand over them. It's an innocent looking garden, but you let a man start in to hoe it once, and you'll see."

"You tested the torpedoes?"

"Well, I was going to, but—"

"But what? Why, it's an immense oversight not to apply a—"

"Test? Yes, I know; but they're all right; I laid a few in the public road beyond our lines and they've been tested."

"Oh, that alters the case. Who did it?"

"A Church committee."

"How kind!"

"Yes. They came to command us to make submission. You see they didn't really come to test the torpedoes; that was merely an incident."

"Did the committee make a report?"

"Yes, they made one. You could have heard it a mile."

"Unanimous?"

"That was the nature of it. After that I put up some signs, for the protection of future committees, and we have had no intruders since."

"Clarence, you've done a world of work, and done it perfectly."

"We had plenty of time for it; there wasn't any occasion for hurry."

We sat silent awhile, thinking. Then my mind was made up, and I said:

"Yes, everything is ready; everything is ship-shape, no detail is wanting. I know what to do, now."

"So do I: sit down and wait."

"No, *sir!* rise up and *strike!*"

"Do you mean it?"

"Yes, indeed! The *de*fensive isn't in my line, and the *of*fensive is. That is, when I hold a fair hand—two-thirds as good a hand as the enemy. Oh, yes, we'll rise up and strike; that's our game."

"A hundred to one, you are right. When does the performance begin?"

"*Now!* We'll proclaim the Republic."

"Well, that *will* precipitate things, sure enough!"

"It will make them buzz, *I* tell you! England will be a hornet's nest before noon to-morrow, if the Church's hand hasn't lost its cunning—and we know it hasn't. Now you write and I'll dictate—thus:

"PROCLAMATION

———

"BE IT KNOWN UNTO ALL. Whereas the king having died and left no heir, it becomes my duty to continue the executive authority vested in me, until a government shall have been created and set in motion. The monarchy has lapsed, it no longer exists. By consequence, all political power has reverted to its original source, the people of the nation. With the monarchy, its several adjuncts died also; wherefore there is no longer a nobility, no longer a privileged class, no longer an Established Church: all men are become exactly equal, they are upon one common level, and religion is free. *A Republic is hereby proclaimed,* as being the natural estate of a nation when other authority has ceased. It is the duty of the British people to meet together immediately, and by their votes elect representatives and deliver into their hands the government."

I signed it "The Boss," and dated it from Merlin's Cave. Clarence said:

"Why, that tells where we are, and invites them to call right away."

"That is the idea. We *strike*—by the Proclamation—then it's their innings. Now have the thing set up and printed and posted, right off; that is, give the order; then, if you've got a couple of bicycles handy at the foot of the hill, ho for Merlin's Cave!"

"I shall be ready in ten minutes. What a cyclone there is going to be to-morrow when this piece of paper gets to work! . . . . . It's a pleasant old palace, this is; I wonder if we shall ever again—but never mind about that."

CHAPTER XLIII

THE BATTLE OF THE SAND-BELT

In Merlin's Cave—Clarence and I and fifty-two fresh, bright, well-educated, clean-minded young British boys. At dawn I sent an order to the factories and to all our great works to stop operations and remove all life to a safe distance, as everything was going to be blown up by secret mines, *"and no telling at what moment— therefore, vacate at once."* These people knew me, and had confidence in my word. They would clear out without waiting to part their hair, and I could take my own time about dating the explosion. You couldn't hire one of them to go back during the century, if the explosion was still impending.

We has a week of waiting. It was not dull for me, because I was writing all the time. During the first three days, I finished turning my old diary into this narrative form; it only required a chapter or so to bring it down to date. The rest of the week I took up in writing letters to my wife. It was always my habit to write to Sandy every day, whenever we were separate, and now I kept up the habit for the love of it, and of her, though I couldn't do anything with the letters, of course, after I had written them. But it put in the time, you see, and was almost like talking; it was almost as if I was saying, "Sandy, if you and Hello-Central were here in the cave, instead of only your photographs, what good times we could have!" And then, you know, I could imagine the baby goo-gooing something out in reply, with its fists in its mouth and itself stretched across its mother's lap on its back, and she a-laughing and admiring and worshipping, and now and then tickling under the baby's chin to set it cackling, and then maybe throwing in a word of answer to me herself—and so on and so on—well, don't you know, I could sit there in the cave with my pen, and keep it up, that way, by the hour with them. Why, it was almost like having us all together again.

I had spies out, every night, of course, to get news. Every report made things look more and more impressive. The hosts were gathering, gathering; down all the roads and paths of England the knights were riding, and priests rode with them, to hearten these original Crusaders, this being the Church's war. All the nobilities, big and little, were on their way, and all the gentry. This was all as was expected. We should thin out this sort of folk to such a degree that the people would have nothing to do but just step to the front with their republic and—

Ah, what a donkey I was! Toward the end of the week I began to get this large and disenchanting fact through my head: that the mass of the nation had swung their caps and shouted for the republic for about one day, and there an end! The Church, the nobles, and the gentry then turned one grand, all-disapproving frown upon them and shrivelled them into sheep! From that moment the sheep had begun to gather to the fold—that is to say, the camps—and offer their valueless lives and their valuable wool to the "righteous cause." Why, even the very men who had lately been slaves were in the "righteous cause," and glorifying it, praying for it, sentimentally slabbering over it, just like all the other commoners. Imagine such human muck as this; conceive of this folly!

Yes, it was now "Death to the Republic!" everywhere—not a dissenting voice. All England was marching against us! Truly this was more than I had bargained for.

I watched my fifty-two boys narrowly; watched their faces, their walk, their unconscious attitudes: for all these are a language— a language given us purposely that it may betray us in times of emergency, when we have secrets which we want to keep. I knew that that thought would keep saying itself over and over again in their minds and hearts, *All England is marching against us!* and ever more strenuously imploring attention with each repetition, ever more sharply realizing itself to their imaginations, until even in their sleep they would find no rest from it, but hear the vague and flitting creatures of their dreams say, *All England*—ALL ENGLAND!—*is marching against you!* I knew all this would happen; I knew that ultimately the pressure would become so great that it would compel utterance; therefore, I must be ready with an answer at that time—an answer well chosen and tranquillizing.

I was right. The time came. They *had* to speak. Poor lads, it was pitiful to see, they were so pale, so worn, so troubled. At first their spokesman could hardly find voice or words; but he presently got both. This is what he said—and he put it in the neat modern English taught him in my schools:

"We have tried to forget what we are—English boys! We have tried to put reason before sentiment, duty before love; our minds approve, but our hearts reproach us. While apparently it was only the nobility, only the gentry, only the twenty-five or thirty thousand knights left alive out of the late wars, we were of one mind, and undisturbed by any troubling doubt; each and every one of these fifty-two lads who stand here before you, said, 'They have chosen—it is their affair.' But think!—the matter is altered—*all England is marching against us!* Oh, sir, consider!—reflect!—these people are our people, they are bone of our bone, flesh of our flesh, we love them—do not ask us to destroy our nation!"

Well, it shows the value of looking ahead, and being ready for a thing when it happens. If I hadn't foreseen this thing and been fixed, that boy would have had me!—I couldn't have said a word. But I *was* fixed. I said:

"My boys, your hearts are in the right place, you have thought the worthy thought, you have done the worthy thing. You are English boys, you will remain English boys, and you will keep that name unsmirched. Give yourselves no further concern, let your minds be at peace. Consider this: while all England *is* marching against us, who is in the van? Who, by the commonest rules of war, will march in the front? Answer me."

"The mounted host of mailed knights."

"True. They are 30,000 strong. Acres deep, they will march. Now, observe: none but *they* will ever strike the sand-belt. Then there will be an episode! Immediately after, the civilian multitude in the rear will retire, to meet business engagements elsewhere. None but nobles and gentry are knights, and *none but these* will remain to dance to our music after that episode. It is absolutely true that we shall have to fight nobody but these thirty thousand knights. Now speak, and it shall be as you decide. Shall we avoid the battle, retire from the field?"

"NO!!!"

The shout was unanimous and hearty.

"Are you—are you—well, afraid of these thirty thousand knights?"

That joke brought out a good laugh, the boys' troubles vanished away, and they went gaily to their posts. Ah, they were a darling fifty-two! As pretty as girls, too.

I was ready for the enemy, now. Let the approaching big day come along—it would find us on deck.

The big day arrived on time. At dawn the sentry on watch in the corral came into the cave and reported a moving black mass under the horizon, and a faint sound which he thought to be military music. Breakfast was just ready; we sat down and ate it.

This over, I made the boys a little speech, and then sent out a detail to man the battery, with Clarence in command of it.

The sun rose presently and sent its unobstructed splendors over the land, and we saw a prodigious host moving slowly toward us, with the steady drift and aligned front of a wave of the sea. Nearer and nearer it came, and more and more sublimely imposing became its aspect; yes, all England was there, apparently. Soon we could see the innumerable banners fluttering, and then the sun struck the sea of armor and set it all aflash. Yes, it was a fine sight; I hadn't ever seen anything to beat it.

At last we could make out details. All the front ranks, no telling how many acres deep, were horsemen—plumed knights in armor. Suddenly we heard the blare of trumpets; the slow walk burst into a gallop, and then—well, it was wonderful to see! Down swept that vast horses-shoe wave—it approached the sand-belt—my breath stood still; nearer, nearer—the strip of green turf beyond the yellow belt grew narrow—narrower still—became a mere ribbon in front of the horses—then disappeared under their hoofs. Great Scott! Why, the whole front of that host shot into the sky with a thunder-crash, and became a whirling tempest of rags and fragments; and along the ground lay a thick wall of smoke that hid what was left of the multitude from our sight.

Time for the second step in the plan of campaign! I touched a button, and shook the bones of England loose from her spine!

In that explosion all our noble civilization-factories went up in the air and disappeared from the earth. It was a pity, but it was necessary. We could not afford to let the enemy turn our own weapons against us.

Now ensued one of the dullest quarter-hours I had ever endured. We waited in a silent solitude enclosed by our circles of wire, and by a circle of heavy smoke outside of these. We couldn't see over the wall of smoke, and we couldn't see through it. But at last it began to to shred away lazily, and by the end of another quarter-hour the land was clear and our curiosity was enabled to satisfy itself. No living creature was in sight! We now perceived that additions had been made to our defences. The dynamite had dug a ditch more than a hundred feet wide, all around us, and cast up an embankment some twenty-five feet high on both borders of it. As to destruction of life, it was amazing. Moreover, it was beyond estimate. Of course we could not *count* the dead, because they did not exist as individuals, but merely as homogeneous protoplasm, with alloys or iron and buttons.

No life was in sight, but necessarily there must have been some wounded in the rear ranks, who were carried off the field under cover of the wall of smoke; there would be sickness among the others—there always is after an episode like that. But there would be no reinforcements; this was the last stand of the chivalry of England; it was all that was left of the order, after the recent annihilating wars. So I felt quite safe in believing that the utmost force that could for the future be brought against us would be but small; that is, of knights. I therefore issued a congratulatory proclamation to my army in these words:

SOLDIERS, CHAMPIONS OF HUMAN LIBERTY AND EQUALITY: Your General congratulates you! In the pride of his strength and the vanity of his renown, an arrogant enemy came against you. You were ready. The conflict was brief; on your side, glorious. This mighty victory having been achieved utterly without loss, stands without example in history. So long as the planets shall continue to move in their orbits, the BATTLE OF THE SAND-BELT will not perish out of the memories of men.   THE BOSS.

I read it well, and the applause I got was very gratifying to me. I then wound up with these remarks:

"The war with the English nation, as a nation, is at an end. The nation has retired from the field and the war. Before it can be persuaded to return, war will have ceased. This campaign is the only one that is going to be fought. It will be brief—the briefest in history. Also the most destructive to life, considered from the standpoint of proportion of casualties to numbers engaged. We are done with the nation; henceforth we deal only with the knights. English knights can be killed, but they cannot be conquered. We know what is before us. While one of these men remains alive, our task is not finished, the war is not ended. We will kill them all." [Loud and long continued applause.]

I picketed the great embankments thrown up around our lines by the dynamite explosion—merely a lookout of a couple of boys to announce the enemy when he should appear again.

Next, I sent an engineer and forty men to a point just beyond our lines on the south, to turn a mountain brook that was there, and bring it within our lines and under our command, arranging it in such a way that I could make instant use of it in an emergency. The forty men were divided into two shifts of twenty each, and were to

relieve each other every two hours. In ten hours the work was
accomplished.

It was nightfall, now, and I withdrew my pickets. The one who had
had the northern outlook reported a camp in sight, but visible with
the glass only. He also reported that a few knights had been feeling
their way toward us, and had driven some cattle across our lines, but
that the knights themselves had not come very near. That was what
I had been expecting. They were feeling us, you see; they wanted to
know if we were going to play that red terror on them again. They
would grow bolder in the night, perhaps. I believed I knew what
project they would attempt, because it was plainly the thing I would
attempt myself if I were in their places and as ignorant as they were.
I mentioned it to Clarence.

"I think you are right." said he; "it is the obvious thing for them
to try."

"Well, then," I said, "if they do it they are doomed."

"Certainly."

"They won't have the slightest show in the world."

"Of course they won't."

"It's dreadful, Clarence. It seems an awful pity."

The thing disturbed me so, that I couldn't get any peace of mind
for thinking of it and worrying over it. So, at last, to quiet my
conscience, I framed this message to the knights:

TO THE HONORABLE THE COMMANDER OF THE INSURGENT
CHIVALRY OF ENGLAND: You fight in vain. We know your strength—if
one may call it by that name. We know that at the utmost you cannot bring
against us above five and twenty thousand knights. Therefore, you have no
chance—none whatever. Reflect: we are well equipped, well fortified, we
number 54. Fifty-four what? Men? No, *minds*—the capablest in the world:
a force against which mere animal might may no more hope to prevail than
may the idle waves of the sea hope to prevail against the granite barriers of
England. Be advised. We offer you your lives; for the sake of your families,
do not reject the gift. We offer you this chance, and it is the last: throw
down your arms; surrender unconditionally to the Republic, and all will be
forgiven.

                                        (Signed).   THE BOSS.

I read it to Clarence, and said I proposed to send it by a flag of
truce. He laughed the sarcastic laugh he was born with, and said:

"Somehow it seems impossible for you to ever fully realize what
these nobilities are. Now let us save a little time and trouble.
Consider me the commander of the knights yonder. Now then, you
are the flag of truce; approach and deliver me your message, and I
will give you your answer."

I humored the idea. I came forward under an imaginary guard of
the enemy's soldiers, produced my paper, and read it through. For
answer, Clarence struck the paper out of my hand, pursed up a

scornful lip and said with lofty disdain—

"Dismember me this animal, and return him in a basket to the base-born knave who sent him; other answer have I none!"

How empty is theory in presence of fact! And this was just fact, and nothing else. It was the thing that would have happened, there was no getting around that. I tore up the paper and granted my mistimed sentimentalities a permanent rest.

Then, to business. I tested the electric signals from the gatling platform to the cave, and made sure that they were all right; I tested and retested those which commanded the fences—these were signals whereby I could break and renew the electric current in each fence independently of the others, at will. I placed the brook-connection under the guard and authority of three of my best boys, who would alternate in two-hour watches all night and promptly obey my signal, if I should have occasion to give it—three revolver-shots in quick succession. Sentry-duty was discarded for the night, and the corral left empty of life; I ordered that quiet be maintained in the cave, and the electric lights turned down to a glimmer.

As soon as it was good and dark, I shut off the current from all of the fences, and then groped my way out to the embankment bordering our side of the great dynamite ditch. I crept to the top of it and lay there on the slant of the muck to watch. But it was too dark to see anything. As for sounds, there were none. The stillness was death-like. True, there were the usual night-sounds of the country— the whir of night-birds, the buzzing of insects, the barking of distant dogs, the mellow lowing of far-off kine—but these didn't seem to break the stillness, they only intensified it, and added a grewsome melancholy to it into the bargain.

I presently gave up looking, the night shut down so black, but I kept my ears strained to catch the least suspicious sound, for I judged I had only to wait and I shouldn't be disappointed. However, I had to wait a long time. At last I caught what you may call indistinct glimpses of sound—dulled metallic sound. I pricked up my ears, then, and held my breath, for this was the sort of thing I had been waiting for. This sound thickened, and approached—from toward the north. Presently I heard it at my own level—the ridge-top of the opposite embankment, a hundred feet or more away. Then I seemed to see a row of black dots appear along that ridge—human heads? I couldn't tell; it mightn't by anything at all; you can't depend on your eyes when your imagination is out of focus. However, the question was soon settled. I heard that metallic noise descending into the great ditch. It augmented fast, it spread all along, and it unmistakably furnished me this fact: an armed host was taking up its quarters in the ditch. Yes, these people were arranging a little surprise for us. We could expect entertainment about dawn, possibly earlier.

I groped my way back to the corral, now; I had seen enough. I

went to the platform and signalled to turn the current onto the two
inner fences. Then I went into the cave, and found everything
satisfactory there—nobody awake but the working-watch. I woke
Clarence and told him the great ditch was filling up with men, and
that I believed all the knights were coming for us in a body. It was
my notion that as soon as dawn approached we could expect the
ditch's ambuscaded thousands to swarm up over the embankment
and make an assault, and be followed immediately by the rest of
their army.

Clarence said:

"They will be wanting to send a scout or two in the dark to make
preliminary observations. Why not take the lightning off the outer
fences, and give them a chance?"

"I've already done it, Clarence. Did you ever know me to be
inhospitable?"

"No, you are a good heart. I want to go and—"

"Be a reception committee? I will go, too."

We crossed the corral and lay down together between the two
inside fences. Even the dim light of the cave had disordered our
eyesight somewhat, but the focus straightway began to regulate itself
and soon it was adjusted for present circumstances. We had had to
feel our way before, but we could make out to see the fence posts
now. We started a whispered conversation, but suddenly Clarence
broke off and said:

"What is that?"

"What is what?"

"That thing yonder?"

"What thing—where?"

"There beyond you a little piece—a dark something—a dull shape
of some kind—against the second fence."

I gazed and he gazed. I said:

"Could it be a man, Clarence?"

"No, I think not. If you notice, it looks a lit—why, it *is* a man!—
leaning on the fence."

"I certainly believe it is; let us go and see."

We crept along on our hands and knees until we were pretty close,
and then looked up. Yes, it was a man—a dim great figure in armor,
standing erect, with both hands on the upper wire—and of course
there was a smell of burning flesh. Poor fellow, dead as a door-nail,
and never knew what hurt him. He stood there like a statue—no
motion about him, except that his plumes swished about a little in
the night wind. We rose up and looked in through the bars of his
visor, but couldn't make out whether we knew him or not—features
too dim and shadowed.

We heard muffled sounds approaching, and we sank down to the
ground where we were. We made out another knight vaguely; he was
coming very stealthily, and feeling his way. He was near enough,

now, for us to see him put out a hand, find an upper wire, then bend and step under it and over the lower one. Now he arrived at the first knight—and started slightly when he discovered him. He stood a moment—no doubt wondering why the other one didn't move on; then he said, in a low voice, "Why dreamest thou here, good Sir Mar—" then he laid his hand on the corpse's shoulder—and just uttered a little soft moan and sunk down dead. Killed by a dead man, you see—killed by a dead friend, in fact. There was something awful about it.

These early birds came scattering along after each other, about one every five minutes in our vicinity, during half an hour. They brought no armor of offence but their swords; as a rule they carried the sword ready in the hand, and put it forward and found the wires with it. We would now and then see a blue spark when the knight that caused it was so far away as to be invisible to us; but we knew what had happened, all the same; poor fellow, he had touched a charged wire with his sword and been elected. We had brief intervals of grim stillness, interrupted with piteous regularity by the clash made by the falling of an iron-clad; and this sort of thing was going on, right along, and was very creepy, there in the dark and lonesomeness.

We concluded to make a tour between the inner fences. We elected to walk upright, for convenience sake; we argued that if discerned, we should be taken for friends rather than enemies, and in any case we should be out of reach of swords, and these gentry did not seem to have any spears along. Well, it was a curious trip. Everywhere dead men were lying outside the second fence—not plainly visible, but still visible; and we counted fifteen of those pathetic statues—dead knights standing with their hands on the upper wire.

One thing seemed to be sufficiently demonstrated: our current was so tremendous that it killed before the victim could cry out. Pretty soon we detected a muffled and heavy sound, and next moment we guessed what it was. It was a surprise in force coming! I whispered Clarence to go and wake the army, and notify it to wait in silence in the cave for further orders. He was soon back, and we stood by the inner fence and watched the silent lightning do its awful work upon that swarming host. One could make out but little of detail; but he could note that a black mass was piling itself up beyond the second fence. That swelling bulk was dead men! Our camp was enclosed with a solid wall of the dead—a bulwark, a breastwork, of corpses, you may say. One terrible thing about this thing was the absence of human voices; there were no cheers, no war cries: being intent upon a surprise, these men moved as noiselessly as they could; and always when the front rank was near enough to their goal to make it proper for them to begin to get a shout ready, of course they struck the fatal line and went down without testifying.

I sent a current through the third fence, now; and almost
immediately through the fourth and fifth, so quickly were the gaps
filled up. I believed the time was come, now, for my climax; I
believed that that whole army was in our trap. Anyway, it was high
time to find out. So I touched a button and set fifty electric suns
aflame on the top of our precipice.

Land, what a sight! We were enclosed in three walls of dead men!
All the other fences were pretty nearly filled with the living, who were
stealthily working their way forward through the wires. The sudden
glare paralyzed this host, petrified them, you may say, with
astonishment; there was just one instant for me to utilize their
immobility in, and I didn't lose the chance. You see, in another
instant they would have recovered their faculties, then they'd have
burst into a cheer and made a rush, and my wires would have gone
down before it; but that lost instant lost them their opportunity
forever; while even that slight fragment of time was still unspent,
I shot the current through all the fences and struck the whole host
dead in their tracks! *There* was a groan you could *hear!* It voiced the
death-pang of eleven thousand men. It swelled out on the night
with awful pathos.

A glance showed that the rest of the enemy—perhaps ten
thousand strong—were between us and the encircling ditch, and
pressing forward to the assault. Consequently we had them *all!* and
had them past help. Time for the last act of the tragedy. I fired the
three appointed revolver shots—which meant:

"Turn on the water!"

There was a sudden rush and roar, and in a minute the mountain
brook was raging through the big ditch and creating a river a
hundred feet wide and twenty-five deep.

"Stand to your guns, men! Open fire!"

The thirteen gatlings began to vomit death into the fated
ten thousand. They halted, they stood their ground a moment
against that withering deluge of fire, then they broke, faced about
and swept toward the ditch like chaff before a gale. A full fourth
part of their force never reached the top of the lofty embankment;
the three-fourths reached it and plunged over—to death by
drowning.

Within ten short minutes after we had opened fire, armed
resistance was totally annihilated, the campaign was ended, we
fifty-four were masters of England! Twenty-five thousand men lay
dead around us.

But how treacherous is fortune! In a little while—say an hour—
happened a thing, by my own fault, which—but I have no heart to
write that. Let the record end here.

CHAPTER XLIV

A POSTSCRIPT BY CLARENCE

I Clarence, must write it for him. He proposed that we two go out and see if any help could be afforded the wounded. I was strenuous against the project. I said that if there were many, we could do but little for them; and it would not be wise for us to trust ourselves among them, anyway. But he could seldom be turned from a purpose once formed; so we shut off the electric current from the fences, took an escort along, climbed over the enclosing ramparts of dead knights, and moved out upon the field. The first wounded man who appealed for help, was sitting with his back against a dead comrade. When The Boss bent over him and spoke to him, the man recognized him and stabbed him. That knight was Sir Meliagraunce, as I found out by tearing off his helmet. He will not ask for help any more.

We carried The Boss to the cave and gave his wound, which was not very serious, the best care we could. In this service we had the help of Merlin, though we did not know it. He was disguised as a woman, and appeared to be a simple old peasant goodwife. In this disguise, with brown-stained face and smooth shaven, he had appeared a few days after Ths Boss was hurt, and offered to cook for us, saying her people had gone off to join certain new camps which the enemy were forming, and that she was starving. The Boss had been getting along very well, and had amused himself with finishing up his record.

We were glad to have this woman, for we were short handed. We were in a trap, you see—a trap of our own making. If we stayed where we were, our dead would kill us; it we moved out of our defences, we should no longer be invincible. We had conquered; in turn we were conquered. The Boss recognized this; we all recognized it. If we could go to one of those new camps and patch up some kind of terms with the enemy—yes, but The Boss could not go, and neither could I, for I was among the first that were made sick by the poisonous air bred by those dead thousands. Others were taken down, and still others. To-morrow—

To-morrow. It is here. And with it the end. About midnight I awoke, and saw that hag making curious passes in the air about The Boss's head and face, and wondered what it meant. Everybody but the dynamo-watch lay steeped in sleep; there was no sound. The woman ceased from her mysterious foolery, and started tip-toeing toward the door. I called out—

"Stop! What have you been doing?"

She halted, and said with an accent of malicious satisfaction:

"Ye were conquerors; ye are conquered! These others are perishing—you also. Ye shall all die in this place—every one—except *him*. He sleepeth, now—and shall sleep thirteen centuries.

I am Merlin!"

Then such a delirium of silly laughter overtook him that he reeled about like a drunken man, and presently fetched up against one of our wires. His mouth is spread open yet; apparently he is still laughing. I suppose the face will retain that petrified laugh until the corpse turns to dust.

The Boss has never stirred—sleeps like a stone. If he does not wake to-day we shall understand what kind of a sleep it is, and his body will then be borne to a place in one of the remote recesses of the cave where none will ever find it to desecrate it. As for the rest of us—well, it is agreed that if any one of us ever escapes alive from this place, he will write the fact here, and loyally hide this Manuscript with The Boss, our dear good chief, whose property it is, be he alive or dead.

END OF THE MANUSCRIPT

FINAL P. S. BY M. T.

The dawn was come when I laid the Manuscript aside. The rain had almost ceased, the world was gray and sad, the exhausted storm was sighing and sobbing itself to rest. I went to the stranger's room, and listened at his door, which was slightly ajar. I could hear his voice, and so I knocked. There was no answer, but I still heard the voice. I peeped in. The man lay on his back, in bed, talking brokenly but with spirit, and punctuating with his arms, which he thrashed about, restlessly, as sick people do in delirium. I slipped in softly and bent over him. His mutterings and ejaculations went on. I spoke—merely a word, to call his attention. His glassy eyes and his ashy face were alight in an instant with pleasure, gratitude, gladness, welcome:

"O, Sandy, you are come at last—how I have longed for you! Sit by me—do not leave me—never leave me again, Sandy, never again. Where is your hand?—give it me, dear, let me hold it—there—now all is well, all is peace, and I am happy again—*we* are happy again, isn't it so, Sandy? You are so dim, so vague, you are but a mist, a cloud, but you are *here*, and that is blessedness sufficient; and I have your hand; don't take it away—it is for only a little while, I shall not require it long. . . . . Was that the child? . . . .Hello-Central! . . . She doesn't answer. Asleep, perhaps? Bring her when she wakes, and let me touch her hands, her face, her hair, and tell her good-bye. . . . . . . Sandy! . . . . . Yes, you are there. I lost myself a moment, and I thought you were gone. . . Have I been sick long? it must be so; it seems months to me. And such dreams!

such strange and awful dreams, Sandy! Dreams that were as real as
reality—delirium, of course, but *so* real! Why, I thought the king
was dead, I thought you were in Gaul and couldn't get home, I
thought there was a revolution; in the fantastic frenzy of these
dreams, I thought that Clarence and I and a handful of my cadets
fought and exterminated the whole chivalry of England! But even
that was not the strangest. I seemed to be a creature out of a remote
unborn age, centuries hence, and even *that* was as real as the rest!
Yes, I seemed to have flown back out of that age into this of ours,
and then forward to it again, and was set down, a stranger and
forlorn in that strange England, with an abyss of thirteen centuries
yawning between me and you! between me and my home and my
friends! between me and all that is dear to me, all that could make
life worth the living! It was awful—awfuler than you can ever
imagine, Sandy. Ah, watch by me, Sandy—stay by me every
moment—*don't* let me go out of my mind again; death is nothing,
let it come, but not with those dreams, not with the torture of those
hideous dreams—I cannot endure *that* again. . . . .
Sandy? . . . . ."

He lay muttering incoherently some little time; then for a time he
lay silent, and apparently sinking away toward death. Presently his
fingers began to pick busily at the coverlet, and by that sign I knew
that his end was at hand. With the first suggestion of the
death-rattle in his throat he started up slightly, and seemed to listen;
then he said:

"A bugle? . . . . . It is the king! The drawbridge, there! Man the
battlements!—turn out the—"

He was getting up his last "effect;" but he never finished it.

FENIMORE COOPER'S LITERARY OFFENSES

FENIMORE COOPER'S LITERARY OFFENSES

The Pathfinder and *The Deerslayer* stand at the head of Cooper's novels as artistic creations. There are others of his works which contain parts as perfect as are to be found in these, and scenes even more thrilling. Not one can be compared with either of them as a finished whole.

The defects in both of these tales are comparatively slight. They were pure works of art.—*Prof. Lounsbury.*

The five tales reveal an extraordinary fulness of invention.

... One of the very greatest characters in fiction, "Natty Bumppo." ...

The craft of the woodsman, the tricks of the trapper, all the delicate art of the forest, were familiar to Cooper from his youth up.—*Prof. Brander Matthews.*

Cooper is the greatest artist in the domain of romantic fiction yet produced by America.—*Wilkie Collins.*

It seems to me that it was far from right for the Professor of English Literature in Yale, the Professor of English Literature in Columbia, and Wilkie Collins, to deliver opinions on Cooper's literature without having read some of it. It would have been much more decorous to keep silent and let persons talk who have read Cooper.

Cooper's art has some defects. In one place in *Deerslayer,* and in the restricted space of two-thirds of a page, Cooper has scored 114 offences against literary art out of a possible 115. It breaks the record.

There are nineteen rules governing literary art in the domain of romantic fiction—some say twenty-two. In *Deerslayer* Cooper violated eighteen of them. These eighteen require:

1. That a tale shall accomplish something and arrive somewhere. But the *Deerslayer* tale accomplishes nothing and arrives in the air.

2. They require that the episodes of a tale shall be necessary parts of the tale, and shall help to develop it. But as the *Deerslayer* tale is not a tale, and accomplishes nothing and arrives nowhere, the episodes have no rightful place in the work, since there was

nothing for them to develop.

3. They require that the personages in a tale shall be alive, except in the case of corpses, and that always the reader shall be able to tell the corpses from the others. But this detail has often been overlooked in the *Deerslayer* tale.

4. They require that the personages in a tale, both dead and alive, shall exhibit a sufficient excuse for being there. But this detail also has been overlooked in the *Deerslayer* tale.

5. They require that when the personages of a tale deal in conversation, the talk shall sound like human talk, and be talk such as human beings would be likely to talk in the given circumstances, and have a discoverable meaning, also a discoverable purpose, and a show of relevancy, and remain in the neighborhood of the subject in hand, and be interesting to the reader, and help out the tale, and stop when the people cannot think of anything more to say. But this requirement has been ignored from the beginning of the *Deerslayer* tale to the end of it.

6. They require that when the author describes the character of a personage in his tale, the conduct and conversation of that personage shall justify said description. But this law gets little or no attention in the *Deerslayer* tale, as "Natty Bumppo's" case will amply prove.

7. They require that when a personage talks like an illustrated, gilt-edged, tree-calf, hand tooled, seven-dollar Friendship's Offering in the beginning of a paragraph, he shall not talk like a negro minstrel in the end of it. But this rule is flung down and danced upon in the *Deerslayer* tale.

8. They require that crass stupidities shall not be played upon the reader as "the craft of the woodsman, the delicate art of the forest," by either the author or the people in the tale. But this rule is persistently violated in the *Deerslayer* tale.

9. They require that the personages of a tale shall confine themselves to possibilities and let miracles alone; or, if they venture a miracle, the author must so plausibly set it forth as to make it look possible and reasonable. But these rules are not respected in the *Deerslayer* tale.

10. They require that the author shall make the reader feel a deep interest in the personages of his tale and in their fate; and that he shall make the reader love the good people in the tale and hate the bad ones. But the reader of the *Deerslayer* tale dislikes the good people in it, is indifferent to the others, and wishes they would all get drowned together.

11. They require that the characters in a tale shall be so clearly defined that the reader can tell beforehand what each will do in a given emergency. But in the *Deerslayer* tale this rule is vacated.

In addition to these large rules there are some little ones. These require that the author shall

12. *Say* what he is proposing to say, not merely come near it.

13. Use the right word, not its second cousin.

14. Eschew surplusage.

15. Not omit necessary details.

16. Avoid slovenliness of form.

17. Use good grammar.

18. Employ a simple and straightforward style.

Even these seven are coldly and persistently violated in the *Deerslayer* tale.

Cooper's gift in the way of invention was not a rich endowment; but such as it was he liked to work it, he was pleased with the effects, and indeed he did some quite sweet things with it. In his little box of stage properties he kept six or eight cunning devices, tricks, artifices for his savages and woodsmen to deceive and circumvent each other with, and he was never so happy as when he was working these innocent things and seeing them go. A favorite one was to make a moccasined person tread in the tracks of the moccasined enemy, and thus hide his own trail. Cooper wore out barrels and barrels of moccasins in working that trick. Another stage-property that he pulled out of his box pretty frequently was his broken twig. He prized his broken twig above all the rest of his effects, and worked it the hardest. It is a restful chapter in any book of his when somebody doesn't step on a dry twig and alarm all the reds and whites for two hundred yards around. Every time a Cooper person is in peril, and absolute silence is worth four dollars a minute, he is sure to step on a dry twig. There may be a hundred handier things to step on, but that wouldn't satisfy Cooper. Cooper requires him to turn out and find a dry twig; and if he can't do it, go and borrow one. In fact the Leather Stocking Series ought to have been called the Broken Twig Series.

I am sorry there is not room to put in a few dozen instances of the delicate art of the forest, as practiced by Natty Bumppo and some of the other Cooperian experts. Perhaps we may venture two or three samples. Cooper was a sailor—a naval officer; yet he gravely tells us how a vessel, driving toward a lee shore in a gale, is steered for a particular spot by her skipper because he knows of an *undertow* there which will hold her back against the gale and save her. For just pure woodcraft, or sailorcraft, or whatever it is, isn't that neat? For several years Cooper was daily in the society of artillery, and he ought to have noticed that when a cannon ball strikes the ground it either buries itself or skips a hundred feet or so; skips again a hundred feet or so—and so on, till it finally gets tired and rolls. Now in one place he loses some "females"—as he always calls women—in the edge of a wood near a plain at night in a fog, on purpose to give Bumppo a chance to show off the delicate art of the forest before the reader. These mislaid people are hunting for a fort. They hear a cannon-blast, and a cannon-ball presently

comes rolling into the wood and stops at their feet. To the females
this suggests nothing. The case is very different with the admirable
Bumppo. I wish I may never know peace again if he doesn't strike
out promptly and *follow the track* of that cannon-ball across the
plain through the dense fog and find the fort. Isn't it a daisy? If
Cooper had any real knowledge of Nature's ways of doing things,
he had a most delicate art in concealing the fact. For instance:
one of his acute Indian experts, Chingachgook (pronounced
Chicago, I think), has lost the trail of a person he is tracking through
the forest. Apparently that trail is hopelessly lost. Neither you nor
I could ever have guessed out the way to find it. It was very different
with Chicago. Chicago was not stumped for long. He turned a
running stream out of its course, and there, in the slush in its old bed,
were that person's moccasin-tracks. The current did not wash them
away, as it would have done in all other like cases—no, even the
eternal laws of Nature have to vacate when Cooper wants to put up
a delicate job of woodcraft on the reader.

We must be a little wary when Brander Matthews tells us that
Cooper's books "reveal an extraordinary fulness of invention."
As a rule, I am quite willing to accept Brander Matthews's literary
judgments and applaud his lucid and graceful phrasing of them;
but that particular statement needs to be taken with a few tons
of salt. Bless your heart, Cooper hadn't any more invention than a
horse; and I don't mean a high-class horse, either; I mean a clothes-
horse. It would be very difficult to find a really clever "situation"
in Cooper's books; and still more difficult to find one of any kind
which he has failed to render absurd by his handling of it. Look
at the episodes of "the caves;" and at the celebrated scuffle between
Maqua and those others on the table-land a few days later; and
at Hurry Harry's queer water-transit from the castle to the ark;
and at Deerslayer's half hour with his first corpse; and at the quarrel
between Hurry Harry and Deerslayer later; and at—but choose for
yourself; you can't go amiss.

If Cooper had been an observer, his inventive faculty would
have worked better, not more interestingly, but more rationally,
more plausibly. Cooper's proudest creations in the way of
"situations" suffer noticeably from the absence of the observer's
protecting gift. Cooper's eye was splendidly inaccurate. Cooper
seldom saw anything correctly. He saw nearly all things as
through a glass eye, darkly. Of course a man who cannot see the
commonest little everyday matters accurately is working at a
disadvantage when he is constructing a "situation." In the
Deerslayer tale Cooper has a stream which is fifty feet wide, where
it flows out of a lake; it presently narrows to twenty as it meanders
along for no given reason, and yet, when a stream acts like that
it ought to be required to explain itself. Fourteen pages later the
width of the brook's outlet from the lake has suddenly shrunk thirty

feet, and become "the narrowest part of the stream." This shrinkage is not accounted for. The stream has bends in it, a sure indication that it has alluvial banks, and cuts them; yet these bends are only thirty and fifty feet long. If Cooper had been a nice and punctilious observer he would have noticed that the bends were oftener nine hundred feet long than short of it.

Cooper made the exit of that stream fifty feet wide in the first place, for no particular reason; in the second place, he narrowed it to less than twenty to accommodate some Indians. He bends a "sapling" to the form of an arch over this narrow passage, and conceals six Indians in its foliage. They are "laying" for a settler's scow or ark which is coming up the stream on its way to the lake; it is being hauled against the stiff current by a rope whose stationary end is anchored in the lake; its rate of progress cannot be more than a mile an hour. Cooper describes the ark, but pretty obscurely. In the matter of dimensions "it was little more than a modern canal boat." Let us guess, then, that it was about 140 feet long. It was of "greater breadth than common." Let us guess, then, that it was about sixteen feet wide. This leviathan had been prowling down bends which were but a third as long as itself, and scraping between banks where it had only two feet of space to spare on each side. We cannot too much admire this miracle. A low-roofed log dwelling occupies "two-third's of the ark's length"—a dwelling ninety feet long and sixteen feet wide, let us say—a kind of vestibule train. The dwelling has two rooms—each forty-five feet long and sixteen feet wide, let us guess. One of them is the bed-room of the Hutter girls, Judith and Hetty; the other is the parlor, in the day time, at night it is papa's bed chamber. The ark is arriving at the stream's exit, now, whose width has been reduced to less than twenty feet to accommodate the Indians—say to eighteen. There is a foot to spare on each side of the boat. Did the Indians notice that there was going to be a tight squeeze there? Did they notice that they could make money by climbing down out of that arched sapling and just stepping aboard when the ark scraped by? No; other Indians would have noticed these things, but Cooper's Indians never notice anything. Cooper thinks they are marvellous creatures for noticing, but he was almost always in error about his Indians. There was seldom a sane one among them.

The ark is 140 feet long; the dwelling is 90 feet long. The idea of the Indians is to drop softly and secretly from the arched sapling to the dwelling as the ark creeps along under it at the rate of a mile an hour, and butcher the family. It will take the ark a minute and a half to pass under. It will take the 90-foot dwelling a minute to pass under. Now, then, what did the six Indians do? It would take you thirty years to guess, and even then you would have to give it up, I believe. Therefore, I will tell you what the Indians did. Their chief, a person of quite extraordinary intellect for a

Cooper Indian, warily watched the canal boat as it squeezed along under him, and when he had got his calculations fined down to exactly the right shade, as he judged, he let go and dropped. And *missed the house!* That is actually what he did. He missed the house, and landed in the stern of the scow. It was not much of a fall, yet it knocked him silly. He lay there unconscious. If the house had been 97 feet long, he would have made the trip. The fault was Cooper's, not his. The error lay in the construction of the house. Cooper was no architect.

There still remained in the roost five Indians. The boat has passed under and is now out of their reach. Let me explain what the five did—you would not be able to reason it out for yourself. No. 1 jumped for the boat, but fell in the water astern of it. Then No. 2 jumped for the boat, but fell in the water still further astern of it. Then No. 3 jumped for the boat, and fell a good way astern of it. Then No. 4 jumped for the boat, and fell in the water *away* astern. Then even No. 5 made a jump for the boat—for he was a Cooper Indian. In the matter of intellect, the difference between a Cooper Indian and the Indian that stands in front of the cigar shop is not spacious. The scow episode is really a sublime burst of invention; but it does not thrill, because the inaccuracy of the details throws a sort of air of fictitiousness and general improbability over it. This comes of Cooper's inadequacy as an observer.

The reader will find some examples of Cooper's high talent for inaccurate observation in the account of the shooting match in *The Pathfinder.* "A common wrought nail was driven lightly into the target, its head having been first touched with paint." The color of the paint is not stated—an important omission, but Cooper deals freely in important omissions. No, after all, it was not an important omission; for this nail head is a *hundred yards* from the marksman and could not be seen by them at that distance no matter what its color might be. How far can the best eyes see a common house fly? A hundred yards? It is quite impossible. Very well, eyes that cannot see a house fly that is a hundred yards away cannot see an ordinary nail head at that distance, for the size of the two objects is the same. It takes a keen eye to see a fly or a nail head at fifty yards—one hundred and fifty feet. Can the reader do it?

The nail was lightly driven, its head painted, and game called. Then the Cooper miracles began. The bullet of the first marksman chipped an edge of the nail head; the next man's bullet drove the nail a little way into the target—and removed all the paint. Haven't the miracles gone far enough now? Not to suit Cooper; for the purpose of this whole scheme is to show off his prodigy, Deerslayer-Hawkeye-Long-Rifle-Leather-Stocking-Pathfinder-Bumppo before the ladies.

"Be all ready to clench it, boys!" cried out Pathfinder, stepping into his friend's tracks the instant they were vacant. "Never mind a new nail; I can see that, though the paint is gone, and what I can see, I can hit at a hundred yards, though it were only a mosquito's eye. Be ready to clench!"

The rifle cracked, the bullet sped its way and the head of the nail was buried in the wood, covered by the piece of flattened lead.

There, you see, is a man who could hunt flies with a rifle, and command a ducal salary in a Wild West show to-day, if we had him back with us.

The recorded feat is certainly surprising, just as it stands; but it is not surprising enough for Cooper. Cooper adds a touch. He has made Pathfinder do this miracle with another man's rifle, and not only that, but Pathfinder did not have even the advantage of loading it himself. He had everything against him, and yet he made that impossible shot, and not only made it, but did it with absolute confidence, saying, "Be ready to clench." Now a person like that would have undertaken that same feat with a brickbat, and with Cooper to help he would have achieved it, too.

Pathfinder showed off handsomely that day before the ladies. His very first feat was a thing which no Wild West show can touch. He was standing with the group of marksmen, observing—a hundred yards from the target, mind: one Jasper raised his rifle and drove the centre of the bull's-eye. Then the quartermaster fired. The target exhibited no result this time. There was a laugh. "It's a dead miss," said Major Lundie. Pathfinder waited an impressive moment or two, then said in that calm, indifferent, know-it-all way of his, "No, Major—he has covered Jasper's bullet, as will be seen if any one will take the trouble to examine the target."

Wasn't it remarkable! How *could* he see that little pellet fly through the air and enter that distant bullet-hole? Yet that is what he did; for nothing is impossible to a Cooper person. Did any of those people have any deep-seated doubts about this thing? No; for that would imply sanity, and these were all Cooper people.

The respect for Pathfinder's skill and for his *quickness and accuracy of sight* (the italics are mine) was so profound and general, that the instant he made this declaration the spectators began to distrust their own opinions, and a dozen rushed to the target in order to ascertain the fact. There, sure enough, it was found that the quartermaster's bullet had gone through the hole made by Jasper's, and that, too, so accurately as to require a minute examination to be certain of the circumstances, which, however, was soon established by discovering one bullet over the other in the stump against which the target was placed.

They made a "minute" examination; but never mind, how could they know that there were two bullets in that hole without digging the latest one out? for neither probe nor eyesight could prove the presence of any more than one bullet. Did they dig? No; as we shall

see. It is the Pathfinder's turn now; he steps out before the ladies,
takes aim, and fires.

But alas! here is a disappointment; an incredible, an
unimaginable disappointment—for the target's aspect is
unchanged; there is nothing there but that same old bullet hole!

"If one dared to hint at such a thing," cried Major Duncan, "I should
say that the Pathfinder has also missed the target."

As nobody had missed it yet, the "also" was not necessary; but
never mind about that, for the Pathfinder is going to speak.

"No, no, Major," said he, confidently, "that *would* be a risky declaration.
I didn't load the piece, and can't say what was in it, but if it was lead, you
will find the bullet driving down those of the Quartermaster and Jasper,
else is not my name Pathfinder."

A shout from the target announced the truth of this assertion.

Is the miracle sufficient as it stands? Not for Cooper. The
Pathfinder speaks again, as he "now slowly advances towards the
stage occupied by the females:"

"That's not all, boys, that's not all; if you find the target touched at all,
I'll own to a miss. The Quartermaster cut the wood, but you'll find no wood
cut by that last messenger."

The miracle is at last complete. He knew—doubtless *saw*—at the
distance of a hundred yards—that his bullet had passed into the hole
without fraying the edges. There were now three bullets in that one
hole—three bullets imbedded processionally in the body of the
stump back of the target. Everybody knew this—somehow or
other—and yet nobody had dug any of them out to make sure.
Cooper is not a close observer, but he is interesting. He is certainly
always that, no matter what happens. And he is more interesting
when he is not noticing what he is about than when he is. This is a
considerable merit.

The conversations in the Cooper books have a curious sound in
our modern ears. To believe that such talk really ever came out of
people's mouths would be to believe that there was a time when time
was of no value to a person who thought he had something to say;
when a man's mouth was a rolling-mill, and busied itself all day long
in turning four-foot pigs of thought into thirty-foot bars of
conversational railroad iron by attenuation; when subjects were
seldom faithfully stuck to, but the talk wandered all around and
arrived nowhere; when conversations consisted mainly of
irrelevances, with here and there a relevancy, a relevancy with an
embarrassed look, as not being able to explain how it got there.

Cooper was certainly not a master in the construction of dialogue.
Inaccurate observation defeated him here as it defeated him in so
many other enterprises of his. He even failed to notice that the man
who talks corrupt English six days in the week must and will talk it
on the seventh, and can't help himself. In the *Deerslayer* story he
lets Deerslayer talk the showiest kind of book talk sometimes, and at

other times the basest of base dialects. For instance, when some one asks him if he has a sweetheart, and if so, where she abides, this is his majestic answer:

"She's in the forest—hanging from the boughs of the trees, in a soft rain—in the dew on the open grass—the clouds that float about in the blue heavens—the birds that sing in the woods—the sweet springs where I slake my thirst—and in all the other glorious gifts that come from God's Providence!"

And he preceded that, a little before, with this:

"It consarns me as all things that touches a fri'nd consarns a fri'nd."

And this is another of his remarks:

"If I was Injin born, now, I might tell of this, or carry in the scalp and boast of the expl'ite afore the whole tribe; or if my inimy had only been a bear"—and so on.

We cannot imagine such a thing as a veteran Scotch Commander-in-Chief comporting himself in the field like a windy melodramatic actor, but Cooper could. On one occasion Alice and Cora were being chased by the French through a fog in the neighborhood of their father's fort:

"Point de quartier aux coquins!" cried an eager pursuer, who seemed to direct the operations of the enemy.

"Stand firm and be ready, my gallant 60ths!" suddenly exclaimed a voice above them; "wait to see the enemy; fire low, and sweep the glacis."

"Father! father!" exclaimed a piercing cry from out the mist; "it is I! Alice! thy own Elsie! spare, O! save your daughters!"

"Hold!" shouted the former speaker, in the awful tones of parental agony, the sound reaching even to the woods, and rolling back in solemn echo. " 'Tis she! God has restored me my children! Throw open the sally-port; to the field, 60ths, to the field; pull not a trigger, lest ye kill my lambs! Drive off these dogs of France with your steel."

Cooper's word-sense was singularly dull. When a person has a poor ear for music he will flat and sharp right along without knowing it. He keeps near the tune, but it is *not* the tune. When a person has a poor ear for words, the result is a literary flatting and sharping; you perceive what he is intending to say, but you also perceive that he doesn't *say* it. This is Cooper. He was not a word-musician. His ear was satisfied with the *approximate* word. I will furnish some circumstantial evidence in support of this charge. My instances are gathered from half a dozen pages of the tale called *Deerslayer*. He uses "verbal," for "oral"; "precision," for "facility"; "phenomena," for "marvels"; "necessary," for "predetermined"; "unsophisticated," for "primitive"; "preparation," for "expectancy"; "rebuked," for "subdued"; "dependent on," for "resulting from"; "fact," for "condition"; "fact," for "conjecture"; "precaution," for "caution"; "explain," for "determine"; "mortified," for "disappointed"; "meretricious," for "factitious"; "materially," for "considerably"; "decreasing," for "deepening"; "increasing," for "disappearing"; "embedded,"

for "enclosed"; "treacherous," for "hostile"; "stood," for
"stooped"; "softened," for "replaced"; "rejoined," for "remarked";
"situation," for "condition"; "different," for "differing";
"insensible," for "unsentient"; "brevity," for "celerity";
"distrusted," for "suspicious"; "mental imbecility," for
"imbecility"; "eyes," for "sight"; "counteracting," for "opposing";
"funeral obsequies," for "obsequies."

There have been daring people in the world who claimed that
Cooper could write English, but they are all dead now—all dead but
Lounsbury. I don't remember that Lounsbury makes the claim in
so many words, still he makes it, for he says that *Deerslayer* is a
"pure work of art." Pure, in that connection, means faultless—
faultless in all details—and language is a detail. If Mr. Lounsbury
had only compared Cooper's English with the English which he
writes himself—but it is plain that he didn't; and so it is likely that
he imagines until this day that Cooper's is as clean and compact as
his own. Now I feel sure, deep down in my heart, that Cooper wrote
about the poorest English that exists in our language, and that the
English of *Deerslayer* is the very worst than even Cooper ever wrote.

I may be mistaken, but it does seem to me that *Deerslayer* is not a
work of art in any sense; it does seem to me that it is destitute of
every detail that goes to the making of a work of art; in truth, it
seems to me that *Deerslayer* is just simply a literary *delirium
tremens*.

A work of art? It has no invention; it has no order, system,
sequence, or result; it has no lifelikeness, no thrill, no stir, no
seeming of reality; its characters are confusedly drawn, and by their
acts and words they prove that they are not the sort of people the
author claims that they are; its humor is pathetic; its pathos is
funny; its conversations are—oh! indescribable; its love-scenes
odious; its English a crime against the language.

Counting these out, what is left is Art. I think we must all
admit that.